A DICTIONARY OF THE HOLY BIBLE,

FOR GENERAL USE

IN

THE STUDY OF THE SCRIPTURES;

WITH

ENGRAVINGS, MAPS, AND TABLES.

PUBLISHED BY THE

AMERICAN TRACT SOCIETY,

NEW YORK: 150 NASSAU-STREET.

MAP OF THE EAST,
SYRIA, ARABIA, CHALDEA, MESOPOTAMIA,
MEDIA, PERSIA, ETC.
English Miles
ARARAT OR ARMENIA MAJOR
Ararat Mt
Euphrates R.
ELLASAR
Charan
Aram Naharaim
PADAN ARAM
Carchemish
NINEVEH
Tadmor
Damascus
Hamath
Zobah
Tyre
Jerusalem
Hebron
Kir
Mt Hor
Rameses
Paphos
Tarsus
Lystra
Derbe
ARABIA DESERTA
BABYLON
SHINAR
Tigris
Halah
Habor
GREATER MEDIA
PARTHIA
SHUSHAN
ELYMEIS
Havilah
Horeb
Sinai
Sin
ARABIA
Longitude East from Greenwich

CANAAN
IN THE TIME OF THE
PATRIARCHS
Scale of Statute Miles
THE GREAT SEA OR MEDITERRANEAN
HAMATHITES
Arvad
ARVADITES
ZEMARITES
ARKITES
Gebal
GIBLITES
Zobah
Mount Lebanon
MAACHATHITES
Mt. Hermon
DAMASCUS
Zidon
Tyre
HIVITES
GESHURITES
Ashtaroth Karnaim
Salchah
Dothan
HIVITES
Shechem
CANAANITES
GIRGASHITES
PERIZZITES
Mahanaim
Japho
Shiloh
Mt. Gilead
Rabbath Ammon
Luz
JEBUSITES
Heshbon
AMMONITES
Mamre
HITTITES
Gaza
ANAKIM
AMORITES
SALT LAKE
MOABITES
Zoar
Rehoboth
River of Egypt
KENITES
Bozrah
Kadesh Barnea
Wilderness of Zin
Mt. Hor
HORIM
T E M A N
Desert of Shur
AMALEKITES
Mount Seir
NEBAIOTH
ISHMAELITES
MIDIANITES
Elath

THE
HOLY LAND
in the
TIME OF SAMUEL.
SCALE OF MILES
Judah
II. Simeon
III Benjamin
IV Dan
V Ephraim
VI Manasseh
VII Issachar
VIII Zebulon
IX Asher
X Naphtali
XI Gad
XII Reuben
THE GREAT SEA
Mt. Hermon
Damascus
Sidon
Mt. Tabor
Shechem
Mt. Ebal
Mt. Gerizim
Mt. Gilead
JERUSALEM
Mt. of Olives
Mt. Pisgah
Hebron
Beersheba
Desert of Paran
E D O M
Longitude East from Greenwich
E. Wells N.Y.

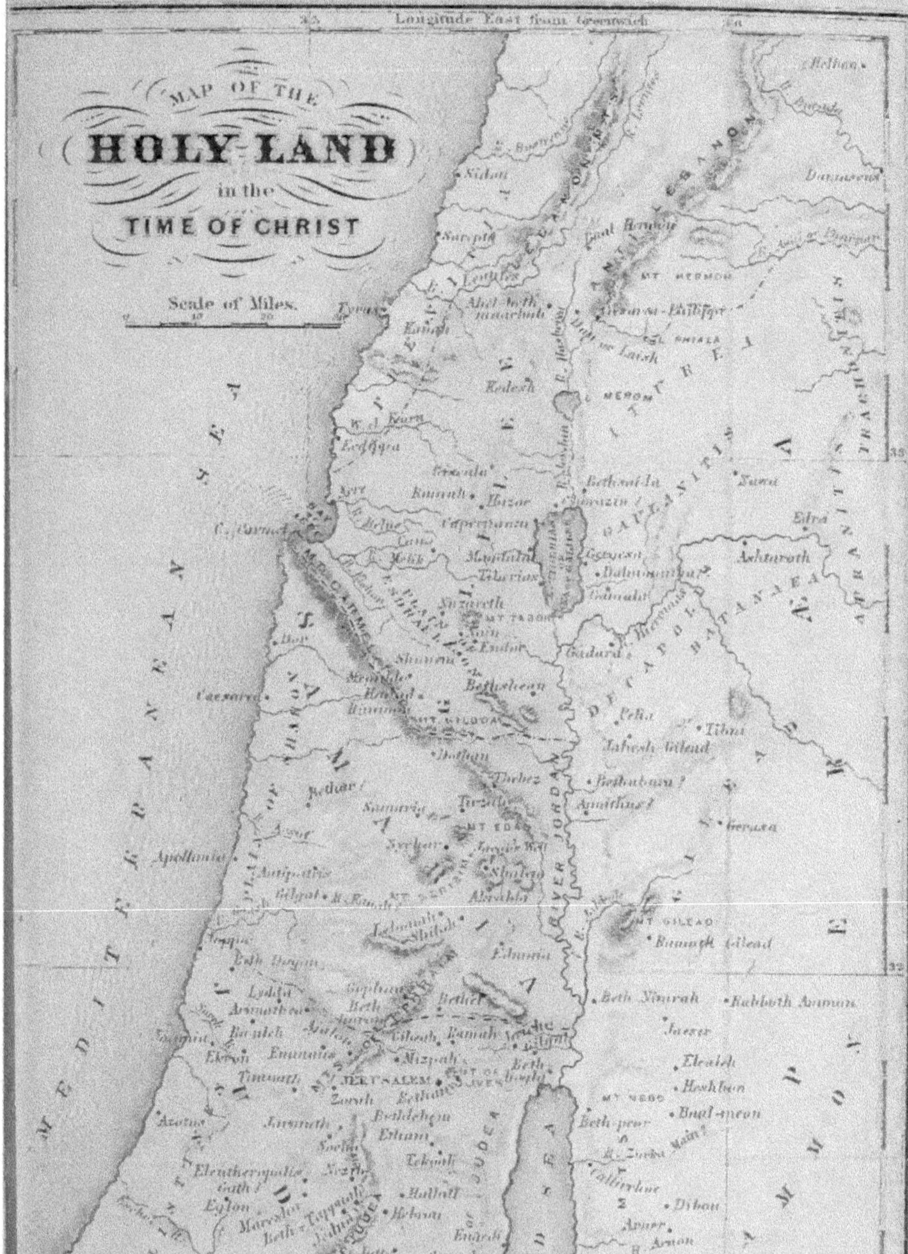
MAP OF THE
HOLY LAND
in the
TIME OF CHRIST
Scale of Miles.
Longitude East from Greenwich
MEDITERRANEAN SEA
Sidon
Sarepta
Tyrus
Damascus
MT HERMON
Kedesh
Caesarea
Samaria
Bethshean
Dothan
Apollonia
Antipatris
Joppa
Lydda
Bethel
Emmaus
Ekron
Azotus
Bethlehem
Eleutheropolis
Eglon
Gaza
Gerar
Beersheba
Arad
Masada
Hebron
Carmel
Maon
Jericho
Gadara
Pella
Gerasa
Rabboth Ammon
Heshbon
Dibon
Aroer
Medeba
Rabbath Moab
Kir Moab
Callirrhoe
MT GILEAD
RIVER JORDAN
DEAD SEA
TRACHONITIS
BATANAEA
GAULANITIS
DECAPOLIS
ITUREA
MOAB
ARABIA PETRÆA
Edra
Ashtaroth
Nazareth
MT TABOR
Endor
MT GILBOA
Capernaum
Tiberias
Magdala
Bethsaida
Chorazin
Hazor
MT NEBO
Akrabbim

MAP
Illustrative of the
TRAVELS & VOYAGES
OF THE
APOSTLE PAUL
ROME
Three Taverns
Appii Forum
Puteoli
Neapolis
Cephallenia
Zacynthus
Amphipolis
Thessalonica
Philippi
Athens
Melita
A D R I A
A D R I A T I C
S E A
T H E
G R E
C Y R E N A I C A

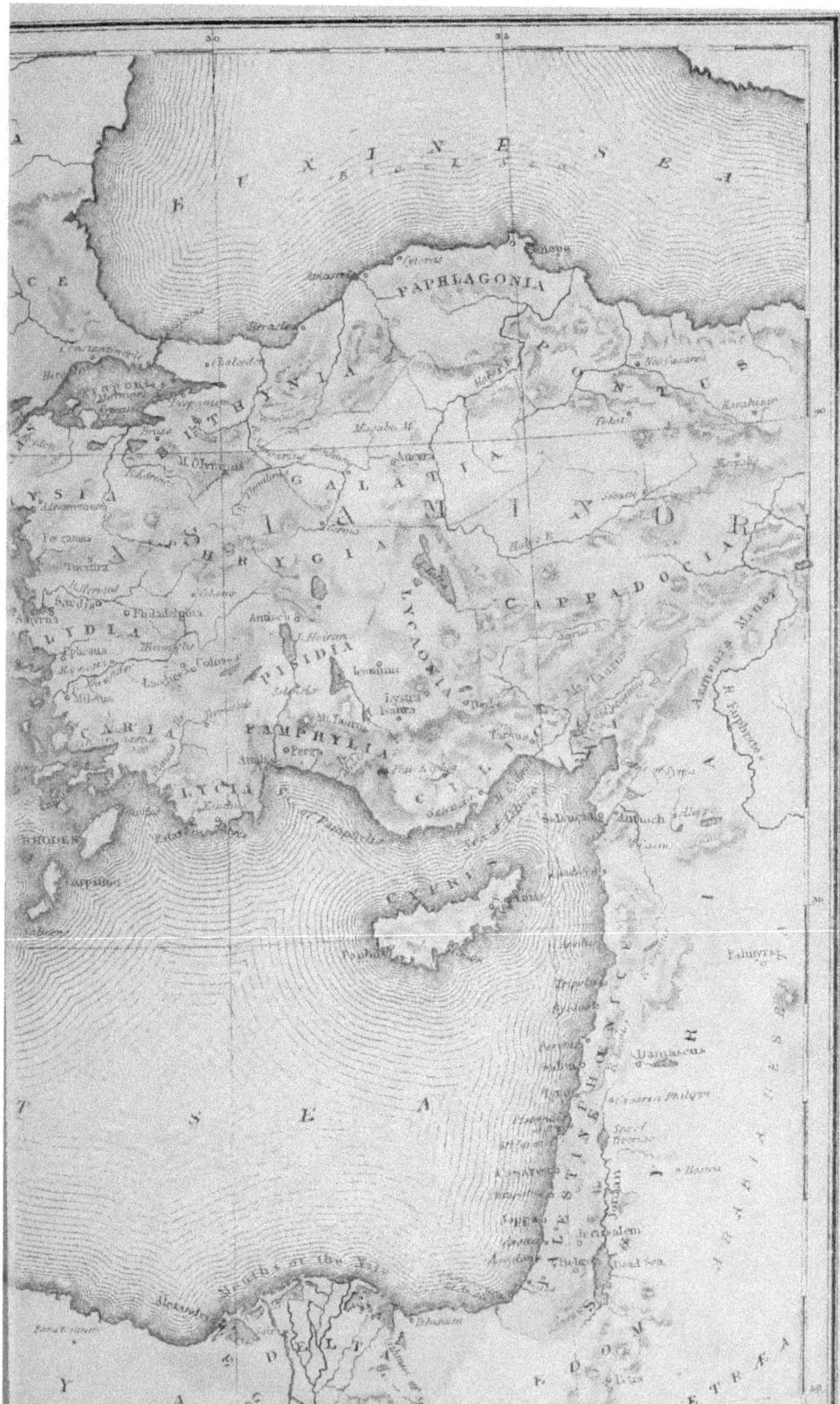

E U X I N E   S E A
Black Sea
PAPHLAGONIA
B I T H Y N I A
P O N T U S
G A L A T I A
A S I A   M I N O R
P H R Y G I A
LYCAONIA
C A P P A D O C I A
LYDIA
PISIDIA
C A R I A
PAMPHYLIA
LYCIA
C I L I C I A
CYPRUS
Ancyra
Sardis
Philadelphia
Smyrna
Ephesus
Miletus
Iconium
Lystra
Tarsus
Perga
Antioch
Seleucia
Rhodes
Carpathus
Paphos
Tripolis
Damascus
Palmyra
Jerusalem
Dead Sea
Joppa
Petra
E D O M
A R A B I A   P E T R Æ A
S E A
DELTA
Mouths of the Nile
Alexandria
Memphis
R. Nile
Euphrates
Armenia Minor
Longitude East from Greenwich

PREFACE.

THIS work is based on "A Dictionary of the Holy Bible, for the use of Schools and Young Persons, by Edward Robinson, D. D.," issued in 1833, by Messrs. Crocker and Brewster, Boston. The use of the copy-right of that volume having been procured from the publishers, about two-thirds of it are embodied in these pages, constituting about one-third of the whole; but without any participation or responsibility on the part of Dr. Robinson. His own later biblical works, including his Researches in Palestine, afford invaluable aids to the Bible student, which have been freely used in the preparation of the present volume. Much aid has also been drawn from the Bible Dictionaries of Rev. John Brown of Haddington, and Professor Eadie of the United Presbyterian Church, Scotland; Bost, of Switzerland; Kitto, and other sources; while the accuracy of all that has been inserted has been studiously tested, in every case as far as possible, by a comparison with the only infallible standard, the inspired word itself.

The aim of this work and the principles on which it has been prepared, cannot be better expressed than in the language of Dr. Robinson in 1833, in his preface to the work on which it is based.

"In the present work," he says, "the Editor has aimed to give only the *results* of his previous investigations; and to present them in such a form as may be attractive and useful to the very large class of young persons and others, who may be supposed to take an interest in this species of knowledge. There are doubtless thousands of such persons, especially females, to whom the information contained in this small volume would be in a high degree interesting and instructive; but who, nevertheless, would never think of seeking for it in the larger and more learned volumes in which it is usually contained.

"It has everywhere been my endeavor, not to omit any results, or any information, which might be useful to the classes of readers for whom this volume is more particularly designed. The processes of induction and reasoning, the allusions to the original Hebrew and Greek of the Scriptures, have of course been passed by; and also all the references to sources and authorities, excepting to the Bible itself. These last I have endeavored to render full and correct.

"If I may be permitted to advise in respect to the mode of using this little volume, I would strongly recommend that it be read and studied chiefly as a companion of the Bible, and always with the Bible in the hand; and that every reference to the sacred volume be immediately looked out, and the passages, or the sense of them, faithfully impressed upon the memory. In this way, not only will a great amount of biblical knowledge be acquired by degrees, but the mind of the learner, by thus comparing the statements of facts with the authorities on which they rest, is ever gaining discipline and strength, and learning to 'prove all things, and hold fast that which is good.'

"That, through this little work the Editor may be useful in his day and generation to his youthful friends, by enlarging and facilitating their acquaintance with that HOLY BOOK in which alone are contained the words of eternal life, and treasures of wisdom that will never fail, is his sincere and fervent prayer."

NEW YORK, 1859.

A
DICTIONARY
OF
THE HOLY BIBLE.

A, the first letter in almost all alphabets. In Hebrew, it is called *aleph;* in Greek, *alpha*, the last letter in the Greek alphabet being *omega.* Both the Hebrews and Greeks used their letters as numerals; and hence A (*aleph* or *alpha*) denoted *one*, or *the first*. So our Lord says, "I am *Alpha* and *Omega*, the beginning and the end, the first and the last;" thus declaring his eternity, and that he is the cause and end of all things, Rev. 1:8, 11; 21:6; 22:13. Compare Isa. 44:6; 48:12; Col. 1:15-18.

AAR'ON, the son of Amram and Jochebed, of the tribe of Levi, and brother of Moses and Miriam, Ex. 6:20; born about the year A. M. 2430; B. C. 1574. He was three years older than Moses, Ex. 7:7; and was the spokesman and assistant of the latter in bringing Israel out of Egypt, Ex. 4:16. His wife was Elisheba, daughter of Amminadab; and his sons, Nadab, Abihu, Eleazar, and Ithamar. He was 83 years old when God summoned him to join Moses in the desert near Horeb. Coöperating with his brother in the exodus from Egypt, Ex. 4-16, he held up his hands in the battle with Amalek, Ex. 17; and ascended mount Sinai with him to see the glory of God, Ex. 24:1, 2, 9-11.

Aaron's chief distinction consisted in the choice of him and his male posterity for the priesthood. He was consecrated the first high-priest by God's directions, Ex. 28, 29; Lev. 8; and was afterwards confirmed in his office by the destruction of Korah and his company, by the staying of the plague at his intercession, and by the budding of his rod, Num. 16, 17. He was faithful and self-sacrificing in the duties of his office, and meekly "held his peace" when his sons Nadab and Abihu were slain, Lev. 10:1-3. Yet he fell sometimes into grievous sins: he made the golden calf at Sinai, Ex. 32; he joined Miriam in sedition against Moses, Num. 12; and with Moses disobeyed God at Kadesh, Num. 20:8-12. God, therefore, did not permit him to enter the promised land; but he died on mount Hor, in Edom, in the fortieth year after leaving Egypt, at the age of about 123 years, Num. 20:22-29; 33:39. In Deut. 10:6, he is said to have died at Mosera, which was probably the station in the valley west of mount Hor, whence he ascended into the mount. The Arabs still pretend to show his tomb on the mount, and highly venerate it. In his office as high-priest, Aaron was an eminent type of Christ, being "called of God," and anointed; bearing the names of the tribes on his breast; communicating God's will by Urim and Thummim; entering the Most Holy place on the Day of Atonement, "not without blood;" and interceding for and blessing the people of God. See PRIEST.

AAR'ONITES, descendants of Aaron the high-priest, so called 1 Chr. 12:27; 27:17. Thirteen cities were assigned to them, in Judah and Benjamin, Josh. 21:13-19; 1 Chr. 6:57-60.

AB, *father*, found in many compound Hebrew proper names: as Abner, father of light; Absalom, father of peace.

AB. The fifth month of the sacred, and the eleventh of the civil year among the Jews. It began, according to the latest authorities, with the new moon of August. It was a sad month in the Jewish calendar. On its first day, a fast was observed for the death of Aaron, Num. 33:38; and on its ninth, another was held in memory of the divine edicts which excluded so many that came out of Egypt from entering the promised land; and also, of the overthrow of the first and second temple. See MONTH.

ABAD'DON, or APOL'LYON. The former name is Hebrew, and the latter Greek, and both signify *the destroyer*, Rev. 9:11. He is called the "angel of the abyss," that is, the angel of death, or the destroying angel.

RIVER ABANA, NOW BARADA, AND DAMASCUS.

AB'ANA, and PHAR'PAR, rivers of Damascus, 2 Kin. 5:12. The Abana, (or, as in the margin, Amana,) was undoubtedly the present Barada, the Chrysorrhoas of the Greeks. It is a clear, cold, and swift mountain stream, rising in Anti-Lebanon, north-east of Hermon, flowing south-east into the plain, and near Damascus turning eastward, skirting the northern wall of the city, and terminating 20 miles east in one of three large lakes. It is a perennial river, and so copious, that though no less than nine or ten branches or canals are drawn off from it to irrigate the plain and supply the city and the villages around it, the stream is a large one to the end.

The only other independent river of any size in the territory of Damascus is the Awaj, which crosses the plain south of Damascus, and enters the southernmost of the three lakes above referred to. This is supposed to be the Pharpar of the Bible. As these rivers of Damascus were never dry, but made the region they watered like the garden of Eden for fertility and beauty, Naaman might well contrast them with most of "the waters of Israel," which dry up under the summer sun. See AMANA.

AB'ARIM, mountains east of the Dead sea and the lower Jordan, "over against Jericho," within the territory of Moab and the tribe of Reuben. It is impossible to define exactly their extent. The mountains Nebo, Pisgah, and Peor were in the Abarim, Num. 27:12; 33:47, 48; Deut. 32:49; 34:1. Ije-abarim, Num. 21:11, seems to denote the southern part of the same chain.

AB'BA, a Syriac word signifying *father*. When the Jews came to speak Greek, this word may have been retained from their ancient language, as being easier to pronounce, especially for children, than the Greek *patĕr*. It expresses the peculiar tenderness, familiarity, and confidence of the love between parent and child, Mark 14:36; Rom. 8:15; Gal. 4:6.

ABED'NEGO, *servant of Nego*; a Chaldee name given to Azariah, one of the three captive young princes of Judah, who were Daniel's companions at the court of the king of Babylon, Dan. 1:7. Their virtue, wisdom, and piety secured their promotion at court, Dan. 1:3–19; 2:17, 49; and their steadfastness in witnessing for God among idolaters, with their deliverance from the fiery furnace by the Angel-Jehovah, led many to acknowledge the true God, and rendered these pious youth for ever illustrious as monuments of the excellence and safety of faith in Him, Dan. 3; Heb. 11:34. See FURNACE.

A'BEL, the second son of Adam and Eve. He became a shepherd, and offered to God a sacrifice from his flocks, at the same time that Cain his brother offered of the fruits of the earth. God had respect to Abel's sacrifice, and not to Cain's; hence Cain in anger killed Abel, Gen. 4. It was "by faith" that Abel offered a more acceptable sacrifice than Cain; that is, his heart was right towards God, and he worshipped Him in trustful obedience to the divine directions. His offering, made by the shedding of blood, was that of a penitent sinner confiding in the atonement ordained of God; and it was accepted, "God testifying of his gifts," probably by fire from heaven; "by which he obtained witness that he was righteous," that is, justified, Heb. 11:4. "The blood of Abel" called from the ground for vengeance, Gen. 4:10; but the blood of Christ claims forgiveness and salvation for his people, Heb. 12:24; 1 John 1:7.

ABEL is also a prefix in the names of several towns. In such cases it signifies a grassy place or meadow.

ABEL-BETH-MA'ACHAH, *meadow of the house of Maachah;* a town in the tribe of Naphtali, north of lake Merom. It was besieged in the rebellion of Sheba, 2 Sam. 20:13–22; eighty years afterwards it was taken by Ben-hadad, 1 Kin. 15:20, and again, after 200 years, by Tiglath-pileser, 2 Kin. 15:29. It is called Abel-maim in 2 Chr. 16:4. Compare 1 Kin. 15:20. Also simply Abel, 2 Sam. 20:18.

ABEL-CARMA'IM, *meadow of vineyards;* a village of the Ammonites, six miles from Rabbath-Ammon; in the history of Jephthah it is called "the plain of the vineyards," Judg. 11:33.

ABEL-MEHO'LAH, or ABEL-MEA, a town of Issachar, near the Jordan, ten miles south of Beth-shean. Near this place Gideon defeated the Midianites, Judg. 7:22; and here Elisha was born, 1 Kin. 19:16.

ABEL-MIZRA'IM, *meadow of the Egyptians;* so called from the seven days' lamentation of Joseph and his company, on bringing up the body of Jacob from Egypt for burial, Gen. 50:10, 11. It lay in the plain of Jericho, between that city and the Jordan.

ABEL-SHIT'TIM, in the plains of Moab, east of the Jordan, and near mount Peor. It was one of the last encampments of Israel before the death of Moses, Num. 33:49; called also Shittim, Josh. 2:1. Here the Israelites were enticed by the women of Moab and Midian into uncleanness and the idolatry of Baal-peor, and 24,000 died of the plague, Num. 25.

ABI'A, in the New Testament the same as ABIJAH in the Old Testament, which see.

ABI'AH, second son of Samuel, who appointed his brother and him judges in Israel. Their corruption and injustice were the pretext upon which the people demanded a king, 1 Sam. 8:1–5.

ABI'ATHAR, son of Ahimelech, and tenth high-priest of the Jews. When Saul sent his emissaries to Nob, to destroy all the priests there, Abiathar, who was young, fled to David in the wilderness, 1 Sam. 22:11–23, with whom he continued in the character of priest, 1 Sam. 23:9; 30:7. Being confirmed in the high-priesthood on David's accession to the throne, he aided in bringing up the ark to Jerusalem, 1 Chr. 15:11, 12, and adhered to David during the rebellion of Absalom, 2 Sam. 15:35, but afterwards was led to follow Adonijah, thus strangely betraying his royal friend in his old age. Solomon succeeding to the throne, degraded him from the priesthood, and sent him to Anathoth, 1 Kin. 2:26, 27; thus fulfilling the prediction made to Eli 150 years before, 1 Sam. 2:27–36. Saul, it would appear, had transferred the dignity of the high-priesthood from the line of Ithamar, to which Eli belonged, to that of Eleazar, by conferring the office upon Zadok. Thus there were, at the same time, two high-priests in Israel: Abiathar with David, and Zadok with Saul. This double priesthood continued from the death of Ahimelech till the reign of Solomon, after which the office was held by Zadok and his race alone.

A difficulty arises from the circumstance that, in 1 Kin. 2:27, Abiathar is said to be deprived of the priest's office by Solomon; while in 2 Sam. 8:17; 1 Chr. 18:16; 24:3, 6, 31, Ahimelech the son of Abiathar is said to be high-priest along with Zadok. The most probable solution is, that both father and son each bore the two names Ahimelech and Abiathar, as was not at all unusual among the Jews. See under ABIGAIL. In this way also we may remove the difficulty arising from Mark 2:26, where Abiathar is said to have given David the show-bread, in allusion to 1 Sam. 21:1–6, where it is Ahimelech.

A'BIB, the first month of the ecclesiastical year of the Hebrews; afterwards called Nisan. It answered nearly to our April. Abib signifies green ears of grain, or fresh fruits. It was so named, because grain, particularly barley, was in ear at that time. On the tenth of this month the passover-lamb was set apart; it was killed on the fourteenth towards sunset, and eaten the same evening after the fifteenth day had begun. The seven days from the fifteenth to the twenty-first inclusive, were "the feast of unleavened bread," closing with a solemn convocation, Ex. 12, 13.

ABIE'ZER, great-grandson of Manasseh, Num. 26:29, 30, and founder of the family to which Gideon belonged, Josh. 17:2; Judg. 6:34; 8:2. In this last verse, "the vintage of Abiezer" means the first rout of the Midianites by the 300, mostly Abiezrites; and "the gleaning of the grapes of Ephraim" means the capture of Oreb and Zeeb, and other fruits of the victory, gathered by the Ephraimites.

AB'IGAIL, I., formerly the wife of Nabal of Carmel, and afterwards of David. Upon receiving information of Nabal's ingratitude to David, 1 Sam. 25:14, she loaded several asses with provisions, and attended by some of her domestics went out to meet him. Her manners and conversation gained for her his esteem, and as soon as the days of mourning for Nabal's death, which happened soon afterwards, were over, he made her his wife. The issue of the marriage was, as some critics suppose, two sons, Chileab and Daniel, 2 Sam. 3:3; 1 Chr. 3:1; but it is most probable that these names were borne by one person.

II. A sister of David, and mother of Amasa, 1 Chr. 2:16, 17.

AB'IHAIL, the wife of Rehoboam, king of Judah, 2 Chr. 11:18; the "daughter"—that is here, the descendant—of Eliab, David's brother.

ABI'HU, the second son of Aaron, consecrated to the priesthood with his three brethren, Exod. 28:21; but consumed shortly after by fire from the Lord, with Nadab his brother, for burning incense with common fire instead of that kept perpetually on the altar of burnt-offering, Lev. 10:1–2; 16:12; Num. 16:46. As this is immediately followed by the prohibition of wine to the priests when ministering in the tabernacle, it is not improbable that Nadab and Abihu were intoxicated when thus transgressing. Their death is a solemn warning not to presume to worship God except with incense kindled at the one altar which Christ hath sanctified, Heb. 10:10–14. It is a dangerous thing, in the service of God, to decline from his own institutions. We have to do with a God who is wise to prescribe his own worship, just to require what he has prescribed, and powerful to avenge what he has not prescribed.

ABI'JAH, I., called, in Luke 1:5, Abia; founder of a family among the posterity of Aaron. When David divided the priests into twenty-four courses, to perform the temple-service in turn, the eighth class was called after him, 1 Chr. 24:10. To this class or course Zacharias belonged.

II. Son of Jeroboam, the first king of Israel. He died young, and much beloved and lamented, for in him there was found some good thing towards the Lord, 1 Kin. 14:1–18.

III. Son of Rehoboam, the first king of Judah; called, in 1 Kin. 15:1, Abijam. He came to the throne A. M. 3046, and reigned only three years. In war with Jeroboam he gained a signal victory, 2 Chr. 13; yet he followed the evil example of his father. His mother Maachah, or Michaiah, was probably the *grand*-daughter of Absalom, 1 Kin. 15:2; 2 Chr. 11:20; 13:2.

IV. The mother of king Hezekiah, 2 Chr. 29:1.

ABILE'NE, the name of a district of country on the eastern declivity of Anti-Lebanon, from twelve to twenty miles north-west of Damascus, towards Heliopolis, or Baalbek; so called from the city ABILA, and also called Abilene of

Lysanias, to distinguish it from others. This territory, in the fifteenth year of Tiberius emperor of Rome, was governed as a tetrarchate by a certain Lysanias, Luke 3:1.

ABIM'ELECH, I., king of Gerar of the Philistines, who took Sarah into his harem; but being warned of God in a dream, he restored her to Abraham, and gave him 1,000 pieces of silver as a "covering of the eyes" for Sarah, that is, as an atoning present, and to be a testimony of her innocence in the eyes of all. He afterwards made a league with Abraham, Gen. 20.

II. Another king of Gerar, probably son of the former, and contemporary with Isaac. He rebuked Isaac for dissimulation in regard to Rebekah, and afterwards made a new league with him at Beersheba, Gen. 26.

III. A son of Gideon by a concubine, made himself king of Shechem after his father's death, and slew his father's seventy sons on one stone, only Jotham the youngest being left. Jotham reproached the Shechemites for their conduct, in his celebrated fable of the trees. Three years afterwards, they rose against Abimelech; he defeated them, and destroyed their city, but as he was attacking Thebez, a woman threw down a piece of a millstone on his head, which so injured him, that he called to his armor-bearer to slay him, Judg. 9.

ABIN'ADAB, the same as Aminadab, *b* and *m* being often interchanged in Hebrew. I. A son of Jesse, one of the three who followed Saul in the war with the Philistines, 1 Sam. 16:8; 17:13.

II. A son of Saul, slain in the battle at Gilboa, 1 Sam. 31:2.

III. A Levite of Kirjath-jearim, in whose house the ark of God, when restored by the Philistines, remained seventy years, 1 Sam. 7:1; 1 Chr. 13:7.

ABI'RAM, a prince of Reuben, who with Korah, Dathan, etc., conspired to overthrow the authority of Moses and Aaron in the wilderness, Num. 16.

AB'ISHAG, a beautiful virgin of Shunem, in Issachar, chosen to marry David in his old age and cherish him. After his death, Adonijah sought her hand to promote his treasonable aspirations, and was punished by death, 1 Kin. 1, 2.

ABISH'AI, a son of Zeruiah, David's sister, brother of Joab and Asahel, one of the bravest of David's mighty men, 1 Chr. 2:16, and always faithful to his royal uncle. He went with him alone to the tent of Saul, 1 Sam. 26:7-11; and was a leader in the war with Ish-bosheth, 2 Sam. 2:18, 24, in the war with the Edomites, 1 Chr. 18:12, 13, and with the Syrians and Ammonites, 2 Sam. 10:10. In a battle with the Philistines, he rescued David, and slew Ishbi-benob the giant, 2 Sam. 21:16, 17. He lifted up his spear against three hundred, and slew them, 2 Sam. 23:18; and was with David in the affairs of Shimei, Absalom, and Sheba, 2 Sam. 16:9; 18:2; 20:6, 7.

ABISH'UA, son of Phinehas, and fourth high-priest, 1 Chr. 6:50. He was probably a contemporary of Eglon and Ehud, Judg. 3.

AB'NER, the son of Ner, Saul's uncle, and the general of his armies, 1 Sam. 14:50. For seven years after Saul's death, he supported Ish-bosheth; but being reproved by him for his conduct towards Rizpah, he undertook to unite the whole kingdom under David. He was, however, treacherously slain by Joab, either to revenge the death of Asahel, Joab's brother, whom Abner had formerly killed, or more probably from jealousy. David abhorred this perfidious act, and composed an elegy on his death, 2 Sam. 2:8; 3:33. He also charged Solomon to punish the crime of Joab with death, 1 Kin. 2:5, 6.

ABOMINA'TION, a term applied in Scripture to objects of great detestation. Idols and their worship were so named, because they robbed God of his honor, while the rites themselves were impure and cruel, Deut. 7:25, 26; 12:31. The term was used respecting the Hebrews in Egypt, Gen. 43:32, Ex. 8:26, either because they ate and sacrificed animals held sacred by the Egyptians, or because they did not observe those ceremonies in eating which made a part of the religion of Egypt; and in Gen. 46:34, because they were "wandering shepherds," a race of whom had grievously oppressed Egypt.

The ABOMINATION OF DESOLATION foretold by Daniel, 9:27, denotes, probably, the image of Jupiter, erected in the temple of Jerusalem by command of Antiochus Epiphanes, 2 Mac. 6:2; 1 Mac. 6:7. But by the Abomination of Desolation spoken of by our Lord, Matt. 24:15; Mark 13:14, and foretold as about to be seen at Jerusalem during the last siege of that city by the Romans under Titus, is probably meant the Roman army, whose standards had the images of their gods and emperors upon them, and were

worshipped in the precincts of the temple when that and the city were taken. Luke 21:20. See ARMOR.

A'BRAM, *high father*, afterwards named A'BRAHAM, *father of a multitude*, Gen. 17:4, 5; the great founder of the Jewish nation. He was a son of Terah, a descendant of Shem, and born in Ur, a city of Chaldea, A. M. 2008, B. C. 1996, Gen. 11:27, 28. Here he lived seventy years, when at the call of God he left his idolatrous kindred, and removed to Haran, in Mesopotamia, Acts 7:2-4, accompanied by his father, his wife Sarai, his brother Nahor, and his nephew Lot. A few years after, having buried his father, he again removed at the call of God, with his wife and nephew, and entered the land of promise as a nomade or wandering shepherd. Sojourning for a time at Shechem, he built here, as was his custom, an altar to the Lord, who appeared to him, and promised that land to his seed. Removing from place to place for convenience of water and pasturage, he was at length driven by a famine into Egypt, where he dissembled in calling his wife his sister, Gen. 12. Returning to Canaan rich in flocks and herds, he left Lot to dwell in the fertile valley of the lower Jordan, and pitched his own tents in Mamre, Gen. 13. A few years after, he rescued Lot and his friends from captivity, and received the blessing of Melchizedek, Gen. 14. Again God appeared to him, promised that his seed should be like the stars for number, and foretold their oppression in Egypt 400 years, and their return to possess the promised land, Gen. 15. But the promise of a son being yet unfulfilled, Sarai gave him Hagar her maid for a secondary wife, of whom Ishmael was born, Gen. 16. After thirteen years, God again appeared to him, and assured him that the heir of the promise should yet be born of his wife, whose name was then changed to Sarah. He established also the covenant of circumcision, Gen. 17. Here, too, occurred the visit of the three angels, and the memorable intercession with the Angel-Jehovah for the inhabitants of Sodom, Gen. 18. After this, Abraham journeyed south to Gerah, where he again called Sarah his sister. In this region Isaac was born; and soon after, Hagar and Ishmael were driven out to seek a new home, Gen. 21. About twenty-five years after, God put to trial the faith of Abraham, by commanding him to sacrifice Isaac, his son and the heir of the promise, upon mount Moriah, Gen. 22. Twelve years after, Sarah died, and the cave of Machpelah was bought for a burial-place, Gen. 23. Abraham sent his steward, and obtained a wife for Isaac from his pious kindred in Mesopotamia, Gen. 24. He himself also married Keturah, and had six sons, each one the founder of a distinct people in Arabia. At the age of 175, full of years and honors, he died, and was buried by his sons in the same tomb with Sarah, Gen. 25.

The character of Abraham is one of the most remarkable in Scripture. He was a genuine oriental patriarch, a prince in the land; his property was large, his retinue very numerous, and he commanded the respect of the neighboring people: and yet he was truly a stranger and a pilgrim, the only land he possessed being the burial-place he had purchased. Distinguished by his integrity, generosity, and hospitality, he was most of all remarkable for his simple and unwavering faith, a faith that obeyed without hesitation or delay, and recoiled not from the most fearful trial ever imposed upon man, so that he is justly styled "the father of the faithful," that is, of believers. No name in history is venerated by so large a portion of the human race. Mohammedans as well as Jews and Christians. As the ancestor of Christ, in whom all the nations are blessed, and as the father of all believers, the covenant is abundantly fulfilled to him: his seed are as the stars of heaven, and with them he shall inherit the heavenly Canaan.

ABRAHAM'S BOSOM. In Luke 16:22, Lazarus is said to have been carried to Abraham's bosom, that is, to the state of bliss in paradise which the father of the faithful was enjoying. This is often represented by a feast, by sitting down to a banquet, Matt. 8:11; Luke 13:29. *To lie on one's bosom* refers to the oriental mode of reclining at table, John 13:23. See EATING.

AB'SALOM, only son of David by Maacah, 2 Sam. 3:3. He was remarkable for his beauty and for his fine head of hair, 2 Sam. 14:25, which being cut from time to time when it incommoded him, used to weigh 200 shekels by the king's standard, that is, probably about thirty ounces, an extraordinary, but not incredible weight. Amnon, another of the king's sons, having violated his sister Tamar, Absalom caused him to be slain, and then fled to Geshur, where Talmai his grandfather was king. After three years, at the intercession of Joab, David permitted him to return to Jerusalem, and at length received him again into favor, 2 Sam. 14. Absalom, however, grossly abused his father's kindness; he soon began to play the demagogue, and by many artful devices "stole the hearts of the people," and got himself proclaimed king in Hebron. David retired from Jerusalem; Absalom followed him; and in the battle which ensued, the troops of the latter were defeated, and he himself, being caught by his head in a tree, was found and slain by Joab. David was much affected by his death, and uttered bitter lamentations over him, 2 Sam. 18:33.

His history affords instructive lessons to the young against the sins to which they are prone, particularly vanity, ambition, lawless passions, and filial disobedience.

AC'CAD, one of the four cities built in the plain of Shinar by Nimrod, founder of the Assyrian empire, Gen. 10:10. Its site is identified by some travellers with ruins which lie from six to nine miles west of Bagdad. There is here a ruinous structure called Tell-i-nimrood, Hill of Nimrod, consisting of a mass of brickwork 400 feet in circumference at the base, and 125 feet high, standing on a mound of rubbish. More recently, Col. Rawlinson claims that the site of Accad was at a place now called Niffer, amid the marshes of Southern Babylonia.

AC'CHO, a city of the tribe of Asher, Judg. 1:31. In the New Testament, Accho is called Ptolemais, Acts 21:7, from one of the Ptolemies, who enlarged and beautified it. The crusaders gave it the name of Acre, or St. John of Acre. It is still called Akka by the Turks. It sustained several sieges during the crusades, and was the last fortified place wrested from the Christians by the Turks.

The town is situated on the coast of the Mediterranean sea, thirty miles south of Tyre, on the north angle of a bay to which it gives its name, and which extends in a semicircle of three leagues, as far as the point of mount Carmel, south-west of Acre. After its memorable siege by Buonaparte, when he was repulsed by Sir Sidney Smith, in 1799, Accho was much improved and strengthened, and its population was estimated at from 18,000 to 20,000. It has since then suffered greatly, having been besieged six months by Ibrahim Pacha, in 1832, and bombarded by an English fleet in 1840. Present population, (1859,) 10,000 or 12,000.

Accho, and all the sea-coast beyond it northwards, was considered as the heathen land of the Jews.

ACEL'DAMA, *field of blood*, a small field south of Jerusalem, which the priests purchased with the thirty pieces of silver that Judas had received as the price of our Saviour's blood, Matt. 27:8; Acts 1:19. Pretending that it was not lawful to appropriate this money to sacred uses, because it was the price of blood, they purchased with it the so called potter's field, to be a burying-place for strangers. Judas is said, Acts 1:8, to have purchased the field, because it was bought with his money. Tradition points out this field on the steep side of the hill of Evil Counsel overhanging the valley of Hinnom on the south. It appears to have been used, since the time of the crusaders, as a sepulchre for pilgrims, and subsequently by the Armenians. At present it is not thus used.

ACHA'IA is used in the New Testament for the whole region of Greece south of

Macedonia, including the Peloponnesus, or Morea, and some territory north of the gulf of Corinth, Acts 18:12; 19:21; 2 Cor. 11:10. Achaia Proper, however, was a province of Greece, of which Corinth was the capital, and embraced the north-western part of the Peloponnesus. See GREECE.

A'CHAN, the son of Carmi, who disobeyed the strict charge of the Lord, and purloined some of the spoils of Jericho which were doomed to destruction. This brought a curse and defeat upon the people. He was discovered by lot, and stoned with all his family in the valley of Achor, north of Jericho, Josh. 6:18; 7:1-26. He is called Achar in 1 Chr. 2:7.

A'CHISH, king of Gath, a city of the Philistines, to whom David twice fled for protection from Saul. On the first occasion, being recognized by the king's officers, and thinking his life in danger, he feigned madness, and by this device escaped, 1 Sam. 21:10. Several years after, he returned with a band of 600 men, and was welcomed by Achish as an enemy of Saul and of Israel. Achish gave him Ziklag for a residence; and being deceived as to the views and operations of David, expected his assistance in a war with Israel, but was persuaded by his officers to send him home to Ziklag, 1 Sam. 27-29.

ACH'METHA, Ezra 6:2, supposed to mean Ecbatana, a city of Media, inferior to none in the East but Babylon and Nineveh. It was surrounded by seven walls, of different heights and colors, and was a summer residence of the Persian kings after Cyrus. Travellers identify it with the modern Hamadan, in which many Jews still reside, and where they profess to point out the tomb of Mordecai and Esther.

A'CHOR, *trouble*, a valley north of Jericho; so called, perhaps, from the troubles occasioned by the sin of Achan, who was here put to death, Josh. 7:26. The prophets allude to it with promises of hope and joy in the gospel era, Isa. 65:10; Hos. 2:15.

ACH'SAH, the daughter of Caleb, given in marriage with a large dowry to his nephew Othniel, as a prize for taking the city Debir, Josh. 15:15-17; Judg. 1:12,13.

ACH'SHAPH, a royal city of the Canaanites, Josh. 11:1, conquered by Joshua, and assigned to the tribe of Asher, Josh. 12:20; 19:25.

ACH'ZIB, a city of Asher, from which, however, the Jews were unable to expel the Canaanites, Judg. 1:31. It was afterwards called by the Greeks, Ecdippa, and is now named Zib; it lay on the seacoast, ten miles north of Acre.

ACTS OF THE APOSTLES, a canonical book of the New Testament, written by Luke as a sequel to his gospel, and a history in part of the early church. It is not, however, a record of the acts of all the apostles, but chiefly of those of Peter and Paul. In his gospel, Luke described the *founding* of Christianity in what Christ did, taught, and suffered: in the Acts he illustrates its *diffusion*, selecting what was best fitted to show how the Holy Spirit guided and blessed the first followers of Christ in building up his church. Beginning where his gospel ended, he narrates the ascension of the Saviour and the conduct of the disciples thereupon; the outpouring of the Holy Spirit according to Christ's promise; the miraculous preaching of the apostles, their amazing success, and the persecutions raised against them; with other events of moment to the church at Jerusalem, till they were scattered abroad. He then shows how Judaism was superseded, and how Peter was led to receive to Christian fellowship converts from the Gentiles. The remainder of the narrative is devoted to the conversion and calling of the apostle Paul, his missionary zeal, labors, and sufferings, and ends with his two years' imprisonment at Rome.

Luke himself witnessed, to a great extent, the events he narrates. His Greek is the most classical in the New Testament; and the view he gives of the spirit of the early church, so many of whose members had "been with the Lord," is invaluable. The book was probably written about A. D. 64, that is, soon after the time at which the narration terminates. The place where it was written is not known.

In order to read the Acts of the Apostles with intelligence and profit, it is necessary to have a sufficient acquaintance with geography, with the manners of the times and people referred to, and with the leading historical events. The power of the Romans, with the nature and names of the public offices they established, and the distinctions among them, must be understood, as well as the disposition and political opinions of the unconverted Jewish nation, which were too prevalent among the Christianized Hebrews.

AD'AM, the progenitor and representative head of our race; formed of the dust of the ground, and made a living soul by the Creator's breath. He was the last work of the creation, and received dominion over all that the earth contained. That he might not be alone, God provided Eve as a helpmeet for him, and she became his wife. Marriage is thus a divine institution, first in order of time, as well as of importance and blessedness to mankind. Adam was made a perfect man—complete in every physical, mental, and spiritual endowment; and placed in the garden of Eden on probation, holy and happy, but liable to sin. From this estate he fell by breaking the express command of God, through the temptations of Satan and the compliance of Eve; and thus brought the curse upon himself and all his posterity. Sovereign grace interposed; a Saviour was revealed, and the full execution of the curse stayed; but Adam was banished from Eden and its tree of life, and reduced to a life of painful toil. His happiness was farther imbittered by witnessing the fruits of his fall in his posterity. Cain his first-born son, and Abel the second, born in the likeness of their fallen parents, were ere long lost to them—the one slain, and the other a fugitive. They probably had many other sons and daughters, but the name of Seth alone is given. Adam lived to the age of nine hundred and thirty years, and saw the earth rapidly peopled by his descendants; but "the wickedness of man was great upon the earth." At the time of his death, Lamech, the father of Noah, was fifty-six years of age; and being in the line of those who "walked with God," had probably heard the early history of the race from the lips of the penitent Adam.

The curse pronounced on man includes not only physical labor and toil on a barren and thorny earth, and the physical dissolution of the body, but also the exposure of the soul, the nobler part, to "everlasting death." In that very day he should lose the moral image of his Maker, and become subject not only to physical death, but also to God's eternal wrath and curse, which is death in the highest sense of the word, and is the doom which has fallen upon all his race. Such is the view of the apostle Paul; who everywhere contrasts the *death* introduced into the world through Adam, with the *life* which is procured for our race through Jesus Christ, Rom. 5. This life is spiritual; and the death, in its highest sense, is also spiritual. So far as the penalty is temporal and physical, no man is or can be exempt from it; but to remove the spiritual and eternal punishment, Christ has died; and he who comes to him in penitence and faith will avoid the threatened death, and enter into life eternal, both of the body and the soul.

The Redeemer is called "the second Adam," 1 Cor. 15:45, as being the head of his spiritual seed, and the source of righteousness and life to all believers, as the first Adam was the source of sin and death to all his seed.

II. A city near the Jordan, towards the sea of Tiberias, at some distance from which the waters of the Jordan were heaped up for the passage of the Jews, Josh. 3:16.

AD'AMANT, a name anciently used for the diamond, the hardest of all minerals. It is used for cutting or writing upon glass and other hard substances, Jer. 17:1. It is also employed figuratively, Ezek. 3:9; Zech. 7:12. Others suppose the *smiris*, or emery, to be meant.

AD'DER, a species of serpent, more commonly called viper. The word adder

is used five times in the Bible, as a translation of four different Hebrew words, denoting different serpents of the venomous sort. In Gen. 49:17, it seems to mean the cerastes, or horned viper, of the color of sand, and very deadly bite; accustomed to lie hidden in the tracks in the sand, and dart up on the unwary traveller. In Psa. 58:4; 91:13, it is probably the asp. In Psa. 140:3 perhaps the tarantula, or some serpent that strikes backward. See SERPENT, VIPER.

A'DAR, the twelfth month of the Hebrew ecclesiastical year, and the sixth of the civil year. In this month occurred the celebrated feast of Purim. It nearly answers to our March. As the lunar year, which the Jews follow, is shorter than the solar year by eleven days, which, after three years, make about a month, they then insert a thirteenth month, which they call *Ve-Adar*, or a second Adar. See MONTH.

AD'MAH, one of the four cities in the plain of Siddim, destroyed by fire from heaven and covered by the Dead sea, Gen. 14:2; 19:24, 25; Hos. 11:8.

ADONI-BE'ZEK, *lord of Bezek*, a Canaanite tyrant of Bezek, east of Shechem. Having taken seventy of the neighboring petty chiefs, he disabled them by cutting off their thumbs and great toes, and fed them like dogs. The same barbarous treatment was meted out to him, when defeated at the head of an army of Canaanites and Perizzites, by Judah and Simeon, Judg. 1:4-7.

ADONI'JAH, the fourth son of David, by Haggith, 2 Sam. 3:4. After the death of Amnon and Absalom, he aspired to the throne, although it was promised to Solomon, his younger brother. Having gained over Joab and Abiathar and other adherents, he at length openly revolted and claimed the crown while David was yet living. The news of this revolt being brought to the king, he caused Solomon to be crowned king at once; upon which the friends of Adonijah dispersed, and he took refuge at the horns of the altar. Solomon dismissed him with only an admonition. But soon after the death of David, he applied for the hand of Abishag, thus renewing his pretensions to the throne, for which he was put to death, 1 Kin. 1, 2.

ADONI-ZE'DEK, a king of Jerusalem, who made an alliance with four other kings against Joshua. A great battle was fought at Gibeon, where the Lord aided Israel by a terrific hailstorm, and by miraculously prolonging the day. The five kings were utterly routed, and hid themselves in a cave at Makkedah; but were taken by Joshua, and put to death, Josh. 10.

ADONI'RAM, a receiver of tributes under David and Solomon, and director of the thirty thousand men sent to Lebanon to cut timber, 1 Kin. 5:14. The same person is also called Adoram, by contraction, 2 Sam. 20:24; 1 Kin. 12:18; and also Hadoram, 2 Chr. 10:18. He was stoned to death by the revolted ten tribes, having been sent to them by Rehoboam, either to induce them to return, or to test them by gathering the taxes.

ADOP'TION is an act by which a person takes a stranger into his family, acknowledges him for his child, and constitutes him heir of his estate. Jacob's adoption of his two grandsons, Ephraim and Manasseh, Gen. 48:5, was a kind of substitution, whereby he intended that these his grandsons should have each his lot in Israel, as if they had been his own sons: "Ephraim and Manasseh are mine; as Reuben and Simeon, they shall be mine." As he gives no inheritance to their father Joseph, the effect of this adoption was simply the doubling of their inheritance.

But Scripture affords instances of another kind of adoption—that of a father having a daughter only, and adopting her children. Thus, 1 Chr. 2:21, Machir, grandson of Joseph, and father of Gilead, Num. 26:29, gave his daughter to Hezron, "who took her; and he was a son of sixty years," sixty years of age, "and she bare him Segub; and Segub begat Jair, who had twenty-three cities in the land of Gilead," Josh. 13:30; 1 Kin. 4:13. However, as well he as his posterity, instead of being reckoned to the family of Judah, as they would have been by their paternal descent from Hezron, are reckoned as sons of Machir, the father of Gilead. Nay, more, it appears, Num. 32:41, that this Jair, who was in fact the son of Segub, the son of Hezron, the son of Judah, is expressly called "Jair, the son of Manasseh," because his maternal great-grandfather was Machir the son of Manasseh. In like manner we read that Mordecai adopted Esther, his niece; he took her to himself to be a daughter, Esth. 2:7. So the daughter of Pharaoh adopted Moses; and he became her son, Ex. 2:10. So we read, Ruth 4:17, that Naomi had a son—a son is born to Naomi; when indeed it was the son of Ruth.

At the present day, adoption is not

uncommon in the East, where it is made before a public officer with legal forms.

In the New Testament, adoption denotes that act of God's free grace by which, on being justified through faith, we are received into the family of God, and made heirs of the inheritance of heaven. It is "in Christ," and through his atoning merits, that believers "receive the adoption of sons," Gal. 4:4, 5. Some of the privileges of this state are, deliverance from a fearful and servile spirit; the special love and care of our heavenly Father; conformity to his image; a filial confidence in him; free access to him at all times; the witness of the Holy Spirit, whereby we cry, "Abba, Father;" and a title to our heavenly home, Rom. 8:14–17; Eph. 1:4, 5.

ADORA'IM, a town in the south of Judah, fortified by Rehoboam, 2 Chr. 11:9. Robinson has identified it with the modern Dura, a large village five miles west by south from Hebron.

ADO'RAM, see ADONIRAM.

ADRAM'MELECH, I., son of Sennacherib, king of Assyria, Isa. 37:38, 2 Kin. 19:37, who, upon returning to Nineveh after his fatal expedition against Hezekiah, was killed by his two sons, Adrammelech and Sharezer, through fear, according to a Jewish tradition, of being sacrificed to his idol Nisroch. They then fled to the mountains of Armenia, B. C. 713.

II. One of the gods adored by the inhabitants of Sepharvaim, who settled in Samaria, in the stead of those Israelites who were carried beyond the Euphrates. They made their children pass through fire, in honor of this false deity, and of another called Anammelech, 2 Kin. 17:31. Some think that Adrammelech represented the sun, and Anammelech the moon.

ADRAMYT'TIUM, a maritime town of Mysia, in Asia Minor, opposite to the island of Lesbos, Acts 27:2. It is now called Adramyt.

A'DRIA, in Acts 27:27, is the Adriatic sea. This term now denotes only the Gulf of Venice; but in St. Paul's time it included the whole sea lying between Italy and Greece, and extending on the south from Crete to Sicily, within which the island of Malta or Melita lies. So Ptolemy and Strabo.

A'DRIEL, a son of Barzillai, married Merab, daughter of Saul, who had been promised to David, 1 Sam. 18:19. Adriel had five sons by her, who were delivered up to the Gibeonites, to be put to death before the Lord, to avenge the cruelty of Saul their grandfather against the Gibeonites. In 2 Sam. 21:8, these are said to be the sons of Michal, whom she "brought up" for Adriel; but unless this is a copyist's error, Michal had adopted the children of her sister Merab, who was perhaps dead; or possibly both sisters may have borne the name Michal. Compare under ABIATHAR.

ADUL'LAM, an ancient city in the plain of Judah, south-west of Jerusalem, Gen. 38:1; Josh. 15:35. Its king was slain by Joshua, Josh. 12:15. It was one of the cities rebuilt and fortified by Rehoboam, 2 Chr. 11:7; Mic. 1:15, and was reoccupied by the Jews after the captivity, Neh. 11:30.

When David withdrew from Achish, king of Gath, he retired to the "cave of Adullam," 1 Sam. 22:1; 2 Sam. 23:13. The location of this cave, however, is uncertain. Tradition places it in the hill country, about six miles south-east of Bethlehem, the city of David; a large and fine cave, visited by many travellers. It is capable of holding thousands.

ADUL'TERY is a criminal connection between persons who are engaged, one or both, to keep themselves wholly to others; and thus it exceeds the guilt of fornication, which is the same intercourse between unmarried persons. As the highest sin of its kind, and so including all other sins of the flesh, it is forbidden in the seventh commandment. Where polygamy was allowed, as among the ancient Jews, illicit intercourse between a married man and a woman who was not married, nor betrothed, constituted not adultery, but fornication.

Fornication may be, in some sense, covered by a subsequent marriage of the parties; but adultery cannot be so healed. Hence God often compares himself to a husband jealous of his honor, Jer. 31:32; and hence the forsaking of the true God is compared to fornication and adultery of the vilest kind, Jer. 3:9; Ezek. 23:36–49.

By the law of Moses, both the man and the woman who had committed adultery were punished with death, Lev. 20:10; 21:9; John 8:5. A woman suspected of this crime might, in order to clear herself, drink the "water of jealousy," as prescribed in Num. 5.

ADUM'MIM, a border town of Benjamin and Judah, not far from Jericho on the road to Jerusalem. This road ascends through a desolate and rocky region, "the ascent of Adummim," Josh. 15:7; 18:17; it furnished many lurking places for robbers, and was the scene of our Saviour's parable, The good Samaritan, Luke 10.

AD'VOCATE, or PAR'ACLETE, one that pleads the cause of another. In its technical sense, the office was unknown to the Jews till they became subject to the Romans. It is applied to Christ as our intercessor, 1 John 2:1; compare Rom. 8:34; Heb. 7:25; and to the Holy Spirit, as our teacher and comforter, John 14:16; 15:26.

Æ'NON, see ENON.

AFFIN'ITY, 1 Kin. 3:1; relationship by marriage; as consanguinity is relationship by blood. The degrees within which relatives were forbidden by the Levitical law to intermarry, may be found in Lev. 18.

AG'ABUS, "a prophet" of the early church, perhaps one of "the seventy" disciples of Christ. He foretold the famine, of which Suetonius and others speak, in the days of Claudius, A. D. 44. It was very severe in Judea; and aid was sent to the church at Jerusalem from Antioch, Acts 11:27. Many years after, Agabus predicted the sufferings of Paul at the hands of the Jews, Acts 21:10.

A'GAG, a general name of the kings of the Amalekites; apparently like Pharaoh for the Egyptian kings, Num. 24:7; 1 Sam. 15:8. The last one mentioned in Scripture was "hewed in pieces" by Samuel, before the Lord, because Saul had sinfully spared him and the flocks and herds, when ordered utterly to exterminate them. He seems to have incurred an uncommon punishment by infamous cruelties, 1 Sam. 15:33.

Agagite, in Esther 3:1, 10; 8:3, 5, is used to mark the nation whence Haman sprung. Josephus explains the word by Amalekite.

AG'ATE, a precious stone, said to take its name from the river Achates in Sicily, where it abounded. Agates, which are of several kinds, are likewise procured in India, in various parts of Europe, and at the Cape of Good Hope. They are semi-transparent, and often are beautifully veined and clouded, and present in miniature the picture of many natural objects. The agate was the second stone in the third row of the high-priest's breastplate, Ex. 28:19; 39:12.

AGRIP'PA, see HEROD III., IV.

A'GUR, an inspired Hebrew, author of the thirtieth chapter of Proverbs, incorporated with those of Solomon.

A'HAB, I., the sixth king of Israel, succeeded his father Omri B. C. 918, and reigned twenty-two years. His wife was Jezebel, daughter of Ethbaal king of Tyre; an ambitious and passionate idolatress, through whose influence the worship of Baal and Ashtoreth was introduced in Israel. Ahab erected in Samaria a house of Baal, and set up images of Baal and Ashtoreth; idolatry and wickedness became fearfully prevalent, and the king "did more to provoke the Lord to anger than all the kings that were before him." In the midst of this great apostasy, God visited the land with three years of drought and famine; and then, at mount Carmel, reproved idolatry by fire from heaven, and by the destruction of four hundred and fifty prophets of Baal. About six years later, Ben-hadad, king of Syria, invaded Israel with a great army, but was ignominiously defeated; and still more disastrously the year after, when Ahab took him captive, but soon released him, and thus incurred the displeasure of God. In spite of the warnings and mercies of Providence, Ahab went on in sin; and at length, after the murder of Naboth, his crimes and abominable idolatries were such that God sent Elijah to denounce judgments upon him and his seed. These were in part deferred, however, by his apparent humiliation. Soon after, having gone with Jehoshaphat, king of Judah, to regain Ramoth-gilead from the Syrians, and joined battle with them in defiance of Jehovah, he was slain, and dogs licked up his blood at the pool of Samaria, 1 Kin. 16:29 to 22:40.

II. A false prophet, who seduced the Israelites at Babylon, and was denounced by Jeremiah, Jer. 29:21, 22.

AHASUE'RUS, a royal title, common to several Median and Persian kings named in Scripture. I. The father of Darius the Mede, Dan. 9:1. The most probable opinion is, that the name here designates Astyages, the grandfather of Cyrus. See below, and DARIUS I.

II. Mentioned Ezra 4:6, the son and successor of Cyrus; probably Cambyses, who reigned seven and a half years from B. C. 529.

III. The husband of Esther, most probably Xerxes. Commentators have been much divided, and have understood under this name all the Persian kings in succession. But the other kings of Persia are all mentioned in Scripture by their own names, or at least definitely pointed out; while Xerxes is not mentioned, unless under this name. Besides, recent researches show that the Hebrew word for Ahasuerus is readily formed from the Persian name of Xerxes, the name Xerxes being only a Greek corruption of the Persian. See ESTHER.

AHA'VA, a town in Chaldea, which gave name to the stream on the banks of which the exiled Jews assembled their second caravan under Ezra, when returning to Jerusalem, Ezra 8:15, 21, 31. It may be the modern Hib on the Euphrates, in the latitude of Bagdad.

A'HAZ, son of Jotham, and twelfth king of Judah. He ascended the throne at twenty years of age, and reigned sixteen years, 2 Kin. 16:1, 2, 20. B. C. 738. He was distinguished for his idolatry and contempt of the true God; and against him many of the prophecies of Isaiah are directed, Isa. 7. He made his own children pass through the fire to idols; he introduced the Syrian gods into Jerusalem, altered the temple after the Syrian model, and even closed it altogether. Having thus forfeited the aid of Jehovah, he met various repulses in battle with Pekah and Rezin; the Edomites revolted, and the Philistines harassed his borders. He turned yet more away from God in his distress, and sought aid from Pul, king of Assyria. This fatal step made him tributary to Pul, and to Tiglath-pileser his successor. Ahaz was reduced to great extremities, in buying off the Assyrians; but became more infatuated still in idolatry, and dying in his impiety at the age of thirty-six, was refused a burial with the kings his ancestors, 2 Chr. 28.

AHAZI'AH, I., son and successor of Ahab, king of Israel, 1 Kin. 22:40, 51; 2 Kin. 1. He reigned two years, alone and with his father, who associated him in the kingdom the year before his death, B. C. 894. Ahaziah imitated Ahab's impiety, and worshipped Baal and Astarte, whose rites had been introduced into Israel by Jezebel his mother. During his reign the Moabites revolted. Having joined king Jehoshaphat in a commercial enterprise on the Red sea, his impiety blasted the whole. After a fall from the gallery of his house, he sent to consult a god of the Philistines as to his recovery. Elijah the prophet foretold his speedy death—first to the messengers, and again to Ahaziah himself, after two companies of fifty had been consumed by fire from heaven.

II. Otherwise Jehoahaz, or Azariah, king of Judah, son of Jehoram and Athaliah; he succeeded his father B. C. 881, 2 Kin. 8:25; 2 Chr. 22:2. He was twenty-two years of age when he ascended the throne, and reigned but one year at Jerusalem. He followed the house of Ahab, to which he was allied by his mother, and did evil. He met his death at the hand of Jehu, while in company with Joram, son of Ahab.

AHI'AH, son of Ahitub, and high-priest in the reign of Saul, 1 Sam. 14:3. He was probably the brother of his successor Ahimelech, slain by Saul, 1 Sam. 22:9.

AHI'JAH, a prophet and chronicler of the times of Solomon and Jeroboam, 1 Kin. 11:29; 2 Chr. 9:29. He is thought to be the person who spoke in God's name to Solomon while building the temple, 1 Kin. 6:11; and again after he fell into sin, 1 Kin. 11:11. He notified Jeroboam of the separation of Israel from Judah, and of the foundation of his house—the ruin of which he afterwards foretold, 1 Kin. 14:1-14.

AHI'KAM, sent by Josiah to Huldah the prophetess, when the book of the law was found in the temple, 2 Kin. 22:12. He afterwards nobly befriended the prophet Jeremiah, Jer. 26:24; 39:14.

AHIM'AAZ, the son and successor of Zadok, became high-priest in the reign of Solomon. During the reign of David, he revealed to him the counsels of Absalom and his advisers in rebellion, 2 Sam. 17:15-21; and conveyed to him also the tidings of Absalom's defeat and death, 2 Sam. 18.

AHIM'ELECH, I., son of Ahitub, and brother of Ahiah, whom he succeeded in the high-priesthood. Some think, however, that both names belong to the same person. During his priesthood the tabernacle was at Nob, where Ahimelech dwelt, with many priests. Here he received David when fleeing from Saul, and gave him the show-bread and Goliath's sword. This act, as reported by Doeg the Edomite, Saul viewed as treasonous; and by the hand of this idolatrous and malignant foreigner, he put Ahimelech and eighty-five other priests of Jehovah to death, 1 Sam. 22—a crime sufficient of itself to forfeit the throne and the favor of God.

II. Also called Abimelech, 1 Chr. 18:16, probably the same as Abiathar, which see, 1 Chr. 24:3, 6, 31.

AHIN'OAM, I., daughter of Ahimaaz and wife of Saul, 1 Sam. 14:50.

II. A woman of Jezreel, wife of David and mother of Amnon. She was taken captive by the Amalekites, at Ziklag, 1 Sam. 30:5; but was recovered by David, and accompanied him to Hebron, 2 Sam. 2:2; 3:2.

AHI'O, a son of Abinadab, who went before the ark of God on its way to Jerusalem from his father's house; thus escaping the fate of Uzzah his brother, 2 Sam. 6:3-7.

AHITH'OPHEL, a native of Giloh, originally one of David's most intimate and valued friends; but upon the defection and rebellion of Absalom, he espoused the cause of that prince, and became one of David's bitterest enemies. Being disappointed that Absalom did not follow his sagacious advice, and foreseeing the issue of the rebellion, he hanged himself, 2 Sam. 15:12; ch. 17; Psa. 55:12-14. Ahithophel seems to have been the grandfather of Bathsheba. 2 Sam. 23:34, compared with 11:3.

AHI'TUB, I., grandson of Eli, and son of Phinehas, in whose place he succeeded to the high-priesthood on the death of Eli, Phinehas having perished in battle, B. C. 1141, 1 Sam. 4:11.

II. Son of Amariah, and father of Zadok, 2 Sam. 8:17; 1 Chr. 6:8.

AHO'LAH, and AHOL'IBAH, two symbolical names, adopted by Ezekiel, 23:4, to denote the two kingdoms of Judah and Samaria. They are represented as sisters, and of Egyptian extraction. Aholah stands for Samaria, and Aholibah for Jerusalem. The allegory is a history of the Jewish church.

A'I, called also Hai, Gen. 12:8; Aija, Neh. 11:31; and Aiath, Isa. 10:28. A royal city of the Canaanites, east of Bethel, near which Abraham once sojourned and built an altar, Gen. 12:8; 13:3. It is memorable for Joshua's defeat on account of Achan, and his subsequent victory, Josh. 7:2-5; 8:1-29. It was rebuilt, and is mentioned by Isaiah. Its ruins are spoken of by Eusebius and Jerome, but the exact site cannot now be fixed with certainty.

A'IN, *fountain*, spelt EN in the English Bible, in compound words, as En-rogel. It is the name of a city of Judah, afterwards assigned to Simeon, Josh. 15:32; 1 Chr. 4:32. Also of a place in the north of Canaan, Num. 34:11.

AIR. The air or atmosphere surrounding the earth is often denoted by the word heaven; so "the fowls of heaven" means the birds of the air.

To "beat the air," and to "speak in the air," 1 Cor. 9:26; 14:9, are modes of expression used in most languages, signifying to speak or act without judgment or understanding, or to no purpose. "The powers of the air," Eph. 2:2, probably means devils.

AJ'ALON, or Aijalon. I. A town in the tribe of Dan, assigned to the Levites, sons of Kohath, Josh. 21:24. It was not far from Timnath, and was taken by the Philistines from Ahaz, 2 Chr. 28:18. It lay in or near a valley, not far from the valley of Gibeon, and is recognized in the modern village of Yalo. The valley lies towards the north, and is the place where Joshua commanded the sun and moon to stand still, and they obeyed him, Josh. 10:12.

II. A town in Benjamin, some three miles east of Bethel. It was fortified by Rehoboam, 2 Chr. 11:10.

III. In the tribe of Zebulun, the place of Elon's burial, Judg. 12:12.

AKRAB'BIM, *scorpions*, a point in the frontier line of the promised land, Judg. 1:36, and in a region infested with serpents and scorpions, Deut. 8:15. It is to be found probably in the mountains near the Dead sea, on its south-west side. In Josh. 15:3, it is translated Maaleh-akrabbim, the ascent of Akrabbim.

AL'ABASTER, a sort of stone, of fine texture, either the white gypsum, a sulphate of lime, or the onyx-alabaster, a hard carbonate of lime, having the color of the human nail, and nearly allied to marble. This material being very generally used to fabricate vessels for holding unguents and perfumed liquids, many vessels were called alabaster though made of a different substance, as gold, silver, glass, etc. In Matt. 26:6, 7, we read that Mary, sister of Lazarus, John 12:3, poured an alabaster box of precious ointment on Christ's head. Mark says "she brake the box," signifying probably, that the seal upon the box, or upon the neck of the vase or bottle, which kept the perfume from evaporating, had never been removed; it was on this occasion first opened. See SPIKENARD.

AL'AMOTH, a musical term, indicating probably music for female voices, Psa. 46, title; 1 Chr. 15:20.

ALEXAN'DER, I., the Great, the famous son and successor of Philip, king of Macedon. He is alluded to in Dan. 7:6; 8:4-7, under the figures of a leopard with four wings, and a one-horned he-goat, representing the swiftness of his conquests and his great strength. He was appointed by God to destroy the Persian empire and substitute the Grecian. In the statue seen by Nebuchadnezzar in his dream, Dan. 2:39, the belly of brass was the emblem of Alexander. He succeeded his father B. C. 336, and within twelve years overran Syria, Palestine, and Egypt, founded Alexandria, conquered the Persians, and penetrated far into the Indies. He died at the age of thirty-two, from the effects of intemperance, and left his vast empire to be divided among his four generals.

II. Son of Simon the Cyrenian, Mark 15:21, apparently one of the more prominent early Christians.

III. One of the council who condemned Peter and John, Acts 4:6.

IV. A Jew of Ephesus, who sought in vain to quiet the popular commotion respecting Paul, Acts 19:33.

V. A coppersmith, and apostate from Christianity, 1 Tim. 1:20; 2 Tim. 4:14.

ALEXAN'DRIA, a celebrated city in Lower Egypt, situated between the Mediterranean sea and the lake Mareotis, not far from the most westerly mouth of the Nile. It was founded by Alexander the Great, B. C. 332, and peopled by colonies of Greeks and Jews. Alexandria rose rapidly to a state of prosperity, becoming the centre of commercial intercourse between the East and the West, and in process of time was, in point both of magnitude and wealth, second only to Rome itself. The ancient city was about fifteen miles in circuit, peopled by 300,000 free citizens and as many slaves. From the gate of the sea ran one magnificent street, 2,000 feet broad, through the entire length of the city, to the gate of Canopus, affording a view of the shipping in the port, whether north in the Mediterranean, or south in the noble basin of the Mareotic lake. Another street of equal width intersected this at right angles, in a square half a league in circumference.

Upon the death of Alexander, whose body was deposited in this new city, Alexandria became the regal capital of Egypt, under the Ptolemies, and rose to its highest splendor. During the reign of the first three princes of this name, its glory was at the highest. The most celebrated philosophers from the East, as well as from Greece and Rome, resorted thither for instruction; and eminent men, in every department of knowledge, were found within its walls. Ptolemy Soter, the first of that line of kings, formed the museum, the library of 700,000 volumes, and several other splendid works. At the death of Cleopatra, B. C. 26, Alexandria passed into the hands of the Romans; and after having enjoyed the highest fame for upwards of a thousand years, it submitted to the arms of the caliph Omar, A. D. 646.

The present Alexandria, or according to the pronunciation of the inhabitants, Skanderia, occupies only about the eighth part of the site of the ancient city. The splendid temples have been exchanged for wretched mosques and miserable churches, and the magnificent palaces for mean and ill-built dwellings. The city, which was of old so celebrated for its commerce and navigation, is now merely the port of Cairo, a place where ships may touch, and where wares may be exchanged. The modern city is built with the ruins of the ancient. The streets are so narrow, that the inhabitants can lay mats of reeds from one roof to the opposite, to protect them from the scorching sun. The population consists of Turks, Arabs, Copts, Jews, and Armenians. Many Europeans have counting-houses here, where the factors' exchange European for oriental merchandise.

The Greek or Alexandrine version of the Scriptures was made here by learned Jews, seventy-two in number, and hence it is called the Septuagint, or version of the Seventy. The Jews established themselves in great numbers in this city very soon after it was founded. Josephus says that Alexander himself assigned to them a particular quarter of the city, and allowed them equal rights and privileges with the Greeks. Philo, who himself lived there in the time of Christ, affirms that, of five parts of the city, the Jews inhabited two. According to his statements, also, there dwelt in his time, in Alexandria and the other Egyptian cities, not less than a million Jews; but this would seem exaggerated.

AL'GUM, the same as ALMUG, which see.

AL'LEGORY, a figurative mode of discourse, which employs terms literally belonging to one thing, in order to express another. It is strictly a prolonged metaphor. Such are Nathan's address to David, 2 Sam. 12:1-14, Psa. 80, and our Lord's parable of the sower, Luke 8:5-15. The expression, "which things are an allegory," Gal. 4:24, means that the events in the life of Isaac and Ishmael, mentioned in previous verses, have been allegorically applied.

ALLELU'IA, see HALLELU'JAH.

AL'LON-BACHUTH', *oak of weeping;* the spot where Rebekah's nurse was buried, Gen. 35:8.

AL'MON-DIBLATHA'IM, one of the encampments of the Israelites on their way from mount Hor to the plains of Moab; location unknown, Num. 33:46.

ALMOND-TREE. This tree resembles a peach-tree, but is larger. In Palestine, it blossoms in January, and in March has fruit. Its blossoms are white. Its Hebrew name signifies *a watcher*, and to this there is an allusion in Jer. 1:11. In Eccl. 12:5, the hoary head is beautifully compared with the almond-tree, both on account of its snowy whiteness and its winter blossoming.

AL'MUG, a kind of tree or wood, which Hiram brought from Ophir for the use of Solomon in making pillars for the temple and his own house, and also musical instruments, 1 Kin. 10:11; 2 Chr. 2:8. The rabbins call it *coral;* but it could not be this. It was more probably the tree which furnishes what is now commonly called Brazil wood, which is also a native of the East Indies, Siam, the Molucca islands, and Japan, and has several species. Its wood is very durable, and is used in fine cabinet work. It yields also a dye of a beautiful red color, for which it is much used. Its resemblance in color to coral may have given occasion for the name almug, which in rabbinic still signifies coral; and thus the meaning of the name would be coral-wood.

AL'OES, or more properly, ALOE, an East Indian tree, that grows about eight or ten feet high, and yields a rich perfume, Psa. 45:8; Prov. 7:17; Song 4:14. This tree or wood was called by the Greeks Agallochon, and has been known to moderns by the names of lign-aloe, aloe-wood, paradise-wood, eagle-wood, etc. Modern botanists distinguish two kinds: the one grows in Cochin-China, Siam, and China, is never exported, and is of so great rarity in India, as to be worth its weight in gold. The tree is represented as large, with an erect trunk and lofty branches. The other or more common species is called *garo* in the East Indies, and is the wood of a tree growing in the Moluccas, the Excæcaria Agallocha of Linnæus. The leaves are like those of a pear-tree; and it has a milky juice, which, as the tree grows old, hardens into a fragrant resin. The trunk is knotty, crooked, and usually hollow. Aloe-wood is said by Herodotus to have been used by the Egyptians for embalming dead bodies, and Nicodemus brought it, mingled with myrrh, to embalm the body of our Lord, John 19:39. This perfume, it will be seen, is something altogether different from the aloes of the apothecaries, which is a bitter resin, extracted from a low herb.

AL'PHA, see the letter A.

ALPHÆ'US, I., father of James the Less, Matt. 10:3, Luke 6:15, and husband of the Mary usually regarded as sister to the mother of Christ, John 19:25. See MARY, I. and III. By comparing John 19:25 with Luke 24:18 and Matt. 10:3, it is evident that Alphæus is the same as Cleophas; Alphæus being his Greek name, and Cleophas his Hebrew or Syriac name.

II. Father of Matthew, or Levi, the evangelist, Mark 2:14.

AL'TAR, a table-like structure on which sacrifices and incense were offered, built of various materials, usually of stone, but sometimes of brass, etc. It is evident that sacrifices were offered long before the flood; but the first mention of an altar in Scripture is when Noah left the ark. Mention is made of altars reared by Abraham, Isaac, Jacob, and Moses. The latter was commanded to build an altar of earth, Ex. 20:24. If stone was employed, it must be rough and unhewn, probably lest the practice of sculpture should lead them to violate the second commandment. It was not to be furnished with steps, Deut. 27:2-6.

The altars in the Jewish tabernacle, and in the temple at Jerusalem, were the following: 1. The altar of burnt-offerings. 2. The altar of incense. 3. The table of show-bread, for which see BREAD.

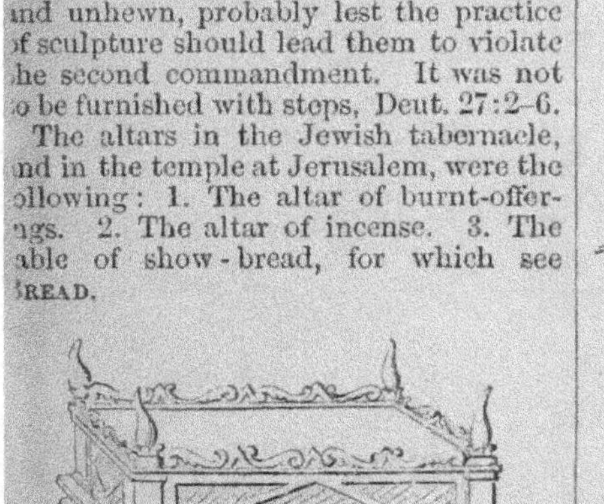

1. THE ALTAR OF BURNT-OFFERINGS was a kind of coffer of shittim-wood covered with brass plates, about seven feet six inches square, and four feet six inches in height. At the four corners were four horns, or elevations. It was portable, and had rings and staves for bearing it, Ex. 27, 38. It was placed in the court before the tabernacle, towards the east. The furniture of the altar was of brass, and consisted of a pan, to receive the ashes that fell through the grating; shovels; basins, to contain the blood with which the altar was sprinkled; and forks, to turn and remove the pieces of flesh upon the coals. The fire was a perpetual one, kindled miraculously, and carefully cherished. Upon this altar the lamb of the daily morning and evening sacrifice was offered, and the other stated and voluntary blood-sacrifices and meat and drink-offerings. To this also certain fugitives were allowed to flee and find protection. The altar in Solomon's temple was larger, being about thirty feet square and fifteen feet high, 2 Chr. 4:1. It is said to have been covered with thick plates of brass and filled with stones, with an ascent on the east side. It is often called "the brazen altar."

2. THE ALTAR OF INCENSE was a small table of shittim-wood, covered with plates of gold; it was eighteen inches square, and three feet high, Ex. 30; 37:25, etc. At the four corners were four horns, and all around its top was a little border or crown. On each side were two rings, into which staves might be inserted for the purpose of carrying it. It stood in the *Holy* place; not in the Holy of Holies, but before it, between the golden candlestick and the table of show-bread, and the priests burned incense upon it every morning and evening. So Zacharias, Luke 1:9, 11. See TEMPLE.

ALTAR at Athens, inscribed "to the unknown God," Acts 17:23. It is certain, both from Paul's assertion and the testimony of Greek writers, that altars to an unknown god or gods existed at Athens. But the attempt to ascertain definitely whom the Athenians worshipped under this appellation, must ever remain fruitless for want of sufficient data. The inscription afforded to Paul a happy occasion of proclaiming the gospel; and those who embraced it found indeed that the Being whom they had thus ignorantly worshipped was the one only living and true God.

AM'ALEK, son of Eliphaz, and grandson of Esau, Gen. 36:12. It is not certain that any distinct mention is made in the Bible of his posterity, people called Amalekites being in existence long before, Gen. 14:7; Num. 24:20.

AM'ALEKITES, a powerful people, who dwelt in Arabia Petraea, between the Dead sea and the Red sea, perhaps in moving troops. We cannot assign the place of their habitation, except in general it is apparent that they dwelt south of Palestine, between mount Seir and the border of Egypt; and it does not appear that they possessed many cities, though one is mentioned in 1 Sam. 15:5. They lived generally in migrating parties, in caves or in tents, like the Bedaween Arabs of the present day. The Israelites had scarcely passed the Red sea, when the Amalekites attacked them in the desert of Rephidim, and slew those who, through fatigue or weakness, lagged behind; and for this unprovoked assault on the people of God, the doom of extermination was passed upon them, Ex. 17:8-16. They came again into conflict with a part of the Israelites on the border of the promised land, Num. 14:45; and after 400 years, Saul attacked and destroyed them at the command of the Lord, 1 Sam. 15. A remnant, however, escaped and subsisted afterwards; David defeated them on several occasions, 1 Sam. 27:8; 30:1; 2 Sam. 8:12; and they were finally blotted out by the Simeonites, in the time of Hezekiah, 1 Chr. 4:43, thus fulfilling the prediction of Balaam, Num. 24:20. Haman, the last of the race mentioned in Scripture, perished like his fathers, in conflict with the Jews. See the book of Esther.

AM'ANA, the southern part or summit of Anti-Lebanon, adjacent to and north of Hermon, from which the river Amana or Abana poured down towards Damascus, Song 4:8.

AMARI'AH, I., son of Meraioth, a descendant of Aaron in the line of Eleazar. He was the father of Ahitub, (II.,) and grandfather of Zadok, in whose person the high-priesthood was restored to that line, 1 Chr. 6:7.

II. High-priest at a later period, a son of Azariah, and father of another Ahitub, 1 Chr. 6:11. In like manner, in the same list there are three persons named Azariah.

AM'ASA, I., David's nephew, the son of Abigail, David's sister, and Jether an Ishmaelite. His parentage may have led David to show him less favor than his other nephews, and this may have disposed him to join in the rebellion of Absalom. He was the general of Absalom's army, and was defeated by his cousin Joab, 2 Sam. 17, 18. David afterwards offered him a pardon and the command of his troops in the place of Joab, whose overbearing conduct he could no longer endure, 2 Sam. 19:13. But in the confusion of Sheba's rebellion, Amasa was treacherously murdered by his powerful rival, 2 Sam. 20:4-10. B. C. 1022.

II. A chief of Ephraim, who opposed retaining as bondsmen the men of Judah taken captive in a war with Pekah king of Israel, 2 Chr. 28:12.

AMAS'AI, a Levite, who joined David with thirty gallant men, while in the desert flying from Saul, 1 Chr. 6:25; 12:16-18.

AMAZI'AH, I., eighth king of Judah, son of Joash, began to reign B. C. 835, and reigned twenty-nine years in Jerusalem. He did good in the sight of the Lord, but not with a perfect heart. Having established himself in his throne and slain the murderers of his father, he mustered a host of 300,000 men of Judah, and hired 100,000 men of Israel, for a war upon Edom. These hired forces he reluctantly dismissed at the command of God, who gave him the victory without their aid. But this did not prevent him from carrying home with him the idols of Edom, and setting them up to be his gods. For this defiance of Jehovah, he was threatened with destruction by a prophet of the Lord; and soon after, went headlong into war with Israel, in which he was defeated and humbled. Fifteen years after, he was slain by conspirators, after flying to Lachish to escape them, 2 Kin. 14:1-20; 2 Chr. 25.

II. A priest of the golden calf at Bethel, who denounced the prophet Amos to Jeroboam, and sought to banish him into Judah for his fidelity, Amos 7:10–17.

AM'BER is a yellow or straw-colored gummy substance, originally a vegetable production, but reckoned in the mineral kingdom. It is found in lumps in the sea and on the shores of Prussia, Sicily, Turkey, etc. Externally it is rough; it is very transparent, and on being rubbed, yields a fragrant odor. It was formerly supposed to be medicinal, but is now employed only in the manufacture of trinkets, ornaments, etc.

The Hebrew word *chasmil* is translated by the Septuagint and Vulgate *electrum*, that is, amber, because the Hebrew denotes a very brilliant amber-like metal, composed of silver and gold, which was much prized in antiquity, Ezek. 1:4, 27; 8:2. Others, as Bochart, refer here to the mixture of gold and brass, of which the ancients had several kinds, some of which exhibited a high degree of lustre. Something similar to this was probably also the "fine brass," in Ezra 8:27; Rev. 1:15.

AMEN is strictly an adjective, signifying firm, and by a metaphor, faithful. So in Rev. 3:14, our Lord is called "the Amen, the faithful and true Witness," where the last words explain the preceding appellation. In its adverbial use it means certainly, truly, surely. It is used at the beginning of a sentence by way of emphasis, frequently by our Saviour, and is there commonly translated Verily. In John's gospel alone, it is often used by him in this way double, Verily, verily. At the end of a sentence it is often used, singly or repeated, especially at the end of hymns and prayers; as, "Amen and Amen," Psa. 41:13; 72:19; 89:52. The proper signification of it here is, to confirm the words which have preceded, assert the sincerity and invoke the fulfilment of them: so it is, so be it, let it be done. Hence, in oaths, after the priest has repeated the words of the covenant or imprecation, all those who pronounce the Amen, bind themselves by the oath, Num. 5:22; Deut. 27:15, etc.; Neh. 5:13; 8:6; 1 Chron. 16:36. Compare Psa. 106:48.

AM'ETHYST, a precious stone of a violet blue color, verging towards a bluish or reddish white. It is seldom uniform in color, and is generally cloudy and spotted with zigzag stripes. The most beautiful specimens come from Ceylon, the East Indies, Siberia, and Saxony. It is very highly prized, Ex. 28:19; Rev. 21:20.

AMMIN'ADAB, I., a son of Aram, of the tribe of Judah, and father of Naashon. He was one of the ancestors of Christ; and his daughter Elisheba was the wife of Aaron, Ex. 6:23; Ruth 4:20; Matt. 1:4. "The chariots of Amminadib," Song 6:12, were very light and swift, in allusion perhaps to some noted charioteer of that day.

II. A son of Kohath, 1 Chr. 6:33.

AM'MONITES, the descendants of Ammon, or Ben-Ammi, a son of Lot. They destroyed an ancient race of giants called Zamzummim, and seized their country, which lay east of Judea, Deut. 2:19–21. Their territory extended from the Arnon to the Jabbok, and from the Jordan a considerable distance into Arabia. Their capital city was Rabbah, (also called Rabbath Ammon, and afterwards Philadelphia,) which stood on the Jabbok. Yet in the time of Moses they had been driven out of this region, towards the east, by the Amorites, Num. 21:21–35; 32:33. Moses was forbidden to assail them, Deut. 2:19. They were gross idolaters; their chief idol being Moloch, supposed to be the same with Saturn, 1 Kin. 11:5-7; 2 Kin. 23:13. They oppressed Israel in the time of Jephthah, and were defeated by him with great slaughter, Judg. 11. The children of Ammon afterwards, at various times, troubled the Israelites, for which the prophets threatened them with divine judgments, Jer. 49:1–6; Ezek. 25:2–10; and they were at last totally subdued by Judas Maccabeus, 1 Macc. 5:6–44.

AM'MON, or NO-AMMON, or NO, a city of Egypt. The name of the city is properly No-Ammon, that is, the seat or dwelling of the god Ammon, Nah. 3:8, in the Hebrew. Similar is its Greek name Diospolis, *the city of Jupiter*-Ammon. In Ez. 30:14, 15, 16, it is called simply No; and in Nah. 3:8 and Jer. 46:25, the English version has also only No. In the latter passage, "the multitude of No" would be better "Ammon of No." The name designates, beyond all reasonable doubt, the city of Thebes, the ancient and renowned capital of Upper Egypt. Homer describes her as

"The world's great empress on the Egyptian plains,

LUXOR, FROM THE RIVER NILE.

That spreads her conquests o'er a thousand states,
And pours her heroes through a hundred gates."

The vast ruins of the temples of Luxor and Carnac still proclaim the grandeur and magnificence with which the worship of Jupiter-Ammon was conducted. The ruins of the ancient city of Thebes are the wonder and delight of modern travellers, for their extent, their vastness, and their sad and solitary grandeur. They are covered with ancient hieroglyphics and historical sculptures, among which one interesting scene is thought to record the exploits of Shishak against Jerusalem in the fifth year of Rehoboam, 1 Kin. 14:25. See Wilkinson, Robinson, and Olin. Also Missionary Herald, 1823, p. 347, and SHISHAK.

AM'NON, the eldest son of David, by Ahinoam of Jezreel. He is known only by his guilt in violating his sister; for which Absalom, two years after, caused him to be assassinated, 2 Sam. 13.

A'MON, the fourteenth king of Judah, son of Manasseh, began to reign B. C. 639, at the age of twenty-two, and reigned only two years at Jerusalem. He did evil in the sight of the Lord, as his father Manasseh had done, by forsaking Jehovah and worshipping idols. His servants conspired against him, and slew him in his own house; but the people killed all the conspirators, and established his son Josiah on the throne. He was buried in the garden of Uzzah, 2 Kin. 21:18–26; 2 Chr. 33:21–25.

AM'ORITES, a people descended from Emer, the fourth son of Canaan, Gen. 10:16. They first peopled the mountains west of the Dead sea, near Hebron; but afterwards extended their limits, and took possession of the finest provinces of Moab and Ammon, on the east between the brooks Jabbok and Arnon, Num. 13:29; 21:21–31; Josh. 5:1; Judg. 11:13. Moses took this country from their king, Sihon. The lands which the Amorites possessed on this side Jordan were given to the tribe of Judah, and those beyond the Jordan to the tribes of Reuben and Gad. The name Amorite is often taken in Scripture for Canaanite in general, Gen. 15:16; Amos 2:9. See CANAANITES.

By the expression, "Thy father was an Amorite and thy mother a Hittite," Ezek. 16:3, God reminds the Jews that they were naturally no more worthy of divine favor than the worst of the heathen Canaanites.

A'MOS, the fourth of the minor prophets, was a herdsman of Tekoah, a small town of Judah, about twelve miles south of Jerusalem. He prophesied, however, concerning Israel, at Bethel, in the days of Uzziah, king of Judah, and Jeroboam II., king of Israel, about B. C. 787, and was thus a contemporary of Hosea, Joel, and Isaiah. The first two chapters contain predictions against the surrounding nations, enemies of the people of God. But the ten tribes of Israel were the chief subjects of his prophecies. Their temporary prosperity under Jeroboam led to gross idolatry, injustice, and corruption; for which sins he denounces the judgments of God upon them: but he closes with cheering words of consolation. His holy boldness in reproving sin drew on him the wrath of the priests, who labored to procure his banishment, Amos 7:10-17. In regard to style, Amos takes a high rank among the prophets. He is full of imagery, concise, and yet simple and perspicuous.

II. One of the ancestors of our Lord, Luke 3:25.

A'MOZ, the father of Isaiah, 2 Kin. 19:2; Isa. 1:1.

AMPHIP'OLIS, a city of Macedonia, situated not far from the mouth of the river Strymon, which flowed "around the city," and thus occasioned its name. The village which now stands upon the site of the ancient city is called Empoli or Yamboli, a corruption of Amphipolis. It was visited by Paul and Silas, Acts 17:1.

AM'RAM, the father of Aaron, Miriam, and Moses. He died in Egypt, aged one hundred and thirty-seven, Exod. 6:18, 20.

AM'RAPHEL, king of Shinar in the time of Abraham. With three other petty kings, he made war upon the tribes around the Dead sea, and the cities of the plain, Gen. 14:1.

A'NAH, the father of Aholibamah, one of Esau's wives. While feeding his father's asses in the desert, he is said to have found the "mules," Gen. 36:24. But the Hebrew word is supposed to mean rather "warm springs;" and such springs are found on the eastern coast of the Dead sea, which was not far from the dwelling of the Seirites, to whom Anah belonged. In this region was a place afterwards celebrated among the Greeks and Romans for its warm springs, and called by them Callirrhoë.

A'NAK, plural AN'AKIM, famous giants in Palestine, descended from Arba, founder of the city Hebron. They spread themselves over the south of Judah, the hill country, and several cities of the Philistines. The Hebrew spies were terrified at their sight, Num. 13:33; but in the conquest of Canaan they were destroyed or expelled, Josh. 11:22; 15:14; Judg. 1:20.

ANAM'MELECH, see ADRAMMELECH.

ANANI'AS, I., a Jew of Jerusalem, the husband of Sapphira, who attempted to join the Christians, and pretended to give them the entire price of his lands, but died instantly on being convicted of falsehood by Peter, Acts 5:1-10.

II. A Christian of Damascus, who restored the sight of Paul, after his vision of the Saviour, Acts 9:10-17; 22:12.

III. A high-priest of the Jews, the son of Nebedæus. He was sent as a prisoner to Rome by Quadratus, the governor of Syria, and Jonathan was appointed in his place; but being discharged by the emperor Claudius, he returned to Palestine, and Jonathan being murdered through the treachery of Felix, Ananias appears to have performed the functions of the high-priest as a substitute, until Ismael was appointed by Agrippa. It was he before whom with the Sanhedrim Paul was summoned, under Felix, and who ordered an attendant to smite Paul on the mouth. The apostle's prophetic denunciation in reply seems to have been fulfilled when, in the commencement of the siege of Jerusalem, the assassins burned the house of Ananias, and afterwards discovered his place of retreat in an aqueduct, and slew him, Acts 23:2; 24:1.

ANATH'EMA, that is, a curse, a ban, signifies properly something set apart, separated, devoted. It is understood principally to denote the absolute, irrevocable, and entire separation of a person from the communion of the faithful, or from the number of the living, or from the privileges of society; or the devoting of any man, animal, city or thing, to be extirpated, destroyed, consumed, and, as it were, annihilated, Lev. 27. Thus Jericho, Josh. 6:17-21, and Achan were accursed, Josh. 7.

Another kind of anathema, very peculiarly expressed, occurs 1 Cor. 16:22; "If any man love not the Lord Jesus Christ, let him be Anathema, Maranatha." This last word is made up of two Syriac words, signifying, "The Lord cometh," that is, the Lord will surely come, and will execute this curse, by condemning those who love him not. At the same time, the opposite is also implied, that is, the Lord cometh also to reward those who love him. See EXCOMMUNICATION.

AN'ATHOTH, one of the cities given to the priests, in Benjamin; identified by Robinson in Anata, some four miles north by east of Jerusalem, Josh. 21:18; 1 Chr. 6:60. It was the birthplace of the prophet Jeremiah, Jer. 1:1; 32:7. Its people, however, rejected his words, and sought his life, Jer. 11:21.

AN'DREW, one of the twelve apostles, was of Bethsaida, and the brother of Peter, John 1:40, 44. Being a disciple of John the Baptist, he understood the intimations of his master as to the Lamb of God, and was the first of the apostles to follow him, John 1:35-40, and come to the knowledge of the Messiah. Compare Jas. 4:8. He was afterwards called as an apostle, on the shore of the sea of Galilee, Matt. 4:18; and thenceforth followed Christ to the end, Mark 13:3; John 6:7; 12:22. Of his later history nothing is known with certainty. It seems probable, however, that after preaching the gospel in Greece, and perhaps Thrace and Scythia, he suffered crucifixion at Patras in Achaia, on a cross of peculiar form (X,) hence commonly known as "St. Andrew's cross."

ANDRONI'CUS, a Jewish Christian, and fellow-prisoner of Paul, Rom. 16:7.

A'NER, I., one of Abraham's allies in the pursuit of Chedorlaomer and the rescue of Lot, Gen. 14:13.

II. A Levitical city, in Manasseh, 1 Chr. 6:70.

AN'GEL. The original word, both in Hebrew and Greek, means messenger, and is so translated, Matt. 11:10; Luke 7:24, etc. It is often applied to an ordinary messenger, Job 1:14; 1 Sam. 11:3; Luke 9:52; to prophets, Isa. 42:19; Hag. 1:13; to priests, Eccl. 5:6; Mal. 2:7; and even to inanimate objects, Psa. 78:49; 104:4; 2 Cor. 12:7. Under the general sense of messenger, the term angel is properly applied also to Christ, as the great Angel or Messenger of the covenant, Mal. 3:1, and to the ministers of his gospel, the overseers or angels of the churches, Rev. 2:1, 8, 12, etc. In 1 Cor. 11:10, the best interpreters understand by the term "angels" the holy angels, who were present in an especial sense in the Christian assemblies; and from reverence to them it was proper that the women should have power (veils, as a sign of their being in subjection to a higher power) on their heads. See under VEIL.

But generally in the Bible the word is applied to a race of intelligent beings, of a higher order than man, who surround the Deity, and whom he employs as his *messengers* or agents in administering the affairs of the world, and in promoting the welfare of individuals, as well as of the whole human race, Matt. 1:20; 22:30; Acts 7:30, etc. Whether pure spirits, or having spiritual bodies, they have no bodily organization like ours, and are not distinguished in sex, Matt. 22:30. They were doubtless created long before our present world was made, Job 38:7. The Bible represents them as exceedingly *numerous*, Dan. 7:10; Matt. 26:53; Luke 2:13; Heb. 12:22, 23; as remarkable for *strength*, Psa. 103:20; 2 Pet. 2:11; Rev. 5:2; 18:21; 19:17; and for *activity*, Judg. 13:20; Isa. 6:2-6; Dan. 9:21-23; Matt. 13:49; 26:53; Acts 27:23; Rev. 8:13. They appear to be of *divers orders*, Isa. 6:2-6; Ezek. 10:1; Col. 1:16; Rev. 12:7. Their name indicates their agency in the dispensations of Providence towards man, and the Bible abounds in narratives of events in which they have borne a visible part. Yet in this employment they act as the mere instruments of God, and in fulfilment of his commands, Psa. 91:11; 103:20; Heb. 1:14. We are not therefore to put trust in them, pay them adoration, or pray in their name, Rev. 19:10; 22:8, 9. Though Scripture does not warrant us to believe that each individual has his particular guardian angel, it teaches very explicitly that the angels minister to every Christian, Matt. 18:10; Luke 16:22; Heb. 1:14. They are intensely concerned in the salvation of men, Luke 2:10-12; 15:7, 10; 1 Pet. 1:12; and will share with saints the blessedness of heaven for ever, Heb. 12:22.

Those angels "who kept not their first estate," but fell and rebelled against God, are called the angels of Satan or the devil, Matt. 25:41; Rev. 12:9. These are represented as being "cast down to hell, and reserved unto judgment," 2 Pet. 2:4. See SYNAGOGUE, ARCHANGEL.

ANGEL OF THE LORD, THE ANGEL-JEHOVAH, the usual title of Christ in the Old Testament. Compare Gen. 16:7-13; 22:11-18; 31:11-13; 32:24-30; Ex. 3:2-6, 14; 23:20; Judg. 2; 13:16-22; Acts 7:30-38. Christ thus appears in the Patriarchal, the Mosaic, and the Christian dispensation as the same Jehovah, revealing the Father to men, and carrying forward the same great plan for the redemption of his people, Isa. 63:9.

AN'GER, a violent emotion of a painful nature, sometimes arising spontaneously upon just occasion, but usually characterized in the Bible as a great sin, Matt. 5:22; Eph. 4:31; Col. 3:8. Even when just, our anger should be mitigated by a due consideration of the circumstances of the offence and the state of mind of the offender; of the folly and ill-results of this passion; of the claims of the gospel, and of our own need of forgiveness from others, but especially from God, Matt. 6:15. Anger is in Scripture frequently attributed to God, Psa. 7:11; 90:11; not that he is liable to those violent emotions which this passion produces, but figuratively speaking, that is, after the manner of men; and because he punishes the wicked with the severity of a superior provoked to anger.

AN'ISE, a well-known plant, resembling dill, carraway, etc., but more fragrant. The seeds are kept by apothecaries. The plant mentioned in Matt. 23:23 was no doubt the *dill*, which

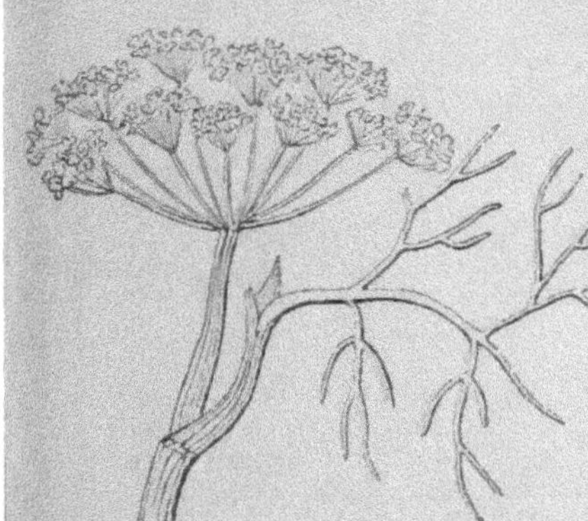

grows in Palestine, and was tithed by the Jews.

AN'NA, a daughter of Phanuel, of the tribe of Asher, early married, but left a widow after seven years, and thenceforth devoted to the service of God. She was constant in attendance at the morning and evening sacrifices at the temple; and there, at the age of eighty-four years, was blessed with a sight of the infant Saviour, and inspired to announce the coming of the promised Messiah to many who longed to see him, Luke 2:36-38.

AN'NAS, a high-priest of the Jews, Luke 3:2; John 18:13, 24; Acts 4:6. He is mentioned in Luke as being high-priest along with Caiaphas, his son-in-law. He was first appointed to that office by Cyrenius, or Quirinus, proconsul of Syria, about A. D. 7 or 8, but was afterwards deprived of it. After various changes, the office was given to Joseph, also called Caiaphas, the son-in-law of Annas, about A. D. 25, who continued in office until A. D. 35 or 36. In the passages of the New Testament above cited, therefore, it is apparent that Caiaphas was the only actual and proper high-priest; but Annas being his father-in-law, and having been formerly himself high-priest, and being also perhaps his substitute, had great influence and authority, and could with propriety be still termed high-priest along with Caiaphas. It was before him that Christ was first taken on the night of his seizure. He also assisted in presiding over the Sanhedrim which sat in judgment upon Peter and John, Acts 4:6.

ANOINT'ING was a custom in general use among the Hebrews and other oriental nations, and its omission was one sign of mourning, Isa. 61:3. They anointed the hair, head, and beard, Psa. 104:15; 133:2. At their feasts and rejoicings they anointed the whole body; but sometimes only the head or the feet, Psa. 23:5; Matt. 6:17; John 12:3. It was a customary mark of respect to guests, Luke 7:38, 46. The use of oil upon the skin was thought to be conducive to health. Anointing was then used, and is still, medicinally, Mark 6:13; Jas. 5:14; but the miraculous *cures* thus wrought by the apostles furnish no warrant for the ceremony just before *death* called "extreme unction." The anointing of dead bodies was also practised, to preserve them from corruption, Mark 14:8; 16:1; Luke 23:56. They anointed kings and high-priests at their inauguration, Ex. 29:7, 29, Lev. 4:3, Judg. 9:8, 1 Sam. 9:16, 1 Kings 19:15, 16, as also the sacred vessels of the tabernacle and temple, Ex. 30:26. This anointing of sacred persons and objects signified their being set apart and consecrated to the service of God; and the costly and fragrant mixture appointed for this purpose was forbidden for all others, Ex. 30:23-33; Ezek. 23:41.

The custom of anointing with oil or perfume was also common among the Greeks and Romans; especially the anointing of guests at feasts and other entertainments.

ANSWER. Besides the common use of this word in the sense of *to reply*, it is very often used in the Bible, following the Hebrew and Greek idioms, in the sense of *to speak;* meaning simply that one begins or resumes his discourse, Zech. 3:4; 6:4; Matt. 11:25; 12:38; Luke 7:40. It also means, to sing in choruses or responses, 1 Sam. 18:7; and to give account of one's self in judgment, Gen. 30:33; Job 9:3.

ANT, a small insect, famous for its industry and economy, for its social habits and skill in building. Some species build habitations truly immense compared with themselves, and able to contain a dozen men. Their roofs are impervious to rain, and they contain numerous stories, galleries, etc., the result of skilful and incessant labor. Ants lavish the utmost care and pains upon their young, both in the egg and the crysalis state. The *termites* or white ants are large and very destructive. Most varieties of ants are known to choose animal or saccharine food; and no species has yet been found laying up stores of grain for winter use, for while the frost continues they all lie torpid. The language of Solomon, Prov. 6:6, commends them for toiling as soon and as long as the season permits and rewards their labor, and bids us make the same diligent use of life and opportunities, Prov. 30:24, 25. The inferior animals are in many respects wiser than sinful man, Job 12:7, 8.

ANTELOPE, see under Roe.

ANTICHRIST strictly means one opposed to Christ. In this sense, John says there were already in his time many antichrists, many having the spirit of antichrist; unbelievers, heretics, and persecutors, 1 John 2:18; 4:3. They were characterized by the denial of the Father and the Son, and of Christ's coming in the flesh, 1 John 2:22; 4:3. But the apostles and early Christians seem to have looked forward to some one great antichrist, who should precede the second coming of our Lord, and whom Paul calls "the man of sin, the son of perdition," 2 Thess. 2:3. To this passage John alludes, 1 John 2:18. Able interpreters agree that antichrist denotes an organized body of men, perpetuated from age to age, opposed to Christ, and which he will destroy, Rev. 11; 13; 17.

ANTIOCH IN SYRIA, ON THE ORONTES.

AN'TIOCH, the name of two cities mentioned in the New Testament. The first was situated on the river Orontes, twenty miles from its mouth, and was the metropolis of all Syria. It was founded by Seleucus Nicator, and called by him after the name of his father Antiochus. This city is celebrated by Cicero, as being opulent and abounding in men of taste and letters. It was at one time a place of great wealth and refinement, and ranked as the third city in the Roman empire. Its situation, amid innumerable groves and small streams, midway between Alexandria and Constantinople, rendered it a place of great beauty and salubrity, as well as commercial importance. It was also a place of great resort for the Jews, and afterwards for Christians, to all of whom invitations and encouragements were held out by Seleucus Nicator. The distinctive name of "Christians" was here first applied to the followers of Jesus, Acts 11:19, 26; 13:1; Gal. 2:11. Antioch was highly favored by Vespasian and Titus, and became celebrated for luxury and vice. Few cities have suffered greater disasters. Many times it has been nearly ruined by earthquakes, one of which, in 1822, destroyed one-fourth of its population, then about twenty thousand. It is now called Antakia.

The other city, also founded by Seleucus Nicator, was called Antioch of Pisidia, because it was attached to that province, although situated in Phrygia, Acts 13:14; 14:19, 21; 2 Tim. 3:11.

AN'TIPAS, I. See HEROD ANTIPAS.

II. A faithful martyr, in Pergamos, Rev. 2:13.

ANTIP'ATRIS, the name of a city of Palestine, situated seven or eight miles from the coast, in a fertile and well watered plain between Cæsarea and Jerusalem, on the site of the former city Caphar-Saba. It was founded by Herod the Great, and called Antipatris, in honor of his father Antipater. This place was visited by Paul, Acts 23:31. An Arab village, called Kefr Sâba, now occupies its site.

ANTO'NIA, a square fortress on the east side of Jerusalem, north of the temple area, with which it had a covered communication. There was a tower at each corner, and it was isolated by high walls and trenches. It was rebuilt by Herod the Great, and named after Mark Antony. Josephus often speaks of it. It was "the castle" from which soldiers came down to rescue Paul from the Jews in the temple; and from its stairs he addressed the multitude, Acts 21:31–40.

APE, an animal rudely resembling the human race. The tribe may be familiarly distinguished as monkeys, apes, and baboons. Solomon imported them from Ophir, 1 Kin. 10:22; 2 Chr. 9:21. They were at one time worshipped in Egypt; and still are adored in some parts of India, where one traveller describes a magnificent temple dedicated to the monkey. There may be an allu-

sion to large apes or baboons, literally "hairy ones," in Lev. 17:7: Isa. 13:21; 34:14.

APHAR'SACHITES, etc., Ezra 4:9; 5:6; named among the heathen subjects of the king of Assyria, transplanted into Samaria. The Apharsites, also named in Ezra 4:9, are regarded by Luther as Persians.

A'PHEK, *strength*, I., a city in Lebanon, assigned to the tribe of Asher, Josh. 13:4; 19:30; but not subdued, Judg. 1:31. Its site may be still found in mount Lebanon, called Aphka.

II. A city of the tribe of Issachar, in the valley of Jezreel, noted in the wars with the Philistines, 1 Sam. 4:1; 29:1.

III. A city five miles east of the sea of Galilee, the walls of which fell upon twenty-seven thousand Syrians under Benhadad, after his defeat by the Israelites, 1 Kin. 20:26-34.

APOC'ALYPSE signifies revelation, but is particularly referred to the revelations which John had in the isle of Patmos, whither he was banished by Domitian. Hence it is another name for the book of Revelation. This book belongs, in its character, to the *prophetical* writings, and stands in intimate relation with the prophecies of the Old Testament, and more especially with the writings of the later prophets, as Ezekiel, Zechariah, and particularly Daniel, inasmuch as it is almost entirely symbolical. This circumstance has surrounded the interpretation of this book with difficulties, which no interpreter has yet been able fully to overcome. As to the author, the weight of testimony throughout all the history of the church is in favor of John, the beloved apostle. As to the time of its composition, most commentators suppose it to have been written after the destruction of Jerusalem, about A. D. 96; while others assign it an earlier date.

It is an expanded illustration of the first great promise, "The seed of the woman shall bruise the head of the serpent." Its figures and symbols are august and impressive. It is full of prophetic grandeur, and awful in its hieroglyphics and mystic symbols: seven seals opened, seven trumpets sounded, seven vials poured out; mighty antagonists and hostile powers, full of malignity against Christianity, and for a season oppressing it, but at length defeated and annihilated; the darkened heaven, tempestuous sea, and convulsed earth fighting against them, while the issue of the long combat is the universal reign of peace and truth and righteousness—the whole scene being relieved at intervals by a choral burst of praise to God the Creator, and Christ the Redeemer and Governor. Thus its general scope is intelligible to all readers, or it could not yield either hope or comfort. It is also full of Christ. It exhibits his glory as Redeemer and Governor, and describes that deep and universal homage and praise which the "Lamb that was slain" is for ever receiving before the throne. Either Christ is God, or the saints and angels are guilty of idolatry.

"To explain this book perfectly," says Bishop Newton, "is not the work of one man, or of one age; probably it never will be clearly understood till it is all fulfilled."

APOC'RYPHA signifies properly hidden, concealed; and as applied to books, it means those which assume a claim to a sacred character, but are really uninspired, and have not been publicly admitted into the canon. These are of two classes: namely,

1. Those which were in existence in the time of Christ, but were not admitted by the Jews into the canon of the Old Testament, because they had no Hebrew original and were regarded as not divinely inspired. The most important of these are collected in the Apocrypha often bound up with the English Bible; but in the Septuagint and Vulgate they stand as canonical.

These apocryphal writings are ten in number: namely, Baruch, Ecclesiasticus, Wisdom of Solomon, Tobit, Judith, two books of the Maccabees, Song of the Three Children, Susannah, and Bell and the Dragon. Their style proves that they were a part of the Jewish-Greek literature of Alexandria, within three hundred years before Christ; and as the Septuagint Greek version of the Hebrew Bible came from the same quarter, it was often accompanied by these uninspired Greek writings, and they thus gained a general circulation. Josephus and Philo, of the first century, exclude them from the canon. The Talmud contains no trace of them; and from the various lists of the Old Testament Scriptures in the early centuries, it is clear that then as now they formed no part of the Hebrew canon. None of them are quoted or endorsed by Christ or the apostles; they were not acknowledged by the Christian fathers; and their own contents condemn them, abounding with errors and absurdities. Some of them, however, are of value for the historical information they furnish, for their moral and prudential maxims, and for the illustrations they afford of ancient life.

2. Those which were written after the time of Christ, but were not admitted by the churches into the canon of the New Testament, as not being divinely inspired. These are mostly of a legendary character. They have all been collected by Fabricius in his Codex Apoc. New Testament.

APOLLO'NIA, a city of Macedonia, situated between Amphipolis and Thessalonica, about a day's journey on foot from the former place, Acts 17:1.

APOL'LOS, a Jew of Alexandria, a learned and eloquent man, who through the Scriptures and the ministry of John the Baptist became a Christian. He visited Ephesus about A. D. 54, and publicly proclaimed his faith in Christ; whereupon he was further instructed in gospel truth. Passing thence into Achaia, he preached with great power and success, especially among the Jews, Acts 18:24-28. At Corinth, he for a time watered what Paul had planted, Acts 19:1; 1 Cor. 3:6. His character was not unlike that of Paul; they were equally grieved at the dissensions of the Corinthians, and at those personal partialities which led many away from Christ, 1 Cor. 3:4-22; 16:12; and they coöperated to the end in serving him, Titus 3:13. Jerome is of opinion that Apollos afterwards returned to Corinth from Crete.

APOL'LYON, see ABADDON.

APOS'TLE, a messenger or envoy. The term is applied to Jesus Christ, who was God's envoy to save the world, Heb. 3:1; though, more commonly, the title is given to persons who were envoys commissioned by the Saviour himself.

The apostles of Jesus Christ were his chief disciples, whom he invested with authority, filled with his Spirit, entrusted particularly with his doctrines and services, and chose to raise the edifice of his church. They were twelve in number, answering to the twelve tribes, Matt. 19:28, and were plain, unlearned men, chosen from the common people. After their calling and charge, Matt. 10:5-42, they attended their divine Master, witnessing his works, imbibing his spirit, and gradually learning the facts and doctrines of the gospel. After his resurrection, he sent them into all the world, commissioned to preach, to baptize, to work miracles, etc. See John 15:27; 1 Cor. 9:1; 15:8; 2 Cor. 12:12; 1 Thess. 2:13. The names of the twelve are, Simon Peter; Andrew, his brother; James, the son of Zebedee, called also "the greater;" John, his brother; Philip; Bartholomew; Thomas; Matthew, or Levi; Simon the Canaanite; Lebbeus, surnamed Thaddeus, also called Judas or Jude; James, "the less," the son of Alphæus; and Judas Iscariot, Matt. 10:2-4; Mark 3:16; Luke 6:14. The last betrayed his Master, and then hanged himself, and Matthias was chosen in his place, Acts 1:15-26. In the Acts of the Apostles are recorded the self-sacrificing toils and sufferings of these Christlike men, who did that which was "right in the sight of God" from love to their Lord; and gave themselves wholly to their work, with a zeal, love, and faith Christ delighted to honor—teaching us that apostolic graces alone can secure apostolic successes.

APPHI'A, Phile. 2, supposed by some to have been the wife of Philemon.

APPLE-TREES, mentioned in Song 2:3; 8:5; Joel 1:12. Many suppose the *citron-tree* to be here meant. The rich color, fragrant odor and handsome appearance of this tree, both in flower and in fruit, agree well with the above passages. Thoughts of wise men, well expressed, are like "apples of gold in pictures of silver," that is, like ripe and golden fruit in finely wrought silver baskets, Prov. 25:11.

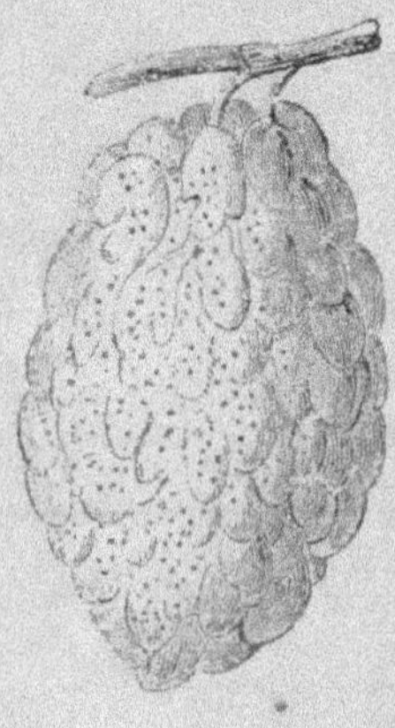

CITRON.

AP'PII-FO'RUM, *market-place of Appius*, a village or market-town, founded by Appius Claudius on the great road (via Appia) which he constructed from Rome to Capua. It is most probably to be found in the present Casarillo di Santa Maria, situated forty miles from Rome, in the borders of the Pontine marshes, where are the remains of an ancient town. Three Taverns was a village about ten miles nearer Rome, Acts 28:15.

AQ'UILA, a Jew born in Pontus, a tent-maker by occupation, who with his wife Priscilla joined the Christian church at Rome. When the Jews were banished from that city by the emperor Claudius, Aquila and his wife retired to Corinth. They afterwards became the companions of Paul in his labors, and are mentioned by him with much commendation, Acts 18:2, 3, 24-26; Rom. 16:3, 4; 1 Cor. 16:19; 2 Tim. 4:19.

AR, called also Rabbah and Rabbath-Moab, the capital of Moab, Num. 21:28; Deut. 2; Isa. 15:1. Its site, still called Rabbah, is found upon a hill some fifteen miles east of the Dead sea, and south of the Arnon, midway between it and Kir Moab.

ARA'BIA is a country of Western Asia, lying south and east of Judea. It extends 1,500 miles from north to south, and 1,200 from east to west. On the north it is bounded by part of Syria, on the east by the Persian gulf and the Euphrates, on the south by the Arabian sea and the straits of Babelmandel, and on the west by the Red sea, Egypt, and Palestine. Arabia is distinguished by geographers into three parts—Deserta, Petræa, and Felix.

ARABIA DESER'TA, *the desert*, a vast steppe, or elevated expanse of sand, with occasional hills and a sparse vegetation. It has the mountains of Gilead on the west, and the river Euphrates on the east, and extends far to the south. It comprehends the country of the Itureans, the Ishmaelites, the people of Kedar, and others, who led a wandering life, having no cities, houses, or fixed habitations, but wholly dwelling in tents; in modern Arabic, such are called *Bedawîn*. When Paul says he "went into Arabia and returned again to Damascus," he meant doubtless the northern part of Arabia Deserta, which lay adjacent to the territories of Damascus, Gal. 1:17.

ARABIA PETRÆ'A lies south of the Holy Land, and had Petra for its capital. See SELA. This region contained the southern Edomites, the Amalekites, the Hivites, etc., people at present known under the general name of Arabs. In this country was Kadesh-barnea, Gerar, Beersheba, Paran, Arad, Hasmona, Oboth, Dedan, etc., also the peninsula of mount Sinai and the land of Midian. This portion of Arabia, though smaller than the others, is rich in historical associations. The patriarch Job was familiar with its scenery. At Horeb, Moses saw the burning bush, and Elijah heard the "still small voice." In this "great and terrible wilderness," from mount Sinai to the promised land, the Hebrews spent their forty years of wanderings.

ARABIA FE'LIX, *the happy*, lies still farther south and east, being bounded east by the Persian gulf, south by the ocean between Africa and India, and west by the Red sea. As this region did not immediately adjoin the Holy Land, it is not so frequently mentioned as the former ones. The queen of Sheba, who visited Solomon, 1 Kings 10:1, was probably queen of part of Arabia Felix. This

A SCENE IN ARABIA.

country abounded with riches, and particularly with spices, and is now called Hedjaz, Yemen, etc. It is much celebrated in modern times by reason of the cities of Mecca and Medina being situated in it.

There are, according to native historians, two races of Arabs: those who derive their descent from the primitive inhabitants of the land, Joktan, etc., and those who claim Ishmael as their ancestor. Southern Arabia was settled in part by Cush and his sons, descendants of Ham, who also peopled the adjoining coast of Africa, and in part by descendants of Shem, particularly Joktan, Gen. 10:25, 26. Ishmael, Gen. 25:13-15, and the six sons of Abraham by Keturah, Gen. 25:2, together with the seed of Esau and of Lot, occupied the parts of Arabia nearer Judea. The changes of forty centuries render it impossible to distinguish either of these parent sources in the numerous Arab tribes descended from them. These tribes have traditions and peculiarities of their own, and incessant feuds; yet as a whole they are but one people, distinct from all others. The only general division is into those who dwell in cities, as in Southern Arabia, and those who live in the fields and deserts. The latter are migratory, dwelling in tents and removing according to the convenience of water and pasturage, and are often robbers. Each tribe is divided up into little communities, of which a *sheikh* or patriarch is the head. Such are the *Bedaween*.

In ancient times the Arabs were idolaters and star-worshippers. They are now nominally Mohammedans, but their religion sits but lightly on them. Isolated from other nations, and with slight exceptions free from all foreign control they preserve their ancient manners with singular fidelity, and the study of these throws much light upon Bible narratives. Their language also is still spoken with great purity; and as it is near akin to the Hebrew, it furnishes invaluable aid in the study of the Old Testament.

A'RAD, a Canaanitish city on the extreme south of Judea, the inhabitants of which drove back the Hebrews as they attempted to enter the promised land from Kadesh, Num. 21:1; it was afterwards subdued, Josh. 10:41; 12:14; Judg. 1:16. Robinson found its site on a hill about fifteen miles south of Hebron.

A'RAM, I., the name of three men in the Bible: a son of Shem, Gen. 10:22, a grandson of Nahor, Gen. 22:21, and an ancestor of our Lord, Ruth 4:19; 1 Chr. 2:10; Matt. 1:3; Luke 3:33.

II. Nearly synonymous with Syria; the Hebrew name of the whole region north-east of Palestine, extending from the Tigris on the east nearly to the Mediterranean on the west, and to the Taurus range on the north. It was named after Aram the son of Shem. Thus defined, it includes also Mesopotamia, which the Hebrews named Aram-naharaim, *Aram of the two rivers*, Gen. 24:10, or Padan-aram, *the plain of Aram*, Gen. 25:20; 48:7. Various cities in the western part of Aram gave their own names to the regions around them: as Damascus, (Aram-Dammesek,) 2 Sam. 8:6; Maachah, near Bashan, 1 Chr. 19:6; Geshur, Josh. 12:5; 2 Sam. 15:8; Zobah, and Beth-rehob, 2 Sam. 10:6, 8. Several of these were powerful states, and often waged war against Israel. David subdued them and made them tributaries, and Solomon preserved this supremacy. After him it was lost, except perhaps under Jeroboam II. See SYRIA, PADAN-ARAM. The Aramæan language, nearly resembling the Hebrew, gradually supplanted the latter as a spoken language, and was in use in Judea at the time of Christ. It is still used by Syrian Christians around Mosul.

MOUNT ARARAT, IN ARMENIA.

AR'ARAT, the name of a province in the centre of Armenia, between the river Araxes and the lakes Van and Ooroomiah. 2 Kings 19:37, Isaiah 37:38, and sometimes used to denote the whole country, Jer. 51:27. On the mountains of Ararat the ark rested, Gen. 8:4. In 1831, Messrs. Smith and Dwight, American missionaries, visited Armenia, and traversed the province of Ararat. Mr. Smith describes the mountains as follows:

"We passed very near the base of that noble mountain, which is called by the Armenians Masis, and by Europeans generally Ararat; and for more than twenty days had it constantly in sight, except when obscured by clouds. It consists of two peaks, one considerably higher than the other, and is connected with a chain of mountains running off to the north-west and west, which, though high, are not of sufficient elevation to detract at all from the lonely dignity of this stupendous mass. From Nakhchewan, at the distance of at least 100 miles to the south-east, it appeared like an immense isolated cone, of extreme regularity, rising out of the valley of the Araxes. Its height is said to be 16,000 feet. The eternal snows upon its summit occasionally form vast avalanches, which precipitate themselves down its sides with a sound not unlike that of an earthquake. When we saw it, it was white to its very base with snow. And certainly not among the mountains of Ararat or of Armenia generally, nor those of any part of the world where I have been, have I ever seen one whose majesty could plead half so powerfully its claims to the honor of having once been the stepping-stone between the old world and the new. I gave myself up to the feeling, that on its summit were once congregated all the inhabitants of the earth, and that, while in the valley of the Araxes, I was paying a visit to the second cradle of the human race."

Mount Ararat was visited in 1829 by Prof. Parrot, who after several attempts reached the summit, more than 17,200 feet above the level of the sea. It bears traces of volcanic action, and in 1840 was shaken by a disastrous earthquake.

ARAU'NAH, a Jebusite, residing on mount Moriah after the Jebusites were dispossessed by David, 2 Sam. 5:6; 24:18. In 1 Chr. 21:18, he is called ORNAN. The divine choice of his land for the temple site, 2 Chr. 3:1, and his readiness to give it freely for this purpose, suggest the probability that he was a convert to the true religion.

AR'BA, an ancestor of the Anakim, and founder of Hebron, to which he gave its ancient name, Josh. 15:13.

ARCHAN'GEL. This word is only twice used in the Bible, 1 Thess. 4:16; Jude 9. In this last passage it is applied to Michael, who, in Dan. 10:13, 21; 12:1, is described as having a special charge of the Jewish nation, and in Rev. 12:7-9 as the leader of an angelic army. So exalted are the position and offices ascribed to Michael, that many think the Messiah is meant.

ARCHELA'US, a son of Herod the Great, by his Samaritan wife Malthace. He was educated with his brother Antipas at Rome, and after his father's death was placed over Judea, Idumea, and Samaria, (the cities Gaza, Gadara, and Hippo excepted,) with the title of *ethnarch* or *tetrarch;* whence he is said to *reign*, Matt. 2:22. This passage implies that he inherited the tyrannical and cruel disposition of his father; and history informs us that after enjoying his power for ten years, he was accused before the emperor on account of his cruelties, and banished to Vienne on the Rhone, in Gaul, where he died.

ARCHIP'PUS, saluted by Paul as his "fellow-soldier," Phile. 2, and exhorted to take heed to his ministry at Colosse, and fulfil it, Col. 4:17.

ARCTU'RUS signifies, properly, *the Bear's Tail*, and denotes a star in the tail of the Great Bear, or constellation Ursa Major. The "sons" of Arcturus are probably the smaller stars adjacent, Job 9:9; 38:32.

AREOP'AGUS, *the hill of Mars*, the seat of the ancient and venerable supreme court of Athens, called the Areopagites, Acts 17:19-34. It was composed entirely of ex-archons, of grave and blameless character, and their wise and just decisions made it famous far beyond the bounds of Greece. Their numbers and authority varied greatly from age to age. They held their sessions by night. They took cognizance of murders, impieties, and immoralities; punished vices of all kinds, idleness included; rewarded or assisted the virtuous; and were peculiarly attentive to blasphemies against the gods, and to the performance of the sacred mysteries. The case of Paul, therefore, would naturally come before them, for he sought to subvert their whole system of idolatry, and establish Christianity in its place. The

Bible narrative, however, rather describes an informal popular movement. Having heard Paul discoursing from day to day in the market-place, the philosophic and inquisitive Athenians took him one day up into the adjacent hill, for a more full and quiet exposition of his doctrine. The stone seats of the Areopagus lay open to the sky; in the court stood Epicureans, Stoics, etc.; around them spread the city, full of idolaters and their temples; and a little southeast rose the steep height of the Acropolis, on whose level summit were crowded more and richer idolatrous structures than on any other equal space in the world. Amid this scene, Paul exhibited the sin and folly of idol-worship with such boldness and power, that none could refute him, and some were converted.

RUINS OF THE AREOPAGUS AND ACROPOLIS.

AR'ETAS, the name of several kings of north-western Arabia. The only one mentioned in Scripture gave his daughter in marriage to Herod Antipas; but she being repudiated by Herod, Aretas made war upon him and destroyed his army. In consequence of this, the emperor Tiberius directed Vitellius, then proconsul of Syria, to make war upon the Arabian king, and bring him alive or dead to Rome. But while Vitellius was in the midst of preparation for the war, he received intelligence of the death of Tiberius, A. D. 37; on which he immediately recalled his troops, dismissed them into winter quarters, and then left the province. Aretas, taking advantage of this supineness, seems to have made an incursion and got possession of Damascus, over which he appointed a governor or ethnarch, who, A. D. 39, at the instigation of the Jews, attempted to put Paul in prison, 2 Cor. 11:32. Compare Acts 9:24, 25.

AR'GOB, a city in Bashan and Manasseh east of the Jordan; also the region around it. This was very fertile, and contained at one time sixty walled towns, which were taken by Jair the son of Manasseh, and called after him, Deut. 3:4, 13, 14; 1 Kin. 4:13.

A'RIEL, *the lion of God*, one of Ezra's chief men, Ezra 8:16. This word is used, in 2 Sam. 23:20, 1 Chr. 11:22, as a descriptive or perhaps a family name of two lion-like men of Moab. In another sense, Ezekiel applies it to the altar of God, Ezek. 43:15, and Isaiah to Jerusalem, as the hearth on which both the burnt-offerings and the enemies of God should be consumed, Isa. 29:1, 2, 7. See also Gen. 49:9.

ARIMATHE'A, or RA'MAH, (dual, Ramathaim,) a city whence came Joseph the counsellor, in whose new tomb the body of Jesus was laid, Matt. 27:57; John 19:38. We learn from Eusebius and Jerome that this city was near Lydda, a town twenty-four miles north-west of Jerusalem. It has generally been located at the modern Ramleh, a town near Lydda, of 3,000 inhabitants, in which the route from Egypt to Syria crosses that from Jerusalem to Joppa. But its site is rather to be sought a few miles east of Lydda, in the hills which skirt the plain of Sharon. The first book of Maccabees, 11:34, speaks of it as transferred, together with Lydda, from Samaria to Judea, which may account for Luke's calling it "a city of the Jews," Luke 23:51. It has been supposed to be the same place as the Ramah of mount Ephraim, the birthplace and residence of Samuel. This was called also Ramathaim-Zophim, 1 Sam. 1:1, 19, from which name the form Arimathea is readily derived. See RAMAH.

A'RIOCH, I., king of Ellasar, and ally of Chedorlaomer, Gen. 14:1.

II. A captain of Nebuchadnezzar's guard, Dan. 2:14.

ARISTAR'CHUS, a native of Thessalonica, a faithful fellow-laborer with Paul, Acts 20:4; 27:2; Phile. 24. His life was endangered in the riot at Ephesus, excited by the silversmiths, Acts 19:29; but having escaped, he continued with Paul, and was a prisoner with him at Rome, Col. 4:10.

ARK OF NOAH, the vessel in which the family of Noah was preserved during the deluge, when all the rest of our race perished for their sins. The ark is called in Hebrew, in the Septuagint, and by Josephus, a *chest;* and the same word is used in the history of the infant Moses, Ex. 2:3. So far as this name affords any evidence, it goes to show that the ark of Noah was not a regular sailing-vessel, but merely intended to float at large upon the waters. We may therefore regard it as a large, oblong, floating house, with a roof either flat or only slightly inclined. It was constructed with three stories, and had a door in the side. There is no mention of windows in *the side,* but "above," probably in the roof, where Noah was commanded to make them of a cubit in height, Gen. 5:16; 8:13.

The dimensions of the ark, taking the cubit as eighteen inches, were 450 ft. in length, 75 in breadth and 45 in height. It was built of gopher-wood, and made water-proof with bitumen, and was no doubt large enough to accommodate the eight persons of Noah's family and the animals to be saved in it—namely, of all birds and clean beasts seven each, and of unclean beasts two each, male and female. Many questions have been raised, and discussed at great length by sceptics and others, respecting the form and dimensions of the ark; the number of animals saved in it—whether including all species then existing in the world, except such as live in water or lie dormant, or only the species living in the parts of the world then peopled by man; and as to the possibility of their being all lodged in the ark, and their food during the year, etc. Some of these questions the Bible clearly settles. Others it is vain to discuss, since we have no means of deciding them. Certain it is, that while the Bible eulogizes the faith and obedience of Noah, it shows that his salvation was a miracle of Providence. It was by miracle that he was forewarned, and directed to prepare for the flood; and the same miraculous power accomplished all that Noah was unable to do in designing, building, and filling the ark, and preserving and guiding it through the deluge. It has been commonly supposed that the warning came to Noah 120 years before the flood. Compare Gen. 5:32 with 7:6, and Gen. 6:3 with 1 Pet. 3:20. Traditions of the ark are found in most nations all over the globe. See DELUGE.

ARK OF THE COVENANT, the sacred chest or coffer in which the tables of the law were deposited, written by the finger of God, and witnessing to his covenant with his people, Ex. 25:22; 34:29. It

was of shittim-wood, covered within and without with plates of gold, nearly four feet in length, and two feet three inches in width and height. On the top of it, all around, ran a kind of gold crown. It had four rings of gold, two on each side, through which staves were put, by which it was carried. These also were overlaid with the finest gold, and were not to be removed from the rings, Ex. 25:10-22. The lid of the ark, all of gold, was called *the mercy-seat;* and upon its opposite ends were two golden cherubim, fronting each other and the mercy-seat, which they covered with their outspread wings, Ex. 37:1-9. Here God specially dwelt, 2 Kin. 19:15, 1 Chr. 13:6, and shone forth, perhaps by some sensible manifestations,

Lev. 16:2; Psa. 80:1. Here he received the homage of his people, and dispensed his living oracles, Num. 7:89. The great yearly sacrifice of expiation was here offered by the high-priest, Heb. 9:7, in the Holy of Holies. Hence there was no object held more sacred by the Jews than "the ark of God." During their journeys in the wilderness, it was borne by the priests under a purple canopy and with great reverence before the host of Israel, Num. 4:5, 6. Before it the Jordan was divided, and behind it the waters flowed on again, Josh. 3, 4. The walls of Jericho fell down before it, Josh. 6:4–12.

After this, the ark continued some time at Gilgal, whence it was removed to Shiloh, Josh. 4:19; 10:43; 18:1. Hence the Israelites took it to their camp; but when they gave battle to the Philistines, it was taken by the enemy, 1 Sam. 4. The Philistines, oppressed by the hand of God, returned the ark, and it was lodged at Kirjath-jearim, 1 Sam. 7:1. It was afterwards, in the reign of Saul, at Nob. David conveyed it from Kirjath-jearim to the house of Obed-Edom, and from thence to his palace on Zion, 2 Sam. 6; and lastly, Solomon brought it into the temple at Jerusalem, 2 Chr. 5:2. It remained in the temple, with all suitable respect, till the times of the later idolatrous kings of Judah, who profaned the Most Holy place by their idols, when the priests appear to have removed the ark from the temple. At least, Josiah commanded them to bring it back to the sanctuary, and forbade them to carry it about, as they had hitherto done, 2 Chr. 35:3. The ark appears to have been destroyed at the captivity, or perhaps concealed by pious Jews in some hiding-place afterwards undiscoverable, as we hear nothing more of it; and the want of it made the second temple less glorious than the first.

Besides the tables of the covenant, placed by Moses in this sacred coffer, God appointed the blossoming rod of Aaron to be lodged there, Num. 17:10; Heb. 9:4; a golden vase of manna gathered in the wilderness, Ex. 16:33, 34, and a copy of the book of the law, Deut. 31:26.

AR'KITES, descendants of Canaan, of the Zidonian branch, who settled a town called Arka, at the north-west foot of mount Lebanon, Gen. 10:17; 1 Chr. 1:15. The ruins of Arka have been found by Burckhardt and others about fourteen miles north-east of Tripolis.

ARMAGED'DON, *mountain of Megiddo*, a place mentioned Rev. 16:16. Megiddo is a city in the great plain at the foot of mount Carmel, which had been the scene of much slaughter. Under this character it is referred to in the above text as the place in which God will collect together his enemies for destruction.

ARME'NIA, a large country of Asia, having Media on the east, Cappadocia on the west, Colchis and Iberia on the north, Mesopotamia on the south, and the Euphrates and Syria on the southwest. It is an elevated table-land, with a cool and salubrious climate. Lying between the Caucasus and the Taurus range, with mount Ararat towering in its central province, it gives rise to three notable rivers, the Euphrates, Tigris, and Araxes. It is only named in Scripture as the place of refuge of two Assyrian parricides, 2 Kin. 19:37. The modern Armenian church resembles strongly the Greek church, and is sadly debased and corrupt. See ARARAT, MINNI, and TOGARMAH.

ARMS and ARMOR. The Hebrews used in war offensive arms of the same kinds as were employed by other people of their time and of the East—swords, lances, spears, darts, javelins, bows, arrows, and slings. For defensive armor, they used helmets, cuirasses, bucklers, armor for the thighs, etc. See WAR.

In the accompanying engravings are represented specimens of the various weapons anciently used; also of the sev-

eral parts of the armor for defence, and the manner in which they were worn: 1. the cuirass, or defence of the body—this is called in Scripture the coat of mail, habergeon, and breastplate; it appears to have been made of leather or some pliant material, sometimes covered with metallic scales, and capable of taking the form of the parts of the body it protected; 2. the helmet, usually of metal, with its flowing crest; 3. the shield, target, or buckler, either of wood covered with tough hides,

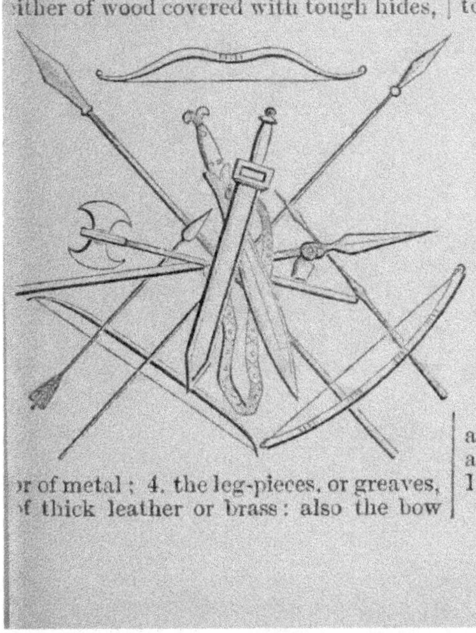

or of metal; 4. the leg-pieces, or greaves, of thick leather or brass: also the bow and arrow; the battleaxe; the spear, dart, and javelin or short spear; and the sword with its sheath, the ancient sword being short, straight, and twoedged.

Each Jewish tribe had its own banner. Under ABOMINATION is a cut representing the ensigns of the Roman legions, which the Jews regarded as idolatrous, not only because they had been consecrated to idols, and by heathen priests, but as they had images on them, and were objects of adoration. Exod. 20:4.

AR'NON, a river rising in the mountains east of the Dead sea, into which it flows. It is now called Wady Modjeb, and anciently divided the territories of the Moabites in turn from those of the Ammonites, Amorites, and Reubenites, Num. 21:13; Josh. 13:16. It flows in a deep and wild ravine of the same name. Burckhardt, after reaching the ruins of Aroer, which stand on the edge of the precipice at the foot of which the Arnon flows, says, "From hence a footpath leads down to the river. The view which the Modjeb presents is very striking. From the bottom, where the river runs through a narrow stripe of verdant level about forty yards across, the steep and barren banks arise to a great height, covered with immense blocks of stone which have rolled down from the upper strata; so that, when viewed from above, the valley looks like a deep chasm, formed by some tremendous convulsion of the earth, into which there seems to be no possibility of descending to the bottom. The distance from the edge of one precipice to that of the opposite one, is about two miles in a straight line."

He was thirty-five minutes in descending to the river bed. Here the heat of midsummer is extreme, and the river becomes almost dried up; but in the rainy season there is an impetuous torrent.

AR'OER, I., an ancient city on the north side of the Arnon, in the southern border of the tribe of Reuben, Deut. 2:36; 4:48; Josh. 13:9. It was in the territory of the Amorites, Josh. 12:2, but seems to have fallen at a later day into the hands of Moab, Jer. 48:19. See ARNON.

II. A town in the tribe of Gad, probably east of Rabbath-Ammon, Josh. 13:25, and perhaps on the Jabbok, 2 Sam. 24:5. It is mentioned in Judg. 11:33.

III. A town of Judah, to which David

sent presents, 1 Sam. 30:28; 1 Chr. 11:44. Robinson found traces of it about sixteen miles south by west from Hebron.

AR'PAD, a Syrian city, associated with Hamath, 2 Kin. 18:34; 19; Isa. 10:9; 36:19, and with Damascus, Jer. 49:23. Its site is unknown.

ARPHAX'AD, a son of Shem, two years after the flood, Gen. 10:22; 11:10. Seven generations followed him before Abraham, while he lived till after the settlement of Abraham in the land of promise and the rescue of Lot from the four kings. He died A. M. 2096, aged four hundred and thirty-eight.

AR'ROW, used by the Jews both in hunting and in war; sometimes merely a sharpened reed, sometimes feathered, barbed, and even poisoned, Job 6:4. The bow was of various forms and materials, and many could be used only by the strongest men, Psa. 18:34. Arrows were used to convey fire to an enemy's house, and for divination, Ezek. 21:21. The word is applied symbolically to children, Psa. 127:4, 5; to the lightning, Psa. 18:14; Hab. 3:11; to sudden calamities, Job 6:4; Psa. 38:2; 91:5; Ezek. 5:15; and to the deceitful and bitter words of an evil tongue, Psa. 64:3; 120:4.

ARTAXER'XES, *great king*, the name or title of several kings of Persia. I. It is given in Ezra 4:7–24, to Smerdis the Magian, who usurped the throne after the death of Cambyses, B. C. 522, pretending to be Smerdis, the son of Cyrus, whom Cambyses had put to death. His usurped power was used, at the instigation of Rehum, etc., to stop the rebuilding of the temple. He was murdered, after a reign of eight months, and was succeeded by Darius son of Hystaspes.

II. The king of this name mentioned in Ezra 7, is most probably Artaxerxes Longimanus, the son and successor of Xerxes, who ascended the throne B. C. 464, and died B. C. 425, after a mild reign of thirty-nine years. In the seventh year of his reign, Ezra led a second company of the Jewish exiles back to Jerusalem. In the twentieth year of Artaxerxes Longimanus, Nehemiah was sent to Jerusalem as governor, Neh. 2:1; 5:14, etc.

AR'TEMAS, apparently a faithful minister, coöperating with Paul, Titus 3:12, who thought him worthy to take the place of Titus at Crete, while the latter spent the winter with the apostle at Nicopolis.

AR'VAD, a Phœnician city, on a small rocky island at the mouth of the river Eleutherus, twenty-two miles north of Tripolis. It is now called Ruad, and is but a ruin. The Arvadites also occupied the adjacent coast. They were descendants of Canaan, Gen. 10:18; 1 Chr. 1:16; and were noted mariners, Ezek. 27:8, 11.

A'SA, the third king of Judah after Solomon, son and successor of Abijam, 1 Kin. 15:8. He began to reign B. C. 951, and reigned forty-one years at Jerusalem. The first part of his reign was comparatively peaceful and prosperous. He restored the pure worship of God; expelled those who, from sacrilegious superstition, prostituted themselves in honor of their false gods; purified Jerusalem from the infamous practices attending the worship of idols; and deprived his mother of her office and dignity of queen, because she erected an idol to Astarte. In the eleventh year of his reign, God gave him the victory over the vast army of the Cushite king Zerah; and the prophet Azariah encouraged him to go on in his work of reform. And yet, when Baasha king of Israel opposed this very work, he sought aid not from God, but from heathen Syria. In the latter part of his life, he became diseased in his feet; and Scripture reproaches him with having had recourse to the physicians, rather than to the Lord, 2 Chr. 16:12. Yet his reign was, on the whole, one of the happiest which Judah enjoyed, and the Bible repeatedly commends his piety as an example. 1 Kin. 22:43; 2 Chr. 20:32; 21:12. His funeral rites were celebrated with special magnificence. There was ill-will and strife between Asa and Baasha all their days, as between Rehoboam and Israel, 1 Kin. 15:6, 16.

AS'AHEL, son of David's sister Zeruiah, and brother of Joab; one of David's thirty heroes, and extremely swift of foot; killed by Abner, at the battle of Gibeon, 2 Sam. 2:18, 23.

A'SAPH, I., *assembler*, a celebrated musician in David's time, and one of the leaders of the temple music. 1 Chr. 16:5; 25:1, 2. This service appears to have been hereditary in his family, Neh. 7:44; 11:22. He is also called a seer, 2 Chr. 29:30; and his name is prefixed to twelve Psalms, (50, 73–83,) but whether they were written by him, or for him or his family to sing, is unknown. See MUSIC.

II. A recorder of king Hezekiah, 2 Kin. 18:18; Isa. 36:3.

III. Keeper of forests under Artaxerxes, Neh. 2:8.

ASCEN'SION, the visible ascent of Christ to heaven. When our Saviour had repeatedly conversed with his apostles during forty days, after his resurrection, and afforded them infallible proofs of its reality, he led them out to the mount of Olives, and was raised up to heaven in their sight, there to continue till he shall come again at the last day to judge the quick and the dead, Acts 1:9, 11. The ascension was demonstrated by the descent of the Holy Ghost, John 16:7-14; Acts 2. It was Christ's real human nature that ascended; and he thus triumphed gloriously over death and hell, as head of his body the church. While he blessed his disciples he was parted from them, and multitudes of the angelic hosts accompanied and welcomed him, Psa. 24:9; 68:17. The consequences resulting from his ascension are: the fulfilment of types and prophecies concerning it; his appearance as a priest in the presence of God for us; his more open and full assumption of his kingly office; his receiving gifts for men; his opening the way to heaven for his people, Heb. 10:19, 20; and assuring his saints of their ascension to heaven after the resurrection of the dead, John 14:1, 2.

AS'ENATH, daughter of Potipherah, priest or prince of On; given in marriage by Pharaoh to Joseph, as adding honor and strength to his high office. She was the mother of Ephraim and Manasseh, Gen. 41:45; 46:20.

ASH'DOD, one of the five chief cities of the Philistines, assigned to the tribe of Judah, but never conquered by them, Josh. 13:3; 15:47; 1 Sam. 5:1; 6:17; Neh. 4:7. Here stood the temple of Dagon; and hither the ark was first brought, after the fatal battle at Ebenezer, 1 Sam. 5:1. It was called by the Greeks Azotus, and belonged to Judea in the time of Christ. Here Philip preached the gospel, Acts 8:40. At the present day, it is a miserable village, still called Esdud.

ASH'ER, the eighth son of Jacob and second of Zilpah, Gen. 30:13; 35:26. On entering Canaan his tribe was the fifth in order, numbering fifty-three thousand four hundred. The portion of Asher lay along the seaboard, having Lebanon and Zidon on the north, Carmel and the tribe of Issachar on the south, and Zebulun and Naphtali on the east. It was fruitful in grain, wine, oil, and minerals, Gen. 49:20; Deut. 33:24, 25. How much of the Phœnician coast was included is uncertain, Josh. 19:25, 28; but the Asherites were unable to expel the Canaanites, and dwelt in part among them, Judg. 1:31, 32. They are honorably mentioned in the history of David, 1 Chr. 12:36, and of Hezekiah, 2 Chr. 30:11.

ASH'ES. To repent in sackcloth and ashes, or to lie down among ashes, was an external sign of self-affliction for sin, or of grief under misfortune. We find it adopted by Job, 2:8; by many Jews when in great fear, Esth. 4:3; and by the king of Nineveh, Jonah 3:6. The ashes of a red heifer were used in ceremonial purification, Num. 19.

ASH'IMA, a deity adored by the men of Hamath, who were settled in Samaria, 2 Kin. 17:30.

ASH'KENAZ, a son of Gomer and grandson of Japheth, Gen. 10:3. The region peopled by his descendants is named in Jer. 51:27 with Minni and Ararat, provinces of Armenia. It probably lay towards the Black sea.

ASH'PENAZ, chief of the eunuchs of king Nebuchadnezzar, who had the charge of Daniel and his young companions, and was led to show them favor at his own peril, Dan. 1:3-18.

ASHTORETH, FROM A TYRIAN COIN.

ASH'TORETH, plural ASH'TAROTH, called by the Greeks Astarte, was a goddess of the Phœnicians, 2 Kin. 23:13, whose worship was also introduced among the Israelites and Philistines, 1 Kin. 11:5, 33; 1 Sam. 7:3; 31:10. She is commonly named in connection with Baal, Judg. 2:13; 10:6; 1 Sam. 7:4; 12:10. Another Hebrew name for the same goddess is Asherah, the happy, the fortunate; or more simply, fortune. This last name is commonly rendered in the English version "grove;" but eminent Hebrew scholars think this meaning is unsupported either by the etymology or the context. Both these Hebrew names of Astarte, when used in the plural, often signify images or statues of Astarte; which are said to be set up, broken down, destroyed, etc. In connection with the worship of Astarte there was much of dissolute licentiousness; and the public prostitutes of both sexes were regarded as consecrated to her. See 2 Kin. 23:7. Compare Lev. 19:29; Deut. 23:18.

As Baal or Bel denotes, in the astrological mythology of the East, the male star of fortune, the planet Jupiter; so Ashtoreth signifies the female star of fortune, the planet Venus. As to the opinion that Baal designates the sun, and Ashtoreth the moon, see under BAAL. Compare Jer. 7:18; 11:13; 44:17, 18; Ezek. 16.

ASHTAROTH-KARNAÏM, *two-horned Astartes*, Gen. 14:5, or simply Ashtaroth, Deut. 1:4, a city of Og, king of Bashan, beyond Jordan. The name is doubtless derived from the goddess Ashtoreth or Astarte, whose images were adored there under the figure of a female with a crescent, or horns. It was in the limits of the half tribe of Manasseh, Josh. 13:31; and was a Levitical city, 1 Chr. 6:71. It is also called Beeshterah, Josh. 21:27.

ASIA, one of the great divisions of the eastern continent, lying east of Europe. The Asia spoken of in the Bible is Asia Minor, a peninsula which lies between the Euxine or Black sea and the eastern part of the Mediterranean, and which formerly included the provinces of Phrygia, Cilicia, Pamphylia, Caria, Lycia, Lydia, Mysia, Bithynia, Paphlagonia, Cappadocia, Galatia, Lycaonia, and Pisidia. On the western coast were anciently the countries of Æolia, Ionia, and Doris, the names of which were afterwards retained, although the countries were included in the provinces of Mysia, Lydia, and Caria. Many Jews were scattered over these regions, as appears from the history in Acts, and from Josephus. The writers of the New Testament comprehend, under the name of Asia, either (1) the whole of Asia Minor, Acts 19:26, 27; 20:4, 16, 18; or (2) only proconsular Asia, that is, the region of Ionia, of which Ephesus was the capital, and which Strabo also calls Asia, Acts 2:9; 6:9; 16:6; 19:10, 22. Cicero speaks of proconsular Asia as containing the provinces of Phrygia, Mysia, Caria, and Lydia.

AS'KELON, a city in the land of the Philistines, between Ashdod and Gaza, on the coast of the Mediterranean. After the death of Joshua, the tribe of Judah took Askelon; but it subsequently became one of the five governments belonging to the Philistines, Judg. 1:18; 1 Sam. 6:17. Dr. Richardson thus describes its present state: "Askelon was one of the proudest satrapies of the Philistines; now there is not an inhabitant within its walls; and the prophecy of Zechariah is fulfilled: 'The king shall perish from Gaza, and Askelon shall not be inhabited,'" Zech. 9:5.

ASNAP'PER, the Assyrian king or satrap, under whose direction the territory of the ten tribes was peopled by emigrants from beyond the Euphrates, 2 Kin. 17:24; Ezra 4:10. Some identify him with Esar-haddon, and some with Shalmaneser. Ezra styles him "great and noble;" but no other trace of him is left.

ASP, Hebrew Pethen, a kind of serpent, whose poison is of such rapid operation, that it kills almost the instant it penetrates, without a possibility of remedy. It is said to be very small, not more than a foot in length. Forskal supposes it to be the Baetan, or Coluber Lebetina of Linnæus; but the true asp of the ancients seems to be unknown. It is frequently mentioned by ancient writers; but in such an indefinite manner, that it is impossible to ascertain the species with precision. It is mentioned in Deut. 32:33; Job 20:14, 16; Psa. 58:4; 91:13; Isa. 11:8; Jer. 8:17; Rom. 3:13. A traveller in the desert south of Judah describes it as still infested with serpents; and adds as an instance, "One day we saw in our path an asp, a foot long, coiled up in the attitude of springing. Our Arabs killed it, saying it was exceedingly venomous."

ASS, an animal well known for domestic uses; and frequently mentioned in Scripture. People of the first quality in Palestine rode on asses. Deborah, in her song, describes the nobles of the land as those who "ride on white asses,"

Judg. 5:10. Compare Judg. 10:4; 12:14. The oriental asses are not to be compared with those of northern countries; but are far more stately, active, and lively. Indeed, they were anciently, as still, highly prized; and were also preferred for riding, especially the she-asses, on account of their sure-footedness. Hence we so often find mention of she-asses alone.

The Wild Ass is a well-known oriental animal, often mentioned in Scripture, and is a much handsomer and more dignified animal than the common ass. These animals were anciently found in Palestine, Syria, Arabia Deserta, Mesopotamia, Phrygia, and Lycaonia; but they rarely occur in those regions at the present time, and seem to be almost entirely confined to Tartary, some parts of Persia and India, and Africa. Their manners greatly resemble those of the wild horse. They assemble in troops under the conduct of a leader or sentinel, and are extremely shy and vigilant. They will, however, stop in the midst of their course, and even suffer the approach of man for an instant, and then dart off with the utmost rapidity. They have been at all times celebrated for their swiftness. Their voice resembles that of the common ass, but is shriller. Mr. Morier says, "We gave chase to two wild asses, which had so much more speed than our horses, that when they had got at some distance, they stood still and looked behind at us, snorting with their noses in the air, as if in contempt of our endeavors to catch them."

AS'SOS, a seaport in Mysia, opposite to the island of Lesbos on the north. Here Paul took ship for Mitylene, Acts 20:13. It is now a poor village, called Beiram.

ASSYR'IA, a celebrated country and empire, had its name from Ashur, or Assur, the second son of Shem, who settled in that region, Gen. 10:22. In the Bible the name Assyria is employed in three different significations: namely,

1. Assyria *ancient* and *proper* lay east of the Tigris, between Armenia, Susiana, and Media, and appears to have comprehended the six provinces attributed to it by Ptolemy, namely, Arrapachis, Adiabene, Arbelis, (now Erbil,) Calachene, (Heb. Halah? 2 Kin. 17:6,) Apollonias, and Sittacene. It is the region which mostly comprises the modern Kurdistan and the pashalik of Mosul. Of these provinces, Adiabene was the most fertile and important; in it was situated Nineveh the capital; and the term *Assyria*, in its most narrow sense, seems sometimes to have meant only this province.

2. Most generally, Assyria means the Kingdom of Assyria, including Babylonia and Mesopotamia, and extending to the Euphrates, which is therefore used by Isaiah as an image of this empire, Isa. 7:20; 8:7. In one instance, the idea of the *empire* predominates so as to exclude that of Assyria proper, namely, Gen. 2:14, where the Hiddekel or Tigris is said to flow *eastward* of Assyria.

3. After the overthrow of the Assyrian state, the name continued to be applied to those countries which had been formerly under its dominion, namely, (*a*) To Babylonia, 2 Kin. 23:29; Jer. 2:18. (*b*) To Persia, Ezra 6:22, where Darius is also called king of Assyria.

The early history of Assyria is involved in obscurity. We know from the sacred narrative that it was a powerful nation. Israel was subjugated by one of its monarchs in the period of the Judges, and during the reign of the kings the Assyrian power was an object of perpetual dread. Pul, king of Assyria, invaded Israel in the reign of Menahem. Tiglath-pileser assisted Ahaz against a confederate army formed of the Syrian forces in league with those of the ten tribes. Shalmanezer invaded Israel, conquered Hoshea, and made him a vassal, bound to pay a yearly tribute. Hoshea wishing however to throw off the yoke, attempted to form a league with Egypt, and refused the tribute. On ascertaining this secret design of the Israelitish prince, Shalmanezer again invaded Israel, reduced Samaria, loaded its king with fetters, and transported the people of the land into Media, and put an end to the separate kingdom of the ten tribes. The three tribes located east of Jordan had already been deported into Media by Tiglath-pileser, when he ravaged Israel to save Ahaz and the kingdom of Judah. Sennacherib of Assyria came into Judah with a powerful army in the reign of Hezekiah, but was miraculously defeated. Esarhaddon, his son and successor, ravaged Judah in the days of Manasseh, and carried the conquered sovereign in chains to Babylon. After this period the empire of Assyria suddenly waned, and its last monarch was the effeminate Sardanapalus, Num. 24:22. Its capital was one of the most renowned of the eastern world. See NINEVEH. But the kingdom fell at length into the hands of the Medes, the monarchy was divided between them and the Babylonians, and the very name of Assyria was thenceforth forgotten.

ASTROL'OGERS, men who pretended to foretell future events by means of astronomical observations. It was fancied that the stars and planets had an influence, for good or for evil, on human affairs, and that certain aspects and relative positions of the heavenly bodies were full of meaning to those who had skill to interpret them, Dan. 2:2. These superstitions were prevalent among the Chaldeans, Assyrians, Egyptians, Phœnicians, and Arabians, and were closely connected with the worship of the sun, moon, and stars, Deut. 4:19; 17:3; 2 Kin. 23:5, 12; Jer. 19:13; Ezek. 8:16; Zeph. 1:5. They were thus idolatrous in their spirit, robbed God of his glory, and were highly offensive in his sight.

ASTRON'OMY, the science which treats of the heavenly bodies, was much studied in Asia in ancient times. The Chaldeans excelled in it. The Hebrews do not appear to have made great proficiency in it, though their climate and mode of life invited to the contemplation of the heavens. Revelation had taught them who created and governed all the worlds, Gen. 1, and the infinite presence of the one living and true God filled the universe, to their minds, with a glory unknown to others, Psa. 19; Isa. 40:26; Amos 5:8. The Bible does not aim to teach the science of astronomy, but speaks of the sun, moon, and stars in the familiar language of mankind in all ages. The following heavenly bodies are alluded to particularly in Scripture: Venus, the morning star, Isa. 14:12; Rev. 2:28; Orion, and the Pleiades, Job 9:9; 38:31; Amos 5:8; the Great Bear, called "Arcturus," Job 9:9; 38:32; Draco, "the crooked serpent," Job 26:13; and Gemini, "the twins," 2 Kin. 23:5; Acts 28:11. The planets Jupiter and Venus were worshipped under various names, as Baal and Ashtoreth, Gad and Meni, Isa. 65:11. Mercury is named as Nebo, in Isa. 46:1; Saturn as Chiun, in Amos 5:26; and Mars as Nergal, in 2 Kin. 17:30. See IDOLATRY and STARS.

ASUP'PIM, *collections*. The "house of Asuppim" was probably a storehouse in connection with the temple, 1 Chr. 26:15.

A'TAD, a Canaanite, at whose threshing-floor a solemn mourning was held over the remains of Jacob, on their way from Egypt to Hebron, Gen. 50:10, 11. See ABEL-MIZRAIM.

AT'AROTH. Several places of this name occur in Scripture: one in the tribe of Judah, 1 Chr. 2:54; one or two in Ephraim, Josh. 16:2, 5, 7; 18:13; and one or two in Gad, Num. 32:3, 34, 35. Robinson found traces of one of those in Ephraim, on a high hill about six miles north by west from Bethel.

ATHALI'AH, a granddaughter of Omri, 2 Chr. 22:2, and daughter of Ahab and Jezebel, 2 Kin. 11:1. Strangely enough, she was chosen as the wife of Jehoram, son of the pious Jehoshaphat king of Judah. Her pernicious influence drew into idolatry and crime both her husband and her son Ahaziah, 2 Chr. 21:6; 22:3. After their premature death, she usurped the throne, and sought to secure herself in it by the murder of all the seed royal. Only Joash her grandson, then an infant, was saved by his aunt Jehosheba. Six years afterwards he was brought from his place of refuge, and crowned by the bold and faithful high-priest Jehoiada, who at the same time caused the blood-stained Athaliah to be put to death, 2 Kin. 11; 2 Chr. 23.

THE ACROPOLIS AT ATHENS, AS IT WAS.

ATH'ENS, *the city of Minerva*, the chief city of Attica in Greece, situated on the Saronic gulf, forty-six miles east of Corinth, and about five miles from the coast. The city was in a plain extending to the sea on the south-west, where it had three ports, the passage to which was defended by long and broad walls. Several rocky hills rose in the plain, the largest of which was the citadel, or Acropolis. Around this the city was built, most of the buildings spreading towards the sea. The summit of the hill was nearly level, about eight-hundred feet long and four hundred wide. The only way to the Acropolis was through the Propylæa, a magnificent gateway on the western side, adorned with two temples decorated with the finest pieces of sculpture and painting. These splendid portals crowned an ascent by marble steps to the summit of the hill, on which were erected the temples of the guardian divinities of Athens. On the left was the temple of Pallas Athene, (Minerva,) regarded as the protectress of the city. Under the same roof was the temple of Neptune. In the area, on a high pedestal, stood a bronze statue of Minerva seventy feet high. On the right arose the Parthenon, the glory of Athens, the noblest triumph of Grecian architecture. From whatever quarter the traveller arrived, the first thing he saw was the Parthenon rearing its lofty head above the city and the citadel. Its ruins, still sublime in decay, are the first object that attracts the eye of a stranger. It was of the Doric order of architecture, built of beautiful white marble, and was about one hundred feet wide, two hundred and twenty-six feet deep, and seventy feet high. There was a double portico of columns at the two fronts, and a single row along each side. There was an architrave, or frieze, along the exterior of the nave, beautifully sculptured, with the representation of a procession in honor of Minerva. Within the temple was a statue of Minerva, by Phidias, celebrated for its exquisite beauty. It was made of gold and ivory, and was nearly forty feet high. The goddess was represented erect, covered with her ægis, holding in one hand a lance, and in the other a figure of victory. At the foot of the Acropolis, on one side was the Odeum, or music-hall, and the theatre of Bacchus: on the other side was the Prytaneum, where the chief magistrates and most meritorious citizens were entertained at a table furnished at the public expense. A small valley lay between the Acropolis and the hill on which the Areopagus held its sessions; it also separated the Areopagus from the Pnyx, a small rocky hill on which the general assemblies of the people were held. Here the spot is yet pointed out from which the eminent orators addressed the people. It is cut in the natural rock. In this vicinity also was the *agora*, or market-place, Acts 17:17, an open square surrounded by beautiful structures; while on every side altars, shrines, and temples were seen, some of them exceedingly magnificent. This beautiful city was also celebrated for the military talents and the learning, eloquence, and politeness of its inhabitants. It was the very flower of ancient civilization; its schools of philosophy were the most illustrious in the world, and its painters, sculptors, and architects have never been surpassed. Yet no city was so "wholly given to idolatry." The apostle Paul visited it about the year A. D. 52, and though alone among its proud philosophers, preached Jesus and the resurrection to them with fidelity and success, Acts 17:15–34. See AREOPAGUS. At present Athens is comparatively in ruins, and has a population of about 28,000 addicted to the superstitions of the Greek church.

ATONE'MENT is the satisfaction offered to divine justice for the sins of mankind by the death of Jesus Christ; by virtue of which all true penitents believing in Christ are reconciled to God, are freed from the penalty of their sins, and entitled to eternal life. The atonement by Jesus Christ is the great distinguishing peculiarity of the gospel, and is presented in a great variety of terms and illustrations in both the Old Testament and the New. See REDEMPTION, SACRIFICES. The English word atonement originally denoted the reconciliation of parties previously at variance. It is used in the Old Testament to translate a Hebrew word which means a covering; implying that by a Divine propitiation the sinner is covered from the just anger of God. This is actually effected by the death of Christ; while the ceremonial offerings of the Jewish church only secured from impending temporal judgments, and typified the blood of Jesus Christ which "cleanseth us from all sin."

ATONEMENT, DAY OF. See EXPIATION.

ATTA'LIA, a seaport in Pamphylia, at the mouth of the river Catarrhactes, visited by Paul and Barnabas on their way from Perga to Antioch, Acts 14:25. There is still a village there of a similar name, with extensive ruins in the vicinity.

AUGUS'TUS, *venerable*, the first peacefully acknowledged emperor of Rome, began to reign B. C. 19. Augustus was the emperor who appointed the enrolment, Luke 2:1, which obliged Joseph and the Virgin to go to Bethlehem, the place where the Messiah was to be born. He died A. D. 14.

A'VEN, see HELIOPOLIS.

AVEN'GER OF BLOOD. See BLOOD, REFUGE.

A'VIM, or A'VITES, descendants of Canaan, Gen. 10:17, who occupied a portion of the coast of Palestine from Gaza towards the river of Egypt, but were expelled and almost destroyed by invading Philistines or Caphtorim, before the time of Moses, Deut. 2:23. Some yet remained in the time of Joshua, Josh. 13:3. They are conjectured to have been the same people with the Hivites, of whom traces were found in various parts of Canaan, Gen. 34:2; Josh. 9:7; 11:3.

AZARI'AH, a king of Judah, 2 Kin. 15:1–7. In 2 Chr. 26, and elsewhere, he is called *Uzziah*. He began to reign at sixteen years of age, B. C. 806. The first part of his reign was prosperous and happy; but afterwards, presuming to offer incense in the temple, he was smitten with leprosy, and continued a leper till his death, 2 Chr. 26:16–23. This name was very common among the Jews, and was borne by many briefly referred to in Scripture.

AZE'KAH, a town in the tribe of Judah, about fifteen miles south-west of Jerusalem; mentioned in the narratives of Joshua and Saul, Josh. 10:10; 1 Sam. 17:1; taken by Nebuchadnezzar, Jer. 34:7, but afterwards repeopled by the Jews, Neh. 11:30.

AZ'ZAH, the same as GAZA.

AZO'TUS. See ASHDOD.

B.

BA'AL, *lord*, I., in the Old Testament denotes an idol of the Phœnicians, and particularly of the Tyrians, whose worship was also introduced with great solemnities among the Hebrews, and especially at Samaria, along with that of Astarte, Judg. 6:25–32; 2 Kin. 10:18, 28. See ASHTORETH. The plural, Baalim, signifies images or statues of Baal, Judg. 2:11; 10.10. Of the extent to which the worship of this idol was domesticated

HEAD OF BAAL, FROM A TYRIAN COIN.

among the Phœnicians and Carthaginians, we have an evidence in the proper names of persons; as, among the former, Ethbaal, Jerubbaal; and among the latter, Hannibal, Asdrubal, etc. Among the Babylonians, the same idol was worshipped under the name of BEL, which is only another form of the word *Baal*, Isa. 46:1; Jer. 50:2; 51:44. The worship of Baal was established in Babylon in the famous tower of Babel, the uppermost room of which served at the same time as an observatory, and as the repository of a collection of astronomical observations.

That in the astronomical, or rather, astrological mythology of the East, we are to look for the origin of this worship in the adoration of the heavenly bodies, is conceded by all critics. The more common opinion has been, that Baal, or Bel, is the sun; and that, under this name, this luminary received divine honors. But the Greek and Roman writers give to the Babylonian Bel the name of Jupiter Belus, meaning the *planet* Jupiter, which was regarded, along with the planet Venus, as the guardian and giver of all good fortune; and formed, with Venus, the most fortunate of all constellations, under which alone fortunate sovereigns could be born. This planet, therefore, many suppose to have been the object of worship under the name of Baal, as also the planet Venus under that of Astarte. Not that the sun was not an object of idolatrous worship among these nations, but in that case he is represented under his own name; as 2 Kin. 23:11.

The temples and altars of Baal were generally on eminences. Manasseh placed in the two courts of the temple at Jerusalem altars to all the host of heaven, and in particular to Astarte, 2 Kin. 21:5, 7. Jeremiah threatens the Jews who had sacrificed to Baal on the house-top, Jer. 32:29; and Josiah destroyed the altars which Ahaz had erected on the terrace of his palace, 2 Kin. 23:12.

Human victims were offered to Baal, as they were also to the sun. Jeremiah reproaches the inhabitants of Judah and Jerusalem with "building the high places of Baal, to burn their sons with fire for burnt-offerings unto Baal," Jer. 19:5; an expression which appears to be decisive as to the actual slaying by fire of the unhappy victims to Baal. See MOLOCH.

The children of Israel were prone to serve Baal. See Num. 25:3; Judg. 2:13; 3:7. Under Samuel they put away their idols, 1 Sam. 7:4. This continued under David and Solomon; but under Ahab, whose wife Jezebel was a daughter of the Zidonian king Ethbaal, the worship of Baal was restored with great pomp, 1 Kin. 16:31.

Joined with other words, Baal signifies also other false gods. Baal-Berith, or the "lord of the covenant," was a god of the Shechemites, Judg. 8:33; 9:4. Baal-Peor, or "the lord of Peor," was a filthy idol of the Moabites, Num. 25:3, 5; Hos. 9:10. Baal-Zebub, "lord of flies," was a god of the Philistines at Ekron. See BEELZEBUB.

II. The word BAAL also occurs in many compound names of places, not always having any reference to the idol.

BA'ALAH, a town in the tribe of Simeon, Josh. 15:29; 19:3; called also Bilhah, 1 Chr. 4:29. The same as Kirjathjearim.

BA'ALATH, a town in the tribe of Gad, Josh. 19:44. This lay not far from Bethhoron. It is uncertain whether it is the same as the Baalath rebuilt by Solomon, 1 Kin. 9:18; 2 Chr. 8:6.

BAAL-GAD', a city in the valley of Lebanon, at the foot of Hermon; the northernmost point to which the wars of Joshua reached, Josh. 11:17; 12:7; 13:5. It was perhaps the same as Baalhermon. Some have supposed it was Baalbek; but this lay further north.

BAAL-HA'ZOR, where Absalom kept his flocks, 2 Sam. 13:23, was near Ephraim, a city of Judah, some eight miles east of Jerusalem.

BA'ALIS, king of the Ammonites in the time of the captivity. He caused the assassination of Gedaliah, then governor of Judah, Jer. 40:14; 41:1-10.

BAAL-ME'ON, in Reuben beyond the Jordan, Num. 32:38; called also Beth-meon, Jer. 48:23, and Beth-baal-meon, Josh. 13:17. Its ruins are found two miles southeast of Heshbon. Ezekiel, 25:9, speaks of it as then a Moabitish town.

BAAL-PERA'ZIM, *place of breaches*, a name given by David to the scene of a battle with the Philistines, 2 Sam. 5:20; 1 Chr. 14:11; Isa. 28:21. It was in the valley of Rephaim, not far south-west of Jerusalem.

BAAL-ZEPH'ON, a town in Egypt, probably near the modern Suez. Its location is unknown, as are the details of the route of the Hebrews on leaving Egypt. They encamped "over against" and "before" Baal-zephon before crossing the Red sea, Ex. 14:2; Num. 33:7.

BA'ANAH and RECHAB, sons of Rimmon, in the service of Ish-bosheth the son of Saul. Thinking to obtain a reward from David, they secretly slew their master while reposing at noon, and carried his head to David at Hebron. They suffered, however, the punishment suitable for those whose "feet are swift to shed blood," 2 Sam. 4:1-12.

BA'ASHA, son of Ahijah, and commander of the armies of Nadab, king of Israel. He killed his master treacherously at the siege of Gibbethon, and usurped the kingdom, B. C. 953, which he possessed twenty-three years. He exterminated the whole race of Jeroboam, as had been predicted, 1 Kin. 14:7-14; but by his bad conduct and idolatry incurred God's indignation, 1 Kin. 15; 16:1-7, 12. God sent him a warning by the mouth of Jehu the prophet; which was fulfilled in the extermination of his family two years after his own death.

BIRS NIMROUD.

BA'BEL, *confusion*, the name of a lofty tower, begun to be built by the descendants of Noah among whom Nimrod was a leader, about one hundred and twenty years after the flood; so called because God there *confounded* the language of those who were employed in the undertaking, Gen. 10:10; 11:9. Their object in building the city and tower, was to concentrate the population and the dominion at that spot; and as this was contrary to the divine purpose of replenishing the earth with inhabitants, and betrayed an ungodly and perhaps idolatrous disposition, God frustrated their design by miraculously giving to different portions of the people different languages or different modes of pronunciation and divergent dialects of the original language of man, thus causing them to disperse over the globe. Compare Acts 2:1-11. The tower was apparently left incomplete, but the foundation of the city was probably laid, and a portion no doubt of the builders continued to dwell there. The place became afterwards the celebrated city of Babylon. It has been supposed that the tower of Babel was afterwards finished, and called the tower of Belus, within the city of Babylon. Herodotus visited this tower, and describes it as a square pyramid, measuring half a mile in circumference at the base; from this rose eight towers one above another gradually decreasing to the summit, which was reached by a broad road winding up around the outside. This tower was used for astronomical purposes, but was chiefly devoted to the worship of Bel, whose temple contained immense treasures, including several statues of massive gold, one of which was forty feet in height. Here were deposited the sacred golden vessels brought from Jerusalem, 2 Chr. 36:7; Jer. 51:44. Its ruins are supposed to be the present Birs Nimroud, six miles south-west of Hilleh, the modern Babylon: an immense mound of coarse sun-dried bricks, laid with bitumen. It is a ruinous heap, shattered by violence, furrowed by storms, and strown with fragments of brick, pottery, etc., fused and vitrified by some intense heat. It is 190 feet high, and on the top rises an irregular tower 90 feet in circumference and 35 feet high, built of a fine brick—with which the whole mound appears to have been faced. The tower is rent asunder and mutilated at the top, and scathed as if by lightning—a monument, some have thought, of the just wrath of God. See NEBUCHADNEZZAR.

BAB'YLON, I., a celebrated city situated on the Euphrates, the original foundation of which is described under the word Babel. With this coincide many ancient traditions, while some speak of Semiramis as the founder, and others of Nebuchadnezzar. These accounts may all be reconciled, by supposing that Semiramis rebuilt the ancient city, and that Nebuchadnezzar afterwards greatly enlarged and adorned it.

Babylon lay in a vast and fertile plain watered by the Euphrates, which flowed through the city. Its walls are described as 60 miles in circumference, 300 feet high, and 75 feet wide, Jer. 51:44-58. A deep trench ran parallel with the walls. In each of the four sides were 25 brazen gates, from which roads crossed to the opposite gates. On the squares thus formed, countless houses and gardens were made. Nebuchadnezzar's palace was in an inclosure six miles in circumference. Within this were also "the hanging gardens," an immense artificial mound 400 feet high, sustained by arches upon arches, terraced off for trees and flowers, the water for which was drawn from the river by machinery concealed in the mound, Dan. 4:29, 30.

Under Nebuchadnezzar, Babylon reached the summit of her greatness and splendor. She was renowned for learning, especially in astronomy, and for skill in various arts, as the making of carpets and cloths, of perfumes, jewelry, etc. Her location gave her to a great extent the control of the traffic, by the Euphrates and by caravans, between Central Asia and Arabia and Egypt. She was "a city of merchants," Isa. 43:14; Ezek. 17:4; and into her lap flowed, either through conquest or commerce, the wealth of almost all known lands. Justly therefore might the prophets call her "the great," Dan. 4:20; "the praise of the whole earth," Jer. 51:41; "the beauty of the Chaldees' excellency," Isa. 13:19; "the lady of kingdoms," Isa. 47:5; but also "the tender and delicate," and "given to pleasures," Isa. 47:1, 8. In consequence of the opulence and luxury of the inhabitants, corruptness and licentiousness of manners and morals were carried to a frightful extreme. Bel, Nebo, Nergal, Merodach, Succoth-benoth, and other idols, were there worshipped with rites in which impurity was made a matter of religion. Well might we expect Jehovah to bring down vengeance on her crimes. Indeed, the woes denounced against Babylon by the prophets constitute some of the most awfully splendid and sublime portions of the whole Bible, Isa. 13:1-22; 14:22; 21:9; 47; Jer. 25; 50; 51, etc.

The city did not long remain the capital of the world. Under the reign of Nebuchadnezzar's grandson, Nabonnidus, the Belshazzar of the Scriptures, it was besieged and taken by Cyrus. The accounts of Greek historians harmonize here with that of the Bible: that Cyrus made his successful assault on a night when the whole city, relying on the strength of the walls, had given themselves up to the riot and debauchery of a grand public festival, and the king and his nobles were revelling at a splendid entertainment. Cyrus had previously caused a canal, which ran west of the city, and carried off the superfluous water of the Euphrates into the lake of Nitocris, to be cleared out, in order to turn the river into it; which, by this means, was rendered so shallow, that his soldiers were able to penetrate along its bed into the city, Dan. 5. 538 B. C. From this time its importance declined, for Cyrus made Susa the capital of his kingdom. It revolted against Darius Hystaspis, who again subdued it, broke down all its gates, and reduced its walls to the height of fifty cubits. According to Strabo, Xerxes destroyed the tower of Belus. Under the Persians, and under Alexander's successors, Babylon continued to decline, especially after Seleucus Nicator had founded Seleucia, and made it his residence. A great portion of the inhabitants of Babylon removed thither; and in Strabo's time, that is, under Augustus, Babylon had become so desolate, that it might be called a vast desert. There was a town on its site until the fourth century, and many Jews dwelt there, 1 Pet. 5:13. But from this time onward, Babylon ceases almost to be mentioned; even its ruins have not been discovered until within the last two centuries; and it is only within the present century that these ruins have been traced and described. These consist of numerous mounds, usually of brick, deeply furrowed and decayed by time, strown with fragments of brick, bitumen, pottery, etc. One of these is described above. See BABEL. Another, four miles north-west of Hilleh, and called by the natives Kasr, is thought to mark the site of the hanging gardens. These ruins are 2,400 feet long, and 1,800 broad. Another near by, called Mujellibah, is of similar dimensions. From these mounds thousands of bricks have been dug, bearing arrow-headed inscriptions as ancient as the time of Nebuchadnezzar, whose name often occurs. The aspect of the whole region is dreary and forlorn. It is infested by noxious animals, and perhaps in no place under heaven is the contrast between ancient magnificence and present desolation greater than here. The awful prophecy of Isaiah, uttered more than a century before, has been most literally fulfilled, Isa. 13: 14.

The name of Babylon is used symbolically in Rev. 14:8; 16; 17; 18, to mark the idolatry, superstition, lewdness, luxury, and persecution of the people of God, which characterized heathen Rome and modern Antichrist. Some thus interpret 1 Pet. 5:13.

A BABYLONIAN BRICK.

II. There was also a Babylon in Egypt, a city not far from Heliopolis. Some suppose this to be the Babylon mentioned 1 Pet. 5:13; but this is not probable.

BABYLO'NIA, the province of which Babylon was the capital; now the Babylonian or Arabian *Irak*, which constitutes the pashalic of Bagdad. This celebrated province included the tract of country lying on the river Euphrates, bounded north by Mesopotamia and Assyria, and south by the Persian gulf. This gulf was indeed its only definite and natural boundary; for towards the north, towards the east or Persia, and towards the west or desert Arabia, its limits were quite indefinite. Both in ancient and modern times, important tracts on the eastern bank of the Tigris, and on the western bank of the Euphrates, and still more on both banks of their united streams, were reckoned to Babylonia, or Irak el-Arab.

The most ancient name of the country is Shinar, Gen. 10:10; Dan. 1:2. Afterwards Babel, Babylon, and Babylonia became its common appellation, with which, at a later period, Chaldea, or the land of the Chaldeans, was used as synonymous, after this people had got the whole into their possession.

Babylonia is an extensive plain, interrupted by no hill or mountain, consisting of a fatty, brownish soil, and subject to the annual inundations of the Tigris and Euphrates, more especially of the latter, whose banks are lower than those of the Tigris. The Euphrates commonly rises about twelve feet above its ordinary level, and continues at this height from the end of April till June. These inundations of course compelled the earliest tillers of the soil to provide means for drawing off the superabundant water, and so distributing it over the whole surface, that those tracts which were in themselves less watered might receive the requisite irrigation. From this cause, the whole of Babylonia came to be divided up by a multitude of larger and smaller canals; in part passing entirely through from one river to the other; in part also losing themselves in the interior, and serving only the purposes of irrigation. These canals seem to be the "rivers of Babylon" spoken of in Psa. 137:1. Besides this multitude of canals, which have long since vanished without trace, Babylonia contained several large lakes, partly the work of art and partly formed by the inundations of the two rivers. Babylonia, therefore, was a land abounding in water; and Jeremiah might therefore well say of it, that it "dwelt upon many waters," Jer. 51:13.

The Babylonians belonged to the Shemitic branch of the descendants of Noah, and their language had an affinity with the Arabic and Hebrew, nearly resembling what is now called Chaldee. The Babylonian empire was founded by Nimrod twenty centuries before Christ, and then embraced the cities Babel, Erech, Accad, and Calneh, Gen. 10:10. After the building of Nineveh by Ninus, 1237 B. C., that city became the seat of power, and continued so until about 606 B. C., when the Assyrian empire gave way to the Chaldean, and Babylon reached its highest point in fame and power. Upon the return of the Jews from captivity, many still remained in Babylonia, and to their posterity the gospel was early conveyed. Peter is supposed by many to have written his first epistle there, 1 Pet. 5:13. The Jews had thriving synagogues in Babylonia, and one of their Talmuds was there composed. See CHALDEANS.

BA'CA, *tears*, or *weeping*, Psa. 84:6. It is not necessary to understand here that there was really a valley so called. The psalmist, at a distance from Jerusalem, is speaking of the happiness of those who are permitted to make the usual pilgrimages to that city in order to worship Jehovah in the temple: they love the ways which lead thither; yea, though they must pass through rough and dreary paths, even a vale of tears, yet such are their hope and joy of heart, that all this is to them as a well-watered country, a land crowned with the blessings of the early rain.

BAD'GER, a small inoffensive animal, of the bear genus, which remains torpid all winter. It is an inhabitant of cold countries, and is not found in Palestine. Hence many think the "badgers' skins" mentioned Exod. 25:5; 26:14; Ezek. 16:10, and elsewhere, as being used for covering the tabernacle and for shoes, were the skins not of this animal, but of a species of seal found in the Red sea. Burckhardt remarks that he "saw parts of the skin of a large fish, killed on the coast, which was an inch in thickness, and is employed by the Arabs instead of leather for sandals." Others think it was an animal of the antelope species, the skins of which the Jews had obtained in Egypt.

BAG, Deut. 25:13; Luke 12:33. Eastern money was often sealed up in bags containing a certain sum, for which they passed current while the seal remained unbroken, 2 Kin. 12:10.

BAHU'RIM, a town of Benjamin, near Jerusalem, on the road to the Jordan. It is several times mentioned in the history of David, 2 Sam. 3:16; 16:5; 17:18.

BA'JITH, the site of a temple in Moab, where the king offered vain supplications against the Assyrians, Isa. 15:2.

BA'LAAM, a celebrated diviner, of the city Pethor, on the Euphrates, Num. 22:5. Balak, king of Moab, having seen the multitudes of Israel, and fearing they would attack his country, sent for Balaam, who was famous for his supposed supernatural powers, to come and curse them. Balaam, though eager for gain, was led to ask counsel of God, who forbade his going. Balak afterwards sent other deputies, whom Balaam finally accompanied without the approval of God, who sent an angel to meet and warn him in the way. Here occurred the miracle of Balaam's ass, Num. 22:22, 35. But instead of cursing, he was constrained by the Spirit of God to bless the children of Israel. This he did a second and a third time, to the extreme mortification of Balak, who dismissed him in great anger. Balaam subsequently foretold what Israel should in future times do to the nations round about; and after having advised Balak to engage Israel in idolatry and whoredom, that they might offend God and be forsaken by him, quitted his territories for his own land. This bad counsel was pursued; the young women of Moab inveigled the Hebrews to the impure and idolatrous worship of Baal-Peor, for which 24,000 Israelites were slain, Num. 25:1-9; 31:16; 2 Pet. 2:15; Jude 11; Rev. 2:14.

Balaam was probably a descendant of Shem, and possessed many just ideas of the true God. He calls Him "the LORD my God," Num. 22:18; and yet he seems to have been only an enchanter and false prophet, like many in the times of the kings of Israel, until he came in collision with the people of God. In this transaction he was made a bearer, against his own will, of the sublime messages of Jehovah; yet his heart remained unchanged, and he died not "the death of the righteous," Num. 31:8; Josh. 13:22.

BA'LAK, king of Moab, when the Israelites were drawing near the promised land. He was filled with terror lest they should attack and destroy him, as they had Sihon and Og, and implored the soothsayer Balaam to come and curse them. His fears and his devices were both in vain, Deut. 2:9. See BALAAM. He found he had nothing to fear from Israel if at peace with them, and nothing to hope if at war with them.

BALD'NESS was either natural or artificial. It was customary among eastern nations to cut off the hair of the head, or to shave the head, as a token of mourning, on the death of a relative, Job 1:20; Jer. 16:6. This was forbidden to the Israelites, in consequence of its being a heathen custom, Deut. 14:1. Natural baldness was treated with contempt, because it exposed a man to the suspicion of leprosy. The children at Bethel cried after Elisha, "Go up, thou bald-head," 2 Kin. 2:23. While they indicated by this epithet great contempt for him as a prophet of the Lord, they probably scoffed at the same time at the miracle of Elijah's ascension.

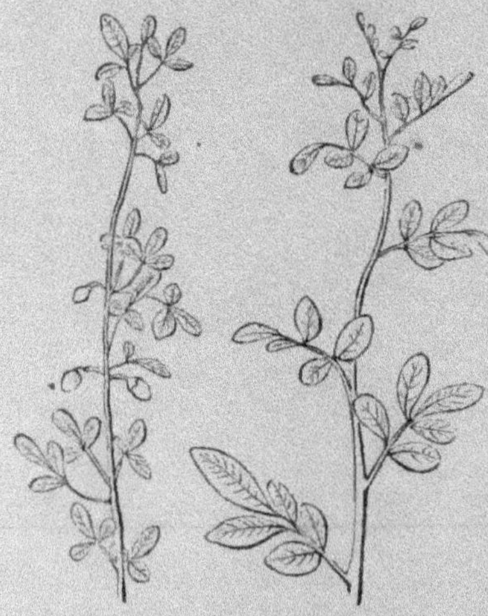

BALM, or more properly, BALSAM, the gum or inspissated juice which exudes from the balsam-tree, the Opobalsamum, which was anciently frequent in Judea, and particularly in Gilead; hence called the balm or balsam of Gilead, Jer. 8:22; 46:11. It was reckoned very valuable in the cure of external wounds. The true balsam-tree is an evergreen, a native of Southern Arabia and Abyssinia, and is about fourteen feet high. It yields its gum in very small quantities. At the present day, this is collected chiefly in Arabia, between Mecca and Medina, and is therefore sometimes called the balm of Mecca. Its odor is exquisitely fragrant and pungent. It is very costly, and is still in the highest esteem among the Turks and other oriental nations, both as a medicine and as a cosmetic for beautifying the complexion, Gen. 37:25; Jer. 51:8; Ezek. 27:17.

BA'MAH, plur. BAMOTH, *high places*, Ezek. 20:29. Bamoth-baal was a station of the Hebrews, in the border of Moab, Num. 21:20; 22:41; afterwards assigned to the tribe of Reuben, Josh. 13:17. Baal was worshipped there, and it was perhaps the "high places" referred to in Isa. 15:2. See HIGH PLACES.

BAP'TISM is the holy ordinance by which persons are admitted as members of the Christian community. It is administered in the name of the Father, the Son, and the Holy Ghost; and is a visible and public profession of faith in Christ and his salvation, of vital union with him, of the obligation to live a new life according to his precepts and in his service, and of the expectation of sharing in his glorious and heavenly immortality. It is not by any means to be regarded as a regenerating ordinance, though significant of regeneration. It was established in the Christian church by Christ and his apostles, and is binding on his followers to the end of time. The use of water in this ordinance is grounded in part on its qualities as the great element of purification, and on the rites of the ancient dispensation, in which "water and blood" were the divinely appointed symbols of moral renovation and atonement.

BAPTISM "WITH THE HOLY GHOST AND WITH FIRE," Matt. 3:11; Luke 3:16. Christ is speaking in these places of the wheat and the chaff—the men who receive him and those who reject him. The former class shall be abundantly endued with the teachings and consolations of the Holy Spirit, but "the chaff he will burn with fire unquenchable." Many here understand "fire" in the widest sense of purification: the purification of Christ's people by the destruction of the ungodly from among them, and their purification from sin by the discipline to which he subjects them. "He shall sit as a refiner's fire."

BARAB'BAS, a noted robber in Christ's time, who was imprisoned and awaiting death for the crimes of sedition and murder. It was a custom of the Roman government, for the sake of conciliating the Jews, to release one Jewish prisoner, whom they might choose, at the yearly Passover. Pilate desired thus to release Jesus, but the Jews demanded Barabbas, Matt. 27:16–26.

BA'RAK, the son of Abinoam, of Kedesh in the tribe of Naphtali. God summoned him, by means of Deborah the prophetess, to release Israel from the yoke of Jabin king of Canaan. Having first secured the attendance of the prophetess, he gathered 10,000 men, and stationed them on mount Tabor, perhaps to avoid the enemies' 900 chariots of iron, Judg. 4:3. God fought for Israel in the battle which ensued, and the song of Deborah and Barak, Judg. 5, chronicles their victory. The name of Barak is enrolled among those illustrious for faith, Heb. 12:32.

BARBA'RIAN. According to the Greek idiom, all other nations, however learned and polite they might be, were "barbarians." Hence Paul comprehends all mankind under the names of "Greeks and barbarians," Rom. 1:14. Luke calls the inhabitants of the island of Malta, "barbarians," Acts 28:2, 4. Indeed, "barbarian" is used in Scripture for every stranger or foreigner who does not speak the native language of the writer, Psa. 114:1, and includes no implication whatever of savage nature or manners in those respecting whom it is used.

BAR-JE'SUS. See ELYMAS.

BAR'LEY was sown in Palestine in autumn, and reaped in the spring, that is, at the Passover. The Hebrews frequently used barley bread, 2 Sam. 17:28; 2 Kin. 4:42; John 6:9. Barley also was much used as food for cattle, 1 Kin. 4:28.

BAR'NABAS, *son of consolation*, or JOSES, a disciple of Jesus, and a companion of the apostle Paul. He was a Levite, and a native of the isle of Cyprus, and is said to have sold all his property, and laid the price of it at the apostles' feet, Acts 4:36, 37. When Paul came to Jerusalem, three years after his conversion, about A. D. 38, Barnabas introduced him to the other apostles, Acts 9:26, 27. Five years afterwards, the church at Jerusalem, being informed of the progress of the gospel at Antioch, sent Barnabas thither, who beheld with great joy the wonders of the grace of God, Acts 11:20–24. He afterwards went to Tarsus, to seek Paul and bring him to Antioch, where they dwelt together two years, and great numbers were converted. They left Antioch A. D. 45, to convey alms from this church to that at Jerusalem, and soon returned, bringing with them John Mark, Acts 11:28–30; 12:25. While they were at Antioch, the Holy Ghost directed that they should be set apart for those labors to which he had appointed them, the planting of new churches among the Gentiles. They visited Cyprus and some cities of Asia Minor, Acts 13:2–14, and after three years returned to Antioch. In A. D. 50, he and Paul were appointed delegates from the Syrian churches to consult the apostles and elders at Jerusalem respecting certain questions raised by Jewish zealots; and having obtained the judgment of the brethren at Jerusalem, they returned with it, accompanied by Silas and Barnabas. At Antioch he was led into dissimulation by Peter, and was, in consequence, reproved by Paul. While preparing for a second missionary tour, Paul and Barnabas having a dispute relative to Mark, Barnabas' nephew, they separated, Paul going to Asia, and Barnabas with Mark to Cyprus, Acts 13–15; Gal. 2:13. Nothing is known of his subsequent history. There is a spurious gospel, in Arabic, ascribed to him; and an epistle, treating mainly of the connection of the Mosaic dispensation with the gospel, but evidently written by some other hand. The name of Barnabas stands high in the annals of the early church. When he gave all his estates to Christ, he gave himself also, as his life of generous self-devotion and missionary toil clearly shows. He was a beloved fellow-laborer with Paul, somewhat as Melancthon was with Luther, and a true "son of consolation" to the church.

BAR'RENNESS was an affliction peculiarly lamented throughout the East, Gen. 16:1; 30:1–23; 1 Sam. 1:6, 19; Isa. 47:9; 49:21; Luke 1:25, especially by the Jewish women, who remembered the promised Messiah, Gen. 3:15, and hoped for the honor of his parentage. The strength of this feeling is evinced by the extraordinary and often unjustifiable measures it led them to adopt, Gen. 16:2; 19:31; 38:14; Deut. 25:5–10. Professed Christians are charged with barrenness, if they are destitute of the fruits of the Spirit, and do not abound in good works, Luke 13:6–9; 2 Pet. 1:8.

BAR'SABAS, I. Joseph Barsabas, surnamed *The Just*, was one of Christ's early disciples, and probably among the seventy. He was one of the two candidates nominated to fill the vacancy left by Judas Iscariot in the apostleship, Acts 1.

II. Judas Barsabas was "a prophet," and a distinguished member of the Jerusalem church. He was deputed, with Silas, to accompany Paul and Barnabas in a mission of importance to the Gentile converts in the Syrian churches, Acts 15:22–33.

BARTHOL'OMEW, one of the twelve apostles, Matt. 10:3; Mark 3:18; Luke 6:14; Acts 1:13. He is named in connection with Philip, and seems to have been the same person whom John calls Nathanael, John 1:45–51, and mentions among the other apostles, John 21:2. Nathanael may have been his real name, and Bar-tholomew, that is, *son of Tolmai*, his patronymic and best known name. See APOSTLE and NATHANAEL.

BARTIME'US, *son of Timeus*, a blind man, to whom Christ gave sight, by the wayside near Jericho, Matt. 20:29–34; Mark 10:46–52; Luke 18:35–43. There were two healed, according to Matthew; but Mark and Luke only mention Bartimeus, who bore his father's name, as though of a well known family. There is an apparent disagreement as to the *time* of the occurrence, which has led some to suppose there were two cases at different times, one as Christ entered Jericho and the other as he left it. We may rather suppose that Bartimeus heard the approach of Christ, Luke 18:35, and learned who he was on the first day; and encouraged by the mercy of the Saviour to Zaccheus, and being joined by another blind man, called to him for help as he again passed by on his way to Jerusalem. The touching narrative of his steadfast faith, and Christ's ready compassion, should encourage all to go boldly unto Jesus.

BA'RUCH, I., the son of Neriah, of a distinguished family in the tribe of Judah. He was the faithful friend of Jeremiah. About 605 B.C. he wrote down, from the lips of Jeremiah, all the divine messages to that prophet, and subsequently read them to the people, and again to certain princes. These last took the book, and soon made known its contents to king Jehoiakim, who impiously destroyed it. Baruch wrote it down a second time as before, with some additions, Jer. 36. He is supposed by some to have accompanied his brother Seraiah to Babylon, with the predictions of Jeremiah respecting that city, Jer. 51:59–64. He afterwards shared the persecutions of the prophet, was imprisoned with him, and forced to go to Egypt with the rebellious Jews, Jer. 43. After the death of Jeremiah, the rabbins say, he returned to Babylon. An apocryphal book is ascribed to him.

II. Another Baruch is mentioned among the friends of Nehemiah, Neh. 3:20; 10:6; 11:5.

BARZIL'LAI, I., of Meholah in Simeon; father of Adriel, who married Merab the daughter of Saul, 1 Sam. 18:19; 2 Sam. 21:8.

II. An aged and wealthy Gileadite, a friend of David when he was in exile during Absalom's rebellion. He sent a liberal supply of provisions, beds, and other conveniences for the use of the king's followers, 2 Sam. 17:27; 19:32. On David's return, Barzillai accompanied him as far as Jordan, but declined, in consequence of his great age, to proceed to Jerusalem, and receive the favors the king had intended for him. David, in his final charge to Solomon, enjoined upon him to show kindness to Barzillai's family, and to make them members of the royal household, 1 Kin. 2:7.

III. A priest who married a daughter of the above, Ezra 2:61; Neh. 7:63.

BAS'HAN, *fat, fruitful*, Num. 21:33, a rich hilly district lying east of the Jordan, and between the mountains of Hermon on the north, and those of Gilead and Ammon on the south. The country takes its name from its soft and sandy soil. It is celebrated in Scripture for its stately oaks, its fine breed of cattle, and its rich pasturage: "Rams of the breed of Bashan," Deut. 32:14; "Rams, bulls, goats, all of them fatlings of Bashan," Ezek. 39:18. The oaks of Bashan are mentioned in connection with the cedars of Lebanon, Isa. 2:13. Modern travellers describe the country as still abounding with verdant and fertile meadows, valleys traversed by refreshing streams, hills crowned with forests, and pastures offering an abundance to the flocks that wander through them. In the time of Joshua, Argob, one of its chief districts, contained sixty walled towns, Deut. 4:43; Josh. 20:8; 21:27. Bashan was assigned, after the conquest of Og and his people, Josh. 12:4, to the half tribe of Manasseh. David drew supplies from this region, 1 Kin. 4:13. It was conquered by Hazael, but Joash recovered it, 2 Kin. 10:33; 13:25. From Bashan came the Greek name Batanæa, in modern Arabic El-Bottein. But this latter only included its southern part. The ancient Bashan covered the Roman provinces named Gaulonitis, Trachonitis, Auranitis, Batanæa, and Ituræa.

BA'TH, or EPHAH, a Hebrew measure, containing seven gallons, four pints, liquid measure; or three pecks, three pints, dry measure.

BATH'-SHEBA, the wife of Uriah, and probably granddaughter of AHITHOPHEL, which see. David first committed adultery with her, then caused her husband to be slain, and afterwards took her to wife. These sins displeased Jehovah, who sent the prophet Nathan to David, with the parable of the ewe lamb, 2 Sam. 12:1. David bitterly repented, but was yet punished, 2 Sam. 11; 12. Bath-sheba was the mother of Solomon, whose succession to the throne she took pains to secure, 1 Kin. 1:15. She is afterwards mentioned in the history of Adonijah, 1 Kin. 2:13, in the title of Psa. 51, and among the ancestors of Christ, Matt. 1:6.

BATTERING-RAM AND TOWER.

BATTERING-RAM, a military engine for battering walls. A long and solid beam, armed at one end with a metallic ram's-head, was suspended by the middle, and swung violently and repeatedly against the walls of a city or castle, till a breach was made. It was sometimes in the lower part of a wooden tower built upon wheels, and was worked by more than a hundred men; while the upper part of the tower was filled with archers and slingers, Ezek. 4:2; 21:22.

BATTLEMENT, a balustrade around the roofs of ancient houses, which were flat, and were much resorted to for fresh air, amusement, or retirement by day, and for sleep at night. The Mosaic law required a battlement for each house, Deut. 22:8.

BAY-TREE. The bay-tree is the Laurel of North Africa and the south of Europe; an evergreen tree, a wreath from which has been from time immemorial the symbolical crown of poets and warriors. The word rendered "bay-tree" in Psa. 37:35, seems to mean simply a native tree, green and vigorous.

BDEL'LIUM is commonly supposed to mean the aromatic gum of a tree growing near the Persian gulf, etc. It is transparent, and bitter to the taste, yet very fragrant while burning. But the substance so called, whatever it was, is mentioned in connection with gold and gems; while a *gum* is certainly not so remarkable a gift of nature as to deserve this classification, or as that the production of it should confer on Havilah a peculiar celebrity, Gen. 2:12. Hence the opinion of the Jewish writers is not to be contemned, namely, that *pearls* are to be here understood, of which great quantities are found on the shores of the Persian gulf and in India, and which might not inaptly be compared with manna, as in Num. 11:7.

THE SYRIAN BEAR.

BEAR. That bears were common in Palestine appears from several passages in the Old Testament, 1 Sam. 17:34, 36, 37; 2 Sam. 17:8; 2 Kin. 2:24. The species known in Syria resembles the common brown bear; it is still met in the recesses of Lebanon. To a sullen and ferocious disposition, the bear joins immense strength, considerable sagacity, and the power of climbing trees. Her ferocity, especially when her young are injured, is proverbial. See 2 Sam. 17:8; Prov. 17:12; Isa. 11:7; Hos. 13:8.

BEARD. The Hebrews regarded a thin, scanty beard as a great deformity; while a long, full, flowing beard was esteemed the noblest ornament of personal beauty and dignity. A man's honor was lodged, as it were, in his beard. To

ORIENTAL HEADS, WITH BEARDS.

insult it by word or act was the grossest indignity; to take it respectfully in the right hand and kiss it, was a mode of expressing high esteem and love permit-

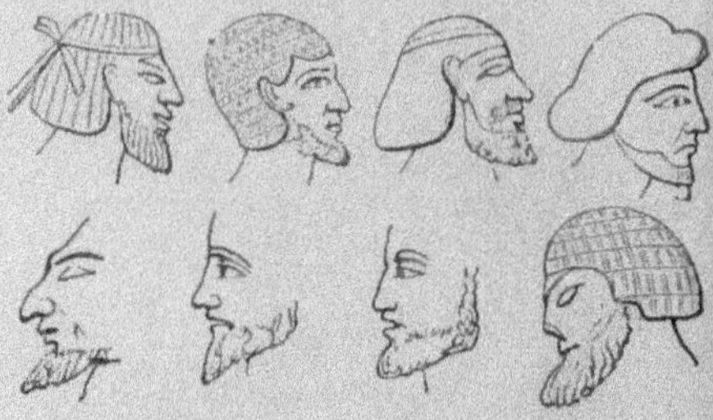

BEARDS FROM EGYPTIAN PAINTINGS.

ted only to the nearest friends. It was cherished with great care, Psa. 133:2; Dan. 10:3. To neglect, tear, or cut it, indicated the deepest grief, Ezra 9:3; Isa. 15:2; Jer. 41:5; 48:37; while to be deprived of it was a mark of servility and infamy. Many would prefer death to such a mutilation. These facts explain many passages of Scripture: as the gross insult offered to David's ambassadors, 2 Sam. 10:4-14; the zealous indignation of Nehemiah, Neh. 13:25; the mode in which the feigned insanity of David was expressed, 1 Sam. 21:13, and the grief of Mephibosheth, 2 Sam. 19:24; the treachery of Joab, 2 Sam. 20:9, and perhaps of Judas; also several passages in the prophets, Isa. 7:20; 50:6; Ezek. 5:1-5. See SHAVING.

BEASTS. This word, used in contradistinction to man, denotes all animals besides, Psa. 36:6; sometimes it means quadrupeds, and not creeping things,

Lev. 11:2-7; and sometimes domestic cattle, in distinction from wild creatures, Gen. 1:25. They were all brought to Adam to be named. Few are mentioned in the Bible but such as lived in Palestine and the countries adjacent. Beasts suffer with man under the penalties of the fall, Gen. 3:14; Ex. 9:6; 13:15; Ezek. 38:20; Hos. 4:3. Yet various merciful provisions for them were made in the Jewish law, Ex. 20:10; 23:11, 12; Lev. 22:28; 25:7. Animals were classed in the law as clean or unclean, with a primary reference to animal sacrifices, Gen. 7:2; Lev. 11. See CLEAN.

The word beasts is figuratively used to symbolize various kings and nations, Psa. 74:14; Isa. 27:1; Ezek. 29:3; Dan. 7, 8; Rev. 12; 13. It also describes the character of violent and brutal men, Psa. 22:12, 16; 1 Cor. 15:32; 2 Pet. 2:12. The Hebrew word commonly rendered beast signifies *living creatures.* In Ezekiel's vision, Ezek. 1, this is applied to human beings or their symbols. In the book of Revelation two distinct words are employed symbolically, both rendered "beast" in our version. One is applied to persecuting earthly powers, Rev. 11:7; 13:1, etc.; the other to superhuman beings or their symbols, Rev. 4:6, etc. This latter might be appropriately rendered, "living creature," as the corresponding Hebrew word is in Ezekiel.

AN EASTERN DIVAN, OR BED.

BED, in the East, is, and was anciently, a divan, or broad low step around the sides of a room, like a low sofa, which answered the purpose of a sofa by day for reclining, and of a bed by night for sleeping, Ex. 8:3; 2 Sam. 4:5-7. Sometimes it was raised several steps above the floor, 2 Kin. 1:4; Psa. 132:4. It was covered very differently, and with more or less ornament, according to the rank of the owner of the house. The poor had but a simple mattress or sheep-skin; or a cloak or blanket, which also answered to wrap themselves in by day, Ex. 22:2? ; Deut. 24:13. Hence it was easy for the persons whom Jesus healed, to take up their bed and walk, Mark 4:21. Bedsteads, however, were not unknown, though unlike those of modern times. See Deut. 3:11; 1 Sam. 19:15; Amos 6:4. The Jews only laid off their sandals and outer garments at night.

BEEL'ZEBUB, "the prince of the devils," Matt. 12:24. This name is derived from Baal-zebub, an idol deity among the Ekronites, signifying lord of flies, fly-baal, fly-god, whose office was to protect his worshippers from the torment of the gnats and flies with which that region was infested, 2 Kin. 1:2, 3, 16. It is also sometimes written *Beel-zebul*, which signifies probably the *dung-god*. The Jews seem to have applied this appellation to Satan, as being the author of all the pollutions and abominations of idol-worship.

BE'ER, *a well*, I., a station of the Hebrews in Moab, where God gave them water, Num. 21:16-18; Isa. 15:8.

II. A town in Judah, according to Eusebius and Jerome a few miles west of Jerusalem, near Beth-shemesh. Jotham took refuge there from his brother Abimelech, Judg. 9:21.

BE'ER-LAHAI'-ROI, *well of him living, and seeing me*, on the south-west border of Canaan, where Hagar was visited by an angel, Gen. 16:14.

BEE'ROTH, *wells*, a city of Benjamin, near Gibeon, Josh. 9:17; 2 Sam. 4:2, 3. It is now El-Bireh, a village of 700 inhabitants, on a ridge seven miles north of Jerusalem.

BE'ER-SHE'BA, *the well of the oath*, Gen. 21:31; 26:31, 33, a city twenty-eight miles south-west of Hebron, at the southern extremity of the Holy Land. Dan lay at the northern extremity; so that the phrase, "from Dan to Beersheba," means, the whole length of the land, Judg. 20:1. At Beersheba, Abraham, Isaac, and Jacob often dwelt, Gen. 21:31; 22:19; 26:23; 28:10; 46:1. The town that afterwards rose here was first assigned to Judah, and then to Simeon, Josh. 15:28; 19:2. Here Samuel established his sons as judges, 1 Sam. 8:2. Elijah rested here on his way to Horeb, 1 Kin. 19:3. It was a seat of idolatry in the time of Uzziah, Amos 5:5; 8:14. After the captivity, it was repeopled by the Jews, Neh. 11:27, 30, and continued a large village many centuries after the coming of Christ. Dr. Robinson found its site at Bir-es-Seba, on the border of the great desert south of Canaan—the ruins of a small straggling city, and two deep stone wells of excellent water, surrounded by stone troughs, and bearing the marks of great antiquity.

BEESH'TERAH, a Levitical city, in Manasseh beyond the Jordan, Josh. 21:27. It is also called Ashtaroth, 1 Chr. 6:71, and is perhaps a contraction of Beth-Ashtaroth.

BEETLE, in Lev. 11:22, a species of locust.

BEEVES, cattle, including the larger antelopes, Lev. 22:19. It is the old plural of *beef*. See CATTLE.

HIPPOPOTAMUS, OR BEHEMOTH.

BEHE'MOTH, a huge amphibious animal, described in Job 40:15-24. Commentators are now generally agreed that it is the hippopotamus, or river-horse, which is found only in the Nile and other great rivers of Africa. This is a very large, powerful, and unwieldy animal, which lives in the water, but comes out upon the banks to feed on grass, grain, green herbs, and branches of trees. The appearance of the hippopotamus when on the land is altogether uncouth, the body being extremely large, flat, and round, the head enormously large in proportion, and the legs as disproportionately short. The length of a male has been known to be seventeen feet, the height seven feet, and the circumference fifteen; the head three feet and a half, and the girt nine feet; the mouth in width about two feet. The general color of the animal is brownish; the ears small and pointed; the eyes small and black; the lips very thick and broad; the nostrils small. The armament of teeth in its mouth is truly formidable; more particularly the tusks of the lower jaw, which are of a curved form, somewhat cylindrical: these are so strong and hard that they will strike fire with steel, are sometimes more than two feet in length, and weigh upwards of six pounds each. The other teeth are much smaller. The tail is short and thick; and the whole body is protected by a thick and tough hide, which swords and arrows cannot penetrate, thickly covered with short hair.

Mr. Rüppell gives the following graphic account of a combat on the upper Nile.

"One of the hippopotami which we killed was a very old male, and seemed to have reached his utmost growth. He measured, from the snout to the end of the tail, about fifteen feet; and his tusks, from the root to the point, along the external curve, twenty-eight inches. We had a battle with him four hours long, and that too in the night. Indeed, he came very near destroying our large bark; and with it, perhaps, all our lives. The moment he saw the hunters in the small canoe, as they were about to fasten the long rope to the buoy in order to draw him in, he threw himself with one rush upon it, dragged it with him under water, and shattered it to pieces. Out of twenty-five musket balls, which were fired into the monster's head at the distance of five feet, only one penetrated the hide and the bones near the nose; so that, every time he breathed, he snorted a stream of blood upon the bark. All the other balls remained sticking in the thickness of the hide. We had at last to employ a small cannon; but it was only after five of its balls, fired at the distance of a few feet, had mangled most shockingly the head and body of the monster, that he died. This gigantic hippopotamus dragged our large bark at his will, in every direction of the stream."

BE'KAH, a half-shekel: in weight, five pennyweights; in money, about twenty-five cents. This sum each Israelite over twenty years old was to pay as a poll-tax for the temple service, Ex. 30:13.

BEL, the chief idol of the Babylonians. See BAAL.

BE'LA, Gen. 14:2. See ZOAR.

BE'LIAL, *worthlessness*, always so used in a moral sense. A man or son of Belial is a wicked, worthless man; one resolved to endure no subjection; a rebel; a disobedient, uncontrollable fellow, Judg. 19:22; 1 Sam. 2:12. In later writings, Belial is put for the power or lord of evil, Satan, 2 Cor. 6:15.

BELSHAZ'ZAR, the last king of the Chaldees at Babylon, B. C. 538, who made an impious feast, at which he and his courtiers drank out of the sacred vessels which had been carried away from the temple at Jerusalem by Nebuchadnezzar his grandfather. He was terrified by the apparition of the hand which wrote upon the wall; and in the same night was slain, and the city taken by the Medes, under Darius and Cyrus, Dan. 5. See BABYLON, MENE.

BELTESHAZ'ZAR, *prince of Bel*, the Chaldean name given to Daniel at the court of Nebuchadnezzar, Dan. 1:7; 4:8.

BENAI'AH, son of Jehoiada, and commander of David's body-guards. Several instances of his rare bravery are recorded, 2 Sam 8:18; 23:20-23. He adhered to Solomon when some favored the pretensions of Adonijah, slew Joab at the command of Solomon, and was made general of the army in his stead, 1 Kin. 1:36; 2:29-35.

BEN-HA'DAD, I., a king of Damascene Syria, hired by Asa king of Judah to make war upon Baasha king of Israel, 1 Kin. 15:18-22. He ravaged a large part of Naphtali.

II. Son and successor of the preceding In two successive years he raised large armies, and made war upon Ahab king of Israel. He was utterly routed, by the aid of Jehovah, God of the hills and the plains also, 1 Kin. 20 Ahab spared him, contrary to the command of God, and gave him conditions of peace. These do not seem to have been fulfilled; for three years after, Ahab renewed the war and was slain, 1 Kin. 22. After about nine years, Ben-hadad again invaded Israel, and the prophet Elisha was instrumental in frustrating his plans, 2 Kin. 6:8-23. But once more renewing the war, he laid siege to Samaria, and reduced it to extremities by famine. God sent a sudden panic upon his army by night, and they fled precipitately, 2 Kin. 6:17; 7:6; Prov. 28:1. Shortly before his death, Ben-hadad, being sick, sent Hazael to ask the prophet Elisha, then at Damascus, what the issue would be. The prophet answered that the disease was not mortal, and yet he would surely die; a paradox which Hazael soon after solved, by stifling his master in bed, 2 Kin. 8:7-15.

III. Son of the Hazael just named. His father had greatly afflicted and oppressed Israel; but he lost all that his father had gained, being thrice defeated by king Jehoash, 2 Kin. 13.

BEN'JAMIN, the youngest son of Jacob and Rachel, Gen. 35:16-18. Rachel died immediately after he was born, and with her last breath named him Ben-oni, the son of my sorrow; but Jacob called him Benjamin, son of my right hand. He was a great comfort to his father, who saw in him the beloved wife he had buried, and Joseph whose loss he mourned. He could hardly be persuaded to let him go with his brethren to Egypt, Gen. 42; 43. The tribe of Benjamin was small at first, and was almost exterminated in the days of the Judges, Judg. 20, but afterwards greatly increased, 2 Chr. 14:8; 17:17. It was valiant, Gen. 49:27, and "beloved of the Lord," dwelling safely by him, Deut. 33:12; for its territory adjoined Judah and the Holy City on the north. At the revolt of the ten tribes, Benjamin adhered to the cause of Judah; and the two tribes were ever afterwards closely united, 1 Kin. 11:13; 12:20; Ezra 4:1; 10:9. King Saul and Saul of Tarsus were both Benjamites, Phil. 3:5.

BE'RA, king of Sodom in the days of Abraham, Gen. 14.

BERA'CHAH, *blessing*, a beautiful valley between Tekoa and Etham, where Jehoshaphat and all Judah held a thanksgiving for their miraculous victory over the Moabites and Ammonites, 2 Chr. 20:26.

BERE'A, a city of Macedonia, not far from Pella towards the south-west, and near mount Bermius. It was afterwards called Irenopolis, and is now called by the Turks, Boor; by others, Cara Veria. Paul preached the gospel here with success; the ingenuous Bereans examined his doctrine by the Old Testament scriptures, and many believed, Acts 17:10, 14; 20:4.

BERNI'CE, or BERENI'CE, eldest daughter of king Herod Agrippa I., and sister to the younger Agrippa, Acts 25:13, 23; 26:30. She was first married to her uncle Herod, king of Chalcis; and after his death, in order to avoid the merited suspicion of incest with her brother Agrippa, she became the wife of Polemon, king of Cilicia. This connection being soon dissolved, she returned to her brother, and afterwards became mistress of Vespasian and Titus.

BERO'THAH, BERO'THAI, a Syrian town, conquered by David, 2 Sam. 8:8; 1 Chr. 18:8; Ezek. 47:16. Some find it in the modern Beyrout; but aside from the similarity of the name, the indications point to an inland site, nearer Hamath or Damascus.

BER'YL, the name of a precious stone of a sea-green color, found principally in India, Dan. 10:6; Rev. 21:20.

BE'SOM, a broom or brush for sweeping. Before "the besom of destruction," the hosts of God's enemies are like the dust of the floor, Isa. 14:23.

BE'SOR, a brook flowing into the Mediterranean five miles south of Gaza. A part of David's troops in pursuit of Amalekites halted there, 1 Sam. 30:9-21. The stream dries up in spring.

BE'TAH, or TIB'HATH, a city of Syria-Zobah, taken by David, 2 Sam. 8:8; 1 Chr. 18:8; perhaps the modern Taibeh, between Aleppo and Tadmor.

BETH, *house*, forms a part of many compound names of places, and sometimes means *the place* or *dwelling*; and at others *the temple*. This word becomes *Beit* in modern Arabic.

BETH-AB'ARA, *place of the ford*, a town on the east bank of the Jordan, where John baptized, John 1:28. It was perhaps the same as Beth-barah, Judg. 7:24; but the true site is unknown. Many of the best Greek manuscripts and recent editions have Bethany, also unknown, instead of Beth-abara.

BETH'ANY, a village on the eastern slope of mount Olivet, about two miles east-south-east of Jerusalem, and on the road to Jericho. It was often visited by Christ, Matt. 21:17; Mark 11:1, 12; Luke 19:29. Here Martha and Mary dwelt, and Lazarus was raised from the dead, John 11. Here Mary anointed the Lord against the day of his burying, John 12; and from the midst of his disciples, near this village which he loved, he ascended to heaven, Matt. 24:50. Its modern name, Aziriyeh, is derived from Lazarus. It is a poor village of some twenty families.

BETH-AR'BEL, probably Arbela, now Irbid. One place of this name lay twenty-five miles south-east of the sea of Galilee. Another was in Galilee, near Magdala. Here were some large and almost inaccessible fortified caverns, in the sides of precipices, Hos. 10:14.

BETH-A'VEN, a place and desert near Bethel on the east, Josh. 7:2; 18:12; 1 Sam. 13:5; 14:23. It seems to be reproachfully used at times for Bethel itself, after the golden calves were there set up, Hos. 4:15; 10:5: Beth-el meaning the house of God; and Beth-aven, the house of sin, or of an idol.

BETH-CAR', in Dan, near Mizpeh; noted for the defeat of the Philistines, and the Eben-Ezer set up by Samuel, 1 Sam. 7:11.

BETH'EL, *house of God*, the name of a city west of Hai, on the confines of the tribes of Ephraim and Benjamin, Gen. 12:8; 28:10-22, and occupying the spot where Jacob slept and had his memorable dream, the name he then gave it superseding the old name Luz, Judg. 1:23. Thirty years after, he again pitched his tent there, Gen. 35:1-15. It was captured by Joshua, and given to Benjamin, Josh. 12:9; 18:22. The Ephraimites, however, expelled the Canaanites, Judg. 1:22-26. Here the ark of the covenant, and probably the tabernacle, long remained, Judg. 20:26; 1 Sam. 10:3. Samuel held his court here in turn, 1 Sam. 7:16. After Solomon, it became a seat of gross idolatry; Jeroboam choosing it as the place for one of his golden calves, from the sacredness previously attached to it, 1 Kin. 12:29. The prophets were charged with messages against Bethel, 1 Kin. 13:1, 2; Jer. 48:13; Amos 3:14; 7:10. The first of these was fulfilled by Josiah, 2 Kin. 23:13; and the others in the later desolation of Bethel, where nothing but ruins can now be found. Its site was identified by Dr. Robinson, in the place now called Beitin. It is twelve miles from Jerusalem towards Shechem, on the southern side of a hill, with a narrow and fertile valley on the east, and the long-travelled road on the west. At the bottom of the hill are the remains of a vast stone reservoir, of an ancient Hebrew age. See BETHAVEN.

BETHES'DA, *house of mercy*, the name of a pool or fountain near the temple in Jerusalem, with an open building over or near it, for the accommodation of the sick who came to try the healing efficacy of the water, John 5:2. Tradition locates this pool in what is now a large dry reservoir, along the outside of the north wall of the temple area. Robinson, however, shows the probability that this is but a portion of the trench, which separated mount Moriah from the adjacent hill on the north. He suggests that the true Bethesda may perhaps be "The Fountain of the Virgin," so called, in the lower part of the valley of Jehoshaphat, eight hundred and fifty feet south of the temple area. This pool is of great antiquity, and seems to be fed from ancient reservoirs under the temple. Two flights of steps, sixteen and thirteen in number, with a platform of twelve feet between them, lead down to the pool; this is fifteen feet long, and five or six feet wide. Its waters rise and fall at irregular intervals, and flow down by a subterraneous channel to the pool of Siloam. It is supposed to be the "king's pool" of Neh. 2:14. Bethesda, even if known and accessible to us, has lost its healing power; but the fountain Christ has opened for sin, guilt, and death, is nigh to all and of never failing virtue. See SILOAM.

BETH-HAC'CEREM, conjectured to be the Frank mountain, between Tekoa and Bethlehem, Neh. 3:14; Jer. 6:1. This is a solitary conical hill, on which the crusaders had a strong fortress.

BETH-HOG'LAH, a town of Benjamin, on the border of Judah, Josh. 15:6; 18:19, 21. Robinson traced this name at a place three miles from the mouth of the Jordan, on the way to Jericho; here was a fine grove, watered by a sweet and limpid fountain the best in the valley of the Jordan.

BETH-HO'RON, now Beit-ur, the name common to two neighboring towns in the north-west corner of Benjamin, still distinguished as the Upper and the Lower. These lay on two ridges, with valleys on each side; Beth-horon the Nether being separated from the Upper by a small valley, and a rocky and rough pass up the ridge on which Upper Beth-horon stood. The latter was nearest to Jerusalem, about twelve miles from it; and both were on the usual route to the seacoast. Down this pass Joshua drove the Amorites, and here Paul passed by night on his way to Antipatris, Josh. 10:1-11; Acts 23:31, 32.

BETH-JESH'IMOTH, a city of Reuben, taken from the Moabites, Num. 33:49; Josh. 12:3; 13:20; but retaken by them after the captivity, Ezek. 25:9. It lay not far east of the mouth of the Jordan.

BETH'LEHEM, *house of bread*, 1., a celebrated city, the birthplace of David and of Christ. It was in the tribe of Judah, six miles south by west of Jerusalem, and probably received its appellation from the fertility of the circumjacent country. This also gave it its ancient name Ephrath, *fruitful*, Gen. 48:7; Mic. 5:2. It was beautifully situated on an oblong ridge, twenty-seven hundred feet above the level of the sea, and affording a fine view in every direction. The hills around it were terraced, and clothed with vines, fig-trees, and almonds; and the valleys around it bore rich crops of grain. It was fortified by Rehoboam, 2 Chr. 11:6, but was comparatively an unimportant place, Mic. 5:1, and is not mentioned by Joshua or Nehemiah among the cities of

BETHLEHEM, AS IT NOW IS.

Judah. Its memory is delightfully associated with the names of Boaz and Ruth; it is celebrated as the birthplace and city of David, 1 Sam. 17:12, 15; 20:6; 2 Sam. 23:14–17; but above all, it is hallowed as the place where the Redeemer was born. Over that lovely spot the guiding star hovered; there the eastern sages worshipped the King of kings, and there where David watched his flock and praised God, were heard the songs of the angelic host at the Saviour's birth, Luke 2:8. Bethlehem is now called Beit-lahm, and contains about three thousand inhabitants, almost exclusively nominal Christians. Half a mile north is the spot pointed out by tradition as Rachel's tomb, Gen. 35:16–20; and about two miles south-west are the great reservoirs described under SOLOMON'S POOLS.

II. An unknown place in Zebulun, Josh. 19:15; Judg. 12:10, in distinction from which the city of David was often called Bethlehem-Judah.

BETH-NIM'RAH, Num. 32:3, 36; Josh. 13:27, and NIMRIM, Isa. 15:6; Jer. 48:34; a town in Gad, a little east of the Jordan, on a water-course leading, from near Ramoth-Gilead, south-west into that river.

BETH-PE'OR, a town of Moab, in the limits assigned to Reuben, and conquered from the Amorites, Josh. 13:20. It was infamous for the worship of Baal-peor. In the adjacent valley Moses rehearsed the law to Israel, and was buried, Deut. 4:44–46; 34:6.

BETH'PHAGE, *place of figs*, a little village at the eastern foot of the mount of Olives, near to Bethany, Matt. 21:1; Mark 11:1; Luke 19:29.

BETHSAI'DA, *place of fishing*, I., a city in Galilee, on the western shore of the lake of Gennesareth, a little north of Capernaum; it was the birthplace of the apostles Philip, Andrew, and Peter, and was often visited by our Lord, Matt. 11:21; Mark 6:45; 8:22.

II. A city in Gaulonitis, north of the same lake, and east of the Jordan. Near this place Christ fed the five thousand. It lay on a gentle hill near the Jordan, separated from the sea of Galilee by a plain three miles wide, of surpassing fertility, Luke 9:10. Compare Matt. 14:13–22; Mark 6:31–45. This town was enlarged by Philip, tetrarch of that region, Luke 3:1, and called Julias in honor of Julia, the daughter of Augustus. It is now little but ruins.

BETH-SHEAN, or BETH-SHAN, more generally known by the name of Scythopolis, was situated two miles west of the Jordan, at the extremity of the valley of Jezreel, an arm of the great plain of Esdrælon, running down from it to the valley of the Jordan in a south-easterly direction. It stood on the brow, just where the former valley drops down by a rather steep descent to the level of the latter. Bethshean was assigned to Manasseh, though not at once subdued, Josh. 17:11, 16; Judg. 1:27. The dead body of Saul was fastened to its walls, 1 Sam. 31:10, 12; 2 Sam. 21:12; 1 Kin. 4:12. The place is now called Beisan, and is about twenty-four miles south of Tiberias. The present village contains seventy or eighty houses, the inhabitants of which are in a miserable condition, owing to the depredations of the Bedaween. The ruins of the ancient city are of considerable extent, along the banks of the rivulet which ran by it, and on the side of the valley; and bespeak it to have been nearly three miles in circuit.

BETH-SHE'MESH, *house of the sun*, I., a city of Judah given to the priests, Josh. 21:16; 1 Chr. 6:59; 1 Sam. 6:15. It lay fifteen miles west of Jerusalem, near the border of Dan and of the Philistines, Josh. 15:10; 1 Sam. 6:12. Probably the same as Irshemesh, Josh. 19:41. It is memorable for a battle between Judah and Israel, in which Amaziah was defeated, 2 Kin. 14:12-14; and for the return of the ark from among the Philistines, and the punishment of those who then profaned it, 1 Sam. 6. There is reason to suppose the numbers in ver. 19 should be translated "threescore and ten men, even fifty out of one thousand," or one in two hundred of the men of the city.

II. A celebrated city in Egypt, Jer. 43:13. See HELIOPOLIS.

BETHU'EL, son of Abraham's uncle Nahor, and father of Rebekah, Gen. 22:22, 23; 24:50.

BETH-ZUR', a city in the hill country of Judah, near Hebron, Josh. 15:58. It was fortified by Rehoboam, 2 Chr. 11:7, and assisted in rebuilding Jerusalem, Neh. 3:16. Josephus calls it one of the strongest fortresses in Judea; but its site has not yet been identified.

BETROTHING, the engagement of a man and woman to marry each other at a future time. Parents anciently often betrothed their daughters without their consent, and even while very young, as is still the case in oriental countries. Sometimes a regular written contract was made, in which the bridegroom bound himself to give a certain sum as a portion to his bride. The marriage was not completed until the bride was at least twelve years old; yet the betrothal could be dissolved only by divorce or death, Matt. 1:18-25; Luke 2:27. God speaks of betrothing his people to himself, in bonds of tender affection, and pledging his word that all his gracious promises will be fulfilled to them, Jer. 2:2; Hos. 2:19, 20. Of this, ministers are the instruments, through the preaching of the gospel, 2 Cor. 11:2. Hence the following word,

BEU'LAH, *married*, a term applied to the Israel of God, in Isa. 62:4, to signify his intimate and vital union with them.

BEZALEEL', an artificer, endued by God with special skill for constructing and adorning the tabernacle, Ex. 31:2; 35:30.

BE'ZEK, a city of the Canaanites, of which Adoni-zedek was king. The account of its capture by Judah is in Judg. 1:1-8. Here Saul reviewed his forces, before going to raise the siege of Jabesh-gilead, 1 Sam. 11:8.

BE'ZER, a city of refuge, in the plain country of Reuben beyond Jordan. Its exact site is not known, Deut. 4:43; Josh. 20:8; 21:36.

BIBLE. This word signifies the Book, by way of distinction, the Book of all books. It is also called Scripture, or the Scriptures, that is, the writings. It comprises the Old and New Testaments, or more properly, Covenants, Ex. 24:7; Matt. 26:28. The former was written mostly in Hebrew, and was the Bible of the ancient Jewish church; a few chapters of Daniel and Ezra only were written in Chaldee. The latter was wholly written in Greek, which was the language most generally understood in Judea and the adjacent countries first visited by the gospel. The entire Bible is the rule of faith to all Christians, and not the New Testament alone; though this is of especial value as unfolding the history and doctrines of our divine Redeemer and of his holy institutions. The fact that God gave the inspired writings to men in the languages most familiar to the mass of the people who received them, proves that he intended they should be read not by the learned alone, but by all the people, and in their own spoken language.

The Old Testament contains thirty-nine books. Josephus and the church fathers mention a division into twenty-two books, corresponding with the twenty-two letters of the Hebrew alphabet. But we have no sufficient evidence that such a division obtained among the Jews themselves. They arranged the books of the Old Testament in three divisions, called, the Law, the Prophets, and the Writings, that is, the Holy Writings. The Law embraces the five books of Moses. These are divided into convenient sections to be read through once a year in their synagogues. The second division, the Prophets, is subdivided into the former prophets, namely, the historical books of Joshua, Judges, Samuel, and Kings; and the later, that is, the prophets proper, with the exception of the book of Daniel. The later prophets are once more distributed into the greater — Isaiah, Jeremiah, (not including Lamentations,) and Ezekiel; and the less—the twelve minor prophets. Selections from both the earlier and the later prophets are read in the synagogues along with the sections of the Law; but these do not embrace the whole of the prophets, and the arrangement of them differs among different divisions of the Jews. The Holy Writings (Hagiographa) embrace all the remaining books of the Old Testament, namely, (according to the Masoretic arrangement,) Psalms, Proverbs, Job, Canticles, Ruth, Lamentations, Ecclesiastes, Esther, Daniel, Ezra, Nehemiah, Chronicles. In the arrangement of the Old Testament books now prevalent, the historical books come first, then the devotional and didactic, and lastly the prophetical. The Jews ascribe to Ezra the honor of arranging and completing the canon of the Old Testament books, being inspired for this work by the Spirit of God, and aided by the learned and pious Jews of his day. The New Testament writings were received each one by itself from the hands of the apostles, and were, as their inspired works, gradually collected into one volume to the exclusion of all others.

The division into chapters and verses was not made until comparatively modern times, though there appears to have been a more ancient separation into short sections or paragraphs. The chapters now used were arranged probably by Cardinal Hugo, about the year 1240. The division into verses was made in the Old Testament in 1450, and recognized in the Hebrew Concordance of Rabbi Nathan. The arrangement of the verses of the New Testament as we now have them was perfected in the Latin Vulgate, an edition of which with verses was published by Robert Stephens, a learned French printer, in 1551. He also modified and completed the division of the Old Testament into verses, in an edition of the whole Bible, the Vulgate, in 1555. This division into verses, and even into chapters, having regard more to convenience of reference than to the meaning, must often be disregarded in reading in order to get the true sense.

The genuineness, authenticity, and divine origin of the Scriptures cannot be here discussed. The reader is referred to the treatises of Bogue, Gregory, Keith, McIlvaine, Nelson, Spring, etc., published by the American Tract Society, and numerous other valuable and standard works.

The first well-known English translation of the New Testament was that of Wicliffe, made about 1370, before the invention of printing; though others had been made, one as early as king Alfred, of parts of the Bible into Saxon. In the time of Edward I., 1250, it required the earnings of a day-laborer for fifteen years to purchase a manuscript copy of the entire Bible. Now, a printed copy may be had for the earnings of a few hours. The first printed English Testament was that of Tyndal, in 1526, which was afterwards followed by his translation of the Pentateuch. The first complete English Bible is that of Myles Coverdale, in 1535. Matthew's Bible appeared in 1537. Coverdale and some other prelates, who resided at Geneva during the bloody reign of Mary, published there another edition in 1560, hence called the Geneva Bible. At the accession of queen Elizabeth a new revision was made, which appeared in 1568, and is called the Bishop's Bible. This continued in use till our present English version, made by order of James I., was published in 1611. The first copy of this was made by forty-seven of the most learned men in England, divided into six companies. This first copy was then revised by a committee of twelve, or two from each of the six companies; and then again by two others. The work of translation and revision occupied between four and five years; and the faithful, clear, and vigorous standard Bible thus secured, is an enduring monument of the learning, wisdom, and fidelity of the translators.

One of the most remarkable movements of modern times, and that which holds out the greatest promise of good for the coming triumphs of the Redeemer's kingdom, and the temporal as well as spiritual welfare of future generations, is the mighty effort which is making to circulate the holy Scriptures, not only in Christian, but also in heathen lands. In the year 1804, the British and Foreign Bible Society was formed; and the success which has attended this glorious object has by far exceeded the most sanguine expectations of its founders and supporters. "Their voice has gone out through all the earth, and their words to the end of the world." During the first fifty years of this society, it printed or assisted in printing the Scriptures in 148 languages, in about sixty of which they had never before been printed, and issued upwards of 29,000,000 copies of the sacred writings. The Scriptures have now been published in about 220 different languages and dialects. Other similar associations have followed nobly this glorious example; and of these none has labored with more effect than the American Bible Society, which was formed in 1816, and has now, 1859, issued thirteen millions of Bibles and Testaments.

BIG'THAN, a eunuch at the court of Ahasuerus, whose conspiracy against that king was frustrated by the vigilance of Mordecai, Esther 2:21.

BIL'DAD, a descendant of Abraham by Keturah, Gen. 25:1, 2. Shuah and his brethren were located in Arabia Petræa; and thus Bildad the Shuhite was a neighbor and friend of Job, and came to condole with him in his affliction, Job 2:11; 8; 18; 25. His chief topics are, the suddenness, swiftness, and terribleness of God's wrath upon hypocrites and oppressors.

BIL'HAH, the handmaid of Rachel, given by her to her husband Jacob when herself childless, that she might become a mother through her handmaid. Bilhah was the mother of Dan and Naphtali, Gen. 30:1-8.

BIRDS, like other animals, were divided by Moses into *clean* and *unclean*; the former might be eaten, the latter not. The general ground of distinction is, that those which feed on grain or seeds are clean; while those which devour flesh, fish, or carrion, are unclean. Turtledoves, young pigeons, and perhaps some other kinds of birds, were prescribed in the Mosaic law as offerings, Lev. 5:7-10; 14:4-7; Luke 2:24.

There is great difficulty in accurately determining the different species of birds prohibited in Levit. 11:13-19; Deut. 14:11-20, and the proper version of the Hebrew names. The information we have respecting them may be found under the names by which they are translated in our Bible.

Moses, to inculcate humanity on the Israelites, ordered them, if they found a bird's nest, not to take the dam with the young, but to suffer the old one to fly away, and to take the young only, Deut. 22:6, 7.

Cages for singing-birds are alluded to in Jer. 5:27; and snares in Prov. 7:23; Eccl. 9:12. Birds of prey are emblems of destroying hosts, Isa. 46:11; Jer. 12:9; Ezek. 32:4; Rev. 19:17-19; and the Lord comes to the defence of his people with the swiftness of the eagle, Isa. 31:5.

BIRTH'RIGHT, the privilege of the first-born son. Among the Hebrews, as indeed among most other nations, the first-born enjoyed particular privileges; and wherever polygamy was tolerated, it was highly necessary to fix them, Deut. 21:15-17. Besides the father's chief blessing, Gen. 27, and various minor advantages, the first-born son was, first, specially consecrated to the Lord, Ex. 13:11-16; 22:29; and the first-born son of a priest succeeded his father in the priestly office. Among the sons of Jacob, Reuben the first-born forfeited the right of the first-born, Gen. 35:22; 49:3, 4, and God gave it to Levi, Num. 3:12, 13; 8:18. Secondly, the first-born was entitled to a share of his father's estate twice as large as any of the other brethren received, Deut. 21:17. Thirdly, he succeeded to the official dignities and rights of his father, 2 Chr. 21:3. In some of these privileges there is an allusion to Him who is "the first-born among many brethren," Rom. 8:29; Col. 1:18; Heb. 1:2–6. Universal dominion is his, and an everlasting priesthood. See FIRST-BORN.

BISH'OP, *an overseer*, one who has the charge and direction of any thing. The most common acceptation of the word in the New Testament is that which occurs Acts 20:28; Phil. 1:1, where it signifies the pastor of a church. Peter calls Jesus Christ "the Shepherd and Bishop of your souls," 1 Pet. 2:25. Paul describes the qualities requisite in bishops, 1 Tim. 3:2; Tit. 1:7, etc.; Christ himself is their great exemplar.

BIT'TERN, a fowl about the size of a heron, and of the same genus. Nineveh and Babylon became a possession for "the bittern" and other wild birds, Isa. 14:23; 34:11; Zeph. 2:14. According to some critics, the more probable meaning of the Hebrew word is hedge-hog, or porcupine; and Mr. Rich says he found "great quantities" of porcupine quills among the ruins of Babylon; but others think this inconsistent with Zeph. 2:14, and understand the word as referring to the common night-heron, a bird like the bittern found among the marshes of Western Asia, resorting to ruined buildings, and uttering a peculiar harsh cry before and after its evening flight.

BITHYN'IA, 1 Pet. 1:1, a province in the northern part of Asia Minor, on the shore of the Black sea, having Paphlagonia on the east, Phrygia and Galatia on the south, and Mysia on the southwest. It was directly opposite to Constantinople. It is famous as being one of the provinces to which the apostle Peter addressed his first epistle; also as having been under the government of Pliny, who, in a letter to the emperor Trajan, makes honorable mention of the number, character, and customs of the persecuted Christians there, about A. D. 106; also for the holding of the most celebrated council of the Christian church in the city of Nice, its metropolis, about A. D. 325. It may be, with some justice, considered as a province taught by Peter; and we read that when Paul attempted to go into Bithynia, the Spirit suffered him not, Acts 16:7.

BLAINS, Ex. 9:8–10, burning ulcerous eruptions, miraculously caused by the ashes which Moses threw up among the Egyptians. If these ashes came from the brick-kilns where the Hebrews had toiled, the pains which the Egyptians suffered would naturally remind them of those which they had inflicted.

BLAS'PHEMY. A man is guilty of blasphemy, when he speaks of God, or his attributes, injuriously; when he calumniously ascribes such qualities to him as do not belong to him, or robs him of those which do. The law sentenced blasphemers to death, Lev. 24:12–16. In a lower sense, men are said to be blasphemed when abused by calumnious and reviling words, 1 Kin. 21:10; Acts 6:11.

BLASPHEMY AGAINST THE HOLY GHOST, Matt. 12:31, 32; Mark 3:28; Luke 12:10. This sin was committed by the Pharisees when they, in violation of their own convictions, wilfully and maliciously ascribed the miracles of the Son of God and the work of the Holy Spirit to the evil one. It is often inquired whether this was the "sin unto death" spoken of 1 John 5 16, and whether it is committed in these days. However these questions may be answered, certain it is that when one can ridicule religion and its ordinances, when he can make sport with the work of the Holy Ghost in the human heart, when he can persist in a wilful disbelief of the Gospel, and cast contempt upon Christianity and "the ministration of the Spirit," he is going to a fearful extremity of guilt, and provoking the final withdrawment of divine grace. While on the other hand the vilest blasphemer, who feels the relentings of godly sorrow for his sins, and the desire to confess them at the Saviour's feet, may be sure of realizing the truth of Christ's word. "Him that cometh unto me I will in no wise cast out."

BLAS'TUS, a chamberlain of Herod Agrippa, bribed to favor the men of Tyre and Sidon, Acts 12:20.

BLEM'ISHES, imperfections or deformities which unfitted men for the priesthood, and animals for sacrifice. Of these we have a particular enumeration in Lev. 21:18-20; 22:20-24. In this provision of the law there was an allusion to the great High-priest of our profession, who offered himself without spot to God.

BLESS'ING is referred both to God and to man. When God blesses, he bestows that efficacy which renders his blessing effectual. His blessings are either temporal or spiritual, bodily or mental; but in every thing they really convey the good which they import, Num. 6:23-27. The blessings of men to other men, unless they be inspired prophecies, as in Gen. 32, 49; Deut. 33, are only good wishes, personal or official, and as it were a peculiar kind of prayer to the Author of all good for the welfare of the subject of them. Blessing, on the part of man towards God, is an act of thanksgiving for his mercies, Psa. 103:1; or rather, for that special mercy which at the time occasions the act of blessing: as for food, for which thanks are rendered to God, or for any other good, Psa. 116:13; 1 Cor. 10:16.

BLIND'NESS. This distressing malady is very prevalent in the East. Many physical causes in those countries unite to injure the organs of vision. The sun is hot, and in the atmosphere floats a very fine dust, which enters and frets the eye. The armies of France and England, which were so long in Egypt during the French war, suffered severely from ophthalmic disease. In the cities of Egypt, blindness is perpetuated as a contagious disease by the filthy habits of the natives. It is of frequent occurrence also on the coast of Syria. In ancient times, the eyes of persons hated or feared were often torn out, Judg. 16:21; 1 Sam. 11:2; 2 Kin. 25:7. Blindness was sometimes inflicted as a punishment, Gen. 19:11; Acts 13:6; and it was often threatened as a penalty, Deut. 28:28. The Jews were enjoined by the humane laws of Moses to show all kindness and consideration to the blind, Lev. 19:14; Deut. 27:18. No one affected with this infirmity could officiate as priest, Lev. 21:18.

Our Saviour miraculously cured many cases of blindness, both that which was caused by disease and that which had existed from birth. In these cases there was a double miracle; for not only was the organ of sight restored, but also the faculty of using it, which is usually gained only by long experience, Mark 8:22-25. The touching of the eyes of the blind, and anointing them with clay, Matt. 9:29; John 9:6, can not have had any medicinal or healing effect. The healing was miraculous, by the power of God.

"Blindness" is often used for ignorance and error, especially our sinful want of discernment as to spiritual things, Matt. 15:14; 2 Cor. 4:4. The abuse of God's mercy increases this blindness, John 12:40. Blessed are the eyes that fix their adoring gaze first of all on their Redeemer.

BLOOD. The life of all animals was regarded as especially in the blood, which was a sacred and essential part of the sacrifices offered to God, Heb. 9:22. It was solemnly sprinkled upon the altar and the mercy-seat, "for it is the blood that maketh atonement for the soul," Lev. 17—the life of the victim for the life of the sinner. It was therefore most sacredly associated with the blood of the Lamb of God, which "cleanseth us from all sin," Eph. 1:7; 1 John 1:7. Hence the strict prohibition of the Israelites to eat blood, or any meat in which blood remained; a prohibition renewed in Acts 15:29. In direct opposition to this are the heathen customs of drinking the blood of animals and even of men—of eating raw flesh, with the blood, and even fresh cut from the living animal, 1 Sam. 14:32; Psa. 16:4; Ezek. 33:25.

Besides the ordinary meaning of the word blood, it often signifies the guilt of murder, 2 Sam. 3:28; Acts 27:25; also relationship or consanguinity. "Flesh and blood" are placed in contrast with a spiritual nature, Matt. 16:17, the glorified body, 1 Cor. 15:50, and evil spirits, Eph. 6:12. The cause "between blood and blood," Deut. 17:8, was one where life was depending on the judgment rendered.

BLOOD-AVEN'GER. The sacredness of human life, and the justice of punishing a murderer by death, are grounded on the fact that man was made in the image of God, Gen. 9:6. With justice, the passion for revenge often conspired to secure the death of the criminal. Among the Arabs, the nearest male relative of a murdered person was to pursue the homicide until by force or craft he put him to death. The law of Moses expressly forbade the acceptance of any ransom for a life thus forfeited, Num. 35:31; but it interfered between an accused person and his pursuer, by providing a sanctuary—at the altar of God and in the cities of refuge—where the accused might be safe until it was proved that he had committed the act, wilfully or accidentally, Josh. 20:6, 9. In the former case, he was at once given up to his pursuer for death, Ex. 21:14; 1 Kin. 2:29, 34. In the latter case, he might dwell with safety in the city of refuge; but should he go elsewhere before the death of the high-priest, he was liable to be slain by the avenger of blood, Num. 35:25–28. See Refuge.

BLUE. See Purple.

BOANER'GES, *sons of thunder*, a name given by our Saviour to James and John the sons of Zebedee, Mark 3:17, perhaps on account of their power as preachers. Some suppose it was given on the occasion of their request that Christ would call for fire from heaven, and destroy a village of the Samaritans, which had refused to entertain them, Luke 9:53, 54.

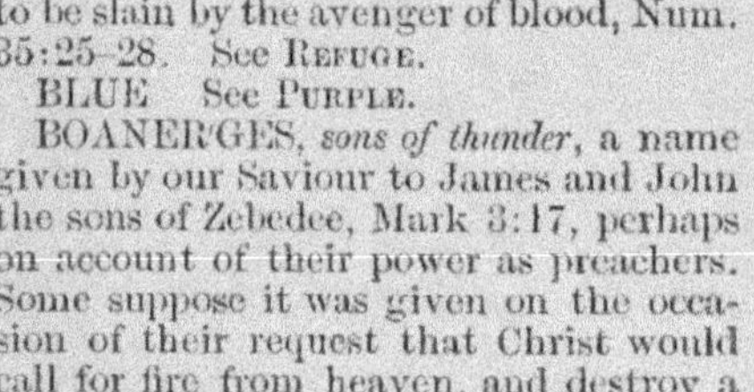

BOAR. The wild boar is considered as the parent stock of the common hog. He is a furious and formidable animal. The tusks are larger and stronger than in the tame herds. The color is iron-grey, inclining to black. His snout is long, and his ears are short. At present wild boars frequent the marshes around the upper Jordan, and have been found on mount Carmel, and in large herds near the sea of Tiberias. They were frequent in the time of the Crusades. Richard Cœur de Lion encountered one, ran him through with a lance, and while the animal was still endeavoring to gore his horse, leaped over him, and slew him with his sword. The destructive ravages of the animal are referred to in Psa. 80:13.

BO'AZ, Ruth 2:1, a wealthy Bethlehemite, a descendant of Judah, through whom is traced the regular succession of Jewish kings, Matt. 1:5. His conduct in the case of Ruth proves him to have been a man of fine spirit and of strict integrity. He admitted the claim which Ruth had upon him as a near kinsman: under the obligations of the Levitical law, he married the poor gleaner, and thus became one of the ancestors of David, and also of David's Son and Lord. He was the father of Obed, Obed was the father of Jesse, and Jesse of David. The whole narrative is a beautiful picture of the simplicity of the age, when artificial courtesies had not usurped the place of natural and sincere expressions of love.

Boaz was also the name of one of the two brazen pillars which Solomon erected in the porch of the temple, the other being called Jachin. These columns were about thirty-five feet high, 1 Kin. 7:15, 16, 21.

BO'CHIM, *weepings*, a place near Gilgal, where the angel of the Lord reproved Israel for their remissness, Judg. 2:1–5.

BOOK. Several sorts of materials were anciently used in making books. Plates of lead or copper, the bark of trees, brick, stone, and wood, were originally employed to engrave such things and documents upon as men desired to transmit to posterity, Deut. 27:2, 3; Job 19:23, 24. God's laws were written on stone tablets. Inscriptions were also made on tiles and bricks, which were afterwards hardened by fire. Many of these are found in the ruins of Babylon. See Babylon, Nebuchadnezzar. Tablets of wood, box, and ivory were common among the ancients: when they were of wood only,

ANCIENT BOOKS, PENS, AND INKSTAND.

they were oftentimes coated over with wax, which received the writing inscribed on them with the point of a style, or iron pen, Jer. 17:13; and what was written might be effaced by the broad end of a style, Luke 1:63. Afterwards, the leaves of the palm-tree were used instead of wooden tablets, and also the finest and thinnest bark of trees, such as the lime, the ash, the maple, the elm: hence the word *liber*, which denotes the inner bark of trees, signifies also a book. As these barks were rolled up, to be more readily carried about, the united rolls were called *volumen*, a volume; a name given likewise to rolls of paper or of parchment. The ancients wrote likewise on linen. But the oldest material commonly employed for writing upon, appears to have been the *papyrus*, a reed very common in Egypt and other places, and still found in Sicily and Chaldea. From this comes our word paper. At a later period, *parchment* from skins was invented in Pergamos, and was there used for *rolls* or *volumes*. The pen for writing on these soft materials was a small brush, or a reed split at the end, Jer. 36:23. The ink was prepared with lampblack, coal of ivory, various gums, etc., and the writing was sometimes permanently fixed by fire. Scribes carried their inkhorns hanging to their girdles, Ezek. 9:2. The making of paper from *linen*, in its modern form, was first known in Europe about A. D. 1300. The art of printing was introduced about one hundred and fifty years later.

An ancient book therefore had the appearance of a thick roll of some paper-like substance, written usually in parallel columns on one side only, and read by gradually unrolling it by means of two small rollers, one at the beginning and the other at the end of the volume. A roll was sometimes sealed, being first tied or wrapped about with a cord, on which the wax was dropped, and stamped by a signet, Isa. 29:11; Rev. 5:1–3.

That writing was practised very early, may be inferred from allusions to the art in Gen. 5:1; Ex. 17:14; Job 9:25; 19:23; 31:5. The Egyptians were accustomed to it from the earliest ages.

Ancient writers, instead of writing their books, etc., with their own hand, often employed amanuenses. St. Paul notes it as a particular circumstance, in the epistle to the Galatians, that he had written it with his own hand, Gal. 6:11. To other letters he only affixed his salutation with his own hand, 1 Cor. 16:21; Col. 4:18; 2 Thess. 3:17. The amanuensis who wrote the epistle to the Romans, has mentioned himself at the close, Rom. 16:22. See LETTER.

BOOK OF THE GENERATION, is used in Gen. 5:1; Matt. 1:1, in the sense of a genealogical record. See GENERATION.

BOOK OF THE WARS OF THE LORD, Num. 21:14, was probably a sort of military journal, formed of detached odes.

THE BOOK OF JASHER, 2 Sam. 1:18, may perhaps have been a collection of national ballads, one of the forms most used for perpetuating the history of ancient times.

THE BOOKS OF THE CHRONICLES of the kings of Judah and Israel were apparently public journals, 1 Kin. 14:19, 29.

BOOK OF LIFE, OR OF THE LIVING, Psa. 69:28. It is probable that these descriptive phrases are taken from the custom observed in the courts of princes, of keeping a list of persons who are in their service, of the provinces which they govern, of the officers of their armies, of the number of their troops, and sometimes even of the names of their soldiers. In the figurative style of oriental poetry, God is represented as inscribing the names, acts, and destinies of men in volumes; and the volume in which are thus entered the names of those who are chosen to salvation, is "the book of life," Phil. 4:3.

BOOTH, a shelter, made usually of poles fixed upright in the ground, and covered over with green boughs, Gen. 33:17. The great feast of tabernacles, or booths, had its name from the circumstance that the Jews were directed by their law to dwell in booths during the seven days of this feast, Lev. 23:40–42; Neh. 8:14. See TABERNACLE.

BOO'TY. Spoils taken in war were to be shared equally by those who fought and those who guarded the camp, Num. 31:27–32. The Lord's portion was first deducted from the whole; and in after-times the king appropriated a large part to himself.

BOR'ROW. The Hebrews are said to have "borrowed" of the Egyptians, Ex. 3:22; 12:35. The original word denotes simply *asked*. As they were known to be taking a final leave of Egypt, it is plain that the Egyptians did not expect the thing asked for to be returned. They asked for them by divine direction, and they undoubtedly received no more than a fair compensation for their many years of hard service.

BO'SOM, the front of the upper part of the body, the breast. The orientals generally wore long, wide, and loose garments; and when about to carry any thing away that their hands would not contain, they used for the purpose a fold in the bosom of their robe above the girdle, Luke 6:38. Our Saviour is said to carry his lambs in his bosom, which beautifully represents his tender care and watchfulness over them, Isa. 40:11. See ABRAHAM'S BOSOM.

BOS'SES, the thickest and strongest parts, the projecting points, of a shield. Job 15:26.

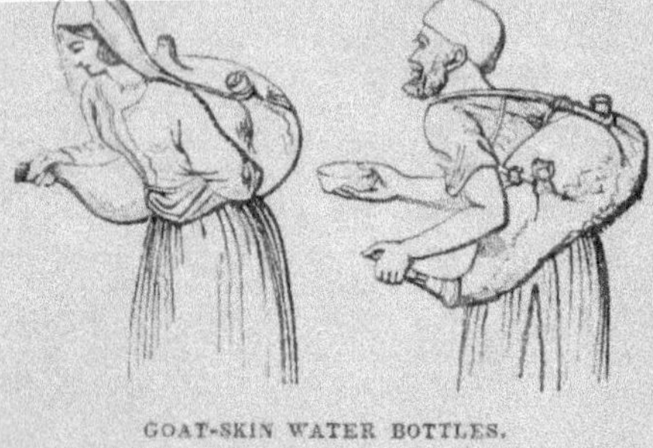

GOAT-SKIN WATER BOTTLES.

BOT'TLE. The accompanying engraving shows the form and nature of an ancient goat-skin bottle, out of which a water-carrier is offering to sell a draught of water. After the skin has been stripped off from an animal, and properly dressed, the places where the legs had been are closed up; and where the neck was, is the opening left for receiving and discharging the contents of the bottle. These were readily borne upon the shoulder, Gen. 21:14. See also Josh. 9:4, 13; Psa. 119:83; Jer. 13:12.

By receiving the liquor poured into it, a skin bottle must be greatly swelled and distended; and still more, if the liquor be wine, by its fermentation while advancing to ripeness; so that if no vent be given to it, the liquor may overpower the strength of the bottle, or if it find any defect, it may ooze out by that. Hence the propriety of putting *new* wine into *new* bottles, which being in the prime of their strength, may resist the expansion of their contents, and preserve the wine to maturity; while old bottles may, without danger, contain old wine, whose fermentation is already past, Matt. 9:17; Luke 5:38; Job 32:19.

Such bottles, or skins, are still universally employed in travelling in the East, as well as by the public water-carriers, and for domestic uses. They were made, for storage in wine-cellars, of the hides of oxen or camels. But the smaller ones of goat-skins were more generally used for water as well as wine. The ancients, however, were acquainted with the art of making earthenware, and had a variety of elegant small bottles and vases for toilet purposes, made of the precious metals, of stone, glass, porcelain, and alabaster, Jer. 19:1, 10, 11. See CRUSE, VINE, TEARS.

BOW, a weapon much used in ancient times, both for hunting and for war. It was made of wood, horn, or steel, Gen. 27:3; Psa. 18:34; and the foot was sometimes used in bending it. It was carried in a case, when not used, Hab. 3:19. The Benjamites were celebrated for their skill in the use of this weapon, 1 Chr. 12:2; 2 Chr. 14:8; 17:17. See ARMS. The phrase, "a deceitful bow," to which the people of Israel are compared, Psa. 78:57; Hos. 7:16, means an ill-made or twisted bow, which does not shoot the arrow as it is aimed. In 2 Sam. 1:18, we read, "Also he bade them teach the children of Judah the use of the bow." Here the words, "the use of," are not in the Hebrew. The use of the bow in war had long been common among the Jews, Gen. 48:22; and to "teach them the bow," is by some supposed to mean, teach them the song of THE BOW, the lamentation over Saul and Jonathan, which follows;

so called from the mention of the weapon in verse 22, as the first four books in the Bible take their title in Hebrew from the first word in each. See ARROW.

BOWELS are often put by the Hebrew writers for the internal parts generally, the inner man, just as we often use the word heart. Hence the bowels are often represented as the seat of mercy, tenderness, compassion, etc., 1 Kin. 3:26; Isa. 63:15; Jer. 31:20; Col. 3:12; 1 John 3:17.

BOX-TREE, a well-known beautiful evergreen, growing in many parts of Europe and Asia. Its wood is highly prized by engravers. The word employed in Isa. 60:13, is thought by many to have been a species of cedar. It is used as an emblem of the abiding grace and prosperity of the church of God.

BOZ'RAH, Gen. 36:33, a city of Edom, Isa. 34:6; 63:1, and the region around it, Jer. 49:13, 22. It is associated with Teman, and with the Red sea, Jer. 49:20-22; Amos 1:12. Its site is found in the modern El-Busaireh, midway between Kir Moab and mount Hor, south by east of the Dead sea. This is a village of about fifty houses, on a hill crowned by a small castle. The ruins are those of a considerable city. Bozrah of Moab, Jer. 48:24, may be the same place with this, or perhaps with Bezer.

BRACE'LET, properly an ornament for the wrist, or for the arm above or below the elbow; but sometimes used also in the Bible to signify an ornament worn on the leg, Num. 31:50; Isa. 3:19. Armlets were worn by men, sometimes as a badge of royalty, 2 Sam. 1:10. Bracelets were of a great variety of materials and forms; were usually large, and often of great value, Gen. 24:22.

The women of Syria and Arabia at this day wear rings round their legs, to which are fastened many other lesser rings, which make a tinkling noise, like little bells, when they walk. These rings are fixed above the ankle, and are of gold, silver, copper, glass, or even of varnished earth, according to the condition of the wearer. The princesses wear large hollow rings of gold, within which are enclosed little pebbles, that tinkle. See RINGS.

BRANCH. As trees denote, in figurative language, great men and princes, so branches, boughs, and plants denote their offspring. Christ is called "the Branch," the "rod out of the stem of Jesse," and the "branch out of his roots," Isa. 11:1; 53:2; Zech. 3:8; 6:12; being a royal descendant of the princely house of David, Jer. 23:5; 33:15. The word branch also illustrates the union of believers with Christ, John 15:5, 6. It is used in Ezek. 8:17 as a symbol of idolatrous worship, probably in allusion to the carrying of fragrant boughs in honor of idols.

BRASS is frequently mentioned in the English Bible, Gen. 4:22; Deut. 8:9; but there is little doubt that copper is intended, brass being a mixed metal—two-thirds copper and one-third zinc—for the manufacture of which we are indebted to the Germans. The ancients knew nothing of that particular compound, though well acquainted with bronze, of which arms, mirrors, and ornaments were made. Copper was used for many purposes about the temple, Lev. 6:28; Num. 16:39; 2 Chr. 4:16; for filters, Judg. 16:21; 2 Kin. 25:7; for armor, 1 Sam. 17:5, 6, 38; for musical instruments, 1 Chr. 15:19; and for money, Matt. 10:9. "Brass" is used to describe drought, insensibility, baseness, and obstinacy in sin, Lev. 26:19; Deut. 28:23; Isa. 48:4; Jer. 6:28; Ezek. 22:18. It is also a symbol of strength, Psa. 107:16; Dan. 2:39; Zech. 6:1. See COPPER.

BRA'ZEN SER'PENT, an image in brass prepared by Moses, resembling the fiery serpents so destructive to Israel in the desert, and set up in the midst of the camp in the view of all, that whosoever would evince penitence, faith, and obedience by looking to it, might live, Num. 21:6-9. Our Saviour has shown us that this was typical of himself and of salvation through him—a gratuitous salvation, free to all, on the easy terms of faith and obedience, John 3:14, 15. The brazen serpent was long preserved, as a memorial of the gracious miracle wrought in connection with it; but being regarded as an object of worship, it was broken to pieces by king Hezekiah, as Nehushtan—a mere piece of brass, 2 Kin. 18:4.

BREAD, a word which in Scripture is often put for *food* in general, Gen. 3:19; 18:5; 28:20; Ex. 2:20; Lev. 11:3. Manna is called *bread* from heaven, Ex. 16:4. Bread, in the proper and literal sense, usually means cakes made of wheaten flour; barley being used chiefly by the poor and for feeding horses. The wheat was ground daily, in small stone mills; the flour was made into dough in a wooden trough, and subsequently leavened, Ex. 12:34; Hos. 7:4. It was then made into cakes, and baked.

The ancient Hebrews had several ways of baking bread: they often baked it under the ashes upon the earth, upon round copper or iron plates, or in pans or stoves made on purpose. The Arabians and other oriental nations, among whom wood is scarce, often bake their bread between two fires made of cow-dung, which burns slowly. The bread is good, if eaten the same day, but the crust is black and burnt, and retains a smell of the fuel used in baking it. This explains Ezek. 4:9, 15.

The Hebrews, in common with other eastern people, had a kind of oven, (*tannoor*,) which is like a large pitcher, open at top, in which they made a fire. When it was well heated, they mingled flour in water, and this paste they applied to the outside of the pitcher. Such bread is baked in an instant, and is taken off in thin, fine pieces, like our wafers, Lev. 2. Bread was also baked in cavities sunk in the ground, or the floor of the tent, and well lined with compost or cement. A fire was built on the floor of this oven; and the sides being sufficiently heated, thin cakes were adroitly stuck upon them, and soon baked. In the large towns there were public ovens, and bakers by trade, Jer. 37:21; Hos. 7:4.

As the Hebrews generally made their bread thin, and in the form of flat cakes, or wafers, they did not cut it with a knife, but broke it, Lam. 4:4, which gave rise to that expression so usual in Scripture, of "breaking bread," to signify eating, sitting down to table, taking a repast. In the institution of the Lord's supper, our Saviour broke the bread which he had consecrated; whence "to break bread," and "breaking of bread," in the New Testament are used for celebrating the Lord's supper. See under Eating.

Show-bread, Heb. bread of presence, was bread offered every Sabbath-day to God on the golden table which stood in the holy place, Ex. 25:30; twelve cakes of unleavened bread, offered with salt and frankincense, Lev. 2:13; 24:5-9. The show-bread could be lawfully eaten by none but the priests; nevertheless, David having received some of these

THE TABLE OF SHOW-BREAD.

loaves from the high-priest Abimelech, ate of them without scruple in his necessity, 1 Sam. 21:1-6; and our Saviour quotes his example to justify the disciples, who had bruised ears of corn, and were eating them on the Sabbath-day, Matt. 12:1-4.

BREASTPLATE, a piece of embroidery, about ten inches square, Ex. 28:15-30, of very rich work, which the high-priest wore on his breast. It was made of two pieces of the same rich embroidered stuff of which the ephod was made, having a front and a lining, and forming a kind of purse or bag, in which, according to the rabbins, the Urim and Thummim were enclosed. The front of it was

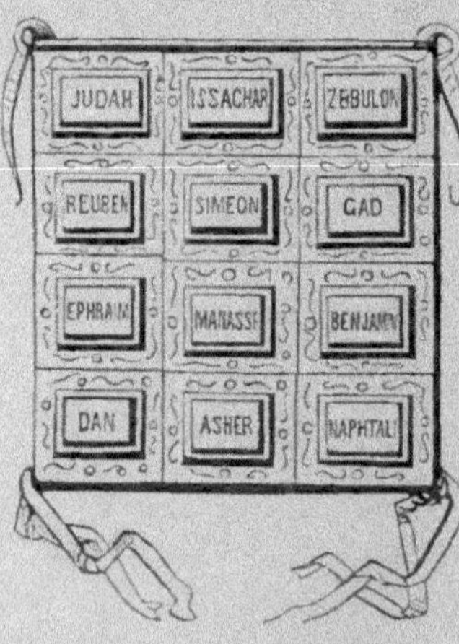

set with twelve precious stones, on each of which was engraved the name of one of the tribes. They were placed in four rows, and divided from each other by the little golden squares or partitions in which they were set. At each corner was a gold ring answering to a ring upon the ephod, these four pairs of rings serving to hold the breastplate in its place on the front of the ephod, by means of four blue ribands, one at each corner.

BRICKS were usually made of clay, dried and hardened in the sun, Gen. 11:3, though brick-kilns were sometimes used, 2 Sam. 12:31; Nah. 3:14. The tower of Babel was constructed of brick, cemented with bitumen. The bricks used were often a foot square; and great numbers of them are found, both in Babylonia and Egypt, impressed with some royal or priestly stamp. The principal subject of interest connected with brick-making is the fact that it was the labor in which the Hebrews in Egypt were most oppressed. On the monuments of Egypt, all the parts of this hard and ancient task-work are painted—the carrying, tempering, and moulding of the clay, and the drying and piling of the bricks—all done by foreigners under the orders of taskmasters. The straw was probably mixed with the clay to compact it. See Wilkinson's "Ancient Egyptians."

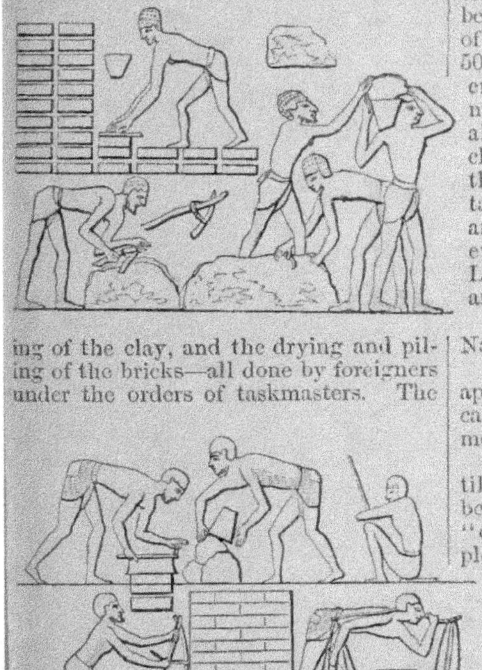

BRICKMAKING, UNDER A TASKMASTER.

BRIDE and BRIDE'GROOM, see MARRIAGE and SOLOMON'S SONG.

BRIG'ANDINE, a coat of mail, Jer. 46:4; 51:3.

BRIM'STONE, a mineral substance, highly inflammable, and burning with a suffocating smell. Sodom and the other cities of the plain were destroyed "by brimstone and fire," Gen. 19:24; and this awful catastrophe is often used in Scripture, as an emblem of temporal and eternal judgments of God upon the wicked, Job 18:15; Psa. 11:6; Isa. 30:33; 34:9; Rev. 21:8.

BROOK, see RIVER.

BROTH'ER signifies in Scripture the son of the same parent or parents, Matt. 1:2; Luke 6:14; a cousin or near kinsman, Gen. 13:8; 14:16; John 7:3; Acts 1:14; one of the same stock or country, Matt. 5:47; Acts 3:22; Heb. 7:5; a fellow-man, an equal, Matt 5:23; 7:3; one beloved, 2 Sam. 1:26; Christians, as sons of God, Acts 9:30; 11:29. In Matt. 12:46–50; 13:55, 56; Mark 3:31–35, the brothers of Christ are so mentioned, in connection with his mother and sisters, as almost to require us to believe they were children of Joseph and Mary, younger than Jesus. Yet this is not quite certain, as it may be that the James, Joses, and Judas in Matt. 13:55, are the nephews of Christ alluded to in Matt. 27:56; Luke 6:15, 16; John 19:25; Cleophas and Alphæus being probably the same.

BRUIT, rumor or report, Jer. 10:22; Nah. 3:19.

BUL, occurring only in 1 Kin. 6:38, applied to the eighth month, usually called Marcheshvan, which see. Solomon's temple was finished in Bul.

BULLS of Bashan, pasturing in a fertile region and with but few keepers, became strong and fierce, and might "compass about" an intruder, and trample him under foot. They are symbols of powerful, fierce, and numerous foes, Psa. 22:12; 68:30; Isa. 34:7. See Ox.

BUL'RUSH, see next page.

BUR'DEN, a weight or load, on body or soul; often used figuratively, to denote afflictions, failings, sins, Psa. 38:4; 55:22; Gal. 6:2; services under the law, Matt. 23:4; official responsibilities, Ex. 18:22; Deut 1:12; and especially prophetic messages, not always of a threatening character, Isa. 19:1. In this last sense the Hebrew word may be rendered "oracle," "divine declaration," or "prophecy," as in Prov. 30:1; 31:1.

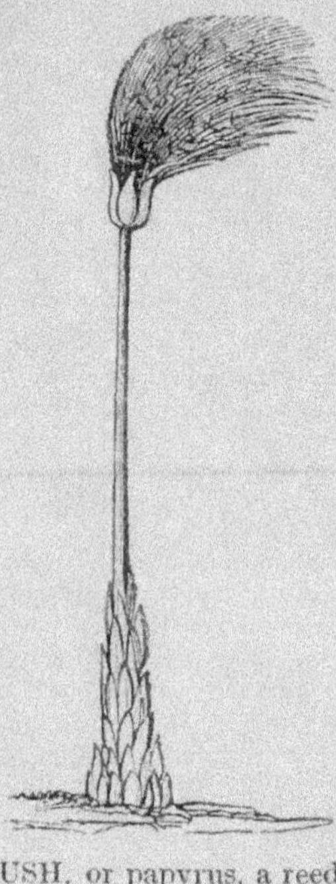

BUL'RUSH, or papyrus, a reed growing on the banks of the Nile, in marshy ground, Job 8:11, to the height of twelve or fifteen feet, Isa. 35:7. The stalks are pliable, and capable of being interwoven very closely, as is evident from their being used in the construction of arks, Ex. 2:3, 5; and also vessels of larger dimensions, Isa. 18:2. Boats of this material were very common in Egypt. Being exceedingly light and small, they sailed with great velocity, and might easily be borne on the shoulders around rapids and falls. The inner bark of this plant, platted and cemented together, furnished a writing material; and the pith was sometimes used for food. See Book.

BUR'IAL. The Hebrews were at all times very careful in the burial of their dead, Gen. 25:9; 35:29. To be deprived of burial was thought one of the greatest marks of dishonor, or causes of unhappiness, Eccl. 6:3; Jer. 22:18, 19; it being denied to none, not even to enemies. Good men made it a part of their piety to inter the dead. Indeed, how shocking must the sight of unburied corpses have been to the Jews, when their land was thought to be polluted if the dead were in any manner exposed to view, 2 Sam. 21:14; and when the very touch of a dead body, or of any thing that had touched a dead body, was esteemed a defilement, and required a ceremonial ablution, Num. 19:11–22.

Only two cases of burning the bodies of the dead occur in Scripture: the mangled remains of Saul and his sons, 1 Sam. 31:12, and the victims of some plague, Amos 6:10. It was customary for the nearest relatives to close the eyes of the dying and give them the parting kiss, and then to commence the wailing for the dead, Jer. 46:4; 50:1; in this wailing, which continued at intervals until after the burial, they were joined by other relatives and friends, John 11:19, whose loud and shrill lamentations are referred to in Mark 5:38. It is also a custom still prevailing in the East to hire wailing women, Jer. 9:17; Amos 5:16, who praised the deceased, Acts 9:39, and by doleful cries and frantic gestures, aided at times by melancholy tones of music, Matt. 9:23, strove to express the deepest grief, Ezek. 24:17, 18.

Immediately after death the body was washed, and laid out in a convenient room, Acts 9:39; it was wrapped in many folds of linen, with spices, and the head bound about with a napkin, Matt. 27:59; John 11:44. Unless the body was to be embalmed, the burial took place very soon, both on account of the heat of the climate and the ceremonial uncleanness incurred. Rarely did twenty-four hours elapse between death and burial, Acts 5:6, 10. The body being shrouded, was placed upon a bier—a board resting on a simple handbarrow borne by men—to be conveyed to the tomb, 2 Sam. 3:31; Luke 7:14. Sometimes a more costly bier or bed was used, 2 Chr. 16:14; and the bodies of kings and some others may have been laid in coffins of wood, or stone sarcophagi. The relatives attended the bier to the tomb, which was usually without the city. A banquet sometimes followed the funeral, Jer. 16:7, 8; and during subsequent days the bereaved friends were wont to go to the grave from time to time, to weep and to adorn the place with fresh flowers, John 11:31, a custom observed even at this day. See Embalming, Sepulchre.

BURNT-OFFERINGS. See SACRIFICE.

BUSH'EL, used in the New Testament to express the Greek modius, which was about a peck by our measure.

BUTTER. The Hebrew word usually rendered *butter* denotes, properly, sour or curdled milk, Gen. 18:8; Judg. 5:25; Job 20:17. This last is a favorite beverage in the East to the present day. Burckhardt, when crossing the desert from the country south of the Dead sea to Egypt, says, "Besides flour, I carried some butter and dried *leben*, (sour milk,) which, when dissolved in water, not only forms a refreshing beverage, but is much to be recommended as a preservative of health when travelling in summer." Yet butter may have been known to the Hebrews. It is much used by the Arabs and Syrians at the present day, and is made by pouring the milk into the common goat-skin bottle, suspending this from the tent-poles, and swinging it to and fro with a jerk, until the process is completed. Still it is not certain that the Hebrew word rendered butter ever denotes that article. Even in Prov. 30:33 we may render, "The pressing of milk bringeth forth cheese;" and everywhere else the rendering "curd," or "curdled milk," would be appropriate.

BUZ, son of Nahor and Milcah, and ancestor of the Buzites, who lived in Mesopotamia or Ram, and afterwards perhaps in Arabia Deserta, Gen. 22:21; Job 32:2; Jer. 25:23.

C.

CAB, a Hebrew measure, the sixth part of a seah, and the eighteenth part of an ephah. A cab contained three pints and one third, of our wine measure, or two pints and five sixths, of our corn measure, 2 Kin. 6:25.

CA'BUL, probably meaning *displeasing*, I., a name given by Hiram king of Tyre to a district in Northern Galilee containing twenty cities, which Solomon gave him for his help in building the temple, 1 Kin. 9:13; the term implying his dissatisfaction with the gift.

II. A city of Asher, Josh. 19:27.

CÆ'SAR, originally the surname of the Julian family at Rome. After being dignified in the person of Julius Cæsar, it became the usual appellation of those of his family who ascended the throne. The last of these was Nero, but the name was still retained by his successors as a sort of title belonging to the imperial dignity. The emperors alluded to by this title in the New Testament, are Augustus, Luke 2:1; Tiberius, Luke 3:1; 20:22; Claudius, Acts 11:28; and Nero, Acts 25:8; Phil. 4:22. Caligula, who succeeded Tiberius, is not mentioned.

CÆSARE'A, often called Cæsarea of Palestine, situated on the coast of the Mediterranean sea, between Joppa and Tyre. It was anciently a small place, called the Tower of Strato, but was rebuilt with great splendor, and strongly fortified by Herod the Great, who formed a harbor by constructing a vast breakwater, adorned the city with many stately buildings, and named it Cæsarea, in honor of Augustus. It was inhabited chiefly by Greeks, and Herod established in it quinquennial games in honor of the emperor. This city was the capital of Judea during the reign of Herod the Great and of Herod Agrippa I., and was also the seat of the Roman power while Judea was governed as a province of the empire. It was subject to frequent commotions between the Greeks, Romans, and Jews, so that on one occasion 20,000 persons are said to have fallen in one day.

It is noted in gospel history as the residence of Philip the evangelist, Acts 8:40; 21:8; and of Cornelius the centurion, the first-fruits from the Gentiles, Acts 10; 11:1-18. Here Herod Agrippa was smitten by the angel of God, Acts 12:20-23. Paul several times visited it, Acts 9:30; 18:22; 21:8, 16; here he appeared before Felix, who trembled under his appeals, Acts 23:23; 24; here he was imprisoned for two years; and after pleading before Festus and Agrippa, he sailed hence for imperial Rome, Acts 25:26; 27:1. It is now a heap of ruins.

CÆSARE'A-PHILIP'PI, a city three or four miles east of Dan, near the eastern source of the Jordan; anciently called Paneas, now Banias, from an adjacent grotto dedicated to Pan, from which one of the sources of the Jordan flowed. It stood where the mountains south-west of Hermon join the plain above lake Huleh, on an elevated plateau surrounded by ravines and water-courses; and its walls were thick and strong. It was enlarged and embellished by Philip the tetrarch of Trachonitis, and called Cæsarea in honor of Tiberius Cæsar; and the name Philippi was added to distinguish it from Cæsarea on the Mediterranean. Our Saviour visited this place shortly before his transfiguration, Matt. 16:13–28; Mark 8:27–38; Luke 9:18, 27. After the destruction of Jerusalem, Titus here made the captive Jews fight and kill each other in gladiatorial shows. In the time of the crusades it underwent many changes, and is now a paltry village amid extensive ruins.

CAI'APHAS, high-priest of the Jews, A. D 27 to 36. He was a Sadducee, and a bitter enemy of Christ. At his palace the priests, etc., met after the resurrection of Lazarus, to plot the death of the Saviour, lest all the people should believe on him. On one of these occasions, John 11:47–54, he counselled the death of Christ for the political salvation of the nation; and his words were, unconsciously to him, an inspired prediction of the salvation of a lost world. These plots against Christ, Matt. 26:1–5; Mark 14:1; Luke 22:2, led to his seizure, and he was brought first before Annas, formerly high-priest, who sent him to Caiaphas his son-in-law. See ANNAS. Caiaphas examined Christ before the assembling of the Sanhedrim, after which the trial went on, and Christ was condemned, mocked, and transferred to Pilate for sentence and execution, Matt. 26:57–68; Mark 14:53–72; Luke 22:54–71; John 18:13–27. Not content with procuring the death of the Saviour, Caiaphas and his friends violently persecuted his followers, Acts 4:1–6; 5:17, 33. But a few years after the ascension of Christ, and soon after the degradation of Pilate, Caiaphas also was deposed from office by the Roman proconsul Vitellius. Like Balaam of the Old Testament, he is a melancholy instance of light resisted, privilege, station, and opportunity abused, and prophetic words concerning Christ joined with a life of infidelity and crime and a fearful death.

CAIN, the first-born of the human race, Gen. 4:1, and the first murderer. See ABEL. His crime was committed against the warnings of God, and he despised the call of God to confession and penitence, Gen. 4:6–9. The punishment inflicted upon him included an increase of physical wants and hardships, distress of conscience, banishment from society, and loss of God's manifested presence and favor, Gen. 4:16. But God mingled mercy with judgment; and appointed for Cain some sign that he should not suffer the death-penalty he had incurred at the hand of man, thus signifying that God only was his judge. He withdrew into the land of Nod, east of Eden, and built a city which he named Enoch, after one of his sons.

CAIN'AN, I., son of Enos, and father of Mahalaleel, Gen. 5:9; 1 Chr. 1:2.

II. Son of Arphaxad and father of Salah, Luke 3:36. This Cainan, however, is not named in the three Old Testament genealogies, Gen. 10:24; 11:12; 1 Chr. 1:24, nor in any ancient version. The name occurs in two places in the Septuagint, an early Greek version; and some suppose that copyists of Luke's gospel inserted the name, in order to agree with the Septuagint.

CA'LAH, a city of Assyria, built by Ashur or by Nimrod, Gen. 10:11, 12. It was at some distance from Nineveh, and Resen lay between them. It is thought to have been near the river Lycus, the great Zab, which empties into the Tigris.

CAL'AMUS. See CANE.

CA'LEB, I., son of Jephunneh, of the tribe of Judah, who was sent, with one man from each of the other tribes, to search out the promised land, Num. 13; 14. Of all the twelve, Caleb and Joshua acted the part of true and faithful men; and they only, of all the grown men of Israel, were permitted to enter Canaan, Num. 14:6–24, 38; 26:65. He was one of the princes appointed to divide the conquered territory among the tribes, Num. 34:19. Hebron was given to him as a reward of his fidelity, according to the promise of God, Deut. 1:36; Josh. 14. Though eighty-five years old, he still retained his vigor, and soon drove out the Anakim from his inheritance. He gave a portion also with his daughter Achsah to Othniel his nephew, who had earned the reward by his valor in the capture of Debir, Josh. 15:13–19; 21:12. This region was for some time called by his name, 1 Sam. 30:14.

II. Son of Hur, whose children peopled the country about Bethlehem, etc., 1 Chr. 2:50–55.

CALF, the young of the cow, a clean animal much used in sacrifice; hence the expression, "So will we render the calves of our lips," Hos. 14:2, meaning, we will offer as sacrifices the prayers and praises of our lips, Heb. 13:15. The fatted calf was considered the choicest animal food, Gen. 18:7; Amos 6:4; Luke 15:23.

In Jer. 34:18, "they cut the calf in twain, and passed between the parts thereof," there is an allusion to an ancient mode of ratifying a covenant; the parties thus signifying their willingness to be themselves cut in pieces if unfaithful, Gen. 15:9–18.

THE GOLDEN CALF worshipped by the Jews at mount Sinai, while Moses was absent in the mount, was cast by Aaron from the earrings of the people. Its worship was attended with degrading obscenities, and was punished by the death of three thousand men.

The golden calves of Jeroboam were erected by him, one at each extreme of his kingdom, that the ten tribes might be prevented from resorting to Jerusalem to worship, and thus coalescing with the men of Judah, 1 Kin. 12:26–29. Thus the people "forgot God their Saviour," and sank into gross idolatry. Jeroboam is scarcely ever mentioned in Scripture without the brand upon him, "who made Israel to sin," 2 Kin. 17:21. The prophet Hosea frequently alludes to the calf at Bethel, to the folly and guilt of its worshippers, and to the day when both idol and people should be broken in pieces by the Assyrians.

CAL'NEH, called Calno, Isa. 10:9, and Canneh, Ezek. 27:23, one of Nimrod's cities, Gen. 10:10, afterwards called Ctesiphon; it lay on the east bank of the Tigris opposite Seleucia, twenty miles below Bagdad. Ctesiphon was a winter residence of the Parthian kings. Nothing now remains but the ruins of a palace and mounds of rubbish.

CAL'VARY, or GOL'GOTHA, the latter being the Hebrew term, *place of a skull*, the place where our Saviour was crucified, near by Jerusalem, John 19:20, but outside of its walls, Matt. 27:33; Mark 15:22; John 19:17; Heb. 13:12. In the same place was a private garden, and a tomb in which the body of Christ lay until the resurrection, John 19:41, 42. The expression, "*mount* Calvary," has no evidence to support it beyond what is implied in the name Golgotha which might well be given to a slight elevation shaped like the top of a skull, and the probability that such a place would be chosen for the crucifixion. It is very doubtful whether the true localities of Calvary and the tomb are those covered by the present "Church of the Holy Sepulchre," a vast structure north of mount Zion and within the modern city, built on the site which was fixed under the empress Helena, A. D. 335, by tradition and a pretended miracle. Some biblical geographers adhere to this location; but Robinson and many others strongly oppose it, on the ground of the weakness of the tradition, and the difficulty of supposing that this place lay outside of the ancient walls. See JERUSALEM. Dr. Fisk, while visiting the spot under the natural desire to identify the scene of these most sacred events, felt it to be just possible, and that was all, that the spot shown him might be the actual scene of the crucifixion; that the rock shown him might be a part of the rock riven by the earthquake; that the stone column he saw, half concealed by iron-work, might have been that to which our Lord was bound when scourged; that the small fragment of rude stone seen by the light of a small taper, through a kind of iron filigree, might have been the stone on which he sat to be crowned with thorns; that the spot overhung with lamps, and covered with a white marble sarcophagus, with a kind of domed structure in the centre, might have been the place of our Lord's burial and resurrection: but when he saw the near juxtaposition of all these things, and knew that in order to provide for the structure of the church the site had to be cut down and levelled; when he reflected that on the very spot a heathen temple had stood, till removed by the empress Helena, to make room for this church; and, moreover, when he considered the superstitious purpose all these things were to serve, and the spirit of that church which thus paraded these objects of curiosity, he could not bring himself to feel they were what they professed to be.

Let us be thankful that though the exact scene of Christ's death is now unknown, there can be no doubt as to the fact. "He died, and was buried, and the third day rose again, according to the Scriptures." Then the old ritual passed away, Satan was despoiled, man was redeemed, God reconciled, and heaven opened to all believers.

THE SWIFT CAMEL, OR DROMEDARY.

CAMEL, *carrier*, a beast of burden very common in the East, where it is called "the land-ship," and "the carrier of the desert." It is six or seven feet high, and is exceedingly strong, tough, and enduring of labor. The feet are constructed with a tough elastic sole, which prevents the animal from sinking in the sand; and on all sorts of ground it is very sure-footed. The Arabian species, most commonly referred to in Scripture, has but one hump on the back; while the Bactrian camel, found in central Asia, has two. While the animal is well fed, these humps swell with accumulated fat, which is gradually absorbed under scarcity and toil, to supply the lack of food. The dromedary is a lighter and swifter variety, otherwise not distinguishable from the common camel, Jer. 2:23. Within the cavity of the stomach is a sort of paunch, provided with membranous cells to contain an extra provision of water: the supply with which this is filled will last for many days while he traverses the desert. His food is coarse leaves, twigs, thistles, which he prefers to the tenderest grass, and on which he performs the longest journeys. But generally, on a march, about a pound weight of dates, beans, or barley, will serve for twenty-four hours. The camel kneels to receive its load, which varies from 500 to 1,000 or 1,200 pounds. Meanwhile it is wont to utter loud cries or growls of anger and impatience. It is often obstinate and stupid, and at times ferocious; the young are as dull and ungainly as the old. Its average rate of travel is about two and one third miles an hour; and it jogs on with a sullen pertinacity hour after hour without fatigue, seeming as fresh at night as in the morning. No other animal could endure the severe and continual hardships of the camel, his rough usage, his coarse and scanty food. The Arabians well say of him, "Job's beast is a monument of God's mercy."

This useful animal has been much employed in the East, from a very early period. The merchants of those sultry climes have found it the only means of exchanging the products of different lands, and from time immemorial long caravans have traversed year after year the almost pathless deserts, Gen. 37:25. The number of one's camels was a token of his wealth. Job had 3,000, and the Midianites' camels were like the sand of the sea, Judg. 7:12; 1 Chr. 5:21; Job 1:3. Rebekah came to Isaac riding upon a camel, Gen. 24:64; the queen of Sheba brought them to Solomon, and Hazael to Elisha, laden with the choicest gifts, 1 Kin. 10:2; 2 Kin. 8:9; and they were even made serviceable in war, 1 Sam. 30:17. The camel was to the Hebrews an unclean animal, Lev. 11:4; yet its milk has ever been to the Arabs an important article of food, and is highly prized as a cooling and healthy drink. Indeed, no animal is more useful to the Arabs, while living or after death. Out of its hair they manufacture carpets, tent cloth, and large sacks for corn. Of its skin they make huge water-bottles and leather sacks, also sandals, ropes, and thongs. Its dung, dried in the sun, serves them for fuel.

CAMELS' HAIR was woven into cloth in the East, some of it exceedingly fine and soft, but usually coarse and rough, used for making the coats of shepherds and camel-drivers, and for covering tents. It was this that John the Baptist wore, and not "soft raiment," Matt. 11:8. Modern dervishes wear garments of this kind; and this appears to be meant in 2 Kin 1 8.

The expression, "It is easier for a camel to go through the eye of a needle," etc., Matt. 19:24, was a proverb to describe an impossibility. The same phrase occurs in the Koran; and a similar one in the Talmud, respecting an elephant's going through a needle's eye.

See also the proverb in Matt 23: 24, which illustrates the hypocrisy of the Pharisees by the custom of passing wine through a strainer. The old versions of the New Testament, instead of, "strain *at*" a gnat, have, "strain *out*," which conveys the true meaning.

CAMP, ENCAMP'MENTS. These terms usually refer to the movements of the Israelites between Egypt and Canaan; and many passages of the Levitical law relate to things done "within" or "without the camp." The whole body of the people consisted of six hundred thousand fighting men, besides women and children, Num. 1:2; and was disposed into four battalions, so arranged as to enclose the tabernacle in a square, and each under one general standard, Num. 2: 3. The mode in which this vast mass of people was arranged, with the most perfect order and subordination, must excite general surprise. Balaam, standing on the heights of Moab, viewed the imposing spectacle with admiration and awe: "How goodly are thy tents, O Jacob! the Lord his God is with him," Num. 23; 24.

The order appointed for the removal of the hosts of Israel from one encampment to another is detailed in Num. 9; 10. The names of forty-one encampments are given in Num. 33; from the first in Rameses, in the month April, B. C. 1491, to the last on the brink of the Jordan forty years later. See EXODUS, and WANDERINGS

Travellers in the desert were wont to pitch their tents in the centre of a circle formed by their camels and baggage, which served as a barrier against an assault. A similar mode of encamping was practised by large caravans, and by armies, 1 Sam. 26:5, margin.

CAM'PHIRE, in Sol. Song 1:14; 4:13, is not the gum Camphor of our apothecaries, but the Cyprus-flower, as it is sometimes called, the Alhenna of the Arabs, a whitish fragrant flower, hanging in clusters like grapes. Oriental ladies make use of the dried and powdered leaves to give their nails, feet, and hands a reddish orange tinge. The nails of Egyptian mummies are found thus dyed. See EYELIDS. The flowers of the Alhenna are fragrant; and being disposed in clusters, the females of Egypt are fond of carrying it in their bosoms.

CA'NA, the birthplace of Nathanael, the city in which our Lord performed his first miracle, and from which he soon after sent a miraculous healing to the nobleman's son at Capernaum, eighteen miles off, John 2:1-11; 4:46-54; 21:2. It was called Cana of Galilee, now Kana-el-Jelil, and lay seven miles north of Nazareth. This is Robinson's view. The commonly received site is nearer Nazareth. Cana is now in ruins.

CA'NAAN, I., the son of Ham, and grandson of Noah, Gen. 9:18. His numerous posterity seem to have occupied Zidon first, and thence spread into Syria and Canaan, Gen. 10: 15-19; 1 Chr. 1:13-16 The Jews believe that he was implicated with his father in the dishonor done to Noah, Gen. 9:20-27, which was the occasion of the curse under which he and his posterity suffered, Josh. 9:23, 27; 2 Chr. 8:7, 8.

II. The land peopled by Canaan and his posterity, and afterwards given to the Hebrews. This country has at different periods been called by various names, either from its inhabitants or some circumstances connected with its history. (1.) "The land of Canaan," from Canaan, the son of Ham, who divided it among his sons, each of whom became the head of a numerous tribe, and ultimately of a distinct people, Gen. 10:15-20; 11:31. This did not at first include any land east of the Jordan. (2.) "The land of Promise," Heb. 11:9, from the promise given to Abraham, that his posterity should possess it, Gen. 12:7; 13:15. These being termed Hebrews, the region in which they dwelt was called, (3.) "The land of the Hebrews, Gen. 40:15; and (4.) "The land of Israel," from the Israelites, or posterity of Jacob, having settled there. This name is of frequent occurrence in the Old Testament. It comprehends all that tract of ground on each side of the Jordan, which God gave for an inheritance to the Hebrews. At a later age, this term was often restricted to the territory of the ten tribes, Ezek. 27:17. (5.) "The land of Judah." This at first comprised only the region which was allotted to the tribe of Judah. After the separation of the ten tribes, the land which belonged to Judah and Benjamin, who formed a separate kingdom, was distinguished by the appellation of "the land of Judah," or Judea; which latter name the whole country retained during the existence of the second temple, and under the dominion of the Romans. (6.) "The Holy Land." This name appears to have been used by the Hebrews after the Babylonish captivity, Zech. 2:13. (7.) "Palestine," Ex. 15:14, a name derived from the Philistines, who migrated from Egypt, and having expelled the aboriginal inhabitants, settled on the borders of the Mediterranean. Their name was subsequently given to the whole country, though they in fact possessed only a small part of it. By heathen writers, the Holy Land has been variously termed Palestine, Syria, and Phœnicia.

Canaan was bounded on the west by the Mediterranean sea, north by mount Lebanon and Syria, east by Arabia Deserta, and south by Edom and the desert of Zin and Paran. Its extreme length was about one hundred and eighty miles, and its average width about sixty-five. Its general form and dimensions Coleman has well compared to those of the state of New Hampshire. At the period of David, vast tributary regions were for a time annexed to the Holy Land. These included the bordering nations on the east, far into Arabia Deserta; thence north to Tiphsah on the Euphrates, with all Syria between Lebanon and the Euphrates. On the south it included Edom, and reached the Red sea at Ezion-geber.

The land of Canaan has been variously divided. Under Joshua it was apportioned out to the twelve tribes. Under Rehoboam it was divided into the two kingdoms of Israel and Judah. It afterwards fell into the hands of the Babylonians, the Greeks, the Syrians, and the Romans. During the time of our Saviour, it was under the dominion of the last-mentioned people, and was divided into five provinces: Galilee, Samaria, Judea, Peræa, and Idumæa. Peræa was again divided into seven cantons: Abilene, Trachonitis, Iturea, Gaulonitis, Batanæa, Peræa, and Decapolis. At present, Palestine is subject to the sultan of Turkey, under whom the pashas of Acre and Gaza govern the seacoast, and the pasha of Damascus the interior of the country.

The surface of the land of Canaan is beautifully diversified with mountains and plains, rivers and valleys. The principal mountains are Lebanon, Carmel, Tabor, Gilead, Hermon, the mount of Olives, etc. The plain of the Mediterranean, of Esdraelon, and of Jericho, are celebrated as the scenes of many important events. The chief streams are the Jordan, the Arnon, the Sihor, the Jabbok, and the Kishon. The lakes are the Asphaltites or Dead sea, the lake of Tiberias or sea of Galilee, and lake Merom. These are elsewhere described, each in its own place.

The general features of the country may here be briefly described. The northern boundary is at the lofty mountains of Lebanon and Hermon, some peaks of which are ten thousand feet high. Around the base of mount Hermon are the various sources of the Jordan. This river, passing through lake Merom and the sea of Galilee, flows south with innumerable windings into the Dead sea. Its valley is deeply sunk, and from its source to the Dead sea it has a descent of two thousand feet. The country between the Jordan valley and the Mediterranean sea is in general an elevated table-land, broken up by many hills, and by numerous deep valleys through which the wintry torrents flow into Jordan and the sea. The tableland of Galilee may be nine hundred or one thousand feet above the Mediterranean. In lower Galilee we find the great and beautiful plain of Esdraelon, extending from mount Carmel and Acre on the west to Tabor and Gilboa, and even to the Jordan on the east. From this plain the land again rises towards the south; mount Gerizim being 2,300 feet, Jerusalem 2,400, and Hebron 2,600 above the sea. On the sea-coast, below mount Carmel, a fertile plain is found; towards the south it becomes gradually wider, and expands at last into the great desert of Paran. From this plain of the sea-coast the ascent to the high land of the interior is by a succession of natural terraces; while the descent to the Jordan, the Dead sea, and Edom, is abrupt and precipitous. The country beyond the Jordan is mountainous; a rich grazing land, with many fertile valleys. Still farther east is the high and desolate plateau of Arabia Deserta.

The soil and climate of Canaan were highly favorable. The heat was not extreme except in the deep river beds, and on the sea-coast; and the climate was in general mild and healthful. The variations of sunshine, clouds, and rain, which with us extend throughout the year, are in Palestine confined chiefly to the winter or rainy season. The autumnal rains usually commence in the latter part of October, and soon after the first showers wheat and barley are sowed. Rain falls more heavily in December; and continues, though with less frequency, until April. From May to October no rain falls. The cold of winter is not severe, and the ground does not freeze. Snows a foot or more deep sometimes occur, and there are frequent hailstorms in winter. The barley harvest is about a fortnight earlier than the wheat, and both are earlier in the plains than on the high land; altogether the grain harvest extends from April to June. The first grapes ripen in July, but the vintage is not over till September. In this month and October the heat is great; the ground becomes dry and parched; verdure has long before disappeared; pools and cisterns begin to dry up; and all nature, animate and inanimate, looks forward with longing for the return of the rainy season.

The soil of Canaan was highly productive. The prevailing rock is a chalky limestone, abounding in caverns. It readily formed, and was covered with, a rich mould, which produced, in the various elevations and climates so remarkably grouped together in that small region of the world, an unequalled variety of the fruits of the ground Olives, figs, vines, and pomegranates grew in abundance; the hills were clothed with flocks and herds, and the valleys were covered with corn. The land of promise was currently described as "flowing with milk and honey." Yet the glowing description given by Moses, Deut. 8:7–9, and the statements of history as to the vast population formerly occupying it, are in striking contrast with its present aspect of barrenness and desolation. The curse brought down by the unbelief of the Jews still blights their unhappy land. Long ages of warfare and misrule have despoiled and depopulated it. Its hills, once terraced to the summit, and covered with luxuriant grain, vines, olives, and figs, are now bare rocks. Its early and latter rains, once preserved in reservoirs, and conducted by winding channels to water the ground in the season of drought, now flow off unheeded to the sea. The land, stripped of its forests, lies open to the sun—which now scorches where it once fertilized. And yet some parts of Palestine still show an astonishing fertility; and wherever the soil is cultivated, it yields a hundredfold. Indian corn grows there eleven feet high, and grapes are still produced that almost rival the clusters of Eshcol. Intelligent travellers agree in confirming the statements of Scripture as to its ancient fertility. See HEBREWS, JUDEA.

CONQUEST OF CANAAN. Various arguments have been adduced to justify the conquest of Canaan, and the extermination of its inhabitants by the Israelites: as, that the land had been allotted to Shem and his sons after the flood, and the sons of Ham were usurpers; that they first assaulted the Jews; that Abraham had taken possession of the land ages before; that the Canaanites were akin to the Egyptians, and implicated in their guilt and punishment as oppressors of the Hebrews. Whatever justice there may be in any of these reasons, they are not those which the Bible assigns. The only true warrant of the Jews was, the special command of the Lord of all They were impressively taught that the wickedness of those nations was the reason of their punishment, which the forbearance of God had long delayed, and which was designed as a warning to them and all mankind against idolatry and its kindred sins. It was these sins the Jews were to abhor and exterminate; they were to act as agents of God's justice, and not for the gratification of their own avarice, anger, or lust, the spoil and the captives being all devoted to destruction. The narrative of the conquest is given in Num. 1–4; Joshua; and Judges 1. The Canaanites were not wholly destroyed. Many of them escaped to other lands; and fragments of almost all the nations remained in Judea, subject to the Israelites, but snares to their feet and thorns in their sides. It must be observed also, that full notice was previously given them to quit their forfeited possessions; a solemn writ of ejectment had been issued by the great Proprietor, and if they resisted, they incurred the consequences.

CA'NAANITES, the descendants of Canaan. Their first habitation was in the land of Canaan, where they multiplied extremely, and by trade and war acquired great riches, and sent out colonies all over the islands and coasts of the Mediterranean. When the measure of their idolatries and abominations was completed, God delivered their country into the hands of the Israelites, who conquered it under Joshua. See the previous article. The following are the principal tribes mentioned.

1. The HIVITES dwelt in the northern part of the country, at the foot of mount Hermon, or Anti-Lebanon, according to Josh. 11:3, where it is related that they, along with the united forces of northern Canaan, were defeated by Joshua. They were not, however, entirely driven out of their possessions, Judg. 3:3; 2 Sam. 24:7; 1 Kin. 9:20. There were also Hivites in middle Palestine, Gen. 34:2; Josh. 19:1, 7; 11:19.

2. The CANAANITES, in a restricted sense, inhabited partly the plains on the west side of the Jordan, and partly the plains on the coast of the Mediterranean sea, Num. 13:29; Josh. 11:3.

3. The GIRGASHITES dwelt between the Canaanites and the Jebusites; as may be inferred from the order in which they are mentioned in Josh. 24:11.

4. The JEBUSITES had possession of the hill country around Jerusalem, and of that city itself, of which the ancient name was Jebus, Josh. 15 8, 63; 18:28. The Benjamites, to whom this region was allotted, did not drive out the Jebusites, Judg. 1:21 David first captured the citadel of Jebus, 2 Sam. 5:6.

5 The AMORITES inhabited, in Abraham's time, the region south of Jerusalem, on the western side of the Dead sea, Gen. 14:7. At a later period, they spread themselves out over all the mountainous country which forms the south-eastern part of Canaan, and which was called from them the "mountain of the Amorites," and afterwards the "mountain of Judah," Deut. 1:19, 20; Num. 13:29; Josh. 11:3. On the east side of the Jordan also they had, before the time of Moses, founded two kingdoms, that of Bashan in the north, and another, bounded at first by the Jabbok, in the south. But under Sihon they crossed the Jabbok, and took from the Ammonites and Moabites all the country between the Jabbok and the Arnon; so that this latter stream now became the southern boundary of the Amorites, Num. 21:13, 14, 26; 32:33, 39; Deut. 4:46, 47; 31:4. This last tract the Israelites took possession of after their victory over Sihon. See AMORITES.

6. The HITTITES, or children of Heth, according to the report of the spies, Num. 1:29, dwelt among the Amorites in the mountainous district of the south, afterwards called the "mountain of Judah." In the time of Abraham they possessed Hebron; and the patriarch purchased from them the cave of Machpelah as a sepulchre, Gen. 23; 25:9, 10. After the Israelites entered Canaan, the Hittites seem to have moved farther northward. The country around Bethel is called "the land of the Hittites," Judg. 1:26. See HITTITES.

7. The PERIZZITES were found in various parts of Canaan. The name signifies inhabitants of the plains, from their original abode. According to Gen. 13:7, they dwelt with the Canaanites, between Bethel and Ai; and according to Gen. 34:30, in the vicinity of Shechem. See PERIZZITES.

Besides these seven tribes, there were several others of the same parentage, dwelling north of Canaan. These were the Arkites, Arvadites, Hamathites, and Zemarites. There were also several other tribes of diverse origin within the bounds of Canaan, destroyed by the Israelites; such as the Anakim, the Amalekites, and the Rephaim or giants.

CAN'DACE, the name of an Ethiopian queen, whose high treasurer was converted to Christianity under the preaching of Philip the evangelist, Acts 8:27. The Ethiopia over which she ruled was not Abyssinia, but that region of Upper Nubia called by the Greeks Meroe; and is supposed to correspond with the present province of Atbara, lying between thirteen and eighteen degrees north latitude. Extensive ruins found in this neighborhood, and along the upper valley of the Nile, indicate high civilization among the ancient Ethiopians. Pliny and Strabo inform us that for some time before and after the Christian era, Ethiopia Proper was under the government of female sovereigns, who all bore the appellation of Candace. Irenæus and Eusebius ascribe to Candace's minister her own conversion to Christianity, and the promulgation of the gospel through her kingdom.

CAN'DLESTICK. In the tabernacle, the golden candlestick stood on the left hand of one entering the Holy Place, opposite the table of show-bread. It consisted of a pedestal; an upright shaft;

SPOILS OF JERUSALEM, FROM THE ARCH OF TITUS AT ROME.

six arms, three on one side, and three on the opposite side of the shaft; and seven lamps surmounting the shaft and arms. The arms were adorned with three kinds of carved ornaments, called cups, globes, and blossoms. Its lamps were supplied with pure olive oil, and lighted every evening, Ex. 25:31-40; 30:7, 8; 37:17-24; Lev. 24:1-3; 1 Sam. 3:3; 2 Chr. 13:11. In the first temple there were ten candelabra of pure gold, half of them standing on the north, and half on the south side, within the Holy Place, 1 Kin. 7:49, 50; 2 Chr. 4:7; Jer. 52:19. In the second temple there was but one, resembling that of the tabernacle. This was carried to Rome, on the destruction of Jerusalem; it was lodged in Vespasian's temple to Peace, and copied on the triumphal arch of Titus, where its mutilated image is yet to be seen. See the beautiful and significant visions of the candlestick by Zechariah and John, Zech. 4:2-12; Rev. 1:12, 20.

CANE, or CAL'AMUS, SWEET, Song 4:14, an aromatic reed mentioned among the drugs of which the sacred perfumes were compounded, Ex. 30:23. The true odoriferous calamus or grass came from India; and the prophets speak of it as a foreign commodity of great value, Isa. 43:24; Jer. 6:20; Ezek. 27:19.

CAN'KER-WORM, in our English Bible, is put where the Hebrew means a species of locust, Joel 1:4; Nah. 3:15, 16.

CAN'ON. The Greek word denotes, primarily, *a straight rod*; hence a *rule* or *standard*, by a reference to which the rectitude of opinions or actions may be decided. In the latter sense it is used in Gal. 6:16; Phil. 3:16. In the same sense it was used by the Greek fathers. As the standard to which they sought to appeal on all questions was the will of God contained in the Scriptures of the Old and New Testaments, they came naturally to apply this term to the collective body of those writings, and to speak of them as the *canon* or *rule*. Canon is also equivalent to a list or catalogue, in which are inserted those books which contain the inspired rule of faith.

In order to establish the canon of Scripture, it must be shown that all the books are of divine authority; that they are entire and incorrupt; that it is complete without addition from any foreign source; and that the whole of the books for which divine authority can be proved are included. See BIBLE.

CAPER'NAUM, a chief city of Galilee in the time of Christ, not mentioned before the captivity in Babylon. It lay on the north-west shore of the sea of Galilee, about five miles from the Jordan, and on the frequented route from Damascus to the Mediterranean. This seems to have been the residence of Christ, during the three years of his ministry, more than any other place. The brothers Andrew and Peter dwelt there; Christ often taught in the synagogue, and wrought mighty works there, Matt. 17:23; Mark 1:21-35; John 6:17, 59; and it is called "his own city," Matt. 4:12-16; 9:1; Mark 2:1. Its inhabitants were thus "exalted unto heaven;" but their unbelief and impenitence cast them down to destruction, Matt. 11:20-24. The very name and site of Capernaum have been lost. Dr. Robinson, however, finds them at Khan Minyeh, on the northern border of the fine plain of Gennesareth, where ruins of some extent still remain, and a copious fountain not far from the sea.

CAPHTORIM, descendants of Mizraim, and kindred to the Casluhim, near whom they were probably located on the north-east coast of Africa. These last two people are both named as ancestors of the Philistines, Gen. 10:14; Deut. 2:23; Amos 9:7; and it is probable that a colony made up from both drove out the Avim from the country on the south-east coast of the Mediterranean, and occupied it under the name of Philistines, which it is generally agreed means strangers. But whether they came from Cyprus, Crete, or Cappadocia, is not agreed.

CAPPADO'CIA, the largest ancient province of Asia Minor; having Pontus on the north, mount Taurus, separating it from Cilicia and Syria, on the south, Galatia on the west, and the Euphrates and Armenia on the east. It was watered by the river Halys, and was noted for its fine pastures and its excellent breed of horses, asses, and sheep. There were many Jews residing in it, Acts 2:9. Christianity was early introduced there, 1 Pet. 1:1, among a people proverbial for dulness, faithlessness, and vice. See CRETE. Several celebrated Christian fathers flourished in this province, as Basil and the three Gregories; and their churches may be traced as late as the tenth century.

CAP'TIVES, taken in war, seem anciently to have been looked upon as justly liable to death, and hence to any treatment less dreadful than death. Their necks were trodden upon, Josh. 10:24, in token of abject subjection, which illustrates Psa. 110:1. They were sold into servitude, like Joseph. They were mutilated, like Samson, or Adonizedek. They were stripped of all clothing, and driven in crowds to adorn the victor's triumph. Large numbers of them were selected, often by a measuring line, 2 Sam. 8:2, and slain, 2 Chr. 25:12. This was sometimes done with designed cruelty, 2 Sam. 12:31; 1 Chr. 20:3. The Romans in some cases bound a living captive to a dead body, and left them to perish together; a practice which may be applied to illustrate the apostle's cry, "O wretched man that I am! who shall deliver me from the body of this death?" Rom. 7:24.

CAPTIVITY. God often punished the sins of the Jews by captivities or servitudes, according to his threatenings, Deut. 28. Their first captivity, however, from which Moses delivered them, should be considered rather as a permission of Providence, than as a punishment for sin. There were six subjugations of the twelve tribes during the period of the judges. But the most remarkable captivities, or rather expatriations of the Hebrews, were those of Israel and Judah under the regal government. Israel was first carried away in part about B. C. 740, by Tiglath-pileser, 2 Kin. 15:29. The tribes east of the Jordan, with parts of Zebulun and Naphtali, Isa. 9:1, were the first sufferers. Twenty years later, Shalmanezer carried away the remainder, 2 Kin. 17:6, and located them in distant cities, many of them probably not far from the Caspian sea; and their place was supplied by colonies from Babylon and Persia, 2 Kin. 17:6–24. Aside from certain prophecies, Isa. 11:12, 13; Jer. 31:7–9, 16–20; 49:2; Ezek. 37:16; Hos. 11:11; Amos 9:14; Obad. 18, 19, etc., which are variously interpreted to mean a past or a future return, a physical or a spiritual restoration, there is no evidence that the ten tribes as a body ever returned to Palestine.

To Judah are generally reckoned three captivities: 1. Under Jehoiakim, in his third year, B. C. 606, when Daniel and others were carried to Babylon, 2 Kin. 24:1, 2; Dan. 1:1. 2. In the last year of Jehoiakim, when Nebuchadnezzar carried 3,023 Jews to Babylon; or rather, under Jehoiachin, when this prince also was sent to Babylon, that is, in the seventh and eighth years of Nebuchadnezzar, B. C. 598, 2 Kin. 24:2, 12; 2 Chr. 36:8, 10; Jer. 52:28. 3. Under Zedekiah, B. C. 588, when Jerusalem and the temple were destroyed, and most that was valuable among the people and their treasures was carried to Babylon, 2 Kin. 25; 2 Chr. 36. The seventy years during which they were to remain in captivity, Jer. 25:11; 29:10, are reckoned probably from the date of the first captivity, B. C. 606. While at Babylon the Jews had judges and elders who governed them, and decided matters in dispute juridically according to their laws. The book of Daniel shows us a Jew in a high position at court, and the book of Esther celebrates their numbers and power in the Persian empire. The prophets labored, not in vain, to keep alive the flame of true religion.

At length the seventy years were fulfilled, and Cyrus, in the first year of his reign at Babylon, B. C. 536, made a proclamation throughout his empire permitting the people of God to return to their own country, and rebuild the temple, Ezra 1:11. Nearly 50,000 accepted the invitation, Ezra 2:2; Neh. 7:7 This company laid the foundation of the second temple, which was completed in the sixth year of Darius, B. C. 516. Fifty-eight years after, Ezra led a small company of 7,000 from Babylon to Judea. He was succeeded as governor by Nehemiah, who labored faithfully and successfully to reform the people, and many of the good fruits of his labors remained until the time of Christ.

Probably none among the posterity of Jacob can now prove from which of his twelve sons they are descended. Both Judah and Israel being removed from "the lot of their inheritance" in Canaan, and dispersed among strangers, the various tribes would naturally amalgamate with each other, the envy of Judah and Ephraim would depart, and the memory of Abraham, Moses, and David would revive, Ezra 6:16, 17; 8:35; Ezek. 37:26-28.

The last captivity of the Jews, A. D. 71, after they had filled up the measure of their iniquity by rejecting Christ and the gospel, was a terrible one. According to Josephus, 1,100,000 perished at the

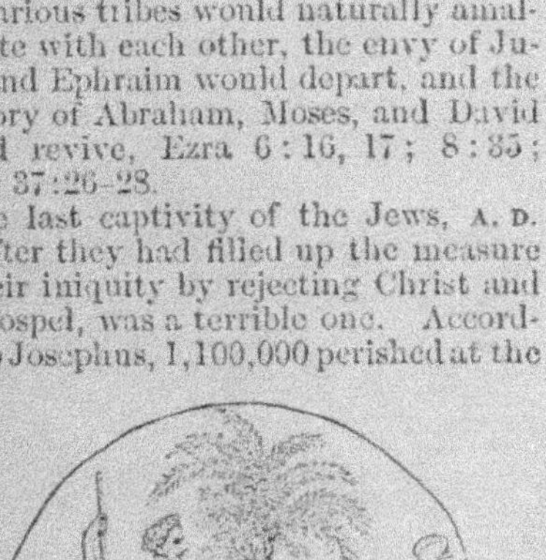

siege of Jerusalem by Titus, and nearly 100,000 captives were scattered among the provinces to perish in gladiatorial shows, doomed to toil as public slaves, or sold into private bondage. The cut represents the medal of the emperor Vespasian, A. D. 71, in memory of the capture of Jerusalem. Under the emperor Hadrian, A. D. 133, a similar crushing blow fell on the Jews who had again assembled in Judea; and at this day they are scattered all over the world, yet distinct from the people among whom they dwell, suffering under the woe which unbelief has brought upon their fathers and themselves, and awaiting the time when Christ "shall turn away ungodliness from Jacob," Rom. 11:25, 26.

CARBUNCLE, a precious stone, like a large ruby or garnet, of a dark, deep red color, said to glitter even in the dark, and to sparkle more than the ruby. The word is put to represent two different Hebrew words, one of which, Ex. 28:17; Ezek. 28:13, is commonly thought to mean the emerald; and the other, Isa. 54:12, may mean a brilliant species of ruby.

CARCHEMISH, probably the same with Circesium or Circusium, a fortified city on the west side of the Euphrates, where the river Chaboras enters it. In Isa. 10:9, it appears as taken by some king of Assyria. It was attacked by Pharaoh-necho king of Egypt, near the close of king Josiah's reign, 2 Chr. 35:20. Five years afterwards Necho was signally defeated by Nebuchadnezzar, Jer. 46:1-12. In later times it was held as a frontier post of the Roman empire on the east.

CARMEL, *a fruitful field*, I., a city of Judah, on a mountain of the same name, eight miles south by east of Hebron, Josh. 15:55. On this mountain Saul, returning from his expedition against Amalek, erected a trophy; and here Nabal the Carmelite, Abigail's husband, dwelt, 1 Sam. 15:12, 25. Its ruins indicate that it was a large place.

II. A celebrated range of hills running north-west from the plain of Esdraelon, and ending in the promontory which forms the bay of Acre. Its greatest height is about 1,500 feet; at its north-eastern foot runs the brook Kishon, and a little farther north, the river Belus. On its northern point stands a convent of the Carmelite friars, an order established in the twelfth century, and, having at the present day various branches in Europe. Mount Carmel is the only great promontory upon the coast of Palestine. The foot of the northern part approaches the water, so that, seen from the hills north-east of Acre, mount Car-

MT. CARMEL AND HAIFA, FROM THE N. E.

mel appears as if "dipping his feet in the western sea;" farther south it retires more inland, so that between the mountain and the sea there is an extensive plain covered with fields and olive-trees. Mariti describes it as a delightful region, and says the good quality of its soil is apparent from the fact that so many odoriferous plants and flowers, as hyacinths, jonquilles, tazettos, anemones, etc., grow wild upon the mountain. Von Richter says, "Mount Carmel is entirely covered with green; on its summit are pines and oaks, and farther down olive and laurel trees. It gives rise to a multitude of crystal brooks, the largest of which issues from the so-called 'fountain of Elijah;' and they all hurry along, between banks thickly overgrown with bushes, to the Kishon. Every species of tillage succeeds admirably under this mild and cheerful sky. The prospect from the summit of the mountain out over the gulf of Acre and its fertile shores, to the blue heights of Lebanon and to the White cape, is enchanting." Mr. Carne also ascended the mountain, and traversed the whole summit, which occupied several hours. He says, "It is the finest and most beautiful mountain in Palestine, of great length, and in many parts covered with trees and flowers. On reaching, at last, the opposite summit, and coming out of a wood, we saw the celebrated plain of Esdrælon beneath, with the river Kishon flowing through it; mounts Tabor and Little Hermon were in front, (east); and on the right, (south,) the prospect was bounded by the hills of Samaria." From the south-east side of this ridge, a range of low wooded hills on the south spreads and rises into the high lands of Samaria. Those who visit mount Carmel in the last part of the dry season, find every thing parched and brown; yet enough remains to show how just were the allusions of ancient writers to its exceeding beauty, Isa. 35:2, its verdure of drapery and grace of outline, Song 7:5, and its rich pastures, Isa. 33:9; Jer. 50:19; Amos 1:2. The rock of the mountain is a hard limestone, abounding in natural caves, Amos 9:3. These have in many cases been enlarged, and otherwise fitted for human habitation; and the mountain has been in various ages a favorite residence for devotees. It is memorable for frequent visits of the prophets Elijah and Elisha, 2 Kin. 2:25; 4:25, and especially for the destruction of the priests of Baal upon it, 1 Kin. 18.

CAR'PUS, a disciple and friend of Paul, who lived at Troas, 2 Tim. 4:13.

CAR'RIAGE, in the Bible, usually means the baggage which formed the burden of a man or beast, Acts 21:15. Once it seems to indicate a circular trench or rampart of baggage, etc., around a camp, 1 Sam. 17:20.

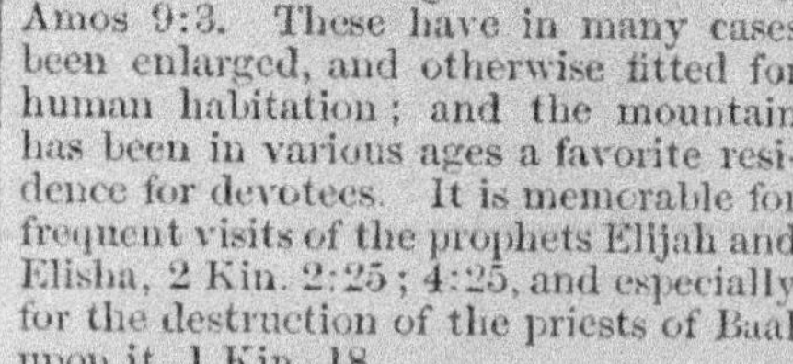

A MODERN SYRIAN CART.

CARTS or wagons were used in Palestine formerly, though now almost unknown. The roads are generally impassable by any wheeled vehicle; and the chief use of the cart was on a limited scale for agricultural purposes, such as forcing the ripe grain out of the ear, bruising the straw, removing the produce of the fields, etc., Isa. 5:18; 28:27, 28. Wagons were used to carry Israel into Egypt, and for the conveyance of the ark, Gen. 45:27; Num. 7:3-9 They were often drawn by heifers, etc., 1 Sam. 6:7, and were usually low, and on solid wooden wheels, sometimes iron-shod.

CASIPH'IA, the home of many of the exiled Jews, was probably in the vicinity of the Caspian sea, Ezra 8:17.

CAS'LUHIM, descendants of Mizraim See CAPHTORIM.

CAS'SIA, the bark of an odoriferous tree, from which came one ingredient of the holy oil or ointment, Ex. 30:24; Psa. 45:8; Ezek. 27:19.

CAS'TOR and POL'LUX, twin sons of Jupiter, and guardians of seamen, according to heathen mythology. Ships often bore their images on the prow, and were distinguished by their names, Acts 28:11.

CAT'ERPILLAR, some locust-like insect, now undistinguishable, Deut. 28:38; 1 Kin. 8:37; Psa. 78:46; 105:34; Isa. 33:4. See LOCUST.

CATH'OLIC. This term is Greek, signifying *universal* or *general* The church of Christ is called *catholic*, because it extends throughout the world, and during all time. In modern times the church of Rome has usurped this title, improperly applying it exclusively to itself.

The "Catholic epistles" are seven, so called because they were addressed to the church or Christians *in general*, and not to any particular church. They are, one epistle of James, two of Peter, three of John, and one of Jude.

CAVE. The geological structure of Judea is highly favorable to the formation of caves; and the whole region abounds with subterranean caverns of various dimensions, often giving rise to small rivulets. These were used as dwellings, places of refuge, and tombs. It was in a cave that Lot resided after the destruction of Sodom, Gen. 19:30 Petra, in Idumea, was a city of caves, Num. 24:21; Song 2:14; Jer 49:16; Obad. 3. In the vicinity of Hebron, the poor still live in caves while pasturing their flocks. Natural cavities were sometimes enlarged, and artificial ones made for refuge and defence, Judg. 6:2; 1 Sam. 13:6; Isa. 2:19; Jer. 41:9. The caves of Machpelah, of Adullam, of Engedi, of Carmel, and of Arbela, still exist. See SEPULCHRE.

CE'DAR, a noble evergreen-tree greatly celebrated in the Scriptures, Psa. 92:12; Ezek. 31:3-6. These trees are remarkably thick and tall; some among them are from thirty-five to forty feet in girth, and ninety feet in height. The cedar-tree shoots out branches at ten or twelve feet from the ground, large and almost horizontal; its leaves are an inch long, slender and straight, growing in tufts. The tree bears a small cone, like that of the pine. This celebrated tree is not peculiar to mount Lebanon, but grows also upon mounts Amanus and Taurus in Asia Minor, and in other parts of the Levant, but does not elsewhere reach the size and height of those on Lebanon It has also been cultivated in the gardens of Europe; two venerable individuals of this species exist at Chiswick in England; and there is a very beautiful one in the Jardin des Plantes in Paris. The beauty of the cedar consists in the proportion and symmetry of its wide-spreading branches and cone-like top. The gum, which exudes both from the trunk and the cones or fruit, is soft like balsam; its fragrance is like that of the balsam of Mecca. Every thing about this tree has a strong balsamic odor; and hence the whole grove is so pleasant and fragrant, that it is delightful to walk in it, Song 4:11; Hos. 14:6. The wood is peculiarly adapted to building, because it is not subject to decay, nor to be eaten of worms; hence it was much used for rafters, and for boards with which to cover houses and form the floors and ceilings of rooms. It was of a red color, beautiful, solid, and free from knots. The palace of Persepolis, the temple at Jerusalem, and Solomon's palace, were all in this way built with cedar; and "the house of the forest of Lebanon," was perhaps so called from the quantity of this wood used in its construction, 1 Kin. 7:2; 10:17

Of the forests of cedars which once covered Lebanon, comparatively few are now left, Isa. 2:13; 10:19; though there are still many scattered trees in various parts, resembling the genuine cedar. The largest and most ancient trees, generally thought to be the only ones, are found in a grove, lying a little off from the road which crosses mount Lebanon from Baalbek to Tripoli, at some distance below the summit of the mountain on the western side, at the foot indeed of the highest summit or ridge of Lebanon. This grove consists of a few very old trees, perhaps as old as the time of Christ, intermingled with 400 or 500 younger ones. See LEBANON.

Besides the true cedar of Lebanon, the word cedar in the Bible appears to mean sometimes the juniper and sometimes the pine.

CE'DRON, see KIDRON.

CEIL'ING. The ancients took great pains to ornament the ceilings of their best apartments; making them sometimes of a sort of wainscoting, in squares or complicated figures; and sometimes of a fine plaster with beautiful mouldings, tinted and relieved by gilding, small mirrors, etc., 1 Kin. 6:15; 2 Chr. 3:5; Jer. 22:14.

CEN'CHREA, a port of Corinth, now called Kikries, whence Paul sailed for Ephesus, Acts 18.18. It was a place of some commercial note, and the seat of an early church, Rom. 16:1. It was situated on the eastern side of the isthmus, eight or nine miles east of the city. The other port, on the western side of the isthmus, was Lechæum.

CEN'SER, a vessel in which fire and incense were carried, in certain parts of the Hebrew worship. Little is known of its form. The censer for the daily offering was at first made of copper, Num. 16:39. That used on the great day of atonement, (and perhaps others also,) was made of pure gold, 1 Kin. 7:50; Heb. 9:4. In the daily offering, the censer was filled with coals from the perpetual fire, and placed on the altar of incense, where the incense was thrown upon the coals, Ex. 30:1, 7-10 On the day of atonement, in the Holy of Holies, the censer must have been held in the hand, and probably by a handle, Lev. 16:12, 13

There are two Hebrew words, which

are translated censer in our English Bibles. The one signifies strictly fire-pan. The other signifies incense-pan, a vessel for burning incense; but we do not know its exact shape.

The censers of the Egyptians had long handles, like a human arm and hand, upon the palm of which the incense-cup stood. Those of the Greeks and Romans had chains, by which they were carried, like those now used in the Romish service.

In the New Testament, where the twenty-four elders are said to have golden "vials" full of odors, Rev. 5:8, the meaning is vessels of incense, censers, not vials in the present sense of the word.

CENTU'RION, a Roman officer commanding a hundred soldiers; similar to "captain" in modern times. Several centurions are mentioned with honor in the New Testament, Mark 15:39; Luke 7:1-10; and the first-fruits to Christ from the Gentiles was the generous and devout Cornelius, Acts 10.

CE'PHAS, *a rock*, a Syriac or later Hebrew name given to Peter by Christ, John 1:42. The Greek *Petros* and the Latin *Petrus* have the same meaning. See PETER.

CESAR, see CÆSAR.

CHALCED'ONY, a precious stone, resembling the agate; of various colors, but often a light brown or blue, Rev. 21:19. It is found in most parts of the world, though named after Chalcedon, in Bithynia opposite Constantinople; and is much used as a material for cups, vases, and other articles of taste. Carnelian is said to be one of its varieties.

CHALDE'A, a country in Asia, the capital of which, in its widest extent, was Babylon. It was originally of small extent; but the empire being afterwards very much enlarged, the name is generally taken in a more extensive sense, and includes Babylonia, which see.

CHALDE'ANS. This name is taken, 1. for the people of Chaldea, and the subjects of that empire generally; 2. for philosophers, naturalists, or soothsayers, whose principal employment was the study of mathematics and astrology, by which they pretended to foretell the destiny of men born under certain constellations.

The Chaldeans were originally a warlike people, who at first inhabited the Carduchian or Koordish mountains north of Assyria and Mesopotamia, Jer. 50:17. As the Assyrian monarchs extended their conquests towards the north and west, the Chaldeans also came under their dominion; and this rough and energetic people appear to have assumed, under the sway of their conquerors, a new character, and to have been transformed from a rude horde into a civilized people. A very vivid and graphic description of the Chaldean warriors is given by the prophet Habakkuk, who probably lived about the time when they first made incursions into Palestine or the adjacent regions, Hab. 1:6-11. Of the date of their location in Babylonia nothing is now known. In the reign of king Hezekiah, B. C. 713, a king of Babylon is mentioned, the first of whom we read after Nimrod and Amraphel. About one hundred years later we find the Chaldeans in possession of the kingdom of Babylon. The first sovereign in the new line appearing in history was Nabopolassar. His son Nebuchadnezzar invaded Palestine, as foretold by Jeremiah and Habakkuk, Ezra 5.12; Jer. 39:5. He was succeeded by his son Evil-merodach, 2 Kin. 25:27; Jer. 52:31. After him came, in quick succession, Neriglissar, Laborosoarchod, and Nabonnidus or Belshazzar, under whom this empire was absorbed in the Medo-Persian. The Chaldeo-Babylonian dynasty continued probably not more than one hundred years.

CHAL'DEE LANGUAGE, see LANGUAGE.

CHAM'BERLAIN, 2 Kin. 23:11, an officer who had charge of a king's lodgings and wardrobe. In eastern courts eunuchs were generally employed in this office, Esth. 1:10, 12, 15. This title in Rom. 16:23 probably denotes the steward or treasurer of the city.

CHAME'LEON, Lev. 11:30, a kind of lizard. Its body is about six inches long; its feet have five toes each, arranged like two thumbs opposite to three fingers; its eyes turn backwards or forwards independently of each other. It feeds upon flies, which it catches by darting out its long, viscous tongue. It has the faculty of inflating itself at pleasure with air; and of changing its color, from its ordinary gray to green, purple, and even black when enraged.

CHAM'OIS, not the well-known mountain goat of southern Europe, but probably a variety of wild sheep, resembling a goat, and still found in Arabia Petræa, Deut. 14:5.

CHAP'MEN, merchants, 2 Chr. 9:14.

CHAP'TER, see Bible.

CHAR'GER, a large, shallow dish, Num. 7:13; Matt. 14:8.

CHAR'IOTS. Scripture speaks of two sorts of these: one for princes and generals to ride in, Gen. 41:43; the other to break the enemy's battalions, by rushing in among them, being "chariots of iron," that is, armed with iron scythes or hooks, projecting from the ends of the axletrees. These made terrible havoc. The Canaanites, whom Joshua engaged at the waters of Merom, had horsemen, and a multitude of chariots, Josh. 11:4; Judg. 1:19. Sisera, general of Jabin king of Hazor, had nine hundred chariots of iron, Judg. 4:3. See Litter.

CHARM'ERS, Psa. 58:4, 5; Eccl. 10:11; Jer. 8:17, persons very common throughout India and Egypt, who claim to have the faculty of catching, taming, and controlling serpents, even the most venomous.

CHE'BAR, a river which rises in the northern part of Mesopotamia, and flows first south-east, then south and south-west, into the Euphrates. It was called Chaboras by the Greeks; now Khabour. On its fertile banks Nebuchadnezzar located a part of the captive Jews, and here the sublime visions of Ezekiel took place, Ezek. 1:3; 3:15; 10.15; 43:3.

CHEDORLA'OMER, king of Elam, in Persia, in the time of Abraham. He made the cities in the region of the Dead sea his tributaries; and on their rebelling, he came with four allied kings and overran the whole country south and east of the Jordan. Lot was among his captives, but was rescued by Abraham; who promptly raised a force from his own dependents and his neighbors, pursued the enemy, and surprised and defeated them, Gen. 14:1–24. Compare Psa. 110.

CHEESE, several times alluded to in Scripture, and still an important article of food in the East, 1 Sam. 17:18; 2 Sam. 17:29. It is usually white and very salt; soft, when new, but soon becoming hard and dry. The cheese was like a small saucer in size, Job 10:10.

CHEM'ARIM, occurring once only in the English version, Zeph. 1:4, but frequently in the Hebrew, translated "idolatrous priests," 2 Kin. 23:5; Hos. 10:5. The word is supposed to be derived from a root signifying *to burn*, and may perhaps denote fire-priests. worshippers of the sun.

CHE'MOSH, the national god of the Moabites, and of the Ammonites, worshipped also under Solomon at Jerusalem, Num. 21:29; Judg. 11:24; 1 Kin. 11:7; 2 Kin. 23:13; Jer. 48:7. Some erroneously identify Chemosh with Ammon.

CHER'ETHITES, or Cher'ethim, I., a portion of the Philistines, supposed by many to have originated in Crete, 1 Sam. 30:14; Ezek. 25:16; Zeph. 2:5.

II. A portion of David's body-guard, always mentioned with the Pelethites, 2 Sam. 8:18; 15:18; 20:7; 1 Chr. 18:17. Some suppose that they were foreigners, whom David took into his service while among the Philistines. The Gittites mentioned with them in 2 Sam. 15:18, were plainly such. Others think they had their name from their office—executioners and runners. See Pelethites.

CHE'RITH, a small brook flowing into the Jordan, to which Elijah once withdrew, and where ravens brought him supplies of bread and flesh, 1 Kin. 17:3–5. Robinson suggests that it may be the present Wady Kelt, which drains the hills west of Jericho, and flows near that town on its way to the Jordan. This brook is dry in summer.

CHER'UB, plural CHER'UBIM, an order of celestial beings or symbolical representations often referred to in the Old Testament and in the book of Revelation. The cherubim are variously represented as living creatures, Ezek. 1; Rev. 4; or as images wrought in tapestry, gold, or wood, Ex. 36:35; 37:7; Ezek. 41:25; as having one, two, or four faces, Ex. 25:20; Ezek. 10:14; 41:18; as having two, four, or six wings, 1 Kin. 6:27; Ezek. 1:6; Rev. 4:8; in the simplest form, as in the golden figures above the ark of the covenant; or in the most complex and sublime form, as in Ezekiel's wonderful visions of the glory of God—discerning and ruling all things, and executing irresistibly and with the speed of thought all his wise and just decrees, Ezek. 1 and 10. The fullest of these descriptions represents the cherub as a winged figure, like a man in form, full of eyes, and with a fourfold head—of a man, a lion, an ox, and an eagle—with wheels turning every way, and speed like the lightning; presenting the highest earthly forms and powers of creation in harmonious and perfect union, Ezek. 1; 10; 41; Rev. 4. Usually also the cherubim stand in a special nearness to God; they are engaged in the loftiest adoration and service, moving in instant accordance with his will, Psa. 18:10; Ezek. 1:26; 10:20; Rev. 4; they are seen in the temple inseparably associated with the *mercy-seat*—made of the same mass of pure gold, Ex. 25:19, bending reverently over the place of God's presence, Psa. 99:1, where he met his people, Num. 7:89, accepted the blood of atonement, Lev. 16:14–16, and shone forth as their Saviour, Psa. 80:1.

CHEST'NUT-TREE, Gen. 30:37, called by the Septuagint and Vulgate the plane-tree, with which most modern expositors agree. The plane-tree has a tall and stately trunk, with smooth bark, and branches spreading in every direction, covered with a profusion of glossy green leaves. It is nowhere more abundant and noble than in the plains of Assyria, Ezek. 31:8.

CHESUL'LOTH, or CHISLOTH-TABOR, a town on the border of Zebulun and Issachar, about four miles west of mount Tabor; the village called Iksal now marks its site, together with numerous excavated tombs, Josh. 19:12, 18, 22; 1 Chr. 6:62.

CHIL'DREN. A numerous offspring was regarded as a signal blessing, Psa. 127:3–5, and childless wives sought various means to escape the reproach of barrenness, which was deprecated in the blessing given to a newly married couple, Ruth 4:11. The pangs of childbirth, in their suddenness and sharpness, are often alluded to in Scripture. The apostle Paul speaks of them as fruits and evidences of the fall; but assures those who abide in faith, that, amid all the suffering that reminds them that woman was first in the transgression, Gen. 3:16, they may yet look trustfully to God for acceptance and salvation, 1 Tim. 2:15.

A new-born child was washed, rubbed with salt, and wrapped in swaddling clothes, Ezek. 16:4; Luke 2:7–11. On the eighth day he was circumcised and named. At his weaning a feast was often made, Gen. 21:8. The nurse of a female child often attended her through life, Gen. 24:59; 35:8. Children were to be instructed with great diligence and care, Deut. 6:20–23. They were required to honor and obey their parents, and were subject to the father's control in all things, Gen. 22:21; Num. 30:5; they were even liable to be sold into temporary bondage for his debts, Lev. 25:39–41; 2 Kin. 4:1; Matt. 18:25.

The first-born son received, besides other privileges, (see BIRTHRIGHT,) two portions of his father's estate; the other sons, one portion each. The sons of concubines received presents, and sometimes an equal portion with the others, Gen. 21:8–21; 25:1–6; 49:1–27; Judg. 11:1–7. The daughters received no portion, except in cases provided for in Num. 27:1–11.

The term child or children, by a Hebrew idiom, is used to express a great variety of relations: the good are called children of God, of light, of the kingdom, etc.; the bad are named children of the devil, of wrath, of disobedience, etc. A strong man is called a son of strength; an impious man, a son of Belial; an arrow, the son of a bow, and a branch the son of a tree. The posterity of a man are his "sons," for many generations.

CHIM'HAM, probably a son of Barzillai, 2 Sam. 19:37; 1 Kin. 2:7. He may have received from David the place near Bethlehem called Chimham, Jer. 41:17.

CHIN'NERETH, or CINNEROTH, a town

on the west shore of the sea of Galilee, Num. 34:11; Deut. 3:17; Josh. 11:2; 19:35; 1 Kin. 15:20. It was a "fenced city" of Naphtali, and gave its name to the lake on which it stood. Tiberias is supposed by Jerome to have afterwards occupied its site.

CHI'OS, an island in the Archipelago, between Lesbos and Samos, on the coast of Asia Minor, now called Scio. It is thirty miles long and ten wide. Paul passed this way as he sailed southward from Mitylene to Samos, Acts 20:15.

CHIS'LEU, the ninth month of the Hebrews, beginning with the new moon of December, Neh. 1:1; Zech. 7:1.

CHIT'TIM, or KITTIM, descendants of Javan, son of Japheth; and the land settled by them, Gen. 10:4. Chittim seems to denote primarily the island Cyprus, and also to be employed, in a wider sense, to designate other islands and countries adjacent to the Mediterranean, as for instance, Macedonia, Dan. 11:30, and Rome, Num. 24:24.

CHI'UN, the name of an idol worshipped by the Israelites in the desert, Amos 5:26; Acts 7:43. It was most probably the planet Saturn, worshipped by eastern nations as an evil spirit to be propitiated by sacrifices. See REMPHAN.

CHORA'ZIN, a town in Galilee, near to Capernaum and Bethsaida, on the north-west shore of the sea of Galilee. Jerome says it was two miles from Capernaum. No traces of its name remain; but Robinson with strong probability locates it at the modern Tell-hûm, on the northern shore of the sea of Galilee, three miles north-east of Capernaum. It was upbraided by Christ for its impenitence, Matt. 11:21; Luke 10:13.

CHRIST, *anointed*, a Greek word, answering to the Hebrew MESSIAH, the consecrated or anointed one, and given preëminently to our blessed Lord and Saviour. See MESSIAH and JESUS.

The ancient Hebrews, being instructed by the prophets, had clear notions of the Messiah; but these became gradually depraved, so that when Jesus appeared in Judea, the Jews entertained a false conception of the Messiah, expecting a temporal monarch and conqueror, who should remove the Roman yoke and subject the whole world. Hence they were scandalized at the outward appearance, the humility, and seeming weakness of our Saviour. The modern Jews, indulging still greater mistakes, form to themselves ideas of the Messiah utterly unknown to their forefathers.

The ancient prophets had foretold that the Messiah should be God, and man: exalted, and abased; master, and servant; priest, and victim; prince, and subject; involved in death, yet victor over death; rich, and poor; a king, a conqueror, glorious—and a man of griefs, exposed to infirmities, unknown, in a state of abjection and humiliation. All these contrarieties were to be reconciled in the person of the Messiah; as they really were in the person of Jesus.

It is not recorded that Christ ever received any external official unction. The unction that the prophets and the apostles speak of is the spiritual and internal unction of grace and of the Holy Ghost, of which the outward unction, with which kings, priests, and prophets were anciently anointed, was but the figure and symbol.

The name CHRIST is the official title of the Redeemer; and is not to be regarded as a mere appellative, to distinguish our Lord from other persons named Jesus. The force of many passages of Scripture is greatly weakened by overlooking this. We may get the true sense of such passages by substituting for "Christ," "the Anointed," and where Jews were addressed, "THE MESSIAH." Thus in Matt. 2:4, Herod "demanded of them," the priests and scribes, "where Christ should be born," that is, the Old Testament Messiah. Peter confessed, "thou art the Messiah," Matt. 16:16. The devils did the same, Luke 4:41. In later times the name JESUS was comparatively disused; and CHRIST, as a proper name, was used instead of JESUS.

When we consider the relation of Christ's person, as God and man, to his official work as our Prophet, Priest, and King, and to his states of humiliation and glory; when we consider how God is in and with him—how all the perfections of God are displayed, and all the truths of God exemplified in him; when we consider his various relations to the purposes, covenants, word, and ordinances of God, and to the privileges, duties, and services of saints, in time and to eternity, we have a delightful view of him as ALL and IN ALL, Col. 3:11.

CHRISTS, FALSE. Our Saviour predicted that many pretended Messiahs would come, Matt. 24:24, and his word has been abundantly fulfilled. One of them named Coziba lived within one hundred years of Christ, had many followers, and occasioned the death of more than half a million of Jews. Others have continued to appear, even down to modern times.

CHRIS'TIANS, a name given at Antioch to those who believed Jesus to be the Messiah, A. D. 42, Acts 11:26. It seems to have been given to them by the men of Antioch as a term of convenience rather than of ridicule, to designate the new sect more perfectly than any other word could do. They generally called each other "brethren," "the faithful," "saints," "believers;" and were named by the Gentiles, Nazarenes and Galileans. He only is a real Christian who heartily accepts Christ as his teacher, guide, and master, the source of his highest life, strength, and joy, his only Redeemer from sin and hell, his Lord and his God. They who rightly bear Christ's name and partake of his nature, and they only, shall finally share in his glory.

CHRON'ICLES, the name of two historical books of the Old Testament, the author of which is not known, though the general opinion ascribes them to Ezra, B. C. 457. In writing them the inspired penman made use, not only of the earlier books of Scripture, but of numerous other public annals, now lost, 2 Chr. 9:29; 16:11; 20:34. The first book contains a recapitulation of sacred history, by genealogies, from the beginning of the world to the death of David. The second book contains the history of the kings of Judah, without those of Israel, from the beginning of the reign of Solomon only, to the return from the captivity of Babylon. In this respect it differs from the books of Kings, which give the history of the kings of both Judah and Israel. In many places, where the history of the same kings is related, the narrative in Chronicles is almost a copy of that in Kings; in other places, the one serves as a supplement to the other. In the Septuagint, these books are called *Paraleipomena*, that is, things omitted. The two books of Chronicles dwell more on ecclesiastical matters than the books of Kings; they enlarge upon the ordinances of public worship; and detail minutely the preparations of David for the building of the temple, and its erection and dedication by Solomon; the histories of the other kings also are specially full in respect to their religious character and acts, 1 Chr. 13:8–11; 2 Chr. 11:13; 19:8–11; 26:16–19, etc. The Chronicles should be read in connection with the books of Samuel and the Kings; treating of the same periods, they illustrate each other, and form a continuous and instructive history, showing that religion is the main source of national prosperity, and ungodliness of adversity, Prov. 14:34. The details of these books may be studied with interest, in view of their bearing upon the coming and the kingdom of our Lord Jesus Christ. The whole period treated of in the Chronicles is about 3,500 years.

CHRYS'OLITE, a transparent precious stone, having the color of gold with a mixture of green, and a fine lustre, Rev. 21:20. Many suppose it to be the topaz of the moderns.

CHRYSOP'RASUS, the tenth of those precious stones which adorned the foundation of the heavenly Jerusalem, as seen by John the Evangelist. Its color was green, inclining to gold, as its name imports, Rev 21:20.

CHUN, elsewhere called BEROTHAH, which see.

CHURCH. The Greek word translated church signifies generally an assembly, either common or religious; and it is sometimes so translated, as in Acts 19:32, 39. In the New Testament it usually means a congregation of religious worshippers, either Jewish, as Acts 7:38, or Christian, as Matt. 16:18; 1 Cor. 6:4. The latter sense is the more common one; and it is thus used in a twofold manner, denoting,

1. The universal Christian church: either the invisible church, consisting of those whose names are written in heaven, whom God knows, but whom we cannot infallibly know, Heb. 12:23; or the visible church, made up of the professed followers of Christ on earth, Col. 1:24; 1 Tim. 3:5, 15.

2. A particular church or body of professing believers, who meet and worship together in one place; as the churches of Rome, Corinth, Ephesus, Philippi, etc., to which Paul addressed epistles.

CHURN'ING, Prov. 30:33. See BUTTER.

CHU'SHAN-RISHATHA'IM, a king of

Mesopotamia, who oppressed the Israelites eight years, A. M. 2591–9, but was defeated by Othniel, Caleb's nephew, Judg. 3:8–10.

CHU'ZA, see JOANNA.

CILI'CIA, the south-eastern province of Asia Minor, bounded north by the Taurus range, separating it from Cappadocia, Lycaonia, and Isauria, south by the Mediterranean, east by Syria, and west by Pamphylia. The western part had the appellation of Aspera, or rough; while the eastern was called Campestris, or level. This country was the province of Cicero when proconsul; and its chief town, Tarsus, was the birthplace of the apostle Paul, Acts 6:9. Many Jews dwelt in Cilicia, and maintained frequent intercourse with Jerusalem, where they joined the other Jews in opposing the progress of Christianity. Paul himself may have taken part in the public discussion with Stephen, Acts 6:9; 7:58. After his conversion he visited his native province, Acts 9:30; Gal. 1:21, and established churches, which were addressed in the letter of the council at Jerusalem, Acts 15:23. The apostle once afterwards made a missionary tour among these churches, his heart yearning to behold and to increase their prosperity, Acts 15:36, 41.

CIN'NAMON, one of the ingredients in the perfumed oil with which the tabernacle and its vessels were anointed, Ex. 30:23; Prov. 7:17; Song 4:14. It is the inner bark of a tree growing about twenty feet high, and being peeled off in thin strips curls as it is found in market. It is of a dark red color, of a poignant taste, aromatic, and very agreeable. That of the finest quality comes from Ceylon, Rev. 18:13.

CIRCUMCIS'ION, *a cutting around*, because in this rite the foreskin was cut away. God commanded Abraham to use circumcision, as a sign of his covenant; and in obedience to this order, the patriarch, at ninety-nine years of age, was circumcised, as also his son Ishmael, and all the males of his household, Gen. 17:10–12. God repeated the precept to Moses, and ordered that all who intended to partake of the paschal sacrifice should receive circumcision; and that this rite should be performed on children on the eighth day after their birth, Ex. 12:44; Lev. 12:3; John 7:22. The Jews have always been very exact in observing this ceremony, and it appears that they did not neglect it when in Egypt, Josh. 5:1–9.

All the other nations sprung from Abraham besides the Hebrews, as the Ishmaelites, the Arabians, etc., also retained the practice of circumcision. At the present day it is an essential rite of the Mohammedan religion, and though not enjoined in the Koran, prevails wherever this religion is found. It is also practised in some form among the Abyssinians, and various tribes of south Africa, as it was by the ancient Egyptians. But there is no proof that it was practised upon infants, or became a general, national, or religious custom, before God enjoined it upon Abraham.

The Jews esteemed uncircumcision as a very great impurity; and the greatest offence they could receive was to be called "uncircumcised." Paul frequently mentions the Gentiles under this term, not opprobriously, Rom. 2:26, in opposition to the Jews, whom he names "the circumcision," etc.

Disputes as to the observance of this rite by the converts from heathenism to Christianity occasioned much trouble in the early church, Acts 15; and it was long before it was well understood that "in Christ Jesus neither circumcision availeth any thing, nor uncircumcision, but a new creature," Gal. 5:2, 3; 6:15.

The true circumcision is that of the heart; and those are "uncircumcised in heart and ears," who will not obey the law of God nor embrace the gospel of Christ.

CIS'TERNS and reservoirs were very common in Palestine, both in the country and in cities. During half the year no rain falls, and never-failing streams and springs are rare indeed. The main dependence of a large portion of the population was upon the water which fell in the rainy season and was preserved in cisterns, 2 Sam. 17 : 18. Dr. Robinson alludes to immense reservoirs within and under the area of the temple, supplied by rainwater and by the aqueduct from Solomon's pools, and says, "These of themselves, in case of a siege, would furnish a tolerable supply. But in addition to these, almost every house in Jerusalem, of any size, is understood to have at least one or more cisterns, excavated in the soft limestone rock on which the city is built. The house of Mr. Lanneau, in which we resided, had no less than four cisterns; and as these are but a specimen of the manner in which all the better class of houses are supplied, I subjoin here the dimensions:

	LENGTH.	BREADTH.	DEPTH.
I.	15 feet.	8 feet.	12 feet.
II.	8 "	4 "	15 "
III.	10 "	10 "	15 "
IV.	30 "	30 "	20 "

The water is conducted into them during the rainy season, and with proper care remains pure and sweet during the whole summer and autumn." Such cisterns, and others more properly called tanks and pools, were provided in the fields for irrigation, and at intervals along the highways, for the accommodation of travellers, Psa. 84 : 6. The same causes led to the erection, near all the chief cities, of large open reservoirs for public use. These were built of massive stones, and in places where the winter rains could be easily conducted into them. Many such reservoirs, and ruins of others, yet remain. See BETHESDA, SILOAM, SOLOMON'S POOLS.

CITY. The towns and cities of Palestine were commonly built on heights, for better security against robbers or invaders. These heights, surrounded by walls, sometimes formed the entire city. In other cases, the citadel alone crowned the hill, around and at the base of which the town was built; and in time of danger the surrounding population all took refuge in the fortified place. Larger towns and cities were often not only defended by strong outer walls, with towers and gates, but by a citadel or castle within these limits—a last resort when the rest of the city was taken, Judg. 9:46, 51. The "fenced cities" of the Jews, Deut. 3 : 5, were of various sizes and degrees of strength; some being surrounded by high and thick stone walls, and others by feebler ramparts, often of clay or sun-dried bricks, and sometimes combustible, Isa. 9 : 10; Amos 1 : 7-14. They were also provided with watchmen, Psa. 127:1; Song 5:7. The streets of ancient towns were usually narrow, and often unpaved. Some cities were adorned with vast parks and gardens; this was the case with Babylon, which embraced an immense space within its walls. It is impossible at this day to form any reliable estimate of the population of the cities of Judea. Jerusalem is said by Josephus to have had 150,000 inhabitants, and to have contained, at the time of its siege by the Romans, more than a million of persons crowded in its circuit of four miles of wall. See GATE, REFUGE, WATCHMEN.

CITY OF DAVID, usually denotes mount Zion, the south-west section of Jerusalem, which David took from the Jebusites, and occupied by a palace and city called by his own name. In Luke 2:11, Bethlehem his native city is meant.

CITY OF GOD, Deut. 12:5; Psa. 46:4, and THE HOLY CITY, Neh. 11:1, names of Jerusalem. Its modern name is El-Kuds, the Holy.

CLAU'DA, a small island near the south-west shore of Crete, approached by Paul in his voyage to Jerusalem, Acts 27:16. It is now called Gozzo, and is occupied by about thirty families.

CLAU'DIA, a Christian woman, probably a convert of Paul at Rome, 2 Tim. 4:21.

CLAU'DIUS CÆSAR, fifth emperor of Rome, succeeded Caius Caligula, A. D. 41, and was followed by Nero, after a reign of thirteen years. He endowed Agrippa with royal authority over Judea, which on the death of Agrippa again became a province of Rome, A. D. 45. About this time probably occurred the famine foretold by Agabus, Acts 11:28. In the ninth year of his reign, he banished all Jews from Rome, Acts 18:2. In A. D. 43-44, he made a military expedition to Britain. His death was caused by poison, from the hand of his wife and niece Agrippina.

CLAU'DIUS FE'LIX. See FELIX.

CLAU'DIUS LYS'IAS. See LYSIAS.

CLAY designed for earthenware was trodden by the feet to mix it well, Isa. 41:25, was moulded on a wheel, and then baked in a kiln, Jer. 18:3; 43:9. The potter's art is referred to in Scripture to illustrate man's dependence upon God, Isa. 64:8; Rom. 9:21. See POTTER. Clay seems to have been also used in sealing, as wax is with us, Job 38:14. The bricks of Babylon are found marked with a large seal or stamp, and modern travellers find the locks of doors in eastern khans and granaries sealed on the outside with clay.

CLEAN and UNCLEAN, terms often used in the Bible in a ceremonial sense; assigned to certain animals, and to men in certain cases, by the law of Moses, Lev. 11-15; Num. 19; Deut. 14. A distinction between clean and unclean animals existed before the deluge, Gen. 7:2. The Mosaic law was not merely arbitrary, but grounded on reasons connected with animal sacrifices, with health, with the separation of the Jews from other nations, and their practise of moral purity, Lev. 11:43-45; 20:24-26; Deut. 14:2, 3, 21. The ritual law was still observed in the time of Christ, but under the gospel is annulled, Acts 10:9-16.

Ceremonial uncleanness was contracted by the Jews in various ways, voluntarily and involuntarily. It was removed, usually at the evening of the same day, by bathing. In other cases a week, or even forty or fifty days, and some sacrificial offerings, were required.

CLEM'ENT, mentioned in Phil. 4:3. It is conjectured, though without evidence, that this is the same Clement who was afterwards a bishop at Rome, commonly called Clemens Romanus. The church at Corinth having been disturbed by divisions, Clement wrote a letter to the Corinthians, which was so much esteemed by the ancients, that they read it publicly in many churches.

CLE'OPHAS, the husband of Mary, John 19:25, called also ALPHEUS, which see. The Cleopas mentioned in Luke 24:18, probably was a different person.

CLOTHES. See GARMENTS.

CLOUD, PILLAR OF, the miraculous token of the divine presence and care, Ex. 14:24; 16:10; Num. 12:5, which guided the Israelites in the desert; it was a means of protection and perhaps of shade by day, and gave them light by night, Ex. 13:21, 22; 14:19, 20. By it God directed their movements, Num. 9:15-23; 14:14; Deut. 1:33. See the beautiful application of the image to the future church in Isa. 4:5.

CLOUDS, in the summer season of Palestine, were an unlooked-for phenomenon, 1 Sam. 12:17, 18, and rising from off the Mediterranean, betokened rain, 1 Kin. 18:44; Luke 12:54. Clouds are the symbol of armies and multitudes, probably by their grand and majestic movements, Isa. 60:8; Jer. 4:13; Heb. 12:1. They betokened the presence of Jehovah, as on mount Sinai, Ex. 19:9; 24:12-18; in the temple, Ex. 40:34; 1 Kin. 8:10; in the cloudy pillar, and on the mount of Transfiguration. They are found in many representations of the majesty of God, Psa. 18:11, 12; 97:2, and of Christ, Matt. 24:30; Rev. 14:14-16.

CNI'DUS, a town and peninsula of Doris in Caria, jutting out from the south-west corner of Asia Minor, between the islands of Rhodes and Cos. It had a fine harbor, and was celebrated for the worship of Venus. Paul passed by it in his voyage to Rome, Acts 27:7.

COAL, usually in Scripture, charcoal, or the embers of fire. Mineral coal is now procured in mount Lebanon, eight hours from Beirut; but we have no certainty that it was known and used by the Jews. The following passages are those which most strongly suggest this substance, 2 Sam. 22:9, 13; Job 41:21.

COCK'ATRICE, an old English word of obscure origin, used by our translators to designate the Hebrew Tzepha, or Tsiphoni, a serpent of a highly venomous character, Isa. 14:29; 59:5; Jer. 8:17. See SERPENT.

COCK-CROWING, the third watch of the night, in the time of Christ. See HOUR.

COCK'LE, a plant growing among wheat, Job 31:40. The Hebrew word seems to denote some noisome weed which infests cultivated grounds.

COLOS'SE, a city of Phrygia, situated on a hill near the junction of the Lycus with the Meander, and not far from the cities Hierapolis and Laodicea, Col. 2:1; 4:13, 15. With these cities it was destroyed by an earthquake in the tenth year of Nero, about A. D. 65, while Paul was yet living. It was soon rebuilt. The church of Christians in this city, to whom Paul wrote, seems to have been gathered by Epaphras, Col. 1:2. Compare 1:7, 8, 9, and 4:12, 13. In modern times the place is called Chonos.

COLOS'SIANS, EPISTLE TO THE, was written by Paul, from Rome, A. D. 62. The occasion of the letter was the intelligence brought him by Epaphras, Col. 1:6–8, respecting the internal state of the church, which apparently he himself had not yet visited, Col. 2:1, though familiar with their history and affairs, Acts 16:6; 18:23. Some Jewish philosopher professing Christianity, but mingling with it a superstitious regard for the law and other errors, seems to have gained a dangerous ascendancy in the church. Paul shows that all our hope of salvation is in Christ the only mediator, in whom all fulness dwells; he cautions the Colossians against the errors introduced among them, as inconsistent with the gospel, and incites them by most persuasive arguments to a temper and conduct worthy of their Christian character. The epistle was written at the same time with that to the Ephesians, and was sent by the same bearer. The two closely resemble each other, and should be studied together.

COM'FORTER, Greek PAR'ACLETE, an advocate, teacher, or consoler. This title is given to our Saviour: "We have an advocate (*paraclete*) with the Father, Jesus Christ the righteous," 1 John 2:1. But more frequently it designates the Holy Spirit. He is the "other Comforter," succeeding Christ, the great promised blessing of the Christian church, John 14:16, 17, 26; 15; 16; Luke 24:49; Acts 1:4. The English word Comforter does not adequately describe the office of the Paraclete, who was not only to console, but to aid and direct them, as Christ had done. The disciples found the promise fulfilled to them. The Comforter aided them when called before councils; guided them into all truth respecting the plan of salvation; brought to their remembrance the words and deeds of Christ; and revealed to them things to come. His presence was accompanied by signal triumphs of grace, and made amends for the absence of Christ. The church is still under the dispensation of the Comforter, and still he convinces the world of sin, of righteousness, and of the judgment to come.

COM'MON, profane, ceremonially unclean, Mark 7. 2, 5; Acts 10:14, 15; Rom. 14:14.

CONCIS'ION, *cutting*, a term of reproach, applied to certain Judaizing teachers at Philippi, as mere cutters of the flesh; in contrast with the true circumcision, those who were created anew in Christ Jesus unto righteousness and true holiness, Phil. 3:2.

CON'CUBINE, a term which, in modern authors, commonly signifies a woman who, without being married to a man, lives with him as his wife; but in the Bible the word *concubine* is understood in another sense—meaning a lawful wife, but of a secondary rank. She differed from a proper wife in that she was not married by solemn stipulation, but only betrothed; she brought no dowry with her, and had no share in the government of the family She was liable to be repudiated, or sent away with a gift, Gen. 21:14, and her children might be treated in the same way, and not share in their father's inheritance, Gen. 25:6. One cause of concubinage is shown in the history of Abraham and Jacob, Gen. 16; 30. Concubinage, however, became a general custom, and the law of Moses restricted its abuses, Ex. 21:7–9; Deut. 21:10–14, but never sanctioned it. The gospel has restored the original law of marriage, Gen. 2:24; Matt. 19:5; 1 Cor. 7:2, and concubinage is ranked with fornication and adultery.

CO'NEY, an old English name for the rabbit; used in Scripture to translate the Hebrew SHAPHAN, which agrees with the Ashkoko or Syrian Hyrax, Lev. 11:5; Deut. 14:7; Psa. 104:18; Prov. 30:26. This animal is externally of the size and form of the rabbit, and of a brownish color. It is, however, much clumsier in its structure, without tail, and having long bristly hairs scattered through the fur. The feet are naked below, and the nails flat and rounded, except those on the inner toe of the hind feet, which are long and awl-shaped. They cannot dig, but reside in the clefts of rocks. They are called by Solomon, "wise," and "a feeble folk;" they are timid and gregarious in their habits, and so gentle and quiet, that they shrink from the shadow of a passing bird. The name of Spain is said to have been given to it by Phœnician voyagers, who seeing its western coast overrun with animals resembling the shaphan, called it Hispania, or Coney-land. Some eminent interpreters think the SHAPHAN means the Jerboa.

CONI'AH. See JEHOIACHIN.

CON'SCIENCE is that faculty common to all free moral agents, Rom. 2:13-15, in virtue of which we discern between right and wrong, and are prompted to choose the former and refuse the latter. Its appointed sphere is in the regulation, according to the will of God revealed in nature and the Bible, of all our being and actions so far as these have a moral character. The existence of this faculty proves the soul accountable at the bar of its Creator, and its voice is in an important sense the voice of God. We feel that when pure and fully informed, it is an unerring guide to duty, and that no possible array of inducements can justify us in disregarding it. In man, however, though this conviction that we must do what is right never fails, yet the value of conscience is greatly impaired by its inhering in a depraved soul, whose evil tendencies warp and pervert our judgments on all subjects. Thus Paul verily thought that he ought to persecute the followers of Christ, Acts 26:9. His sin was in his culpable neglect to enlighten his conscience by all the means in his power, and to purify it by divine grace. A terrible array of conscientious errors and persecutions, which have infested and afflicted the church in all ages, warns us of our individual need of perfect light and sanctifying grace. A "good" and "pure" conscience, 1 Tim. 1:5; 3:9, is sprinkled with Christ's blood, clearly discerns the will of God, and urges us to obey it from gospel motives; in proportion as we thus obey it, it is "void of offence," Acts 24:16, and its approbation is one of the most essential elements of happiness. A "weak," or irresolute and blind conscience, 1 Cor. 8:7; a "defiled" conscience, the slave of a corrupt heart, Tit. 1:15; Heb. 10:22; and a "seared" conscience, 1 Tim. 4:2, hardened against the law and the gospel alike, unless changed by grace, will at length become an avenging conscience, the instrument of a fearful and eternal remorse. The case of Judas shows its terrific power. No bodily tortures can equal the agony it inflicts; and though it may slumber here, it will hereafter be like the worm that never dies and the fire that never can be quenched.

CONVEN'IENT, suitable and right, Rom. 1:28.

CONVERSA'TION, in the Bible, usually means the whole tenor of one's life, in intercourse with his fellow-men, Gal. 1:13; Eph. 4:22; 1 Pet. 1:15. Another word is employed in Phil. 3:20, which means, "our *citizenship* is in heaven." For conversation in the modern sense of discourse, the English version generally has communication, 2 Kin. 9:11; Matt. 5:37; Eph. 4:29, etc.

CO'OS, a small island of the Grecian archipelago, at a short distance from the south-west point of Asia Minor. Paul passed it in his voyage to Jerusalem, Acts 21:1. It is now called Stanchio. It was celebrated for its fertility, for wine and silkworms, and for the manufacture of silk and cotton of a beautiful texture.

COP'PER, one of the primitive metals, and the most ductile and malleable after gold and silver. Of this metal and zinc is made brass, which is a modern invention. There is little doubt but that copper is intended in those passages of our translation of the Bible which speak of brass. Copper was known prior to the flood, and was wrought by Tubal-cain, Gen. 4:22. Hiram of Tyre was a celebrated worker in copper, 1 Kin. 7:14. Palestine abounded in it, Deut. 8:9, and David amassed great quantities to be employed in building the temple, 1 Chr. 22:3-14. In Ezra 8:27, two vessels are mentioned "of fine copper, precious as gold." This was probably a metal compounded of copper, with gold or silver, or both. It was extolled for its beauty, solidity, and rarity, and for some uses was preferred to gold itself. Some compound of this kind may have been used for the small mirrors mentioned in Ex. 38:8; Job 37:18. See BRASS.

COR'AL, a hard, calcareous, marine production, produced by the labors of millions of insects, and often resembling in figure the stem of a plant, divided into branches. It is of various colors, black, white, and red. The latter is the most valuable. It is ranked by Job, 28:18, and Ezekiel, 27:16, among precious stones. It abounds in the Red sea; and the islands of the South seas are often coral reefs, covered over with earth. The word "rubies" in Prov. 3:15; 8:11; 20:15; 31:10, is thought by many to mean ornaments of coral.

COR'BAN, a sacred gift, a present devoted to God, or to his temple, Matt. 23:18. Our Saviour reproaches the Jews with cruelty towards their parents, in making a *corban* of what should have been appropriated to their use. The son would say to his needy parents, "It is a gift—whatsoever thou mightest be profited by me," that is, I have already devoted to God that which you request of me, Mark 7:11; and the traditionary teachings of the Jewish doctors would enforce such a vow, and not suffer him to do aught for his parents against it, although it was contrary to nature and reason, and made void the law of God as to honoring parents, Matt. 15:3-9. The Pharisees, and the Talmudists their successors, permitted even debtors to defraud their creditors by consecrating their debt to God; as if the property were their own, and not rather the right of their creditor.

CORIAN'DER, a small round seed of an aromatic plant. The plant is a native of China, and is widely diffused in Asia and the south of Europe. Its seeds are planted in March. They are employed as a spice in the East, and are much used by druggists, confectionarists, etc. The manna which fell in the wilderness was like coriander-seed, Exod. 16:31; Num. 11:7. See MANNA.

COR'INTH, see page 100.

CORIN'THIANS, EPISTLE I. This was written by Paul at Ephesus, about A. D. 57, upon the receipt of intelligence respecting the Corinthian church, conveyed by members of the family of Chloe, chap. 1:11, and by a letter from the church requesting advice, chap. 7:1, probably brought by Stephanus, etc., chap. 16:17. Certain factions had arisen in the church, using his name and those of Peter, Apollos, and of Christ himself, in bitter partisan contentions. In the first part of this letter he endeavors to restore harmony among them, by reuniting them to the great and sole Head of the church. He then takes occasion to put them on their guard against teachers of false philosophy, and resting their faith on the wisdom of men instead of the simple but mighty word of God. He proceeds, in chap. 5, to reprove them for certain gross immoralities tolerated among them, such as they had formerly practised like all around them, but which he charges them to banish from the church of Christ. He replies to their queries respecting celibacy and marriage, and the eating of food offered to idols; and meets several errors and sins prevalent in the church by timely instructions as to disputes among brethren, decorum in public assemblies, the Lord's supper, the resurrection of believers, true charity, and the right use of spiritual gifts, in which the Corinthian Christians excelled, but not without a mixture of ostentation and disorder. He directs them as to the best method of Christian beneficence, and closes with friendly greetings.

EPISTLE II. This was occasioned by intelligence received through Titus, at Philippi. Paul learned of the favorable reception of his former letter, and the good effects produced, and yet that a party remained opposed to him—accusing him of fickleness in not fulfilling his promise to visit them; blaming his severity towards the incestuous person; and charging him with an arrogance and assumption unsuited to his true authority and his personal appearance. In the course of his reply he answers all these objections; he enlarges upon the excellence of the new covenant, and the duties and rewards of its ministers, and on the duty of the Corinthian Christians as to charitable collections. He then vindicates his own course, his dignity and authority as an apostle, against those who assailed him. His last words invite them to penitence, peace, and brotherly love. This epistle seems to have been written soon after the first.

MODERN CORINTH.

COR'INTH, called anciently Ephyra, the capital of Achaia, and seated on the isthmus which separates the Ionian sea from the Ægean, and hence called *bimaris*, "on two seas." The city itself stood a little inland; but it had two ports, Lechæum on the west, and Cenchrea on the east. Its position gave it great commercial and military importance; for while the traffic of the east and west poured through its gates, as over the isthmus of Darien the commerce of two oceans, it was also at the gate of the Peloponnesus, and was the highway between Northern and Southern Greece. Its defence, besides the city walls, was in the Acro-corinth, a mass of rock, rising 2,000 feet above the sea, with precipitous sides, and with room for a town upon its summit. Corinth thus became one of the most populous and wealthy cities of Greece; but its riches produced pride, ostentation, effeminacy, and all the vices generally consequent on plenty. Lasciviousness, particularly, was not only tolerated, but consecrated here, by the worship of Venus, and the notorious prostitution of numerous attendants devoted to her. Corinth was destroyed by the Romans, B. C. 146. It was afterwards restored by Julius Cæsar, who planted in it a Roman colony; but though it soon regained its ancient splendor, it also relapsed into all its former dissipation and licentiousness. Paul arrived at Corinth, A. D. 52, Acts 18:1, and lodged with Aquila and his wife Priscilla, who, as well as himself, were tentmakers. Supporting himself by this labor, he remained at Corinth a year and a half, preaching the gospel at first to the Jews, and afterwards more successfully to the Gentiles. During this time he wrote the epistles to the Thessalonians; and in a subsequent visit, the epistles to the Galatians and Romans. Some suppose he made a short intervening visit, not narrated in the Bible. Compare 2 Cor. 13:1 with 2 Cor. 1:15; 2:1; 12:14, 21; 13:2. Apollos followed him in his labors at Corinth, and Aquila and Sosthenes were also among its early ministers, Acts 18:1; 1 Cor. 1:1; 16:19. Its site is now unhealthy and almost deserted, with few vestiges of its former greatness.

CORMORANT, a water-bird, about the size of a goose. It lives on fish, which it catches with great dexterity; and is so voracious and greedy, that its name has passed into a kind of proverbial use. The Hebrew word translated "cormorant" in Isa. 34:11; Zeph. 2:14, should rather be translated, as it is in other passages, "pelican," Lev. 11:17.

CORN, in the Bible, is the general word for *grain* of all kinds, including various seeds, peas, and beans. It never means, as in America, simply *maize*, or Indian corn. Palestine was anciently very fertile in grain, which furnished in a great measure the support of the inhabitants. "Corn, wine, and oil-olive" were the staple products, and wheat and barley still grow there luxuriantly, when cultivated. Wheat was often eaten in the field, the ripe ear being simply rubbed in the hands to separate the kernels, Deut. 23:25; Matt. 12:1. Parched wheat was a part of the ordinary food of the Israelites, as it still is of the Arabs, Ruth 2:14; 2 Sam. 17:28, 29. Their methods of preparing grain for the manufacture of bread were the following: The threshing was done either by the staff or the flail, Isa. 28:27, 28; by the feet of cattle, Deut. 25:4; or by "a sharp threshing instrument having teeth," Isa. 41:15, which was something resembling a cart, drawn over the corn by means of horses or oxen. See THRESHING. When the grain was threshed, it was separated from the chaff and dust by throwing it forward across the wind, by means of a winnowing fan, or shovel, Matt. 3.12; after which the grain was sifted, to separate all impurities from it, Amos 9:9; Luke 22:31. Hence we see that the threshing-floors were in the open air, and if possible on high ground, as travellers still find them in actual use, Judg. 6:11; 2 Sam. 24:18. The grain thus obtained was sometimes pounded in a mortar, Num. 11:8; Rev. 18:22, but was commonly reduced to meal by the hand-mill. This consisted of a lower

millstone, the upper side of which was slightly concave, and an upper millstone, the lower surface of which was convex. These stones were each about two feet in diameter, and half a foot thick; and were called "the nether millstone," and the rider, Job 41:24; Judg. 9:53; 2 Sam. 11:21. The hole for receiving the corn was in the centre of the upper millstone; and in the operation of grinding, the lower was fixed, and the upper made to move round upon it with considerable velocity by means of a handle. The meal came out at the edges, and was received on a cloth spread under the mill on the ground. Each family possessed a mill, and the law forbade its being taken in pledge, Deut. 24:6; one among innumerable examples of the humanity of the Mosaic legislation. These mills are still in use in the East, and in some parts of Scotland. Dr. E. D. Clarke says, "In the island of Cyprus I observed upon the ground the sort of stones used for grinding corn, called *querns* in Scotland, common also in Lapland, and in all parts of Palestine. These are the primeval mills of the world; and they are still found in all corn countries where rude and ancient customs have not been liable to those changes introduced by refinement. The employment of grinding with these mills is confined solely to females, who sit on the ground with the mill before them, and thus may be said to be "behind the mill," Ex. 11:5; and the practice illustrates the prophetic observation of our Saviour concerning the day of Jerusalem's destruction: "Two women shall be grinding at the mill; one shall be taken and the other left," Matt. 24:41. To this feminine occupation Samson was degraded, Judg. 16:21. The women always accompany the grating noise of the stones with their voices; and when ten or a dozen are thus employed, the fury of the song rises to a high pitch. As the grinding was usually performed in the morning at daybreak, the noise of the females at the hand-mill was heard all over the city, and often awoke their more indolent masters. The Scriptures mention the want of this noise as a mark of desolation, Jer. 25:10; Rev. 18:22.

CORNE'LIUS, a Roman centurion, stationed at Cæsarea in Palestine, supposed to have been of a distinguished family in Rome. He was "the first gentile convert;" and the story of his reception of the gospel shows how God broke down the partition-wall between Jews and Gentiles. When first mentioned, Acts 10:1, he had evidently been led by the Holy Spirit to renounce idolatry, to worship the true God, and to lead, in the midst of profligacy, a devout and beneficent life; he was prepared to receive the Saviour, and God did not fail to reveal Him. Cornelius was miraculously directed to send for Peter, who was also miraculously prepared to attend the summons. He went from Joppa to Cæsarea, thirty-five miles, preached the gospel to Cornelius and his friends, and saw with wonder the miraculous gifts of the Spirit poured upon them all. Providence thus explained his recent vision in the trance; he nobly discarded his Jewish prejudices, and at once began his great work as apostle to the Gentiles by receiving into the church of Christ those whom Christ had so manifestly accepted, Acts 10;11.

COR'NER-STONE, a massive stone, usually distinct from the foundation, Jer. 51:26; and so placed at the corner of the building as to bind together the two walls meeting upon it. Such a stone is found at Baalbek, twenty-eight feet long, six and a half feet wide, and four feet thick.

Our Lord is compared in the New Testament to a corner-stone in three different points of view. First, as this stone lies at the foundation, and serves to give support and strength to the building, so Christ, or the doctrine of a Saviour, is called the chief corner-stone, Eph. 2:20, because this doctrine is the most important feature of the Christian religion—as a system of truths, and as a living power in the souls of men. Further, as the corner-stone occupies an important and conspicuous place, Jesus is compared to it, 1 Pet. 2:6, because God has given him, as the Mediator, a dignity and conspicuousness above all others. Lastly, since men often stumble against a projecting corner-stone, Christ is so called, Matt. 21:42, because his gospel will be the cause of aggravated condemnation to those who reject it.

COR'NET, a wind instrument of music, of a curved form, 1 Chr. 15:28; Dan. 3:5, 7. See MUSIC.

COTES, inclosures for the safe keeping of sheep, 2 Chr. 32:28. See SHEEP.

COT'TAGE, a rustic tent or shelter, made perhaps of boughs, Isa. 24:20.

COT'TON was a native product of India, and perhaps of Egypt, and is supposed to be intended in some of the passages where the English version has "fine linen." It has been much disputed whether cotton cloth was used by the ancient Hebrews and Egyptians, or not; but minute examination of the cloths in which Egyptian mummies were wrapped, proves that this material was sometimes used, especially for children. See FLAX, LINEN.

COUCH. See BED.

COUN'CIL is occasionally taken for any kind of assembly; sometimes for that of the Sanhedrim; at others, for a convention of pastors met to regulate ecclesiastical affairs. Thus the assembly of the apostles, etc., at Jerusalem, Acts 15, to determine whether the yoke of the law should be imposed on gentile converts, is commonly reputed to be the first council of the Christian church. See SANHEDRIM.

COUR'SES, the order in which the priests were on duty at the temple. See ABIA.

COURT, an inclosed space or yard within the limits of an oriental house, 2 Sam. 17:18. For the *courts of the temple*, see TEMPLE. The tabernacle also had a court. All oriental houses are built in the form of a hollow square around a court. See HOUSE.

COV'ENANT. The word *testamentum* is often used in Latin to express the Hebrew word which signifies covenant; whence the titles, Old and New Testaments, are used to denote the old and new covenants. See TESTAMENT.

A covenant is properly an agreement between two parties. Where one of the parties is infinitely superior to the other, as in a covenant between God and man, there God's covenant assumes the nature of a promise, Isa. 59:21; Jer. 31:33, 34; Gal. 3:15-18. The first covenant with the Hebrews was made when the Lord chose Abraham and his posterity for his people; a second covenant, or a solemn renewal of the former, was made at Sinai, comprehending all who observe the law of Moses. The "new covenant" of which Christ is the Mediator and Author, and which was confirmed by his blood, comprehends all who believe in him and are born again, Gal. 4:24; Heb. 7:22; 8:6-13; 9:15-23; 12:24. The divine covenants were ratified by the sacrifice of a victim, to show that without an atonement there could be no communication of blessing and salvation from God to man, Gen. 15:1-18; Ex. 24:6-8; Heb. 9:6. Eminent believers among the covenant people of God were favored by the establishment of particular covenants, in which he promised them certain temporal favors; but these were only renewals to individuals of the "everlasting covenant," with temporal types and pledges of its fulfilment. Thus God covenanted with Noah, Abraham, and David, Gen. 9:8, 9; 17:4, 5; Psa. 89:3, 4; etc., and gave them faith in the Saviour afterwards to be revealed, Rom. 3:25; Heb. 9:15.

In common discourse, we usually say the old and new testaments, or covenants—the covenant between God and the posterity of Abraham, and that which he has made with believers by Jesus Christ; because these two covenants contain eminently all the rest, which are consequences, branches, or explanations of them. The most solemn and perfect of the covenants of God with men is that made through the mediation of our Redeemer, which must subsist to the end of time. The Son of God is the guarantee of it; it is confirmed with his blood; the end and object of it is eternal life, and its constitution and laws are more exalted than those of the former covenant.

Theologians use the phrase "covenant of works" to denote the constitution established by God with man before the fall, the promise of which was eternal life on condition of obedience, Hos. 6:7; Rom. 3:27; Gal. 2:19. They also use the phrase, "covenant of grace or redemption," to denote the arrangement made in the counsels of eternity, in virtue of which the Father forgives and saves sinful men redeemed by the death of the Son.

CRACK'NELS, a sort of hard brittle cakes, 1 Kin. 14:3.

CRANE, see next page.

CREA'TION, (1,) the act by which God calls into existence things not previously in being—material or spiritual, visible or invisible, Psa. 148:5; Rev. 4:11; (2,) the moulding or reconstituting things, the elements of which previously existed; and (3,) the things thus "created and made," 2 Pet. 3:4; Rev. 3:14; 5:13. It is probably in the first of these senses the word "created" is to be understood in Gen. 1:1, though some understand it in the second sense. In either case the idea of the eternity of matter is to be rejected, as contrary to sound reason and to the teachings of Scripture, Prov. 8:22-31; John 1:1-3; Heb. 11:3.

Creation is exclusively the work of God. The Father, the Son, and the Spirit are each in turn named as its author, Isa. 40:28; Col. 1:16; Gen. 2:2. It is a work the mysteries of which no finite mind can apprehend; and yet, as it reveals to us the invisible things of God, Rom. 1:20, we may and ought to learn what he reveals respecting it not only in revelation, but in his works. These two volumes are from the same divine hand, and cannot but harmonize with each other. The Bible opens with an account of the creation unspeakably majestic and sublime. The six days there spoken of have usually been taken for our present natural days; but modern geological researches have given rise to the idea that "day" here denotes a longer period. The different rocks of our globe lie in distinct layers, the comparative age of which is supposed to have been ascertained. Only the most recent have been found to contain human remains. Older layers present in turn different fossil remains of animals and plants, many of them supposed to be now extinct. These layers are deeply imbedded beneath the present soil, and yet appear to be formed of matter washed into the bed of some primeval sea, and hardened into rock. Above this may lie numerous other strata of different materials, but which appear to have been deposited in the same manner, in the slow lapse of time. These layers are also thrown up and penetrated all over the world by rocks of still earlier formations, apparently once in a melted state.

There are several modes of reconciling these geological discoveries with the statements of Scripture: First, that the six days of Gen. 1 denote six long epochs—periods of alternate progressive formation and revolution on the surface of the earth. To the Lord "a thousand years are as one day," Psa. 90:2, 4; 2 Pet. 3:5–10; Rev. 20. Secondly, that the long epochs indicated in the geological structure of the globe occurred before the Bible account commences, or rather in the interval between the first and second verses of Gen. 1. According to this interpretation, verse 2 describes the state of the earth at the close of the last revolution it experienced, preparatory to God's fitting it up for the abode of man as described in the verses following. Thirdly, that God compressed the work of those untold ages into six short days, and created the world as he did Adam, in a state of maturity, embodying in its rocks and fossils those rudimental forms of animal and vegetable life which seem naturally to lead up to the existing forms.

The "creature" and "the whole creation," in Rom. 8:19–22, may denote the irrational and inferior creation, which shall be released from the curse, and share in the glorious liberty of the sons of God, Isa. 11:6; 35:1; 2 Pet. 3:7–13. The bodies of believers, now subject to vanity, are secure of full deliverance at the resurrection—"the redemption of our body," Rom. 8:23.

THE DEMOISELLE, OR NUMIDIAN CRANE.

CRANE. In Isa. 38:14, and Jer. 8:7, two birds are mentioned, the SUS and the AGUR, the first rendered in our version crane, the second swallow. Bochart says the sus, or sis, is the swallow; the agur, the crane. The Numidian crane, supposed to be referred to, is about three feet in length, is bluish-grey, with the cheeks, throat, breast, and tips of the long hinder feathers black, with a tuft of white feathers behind each eye. "Like a crane, or a swallow, so did I chatter:" there is peculiar force and beauty in the comparison here made between the dying believer and migratory birds about to take their departure to a distant but more genial clime. They linger in the scenes which they have frequented, but instinct compels them to remove.

CRES'CENS, an assistant of the apostle Paul, and probably one of the seventy disciples; supposed to have exercised his ministry in Galatia, 2 Tim. 4:10.

CRETE, a large island, now called Candia, in the Mediterranean, originally peopled probably by a branch of the Caphtorim. It is celebrated by Homer for its hundred cities. Being surrounded by the sea, its inhabitants were excellent sailors, and its vessels visited all coasts. They were also famous for archery, which they practised from their infancy. The Cretans were one of the three K's against whose unfaithfulness the Grecian proverb cautioned—Kappadocia, Kilicia, and Krete. In common speech, the expression, "to Cretanize," signified to tell lies; which helps to account for that detestable character which the apostle has given of the Cretans, that they were "always liars," brutes, and gormandizers, as Epimenides, a Cretan poet, described them, Tit. 1:12, 13.

Crete is famous as the birthplace of the legislator Minos; and in the Bible, for its connection with the voyage of Paul to Rome, Acts 27. The ship first made Salmone, the eastern promontory of the island, and took shelter at Fair Havens, a roadstead on the south side, east of cape Matala. After some time, and against Paul's warning, they set sail for Phenice, a more commodious harbor on the western part of the island; but were overtaken by a fierce wind from the east-north-east, which compelled them to lie to, and drifted them to Malta. Paul is supposed to have visited Crete afterwards, in connection with one of his visits to Asia Minor, 1 Tim. 1:3; Phile. 22. Here he established gospel institutions, and left Titus in the pastoral charge, Tit. 1:5.

CRIM'SON, 2 Chr. 2:7-14; 3:14. See PURPLE.

CRISP'ING-PINS irons for curling the hair, Isa. 3:22.

CRIS'PUS, president of the synagogue at Corinth, converted under the preaching of Paul, Acts 18:8, and baptized by him, 1 Cor. 1:14.

CROSS, a kind of gibbet made of pieces of wood placed transversely, whether

crossing at right angles, one at the top of the other, T, or below the top, †, or diagonally, X. Death by the cross was a punishment of the meanest slaves, and was a mark of infamy, Deut. 21:23; Gal. 3:13. This punishment was so common among the Romans, that pains, afflictions, troubles, etc., were called "crosses." Our Saviour says, that his disciples must take up the cross and follow Him. Though the cross is the sign of ignominy and sufferings, yet it is the badge and glory of the Christian.

The common way of crucifying was by fastening the criminal with nails, one through each hand, and one through both his feet, or through each foot. Sometimes they were bound with cords, which, though it seems gentler, because it occasions less pain, was really more cruel, because the sufferer was hereby made to languish longer. Sometimes they used both nails and cords for fastenings; and when this was the case, there was no difficulty in lifting up the person, together with his cross, he being sufficiently supported by the cords; near the middle of the cross also there was a wooden projection, which partially supported the body of the sufferer. Before they nailed him to the cross, they generally scourged him with whips or leathern thongs, which was thought more severe and more infamous than scourging with cords. Slaves who had been guilty of great crimes were fastened to a gibbet or cross, and were thus led about the city, and beaten. Our Saviour was loaded with his cross, and as he sunk under the burden, Simon the Cyrenian was constrained to bear it after him and with him, Mark 15:21.

After the person had been nailed to the cross, a stupefying draught was sometimes administered, in order to render him less sensible to pain, an alleviation which our Saviour did not accept, Matt.

27 : 34 ; Mark 15 : 23 ; though he seems afterwards to have taken a little of the common beverage of the soldiers. Sent by the Father to bear the heavy load of penal suffering for a lost race, he felt that he had no right to the palliatives resorted to in ordinary cases, and perfectly lawful except in his own. "The cup which my Father hath given me, shall I not drink it?" John 18:11. He drank it, and to the very dregs. The cross being erected under the burning sun, the wounds made by the scourge and the nails soon occasioned a general fever and an intolerable thirst. The blood, interrupted in its regular flow, accumulated in various parts of the body, and caused painful congestions. Every slight writhing of the sufferer increased his anguish, which found no relief but in final mortification and death. Those who were fastened upon the cross lived in that condition several days, and sometimes a week or more. Hence Pilate was amazed at our Saviour's dying so soon, because naturally he must have lived longer, Mark 15.44. The legs of the two thieves were broken, to hasten their death, that their bodies might not remain on the cross on the Sabbath day, Deut. 21:23 ; Josh. 8:29 ; but the crucified were usually left hanging, under the eye of guards, till their bodies fell to the ground, or were devoured by birds and beasts of prey.

CROWN. There are two distinct Hebrew terms rendered crown. The one represents such headdresses as we should designate coronet, band, mitre, tiara, garland, etc. The other is generally applied to the headdresses of kings. The former was a simple fillet or diadem around the head, variously ornamented. Newly-married persons of both sexes wore crowns on their wedding-day, Song 3:11 ; Ezek. 16:12. The crowns of kings were sometimes white fillets, bound round the forehead, the ends falling back on the neck ; or were made of gold tissue, adorned with jewels. That of the Jewish high-priest was a fillet, or diadem, tied with a ribbon of a hyacinth color, Ex. 28:36 ; 39 : 30. Occasionally the crown was of pure gold, and was worn by kings, 2 Chr. 23:11, sometimes when they went to battle, 2 Sam. 1:10 ; 12:30. It was also worn by queens, Esth. 2:17. The crown is a symbol of honor, power, and eternal life, Prov. 12:4 ; Lam. 5:16 ; 1 Pet. 5:4. Crowns

ANTIQUE GARLANDS, DIADEMS, AND CROWNS.

or garlands were given to the successful competitors at the Grecian games, to which frequent allusion is made in the Epistles, 2 Tim. 4:7, 8.

CRUSE, a small vessel for holding water and other liquids, 1 Sam. 26:11. The above cut represents various antique cups, travelling flasks, and cruses, like those still used in the East.

CRYSTAL. The same Hebrew word is rendered by our translators, crystal, Ezek. 1:22 ; frost, Gen. 31:40 ; and ice, Job 6:16. The word primarily denotes ice ; and the name is given to a perfectly transparent and glass-like gem, from its resemblance to this substance, Job 28:17; Rev. 4:6; 21:11.

CU'BIT, a measure used among the ancients. A cubit was originally the distance from the elbow to the extremity of the middle finger, which is the fourth part of a well-proportioned man's stature. The Hebrew cubit, according to some, is twenty-one inches; but others fix it at eighteen. The Talmudists observe that the Hebrew cubit was larger by one quarter than the Roman.

CU'CUMBER, a vegetable very plentiful in the East, especially in Egypt, Num. 11:5, where they are esteemed delicacies, and form a great part of the food of the lower class of people, especially during the hot months. The Egyptian cucumber is similar in form to ours, but larger, being usually a foot in length. It is described by Hasselquist as greener, smoother, softer, sweeter, and more digestible than our cucumber.

CUM'MIN, a plant much like fennel, and which produces blossoms and branches in an umbellated form. Its seeds yield an aromatic oil, of a warm, stimulating nature, Isa. 28:25–27. Our Lord reproved the scribes and Pharisees for so very carefully paying tithe of mint, anise, and cummin, and yet neglecting good works and obedience to God's law, Matt. 23:23.

CUP. This word is taken in Scripture both in a proper and in a figurative sense. In a proper sense, it signifies a common cup, of horn, or some precious metal, Gen. 40:13; 44:2; 1 Kin. 7:26, such as is used for drinking out of at meals; or a cup of ceremony, used at solemn and religious meals—as at the passover, when the father of the family pronounced certain blessings over the cup, and having tasted it, passed it round to the company and his whole family, who partook of it, 1 Cor. 10:16. In a figurative sense, a cup is spoken of as filled with the portion given to one by divine providence, Psa 11:6; 16:5; with the blessings of life and of grace, Psa. 23:5; with a thank-offering to God, Ex. 29:40; Psa. 116:13; with liquor used at idolatrous feasts, 1 Cor. 10:21; with love-potions, Rev. 17:4; with sore afflictions, Psa. 65:8; Isa. 51:17; and with the bitter draught of death, which was often caused by a cup of hemlock or some other poison, Psa. 75:8. See Matt. 16:28; Luke 22:42; John 18:11. See CRUSE.

CUSH, I., the eldest son of Ham, and father of Nimrod, Seba, Havilah, Sabtah, Raamah, and Sabtecha, most of whom settled in Arabia Felix, Gen. 10:6–8.

II. The countries peopled by the descendants of Cush, and generally called in the English Bible, Ethiopia, though not always. But under this name there seem to be included not less than three different countries:

1. The oriental Cush, comprehending the regions of Persis, Chusistan, and Susiana, in Persia. It lay chiefly to the eastward of the Tigris. Hither we may refer the river Gihon, Gen. 2:13; Zeph. 3:10. See EDEN.

2. The Hebrews also, in the opinion of many, used Cush and Cushan, Hab. 3:7, to designate the southern parts of Arabia, and the coast of the Red sea. From this country originated Nimrod, who established himself in Mesopotamia, Gen. 10:8. The "Ethiopian woman," too, whom Moses married during the march of the Israelites through the desert, came probably from this Cush, Exod. 2:16–21; Num. 12:1; 2 Chr. 21:16.

3. But, more commonly, Cush signifies Ethiopia proper, lying south and southeast of Egypt, and now called Abyssinia, Isa. 18:1; 20:3–5; Jer. 13:23; Ezek. 29:10; Dan. 11:43.

CUTH'ITES, a people who dwelt beyond the Euphrates, and were thence transplanted into Samaria, in place of the Israelites who had before inhabited it. They came from the land of Cush, or Cutha, in the East; their first settlement being in the cities of the Medes, subdued by Shalmaneser and his predecessors. See CUSH. The Israelites were substituted for them in those places, 2 Kin. 17:24, 30.

CYM'BAL, a musical instrument consisting of two broad plates of brass, of a convex form, which being struck together, produce a shrill, piercing sound. From Psa. 150:5, it would appear that both hand-cymbals and finger-cymbals, or castagnets, were used. They were used in the temple, and upon occasions of public rejoicings, 1 Chr. 13:8; 16:5, as they are by the Armenians at the present day. In 1 Cor. 13:1, the apostle deduces a comparison from sounding brass and "tinkling" cymbals; perhaps the latter words had been better rendered clanging or clattering cymbals,

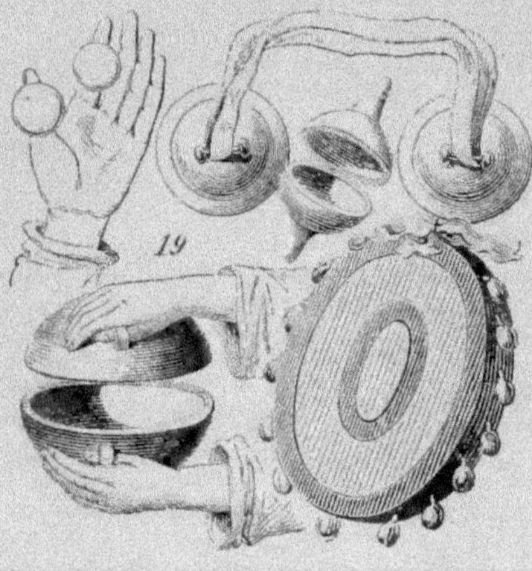

HAND AND FINGER CYMBALS, AND TAMBOURINE

since such is the nature of the instrument. See MUSIC.

CY'PRESS, an evergreen tree, resembling in form and size the Lombardy poplar. Its wood is exceedingly durable, and seems to have been used for making idols, Isa. 44:14. The cypress is thought to be intended in some of the passages where "fir-tree" occurs, 2 Sam. 6 : 5, etc.

CY'PRUS, a large island in the Mediterranean, situated in the north-east part of that sea between Cilicia and Syria. It is about one hundred and forty miles long, and varies from five to fifty miles in breadth. Its inhabitants were plunged in all manner of luxury and debauchery. Their principal deity was Venus, who had a celebrated temple at Paphos. The island was extremely fertile, and abounded in wine, oil, honey, wool, copper, agate, and a beautiful species of rock crystal. There were also large forests of cypress-trees. Of the cities in the island, Paphos on the western coast, and Salamis at the opposite end, are mentioned in the New Testament. The gospel was preached there at an early day, Acts 11:19. Barnabas and Mnason, and other eminent Christians, were natives of this island, Acts 11 : 20; 21 : 16. The apostles Paul and Barnabas made a missionary tour through it, A. D. 44, Acts 13:4-13. See also Acts 15:39; 27:4.

CYRE'NE, a city and province of Libya, west of Egypt, between the Great Syrtis and the Mareotis, at present called Caïroan, in the province of Barca. It was sometimes called PENTAPOLIS, from the five principal cities which it contained—Cyrene, Apollonia, Arsinoë, Berenicé, and Ptolemais. From hence came Simon the Cyrenian, father of Alexander and Rufus, on whom the Roman soldiers laid a part of our Saviour's cross, Matt. 27:32; Luke 23:26. There were many Jews in the province of Cyrene, a great part of whom embraced the Christian religion, though others opposed it with much obstinacy, Acts 11:20; 13:1. Also Acts 6:9.

CYRE'NIUS, or Publius Sulpitius QUIRINUS, according to his Latin appellation, governor of Syria, Luke 2:2. According to history, Quirinus was not properly governor of Syria till some years after this date; and the only census of that time mentioned by secular historians took place when Christ was eight or ten years old. The passage in Luke may be translated, "This enrolment took place first under Cyrenius governor of Syria." Compare Acts 5:37.

CY'RUS, son of Cambyses king of Persia, and Mandane, daughter of Astyages king of the Medes. He aided his uncle Cyaxares (called "Darius the Mede" in the Bible) in conquering Asia Minor, and afterwards their joint forces captured Babylon and overran the Assyrian empire. He married his cousin, the daughter of Cyaxares, and thus at length inherited and united the crowns of Persia and Media. Cyrus was foretold by the prophet Isaiah, 44 : 28; 45 : 1-7, as the deliverer and restorer of Judah, as he proved to be, 2 Chr. 36:22, 23; Ezra 1:1-4. The prophet Daniel was his favorite minister, Dan. 6:28.

D.

DAB'ERATH, a Levitical town in the borders of Zebulun and Issachar, Josh. 19:12; 21:28; 1 Chr. 6:72. Its site is probably that of the modern Deburieh, a small village at the foot of mount Tabor on the north-west.

DA'GON, *fish-god*, a national idol of the Philistines, with temples at Gaza, Ashdod, etc., 1 Chr 10:10. The temple at Gaza was destroyed by Samson, Judg. 16:21-30. In that at Ashdod, Dagon twice miraculously fell down before the ark of God; and in the second fall his head and hands were broken off, leaving

only the body, which was in the form of a large fish, 1 Sam. 5:1-9. See Josh. 15:41; 19:27. There were other idols of like form among the ancients, particularly the goddess Derceto or Atergatis; and a similar form or "incarnation" of Vishnu is at this day much worshipped in India, and like Dagon is destined to be prostrated in the dust before the true God.

DALMANUTHA, a town or village near the city of Magdala, Mark 8:10. Compare Matt. 15:39. The exact situation of this place is uncertain; it lay, however, on the western shore of the sea of Galilee, north of Tiberias.

DALMATIA, a province of Europe on the east of the Adriatic sea, and forming part of Illyricum. It was contiguous to Macedonia, Upper Mœsia, and Liburnia, from which latter it was divided by the river Titius. Hither Titus was sent by Paul to spread the knowledge of Christianity, 2 Tim. 4:10.

DAM'ARIS, an Athenian lady, honorably distinguished as one of the few who embraced Christianity at Athens under the preaching of Paul, Acts 17:34.

DAMAS'CUS, a celebrated metropolis of Syria, first mentioned in Gen. 14:15; 15:2, and now probably the oldest city on the globe. It stands on the river Barada, the ancient Chrysorrhoas, in a beautiful and fertile plain on the east and south-east of Anti-Lebanon. See Abana. This plain is about fifty miles in circumference; it is open to the desert of Arabia on the south and east, and is bounded on the other sides by the mountains. The region around and north of Damascus, including probably the valley between the ridges of Lebanon and Anti-Lebanon, is called in the Scriptures, "Syria of Damascus," 2 Sam. 8:5, and by Strabo, Cœlesyria. This city, which at first had its own kings, was taken by David, 2 Sam. 8:5, 6, and by Jeroboam II., 2 Kings 14:28. Its history at this period is to be found in the accounts given of Naaman, Ben-hadad, Hazael, and Rezin. It was subdued by Tiglath-pileser, 2 Kin. 16:9; and was afterwards subject to the Assyrians, Babylonians, Persians, Seleucidæ, and Romans. In the days of Paul it appears to have been held, for a time at least, by Aretas, king of Arabia Petræa, the father-in-law of Herod Antipas. At this period the city was so much thronged by the Jews, that, according to Josephus, ten thousand of them, by command of Nero, were put to death at once. It is memorable to Christians as the scene of the miraculous conversion of that most illustrious "servant of the Lord Jesus Christ," the apostle Paul, Acts 9:1-27; 22:1-16. Since 1506, Damascus has been held by the Turks; it is the metropolis of "the Pashalic of Damascus," and has a population of about one hundred and fifty thousand. The Arabs call it Esh-shams. It is still celebrated, with the surrounding country, by all travellers, as one of the most beautiful and luxuriant regions in the world. The orientals themselves call it the "Paradise on earth," and it is pretended that Mohammed refused to enter it, lest he should thereby forfeit his heavenly Paradise. The plain around the city is well watered and of exuberant fertility; and the eye of the traveller from any direction is fascinated by the view—a wilderness of verdure, interspersed with innumerable villas and hamlets, with gardens, fountains, and groves. A nearer view of the city discloses much that is offensive to the senses, as well as to the spirit. It is the most purely oriental city yet remaining of all that are named in the Bible. Its public buildings and bazaars are fine; and many private dwellings, though outwardly mean, are decorated within in a style of the most costly luxury. Its position has made it from the very first a commercial city, Ezek. 27:18. The cloth called Damask is supposed to have originated here, and Damascus steel has never been equalled. It still carries on an extensive traffic in woven stuffs of silk and cotton, in fine inlaid cabinet work, in leather, fruits, sweetmeats, etc. For this purpose huge caravans assemble here at intervals, and traverse, just as of old, the desert routes to remote cities. Here too is a chief gathering-place of pilgrims to Mecca. People from all the nations of the East resort to Damascus, a fact which shows its importance as a missionary station. An encouraging commencement has been made by English Christians, and the fierce and bigoted intolerance of its Mussulman population has begun to give way. A street is still found here called "Straight," probably the same referred to in Acts 9:11. It runs a mile or more through the city from the eastern gate.

DAMNA'TION, the state of being excluded from God's mercy, and condemned to the everlasting punishment of the wicked. This is now the sense of the word damnation, in our language; but at the time when the Bible was translated, it signified the same as condemnation. The words damn and damnation ought therefore to be still so understood, in such passages as Rom. 13:2; 14:23; 1 Cor. 11:29.

DAN, *a judge*, I., a son of Jacob by Bilhah, Gen. 30:3; 35.25. The tribe of Dan was second only to that of Judah in numbers before entering Canaan, Num. 1:39; 26:43. A portion was assigned to Dan, extending south-east from the seacoast near Joppa. It bordered on the land of the Philistines, with whom the tribe of Dan had much to do, Judg. 13–16. Their territory was fertile, but small, and the natives were powerful. A part of the tribe therefore sought and conquered another home, Josh. 19; Judg. 18.

II. A city originally called Laish, Judg. 18:29, at the northern extremity of Israel, in the tribe of Naphtali. "From Dan to Beersheba" denotes the whole extent of the land of promise, Dan being the northern city, and Beersheba the southern one. Dan was seated at the foot of mount Hermon, four miles west of Paneas, near one source of the Jordan, on a hill now called Tell-el-Kady. Laish at one time belonged to Zidon, and received the name of Dan from a portion of that tribe who conquered and rebuilt it, Judg. 18. It was an idolatrous city even then, and was afterwards the seat of one of the golden calves of Jeroboam, 1 Kin. 12:28; Amos 8:14. Though once and again a very prosperous city, Judg. 18:10; Ezek. 27:19, only slight remains of it now exist.

DANC'ING. The Hebrew word signified "to leap for joy," Psa. 30:11; and the action of the lame man healed by Peter and John, Acts 3:8, more nearly resembled the Hebrew dancing than the measured artificial steps of modern times do. The Jewish dances were expressive of religious joy and gratitude. Sometimes they were in honor of a conqueror, as in the case of David, 1 Sam. 18:6, 7; when he had slain the Philistine giant, "the women came out of all the cities of Israel singing and dancing." It was practised on occasions of domestic joy. See the case of the prodigal son's return. In the religious dance, the timbrel was used to direct the ceremony, and some one led, whom the rest followed with measured step and devotional songs; thus Miriam led the women of Israel, Ex. 15:20, 21, and king David the men, 2 Sam. 6:14; Psa. 150:4. Several important conclusions have been drawn from a careful comparison of the portions of Scripture in which there is allusion to dancing. It was religious in its character; practised exclusively on joyous occasions; only by one of the sexes; usually in the daytime, and in the open air: no instances are on record in which the two sexes united in the exercise; and it was not practised for amusement. The exceptions to this latter assertion are the "vain fellows," alluded to by Michal, 2 Sam. 6:20, the ungodly rich families referred to by Job, 21:11, and the daughter of Herodias, Mark 14:6. Among the Greeks and Romans dancing was a common pastime, resorted to in order to enliven feasts, and also on occasions of domestic joy. Still Cicero says, "No one dances, unless he is either drunk or mad;" and these words express the prevailing sense as to the impropriety of respectable individuals taking part in the amusement. Hence the gay circles of Rome, as is the case in the East at the present time, derived their entertainment from the performances of professional dancers. These were women of abandoned character; and their dances, like those in heathen temples, were often grossly indecent, Isa. 23:16.

DAN'IEL, I., called Belteshazzar by the Chaldeans, a prophet descended from the royal family of David, who was carried captive to Babylon, when very young, in the fourth year of Jehoiakim king of Judah, B. C. 606. He was chosen, with his three companions, Hananiah, Mishael, and Azariah, to reside at Nebuchadnezzar's court, where he received a suitable education, and made great progress in all the sciences of the Chaldeans, but declined to pollute himself by eating provisions from the king's table, which would often be ceremonially unclean to a Jew, or defiled by some connection with idol-worship. At the end of their three years' education, Daniel and his companions excelled all others, and received honorable appointments in the royal service. Here Daniel soon displayed his prophetic gifts in interpreting a dream of Nebuchadnezzar, by whom he was made governor of Babylon, and head of the learned and priestly class. He seems to have been absent, perhaps on some foreign embassy, when his three companions were cast into the fiery furnace. At a later period he interpreted another dream of Nebuchadnezzar, and afterwards the celebrated vision of Belshazzar—one of whose last works was to promote Daniel to an office much higher than he had previously held during his reign, Dan. 5:29; 8:27.

After the capture of Babylon by the Medes and Persians, under Cyaxares and Cyrus, Daniel was continued in all his high employments, and enjoyed the favor of these princes until his death, except at one short interval, when the envy of the other officers prevailed on the king to cast him into the lions' den, an act which recoiled on his foes to their own destruction. During this period he earnestly labored, by fasting and prayer as well as by counsel, to secure the return of the Jews to their own land, the promised time having come, Dan. 9. He lived to see the decree issued, and many of his people restored; but it is not known that he ever revisited Jerusalem. In the third year of Cyrus, he had a series of visions disclosing the state of the Jews till the coming of the promised Redeemer; and at last we see him calmly awaiting the peaceful close of a well-spent life, and the gracious resurrection of the just. Daniel was one of the most spotless characters upon record. His youth and his age were alike devoted to God. He maintained his integrity in the most difficult circumstances, and amid the fascinations of an eastern court he was pure and upright. He confessed the name of God before idolatrous princes; and would have been a martyr, but for the miracle which rescued him from death. His history deserves the careful and prayerful study of the young, and the lessons which it inculcates are weighty and rich in instruction.

II. The second son of David, also called Chileab, 1 Chr. 3:1; 2 Sam. 3:3.

III. A descendant of Ithamar, the fourth son of Aaron. He was one of the chiefs who accompanied Ezra from Babylon to Judea, and afterwards took a prominent part in the reformation of the people, Ezra 8:2.

DAN'IEL, BOOK OF. This is a mixture of history and prophecy. The first six chapters are chiefly historical, and the remainder prophetical. It was completed about B. C. 534. The wonders related are of a peculiar and striking character, and were designed to show the people of God that, amid their degeneracy, the Lord's hand was not shortened that it could not save; and also to exhibit to their enemies that there was an essential difference between Jehovah and idols, between the people of God and the world. The prophecies contained in the latter part of the book extend from the days of Daniel to the general resurrection. The Assyrian, the Persian, the Grecian, and the Roman empires are described under appropriate imagery. The precise time of Christ's coming is told; the rise and fall of antichrist, and the duration of his power, are accurately determined; the victory of Christ over his enemies, and the universal prevalence of his religion are clearly pointed out. The book is filled with the most exalted sentiments of piety and devout gratitude. Its style is simple, clear, and concise, and many of the prophecies are delivered in language so plain and circumstantial, that some infidels have asserted that they were written after the events they describe had taken place. Sir Isaac Newton regards Daniel as the most distinct and plain of all the prophets, and most easy to be understood; and therefore considers that in things relating to the last times, he is to be regarded as the key to the other prophets.

With respect to the genuineness and authenticity of the book, there is the strongest evidence, both internal and external. We have the testimony of Christ himself, Matt. 24:15; of St. John and St. Paul, who have copied his prophecies; of the Jewish church and nation, who have constantly received this book as canonical; of Josephus, who recommends him as the greatest of the prophets; and of the Jewish Targums and Talmuds, which frequently cite his authority. As to the internal evidence, the style, the language, the manner of writing, perfectly agree with the age; and especially, he is proved to have been a prophet by the exact fulfilment of his predictions. This book, like that of Ezra, is written partly in Hebrew, and partly in Chaldee, the prevailing language of the Babylonians.

I. DARI'US THE MEDE, Dan. 5:31; 9:1; 11:1, was son of Astyages king of the Medes, and brother of Mandane mother of Cyrus, and of Amyit the mother of Evil-merodach and grandmother of Belshazzar: thus he was uncle, by the mother's side, to Evil-merodach and to Cyrus. The Hebrew generally calls him Darius; the Septuagint, Artaxerxes; and Xenophon, Cyaxares. Darius dethroned Belshazzar king of the Chaldeans, and occupied the throne till his death two years after, when it reverted to the illustrious Cyrus. In his reign Daniel was cast into the lions' den, Dan. 6.

II. DARI'US HYSTAS'PIS, spoken of in Ezra 4-7, Haggai, and Zechariah, as the king who renewed the permission to rebuild the temple, given to the Jews by Cyrus and afterwards recalled. He succeeded Smerdis, the Magian usurper, B. C. 521, and reigned thirty-six years. He removed the seat of government to Susa, whereupon Babylon rebelled against him; but he subdued the rebellion and broke down the walls of Babylon, as was predicted, Jer. 51:58.

III. DARI'US CODOMA'NUS, Neh. 12:22, was one of the most brave and generous of the Persian kings. Alexander the Great defeated him several times, and at length subverted the Persian monarchy, after it had been established two hundred and six years. Darius was killed by his own generals, after a short reign of six years. Thus were verified the prophecies of Daniel, ch. 8, who had foretold the enlargement of the Persian monarchy, under the symbol of a ram, butting with its horns westward, northward, and southward, which nothing could resist; and its destruction by a goat having a very large horn between his eyes, (Alexander the Great,) coming from the west, and overrunning the world without touching the earth. Nothing can be added to the clearness of these prophecies, so exactly describing what in due time took place and is matter of history.

DARK'NESS, the absence of natural light, Gen. 1:2, and hence figuratively a state of misery and adversity, Job 18:6; Psa. 107:10; Isa. 8:22; 9:1; also the absence of the sun and stars, and hence the fall of chief men and national convulsions, Isa. 13:10; Acts 2:20. "Works of darkness," are the impure mysteries practised in heathen worship, Eph. 5:11. "Outer darkness" illustrates the gloom of those on whom the gates of heaven are closed, Matt. 8:12. The darkness in Egypt, Ex. 10:21-23, was miraculous; also that which covered all Judea with sympathetic gloom at the crucifixion of Christ, Luke 23:43. This could not have been caused by an eclipse of the sun; for at the Passover the moon was full, and on the opposite side of the earth from the sun.

DATE, the fruit of the palm-tree. See PALM.

DA'THAN, one of the rebels, in company with Korah, against the authority of Moses and Aaron, Num. 16.

DA'VID, *beloved*, the youngest son of Jesse, of the tribe of Judah, born in Bethlehem B. C. 1085; one of the most remarkable men in either sacred or secular history. His life is fully recorded in 1 Sam. 16 to 1 Kin. 2. He was "the Lord's anointed," chosen by God to be king of Israel instead of Saul, and consecrated to that office by the venerable prophet Samuel long before he actually came to the throne, 1 Sam. 16:1-13, for which God prepared him by the gift of his Spirit, and a long course of vicissitudes and dangers. In his early pastoral life he distinguished himself by his boldness, fidelity, and faith in God; and while yet a youth was summoned to court, as one expert in music, valiant, prudent in behavior, and comely in person. He succeeded in relieving from time to time the mind of king Saul, oppressed by a spirit of melancholy and remorse, and became a favorite attendant, ver. 21; but on the breaking out of war with the Philistines he seems to have been released, and to have returned to take care of his father's flock. Providence soon led him to visit the camp, and gave to his noble valor and faith the victory over the giant champion Goliath. He returned to court crowned with honor, received a command in the army, acquitted himself well on all occasions, and rapidly gained the confidence and love of the people. The jealousy of Saul, however, at length drove him to seek refuge in the wilderness of Judea; where he soon gathered a band of six hundred men, whom he kept in perfect control and employed only against the enemies of the land. He was still pursued by Saul with implacable hostility; and as he would not lift his hand against his king, though he often had him in his power, he at length judged it best to retire into the land of the Philistines. Here he was generously received; but had found the difficulties of his position such as he could not honorably meet, when the death of Saul and Jonathan opened the way for him to the promised throne.

He was at once chosen king over the house of Judah, at Hebron; and after about seven years of hostilities was unanimously chosen king by all the tribes of Israel, and established himself at Jerusalem—the founder of a royal family which continued till the downfall of the Jewish state. His character as a monarch is remarkable for fidelity to God, and to the great purposes for which he was called to so responsible a position. The ark of God he conveyed to the Holy City with the highest demonstrations of honor and of joy. The ordinances of worship were remodelled and provided for with the greatest care. He administered justice to the people with impartiality, and gave a strong impulse to the general prosperity of the nation. His wisdom and energy consolidated the Jewish kingdom; and his warlike skill enabled him not only to resist with success the assaults of invaders, but to extend the bounds of the kingdom over the whole territory promised in prophecy—from the Red sea and Egypt to the Euphrates, Gen. 15:18; Josh. 1:3. With the spoils he took in war he enriched his people, and provided abundant materials for the magnificent temple he purposed to build in honor of Jehovah, but which it was Solomon's privilege to erect.

David did not wholly escape the demoralizing influences of prosperity and unrestricted power. His temptations were numerous and strong; and though his general course was in striking contrast with that of the kings around him, he fell into grievous sins. Like others in those days, he had numerous wives, and his later years were imbittered by the evil results of polygamy. His crimes in the case of Uriah and Bathsheba were heinous indeed; but on awaking from his dream of folly, he repented in dust and ashes, meekly submitted to reproof and punishment, and sought and found mercy from God. Thenceforth frequent afflictions reminded him to be humble and self distrustful. There were discords, profligacy, and murder in his own household. The histories of Tamar, Amnon, and Absalom show what anguish must have rent their father's heart. The rebellions of Absalom, Sheba, and Adonijah, the famine and plague that afflicted his people, the crimes of Joab, etc., led him to cry out, "O that I had wings, like a dove; then would I fly away, and be at rest." Yet his trials bore good fruit. His firmness and decision of character, his humility, nobleness, and piety shine in his last acts, on the occasion of Adonijah's rebellion. His charge to Solomon respecting the forfeited lives of Joab and Shimei, was the voice of justice and not of revenge. His preparations for the building of the temple, and the public service in which he devoted all to Jehovah, and called on all the people to bless the Lord God of their fathers, crown with singular beauty and glory the life of this eminent servant of God. After a reign of forty years, he died at the age of seventy-one.

The mental abilities and acquirements of David were of a high order; his general conduct was marked by generosity, integrity, fortitude, activity, and perseverance; and his religious character eminently adorned by sincere, fervent, and exalted piety. He was statesman, warrior, and poet all in one. In his Psalms he frankly reveals his whole heart. They are inspired poems, containing many prophetic passages, and wonderfully fitted to guide the devotions of the people of God so long as he has a church on earth. Though first sung by Hebrew tongues in the vales of Bethlehem and on the heights of Zion, they sound as sweetly in languages then unknown, and are dear to Christian hearts all round the world In introducing them into the temple service, David added an important means of instruction and edification to the former ritual.

In his kingly character, David was a remarkable type of Christ; and his conquests foreshadowed those of Christ's kingdom. His royal race was spiritually revived in the person of our Saviour, who was descended from him after the flesh, and who is therefore called "the Son of David," and is said to sit upon his throne.

DAY. The day is distinguished into natural, civil, and artificial. The *natural* day is one revolution of the earth on its axis. The *civil* day is that, the beginning and end of which are determined by the custom of any nation. The Hebrews began their day in the evening, Lev. 23:32; the Babylonians at sunrise; and we begin at midnight. The *artificial* day is the time of the sun's continuance above the horizon, which is unequal according to different seasons, on account of the obliquity of the equator. The sacred writers generally divide the day into twelve hours. The sixth hour always ends at noon throughout the year; and the twelfth hour is the last hour before sunset. But in summer, all the hours of the day were longer than in winter, while those of night were shorter. See HOURS, and THREE.

The word day is also often put for an indeterminate period, for the time of Christ's coming in the flesh, and of his second coming to judgment, Isa. 2:12; Ezek. 13:5; John 11:24; 1 Thess. 5:2. The prophetic "day" usually is to be understood as one year, and the prophetic "year" or "time" as 360 days, Ezek. 4:6. Compare the three and a half years of Dan. 7:25, with the forty-two months and twelve hundred and sixty days of Rev. 11:2, 3.

DEA'CON. The original meaning of this word is an attendant, assistant, helper. It is sometimes translated minister, that is, servant, as in Matt. 20:26; 2 Cor. 6:4; Eph. 3:7. Deacons are first mentioned as officers in the Christian church in Acts 6, where it appears that their duty was to collect the alms of the church, and distribute them to such as had a claim upon them, visiting the poor and sick, widows, orphans, and sufferers under persecution, and administering all necessary and proper relief. Of the seven there named, Philip and Stephen are afterwards found laboring as evangelists. The qualifications of deacons are specified in 1 Tim. 3:8-12.

DEA'CONESS. Such women were called deaconesses as served the church in those offices in which the deacons could not with propriety engage; such as keeping the doors of that part of the church where the women sat, privately instructing those of their own sex, and visiting others imprisoned for the faith. In Rom. 16:1, Phebe is said to be a "servant" of the church at Cenchrea; but in the original Greek she is called *deaconess.*

DEAD SEA. See SEA.

DEATH is taken in Scripture, first, for the separation of body and soul, the *first death*, Gen. 25:11; secondly, for alienation from God, and exposure to his wrath, 1 John 3:14, etc.; thirdly, for the *second death*, that of eternal damnation. Death was the penalty affixed to Adam's transgression, Gen. 2:17; 3:19; and all his posterity are transgressors, and share the curse inflicted upon him. CHRIST is "our life." All believers share his life, spiritually and eternally; and though sin and bodily death remain to afflict them, their sting is taken away, and in the resurrection the last enemy shall be trampled under foot, Rom. 5:12-21; 1 Cor. 15.

Natural death is described as a yielding up of the breath, or spirit, *expiring*, Psa. 104:29; as a return to our original dust, Gen. 3:19; Eccl. 12:7; as the soul's laying off the body, its clothing, 2 Cor. 5:3, 4, or the tent in which it has dwelt, 2 Cor. 5:1; 2 Pet. 1:13, 14. The death of the believer is a departure, a going home, a falling asleep in Jesus, Phil. 1:23; Matt. 26:24; John 11:11.

The term death is also sometimes used for any great calamity, or imminent danger threatening life, as persecution, 2 Cor. 1:10. "The gates of death," Job 38:17, signify the unseen world occupied by departed spirits. Death is also figuratively used to denote the insensibility of Christians to the temptations of a sinful world, Col. 3:3.

DE'BIR, *a word, an oracle*, Judg. 1:11, a place called also KIRJATH-SEPHER, a city of books; and KIRJATH-SANNAH, a city of literature, Josh. 15:15, 49. Judging from the names, it appears to have been some sacred place among the Canaanites, and a repository of their records. It was a city in the south-west part of Judea, conquered from the Anakim by Joshua, but recaptured by the Canaanites, and resubdued by Othniel, and afterwards given to the priests, Josh. 10:38, 39; 15:15–17; 21:15. Its site is wholly lost. There was another Debir in Gad, and a third on the border of Benjamin, Josh. 13:26; 15:7.

DEB'ORAH, I., a prophetess, and wife of Lapidoth, judged the Israelites, and dwelt under a palm-tree between Ramah and Bethel, Judg. 4:4, 5. She sent for Barak, directed him to attack Sisera, and promised him victory. Barak, however, refused to go unless she accompanied him, which she did, but told him that the success of the expedition would be imputed to a woman and not to him. After the victory, Deborah composed a splendid triumphal song, which is preserved in Judg. 5.

II. The nurse of Rebekah, whom she accompanied from Aram into Canaan, Gen. 24. At her death, near Bethel, she was buried with honorable marks of affection, Gen. 35:8. There is something very beautiful in this simple and artless record, which would scarcely find a place in our grand histories, treating only of kings, statesmen, and renowned warriors. They seldom take the trouble of erecting a memorial to obscure worth and a long life of humble usefulness.

DEBTOR, one under obligations, whether pecuniary or moral, Matt. 23:16; Rom. 1:14; Gal. 5:3. If the house, cattle, or goods of a Hebrew would not meet his debts, his land might be appropriated for this purpose until the year of Jubilee, or his person might be reduced into servitude till he had paid his debt by his labor, or till the year of Jubilee, which terminated Hebrew bondage in all cases, Lev. 25:29–41; 2 Kin. 4:1; Neh. 5:3–5.

DEC'ALOGUE, the ten principal commandments, Exod. 20:3–17, from the Greek words *deka*, ten, and *logos*, word. The Jews call these precepts, The Ten Words. The usual division of the ten commandments among Protestants, is that which Josephus tells us was employed by the Jews in his day.

DECAP'OLIS, (from the Greek words, *deka*, ten, and *polis*, a city,) a country in Palestine, which contained ten principal cities, on both sides of the Jordan, chiefly the east, Matt. 4:25; Mark 5:20; 7:31. According to Pliny, they were, Scythopolis, Philadelphia, Raphanæ, Gadara, Hippos, Dios, Pella, Gerasa, Canatha, and Damascus. Josephus inserts Otopos instead of Canatha. Though within the limits of Israel, the Decapolis was inhabited by many foreigners, and hence it retained a foreign appellation. This may also account for the numerous herds of swine kept in the district, Matt. 8:30; a practice which was forbidden by the Mosaic law.

DE'DAN, I., the grandson of Cush, Gen. 10:7; and II., the son of Jokshan, Abraham's son by Keturah, Gen. 25:3. Both were founders of tribes frequently named in Scripture. The descendants of the Cushite Dedan are supposed to have settled in southern Arabia, near the Persian gulf, in which there is an island called by the Arabs Daden. The descendants of the Abrahamite Dedan lived in the neighborhood of Idumæa, Jer. 49:8. It is not clear, in all cases where the name occurs, which of the tribes is intended. It was probably the Cushite tribe which was employed in trade. The "travelling companies" of Dedan are mentioned by Isaiah, 21:13. They are also named with the merchants of Tarshish by Ezekiel, 38:13, and were celebrated on account of their trade with the Phœnicians.

DEDICA'TION, a religious ceremony by which any person, place, or thing was devoted to a holy purpose. Thus the tabernacle and the first and second temples were dedicated to God, Ex. 40; I Kin. 8; Ezra 6. The Jews also practised a certain dedication of walls, houses, etc., Deut. 20:5; Neh. 12:27. The "feast of the dedication" was a yearly commemoration of the cleansing and rededication of the temple, when polluted by Antiochus Epiphanes, John 10:22.

DEEP and DEPTHS. The *deep*, or the *great deep*, signifies in Scripture, hell, the place of punishment, the bottomless pit, Luke 8:31, compare Rev. 9:1; 11:7; the grave, Rom. 10:7; the deepest parts of the sea, Psa. 69:15; 107:26; chaos in the beginning of the world, Gen. 1:2. See HELL.

DEER, a wild quadruped, of a middle

THE FALLOW-DEER.

size between the stag and the roebuck; its horns turn inward, and are large and flat. The fallow-deer is naturally very timorous: it was reputed clean, and good for food, Deut. 14:5. Young deer are noticed in Proverbs, Songs, and Isaiah, as beautiful creatures, and very swift, Prov. 5:19. See HIND.

DEFILE', DEFILE'MENT. Many were the blemishes of person and conduct which, under the Jewish ceremonial law, were esteemed defilements; some were voluntary, some involuntary; some were inevitable, being defects of nature, others the consequences of personal transgression. Under the gospel, defilements are those of the heart, of the mind, the temper, the conduct. Moral defilements are as numerous, and as strongly prohibited under the gospel as ever, though ceremonial defilements have ceased, Matt. 15:18; Rom. 1:24. See CLEAN.

DEGREES', PSALMS OF, is the title prefixed to fifteen psalms, from Psa. 120 to Psa. 134 inclusive. Of this title commentators have proposed a variety of explanations. The most probable are the following: First, *pilgrim songs*, sung by the Israelites while going up to Jerusalem to worship; compare Psa. 122:4; but to this explanation the contents of only a few of these psalms are appropriate, as for instance, of Psa. 122. Secondly, others suppose the title to refer to a species of rhythm in these psalms; by which the sense *ascends*, as it were, by degrees, one member or clause frequently repeating the words with which the preceding member closes. Thus in Psa. 121,

1. I will lift up mine eyes unto the hills,
From whence cometh *my help*.

2. *My help* cometh from the Lord,
Who made heaven and earth.

3. He will not suffer thy foot to be moved;
Thy *keeper* will *not slumber*.

4. Lo, *not slumber* nor sleep will the *keeper* of Israel.

But this solution does not well apply to all these psalms.

DEHA'VITES, a people beyond the Euphrates, who furnished colonists for Samaria, 2 Kin. 17:24; Ezra 4:9; supposed to be the Dahæ, on the east of the Caspian sea, and under the Persian government.

DELI'LAH, a Philistine woman, whom Samson loved, and who betrayed him to the enemies of Israel, Judg. 16.

DEL'UGE, that universal flood which was sent upon the earth in the time of Noah, and from which there were but eight persons saved. Moses' account of this event is recorded in Gen. 6-8. See ARK OF NOAH. The sins of mankind were the cause of the deluge; and most commentators agree to place it A. M. 1656, B. C. 2348. After the door of the ark had been closed upon those that were to be saved, the deluge commenced: it rained forty days; "the fountains of the great deep were broken up, and the windows of heaven were opened." All men and all creatures living on the land perished, except Noah and those with him. For five months the waters continued to rise, and reached fifteen cubits above the highest summits to which any could fly for refuge; "a shoreless ocean tumbled round the world." At length the waters began to abate; the highest land appeared, and the ark touched ground upon mount Ararat. In three months more the hills began to appear. Forty days after, Noah tested the state of the earth's surface by sending out a raven; and then thrice, at intervals of a week, a dove. At length he removed the covering of the ark, and found the flood had disappeared; he came forth from the ark, reared an altar, and offered sacrifices to God, who appointed the rainbow as a pledge that he would no more destroy mankind with a flood.

Since all nations have descended from the family then preserved in the ark, it is natural that the memory of such an event should be perpetuated in various national traditions. Such is indeed the fact. These traditions have been found among the Egyptians, Chaldeans, Phœnicians, Greeks, Hindoos, Chinese, Japanese, Scythians, and Celts, and in the western hemisphere among the Mexicans, Peruvians, and South sea islanders. Much labor has been expended in searching for natural causes adequate to the production of a deluge; but we should beware of endeavoring to account on natural principles for that which the Bible represents as *miraculous*.

In the New Testament, the deluge is spoken of as a stupendous exhibition of divine power, like the creation and the final burning of the world. It is applied to illustrate the long suffering of God, and assure us of his judgment on sin, 2 Pet. 3:5–7, and of the second coming of Christ, Matt. 24:38.

DE'MAS, a fellow-laborer with Paul at Thessalonica, who afterwards deserted him, either discouraged by the hardships of the work, or allured by the love of the world, Col. 4 : 14; 2 Tim. 4 : 10; Phile. 24.

DEME'TRIUS, I., a goldsmith of Ephesus, who made models of the famous temple of Diana at Ephesus, which he sold to foreigners, Acts 19 : 24–41. Observing the progress of the gospel, not in Ephesus only, but in the regions around, he assembled his fellow-craftsmen, and represented that, by this new doctrine, not only their trade would suffer, but the worship of the great Diana of Ephesus was in danger of being entirely forsaken. This produced an uproar and riot in the city, which the town-clerk with difficulty appeased by firmness and persuasion.

II. A disciple, and probably a minister, of high repute, 3 John 12. He may have been formerly the silversmith of Ephesus; but this can be neither proved nor disproved.

DER'BE, a small town of Lycaonia, in Asia Minor, to which Paul and Barnabas fled from Lystra, A. D. 41, Acts 14 : 20. It lay at the foot of the Taurus mountains on the north, sixteen or twenty miles east of Lystra. The two missionaries gained many disciples here, and among them perhaps Gaius, who afterwards labored with Paul, Acts 14:21; 20:4.

DES'ERT. The Scriptures, by "desert," generally mean an uncultivated place, a wilderness, or grazing tract. Some deserts were entirely dry and barren; others were beautiful, and had good pastures. David speaks of the beauty of the desert, Psa. 65 : 12, 13. Scripture names several deserts in the Holy Land. Other deserts particularly mentioned, are "that great and terrible wilderness" in Arabia Petræa, south of Canaan, Num. 21 : 20; also the region between Canaan and the Euphrates, Ex. 23 : 31; Deut. 11 : 24. The pastures of this wilderness are clothed in winter and spring with rich and tender herbage; but the heat of summer soon burns this up, and the Arabs are driven to seek pasturage elsewhere.

DEUTERON'OMY, or the repetition of the law, the fifth book of the Pentateuch, so called by the Greeks, because in it Moses recapitulates what he had ordained in the preceding books, Deut. 1:1–6; 29:1; 31:1; 33. This book contains the history of what passed in the wilderness from the beginning of the eleventh month, to the seventh day of the twelfth month, in the fortieth year after the Israelites' departure from Egypt, that is, about six weeks, B. C. 1451. That part which mentions the death of Moses was added afterwards, very probably by Joshua.

The book of Deuteronomy is the sublime and precious valedictory address of the inspired "man of God," now venerable for his age and experience, and standing almost in the gate of heaven. He gives the people of God his fatherly counsel and blessing, and then goes up into mount Pisgah alone to die. He recounts the dealings of God with them; recapitulates his laws; shows them why they should love him, and how they should serve him. It is full of tender solicitude, wise instruction, faithful warning, and the zealous love of a patriot and a prophet for the people of God, whom he had borne on his heart so long. It is often quoted by later inspired writers, and by our Lord, Matt. 4:4, 7, 10.

DEV'IL, a fallen angel; and particularly the chief of them, *the devil*, or Satan. He is the great principle of evil in the world; and it is his grand object to counteract the good which God desires to do. He exerts himself, especially with his angels, to draw away the souls of men from embracing salvation through Jesus Christ.

His name signifies the calumniator, or false accuser; as the Hebrew Satan means the adversary. But the Scriptures give him various other appellations descriptive of his character. He is called, "The prince of this world," John 12:31; "The prince of the power of the air," Eph. 2:2; "The god of this world," 2 Cor. 4:4; "The dragon, that old serpent, the devil," Rev. 20:2; "That wicked one," 1 John 5:18; "A roaring lion," 1 Pet. 5:8; "A murderer," "a liar," John 8:44; "Beelzebub," Matt. 12:24; "Belial," 2 Cor. 6:15; "The accuser of the brethren," Rev. 12:10. He is everywhere shown to be full of malignity, cruelty, and deceit, hating God and man. He is ceaselessly active in his efforts to destroy souls, and uses innumerable devices and wiles to adapt his temptations to the varying characters and conditions of men, enticing wicked men, and even good men at times, as well as his own angels, to aid in his work. Almost the whole world has been under his sway. But he is a doomed foe. Christ shall bruise the serpent's head; shall dispossess him from the world, as he has done from individuals, and at length confine him for ever in the place prepared for him and his angels, Matt. 25:41.

The word "devils" occurs frequently in the gospels; but it is the translation of a different Greek word from that used to denote the devil, and might be rendered "demons." The Bible applies the other word only to Satan—"the devil, and his angels," who are like their leader in nature and in actions. There are many examples in the New Testament of persons *possessed* by demons. These are often called *demoniacs*. Some have argued that these were afflicted by natural diseases, such as epilepsy, insanity, etc., and were not possessed by evil spirits. But our Saviour speaks to and commands the demons who actuated the possessed, which demons answered and obeyed, and gave proofs of their presence by tormenting those whom they were obliged to quit. Christ alleges, as proof of his mission, that the demons are cast out; he promises his apostles the same power that he himself exercised against those wicked spirits. Campbell says, "When I find mention made of the number of demons in particular possessions, their actions so particularly distinguished from the actions of the man possessed, conversations held by the former in regard to the disposal of them after their expulsion, and accounts given how they were actually disposed of—when I find desires and passions ascribed particularly to them, and similitudes taken from the conduct which they usually observe, it is impossible for me to deny their existence."

DEW. The dews in Palestine and some other oriental countries are very copious, and serve very greatly to sustain and promote vegetation in seasons when little or no rain falls. Maundrell tells us that the tents of his company, when pitched on Tabor and Hermon, "were as wet with dew as if it had rained on them all night," Judg. 6:38; Song 5:2. Dew was especially heavy near the mountains, and just before and after the rainy season. It was prized as a precious boon of Providence, Gen. 27:28; Deut. 33:28; 1 Kin. 17:1; Job 29:19; Hag. 1:10; Zech. 8:12. The dew furnishes the sacred penmen with many beautiful allusions, Deut. 32:2; 2 Sam. 17:12; Psa. 110:3; Prov. 19:12; Hos. 14:5; Mic. 5:7.

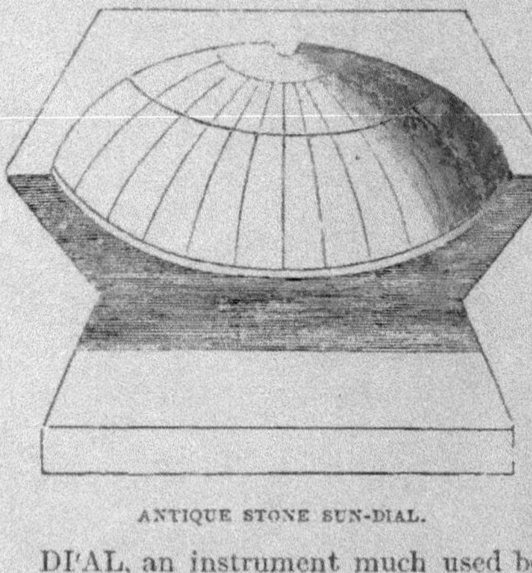

ANTIQUE STONE SUN-DIAL.

DI'AL, an instrument much used before the invention of clocks, to tell the time of day by the progress of the sun's shadow. The dial of Ahaz, 2 Kin. 20:11; Isa. 38:1–9, seems to have been peculiar either in structure or size, and was perhaps borrowed from Babylon or Damascus, 2 Kin. 16:10. The causing the shadow upon it to go back ten degrees, to assure king Hezekiah of his recovery from sickness, was probably effected not by arresting and turning backwards the revolution of the earth, but by a miraculous refraction of the sun's rays, observed only in Judea, though the fame of it reached Babylon, 2 Chr. 32:31.

DI'AMOND, the hardest and most brilliant of gems, very rare and costly. The largest diamonds known in the world, procured from India and Brazil, are guarded among the royal treasures of England, Russia, etc., and valued at immense sums. Common diamonds are used not only for ornaments, but for cutting and graving hard substances, Jer. 17:1. The Hebrew word here used is called "adamant" in Ezek. 3:9; Zech. 7:12. See ADAMANT. There is another Hebrew word also translated "diamond," Ex. 28:18; 39:11; Ezek. 28:13, and thought by some to mean the topaz. The diamond is *carbon* in its purest and crystalline form.

DIAN'A, or AR'TEMIS, a celebrated goddess of the Romans and Greeks, and one of their twelve superior deities. In the heavens she was Luna, (the moon,) on earth Diana, in the unseen world Hecate. She was invoked by women in childbirth under the name of Lucina. She was usually represented with a crescent on her head, a bow in her hand, and dressed in a hunting-habit, because she was said to preside over forests and hunting. Diana was said to be the daughter of Jupiter by Latona, and twin sister of Apollo. As Hecate, she was regarded as sanguinary and pitiless; as goddess of hunting and the forests, she was chaste, but haughty and vindictive; as associated with the moon, she was capricious and wanton. The Diana of Ephesus was like the Syrian goddess Ashtoreth, and appears to have been worshipped with impure rites and magical mysteries, Acts 19:19. Her image, fabled to have fallen down from Jupiter in heaven, seems to have been a block of wood tapering to the foot, with a female bust above covered with many breasts, the head crowned with turrets, and each hand resting on a staff. It was of great antiquity, and highly venerated.

The temple of this goddess was the pride and glory of Ephesus. It was 425 feet long, and 220 broad, and had 127 columns of white marble, each 60 feet high. Its treasures were of immense value. It was 220 years in building, and was one of the seven wonders of the world. In the year when Alexander the Great was born, B. C. 356, it was burned down by one Herostratus, in order to immortalize his name, but was afterwards rebuilt with even greater splendor. The "silver shrines for Diana," made by Demetrius and others, were probably small models of the same for domestic use, and for sale to travellers and visitors. Ancient coins of Ephesus represent the shrine and statue of Diana, with a Greek inscription, meaning "of the Ephesians," Acts 19:28, 34, 35.

DI'BON, DI'MON, Isa. 15:9, and DIBON-GAD', Num. 33:45, 46, a town of Gad, Num. 32:34, but afterwards of Reuben, Josh. 13:17. It lay in a plain just north of the Arnon, and was the first encampment of the Israelites upon crossing that river. Later we find it in the hands of the Moabites, Isa. 15:2; Jer. 48:22. Traces of it remain at a place now called Diban.

DIK'LAH, a tribe descended from Joktan, Gen. 10:27, and dwelling in Southern Arabia, or perhaps near the head of the Persian gulf.

DI'NAH, daughter of Jacob by Leah, Gen. 30:21, his only daughter named in Scripture. While the family were sojourning near Shalem, she heedlessly associated with the Canaanitish maidens, and fell a victim to the seductive arts of Shechem, a young prince of the land; but was perfidiously and savagely avenged by Simeon and Levi, her full brothers, to the great grief of Jacob their father, Gen. 34; 49:5, 7. She seems to have gone with the family to Egypt, Gen. 46:15.

DIONYS'IUS, a member of the court of the Areopagus at Athens, converted under the preaching of Paul, Acts 17:34. Tradition says that he was eminent for learning, that he was ordained by Paul at Athens, and after many labors and trials, suffered martyrdom by fire. The works ascribed to him are spurious, being the product of some unknown writer in the fourth or fifth century.

DIOT'REPHES, an influential member, perhaps minister, of some early church, censured by John for his jealous ambition, and his violent rejection of the best Christians, 3 John 9, 10.

DISCERN'ING OF SPIRITS, 1 Cor. 12:10, a miraculous gift of the Holy Ghost to certain of the early church, empowering them to judge of the real character of those who professed to love Christ, and to be inspired to teach in his name, 1 John 4:1; 2 John 7. Compare Acts 5:1–10; 13:6–12.

DISCI'PLE, *a scholar*, Matt. 10:24. In the New Testament it is applied principally to the followers of Christ; sometimes to those of John the Baptist, Matt. 9:14, and of the Pharisees, Matt. 22:16. It is used in a special manner to point out the twelve, Matt. 10:1; 11:1; 20:17. A disciple of Christ may now be defined as one who believes his doctrine, rests upon his sacrifice, imbibes his spirit, imitates his example, and lives to do his work.

DISCOV'ER, Mic. 1:6, to uncover, or lay bare.

DISEAS'ES were introduced into the world by sin, and have been greatly increased by the prevalence of corrupt, indolent, and luxurious habits. Besides the natural causes of diseases, evil spirits were charged with producing them among the Hebrews, Job 2:7; Mark 9:17; Luke 13:16; 2 Cor. 12:7. The pious Jews recognized the hand of God in sending them, Psa. 39:9–11; 90:3–12; and in many cases special diseases were sent in punishment of particular sins, as Abimelech, Gehazi, Jehoram, Uzziah, Miriam, Herod, the Philistines, etc., and those who partook of the Lord's supper unworthily, 1 Cor. 11:30. Christ manifested his divine goodness and power by healing every form of disease; and in these cases, as in that of king Asa, 2 Chr. 16:12, it is shown that all the skill of physicians is in vain without God's blessing. The prevalent diseases in Bible lands were malignant fevers, cutaneous diseases, palsy, dysentery, and ophthalmia. Almost every form of bodily disease has a counterpart in the maladies of the soul.

DISPENSA'TION, the charge of proclaiming the gospel of Christ, 1 Cor. 9:17; Eph. 3:2. Also the scheme or plan of God's dealings with men. In the Patriarchal, Mosaic, and Christian dispensations, God has commenced, enlarged, and perfected his revelation of himself and his grace to this world, Eph. 1:10; Col. 1:25. The whole development of his great plan has been gradual, and adapted at every stage to the existing state of the human family.

DIVINA'TION. The Eastern people were fond of divination, magic, and the pretended art of interpreting dreams and acquiring a knowledge of futurity. When Moses published the law, this disposition had long been common in Egypt and the neighboring countries; and to correct the Israelites' inclination to consult diviners, wizards, fortune-tellers, and interpreters of dreams, it was forbidden them under very severe penalties, and the true spirit of prophecy was promised to them as infinitely superior, Ex. 22:18; Lev. 19:26, 31; 20:27. Those were to be stoned who pretended to have a familiar spirit, or the spirit of divination, Deut. 18:9–12; and the prophecies are full of invectives against the Israelites who consulted such, as well as against false prophets, who seduced the people, Isa. 8:19; 47:11–14; Ezek. 13:6–9. A fresh impulse to these superstitions was gained from intercourse with the Chaldeans, during the reign of the later kings of Judah and the captivities in Babylon, 2 Kin. 21:6; 2 Chr. 33:6. See MAGIC, SORCERERS.

Divination was of several kinds: by water, fire, earth, air; by the flight of birds, and their singing; by lots, dreams, arrows, clouds, entrails of sacrifices, pretended communication with spirits, etc., Ezek. 21:21.

DIVORCE' was tolerated by Moses for sufficient reasons, Deut. 24:1–4; but our Lord has limited it to the single case of adultery, Matt. 5:31, 32.

DOC'TOR OF THE LAW may perhaps be distinguished from SCRIBE, as rather teaching orally, than giving written opinions, Luke 2:46. It implies one learned in the *divine* law. Doctors of the law were mostly of the sect of the Pharisees, but are distinguished from that sect in Luke 5:17, where it appears that the novelty of our Saviour's teaching drew together a great company both of Pharisees and doctors of the law.

DOD'ANIM, or RODANIM, 1 Chr. 1:7, a people descended from Japhet through Javan, Gen. 10:4. They are associated, by the above passage, and by dim etymological inferences, with the island of Rhodes or some location on the north coast of the Mediterranean.

DO'EG, an Edomite, overseer of Saul's flocks. At Nob he witnessed the relief kindly furnished to David when fleeing from Saul, by Ahimelech the high-priest, and carried a malicious and distorted report of it to his master. The king gladly seized the opportunity to wreak his passion on a helpless victim; and when the Jews around him refused to slay the priests of God, infamously used the willing services of this alien and heathen. Doeg not only slew Ahimelech and eighty-four other priests, but put the town in which they dwelt to the sword, 1 Sam. 21; 22. David forebodes his wretched fate, Psa. 52; 120; 140.

DOGS were held in great contempt by the Jews, but were worshipped, as well as cats, by the Egyptians. Among the Jews, to compare a person to a dog was the most degrading expression possible, 1 Sam. 17:43; 24:14; 2 Sam. 9:8. The state of dogs among the Jews was the same that now prevails in the East, where, having no owners, they run about the streets in troops, and are fed by charity or caprice, or live on such offal as they can pick up. As they are often on the point of starvation, they devour corpses, and in the night even attack living men, Psa. 59:6, 14, 15; 1 Kin. 14:11. In various places in Scripture the epithet "dogs" is given to certain classes of men, as expressing their insolent rapacity, Matt. 7:6; Psa. 22:16; Phil. 3:2, and their beastly vices, Deut. 23:18; 2 Pet. 2:22; Rev. 22:15.

DOR, a royal city of the Canaanites, on the Mediterranean between Cæsarea and mount Carmel; after the conquest it was assigned to Manasseh, Josh. 11:2; 12:23; 17:11; 1 Kin. 4:11; 1 Chr. 7:29. There is now a small port there, with about 500 inhabitants.

DOR'CAS in Greek, the same as TABITHA in Syriac, that is, *gazelle*, the name of a pious and charitable woman at Joppa, whom Peter raised from the dead, Acts 9:36-42.

DO'THAN, or DOTHA'IN, the place where Joseph was sold to the Ishmaelites, Gen. 37:17, and where the Syrians were smitten with blindness at Elisha's word, 2 Kin. 6:13. It was on the caravan-route from Syria to Egypt, about eleven miles north of Samaria.

DOVES were clean according to the Mosaic ritual, and were offered in sacrifice, especially by the poor, Gen. 15:9; Lev. 5:7; 12:6-8; Luke 2:24. Several kinds of doves or pigeons frequented the

THE EASTERN CARRIER-DOVE.

Holy Land; and the immense flocks of them sometimes witnessed illustrate a passage in Isaiah, 60:8. They are symbols of simplicity, innocence, and fidelity, Hos. 7:11; Matt. 10:16. The dove was the chosen harbinger of God's returning favor after the flood, Gen. 8, and was honored as an emblem of the Holy Spirit, Matt. 3:16. See TURTLEDOVE.

DOVES' DUNG. It is said, 2 Kin. 6:25, that during the siege of Samaria, "the fourth part of a cab," little more than half a pint, "of doves' dung was sold for five pieces of silver," about two and a half dollars. As doves' dung is not a nourishment for man, even in the most extreme famine, the general opinion is, that it was a kind of chick-pea, lentil, or tare, which has very much the appearance of doves' dung. Great quantities of these are sold in Cairo to the pilgrims going to Mecca; and at Damascus there are many shops where nothing else is done but preparing chick-peas. These, parched in a copper pan, and dried, are of great service to those who take long journeys.

DOW'RY. In eastern countries the bridegroom was required to pay the father of his betrothed a stipulated portion, in money or other valuables, proportioned to the rank and station of the family to which she belonged; this was the dowry. Jacob purchased his wives by his services to their father, Gen. 29:18-27; 34:12; Ex. 22:16-17; 1 Sam. 18:25; Hos. 3:2.

DRAG'ON answers, in the English Bible, to the Hebrew word signifying a sea-monster, huge serpent, etc. Thus in Deut. 32:33, Jer. 51:34, and Rev. 12, it evidently implies a huge serpent; in Isa. 27:1; 51:9; Ezek. 29:3, it may mean the crocodile, or any large sea-monster; while in Job 30:29; Lam. 4:3; Mic. 1:8, it seems to refer to some wild animal of the desert, most probably the jackal. The animal known to modern naturalists under the name of dragon, is a harmless species of lizard, found in Asia and Africa.

DRAG'ON-WELL, Neh. 2:13; probably the fountain of Gihon, on the west side of Jerusalem.

DRAM, Ezra 2:69, a gold coin of Persia, worth about five dollars.

DRAUGHT, a cess-pool or receptacle for filth, 2 Kin. 10 : 27; Matt. 15 : 17. Also, all the fishes taken at one drawing of a net, Luke 5:9.

DREAM. The orientals, and in particular the Jews, greatly regarded dreams, and applied for their interpretation to those who undertook to explain them. We see the antiquity of this custom in the history of Pharaoh's butler and baker, Gen. 40; and Pharaoh himself and Nebuchadnezzar are also instances. God expressly forbade his people to observe dreams, and to consult explainers of them. He condemned to death all who pretended to have prophetic dreams, even though what they foretold came to pass, if they had any tendency to promote idolatry, Deut. 13:1-3. But they were not forbidden, when they thought they had a significant dream, to address the prophets of the Lord, or the high-priest in his ephod, to have it explained. The Lord frequently made known his will in dreams, and enabled persons to explain them, Gen. 20:3-7; 28:12-15; 1 Sam. 28:6; Dan. 2; Joel 2:28; Matt. 1:20; Acts 27:22. Supernatural dreams are distinguished from visions, in that the former occurred during sleep, and the latter when the person was awake. God spoke to Abimelech in a dream, but to Abraham by vision. In both cases he left on the mind an assurance of the certainty of whatever he revealed. Both are now superseded by the Bible, our sure and sufficient guide through earth to heaven.

DREGS. See LEES.

DRESS'ES. See GARMENTS.

DRINK'-OFFERING, a small quantity of wine, part of which was to be poured on the sacrifice or meat-offering, and the residue given to the priests, Ex. 29:40; Lev. 23:18; Num. 15:5, 7. It may have been appointed as an acknowledgment that all the blessings of the earth are from God, Gen. 35:14.

DROM'EDARY. See CAMEL.

DROUGHT was an evil to which Palestine was naturally subject, as no rain fell from May to September. During these months of summer, the ground became parched and cleft, the streams and springs became dry, and vegetation was kept from extinction by the dews at night and by artificial irrigation. If rain did not come in its season and abundantly, the distress was general and dreadful. A drought therefore is threatened as one of God's sorest judgments, Job 24:19; Jer. 50:38; Joel 1:10-20; Hag. 1:11; and there are many allusions to its horrors in Scripture, Deut. 28:23; Psa. 32:4; 102:4.

DRUNK'ENNESS is referred to in the Bible both in single instances and as a habit. Its folly is often illustrated, Psa. 107:27; Isa. 19:14; 24:20; 28:7, 8, its guilt denounced, Isa. 5:22, its ill results traced, 1 Sam. 25:36; 1 Kin. 16:9; 20:16, and its doom shown, 1 Cor 6:9, 10. It is produced by wine, Gen. 9:21; 21:33; Jer. 23:9; Eph. 5:18, as well as by "strong drink," 1 Sam. 1:13-15; Isa. 5:11. Hence the use of these was forbidden to the priests at the altar, Lev. 10:9; and all are cautioned to avoid them, Prov. 20:1; 23:30. To tempt others to drunkenness is a sin accursed of God, 2 Sam. 11:13; Hab. 2:15, 16. Its prevalence in a community is inseparable from the habitual use of any inebriating liquor. Hence the efforts made by the wise and good to secure abstinence from all intoxicating drinks, 1 Cor. 8:13. See WINE.

DRUSIL'LA, the youngest daughter of Herod Agrippa I., and sister of the younger Agrippa and Bernice, celebrated for her beauty and infamous for her licentiousness. She was first espoused to Epiphanes, son of Antiochus king of Comagena, on condition of his embracing the Jewish religion; but as he afterwards refused to be circumcised, Drusilla was given in marriage by her brother to Azizus king of Emessa. When Felix came as governor of Judea, he persuaded her to abandon her husband and her religion, and become his wife. Paul bore testimony before them to the truth of the Christian religion, Acts 24:24. She and her son afterwards perished in an eruption of Vesuvius.

DUKE. In Gen. 36:15–43, is a long list of "dukes" of Edom; but the word duke, from the Latin *dux*, merely signifies a leader, and not an order of nobility; and the word chief or sheikh would have been preferable in our translation, 1 Chr. 1:51.

DUL'CIMER, Dan. 3:5, 10, an instrument of music, which the rabbins describe as a sort of bagpipe, composed of two pipes connected with a leathern sack, and of a harsh, screaming sound. The modern dulcimer is an instrument of a triangular form, strung with about fifty wires, and struck with an iron key while lying on the table before the performer. See MUSIC.

DU'MAH, a tribe and country of the Ishmaelites in Arabia, Gen. 25:14; 1 Chr. 1:30; Isa. 21:11. This is doubtless the same which is still called by the Arabs "Duma the stony" and "the Syrian Duma," situated on the confines of the Arabian and Syrian desert, with a fortress.

DUNG. Among the Israelites, the dung of animals was used not only for manure, but, when dried, for fuel. In districts where wood is scarce, the inhabitants are very careful in collecting the dung of camels or asses; it is mixed with chopped straw, and dried. It is not unusual to see a whole village with portions of this material adhering to the walls of the cottages to dry; and towards the end of autumn it is piled in conical heaps or stacks on the roof. It is employed in heating ovens, and for other similar purposes, Ezek. 4:12–16. The use of dung for manure is intimated in Isa. 25:10.

DU'RA, the plain in Babylon where Nebuchadnezzar set up his golden image, Dan. 3:1.

DUST, Josh. 7:6. Dust or ashes put upon the head was a sign of mourning; sitting in the dust, a sign of affliction, Lam. 3:29; Isa. 47:1. "Dust" is also put for the grave, Gen. 3:19; Job 7:21. It signifies a multitude, Gen. 13:16, and a low and mean condition, 1 Sam. 2:8. We have two remarkable instances of casting dust recorded in Scripture, and they seem to illustrate a practice common in Asia: those who demanded justice against a criminal were accustomed to throw dust upon him, signifying that he deserved to be cast into the grave. Shimei cast dust upon David when he fled from Jerusalem, 2 Sam. 16:13. The Jews treated the apostle Paul in a similar manner in the same city: "They cried out, 'Away with such a fellow from the earth; for it is not fit that he should live.' And as they cried out, and cast off their clothes, and threw dust into the air, the chief captain commanded him to be brought into the castle," Acts 22:22–24. To shake off the dust of the feet against another was expressive of entire renunciation, Matt. 10:14; Mark 6:11; Acts 13:51. The threatening of God, recorded in Deut. 28:24, "The Lord shall make the rain of thy land powder and dust: from heaven shall it come down upon thee, until thou be destroyed," means that instead of fertilizing rains, clouds of fine dust, raised from the parched ground and driven by fierce and burning winds, shall fill the air. Of such a rain of dust, famine and disease would be the natural attendants. See WIND.

E.

EA'GLE, Job 39:27-30, a large and very powerful bird of prey, hence called the King of birds. There are several species of eagle described by naturalists,

and it is probable that this word in the Bible comprehends more than one of these. The noble eastern species, called by Mr. Bruce "the golden eagle," measures eight feet four inches from wing to wing; and from the tip of his tail to the point of his beak, when dead, four feet seven inches. Of all known birds, the eagle flies not only the highest, Prov. 23:5; Jer. 49:16; Obad. 4, but also with the greatest rapidity. To this circumstance there are several striking allusions in the sacred volume, 2 Sam. 1:23; Job 9:26; Lam. 4:19. Among the evils threatened to the Israelites in case of their disobedience, the prophet names one in the following terms: "The Lord shall bring a nation against thee from far, from the end of the earth, as swift as the eagle flieth," Deut. 28:49. The march of Nebuchadnezzar against Jerusalem, is predicted in similar terms: "Behold, he shall come up as clouds, and his chariots as a whirlwind: his horses are swifter than eagles," Jer. 4:13; 48:40; 49:22; Hos. 8:1. This bird was a national emblem on Persian and Roman standards, as it now is on United States' coins.

The eagle, it is said, lives to a great age; and like other birds of prey, sheds his feathers in the beginning of spring, after which his old age assumes the appearance of youth. To this David alludes, when gratefully reviewing the mercies of Jehovah: "Who satisfieth thy mouth with good things, so that thy youth is renewed like the eagle's," Psa. 103:5; Isa. 40:31. The careful pains of the eagle in teaching its young to fly, beautifully illustrate God's providential care over Israel, Ex. 19:4; Deut. 32:11, 12.

The eagle is remarkable for its keen sight and scent. Its flesh, like that of all birds of prey, was unclean to the Jews; and is never eaten by any body, unless in cases of necessity, Matt. 24:28; Luke 17:37.

EAR'ING, an old agricultural term for ploughing. Thus, in Isa. 30:24, it is said, "The oxen also, and the young asses which *ear*," that is, *plough*, "the ground." So also in Gen. 45:6; Exod. 34:21; Deut. 21:4; 1 Sam. 8:12.

EAR'NEST, a pledge of the performance of a promise; or part of a debt, paid in assurance of the payment of the whole; or part of the price, paid down to confirm a bargain; or part of a servant's wages, paid at the time of hiring, to ratify the engagement. In the New Testament it describes the gifts of God to his people here, as the assurance and commencement of the far superior blessings of the life to come, 2 Cor. 1:22; 5:5; Eph. 1:13, 14.

EAR'-RINGS. See RINGS.

EARTH. In both Hebrew and Greek the same word is used to denote the earth as a whole, and a particular land. Only the context can enable us to decide in which of these senses it is to be taken in a given passage. Thus in Matt. 27:45 we might, so far as the original word is concerned, render either "there was darkness over all the land," or over all the earth. The expression "all the earth" is sometimes used hyperbolically for a large portion of it, Ezra 1:2. The word is used of the whole world, or its surface, in distinction from the heavens; of the mould or arable land of the world; of the people who inhabit the world, etc. In a moral sense, earthly is opposed to what is heavenly, spiritual and holy, John 3:31; 1 Cor. 15:47; Col. 3:2; James 3:15. "The lower parts of the earth," means the unseen world of the dead, Psa. 63:9; Isa. 44:23; Eph. 4:9.

EARTH'QUAKE, a convulsion of the earth common in volcanic regions, and well known in all parts of the world; probably occasioned by the action of internal heat or fire. Scripture speaks of several earthquakes, Num. 16; 1 Kin. 19:11, 12. One occurred in the twenty-seventh year of Uzziah king of Judah, and is mentioned in Amos 1:1; Zech. 14:5. A very memorable earthquake was that at our Saviour's death, Matt. 27.51, which some suppose extended throughout the world. Palestine has been often visited by earthquakes. So late as 1837 one occurred in the vicinity of the sea of Galilee, by which about a third part of Tiberias was destroyed, and thousands of people perished there and in the towns near by. Earthquakes were among the calamities foretold as connected with the destruction of Jerusalem, Matt. 24:7; and history proves the truth of the prediction.

The word earthquake is also used figuratively to denote God's power and wrath, as in Psa. 18:7; 46:2; 104:32, etc.; and as an emblem of a great civil or national catastrophe, Matt. 24:7, 29; Rev. 16:18, 19.

EAST. The Hebrews, in speaking of the different quarters of the heaven, always suppose the face to be turned towards the east. Hence "before," or "forwards," means the east; "behind" is the west, the right-hand is south, and the left-hand, north. Besides the ordinary meanings of the word east, Josh. 4:19; Psa. 103:12, the Jews often used it to designate a large region lying north-east and south-east as well as east of Palestine, including Syria and Arabia near at hand, and Babylonia, Assyria, Armenia, etc., with the whole region from the Caspian sea to the Arabian gulf, Gen. 29:1; Num. 23:7; Judg. 6:3; 7:12; 8:10. The wise men who visited the infant Saviour dwelt somewhere in this region; and being "in the east," saw his star—not east of them, but in the direction to guide them to Jerusalem, Matt. 2:1, 2.

EAST WIND. See WIND.

EASTER is improperly put for PASSOVER, Acts 12:4; Passover being the name of the ancient Jewish festival here referred to; while Easter, from the Saxon goddess Eostre, is the modern name of a Christian festival, in commemoration of the events of Passover-week, and fixed at the same period of the year.

EATING. The Jews would have considered themselves polluted by eating with people of another religion, or with any who were ceremonially unclean or disreputable—as with Samaritans, John 4:9, publicans, Matt. 9:11, or Gentiles, Acts 10:28; Gal. 2:12. Eating together was an established token of mutual confidence and friendship, a pledge of friendly relations between families, which their children were expected to perpetuate. The rites of hospitality were held sacred; and to this day, among the Arabs, a fugitive is safe for the time, if he gains the shelter of even an enemy's tent. The abuse of hospitality was a great crime, Psa. 41:9.

To "eat" a book, is to make its precepts, promises, and spirit one's own, Jer. 15:16; Ezek. 3:1; John 4:14; Rev. 10:9. So to eat Christ's flesh and drink his blood, is to receive him as a Saviour, and by a living faith to be imbued with his truth, his Spirit, and his heavenly life, John 6:32-58.

EATING, MODE OF. The Hebrews anciently *sat* at their meals, Gen. 43:33; 1 Sam. 9:22; 20:25; Psa. 128:3; but afterwards adopted the practice of reclining on table-beds or divans, like the Persians, Chaldeans, Romans, etc., Amos 6:4. The accompanying engraving of a

Roman triclinium, *three beds*, will illustrate several points obscure to the modern reader of the Bible. It will be seen that three low tables are so placed as to form three sides of a hollow square accessible to the waiters. Around these tables are placed, not seats, but couches, or beds, one to each table, formed of mattresses stuffed, and often highly ornamented, Est. 1:6; 7:1, 8. The guests reclined with their heads to the table, each one leaning on his left elbow, and therefore using principally his right hand in taking food. Observe also that the feet of the person reclining being towards the external edge of the bed, they were much more readily reached by any one passing than any other part of the person so reclining, Luke 7:36–50; John 12:3.

This mode of reclining at table rendered it easy for our Lord to wash the feet of his disciples at the last supper, John 13:5-12, and "wipe them with the towel wherewith he was girded." It also explains the position of John at the same supper; for if he reclined next in front of the SAVIOUR, he lay as it were in his bosom, John 13:23, 25, and might readily lean back his head upon the Saviour's breast.

It is unknown, however, how far or how long this custom displaced the primitive eastern mode still prevalent in Palestine and vicinity. The ordinary table was no more than a circular skin or carpet spread upon the floor, around which the family sat on the floor, or on rugs or cushions. Sometimes there was a small table in the centre, raising the principal dish a little above the floor.

The meals of the Jews were generally two, loosely distinguished as dinner and supper, Luke 14:12; John 21:12. The first meal was usually light, consisting of milk, cheese, bread, or fruits, and eaten at various hours from early morning to the middle of the forenoon. In the early history of the Hebrews, the principal meal, corresponding with our dinner, was eaten about noon, Gen. 43:25; 1 Kin. 20:16. At a later period, at least on festive occasions, it was taken after the heat of the day was over. This was the "supper." The Jews were wont to wash their hands before eating, a custom rendered necessary by their mode of eating, but made by the Pharisees a test of piety, Mark 7:2, 3; Luke 11:38. Devout Jews, not only in their sacred feasts, but in their daily enjoyments at the family meal, recognized the Giver of all good, and implored his blessing on their food, 1 Sam. 9:13; Matt. 14:19; 15:36; 26:26; Luke 9:16; John 6:11; 1 Tim. 4:3. Some families repeated the twenty-third Psalm as they seated themselves at meals. The food consisted of flesh, fish, or fowls, butter, honey, bread, and fruits. See FOOD. Animal food was often cut into small pieces, or stewed, and served up in one large dish with melted butter, vegetables, etc.

MODERN SYRIANS AT DINNER.

Knives, forks, and spoons were unknown as table-furniture; and the food was conveyed to the mouth by the right hand, Prov. 19:24. Each person took a portion from the dish either with his thumb and fingers, or with the help of a small piece of thin bread. Several hands were occasionally plunged into the same dish at once, John 13:26. The head of the family was wont to send a double portion of food to a stranger, as an honor, and to furnish him a greater variety, Gen. 43:31; 1 Sam. 1:4; 9:22–24; and often would select the choicest morsels and present them to his guest with his own fingers. Compare Ruth 2:14, and John 13:26. This is still customary in the East. After eating, the hands were again cleansed by pouring water upon them, 2 Kin. 3:11. See FEAST, WASHING.

The following description of a dinner at Hebron is from Dr. Robinson. "They were dining in the true oriental style. A very large circular tray of tinned copper, placed upon a coarse wooden stool about a foot high, served as the table. In the centre of this stood a large dish with a mountain of pillaw, composed of rice boiled and buttered, with small pieces of meat strewed through and upon it. This was the chief dish, although there were also other smaller dishes, both of meat and vegetables.

Around this table ten persons, including the three governors—of Gaza, Hebron, and Jerusalem—were seated, or rather, squatted on their feet. Each had before him a plate of tinned copper and a wooden spoon. Some used the spoon without the plate; but the most preferred to eat with the fingers of the left hand, without either spoon or plate. When any one had finished, he immediately rose, and went and washed his hands by having water poured over them in an adjoining room. The vacant place at table was immediately filled by a new comer."

E'BAL, Deut. 27; 28; a mountain in Ephraim, over against mount Gerizim, from which it is separated by a valley about five hundred yards wide and three miles long, in which stands the town of Shechem. Both mountains are much alike in length, height, and form, and their altitude is stated not to exceed seven hundred and fifty or eight hundred feet from the level of the valley. As you journey from Jerusalem, and turn to pass through the valley west-north-west to Shechem, mount Ebal is on the right hand and mount Gerizim on the left. Some have described the mount of cursing as sterile and desolate, and Gerizim as smiling and fertile. But at present there is little difference between their opposing fronts, which are alike steep and barren. Mount Gerizim, however, is said to have a more fertile background, and to be a little higher than mount Ebal. The base of the latter is full of sepulchral excavations. See GERIZIM, SHECHEM.

EBED'-MELECH, an Ethiopian servant of king Zedekiah, who was instrumental in saving the prophet Jeremiah from famishing in a filthy dungeon, and was therefore preserved when Jerusalem was taken by Nebuzaradan, Jer. 38:7-13; 39:15-18. The Lord knoweth them that are his.

EBENE'ZER, *stone of help*, the place where Samuel erected a monument, in grateful remembrance of the divine help, given in answer to prayer, in a great battle with the Philistines. The same place had before witnessed the defeat of Israel and the capture of the ark, 1 Sam. 4:1; 5:1; 7:5-12.

E'BER. See HEBER.

EB'ONY, the wood of a tree of no great size, growing in India and Africa; it is black, hard, heavy, and fine-grained, and receives a beautiful polish. It was anciently highly prized, Ezek. 27:15, and is still much used for musical instruments and fancy articles.

ECCLESIASTES, *the preacher*, the name of a book of the Old Testament, usually ascribed to Solomon. Compare 1 Kin. 3:12 and Eccl. 1:16; 1 Kin. 10:21, 27 and Eccl. 2:4-9; 1 Kin. 11:3, 4 and Eccl. 7:26, 28. It appears to have been written by Solomon in his old age, when freed from the entanglements of idolatry, luxury, and lust, B. C. 977. It is a discourse upon the true wisdom; with many isolated precepts, illustrated from his own unexampled experience and from the most sagacious observation of the course of life; the whole demonstrating the vanity of all earthly good, and showing that there is a better life to come, and that the only true wisdom is to "fear God and keep his commandments." This, he says, is the conclusion of the whole matter, Eccl. 12:13. In reading this book, care should be taken not to deduce opinions from detached sentiments, but from the general scope and combined force of the whole.

E'DEN, a province in Asia, in which was Paradise. "The Lord God planted a garden eastward in Eden, and there he put the man whom he had formed," Gen. 2:8. The topography of Eden is thus described: "And a river went out of Eden to water the garden, and from thence it was parted, and became into four heads. The name of the first is Pison," etc.

This obscure passage has received many different explanations and applications, none of which are fully satisfactory; and now it is impossible to say with certainty where Eden lay. Most writers have sought for it in some elevated and central region, the heights of which would give rise to various rivers flowing off in different directions through lower grounds to their outlets. Such a region exists in the high lands of Armenia, west of mount Ararat and 5,000 feet above the sea. Here, within a circle but a few miles in diameter, four large rivers rise: the Euphrates, and Tigris, or Hiddekel, flowing south into the Persian gulf; the Araxes, flowing north-east into the Caspian sea; and the Phasis, or the Halys, flowing north-west into the Black sea. This fouth river may have been the Pishon of Eden; and the Araxes may well be the Gihon, since both words mean the same, and describe its dart-like swiftness. This elevated country, still beautiful and fertile, may have been the land of Eden; and in its choicest portion, towards the east, the garden may once have smiled.

Another location of Eden is now preferred by many interpreters—near the spot where the Euphrates and Tigris form a junction after their long wanderings, a hundred and twenty miles north of the Persian gulf, and where the river Ulai flows in from the north-east. This region may have been greatly changed by the lapse of many thousand years, and may now bear little resemblance to the luxuriant and beautiful plain of primeval times. Yet long after the flood the plain of Shinar in the same region attracted the admiration of the sons of Cush, Gen. 10:8-10; 11:2. As two of the rivers of Eden bear the familiar names of the Euphrates and Tigris, it seems probable that it was in one or the other of the regions above named. Wherever it was, it is there no more since the fall and the curse. The first chapters of the Bible show Paradise withdrawn from man's view, and no pilgrimage can discover it upon earth. The last chapters of the Bible restore to our view a more glorious and enduring Paradise: "Blessed are they that do his commandments, that they may have right to the tree of life."

E'DOM, *red*, a name of Esau, Isaac's eldest son, appropriate on account of his natural complexion, but given, it would seem, from the current name of the food for which he sold his birthright—"that same red," Gen. 25:25, 30. See ESAU and IDUMEA.

ED'REI, one of the capitals of Bashan, near which Og and his forces were destroyed, Num. 21:33-35: Deut. 1:4; 3:1-3. It afterwards fell within the limits of Manasseh, Josh. 13:31. Its ruins cover a large space; it was a place of some note in the early ages of Christianity and in the era of the crusades. It is now called Draa, and lies about thirty-five miles east of the outlet of the sea of Galilee.

EG'LON, a king of Moab, who, with the help of Ammon and Amalek, subdued the southern and eastern tribes of the Jews. He made Jericho his seat of government, and held his power eighteen years, but was then slain by Ehud, and his people expelled, Judg. 3:12-33.

E'GYPT, a celebrated country in the north of Africa, at the eastern part of the Mediterranean sea. The Hebrews called it Mizraim, Gen. 10:6, and hence it is now called by the Arabs, Mizr. The Greeks and Romans called it Ægyptus, whence Egypt; but the origin of this name is unknown.

The habitable land of Egypt is for the most part a great valley, through which the river Nile pours its waters, extending in a straight line from north to south, and skirted on the east and west by ranges of mountains, which approach and recede from the river more or less in different parts. Where this valley terminates, towards the north, the Nile divides itself, about forty or fifty miles from the seacoast, into several arms, which inclose the so called Delta. The ancients numbered seven arms and mouths; the eastern was that of Pelusium, now that of Tineh; and the western that of Canopus, now that of Aboukir. As these branches all separate from one point or channel, that is, from the main stream, and spread themselves more and more as they approach the coast, they form with the latter a triangle, the base of which is the seacoast; and having thus the form of the Greek letter Δ, *delta*, this part of Egypt received the name of the Delta, which it has ever since retained. The prophet Ezekiel describes Egypt as extending from Migdol, that is, Magdolum, not far from the mouth of the Pelusian arm, to Syene, now Essuan, namely, to the border of Ethiopia, Ezek. 29:10; 30:6, margin. Essuan is also assigned by Greek and Arabian writers as the southern limit of Egypt. Here the Nile issues from the granite rocks of the cataracts, and enters Egypt proper. The length of the country, therefore, in a direct line, is about four hundred and fifty miles, and its area about eleven thousand square miles. The breadth of the valley, between Essuan and the Delta, is very unequal; in some places the inundations of the river extend to the foot of the mountains; in other parts there remains a strip of a mile or two in breadth which the water never covers, and which is therefore always dry and barren. Originally the name Egypt designated only the valley and the Delta; but at a later period it came to include also the region between this and the Red sea.

ANCIENT STATUES OF MEMNON, IN THE PLAIN OF THEBES

The country around Syene and the cataracts is highly picturesque; the other parts of Egypt, and especially the Delta, are uniform and monotonous. The prospect, however, is extremely different, according to the season of the year. From the middle of spring, when the harvest is over, one sees nothing but a grey and dusty soil, so full of cracks and chasms that he can hardly pass along. At the time of the autumnal equinox, the country presents nothing but an immeasurable surface of reddish or yellowish water, out of which rise date-trees, villages, and narrow dams, which serve as a means of communication. After the waters have retreated, and they usually remain only a short time at this height, you see, till the end of autumn, only a black and slimy mud. But in winter, nature puts on all her splendor. In this season, the freshness and power of the new vegetation, the variety and abundance of vegetable productions, exceed every thing that is known in the most celebrated parts of the European continent; and Egypt is then, from one end of the country to the other, like a beautiful garden, a verdant meadow, a field sown with flowers, or a waving ocean of grain in the ear. This fertility, as is well known, depends upon the annual and regular inundations of the Nile. Hence Egypt was called by Herodotus, "the gift of the Nile." See NILE.

The sky is not less uniform and monotonous than the earth; it is constantly a pure unclouded arch, of a color and light more white than azure. The atmosphere has a splendor which the eye can scarcely bear, and a burning sun, whose glow is tempered by no shade, scorches through the whole day these vast and unprotected plains. It is almost a peculiar trait in the Egyptian landscape, that although not without trees, it is yet almost without shade. The only tree is the date-tree, which is frequent; but with its tall, slender stem, and bunch of foliage on the top, this tree does very little to keep off the light, and casts upon the earth only a pale and uncertain shade. Egypt, accordingly, has a very hot climate; the thermometer in summer standing usually at eighty or ninety degrees of Fahrenheit; and in Upper Egypt still higher. The burning wind of the desert, Simoom, or Camsin, is also experienced, usually about the time of the early equinox. The country is not unfrequently visited by swarms of locusts. See LOCUSTS.

In the very earliest times, Egypt appears to have been regarded under three principal divisions; and writers spoke of Upper Egypt or Thebais; Middle Egypt, Heptanomis or Heptapolis; and Lower Egypt or the Delta, including the districts lying east and west of the river. The provinces and cities of Egypt mentioned in the Bible may, in like manner, be arranged under these three great divisions:

1. LOWER EGYPT. The north-eastern point of this was "the river of Egypt," (see below,) on the border of Palestine. The desert between this point, the Red sea, and the ancient Pelusium, seems to have been the desert of Shur, Gen 20:1, now El-Djefer. Sin, "the strength [key] of Egypt," Ezek. 30:15, was probably Pelusium. The land of GOSHEN appears to have lain between Pelusium, its branch of the Nile, and the Red sea, having been skirted on the north-east by the desert of Shur; constituting perhaps a part of the province Rameses, Gen. 47:11. In this district, or adjacent to it, are mentioned also the cities Pithom, Raamses, Pi-Beseth, and On or Heliopolis. In the proper Delta itself, lay Tahapanes, that is, Taphne or Daphne; Zoan, the Tanis of the Greeks; Leontopolis, alluded to perhaps in Isa. 19:18. West of the Delta was Alexandria.

2. MIDDLE EGYPT. Here are mentioned Moph or Memphis, and Hanes, the Heracleopolis of the Greeks.

3. UPPER EGYPT. The southern part of Egypt, the Hebrews appear to have called Pathros, Jer. 44:1, 15. The Bible

TEMPLE OF ABOO-SIMBEL, NUBIA, HALF BURIED IN SAND, STATUES SIXTY FEET HIGH

mentions here only two cities, namely, No, or more fully No-Ammon, for which the Seventy put Diospolis, the Greek name for Thebes, the most ancient capital of Egypt, (see AMMON;) and Syene, the southern city and limit of Egypt.

The chief agricultural productions of Egypt are wheat, durrah, or small maize, Turkish or Indian corn or maize, rice, barley, beans, cucumbers, water-melons, leeks, and onions; also flax and cotton. The date-tree and vine are frequent. The papyrus is still found in small quantity, chiefly near Damietta; it is a reed about nine feet high, as thick as a man's thumb, with a tuft of down on the top. See Book, Bulrush. The animals of Egypt, besides the usual kinds of tame cattle, are the wild ox or buffalo in great numbers, the ass and camel, dogs in multitudes without masters, the ichneumon, the crocodile, and the hippopotamus.

The inhabitants of Egypt may be considered as including three divisions: 1. The Copts, or descendants of the ancient Egyptians. 2. The Fellahs, or husbandmen, who are supposed to represent the people in Scripture called Phul. 3. The Arabs, or conquerors of the country, including the Turks, etc. The Copts are nominal Christians, and the clerks and accountants of the country. They have seen so many revolutions in the governing powers, that they concern themselves very little about the successes or misfortunes of those who aspire to dominion. The Fellahs suffer so much oppression, and are so despised by the Bedaween or wandering Arabs, and by their despotic rulers, that they seldom acquire property, and very rarely enjoy it in security; yet they are an interesting race, and devotedly attached to their native country and the Nile. The Arabs hate the Turks; yet the Turks enjoy most offices of government, though they hold their superiority by no very certain tenure.

The most extraordinary monuments of Egyptian power and industry were the pyramids, which still subsist, to excite the wonder and admiration of the world. No work of man now extant is so ancient or so vast as these mysterious structures. The largest of them covers a square area of thirteen acres, and is still four hundred and seventy-four feet high. They have by some been supposed to have been erected by the Israelites during their bondage in Egypt. But the tenor of ancient history in general, as well as the results of modern researches, is against this supposition. It is generally believed that they were erected more than two thousand years before Christ, as the sepulchres of kings.

But besides these imperishable monuments of kings long forgotten, Egypt abounds in other structures hardly less wonderful; on the beautiful islands above the cataracts, near Syene, and at other places in Upper Egypt; and especially in the whole valley of the Nile near Thebes, including Carnac, Luxor, etc. The temples, statues, obelisks, and sphinxes that cover the ground astonish and awe the beholder with their colossal height, their massive grandeur, and their vast extent: while the dwellings of the dead, tombs in the rock occupied by myriads of mummies, extend far into the adjacant mountains. The huge columns of these temples, their vast walls, and many of the tombs, are covered with sculptures and paintings which are exceedingly valuable as illustrating the public and the domestic life of the ancient Egyptians. See Shishak. With these are mingled many hieroglyphic records, which have begun to yield their long-concealed meaning to the inquisitions of modern science. Some of these are mere symbols, comparatively easy to understand. But a large portion of them are now found to be written with a sort of pictorial alphabet—each symbol representing the sound with which its own name commences. Thus osir, the name of the Egyptian god Osiris, would be represented by the picture of a reed, a child, and a mouth; because the initial sounds of the Coptic words for these three objects, namely, Oke, Si, and Ro, make up the

AVENUE IN THE GREAT HALL OF COLUMNS, AT KARNAC, THEBES.

SCULPTURED TABLET, ON A TEMPLE IN UPPER EGYPT.

name OSIR. There is, however, great ambiguity in the interpretation of these records; and in many cases the words, when apparently made out, are as yet unintelligible, and seem to be part of a priestly dialect understood only by the learned.

The early history of ancient Egypt is involved in great obscurity. All accounts, however, and the results of all modern researches, seem to concur in representing culture and civilization as having been introduced and spread in Egypt from the south, and especially from Meroë; and that the country in the earliest times was possessed by several contemporary kings or states, which at length were all united into one great kingdom. The common name of the Egyptian kings was Pharaoh, which signified sovereign power. History has preserved the names of several of these kings, and a succession of their dynasties. But the inclination of the Egyptian historians to magnify the great antiquity of their nation, has destroyed their credibility. See PHARAOH.

This ancient and remarkable land is often mentioned in Scripture. A grandson of Noah seems to have given it his name, Gen. 10:6. In the day of Abraham it was the granary of the world, and the patriarch himself resorted thither in a famine, Gen. 12:10. His wife had an Egyptian handmaid, Hagar the mother of Ishmael, who also sought a wife in Egypt, Gen. 21:9, 21. Another famine, in the days of Isaac, nearly drove him to Egypt, Gen. 26:2; and Jacob and all his household ended their days there, Gen. 39–50. After the escape of Israel from their weary bondage in Egypt, we read of little intercourse between the two nations for many years. In the time of David and Solomon, mention is again made of Egypt. Solomon married an Egyptian princess, 1 Kin. 3:7; 9; 11. But in the fifth year of his son Rehoboam, Judah was humbled at the feet of Shishak, king of Egypt, 2 Chr. 12; and for many generations afterwards the Jews were alternately in alliance and at war with that nation, until both were subjugated to the Assyrian empire, 2 Kin. 17; 18:21; 23:29; 24; Jer. 25; 37:5; 44; 46.

Egypt was conquered by Cambyses,

and became a province of the Persian empire about 525 B. C. Thus it continued until conquered by Alexander, 350 B. C., after whose death it formed, along with Syria, Palestine, Lybia, etc., the kingdom of the Ptolemies. After the battle of Actium, 30 B. C., it became a Roman province. In the time of Christ, great numbers of Jews were residents of Alexandria, Leontopolis, and other parts of Egypt; and our Saviour himself found an asylum there in his infancy, Matt. 2:13. Since that time it has ceased to be an independent state, and its history is incorporated with that of its different conquerors and possessors. In A. D. 640, it was conquered by the Arabs; and in later periods has passed from the hands of the caliphs under the power of Turks, Arabs, Kurds, Mamelukes; and since 1517, has been governed as a province of the Turkish empire. Thus have been fulfilled the ancient predictions recorded in God's word, Ezek. 29:14, 15; 30:7, 12, 13; 32:15. Its present population is about two millions.

The religion of Egypt consisted in the worship of the heavenly bodies and the powers of nature; the priests cultivated at the same time astronomy and astrology, and to these belong probably the wise men, sorcerers, and magicians mentioned in Ex. 7:11, 22. They were the most honored and powerful of the castes into which the people were divided. It was probably this wisdom, in which Moses also was learned, Acts 7:22. But the Egyptian religion had this peculiarity, that it adopted living animals as symbols of the real objects of worship. The Egyptians not only esteemed many species of animals as sacred, which might not be killed without the punishment of death, but individual animals were kept in temples and worshipped with sacrifices, as gods.

"The river of Egypt," Num. 34:5; Josh. 15:4, 47; 1 Kin. 8:65; 2 Kin. 24:7; Isa. 27:12; Ezek. 47:19; 48:28, (and, according to some, Gen. 15:18, though in this passage a different word is used signifying a permanent stream,) designates the brook El-Arish, emptying into the south-east corner of the Mediterranean at Rhinocolura.

E'HUD, a Benjamite, who delivered Israel from the Moabites, by first slaying Eglon their king, and then raising an army and defeating his people. He judged Israel with honor for many years, Judg. 3:12-31; 4:1.

EK'RON, the most northern city of the Philistines, allotted to Judah by Joshua, 15:45, but afterwards given to Dan, 19:43, though it does not appear that the Jews ever peaceably possessed it. It is memorable for its connection with the captivity of the ark and its restoration to the Jews, 1 Sam. 5:10; 6:1-18. The fly-god was worshipped here, 2 Kin. 1:2. Its ruin was foretold, Amos 1:8; Zeph. 2:4; Zech. 9:5, 7. Robinson found its site at the Moslem village Akir, some ten miles north-east of Ashdod. There are no ruins.

EL, *strength*, one of the names of God, especially in poetry, Gen. 33:18-20. It is very often found in proper names, as Bethel, Daniel, Elijah, etc. Eloi, like Eli, means, My God.

E'LAH, I., a valley in which David slew Goliath, 1 Sam. 17:2, 3, 19. It was probably about eleven miles southwest from Jerusalem.

II. Son and successor of Baasha, king of Israel, B. C. 926. After reigning two years, he was slain while intoxicated, by Zimri, one of his officers, who succeeded him as king. Zimri destroyed all the family of Baasha, according to the prediction of Jehu, 1 Kin. 16:6-10.

E'LAM, the region afterwards called Persia, Gen. 14:1. It was called Elam after a son of Shem, Gen. 10:22. It corresponded to the Elymais of Greek and Roman writers, which comprehended a part of Susiana, now Khusistan, or more probably included the whole of Susiana. The city Susa, or Shushan, was in it, Dan. 8:2. See also Acts 2:9.

E'LATH, or E'LOTH, a city of Idumea, situated at the northern extremity of the eastern gulf of the Red sea, which was anciently called the Elanitic gulf, and now the gulf of Akaba. Ezion-Gaber was also situated here, and very near Elath, Deut. 2:8; 1 Kin. 9:26. This gulf, although known to the ancients, has been almost unknown to modern geographers until the time of Burckhardt. This enterprising traveller explored it, and gave the first full account of it. The great sand valley called El-Arabah, and towards the north El-Ghor, runs from this gulf to the Dead sea. Elath was annexed to Judah by David, who established there an extensive commerce, 2 Sam. 8:14. Solomon also built ships there, 2 Chr. 8:17, 18. In the reign of Joram the Edomites recovered it, but lost it again to Uzziah, 2 Kin. 8:20; 14:22; and he to Rezin, 16:6. Under the rule of the Romans it was a flourishing commercial town, with the ordinances of Christianity. In 630 A. D. it fell under the power of Mohammed, and is now in ruins. The fortress of Akaba, near by, now often visited by travellers from mount Sinai to Palestine, is only important for the protection of pilgrims to Mecca.

EL'DAD, and ME'DAD, two of the seventy elders appointed to aid Moses in governing the people. The spirit of prophecy coming upon them, they prophesied in the camp at a distance from Moses. Joshua censured them for this as an irregularity, but they were nobly vindicated by Moses, Num. 11:24-29.

EL'DERS OF ISRAEL, the heads of tribes, who, before the settlement of the Hebrew commonwealth, had a government and authority over their own families and the people. Moses and Aaron treated the elders as representatives of the nation, Ex. 3:16; 4:29; 12:21. When the law was given, God directed Moses to take the seventy elders, as well as Aaron, and Nadab and Abihu his sons, that they might be witnesses, Ex. 24:1, 9. Ever afterwards we find this number of seventy, or rather, seventy-two, elders; six from each tribe.

In allusion to the Jewish elders, the ordinary governors and teachers of the Christian church are called elders, or presbyters, Acts 20:17, 28; Titus 1:5, 7; 1 Pet. 5:1; 2 John 1.

ELEA'LEH, a town of the Amorites, near Heshbon their capital, assigned to the tribe of Reuben, Num. 32:3, 37, and long afterwards threatened as a city of Moab, Isa. 15:4; 16:9; Jer. 48:34. Its ruins, now El-Aal, are a mile or more north-east of Heshban.

ELEA'ZAR, I., the third son of Aaron, and high-priest after him, Ex. 6:23; Num. 20:25-28. The high-priesthood continued in his family through seven generations; till the time of Eli, when we find it transferred to the line of Ithamar. In the reigns of Saul and David, it was restored to the line of Eleazar, and so continued till after the captivity.

II. A son of Abinadab, honored with the charge of the ark while it was in his father's house, 1 Sam. 7:1.

III. One of David's champions, 2 Sam. 23:9; 1 Chr. 11:11-18.

E'LI, a high-priest of the Jews, the first in the line of Ithamar, 1 Sam. 2:27. He was also a judge of Israel forty years, and was eminent for piety and usefulness, but criminally negligent of family discipline. For this the judgments of God fell upon his house, 1 Sam. 3:11-18 In battle with the Philistines his two sons were slain, and Israel defeated; but it was the capture of the ark of God that broke his heart, 1 Sam. 4. The divine threatening was fully performed in the day of Abiathar, which see.

ELI'AB, the oldest brother of David, towards whom his conduct was passionate and jealous, thus confirming the judgment of Him who looks not on the appearance, but the heart, 1 Sam. 16:6, 7; 17:28.

ELI'AKIM, I., a king of Judah, 2 Kin. 23:34. See JEHOIAKIM.

II. An officer of king Hezekiah's court, appointed with others to treat with Rabshakeh, general of the Assyrian forces then besieging Jerusalem, 2 Kin. 18; 19; Isa. 36; 37. See SENNACHERIB.

ELI'AS, see ELIJAH.

ELI'ASHIB, a high-priest in the days of Nehemiah, who took part in rebuilding the wall of Jerusalem, Neh. 3:1. The same person probably was afterwards censured for profaning the temple, by giving the use of one of its chambers to a heathen and an Ammonite, his relative, Deut. 23:3, 4; Neh. 12:10; 13:1-9.

ELIE'ZER, I., of Damascus, the lawful heir of Abraham, should he die childless, Gen. 15:2. He is generally assumed to be the "eldest servant," who was sent, sixty-five years afterwards, to obtain a wife for Isaac, Gen. 24. But as the name of the latter is not given; as Abraham had near relatives, Lot and others; and as there is no evidence that he ever lived in Damascus, some think Eliezer must have been a near relative of Abraham residing at Damascus; and that "steward of my house" and "born in my house"—literally son of my house, Gen. 15:2, 3—mean the same thing, the lawful family heir.

II. Several others of this name are mentioned, Ex. 18:4; 1 Chr. 15:24; 27:16; 2 Chr. 20:37; Luke 3:29.

ELI'HU, a native of Buz, Gen. 22:21, which was probably a city of Edom, Jer.

25:23, perhaps Bozrah, Jer. 49:7, 8, 13. He came to condole with Job in his calamities. Young, ardent, sagacious, and devout, he listened attentively to the discourses of Job and his three friends; and at length broke in, with profuse apologies, to set them all right, Job 32. His address to Job is friendly and soothing, yet faithful; he censures him for justifying himself, rather than God. The adversaries of Job he blames for condemning him as a hypocrite, in their ignorance of the wonders of God's providence. In several sentences he beautifully expresses his faith in the pardoning and restoring grace of God towards sinners, Job 33:23, 24, 27–30, passages in probably the oldest book of the Bible in the very spirit of the parable of the prodigal son.

ELI'JAH, the prophet, a native of Tishbeh in Gilead, 1 Kin. 17:1. His parentage and early history are unknown. His bold faithfulness provoked the wrath of Ahab and Jezebel, especially when he threatened several years of drought and famine as a punishment for the sins of Israel, B. C. 908. By the divine direction the prophet took refuge on the bank of the brook Cherith, where he was miraculously fed by ravens. Thence he resorted to Zarephath, in Phœnicia; where one miracle provided him with sustenance, and another restored to life the child of his hostess. Returning to king Ahab, he procured the great assembling at mount Carmel, where God "answered by fire," and the prophets of Baal were destroyed. Now too the long and terrible drought was broken, and a plentiful rain descended at the prophet's prayer. Finding that not even these mighty works of God would bring the nation and its rulers to repentance, Elijah was almost in despair. He fled into the wilderness, and was brought to Horeb, the mount of God, where he was comforted by a vision of God's power and grace. Again he is sent on a long journey to Damascus, to anoint Hazael as king of Syria. Jehu also he anoints to be king of Israel, and Elisha he summons to become a prophet. Six years later, he denounces Ahab and Jezebel for their crimes in the matter of Naboth; and afterwards again is seen foretelling the death of king Ahaziah, and calling fire from heaven upon two bands of guards sent to arrest him. Being now forewarned of the approach of his removal from earth, he gives his last instructions to the school of the prophets, crosses the Jordan miraculously, and is borne to heaven in a fiery chariot without tasting death, leaving his mantle and office to Elisha, 1 Kin. 17–19; 21; 2 Kin. 1;2.

His translation occurred about B. C. 896. Previously, it is supposed, he had written the letter which, eight years afterwards, announced to king Jehoram his approaching sickness and death, 2 Chr. 21:12–19.

Elijah was one of the most eminent and honored of the Hebrew prophets. He was bold, faithful, stern, self-denying, and zealous for the honor of God. His whole character and life are marked by peculiar moral grandeur. He bursts upon our view without previous notice; he disappears by a miracle. He bears the appearance of a supernatural messenger of heaven, who has but one work to do, and whose mind is engrossed in its performance. His history is one of the most extraordinary on record, and is fraught with instruction. It was a high honor granted to Moses and Elijah, that they alone should appear on the mount of Transfiguration, many centuries after they had gone into heaven—to bear witness of its existence, and commune with the Saviour concerning his death, Luke 9:28–35.

John the Baptist was foretold under the name of Elias, or Elijah, from his resemblance in character and life to the ancient prophet of Israel, Mal. 4:5, 6; Matt. 17:10–13.

E'LIM, a station of the Israelites, on their way to mount Sinai, Ex. 15:27; 16:1; Num. 33:9, generally taken to be the present Wady Ghurundel, a broad valley running south-west to the sea, about forty miles south-east of Suez. Here are fountains and a brook, many bushes and shrubs, and a few tamarisks and palms.

ELIM'ELECH, a Bethlehemite, husband of Naomi, Ruth 1:2.

EL'IPHAZ, a native of Teman, and friend of Job, Job 2:11. Compare Gen. 36:10. He seems to have been older than Bildad and Zophar, and was the first to address Job, chs. 4, 5, 15, 22.

ELIS'ABETH, a devout woman, "of the daughters of Aaron," the wife of Zacharias, and mother of John the Baptist, Luke 1:5–25, 36, 39–80.

ELI'SHA, the pupil and successor of Elijah, a prophet of Israel during the reign of Jehoram, Jehu, Jehoahaz, and Joash, B. C. 903–838. He was a native of Abel-meholah, where he was at work ploughing when Elijah called him to become a prophet, 1 Kin. 19:16. Some years afterwards he witnessed the miraculous ascension of Elijah, divided the Jordan with his mantle, and took his place at the head of the schools of the prophets. During his long ministry he acted an important part in the public affairs of Israel. Many miracles also were wrought at his word; some of these were, healing the waters of Jericho; supplying the widow's cruse with oil, and the allied armies of Judah, Israel, and Edom with water; gaining a son for the woman of Shunem, and restoring him to life; healing the leprosy of Naaman; detecting and punishing Gehazi. His history is recorded in 2 Kin. 2–9; 13:14–21. He died lamented by king Joash and the people; and a year afterwards, a corpse deposited in the same sepulchre was at once restored to life.

ELI'SHAH, a son of Javan, Gen. 10:4. "The isles of Elishah," which sent purple and scarlet stuffs to Tyre, Ezek. 27:7, are supposed to mean Greece and the adjacent islands.

ELISH'EBA, the wife of Aaron, Ex. 6:23. Elisabeth is the same name in Greek, Luke 1.5.

EL'LASAR, Gen. 14:1, 9, perhaps the same country as Thelassar, 2 Kin. 19:12; Isa. 37:12. The Arabic version calls it Armenia.

ELM, Hos. 4:13. The original Hebrew word here, elsewhere translated oak, probably denotes the terebinth. See OAK.

E'LOI, see EL.

E'LUL, a Hebrew month, the twelfth of the civil year, and sixth of the ecclesiastical, Neh. 6:15. It included the time from the new moon of September to that of October.

EL'YMAS, a Jewish sorcerer in the retinue of Sergius Paulus, the Roman proconsul at Paphos in Cyprus. He was sharply reproved by Paul, and struck with instant blindness for opposing the religious inquiries of the proconsul, who was abandoning idolatry and superstition, and embracing the gospel, Acts 13:6–12. His blindness was to continue "for a season," and may have led to his spiritual illumination.

EMBALM'ING. The process of embalming dead bodies among the Egyptians was as follows: The embalmers, who were looked upon as sacred officers, drew the brains through the nostrils with a hooked piece of iron, and filled the skull with astringent drugs; they drew all the entrails, except the heart and kidneys, through a hole cut in the left side, washed them in palm-wine, and replaced them, filling the cavity with astringent and preservative drugs. The body was anointed repeatedly with oil of cedar, myrrh, cinnamon, etc., about thirty days, and was then put into nitre for about forty days; by which process it was preserved from decay, retaining at the same time a lifelike appearance. When Moses says that forty days were employed in embalming Jacob, he probably speaks of the forty days of his continuing in the salt of nitre, not including the thirty days spent in the previous ceremonies; so that, in the whole, they mourned seventy days for him in Egypt, Gen. 50:2, 3.

The body was afterwards taken out of the salt, washed, wrapped up in long linen bandages, dipped in myrrh, and closed with gum. It was then restored to the relatives, who inclosed it in a coffin, and kept it in their houses, or deposited it

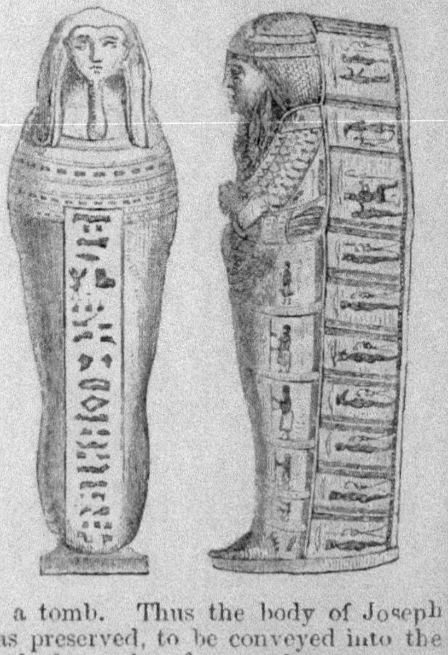

in a tomb. Thus the body of Joseph was preserved, to be conveyed into the land of promise af er nearly two centuries, Gen. 50:26. Great numbers of mummies are still found in Egypt, in the subterraneous vaults where they were deposited two or three thousand years ago.

The common people of that country were embalmed by means of bitumen, a cheap material and easily managed. With this the corpse and its envelopes were smeared, with more or less care and diligence. Sepulchres have been opened in which thousands of bodies had been deposited in rows, one on another, without coffins, preserved in this manner.

The usual embalming of the Jews was less elaborate and effectual. It consisted mainly in wrapping the body in many folds of linen, with a profusion of aromatic spices—myrrh, aloes, etc. Thus the body of the Saviour was embalmed entire by Joseph and Nicodemus, while, ignorant of this, the two Marys and their friends were prepared to render him a similar honor when the Jewish Sabbath was past, John 19:38–40. The practice, even in this form, does not appear to have been prevalent among the Jews. See BURIAL.

EM'ERALD, a precious stone of a fine green color, found anciently in Ethiopia, but in modern times only in South America, Ex. 28:18; Ezek. 27:16; 28:13. Josephus, however, and the Seventy make it a gem like a burning coal—the Indian ruby.

EM'ERODS, that is, hemorrhoids, the name of a painful disease occasioned by tumors, probably the piles, Deut. 28:27; 1 Sam. 5:12.

E'MIM, a gigantic and warlike race, who in the time of Abraham occupied the country beyond the Jordan, afterwards possessed by the Moabites, Gen. 14:5; Deut. 2:10.

EMMAN'UEL, a compound Hebrew word or name, signifying *God with us*. It is applied to the Messiah, our Saviour, who, as having united the divine with the human nature, and having come to dwell with men, is *God with us*, Isa. 7:14; 8:8; Matt. 1:23.

EM'MAUS, the village where our Lord revealed himself to two of his disciples, on the afternoon of his resurrection-day. It lay about seven and a half miles, sixty furlongs, north-west from Jerusalem, Luke 24:13–33. Some manuscripts, however, read one hundred and sixty furlongs, instead of sixty; and Eusebius and Jerome locate Emmaus at the ancient Nicopolis, twenty miles west-north-west of Jerusalem, where a village called Amwâs still exists. Dr. Robinson inclines to this location.

EN, *a fountain*, compounded with many names of towns and places; as En-dor, En-gedi, En-eglaim, En-shemesh, that is, the fountain of Dor, etc.

ENCHANT'MENTS, deceptive arts and charms practised by designing men, and classed in the Bible with sorcery, magic, divination, witchcraft, and necromancy, or professed communication with departed spirits. All these are expressly forbidden and denounced in Scripture, Ex. 22:18; Lev. 19:26, 31; 20:27; Deut. 18:10, 11. The pretended power and skill of enchanters was ascribed to infernal agency, and the art was essentially hostile to true religion. Their seeming wonders were usually wrought by juggling tricks or sleight of hand, or by mysteries of science, known to but few. The magicians of Egypt are said to have done several things "with their enchantments," Ex. 7–9; Acts 19:19.

EN'-DOR, a city of Manasseh, Josh. 17:11, four miles south of mount Tabor, near Nain, in the way to Scythopolis, Psa. 83:9, 10. Here the witch lived whom Saul consulted, 1 Sam. 28. The pretence of this sorceress that she could call up the spirits of the dead from their repose, was evidently false. She was amazed and appalled when the form of Samuel really appeared, sent by God himself to put her to shame, and bring to king Saul his last warning.

EN-EGLA'IM, Ezek. 47:10, a town on the Dead sea, west of the Jordan's mouth.

EN-GAN'NIM, I., a town of Judah, probably near Bethel, Josh. 15:34.

II. A city of the priests, in Issachar, now Jenin, fifteen miles south of mount Tabor, Josh. 19:21; 21:29.

EN-GED'I, *fountain of the kid*, 1 Sam. 24:1, 2; called also Hazezon-Tamar, that is, *the city of palm-trees*, there being great numbers of palm-trees around it, Gen. 14:7; 2 Chr. 20:1, 2. It stood near the middle of the western shore of the Dead sea, twenty-five or thirty miles south-east of Jerusalem, in the edge of the loftiest part of the wilderness of Judea, a region full of rocks and caverns, 1 Sam. 23:29; Ezek. 47:10. See cut in SEA, 117

The heights of En-gedi are fifteen hundred feet above the Dead sea. At four hundred feet from the sea a fine and copious fountain, still bearing its ancient name, flows down to the sea, watering in its course a fruitful valley and a plain half a mile square, in both of which ruins are found. The mountain side was formerly terraced, and the whole spot was an oasis of fertility, Song 1:14.

E'NOCH, I., a son of Cain, in honor of whom the first city named in the Bible was called Enoch, Gen. 4:17.

II. "The seventh from Adam," and the father of Methuselah; eminent as a patriarch who lived near to God, through faith in a Redeemer to come, Heb. 11:5, 13. It was a testimony to his rare piety in an ungodly age that he was translated without seeing death, like Elijah. He had lived only three hundred and sixty-five years, A. M. 622–987, Gen. 5:18-24. Jude, ver. 14, 15, quotes a traditionary prophecy of Enoch, showing his belief in a judgment to come. There is an apocryphal book bearing the name of Enoch, in which similar language occurs. It was probably written by some devout Christian of the first century, and is only valuable for the light it throws on the belief of the early church. It was never received as canonical.

E'NON, the place where John baptized, was near Salim, on the west side of the Jordan, John 1:28; 3:26. It is supposed to have been eight or ten miles south of Beth-shean, and near the Jordan.

E'NOS, the grandson of Adam. He lived nine hundred and five years, A. M. 235-1140. Adam, Seth, and Enoch died before him; and Noah was contemporary with him eighty-four years, Gen. 4:26; 5:6-11; Luke 3:38. In his days "began men to call upon the name of the Lord" in organized and systematic public worship; or according to the marginal reading, then began men to call themselves by the name of the Lord; that is, for the purpose of marking the distinction between men of God and the ungodly.

EN-RO'GEL, *fuller's fountain*, so named because here the fullers were wont to cleanse their cloths by treading them with their feet. This is believed to be the "well of Nehemiah," now called Bir Eyûb, Job's well. It is in the valley of the Kidron, just below its junc-

tion with the valley of the son of Hinnom, on the south-east corner of Jerusalem, Josh. 15:7; 18:16. It is mentioned in the Bible in connection with the conspiracy of Absalom, 2 Sam 17:17, and afterwards with that of Adonijah, 1 Kin. 1:9. This well is situated in what is now the prettiest and most fertile spot around Jerusalem. It is one hundred and twenty-five feet deep; is walled up with large squared stones, which on one side rise and form an arch, and is apparently of great antiquity.

EP'APHRAS, supposed to have founded the church at Colosse, and denominated by Paul his "dear fellow-servant," and "a faithful minister of Jesus Christ," Col. 1:7; 4:12. He was for a time an inmate of Paul's house of imprisonment at Rome.

EPAPHRODI'TUS, a member of the church at Philippi, charged with the supplies which that church contributed for the relief of Paul while imprisoned at Rome, Phil. 2:25; 4:18. This labor of love brought on him a serious illness at Rome, on which occasion we see how much he was esteemed and beloved both by Paul and the Philippians, Phil. 2:25-30. On his return he was the bearer of the epistle to them.

EPE'NETUS, saluted by Paul in his epistle to Rome, Rom. 16:5, and called "the first-fruits of Achaia," that is, one of his first converts there. Many manuscripts and versions read Asia instead of Achaia.

E'PHAH, I., a measure of capacity

used among the Hebrews, containing three pecks and three pints. The ephah was a dry measure, as of barley, Ruth 2:17; and meal, Num. 5:15; Judg. 6:19; and was of the same capacity with the bath in liquids. See BATH.

II. The son of Midian, and grandson of Abraham, Gen. 25:4, who settled and gave his name to a region in Arabia supposed to have been near Midian, Isa. 60:6.

E'PHER, a son of Midian, Gen. 25:4, located beyond the Jordan, 1 Kin. 4:10.

EPHE'SIANS, EPISTLE TO THE. This epistle was written by Paul, at Rome, probably A. D. 62. The ablest modern critics are not agreed as to the church to whom it was addressed, whether to that in Ephesus, that in Laodicea, or to both of these in connection with the other churches in that region. It does not appear, however, that any important point of doctrine or instruction depends on the decision of this question. The epistle is now addressed to and is intelligible by every one who studies it. The first part of it is a grateful discourse upon the vast scheme of divine grace, and the blessings flowing from it. The latter part inculcates Christian consistency and steadfastness, and a faithful discharge of all relative duties. It is one of the richest and most valuable of the epistles, having a singular fulness of matter, depth of doctrine, sublimity of style, and warmth of emotion, which render it precious to the Christian of every land.

EPH'ESUS, the capital of Ionia, a celebrated city of Asia Minor, situated near the mouth of the Cayster, about forty miles south-east of Smyrna. It was chiefly celebrated for the worship and temple of Diana, which last was accounted one of the seven wonders of the world. See DIANA. Paul first visited Ephesus about A. D. 54, Acts 18:19, 21. This first brief visit was followed by a longer one towards the close of the same year, and continuing through the two following years, Acts 19:10; 20:31. The church thus early established, enjoyed the labors of Aquila and Priscilla, of Tychicus and Timothy. It was favored with one of the best of Paul's epistles; its elders held an interview with him at Miletus, before he saw Rome, and he is supposed to have visited them after his first imprisonment. Here the apostle John is said to have spent the latter part of his life, and written his gospel and epistles; and having penned Christ's message to them in the isle of Patmos, to have returned and died among them. Christ gives the church at Ephesus a high degree of praise, coupled with a solemn warning, Rev. 2:1–5, which seems not to have prevented its final extinction, though it remained in existence six hundred years. But now its candlestick is indeed removed out of its place. The site of that great and opulent city is desolate. Its harbor has become a pestilential marsh; the lovely and fertile level ground south of the Cayster now languishes under Turkish misrule; and the heights upon its border bear only shapeless ruins. The outlines of the immense theatre, Acts 19:29, yet remain in the solid rock; but no vestige of the temple of Diana can be traced.

EPH'OD, an ornamental part of the dress worn by the Hebrew priests. It was worn above the tunic and the robe, (*meîl;*) was without sleeves, and open below the arms on each side, consisting of two pieces, one of which covered the front of the body and the other the back, joined together on the shoulders by golden buckles set with gems, and reaching down to the middle of the thigh. A girdle was inwoven with it, by which it was fastened around the body, Ex. 28:6–12. There were two kinds of ephod: one plain, of linen, for the priests, 1 Sam. 22:18; another embroidered, for the high-priest. Young Samuel wore an ephod, though only a Levite and a child, 1 Sam. 2:18. David, in transferring the ark to Jerusalem, was "girt with a linen ephod," 2 Sam. 6:14. The Jews had a peculiar superstitious regard for this garment, and employed it in connection with idolatrous worship. Gideon's ephod became a snare to Israel; and Micah made one, that his idol might be duly worshipped, Judg. 8:27; 17:5; 18:17.

EPH'PHATHA, *be opened*, a Syro-chaldaic word, which our Saviour pronounced when he cured one deaf and dumb, Mark 7:34.

E'PHRAIM, the second son of Joseph, born in Egypt, Gen. 41:52. Although the youngest, he yet had the chief blessing of his grandfather Jacob, and the tribe was always more distinguished than that of Manasseh, Gen. 48:8–20;

Num. 2:18-21. The portion of Ephraim was large and central, and embraced some of the most fertile land in all Canaan. It extended from the Mediterranean across to the Jordan, north of the portions of Dan and Benjamin, and included Shiloh, Shechem, etc. A range of mountainous country, which runs through it, is called "the mountains of Ephraim," or "mount Ephraim." This extends also farther south into the portion of Judah, and is there called "the mountains of Judah." Samaria, the capital of the ten tribes, being in Ephraim, this latter name is often used for the kingdom of Israel, Isa. 11:13; Jer. 31:6; 50:19.

The FOREST of Ephraim, where Absalom lost his life, was on the east side of the Jordan, near Mahanaim, 2 Sam. 18:6-8.

The TOWN called Ephraim, to which the Saviour withdrew from his enemies, John 11:54, was probably the same place mentioned in 2 Chr. 13:19, and called Ophrah in Josh. 18:23; 1 Sam. 13:17. See also 2 Sam. 13:23. It is supposed to be the present Taiyibeh, on a hill overlooking the Jordan valley, five miles north-east of Bethel.

EPH'RATH, or EPH'RATAH, I., the second wife of Caleb, and mother of Hur, 1 Chr 2:19; supposed by some to have given her name to the city of Ephrath or Beth-lehem, 1 Chr. 2:50, 51; 4:4. Compare Gen. 35:16, 19. Elimelech was an Ephrathite of Bethlehem, Ruth 1:2; 4:11; so also was David, 1 Sam. 17:12.

II. A name of Ephraim and Ephraimites, 1 Sam. 1:1; 1 Kin. 11:26; Psa. 132:6.

EPH'RON, a Hittite, dwelling at Hebron in the time of Abraham, Gen. 23. The charming account of his transaction with Abraham, and the frequent subsequent mention of his name, point him out as a prince in the land.

EPICURE'ANS, a celebrated sect of ancient philosophers. They were materialists, and virtually atheists—believing that the atoms of nature existed from eternity, and that from their incidental union all things are formed, both visible and invisible. They denied a divine Providence and man's immortality, and believed there was no after-judgment, and no soul but what was material, like the body, and perishable with it at death. Their rule of life was self-gratification—the pursuit of pleasure, properly regulated and governed. Vicious indulgences were condemned only inasmuch as they on the whole lessen one's happiness. The philosopher Epicurus, their founder, was a learned and moral man, who lived in exemplary harmony with his principles, and died at Athens, B. C. 271, at the age of seventy-three. His followers, however, easily disregarded the limitations he imposed, and pursued pleasure without restraint. At Paul's time they had become exceedingly corrupt, and of course their philosophy and their life both led them to oppose with violence his great truths concerning God, the resurrection, and the judgment everlasting, Acts 17.16-34.

EPIS'TLE, a letter; but the term is applied particularly to the inspired letters in the New Testament, written by the apostles on various occasions, to approve, condemn, or direct the conduct of Christian churches. The Holy Spirit has thus provided that we should have the great doctrines of the true gospel not only historically stated by the evangelists, but applied familiarly to the various emergencies of daily life. It is not to be supposed that every note or memorandum written by the hands of the apostles, or by their direction, was divinely inspired, or proper for preservation to distant ages. Compare 1 Cor. 5:9; Col. 4:16. Those only have been preserved by the overruling hand of Providence which were so inspired, and from which useful directions had been drawn, and might in after-ages be drawn, as from a perpetual directory, for faith and practice—always supposing that similar circumstances require similar directions. In reading an Epistle, we ought to consider the occasion of it, the circumstances of those to whom it was addressed, the time when written, the general scope and design of it, as well as the intention of particular arguments and passages. We ought also to observe the style and manner of the writer, his mode of expression, the peculiar effect he designed to produce on those to whom he wrote, to whose temper, manners, general principles, and actual situation, he might address his arguments, etc.

Of the books of the New Testament, twenty-one are epistles; fourteen of them by Paul, one by James, two by Peter, three by John, and one by Jude. Being placed in our canon without reference to their chronological order, they are perused under considerable disadvantages; and it would be well to read them occasionally in connection with what the history in the Acts of the Apostles relates respecting the several churches to which they are addressed. This would also give us nearly their order of time, which should also be considered, together with the situation of the writer; as it may naturally be inferred that such compositions would partake of the writer's recent and present feelings. The epistles addressed to the dispersed Jews by John and James, by Peter and Jude, are very different in their style and application from those of Paul written to the Gentiles; and those of Paul no doubt contain expressions and allude to facts much more familiar to their original readers than to later ages.

ERAS'TUS, a Christian friend and fellow-laborer of Paul, a Corinthian, and chamberlain—that is, steward or treasurer—of the city. He followed Paul to Ephesus, and attended Timothy in a mission to Macedonia, Acts 19:22. He was again at Corinth when Paul wrote to the Romans, 16. 23; and remained there when Paul went as a prisoner to Rome, 2 Tim. 4:20.

E'RECH, one of Nimrod's cities in the plain of Shinar, Gen. 10:10. A recent explorer finds its probable site in the mounds of primeval ruins now called Irka or Irak, a few miles east of the Euphrates, midway between Babylon and the junction of the Euphrates and Tigris.

E'SAR-HAD'DON, son of Sennacherib, and his successor as king of Assyria, 2 Kin. 19:37; Isa. 37:38, B. C. 896. It is only said of him in Scripture that he sent colonists to Samaria, Ezra 4:2. He is supposed to be the Sardanapalus of profane historians, the last king of Assyria, infamous for his luxury and effeminacy. The city being besieged and nearly taken, he collected his favorites and treasures in his palace and set it on fire, so that all perished together in the flames.

E'SAU, the son of Isaac, and twin brother of Jacob, Gen. 25. He was the elder of the two, and was therefore legally the heir, but sold his birthright to Jacob. We have an account of his ill-advised marriages, Gen. 26:34; of his loss of his father's chief blessing, and his consequent anger against Jacob, Gen. 27; of their subsequent reconciliation, Gen. 32; 33; and of his posterity, Gen. 36. He is also called Edom; and settled in the mountains south of the Dead sea, extending to the gulf of Akaba, where he became very powerful. This country was called from him the land of Edom, and afterwards Idumaea, which see.

ESDRAE'LON, PLAIN OF. See JEZREEL.

ESH'BAAL, 1 Chr. 8:33, the fourth son of Saul, generally called Ishbosheth. The word BAAL, the name of an idol, was not pronounced by scrupulous Jews; they substituted BOSHETH, *confusion*. For Meribbaal, they said Mephibosheth, etc. See ISHBOSHETH.

ESH'COL, I., an Amorite prince near Hebron, who joined Abraham in pursuing the eastern host who had ravaged Sodom and taken Lot captive, Gen. 14:13-14.

II. The small and well-watered valley from which the Hebrew spies obtained the specimen of grapes, which they suspended from a staff borne by two men for safe carriage to Moses, Num. 13:22-27; 32.9; Deut. 1:24. This valley is believed to be one which closely adjoins Hebron on the north, and still furnishes the finest grapes in the country, as well as pomegranates, figs, olives, etc.

ESH'TAOL, a town on the western border of Judah, afterwards given to Dan, Josh. 15:33; 19:41 It is named in the history of Samson, Judg. 13:25; 16:31.

ESHTEM'OA, a city of the priests in Judah, Josh. 15:50; 21:14; 1 Sam. 30:28; traced by Robinson in the modern village Semua, south of Hebron.

ESPOU'SALS. See BETROTHING, MARRIAGE.

ES'THER, a Persian name given to Hadassah, a daughter of Abihail, of the tribe of Benjamin. The family had not returned to Judea after the permission given by Cyrus, and she was born probably beyond the Tigris, and nearly five hundred years before Christ. Her parents being dead, Mordecai, her father's brother, took care of her education. After Ahasuerus had divorced Vashti, search was made throughout Persia for the most beautiful women, and Esther was one selected. She found favor in the eyes of the king, and he married her with royal magnificence, bestowing largesses and remissions of tribute on his people. She was thus in a position which enabled her to do a signal favor to her people, then very numerous in Persia. Their deliverance is still celebrated by the Jews in the yearly festival called Purim, which was instituted at that time. The husband of Esther is supposed to have been the Xerxes of secular history.

ESTHER, THE BOOK OF, has always been esteemed canonical, both by Jews and Christians, though certain additions to it, found in some versions and manuscripts, are apocryphal. Who was its writer is not certainly known. It has been ascribed to Ezra, to a high-priest named Jehoiakim, and to Mordecai. This last opinion is supported by the internal evidence; the book having every appearance of having been written in Persia, by an eye-witness of the scenes it describes, B. C. 509. It presents a graphic picture of the Persian court and customs, and is intensely Jewish in its spirit. The chief value of the book is to illustrate the wonder-working providence of God, his control of human passions, his righteous judgment of sinners, and his care for his covenant people—whom, even when captives in a strange land, he can exalt above all their foes.

E'TAM, a town in Judah near Bethlehem and Tekoa; a favorite resort of Solomon, and fortified by Rehoboam, 1 Chr. 4:3, 32; 2 Chr. 11:6. Its supposed site is now occupied by a ruined village called Urtas, a mile and a half south-west of Bethlehem, not far from Solomon's Pools. "The rock Etam" to which Samson withdrew, Judg. 15:8-19, may have been in this vicinity, perhaps the Frank mountain two miles east.

E'THAM, a station of the Israelites soon after leaving Egypt, Ex. 13:20; Num. 33:6. It lay near the head of the west gulf of the Red sea, and the wilderness east of it was often called by the same name.

E'THAN, I., one of four men renowned for wisdom, though excelled by Solomon, 1 Kin. 4:31; 1 Chr. 2:6. He appears to have been a son of Zerah or Ezra, and grandson of the patriarch Judah.

II. A Levite, son of Kishi, and one of the three masters of the temple music, 1 Chr. 6:44; 15:17-19. He would seem to be the same as Jeduthun, 1 Chr. 25:1; 2 Chr. 35:15.

III. A person to whom Psa. 89 is inscribed.

ETH'ANIM, *constantly flowing*, a month so named before the captivity, because the autumnal rains then begin to fill the dry river channels. It was afterwards called Tishri, and answers nearly to our October. On this month Solomon's temple was dedicated, 1 Kin. 8:2.

ETHIO'PIA, one of the great kingdoms in Africa, frequently mentioned in Scripture under the name of Cush, the various significations of which in the Old Testament have been mentioned under the article CUSH, which see. Ethiopia proper lay south of Egypt, on the Nile; and was bounded north by Egypt, at the cataracts near Syene; east by the Red sea, and perhaps a part of the Indian ocean; south by unknown regions of the interior of Africa; and west by Libya and deserts. It comprehended of course the modern countries of Nubia or Sennaar, and Abyssinia. The chief city in it was the ancient Meroë, situated on the island or tract of the same name, between the Nile and the Astaboras, now the Tacazzé, not far from the modern Shendi, Isa. 18; Zeph. 3:10.

The name of Seba was given to the northern part of Ethiopia, afterwards Meroë, by the eldest son of Cush, Gen. 10:7. This country was in some parts mountainous, and in others sandy; but was to a great extent well-watered and fertile. Ebony, ivory, spices, gold, and precious stones were among its articles of traffic. Its history is much involved with that of Egypt, and the two countries are often mentioned together in the Bible, Isa. 20:3-6; 43:3; 45:14; Ezek. 30; Dan. 11:43.

Zerah "the Ethiopian" who invaded Judah in the reign of Asa, B. C. 944, 2 Chr. 14:9-15, is thought by some to have been an Egyptian king of an Ethiopian dynasty; by others, to have been a king of Ethiopia on both sides of the Red sea; that is, of the Arabian as well as African Cush. This would explain how he could obtain access to the land of Palestine without passing through Egypt. But the whole question is involved in uncertainty. The Ethiopian queen Candace, whose treasurer is mentioned in Acts 8:27, was probably queen of Meroë, where a succession of females reigned who all bore this name. As this courtier is said to have gone up to Jerusalem "to worship," he was probably a Jew by religion, if not by birth. There appear to have been many Jews in that country. The gospel gained adherents among them; and early in the fourth century the entire Bible was translated into the ancient Ethiopic language, from the Greek.

EU'NICE, the mother of Timothy and daughter of Lois; she was a Jewess, though her husband was a Greek, Acts 16:1; 2 Tim. 1:5. She transmitted to her son the lessons of truth she herself had received from a pious mother; and Paul, on his arrival at Lystra, found them rooted and grounded in the truth as it is in Christ.

EU'NUCH. In the courts of oriental monarchs, the charge of the female and interior apartments is committed to eunuchs. Hence the word came to signify merely a court officer. Such were Potiphar, Joseph's master, Gen. 39:17, and the treasurer of queen Candace, Acts 8:27. Our Saviour speaks of some who "have made themselves eunuchs for the kingdom of heaven's sake;" that is, who have voluntarily abstained from marriage, in order more effectually to labor for the kingdom of God, Matt. 19:12; and the apostle Paul commends the same abstinence in certain exceptional cases in times of persecution, 1 Cor. 7:26, 27. See GAZA.

EUO'DIAS. See SYNTYCHE.

EUPHRA'TES, a famous river of Asia, which has its source in the mountains of Armenia, runs along the frontiers of Cappadocia, Syria, Arabia Deserta, Chaldea, and Mesopotamia, and falls into the Persian gulf. According to the recent researches of Chesney, it receives the Tigris at a place called Kurnah, the united stream being called Shat-el-Arab. Five miles below the junction of these two mighty rivers, the Shat-el-Arab receives from the north-east the Kerkhah, which has a course of upwards of five hundred miles. Sixty-two miles below the mouth of the Kerkhah, another large river, the Kuran, comes in from the east. At present it enters the Shat-el-Arab forty miles above its mouth; but formerly it flowed into the Persian gulf by a separate channel, east of the main stream. According to that view which places the garden of Eden near the junction of the Tigris with the Euphrates, these might be regarded as the four rivers of Paradise. We might well suppose that the Kuran, in very ancient times, as now, entered the Shat-el-Arab; and perhaps still farther from its mouth. Scripture often calls the Euphrates simply "the river," Ex. 23:31; Isa. 7:20; 8:7; Jer. 2:18; or "the great river," and assigns it for the eastern boundary of that land which God promised to the Hebrews, Deut. 1:7; Josh. 1:4. It overflows in summer like the Nile, when the snow on the mountains of Armenia begins to melt. The source of the Euphrates, as well as that of the Tigris, being in the mountains of Armenia, the nearest springs of both are but a few miles apart.

The Euphrates is a river of consequence in Scripture geography, being the utmost limit, east, of the territory of the Israelites. It was indeed only occasionally that the dominion of the Hebrews extended so far; but it would appear that even Egypt, under Pharaoh Necho, made conquests to the western bank of the Euphrates. The river is about eighteen hundred miles long. Its general direction is south-east; but in a part of its course it runs westerly, and approaches the Mediterranean near Cilicia. It is accompanied in its general course by the Tigris. There are many towns on its banks, which are in general rather level than mountainous. The river does not appear to be of very great breadth, varying, however, from sixty to six hundred yards. Its current, after reaching the plains of Mesopotamia, is somewhat sluggish, and in this part of its course many canals, etc., were dug, to prevent injury and secure benefit from the yearly overflows. At Seleucia, and Hilleh the ancient Babylon, it approaches near the Tigris, and some of its waters are drawn off by canals to the latter river. Again, however, they diverge, and only unite in the same channel about one hundred and twenty miles from the Persian gulf. It is not well adapted for navigation, yet light vessels go up about one thousand miles, and the modern steam-boat which now ascends from the ocean, meets the same kind of goat-skin floats on which produce was rafted down the river thousands of years ago.

EUROC'LYDON, *the wave-stirring easter*, a tempestuous wind which came down on Paul's ship on the south shore of Crete, and at length wrecked her upon Malta, Acts 27. The small island Clauda, south of which she passed, and the "Syrtis" on the African coast, into which the seamen feared she would be driven, ver. 17, lay south-west of Crete. The result shows that the general course of the wind was east-north-east. It would now be called there a Levanter.

EU'TYCHUS, a young man who was killed at Troas by falling from the window of a room in the third story, where Paul was preaching. His life was miraculously restored, Acts 20:6-12.

EVAN'GELIST, one who proclaims good news, either by preaching or writing. There were originally evangelists or preachers who, without being fixed to any church, preached wherever they were led by the Holy Spirit, like some missionaries in our own day, Eph. 4:11. Such was Philip, Acts 21:8. Timothy also is exhorted to "do the work of an evangelist," 2 Tim. 4:5. We commonly call Matthew, Mark, Luke, and John, "the Evangelists," because they were the writers of the four gospels, which bring to all men the glad tidings of eternal salvation.

EVE, the first mother of our race, and the cause of our fall. Her history is so closely connected with that of Adam, that the remarks made in the article ADAM apply also to her. Her name Eve is from a word signifying *life*, Gen. 3:20. She was made, we are told in Gen. 2:18-22, both *for* man and *of* him; subordinate and weaker, and yet to be loved as his own body. The history of woman in all ages has been a striking fulfilment of the distinct penalties pronounced upon her, Gen. 3:16.

EVE'NING. The Hebrews reckoned two evenings in each day; as in the phrase, "between the two evenings," Ex. 12:6; Num. 9:3; 28:4, margin. In this interval the passover was to be killed, and the daily evening sacrifice offered, Ex. 29:39-41, Hebrew. According to the Caraïtes, this time between the evenings is the interval from sunset to complete darkness, that is, the evening twilight. Compare Deut. 16:6. According to the Pharisees and the rabbins, the first evening began when the sun inclined to descend more rapidly, that is, at the ninth hour; while the second or real evening commenced at sunset. See DAY.

E'VIL-MERO'DACH, the son and successor of Nebuchadnezzar, king of Babylon, B. C. 561. His friendly treatment of Jehoiachin the captive king of Judah, in releasing him from prison and variously distinguishing him above other captives, is mentioned to his praise, 2 Kin. 25:27; Jer. 52:31-34. His reign and life were cut short by a conspiracy, headed by Neriglissar his sister's husband, who succeeded him.

EXCOMMUNICA'TION, an ecclesiastical penalty, by which they who incur the guilt of any heinous sin, are separated from the church, and deprived of its spiritual advantages. Thus the Jews "put out of the synagogue" those they deemed unworthy, John 9:22; 12:42; 16:2. There were two degrees of excommunication among them: one a temporary and partial exclusion from ecclesiastical privileges, and from society; the other a complete excision from the covenant people of God and their numerous privileges, and abandonment to eternal perdition. See ANATHEMA.

The right and duty of excommunication when necessary were recognized in the Christian church by Christ and his apostles, Matt. 18:15-18; 1 Cor. 5:1-13; 16:22; Gal. 5:12; 1 Tim. 1:20; Titus 3:10. The offender, found guilty and incorrigible, was to be excluded from the Lord's supper and cut off from the body of believers. This excision from Christian fellowship does not release one from any obligation to obey the law of God and the gospel of Christ; nor exempt him from any relative duties, as a man or a citizen. The censure of the church, on the other hand, is not to be accompanied, as among papists, with enmity, curses, and persecution. Our Saviour directs that such an offender be regarded "as a heathen man and a publican;" and the apostles charge the church to "withdraw from" those who trouble them, and "keep no company with them," "no, not to eat;" but this is to be understood of those offices of civility and fraternity which a man is at liberty to pay or to withhold, and not of the indispensable duties of humanity, founded on nature, the law of nations, and the spirit of Christianity, 2 Thess. 3:6, 15; 2 John 10, 11.

EX'ODUS, *going out*, the name of the second book of Moses and of the Bible; so called because it narrates the departure of the Israelites from Egypt. It comprises a period of about one hundred and forty-five years, from the death of Joseph to the erection of the tabernacle in the desert, A. M. 2369–2514. The various topics of the book may be thus presented: (1.) The oppression of the Israelites, under the change of dynasty which sprung up after the death of Joseph: "There arose up another king, who knew not Joseph," chap. 1:8. The reference many believe is to the invasion of Egypt by the Hyksos, who are spoken of in secular history as having invaded Egypt probably about this period, and who held it in subjection for many years. They are termed shepherd-kings, and represented as coming from the east. (2.) The youth, education, patriotism, and flight of Moses, chap. 2–6. (3.) The commission of Moses, the perversity of Pharaoh, and the infliction of the ten plagues in succession, chap. 7–11. (4.) The institution of the Passover, the sudden departure of the Israelites, the passage of the Red sea, and the thanksgiving of Moses and the people on the opposite shore, after the destruction of Pharaoh and his host, chap. 12–15. (5.) The narration of various miracles wrought in behalf of the people during their journeyings towards Sinai, chap. 15–17. (6.) The promulgation of the law on mount Sinai. This includes the preparation of the people by Moses, and the promulgation, first of the moral law, then of the judicial law, and subsequently of the ceremonial law, including the instructions for the erection of the tabernacle and the completion of that house of God, chap. 19–40.

The scope of the book is not only to preserve the memorial of the departure of the Israelites from Egypt, but to present to view the church of God in her afflictions and triumphs; to point out the providential care of God over her, and the judgments inflicted on her enemies. It clearly shows the accomplishment of the divine promises and prophecies delivered to Abraham: that his posterity would be numerous, Gen. 15:5; 17:4–6; 46:27; Num. 1:1–3, 46; and that they should be afflicted in a land not their own, whence they should depart in the fourth generation with great substance, Gen. 15:13–16; Exod. 12:40, 41. Their exodus in many particulars well illustrates the state of Christ's church in the wilderness of this world, until her arrival in the heavenly Canaan. See 1 Cor. 10; and also the epistle to the Hebrews. The book of Exodus brings before us many and singular types of Christ: Moses, Deut. 18:15; Aaron, Heb. 4:14–16; ver. 4, 5; the paschal lamb, Ex. 12:46; John 19:36; 1 Cor. 5:7, 8; the manna, Ex. 16:15; 1 Cor. 10:3; the rock in Horeb, Ex. 17:6; 1 Cor. 10:4; the mercy-seat, Ex. 37:6; Rom. 3:25; Heb. 4:16; the tabernacle, Ex. 40, "The Word *tabernacled* among us," John 1:14.

This departure from Egypt, and the subsequent wanderings of the children of Israel in the desert, form one of the great epochs in their history. They were constantly led by Jehovah, and the whole series of events is a constant succession of miracles. From their breaking up at Rameses, to their arrival on the confines of the promised land, there was an interval of forty years, during which one whole generation passed away, and the whole Mosaic law was given, and sanctioned by the thunders and lightnings of Sinai. There is no portion of history extant which so displays the interposition of an overruling Providence in the affairs both of nations and of individuals, as that which recounts these wanderings of Israel.

The four hundred and thirty years referred to in Ex. 12:40, date, according to the received chronology, from the time when the promise was made to Abraham, Gen. 15:13. From the arrival of Jacob in Egypt to the exodus of his posterity, was about two hundred and thirty years. The threescore and fifteen souls had now become 600,000, besides children. They took with them great numbers of cattle, and much Egyptian spoil. It was only by the mighty hand of God that their deliverance was effected; and there seems to have been a special vindication of his glory in the fact that the Nile, the flies, the frogs, fishes, cattle, etc., which were made the means or the subjects of the plagues of Egypt, were there regarded with idolatrous veneration.

After the tenth and decisive plague had been sent, the Israelites were dismissed from Egypt in haste. They are supposed to have been assembled at Rameses, or Heroöpolis, in the land of Goshen, about thirty-five miles north-west of Suez, on the ancient canal which united the Nile with the Red sea. They set off on the fifteenth day of the first month,

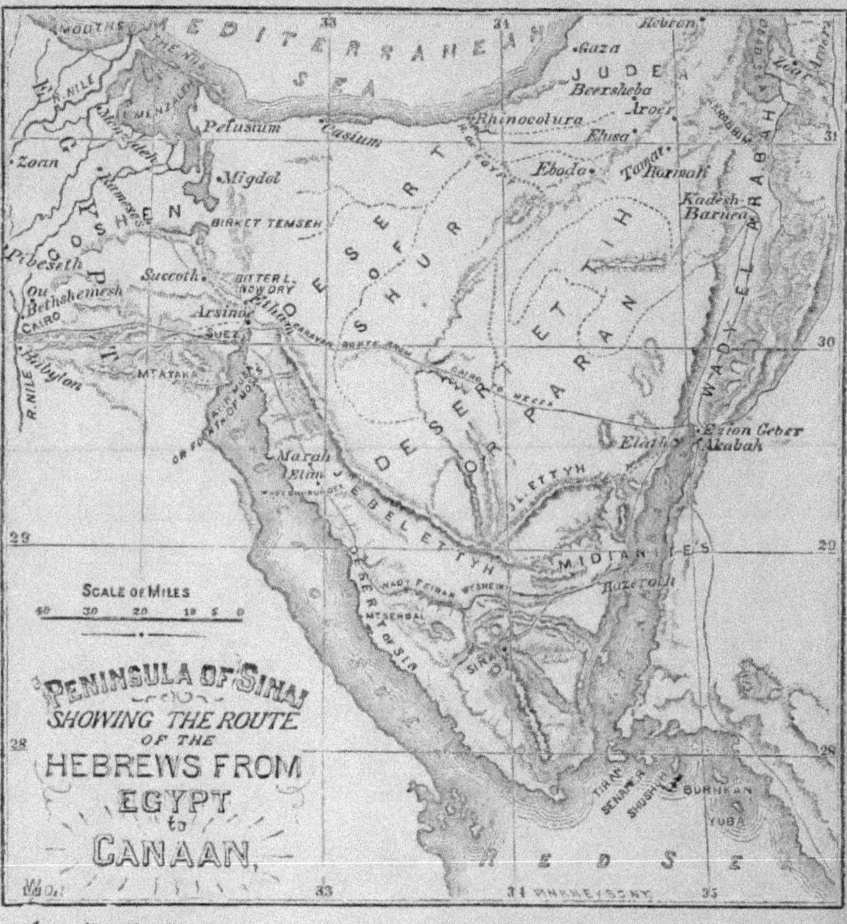

the day after the Passover, that is, about the middle of April. Their course was south-east as far as Etham; but then, instead of keeping on directly to Sinai, they turned to the south, Ex. 14:2, on the west side of the Red sea, which they reached three days after starting, probably near Suez. Here, by means of a strong east wind, God miraculously divided the waters of the sea in such a way that the Israelites passed over the bed of it on dry ground; while the Egyptians, who attempted to follow them, were drowned by the returning waters. The arm of the sea at Suez is now only three or four miles wide, and at low water may be forded. It is known to have been formerly wider and deeper; but the drifting sands of ages have greatly filled and altered it. The miracle here wrought was an amazing one, and revealed the hand of God more signally than any of the ten plagues had done. According to the Bible, God caused a "strong east wind" to blow; the deep waters were sundered, and "gathered together;" "the floods stood upright as a heap;" "the children of Israel walked upon dry land in the midst of the sea, and the waters were a wall unto them on their right hand and on their left." These effects continued all night till the morning watch, and without obstructing the progress of the Hebrews; whereas in the morning the pursuing Egyptians were covered by the sea, and "sank like lead in the mighty waters." These were wonders towards the effecting of which any wind must have been as insufficient as Naaman's mere washing in Jordan would have been to the healing of his leprosy. It should here be stated also, that some geographers think this miracle took place below mount Atakah, ten or twelve miles south of Suez, where the sea is about twelve miles wide. This opinion is liable to several objections, though it cannot be *proved* to be false. At this late day the precise locality may be undiscoverable, like the point of a soul's transition from the bondage of Satan into the kingdom of God; but in both cases the work is of God, and the glory of it is his alone.

Having offered thanksgiving to God for their wonderful deliverance, the Israelites advanced along the eastern shore of the Red sea and through the valleys and desert to mount Sinai. This part of their route may be readily traced, and Marah, Elim, and the desert of Sin have been with much probability identified. They arrived at mount Sinai in the third month, or June, probably about the middle of it, having been two months on their journey. Here the law was given, and here they abode during all the transactions recorded in the remainder of Exodus, in Leviticus, and in the first nine chapters of Numbers, that is, until the twentieth day of the second month (May) in the following year, a period of about eleven months.

Breaking up at this time from Sinai, they marched northwards through the desert of Paran, or perhaps along the eastern arm of the Red sea and north through El-Arabah, to Kadesh-barnea, near the south-east border of Canaan. Rephidim near mount Sinai, and Taberah, Kibroth-hattaaveh, and Hazeroth, on their journey north, were the scenes of incidents which may be found described under their several heads. From Kadesh-barnea, spies were sent out to view the promised land, and brought back an evil report, probably in August of the same year. The people murmured, and were directed by Jehovah to turn back and wander in the desert, until the carcasses of that generation should all fall in the wilderness, Num. 14:25. This they did, wandering from one station to another in the great desert of Paran, lying south of Palestine, and also in the great sandy valley called El-Ghor and chiefly El-Arabah, which extends from the Dead sea to the gulf of Akaba, the eastern arm of the Red sea. See JORDAN. Where and how these long years were spent we are not informed, nor by what routes they traversed the desert, nor how they were furnished with food except manna. Moses says they "compassed mount Seir many days," always under the guidance of the pillar of fire and cloud, Num. 9:22; he also gives a list of seventeen stations, mostly unknown, where they rested or dwelt before reaching Ezion-gaber, Num. 33:19–35; and then mentions their return to Kadesh, ver. 36, 37, in the first month, Num. 20:1, after an interval of almost thirty-eight years. While thus a second time encamped at Kadesh, Moses sent to the king of Idumæa, to ask liberty to pass through his dominions, that is, through the chain of mountains (mount Seir) lying along the eastern side of the great valley El-Arabah. See IDUMÆA. This was refused; and Israel, feeling too weak to penetrate into Palestine from the south, in face of the powerful tribes of Canaanites dwelling there, was compelled to take the southern passage around Edom, Num. 21:4. Soon after turning, they came to mount Hor, where Aaron died and was buried, Num. 20:20–28. Proceeding southward along the valley El-Arabah to Ezion-gaber, at the head of the eastern gulf of the Red sea, they here passed through the eastern mountains, and then turned north along the eastern desert, by the route which the great Syrian caravan of Mohammedan pilgrims now passes in going to Mecca. They arrived at the brook Zered, on the southern border of Moab, just forty years after their departure from Egypt.

See a tabular view of the various encampments of the Israelites, under WANDERINGS.

EXOR'CISTS, from a Greek word signifying *to conjure*, to use the name of God or certain magical ceremonies with design to expel devils from places or bodies which they possess. The apostles were enabled to cast out evil spirits in Christ's name, Matt. 10:1; Mark 16:17; Luke 10:17; and designing men, both before and after the Saviour's death, pretended to exercise the same power, Matt. 12:27; Mark 9:38; Luke 9:49, 50; Acts 19:13–17. Exorcists were thought to have gained this power by secret studies respecting the nature of demons, and the powers of certain herbs, drugs, and stones, and were accustomed to use various forms of adjuration and incantation in their unlawful art; but the whole was delusion and imposture, and strictly forbidden. See DIVINATION.

EXPIATION, an act by which satisfaction is made for a crime, and the liability to punishment for it is cancelled. It supposes penitence and faith on the sinner's part. Among the Jews, expiation was effected by a divinely appointed and typical system of sacrifices, all pointing to Christ. The New Testament shows Him to be the true sin-offering for mankind, "the Lamb of God," "our Passover," offering "his own blood," and putting away "sin by the sacrifice of himself," John 1:29; 1 Cor. 5:7; Eph. 1:7; Heb. 9:26.

THE DAY OF EXPIATION, OR ATONEMENT, was a yearly solemnity, observed with rest and fasting on the tenth day of Tisri, five days before the feast of tabernacles, Lev. 23:7; 25:9. The ceremonies of this all-important day are minutely described in Lev. 16. On this day alone the high-priest entered the Most Holy Place, Heb. 9:7; but the various rites of the day required him to enter several times. First with the golden censer and a vessel filled with incense. Then with the blood of the bullock, which he had offered for his own sins and those of all the priests, in which he dipped his finger, and sprinkled it seven times below and once above the mercy-seat. This done, he left the basin of blood behind, and withdrew again. The third time he entered with the blood of the ram which he had offered for the sins of the nation, with which he sprinkled towards the veil of the tabernacle eight times; and having mixed it with the blood of the bullock, he sprinkled again towards the horns of the altar of incense seven times, and once above it towards the east; after which, having again left the sanctuary and taken with him the basins of blood, he poured out the whole on the floor of the altar of burnt-offering. The fourth time he entered to bring out the censer and vessel of incense; and having returned, he washed his hands and performed the other services of the day. The ceremony of the scape-goat also took place on this day. Two goats were set apart, one of which was sacrificed to the Lord, while the other, called the azazel or scape-goat, which was determined by lot to be set at liberty, was sent into the desert burdened with the sins of the people. All these solemn rites pointed to Christ, and in every age there were many believers who had spiritual discernment of their sacred meaning, Heb. 9-11. They looked unto Him whom they had pierced, and mourned. As this day of expiation was the great fast-day of the Jewish church, so godly sorrow for sin characterizes the Christian's looking unto the Lamb of God, and "the rapture of pardon" is mingled with "penitent tears."

EYE. The same Hebrew word means both eye and fountain. Besides its common use, to denote the organ of sight, it is often used figuratively in the Bible. Most of these passages, however, require no explanation. The custom of sealing up the eyes of criminals, still practised in the East, is thought to be alluded to in Isa. 6:10; 44:18. The expression, "As the eyes of servants look unto the hand of their masters," Psa. 123:2, is elucidated by a knowledge of the fact that many eastern servants are taught to stand always upon the watch, and are in general directed by a nod, a wink, or some slight motion of the fingers imperceptible to strangers. Many Scripture phrases intimate the soul-like nature of the eye, quickly and truly expressing the thoughts of the heart: such as "the bountiful eye" and the "evil eye," Prov. 22:9; 23:6; "haughty eyes" and "wanton eyes," Prov. 6:17; Isa. 3:16. "The lust of the eyes," 1 John 2:16, expresses a craving for any of the gay vanities of this life. The threatening against "the eye that mocketh at his father," Prov. 30:17, is explained by the habit of birds of prey, which attack the eyes of a living enemy, and quickly devour those of the dead. A "single" eye, Matt. 6:22, is one which is clear, and sees every object as it is.

There are allusions in the Bible, and in many ancient and modern writers, to the practice of painting the eyelids, to make the eyes appear large, lustrous, and languishing. Jezebel, 2 Kin. 9:30, is said to have "painted her face," literally, "put her eyes in paint." This was sometimes done to excess, Jer. 4:30; and was practised by abandoned women, Prov. 6:25. A small probe of wood, ivory, or silver, is wet with rose-water, and dipped in an impalpable powder; this is then drawn between the lids of the eye nearly closed, and leaves a narrow black border which is thought a

great ornament. The powder for this purpose, called kohol, is made by burning a kind of aromatic resin, and sometimes of lead ore and other substances, for the benefit of the eyes. In Persia this custom is as common among the men as among the women; so also in ancient Egypt, as the Theban monuments show. "The females of Arabia," Niebuhr says, "color their nails blood-red, and their hands and feet yellow, with the herb Al-henna. (See CAMPHIRE.) They also tinge the inside of their eyelids coal-black with *köchel*, a coloring material prepared from lead ore. They not only enlarge their eyebrows, but also paint other figures of black, as ornaments, upon the face and hands. Sometimes they even prick through the skin, in various figures, and then lay certain substances upon the wounds, which eat in so deeply, that the ornaments thus impressed are rendered permanent for life. All this the Arabian women esteem as beauty."

EZE'KIEL, son of Buzi, a prophet of the sacerdotal race, was carried captive to Babylon by Nebuchadnezzar, with Jehoiachin king of Judah, B. C. 598, and placed by the river Chebar. See NINEVEH. He began his ministry in the thirtieth year of his age, according to the general account; but perhaps in the thirtieth year after the covenant was renewed with God in the reign of Josiah, Ezek. 1:1, which answers to the fifth year of Ezekiel's captivity. The elders of Israel resorted to him for direction, Ezra 8:1; 14:1; 20:1; 33:31. He prophesied twenty years, B. C. 595–575, till the fourteenth year after the final captivity of Jerusalem. During the first eight years he was contemporary with Jeremiah. Daniel also lived at the same time, Ezek. 14:14, 16; 28:3, though most of his predictions are of a later date.

The BOOK OF EZEKIEL abounds with sublime visions of the divine glory, and awful denunciations against Israel for their rebellious spirit against God, and the abominations of their idolatry, chap. 1–24. It contains also similar denunciations against Tyre and other hostile nations, chap. 25–32. The latter part of the book contains oracles respecting the return and restoration of the people of God, chap. 33–48.

EZ'ION-GE'BER, or EZION-GABER, a city at the northern extremity of the Elanitic or eastern gulf of the Red sea, and close by Elath. The Israelites rested here in the last year of their wanderings from Egypt to Canaan, Num. 33:35; Deut. 2:8. At this port Solomon equipped his fleets for the voyage to Ophir, 1 Kin. 9:26. A similar enterprise of Jehoshaphat failed, 1 Kin. 22:48; 2 Chr. 20:36. See ELATH and EXODUS.

EZ'RA, a celebrated priest and leader of the Jewish nation. He was "a ready scribe in the law," a learned, able, and faithful man, and appears to have enjoyed great consideration in the Persian court. During the eighty years embraced in his narrative, most of the reign of Cyrus passed, and the whole reign of Cambyses, Smerdis, Darius Hystaspis, Xerxes, and eight years of Artaxerxes Longimanus. From this last king he received letters, money, and every desirable help, and went at the head of a large party of returning exiles to Jerusalem, B. C. 457. Here he instituted many reforms in the conduct of the people, and in the public worship, Ezra 8–10; Neh. 8. After this he is generally believed to have collected and revised all the books of the Old Testament Scripture, which form the present canon.

The BOOK OF EZRA contains a history

of the return of the Jews from the time of Cyrus; with an account of his own subsequent proceedings, B. C. 450. There are two apocryphal books ascribed to him under the name of Esdras, which is only the Greek form of the name Ezra.

F.

FA'BLE, an idle, groundless, and worthless story, like the mythological legends of the heathen and the vain traditions of the Jews. These were often not only false and weak, but pernicious, 1 Tim. 4:7; Tit. 1:14; 2 Pet. 1:16.

FACE, and presence, expressed by the same word in Hebrew, are often put for the person himself, Gen. 48:11; Exod. 33:14; Isa. 63:9. No man has seen the face of God, that is, had a full revelation of his glory, Exod. 33:20; John 1:18; 1 Tim. 6:16. To see him "face to face," is to enjoy his presence, Gen. 32:30; Num. 14:14; Deut. 5:4, and have a clear manifestation of his nature and grace, 1 Cor. 13:12.

FAIR-HA'VENS, a roadstead or small bay, near the town of Lasea, midway on the southern coast of Crete, where Paul wished to winter when on the voyage to Rome, Acts 27:8. The sailors preferred Phenice as safer, and were wrecked in consequence. It still retains nearly its old name.

FAITH is the assent of the understanding to any truth. Religious faith is assent to the truth of divine revelation and of the events and doctrines contained in it. This may be merely historical, without producing any effect on our lives and conversation; and it is then a dead faith, such as even the devils have. But a living or saving faith not only believes the great doctrines of religion as true, but embraces them with the heart and affections; and is thus the source of sincere obedience to the divine will, exhibited in the life and conversation. Faith in Christ is a grace wrought in the heart by the Holy Spirit, whereby we receive Christ as our Saviour, our Prophet, Priest, and King, and love and obey him as such. This living faith in Christ is the means of salvation—not meritoriously, but instrumentally. Without it there can be no forgiveness of sins, and no holiness of life; and they who are justified by faith, live and walk by faith, Mark 16:16; John 3:15, 16; Acts 16:31; 1 John 5:10.

True faith is an essential grace, and a main-spring of Christian life. By it the Christian overcomes the world, the flesh, and the devil, and receives the crown of righteousness, 1 Tim. 4:7, 8. In virtue of it, worthy men of old wrought great wonders, Heb. 11; Acts 14:9; 1 Cor. 13:2, being sustained by Omnipotence in doing whatever God enjoined, Matt. 17:20; Mark 9:23; 11:23, 24. In Rom. 1:8, faith is put for the exhibition of faith, in the practice of all the duties implied in a profession of faith.

FAITH'FUL, in many passages in the Bible, means "believing." Thus in Gal. 3:9, believers are said to be blessed with Abraham, because of his preëminent distinction above all men for steadfast faith in God. This appellation is given in Scripture to true Christians, to indicate not only their saving faith in Christ, but their trustworthy and consistent Christian character, Acts 16:15; 1 Cor. 4:17; Eph. 6:21; Col. 4:9; 1 Pet. 5:12. "A faithful saying" is one that cannot prove false, 1 Tim. 1:15; 2 Tim. 2:11.

FAITH'FULNESS is an infinite attribute of Jehovah; adapted to make perfect both the confidence of those who believe his word and rely on his promises, and the despair of those who doubt his word and defy his threatenings, Deut. 28:26; Num. 23:19; Psa. 89:33, 34; Heb. 10:23.

FAM'INE. Scripture records several famines in Palestine, and the neighboring countries, Gen. 12:10; 26:1; Ruth 1:1; 2 Kin. 6:25; Acts 11:27. The most remarkable one was that of seven years in Egypt, while Joseph was governor, Gen. 41. It was distinguished for its duration, extent, and severity; particularly as Egypt is one of the countries least subject to such a calamity, by reason of its general fertility. Famine is sometimes a natural effect, as when the Nile does not overflow in Egypt, or rains do not fall in Judea, at the customary season; or when caterpillars, locusts, or other insects, destroy the fruits. But all natural causes are under the control of God; and he often so directs them as to chastise the rebellious with want, 2 Kin. 8:1, 2; Ezek. 6:11; Matt. 24:7. The worst famine is a spiritual one, Amos 8:11.

FAN, an instrument used for winnowing grain. In the East, fans are of two kinds: one a sort of fork, having three or four prongs, and a handle four feet long; with this they throw up the grain to the wind, that the chaff may be blown away: the other sort of fan is formed to produce wind when the air is calm, Isa. 30:24. This process illustrates the complete separation which Christ the Judge will effect between the righteous and the wicked, Jer. 15:7; Matt. 3:12. See THRESHING.

FARTHING. Two different Roman brass coins are translated by this word: one of these, the *assarion*, Matt. 10:29, Luke 12:6, was worth less than a cent; the other, the *kodrantes*, Matt. 5:26, was probably nearly four mills.

FASTING has, in all ages, and among all nations, been practised in times of sorrow, and affliction, Jonah 3:5. It may be regarded as a dictate of nature, which under these circumstances refuses nourishment, and suspends the cravings of hunger. In the Bible no example is mentioned of fasting, properly so called, before Moses. His forty days' fast, like that of Elijah and of our Lord, was miraculous, Deut. 9:9; 1 Kin. 19:8; Matt. 4:2. The Jews often had recourse to this practice, when they had occasion to humble themselves before God, to confess their sins and deprecate his displeasure, Judg. 20:26; 1 Sam. 7:6; 2 Sam. 12:16; Neh. 9:1; Jer. 36:9. Especially in times of public calamity, they appointed extraordinary fasts, and made even the children at the breast fast, Joel 2:16; but see Dan. 10:2, 3. They began the observance of their fasts at sunset, and remained without eating until the same hour the next day. The great day of expiation was probably the only annual and national fast-day among them.

It does not appear by his own practice or by his commands, that our Lord instituted any particular fast. On one occasion, he intimated that his disciples would fast after his death, Luke 5:34, 35. Accordingly, the life of the apostles and first believers was a life of self-denials, sufferings, and fastings, 2 Cor. 5:7; 11:27. Our Saviour recognized the custom, and the apostles practised it as occasion required, Matt. 6:16-18; Acts 13:3; 1 Cor. 7:5.

FAT. The fat portions of animals offered in sacrifice were always to be consumed, as being the choice part and especially sacred to the Lord. The blood was also sacred, as containing the life of the animal. The Jews were forbidden to eat either, Lev. 3:16, 17; 7:23-27.

FATHER, is often synonymous with ancestor, founder, or originator, as Gen. 4:20, 21; John 8:56; Rom. 4:16. Joseph was a father to Pharaoh, Gen. 45:8, as his counsellor and provider. God is the FATHER of men, as their Creator, Deut. 32:6; Isa. 63:16; 64:8; Luke 3:38. But as we have forfeited the rights of children by our sins, it is only through Christ that we can call God by that endearing name, "our Father," John 20:17; Rom. 8:15-17.

In patriarchal times, a father was master and judge in his own household, and exercised an authority almost unlimited over his family. Filial disobedience or disrespect was a high offence. Under the law, certain acts of children were capital crimes, Ex. 21:15, 17; Lev. 20:9; and the father was required to bring his son to the public tribunal, Deut. 21:18-21. See MOTHER.

FEASTS. God appointed several festivals, or days of rest and worship, among the Jews, to perpetuate the memory of great events wrought in favor of them: the Sabbath commemorated the creation of the world; the Passover, the departure out of Egypt; the Pentecost, the law given at Sinai, etc. At the three great feasts of the year, the Passover, Pentecost, and that of Tabernacles, all the males of the nation were required to visit the temple, Ex. 23:14-17; Deut. 16:16, 17; and to protect their borders from invasion during their absence, the shield of a special providence was always interposed, Ex. 34:23, 24. The other festivals were the Feast of Trumpets, or New Moon, Purim, Dedication, the Sabbath year, and the year of Jubilee. These are described elsewhere. The observance of these sacred festivals was adapted not merely to freshen the remembrance of their early history as a nation, but to keep alive the influence of religion and the expectation of the Messiah, to deepen their joy in God, to dispel animosities and jealousies, and to form new associations between the different tribes and families. See also Day of EXPIATION.

In the Christian church, we have no festival that clearly appears to have been instituted by our Saviour, or his apostles; but as we commemorate his death as often as we celebrate his supper, he has hereby seemed to institute a perpetual feast. Christians have always celebrated the memory of his resurrection by regarding the Sabbath, which we see, from Rev. 1:10, was in John's time commonly called "the Lord's day."

Feasts of love, Jude 12, were public banquets of a frugal kind, instituted by the primitive Christians, and connected by them with the celebration of the Lord's supper. The provisions were contributed by the more wealthy, and were common to all Christians, whether rich or poor, who chose to partake. Portions were also sent to the sick and absent members. These love-feasts were intended as an exhibition of mutual Christian affection; but they became subject to abuses, and were afterwards generally discontinued, 1 Cor. 11:17–34.

The Hebrews were a hospitable people, and were wont to welcome their guests with a feast, and dismiss them with another, Gen. 19:3; 31:27; Judg. 6:19; 2 Sam. 3:20; 2 Kin. 6:23. The returning prodigal was thus welcomed, Luke 15:23. Many joyful domestic events were observed with feasting: birthdays, etc., Gen. 21:8; 40:20; Job 1:4; Matt. 14:6; marriages, Gen. 29:22; Judg. 14:10; John 2:1–10; sheep-shearing and harvesting, Judg. 9:27; 1 Sam. 25:2, 36; 2 Sam. 13:23. A feast was also provided at funerals, 2 Sam. 3:35; Jer. 16:7. Those who brought sacrifices and offerings to the temple were wont to feast upon them there, with joy and praise to God, Deut. 12:6, 7; 1 Sam. 16:5; 2 Sam. 6:19. They were taught to invite all the needy to partake with them, Deut. 16:11; and even to make special feasts for the poor, Deut. 12:17–19; 14:28, 29; 26:12–15; a custom which the Saviour specially commended, Luke 14:12–14.

The manner of holding a feast was anciently marked with great simplicity. But at the time of Christ many Roman customs had been introduced. The feast or "supper" usually took place at five or six in the afternoon, and often continued to a late hour. The guests were invited some time in advance; and those who accepted the invitation were again notified by servants when the hour arrived, Matt. 22:4–8; Luke 14:16–24. The door was guarded against uninvited persons; and was at length closed for the day by the hand of the master of the house, Matt. 25:10; Luke 13:24. Sometimes very large numbers were present, Esth. 1:3, 5; Luke 14:16–24; and on such occasions a "governor of the feast" was appointed, whose social qualities, tact, firmness, and temperance fitted him to preside, John 2:8. The guests were arranged with a careful regard to their claims to honor, Gen. 43:33; 1 Sam. 9:22; Prov. 25:6, 7; Matt. 23:6; Luke 14:7; in which matter the laws of etiquette are still jealously enforced in the East. Sometimes the host provided light, rich, loose robes for the company; and if so, the refusing to wear one was a gross insult, Ecc. 9:8; Matt. 22:11; Rev. 3:4, 5. The guests reclined around the tables; water and perfumes were served to them, Mark 7:2; Luke 7:44–46; and after eating, the hands were again washed, a servant pouring water over them. See illustration in BED. During the repast and after it various entertainments were provided; enigmas were proposed, Judg. 14:12; eastern tales were told; music and hired dancers, and often excessive drinking, etc., occupied the time, Isa. 5:12; 24:7–9; Amos 6:5. See EATING, FOOD.

FE'LIX, a Roman governor of Judea; originally a slave, but manumitted and promoted by Claudius Cæsar, from whom he received the name of Claudius. He is described by the historian Tacitus as cruel, licentious, and base. In Judea he married Drusilla, sister of the younger Agrippa, having enticed her from her second husband Azizus. Paul having been sent by Lysias to Cæsarea, then the seat of government, Felix gave him an audience, and was convinced of his innocence. Nevertheless he kept him a prisoner, though with many alleviations, in hopes that his friends would purchase his liberty by a heavy bribe. Meanwhile his wife Drusilla, who was a Jewess, desired to hear Paul explain the new religion; and the apostle being summoned before them, discoursed with his usual boldness on justice, chastity, and the final judgment. Felix trembled, but hastily remanded Paul to confinement, and stifled his convictions—a melancholy instance of the power of lust and the danger of delay. Two years after, A. D. 60, he was recalled to Rome; and left Paul in prison, in order to appease the Jews. He was brought to trial, however, for maladministration, found guilty, and barely escaped death through the intercession of his brother Pallas, another royal favorite, Acts 23:26; 24.

FER'RET, a sort of weasel, Lev. 11:30. The Hebrew word means rather a species of lizard, the gecko, which Moses forbids as unclean.

FES'TUS, PORTIUS, succeeded Felix in the government of Judea, A. D. 60. To oblige the Jews, Felix, when he resigned his government, left Paul in bonds at Cæsarea in Palestine, Acts 24:27; and when Festus arrived, he was entreated by the principal Jews to condemn the apostle, or to order him up to Jerusalem—they having conspired to assassinate him in the way. Festus, however, answered that it was not customary with the Romans to condemn any man without hearing him; and promised to hear their accusations at Cæsarea. Five days after, on hearing Paul and learning the nature of the charges against him, he proposed to him to abide the issue of a trial before the Jewish Sanhedrim. But Paul appealed to Cæsar; and so secured himself from the prosecution of the Jews, and the intentions of Festus. The governor gave him another hearing during a congratulatory visit of king Agrippa, in order to make out a statement to be forwarded with him to Rome. Finding how greatly robberies abounded in Judea, Festus very diligently pursued the thieves; and he also suppressed a magician, who drew the people after him into the desert. Josephus speaks well of his brief administration. He died in Judea, A. D. 62, and was succeeded by Albinus.

FIG. The fig-tree is common in Palestine and the East, and flourishes with the greatest luxuriance in those barren and stony situations where little else will grow. Its large size, and its abundance of five-lobed leaves, render it a pleasant shade-tree; and its fruit furnished a wholesome food, very much used in all the lands of the Bible. Thus it was a symbol of peace and plenty, 1 Kin. 4:25; Mic. 4:4; Zech. 3:10; John 1:49-51. Figs are of two sorts, the "boccore," and the "kermouse." The black and white boccore, or early fig, is produced in June; though the kermouse, the fig properly so called, which is preserved, and made up into cakes, is rarely ripe before August. There is also a long

dark-colored kermouse, that sometimes hangs upon the trees all winter.

The fruit of the fig-tree is one of the delicacies of the East, and is very often spoken of in Scripture. The early fig was especially prized, Isa. 28:4; Jer. 24:2; Nah. 3:12, though the summer fig is most abundant, 2 Kin. 20:7; Isa. 38:21. It is a peculiarity of the fig-tree that its fruit begins to appear before the leaves, and without any show of blossoms. It has, indeed, small and hidden blossoms, but the passage in Hab. 3:17, should read, according to the original Hebrew, "Although the fig-tree should not *bear*," instead of "blossom." Its leaves come so late in the spring as to justify the words of Christ, "Ye know that summer is nigh," Matt. 24:32; Song 2:13. The fresh fruit is shaped like a pear. The dried figs of Palestine were probably like those which are brought to our own country; sometimes, however, they are dried on a string. We likewise read of "cakes of figs," 1 Sam. 25:18; 2 Kin. 20:7; 1 Chr. 12:40. These were probably formed by pressing the fruit forcibly into baskets or other vessels, so as to reduce them to a solid cake or lump. In this way dates are still prepared in Arabia.

The barren fig-tree which was withered at our Saviour's word, as an awful warning to unfruitful professors of religion, seems to have spent itself in leaves. It stood by the way-side, free to all; and as the time for stripping the trees of their fruit had not come, Mark 11:14, it was reasonable to expect to find it covered with figs in various stages of growth.

Yet there was "nothing thereon, but leaves only," Matt. 21:19.

FIR, an evergreen tree, of beautiful appearance, whose lofty height and dense foliage afford a spacious shelter and shade. The Hebrew word often seems to mean the CYPRESS, which see. It was used for ship-building, Ezek. 27:5; for musical instruments, 2 Sam. 6:5; for beams and rafters of houses, 1 Kin. 5:8, 10; 9:11; Song 1:17.

FIRE, in Scripture, is often connected with the presence of Jehovah; as in the burning bush, and on mount Sinai, Ex. 3:2; 19:18; in Psalm 18, and the ode of Habakkuk. The second coming of Christ will be "in flaming fire," 2 Thess. 1:8. In the New Testament it illustrates the enlightening, cheering, and purifying agency of the Holy Spirit, Matt. 3:11; Acts 2:3. By sending fire from heaven to consume sacrifices, God often signified his acceptance of them: as in the case of Abel, Gen. 4:4; Abraham, Gen. 15:17; Manoah, Judg. 13:19, 20; Elijah, 1 Kin. 18:38; and at the dedication of the tabernacle and the temple, Lev. 9:24; 2 Chr. 7:1. This sacred fire was preserved by the priests with the utmost care, Isa. 31:9. In many ancient religions fire was worshipped; and children were made to pass through the fire to Moloch, 2 Kin. 17:17; Jer. 7:31; Ezek. 16:21; 23:37. The Jews had occasion for fires, except for cooking, only during a small part of the year. Besides their ordinary hearths and ovens, they warmed their apartments with "a fire of coals" in a brazier, Jer. 36:22, 23; Luke 22:30. They were forbidden to kindle a fire on the Sabbath, Ex. 35:3—a prohibition perhaps only of cooking on that day, but understood by many Jews even now in the fullest extent; it is avoided by employing gentile servants. Another provision of the Mosaic law was designed to protect the standing corn, etc., in the dry summer season, Ex. 22:6. The earth is to be destroyed by fire, 2 Pet. 3:7; of which the destruction of Sodom, and the volcanoes and earthquakes which so often indicate the internal commotions of the globe, may serve as warnings.

FIR'KIN, John 2:6, a Greek measure, equivalent to the Hebrew *bath*, and containing seven and a half gallons. The quantity of wine produced by the miracle at Cana was large; but the assemblage was also large; the festivities continued, it may be, a whole week, Judg. 14:12; and many would be drawn to the scene by hearing of the miracle.

FIR'MAMENT, Gen. 1:17, the expanse of the heavens immediately above the earth. The Hebrews seem to have viewed this as an immense crystalline dome, studded with stars, resting on the far distant horizon all around the spectator, and separating the waters above us from those on the earth. Through its windows the rain descended. It is not necessary to suppose they thought it was solid, Psa. 19:1; Isa. 40:22. It is not the aim of Scripture to give scientific statements of natural phenomena. Teaching religion, not astronomy or physics, it does not anticipate modern discoveries, but speaks of natural objects and occurrences in the common language of men everywhere. Hence, in part, its attractiveness in all ages as a book for the people.

FIRST-BORN. This phrase is not always to be understood literally; it is sometimes taken for the prime, most excellent, most distinguished of things, Psa. 89:27; Rom. 8:29; Heb. 1:4-6. Thus Jesus Christ is "the first-born of every creature," Col. 1:15, inasmuch as he was the "Only-begotten" of the Father before any creature was produced. He is "the first-born from the dead," Col. 1:18, because he is the beginning, and the author of the resurrection of all who die in faith.

After the destroying angel had slain the first-born of the Egyptians, God ordained that all the Jewish first-born, both of men and of beasts for service, should be consecrated to him; but the male children only were subject to this law. If a man had several wives, he was obliged to offer the first-born son by each one of them to the Lord. The first-born were offered at the temple, and redeemed for five shekels. The firstling of a clean beast was offered at the temple, not to be redeemed, but to be killed; an unclean beast, a horse, an ass, or a camel, was either redeemed or exchanged; an ass was redeemed by a lamb or five shekels; if not redeemed, it was killed, Ex. 13:2, 11, etc. The first-born son among the Hebrews, as among all other nations, enjoyed particular privileges. See BIRTHRIGHT.

FIRST-FRUITS were presents made to God of part of the fruits of the harvest, to express the submission, dependence, and thankfulness of the offerers. The portion given was instead of the whole, in acknowledgment that all was due to God. They were offered in the temple before the crop was gathered, and when the harvest was over, before the people began to use their corn. The first of these first-fruits, offered in the name of the nation, was a sheaf of barley, gathered on the fifteenth of Nisan, in the evening, and threshed in a court of the temple. After it was well cleaned, about three pints of it were roasted, and pounded in a mortar. Over this was thrown a measure of olive-oil and a handful of incense; and the priest, taking the offering, waved it before the Lord towards the four cardinal points, throwing a handful of it into the fire on the altar, and keeping the rest. After this, all were at liberty to get in the harvest. When the wheat harvest was over, on the day of Pentecost they offered as first-fruits of another kind, in the name of the nation, two loaves, of about three pints of flour each, made of leavened dough, Lev. 23:10, 17. In addition to these first-fruits, every private person was obliged to bring his first-fruits to the temple, but Scripture prescribes neither the time nor the qantity.

There was, besides this, another sort of first-fruits paid to God, Num. 15:19, 21; Neh. 10:37: when the bread in the family was kneaded, a portion of it was set apart, and given to the priest or Levite of the place; if there were no priest or Levite, it was cast into the oven and there consumed.

Those offerings are also often called first-fruits, which were brought by the Israelites from devotion, to the temple, for the feast of thanksgiving, to which they invited their relations and friends, and the Levites of their cities. The first-fruits and tenths were the most considerable revenue of the priests and Levites.

Christians have "the first-fruits of the Holy Spirit," Rom. 8:23; that is, more abundant and more excellent gifts than the Jews; these were also a foretaste of the full harvest. "Christ is risen from the dead, and become the first-fruits of them that slept," 1 Cor. 15:20, the forerunner of all those who, because he lives, shall live also, John 14:19.

FISH, FISHER. The Hebrews have very few names of particular species of fish. Moses says in general, that all sorts of river, lake, or sea fish, which have scales and fins, may be eaten; all others shall be to the Hebrews an abomination, Lev. 11:9–12; Deut. 14:9, 10. The Nile had an early celebrity, which it still retains, for the abundance and excellence of its fish, Ex. 7:18–21; Num. 11:5. The sea of Tiberias also still abounds in fish, Luke 5:5; John 21:6–11. They were a common article of food among the Jews, Matt. 7:10, and were obtained from the Mediterranean, Neh. 13:16, and from the Jordan. They were caught with hooks, Amos 4:2, spears, Job 41:7, and nets, Isa. 19:8–10. The "great fish," Jon. 1:17, which swallowed Jonah, may have been of the shark genus, as this animal is common in the Mediterranean. The original word, both in Hebrew and Greek, Matt. 12:40, means a fish, and not specifically a "whale." See WHALE. Fishermen are often spoken of in the Bible, and a large proportion of the twelve apostles of our Lord were of that occupation. Christ made them "fishers of men," Matt. 4:18–22.

The early Christians, in times of persecution, used to engrave the form of a fish on their medals, seals, and tombs, as a tacit confession of their faith; as the five letters of the Greek word for fish, ἰχθυς, are the initial letters of five words, signifying "Jesus Christ, the Son of God, the Saviour." This symbol has thus become the subject of a superstitious regard.

FITCH'ES, or VETCH'ES, a species of wild pea. Two Hebrew words are translated "fitches," one of which probably means *spelt*, Ezek. 4:9, and the other *gith*, a plant resembling fennel, and very pungent, Isa. 28:25. The seed is black, and aromatic.

FLAG'ON. The Hebrew word everywhere rendered in the English version flagon, 2 Sam. 6:19; 1 Chr. 16:3; Song 2:5; Hos. 3:1, means rather a *cake*, especially of dried grapes or raisins, pressed into a particular form. These are mentioned as delicacies, by which the weary and languid are refreshed; they were also offered to idols, Hos. 3:1. They differed from the dried clusters of grapes not pressed into any form, 1 Sam. 25:18, and also from the "cakes of figs." We may refer, in illustration, to the manner in which with us cheeses are pressed in various forms, as of pine-apples, etc., and also the manner in which dates are prepared at the present day by the Arabs. See Figs.

FLAX, a well-known plant, upon which the industry of mankind has been exercised with the greatest success and utility, Josh. 2:6; Prov. 31:13. Moses speaks of the flax in Egypt, Ex. 9:31, which country has been celebrated, from time immemorial, for its production and manufacture. The "fine linen of Egypt," which was manufactured from this article, is spoken of for its superior excellence, in Scripture, Prov. 7:16; Ezek. 27:7. It is, however, probable that fine cotton is sometimes to be understood when the Byssus is spoken of. Most of the linen found wrapped around Egyptian mummies will hardly compare with our common sheetings. But some specimens are found of most remarkable fineness; one containing 152 threads in the warp, and 71 in the woof, to each square inch; and another, 270 double threads in the warp, and 110 in the woof, per inch. See Cotton and Linen.

The prophet Isaiah, in speaking of the gentleness of the Messiah, makes use of a proverbial expression, which is also quoted by Matthew and applied to Jesus: "The bruised reed he shall not break, and the smoking flax he shall not quench," Isa. 42:3; Matt. 12:20. Here "flax" is used for the wick of a lamp or taper, which was usually made of flax. He will not break a reed already bruised and ready to be broken, nor extinguish a flickering, dying lamp, just ready to expire; that is, he will not oppress his humble and penitent followers, but cherish the feeblest beginnings of true grace.

FLESH, the substance of which the bodies of men and animals are composed. In the Bible, besides the ordinary sense, Job 33:25, it denotes mankind as a race, Gen. 6:12; Psa. 145:21; Isa. 40:5, 6; and all living creatures on the earth, Gen. 6:17, 19. It is often used in opposition to "spirit," as we use body and soul, Job 14:22; and sometimes means the body as animated and sensitive, Matt. 26:41, and the seat of bodily appetites, Prov. 5:11; 2 Cor. 7:1. In the New Testament, "flesh" is very often used to designate the bodily appetites, propensities, and passions, which draw men away from yielding themselves to the Lord and to the things of the Spirit. The flesh, or carnal principle, is opposed to the spirit, or spiritual principle, Rom. 8; Gal. 5:17.

FLOCKS. See Sheep.

FLOOD. See Deluge.

FLUTE, a soft, sweet-toned wind instrument of music. The word flute is used only in Dan. 3, and is supposed to mean a pipe with two reeds, such as are still to be found in the East. It is blown at the end. See Music, Pipe.

FLY, a genus of insects, of which there are a great many species. Moses declares them and most other insects to be unclean, Lev. 11:42. They abound in Egypt, and are annoying and vexatious in the extreme, attacking the eyelids, etc., in swarms and with the utmost pertinacity. How intolerable a plague of flies may be, is evident from the fact that whole districts in the Levant have been for a time depopulated by them, the inhabitants being unable to stand against their incessant attacks, Ex. 8:24. The Philistines and Canaanites adored Beelzebub, the fly-god, probably as a patron to protect them against these tormenting insects.

In Isa. 7:18, the prophet describing the armies of Egypt and Assyria, each under the symbol of one of the prevalent insects in those countries, says, "And it shall come to pass in that day that the Lord shall hiss for the fly that is in the uttermost part of the rivers of Egypt;" (or rather, as the same Hebrew word is rendered in Ex. 16:35, the fly that is in the borders of the streams of Egypt,) "and for the bee that is in the land of Assyria." It is thought by some that the fly here spoken of is the zimb, or Ethiopian fly, of which Mr. Bruce says, "It is, in size, very little larger than a bee, of a thicker proportion, and has wings which are broader than those of a bee, placed separate, like those of a fly; they are of pure gauze, without color or spot upon them; the head is

large. As soon as this plague appears, and their buzzing is heard, all the cattle forsake their food, and run wildly about the plain till they die, worn out with fatigue, fright, and hunger. No remedy remains but to leave the black earth, and hasten down to the sands of the desert; and there they remain while the rains last, this cruel enemy never daring to pursue them farther." The camel also is obliged to fly before these insects; and the elephant and rhinoceros coat themselves with a thick armor of mud.

FOOD. In ancient times the food of a people was more entirely the product of their own country than in our day. Palestine was favored with an abundance of animal food, grain, and vegetables. But throughout the East, vegetable food is more used than animal. Bread was the principal food. Grain of various kinds, beans, lentils, onions, grapes, together with olive oil, honey, and the milk of goats and cows were the ordinary fare. The wandering Arabs live much upon a coarse black bread. A very common dish in Syria is rice, with shreds of meat, vegetables, olive oil, etc., intermixed. A similar dish, made with beans, lentils, and various kinds of pulse, was in frequent use at an earlier age, Gen. 25 : 29–34 ; 2 Kin. 4 : 38–41. Fish was a common article of food, when accessible, and was very much used in Egypt. This country was also famous for cucumbers, melons, leeks, onions, and garlics, Num. 11:5. Such is the food of the Egyptians still. See EATING.

Animal food was always used on festive occasions; and the hospitable patriarchs lost little time in preparing for their guests a smoking dish from their flocks of sheep and goats, their herds of cattle, or their dove-cotes, Gen. 18:7 ; Luke 15:23. The rich had animal food more frequently, and their cattle were stalled and fattened for the table, 1 Sam. 16:20 ; Isa. 1:11 ; 11:6 ; Mal. 4:2. Among the poor, locusts were a common means of sustenance, being dried in the sun, or roasted over the fire on iron plates.

Water was the earliest and common drink. Wine of an intoxicating quality was early known, Gen. 9:20 ; 14:18 ; 40:1. Date-wine and similar beverages were common ; and the common people used a kind of sour wine, called vinegar in Ruth 2:14 ; Matt. 27:48.

FOOL, any person who does not act wisely, that is, does not follow the warnings and requirements of God, which are founded in infinite wisdom. Hence "a fool" is put for a wicked man, an enemy or neglecter of God, Psa. 14:1 ; Prov. 19:1. So folly is put for wickedness, 2 Sam. 13:12, 13 ; Psa. 38:5, foolish lusts for wicked lusts, etc. Foolish talking, foolish questions, are vain, empty, unprofitable conversation, 2 Tim. 2:23.

FOOT. The expressions in Deut. 32:35, "their foot shall slide in due time," and in the traveller's song, Psa. 121:3, "he will not suffer thy foot to be moved," Psa. 66:9, Jer. 13:16, have reference to the dangerous character of the narrow roads or paths of the East, over rocks and beside precipices where a sliding foot was often fatal. See also Isa. 8:14 ; Luke 2 : 34. Nakedness of feet was a sign of mourning. God says to Ezekiel, "Make no mourning for the dead, and put on thy shoes upon thy feet," Ezek. 24:17. It was likewise a mark of respect. Moses put off his shoes to approach the burning bush ; and most commentators are of opinion that the priests served in the tabernacle with their feet naked, as they did afterwards in the temple. The Turks never enter their mosques till after they have washed their feet and their hands, and have put off the outward covering of their legs. The Christians of Ethiopia enter their churches with their shoes off, and the Indian Brahmins and others have the same respect for their pagodas and temples. Eastern conquerors used to set their feet on the necks of conquered princes, Josh. 10 : 22, an action often figured in ancient sculptures, Psa. 8:6 ;

Isa. 49:23; 1 Cor. 15:25; Heb. 2:8. See NINEVEH.

The orientals used to wash the feet of strangers who came off a journey, because they commonly walked with their legs bare, and their feet defended only by sandals, Gen. 24:32; 43:24. So Abraham washed the feet of the three angels, Gen. 18:4. This office was usually performed by servants and slaves; and hence Abigail answers David, who sought her in marriage, that she should think it an honor to wash the feet of the king's servants, 1 Sam. 25:41. Paul would have a widow assisted by the church, to be one who had hospitably washed the feet of saints, 1 Tim. 5:10. The practice is still met with in Palestine. Says Dr. Robinson, at Ramleh, "Our youthful host now proposed, in the genuine style of ancient oriental hospitality, that a servant should wash our feet. This took me by surprise; for I was not aware that the custom still existed here. Nor does it indeed towards foreigners, though it is quite common among the natives. We gladly accepted the proposal, both for the sake of the refreshment and of the scriptural illustration. A female Nubian slave accordingly brought water, which she poured upon our feet over a large shallow basin of tinned copper, kneeling before us and rubbing our feet with her hands, and wiping them with a napkin. It was one of the most gratifying minor incidents of our whole journey." Our Saviour, after his last supper, gave a striking lesson of humility, by washing his disciples' feet, John 13:5, 6, though the eighth verse shows that he had also a deeper meaning. See SANDALS.

FOOT'MEN, or runners, were attendants on Eastern princes, trained to run before their chariots, 1 Sam. 8:11. So Elijah ran before Ahab, 1 Kin. 18:46. The speed and endurance of some of these couriers is almost beyond belief, Jer. 42:5.

FORE'HEAD, Ezek. 9; Rev. 7:3. The devotees of different idols in India receive at this day different marks on the forehead, distinguishing them one from another. By a similar method the slaves claimed by different owners were sometimes designated.

FORNICA'TION. This word is used in Scripture not only for the sin of impurity between unmarried persons, but for idolatry, and for all kinds of infidelity to God. In Ezek. 16, the Jewish church is symbolized as a female infant, growing up to womanhood, and then wedded to Jehovah by covenant. When she breaks her covenant by going after idols, she is justly reproached as an adulteress and a harlot, Jer. 2:20; 3:8, 9; Hos. 3:1. Adultery and fornication are frequently confounded. Both the Old and New Testaments condemn all impurity and fornication, corporeal and spiritual—idolatry, apostasy, heresy, and infidelity. See ADULTERY.

FORTUNA'TUS, 1 Cor. 16:17, came from Corinth to Ephesus, to visit Paul. Paul speaks of Stephanus, Fortunatus, and Achaïcus as the first-fruits of Achaia, and as set for the service of the church and saints. They carried Paul's first epistle to Corinth.

FOUN'TAINS, or perennial springs of good water, were of inestimable value in Palestine, and numerous places took their name from some fountain in their vicinity. They have furnished to the sacred writers some of their finest illustrations of spiritual things. Thus, God is "the Fountain of living waters," Jer. 2:13. The atonement is a precious fountain of cleansing, healing, life-giving power, Joel 3:18; Zech. 13:1. The consolations of the gospel and the felicity of heaven are also described by this similitude, Psa. 36:7-9; Rev. 7:17. See WELLS.

FOWL. See BIRDS.

FOX. Two words in Hebrew are translated "fox" in the Bible; and it is not easy in every case to determine what animal is referred to. There were several varieties of fox in Palestine, all like the common fox in form and habits. The fox is cunning, voracious, and mischievous, Ezek. 13:4; Luke 13:32. He is fond of grapes, and does much harm in vineyards, Song 2:15. The fable of the fox and the sour grapes is well known. He is solitary in his habits, and burrows a home for himself in the ground, Luke 9:58. The *jackal*, at the present day, is much more numerous in Palestine, and is probably referred to in many texts where the word "foxes" occurs. It is like a medium-sized dog, with a head like the wolf's, and a tail like the fox's; of a bright yellow color. To the fierceness of the wolf it joins the impudent familiarity of the dog. It differs from the fox in its habit of hunting its prey

in large packs, and in its cry—a mournful howl, mixed with barking, which they keep up all night, to the annoyance of all within hearing. They live in holes; prowl around villages; ravage poultry-yards; feed upon game, lizards, insects, grapes, garbage; and when they can find nothing else, old leather and any thing that has once had animal life. They follow after caravans and armies, and devour the bodies of the dead, and even dig them up from their graves, Psa. 63:10; Lam. 5:18. The incident in the life of Samson, where foxes, or perhaps jackals, are referred to, Judg. 15:4, 5, has a parallel in the ancient Roman feast of Ceres, goddess of corn; when torches were bound to the tails of numbers of foxes, and they ran round the circus till the fire stopped and consumed them. This was in revenge for their once burning up some fields of corn.

FRANK'INCENSE. See INCENSE.

FRIEND. Abraham is signally honored in being called "the friend of God," Isa. 41:8; James 2:23. Christ granted a similar honor and blessing to his disciples, John 15:15. It is a different word, however, in Greek, by which he addressed Judas, Matt. 26:50; the word there translated friend, means simply companion, and appears to have been used as a conversational term not implying friendship. The same word occurs in Matt. 20:13; 22:12.

FROG, a well-known amphibious animal, famous in connection with the plagues in Egypt, Ex. 8:1-14. The magicians are said to have brought up frogs upon the land by their enchantments; but as they could not remove them, it is clear that they did not actually produce them. They penetrated everywhere—to the beds of the Egyptians, which were near the ground; and to their ovens, which were cavities in the ground.

FRONTLETS are thus described by Leo of Modena: the Jews take four pieces of parchment, and write with an ink made on purpose, and in square letters, these four passages, one on each piece: (1.) "Sanctify unto me all the first-born," etc., Ex. 13:2-10. (2.) "And when the Lord shall bring thee into the land of the Canaanites," etc., ver. 11-16. (3.) "Hear, O Israel; the Lord our God is one Lord," etc., Deut. 6:4-9. (4.) "If you shall hearken diligently unto my commandments," etc., ver. 13-21. This they do in obedience to the words of Moses: "These commandments shall be for a sign unto thee upon thy hand, and for a memorial between thine eyes."

These four pieces are fastened together, and a square formed of them, on which the Hebrew letter ש Shin is written;

then a little square of hard calf-skin is put at the top, out of which come

two leathern strings. This square is put on the middle of the forehead, and the strings being girt about the head, are then brought before, and fall on the breast. It is called the Tephila of the head. The most devout Jews put it on both at morning and noon-day prayer; but it is generally worn only at morning prayer. See PHYLACTERIES.

FULFILLED'. The ordinary meaning of this word is sufficiently obvious. It will ultimately be recorded over against all the predictions and promises of Jehovah, every one having been fully accomplished at the proper time and place, Josh. 23:14; Matt. 2:17; 8:17; 12:17. There are in the New Testament many instances of such an accomplishment, where the purposes of men were very different, and those who figured in the transaction did not dream of any thing but some evil project of their own. Thus in John 19:24, 28, 36, the actual agents in Christ's crucifixion had no thought that they were fulfilling the purposes of God. Sometimes also the phrase, "that it might be fulfilled," signifies that the occurrence to which it is applied is a secondary fulfilment, a verification, or simply an illustration of the original prophetic passage—yet foreknown and foreordained of God. Thus the words of Hosea 11:1, "I called my son out of Egypt," refer directly to the exodus of Israel from that land of bondage; but, as we learn from Matt. 2:15, they were not suggested by the Holy Spirit to the prophet without a regard to their foreseen application to the case of Christ. Compare also Matt. 13:14, with Isa. 6:9; Luke 4:18-21, with Isa. 61:1-3; Acts 1:16, 20, with Psa. 109:8.

FUL'LER, a cleanser of cloth. His process is unknown. Christ's robes at the transfiguration were white "so as no fuller on earth can white them," Mark 9:3. We read also of fullers' soap, Mal. 3:2, and of the fullers' fountain. See EN-ROGEL.

FU'NERAL. See BURIAL and SEPULCHRE.

FUR'LONG is put, in the New Testament, for the Greek, or rather, Roman stadium, which contained about 201 45-100 yards. The English furlong, one-eighth of a mile, contains 220 yards; and is thus one-twelfth longer than the Roman stadium, Luke 24:13.

FUR'NACES were often portable, Gen. 15:17. They were used for melting the precious metals, Prov. 17:3. The furnace into which Daniel's three friends were cast was large, and remained open after they were cast in, Dan. 3. The fearful punishment spoken of in Jer. 29:22 is still used in the East. The word furnace is used to illustrate a state of oppression, Deut. 4:20, and of affliction, Isa. 48:10.

FU'RY is attributed to God metaphorically, or speaking after the manner of men; that is, God's providential actions are such as would be performed by a man in a state of anger; so that, when he is said to pour out his fury on a person, or on a people, it is a figurative expression for dispensing afflictive providences. But we must be cautious not to attribute human infirmities, passions, or malevolence to the Deity.

G.

GA'AL, Judg. 9:26-41, son of Ebed, perhaps a descendant of Hamor, the father of Shechem, Gen. 34:2-6. He joined the Shechemites when revolting against Abimelech, son of Gideon, inflamed their passions, and led them to battle, but was defeated, and excluded from the city.

GA'ASH, a hill of Ephraim, north of which stood Timnath-seres, celebrated for Joshua's tomb, Josh. 24:30. The brooks, or valleys of Gaash, 2 Sam. 23:30; 1 Chr. 11:32, were probably at the foot of the hill.

GAB'BATHA, *an elevated place*, the name of a place in front of Pilate's palace, whence he pronounced sentence against our Saviour, John 19:13. In Greek it was called the pavement. It was not the usual judgment-hall, which the Jews could not then enter, but some place in the vicinity of the crowd without, John 18:28; 19:4, 9, 13. It appears to have been a checkered marble pavement, or mosaic floor, on which his seat of judgment was erected. Such ornamented pavements had become common at that day among the wealthy Romans.

GA'BRIEL, a principal angel. He was sent to the prophet Daniel to explain his visions; also to Zacharias, to announce to him the future birth of John the Baptist, Dan. 8:16; 9:21; Luke 1:11, 19. Six months afterwards, he was sent to Nazareth, to the Virgin Mary, Luke 1:26-38.

GAD, *prosperity, fortune*, I., son of Jacob and Zilpah, Leah's servant, Gen. 30:11. Leah called him Gad, and said, "A troop cometh." Compare Gen. 49:19; but many Hebrew scholars prefer the rendering, good fortune or prosperity cometh. The tribe of Gad came out of Egypt in number forty-five thousand six hundred and fifty, Gen. 46:16; Num. 1:24. After the defeat of the kings Og and Sihon, Gad and Reuben desired to have their allotment east of Jordan, alleging their great number of cattle. Moses granted their request, on condition that they should accompany their brethren, and assist in conquering the land west of Jordan, Num. 32. The inheritance of the tribe of Gad lay between Manasseh on the north, Reuben on the south, the Jordan on the west, and the Ammonites on the east. The north-west point stretched to the sea of Galilee. It was a fine pastoral region, though its exposure to the incursions of eastern Arabians compelled the Gadites to be well armed and on the alert, Gen. 49:19; Deut. 33:20; 1 Chr. 5:18–22, 25, 26; 12:8. The principal cities of Gad are called cities of Gilead, Josh. 13:25.

II. David's friend, who followed him when persecuted by Saul, and was often sent with a divine message to David, 1 Sam. 22:5; 2 Sam. 24:11–19; 1 Chr. 21:9–19; 2 Chr. 29:25. Scripture styles him a prophet, and David's seer. He appears to have written a history of David's life; which is cited in 1 Chr. 29:29.

III. Rendered "troop" in Isa. 65:11, but generally supposed to be the name of a heathen god of Fortune; and perhaps of the planet Jupiter, the star of good fortune. Compare Josh. 11:17; 15:37. MENI in the same verse, translated "number," is supposed by some to mean destiny; by others, the planet Venus, the goddess of good fortune.

GAD'ARA, now Um-keis, a fortified chief city of Decapolis, of considerable importance in the time of Christ, and having many Greek inhabitants. It lay south of the river Hieromax, seven miles south-east of the sea of Galilee, upon the level summit of a steep limestone hill. A few ruins are found on the top of the hill; many excavated tombs on its sides, still partly occupied as residences; and warm-springs at its base. The country of the Gadarenes extended to the Jordan and the sea of Galilee; and in the part of it bordering on the lake occurred the miracle recorded in Matt. 8:28; 9:1; Mark 5:1–20; Luke 8:26–39. A legion of demons were cast out of two men, and entered a herd of swine, causing their destruction. See GERGESENES.

GA'IUS, or CAIUS, I., a Macedonian, who accompanied Paul in his travels, and whose life was in danger at Ephesus, Acts 19:29.

II. A Corinthian convert of Paul, who hospitably entertained the apostle while laboring at Corinth, Rom. 16:23; 1 Cor. 1:14.

III. Of Derbe; an attendant of Paul from Corinth, in his last journey to Jerusalem, Acts 20:4.

The third epistle of John is addressed "to the well-beloved Gaius;" whose character for hospitality comports well with that of II. above. The name was a common one wherever the Romans lived; and yet it is not certain that more than one or two different individuals of this name are spoken of in Scripture.

GALA'TIA, a province of Asia Minor, lying south and south-east of Bithynia and Paphlagonia, west of Pontus, north and north-west of Cappadocia, and north and north-east of Lycaonia and Phrygia. Its name was derived from the Gauls; of whom two tribes, (Trocmi and Tolistoboii,) with a tribe of the Celts, (Tectosages,) migrated thither after the sacking of Rome by Brennus; and mingling with the former inhabitants, the whole were called Gallogræci, B. C. 280. The Celtic language continued to be spoken by their descendants at least until the time of Jerome, six hundred years after the migration; and these Gauls of Asia also retained much of the mercurial and impulsive disposition of the Gallic race. Compare Gal. 1:6; 4:15; 5:7. Under Augustus, about B. C. 26, this country was reduced to the form of a Roman province, and was governed by a proprætor. Galatia was distinguished for the fertility of its soil and the flourishing state of its trade. It was also the seat of colonies from various nations, among whom were many Jews; and from all of these Paul appears to have made many converts to Christianity, 1 Cor. 16:1. His first visit, Acts 16:6, probably took place about A. D. 51–2; and the second, Acts 18:23, after which his epistle to the Galatians appears to have been written, was several years later. At his first visit he was sick; yet they received him "as an angel of God," and most heartily embraced the gospel. Four or five years afterwards Jewish teachers, professing Christianity, came among them; they denied Paul's apostolic authority, exalted the works of the law, and perverted the true gospel by intermixing with it the rites of Judaism. Paul, learning their state, probably at Corinth, A. D. 57-8, wrote his epistle to the Galatians. He indignantly rebukes his children in Christ for their sudden alienation from him and from the truth; vindicates his authority and his teachings as an apostle, by showing that he received them from Christ himself; and forcibly presents the great doctrine of Christianity—justification by faith—with its relations to the law on the one hand, and to holy living on the other. The general subject of the epistle is the same as of the epistle to the Romans, and it appears to have been written at about the same time with that. The churches of Galatia are mentioned in ecclesiastical history for about nine hundred years.

GAL'BANUM, an ingredient in the incense burned at the golden altar, in the Holy Place, Ex. 30:34. It is the gum of a plant growing in Abyssinia, Arabia, and Syria, called by Pliny stagonitis, but supposed to be the same as the Bubon Galbanum of Linnæus. The gum is unctuous and adhesive, of a strong and somewhat astringent smell.

GAL'ILEE, in the time of Christ, included all the northern part of Palestine lying west of the Jordan and north of Samaria. Before the exile the name seems to have been applied only to a small tract bordering on the northern limits, 1 Kin. 9:11. Galilee, in the time of Christ, was divided into Upper and Lower, the former lying north of the territory of the tribe of Zebulun, and abounding in mountains; the latter being more level and fertile, and very populous; the whole comprehending the four tribes of Issachar, Zebulun, Naphtali, and Asher. Lower Galilee is said to have contained four hundred and four towns and villages, of which Josephus mentions Tiberias, Sepphoris, and Gabara, as the principal; though Capernaum and Nazareth are the most frequently mentioned in the New Testament, Mark 1:9; Luke 2:39; John 7:52, etc. "Galilee of the Gentiles" is supposed to be Upper Galilee, either because it bordered on Tyre and Zidon, or because Phenicians, Syrians, Arabs, and other heathen were numerous among its inhabitants. The Galileans were accounted brave and industrious; though other Jews affected to consider them as not only stupid and unpolished, but also seditious, and therefore proper objects of contempt, Luke 13:1; 23:6; John 1:47; 7:52. They appear to have used a peculiar dialect, by which they were easily distinguished from the Jews of Jerusalem, Mark 14:70. Many of the apostles and first converts to Christianity were men of Galilee, Acts 1:11; 2:7, as well as Christ himself; and the name Galilean was often given as an insult, both to him and his followers. The apostate emperor Julian constantly used it, and in his dying agony and rage cried out, "O Galilean, thou hast conquered!" Our Saviour resided here from infancy till he was thirty years of age, and during much of his public ministry; and the cities of Nazareth, Nain, Cana, Capernaum, with the whole region of the sea of Galilee, are sacredly endeared to all his people by the words he there spoke, and the wonders he wrought. For the sea of Galilee, see SEA III.

GALL, a general name for any thing very bitter. In Job 16:13; 20:14, 25, it means the animal secretion usually called the bile. In many other places, where a different word is used in the original, it refers to some bitter and noxious plant, according to some, the poppy. See Deut. 29:18; Jer. 9:15; 23:15. In Hos. 10:4; Amos 6:12, the Hebrew word is translated "hemlock." In Matt. 27:34, it is said they gave Jesus to drink, vinegar mixed with gall, which in Mark 15:23, is called wine mingled with myrrh. It was probably the sour wine which the Roman soldiers used to drink, mingled with myrrh and other bitter substances, very much like the "bitters" of modern times, Psa. 69:21. The word gall is often used figuratively for great troubles, wickedness, depravity, etc., Jer. 8:14; Amos 6:12; Acts 8:23.

GAL'LEY, Isa. 33:21. See SHIP.

GAL'LIO, a proconsul of Achaia, under the emperor Claudius, in the time of Paul, Acts 18:12-17. He was the elder brother of the philosopher Seneca, who describes him as uncommonly amiable and upright. His residence was at Corinth; and when the Jews of that city made an insurrection against Paul, and dragged him before the judgment-seat, Gallio refused to entertain their clamorous and unjust demands. The Greeks who were present, pleased with the rebuff the persecuting Jews had received, fell upon Sosthenes their leader, and beat him upon the spot, a mode of retribution which Gallio ought not to have allowed. Like his brother Seneca, he suffered death by order of the tyrant Nero.

GAMA'LIEL, a celebrated Pharisee in the generation after Christ, a doctor of the law, and member of the Sanhedrim. He possessed great influence among the Jews, and is said by some to have presided over the Sanhedrim during the reigns of Tiberius, Caius, and Claudius. The Talmudists say that he was the son of rabbi Simeon, and grandson of Hillel, the celebrated teacher of the law, and that upon his death the glory of the law departed. His noble intervention before the Sanhedrim saved the apostles from an ignominious death, and shows that he was gifted with great wisdom and tolerance, if not strongly inclined towards the gospel, Acts 5:33-40. The apostle Paul thought it a high honor to have been one of his pupils, Acts 22:3, and no doubt received from him not only a zealous enthusiasm for the Jewish law, but many lessons of candor, impartiality, and liberality. His high renown, however, among the Jewish rabbins of later ages, seems inconsistent with the tradition that he embraced Christianity.

GAM'MADIM is used in the English Bible, Ezek. 27:11, as the name of a people; but it rather means simply the brave, the warlike.

GAR'DENS are often mentioned in Scripture, though in a sense somewhat peculiar; for in the language of the Hebrews, every place where plants and trees were cultivated with greater care than in the open field, was called a garden. Fruit and shade trees, with aromatic shrubs, sometimes constituted the garden; though roses, lilies, and various flowers were often cultivated, and some gardens were used only for table vegetables, Gen. 2:8-10, 15; 1 Kin. 21:2; Est. 1:5; 7:7, 8; Eccl. 2:5, 6. They were located, if possible, beside a river or fountain, Gen. 13:10; Num. 24:6. In other places reservoirs were provided, from which the water was distributed in various ways, as occasion required, Prov. 21:1; Song 4:12-16; Isa. 58:11. Gardens were inclosed by walls, or by hedges of rose-bushes, wild pomegranate-trees, or other shrubs, many of which in Palestine have long and sharp thorns, 2 Sam. 23:6, 7; Job 1:10; Prov. 15:19; Hos. 2:6. Often, however, they were left uninclosed, and were watched when their fruits began to ripen, Isa. 1:8; Jer. 4:16, 17. It is still customary in Egypt, Arabia, and Hindostan, to plant a large level tract with melons, cucumbers, etc., and place a small hut or booth on a mound in the centre. In this a solitary keeper is stationed, who remains day and night until the fruits are gathered, Job 27:18; Isa. 1:8. Gardens and groves were often furnished with pavilions, seats, etc., and were resorted to for banqueting and mirth, Isa. 51:3; for retirement and meditation, John 18:4; for devotional purposes, Matt. 26:30; John 1:48; 18:1, 2; and for idolatrous abominations, 1 Kin. 14:23; Isa. 1:29; 65:3; 66:17; Jer. 2:20; 3:6. A family tomb was often prepared in a garden, John 19:41.

GAR'LIC, a bulbous vegetable, of pungent smell and taste, and highly prized in the East. The Jews acquired a liking for it in Egypt, Num. 11:5. One variety, called the eschalot, or shallot, was introduced into Europe from Ascalon.

GAR'MENTS. The chief garments of the Hebrews were the tunic or inner garment, and the mantle or outer garment. These seem to have constituted a "change of raiment," Judg. 14:13; 19; Acts 9:39. The tunic was of linen, and was worn next to the skin, fitting close to the body; it had armholes, and sometimes wide and open sleeves, and reached below the knees; that worn by females reached to the ankles. The tunic was sometimes woven without seam, like that of Jesus, John 19:23. The upper garment or mantle was a piece of cloth nearly square, and two or three yards in length and breadth, which was wrapped round the body, or tied over the shoulders. A man without this robe on was sometimes said to be "naked," Isa. 20:2–4; John 21:7. This could be so arranged as to form a large *bosom* for carrying things; and the mantle also served the poor as a bed by night, Ex. 22:26, 27; Job 22:6. See Bosom and Bed.

Between these two garments, the Hebrews sometimes wore a third, called *me-il*, a long and wide robe or tunic of cotton or linen, without sleeves.

The head was usually bare, or covered from too fierce a sunshine, or from rain, by a fold of the outer mantle, 2 Sam. 15:30; 1 Kin. 19:13; Esth. 6:12. The priests, however, wore a mitre, bonnet, or sacred turban; and after the captivity, the Jews adopted to some extent the turban, now so universal in the East. Women wore a variety of plain and ornamented headdresses. Veils were also an article of female dress, Isa. 3:19. They were of various kinds, and were used alike by married and unmarried women; generally as a token of modesty, or of subjection to the authority of the husband, Gen. 24:65; 1 Cor. 11:3–10; but sometimes for the purpose of concealment, Gen. 38:14.

As the Hebrews did not change the fashion of their clothes, as we do, it was common to lay up stores of raiment beforehand, in proportion to their wealth, Isa. 3:6. To this Christ alludes when he speaks of treasures which the moth devours, Matt. 6:19; James 5:1, 2. But though there was a general uniformity in dress from age to age, no doubt various changes took place in the long course of Bible history; and at all times numerous and increasing varieties existed among the different classes, especially in materials and ornaments. In early ages, and where society was wild and rude, the skins of animals were made into clothing, Gen. 3:21; Heb. 11:37. Spinning, weaving, and needlework soon began to be practised, Ex. 35:25; Judg. 5:30. A coarse cloth was made of goats' or camels' hair, and finer cloths of woollen, linen, and probably cotton. Their manufacture was a branch of domestic industry, Prov. 31:13–24.

The great and wealthy delighted in white raiment; and hence this is also a mark of opulence and prosperity, Eccl. 9:8. Angels are described as clothed in pure and cheerful white; and such was the appearance of our Saviour's raiment during his transfiguration, Matt. 17:2. The saints, in like manner, are described as clothed in white robes, Rev. 7:9, 13, 14; the righteousness of Christ in which they are clothed is more glorious than that of the angels.

The garments of mourning among the Hebrews were sackcloth and haircloth, and their color dark brown or black, Isa. 50:3; Rev. 6:12. As the prophets were penitents by profession, their common clothing was mourning. Widows also dressed themselves much the same. The Hebrews, in common with their neighbors, sometimes used a variety of colors for their gayer and more costly dresses, Judg. 5:30. So also according to our version, Gen. 37:3, 23; 2 Sam. 13:18; though in these passages some understand a tunic with long sleeves. Blue, scarlet, and purple are most frequently referred to, the first being a sacred color. Embroidery and fine needlework were highly valued among them, Judg. 5:30; Psa. 45:14.

The dress of females differed from that of males less than is customary among us. Yet there was a distinction; and Moses expressly forbade any exchange of apparel between the sexes, Deut. 22:5, a custom associated with immodesty, and with the worship of certain idols. It is not clear for what reason clothing in which linen and woolen were woven together was prohibited, Deut. 22:11; but probably it had reference to some superstitious usage of heathenism. In Isa. 3:16-23, mention is made of the decorations common among the Hebrew women of that day; among which seem to be included tunics, embroidered vests, wide flowing mantles, girdles, veils, caps of network, and metallic ornaments for the ears and nose, for the neck, arms, fingers, and ankles; also smelling-bottles and metallic mirrors. In Acts 19:12, mention is made of handkerchiefs and aprons. Drawers were used, Ex. 28:42, but perhaps not generally. See GIRDLES, RINGS, and SANDALS.

Presents of dresses are alluded to very frequently in the historical books of Scripture, and in the earliest times. Joseph gave to each of his brethren a change of raiment, and to Benjamin five changes, Gen. 45:22. Naaman gave to Gehazi two changes of raiment; and even Solomon received raiment as presents, 2 Chr. 9:24. This custom is still maintained in the East, and is mentioned by most travellers. In Turkey, the appointment to any important office is accompanied with the gift of a suitable official robe. In the parable of the wedding garment, the king expected to have found all his guests clad in robes of honor of his own providing, Matt. 22:11.

GATE. The gates of eastern walled towns were usually of wood, Judg. 16:3, often covered with thick plates of iron or copper, Psa. 107:16; Isa. 45:2; Acts 12:10, secured by bolts and bars, Deut. 3:5; 1 Kin. 4:13, and flanked by towers, 2 Sam. 18:24, 33. A city was usually regarded as taken when its gates were won, Deut. 28:52; Judg. 5:8. Hence "gate" sometimes signifies power, dominion; almost in the same sense as the Turkish sultan's palace is called the Porte, or Gate. God promises Abraham that his posterity shall possess the gates of their enemies—their towns, their fortresses, Gen. 22:17. So too, "the gates of hell," that is, the power of hell, or hell itself.

In oriental cities there was always an open space or place adjacent to each gate, and these were at the same time the market-places and the place of justice, Gen. 23:10-18; Ruth 4:1-12; Deut. 16:18; 21:19; 25:6, 7; Prov. 22:22; Amos 5:10, 12, 15. There too people assembled to spend their leisure hours, Gen. 19:1. Hence "they that sit in the gate" is put for idlers, loungers, who are coupled with drunkards, Psa. 69:12. The woes of a city were disclosed in the mourning or loneliness of these places of resort, Isa. 14:31; Jer. 14:2. Here too the public proclamations were made, and the messages of prophets delivered, Prov. 1:21; 8:3; Isa 29:21; Jer. 17:19; 26:10. Near the gate of a city, but without it, executions took place, 1 Kin. 21:13; Acts 7:58; Heb. 13:12. To exalt the gate of a house through pride, increased one's exposure to robbery, Prov. 17:19. To open it wide and high was significant of joy and welcome, as when the Saviour ascended to heaven, Psa. 24:7, 9; and the open gates of the new Jerusalem, in contrast with those of earthly cities carefully closed and guarded at nightfall, indicate the happy security of that world of light, Rev. 21:25.

GATH, a city of the Philistines, and one of their five principalities, 1 Sam. 5:8; 6:17. It was a notable city, in the border of the Philistines nearest to Jerusalem; but its site has long been lost. It was the home of Goliath, 1 Sam. 17:4. Compare Josh. 11:22; 2 Sam. 21:19-22. Here David sought a refuge from Saul, 1 Sam. 21:10; 27:2-7. It came under his power in the beginning of his reign over all Israel, 1 Chr. 18:1, and continued subject to his successors till the declension of the kingdom of Judah. Rehoboam rebuilt or fortified it, 2 Chr. 11:8. It was afterwards recovered by the Philistines, but Uzziah reconquered it, 2 Chr. 26:6. Its inhabitants were called Gittites, Josh. 13:3; and David had two of them in his service, who faithfully adhered to him during the rebellion of Absalom, 2 Sam. 15:18-22.

GATH-HE'PHER, in Zebulun, was the birthplace of Jonah, 1 Kin. 4:10; 2 Kin. 14:25. It lay near Sepphoris, on a road leading to Tiberias.

GAU'LAN, or GO'LAN, a Levitical town of Bashan, in Manasseh beyond Jordan. From it was named the small province of Gaulonitis, Deut. 4:43; Josh. 20:8; 21:27; 1 Chr. 6:71.

GA'ZA, or AZZAH, now Ghuzzeh, an ancient city in the south-west corner of

Canaan, Gen. 10:19, belonging to the Avim, Deut 2:23, and afterwards to the Philistines. Joshua assigned it to the tribe of Judah, but did not conquer it, Josh 10:41; 11:21, 22; 13:3; 15:47 Judah seems to have held possession of it for a while; but in the time of the judges it was independent, and one of the five chief cities of the Philistines, Judg. 1:18; 3:3; 13:1; 16. Samson carried away its gates, and afterwards perished under the ruins of its vast temple. The ark of God was there in the days of Eli, 1 Sam. 6. It yielded allegiance to David and Solomon, recovered its liberty in the reigns of Jotham and Ahaz, but was reconquered by Hezekiah, 2 Kin. 18:8. At subsequent periods it was occupied by Chaldeans, Persians, and Egyptians, Jer. 47:1. About 96 B. C. the Jewish king Alexander Jannæus captured and destroyed it. The Roman general Gabinius rebuilt it; and not long after the ascension of the Saviour, a Christian church was planted there to struggle with the prevailing idolatry. In A. D. 634 it came under the Mohammedan yoke; and in the era of the Crusades had fallen into ruins. It was partially rebuilt and fortified, and is now a city of some 15,000 inhabitants. The few remains of the old city cover a large but low hill, two or three miles from the sea, once so strongly fortified as to withstand Alexander the Great for five months. The modern city lies more in the plain, which is exceedingly fertile, and abounds in gardens, date-trees, and olive-trees. There was a landing-place and "port" for ancient Gaza, but no harbor worthy of the name. It was often referred to by the prophets, Jer. 25:20; 47:5; Amos 1:6, 7; Zeph. 2:4; Zech. 9:5. The southern route from Jerusalem to Gaza, memorable in the history of the Ethiopian eunuch, is called "desert" in Acts 8:26, as passing through a region then destitute of villages.

GAZELLE'. See ROE.

GE'BA, a Levitical town of Benjamin, Josh. 18:24; 21:17; 1 Chr. 8:6, near Ramah, Neh. 7:30; Isa. 10:29, and not far from the northern border of the kingdom of Judah, 2 Kin. 23:8; Zech. 14:10. Near Geba David defeated the Philistines, 2 Sam. 5:25. Asa renewed it from the ruins of Ramah, 1 Kin. 15:22. It was six or seven miles from Jerusalem, and was separated from Michmash on the north by a deep valley. See GIBEAH.

GE'BAL, I., the Gebalene of the Romans, was a district of Idumæa, called also at the present day Djebal, signifying mountains. It is the northern part of the range of mountains skirting the eastern side of the great valley El-Arabah, which runs from the Dead sea to the Elanitic gulf of the Red sea, Psa. 83:7.

II. A seaport and district of Phœnicia, north of Beyroot, called Byblos by the Greeks, now Jebail; population, 2,000. The inhabitants were called Giblites, and are denoted in the Hebrew word rendered "stone-squarers" in 1 Kings 5:18. Their land and all Lebanon were assigned to the Israelites, but never fully possessed, Josh. 13:5. It was an important place, Ezek. 27:9, and the seat of the worship of Thammuz.

GEDALI'AH, son of Ahikam, appointed by Nebuchadnezzar to govern Judæa after the destruction of Jerusalem. Like his father, he honored and befriended Jeremiah, Jer. 40:5. He began the administration of his government at Mizpeh with wisdom, but in two months was treacherously murdered by one Ishmael, 2 Kin. 25:22-26; Jer. 39:14; 40:5-41:18.

GE'DER. This word signifies a *wall, inclosure, fortified place*; as do also the two names following, which are derived from it. Geder itself was an ancient Canaanitish place, in the plain of Judah, Josh. 12:13, and was probably the same with the following Gederah.

GEDE'RAH, a city in the plain of Judah, Josh. 15:36, probably the same with the preceding Geder, and with Beth-Gader, 1 Chr. 2:51. It would thence seem to have pertained to the family of Caleb.

GE'DOR, a city in the mountains of Judah, surrounded by fat pastures, and formerly occupied by the Amalekites, 1 Chr. 4:39; 12:7; Josh. 15:58. It is now called Jedur, and lies about eight miles south-west of Bethlehem. Gedor is also the name of a man, 1 Chr. 8:31; 9:37.

GEHA'ZI, a confidential attendant of Elisha. He appears in the story of the Shunammite woman, 2 Kin. 4:14-37, and in that of Naaman the Syrian, from whom he fraudulently obtained a portion of the present his master had refused. His covetousness and falsehoods were punished by a perpetual leprosy, 2 Kin. 5:20-27, B. C. 894. We afterwards find him recounting to king Jehoram the wonderful deeds of Elisha, at the moment when the providence of God brought the woman of Shunem before the king, to claim the restoration of her lands, 2 Kin. 8:1-6.

GEHEN'NA. See HINNOM.

GEMARI'AH, I., the son of Shaphan, a scribe of the temple in the time of Jehoiakim. In his apartment Baruch read aloud the prophecies of Jeremiah; and he, with others, secured a second and more public reading, and brought the roll to be read to the king, who caused it to be burned, Jer. 36.

II. The son of Hilkiah, sent to Babylon by king Hezekiah with tribute-money for Nebuchadnezzar. He was also the bearer of a letter in which Jeremiah warned the captive Jews against false prophets who promised them a speedy return, Jer. 29:3, 4.

GENEAL'OGY, a record of one's ancestors, either the line of natural descent from father to son, or the line in which, by the laws, the inheritance descended, or that preserved in the public records. Never was a nation more careful to preserve their genealogies than the Hebrews, for on them rested the distinction of tribes, the ownership of lands, and the right to the highest offices and privileges, 1 Chr. 5:1, 17; 9:1; 2 Chr. 12:15; Ezra 2:62. Hence their public tables of genealogies were kept secure amid all vicissitudes. We find in the Bible a record carried on for more than 3,500 years, 1 Chr. 1; 3; 6; and thus were guarded the proofs that Christ was born according to prophecy of the seed of Abraham, and heir to the throne of his father David, Luke 1:32; 2 Tim. 2:8; Heb. 7:14. In the evangelists we have the genealogy of Christ for 4,000 years. The two accounts in Matthew 1 and Luke 3, differ from each other; one giving probably the genealogy of Christ's reputed father Joseph, and the other that of his mother Mary. The two lines descend from Solomon and Nathan, David's sons; they unite in Salathiel, and again in Christ. Joseph was the *legal* father of Christ, and of the same family connections with Mary; so that the Messiah was a descendant of David both by law and "according to the flesh." The discrepances between the various genealogies may be reconciled in accordance with peculiar Jewish laws. The public records, which Josephus says were scrupulously kept down to his day, perished with the ruin of the Jews as a nation. It is now, therefore, impossible for any pretended Messiah to prove his descent from David.

Melchizedek was "without descent," Heb. 7:3, as regards the Jewish race. No sacred records proved his right to be numbered among that people of God. His priesthood was of a different kind from that of Aaron and his sons. Compare Ezra 2:62.

GENERA'TION. Besides the common acceptation of this word, as signifying race, descent, lineage, it is used for the history and genealogy of a person, as in Gen. 5:1, "The book of the generations of Adam," that is, the history of Adam's creation and of his posterity. So in Gen. 2:4, "The generations of the heavens and of the earth," that is, their genealogy, so to speak, the history of the creation of heaven and earth; also in Matt. 1:1, "The book of the generation of Jesus Christ," that is, the genealogy of Jesus Christ, the history of his descent and life. "The present generation" comprises all those who are now alive; "This generation shall not pass till all be fulfilled," some now living shall witness the event foretold, Matt. 24:34. "Save yourselves from this untoward generation," from the punishment which awaits these perverse men, Acts 2:40.

The Hebrews, like other ancient nations, sometimes computed loosely by generations. Thus in Gen. 15:16, "In the fourth generation thy descendants shall come hither again." The duration of a generation is of course very uncertain; indeed, it is impossible to establish any precise limits. It is, however, generally admitted that a generation in the earliest periods is to be reckoned longer than one in later times. The Greeks regarded a generation as one-third of a century. It is now currently reckoned as thirty years.

GEN'ESIS, the first of the sacred books in the Old Testament, so called from the title given to it in the Septuagint, signifying "the book of the generation," or production, of all things. Moses is generally admitted to have been the writer of this book; and it is supposed that he penned it after the promulgation of the law. Its authenticity is attested by the most indisputable evidence, and it is cited as an inspired record thirty-three times in the course of the Scriptures. The history related in it comprises a period of about 2,369 years, according to the lowest computation, but according to Dr. Hales, a much larger period. It contains an account of the creation; the primeval state and fall of man; the history of Adam and his descendants, with the progress of religion and the origin of the arts; the genealogies, age, and death of the patriarchs until Noah; the general defection and corruption of mankind, the general deluge, and the preservation of Noah and his family in the ark; the history of Noah and his family subsequent to the time of the deluge; the repeopling and division of the earth among the sons of Noah; the building of Babel, the confusion of tongues, and the dispersion of mankind; the lives of Abraham, Isaac, Jacob, and Joseph. The book of Genesis was written, like the rest of Scripture, "by inspiration of God." Yet many of the facts it records must have been well known among the Jews; the account given by Adam himself may have been verbally transmitted through seven of the patriarchs to Moses, and he may also have had ancient historical writings to consult. The book of Genesis lays the foundation for all the subsequent books of the Bible; and its value in the history of the earth, of man, and of religion, is inestimable.

GENNES'ARET, supposed to be a corruption of Chinnereth, which see. "The land of Gennesaret," Matt. 14:34, Mark 6:53, was a tract of land some three or four miles long on the western border of the sea of Galilee. It was a lovely and exceedingly fertile region; in it probably lay Capernaum and Bethsaida of Galilee, places often visited by our Lord. See SEA IV.

GEN'TILES, a name given by the Hebrews to all those that had not received the law of Moses. Foreigners who embraced Judaism, they called proselytes. Since the promulgation of the gospel, the true religion has been extended to all nations; God, who had promised by his prophets to call the Gentiles to the faith, with a superabundance of grace, having fulfilled his promise; so that the Christian church is composed principally of Gentile converts, the Jews being too proud of their privileges to acknowledge Jesus Christ as their Messiah and Redeemer. In the writings of Paul, the Gentiles are generally called Greeks, Rom. 1:14, 16; 1 Cor. 1:22, 24; Gal. 3:28. So also in those of Luke, in the Acts 6:1; 11:20; 18:4. Paul is commonly called the apostle of the Gentiles, Gal. 2:8; 1 Tim. 2:7, because he preached Christ principally to them; whereas Peter, etc., preached generally to the Jews, and are called apostles of the circumcision, Gal. 2:8.

GENTILES, COURT OF THE. Josephus says there was in the court of the temple a wall or balustrade, breast high, having pillars at regular distances, with inscriptions on them in Greek and Latin, importing that strangers were forbidden to approach nearer to the altar, Eph. 2:14. See TEMPLE.

GENTILES, ISLES OF THE, Gen. 10:5, Asia Minor and the whole of Europe, peopled by the descendants of Japheth.

GE'RAH, the smallest weight or coin among the Jews, the twentieth part of a shekel, and worth about two and a half cents, Ex. 30:13.

GE'RAR, an ancient town or place of the Philistines in the times of Abraham and Isaac, Gen. 10:19; 20:1; 26:1, 6, 17. It lay not far from Gaza, in the south of Judah, but its exact site is now unknown. See 2 Chr. 14:13, 14.

GERGESENES', Matt. 8:28; in the parallel passages in Mark and Luke, Gadarenes. See GADARA. Some manuscripts have Gadarenes in Matt. 8:28, and others Gerasenes; but Gerasa lay forty miles south-east of the scene of the miracle. Some have thought that the remnant of the ancient Girgashites gave their name to this district. A recent explorer finds ruins called Cherza or Gersa, midway on the eastern side of the sea of Galilee; and this may be the ancient Gergesa.

GER'IZIM, a mountain in Ephraim, between which and Ebal lay the city of Shechem, Judg. 9:7. The world has beheld few scenes more awful and suggestive than when, having conquered Canaan, all the Israelites were summoned to this place, and six tribes were stationed on mount Gerizim to pronounce blessings on those who should obey God's law, and the other six on mount Ebal to denounce curses on those who should break it; while all the people solemnly said, AMEN, Deut. 11:29; 27:12-26; 28. See view in SHECHEM.

After the captivity, Manasseh, a seceding priest, by permission of Alexander the Great, built a temple on Gerizim, and the Samaritans joined the worship of the true God to that of their idols: "They feared the Lord, and served their own gods, after the manner of the nations whom they carried away from thence," 2 Kin. 17:33. See SAMARITANS and SANBALLAT.

This temple was destroyed by John Hyrcanus; yet its site has always retained its ancient sacredness. In our Saviour's time the true God was worshipped by the Samaritans, though ignorantly, John 4. Herod the Great, having rebuilt Samaria, and called it Sebaste, in honor of Augustus, would have compelled the Samaritans to worship in the temple which he had erected; but they constantly refused, and have continued to this day to guard their sacred Scriptures, to keep the law, to pray towards their holy place on the summit of Gerizim, and to worship God there four times in the year.

GER'SHOM, *a stranger there*, one of the two sons of Moses and Zipporah, in the land of Midian, Ex. 2:22; 18:3. Moses appears to have given them no rank or emoluments but those of simple Levites, 1 Chr. 23:15.

GER'SHON, the eldest son of Levi, and head of one of the three branches of the Levitical tribe, Gen. 46:11; Ex. 6:16. The Gershonites encamped west of the tabernacle in the wilderness, and carried its curtains and other parts from station to station, Num. 3:17, 25; 4:24–28, 38–41; 10:17. Thirteen cities were assigned to them in northern Canaan, Josh. 21:6; 1 Chr. 6:62, 71.

GE'SHEM, or GASH'MU, an Arabian, who opposed the work of the Lord in the time of Nehemiah, by ridicule and plots, Neh. 2:19; 6:1–9; about 445 B. C.

GE'SHUR. See next page.

GARDEN OF GETHSEMANE, AND MOUNT OF OLIVES.

GETHSEM'ANE, *oil-press*, a garden or grove in the valley at the foot of the mount of Olives, over against Jerusalem, to which our Saviour sometimes retired, and in which he endured his agony, and was betrayed by Judas, Matt. 26:36–57. Early tradition locates Gethsemane near the base of mount Olivet, beyond the brook Kidron. The place now enclosed by a low stone wall may be but a part of the original "garden." It is about fifty-two yards square, and contains eight aged olive-trees, whose roots in many places project above the ground, and are protected by heaps of stones. Here, or at most not far off, the Saviour endured that unspeakable "agony and bloody sweat" so nearly connected with his expiatory death; and here in deep submission he mingled and closed his prayers for relief with the cry, "Nevertheless, not my will, but thine, be done." From this garden he could readily see the crowd of men "with lanterns and torches" emerging from the city gate, and hastening, under the guidance of Judas, to seize him. It is the spot which the Christian visitor at Jerusalem first seeks out, and where he lingers longest and last ere he turns homeward. A recent traveller, Professor Hackett, passing by Gethsemane one day, saw a shepherd in the act of shearing a sheep. The animal lay on the ground, with its feet tied, the man's knee pressed rudely against its side, while it seemed as if every movement of the shears would lacerate its flesh; yet during the whole, it struggled not and opened not its mouth—a touching memento, upon that sacred spot, of the Lamb of God, Isa. 53:7.

GE'SHUR, GESH'URI, GESHURITES, the name of a district and people in Syria. Geshur lay upon the eastern side of the Jordan between Bashan, Maachah, and mount Hermon, and within the limits of the Hebrew territory; but the Israelites did not expel its inhabitants, Josh. 12:5; 13:13. They appear to have been brought under tribute, 1 Chr. 2:23, but to have retained their own kings. One of David's wives, Maachah the mother of Absalom, was daughter of Talmai king of Geshur; and it was here that Absalom found refuge after the murder of Amnon, and remained three years with his grandfather, 2 Sam. 3:3; 13:37; 15:8. The word Geshur signifies bridge; and in the border of the region, where, according to the above data, we must place Geshur, between mount Hermon and the lake of Tiberias, there still exists an ancient stone bridge of four arches over the Jordan, called Jisr-Beni-Jakub, that is, the bridge of the children of Jacob. There seems to have been here an important pass on the route to Damascus and the East.

There was also a people of the same name in the south of Palestine, near the Philistines, Josh. 13:2; 1 Sam. 27:8.

GE'ZER, a royal city of the Canaanites, Josh. 10:33; 12:12; between Beth-horon and the Mediterranean, Josh. 16:3; afterwards on the western border of Ephraim, and assigned to the Levites, Josh. 16:3; 21:21. The Canaanites long retained a foothold in it, Josh. 16:10; Judg. 1:29; but were dispossessed by a king of Egypt, and the place given to his daughter, the wife of Solomon, 1 Kin. 9:16, who fortified it.

GHOST, the spirit, or principle of life in man. To "give up the ghost," is to die, to yield the soul to God who gave it, Gen. 25:8; Luke 23:46. See SPIRIT.

GI'ANTS, *earth-born*. It is supposed by many that the first men were of a size and strength superior to those of mankind at present, since a long life is usually associated with a well-developed and vigorous frame. We know also that there were giants and families of giants, even after the average length of human life was greatly abridged. These, however, appear to have been exceptions; and if we judge from the mummies of Egypt, and from the armor and implements of the earliest antiquity, found in ancient tombs, in bogs, and in buried cities, we should conclude that mankind never exceeded, in the average, their present stature. There were, however, giants before the flood, Gen. 6:4; fruits of the union of different families, and extraordinary in stature, power, and crime. After the flood, mention is made of a race called Rephaim, Gen. 14:5; Josh. 17:15; kindred with whom were the Emim, early occupants of the land of Moab, and the Zamzummim in Ammon, Deut. 2:10, 20. Og was one of the last of this race, Deut. 3:11, 13. West of the Dead sea, around Hebron and Philistia, lived the Anakim, whose aspect so terrified the Hebrew spies, Num. 13:33; Josh. 11:21, 22. Of this race were Goliath and his kindred, 1 Sam. 17:4; 1 Chr. 20:4-8. See ANAKIM, GOLIATH, and REPHAIM.

GIANTS, VALLEY OF THE. See REPHAIM.

GIB'BETHON, a city of the Philistines, within the bounds of the tribe of Dan, and assigned to the Levites, Josh. 19:44; 21:23. The Philistines, however, were not excluded; and in the time of Nadab they were its masters, and he was slain by Baasha while besieging it, 1 Kin. 15:27; 16:15. Its after-history, and its site are unknown.

GIB'EAH, *a hill*, I., a city of Benjamin, 1 Sam. 13:15, and the birthplace and residence of Saul king of Israel; whence it is frequently called "Gibeah of Saul," 1 Sam. 11:4; 15:34; 23:19; 26:1; 2 Sam. 21:6; Isa. 10:29. Gibeah was also famous for its sins; particularly for that committed by forcing the young Levite's wife, who went to lodge there; and for the war which succeeded it, to the almost entire extermination of the tribe of Benjamin, Judg. 19. Scripture remarks, that this occurred at a time when there was no king in Israel, and when every one did what was right in his own eyes. Dr. Robinson found traces of Gibeah in the small and ruinous village of Jeba, near Ramah, separated from Michmash on the north by a deep valley, and about six miles north by east from Jerusalem.

II. A town of Judah, Josh. 15:57, which lay about ten miles south-west of Jerusalem. The prophet Habakkuk is said to have been buried here.

III. In mount Ephraim, called Gibeah of Phinehas, where Eleazar the son of Aaron was buried, Josh. 24:33. It is found in the narrow valley El-Jib, midway between Jerusalem and Shechem.

GIB'EON, a considerable city of the Hivites, afterwards a Levitical city in the tribe of Benjamin, Josh. 18:25; 21:17. It lay near Geba and Gibeah, and is sometimes wrongly taken for Geba. Its Canaanite inhabitants secured a treaty with Joshua and the elders of Israel by stratagem, and were made hewers of wood for the sanctuary. Five neighboring kings unitedly fell upon them; but were defeated by the Jews in a great battle, during which "the sun stood still upon Gibeon," Josh. 9; 10. Here the tabernacle was set up for many years, 1 Chr. 16:39; 21:29; 2 Chr. 1:3, 4; and here God communed by night with young king Solomon, 1 Kin. 3:4-15. It is also memorable for two scenes in the life of Joab, 2 Sam. 2:12-32; 20:8-12; Jer. 41:12. It stood on an eminence, six miles north of Jerusalem.

GIBLITES, Josh. 13:5. See GEBAL.

GID'EON, or JERUB'BAAL, of the tribe of Manasseh, a valiant and prudent judge of Israel, particularly the eastern and northern tribes, B. C. 1249 to 1209. He resided in Ophrah, east of the Jordan, a region often ravaged in harvest-time by the wandering tribes on its eastern border. Being called of God to deliver his people, and encouraged by signs from heaven, he defeated the Midianites, and caused Israel to dwell in safety for many years. In punishing the refractory cities Succoth and Penuel, and the fratricides Zeba and Zalmunna—in soothing the jealousy of the Ephraimites, and in declining the crown offered him by the Jews, he evinced those qualities which made him a successful judge. In the matter of the golden ephod, however, he fell into a sin and a snare; for this memorial of the wonders God had wrought became erelong an object of idolatrous veneration, Judg. 6-8; 1 Sam. 12:11; Heb. 11:32.

GIER-EAGLE, probably an Egyptian vulture, horrid and filthy, but very useful as a carrion-bird, Lev. 11:18. See VULTURE.

GIFTS have been common from the earliest times as tokens of affection, honor, or respect. The dues to a king were often rendered in this form, 1 Sam. 10:27; Isa. 36:16; and men of high position were approached with presents, Gen. 43:11; Judg. 6:18; 1 Sam. 9:7; 1 Kin. 14:3. Kings made gifts of garments to those they wished to honor, Gen. 45:22, 23; 1 Sam. 18:4; and of treasures to other princes, out of esteem or of fear, 2 Kin. 16:8; 18:14; 2 Chr. 9:9, 12. Conquerors scattered gifts from their triumphal cars, and special privileges in token of generous joy, Psa. 68:18; Acts 1:2, 4. Prophets received gifts, or declined them, as duty required, 2 Kin. 5:15; 8:9; Dan. 2:48; 5:17. The word gifts often denotes bribes, Ex. 23:8; Psa. 15:5; Isa. 5:23. The same word is also applied to the offerings required by the law, Deut. 16:17; Matt. 5:23, 24; to the blessings of the gospel and eternal life, which are preëminently *gifts*, Acts 8:20; to the Christian graces, for the same reason, Eph. 4:8, 11; and to the miraculous endowments of the apostles, 1 Cor. 12-14. See TONGUES.

GI'HON, I., one of the four rivers of Paradise; as some suppose, the Araxes, Gen. 2:13. See EDEN, and EUPHRATES.

II. A fountain near Jerusalem on the west, beside which Solomon was anointed king, 1 Kin. 1:33, 38. Hezekiah covered it over, and brought its waters by a subterranean channel into the city, 2 Chr. 32:3, 30; 33:14. A pool still exists in the spot referred to, three hundred feet long, two hundred wide, and twenty deep, with steps at two corners; and recently, in digging to lay the foundations of the Anglican church, an immense conduit was discovered running east and west, thirty feet under ground, built of stone and coated with cement, and partly cut out of solid rock. Probably this was connected with the fountain of Gihon.

GILBO'A, a mountainous ridge south-east of the plain of Esdraelon, having on each side a valley connecting the great plain with the Jordan valley. The valley north-east of Gilboa is the proper Jezreel; that on the south-west side separates Gilboa from the hills of Samaria. On the eastern part of Gilboa was the town from which it was named, now Jelbon. In this vicinity Saul and Jonathan were defeated by the Philistines, and died, 1 Sam. 28:4; 31. It is now a dry and barren mountain, 2 Sam. 1:6, 21. Endor lay north from Gilboa, and Beth-shean north-east.

GIL'EAD, or GALEED', Gen. 31:45-48, *the mound of witness*, lay east of the Jordan, in the mountainous tract which runs from mount Hermon southward, between the Jordan and Arabia Deserta. The scenery among these mountains is described as very fine. The plains are covered with a fertile soil, the hills are clothed with forests, and at every new turn beautiful landscapes are presented. The Scripture references to the stately oaks and herds of cattle in this region are well known, Gen. 37:25; Num. 32:1.

The name Gilead is sometimes put for the whole country east of the Jordan. Thus, in Deut. 34:1, God is said to have showed Moses, from mount Nebo, "all the land of Gilead unto Dan" Compare Num. 32:26, 29; Deut. 3:12. The proper region of Gilead, however, lay south of Bashan, but probably without any very definite line of separation. Bashan and Gilead are often mentioned together, Josh. 12:5; 13:11; 17:1, 5; 2 Kin. 10:33. A part of Gilead was the district now called Belka, one of the most fertile in Palestine. See BALM and BASHAN.

Mount Gilead, in the strictest sense, was doubtless the mountain now called Jebel Jelâd or Jelûd, mentioned by Burckhardt, the foot of which lies about two hours' distance, or six miles, south of the Wady Zerka, or Jabbok. The mountain itself runs from east to west, and is about two hours and a half (eight or ten miles) in length. Upon it are the ruined towns of Jelad and Jelûd; probably the site of the ancient city Gilead of Hos. 6:8, elsewhere called Ramoth Gilead. Southward of this mountain stands the modern city of Szalt. It was probably in this mountain that Jacob and Laban set up their monument, Gen. 31:45-48. See also Judg. 7:3.

GIL'GAL, *a rolling*, I., a celebrated place between the Jordan and Jericho, where the Israelites first encamped, after the passage of that river; where also they were circumcised, and kept their first Passover in Canaan, Josh. 4:19; 5:9, 10. It continued to be the head-quarters of the Israelites for several years, while Joshua was occupied in subduing the land, Josh. 9:6; 10:6, 15, 43. A considerable city was afterwards built there, Josh. 15:7, which became famous for many events. Here the tabernacle rested, until its removal to Shiloh; here also, according to the prevalent opinion, Samuel offered sacrifices, and held his court as a judge of Israel; and here Saul was crowned, 1 Sam. 7:16; 10:8; 11:15; 13:7-9; 15:33. A school of the prophets was here established, 2 Kin. 4:38; and yet it afterwards appears to have become a seat of idolatry, Hos. 4:15; 9:15; 12:11; Amos 4:4; 5:5. At this day, no traces of it are found. According to Josephus, it lay within two miles of Jericho.

II. Another Gilgal lay near Antipatris, Josh. 12:23; Neh. 12:29. And perhaps a third in the mountains of Ephraim, north of Bethel, Deut. 11:30; 2 Kin. 2:1-6. There are not wanting those who would make the Gilgal near Antipatris the seat of Samuel's judgeship, and of one of the schools of the prophets.

GI'LOH, a city of Judah, Josh. 15:50; where Ahithophel, David's counsellor, dwelt; and where, after his treason against David, and the rejection of his counsel by Absalom, he hung himself, 2 Sam. 15:12; 17:23.

GIRD, GIR'DLE. The orientals commonly dress in loose robes, flowing down around the feet; so that when they wish to run, or fight, or apply themselves to any business, they are obliged to bind their garments close around them with a sash or girdle. Hence, "to have the loins girded," is to be prepared for action or service, 2 Kin. 4:29; Acts 12:8; to be waiting for the call or coming of one's master or Lord, Luke 12:35. A tightened girdle was also thought to increase the power of endurance, and the simile is used in exhortations to Christian courage and fortitude, Job 38:3; Jer. 1:17; Eph. 6:14; 1 Pet. 1:13. To have the girdle loosed, is to be unnerved and unprepared for action, Isa. 5:27. Girdles of leather were worn by the common people; and also by prophets, 2 Kin. 1:8; Matt. 3:4. They were likewise made of cotton or linen, Jer. 13:1; also of silk, sometimes embroidered. They were often wide and long; and were folded lengthwise, and passed several times around the body. The girdle, moreover, answered the purpose of a purse or pouch, to carry money and other things; see Matt. 10:9; Mark 6:8, where the word purse in the English is put for girdle according to the original Greek. The Arabs and other orientals wear girdles in the same manner at the present day; they also carry a knife or dagger stuck in them; as was also the custom of the Hebrews, 1 Sam. 25:13; 2 Sam. 20:8. Clerks carried their inkhorns, carpenters their rules, etc., in the same way, Ezek. 9:2. See cuts in GARMENTS.

GIR'GASHITES. See CANAANITES.

GIT'TITES. See GATH.

GIT'TITH. The word Gittith signifies *belonging to Gath.* It probably denotes either a musical instrument or a kind of music derived from Gath, where David sojourned for a time during the persecution of Saul, 1 Sam. 27:1-7. The word Gath also signifies in Hebrew *a wine-press.* Hence not a few have supposed that it denotes either an instrument or a melody used in the vintage. It is prefixed to Psalms 8, 81, 84, all of which require an animated strain of music.

GLASS was well known to the ancients, and no doubt to the Jews; its invention is traced to an incident on the coast of Phœnicia, and the arts of blowing, coloring, and cutting it were familiar to the ancient Egyptians. The "looking-glasses" of the Jews, however, were of highly polished metal, usually small and round, Ex. 38:8; Job 37:18; Jas. 1:23. Glass does not appear to have been used at that time for mirrors, nor for windows; but for cups, bottles, vases, ornaments, sacred emblems, etc. It is alluded to in 1 Cor. 13:12; Rev. 4:6; 15:2; 21.18, 21; probably also in Job 28:17, where our English version has the word crystal.

GLEDE, a kind of hawk or kite, Deut. 14:13. The same Hebrew word is translated vulture in Lev. 11:14.

GLO'RY, GLO'RIFY, words of great and manifold significance in the Bible, used with reference to God and his works, the Saviour and his gospel, the heavenly state, etc. "The glory of God" was often visibly revealed in the old dispensation—some dazzling appearance indicative of his special presence, Ex. 16:7-10; 24:9, 10, 16, 17; 33:18-23; 1 Kin. 8:11; Psa. 80:1; Zech. 2:5. God's glory is shown in his works, Psa. 19:1; Rom. 1:19, 20. But it is most fully and illustriously displayed in the work of redemption, "in the face of Jesus Christ." "Here the whole Deity is known," John 1:14; 2 Cor. 4:6; Heb. 1:3. The chief end of the Christian is to live "to the glory of God," so that God may be seen to be most glorious, 1 Cor. 6:20; 1 Pet. 2:9. The adjuration, "give God the glory," means, confess the truth in view of his omniscience, Josh. 7:19; John 9:24. The expression, "my glory," Psa. 16:9; 30:12; 57:8; 108:1, is equivalent to my soul, or myself, as the parallelism shows.

GNAT, a small winged stinging insect, a mosquito, spoken of in the proverbial expression, Matt. 23:24, "Ye strain at a gnat, and swallow a camel," which should read, as it did in the first English translations, "Ye strain *out* a gnat," etc. The expression alludes to the Jewish custom of filtering wine, for fear of swallowing any insect forbidden by the law as unclean, Lev. 11:23; and is applied to those who are superstitiously anxious in avoiding small faults, yet do not scruple to commit great sins.

GOAT, a well-known animal, resembling the sheep, but covered with hair instead of wool. Large flocks of them were kept by the Jews, Gen. 27:9; 1 Sam. 25:2; 2 Chr. 17:11. They were regarded as clean for sacrifice, Ex. 12:5; Lev. 3:12; Num. 15:27; and their milk and the young kids were much used for food, Deut. 14:4; Judg. 6:19; Prov. 27:27; Luke 15:29. The common leather bottles were made of their skins. Several kinds of goats were kept in Palestine: one kind having long hair, like the Angora, and another, long and broad ears. This kind is probably referred to in Amos 3:12, and is still the common goat of Palestine.

HEAD OF THE SYRIAN GOAT.

Herodotus says, that at Mendes, in Lower Egypt, both the male and female goat were worshipped. The heathen god Pan was represented with the face and thighs of a goat. The heathen paid divine honors also to real goats, as appears in the table of Isis. The abominations committed during the feasts of these infamous deities cannot be told.

WILD GOATS are mentioned in 1 Sam. 24:2; Job 39:1; Psa. 104:18. This is

doubtless the *Ibex*, or mountain-goat, a large and vigorous animal still found in the mountains in the peninsula of Sinai, and east and south of the Dead sea.

These goats are very similar to the bouquetin or chamois of the Alps. They feed in flocks of a score or two, with one of their number acting as a sentinel. At the slightest alarm, they are gone in an instant, darting fearlessly over the rocks, and falling on their horns from a great height without injury. Their horns are two or three feet long, and are sold by the Arabs for knife-handles, etc. For SCAPE-GOAT, see EXPIATION.

GOATS' HAIR was used by Moses in making the curtains of the tabernacle, Ex. 25:4; 26:7; 35:6. The hair of the goats of Asia, Phrygia, and Cilicia, is very bright and fine, and hangs to the ground; in beauty it almost equals silk, and is never sheared, but combed off. The shepherds carefully and frequently wash these goats in rivers. The women of the country spin the hair, which is carried to Angora, where it is worked and dyed, and a considerable trade in the article carried on. The natives attribute the quality of the hair to the soil of the country. The ordinary goats-hair cloth of the Arabs, used for the coverings of tents, etc., is coarse and black; and this is the kind of which the garments of the Hebrew prophets and of the poor were made.

GOD. This name, the derivation of which is uncertain, we give to that eternal, infinite, perfect, and incomprehensible Being, the Creator of all things, who preserves and governs all by his almighty power and wisdom, and is the only proper object of worship. The proper Hebrew name for God is JEHOVAH, which signifies *He is*. But the Jews, from a feeling of reverence, avoid pronouncing this name, substituting for it, wherever it occurs in the sacred text, the word ADONAI, Lord; except in the expression, ADONAI JEHOVAH, *Lord Jehovah*, for which they put, ADONAI ELOHIM, *Lord God*. This usage, which is not without an element of superstition, is very ancient, dating its origin some centuries before Christ; but there is no good ground for assuming its existence in the days of the inspired Old Testament writers. The proper word for God is ELOHIM, which is plural in its form, being thus used to signify the manifold perfections of God, or, as some think, the Trinity in the godhead. In Ex. 3:14, God replies to

Moses, when he asks Him His name, I AM THAT I AM; which means either, I am he who I am, or, I am what I am. In either case the expression implies the eternal self-existence of Jehovah, and his incomprehensible nature. The name I AM means the same as JEHOVAH, the first person being used instead of the third.

The Bible assumes and asserts the existence of God, "In the beginning God created the heavens and the earth;" and is itself the most illustrious proof of his existence, as well as our chief instructor as to his nature and will. It puts a voice into the mute lips of creation; and not only reveals God in his works, but illustrates his ways in providence, displays the glories of his character, his law, and his grace, and brings man into true and saving communion with him. It reveals him to us as a Spirit, the only being from everlasting and to everlasting by nature, underived, infinite, perfect, and unchangeable in power, wisdom, omniscience, omnipresence, justice, holiness, truth, goodness, and mercy. He is but one God, and yet exists in three persons, the Father, the Son, and the Holy Spirit; and this distinction of the Three in One is, like his other attributes, from everlasting. He is the source, owner, and ruler of all beings, foreknows and predetermines all events, and is the eternal judge and arbiter of the destiny of all. True religion has its foundation in the right knowledge of God, and consists in supremely loving and faithfully obeying him. See JESUS CHRIST, and HOLY SPIRIT.

GODS. The words god and gods, Hebrew ELOHIM, are several times used in Scripture to express the power, office, or excellence of some created beings, as angels, magistrates, Ex. 22:20, 28; Psa. 86:8; 97:7; often also for the false gods of the heathen. These were exceedingly numerous, and are denoted by various terms, signifying vanity, falsehood, etc. Among the first objects to be deified were the sun, the moon, and the chief powers of nature. Innumerable animals, deceased men, all ages, passions, and conditions of man, and every thing which fear, lust, malice, pride, or caprice could suggest, were made objects of worship. The gods of modern India are numbered by millions.

GOD'LY, that which proceeds from God, and is pleasing to him. It also signifies conformity to his will, and an assimilation to his character, Psa. 12:1; Mal. 2:15; 2 Cor. 1:2; Tit. 2:12. Godliness is the substance of revealed religion, 1 Tim. 3:16; 4:8; 2 Pet. 1:6.

GOG and MA'GOG are usually spoken of together in Scripture. In Gen. 10:2, Magog, which seems to denote a country with its people, is reckoned among the descendants of Japheth. In Ezek. 38, 39, Magog apparently signifies a country with its people, and Gog the king of that people; but critics are much divided as to the people and country intended under these names. The Scythians, the Goths, the Persians, and several other nations, have been specified by interpreters as the Magog of the Scriptures; but most probably it is a name given generally to the northern nations of Europe and Asia, or the districts north of the Caucasus. The names reappear in the later predictions of John as enemies of the people of God, who are to be signally overthrown in Armageddon, Rev. 16:14-16; 20:7-9.

GO'LAN, a Levitical city of refuge, in the north-west portion of Bashan. It lay east or north-east of the sea of Galilee, but its site is now lost. See GAULAN.

GOLD, a well-known valuable metal, found in many parts of the world, and obtained anciently in Ophir, Job 28:16; Parvaim, 2 Chr. 3:6; Sheba, and Raamah, Ezek. 27:22. Job alludes to gold in various forms, Job 22:24; 28:15-19. Abraham was rich in it, and female ornaments were early made of it, Gen. 13:2; 24:22, 35. It is spoken of throughout Scripture; and the use of it among the ancient Hebrews, in its native and mixed state, and for the same purposes as at present, was very common. The ark of the covenant was overlaid with pure gold; the mercy-seat, the vessels and utensils belonging to the tabernacle, and those also of the house of the Lord, as well as the drinking-vessels of Solomon, were of gold.

GOL'GOTHA, the Hebrew name for CALVARY, which see.

GOLI'ATH, a celebrated giant of Gath, who challenged the armies of Israel, and was encountered and slain by David. The history is contained in 1 Sam. 17. His height was nine feet and a half; or, if we reckon the cubit at twenty-one inches, over eleven feet. See GIANTS.

GO'MER, I., Gen. 10:2, 3; 1 Chr. 1:5; Ezek. 38:6, a son of Japheth, and father of Ashkenaz, Riphath, and Togarmah. He is believed to have settled the northern shores of the Black sea, and given name to the ancient Cimmerians and to the Crimea. About 700 B. C. a part of his posterity diffused themselves in Asia Minor. Traces of his name and parentage are also found in the Cymbri, Umbri, and Cambri of historians, in Kumero and Kumeraeg, the names of the Welsh people and language, and among various nations of Europe.

II. A harlot whom the prophet Hosea appears to have married in prophetic vision, as directed by God, that the Jews might be led to reflect on the guilt of their spiritual uncleanness or idolatry, Hos. 1.

GOMOR'RAH, one of the cities in the fruitful vale of Siddim, near the southern part of the ancient Dead sea, miraculously blasted by God. See SODOM.

GO'PHER, the name of the wood of which the ark was built. Many suppose it to be the cypress; others, the pine. Gopher may probably be a general name for such trees as abound with resinous inflammable juices, as the cedar, cypress, fir-tree, pine, etc., Gen. 6:14.

GO'SHEN, I., the name of that tract of country in Egypt which was inhabited by the Israelites from the time of Jacob to that of Moses. It was probably the tract lying east of the Pelusian arm of the Nile, towards Arabia. See EGYPT. It appears to have reached to the Nile, Ex. 1:22; 2:3, since the Jews ate fish in abundance, Num. 11:5, and practised artificial irrigation, Deut. 11:10. It was near Heliopolis and Rameses, and not far from the capital of Egypt, Gen. 45:10; 47:11; Ex. 8-12. It was a part of "the best of the land," at least for the pastoral Hebrews, Gen. 46:34, and was evidently better watered and more fertile than at present. Here they greatly multiplied and prospered, Gen. 47:27, and here they were sorely afflicted, and yet not forgotten of God, Ex. 8:22; 9:26. Many Egyptians dwelt among and around them.

II. A city and the adjacent territory in the mountains of Judah, Josh. 10:41; 11:16; 15:51.

GOS'PEL signifies *good news*, and is that revelation and dispensation which God has made known to guilty man through Jesus Christ our Saviour and Redeemer. Scripture speaks of "the gospel of the kingdom," Matt. 24:14, the gospel "of the grace of God," Acts 20:24, "of Christ," and "of peace," Rom. 1:16; 10:15. It is the "glorious" and the "everlasting" gospel, 1 Tim. 1:11, Rev. 14:6, and well merits the noblest epithets that can be given it. The declaration of this gospel was made through the life and teaching, the death, resurrection, and ascension of our Lord.

The writings which contain the recital of our Saviour's life, miracles, death, resurrection, and doctrine, are called GOSPELS, because they include the best news that could be published to mankind. We have four canonical gospels—those of Matthew, Mark, Luke, and John. These have not only been generally received, but they were received very early as the standards of evangelical history, as the depositories of the doctrines and actions of Jesus. They are appealed to under that character both by friends and enemies; and no writer impugning or defending Christianity acknowledges any other gospel as of equal or concurrent authority, although there were many others which purported to be authentic memoirs of the life and actions of Christ. Some of these apocryphal gospels are still extant. They contain many errors and legends, but have some indirect value.

There appears to be valid objection to the idea entertained by many, that the evangelists copied from each other or from an earlier and fuller gospel. Whether Mark wrote with the gospel by Matthew before him, and Luke with Matthew and Mark both, or not, we know that they "spake as they were moved by the Holy Ghost" while recounting the works and sayings of Christ which they had seen or knew to be true, using no doubt the most authentic written and oral accounts of the same, current among the disciples. They have not at all confined themselves to the strict order of time and place.

GOSPEL OF MATTHEW. The time when this gospel was written is very uncertain. All ancient testimony, however, goes to show that it was published before the others. It is believed by many to have been written about A. D. 38. It has been much disputed whether this gospel was originally written in Hebrew or Greek. The unanimous testimony of ancient writers is in favor of a Hebrew original, that is, that it was written in the language of Palestine and for the use of the Hebrew Christians. But, on the other hand, the definiteness and accuracy of this testimony is drawn into question; there is no historical notice of a *translation* into Greek; and the present Greek gospel bears many marks of being an original; the circumstances of the age, too, and the prevalence of the Greek language in Palestine, seem to give weight to the opposite hypothesis. Critics of the greatest name are arranged on both sides of the question; and some who believe it to have been first written in Hebrew, think that the author himself afterwards made a Greek version. Matthew writes as "an Israelite indeed," a guileless converted Jew instructing his brethren. He often quotes from the Old Testament. He represents the Saviour as the fulfilment of the hopes of Israel, the promised Messiah, King of the kingdom of God.

GOSPEL OF MARK. Ancient writers agree in the statement that Mark, not himself an apostle, wrote his gospel under the influence and direction of the apostle Peter. The same traditionary authority, though with less unanimity and evidence, makes it to have been written at Rome, and published after the death of Peter and Paul. Mark wrote primarily for the Gentiles, as appears from his frequent explanations of Jewish customs, etc. He exhibits Christ as the divine Prophet, mighty in deed and word. He is a true evangelical historian, relating facts more than discourses, in a concise, simple, rapid style, with occasional minute and graphic details.

GOSPEL OF LUKE. Luke is said to have written his gospel under the direction of Paul, whose companion he was on many journeys. His expanded views and catholic spirit resemble those of the great apostle to the Gentiles; and his gospel represents Christ as the compassionate Friend of sinners, the Saviour of the world. It appears to have been written primarily for Theophilus, some noble Greek or Roman, and its date is generally supposed to be about A. D. 63.

GOSPEL OF JOHN. The ancient writers all make this gospel the latest. Some place its publication in the first year of the emperor Nerva, A. D. 96, sixty-seven years after our Saviour's death, and when John was now more than eighty years of age. The gospel of John reveals Christ as the divine and divinely appointed Redeemer, the Son of God manifested in flesh. It is a spiritual, rather than historical gospel, omitting many things chronicled by the other evangelists, and containing much more than they do as to the new life in the soul through Christ, union with him, regeneration, the resurrection, and the work of the Holy Spirit. The spirit of the "disciple whom Jesus loved" pervades this precious gospel. It had a special adaptation to refute the Gnostic heresies of that time, but is equally fitted to build up the church of Christ in all generations.

GOURD. It has been supposed that Jonah's gourd was the Ricinus Communis, or castor-oil plant. It grows in the East to the height of eight to twelve feet, and one species much higher. Its leaves are large, and have six or seven divis-

THE CASTOR-OIL PLANT.

ions, whence its name of Palma Christi. Since, however, it is now known that in the vicinity of the ancient Nineveh, a plant of the gourd kind is commonly trained to run over structures of mud and brush, to form booths in which the gardeners may protect themselves from the terrible beams of the Asiatic sun, this goes far to show that this vine, called in the Arabic *ker'a*, is the true gourd of Jonah. If the expression, "which came up in a night," Jonah 4:10, is to be understood literally, it indicates that God "prepared" the gourd, ver. 6, by miraculously quickening its natural growth.

The WILD GOURD is a poisonous plant, conjectured to mean the colocynth, which has a cucumber-like vine, with several branches, and bears a fruit of the size and color of an orange, with a hard, woody shell, within which is the white meat or pulp, exceedingly bitter, and a drastic purgative, 2 Kin. 4:39. It was very inviting to the eye, and furnished a model for the carved "knops" of cedar in Solomon's temple, 1 Kin. 6:18; 7:24.

GO'ZAN, now the Ozan, a river of Media and the adjacent district, Isa. 37:12, to which Tiglath-pileser and afterwards Shalmanezer sent the captive Israelites, 2 Kin. 17:6; 1 Chr. 5:26. The Kizzil-ozan, or Golden river, is in the north-west part of Persia, and flows north-east, with large curves, into the Caspian sea.

GRACE, *favor, mercy*. Divine grace is the free and undeserved love and favor of God towards man as a sinner, especially as exhibited in the plan of redemption through Jesus Christ, John 1:17; 3:16; Rom. 3:24-26. It is only by the free grace of God that we embrace the offers of mercy, and appropriate to ourselves the blessings graciously purchased by redeeming blood.

The "GRACE OF GOD," spontaneous, unmerited, self-directed, and almighty, is the source of the whole scheme of redemption, Rom. 11:6; 2 Tim. 1:9. With it are united "the grace of our Lord Jesus Christ," who gave himself for sinners; and that of "the Spirit of grace," by whom alone the grace offered by the Father and purchased by the Son is effectually applied. Thus GRACE in man, or all true holiness, 2 Pet. 3:18, is traced up to the grace of God as its only source; and the gospel of Christ and the work of the Spirit—both pure grace—are its only channels of communication. Hence also all the fruits and blessings of the gospel are termed graces, 2 Cor. 8:7; Phil 1:7; not only regeneration, pardon, enlightenment, sanctification, etc., but miraculous, official, and prophetic gifts, the peculiar traits of Christian character, and everlasting salvation, 1 Pet. 1:13. In Gal. 5:4, "grace" means, God's plan of salvation by his mercy, not by our works.

GRAIN. See CORN.

GRAPES, the fruit of the vine. The grapes of Palestine were very fine, of great size and high flavor, Num. 13:24. At present, and probably the same has always been true, the wine that is made requires but a small part of the annual yield of the vines. Dr. Robinson says, "No wine is made from the very extensive vineyards of Hebron, except a little by the Jews." While yet green, grapes are used for food in various ways; and are dried in the sun, or their juice preserved in bottles, to secure a pleasant vegetable tart all the year round, Num. 6:4. Ripe grapes may be had in Syria four or five months, Lev. 26:5; and when the season closes many are hung up in clusters, suitably protected, and remain without drying up all through the winter. Grapes are exceedingly cheap, and form no small part of the ordinary food. Ripe grapes are also dried into raisins; and after the hanging grapes are gone, the raisins are used until the return of new grapes.

Besides the law which protected the first three years' growth of the vine, (see FRUITS.) there was another law requiring the Jews to leave the gleanings of their vineyards for the poor, Lev. 19:10, 23. The law also allowed one who was passing a vineyard to pick a few grapes to eat on the spot, but not to carry any away, Deut. 23:24. Everywhere we encounter proofs of the admirable humanity that characterized the Mosaic legislation. A vineyard nearly stripped of its clustered treasures was a frequent image of desolation, Isa. 17:6; 24:13; Obad. 5. See VINE.

"Wild grapes" were the fruit of a wild vine, probably the Vitis Labrusca of Linnæus, the wild claret-grape. The fruit of the wild vine is called œnanthes, or the flower of wine. They never ripen, and are good only for verjuice. In Isa. 5:2, 4, God complains of his people whom he had planted as a choice vine, an excellent plant, that he had a right to require of them good fruit, but they had brought forth only wild grapes—fruit of a bad smell, and a bad taste.

GRASS sometimes means any green herbage, Isa. 15:6, and sometimes the usual food of cattle, Psa. 104:14. The quick growth of grass, its tenderness, and its rapid combustion when dry, have furnished the sacred writers with some of their most appropriate illustrations, Psa. 90:5, 6; 92:7; 103:15, 16; Isa. 40:6-8; 51:12; James 1:10; 1 Pet. 1:24. All sorts of grass and small shrubs are still used in Syria for fuel, on account of the scarcity of wood, Matt. 6:28-30. Travellers in that country often see grass growing on the housetops, the roofs being flat and coated with earth trodden hard. Such grass quickly withers when the rainy season is over, Psa. 129:6, 7; Isa. 37:27.

GRASS'HOPPER, a kind of locust, and so called in 2 Chr. 7:13. It was sometimes used for food, Lev. 11:22. Individually they are insignificant and timid creatures, Num. 13:33, and their worthlessness furnishes a striking comparison in Isa. 40:22; while the feebleness of age is expressed by inability to endure them, Eccl. 12:5. Yet coming in great numbers, they are destructive to all herbage, Amos 7:1. See LOCUST.

GREECE, in the Old Testament, is put for the Hebrew word Javan, which is equivalent to Ionia, and seems to include not only Greece but western Asia Minor, and the intervening isles, all settled by the Ionian race, Gen. 10:2. Greece proper, however, is chiefly intended. It is not often mentioned in the Old Testament, Dan. 8:21; 10:20; 11:2; Joel 3:6; Zech. 9:13. See JAVAN.

In the New Testament, Greece is called Hellas, a name supposed to have belonged first to a single city, but at length applied to the whole country south of Macedonia. About B. C. 146, the Romans conquered Greece, and afterwards organized two great provinces, namely, Macedonia, including Macedonia proper, Thessaly, Epirus, and Illyricum; and Achaia, including all the country which lies south of the former province. (See ACHAIA.) In Acts 20:2, Greece is probably to be taken in its widest acceptation, as including the whole of Greece proper and the Peloponnesus. This country was bounded north by Macedonia and Illyricum, from which it was separated by mountains, south by the Mediterranean sea, east by the Ægean sea, and west by the Ionian sea. It was generally known under the three great divisions of Peloponnesus, Hellas, and Northern Greece.

Peloponnesus, more anciently called Pelasgia, and Argos, and now the Morea, was the southern peninsula; it included the famous cities, Sparta, Messene, Elis, Corinth, Argos, etc. The division of Hellas, which now constitutes a great part of Livadia, included the following cities: Athens, Megara, Platæa, Delphos, and Actium. Northern Greece included Thessaly and Epirus, with the cities Larissa, Nicopolis, etc. The large islands of Crete and Eubœa belonged to Greece, as well as most of those in the Archipelago and on the west.

The Jews and the Greeks appear to have had little intercourse with each other, until after Alexander the Great overran Egypt, Syria, and the East. They then began to come in contact everywhere, for both races were widely dispersed. The Jews extended the name of Greeks to include the people conquered and ruled by Greeks; and the word is thus nearly synonymous in the New Testament with Gentiles, Mark 7:26; Acts 20:21; Rom. 1:16. The term "Grecian" or Hellenist, on the contrary, denotes a Jew by birth or religion, who spoke Greek. It is used chiefly of foreign Jews and proselytes, in contrast with the Hebrews, that is, those speaking the vernacular Hebrew, or Aramæan, Acts 6:1; 9:29. The Greeks were a vivacious, acute, and polished, but superficial people, compared with the Jews. They excelled in all the arts of war and peace; but were worshippers of beauty, not of duty. Their pride of intellect, and their corruption of morals, were almost insurmountable obstacles to their reception of Christianity. Yet it was among the Greek cities and people that Paul chiefly labored, and with great success. Many flourishing churches were, in early times, established among them; and there can be no doubt that they, for a long time, preserved the apostolic customs with much care. At length, however, opinions fluctuated considerably on points of doctrine; schisms and heresies divided the church; and rancor, violence, and even persecution followed in their train. To check these evils, councils were called and various creeds composed. The removal of the seat of government from Rome to Constantinople, gave a preponderance to the Grecian districts of the empire, and the ecclesiastical determinations of the Greek church were extensively received. In the middle of the eighth century disputes arose, which terminated in a permanent schism between the Greek and Latin churches. The Greek church has a general resemblance to the Roman-catholic, and embraces a population of not far from fifty millions of souls, in Russia, Greece, Turkey, Syria, etc.

THE GREEK LANGUAGE is the original language of all the books of the New Testament, except perhaps the gospel by Matthew; but the sacred authors have followed that style of writing which was used by the Hellenists, or Grecizing Hebrews, adopting many idioms and turns of speech from the Syriac and Hebrew languages, very different from the classical style of the Greek writers. They were also obliged to make use of some new words, and new applications of old words, to express religious ideas before unknown to the Greeks, and for which they had no proper expression. After Alexander the Great, Greek became the language best known throughout the East, and was generally used in commerce. As the sacred authors had in view the conversion not only of the Jews, then scattered throughout the East, but of the Gentiles also, it was natural for them to write to them in Greek, that being a language to which all were of necessity accustomed.

GRIND. See CORN.

GROVES were very early used for religious worship, Gen. 21:33. "The groves were God's first temples," and seem naturally fitted for such purposes. Groves were also resorted to by heathen idolaters. Some elevated spot was generally chosen for this purpose. "They sacrifice upon the tops of mountains, and burn incense upon the hills; under oaks and poplars and elms, because the shadow thereof is good," Hos. 4:13. It should be noticed, however, that the Hebrew word *Asherah*, which occurs in many passages, and is rendered grove in the English version, rather signifies an image of Astarte, 1 Kin. 18:19; 2 Kin. 13:6; etc. See ASHTORETH. The "high places" spoken of in Scripture were used first, for the worship of Jehovah, 1 Kin. 3:3, 4; etc. This was, strictly speaking, an irregularity, since, according to the law of Moses, every sacrifice was required to be brought to the altar of the sanctuary, Lev. 17:8, 9; Deut. 11:13, 16. The "high places" were also used, secondly, for the worship of idols, 2 Kin. 23:15, etc.

H.

HABAK'KUK, one of the minor prophets. Of his life we know nothing, except that he appears to have been contemporary with Jeremiah, and to have prophesied about 610 B. C., shortly before Nebuchadnezzar's first invasion of Judea, 2 Kin. 24:1.

The BOOK OF HABAKKUK consists of three chapters, which all constitute one oracle. In the first chapter, he foretells the woes which the rapacious and terrible Chaldeans would soon inflict upon his guilty nation. In the second, he predicts the future humiliation of the conquerors. The third is a sublime and beautiful ode, in which the prophet implores the succor of Jehovah in view of his mighty works of ancient days, and expresses the most assured trust in him. Nothing, even in Hebrew poetry, is more lofty and grand than this triumphal ode.

HABER'GEON, Neh. 4:16, Job 41:26, a coat of mail; an ancient piece of defensive armor, in the form of a coat or tunic, descending from the neck to the middle of the body, and formed of tough hide, or many quilted linen folds, or of scales of brass overlapping each other like fishes' scales, or of small iron rings or meshes linked into each other, Ex. 28:32; 39:23.

HA'BOR, or CHABOR, a city of Media, near which Tiglath-pileser, and afterwards Shalmanezer located portions of the captive Israelites. It is thought to have stood where the town of Abhar now exists on a branch of the river Gozan, 2 Kin. 17:6; 18:11.

HA'DAD, I., an Idumean prince, who defeated the Midianites in the plains of Moab, Gen. 36:35; 1 Chr. 1:16.

II. A second prince of Edom, mentioned in 1 Chr. 1:51.

III. Another Edomite of the royal family, who fled to Egypt while young, upon David's conquest of Edom, 2 Sam. 8:14; was well received, and married the queen's sister. After the death of David and Joab, he returned to Edom and made an ineffectual effort to throw off the yoke of Solomon, 1 Kin. 11:14-22; 2 Chr. 8:17.

HADADE'ZER, or HADARE'ZER, a powerful king of Syria, reigning in Zobah and the surrounding country, even to the Euphrates, 1 Kin. 11:23. He was thrice defeated and his power overthrown by David, 2 Sam. 8:3, 4; 10:6-14, 16-19; 1 Chr. 18:3; 19:6.

HA'DAD-RIM'MON, a place in the valley of Megiddo, where the good king Josiah lost his life in a battle with the Ethiopians, 2 Kin. 23:29; 2 Chr. 35:20-25. The lamentation over this event was very great, Zech. 12:11.

HADO'RAM. See ADONIRAM.

HA'GAR, *stranger*, an Egyptian bondmaid in the household of Sarah, Gen. 12:16, who, being barren, gave her to Abraham for a secondary wife, that by her, as a substitute, she might have children, in accordance with the customs of the East in that age. The history of Hagar is given in Gen. 16; 17; 21. In an allegory, Paul makes Hagar represent the Jewish church, which was in bondage to the ceremonial law; as Sarah represents the true church of Christ, which is free from this bondage, Gal. 4:24. Her name is much honored among the Arabs claiming to be her descendants.

HAGARENES', or HA'GARITES, 1 Chr. 5:10, 20, descendants of Hagar and Ishmael. In Psa. 83:6, the name seems to be given to a distinct portion of the Ishmaelites.

HAG'GAI, one of the minor prophets, probably accompanied Zerubbabel in the first return of the Jews from Babylon, B. C. 536. He began to prophesy in the second year of Darius Hystaspis, B. C. 520; and the object of his prophesying was to excite his countrymen to begin again the building of the temple, which had been so long interrupted. In this he was successful, Darius having granted a decree for this purpose, Ezra 6. The exceeding glory of the second temple was, as he foretold, that Christ "the Desire of all nations" came into it, and made the place of his feet glorious, Hag. 2:7-9.

HAIL! a salutation, importing a wish for the welfare of the person addressed. It is now seldom used among us; but was customary among our Saxon ancestors, and imported "joy to you," or "health to you," including in the term health all kinds of prosperity.

HAIL-STONES, are drops of rain formed into ice by the power of cold in the upper regions of the atmosphere. Hail was among the plagues of Egypt, Ex. 9:24, and was the more terrible, because it rarely occurred in that country. Hail was also made use of by God for defeating an army of Canaanites, Josh. 10:11; and is used figuratively to represent terrible judgments, Isa. 28:2; Rev. 16:21.

HAIR. The Jewish men, except Nazarites, Num. 6:5, 9, and cases like that of Absalom, 2 Sam. 14:26, cut their hair moderately short, 1 Cor. 11:14, and applied fragrant ointments to it, Ex. 30:30-33; Psa. 23:5; Eccl. 9:8. In mourning they wholly neglected it, or shaved it close, or plucked it out by handfuls, Jer. 7:29. Women prized a fine head of hair, and plaited, perfumed, and decked it in many ways, Isa. 3:18, 24; 1 Cor. 11:15, so much as to call for apostolic interdictions, 1 Tim. 2:9; 1 Pet. 3:9. "Hair like women's" characterized the locusts of antichrist, Rev. 9:8. Lepers, when cleansed, and Levites, on their consecration, shaved the whole body, Lev. 13; 14:8, 9.

HA'LAH, 2 Kin. 17:6. See HABOR.

HALLELU'JAH, and in the New Testament, ALLELUIAH, *Praise ye Jehovah.* This word occurs at the beginning and at the end of many psalms. It was also sung on solemn days of rejoicing, as an expression of joy and praise, and as such it has been adopted in the Christian church, and is still used in devotional psalmody, Rev. 19:1, 3, 4, 6.

HAL'LOW, to render sacred, set apart, consecrate. The English word is from the Saxon, and means *to make holy:* hence hallowed persons, things, places, rites, etc.; hence also the name, power, and dignity of God are hallowed, that is, reverenced as holy.

HAM, *burnt, swarthy, black,* I., a son of Noah, Gen. 5:32; 7:13; 9:18; 10:1. The impiety revealed in his conduct towards his father, drew upon him, or rather, according to the Bible statement, on his son Canaan, a prophetic malediction, Gen. 9:20-27. Ham was the father of Cush, Mizraim, Phut, and Canaan, that is, the ancestor of the Canaanites, Southern Arabians, Ethiopians, Egyptians, and the Africans in general, Gen. 10:6–20.

II. A poetical name for Egypt, Psa. 78:51; 106:22.

III. An unknown place of the Zuzim, Gen. 14:5.

HA'MAN, a favorite of Ahasuerus, king of Persia. In order to revenge himself upon Mordecai the Jew, he plotted the extermination of all the Jews in the kingdom; but in the providence of God he was thwarted by Esther, fell into disgrace with the king, and wrought his own ruin and the upbuilding of the Jews. He is called an Agagite; and as Agag was a common name of the Amalekite kings, the Jews believe he was of that race. This would help to explain his malice against the Jews. See AMALEKITES. Similar wholesale slaughters are still plotted in Asia, and the whole narrative is confirmed and illustrated by the descriptions of eastern life furnished by modern travellers in the same region. The death of Haman took place about 485 B. C. His eventful history shows that pride goes before destruction; that the providence of God directs all things; that his people are safe in the midst of perils; and that his foes must perish.

HA'MATH, a celebrated city of Syria. Hamath, like Jerusalem and Damascus, is one of the few places in Syria and Palestine which have retained a certain degree of importance from the very earliest ages to the present time. The name occurs in Gen. 10:18, as the seat of a Canaanitish tribe; and it is often mentioned as the northern limit of Canaan in its widest extent, Num. 13:21; Josh. 13:5; Judg. 3:3. In David's time, Toi king of Hamath was his ally, 2 Sam. 8:9, 10.

Burckhardt describes Hamath as "situated on both sides of the Orontes; a part of it is built on the declivity of a hill, and a part in the plain. The town is of considerable extent, and must contain at least 30,000 inhabitants. There are four bridges over the Orontes in the town. The river supplies the upper town with water by means of buckets fixed to high wheels, which empty themselves into stone canals, supported by lofty arches on a level with the upper part of the town. There are about a dozen of the wheels; the largest of them is at least seventy feet in diameter. The principal trade of Hamath is with the Arabs, who buy here their tent furniture and clothes. The government of Hamath comprises about one hundred and twenty inhabited villages, and seventy or eighty which have been abandoned. The western part of its territory is the granary of northern Syria, though the harvest never yields more than ten for one, chiefly in consequence of the immense numbers of mice, which sometimes wholly destroy the crops." "The entering in of Hamath" is the northern part of the valley which leads up to it from Palestine, between Lebanon and Anti-Lebanon, Num. 13:21; 1 Kin. 8:65.

HANANEEL', a kinsman of Jeremiah, from whom the prophet bought a piece of ground before the captivity, and had the legal record made, in token of his prophetic assurance that his people would return to their possessions, Jer. 32:6–12.

HANA'NI, I., a seer in the time of Asa, 955–914 B. C., imprisoned for his fidelity. He was also the father of the prophet Jehu, 1 Kin. 16:1–7; 2 Chr. 16:7–10; 19:2; 20:34.

II. A brother of Nehemiah, who brought to Babylon an account of the wretched state of the Jews then at Jerusalem, and afterwards had charge of the gates of the city, Neh. 1:1–3; 7:2, 3, B. C. 455.

HANANI'AH, I., a false prophet of Gibeon, who for his impious hardihood was overtaken with speedy death, according to the word of God, Jer. 28:15–17.

II. The Hebrew name of Shadrach.

III. A pious and faithful officer under Nehemiah, Neh. 7:2.

HAND is often put for *strength, power;* so to be "in the hand" of any one, is to be in his power. Joining hands, or striking hands, is a very common method of pledging one's self to a contract or bargain; just as persons among us often shake hands in token of an agreement. To "lift the hand," means to make oath. "At the right hand of God," is the place of honor, power, and happiness, Psa. 16:11; 45:9; 110:1; Matt. 26:64; Col. 3:1. The right hand meant towards the south, the Jews being wont to speak as if facing the east. The "laying on of hands," signified consecration to office, and the bestowal of a blessing or of divine gifts, Gen. 48:14; Num. 8:10; 27:18; Mark 10:16; Acts 6:6; 19:6; 1 Tim. 4:14. The hands of the high-priest laid upon the scape-goat, as if transferring the guilt of the people to his head, represented the work wrought by Christ in order that the sinner might not be "driven away in his wickedness." See WASHING.

HA'NES, a city of Egypt, Isa. 30:4, thought to be the modern Ehnès, in middle Egypt on the Nile.

HAN'NAH, the pious wife of a Levite of Ramathaim-Zophim, named Elkanah, and mother of Samuel, B. C. 1171. She had earnestly besought the Lord for him, and freely devoted him to serve God according to her vow. She was afterwards blessed with three other sons and two daughters, 1 Sam. 1-2:21.

HA'NUN, a king of the Ammonites, whose father Nahash had befriended David in his early troubles. Upon the death of Nahash, David sent an embassage to condole with his son. The shameful treatment received by these ambassadors led to a destructive war upon the Ammonites, 2 Sam. 10; 1 Chr. 19.

HA'RA, 1 Chr. 5:26, probably a mountainous region in the northern part of Media.

HA'RAN, I., the eldest son of Terah, brother of Abraham, and father of Lot, Milcah, and Iscah. He died before his father Terah, Gen. 11:26-31.

II. An ancient city, called in the New Testament Charran, in the north-west part of Mesopotamia. Here, after leaving Ur, Abraham dwelt till his father Terah died; and to this old homestead Isaac sent for a wife, and Jacob fled from the wrath of Esau, Gen. 11:31, 32; 12:5; 24; 27:43; 28:10; 29:4. Haran was ravaged by the Assyrians in the time of Hezekiah, 2 Kin. 19:12; Isa. 37:12. Here also Crassus the Roman general was defeated and killed by the Parthians. Harran, as it is now called, is situated on a branch of the Euphrates, in 36° 52′ N. lat., and 39° 5′ E. long., in a flat and sandy plain, and is only peopled by a few wandering Arabs, who select it for the delicious water it furnishes.

THE COMMON HARE OF PALESTINE.

HARE, of the same genus as the rabbit, prohibited to the Jews for food, Lev. 11:6, because, though it "cheweth the cud," it "divideth not the hoof." No species of hare is known which strictly chews the cud. There were several varieties of the hare in Syria.

HAR'LOT, an abandoned woman, Prov. 29:3; a type of idolatrous nations and cities, Isa. 1:21; Ezek. 16; Nah. 3:4. Among the Jews, prostitutes were often foreigners; hence their name of "strange women." They were often devoted to heathen idols, and their abominations were a part of the worship, Num. 25:1-5; Hos. 4:14; a custom from the defilement of which the house of God was expressly defended, Deut. 23:18.

HAR'NESS, a suit of defensive armor, 1 Kin. 20:11; 2 Chr. 18:33. The Hebrews went out from Egypt "harnessed," that is, properly equipped or arranged.

HA'ROD, a spring near Jezreel and mount Gilboa, Judg. 7:1; 2 Sam. 23:25.

HARO'SHETH OF THE GENTILES, a city in the north of Canaan, the residence of Sisera, Judg. 4:2; 13; 16. The missionary Thompson finds its ruins at a place still called Harothieh, the Arabic equivalent for Harosheth, on a hill commanding the entrance to the narrow passage of the Kishon from the plain of Esdraelon to the plain of Acre.

HARP, Hebrew KINNÔR, the most ancient and common stringed instrument

ANCIENT HARPS OR LYRES

of the Jews, more properly translated lyre. It was light and portable, and was used on joyful occasions, whether sacred or not. It was invented by Jubal, Gen. 4 : 21; 31 : 27; 1 Chr. 16 : 5; 25:1–5; Psa. 81:2. David was a proficient in its use, 1 Sam. 16:16, 23; 18:10. The instrument most nearly resembling our harp was the Hebrew NEBEL, translated psaltery in the Old Testament, Psa. 57:8; 81:2; 92:3; 108:2. It had a general triangular shape, and seven to twelve strings, Psa. 33 : 2; 144 : 9. It was played with the hand, or with a short iron rod or plectrum, according to its size. The Jews had other stringed instruments, like the guitar and lute, but little can be accurately determined respecting their form, etc. See MUSIC.

HART, or STAG, a species of deer, clean by the Levitical law, Deut. 12:15, and celebrated for its elegance, agility, and grace, Song 2:9; Isa. 35:6. See HIND, and ROE.

HATE often denotes in Scripture only a less degree of love, Gen. 29 : 30, 31; Deut. 21:15; Prov. 13:24; Mal. 1:2, 3; Luke 14 : 26; Rom. 9 : 13. God has a just and perfect abhorrence of sin and sinners, Psa. 5:5. But hatred in general is a malevolent passion, Gal. 5:20, and no one who is not perfect in love, can hate without sin.

HAU'RAN, Ezek. 47:16, was originally a small district south of Damascus, and east of the sea of Tiberias, but was afterwards extended to the south and east, and under the Romans was called Auranitis. It now includes the ancient Trachonitis, the Haouran, Ituræa, and part of Batanæa, and is very minutely described by Burckhardt. Many ruins of cities, with Greek inscriptions, are scattered over its rugged surface.

HAVI'LAH. The Scriptures mention a Havilah descended from Ham, Gen. 10 : 7, and another from Shem, Gen. 11:29. We must assume a double Havilah, corresponding to each of these.

1. The location of one Havilah is connected with that of the garden of Eden. According to one theory, it is to be sought on the south-eastern extremity of the Black sea; according to another, at the head of the Persian gulf. See EDEN.

2. The other Havilah seems to have been in Arabia. From the statement in 1 Sam. 15:7, that "Saul smote the Amalekites from Havilah unto Shur, that is over against Egypt," it would seem to have been somewhere in the north-western part of Arabia; since, from the circumstances of this campaign, we cannot well suppose that it extended over a great tract of country.

HA'VOTH-JAIR', *huts of Jair*, a district in Gilead, containing thirty hamlets belonging to the thirty sons of Jair, judges of Israel, Num. 32 : 41; Judg. 10:3, 4.

HAWK, or FALCON, a strong-winged and rapacious bird, of several species in Syria; unclean for the Hebrews, Lev. 11:16, but sacred among the Greeks and Egyptians. In its migrations, it illustrates the wise providence of the Creator, Job 39:26.

HAY, in Prov. 27:25 and Isa. 15:6, denotes the first shoots of grass. The Jews did not prepare and store up hay for winter use, as is customary in cold climates.

HAZ'AEL, an officer of Benhadad king of Syria, whose future accession to the throne was revealed to the prophet Elijah, 1 Kin. 19 : 15. Many years afterwards he was sent by Benhadad to consult Elisha, then at Damascus, as to his recovery from sickness, and on the next day smothered the king with a wet cloth, 2 Kin. 8 : 7–15, B. C. 885. His discomposure under the eye of the prophet was an indication that he had already meditated this crime. Having usurped the throne, he reigned forty years; and by his successful and cruel wars against Judah and Israel justified the forebodings of Elisha, 2 Kin. 8 : 28; 10 : 32; 12 : 17; 13:3, 7; 2 Chr. 22:5.

HAZ'ERIM, an ancient abode of the Avim, apparently in the north-western part of Arabia Petræa, Deut. 2:23.

HAZ'EROTH, a station of the Israelites, about five days' journey from mount Sinai, Num. 11:35. Here they remained a week or more, Num. 12; and their next station recorded was near Kadesh-barnea, on the borders of Canaan, Num. 12:16; 13:26; Deut. 1:19–21.

HAZE'ZON-TA'MAR. See EN-GEDI.

HA'ZOR, I., a chief city of northern Canaan, whose king Jabin, at the head of an allied host, was defeated by Joshua, Josh. 11:1–13. Hazor revived, however, and for a time oppressed the Israelites; but was subdued by Barak, fortified by Solomon, and remained in the possession of Israel until the invasion of Tiglath-pileser, Josh. 19:36; Judg. 4:2; 1 Kin. 9:15; 2 Kin. 15:29. It lay not far from lake Merom.

II. A region in Arabia, laid waste by Nebuchadnezzar, Jer. 49:28–33. Its location is unknown.

III. Cities in Judah and Benjamin, Josh. 15:23; Neh. 11:33.

HEATH, supposed to be the Juniper, a low tree found in desert and rocky places, and thus contrasted with a tree growing by a water-course, Jer. 17:5–8; 48:6.

HEAV'EN, in the Bible, means primarily the region of the air and clouds, and of the planets and stars, but chiefly the world of holy bliss above the visible heavens. It is called "the third heaven," "the highest heaven," and "the heaven of heavens," expressions nearly synonymous. There holy beings are to dwell, seeing all of God that it is possible for creatures to see. Thither Christ ascended, to intercede for his people and prepare for them a place where all shall at length be gathered, to go no more out for ever, Eph. 4:10; Heb. 8:1; 9:24–28. In this life we can know but little of the location and appearance of heaven, or of the employments and blessedness of its inhabitants. The Scriptures inform us that all sin, and every other evil, are for ever excluded; no fruits of sin will be found there—no curse nor sorrow nor sighing, no tear, no death: the former things are passed away. They describe it figuratively, crowding together all the images which nature or art can supply to illustrate its happiness. It is a kingdom, an inheritance: there are rivers of pleasure, trees of life, glorious light, rapturous songs, robes, crowns, feasting, mirth, treasures, triumphs. They also give us positive representations: the righteous dwell in the presence of God; they appear with Christ in glory. Heaven is life, everlasting life: glory, an eternal weight of glory: salvation, repose, peace, fulness of joy, the joy of the Lord. There are different degrees in that glory, and never-ceasing advancement. It will be a social state, and its happiness, in some measure, will arise from mutual communion and converse, and the expressions and exercises of mutual benevolence. It will include the perfect purity of every saint; delightful fellowship with those we have here loved in the Lord, Matt. 8:11; 17:3, 4; 1 Thess. 2:19; 4:13–18; the presence of Christ, and the consciousness that all is perfect and everlasting. We are taught that the body will share this bliss as well as the soul: the consummation of our bliss is subsequent to the resurrection of the body; for it is redeemed as well as the soul, and shall, at the resurrection of the just, be fashioned like unto Christ's glorious body. By descending from heaven, and reascending thither, he proves to the doubting soul the reality of heaven; he opens its door for the guilty by his atoning sacrifice; and all who are admitted to it by his blood shall be made meet for it by his grace, and find their happiness for ever in his love. See KINGDOM OF HEAVEN.

HE'BER, I., an ancestor of the Hebrews, Luke 3:35. See HEBREWS.

II. A Kenite, descended from Hobab, Moses' father-in-law. He resided in the northern part of Canaan, and seems to have been a man of note in his day. His wife Jael slew Sisera with her own hand, Judg. 4:11, 17; 5:24.

HE'BREWS, that branch of the posterity of Abraham whose home was in the land of promise. The name Hebrew is first applied to Abraham in Gen. 14:13, and is generally supposed to have been derived from Heber, the last of the long-lived patriarchs. Heber outlived six generations of his descendants, including Abraham himself, after whose death he was for some years the only surviving ancestor of Isaac and Jacob. Hebrews appears to have been the name by which the Jewish people were known to foreigners, in distinction from their common domestic name, "the children of Israel." The name of Jews, derived from Judah, was afterwards applied to them as inhabitants of Judea, 2 Kin. 16:6.

Abraham, the founder of the Jewish nation, was a migratory shepherd, whose property consisted mainly in vast flocks and herds, but who had no fixed residence, and removed from place to place as the convenience of water and pasturage dictated. As such a nomad, he had lived in Ur of the Chaldees, and then in Haran, whence he removed and dwelt in the same manner among the Canaanites, in the country which God promised to give to his posterity. His son and grandson, Isaac and Jacob, followed in his steps. By a miraculous arrangement of Providence, Joseph, one of the sons of Jacob, became grand-vizier of Egypt; and in a time of famine invited his family to settle in that land. Here they dwelt four hundred and thirty years; during which time the Egyptians reduced them to a state of bondage. From this they were delivered by Jehovah through Moses, who led them out with great signs and wonders to Sinai, where God gave them his law; and then, after forty years of wanderings, he brought them to the borders of the promised land. Here Moses died, and was succeeded by Joshua, who conquered the desired country, and allotted it to the several tribes. From this time they were governed in the name of Jehovah, by chiefs, judges, or patriarchal rulers, until the time of Samuel; when the government was changed to a monarchy, and Saul anointed king. David, a shepherd youth, but the man after God's own heart, was afterwards king, and founded a family which continued to reign in Jerusalem until the entire subjugation of the country by the Chaldeans. Under his grandson Rehoboam, however, ten tribes revolted and formed a separate kingdom, that of Israel, between which and the kingdom of Judah there were hostile feelings and frequent wars. The termination of the whole was the carrying away of the greater part of both nations to Babylonia, Media, etc. After seventy years of exile, a few small colonies of Hebrews returned, and built another temple at Jerusalem, and attempted to reëstablish their nation; but they had to struggle first, under the Maccabees, against the kings of the Seleucian race, (see JERUSALEM.) and then against the Romans; by whom at length, under Titus, Jerusalem was taken and utterly destroyed, A. D. 70-71. Since that time, although Jerusalem has been rebuilt, the Hebrews have ceased to exist as an independent people; but they are scattered among all the nations of the earth, where they retain their characteristic traits, and live as strangers, and, in a great measure, as outcasts.

The government of the Hebrews is, by Josephus, called a theocracy—a form of government which assigns the whole power to God, with the management of all the national affairs—God, in fact, being the proper King of the state. This government, however, underwent several changes under the legislator Moses, his successor Joshua, the judges, the kings, and the high-priests. But amid all these revolutions, God was considered as the monarch of Israel, though he did not exercise his jurisdiction always in the same manner. In the time of Moses, he dwelt among his people as a king in his palace, or in the midst of his camp; always ready to be consulted, promulgating all needful laws, and giving specific directions in all emergencies. This was, properly, the time of the theocracy, in the strictest sense of the term. Under Joshua and the judges, it continued nearly the same: the former being filled by the spirit which animated Moses, would undertake nothing without consulting Jehovah; and the latter were leaders, raised up by God himself, to deliver the Hebrews and govern in his name. The demand of the people for a king occasioned to Samuel, the prophet-judge, great disquietude; for he regarded it as a rejection of the theocratic government, 1 Sam. 8:6, 7. God complied with the wishes of the people; but he still asserted his own sovereign authority, and claimed the obedience of all.

The religion of the Hebrews may be considered in different points of view, with respect to the different conditions of their nation. Under the patriarchs, they were instructed in the will of God by direct revelation, worshipped him by prayer and sacrifices, opposed idolatry and atheism, used circumcision as the appointed seal of the covenant made by God with Abraham, and followed the laws which the light of grace and faith discovers to those who honestly and seriously seek God, his righteousness, and truth. They lived in expectation of the Messiah, the Desire of all nations, to complete their hopes and wishes, and fully to instruct and bless them. Such was the religion of Abraham, Isaac, Jacob, Judah, Joseph, etc., who maintained the worship of God and the tradition of the true religion. After the time of Moses, the religion of the Hebrews became more fixed, and ceremonies, days, feasts, priests, and sacrifices were determined with great exactness. This whole dispensation only prefigured that more perfect one which should in after-times arise, when the Messiah should come, and bring life and immortality to light in his gospel, and make a full atonement for the sins of the world. See TYPE.

The long abode of the Hebrews in Egypt had cherished in them a strong propensity to idolatry; and neither the miracles of Moses, nor his precautions to withdraw them from the worship of idols, nor the rigor of his laws, nor the splendid marks of God's presence in the Israelitish camp, were able to conquer this unhappy perversity. We know with what facility they adopted the adoration of the golden calf, when they had recently been eye-witnesses of such divine wonders. Saul and David, with all their authority, were not able entirely to suppress such inveterate disorders. Superstitions, which the Israelites did not dare to exercise in public, were practised in private. They sacrificed on the high places, and consulted diviners and magicians. Solomon, whom God had chosen to build his temple, was himself a stone of stumbling to Israel. He erected altars to the false gods of the Phœnicians, Moabites, and Ammonites, and not only permitted his wives to worship the gods of their own country, but himself to some extent adored them, 1 Kin. 11:5-7. Most of his successors showed a similar weakness. Jeroboam introduced the worship of the golden calves into Israel, which took such deep root that it was never entirely extirpated. It was for this cause that God gave the Hebrews over into the hands of their enemies, to captivity and dispersion. See IDOLATRY. After the captivity, they appear to have been wholly free from the worship of idols; but they were still corrupt and far from God, and having filled the cup of their guilt by rejecting and crucifying the Lord of glory, they were extirpated as a nation and became strangers and sojourners over all the earth.

For the language of the Hebrews, see LANGUAGE.

The existence of the Hebrews as a people distinct from all others, to this day, is a miracle of that indisputable kind which may well justify a few remarks.

1. They are spread into all parts of the earth; being found not only in Europe and America, but to the utmost extremity of Asia, even in Thibet and China. They abound in Persia, Northern India, and Tartary, wherever travellers have penetrated. They are, as they assert, descendants of the tribes carried away captive by the Assyrian monarchs. They are also numerous in Arabia, in Egypt, and throughout Africa.

2. In most parts of the world their state is much the same—one of dislike, contempt, and oppression. In past ages innumerable exactions and wrongs have been heaped upon them. Within the last few years they have received more justice at the hands of some of the European states; but they have usually held their possessions by a very precarious tenure.

3. They everywhere maintain observances peculiar to themselves: such as circumcision, performed after the law of their fathers; the great day of expiation; also the observance of a sabbath or day of rest on Saturday, and not on the Christian Sabbath. They have generally retained the observance of the passover in some form.

4. They are divided into various sects. Some of them are extremely attached to the traditions of the rabbins, and to the multiplied observances enjoined in the Talmud. Others, as the Caraïtes, reject these with scorn, and adhere solely to Scripture. The majority of the Jews in Europe, and those with whose works we are mostly conversant, are rabbinists, and may be taken as representatives of the ancient Pharisees.

5. They everywhere consider Judea as their proper country, and Jerusalem as their metropolitan city. Wherever settled, and for however long, they still cherish a recollection of country, unparalleled among other nations. They have not lost it; they will not lose it; and they transmit it to their posterity. However comfortably they may be settled in any residence, they hope to see Zion and Jerusalem revive from their ashes.

6. The number of the Jewish nation was estimated a few years ago, for the information of Buonaparte, at the following amount, but from what documents we know not:

In the Turkish empire	1,000,000
In Persia, China, India, on the east and west of the Ganges	300,000
In the west of Europe, Africa, America	1,700,000
Total	3,000,000

This number is probably very far short of the truth. Maltebrun estimates them at from four to five millions.

HEBREWS, EPISTLE TO THE. The object of this epistle, which ranks among the most important of the New Testament books, was to prove to the Jews, from their own Scriptures, the divinity, humanity, atonement, and intercession of Christ, particularly his preëminence over Moses and the angels of God; to demonstrate the superiority of the gospel to the law, and the real object and design of the Mosaic institution; to fortify the minds of the Hebrew converts against apostasy under persecution, and to engage them to a deportment becoming their Christian profession. In this view, the epistle furnishes a key to the Old Testament Scriptures, and is invaluable as a clear elucidation and an inspired, unanswerable demonstration of the doctrine of the great atoning Sacrifice as set forth in Old Testament institutions. The name of the writer of this epistle is nowhere mentioned. The majority of critics, however, refer it to the apostle Paul. It is also believed to have been written in Greek, at Rome, and about A. D. 63. See PAUL.

HE'BRON, one of the most ancient cities of Canaan, being built seven years before Tanis, the capital of Lower Egypt, Num. 13:22. It was anciently called Kirjath-arba, (see ARBA,) and Mamre, and was a favorite residence of the patriarchs Abraham, Isaac, and Jacob. Here too they were buried, Gen. 14:13-24; 23:2-19; 35:27. Under Joshua and Caleb the Israelites conquered it from the Canaanites and Anakim, and it was afterwards made a Levitical city of refuge, Josh. 14:13-15; 15:13; 21:11, 13; Judg. 1:10, 20. It was David's seat of government during the seven years when he reigned over Judah only, 2 Sam. 2:3; 5:5. Here Absalom raised the standard of revolt, 2 Sam. 15:9, 10. It was fortified by Rehoboam, and is mentioned after the captivity, but not in the New Testament, Neh. 11:25. At present Hebron is an unwalled city of about 8,000 inhabitants, of whom some 600 are Jews, and the remainder Turks and Arabs. It lies in a deep valley and on the adjacent hillside, in the ancient hill-country of Judea, about twenty miles south of Jerusalem, and 2,600 feet above the sea. Its modern name, El-khulil, the friend, is the same which the Moslems give to Abraham, "the friend of God;" and they profess to hold in their keeping the burial-place of the patriarchs, the "cave of Machpelah." It is covered by a small mosque, surrounded by a stone structure 60 feet high, 150 feet wide, and 200 feet long. Within this no Christian is permitted to enter; but it is evidently of very high antiquity, and may well be regarded as inclosing the true site of the ancient tomb. Other relics of antiquity exist in two stone reservoirs, the larger 133 feet square, and 21 feet deep. They are still in daily use; and one of them was probably the "pool in Hebron," above which David hung up the assassins of Ish-bosheth, 2 Sam. 4:12. The city contains nine mosques and two synagogues. Its streets are narrow; the houses of stone, with flat roofs surmounted by small domes. Large quantities of glass lamps and colored rings are here manufactured; also leathern bottles, raisins, and dibs, or grape-syrup. The environs of the city are very fertile, furnishing the finest vineyards in Palestine, numerous plantations of olive and other fruit trees, and excellent pasturage. See ESHCOL, MAMRE.

HEIF'ER. Red heifers were to be offered in sacrifice for the national sins, in the impressive manner described in Num. 19:1-10, illustrating the true sacrifice for sin in the person of Christ, Heb. 9:13, 14. The well-fed heifer was a symbol of wanton wildness, Jer. 46:20; 50:11; Hos. 4:16.

HEL'BON, formerly supposed to be Haleb, or as called in Europe, Aleppo, a city of Syria, about one hundred and eighty miles north of Damascus, and about eighty from the Mediterranean sea. In 1822, Aleppo was visited by a dreadful earthquake, by which it was almost entirely destroyed. Its present population is not one half of the 200,000 it then possessed. But recently a valley has been found on the eastern slope of Anti-Lebanon, north of the Barada, called Helbon, from one of its principal villages. Its grapes and the wine made from them are still remarkable for their fine quality. This valley is probably the Helbon of Ezek. 27:18.

HELIOP'OLIS, *city of the sun*, I., a celebrated city of Egypt, called in Coptic, Hebrew, and the English version, ON, *sun, light*, Gen. 41:45. The Seventy mention expressly, Ex. 1:11, that On is Heliopolis. Jeremiah, 43:13, calls this city Beth-shemesh, that is, house or temple of the sun. In Ezekiel, 30:17, the name is pronounced Aven, which is the same as On. The Arabs called it Ain-Shems, fountain of the sun. All these names come from the circumstance that the city was the ancient seat of the Egyptian worship of the sun. It was in ruins in the time of Strabo, who mentions that two obelisks had already been carried away to Rome. At present its site, six miles north-north-east from Cairo, is marked only by extensive ranges of low mounds full of ruinous fragments, and a solitary obelisk formed of a single block of red granite, rising about sixty feet above the sand, and covered on its four sides with hieroglyphics.

II. Another Heliopolis is alluded to in Scripture under the name of the "plain of Aven," or field of the sun, Amos 1:5. This was the Heliopolis of Cœle-Syria, now Baalbec. Its stupendous ruins have been the wonder of past centuries, and will continue to be the wonder of future generations, till barbarism and earthquakes shall have done their last work. The most notable remains are those of three temples, the largest of which, with its courts and portico, extended 1,000 feet from east to west. A magnificent portico, 180 feet long, with twelve lofty and highly wrought columns, led to a large hexagonal court, and this to a vast quadrangle, 440 feet by 370. Fronting

RUINS OF BAALBEC.

on this, rose ten columns of the peristyle which surrounded the inner temple. There were nineteen columns on each side, or fifty-four in all, only six of which are now standing, and they were seven feet in diameter, and sixty-two feet high, besides the entablature of nearly fourteen feet. This temple rested on an immense vaulted substructure, rising nearly fifty feet above the ground outside, and in this are three stones sixty-three feet long and thirteen feet high, lying twenty feet above the ground. The temples are of Roman origin; and in vastness of plan, combined with elaborateness and delicacy of execution, they seem to surpass all others in the world. "They are like those of Athens for lightness, but far surpass them in vastness; they are vast and massive, like those of Thebes, but far excel them in airiness and grace." (Robinson.)

HEL'KATH-HAZZU'RIM, *field of heroes*, a place near Gibeon, so named from a fatal duel-like combat, preceding a battle between the armies of David and Ish-bosheth, 2 Sam. 2:16.

HELL. The Hebrew SHEOL, and the Greek HADES, usually translated *hell*, often signify the place of departed spirits, Psa. 16:10; Isa. 14:9; Ezek. 31:16. Here was the rich man, after being buried, Luke 16 : 23. The above and many other passages in the Old Testament show the futility of that opinion which attributes to the Hebrews an ignorance of a future state.

The term *hell* is most commonly applied to the place of punishment in the unseen world, and is usually represented in the Greek New Testament by the word Gehenna, *valley of Hinnom*. See HINNOM. In 2 Pet. 2:4, the rebellious angels are said, in the original Greek, to have been cast down into "Tartarus," this being the Grecian name of the lowest abyss of Hades. Other expressions are also used, indicating the dreadfulness of the anguish there to be endured. It is called "outer darkness," "flame," "furnace of fire," "unquenchable fire," "fire and brimstone," etc., Matt. 8:12; 13:42; 22:13; 25:20, 41; Mark 9:43–48; Jude 13; Rev. 20:14. The misery of hell will consist in the privation of the vision and love of God, exclusion from every source of happiness, perpetual sin, remorse of conscience in view of the past, malevolent passions, the sense of the just anger of God, and all other sufferings of body and soul which in the nature of things are the natural results of sin, or which the law of God requires as penal inflictions. The degrees of anguish will be proportioned to the degrees of guilt, Matt. 10:15; 23:14; Luke 12:47, 48. And these punishments will be eternal, like the happiness of heaven. The wrath of God will never cease to abide upon the lost soul, and it will always be "the wrath to come."

HE'MAN, I., a celebrated sage, of the tribe of Judah. The period of his life is unknown, 1 Kin. 4:31.

II. A Kohathite Levite, to whom as a chief musician of the temple the eighty-eighth Psalm is inscribed, 1 Chr. 6:33; 16:41, 42.

HEM'LOCK, Hos. 10:4, Amos 6:12, in Hebrew, ROSH, usually translated gall or bitterness, Deut. 32:32, and mentioned in connection with wormwood, Deut. 29:18; Jer. 9:15; 23:15; Lam. 3:19. It indicates some wild, bitter, and noxious plant, which it is difficult to determine. According to some it is the poisonous hemlock, while others consider it to be the poppy.

HEN. The care of a hen to protect her brood from hawks, etc., illustrates the Saviour's tender care of his people when exposed to the swoop of the Roman eagle, as in all similar perils, Matt. 23:37; 24:22. The common barn-door fowl is not often mentioned in Scripture, Mark 13:35; 14:30; Luke 22:34; but at the present day they and their eggs are more used in Syria than any other food not vegetable.

HE'NA, supposed to have been a city of Mesopotamia afterwards called Ana, at a ford of the Euphrates, 2 Kin. 18:34; 19:13; Isa. 37:13.

HEPH'ZIBAH, *my delight*, the mother of Manasseh, 2 Kin. 21:1, and a name given to the church, Isa. 62:4.

HER'ESY, *choice*, chosen way of life or faith; sect, school, party. The Greek word properly designates any sect or party, without implying praise or censure. So everywhere in the book of Acts, 5:17; 15:5; 26:4, 5. In the epistles it denotes a sect or party in a bad sense, implying a refractory spirit, as well as error in faith and practice, 1 Cor. 11:19; Gal. 5:20; 2 Pet. 2:1. After the primitive age, the word came to signify simply error in doctrine.

HER'MAS, a Christian at Rome, Rom. 16:14; supposed by some to have been the writer of the ancient work called "The Shepherd of Hermas"—a singular mixture of truth and piety with folly and superstition.

HERMOG'ENES, and PHYGEL'LUS, fellow-laborers with Paul in Asia Minor, who deserted him during his second imprisonment at Rome, 2 Tim. 1:15.

HER'MON, a lofty mountain on the north-east border of Palestine, called also Sirion, Shenir, and Sion, (not Zion,) Deut. 3:8; 4:39. It is a part of the great Anti-Lebanon range; at the point where an eastern and lower arm branches off, a little south of the latitude of Damascus, and runs in a southerly direction terminating east of the head of the sea of Galilee. This low range is called Jebel Heish. Mount Hermon is believed to be what is now known as Jebel esh-Sheikh, whose highest summit, surpassing every other in Syria, rises into the region of perpetual snow or ice, ten thousand feet above the sea.

For a view of Hermon, see MEROM. Professor Hackett thus describes its appearance as seen from a hill north of Nazareth: "The mountain was concealed one moment, and the next, on ascending a few steps higher, stood arrayed before me with an imposing effect which I cannot easily describe. It rose immensely above every surrounding object. The purity of the atmosphere caused it to appear near, though it was in reality many miles distant. The snow on its head and sides sparkled under the rays of the sun, as if it had been robed in a vesture of silver. In my mind's eye at that moment it had none of the appearance of an inert mass of earth and rock, but glowed with life and animation. It stood there athwart my path, like a mighty giant rearing his head towards heaven and swelling with the proud consciousness of strength and majesty. I felt how natural was the Psalmist's personification: "The north and the south thou hast created them; Tabor and Hermon shall rejoice in thy name,'" Psa. 89:12.

The "little Hermon" of modern travellers, not mentioned in Scripture, is a shapeless mass of hills north of the smaller valley of Jezreel. "Hermonites," or Hermons, in Psa. 42:6, denotes the peaks of the Hermon range.

HER'OD, the name of four princes, Idumæans by descent, who governed either the whole or a part of Judea, under the Romans, and are mentioned in the New Testament.

I. HEROD THE GREAT, Matt. 2; Luke 1:5. He was the son of Antipater, an Idumæan, who was in high favor with Julius Cæsar. At the age of fifteen years, Herod was constituted by his father procurator of Galilee under Hyrcanus II., who was then at the head of the Jewish nation; while his brother Phasael was intrusted with the same authority over Judea. In these stations they were afterwards confirmed by Antony, with the title of tetrarch, about the year 41 B. C. The power of Hyrcanus had always been opposed by his brother Aristobulus; and now Antigonus, the son of the latter, continued in hostility to Herod, and was assisted by the Jews. At first he was unsuccessful, and was driven by Herod out of the country; but having obtained the aid of the Parthians, he at length succeeded in defeating Herod, and acquired possession of the whole of Judea, about the year 40 B. C. Herod meanwhile fled to Rome; and being there declared king of Judea through the exertions of Antony, he collected an army, vanquished Antigonus, recovered Jerusalem, and extirpated all the family of the Maccabees, B. C. 37. After the battle of Actium, in which his patron Antony was defeated, Herod joined the party of Octavius, and was confirmed by him in all his possessions. He endeavored to conciliate the affections of the Jews, by rebuilding and decorating the temple, (see TEMPLE,) and by founding or enlarging many cities and towns; but the prejudices of the nation against a foreign yoke were only heightened when he introduced quinquennial games in honor of Cæsar, and erected theatres and gymnasia at Jerusalem. The cruelty of his disposition also was such as ever to render him odious. He put to death his own wife Mariamne, with her two sons Alexander and Aristobulus; and when he himself was at the point of death, he caused a number of the most illustrious of his subjects to be thrown into prison at Jericho, and exacted from his sister a promise that they should be murdered the moment he expired, in order, as he said, that tears should be shed at the death of Herod. This promise, however, was not fulfilled. His son Antipater was executed for conspiring to poison his father; and five days after, Herod died, A. D. 2, aged sixty-eight, having reigned as king about thirty-seven years. It was during his reign that Jesus was born at Bethlehem; and Herod, in consequence of his suspicious temper, and in order to destroy Jesus, gave orders for the destruction of all the children of two years old and under in the place, Matt. 2. This is also mentioned by Macrobius. After the death of Herod, half of his kingdom, including Judea, Idumæa, and Samaria, was given to his son Archelaus, with the title of Ethnarch; while the remaining half was divided between two of his other sons, Herod Antipas and Philip, with the title of Tetrarchs; the former having the regions of Galilee and Perea, and the latter Batanea, Trachonitis, and Auranitis.

II. HEROD PHILIP. See PHILIP.

III. HEROD AN'TIPAS, Luke 3:1, was the son of Herod the Great by Malthace his Samaritan wife, and own brother to Archelaus, along with whom he was educated at Rome. After the death of his father, he was appointed by Augustus to be tetrarch of Galilee and Perea, that is, the southern part of the country east of the Jordan, Luke 3:1, whence also the general appellation of king is sometimes given to him, Mark 6:14. The Saviour, as a Galilean, was under his jurisdiction, Luke 23:6-12. He first married a daughter of Aretas, an Arabian king; but afterwards becoming enamoured of Herodias, the wife of his brother Herod Philip, and his own niece, he dismissed his former wife, and induced Herodias to leave her own husband and connect herself with him. At her instigation he afterwards went to Rome to ask for the dignity and title of king; but being there accused before Caligula, at the instance of Herod Agrippa, his nephew and the brother of Herodias, he was banished to Lugdunum (now Lyons) in Gaul, about A. D. 41, and the provinces which he governed were given to Herod Agrippa. It was Herod Antipas who caused John the Baptist to be beheadad, Matt. 14:1-12; Mark 6:14-29. He also appears to have been a follower, or at least a favorer, of the sect of the Sadducees, Mark 8:15. Compare Matt. 16:6. See HERODIANS.

IV. HEROD AGRIPPA MAJOR or I., Acts 12; 23:35, was a grandson of Herod the Great and Mariamne, and son of the Aristobulus who was put to death with his mother, by the orders of his father. (See above, HEROD I.) On the accession of Caligula to the imperial throne, Agrippa was taken from prison, where he had been confined by Tiberius, and received from the emperor, A. D. 38, the title of king, together with the provinces which had belonged to his uncle Philip the tetrarch, (see HEROD I.,) and also to the tetrarch Lysanias. (See ABILENE.) He was afterwards confirmed in the possession of these by Claudius, who also annexed to his kingdom all those parts of Judea and Samaria which had formerly belonged to his grandfather Herod, A. D. 43. In order to ingratiate himself with the Jews, he commenced a persecution against the Christians; but seems to have proceeded no further than to put to death James, and to imprison Peter, since he soon after died suddenly and miserably at Cæsarea, A. D. 44, Acts 12. He is mentioned by Josephus only under the name of Agrippa.

V. HEROD AGRIPPA MINOR or II., Acts 25; 26, was the son of Herod Agrippa I., and was educated at Rome, under the care of the emperor Claudius. On the death of his father, when he was seventeen years old, instead of causing him to succeed to his father's kingdom, the emperor set him over the kingdom of Chalcis, which had belonged to his uncle Herod. He was afterwards transferred (A. D. 53) from Chalcis, with the title of king, to the government of those provinces which his father at first possessed, namely, Batanea, Trachonitis, Auranitis, and Abilene, to which several other cities were afterwards added. He is mentioned in the New Testament and by Josephus only by the name of Agrippa. It was before him that St. Paul was brought by Festus, Acts 25:13; 26. He died in the third year of Trajan's reign, at the age of seventy years.

HERO'DIANS, partisans of Herod Antipas, Matt. 22:16; Mark 3:6. Herod was dependent on the Roman power, and his adherents therefore maintained the propriety of paying tribute to Cæsar, which the Pharisees denied. This explains Matt. 22:16.

HERO'DIAS, a granddaughter of Herod the Great and Mariamne, daughter of Aristobulus, and sister of Herod Agrippa I. She was first married to her uncle Herod Philip, but afterwards abandoned him and connected herself with his brother Herod Antipas. It was by her artifice that Herod was persuaded to cause John the Baptist to be put to death, she being enraged at John on account of his bold denunciation of the incestuous connection which subsisted between her and Herod. When Herod was banished to Lyons, she accompanied him, Matt. 14:3, 6; Mark 6:17; Luke 3:19. See HEROD III.

HER'ON. This name is put in Lev. 11:19, Deut. 14:18, for a Hebrew word of very uncertain meaning. See BIRDS.

HESH'BON, a celebrated city of the Amorites, twenty miles east of the mouth of the Jordan, Josh. 3:10; 13:17. It was given to Reuben; but was afterwards transferred to Gad, and then to the Levites. It had been conquered from the Moabites by Sihon, and became his capital; and was taken by the Israelites a little before the death of Moses, Num. 21:25; Josh. 21:39. After the ten tribes were transplanted into the country beyond the Euphrates, the Moabites recovered it, Isa. 15:4; Jer. 48:2, 34, 45. Its ruins are still called Hesban, and cover the sides of a hill seven miles north of Medeba.

HEZEKI'AH, a pious king of Judah, succeeded his father Ahaz about 726 B. C., and died about 698 B. C. His history is contained in 2 Kin. 18–20; 2 Chr. 29–32. Compare Isa. 36–38. His reign is memorable for his faithful efforts to restore the worship of Jehovah; for his pride and presumption towards the Assyrians; for the destruction of their invading host in answer to his prayer; for his sickness and humiliation, and the prolonging of his life fifteen years of peace. He was succeeded by the unworthy Manasseh.

HID'DEKEL, one of the rivers of Paradise. Its modern name is Tigris. See EDEN, and EUPHRATES.

HI'EL, *God liveth*, a Bethelite, who rebuilt Jericho in despite of the woe denounced five hundred years before, Josh. 6:26. The fulfilment of the curse by the death of his children, proves the truth which his name signified, 1 Kin. 16:34.

HIERAP'OLIS, a city of Phrygia, situated on its western border, near the junction of the rivers Lycus and Meander, and not far from Colosse and Laodicea. It was celebrated for its warm springs and baths. A Christian church was early established here, and enjoyed the ministrations of the faithful Epaphras, Col. 4:12, 13. The city is now desolate, but its ruins still exhibit many traces of its ancient splendor. Among them are the remains of three churches, a theatre, a gymnasium, and many sepulchral monuments. The white front of the cliffs, above which the city lay, has given it its present name of Pambuke-kaleh, the Cotton Castle.

HIGGAI'ON, in Psa. 9:16, is supposed to indicate a pause in the singing of the Psalm, for meditation, probably with an instrumental interlude.

HIGH PLACES. The ancient Canaanites, and other nations, worshipped the heavenly bodies and their idols upon hills, mountains, and artificial elevations. The Israelites were commanded to destroy these places of idol-worship, Deut. 12:2, but instead of this, they imitated the heathen, and at first worshipped Jehovah in high places, 1 Sam. 9:12; 1 Kin. 3:4, and afterwards idols, 1 Kin. 11:7; 2 Kin. 17:10, 11. Here also they built chapels or temples, "houses of the high places," 1 Kin. 13:32; 2 Kin. 17:29, and had regular priests, 1 Kin. 12:32; 2 Kin. 17:32. Different groves were sacred to different gods; and the high places were inseparably linked to idolatry. Hence one reason why Jehovah required the festivals and sacrifices of the Jews to be centred at his temple in Jerusalem; that the people of the living and only true God might be delivered from the temptations of the groves, and witness as one man against idolatry. The prophets reproach the Israelites for worshipping on the high places; the destroying of which was a duty, but the honor of performing it is given to few princes in Scripture, though several of them were zealous for the law. Before the temple was built, the high places were not absolutely contrary to the law, provided God only was adored there. Under the judges, they seem to have been tolerated in some exceptional cases; and Samuel offered sacrifice in several places where the ark was not present. Even in David's time, the people sacrificed to the Lord at Shiloh, Jerusalem, and Gibeon. The high places were much frequented in the kingdom of Israel; and on these hills they often adored idols, and committed a thousand abominations. See BAMOTH and GROVES.

HILKI'AH, a faithful high-priest in the reign of Josiah, 2 Kin. 22; 23.

This was also the name of the fathers of Jeremiah and Eliakim, 2 Kin. 18:18; Jer. 1:1.

HIN, a Hebrew liquid measure; as of oil, Ex. 30:24; Ezek. 45:24, or of wine, Ex. 29:40; Lev. 23:13. It was the sixth part of an ephah or bath, and contained ten or eleven pints.

HIND, the female of the hart or stag, a species of deer, distinguished for the lightness and elegance of its form. The hind is destitute of horns, like all the

HIND AND FAWN.

females of this class, except the reindeer. In Gen. 49:21, Naphtali is compared to a hind roaming at liberty, or quickly growing up into elegance; while the "goodly words" of Naphtali refer to the future orators, prophets, and poets of the tribe. A faithful and affectionate wife is compared to the hind, Prov. 5:19, as also are swift and sure-footed heroes, 2 Sam. 22:34; Hab. 3:19.

HIN'NOM, that is, the valley of Hinnom, or of the son of Hinnom, a narrow valley just south of Jerusalem, running up westward from the valley of the Cedron, and passing into the valley of Gihon, which follows the base of mount Zion north, up to the Joppa gate. It was well watered, and in ancient times most verdant and delightfully shaded with trees. The boundary line between Judah and Benjamin passed through it, Josh. 15:8; 18:6; Neh. 11:30. In its lowest part, towards the south-east, and near the king's gardens and Siloam, the idolatrous Israelites made their children pass through the fire to Moloch, 1 Kin. 11:7; 2 Kin. 16:3; Jer. 32:35. See MOLOCH. The place of these abominable sacrifices is also called *Tophet*, Isa. 30:33; Jer. 7:31. According to some, this name is derived from the Hebrew *toph*, drum, because drums are supposed to have been used to drown the cries of the victims. But this opinion rests only on conjecture. King Josiah defiled the place, 2 Kin. 23:10, probably by making it a repository of filth. It has been a common opinion that the later Jews, in imitation of Josiah, threw into this place all manner of filth, as well as the carcasses of animals and the dead bodies of malefactors; and that with reference to either the baleful idolatrous fires in the worship of Moloch, or to the fires afterwards maintained there to consume the mass of impurities that might otherwise have occasioned a pestilence, came the figurative use of the fire of Gehenna, that is, *valley of Hinnom*, to denote the eternal fire in which wicked men and fallen spirits shall be punished. This supposition, however, rests upon uncertain grounds.

It seems clear that the later Jews borrowed their usage of the fire of the valley of Hinnom (Gehenna) to represent the punishment of the wicked in the future world directly from two passages of Isaiah: "For Tophet is ordained of old; yea, for the king it is prepared; he hath made it deep and large: the pile thereof is fire and much wood; the breath of the Lord, like a stream of brimstone, doth kindle it," chap. 30:33; "And they shall go forth, and look upon the carcasses of the men that have transgressed against me: for their worm shall not die, neither shall their fire be quenched: and they shall be an abhorring unto all flesh," chap. 66:24. These they correctly interpreted figuratively, as representing the vengeance which God would take on his enemies and the oppressors of his people. That the prophet, in this terrible imagery, alluded to any fire kept perpetually burning in the valley of Hinnom, has not been clearly proved. But however this may be, it is certain that the Jews transferred the name Gehenna, that is, valley of Hinnom, to the place in which devils and wicked men are to be punished in eternal fire, and which in the New Testament is always translated *hell*, Matt. 5:22, 29, 30; 10:28; Mark 9:43, 45, 47; Luke 12:5; James 3:6. See HELL.

The rocks on the south side of Hinnom are full of gaping apertures, the mouths of tombs once filled with the dead, but now vacant.

HI'RAM, or HU'RAM, I., a king of Tyre, who sent to congratulate David on his accession to the throne, and aided him in building his palace, 2 Sam. 5:11; 1 Chr. 14:1. He seems to have been the Abibal of secular history.

II. A king of Tyre, probably a son of the former, 2 Chr. 2:13, and like him a friend of David. He congratulated Solomon at the commencement of his reign, and furnished essential aid in building the temple. He provided timber and stones, together with gold to an immense amount, and received in return large supplies of corn, wine, and oil, with twenty cities in Galilee, 1 Kin. 5; 2 Chr. 2. See CABUL. He afterwards joined Solomon in his commercial enterprises in the eastern seas, 1 Kin. 9:26–28; 10:11–22; 2 Chr. 8:18. Josephus relates that he and Solomon were wont to exchange enigmas with each other; that he greatly improved his city and realm, and died after a prosperous reign of thirty-four years, at the age of fifty-two.

III. A skilful artificer of Tyre, whose mother was a Jewess. The interior decorations and utensils of Solomon's temple were made under his direction, 1 Kin. 7:13, 14; 2 Chr. 2:13, 14.

HIS'SING, as a mode of calling an attendant to his master's side, is a custom very prevalent in Palestine. Says Osborne, "Whenever a servant was wanted, the usual '*shee!*' which is so common throughout the land, started two or three in an instant." The same custom is evidently alluded to in Isa. 5:26; 7:18; "The Lord shall hiss for the fly that is in the uttermost part of the rivers of Egypt," etc.

HIT'TITES, descendants of Heth, Gen. 10:15, a Canaanite tribe dwelling near Hebron in the time of Abraham, Gen. 15:20; 23, and subdued in the Israelitish invasion, Ex. 3:8; Josh. 3:10. They were not, however, exterminated: Uriah was a Hittite, 2 Sam. 11:3; Solomon used their services, 1 Kin. 9:20; we read of the "kings of the Hittites" in the south, 1 Kin. 10:29; 2 Kin. 7:6; and they were not lost as a people until after the Jews' return from captivity, Ezra 9:1. See CANAANITES.

HI'VITES. See CANAANITES.

HO'BAB, the son of Raguel or Reuel, Num. 10:29. According to one supposition he was the same as Jethro, Moses' father-in-law, Zipporah being called the daughter of Reuel as one of his descendants. According to another view, he was the brother of Jethro. Those who hold this opinion maintain that the Hebrew word rendered father-in-law, Judg. 4:11, may denote simply a relation by marriage. When the Hebrews were about leaving mount Sinai, Moses requested him to cast in his lot with the people of God, both for his own sake and because his knowledge of the desert and its inhabitants might often be of service to the Jews. It would appear that he acceded to this request, Judg. 1:16; 4:11.

HO'BAH, a place north of Damascus, visited by Abraham, Gen. 14:15; now unknown.

HO'LY, HO'LINESS. These terms sometimes denote outward purity or cleanliness; sometimes internal purity and sanctification. True holiness characterizes outward acts, but still more the motive and intent of the heart. It is an inward principle; not mere rectitude or benevolence, or any one moral excellence, but the harmonious and perfect blending of all, as all the colors of the prism duly blended form pure light. God is holy in a transcendent and infinitely perfect manner, Isa. 1:4; 6:3. The Messiah is called "the Holy One," Psa. 16:10; Luke 4:34; Acts 3:14; and Holy is the common epithet given to the third person of the Trinity, the Holy Spirit. God is the fountain of holiness, innocence, and sanctification. Mankind lost all holiness in the fall; but God makes his people gradually "partakers of his holiness" here, and in heaven they will be found perfectly and for ever sanctified; as an earnest of which, he looks upon them as already in Christ, holy and beloved. The Bible applies the epithet holy in a secondary sense to whatever pertains especially to God—to heaven, to his temple, its parts, utensils, and services; to his day, his ministers, priests, prophets, and apostles. The Jews were called a holy people, because they were separated unto God, to be a religious and consecrated people; and Christians, as a body, are also called holy, because they are in like manner separated unto Christ. But a "holy man," in the ordinary Christian sense, is one who exhibits in his conduct the inward purity, benevolence, and holy devotedness to the Saviour, with which his heart overflows.

HO'LY SPIR'IT, or HOLY GHOST, the third person in the blessed Trinity. He is said to proceed from the Father, and to be sent by the Father and the Son upon disciples, John 14:26; 15:26; to be the Spirit of the Father, Matt. 10:20; 1 Cor. 2:11; and the Spirit of Christ, Gal. 4:6; Phil. 1:19.

That he is a real PERSON, and not merely an attribute or emanation of God, is clear from the numerous passages in the Bible which describe him as exercising the acts, thoughts, emotions, and volitions of a distinct intelligent person. None other could be pleased, vexed, and grieved, could speak, console, and intercede, or divide his gifts severally to every one as he will. So also, in Greek as in English, the personal masculine pronouns are applied to him; whereas, if he were not a person, the neuter pronouns would be necessary.

That he is a DIVINE person, equally with the Father and the Son, is proved from his association with them in a great variety of acts purely divine; as in the work of creation, Gen. 1:2; Psa. 33:6; 104:30. He is honored as they are in the baptismal formula, Matt. 28:19, and in the apostolic benediction, 2 Cor. 13:14. He receives the name, 2 Cor. 3:17, and exercises the attributes of God, Rom. 8:14; 1 Cor. 2:10; 6:19; Heb. 9:14. He is prayed to as God, Rev. 1:4, 5; sin against him is sin against God, Acts 5:3, 4; Eph. 4:30; and blasphemy against him is unpardonable, Matt. 12:31.

The WORK of the Holy Spirit is divine. Of old, he inspired the sacred writers and teachers, and imparted miraculous gifts. Under the Christian dispensation, he applies the salvation of Christ to men's hearts, convicting them of sin, John 16:8, 9; showing them "the things of Christ," illuminating and regenerating them, John 3:5; Eph. 2:1. He is the Comforter of the church, aids believers in prayer, witnesses with and intercedes for them, directs them in duty, and sanctifies them for heaven.

HO'MER, or COR, the largest dry measure of the Hebrews, equal to ten baths or ephahs, and containing about eight of our bushels, Ezek. 45:14.

HONEY was formerly very plentiful in Palestine, and hence the frequent expressions of Scripture which import that that country was a land flowing with milk and honey, Lev. 20:24. Wild bee honey was often found in hollow trees and clefts in the rocks, Deut. 32:13; Psa. 81:16; and on this John the Baptist fed, Matt. 3:4. Honey was highly prized, Psa. 19:10; Prov. 5:3; 27:7. Modern travellers observe that it is still very common there, and that the inhabitants mix it in all their sauces. Forskal says the caravans of Mecca bring honey from Arabia to Cairo, and that he has often seen honey flowing in the woods in Arabia. It would seem that this flowing honey is bee-honey, and this fact illustrates the story of Jonathan, 1 Sam. 14:25, 27. But there is also a vegetable honey that is very plentiful in the East. Burckhardt, speaking of the productions of the Ghor, or valley of the Jordan, says one of the most interesting productions of this place is the Beyrouk honey, as the Arabs call it. It was described to him as a juice dropping from the leaves and twigs of a tree called Gharrab, of the size of an olive-tree, with leaves like those of the poplar, but somewhat broader. The honey collects on the leaves like dew, and is gathered from them, or from the ground under the tree. Another vegetable product is referred to in the Bible as honey, 2 Chr. 31:5. It is a syrup, prepared by boiling down the juice of dates, etc. That made from grapes is called *dibs*, and is much used by the Arabs as a condiment with food. It resembles thin molasses, and is pleasant to the taste, Gen. 43:11.

HOPH'NI. See next page.

HOR, a mountain of a conical form in the range of mount Seir, on the east side of the Arabah, or great valley running from the Dead sea to the Elanitic gulf. It is an irregularly truncated cone, with three rugged peaks, overlooking a wilderness of heights, cliffs, ravines, and deserts. On this mountain Aaron died, alone with his brother and son, Num. 20:22-29; 33:38. It is still called Jebel Neby Haroon, mount of the prophet Aaron; and on its summit stands a Mohammedan tomb of Aaron, on the site of a still more ancient structure, and marking perhaps the place of his burial.

HOPH'NI, and PHIN'EHAS, the guilty and wretched sons of Eli the high-priest. They grossly and continuously abused the influence of their position and sacred office; and their cupidity, violence, and impious profligacy, overbearing the feeble remonstrances of their father, brought disgrace and ruin on their family. The ark, which they had carried to the camp in spite of divine prohibitions, was taken, and they were slain in battle, 1 Sam. 2-4. See ELI. The ark of God protects only those who love and obey him. Men in all ages are prone to rely on a form of religion, while the heart and life are not right with God; and all who thus sin, like the sons of Eli, must perish likewise.

HO'REB. See SINAI.

HOR'ITES, or HO'RIM, a race of early dwellers in mount Seir, whence they were expelled by the Edomites, Gen. 14:6; Deut. 2:12, 22. They are supposed to have lived in caves, like the men referred to in Job 30:6, and to have been divided into several tribes, Gen. 36:20-30.

HOR'MAH, *destruction*, Num. 21:1-3; also called Zephath; a city in the extreme south of Canaan, near which the rebellious Hebrews were defeated, in the second year after leaving Egypt, Num. 14:45; it was afterwards laid waste, Judg. 1:16, 17. The Simeonites repeopled it, Josh. 19:4, and David sent them some of his spoils taken from the Amalekites, 1 Sam. 30:30.

HORNS of animals were used as drinking-vessels, and to hold ointments, perfumes, etc., 1 Sam. 16:1; 1 Kin. 1:39. The "horns of the altar" were its four corners and the elevations on them, Ex. 27:2; 30:2. See ALTAR. The principal defence and ornament of many beasts are in their horns; and hence the horn is often a symbol of strength, honor, and dominion. The Lord exalted the horn of David, and of his people; he breaketh the horn of the ungodly. We read also of raising up a horn of salvation, and of defiling the horn in the dust, Deut. 33:17; 1 Sam. 2:1, 10; Job 16:15; Psa. 75:10; Dan. 7:20-24; Luke 1:69. There may be an allusion in these passages to a very common part of the female dress in some parts of the East. The married women among the Druses of mount Lebanon still wear on their heads silver horns, as in the accompanying cut; the other head is that of an Abyssinian chief.

HOR'NET, a well-known insect, which has a powerful sting. The Lord drove out many of the Canaanites before Israel by means of this insect, Ex. 23:28; Deut. 7:20; Josh. 24:12. The Israelites, being in the sandy wilderness, would escape it. Compare FLY.

HOR'SES were anciently less used for labor, in Bible lands, than oxen and asses. They were used by princes and warriors, both with and without chariots, Ex. 14:9, 23; Esth. 6:8; Eccl. 10:7. The finest description of the war-horse ever written, is found in one of the most ancient books, Job 39:19-25. Horses were common in Egypt, Gen. 47:17; 50:9; Song 1:9; but the Jews were at first forbidden to go there for them, Deut. 17:16, or to keep any large number, Josh. 11:6; 2 Sam. 8:4. The object of this was to restrain them from growing proud, idolatrous, and fond of conquest, Isa. 31:1-3. Solomon, however, procured a large cavalry and chariot force, 2 Chr. 1:14-17; 9:25. Horses were sometimes consecrated to idols, 2 Kin. 23:11, and were often used as symbols of angelic and earthly powers, under the control of God, 2 Kin. 2:11; 6:15-17; Zech. 1:8; 6:2-6; Rev. 2-8.

HORSE'LEECH, the bloodsucker, a well-known water-worm; an apt emblem of avarice and rapacity, Prov. 30:15. Cicero speaks of the horseleeches of the public treasury at Rome.

HOSAN'NA, a word of joyful acclamation in Hebrew, signifying *save now*. The people cried Hosanna as Jesus entered in triumph into Jerusalem; that is, they thus invoked the blessings of heaven on him as the Messiah, Matt. 21:9. This was also a customary acclamation at the joyful feast of tabernacles, in which the Jews repeated Psa. 118:25, 26.

HOSE'A, the first of the twelve minor prophets, as arranged in our Bibles. He prophesied for a long time, from Uzziah to Hezekiah, about 785–725 B. C.

The BOOK OF HOSEA contains properly two parts. The first three chapters contain a series of symbolical actions directed against the idolatries of Israel. It is disputed whether the marriage of the prophet was a real transaction, or an allegorical vision; in all probability the latter is the correct view; but in either case it illustrated the relations of idolatrous Israel to her covenant God. The remaining chapters are chiefly occupied with denunciations against Israel, and especially Samaria, for the worship of idols which prevailed there. Hosea's warnings are mingled with tender and pathetic expostulations. His style is obscure, and it is difficult to fix the periods or the divisions of his various predictions. He shows a joyful faith in the coming Redeemer, and is several times quoted in the New Testament, Matt. 9:13; Rom. 9:25, 26; 1 Pet. 2:10.

HOSHE'A, the last king of Israel, the successor of Pekah, whom he slew, 2 Kin. 15:30, B. C. 730. He reigned nine years, and was then carried away captive by Shalmaneser, 2 Kin. 17 : 1–6; 18 : 9–12, B. C. 721.

HOSPITAL'ITY is regarded by all oriental nations as one of the highest virtues. The following notices by modern travellers serve to illustrate very strikingly many passages of Scripture. Thus De la Roque says, "We did not arrive at the foot of the mountain till after sunset, and it was almost night when we entered the plain; but as it was full of villages, mostly inhabited by Maronites, we entered into the first we came to, to pass the night there. It was the priest of the place who wished to receive us; he gave us a supper under the trees before his little dwelling. As we were at table, there came by *a stranger*, wearing a white turban, who, after having saluted the company, sat himself down to the table without ceremony, ate with us during some time, and then went away, repeating several times the name of God. They told us it was some traveller who no doubt stood in need of refreshment, and who had profited by the opportunity, according to the custom of the East, which is to exercise hospitality at all times and towards all persons." This reminds us of the guests of Abraham, Gen. 18, of the conduct of Job, 31:17, and of that frankness with which the apostles of Christ were to enter into a man's house after a salutation, and there to continue "eating and drinking such things as were set before them," Luke 10:7. The universal prevalence of such customs, and of the spirit of hospitality, may help to explain the indignation of James and John against certain rude Samaritans, Luke 9:52–56, and also the stern retribution exacted for the crime of the men of Gibeah, Judg. 19; 20.

Says Niebuhr, "The hospitality of the Arabs has always been the subject of praise; and I believe that those of the present day exercise this virtue no less than their ancestors did. When the Arabs are at table, they invite those who happen to come, to eat with them, whether they be Christians or Mohammedans, gentle or simple. In the caravans, I have often seen with pleasure a mule-driver press those who passed to partake of his repast; and though the majority politely excused themselves, he gave, with an air of satisfaction, to those who would accept of it, a portion of his little meal of bread and dates; and I was not a little surprised when I saw, in Turkey, rich Turks withdraw themselves into corners, to avoid inviting those who might otherwise have sat at table with them."

We ought to notice here also the obligations understood to be contracted by the intercourse of the table. Niebuhr says, "When a Bedaween sheikh eats bread with strangers, they may trust his fidelity and depend on his protection. A traveller will always do well therefore to take an early opportunity of securing the friendship of his guide by a meal." This brings to recollection the complaint of the psalmist, Psa. 41:9, penetrated with the deep ingratitude of one whom he describes as having been his own familiar friend, in whom he trusted, "who did eat of my bread, even he hath lifted up his heel against me."

Beautiful pictures of primitive hospitality may be found in Gen. 18; 19; Ex. 2:20; Judg. 13:15; 19:1–9. The incidents of the first two narratives may have suggested the legends of the Greeks and Romans, which represent their gods as sometimes coming to them disguised as travellers, in order to test their hospitality, etc., Heb. 13:2.

The primitive Christians considered one principal part of their duty to consist in showing hospitality to strangers, Rom. 12:13; 1 Tim. 5:10; remembering that our Saviour had said, whoever received those belonging to him, received himself; and that whatever was given to such a one, though but a cup of cold water, should not lose its reward, Matt. 10:40–42; 25:34–45. They were, in fact, so ready in discharging this duty, that the very heathen admired them for it. They were hospitable to all strangers, but especially to those of the household of faith. Believers scarcely ever travelled without letters of communion, which testified the purity of their faith, and procured them a favorable reception wherever the name of Jesus Christ was known. Indeed, some suppose that the two minor epistles of John may be such letters of communion and recommendation.

HOUGH, (pronounced hock,) to hamstring, or cut the cords of the hind legs. The horses taken by David from the Syrians were thus disabled, Josh. 11:6, 9; 2 Sam. 8:4.

HOURS. The word hour, in Scripture, signifies one of the twelve equal parts into which each day, from sunrise to sunset, was divided, and which of course were of different lengths at different seasons of the year, Matt. 20:3–6; John 11:9. This mode of dividing the day prevailed among the Jews at least after the exile, and perhaps earlier, Dan. 3:6; 4:19. The third, sixth, and ninth hours were the appointed seasons for prayer, Acts 2:15; 3:1; 10:9. Anciently, however, the usual division of the day was into four parts, namely, the morning—the heat of the day, commencing about the middle of the forenoon—midday, and evening. In a similar manner, the Greeks appear at first to have divided the day into only three parts, to which they afterwards added a fourth division. The ancient Hebrews, as well as the Greeks, appear to have divided the night also into three parts or watches, namely, the first watch, Lam. 2:19; the middle, or second watch, Judg. 7:19; and the morning, or third watch, Ex. 14:24. But after the Jews became subject to the Romans, they adopted the Roman manner of dividing the night into four watches, namely, the evening, or first quarter, after sunset; the midnight, or second quarter, ending at midnight; cock-crowing, or third quarter, from midnight on; and the morning, or fourth quarter, including the dawn, Matt. 14:25; Mark 6:48; 13:35; Luke 12:48. A watch in the night seems but an instant to one who spends it in slumber, Psa. 90:4; equally short does the life of man appear in view of eternity.

HOUSE is often put for dwelling, residence; and hence the temple, and even the tabernacle, are called the house of God.

The universal mode of building houses in the East, is in the form of a hollow square, with an open court or yard in the centre; which is thus entirely shut in by the walls of the house around it. Into this court all the windows open, there being usually no windows towards the street. Some houses of large size require several courts, and these usually communicate with each other. These courts are commonly paved; and in many large houses parts of them are planted with shrubs and trees, Psa. 84:3; 128:3; they have also, when possible, a fountain in them, often with a *jet d'eau*, 2 Sam. 17:18. It is customary in many houses to extend an awning over the whole court in hot weather; and the people of the house then spend much of the day in the open air, and indeed often receive visits there. In Aleppo, at least, there is often on the south side of the court an alcove in the wall of the house, furnished with divans or sofas, for reclining and enjoying the fresh air in the hot seasons.

In the middle of the front of each house is usually an arched passage, leading into the court—not directly, lest the court should be exposed to view from the street, but by turning to one side. The outer door of this passage was, in large houses, guarded by a porter, Acts 12:13. The entrance into the house is either from this passage or from the court itself.

The following extracts from Dr. Shaw will interest the reader, and at the same time serve to illustrate many passages of

INTERIOR OF AN ANCIENT HOUSE.

Scripture. He remarks, "The general method of building, both in Barbary and the Levant, seems to have continued the same from the earliest ages, without the least alteration or improvement. Large doors, spacious chambers, marble pavements, cloistered courts, with fountains sometimes playing in the midst, are certainly conveniences very well adapted to the circumstances of these climates, where the summer heats are generally so intense. The jealousy likewise of these people is less apt to be alarmed, while all the windows open into their respective courts, if we except a latticed window or balcony which sometimes looks into the streets, 2 Kin. 9:30.

"The streets of eastern cities, the better to shade them from the sun, are usually narrow, with sometimes a range of shops on each side. If from these we enter into one of the principal houses, we shall first pass through a porch or gateway with benches on each side, where the master of the family receives visits and despatches business; few persons, not even the nearest relations, having a further admission, except upon extraordinary occasions. From hence we are received into the court, or quadrangle, which, lying open to the weather, is, according to the ability of the owner, paved with marble, or such materials as will immediately carry off the water into the common sewers. When much people are to be admitted, as upon the celebration of a marriage, the circumcising of a child, or occasions of the like nature, the company is rarely or never received into one of the chambers. The court is the usual place of their reception, which is strowed accordingly with mats and carpets for their more commodious entertainment. Hence it is probable that the place where our Saviour and the apostles were frequently accustomed to give their instructions, was in the area, or quadrangle, of one of this kind of houses. In the summer season, and upon all occasions when a large company is to be received, this court is commonly sheltered from the heat or inclemency of the weather by a veil or awning, which, being expanded upon ropes from one side of the parapet wall to the other, may be folded or unfolded at pleasure. The psalmist seems to allude either to the tents of the Bedaween, or to some covering of this kind, in that beautiful expression, of spreading out the heavens like a curtain, Psa. 104:2. The court is for the most part surrounded with a cloister or colonnade; over which, when the house has two or three stories, there is a gallery erected, of the same dimensions with the cloister, having a balustrade, or else a piece of carved or latticed work going round about it, to prevent people from falling from it into the court. From the cloisters and galleries we are conducted into large spacious chambers, of the same length with the court, but seldom or never communicating with one another. One of them frequently serves a whole family; particularly when a father indulges his married children to live with him; or when several persons join in the rent of the same house. From whence it is, that the cities of these countries, which in general are much inferior in bigness to those of Europe, yet are so exceedingly populous, that great numbers of people are always swept away by the plague, or any other contagious distemper."

The chambers of the rich were often hung with velvet or damask tapestry, Esth. 1:6; the upper part adorned with fretwork and stucco; and the ceilings with wainscot or mosaic work of fragrant wood, sometimes richly painted, Jer. 22:14. The floors were of wood, or of painted tiles, or marble; and were usually spread with carpets. Around the walls were mattresses or low sofas, instead of chairs. The beds were often at one end of the chamber, on a gallery several feet above the floor, with steps and a low balustrade, 2 Kin. 1:4, 16. The stairs were usually in a corner of the court, beside the gateway, Matt. 24:17.

"The top of the house," says Dr. Shaw, "which is always flat, is covered with a strong plaster of terrace; from whence, in the Frank language, it has attained the name of the terrace. It is usually surrounded by two walls; the outermost whereof is partly built over the street, partly makes the partition with the contiguous houses, being frequently so low that one may easily climb over it. The other, which I call the parapet wall, hangs immediately over the court, being always breast high; we render it the 'battlements,' Deut. 22:8. Instead of this parapet wall, some terraces are guarded in the same manner the galleries are, with balustrades only, or latticed work; in which fashion probably, as the name seems to import, was the net, or 'lattice,' as we render it, that Ahaziah, 2 Kin. 1:2, might be carelessly leaning over, when he fell down from thence into the court. For upon these terraces several offices of the family are performed; such as the drying of linen and flax, Josh. 2:6, the preparing of figs and raisins; here likewise they enjoy the cool, refreshing breezes of the evening; converse with one another, 1 Sam. 9:25; 2 Sam. 11:2; and offer up their devotions, 2 Kin. 23:12; Jer. 19:13; Acts 10:9. In the feast of Tabernacles booths were erected upon them, Neh. 8:16. When one of these cities is built upon level ground, we can pass from one end of it to the other, along the tops of the houses, without coming down into the street.

"Such, in general, is the manner and contrivance of the eastern houses. And if it may be presumed that our Saviour, at the healing of the paralytic, was preaching in a house of this fashion, we may, by attending only to the structure of it, give no small light to one circumstance of that history, which has given great offence to some unbelievers. Among other pretended difficulties and absurdities relating to this fact, it has been urged that the uncovering or breaking up of the roof, Mark 2:4, or the letting a person down through it, Luke 5:19, supposes the breaking up of tiles, rafters," etc. But it is only necessary here to suppose that the crowd being so great around Jesus in the court below, that those who brought the sick man could not come near him, they went upon the flat roof, and removing a part of the awning, let the sick man down in his mattress over the parapet, quite at the feet of Jesus.

Dr. Shaw proceeds to describe a sort of addition to many oriental houses, which corresponds probably to the upper chamber often mentioned in the Bible. He says, "To most of these houses there is a smaller one annexed, which sometimes rises one story higher than the house; at other times it consists of one or two rooms only and a terrace; while others that are built, as they frequently are, over the porch or gateway, have (if we except the ground floor, which they have not) all the conveniences that belong to the house, properly so called. There is a door of communication from them into the gallery of the house, kept open or shut at the discretion of the master of the family; besides another door, which opens immediately from a privy stairs down into the porch, without giving the least disturbance to the house. These smaller houses are known by the name *alee*, or *oleah*, and in them strangers are usually lodged and entertained; and thither likewise the men are wont to retire, from the hurry and noise of their families, to be more at leisure for meditation or devotion, Matt. 6:6; besides the use they are at other times put to, in serving for wardrobes and magazines."

This then, or something like this, we may suppose to have been the *ali'yah* or upper chamber of the Hebrews. Such was the "little chamber upon the wall," which the Shunammite had built for Elisha, 2 Kin. 4:10; the "summer parlor" of Eglon, Judg. 3:20; and the "chamber over the gate," where David retired to weep, 2 Sam. 18:33; and perhaps in the New Testament the "upper chamber" where Tabitha was laid out, Acts 9:37, and whence Eutychus fell from the window of the third loft into the court, Acts 20:9.

The flat roofs of oriental houses often afford a place of retirement and meditation; here Samuel communed with Saul, 1 Sam. 9:25; and from ver. 26, they would seem also to have slept there, as is still common in the East, 2 Sam. 11:2; Dan. 4:30. Mr. Wood says, "It has ever been a custom with them," the Arabs in the East, "equally connected with health and pleasure, to pass the nights in summer upon the house-tops, which for this very purpose are made flat, and divided from each other by walls. We found this way of sleeping extremely agreeable; as we thereby enjoyed the cool air, above the reach of gnats and vapors, without any other covering than the canopy of heaven, which unavoidably presents itself in different pleasing forms, upon every interruption of rest, when silence and solitude strongly dispose the mind to contemplation, Acts 10:9. The roof of an ancient house was the best and often the only place, from which to get a view of the region around; hence the resort to it in times of peril, Isa. 15:3; 22:1. In many cases roofs were coated with hardened earth, through which, when cracked or soaked through by rain, the water dripped, Prov. 27:15; and in which, when neglected, the grass grows in spring, but soon withers after the rains have ceased, Psa. 129:6, 7; Isa. 37:27.

The common material for building the best oriental houses is stone. Brick is also used. But the houses of the people in the East in general are very bad constructions, consisting of mud walls, reeds, and rushes; whence they become apt illustrations of the fragility of human life, Job 4:19; and as mud, pebbles, and slime, or at best unburnt bricks are used in forming the walls, the expression, "digging through houses," Job 24:16; Matt. 6:19; 24:14, is easily accounted for; as is the behavior of Ezekiel, 12:5, who dug through such a wall in the sight of the people; whereby, as may be imagined, he did little injury to his house; notwithstanding which, the symbol was very expressive to the beholders. See also the striking illustration in Ezek. 13:10-16. On the sites of many ancient cities of Syria and Babylonia only the ruins of public edifices remain, the houses having entirely disappeared ages ago. Travellers near the Ganges and the Nile speak of multitudes of huts on the sandy banks of those rivers being swept away in a night by sudden freshets, leaving not a trace behind. This may illustrate our Saviour's parable, in Matt. 7:24-27. See TENT.

HUL'DAH, a prophetess in the reign of Josiah, consulted respecting the denunciations in the new-found copy of the Book of the Law, 2 Kin. 22:14-20, 2 Chr. 34:22-28, B. C. 623.

HUMIL'ITY, the opposite of pride, in its nature and in the degree of its prevalence. It is often extolled in the Bible, Prov. 15:33; 16:19; and the Saviour especially exalts it, Matt. 18:4, and ennobles and endears it by his own example, John 13:4-17; Phil. 2:5-8. Every created being, however holy, should possess it; but in the character of the sinful sons of men it should become a fundamental and all-pervading trait, to continue for ever.

HUR, a chief man among the Hebrews in the desert, associated with Aaron in upholding the hands of Moses at Rephidim, and in supplying his place while on the summit of Sinai, Ex. 17:10; 24:14.

HU'SHAI, the Archite, David's friend. Being informed of Absalom's rebellion, and that David was obliged to fly from Jerusalem, he met him on an eminence without the city, with his clothes rent and his head covered with earth. David suggested, that if he went with him he would be a burden to him; but that he might do him important service if he should remain in Absalom's suite as an adviser. Hushai therefore returned to Jerusalem, and by defeating the counsel of Ahithophel, and gaining time for David, to whom he sent advices, was the cause of Ahithophel's suicide and of Absalom's miscarriage, 2 Sam. 15 : 32-37 ; 16:16-19 ; 17.

HUSKS. The prodigal son desired to feed on the husks, or pods, given to the hogs, Luke 15 : 16. The Greek word here used, means the kharob-beans, the fruit of a tree of the same name. This fruit is common in all the countries bordering on the Mediterranean: it is suffered to ripen and grow dry on the tree; the poor eat it, and cattle are fattened with it. The tree, the Ceratonia Siliqua, is an evergreen of a middle size, full of

branches, and abounding with round dark green leaves, an inch or two in diameter. The blossoms are little red clusters, with yellowish stalks. The fruits are flat brownish pods, from six to eight inches long, and an inch or more broad: they resemble the pods of our locust-trees; and are composed of two husks, separated by membranes into several cells, and containing flat, shining seeds, and when ripe a sweetish, honey-like kind of juice. In all probability, their crooked figure occasioned their being called, in Greek, keratia, which signifies little horns. The tree is called by the Germans, Johannisbrodbaum, that is, "John's-bread-tree," because John the Baptist was supposed to have lived on its fruit.

HYMENE'US, a member of the church, probably at Ephesus, who fell into the heresy of denying the true doctrine of the resurrection, and saying it had already taken place. When first mentioned, 1 Tim. 1 : 20, he was excluded from the church ; and when again mentioned, 2 Tim. 2:17, 18, was still exerting a pernicious influence.

HYMN. See next page.

HYP'OCRITE, one who, like a stage-player, feigns to be what he is not. The epithet is generally applied to those who assume the appearance of virtue or piety, without possessing the reality. Our Saviour accused the Pharisees of hypocrisy, Luke 12:1.

THE CAPPARIS SPINOSA, OR CAPER-PLANT.

HYS'SOP is often mentioned in Scripture, and is directed to be used in the sprinklings which made part of the Jewish ceremonial law, Ex. 12 : 22 ; Lev. 14:4-6 ; Psa. 51:9 ; Heb. 9:19. It is some low shrub, which is contrasted with the lofty cedar, 1 Kin. 4 : 33. In

John 19:29, the soldiers are said to have "filled a sponge with vinegar, and put it upon hyssop," that is, upon a rod of hyssop, two feet or more in length, which was long enough to enable one to reach the mouth of a person on the cross. Many different plants have been taken for the hyssop of Scripture, and among others, the caper-plant.

HYMN, a religious canticle, song, or psalm, Eph. 5:19; Col. 3:16. Paul requires Christians to edify one another with "psalms and hymns and spiritual songs." Matthew says that Christ and his disciples, having supped, sung a hymn, and went out. They probably chanted a part of the psalms which the Jews used to sing after the Passover, which they called the Hâlâl; that is, the Hallelujah psalms. These are Psa. 113–118, of which the first two are supposed to have been chanted before the Passover was eaten, and the others afterwards.

I.

IB'ZAN, the tenth "judge of Israel," born in Bethlehem. He held office seven years, and was noted for his large and prosperous family, B. C. 1182, Judg. 12:8.

ICH'ABOD, *where is the glory?* a son of Phinehas, and grandson of Eli, both of whom, and his mother also, died on the day of his birth, 1 Sam. 4:19–22; 14:3.

ICO'NIUM, a large and opulent city of Asia Minor, now called Konieh. The provinces of Asia Minor varied so much at different times, that Iconium is assigned by different writers to Phrygia, to Lycaonia, and to Pisidia. Christianity was introduced here by Paul, A. D. 45. But he was obliged to flee for his life from a persecution excited by unbelieving Jews, Acts 13:51; 14:1–6. They pursued him to Lystra, where he was nearly killed, but afterwards, A. D. 51, he revisited Iconium, Acts 14:19–21; 2 Tim. 3:11. The church continued in being here for eight centuries, but under the Mohammedan rule was almost extinguished. At present, Konieh is the capital of Caramania. It is situated in a beautiful and fertile country, 260 miles south-east of Constantinople, and 120 from the Mediterranean. It is very large, and its walls are supported by 108 square towers, forty paces distant from each other. The inhabitants, 40,000 in number, are Turks, Armenians, Greeks, and Jews.

ID'DO, a prophet of Judah, who prophesied against Jeroboam, and wrote the history of Rehoboam and Abijah, 2 Chr. 9:29; 12:15; 13:22. Josephus and others are of opinion that he was sent to Jeroboam, at Bethel, and that it was he who was killed by a lion, 1 Kin. 13. Several other persons of this name are mentioned in Scripture, 1 Chr. 27:21; Ezra 8:17–20; Zech. 1:1.

IDLE, in Matt. 12:36, means empty and fruitless. The "idle word" which Christ condemns is a word morally useless and evil.

THE IDOL JUGGERNAUT.

I'DOL, IDOL'ATRY. The word idol signifies literally a representation or figure. It is always employed in Scripture in a bad sense, for representations of heathen deities of what nature soever. God forbids all sorts of idols, or figures and representations of creatures, formed or set up with intention of paying superstitious worship to them, Ex. 20:3, 4; 34:13; Deut. 4:16–19; 7:25, 26. He also forbids all attempts to represent him by any visible form, Ex. 32:4, 5; Deut. 4:15; Neh. 9:18.

The heathen had idols of all sorts—paintings, bas-reliefs, and all varieties of sculpture—and these of many kinds of materials, as gold, silver, brass, stone, wood, potter's earth, etc. Stars, spirits, men, animals, rivers, plants, and elements were the subjects of them. Scarce

THE HINDOO IDOL PULLIAR.

ly an object or power in nature, scarcely a faculty of the soul, a virtue, a vice, or a condition of human life, has not received idolatrous worship. See STARS. Some nations worshipped a rough stone. Such is the black stone of the ancient Arabs, retained by Mohammed, and now kept in the Caaba at Mecca.

It is impossible to ascertain the period at which the worship of false gods and idols was introduced. No mention is made of such worship before the deluge; though from the silence of Scripture we cannot argue that it did not exist. Josephus and many of the fathers were of opinion, that soon after the deluge idolatry became prevalent; and certainly, wherever we turn our eyes after the time of Abraham, we see only a false worship. That patriarch's forefathers, and even he himself, were implicated in it, as is evident from Josh. 24:2, 14.

The Hebrews had no peculiar form of idolatry; they imitated the superstitions of others, but do not appear to have been the inventors of any. When they were in Egypt, many of them worshipped Egyptian deities, Ezek. 20:8; in the wilderness, they worshipped those of the Canaanites, Egyptians, Ammonites, and Moabites; in Judea, those of the Phœnicians, Syrians, and other people around them, Num. 25; Judg. 10:6; Amos 5:25; Acts 7:42. Rachel, it may be, had adored idols at her father Laban's, since she carried off his teraphim, Gen. 31:30. Jacob, after his return from Mesopotamia, required his people to reject the strange gods from among them, and also the superstitious pendants worn by them in their ears, which he hid under a terebinth near Shechem. He preserved his family in the worship of God while he lived.

Under the government of the judges, "the children of Israel did evil in the sight of the Lord, and served Baalim. They forsook the Lord God of their fathers, and followed other gods—of the gods of the people that were round about them; and they forsook the Lord, and served Baal and Ashtaroth," Judg. 2:11, 12. Gideon, after he had been favored by God with a miraculous deliverance, made an ephod, which ensnared the Israelites in unlawful worship, Judg. 8:27. Micah's teraphim also were the objects of idolatrous worship, even till the captivity of Israel in Babylon, Judg. 17:5; 18:30, 31. See TERAPHIM.

During the times of Samuel, Saul, and David, the worship of God seems to have been preserved pure in Israel. There was corruption and irregularity of manners, but little or no idolatry. Solomon, seduced by complaisance to his strange wives, caused temples to be erected in honor of Ashtoreth goddess of the Phœnicians, Moloch god of the Ammonites, and Chemosh god of the Moabites. Jeroboam, who succeeded Solomon, set up golden calves at Dan and Bethel, and made Israel to sin. The people, no longer restrained by royal authority, worshipped not only these golden calves, but many other idols, particularly Baal and Ashtoreth. Under the reign of Ahab, idolatry reached its height. The impious Jezebel endeavored to extinguish the worship of the Lord, by persecuting his prophets, (who, as a barrier, still retained some of the people in the true religion,) till God, incensed at their idolatry, abandoned Israel to the kings of Assyria and Chaldea, who transplanted them beyond the Euphrates. Judah was almost equally corrupted. The descriptions given by the prophets of their irregularities and idolatries, of their abominations and lasciviousness on the high places and in woods consecrated to idols, and of their human sacrifices, fill us with dismay, and unveil the awful corruption of the heart of man. See Mo-

LOCH. After the return from Babylon, we do not find the Jews any more reproached with idolatry. They expressed much zeal for the worship of God, and except some transgressors under Antiochus Epiphanes, 1 Mac. 1, the people kept themselves clear from this sin.

As the maintenance of the worship of the only true God was one of the fundamental objects of the Mosaic polity, and as God was regarded as the king of the Israelitish nation, so we find idolatry, that is, the worship of other gods, occupying, in the Mosaic law, the first place in the list of crimes. It was indeed a crime, not merely against God, but also against the fundamental law of the state, and thus a sort of high treason. The only living and true God was also the civil legislator and ruler of Israel, and accepted by them as their king; and hence idolatry was a crime against the state, and therefore just as deservedly punished with death, as high treason is in modern times. By the Jewish law, an idolater was to be stoned to death, and an idolatrous city must be wholly destroyed, with all it contained, Deut. 13:12–18; 17:2, 5.

At the present day, idolatry prevails over a great portion of the earth, and is practised by about 600,000,000 of the human race. Almost all the heathen nations, as the Chinese, the Hindoos, the South Sea islanders, etc., have their images, to which they bow down and worship. In some lands professedly Christian, it is to be feared that the adoration of crucifixes and paintings is nothing more nor less than idol-worship. But when we regard idolatry in a *moral* point of view, as consisting not merely in the external worship of false gods, but in the preference of, and devotion to something else than the Most High, how many Christians must then fall under this charge. Whoever loves this world, or the pursuits of wealth or honor or ambition, or selfishness in any form, and for these forgets or neglects God and Christ, such a one is an *idolater* in as bad a sense at least as the ancient Israelites, and cannot hope to escape an awful condemnation, Col. 3:5.

IDUMÆA, the name given by the Greeks to the land of Edom, or mount Seir, which extended originally from the Dead sea to the Elanitic gulf of the Red sea, including a territory about one hundred miles long, and fifteen or twenty wide. Afterwards it extended more into the south of Judah, towards Hebron. A large part of it was occupied by the long chain of mountains lying between the great sandy valley El-Ghor and El-Arabah on the west, (see JORDAN,) and the Arabian desert on the east. The northern part of this chain is now called Djebal, the ancient Gebal, which see; the remainder of the chain takes the name Jebel Shera. The whole chain is intersected with valleys and ravines, running down from the elevated desert on the east to the Arabah on the west. It contains traces of many towns and villages, long since destroyed, and many springs, and fertile valleys with tokens of its former productiveness, Gen. 27:39. But at this day, desolation reigns. The capital of East Idumæa was Bozra; but the chief capital of Edom was Petra, or Sela, that is, the rock, because it was excavated in part from a mountain. It is now called Wady Mousa, the valley of Moses. See SELA.

The original inhabitants of this country were called Horites, and were dispossessed by the Idumæans of history, Gen. 14:6; 36:21; Deut. 12:2. The true Idumæans, or Edomites, were, as their name implies, descendants of Edom, or Esau, elder brother of Jacob, Gen. 36:6–9. They were governed by dukes or princes, ver. 15, and afterwards by their own kings, ver. 31. Compare Exod. 15:15; Num. 20:14. On the approach of the Israelites from Egypt to the western border of Edom, they were refused a peaceful passage through that country to Moab. See EXODUS. They were divinely charged, however, to preserve friendly relations with their "brother" Esau, Num. 20:14–21; Deut. 2:4–7; 23:7. Yet hostilities seemed inevitable. Saul was involved in war with them, 1 Sam. 14:47; but they continued independent till the time of David, who subdued them, in completion of Isaac's prophecy, that Jacob should rule Esau, Gen. 27:29; 2 Sam. 8:14; 1 Kin. 11:15; 1 Chr. 18:11–13. The Idumæans bore their subjection with great impatience, and at the end of Solomon's reign, Hadad, an Edomite prince who had been carried into Egypt during his childhood, returned into his own country, where he procured himself to be acknowledged king, 1 Kin. 11:14–22. It is probable, however, that he reigned only in East Edom, 1 Kin. 22 : 47 ; 2 Chr. 20 : 36 ; for Edom south of Judea continued subject to the kings of Judah till the reign of Jehoram, against whom it rebelled, 2 Chr. 21:8, in fulfilment of the second part of Isaac's prophecy, Gen. 27:40. Amaziah king of Judah also discomfited the Edomites, killed 1,000 men, and cast 10,000 more from a precipice, 2 Kin. 14 : 7 ; 2 Chr. 25 : 11, 12. But these conquests were not permanent. When Nebuchadnezzar besieged Jerusalem, the Idumæans joined him, and encouraged him to raze the very foundations of the city; but their cruelty did not long continue unpunished. Many predictions of the prophets foreshadowed Edom's real doom, Obad. ; Jer. 49 : 7 ; Ezek. 25 ; 35 ; Mal. 1:3, 4. Five years after the taking of Jerusalem, Nebuchadnezzar humbled all the states around Judea, particularly Idumea, though he did not carry them captive ; and subsequently John Hyrcanus drove them from Southern Judea, into which they had penetrated, entirely conquered them, and obliged them to receive circumcision and the law. They continued subject to the later kings of Judea till the destruction of Jerusalem by the Romans. Josephus informs us that 20,000 of them were summoned to aid in the defence of that city, but gave themselves up to rapine and murder. Ultimately, the Idumæans were supplanted and absorbed by the Nabatheans, descendants of Nabaioth, a son of Ishmael. In the time of their prosperity, the Edomites were numerous and powerful, devoted to commerce by land and by sea, and also to agriculture and the raising of cattle, Num. 20:17. But neither their strong rock-fortresses, Jer. 49 : 16, nor their gods, 2 Chr. 25 : 20, could save that rich and salubrious country from becoming a desert, and a striking monument of the truth of prophecy. See KEITH on PROPHECY.

ILLYR'ICUM, a country of Europe, lying east of the Adriatic sea, north of Epirus, and west of Macedonia. It was anciently divided into Liburnia, now Croatia, on the north, and Dalmatia on the south, which still retains its name. See DALMATIA. The limits of Illyricum varied much at different times. It was reached by Paul, preaching the gospel of Christ, and probably traversed in part, A. D. 57, Rom. 15:19.

IM'AGE, an exact and complete copy or counterpart of any thing. Christ is called "the image of God," 2 Cor. 4:4, Col. 1:15, Heb. 1:3, as being the same in nature and attributes. The image of God in which man was created, Gen. 1:27, was in his spiritual, intellectual, and moral nature, in righteousness and true holiness. The posterity of Adam were born in his fallen, sinful likeness, Gen. 5:3 ; and as we have borne the image of sinful Adam, so we should be moulded into the moral image of the heavenly man Christ, 1 Cor. 15 : 47–49 ; 2 Cor. 3:18.

"An image," Job 4 : 16, was that which seemed to the dreamer a reality. The word sometimes appears to include, with the image, the idea of the real object, Psa. 73 : 20 ; Heb. 10 : 1. It is usually applied in the Bible to representations of false gods, painted, graven, etc., Dan. 3. All use of images in religious worship was clearly and peremptorily prohibited, Ex. 20 : 4, 5 ; Deut. 16 : 22 ; Acts 17 : 16 ; Rom. 1 : 23. Their introduction into Christian churches, near the close of the fourth century, was at first strenuously resisted. Now, however, they are universally used by Papists ; by most in a gross breach of the second commandment, and by the best in opposition to both the letter and the spirit of the Bible, Ex. 20:4, 5 ; 32:4, 5 ; Deut. 4:15 ; Isa. 40:18-31 ; John 4:23, 24 ; Rev. 22:8, 9.

The "chambers of imagery," in Ezek. 8 : 7–12, had their walls covered with idolatrous paintings, such as are found on the still more ancient stone walls of Egyptian temples, and such as modern researches have disclosed in Assyrian ruins. See NINEVEH.

IMMAN'UEL. See EMMANUEL.

IMMORTAL'ITY, in God, is underived and absolute : "who only hath immortality." In creatures, it is dependent upon the will of God. The immortality of the soul is argued from its boundless desires and capacities, its unlimited improvement, its desert of future punishment or reward, etc. All arguments, however, are unsatisfying without the testimony of Scripture. Christ "hath brought life and immortality to light through the gospel," 2 Tim. 1:10 ; the immortal blessedness of Christians, including the resurrection of the body, is by virtue of their union with Christ,

John 14:19. The everlasting woe of the wicked, the punishment of their sins, runs parallel with the eternal life of the redeemed, Matt. 25:46.

IN'CENSE, a dry, aromatic gum, exuding from a tree which grows in Arabia and India. It is called also frankincense, from the freedom with which when burning it gives forth its odors. Other spices were mixed with it to make the sacred incense, the use of which for any other purpose was strictly forbidden, Exod. 30:34-38. To offer incense, among the Hebrews, was an office peculiar to the priests; for which purpose they entered into the holy apartment of the temple every morning and evening. On the great day of expiation, the high-priest burnt incense in his censer as he entered the Holy of Holies, and the smoke which arose from it prevented his looking with too much curiosity on the ark and mercy-seat, Lev. 16:13. The Levites were not permitted to touch the censers; and Korah, Dathan, and Abiram suffered a terrible punishment for violating this prohibition. Incense was especially a symbol of prayer. While it was offered, the people prayed in the court without, and their prayers ascended with the sweet odor of the incense, until the priest returned and gave the blessing. So Christ presents his people and their prayers to God, accepted through his merits and intercession, and gives them the blessing, "Your sins are forgiven; go in peace," Psa. 141:2; Luke 2:9; Rev. 5:8; 8:4. "Incense" sometimes signifies the sacrifices and fat of victims, as no other kind of incense was offered on the altar of burnt-offerings, Psa. 66:15. For a description of the altar of incense, see ALTAR.

IN'DIA, Esth. 1:1; 8:9, the country lying east of the ancient Persia and Bactria, so named from the river Indus which passed through it. The India of the ancients extended more to the north and west than modern India; and the southern region, now best known to us, was comparatively unknown until the era of modern navigation.

INHER'ITANCE. The laws of inheritance among the Hebrews were very simple. Land might be mortgaged, but could not be alienated, Num. 36:6-9. See JUBILEE. The only permanent right to property was by heritage, or lineal succession. The eldest son had a double portion. Females had no territorial possession; but if a man left no sons, his daughters inherited—on condition of their marrying into a family within the tribe to which their father belonged. If a man had no children, his land passed to distant relatives, according to a law laid down in Num. 27:8-11. The law of Moses rendered wills unnecessary; they were introduced, however, at a later period, Gal. 3:15; Heb. 9:17. Property was sometimes distributed among children during the lifetime of the father: thus, in the parable of the prodigal son, the father divided his property between the two sons, Luke 15:12.

INK, Jer. 36:18. The ink of the ancients was thick and durable, and resembled our printer's ink. The ordinary materials were powdered charcoal, or ivory-black, water, and gum. The black matter of the scuttle-fish was also used. Writers carried their inkhorns within, or suspended from, their girdles, Ezek. 9:2. See GIRDLE.

INNS. There appear to be three descriptions of these buildings in the East. Some are simply places of rest, (by the side of a fountain, if possible,) which, being at proper distances on the road, are thus named, though they are mere naked walls; others have an attendant, who subsists either by some charitable donation, or the benevolence of passengers; and others are more considerable establishments, where families reside to take care of them, and furnish many necessary provisions.

INSPIRA'TION, that supernatural influence exerted on the minds of the sacred writers by the Spirit of God, in virtue of which they unerringly declared his will. Whether what they wrote was previously familiar to their own knowledge, or, as in many cases it must have been, an immediate revelation from heaven; whether his influence in any given case was dictation, suggestion, or superintendence; and however clearly we may trace in their writings the peculiar character, style, mental endowments, and circumstances of each; yet the whole of the Bible was written under the unerring guidance of the Holy Ghost, 2 Tim. 3:16.

Christ everywhere treats the Old Testament Scriptures as infallibly true, and of divine authority—the word of God. To the New Testament writers inspiration was promised, Matt. 10:19, 20; John 14:26; 16:13; and they wrote and prophesied under its direction, 1 Cor. 2:10-13; 14:37; Gal. 1:12; 2 Pet. 1:21; 3:15; Rev. 1:1, 10-19.

INTERCES'SION, Christ's appearing before the throne in heaven as the Advocate of his people, presenting his finished work as the reason why their prayers should be heard and their persons accepted in him, Isa. 53:12; Rom. 8:34; Heb. 7:25; 9:24; 1 John 2:1. In thus pleading for sinners as the one Mediator, his work is perfect; it precludes all help of virgin, saints, or angels; and will certainly prevail. The Holy Spirit in the hearts of believers is said to intercede for them, Rom. 8:26, when he puts words into their mouths, and holy desires into their hearts, such as they would otherwise fail of, but which are according to the will of God and acceptable to him through Christ.

INTERPRETA'TION, revealing the true meaning of supernatural dreams, Gen. 41, Dan. 2; 4, of unknown tongues, etc., 1 Cor. 12:12, 30; 14:5, 13.

For the right interpretation of the word of God, the chief requisites are, a renewed heart, supremely desirous to learn and do the will of God; the aid of the Holy Spirit, sought and gained; a firm conviction that the word of God should rule the erring reason and heart of man; a diligent comparison of its different parts, for the light they throw upon each other; all reliable information as to the history and geography, the customs, laws, and languages, the public, domestic, and inner life of Bible times. Thus to study the Bible for one's self is the privilege and duty of every one.

IRON was early known and wrought, Gen. 4:22. Moses often alludes to it. He compares the bondage in Egypt to a furnace for smelting iron, and speaks of the iron ore of Canaan, Deut. 3:11; 4:20; 8; 9. Many different articles and tools were anciently made of it. Immense quantities were provided for the building of the temple, 1 Chr. 29:2, 7. "Iron" is used to illustrate slavery, strength, obstinacy, fortitude, affliction, etc., Deut. 28:48; Job 40:18; Isa. 48:4; Jer. 1:18; Ezek. 22:18, 20; Dan. 2:33. "Iron sharpeneth iron," says the wise man, "so a man sharpeneth the countenance of his friend;" that is, the presence of a friend gives us more confidence and assurance. God threatens his ungrateful and perfidious people that he will make the heaven brass and the earth iron; that is, make the earth barren, and the heaven to produce no rain. Chariots of iron are chariots armed with iron spikes and scythes. See CHARIOTS.

I'SAAC, *laughter*, Gen. 17:17; 18:12; 21:6, one of the patriarchal ancestors of the Hebrew nation and of Christ, son of Abraham and Sarah, B. C. 1896-1705. His history is related in Gen. 21; 24-28; 35:27-29. He is memorable for the circumstances attending his birth, as a child of prophecy and promise, in the old age of his parents. Even in childhood he was the object of dislike to his brother Ishmael, son of the bondwoman; and in this, a type of all children of the promise, Gal. 4:29. Trained in the fear of God to early manhood, he showed a noble trust and obedience in his conduct during that remarkable trial of faith which established Abraham as the "father of the faithful;" and in his meek submission to all the will of God, prefigured the only-begotten Son of the Father. At the age of forty he married the pious and lovely Rebekah of Mesopotamia. Most of his life was spent in the southern part of Canaan and its vicinity. At the burial of his father, he was joined by his outcast brother Ishmael. Two sons of Isaac are named in Scripture. The partiality of the mother for Jacob, and of the father for Esau, led to unhappy jealousies, discord, sin, and long separations between the brothers, though all were overruled to accomplish the purposes of God. At the age of one hundred and thirty-seven, Isaac blessed Jacob and sent him away into Mesopotamia. At the age of one hundred and eighty, he died, and was buried in the tomb of Abraham by his two sons. In his natural character, Isaac was humble, tranquil, and meditative; in his piety, devout, full of faith, and eminently submissive to the will of God.

ISAI'AH, the son of Amoz, (not Amos,) one of the most distinguished of the Hebrew prophets. He began to prophesy at Jerusalem towards the close of the reign of Uzziah, about the year 759 B. C., and exercised the prophetical office some sixty years, under the three following monarchs, Jotham, Ahaz, and Hezekiah, Isa. 1:1. Compare 2 Kin. 15-20; 2 Chr. 26-32. The first twelve chapters of his prophecies refer to the kingdom of Judah; then follow chapters 13–23, directed against foreign nations, except chapter 22, against Jerusalem. In chapters 24–35, which would seem to belong to the time of Hezekiah, the prophet appears to look forward in prophetic vision to the times of the exile and of the Messiah. Chapters 36–39 give a historical account of Sennacherib's invasion, and of the advice given by Isaiah to Hezekiah. This account is parallel to that in 2 Kin. 18:13, to 20:19; and indeed chapter 37 of Isaiah is almost word for word the same with 2 Kin. 19. The remainder of the book of Isaiah, chapters 40–66, contains a series of oracles referring to the future times of temporal exile and deliverance, and expanding into glorious views of the spiritual deliverance to be wrought by the Messiah.

Isaiah seems to have lived and prophesied wholly at Jerusalem; and disappears from history after the accounts contained in chapter 39. A tradition among the Talmudists and fathers relates that he was sawn asunder during the reign of Manasseh, Heb. 11:37; and this tradition is embodied in an apocryphal book, called the "ascension of Isaiah;" but it seems to rest on no certain grounds.

Some commentators have proposed to divide the book of Isaiah chronologically into three parts, as if composed under the three kings, Jotham, Ahaz, and Hezekiah. But this is of very doubtful propriety; since several of the chapters are evidently transposed and inserted out of their chronological order. But a very obvious and striking division of the book into two parts exists; the first part, including the first thirty-nine chapters, and the second, the remainder of the book, or chapters 40–66.

The first part is made up of those prophecies and historical accounts which Isaiah wrote during the period of his active exertions, when he mingled in the public concerns of the rulers and the people, and acted as the messenger of God to the nation in reference to their internal and external existing relations. These are single prophecies, published at different times, and on different occasions; afterwards, indeed, brought together into one collection, but still marked as distinct and single, either by the superscriptions, or in some other obvious and known method.

The second part, on the contrary, is occupied wholly with *the future.* It was apparently written in the later years of the prophet, when, having left all active exertions in the theocracy to his younger associates in the prophetical office, he transferred his contemplations from the present to that which was to come. In this part therefore, which was not, like the first, occasioned by external circumstances, it is not so easy to distinguish in like manner between the different single prophecies. The whole is more like a single gush of prophecy. The prophet first consoles his people by announcing their deliverance from the approaching Babylonish exile, which he had himself predicted, chapter 39 : 6, 7; he names the monarch whom Jehovah will send to punish the insolence of their oppressors, and lead back the people to their home. But he does not stop at this inferior deliverance. With the prospect of freedom from the Babylonish exile, he connects the prospect of deliverance from sin and error through the Messiah. Sometimes both objects seem closely interwoven with each other; sometimes one of them appears alone with particular clearness and prominency. Especially is the view of the prophet sometimes so exclusively directed upon the latter object, that, filled with the contemplation of the glory of the spiritual kingdom of God and of its exalted Founder, he loses sight for a time of the less distant future. In the description of this spiritual deliverance also, the relations of time are not observed. Sometimes the prophet beholds the Author of this deliverance in his humiliation and sorrows; and again, the remotest ages of the Messiah's kingdom present themselves to his enraptured vision—when man, so long estranged from God, will have again returned to him; when every thing opposed to God shall have been destroyed, and internal and external peace universally prevail; and when all the evil introduced by sin into the world, will be for ever done away. Elevated above all space and time, the prophet contemplates from the height on which the Holy Spirit has thus placed him, the whole development of the Messiah's kingdom, from its smallest beginnings to its glorious completion.

Isaiah is appropriately named "the

evangelical prophet," and the fathers called his book "the Gospel according to St. Isaiah." In it the wonderful person and birth of "Emmanuel—God with us," his beneficent life, his atoning death, and his triumphant and everlasting kingdom, are minutely foretold, Isa. 7:14-16; 9:6, 7; 11:1-10; 32; 42; 49; 52:13-15; 53; 60; 61:1-3. The simplicity, purity, sweetness, and sublimity of Isaiah, and the fulness of his predictions respecting the Messiah, give him the pre-eminence among the Hebrew prophets and poets.

ISH'BI-BE'NOB, a giant who was on the point of killing David in battle, but was slain by Abishai, 2 Sam. 21:16, 17.

ISH'BOSHETH, son and successor of Saul. Abner, Saul's kinsman and general, so managed that Ishbosheth was acknowledged king at Mahanaim by the greater part of Israel, while David reigned at Hebron over Judah. He was forty-four years of age when he began to reign, and he reigned two years peaceably; after which he was involved in a long and unsuccessful war against David. Being abandoned by Abner, whom he had provoked, he became more and more feeble, and was at last assassinated, 2 Sam. 2:8-11; 3; 4. See ESHBAAL.

ISH'MAEL, I., Gen. 16; 21, son of Abraham and Hagar, B. C. 1910. He was at first regarded as "the son of the promise;" but after the birth and weaning of Isaac he was driven from his father's house, at the age of about seventeen, and took with his mother the way to Egypt her native land. Overcome with heat and thirst, and then miraculously relieved, he remained in the wilderness of Paran, took a wife from Egypt, and was the father of twelve sons, heads of Arab tribes. He seems to have become on friendly terms with Isaac, and to have attended at the bedside of their dying father. At his own death, he was one hundred and thirty-seven years old, Gen. 25:9, 17.

The Ishmaelites, his posterity, were said, in the days of Moses, to dwell "from Havilah unto Shur that is before Egypt," that is, in the north-western part of Arabia. See HAVILAH II. Subsequently they, with the descendants of Joktan, the fourth from Shem, Gen. 10:26-29, and Jokshan, the son of Abraham by Keturah, Gen. 25:3, and perhaps also of some of the brethren of Joktan and Jokshan, occupied the whole peninsula of Arabia. See ARABIA. They became very numerous and powerful, according to the divine promise, Gen. 17:16. The prediction also in Gen. 16:12, has been fully verified in their history. Located near their "brethren" the Jews, they have always led a roving, wild, and predatory life. To a great degree unchanged, they are to this day the untamed though tributary masters of the desert. See MIDIANITES.

II. A prince of Judah, who fled to the Ammonites when Jerusalem was destroyed by the Chaldeans. Soon after, he returned and assassinated Gedaliah the governor and many others; but was obliged to flee for his life, Jer. 40; 41.

ISLE, ISLAND. The Hebrew word which is more commonly translated isle, means strictly dry land, habitable country, in opposition to water, or to seas and rivers, Isa. 42:15. Compare Isa. 50:2. Hence, as opposed to water in general, it means land adjacent to water, either washed or surrounded by it, that is, maritime country, coast, island. Thus it means coast, when used of Ashdod, Isa. 20:6; of Tyre, Isa. 23:2, 6; of Peloponnesus, or Greece, Ezek. 27:7, "the isles of Elishah." It means island when used of Caphtor, for example, or Crete, Jer. 47:4; also Jer. 2:10; so Psa. 97:1; and also Esth. 10:1, where the phrase isles of the sea is in antithesis with the land or continent. The plural of this word, usually translated islands, was employed by the Hebrews to denote distant regions beyond the sea, whether coasts or islands; and especially the islands and maritime countries of the west, which had become indistinctly known to the Hebrews, through the voyages of the Phœnicians, Isa. 24:15; 40:15; 42:4, 10, 12; Psa. 72:10. In Ezek. 27:15, the East Indian Archipelago would seem to be intended.

ISRAEL, *who prevails with God*, a name given to Jacob, after having wrestled with the Angel-Jehovah at Penuel, Gen. 32:1, 2, 28, 30; Hosea 12:3. See JACOB. By the name Israel is sometimes understood all the posterity of Israel, the seed of Jacob, 1 Cor. 10:18; sometimes all true believers, his spiritual seed, Rom. 9:6; and sometimes the kingdom of Israel, or the ten tribes, as distinct from the kingdom of Judah.

IS'RAELITES, the "children of Israel," a name of the twelve tribes unitedly until the separation under Rehoboam, when it became the usual designation of the ten tribes forming the kingdom of Israel. Ephraim, the leading tribe among the ten, seems to have shown an early spirit of rivalry towards Judah; Joshua had belonged to Ephraim, the ark had long rested within its borders at Shiloh, and Jeroboam was also an Ephraimite. After the division, in order to prevent the ten tribes from repairing to Jerusalem to worship, the two golden calves were set up, at Bethel and Dan, and thus idolatry was established in those tribes, and corruption and ungodliness increased more rapidly than in Judah. Israel was chastised by sword, famine, etc.; and at length, having been often reproved and hardening their necks, they were suddenly destroyed, and that without remedy. During the two hundred and fifty-four years of the kingdom of Israel, B. C. 975–721, there were nineteen different kings, of various lines. See KINGS. Shechem, Thirzah, and Samaria were in turn the seats of government. After their captivity by Shalmaneser, the Israelites as a nation never returned. Those who did return were merged in the tribes of Judah and Benjamin, and with them constituted the Jews of our Saviour's day. See CANAAN, HEBREWS, and JUDAH.

IS'SACHAR, *recompense*, so named by Leah his mother, Gen. 30:18, the ninth son of Jacob, born B. C. 1749. The character of his posterity was foretold by Jacob and by Moses, Gen. 49:14, 15; Deut. 33:18, 19.

The TRIBE OF ISSACHAR numbered fifty-four thousand men in the desert, and on entering Canaan was the third in population, Num. 1:28; 26:25. Their portion, having the Jordan on the east, Manasseh on the west, Zebulun north, and Ephraim south, included a considerable part of the fine plain of Esdraelon, the most fertile in the country. They were industrious agriculturists, and are mentioned with honor for their brave and wise patriotism, Judg. 5:15; 1 Chr. 7:1–5; 12:32.

IT'ALY is not mentioned in the Old Testament, unless under general terms, as Chittim, Isles of the sea. In the New Testament, Acts 18:2; 27:1, 6; Heb. 13:24, it is chiefly of interest on account of ROME, which see. The Italian band, mentioned in Acts 10:1, was probably a Roman cohort from Italy, stationed at Cæsarea; so called to distinguish it from the other troops, which were drawn from Syria and the adjacent regions.

ITH'AMAR, the fourth son of Aaron, consecrated to the priesthood, Ex. 6:23; Num. 3:2, 3. His posterity took charge of the tabernacle in the wilderness, Ex. 38:21; Num. 4:28. Some of this line, namely, Eli, Ahitub, Ahiah, Ahimelech, and Abiathar, held the office of high-priest, but under Solomon it reverted to the family of Eleazar, 1 Kin. 2:7. See ABIATHAR.

ITURE'A, a region in the extreme north-east of Palestine, perpetuating the name of Jetur a son of Ishmael, and belonging to the half-tribe of Manasseh, 1 Chr. 1:31; 5:19. The name Jedur still remains there. In the time of Christ, Iturea was in the tetrarchy of Philip, Luke 3:1. It lay about midway between the sea of Galilee and Damascus, but its limits are not well known. Its inhabitants are said to have been skilful archers and dexterous robbers.

IVORY: FROM EGYPTIAN RUINS.

I'VORY is mentioned in the reign of Solomon, and referred to in Psalm 45, as used in decorating palaces. Solomon, who traded to India, brought thence elephants and ivory to Judea. "For the king had at sea a navy of Tarshish, with the navy of Hiram: once in three years came the navy of Tarshish, bringing gold and silver and ivory," 1 Kin. 10:22; 2 Chr. 9:21. Solomon had a throne decorated with ivory, and inlaid with gold, these beautiful materials relieving the splendor and heightening the lustre of each other, 1 Kin. 10:18. Ivory, as is well known, is the substance of the tusks of elephants, and hence it is always called in Hebrew, *tooth*.

As to the "ivory houses," 1 Kin. 22:39, Amos 3:15, they may have had ornaments of ivory, as they sometimes have of gold, silver, or other precious materials, in such abundance as to be named from the article of their decoration; as the emperor Nero's palace was named *aurea*, or golden, because overlaid with gold. This method of ornamenting buildings or apartments was very ancient among the Greeks, and is mentioned by Homer. See Ezek. 27:6, 15; Amos 6:4; Rev. 18:12.

J.

JA'BAL, son of Lamech and Adah, and a descendant of Cain. He is supposed to have been the first to adopt the nomadic mode of life, still practised in Arabia and Tartary, and to have invented portable tents, perhaps of skins, Gen. 4:20.

JAB'BOK, now the Zerka, a perennial stream, flowing into the Jordan midway between the sea of Galilee and the Dead sea, about thirty miles from each, after a westerly course of some sixty miles. It traverses at first an elevated and desert region, and receives a branch from the north and another from the south. This latter branch separated the Ammonites from Israel. The eastern part of the Jabbok is dry in summer. Towards the west, it flows through a deep ravine. Penuel, where Jacob wrestled with the Angel, was a fording-place of the Jabbok, Gen. 32:22. This stream divided the territory of Og from that of Sihon, Josh. 12:2, 5, and traversed the region afterwards assigned to the tribe of Gad.

JA'BESH, a city in the half-tribe of Manasseh east of the Jordan, generally called Jabesh-gilead because situated within the territory commonly called Gilead. Eusebius places it six miles from Pella, towards Gerasa. It was sacked by the Israelites for refusing to aid in chastising the Benjamites, Judg. 21:8-10. At a later day, it was besieged by the Ammonites, and relieved by Saul; in gratitude for which service the men of Jabesh-gilead rescued the dead bodies of Saul and his sons from the insults of the Philistines, 1 Sam. 11; 31:11-13; 2 Sam. 2:5.

JA'BEZ, a descendant of Judah, whose high distinction among his brethren seems to have been owing to his prevalence in prayer, 1 Chr. 4:9, 10.

JA'BIN, I., a powerful king in the time of Joshua, at Hazor in the north of Canaan. The league which he organized to crush Joshua, only made his own ruin more complete, Josh. 11, B. C. 1450.

II. Another king of Hazor, a century and a half later, who sorely oppressed Israel for twenty years, till Deborah and Barak were raised up as deliverers, Judg. 4; Psa. 83:9.

JAB'NEH, afterwards Jamnia, now Jebna, a Philistine city on the Mediterranean coast, some twelve miles south of Joppa. It was conquered by the Jews, 2 Chr. 26:6.

JA'CHIN, *God confirms*, the name of the right-hand brazen column at the entrance of Solomon's temple, 1 Kin. 7:21. See BOAZ.

JA'CINTH, or HYACINTH, a gem of a yellowish red or hyacinth color, nearly related to zircon and to the amethyst. It loses its color by being heated, and resembles the diamond, Rev. 9:17; 21:20.

JA'COB, son of Isaac and Rebekah, and twin-brother to Esau. As at his birth he held his brother's heel, he was called Jacob, that is, the heel-holder, one who comes behind and catches the heel of his adversary, a supplanter, Gen. 25:26. This was a kind of predictive intimation of his future conduct in life. Jacob was meek and peaceable, living a shepherd life at home. Esau was more turbulent and fierce, and passionately fond of hunting. Isaac was partial to Esau, Rebekah to Jacob. Jacob having taken advantage of his brother's absence and his father's infirmity to obtain the blessing of the birthright, or primogeniture, was compelled to fly into Mesopotamia to avoid the consequences of his brother's wrath, Gen. 27; 28. On his journey the Lord appeared to him in a dream, (see LADDER,) promised him His protection, and declared His purpose relative to his descendants' possessing the land of Canaan, and the descent of the Messiah through him, Gen. 28:10, etc. His subsequent days, which he calls "few and evil," were clouded with many sorrows, yet amid them all he was sustained by the care and favor of God. On his solitary journey of six hundred miles into Mesopotamia, and during the toils and injuries of his twenty years' service with Laban, God still prospered him, and on his return to the land of promise inclined the hostile spirits of Laban and of Esau to peace. On the border of Canaan the angels of God met him, and the God of angels wrestled with him, yielded him the blessing, and gave him the honored name of Israel. But sore trials awaited him: his mother was no more; his sister-wives imbittered his life with their jealousies; his children Dinah, Simeon, Levi, and Reuben filled him with grief and shame; his beloved Rachel and his father were removed by death; Joseph his favorite son he had given up as slain by wild beasts; and the loss of Benjamin threatened to bring his gray hairs with sorrow to the grave. But the sunset of his life was majestically calm and bright. For seventeen years, he enjoyed in the land of Goshen a serene happiness: he gave a dying blessing in Jehovah's name to his assembled sons; visions of their future prosperity rose before his eyes, especially the long line of the royal race of Judah, culminating in the glorious kingdom of SHILOH. "He saw it, and was glad." Soon after, he was gathered to his fathers, and his body was embalmed, and buried with all possible honors in the burial-place of Abraham near Hebron, B. C. 1836–1689. In the history of Jacob we observe that in repeated instances he used unjustifiable means to secure promised advantages, instead of waiting, in faith and obedience, for the unfailing providence of God. We observe also the divine chastisement of his sins, and his steadfast growth in grace to the last, Gen. 25–50. His name is found in the New Testament, illustrating the sovereignty of God and the power of faith, Rom. 9:13; Heb. 11:9, 21.

JACOB'S WELL. See SHECHEM.

JA'EL, wife of Heber the Kenite, slew Sisera, general of the Canaanitish army, who had fled to her tent, which was then temporarily on the western border of the plain of Esdraelon. Jael took her opportunity, and while he was sleeping, drove a large nail or tent-pin through his temples, Judg. 4:17–23. The life of Sisera was undoubtedly forfeited to the Israelites by the usages of war, and probably to society by his crimes. Besides this, the life or honor of Jael may have been in danger, or her feelings of hospitality may have been overpowered by a sudden impulse to avenge the oppressed Israelites, with whom she was allied by blood. The song of Deborah celebrates the act as one of justice and heroism, and as a divine judgment which, as well as the defeat of Sisera's host, was the more disgraceful to him for being wrought by a woman, Judg. 5:1, 24–27, 31.

JAH, a Hebrew contraction for JEHOVAH, Psa. 68:4. It is often found in Hebrew compound words, as in Adonijah, Malachia, Hallelujah.

JA'HAZ, JAHA'ZAH, or JAH'ZAH, a city in the north of Moab, near which Moses defeated Sihon, Num. 21:23. It was in the limits of Reuben, and was a Levitical city, Josh. 21:36. In Isa. 15:4, and Jer. 48:21, it appears as again in the hands of Moabites.

JA'IR, I., a leader in the conquest of Bashan, probably before the Jews crossed the Jordan, B. C. 1451. Twenty-three cities near Argob were called after him Havoth-jair, which see.

II. The eighth judge of Israel, in Gilead of Manasseh, B. C. 1210. He seems to have been a descendant and heir of the former, Judg. 10:3–5.

JA'IRUS, a ruler of the synagogue at Capernaum, memorable for his faith in Christ. His deceased daughter, twelve years of age, was restored to life and health by the Saviour, Mark 5:22; Luke 8:41.

JAM'BRES. See JAN'NES.

JAMES, I., surnamed the greater, or the elder, to distinguish him from James the younger, was one of the twelve apostles, brother of John the evangelist, and son of Zebedee and Salome, Matt. 4:21; 27:56. Compare Mark 15:40. James was of Bethsaida in Galilee, and left his earthly occupation to follow Christ, Mark 1:19, 20. His mother Salome was one of those women who occasionally attended our Saviour in his journeys, and one day desired that her two sons might be seated at his right and left hand in his kingdom, Matt. 20:20–23.

James and John were originally fishermen, with Zebedee their father, Mark 1:19. They were witnesses of our Lord's transfiguration, Matt. 17:1, 2; and when certain Samaritans refused to receive him,

James and John wished for fire from heaven to consume them, Luke 9:54. For this reason, or because of their zeal and energy as ministers of Christ, the name of Boanerges, or sons of thunder, was afterwards given to them, Mark 3:17. Together with Peter they appear to have enjoyed special honors and privileges among the disciples, Mark 1 : 29 ; 5 : 37 ; 9 : 2 ; 13 : 3 ; 14 : 33 ; Luke 8 : 51. After the ascension of our Lord, at which James was present, he appears to have remained at Jerusalem, and was put to death by Herod, about A. D. 44, the first martyr among the apostles, Acts 12:1, 2.

II. Another apostle, son of Alphæus, or Cleophas, Matt. 10 : 3 ; Mark 3 : 18 ; Luke 6 : 15. His mother's name was Mary, (III.,) and his brethren were Joses and Judas, (III.,) Matt. 27 : 56 ; Mark 15:40. He is here called THE LESS, or the younger, to distinguish him from James the son of Zebedee.

III. "The Lord's brother," Gal. 1:19 ; either a brother of Christ, being a son of Joseph and Mary ; or as many think, a cousin of Christ, and identical with the James above, II. He resided at Jerusalem, Acts 15 : 13 ; and is called "the Just" by Josephus, and said to have been stoned to death, about A. D. 62. The epistle of James is ascribed to him by those who distinguish him from James the Less. The question of his true relationship to Christ is involved in much doubt. The gospels repeatedly mention James, Joses, Juda, and Simon, as "brothers" of our Lord, and speak in the same connection of his "mother" and his "sisters," Matt. 12 : 46 ; 13 : 56 ; Mark 3:31 ; 6:3 ; Luke 8:19 ; moreover, the inspired writers expressly distinguish the brothers of Christ from the apostles, while they include among the apostles both James the Less and Jude, John 2 : 12 ; 7 : 3–10 ; Acts 1 : 13, 14, thus furnishing strong reasons, as many believe, for the opinion that James the Just was literally a brother of our Lord.

The EPISTLE OF JAMES is generally supposed to have been written at Jerusalem, about A. D. 61, by James the Just, shortly before his death. It is addressed particularly to Jewish converts, but was intended for the benefit of Christians generally. It is hence called catholic. See CATHOLIC and EPISTLE. It has often been regarded as teaching a different doctrine in respect to faith and works, from what Paul teaches in his epistle to the Romans. But the doctrine of the two apostles is at bottom the same, only that Paul dwells more on faith, the sole origin of good works ; and James dwells more on good works, which result from true faith. According to Paul, there can be no true faith which does not manifest itself in good works ; and according to James, there can be no truly good works which do not spring from true faith.

JAN'NES and JAM'BRES were two of the principal Egyptian magicians, who withstood Moses and Aaron by attempting to imitate the miracles which they exhibited. See Exod. 7:11, etc. These names are not found in the Old Testament, but are often mentioned in the rabbinical books, 2 Tim. 3:8.

JA'PHETH, *enlargement*, the eldest of Noah's three sons, Gen. 9 : 24 ; 10 : 21, born one hundred years before the flood. He was perhaps the Iapetos, whom Greek legends represent as the progenitor of the Greek race. His seven sons, Gen. 10:2–5 ; 1 Chr. 1:5, occupied with their posterity the north of Asia and most of Europe. The probable location of each of the seven is described in its place. In later years the Greeks and Romans subdued large portions of Southern and Western Asia, in accordance with the prediction of Noah, Gen. 9 : 27. The "enlargement" of Japheth now extends over America also.

JAPH'O. See JOPPA.

JASH'ER, THE BOOK OF, that is, the book of the upright, or of the excellent, noble-minded. This work is mentioned in Josh. 10 : 13, and 2 Sam. 1 : 18, and would seem to have been a collection of national, historical, triumphal, and elegiac songs, which was still extant in the time of David. Josephus speaks of a book of Jasher as then existing in the temple, but nothing is known respecting it. The books now published under this name are gross forgeries.

JA'SON, a kinsman and host of Paul, at Thessalonica. His person and goods were interposed to shield the apostle from the rabble, A. D. 52, Acts 17:5–10. He seems also to have been with him at Corinth, five years afterwards, Rom. 16:21.

JAS'PER, a precious stone of various colors, as green, purple, etc., often clouded with white, and beautifully striped with red or yellow, Ex. 28:20; Rev. 4:3; 21:11.

JA'VAN, the fourth son of Japheth, Gen. 10:2, 4. This name is the same as the Greek Iön, whence comes Ionia, and it is understood that Javan was the ancestor of the Greeks. See GREECE.

JA'ZER, or JAAZER, Num. 21:32, a city of the Amorites, in Gilead; afterwards a Levitical city in Gad. It lay some fifteen miles north of Heshbon, near a small stream, Num. 32:1; Josh. 21:39; 1 Chr. 26:31; Jer. 48:32.

JEAL'OUSY. See under ADULTERY. The idol of jealousy, Ezek. 8:3, 5, is the same with Thammuz in verse 14. See THAMMUZ.

JEB'USITES. See CANAANITES.

JECONI'AH. See JEHOIACHIN.

JEDIDI'AH, *beloved of the Lord*, a name given to Solomon at his birth, by Nathan the prophet, 2 Sam. 12:25.

JED'UTHUN, a Levite, one of the directors of music at the temple, 1 Chr. 16:38-42. His descendants held the same office, 2 Chr. 35:15; Neh. 11:17; and the name of one of them appears in the title of Psalms 39, 62, 77. See ASAPH.

JE'GAR-SAHADU'THA, *heap of witness*, a Chaldee name, equivalent to Galeed in Hebrew, both marking the scene of the covenant between Jacob and Laban, Gen. 31:47.

JEHO'AHAZ, I., son and successor of Jehu king of Israel, B. C. 856, reigned seventeen years. In punishment for his sins and those of his people, Israel was invaded and reduced to great extremities by the Syrians under Hazael and Benhadad. The king humbled himself before God, and deliverance came by the hand of Joash his son, 2 Kin. 13:19, 25.

II. Also called Shallum, 1 Chr. 3:15, the third son and the successor of Josiah king of Judah, B. C. 609, reigned about three months in Jerusalem. He was deposed by the king of Egypt, 2 Kin. 23:30-34; 2 Chr. 36:1-4. See also Jer. 22:10-13; Ezek. 19:3.

JEHO'ASH. See JOASH.

JEHOI'ACHIN, son and successor of Jehoiakim, king of Judah, B. C. 599, reigned three months, and was then carried away to Babylon, where he was imprisoned for thirty-six years, and then released and favored by Evil-merodach, 2 Kin. 24:6-16; 25:27; 2 Chr. 36:9, 10. In this last passage he is said to have been eight years old at the commencement of his reign. If the text has not here been altered from eighteen years, as it stands in the first passage, we may conclude that he reigned ten years conjointly with his father. He is also called Coniah, and Jeconiah, 1 Chr. 3:16; Jer. 27:20; 37:1. The prediction in Jer. 22:30, signified that no son of his should occupy the throne, 1 Chr. 3:17, 18; Matt. 1:12.

JEHOI'ADA, a high-priest, who preserved the life and throne of the young Josiah against the usurping Athaliah. His wisdom and piety continued to bless the kingdom until he died, B. C. 834, aged 130, and was buried with royal honors, 2 Kin. 11; 2 Chr. 23; 24.

JEHOI'AKIM, or ELI'AKIM, second son of Josiah, brother and successor of Jehoahaz or Shallum, king of Judah, for whom he was substituted by the king of Egypt. He was king during eleven years of luxury, extortion, and idolatry. In the third year, Nebuchadnezzar carried to Babylon a part of his princes and treasures. A year after, his allies the Egyptians were defeated on the Euphrates; yet he despised the warnings of Jeremiah, and cast his book into the fire. At length he rebelled against Nebuchadnezzar, but was defeated and ingloriously slain, B. C. 599, 2 Kin. 23:34; 24:6; 2 Chr. 36:4-8; Jer. 22; 26; 36.

JEHO'RAM. See JORAM.

JEHOSH'APHAT, a pious king of Judah, the son and successor of Asa. He began to reign at the age of thirty-five, about the year 914 B. C., and reigned twenty-five years. His history is found in 1 Kin. 15:24; 22; 2 Chr. 17-20. He was distinguished by his zeal for true religion, and his firm trust in God. He thoroughly cleansed the land from idolatry, restored the divine ordinances, and provided for the religious instruction of the people. His government was highly prospered at home and abroad. The great error of his life was, an entangling alliance with the wicked Ahab, whose infamous daughter Athaliah early began to afflict the kingdom of Judah, of which she was afterwards the queen. Jehoshaphat was beguiled by Ahab into an unsuccessful war with the Syrians, but soon resumed his labors in behalf of religion and justice. Having failed in a commercial enterprise with Ahaziah, he declined a second trial, 1 Kin. 22:48, 49, but united with Joram, his successor, in a war with Moab. This seems to have led to his being assailed by a vast host of Moabites, Ammonites, Edomites, and Syrians; but again he was victorious through his faith in God. He died at the age of sixty years.

JEHOSHAPHAT, VALLEY OF, or valley of *the judgment of God*, a metaphorical name of some place where God would judge the foes of his people, Joel 3:2, 12. There is no ground for applying it to any known locality, or for connecting it, unless for mere illustration, with the great battle of Jehoshaphat described in 2 Chr. 20. Since the third century, however, the name has been appropriated to the deep and narrow glen east of Jerusalem, running north and south between the city and the mount of Olives, called in the Bible the brook Kidron. See JERUSALEM.

JEHOSH'EBA, the aunt of Joash, king of Judah, whose life in infancy and childhood she saved, in spite of the designs of Athaliah, 2 Kin. 11:1–3.

JEHO'VAH, the ineffable name of God among the Hebrews. It never has the article before it, nor is it found in the plural form. The Jews never pronounced this name; and wherever it occurs in the Hebrew Scriptures, they substituted for it, in reading, the word ADONAI, *Lord*, or ELOHIM, *God*. See GOD. In the Hebrew Bible, it is always written with the vowels of one or the other of these words. Its ancient pronunciation is by many thought to have been *Yahveh*, but this is not certain. Its meaning is HE IS, the same as I AM, the person only being changed. Thus it denotes the self-existence, independence, immutability, and infinite fulness of the divine Being, which is a pledge that he will fulfil all his promises. Compare Ex. 3:14, I AM THAT I AM, the meaning of which see under the article GOD. In Ex. 6:3, God says, "I appeared unto Abraham, unto Isaac, and unto Jacob, by the name of God Almighty; but by my name Jehovah was I not known to them;" yet the appellation Jehovah appears to have been known from the beginning, Gen. 4:2. We have reason to believe that God himself, who named man *Adam*, named himself JEHOVAH; but in his revelation to the patriarchs he had not appropriated to himself this name in a peculiar way, as he now did, nor unfolded the deep meaning contained in it. He had said to them, "I am God Almighty," Gen. 17:1; 26:11; or, "I am Jehovah, the God of Abraham," etc.; but never simply, "I am Jehovah." It should be remembered that our English version translates this name by the word LORD, printed in small capitals.

JEHOVAH-JIREH, *Jehovah will provide*, the name given by Abraham to the place where he had been on the point of slaying his son Isaac, Gen. 22:14. He gave this name in allusion to his answer to Isaac's question in verse 8, that God would provide a victim for the sacrifice.

JEHOVAH-NIS'SI, *Jehovah my banner*, Ex. 17:15.

JEHOVAH-SHA'LOM, *Jehovah of peace* or *prosperity*, the name given by Gideon to an altar which he built in the place where the Angel-Jehovah had appeared to him, and saluted him by saying, "Peace be unto thee," Judg. 6:24.

JEHOVAH-SHAM'MAH, *Jehovah is there*, the name given by Ezekiel, 48:35, margin, to a future holy city.

JEHOVAH-TZIDKENU, *Jehovah our righteousness*, a name given to the Saviour, and through him to his church, Jer. 23:6; 33:16, margin.

JE'HU, I., the son of Hanani, a prophet, sent with messages from God to Baasha king of Israel, and many years afterwards, to Jehoshaphat king of Judah, 1 Kin. 16:1–7; 2 Chr. 19:1–3; 20:34.

II. The "son" of Jehoshaphat and grandson of Nimshi, (compare 1 Kin. 19:16, and 2 Kin. 9:2,) a general of the army of Joram, slew his master, and usurped the throne of Israel, B. C. 884. He reigned twenty-eight years. See his history in 1 Kin. 19:16, 17; 2 Kin. 9; 10. He fulfilled the divine purpose in extirpating the family of the impious Ahab, and zealously destroyed the priests of Baal and many other friends of Ahab. But his heart was not right with God. The Syrians possessed themselves of his eastern frontier, and his dynasty was cut short in the fourth generation.

JEPH'THAH, the son of Gilead, was a judge of Israel, and successor to Jair. His history is told in Judg. 11; 12. A most affecting incident in it is his devoting his daughter to God as a sacrifice, in consequence of a rash vow.

The arguments on the question whether Jephthah's daughter was actually sacrificed or not cannot here be cited. The natural repugnance we feel to such a vow and its fulfilment has led many interpreters to adopt the less obvious theory that she was only condemned to live and die unmarried. There is no intimation in Scripture that God approved of his vow, whatever it was. Paul numbers Jephthah among the saints of the Old Testament distinguished for their faith, Heb. 11:32.

JEREMI'AH, one of the chief prophets of the Old Testament, prophesied under Josiah, Jehoiakim, and Zedekiah, and also after the captivity of the latter. He was born at Anathoth, of the race of the priests, and was destined of God to be a prophet, and consecrated for that object before his birth, Jer. 1:1, 5. At an early age he was called to act as a prophet, B. C. 628, in the thirteenth year of king Josiah. This good king no doubt coöperated with him to promote the reformation of the people; but the subsequent life of the prophet was full of afflictions and persecutions. Jehoiakim threw his prophetic roll into the fire, and sought his life. Zedekiah was kindly instructed by him, and warned of the woes impending over his guilty people, and of their seventy years' captivity, but to no purpose. The fidelity of the prophet often endangered his life, and he was in prison when Jerusalem was taken by Nebuchadnezzar. That monarch released him, and offered him a home in Babylon; but he chose to remain with the remnant of the Jews, and was carried by them erelong into Egypt, B. C. 586, still faithfully advising and reproving them till he died. For forty-two years he steadfastly maintained the cause of truth and of God against his rebellious people. Though naturally mild, sensitive, and retiring, he shrank from no danger when duty called; threats could not silence him, nor ill-usage alienate him. Tenderly compassionate to his infatuated countrymen, he shared with them the woes which he could not induce them to avert from their own heads.

The BOOK OF JEREMIAH, in the chronological order of its several predictions and divine messages, is somewhat difficult of arrangement; but may be divided, by a natural and sufficiently accurate method, into four general sections, containing severally the prophecies uttered in the reigns of Josiah, Jehoiakim, Zedekiah, and Gedaliah. The last chapter of the book appears to have been added, perhaps by Ezra; it is taken almost verbatim from 2 Kin. 24:18-20, and ch. 25. See Jer. 51:64.

Jeremiah wrote also the book of LAMENTATIONS, in which he utters the most plaintive and pathetic sentiments over the calamities of his people. See LAMENTATIONS.

JER'ICHO, a city of Benjamin, Josh. 16:7; 18:21, about eighteen miles east-north-east of Jerusalem, and seven miles from the Jordan. It was the first city in Canaan taken by Joshua, who being miraculously aided by the downfall of its walls, totally destroyed it, sparing only Rahab and her household, and pronounced a curse upon the person who should ever rebuild it, which was more than five hundred years afterwards fulfilled on Hiel, Josh. 6:26; 1 Kin. 16:34. Meanwhile a new Jericho had been built on some neighboring site, Judg. 3:13; 2 Sam. 10:5. Jericho was also called the "city of palm-trees," Deut. 34:3, Judg. 1:16, and became afterwards flourishing and second in importance only to Jerusalem. It contained a school of the prophets, and was the residence of Elisha, 2 Kin. 2:4, 18. Here also Christ healed two blind men, Matt. 20:29-34, and forgave Zaccheus, Luke 19:1-10.

The site of Jericho has usually been fixed at Rihah, a mean and foul Arab hamlet of some two hundred inhabitants. Recent travellers, however, show that the probable location of Jericho was two miles west of Rihah, at the mouth of Wady Kelt, and where the road from Jerusalem comes into the plain. The city destroyed by Joshua may have been nearer to the fountain of Elisha, supposed to be the present Ain es-Sultan, two miles north-west of Rihah. On the west and north of Jericho rise high limestone hills, one of which, the dreary Quarantana, 1,200 or 1,500 feet high, derives its name from the modern tradition that it was the scene of our Lord's forty days' fast and temptation. Between the hills and the Jordan lies "the plain of Jericho," Josh. 4:13, over against "the plains of Moab" east of the river. It was anciently well watered and amazingly fruitful. It might easily be made so again, but now lies neglected, and the palm-trees, balsam, and honey, for which it was once famous, have disappeared.

The road from Jericho to Jerusalem

THE PLAIN OF JERICHO, FROM THE HILLS ON THE WEST.

ascends through narrow and rocky passes amid ravines and precipices. It is an exceedingly difficult and dangerous route, and is still infested by robbers, as in the time of the good Samaritan, Luke 10:30-34.

JEROBO'AM, I., the first king of Israel, an Ephraimite, the son of Nebat. During the latter part of Solomon's reign, and while an officer under him, he plotted against him, and was obliged to flee into Egypt. On the death of Solomon, he was summoned by the ten tribes to return and present their demands to Rehoboam; and when these were refused, he was chosen king of the revolted tribes, B. C. 975. He reigned twenty-two years. The only notable act of his reign marked him with infamy, as the man "who made Israel to sin." It was the idolatrous establishment of golden calves at Bethel and Dan, that the people might worship there and not at Jerusalem. He also superseded the sons of Aaron by priests chosen from "the lowest of the people." This unprincipled but effective measure, in which he was followed by all the kings of Israel, was a confession of weakness as well as of depravity. Neither miracles nor warnings, nor the premature death of Abijah his son, could dissuade him. He was at war with Judah all his days, and with the brief reign of Nadab his son the doomed family became extinct, 1 Kin. 12-14:20; 2 Chr. 10; 13.

II. JEROBOAM SECOND, the thirteenth king of Israel, son and successor of Joash, B. C. 825, reigned forty-one years. He followed up his father's successes over the Syrians, took Hamath and Damascus, and all the region east of the Jordan down to the Dead sea, and advanced to its highest point the prosperity of that kingdom. Yet his long reign added heavily to the guilt of Israel, by increased luxury, oppression, and vice. After him, the kingdom rapidly declined, and his own dynasty perished within a year, 2 Kin. 14:23-29; 15:8-12. See also the contemporary prophets, particularly Amos and Hosea.

JERUB'-BAAL, *let Baal plead*, Judg. 6:31, 32. See GIDEON.

JERU'SALEM, the chief city of the Holy Land, and to the Christian the most illustrious in the world. It is situated in 31° 46′ 43″ N. lat., and 35° 13′ E. long., on elevated ground south of the centre of the country, about thirty-seven miles from the Mediterranean, and about twenty-four from the Jordan. Its site was early hallowed by God's trial of Abraham's faith, Gen. 22; 2 Chr. 3:1.

It was on the border of the tribes of Benjamin and Judah, mostly within the limits of the former, but reckoned as belonging to the latter, because conquered by it, Josh. 15:8; 18:16, 28; Judg. 1:1–8. The most ancient name of the city was Salem, Gen. 14:18; Psa. 76:2; and it afterwards was called Jebus, as belonging to the Jebusites, Judg. 19:10, 11. Being a very strong position, it resisted the attempts of the Israelites to become the sole masters of it, until at length its fortress was stormed by David, 2 Sam. 5:6, 9; after which it received its present name, and was also called "the city of David." It now became the religious and political centre of the kingdom, and was greatly enlarged, adorned, and fortified. But its chief glory was, that in its magnificent temple the ONE LIVING AND TRUE GOD dwelt, and revealed himself.

After the division of the tribes, it continued the capital of the kingdom of Judah, was several times taken and plundered, and at length was destroyed at the Babylonian captivity, 2 Kin. 14:13; 2 Chr. 12:9; 21:16; 24:23; 25:23; 36:3, 10, 17–20. After seventy years, it was rebuilt by the Jews on their return from captivity about 536 B. C., who did much to restore it to its former splendor. About 332 B. C., the city yielded to Alexander of Macedon; and not long after his death, Ptolemy of Egypt took it by an assault on the Sabbath, when it is said the Jews scrupled to fight. In 170 B. C., Jerusalem fell under the tyranny of Antiochus Epiphanes, who razed its walls, set up an image of Jupiter in the temple, and used every means to force the people into idolatry. Under the Maccabees, however, the Jews, in 163 B. C., recovered their independence. Just a century later, it was conquered by the Romans. Herod the Great expended vast sums in its embellishment. To the city and temple thus renovated the ever-blessed Messiah came, in the fulness of time, and made the place of his feet glorious. By his rejection and crucifixion Jerusalem filled up the cup of her guilt; the Jewish nation perished from off the land of their fathers, and the city and temple were taken by Titus and totally destroyed, A. D. 70–71. Of all the structures of Jerusalem, only three towers and a part of the western wall were left standing. Still, as the Jews began to return thither, and manifested a rebellious spirit, the emperor Adrian planted a Roman colony there in A. D. 135, and banished the Jews, prohibiting their return on pain of death. He changed the name of the city to Ælia Capitolina, consecrated it to heathen deities, in order to defile it as much as possible, and did what he could to obliterate all traces both of Judaism and Christianity. From this period the name Ælia became so common, that the name Jerusalem was preserved only among the Jews and better informed Christians. In the time of Constantine, however, it resumed its ancient name, which it has retained to the present day. Helena, the mother of Constantine, built two churches in Bethlehem and on mount Olivet, about A. D. 326; and Julian, who, after his father, succeeded to the empire of his uncle Constantine, endeavored to rebuild the temple; but his design, and that of the Jews, whom he patronized, was frustrated, as contemporary historians relate, by an earthquake, and by balls of fire bursting forth among the workmen, A. D. 363.

The subsequent history of Jerusalem may be told in a few words. In 613, it was taken by Chosroes king of Persia, who slew, it is said, 90,000 men, and demolished, to the utmost of his power, whatever the Christians had venerated: in 627, Heraclius defeated Chosroes, and Jerusalem was recovered by the Greeks. Soon after commenced the long and wretched era of Mohammedanism. About 637, the city was taken from the Christians by the caliph Omar, after a siege of four months, and continued under the caliphs of Bagdad till 868, when it was taken by Ahmed, a Turkish sovereign of Egypt. During the space of 220 years, it was subject to several masters, Turkish and Saracenic, and in 1099 it was taken by the crusaders under Godfrey Bouillon, who was elected king. He was succeeded by his brother Baldwin, who died in 1118. In 1187, Saladin, sultan of the East, captured the city, assisted by the treachery of Raymond, count of Tripoli, who was found dead in his bed on the morning of the day in which he was to have delivered up the city. It was restored, in 1242, to the Latin princes, by Saleh Ismael, emir of Damascus; they lost it in 1291 to the sultans of Egypt, who held it till 1382 Selim, the Turkish sultan, reduced Egypt and Syria, including Jerusalem, in 1517, and his son Solyman built or reconstructed the present walls in 1534. Since then it has remained under the dominion of Turkey, except when held for a short time, 1832-4, by Ibrahim Pasha of Egypt. At present, this city is included in the pashalic of Damascus, though it has a resident Turkish governor.

Jerusalem is situated on the central table-land of Judea, about 2,400 feet above the Mediterranean. It lies on ground which slopes gently down towards the east, the slope being terminated by an abrupt declivity, in some parts precipitous, and overhanging the valley of Jehoshaphat or of the Kidron. This sloping ground is also terminated on the south by the deep and narrow valley of Hinnom, which constituted the ancient southern boundary of the city, and which also ascends on its west side, and comes out upon the high ground on the north-west. See GIHON. But in the city itself, there were also two ravines or smaller valleys, dividing the land covered by buildings into three principal parts or hills. ZION, the highest of these, was in the south-west quarter of the city, skirted on the south and west by the deep valley of Hinnom. On its north and east sides lay the smaller valley "of the cheesemongers," or Tyropœon, opening on the south-east into the valley of the Kidron. The Tyropœon also united, near the north-east foot of Zion, with a valley coming down from the north. Zion was also called, The city of David; and by Josephus, "the upper city." Surrounded anciently by walls as well as deep valleys, it was the strongest part of the city, and contained the citadel and the king's palace. The Tyropœon separated it from Acra on the north, and Moriah on the north-east. ACRA was less elevated than Zion, or than the ground to the north-west beyond the walls. It is called by Josephus "the lower city." MORIAH, the sacred hill, lay north-east of Zion, with which it was anciently connected at its nearest corner, by a bridge over the Tyropœon, some remnants of which have been identified by Dr. Robinson. Moriah was at first a small eminence, but its area was greatly enlarged to make room for the temple. It was but a part of the continuous ridge on the east side of the city, overlooking the deep valley of the Kidron; rising on the north, after a slight depression, into the hill Bezetha, the "new city" of Josephus, and sinking away on the south into the hill Ophel. On the east of Jerusalem, and stretching from north to south, lies the mount of Olives, divided from the city by the valley of the Kidron, and commanding a noble prospect of the city and surrounding country. Over against Moriah, or a little further north, lies the garden of Gethsemane, with its olive-trees, at the foot of the mount of Olives. Just below the city, on the east side of the valley of the Kidron, lies the miserable village of Siloa; farther down, this valley unites with that of Hinnom, at a beautiful spot anciently "the king's gardens;" still below, is the well of Nehemiah, anciently En-rogel; and from this spot the united valley winds among mountains southward and eastward to the Dead sea. In the mouth of the Tyropœon, between Ophel and Zion, is the pool of Siloam. In the valley west and north-west of Zion are the two pools of Gihon, the lower being now broken and dry. In the rocks around Jerusalem, and chiefly in the sides of the valleys of the Kidron and Hinnom opposite the city, are many excavated tombs and caves.

Of the WALLS of ancient Jerusalem, the most ancient, that of David and Solomon, encircled the whole of mount Zion, and was also continued around Moriah and Ophel. The depth of the valleys south and east of Jerusalem, rendered it comparatively easy to fortify and defend it on these sides. This southern wall, in the period of the kings and of Christ, traversed the outmost verge of those hills, inclosing the pool of Siloam, Ophel, and portions apparently of the valleys of Hinnom and the Kidron, 2 Chr. 33:14; Neh. 2:14; 3:15.

A second wall, built by Jotham, Hezekiah, and Manasseh, made some changes on the southern line, and inclosed a large additional space on the north. It commenced somewhat east of the tower of Hippicus, on the north-west border of Zion, included Acra and part of Bezetha, and united with the old wall on the east. This wall was destroyed, as well as the first, at the captivity, but both were afterwards reerected, it is believed, on nearly the same lines, and were substantially the same at the time of Christ. The precise course of the second wall

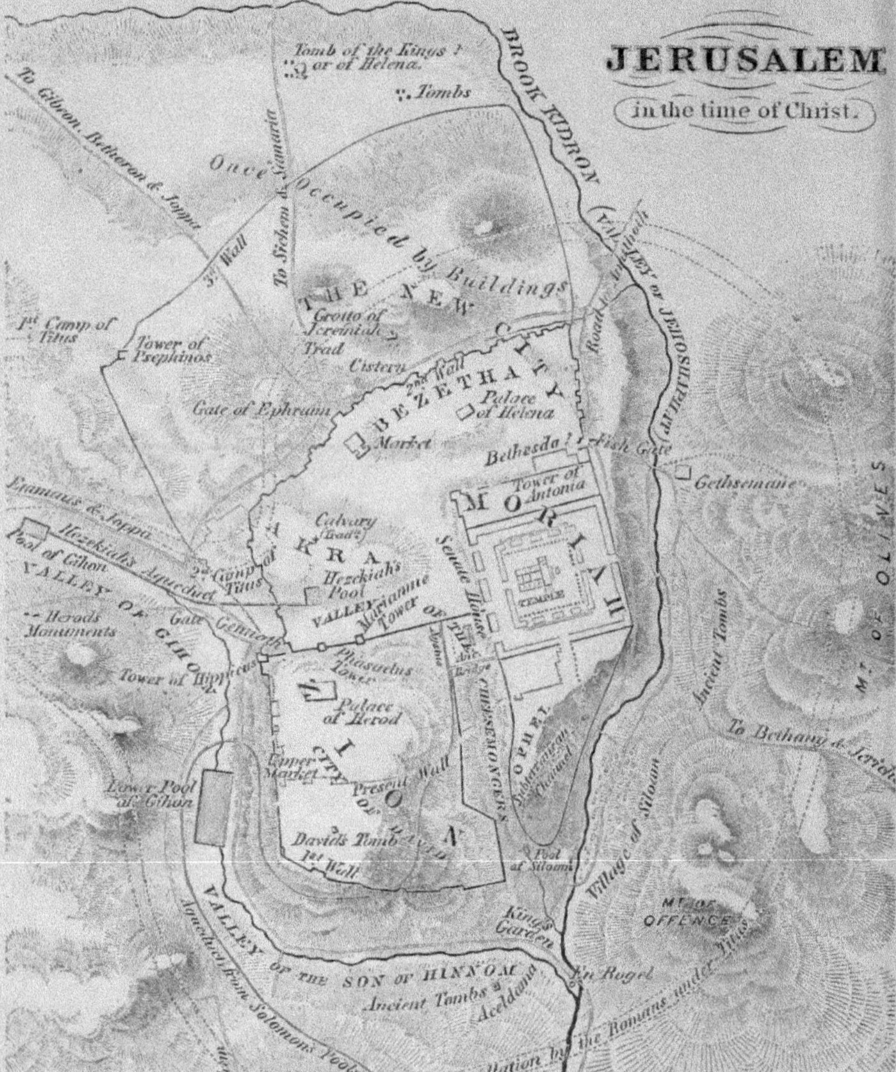

may perhaps be ascertained by future excavations, but is now more disputed than any other point of the topography of Jerusalem. To ascertain the exact location of "the tower Gennath," where this wall began, and trace its course "in a circuit" to Antonia, would show whether the traditional site of Calvary, now far within the city limits, lay within or without the ancient wall. The arguments from topography are strongly against the tradition; and it would seem that this whole region, if not actually within the wall, must have been at least occupied by the city suburbs at that time; for

The third wall, commenced by Herod Agrippa only ten years after the crucifixion of Christ, ran from the tower Hippicus nearly half a mile north-west to the tower of Psephinos, and sweeping round by the "tombs of the kings," passed down east of Bezetha, and joined the old eastern wall. The whole circumference of the city at that time was a little over four miles. Now it is only two and three quarters at the most; and the large space on the north, which the wall of Agrippa inclosed, is proved to have been built upon by the numerous cisterns which yet remain, and the marble fragments which the plough often turns up.

The preceding plan of ancient Jerusalem exhibits the walls, gates, towers, and other prominent objects in and around the city, with as much accuracy as can be secured, now that it has borne the ravages of so many centuries, been nearly a score of times captured, and often razed to the ground. Fuller descriptions of many of the localities referred to may be found under their respective heads.

JERUSALEM FROM THE BETHANY ROAD, ON THE SOUTH PART OF MOUNT OLIVET.

Modern Jerusalem, called by the Arabs El-Kuds, the holy, occupies unquestionably the site of the Jerusalem of the Bible. It is still "beautiful for situation," and stands forth on its well-defined hills "as a city that is compact together," Psa. 48 : 2, 12 ; 122 : 3, 4 ; 125:1, 2. The distant view of its stately walls and numerous domes and minarets is highly imposing. But its old glory has departed ; its thronging myriads are no more ; desolation covers the barren mountains around it, and the tribes go up to the house of the Lord no longer. She that once sat as a queen among them, now sitteth solitary, "trodden down of the Gentiles," "reft of her sons, and mid her foes forlorn." "Zion is ploughed as a field," and the soil is mixed with the rubbish of ages, to the depth in some places of forty feet.

The modern wall, built in 1542, varies from twenty to sixty feet in height, and is about two and a half miles in circuit. On the eastern and shortest side, its course is nearly straight ; and it coincides, in the southern half on this side, with the wall of the sacred area now called El-Haram, the holy. This area, 510 yards long from north to south, and 310 to 350 yards in breadth, is inclosed by high walls, the lower stones of which are in many parts very large, and much more ancient than the superstructure. It is occupied by the great octagonal mosque called Kubbet es-Sukhrah, or Dome of the Rock, and the mosque El-Aksa, with their grounds. It covers the site of the ancient temple and of the great tower Antonia. See Temple. At its south-east corner, where the wall is seventy-seven feet high, the ground at its base is one hundred and fifty feet above the dry bed of the Kidron. From this corner, the wall runs irregularly west by south, crosses mount Zion, leaving the greater part of it uninclosed on the south, and at its western verge turns north to the Jaffa gate, where the lower part of a very old and strong tower still remains. The upper part of this tower is less ancient and massive. It is known as "the Tower of David," and is generally thought to have been the Hippicus of Josephus. Thence the wall sweeps irregularly round to the north-east corner. It is flanked at unequal distances by square towers, and has battlements running all around on its summit, with loop-holes in them for arrows or muskets. There are now in use only four gates: the Jaffa or Bethlehem gate on the west, the Damascus gate on the north, St. Stephen's gate on the east, and Zion gate on the south. In the eastern wall of El-Haram is the Golden gate, long since blocked up, and in the city wall two smaller gates, more recently closed, namely, Herod's gate on the north-east, and Dung gate in the Tyropœon on the south.

Within the city walls are seen narrow and often covered streets, ungraded, ill-paved, and in some parts filthy, though less so than in most oriental cities. The houses are of hewn stone, with few windows towards the streets. Their flat roofs are strengthened and ornamented by many small domes. The most beautiful part of the city is the area of the great mosque—from which until recently all Christians have been rigorously excluded for six centuries—with its lawns and cypress-trees, and the noble dome rising high above the wall. On mount Zion, much of the space within the wall is occupied by the huge Armenian convent, with the Syrian convent, and the church of St. James. Beyond the wall and far to the south is a Mohammedan mosque, professedly over the tomb of David. This is more jealously guarded against Christians than even the mosque of Omar. Near it is the small cemetery of the American missionaries. At the north-west corner of Zion rises the high square citadel above referred to, ancient and grand. Still farther north is the Latin convent, in the most westerly part of Jerusalem; and between it and the centre of the city stands the church of the Holy Sepulchre, over the traditional scenes of the death and the resurrection of our Lord. See CALVARY. In various parts of the city the minarets of eight or ten mosques arise, amid an assemblage of about two thousand dwellings, not a few of which are much dilapidated.

The present population of Jerusalem may be about 12,000 souls, of whom about two-fifths are Mohammedans, and the remainder Jews and Christians in nearly equal numbers. There is also a considerable garrison, 800 to 1,000, stationed there; and in April of each year many thousands of pilgrims from foreign lands make a flying visit to the sacred places. The Moslemim reside in the centre of the city, and towards the north and east. The Jews' quarter is on the north-east side of Zion. The Greek, Latin, Armenian, Syrian, and Coptic Christians are located chiefly around their respective convents, and their burial-places are on mount Zion, as well as that of the American Protestant mission. The Jews bury on mount Olivet, and the Mohammedans in several places, though preferring the eastern brow of Moriah. Jerusalem is but the melancholy shadow of its former self. The nominal Christians residing there are in a state of degraded and ignorant subjection to the Mohammedans, and their petty discords and superstitions are a reproach to the Christian name. The Jews, 3,000 to 5,000 in number, are still more oppressed and abject. Most of them were born in other lands, and have come here to die, in a city no longer their own. Discouraged by endless exactions, they subsist on the charities of their brethren abroad. It is only as a purchased privilege that they are allowed to approach the foundations of the sacred hill where their fathers worshipped the only true God. Here, in a small area near some huge and ancient stones in the base of the western wall of Moriah, they gather, especially on sacred days, to sit weeping and wailing on the ground, taking up the heart-breaking lamentations of Jeremiah—living witnesses of the truth of God's word fulfilled in them. See WALL.

THE NEW JERUSALEM is a name given to the church of Christ, and signifying its firm foundations in the love, choice, and covenant of God; its strong bulwarks, living fountains, and beautiful palaces; its thronging thousands, its indwelling God, and its consummated glory in heaven, Gal. 4:26; Heb. 12:22; Rev. 3:12; 21.

JESH'UA, or JOSHUA, son of Josedech, was high-priest of the Jews at their return from the captivity, and acted well his part in the restoration of the city, the temple, and the divine worship, Ezra 4:3; 5:2. His name occurs in the prophecies of the time, Hag. 1:1; 2:2; Zech. 3; 6:11-15.

JESH'URUN, a poetical name of Israel, probably derived from a root meaning *to be upright*, and applied to the people of God as the objects of his justifying love, which does not "behold iniquity in Jacob," Deut. 32:5; 33:5, 26; Isa. 44:2.

JES'SE, son of Obed and father of David. He was a grandson of Ruth the Moabitess, and in her native land he found an asylum while David was most in danger from the jealous pursuit of Saul, Ruth 4:17; 1 Sam. 16; 17:12; 22:3; Matt. 1:5.

JE'SUS CHRIST, the Son of God, the Messiah and Saviour of the world, the first and principal object of the prophecies; who was prefigured and promised in the Old Testament; was expected and desired by the patriarchs; the hope and salvation of the Gentiles; the glory, happiness, and consolation of Christians. The name JESUS, in Hebrew JEHOSHUAH or Joshua, signifies *Saviour*, or *Jehovah saves*. No one ever bore this name with so much justice, nor so perfectly fulfilled the signification of it, as Jesus Christ, who saves from sin and hell, and has merited heaven for us by the price of his blood. It was given to him by divine appointment, Matt. 1:21, as the proper name for the Saviour so long desired, and whom all the myriads of the redeemed in heaven will for ever adore as their only and all-glorious Redeemer.

JESUS was the common name of the Saviour; while the name CHRIST, meaning The *Anointed* One, The Messiah, was his official name. Both names are used separately, in the gospels and also in the epistles; but JESUS generally stands by itself in the gospels, which are narratives of his life; while in the epistles, which treat of his divine nature and of his redeeming work, he is called CHRIST, CHRIST JESUS, or THE LORD JESUS CHRIST. See CHRIST.

Here, under the Redeemer's human name, belong the facts relating to his human nature and the history of his life upon earth. His true and complete humanity, having the soul as well as the body of man, is everywhere seen in the gospel history. He who is "God over all, blessed for ever," was an Israelite "as concerning the flesh," Rom. 9:5, and took upon him our whole nature, in order to be a perfect Saviour. As a man, Jesus was the King of men. No words can describe that character in which such firmness and gentleness, such dignity and humility, such enthusiasm and calmness, such wisdom and simplicity, such holiness and charity, such justice and mercy, such sympathy with heaven and with earth, such love to God and love to man blended in perfect harmony. Nothing in it was redundant, and nothing was wanting. The world had never produced, nor even conceived of such a character, and its portraiture in the gospels is a proof of their divine origin which the infidel cannot gainsay. Could the whole human race, of all ages, kindreds, and tongues, be assembled to see the crucified Redeemer as he is, and compare earth's noblest benefactors with Him, there would be but one voice among them. Every crown of glory and every meed of praise would be given to Him who alone is worthy—for perfection of character, for love to mankind, for sacrifices endured, and for benefits bestowed. His glory will for ever be celebrated as the Friend of man, the Lamb sacrificed for us.

The visit of JESUS CHRIST to the earth has made it for ever glorious above less favored worlds, and forms the most signal event in its annals. The time of his birth is commemorated by the Christian era, the first year of which corresponds to about the year 753 from the building of Rome. It is generally conceded, however, that the Saviour was born at least four years before A. D. 1, and four thousand years after the creation of Adam. His public ministry commenced when he was thirty years of age; and continued, according to the received opinion, three and a half years. Respecting his ancestors, see GENEALOGY.

The life of the Redeemer must be studied in the four gospels, where it was recorded under the guidance of supreme wisdom. Many efforts have been made, with valuable results, to arrange the narrations of the evangelists in the true order of time. But as neither of the gospels follows the exact course of events, many incidents are very indeterminate, and are variously arranged by different harmonists. No one, however, has been more successful than Dr. Robinson; and we borrow from his valuable "Harmony of the Gospels" the following elaborate table, presenting in a condensed form the various events of our Saviour's life, with the supposed place and period of their occurrence:

PART I.

EVENTS CONNECTED WITH THE BIRTH AND CHILDHOOD OF OUR LORD.

TIME: *About thirteen and a half years.*

An angel appears to Zacharias—*Jerusalem.*
An angel appears to Mary—*Nazareth.*
Mary visits Elisabeth—*Juttah.*
Birth of John the Baptist—*Juttah.*
An angel appears to Joseph—*Nazareth.*
The birth of Jesus—*Bethlehem.*
An angel appears to the shepherds—*Near Bethlehem.*
The circumcision of Jesus, and his presentation in the temple—*Bethlehem; Jerusalem.*
The Magi—*Jerusalem; Bethlehem.*
The flight into Egypt. Herod's cruelty. The return—*Bethlehem; Egypt; Nazareth.*
At twelve years of age Jesus goes to the Passover—*Jerusalem.*

PART II.

ANNOUNCEMENT AND INTRODUCTION OF OUR LORD'S PUBLIC MINISTRY.

TIME: *About one year.*

The ministry of John the Baptist—*The Desert; The Jordan.*
The baptism of Jesus—*The Jordan.*
The temptation—*Desert of Judea.*
Preface to John's gospel.
Testimony of John the Baptist to Jesus—*Bethany beyond Jordan.*
Jesus gains disciples—*The Jordan; Galilee?*
The marriage at Cana of Galilee.

PART III.

OUR LORD'S FIRST PASSOVER, AND THE SUBSEQUENT TRANSACTIONS UNTIL THE SECOND.

TIME: *One year.*

At the Passover Jesus drives the traders out of the temple—*Jerusalem.*
Our Lord's discourse with Nicodemus—*Jerusalem.*
Jesus remains in Judea and baptizes. Further testimony of John the Baptist.
Jesus departs into Galilee after John's imprisonment.
Our Lord's discourse with the Samaritan woman. Many of the Samaritans believe on him—*Shechem* or *Neapolis.*
Jesus teaches publicly in Galilee.
Jesus again at Cana, where he heals the son of a nobleman lying ill at Capernaum—*Cana of Galilee.*
Jesus at Nazareth; he is there rejected, and fixes his abode at Capernaum.
The call of Simon Peter and Andrew, and of James and John, with the miraculous draught of fishes—*Near Capernaum.*
The healing of a demoniac in the synagogue—*Capernaum.*
The healing of Peter's wife's mother, and many others—*Capernaum.*
Jesus with his disciples goes from Capernaum throughout Galilee.
The healing of a leper—*Galilee.*
The healing of a paralytic—*Capernaum.*
The call of Matthew—*Capernaum.*

PART IV.

OUR LORD'S SECOND PASSOVER, AND THE SUBSEQUENT TRANSACTIONS UNTIL THE THIRD.

TIME: *One year.*

The pool of Bethesda; the healing of the infirm man; and our Lord's subsequent discourse—*Jerusalem.*
The disciples pluck ears of grain on the Sabbath—*On the way to Galilee.*
The healing of the withered hand on the Sabbath—*Galilee.*
Jesus arrives at the sea of Tiberias, and is followed by multitudes—*Lake of Galilee.*
Jesus withdraws to a mountain, and chooses the twelve; the multitudes follow him—*Near Capernaum.*
The sermon on the mount—*Near Capernaum.*
The healing of the centurion's servant—*Capernaum.*
The raising of the widow's son—*Nain.*
John the Baptist in prison sends disciples to Jesus—*Galilee; Capernaum?*
Reflections of Jesus on appealing to his mighty works—*Capernaum?*
While sitting at meat with a Pharisee, Jesus is anointed by a woman who had been a sinner—*Capernaum?*
Jesus, with the twelve, makes a second circuit in Galilee.
The healing of a demoniac. The scribes and Pharisees blaspheme—*Galilee.*
The scribes and Pharisees seek a sign. Our Lord's reflections—*Galilee.*
The true disciples of Christ his nearest relatives—*Galilee.*
At a Pharisee's table, Jesus denounces woes against the Pharisees and others—*Galilee.*
Jesus discourses to his disciples and the multitude—*Galilee.*
The slaughter of certain Galileans. Parable of the barren fig-tree—*Galilee.*
Parable of the sower—*Lake of Galilee; Near Capernaum?*
Parable of the tares. Other Parables—*Near Capernaum?*
Jesus directs to cross the lake. Incidents. The tempest stilled—*Lake of Galilee.*
The two demoniacs of Gadara—*South-east coast of the lake of Galilee.*
Levi's feast—*Capernaum.*
The raising of Jairus' daughter. The woman with a bloody flux—*Capernaum.*
Two blind men healed, and a dumb spirit cast out—*Capernaum?*
Jesus again at Nazareth, and again rejected.
A third circuit in Galilee. The twelve instructed and sent forth—*Galilee.*
Herod holds Jesus to be John the Baptist, whom he had just before beheaded—*Galilee? Perea.*

The twelve return, and Jesus retires with them across the lake. Five thousand are fed—*Capernaum; North-east coast of the lake of Galilee.*

Jesus walks upon the water—*Lake of Galilee; Gennesaret.*

Our Lord's discourse to the multitude in the synagogue—*At Capernaum.*

PART V.

FROM OUR LORD'S THIRD PASSOVER UNTIL HIS FINAL DEPARTURE FROM GALILEE AT THE FESTIVAL OF TABERNACLES.

TIME: *Six months.*

Our Lord justifies his disciples for eating with unwashed hands. Pharisaic traditions—*Capernaum.*

The daughter of a Syro Phœnician woman is healed—*Region of Tyre and Sidon.*

A deaf and dumb man healed; also many others. Four thousand are fed—*The Decapolis.*

The Pharisees and Sadducees again require a sign—*Near Magdala, on the west side of the lake.*

The disciples cautioned against the leaven of the Pharisees, etc.—*North-east coast of the lake of Galilee.*

A blind man healed—*Bethsaida (Julias.)*

Peter and the rest again profess their faith in Christ—*Region of Cesarea Philippi.*

Our Lord foretells his own death and resurrection, and the trials of his followers—*Region of Cesarea Philippi.*

The transfiguration. Our Lord's subsequent discourse with the three disciples—*Region of Cesarea Philippi.*

The healing of a demoniac, whom the disciples could not heal—*Region of Cesarea Philippi.*

Jesus again foretells his own death and resurrection—*Galilee.*

The tribute-money miraculously provided—*Capernaum.*

The disciples contend who should be greatest. Jesus exhorts to humility, forbearance, and brotherly love—*Capernaum.*

The seventy instructed and sent out—*Capernaum.*

Jesus goes up to the festival of Tabernacles. His final departure from Galilee. Incidents in Samaria.

Ten lepers cleansed—*Samaria.*

PART VI.

THE FESTIVAL OF TABERNACLES, AND THE SUBSEQUENT TRANSACTIONS UNTIL OUR LORD'S ARRIVAL AT BETHANY, SIX DAYS BEFORE THE FOURTH PASSOVER.

TIME: *Six months, less one week.*

Jesus at the festival of Tabernacles. His public teaching—*Jerusalem.*

The woman taken in adultery—*Jerusalem.*

Further public teaching of our Lord. He reproves the unbelieving Jews, and escapes from their hands—*Jerusalem.*

A lawyer instructed. Love to our neighbor defined. Parable of the good Samaritan—*Near Jerusalem.*

Jesus in the house of Martha and Mary—*Bethany.*

The disciples again taught how to pray—*Near Jerusalem.*

The seventy return—*Jerusalem?*

A man born blind is healed on the Sabbath. Our Lord's subsequent discourses—*Jerusalem.*

Jesus in Jerusalem at the festival of Dedication. He retires beyond Jordan—*Jerusalem; Bethany beyond Jordan.*

The raising of Lazarus—*Bethany.*

The counsel of Caiaphas against Jesus. He retires from Jerusalem—*Jerusalem; Ephraim.*

Jesus beyond Jordan is followed by multitudes. The healing of the infirm woman on the Sabbath—*Valley of Jordan; Perea.*

Our Lord goes teaching and journeying towards Jerusalem. He is warned against Herod—*Perea.*

Our Lord dines with a chief Pharisee on the Sabbath. Incidents—*Perea.*

What is required of true disciples—*Perea.*

Parable of the lost sheep, etc. Parable of the prodigal son—*Perea.*

Parable of the unjust steward—*Perea.*

The Pharisees reproved. Parable of the rich man and Lazarus—*Perea.*

Jesus inculcates forbearance, faith, humility—*Perea.*

Christ's coming will be sudden—*Perea.*

Parables: The importunate widow. The Pharisee and publican—*Perea.*

Precepts respecting divorce—*Perea.*

Jesus receives and blesses little children—*Perea.*

The rich young man. Parable of the laborers in the vineyard—*Perea.*

Jesus a third time foretells his death and resurrection—*Perea.*

James and John prefer their ambitious request—*Perea.*

The healing of two blind men near Jericho.

The visit to Zaccheus. Parable of the ten minæ—*Jericho.*

Jesus arrives at Bethany six days before the Passover—*Bethany.*

PART VII.

OUR LORD'S PUBLIC ENTRY INTO JERUSALEM, AND THE SUBSEQUENT TRANSACTIONS BEFORE THE FOURTH PASSOVER.

TIME. *Five days.*

Our Lord's public entry into Jerusalem—*Bethany, Jerusalem.*

The barren fig-tree. The cleansing of the temple—*Bethany; Jerusalem*

The barren fig-tree withers away—*Between Bethany and Jerusalem.*

Christ's authority questioned. Parable of the two sons—*Jerusalem.*

Parable of the wicked husbandmen—*Jerusalem.*

Parable of the marriage of the king's son—*Jerusalem.*

Insidious question of the Pharisees: Tribute to Cæsar—*Jerusalem.*

Insidious question of the Sadducees: The resurrection—*Jerusalem.*

A lawyer questions Jesus. The two great commandments—*Jerusalem.*

How is Christ the son of David?—*Jerusalem.*

Warnings against the evil example of the scribes and Pharisees—*Jerusalem.*

Woes against the scribes and Pharisees. Lamentations over Jerusalem—*Jerusalem.*

The widow's mite—*Jerusalem.*

Certain Greeks desire to see Jesus—*Jerusalem.*

Reflections upon the unbelief of the Jews—*Jerusalem.*

Jesus, on taking leave of the temple, foretells its destruction and the persecution of his disciples—*Jerusalem; Mount of Olives.*

The signs of Christ's coming to destroy Jerusalem, and put an end to the Jewish state and dispensation—*Mount of Olives*

Transition to Christ's final coming at the day of judgment. Exhortation to watchfulness. Parables: The ten virgins. The five talents—*Mount of Olives.*

Scenes of the judgment-day—*Mount of Olives.*

The rulers conspire. The supper at Bethany. Treachery of Judas—*Jerusalem; Bethany.*

Preparation for the Passover—*Bethany; Jerusalem.*

PART VIII.

THE FOURTH PASSOVER; OUR LORD'S PASSION; AND THE ACCOMPANYING EVENTS UNTIL THE END OF THE JEWISH SABBATH.

TIME. *Two days.*

The Passover meal. Contention among the twelve—*Jerusalem.*

Jesus washes the feet of his disciples—*Jerusalem.*

Jesus points out the traitor. Judas withdraws—*Jerusalem.*

Jesus foretells the fall of Peter, and the dispersion of the twelve—*Jerusalem.*

The Lord's supper—*Jerusalem.*

Jesus comforts his disciples. The Holy Spirit promised—*Jerusalem.*

Christ the true Vine. His disciples hated by the world—*Jerusalem.*

Persecution foretold. Further promise of the Holy Spirit. Prayer in the name of Christ—*Jerusalem.*

Christ's last prayer with his disciples—*Jerusalem.*

The agony in Gethsemane—*Mount of Olives.*

Jesus betrayed, and made prisoner—*Mount of Olives.*

Jesus before Caiaphas. Peter thrice denies him—*Jerusalem.*

Jesus before Caiaphas and the Sanhedrim. He declares himself to be the Christ; is condemned and mocked—*Jerusalem.*

The Sanhedrim lead Jesus away to Pilate—*Jerusalem.*

Jesus before Herod—*Jerusalem.*

Pilate seeks to release Jesus. The Jews demand Barabbas—*Jerusalem.*

Pilate delivers up Jesus to death. He is scourged and mocked—*Jerusalem.*

Pilate again seeks to release Jesus—*Jerusalem.*

Judas repents and hangs himself—*Jerusalem.*

Jesus is led away to be crucified—*Jerusalem.*

The crucifixion—*Jerusalem.*

The Jews mock at Jesus on the cross. He forgives the penitent thief. He commends his mother to John—*Jerusalem.*

Darkness prevails. Christ expires on the cross—*Jerusalem.*

The veil of the temple rent, and graves opened. Judgment of the centurion. The women at the cross—*Jerusalem.*

The taking down from the cross. The burial—*Jerusalem.*

The watch at the sepulchre—*Jerusalem.*

PART IX.

OUR LORD'S RESURRECTION, HIS SUBSEQUENT APPEARANCES, AND HIS ASCENSION.

TIME: *Forty days.*

The morning of the resurrection—*Jerusalem.*

Visit of the women to the sepulchre. Mary Magdalene returns—*Jerusalem.*

Vision of angels in the sepulchre—*Jerusalem.*

The women return to the city. Jesus meets them—*Jerusalem.*

Peter and John run to the sepulchre—*Jerusalem.*

Our Lord is seen by Mary Magdalene at the sepulchre—*Jerusalem.*

Report of the watch—*Jerusalem.*

Our Lord is seen of Peter. Then by two disciples on the way to Emmaus—*Jerusalem; Emmaus.*

Jesus appears in the midst of the apostles, Thomas being absent—*Jerusalem.*

Jesus appears in the midst of the apostles, Thomas being present—*Jerusalem.*

The apostles go away into Galilee. Jesus shows himself to seven of them at the sea of Tiberias—*Galilee.*

Jesus meets the apostles and above five hundred brethren on a mountain in Galilee—*Galilee.*

Our Lord is seen of James; then of all the apostles—*Jerusalem.*

The ascension—*Near Bethany.*

The divine wisdom is conspicuous not only in what is taught us respecting the life of Jesus, but in what is withheld. Curiosity, and the higher motives of warm affection, raise numerous questions to which the gospels give no reply; and in proportion as men resort to dubious traditions, they lose the power of a pure and spiritual gospel. See further, concerning Christ, MESSIAH, REDEEMER, etc.

JESUS was not an uncommon name among the Jews. It was the name of the father of Elymas the sorcerer, Acts 13:6; and of Justus, a fellow-laborer and friend of Paul, Col. 4:11. It is the Greek form of the Hebrew name Joshua, or Jeshua, borne by the high-priest in Ezra's time, and by the well-known leader of the Jews into the promised land. See also 1 Sam. 6:14; 2 Kin. 23:8. The Greek form of the word, Jesus, is twice used in the New Testament when Joshua the son of Nun is intended, Acts 7:45; Heb. 4:8.

JETH'RO, "Moses' father-in-law," a shepherd-prince or priest of Midian, Ex. 3:1; 4:18; 18. When the Hebrews were at mount Sinai, he visited Moses, gave him some wise counsel as to the government of the tribes, and then returned to his own people. See HOBAB and RAGUEL. Jethro was a worshipper of God, Ex. 18:10, 11, and some infer that he was a descendant of Abraham, through Midian, Gen. 25:2.

JEWS, the name borne by the Hebrews among foreign nations, especially after the return from Babylon; from Judah their ancestor. See HEBREWS.

JEZ'EBEL, daughter of Ethbaal king of Tyre and Zidon, and wife of Ahab king of Israel, 1 Kin. 16:31. She spent herself in efforts to establish idolatry in Samaria, and exterminate the worship of God and the lives of his servants. Obadiah saved a hundred of them, at the risk of his own life. Jezebel herself maintained four hundred priests of Astarte. When the prophets of Baal perished at Carmel, at the word of Elijah, she sought to avenge herself on him. Afterwards, she secured the vineyard of Naboth for her husband by perjuries and murder; and her tragical death, the fitting close of a bloody life, took place, according to the prediction of Elijah, near the scene of this crime, 1 Kin. 18; 19; 21; 2 Kin. 9. Her name has become a proverb, and is given by John, probably as a descriptive epithet, to a certain female at Thyatira in his day holding a like bad preëminence in station and profligacy, in malice and in ruin, Luke 20:18; Rev. 2:20.

JEZ'REEL, I., a celebrated city of Issachar, Josh. 19:18, lying westward of Bethshean, 2 Sam. 4:4. Ahab had here a palace; and this city became famous on account of his seizure of Naboth's vineyard, 1 Kin. 21; and the vengeance executed on Ahab, 2 Kin. 9:10, 14–37; 10:1–11. Jezreel was called Esdraela in the time of the Maccabees, and is now replaced by a small and ruinous Arab village, called Zerin, at the north-west point of mount Gilboa. Its elevated site gives one a fine view of the great plain of Esdraelon on the west, and the hills that border it; and towards the east it overhangs the wide and fertile "valley of Jezreel," Josh. 17:16, Judg. 6:33, Hos. 1:5, which runs down east-south-east from the great plain to the Jordan, between Gilboa and little Hermon. In this valley, below and east of Zerin, is the copious "fountain of Jezreel," near which Saul perished, 1 Sam. 29:1; 31:1.

II. The great plain lying between Jezreel and Acre, called from two cities on its border in one part, "the valley of *Megiddo*," 2 Chr. 35:22, and in its western part or branch the "plain or valley of *Jezreel*," afterwards Esdraelon, Judith 1:8. The body of this beautiful plain forms a triangle, rising gradually from the Mediterranean four hundred feet, and being about thirteen or fourteen miles long on the north side, seventeen on the east, and twenty on the south-west. The western part is level; on the east it is more undulating, and is at length broken by mount Gilboa and "little Hermon" into three valleys two or three miles wide, which sink down into the valley of the Jordan. Of these, the middle valley, described above, is the proper "valley of Jezreel." The river Kishon traverses this plain. It was formerly well watered and astonishingly fertile, but is now under the blight of tyranny and insecurity, comparatively uncultivated and deserted. The highways are unoccupied, the villages have ceased in Israel, Judg. 5:6. There are a few small hamlets, particularly on the higher grounds that border it; and the abundant crops which it yields, even with poor cultivation, show that it might again be made the granary of Syria. Across this plain, from Carmel to Jezreel, Elijah ran before the chariot of Ahab, 1 Kin. 18:46. It has been the chosen battle-ground of many armies. Here the hosts of Sisera were swept away, Judg. 4; and here Josiah fell, fighting against Pharaoh-necho, 2 Kin. 23:29. Battles were fought here in the later periods of the Romans, and of the Crusaders; and in our own century, near mount Tabor, fifteen hundred French under General Kleber sustained the assault of twenty-five thousand Turks for half a day, and were succored by Napoleon.

JO'AB, son of Zeruiah, David's sister, and brother of Abishai and Asahel, was the commander of David's army during almost the whole of his reign, 2 Sam. 5:6–10. He was a valiant warrior, and an able general; and his great influence on public affairs was often exerted for good, as in the rebellion of Absalom, and the numbering of Israel, 2 Sam. 18; 19; 24. But as a man he was imperious, revengeful, and unscrupulous: witness his treacherous assassination of Abner, and of his cousin Amasa, 2 Sam. 3:27; 20:9, 10; his bearing towards David, 2 Sam. 3:39; 19:5, and connivance with him in the matter of Uriah; his slaying Absalom, and conspiring with Adonijah against the divinely appointed heir to the throne; for all which he was at length put to death by order of Solomon, 1 Kin. 2.

JOAN'NA, one of the faithful women who ministered to Christ while living, and brought spices to his tomb. Her husband Chuza was a steward of Herod Antipas, Luke 8:3; 24:1–10.

JO'ASH, or JEHO'ASH, I., the father of Gideon, of the family of Abiezer, in Manasseh. For a long time he was a worshipper of Baal; but when his son boldly attacked idolatry, he also came out on the Lord's side, Judg. 6:11, 25–32.

II. An officer, appointed as keeper of the prophet Micaiah, during Ahab's disastrous war with Syria, 1 Kin. 22:26; 2 Chr. 18.

III. The eighth king of Judah, B. C. 878-838. He was the only son of Ahaziah who was not slain by the usurping Athaliah, his grandmother. Being rescued by Jehoshebah his aunt, and secluded six years in the temple, he was raised to the throne when seven years of age through the faithful care of Jehoiada; and while this venerable man survived, Joash served God and prospered. Idols were banished, and the temple was repaired. But afterwards he followed less wholesome counsels; idolatry revived; and when Zechariah the high-priest rebuked the guilty people, the ungrateful king caused this servant of God, the son of his benefactor, to be stoned to death. Misfortunes soon multiplied on his head; he was repeatedly humbled by the Syrians, and gave them the temple treasures as a ransom; a loathsome disease imbittered his life, which was very soon cut short by a conspiracy of his servants, and he was not buried in the sepulchre of the kings, 2 Kin. 11; 12; 2 Chr. 23; 24. The prophet Joel was contemporary with him.

IV. The son and successor of Jehoahaz, king of Israel, B. C. 840-825. There was much in his conduct to commend. He had a great regard for the prophet Elisha, and visited him on his deathbed, where by a divine oracle he was assured of three victories over the Syrians. He was also victorious when forced to give battle to Amaziah king of Judah, and was one of the best of the kings of Israel. The worship of the golden calf, however, still continued during his reign, 2 Kin. 13:9-25; 14:1-8; 2 Chr. 25.

JOB, a patriarch distinguished for his integrity and piety, his wealth, honors, and domestic happiness, whom God permitted, for the trial of his faith, to be deprived of friends, property, and health, and at once plunged into deep affliction. He lived in the land of Uz, lying, it is generally thought, in Eastern Edom, probably not far from Bozrah.

The BOOK OF JOB has originated much criticism, and on many points a considerable diversity of opinion still exists. Sceptics have denied its inspiration, and called it a mere philosophical romance; but no one who respects revelation can entertain this notion, or doubt that Job was a real person. Inspired writers testify to both. See Ezek. 14:14, James 5:11; and compare 1 Cor. 3:19 with Job 5:13. The book itself specifies persons, places, and circumstances in the manner of true history. Moreover, the name and history of Job are spread throughout the East; Arabian writers mention him, and many Mohammedan families perpetuate his name. Five different places claim the possession of his tomb.

The precise period of his life cannot be ascertained, yet no doubt can exist as to its patriarchal antiquity. The book seems to allude to the flood, Job 22:15-17, but not to the destruction of Sodom, to the exodus from Egypt, or the giving of the Law. No reference is made to any order of priesthood, Job himself being the priest of his household, like Noah and Abraham. There is allusion to the most ancient form of idolatry, star-worship, and to the earliest mode of writing, 19:24. The longevity of Job also places him among the patriarchs. He survived his trial one hundred and forty years, and was an old man before his trial began, for his children were established each at the head of his own household, Job 1:4; 42:16. The period of long lives had not wholly passed away, 15:10. Hales places the trial of Job before the birth of Abraham, and Usher, about thirty years before the exodus, B. C. 1521.

As to the authorship of the book, many opinions have been held. It has all the freedom of an original composition, bearing no marks of its being a translation; and if so, it would appear that its author must have been a Hebrew, since it is written in the purest Hebrew. It exhibits, moreover, the most intimate acquaintance with both Egyptian and Arabian scenery, and is in the loftiest style of oriental poetry. All these circumstances are consistent with the views of those who regard Moses as its probable author. It has, however, been ascribed to various other persons. It presents a beautiful exhibition of patriarchal religion. It teaches the being and perfections of God, his creation of all things, and his universal providence; the apostasy and guilt of evil spirits and of mankind; the mercy of God, on the basis of a sacrifice, and on condition of repentance and faith, 33:27-30; 42:6, 8; the immortality of the soul, and the resurrection of the body, 14:7-15; 19:25-27.

The main problem discussed in Job is, the justice of God in suffering the righteous to be afflicted, while the wicked prosper. It is settled, by showing that, while the hand of a just God is manifest in his providential government of human affairs, it is his sovereign right to choose his own time and mode of retribution both to the evil and the good, and to subject the graces of his people to whatever trials he deems best.

The conference of Job and his friends may be divided into three parts. In the first, Eliphaz addresses Job, and Job replies; then Bildad and Job, and Zophar and Job, speak in turn. In the second part, the same order is observed; and in the third also, except that after Job's reply to Bildad, the three friends have no more to urge, and instead of Zophar, a fourth friend named Elihu takes up the word; and the whole is concluded by the decision of Jehovah himself. The friends of Job argue that his remarkable afflictions must have been sent in punishment of highly aggravated transgressions, and urge him to confession and repentance. The pious patriarch, conscious of his own integrity and love to God, cast down and bewildered by his sore chastisements, and pained by the suspicions of his friends, warmly vindicates his innocence, and shows that the best of men are sometimes the most afflicted; but forgets that his inward sins merit far heavier punishment, and though he still maintains faith in God, yet he charges Him foolishly. Afterwards he humbly confesses his wrong, and is cheered by the returning smile of God, while his uncharitable friends are reproved. The whole book is written in the highest style of Hebrew poetry, except the two introductory chapters and part of the last, which are prose. As a poem, it is full of sublime sentiments and bold and striking images.

The DISEASE of Job is generally supposed to have been the elephantiasis, or black leprosy. The word rendered "boils" does not necessarily mean abscesses, but burning and inflammation; and no known disease better answers to the description given, Job 2:7, 8; 7:5, 13, 14; 19:17; 30:17, than the leprosy referred to above. See LEPER.

JOCHEBED, wife of Amram, and mother of Moses, Aaron, and Miriam, Num. 26:59. She was a daughter of Levi, and her husband's aunt, Ex. 6:20, though such marriages were afterwards prohibited, Lev. 18:12.

JO'EL, one of the minor prophets, of whom nothing is known beyond the few hints furnished in his brief but valuable prophecy. He lived in the kingdom of Judah, and at a time when the temple and temple-worship still existed, Joel 1:14; 2:1, 15, 32; 3:1. Different authors assign to his prophecy different dates, but the prevailing opinion is that he prophesied in the reign of Uzziah, nearly 800 B. C.

The BOOK OF JOEL opens with a most graphic and powerful description of the devastation caused by swarms of divers kinds of locusts, accompanied by a terrible drought. The plague of locusts, one of the most dreadful scourges of the East, (see LOCUSTS,) is highly suggestive of an invasion of hostile legions such as have often ravaged Judea; and many have understood, by the locusts of Joel, the Chaldeans, Persians, Greeks, or Romans. The prophet, however, adheres to his figure, if it be one; depicts the land as stripped of its verdure and parched with drought, summons the stricken people to fasting and penitence, and encourages them by promising the removal of the divine judgments and the return of fertility. While describing this returning plenty and prosperity, the prophet casts his view forward on a future still more remote, and predicts the outpouring of the Holy Spirit, and the signs and wonders and spiritual prosperity of the Messiah's reign, Joel 2:28. This passage is quoted by the apostle Peter, in Acts 2:16. The style of Joel is exceedingly poetical and elegant; his descriptions are vivid and sublime, and his prophecy ranks among the gems of Hebrew poetry. It is well fitted to cheer the church militant in all ages.

JOHAN'AN, son of Kareah, a leading

captain of the Jews after the destruction of Jerusalem, B. C. 588, who recognized the authority of Gedaliah, warned him in vain of the plot of Ishmael, and avenged his murder; but afterwards carried the remnant of the people to Egypt against the remonstrances of Jeremiah, who, unable to check his rebellious and idolatrous course, foretold divine judgments, which in due time were fulfilled, 2 Kin. 25:23–26; Jer. 40–44.

JOHN, I., THE BAPTIST, the forerunner of our Lord Jesus Christ, was the son of Zacharias and Elisabeth, and was born about six months before Christ, as Reland and Robinson suppose at Juttah, Josh. 21:16, Luke 1:39, a town some five miles south of Hebron, but according to tradition at a place about four miles west of Jerusalem. Several Old Testament predictions found their fulfilment in him. See Isa. 40:3, and Matt. 3:3; also Mal. 3:1; 4:5, and Matt. 11:14. His birth, name, and office were also foretold by the angel Gabriel to his father Zacharias while ministering at the temple altar. Several other supernatural incidents attended the visit of Mary to Elisabeth, and the birth and naming of John, Luke 1. He passed his early life among the crags of Eastern Judea, and when not far from thirty years of age, appeared as a prophet of the Lord. Being also a priest by birth, and an austere Nazarite in appearance and mode of life, he was like a reproduction of Elijah of old. Crowds flocked from all quarters to hear the word of God from his lips boldly denouncing their sins, and to receive the baptism of repentance preparatory to the full revelation of grace in Christ. Among others, the Saviour at length came, and was baptized as an example of obedience to all divine enjoinments. John was at once satisfied that Jesus was the Messiah, but "knew him not" by any divine intimation till he saw the appointed sign, the descending Spirit. He then stood forth as the representative of "all the law and the prophets," pointing the world to Christ as an atoning Saviour, and thus introduced Him to His public ministry: "Behold the Lamb of God, which taketh away the sin of the world," John 1:29; Gal. 3:24.

John enjoyed at this time a high degree of popular veneration, Luke 3:15; the Sanhedrim sent a deputation to question him, John 1:19–28; king Herod "did many things, and heard him gladly." But he laid all he had at the Saviour's feet, John 1:27; 3:33. We read several times of his "disciples," Matt. 9:14; Luke 5:33; John 3:23–15; 4:1; and meet with subsequent traces of the wide extent of his influence, Acts 18:25; 19:3. We know not why he continued for a time his separate ministry, instead of attending Christ. He persevered, however, in his faithful labors for reformation; and these, in the second year afterwards, led to his imprisonment by Herod Antipas. See HEROD III. It was while in prison that he sent two of his disciples to Christ to inquire, "Art thou he that should come, or do we look for another?" Matt. 11:3. He may have been moved to send this message by some lingering Jewish views as to a temporal Messiah, who would right all their national wrongs, or by some temporary unbelieving haste to have Christ publicly announce his Messiahship. It was on this occasion that Christ calls him greater than any other prophet; because, of all the prophets of the Messiah, he alone saw Him entering on his work whom all "desired to see;" yet he was less than the "least in the kingdom of God," inasmuch as he died without seeing that kingdom established in the death and resurrection of his Lord. But his earthly work was soon done. Herod, according to Josephus, feared his great influence over the people, and Herodias dreaded his bold fidelity to her husband. The dancing of her daughter Salome, and the vow of the besotted king, furnished a pretext. John was beheaded in prison; his disciples buried his remains with honor, and "went and told Jesus," Matt. 14:3–12.

II. THE APOSTLE AND EVANGELIST, son of Zebedee and Salome, was a native of Bethsaida in Galilee. Zebedee and his sons were fishermen, and appear to have been in easy circumstances, Mark 1:20; 15:40; John 18:15; 19:27. In John's character there was an admirable mixture of gentleness and force. The picture the Bible gives of him has a peculiar charm, so much peace, humility, charity, and brotherly love glow in it. His affectionate, meditative, spiritual character had also the elements of vigor and decision, Luke 9:54. Though amiable, he was firm and fearless. He was present at the scene of the Saviour's crucifixion, which he describes as an eye-witness, John 19:35. He was early at the tomb of the Redeemer, and after his ascension, boldly proclaimed the gospel at Jerusalem, Acts 4:13, though imprisoned, scourged, and threatened with death. He was remarkable for devotion to Christ; and it was this, perhaps, as much as ambition, or false views of Christ's kingdom, that led him to request a place at His right hand, Matt. 20:20-24. He is supposed to have been the youngest of the apostles. He had been a disciple of John the Baptist; but on being directed to Christ, at once attached himself to him. For a time he returned to his employment by the sea of Galilee, but was soon called to leave all and attend the Saviour, Luke 5:5-10. Christ had a particular friendship for this lovely and zealous disciple, John 13:23; 19:26; 20:2; 21:7. At the last supper, he reclined next to the Saviour, and to his care the dying Redeemer committed his mother. Together with Peter and James he witnessed the transfiguration, and the agony in the garden. See JAMES. After the ascension of our Lord, John continued to reside at Jerusalem, where he was one of the chief pillars of the church, Gal. 2:9. About A. D. 65, it is thought, he removed to Ephesus, and labored to diffuse the gospel in Asia Minor, where for many years after the death of Paul his great personal and apostolic influence was widely exerted. About A. D. 95, he was banished, probably by Domitian, to the isle of Patmos, where he had the visions described in the Apocalypse. He afterwards returned to Ephesus, where he lived to a very great age, so that he could scarcely go to the assembly of the church without being carried by his disciples. Being now unable to make long discourses, his custom was to say in all assemblies, "Little children, love one another;" and when they wondered at his frequent repetition of this concise exhortation, his answer was, "This is what the Lord commands you; and this, if you do it, is sufficient." Chrysostom, Clement, and Eusebius relate that on his return from Patmos he found that a young man of promise under his charge had been misled, and had joined a band of robbers; and that the aged apostle sought him out in his mountain haunts, and by the blessing of God on his fearless and faithful love, reclaimed his soul from death. He died at Ephesus, in the third year of Trajan, A. D. 100, being then, according to Epiphanius, ninety-four years of age. He was buried near that city, and several of the fathers mention his sepulchre as being there.

Besides the invaluable gospel and the Apocalypse, which bear his name, we have three EPISTLES OF JOHN. The first is a catholic or general letter, designed apparently to go with his gospel, and refute certain Gnostic errors as to the person of Christ; but also and chiefly to build up the church universal in truth and grace, and especially in holy love. The second epistle is addressed "to the elect lady," or the excellent Kuria, who was probably some Christian woman eminent for piety and usefulness. The third is directed to Gaius, the Latin Caius, whom John praises for his fidelity and hospitality, and exhorts to persevere in every good work. The Revelation and epistles of John, it is generally believed, were written about 96-98 A. D. They are the latest books of the New Testament canon, which, as the last surviving apostle, he must have greatly aided in settling.

III. Surnamed MARK. See MARK.

JOK'SHAN, the second son of Abraham and Keturah, ancestor of the Sabeans and Dedanites of Southern Arabia, Gen. 25:1-3.

JOK'TAN, son of Eber, and by him connected with the Hebrews and other Shemite families, Gen. 10.25-30; 1 Chr. 1:19-23. He is believed to be the Kahtan, or Yektan, to whom Arabian writers trace their purest and most ancient genealogies.

JOK'-THEEL, I., a city of Judah, Josh. 15:38.

II. The name given by Amaziah to the capital of Arabia Petræa, 2 Kin. 14:7. See SELA.

JON'ADAB, I., a son of Shimeah, the cunning and unprincipled nephew of David, and friend of Amnon, 2 Sam. 13:3-5. Yet he seems to have been long aware of the purpose of Absalom to avenge his sister's dishonor upon Amnon, and very coolly excused the assassination of his friend, ver. 32-35.

II. A son of Rechab, a Kenite, descended from Hobab the brother of Moses. He was at the head of the Rechabites in the time of Jehu, and seems to have given them a command to abstain from wine, 2 Kin. 10:15; 1 Chr. 2:55; Jer. 35:6-10. See RECHABITES.

JO'NAH, one of the minor prophets, was a native of Gath-hepher, in Zebulun, 2 Kin. 14:25. Being ordered of God to prophesy against Nineveh, probably in or before the reign of Jeroboam II., which begun 825 B. C., he endeavored to avoid the command by embarking at Joppa for Tarshish, in order to fly as far as possible in the opposite direction. But being overtaken by a storm, he was thrown overboard at his own request, and miraculously preserved by being swallowed by a large fish. See WHALE. Several Greek and Roman legends seem to have been borrowed from this source. After three days, typical of our Saviour's stay in the tomb, the fish cast Jonah out upon the shore; the word of the Lord a second time directed him to go to Nineveh, and he obeyed. The allusions of the narrative to the vast extent and population of this city, are confirmed by other ancient accounts and by modern investigations. See NINEVEH. At the warning word of the prophet, the Ninevites repented, and the destruction threatened was postponed; but the feelings of Jonah at seeing his predictions unfulfilled and the enemies of God's people spared, rendered necessary a further exercise of the forbearance of God. See GOURD.

The literal truth of the narrative is established by our Saviour's repeated quotations, Matt. 12:39-41; 16:4; Luke 11:29-32. It is highly instructive, as showing that the providential government of God extends to all heathen nations, and that his grace has never been confined to his covenant people.

JON'ATHAN, I., a Levite, son of Gershom, and grandson of Moses, who after the death of Joshua impiously served as a priest, first to Micah, and then to the Danites in Laish or Dan, where his posterity succeeded him until the captivity, Judg. 17; 18.

II. The eldest son of Saul, and one of the loveliest characters in Old Testament history. The narrative of his brilliant exploit in Michmash, 1 Sam. 13 and 14, illustrates his pious faith, his bravery, (see also 1 Sam. 13:3,) and the favor borne him by the people, who would not suffer him to be put to death in consequence of Saul's foolish vow. This valiant and generous prince loved David as his own soul, 1 Sam. 18:1-4; 19:2; 20; and though convinced that his friend was chosen of God for the throne, nobly yielded his own pretensions, and reconciled fidelity to his father with the most pure and disinterested friendship for David. He perished with his father, in battle with the Philistines at mount Gilboa; and nothing can surpass the beauty and pathos of the elegy in which David laments his friend, 2 Sam. 1, whose son Mephibosheth he afterwards sought out and befriended, 2 Sam. 9.

JOP'PA, Hebrew JAPHO, is one of the most ancient seaports in the world. It was a border town of the tribe of Dan, Josh. 19:46, on the coast of the Mediterranean sea, thirty miles south of Cæsarea, and about thirty-five north-west of Jerusalem. Its harbor is shoal and unprotected from the winds; but on account of its convenience to Jerusalem, it became the principal port of Judea, and is still the great landing-place of pilgrims. Here the materials for building both the first and the second temple, sent from Lebanon and Tyre, were landed, 2 Chr. 3:16; Ezra 3:7. Here Jonah embarked for Tarshish. Here, too, Peter raised Dorcas from the dead; and in the house of Simon the tanner, by the seaside, was taught by a heavenly vision that salvation was for Gentiles as well as Jews, Acts 9-11. Joppa was twice destroyed by the Romans. It was the seat of a Christian church for some centuries after Constantine. During the crusades it several times changed hands; and in modern times, 1799, it was stormed and sacked by the French, and twelve hundred Turkish prisoners, said to have broken their parole, were put to death.

The present town of Jaffa, or Yâfa, is situated on a promontory jutting out into the sea, rising to the height of about one hundred and fifty feet, crowned with a fortress, and offering on all sides picturesque and varied prospects. Towards the west is extended the open sea; towards the south are spread the fertile plains of Philistia, reaching as far as Gaza; towards the north, as far as Carmel, the flowery meads of Sharon present themselves; and to the east, the hills of Ephraim and Judah raise their towering heads. The town is walled round on the south and east, towards the land, and partially so on the north

YAFA, THE MODERN JOPPA, FROM THE NORTH.

and west, towards the sea. Its environs, away from the sand-hills of the shore, are full of gardens and orchards. From the sea, the town looks like a heap of buildings, crowded as closely as possible into a given space; and from the steepness of its site, they appear in some places to stand one on the other. The streets are very narrow, uneven, and dirty, and might rather be called alleys. The inhabitants are estimated at about fifteen thousand, of whom more than half are Turks and Arabs. There are several mosques; and the Latins, Greeks, and Armenians have each a church, and a small convent for the reception of pilgrims.

JO'RAM, or JEHO'RAM, I., son of Ahab king of Israel, succeeded his older brother Ahaziah in the throne, B. C. 896, and reigned twelve years. He discontinued the worship of Baal, but followed the "sin of Jeroboam." During his reign, the Moabites revolted. Joram secured the aid of Jehoshaphat king of Judah, and after receiving for his allies' sake a miraculous deliverance from drought, defeated the Moabites with great slaughter. Not long after he was involved in war with Ben-hadad king of Syria, and Hazael his successor; and in this time occurred the miraculous deliverance of Samaria from siege and famine, and also various miracles of Elisha, including the healing of Naaman. Joram was wounded in a battle with Hazael, and met his death, in the suburbs of Ramoth-gilead, by the hand of Jehu his general. His body was thrown into the field of Naboth at Jezreel, and with him perished the race of Ahab, 1 Kin. 21:18-29; 2 Kin. 1:17; 3:1; 6:9

II. The son and successor of Jehoshaphat king of Judah. He reigned with his father, from B. C. 889, four years, and four years alone; in all eight years. Unhappily he was married to Athaliah, daughter of Ahab and Jezebel, whose evil influence did much to render his reign a curse to the land. He slew his own brothers, five in number, and seized their possessions. He also introduced Phœnician idols and their worship into Judah. The divine wrath was shown in leaving him unaided under a successful revolt of the Edomites, and repeated invasions of the Philistines and Arabians. His country, the city, and his own household were ravaged, his body was afflicted with a frightful dysenteric illness, and after death a burial in the royal sepulchres was denied him, 2 Kin. 8:16-24; 2 Chr. 21.

JOR'DAN, the chief river of Palestine, running from north to south, and dividing the Holy Land into two parts, of which the larger and more important lay on the west. There are two small streams, each of which claims to be its source. One of these, near Banias, anciently Cæsarea Philippi, issues from a large cave in a rocky mountain side, and flows several miles towards the southwest, where it is joined by the second and larger stream, which originates in a fountain at Tell-el-Kady, three miles west of Banias. But besides these, there is a third and longer stream, which rises beyond the northern limit of Palestine, near Hasbeia on the west side of mount Hermon, flows twenty-four miles to the south, and unites with the other streams before they enter the "waters of Merom," now lake Huleh. This marshy lake, when full, is about seven miles long, and receives several other but smaller streams, chiefly from the west. See MEROM. Issuing from lake Huleh, the Jordan flows about nine miles southward to the sea of Tiberias, through which its clear and smooth course may be traced twelve miles to the lower end. Hence it pursues its sinuous way to the south, till its pure waters are lost in the bitter sea of Sodom.

Between these two seas, that of Tiberias and the Dead sea, lies the great valley or plain of the Jordan, 2 Kin. 25:4; 2 Chr. 4:17. It is called by the Arabs El-Ghor. Its average width is about five miles, but near Jericho it is twelve or fifteen miles. It is terminated on both sides, through its whole length, by hills, which rise abruptly on the western border 1,000 or 1,200 feet high, and more gradually on the east, but twice as high. This valley is excessively hot, and except where watered by fountains or rivulets, is sandy and destitute of foliage. It is covered in many parts with innumerable cone-like mounds, and sometimes contains a lower and narrow terrace of similar character, perhaps an eighth of a mile wide. Through this valley the river takes its serpentine course in a channel from fifteen to fifty feet below the general level. Its immediate banks are thickly covered with trees and shrubs, such as the willow, tamarisk, and oleander; and often recede, and leave a larger space for vegetation. In the lower Jordan, the stream is bordered by numerous canebrakes. The thickets adjoining the river were formerly the retreat of wild beasts, which of course would be driven out by a freshet; hence the figure, "He shall come up like a lion from the swelling of Jordan," Jer. 49:19; 50:44. The channel of the river may be deeper sunk than of old, but even now not only the intervales within the banks are overflowed in spring, but in many places the banks themselves, 1 Chr. 12:15. Lieut. Lynch of the United States navy, who traversed the Jordan in 1848, ascertained that, although the distance from the sea of Galilee to the Dead sea is but sixty miles in a straight line, it is two hundred miles by the course of the river, which has innumerable curves. Its width varies at different points from seventy-five to two hundred feet, and its depth from three to twelve feet. Its volume of water differs exceedingly at different seasons and from year to year. The current is usually swift and strong; and there are numerous rapids and falls, of which no less than twenty-seven are specified by Lieut. Lynch as dangerous even to his metallic boats. The sea of Tiberias lies 312 (according to Lynch, 653) feet below the level of the Mediterranean, and the Dead sea 1,316 feet; hence the fall of the Jordan between the two seas is 1,000 feet. The waters of the Jordan are cool and soft, and like the sea of Galilee, it abounds in fish. It is crossed by a stone bridge, below lake Huleh, (see GESHUR;) and the fragments of another, just south of the sea of Tiberias, still remain. Several fords, available in ordinary seasons, are mentioned in Scripture, Judg. 3:28; 12:5; 2 Sam. 17:22-24. Ferry-boats were also used, 2 Sam 19:17, 18, 39. See SEA IV.

It was during the annual "swelling of the Jordan" that Joshua and the Israelites crossed it, Josh. 3:15. Yet the swift and swollen current was arrested in its course, opposite to Jericho; and while the waters below the city rolled on to the sea, those above it were miraculously stayed, and left in the river bed a wide passage for the hosts of Israel. Twice afterwards the Jordan was miraculously crossed, by Elijah and Elisha, 2 Kin. 2:8, 14. In its waters the leprosy of Namaan was healed, and the lost axe-head floated, at the word of Elisha, 2 Kin. 5:14; 6:6. Here, too, our Saviour was baptized, Matt. 3:13; and this event is commemorated, in the middle of April of each year, by thousands of pilgrims of various sects of nominal Christians, who on a given day, and under the protection of a strong Turkish escort, visit the sacred river, drink and bathe in its waters, and after an hour or two return to Jerusalem.

The principal branches of the Jordan are the Yermak, anciently Hieromax, a large stream, and the Jabbok, both on the east. There are several small rivulets and many mountain brooks, which dry up more or less early in the summer. The phrase, "beyond Jordan," usually indicates the east side of the river, but before the conquest by Joshua it meant the west side.

At the present day, the Jordan is lost in the Dead sea; but many have supposed that in very ancient times, before the destruction of the cities in the vale of Sodom, the Jordan passed through the Dead sea and the vale of Siddim, and continued its course southward to the Elanitic gulf of the Red sea. The southern end of the Dead sea is found to be connected with the Elanitic gulf, or gulf of Akaba, by the great valley, called El-Arabah, forming a prolongation of El-Ghor, the valley of the Jordan. See map in EXODUS. The course of this valley is between south and south-south-west. Its length, from the Dead sea to Akaba, is about one hundred miles in a direct line. From the extremity of the Dead sea, a sandy plain extends southward between hills, and on a level with the sea, for the distance of eight or ten miles, where it is interrupted by a chalky cliff, from sixty to eighty feet high, which runs nearly across the valley, but leaves at its western end the opening of a valley nearly half a mile wide, which runs up for many miles to the south *within* the broad and desert valley El-Arabah, upon which it at length emerges, and the water of which it conveys to the Dead sea. The cliff above referred to, probably the Akrabbim of the Bible, marks the termination of El-Ghor and the commencement of El-Arabah, which is thence prolonged without interruption to Akaba. It is skirted on each side by a chain of mountains; but the streams which descend from these, are in summer lost in their gravelly beds before they reach the valley below; so that this lower plain is in summer entirely without water, which alone can produce verdure in the Arabian deserts and render them habitable. There is not the slightest appearance of a road, or of any other work of human art, in any part of the valley. The opinion that the Jordan formerly traversed this great valley is rendered untenable by the fact that the Dead sea lies nearly 1,300 feet lower than the gulf of Akaba, and that most of the intervening region now pours its streams north into the Dead sea. Of course the Jordan must also have stopped there of old, as it does now, unless, according to the somewhat startling theory of Lieut. Lynch and others, the Dead sea—and with it, though less deeply, the whole valley to the north and south—sunk down from a higher level into its present deep chasm, perhaps long before that appalling catastrophe from which Lot found refuge in "the mountain," Gen. 19:17-28, 30. See SEA III.

JO'SEPH, I., the son of Jacob and his beloved Rachel, born in Mesopotamia, Gen. 30:22-24, B. C. 1747 He is memorable for the wonderful providence of God which raised him from a prison to be the grand-vizier of Egypt, and made him the honored means of saving countless human lives. His history is one of the most pleasing and instructive in the Bible; and is related in language inimitably natural, simple, and touching. It is too beautiful for abridgment, and too familiar to need rehearsal. It throws much light on the superintending providence of God, as embracing all things, great and small, in the perpetual unfolding of his universal plan. No narrative in the Bible more strikingly illustrates the protective and elevating power of the fear of God, and its especial value for the young. To behold this lovely image of filial piety and unwavering faith, of self-control in youth and patience in adversity, of discretion and fidelity in all stations of life, serenely walking with God through all, and at death intrusting soul and body alike into his hands, Heb. 11:22, may well lead the young reader to cry, Oh that the God of Joseph were my God, Gen. 37 and 39-50. Joseph died, aged one hundred and ten, B. C. 1637; and when the Israelites, a century and a half later, went up from Egypt, they took his bones, and at length buried them in Shechem, Ex. 13:19; Josh. 24:32. A Mohammedan wely or tomb covers the spot regarded generally, and it may be correctly, as the place of his burial. It is a low stone enclosure, and stands in quiet seclusion among high trees, at the western entrance of the valley of Shechem, at the right of the traveller's path and nearer mount Ebal than mount Gerizim.

II. The husband of Mary, Christ's mother. His genealogy is traced in Matt. 1:1-15, to David, Judah, and Abraham. See GENEALOGY. His residence was at Nazareth in Galilee, where he followed the occupation of a carpenter, to which Christ also was trained, Mark 6:3. He was a pious and honorable man, as appears from his whole course towards Mary and her son. They both attended the Passover at Jerusalem when Christ was twelve years of age, Luke 2:41-51; and as no more is said of him in the sacred narrative, and Christ committed Mary to the care of one of his disciples, he is generally supposed to have died before Christ began his public ministry. He seems to have been well known among the Jews, Mark 6:3; John 6:42.

III. A native of Arimathea, but at the time of Christ's crucifixion a resident at Jerusalem. He was doubtless a believer in the Messiah, and "waited for the kingdom of God." He was a member of the Jewish Sanhedrim, and opposed in vain their action in condemning the Saviour, Luke 23:51. When all was over, he "went in boldly unto Pilate, and craved the body of Jesus." It was now night, and the Jewish Sabbath was at hand. He therefore, with the aid of Nicodemus, wrapped the body in spices, for the time, and laid it in his own tomb, Mark 15:43-46; John 19:38-42.

IV. A disciple of Christ, also named Justus, and Barsabas. See BARSABAS.

JO'SES, I., one of the brethren of our Lord, Matt. 13:55; Mark 6:3. His brethren did not at first believe on him, but after his resurrection they are found among his disciples, John 2:12; 7:5; Acts 1:14.

II. A son of Cleophas and Mary, identified by some with the above, Matt. 27:56. See JAMES III.

III. See BARNABAS.

JOSH'UA, I., the son of Nun, a distinguished leader of the Hebrews, and the successor of Moses. His name at first was Oshea, Num. 13:8, 16; and in the New Testament he is called Jesus, Acts 7:45; Heb. 4:8. Both the names, Joshua and Jesus, signify *saviour*, *deliverer*. See JESUS. Joshua led Israel over the Jordan, and took possession of the promised land; he conquered the Canaanites, and then distributed the country among the tribes. He is first mentioned as the leader of Israel against the Amalekites at Rephidim, Ex. 17:8-16. See also Num. 14:6. At the passage over Jordan he was eighty-four years of age; and after about twenty-six years employed in his appointed work, and then judging Israel at his possession at Timnath-serah, he died, B. C. 1426. His last grand convocation of all Israel, at Shechem, and his solemn address to them and renewal of their covenant with God, form the worthy close of a life on which in the sacred records no blot rests. He seems to have served the Lord with singular fidelity. No man witnessed more or greater miracles than he; and in his life may be found many points of resemblance to that of the greater "Captain of the Lord's host," who establishes his people in the true promised land.

The BOOK OF JOSHUA contains the narrative of all these transactions, and was written by Joshua himself, or under his direction, B. C. 1427. From chap. 24:27 on, was of course added by a later hand; but all was done under the inspiration of the Holy Spirit, 2 Tim. 3:16.

II. The son of Josedech. See JESHUA.

JOSI'AH, son of Amon and great-grandson of Hezekiah, a pious king of Judah, who introduced great reforms in the temple worship, and in the religious character of the nation in general. No king set himself more earnestly to destroy every vestige of idolatry out of the land. Among other things, he defiled the altars of the idols at Bethel by burning upon them the bones from the tombs of their deceased priests; as had been foretold more than three centuries before, I Kin. 13:2. While cleansing and repairing the temple at his command, the priests found the temple copy of the five books of the law, perhaps the original copy from Moses' own hand. The sacred book was too much neglected in those days of declension; and even the pious Josiah seems to have been impressed by the closing chapters of Deuteronomy as though he had never read them before. To avert the judgments there threatened, he humbled himself before God, and sought to bring the people to repentance. He caused them to renew their covenant with Jehovah, and celebrated the Passover with a solemnity like that of its first institution. The repentance of the people was heartless, and did not avert the divine judgments. Josiah, however, was taken away from the evil to come. He met death in battle with Pharaoh-necho, whose passage across his territory to attack the king of Assyria, Josiah felt obliged to resist. The death of this wise and pious king was deeply lamented, by the prophet Jeremiah and all the people, Zech. 12:11. He began to reign B. C. 641, at the age of eight years, and reigned thirty-one years, 2 Kin. 22; 23; 2 Chr. 34; 35.

JOT, a word which comes from the name of the Greek letter *iota* (ι) and the Hebrew *yod* (י). It is the smallest letter of these alphabets; and is therefore put for the smallest thing or particle; which is also its meaning in English, Matt. 5:18. See TITTLE.

JO'THAM, I., the youngest son of Gideon, who escaped the massacre of his brethren by Abimelech, and afterwards boldly and prophetically denounced the Shechemites in the beautiful parable of the bramble and the other trees. He escaped to Beer, and probably lived to see his threatenings fulfilled, Judg. 9. See ABIMELECH III.

II. The son and successor of Uzziah, or Azariah, king of Judah, B. C. 758. He appears to have been for some years regent before the death of Uzziah his leprous father, but ascended the throne at the age of twenty-five years, and reigned sixteen years in the fear of God. The history of his wise and prosperous reign, and of his useful public works, is found in 2 Kin. 15:5, 32-38; 2 Chr. 26:21; 27:9.

JOUR'NEY. A "sabbath-day's journey," among the Jews, seems to have been reckoned at about seven furlongs, or nearly one mile, Matt. 24:20; Acts 1:12. An ordinary day's journey is about twenty miles. Persons starting on a journey in the East frequently make their first stage a short one, that they may the more easily send back for any forgotten articles or necessary supplies. This may perhaps apply to the "day's journey" of the parents of Jesus, mentioned in Luke 2:44.

For the journeyings of the Israelites, see EXODUS, and WANDERINGS.

JU'BAL, *music*, son of Lamech and Adah, and a descendant of Cain. He invented the lyre, and the shepherd's-pipe, Gen. 4:21.

JU'BILEE, a Hebrew festival, celebrated in every fiftieth year, which of course occurred after seven weeks of years, or seven times seven years, Lev. 25:10. Its name Jubilee, *sounding* or *flowing*, was significant of the joyful trumpet-peals that announced its arrival. During this year no one sowed or reaped; but all were satisfied with what the earth and the trees produced spontaneously. Each resumed possession of his inheritance, whether it were sold, mortgaged, or otherwise alienated; and Hebrew servants of every description were set free, with their wives and children, Lev. 25. The first nine days were spent in festivities, during which no one worked, and every one wore a crown on his head. On the tenth day, which was the day of solemn expiation, the sanhedrim ordered the trumpets to sound, and instantly the slaves were declared free, and the lands returned to their hereditary owners. This law was mercifully designed to prevent the rich from oppressing the poor, and getting possession of all the lands by purchase, mortgage, or usurpation; to cause that debts should not be multiplied too much, and that slaves should not continue, with their wives and children, in perpetual bondage. It served to maintain a degree of equality among the Hebrew families; to perpetuate the division of lands and households according to the original tribes, and secure a careful registry of the genealogy of every family. They were also thus reminded that Jehovah was the great Proprietor and Disposer of all things, and they but his tenants. "The land is mine: for ye are strangers and sojourners with me," Lev. 25:23. And this memento met them constantly and pointedly; for every transfer of land was valuable in proportion to the number of years remaining before the jubilee. Isaiah clearly refers to this peculiar and important festival, as foreshadowing the glorious dispensation of gospel grace, Isa. 61:1, 2; Luke 4:17-21.

See also the notice of a similar institution under SABBATICAL YEAR.

JU'DAH, the fourth son of Jacob and Leah, born in Mesopotamia, B. C. 1755, Gen. 29:35. His name appears honorably in the history of Joseph, Gen. 37:26, 27; 44:16-34; but disgracefully in that of Tamar his daughter-in-law, Gen. 38. The dying benediction of Jacob foretells the superior power and prosperity of the family of Judah, and their continuance as chief of the Jewish race until the time of Christ, Gen. 49:8-12. Though not the first-born, Judah soon came to be considered as the chief of Jacob's children, and his tribe was the most powerful and numerous. The south-eastern part of Palestine fell to their lot. See JUDEA. On the border of their territory was Jerusalem, the seat of the Jewish worship; and from Judah sprung David and his royal race, from which descended the Saviour of the world.

After the return from the captivity, this tribe in some sort united in itself the whole Hebrew nation, who from that time were known only as Judæi, Jews, descendants of Judah. Judah—when named in contradistinction to Israel, Ephraim, the kingdom of the ten tribes, or Samaria—denotes the kingdom of Judah, and of David's descendants. See HEBREWS and KINGS. One of the principal distinctions of this tribe is, that it preserved the true religion, and the public exercise of the priesthood, with the legal ceremonies in the temple at Jerusalem; while the ten tribes gave themselves up to idolatry and the worship of the golden calves.

JU'DAS, I., ISCARIOT, that is, man of Carioth or Kerioth, a city of Judah, Josh. 15:25. Being one of the twelve apostles of our Lord, Judas seems to have possessed the full confidence of his fellow-apostles, and was entrusted by them with all the presents which were made them, and all their means of subsistence; and when the twelve were sent out to preach and to work miracles, Judas appears to have been among them, and to have received the same powers. He was accustomed, however, even at this time, to appropriate part of their common stock to his own use, John 12:6; and at length sealed his infamy by betraying his Lord to the Jews for money. For the paltry sum of about $15, he engaged with the Jewish Sanhedrim to guide them to a place where they could seize him by night without danger of a tumult. But when he learned the result, a terrible remorse took possession of him; not succeeding in undoing his fatal work with the priests, he cast down before them the price of blood, crossed the gloomy valley of Hinnom, and hung himself, Matt. 27:3-10. Luke, in Acts 1:18, adds that he fell headlong and burst asunder, probably by the breaking of the rope or branch. The steep hill-side south of the valley of Hinnom might well be the scene of such a twofold death. See ACELDAMA. The remorseful confession of Judas was a signal testimony to the spotless innocence of Christ, Matt. 27:4; and his awful end is a solemn warning against avarice, hypocrisy, and all unfaithfulness, Matt. 26:34; John 17:12; Acts 1:25.

II. One of the apostles, called also Jude, Lebbeus, and Thaddeus, Matt. 10:3, Mark 3:18, Jude 1, the son of Alpheus and Mary, and brother of James the Less. See JAMES II. and III. He was the author of the epistle which bears his name, Mark 6:3; Luke 6:16; Acts 1:13.

III. The brother of our Lord, Matt. 27:56. Supposed by many to have been only a cousin, and the same as Judas II. the apostle. But his "brethren" did not believe in him until near the close of his ministry. See JAMES III.

IV. A Christian teacher, called also Barsabas, sent from Jerusalem to Antioch with Paul and Barnabas, Acts 15:22, 27, 32.

V. Surnamed "the Galilean," called also, by Josephus, the Gaulonite. He was born at Gamala, a city of Gaulonitis near the south-eastern shore of the lake of Tiberias. In company with one Sadoc, he attempted to excite a sedition among the Jews, but was destroyed by Quirinus, or Cyrenius, at that time governor of Syria and Judea, Acts 5:37.

VI. A Jew at Damascus, with whom Paul lodged, Acts 9:11.

JUDE. See JUDAS II.

THE EPISTLE OF JUDE, assigned conjecturally to the year 66 A. D., is a fervid and vehement voice of warning against following certain false teachers in their errors and corruptions, and so sharing their awful doom. It resembles the second epistle of Peter. As to the quotation in ver. 14, 15, see ENOCH II.

JUDE'A, or land of the Jews, a name sometimes given to the southern part of the Holy Land; and sometimes, especially by foreigners, to the whole country. In the general division of Canaan among the tribes, the south-east part fell to the lot of the tribe of Judah. With the increasing ascendency of that tribe the name of Judah covered a more extended territory, 2 Sam. 5:5; and after the secession of the ten tribes, the kingdom of Judah included the territory of the tribes of Judah and Benjamin, with a part of that of Simeon and Dan. Judah thus occupied all the southern portion of Palestine, while the northern part was called Galilee, and the middle Samaria. After the captivity, as most of those who returned were of the kingdom of Judah, the name Judah, or Judea, was applied generally to the whole of Palestine, Hag. 1:1, 14; 2:2; and this use of the word has never wholly ceased. When the whole country fell into the power of the Romans, the former division into Galilee, Samaria, and Judea seems to have again become current, Luke 2:4; John 4:3, 4. Josephus describes Judea in his day as bounded north by Samaria, east by the Jordan, west by the Mediterranean, and south by the territory of the Arabs. These boundaries seem to include a part of Idumæa. Judea in this extent constituted part of the kingdom of Herod the Great, and afterwards belonged to his son Archelaus. When the latter was banished for his cruelties, Judea was reduced to the form of a Roman province, annexed to the proconsulate of Syria, and governed by procurators, until it was at length given as part of his kingdom to Herod Agrippa II. During all this time, the boundaries of the province were often varied, by the addition or abstraction of different towns and cities.

The original territory of the tribe of Judah was an elevated plain, much broken by frequent hills, ravines, and valleys, and sinking into fine plains and pasture-grounds on the west and south, Zech. 7:7. It was a healthy, pleasant, and fruitful land. The valleys yielded large crops of grain; and the hills were terraced, watered, covered with vines, Gen. 49:11, 12, and rich in olives, figs, and many other fruits. See CANAAN. The "hill-country" of Judah lay south and south-east of Jerusalem, Luke 1:39, 65, including Bethlehem, Hebron, etc. "The plain" refers usually to the low ground near the Jordan, 2 Sam. 2:29; 2 Kin. 25:4, 5.

The "wilderness of Judea," in which John began to preach, and where Christ was tempted, seems to have been in the eastern part of Judah, adjacent to the Dead sea, and stretching towards Jericho, 2 Sam. 15:28. It is still one of the most dreary and desolate regions of the whole country, Matt. 3:1; 4:1.

JUDGES, in Hebrew Shophetim, were the rulers, chiefs, or leaders of Israel, from Joshua to Saul. They were very different from the ordinary administrators of justice among the Hebrews, respecting whom, see JUSTICE. The Carthaginians, a colony of the Tyrians, had likewise governors, whom they called Suffetes, or Sophetim, with authority almost equal to that of kings.

The dignity of judge was for life; but the succession was not always constant. There were anarchies, or intervals, during which the commonwealth was without rulers. There were likewise long intervals of foreign servitude and oppression, under which the Hebrews groaned without deliverers. Although God alone regularly appointed the judges, yet the people, on some occasions, chose that individual who appeared to them most proper to deliver them from oppression; and as it often happened that the oppressions which occasioned recourse to the election of a judge were not felt over all Israel, the power of such judge extended only over that province which he had delivered. Thus it was chiefly the land east of the Jordan that Ehud, Jephthah, Elon, and Jair delivered and governed; Barak and Tola governed the northern tribes; Abdon the central; and Ibzan and Samson the southern. The authority of judges was little inferior to that of kings: it extended to peace and war; they decided causes with absolute authority; but had no power to make new laws, or to impose new burdens on the people. They were protectors of the laws, defenders of religion, and avengers of crimes, particularly of idolatry; they were without salary, pomp, or splendor; and without guards, train, or equipage, other than that their own wealth afforded.

The command of Jehovah to expel or destroy all the Canaanites, was but imperfectly executed; and those who were spared infected the Hebrews with the poison of their idolatry and vice. The affair of Micah and the Levite, and the crime at Gibeah which led to the ruinous war against the Benjamites, though recorded at the close of the book of Judges, chap. 17–21, occurred not long after the death of Joshua, and show how soon Israel began to depart from God. To chastise them, he suffered the people of Mesopotamia and of Moab, the Canaanites, Midianites, Ammonites, and Philistines, in turn to oppress by their exactions a part of the tribes, and sometimes the whole nation. But erelong, in pity for their sufferings, he would raise up one of the military and civil dictators above described. Fifteen judges are named in the Bible, beginning with Othniel, some twenty years after Joshua, and continuing till the coronation of Saul. The recorded succession of the judges, and of the periods of oppression, is the following:

	YEARS.
Othniel, about B. C. 1405	40
Under Eglon	18
Ehud, etc.	80
Under the Philistines	unknown
Shamgar	unknown
Under Jabin	20
Deborah and Barak	40
Under Midian	7
Gideon	40
Abimelech	3
Tola	23
Jair	22
Under the Ammonites	18
Jephthah	6
Ibzan	7
Elon	10
Abdon	8
Under the Philistines	40
Samson }	20
Eli }	40
Under the Philistines	20
Samuel, about	12
Saul, the first king, B. C. 1095.	

The time from Othniel to Saul, according to the above table, would be some 500 years; according to the received chronology, it is about 310 years. It is supposed that some of the above periods overlap each other; but chronologists are not agreed as to the mode of reconciling the accounts in Judges with other known dates, and with 1 Kin. 6:1, and Acts 13:20, though several practicable methods are proposed, the examination of which would exceed the limits of this work.

The BOOK OF JUDGES contains the annals of the times in which Israel was ruled by judges, and is often referred to in the New Testament and other parts of the Bible. It appears to have been written before David captured Zion, 1:21, and yet after a regal government was introduced, 17:6; 18:1; 21:25. Who was its author is unknown; the majority of critics ascribe it to Samuel, B. C. 1403, but many regard it as a compilation by Ezra. It illustrates God's care over his people, mingling his long-suffering with timely chastisements. The period of the judges was, on the whole, one of prosperity; and while the providence of God confirmed his word, "If ye refuse and rebel, ye shall be devoured by the sword," it no less faithfully assured them, "If ye be willing and obedient, ye shall eat of the good of the land."

JUDG'MENT is put, in Matt. 5:21, 22, for a court of judgment, a tribunal, namely, the tribunal of seven judges, which Josephus mentions as existing in every city, and which decided causes of minor importance. See under SYNAGOGUE.

For the expression, "judgment-hall," see PRETORIUM.

The DAY OF JUDGMENT, for which the word "judgment" alone is sometimes used, is that great day, at the end of the world and of time, when Christ shall sit as judge over all the universe, and when every individual of the human race will be judged and recompensed according to his works, whether they be good or evil. The time of its coming and its duration are known only to God. It will break upon the world suddenly, and with a glorious but awful majesty. It will witness the perfect vindication of all the ways of God. The revelation of his justice, appalling but unstained, will fill the universe with approving wonder; but the revelation of his yet more amazing goodness will crown him with unutterable glory. The Redeemer especially will then receive his reward, and be glorified in his saints, who shall be raised from the dead in his likeness. He will divide all mankind into two classes: all the righteous will be in one, and all the wicked in the other; all that love God in the one, and all that hate him in the other; all that penitently believed in Christ while they lived in the one, and all that died impenitent and unbelieving in the other. And this judgment and separation will be eternal; the former will rise in holiness and joy, and the latter sink in sin and woe for ever, Eccl. 11:9; Dan. 12:2; Matt. 10:15; 12:36; 25:31-46; 26:64; John 5:22; Acts 17:31; Rom. 14:10-12; 2 Thess. 1:7-10; 2 Pet. 2:9; 3:7; 1 John 4:17; Rev. 20:12-15.

JU'LIUS, a centurion of the cohort of Augustus, to whom Festus, governor of Judea, committed Paul to be conveyed to Rome. Julius had great regard for Paul. He suffered him to land at Sidon, and to visit his friends there; and in a subsequent part of the voyage he opposed the violence of the soldiers, directed against the prisoners generally, in order to save the apostle, Acts 27.

JU'NIPER is found in the English Bible, 1 Kin. 19:4, 5; Job 30:4; Psa. 120:4. The Hebrew word, however, signifies the

plant Genista, or Spanish broom, which is common in the desert regions of Arabia, and has yellowish blossoms and a bitter root.

JU'PITER, the supreme god of the heathen Greeks and Romans. He was called the son of Saturn and Ops, and was said to have been born in Crete. The character attributed to him in pagan mythology was a compound of all that is wicked, obscene, and beastly in the catalogue of human crime. Still he was ever described as of noble and dignified appearance and bearing. Barnabas was supposed by the people of Lystra to represent him, Acts 14:12, 13; 19:35.

JUS'TICE, a principle of righteousness and equity, controlling our conduct, and securing a due regard to all the rights of others—their persons, property, character, and interests. It has to do, not with pecuniary transactions alone, but with all our intercourse with society. It forms a chief element of the character approved in God's word; and a truly just man has but to "love mercy, and walk humbly with God," to fulfil all righteousness. Justice in magistrates, rulers, and judges, must be fearless and impartial, and all its decisions such as will bear revision before the court of heaven, Deut. 1:16–17; 2 Sam. 23:3; 2 Chr. 19:6–10. Judgment is peculiarly the prerogative of God, and every earthly tribunal lies under the shadow of the "great white throne." A just judgment is the voice of God; and hence an unjust one is doubly hateful in his sight.

THE JUSTICE OF GOD is that essential and infinite attribute which makes his nature and his ways the perfect embodiment of equity, and constitutes him the model and the guardian of equity throughout the universe, Deut. 32:4; Psa. 89:14. The justice of God could not leave the world without laws, and cannot fail to vindicate them by executing their penalties; and as all mankind perpetually break them, every human soul is under condemnation, and must perish, unless spared through the accepted ransom, the blood of Christ.

THE ADMINISTRATION OF JUSTICE, among the Hebrews, was characterized by simplicity and promptitude. In early times the patriarch of each family was its judge, Gen. 38:24. Afterwards, in the absence of more formal courts, the elders of a household, tribe, or city, were its judges by natural right. In the wilderness, Moses organized for the Jews a regular system of judges, some having jurisdiction over ten families, others over fifty, one hundred, or one thousand. The difficult cases were referred to Moses, and he often sought divine direction concerning them, Ex. 18:21–26; Lev. 24:12. These judges were perhaps the "princes of the congregation," and the chiefs of the families and tribes of whom we afterwards read, Num. 27:3. In the land of Canaan, local magistrates were appointed for every city and village; and these were instructed to coöperate with the priests, as being all together under the theocracy, the actual government of Jehovah, the supreme Judge of Israel, Deut. 16:18; 17:8–10; 19:17; 21:1–6. Their informal courts were held in the gate of the city, as the most public and convenient place, Deut. 21:9; 22:15; 25:7; and in the same place contracts were ratified, Ruth 4:1, 9; Jer. 32:7–15. Deborah the prophetess judged Israel beneath a palm-tree, Judg. 4:5. Samuel established virtually a circuit court, 1 Sam. 7:16; 8:1; and among the kings, Jehoshaphat made special provision for the faithful administration of justice, 2 Chr. 19. The kings themselves were supreme judges, with almost unlimited powers, 1 Sam. 22:16; 2 Sam. 4:9, 10; 1 Kin. 22:26. They were expected, however, to see that justice was everywhere done, and seem to have been accessible to all who were wronged. Frequent complaints are on record in the sacred books of the maladministration of judges, of bribery and perjury, 1 Sam. 8:3; 1 Kin. 21:8–14; Isa. 1:23; 10:1; Mic. 3:11; 7:3.

There was no class among the Jews exactly corresponding to our lawyers. The accuser and the accused stood side by side before the judge, with their witnesses, and pleaded their own cause. The accuser is named in several places, Satan, that is, the adversary, Psa. 109:6; Zech. 3:1–3. No one could be condemned without the concurring testimony of at least two witnesses, Num. 35:30; and these failing, he was obliged to make oath of his innocence, Ex. 22:11; Heb. 6:16. The sentence of the judge was instantly executed; and in certain cases the witnesses cast the first stone, Deut. 17:5, 7; 25:2; Josh. 7:24; 1 Sam. 22:18; 1 Kin. 2:24; Prov. 16:14. The same frightful celerity still marks the administration of justice in the East. The application of torture to extract evidence is only once mentioned, and that under the authority of Rome, Acts 22:24. See SANHEDRIM and SYNAGOGUE.

JUSTIFICATION, the being regarded and treated as if innocent; or acquittal from the consequences of guilt before the tribunal of God. "Justification by faith" means that a person, on account of true and living faith in Christ as manifested by good works, will be delivered from condemnation on account of his sins; that is, his sins will be forgiven, and he be regarded and treated as if innocent and holy. Thus, besides the remission of sins and their penalty, it includes the restoration and everlasting enjoyment of the favor of God.

We obtain justification by *faith in Christ*. Yet neither this nor any other act of ours, as a work, is any ground of our justification. In acquitting us before his bar, God regards not our works, in whole or in part, but the atoning work and merits of Christ. He was treated as a sinner, that we might be treated as righteous. "There is therefore now no condemnation to them which are in Christ Jesus;" the moment we believe, our justification is as perfect as the infinite worthiness of our Redeemer. Its validity does not depend on the measure of our assurance of hope, nor on spotless holiness of life. Sanctification, indeed, or progressive growth in holiness, commences simultaneously with justification, and must in the end reach the same perfectness. Yet it is important to distinguish between the two, and to observe that, could the believer's holiness become as perfect as an angel's, it could not share with the atoning merits of Christ in entitling him to admission to heaven.

"The best obedience of my hands
Dares not appear before thy throne;
But faith can answer thy demands,
By pleading what my Lord hath done."

True justification, by the gratuitous gift of the Saviour, furnishes the most powerful motive to a holy life. It is followed by adoption, peace of conscience, and the fruits of the Spirit in this life; and by final sanctification, acquittal in the day of judgment, and admittance to heaven, Rom. 3:20-31; 5; 8:1-4; 10:4-10; Gal. 2:16-21; Eph. 2:4-10.

K.

KA'DESH, or KA'DESH-BAR'NEA, called also En-Mishpat, Gen. 14:7, the name of a fountain, a city, and the desert around, Psa. 29:3, in the southern border of the promised land. It is said, in Num. 20:16, to lie in the "uttermost border of Edom," and was probably situated very near the great valley El-Arabah, south of the Dead sea. Dr. Robinson found a watering-place answering well to the indications in Scripture, on the western border of El-Arabah, about twenty-seven miles from the Dead sea. Kadesh was twice visited by the Israelites in their wanderings; once soon after they left mount Sinai, and again thirty-eight years after. At the first visit the mission and return of the twelve spies took place, the rebellion of the people, and their presumptuous effort to enter Canaan by the pass Zephath, immediately north of Kadesh, Num. 13 and 14. At their second visit occurred the death of Miriam, the murmuring of the people for water, the miraculous supply, the sin of Aaron and Moses in smiting the rock, and the fruitless request for a passage through Edom, Num. 20:1-22. The southern border of Judah reached to Kadesh-barnea, Josh. 12:22; 15:3.

KAD'MONITES, Gen. 15:19, a tribe of Canaanites who inhabited the promised land east of the Jordan, about mount Hermon. Some have fancied that Cadmus, the supposed inventor of the Greek alphabet, and who came from the East, was a Kadmonite. If so, he only introduced into Greece the alphabet of his own country, since the Greek letters are obviously derived from the Phœnician or ancient Hebrew letters.

KA'NAH, I., a brook which separated Ephraim and Manasseh, and fell into the Mediterranean north of Joppa, Josh. 16:8; 17:9.

II. A town in the tribe of Asher, Josh. 19:24, 28. See CANA.

KE'DAR, a son of Ishmael, Gen. 25:13, the father of the Kedarenians or Cedrei, mentioned by Pliny, who dwelt in the neighborhood of the Nabatheans, in Arabia Deserta. They were a numerous and powerful tribe, not of the best reputation, Psa. 120:5, and their name is sometimes put for the whole of Arabia Deserta and its wandering inhabitants, Isa. 21:16, 17; 42:11. Their black camel's-hair tents are a picturesque feature in a landscape, Song 1:5.

KEDE'MOTH, a city in the border of Sihon king of Heshbon, whence Moses sent him an embassage of peace. A desert lay near it, Deut. 2:26. It was afterwards a Levitical city of Reuben, Josh. 13:18; 21:37.

KE'DESH, I., a city of refuge, in Naphtali; now Kedis, three miles north-west of lake Merom, Josh. 19:37; 20:7. Barak the judge of Israel was born there, Judg. 4:6.

II. A city in the south of Judah, Josh. 15:23.

III. A city in Issachar, 1 Chr. 6:72.

KE'DRON. See KIDRON.

KEI'LAH, a city in the plains of Judah, which David once relieved from a siege by the Philistines, but which afterwards sought to deliver him up to Saul, 1 Sam. 23:1–13; Neh. 3:17.

KEN'ITES, a people who dwelt west of the Dead sea, and extended themselves far into Arabia Petræa. Jethro, the father-in-law of Moses, was a Kenite, and his family accompanied the Israelites, and settled with other Kenites in various parts of the Holy Land, Judg. 1:16; 4:11; 1 Sam. 30:29; 1 Chr. 2:55. Heber and the Rechabites were their descendants. The Kenites of whom we read appear to have known and served Jehovah, and the whole tribe were friendly to the Hebrews. Saul spared them, when sent to destroy the Amalekites among whom they dwelt, Num. 24:20, 21; 1 Sam. 15:6.

KEN'IZZITES, an ancient people of Canaan, whose land God promised to the descendants of Abraham, Gen. 15:19. They appear to have mingled with other Canaanites, and lost their distinctive name before the time of Joshua. They should be distinguished from the Kenezites, the children of Kenaz. Two men so named are mentioned in Bible history, both subsequent to the Kenizzites, Gen. 36:15, 42; Josh. 14:6; 15:17.

KETU'RAH, the wife of Abraham, after the death of Sarah, Gen. 25:1-6. Though she is called a "concubine," this may have been to distinguish her sons as well as Ishmael from Isaac the son of promise, Gen. 25:6; 1 Chr. 1:32; Gal. 4:22, 30. Her sons were the ancestors of many Arabian tribes.

KIB'ROTH-HATTAA'VAH, *the graves of lust*, one of the encampments of Israel in the wilderness, where they desired of God flesh for their sustenance, declaring they were tired of manna, Num. 11:34, 35; 33:16. Quails were sent in great quantities; but while the meat was in their months, God smote so great a number of them, that the place was called "the graves of those who lusted," Psa. 78:30, 31, a monument to warn mankind against the sin of discontent, 1 Cor. 10:6.

JERUSALEM AND ITS VALLEYS, FROM THE SOUTH; THE KIDRON VALLEY OPENING ON THE RIGHT; AND HINNOM ON THE LEFT.

KID'RON, or CE'DRON, a winter torrent, and the valley in which it flowed, east of Jerusalem. This valley begins a little north-west of the city, passes some two hundred rods north of the present wall, and turns to the south. Here it is wide and open; but as it runs south between the city and mount Olivet, it becomes narrow and deep. Opposite mount Moriah, it is a mere torrent's bed, one hundred and fifty feet below the city wall. It sinks still deeper as it passes

Siloam, the valley of Hinnom, and the well of Nehemiah, and then winds south-east, in a narrow and precipitous gorge, through the horrid wilderness of St. Saba, to the Dead sea. The bed of the Kidron is now dry most of the year; even in the rainy season it has no constant stream, though heavy and continued rains may create an impetuous but short-lived torrent. It is crossed by a causeway and a bridge of a single arch, between St. Stephen's gate and the garden of Gethsemane. By this route probably David fled from Absalom, 2 Sam. 15:23; and the Saviour often passed this way in going to Bethany, mount Olivet, and Gethsemane, John 18:1, 2. In this valley and in that of Hinnom, at their confluence, kings Asa, Josiah, and Hezekiah destroyed the idols and abominations by which Jerusalem was defiled, 1 Kin. 15:13; 2 Kin. 23:4, 6, 12; 2 Chr. 29:16. See HINNOM, and JERUSALEM. A part of the waters of the ancient Kidron were derived from the temple itself, flowing down by several channels to the deep bed of the brook. The prophet Ezekiel makes use of this fact in a beautiful and cheering allegory, foretelling the river of divine grace that shall yet renovate the world. The stream he describes issues from the temple, beside the altar of God; it flows with an ever increasing volume; it carries with it into the dreary wilderness verdure, fruitfulness, and melody; and even heals the bitter waters of the Dead sea itself, Ezek. 47:1-12.

KING, KINGS. In Scripture, the word king does not always imply either a high degree of power or great extent of territory. Many single towns, or towns with their adjacent villages, are said to have had kings; and many persons are called kings in Scripture, whom we should rather denominate chiefs or leaders. Somewhat in this sense, Moses is said to have been "king in Jeshurun," or Israel, Deut. 33:5; he was the chief, the leader, the guide of his people, though not king in the same sense as David or Solomon. These remarks will remove the surprise which some persons have felt at seeing that so small a country as Canaan contained thirty-one kings who were conquered, Josh. 12:9-24, besides many who no doubt escaped the arms of Joshua. Adonizedek, himself no very powerful king, mentions seventy kings whom he had subdued and mutilated. See also 1 Kin. 4.21. These kings, in many cases, were no doubt like the sheikhs of Arab tribes at the present day.

The Israelites had no kings till Saul: having been governed, first by elders, as in Egypt; then by rulers of God's appointment, as Moses and Joshua; then by judges, as Othniel, Ehud, Gideon, Samuel; and lastly by kings, as Saul, David, Solomon. Being peculiarly the people of God, their form of government was essentially a theocracy. God prescribed for them a code of laws; he designated their rulers; these laws and rulers the people were to obey "in the Lord;" and in all cases of doubt, he, as the actual head of the government, was to be consulted, in the spirit of the words, "The Lord is our Judge, the Lord is our Lawgiver, the Lord is our King." Their demand for a king was offensive to him, as an unbelieving and rebellious departure from the more immediate headship of Jehovah, 1 Sam. 8:7. Yet even under the regal government, they were still to regard him as their king. Idolatry was treason against the throne. Their code of laws was still his holy book. It was a prophet or high-priest of Jehovah who anointed the king, and placed the crown upon his head and the sceptre in his hand, Deut. 17:15, 18-20; 1 Sam. 10:1; 12:12-15; 2 Sam. 1:14, 21; 1 Kin. 1:39; 2 Kin. 9:1-6; 11:12; Psa. 21:3. By the instrumentality of his sacred ministers, God gave such directions concerning public affairs as were needed and sought for; and these agents of God, with their instructions and warnings, performed a most important part in the national history. So far as people and kings looked to God as their Head, they prospered; and it was for lack of this, that they were ruined. Of the two kingdoms, Judah and Israel, the latter most rapidly and fully threw off its allegiance, 2 Chr. 13:4-12; and therefore it was the first to perish, having continued two hundred and fifty-four years from the death of Solomon, B. C. 975-721, with nineteen kings of nine different dynasties. The kingdom of Judah continued three hundred and eighty-seven years after the separation, B. C. 975-588, having been held by nineteen successive kings of the line of David.

The following table presents in one

view the kings of Judah and Israel, as given in the Bible, with the year when each one began to reign, and the length of his reign. The chronology is that of Usher and Winer, who nearly coincide.

KINGS OF THE ENTIRE NATION.

Saul	B. C 1095	reigned 40	years.
David	" 1055	" 40	"
Solomon	" 1015	" 40	"

OF JUDAH.	OF ISRAEL.	B C.	REIGNED
Rehoboam		975	17 years.
	Jeroboam	975	22 "
Abijah		958	3 "
Asa		955	41 "
	Nadab	954	2 "
	Baasha	953	23 "
	Elah	930	1 "
	Zimri	929	7 days.
	Omri	929	12 years.
	Ahab	918	22 "
Jehoshaphat		914	25 "
	Ahaziah	897	2 "
	Joram	896	12 "
Jehoram		892	8 "
Ahaziah		885	1 "
(Athaliah, usurper)		884	7 "
Joash		878	40 "
	Jehoahaz	856	17 "
	Joash	840	16 "
Amaziah		838	29 "
	Jeroboam II.	825	41 "
Uzziah		810	52 "
	(Interregnum.)	784	12 "
	Zachariah	772	6 mos
	Shallum	772	1 mo.
	Menahem	771	10 years.
	Pekahiah	760	2 "
	Pekah	758	20 "
Jotham		758	16 "
Ahaz		741	16 "
	(Interregnum.)	738	10 "
	Hosea	729	19 "
Hezekiah		726	29 "
	(Samaria captured.)	721	
Manasseh		697	55 years.
Amon		642	2 "
Josiah		640	31 "
Jehoahaz		609	3 mos.
Jehoiakim		609	11 years.
Jehoiachin		598	3 mos.
Zedekiah		598	11 years.
(Jerusalem captured)		588	

The two BOOKS OF KINGS contain a history of the kings of Judah and Israel intermingled, commencing with Solomon and ending with Zedekiah; unlike the books of Chronicles, which give an account only of the kings of Judah. In the Septuagint and Vulgate, our two books of Samuel are also called books of Kings. The various histories comprising the two books of Kings were evidently the work of a single inspired writer, and not a mere collection. They are believed to have been written before the books of Chronicles, and Jewish tradition makes the prophet Jeremiah their author, B. C. 620. The writer probably drew a part of his materials from the records of each reign left by contemporary prophets and priests, 1 Kin. 11: 41. See CHRONICLES. All these sacred annals are highly instructive. They show us the perfect fulfilment of the divine promises and warnings by Moses; and every page confirms the inspired declaration, "The fear of the Lord is the beginning of wisdom."

KINGDOM OF HEAVEN is an expression used in the New Testament to signify the reign, dispensation, or administration of Jesus Christ. The ancient prophets, when describing the character of the Messiah, Dan. 2 : 44; 7 : 13, 14; Mic. 4 : 1-7, and even when speaking of his humiliation and sufferings, were wont to intersperse hints of his power, his reign, and his divinity. The Jews, overlooking the spiritual import of this language, expected the Messiah to appear as a temporal king, exercising power over his enemies, restoring the throne of David to all its splendor, subduing the nations, and rewarding his friends and faithful servants in proportion to their fidelity and services. Hence the contests among his disciples, ere they had fully learned Christ, about precedency in his kingdom; and hence probably the sons of Zebedee desired the two chief places in it, or those nearest to their endeared Master and Lord. They afterwards learned that his kingdom was not of this world, John 18:36, 37; that its origin, spirit, means, and ends were spiritual and heavenly. It has indeed its outward form, the visible church, Matt. 13:47, and bestows on the world the richest of temporal blessings; but its true dominion is in the souls of men. It embraces all who by the Spirit of Christ are united to him as their divine Head and King, to love, serve, and enjoy him for ever. His work on earth was to establish it, Matt. 3:2. He introduced his disciples into it while on earth, and more fully after his resurrection and ascension, John 20:22; Acts 2:32-36; is "head over all things," in order to make it triumphant and supreme even on earth, Dan. 7 : 27; Eph. 1:20-22. It will be perfected in heaven, Matt. 8 : 11, and will never cease, Luke 1:33, even when the mediatorial reign of the Saviour is accomplished, 1 Cor. 15:28.

KIR, I., a strong city of Moab; called also Kir-hareseth, Kir-haresh, and Kir-heres, Isa. 15:1; 16:7, 11; Jer. 48:31. It was once nearly destroyed by Joram king of Israel, 2 Kin. 3:25. It is now called Kerak, and is a town of three hundred families, on a steep hill at the head of a ravine running up fifteen miles into the mountains of Moab. Three-fourths of its present inhabitants are nominal Christians, greatly oppressed by the Mohammedan Arabs around them.

II. A region to which Tiglath-pileser transported the captive people of Damascus, 2 Kin. 16:9; believed to have been in the vicinity of the river Kur or Cyrus, on the north-east of Armenia. The Kur flows south-east, unites with the Araxes, and empties into the Caspian sea.

KIRJATHA'IM, I., the dual form of Kirjath, *a city*. It was an ancient city of the Emim, east of the Jordan; afterwards inhabited by the Moabites, Amorites, and Israelites in turn, Gen. 14:5; Deut. 2:9-11; Ezek. 25:9. It fell within the limits of the tribe of Reuben, Num. 32:37; Josh. 13:19.

II. A Levitical city in Naphtali, 1 Chr. 6:76; called Kartan, in Josh. 21:32.

KIR'JATH-AR'BA. See HEBRON.

KIR'JATH-JEA'RIM, or KIRJATH-BAAL, Josh. 15:9, 60, a city of the Gibeonites, afterwards given to Judah. It was on the confines of Benjamin, Josh. 18:14, 15, about nine miles from Jerusalem in the way to Lydda. Here the ark was lodged for many years, in the house of Abinadab, till David removed it to Jerusalem, 1 Sam. 7:2; 2 Sam. 6:2; 1 Chr. 13.

KIR'JATH-SAN'NAH, and KIR'JATH-SEPH'ER. See DEBIR.

KI'SHON, now the Mukutta, a brook which rises in the plain of Esdraelon, near the foot of mount Tabor. After passing through the great plain and receiving the waters of various smaller streams, it flows along the foot of mount Carmel, and discharges itself into the Mediterranean, a short distance south of Acre. The supplies it receives from the Carmel ridge, see CARMEL II., make it a perennial stream for about seven miles from its mouth. But all the eastern part of its channel, now that the great plain through which it flows is unwooded, is dry throughout the summer season; and yet, in the winter, and after heavy rains, it swells to a full and rapid torrent. The drowning of Sisera's host, Judg. 4:13; 5:21, is paralleled by a similar destruction of Arabs fleeing from the French after the battle of mount Tabor, April 18, 1799.

KISS. This salutation was customary in the East, to express regard and reverence, as well as affection, Gen. 29:13; Ruth 1:14; Acts 20:37. Sometimes the beard was kissed, 2 Sam. 20:9; and, in token of humble affection, the feet, Luke 7:38. Images and the heavenly bodies were worshipped by kissing the hand towards them, 1 Kin. 19:18; Job 31:27; Hos. 13:2. The expression, "Kiss the Son," Psa. 2:12, may be illustrated by 1 Sam. 10:1, where king Saul receives the kiss of allegiance from Samuel. This salutation being customary in those days between man and man, was used in the early church as a pledge of Christian peace and charity, Rom. 16:16; 1 Pet. 5:14.

KITE, a bird of prey, and therefore placed by Moses among the unclean birds, Lev. 11:14. See BIRDS.

KIT'TIM, son of Javan, and grandson of Noah, Gen. 10:4. See CHITTIM.

KNEAD'ING-TROUGHS. In the description of the departure of the Israelites from Egypt, Exod. 12:34, we read that "the people took their dough before it was leavened, their kneading-troughs being bound up in their clothes upon their shoulders." These were either small wooden bowls, or circular pieces of leather which might be drawn up like a bag, by a cord encircling the edge. The Arabs of the present day use both.

KO'HATH, son of Levi, Gen. 46:11, and father of the Kohathites, who were appointed to carry the ark and sacred utensils of the tabernacle during the journeyings of the Israelites in the desert, Ex. 6:16-24; Num. 4:4-15.

KO'RAH, a Levite, who rebelled against Moses and Aaron, and so against Jehovah. He was a cousin of Moses; for their fathers Izhar and Amram were brothers, Ex. 6:16-21. He was jealous of the civil authority and priestly dignity conferred by God upon Moses and Aaron, his own cousins, while he was simply a Levite; and to obtain a part at least of their power for himself, he stirred up a factious spirit in the people. Too much, alas, of what may seem to be zeal for the honor of God, has its true character displayed in the pride and ambition of this rebellious Levite. The two hundred and fifty Levites whom he had enticed to join him were destroyed by fire from the Lord; while Korah, Dathan, and Abiram were swallowed up by the miraculous opening of the earth, Num. 16. But Korah's children escaped, Num. 26:11; and the Korahites or "sons of Korah," were a celebrated family of singers and poets in the time of David, 1 Chr. 9:19; 26:1. To them are inscribed several Psalms, Psa. 42, 44, 49, 84, 85, 87, 88.

L.

LA'BAN, a rich herdsman of Mesopotamia, son of Bethuel, and grandson of Nahor, Abraham's brother, Gen. 24:28-31. His character is shown in the gladness with which he gave his sister Rebekah in marriage to the only son of his rich uncle, Abraham, Gen. 24:30, 50; and in his deceitful and exacting treatment of Jacob his nephew and son-in-law, against which Jacob defended himself by cunning as well as fidelity. When the prosperity of the one family and the jealousy of the other rendered peace impossible, Jacob, at the command of God, secretly departed, to go to Canaan. Laban pursued him; but being warned by God to do him no harm, returned home after making a treaty of peace. He seems to have known and worshipped God, Gen. 24:50; 30:27; 31:53; but the "gods" or teraphim which Rachel stole from her father, Gen. 31:30, 34, show that he was not without the taint of idolatry.

LA'CHISH, a city in the south-west part of Judah, Josh. 10:3, 5, 31; fortified by Rehoboam, 2 Chr. 11:9, and strong enough to resist for a time the whole army of Sennacherib, 2 Kin. 18:17; 19:8; 2 Chr. 32:1, 9, 21; Mic. 1:13. It was here that king Amaziah was slain, 2 Kin. 14:19. For a wonderful confirmation of the truth of Scripture, see SENNACHERIB.

LAD'DER, Gen. 28:12-17. The comforting vision of the heavenly ladder shown to the fugitive Jacob, assured him of the omnipresent providence of God, and of his communication of all needed good to his people in the desert of this world, Heb. 1:14. It was also an assurance that there was a way open from earth to heaven, as well as from heaven to earth; and we may see in it an illustration of the nature of Christ, in which heaven and earth meet; and of his work, which brings man home to God.

LA'ISH. See DAN.

LAKE. See MEROM and SEA. That most terrible description of hell, as a lake burning with fire and brimstone, Rev. 19:20; 21:8, recalls the fire and sea in which Sodom was consumed and swallowed up.

LAMB, the young of the sheep, and also the kid of the goat, Ex. 12:5. Christ is the Lamb of God, John 1:29, as being the accepted sacrifice for human sin. The sacrifices of the Old Testament were an ordained and perpetual foreshadowing not only of his expiatory death, but of his spotless holiness and his unresisting meekness, Isa. 53:4-9. He is described in Rev. 5:6; 12:11, as wearing the form of a sacrificial lamb in heaven itself. See PASSOVER and SACRIFICES.

LA'MECH, I., Gen. 4:18-24, a descendant of Cain, in the fifth generation, and ancestor of a numerous posterity distinguished for skill in agriculture, music, and several mechanic arts. He is the first polygamist on record. His address to his two wives is the oldest specimen of poetry extant, and is a good illustration of Hebrew parallelism.

"Adah and Zillah,
Hear my voice;
Ye wives of Lamech,
Hearken unto my speech.
I have slain a man
To my wounding,
And [or even] a young man
To my hurt.
If Cain shall be avenged
Seven-fold,
Truly Lamech
Seventy and seven fold."

Many explanations of this abrupt fragment have been suggested. The most satisfactory, perhaps, is that Lamech had accidentally or in self-defence killed a man, and was exposed to the vengeance of "the avenger of blood;" but quiets the fears of his wives by saying, that as God had prohibited the slaying of Cain under heavy penalties, Gen. 4:15, much more would he guard the life of Lamech who was comparatively innocent.

II. The son of Methuselah, and father of Noah; he lived seven hundred and seventy-seven years, and died only five years before the flood, Gen. 5:25-31.

LAMENTA'TIONS OF JEREMIAH, an elegiac poem, composed by the prophet on occasion of the destruction of Jerusalem by Nebuchadnezzar. The first two chapters principally describe the calamities of the siege of Jerusalem; the third deplores the persecutions which Jeremiah himself had suffered; the fourth adverts to the ruin and desolation of the city and temple, and the misfortune of Zedekiah; and the fifth is a kind of form of prayer for the Jews in their captivity. At the close, the prophet speaks of the cruelty of the Edomites, who had insulted Jerusalem in her misery, and threatens them with the wrath of God, B. C. 586.

The first four chapters of the Lamentations are in the acrostic form; every verse beginning with a letter of the Hebrew alphabet, in regular order. The first, second, and fourth chapters contain twenty-two verses each, according to the letters of the alphabet; the third chapter has three successive verses beginning with the same letter, making sixty-six in all. Moreover, all the verses in each chapter are nearly of the same length. The fifth chapter is not acrostic. See LETTERS. The style of Jeremiah's Lamentations is lively, tender, pathetic, and affecting. It was the talent of this prophet to write melancholy and moving elegies, 2 Chr. 35:25; and never was a subject more worthy of tears, nor treated with more tender and affecting sentiments. One would think, as it has often been said, that every letter was written with a tear, and every word was the sob of a broken heart. Yet he does not forget that a covenant God still reigns.

LAMP. The lamps of the ancients, sometimes called "candles" in our Bible, were cups and vessels of many convenient and graceful shapes; and might be carried in the hand, or set upon a stand. See CANDLESTICK. The lamp was fed with vegetable oils, tallow, wax, etc., and was kept burning all night. The poorest families, in some parts of the East, still regard this as essential to health and comfort. A darkened house therefore forcibly told of the extinction of its former occupants, Job 18:5, 6; Prov. 13:9; 20:20; Jer. 25:10, 11; while a constant light was significant of prosperity and perpetuity, 2 Sam. 21:17;

1 Kin. 11:36; Psa. 132:17. Lamps to be carried in the streets presented a large surface of wicking to the air, and needed to be frequently replenished from a vessel of oil borne in the other hand, Matt. 25:3, 4. Torches and lanterns, John 18:3, were very necessary in ancient cities, the streets of which were never lighted.

LAND'MARK. Fences and walls seem to have been little used in Judea, Mark 2:23, though gardens were sometimes inclosed. The ancient and permanent limits, therefore, of individual property in the open field, Ruth 2:3, were marked by trees or heaps of stones at the corners; and as it was easy, by removing these, to encroach on a neighbor's ground, a peculiar form of dishonesty arose, requiring a severe punishment, Deut. 19:14; Prov. 22:28; Hos. 5:10.

LAN'GUAGE, one of the distinguishing gifts of God to man, essential to all high enjoyment and improvement in social life, and to be prized and used in a manner worthy of its priceless value for the glory of God and the benefit of mankind. The original language was not the growth of a mere faculty of speech in man, but a creation and gift of God. Adam and Eve when created knew how to converse with each other and with the Creator. For some two thousand years, "the whole earth was of one language and of one speech," Gen. 11:1. But about one hundred years after the flood, according to the common chronology, and later according to others, God miraculously "confounded the language" of the Cushite rebels at Babel; and peopling the earth by these scattered families of diverse tongues, He frustrated their designs and promoted his own. There are now several hundreds of languages and dialects spoken on the earth, and infidels have hence taken occasion to discredit the Bible doctrine of the unity of the human race. It is found, however, that these languages are distributed in several great classes, which have striking affinities with each other; and as comparative philology extends its researches, it finds increasing evidence of the substantial oneness of the human race and of the truth of Scripture.

The miracle performed at Jerusalem on the day of Pentecost was the reverse of that at Babel, Acts 2:1-18, and beautifully illustrated the tendency of the gospel to introduce peace and harmony where sin has brought discord, and to reunite all the tribes of mankind in one great brotherhood.

To the student of the Bible, one of the most important subjects is the character and history of the original languages in which that holy book was written. In respect to the original Greek of the New Testament, some remarks have been made under the article GREECE. The Hebrew language, in which the Old Testament was written, is but one of the cluster of cognate languages which anciently prevailed in Western Asia, commonly called the Shemitic languages, as belonging particularly to the descendants of Shem. A proper knowledge of the Hebrew, therefore, implies also an acquaintance with these other kindred dialects.

The Shemitic languages may be divided into three principal dialects, namely, the Aramæan, the Hebrew, and the Arabic. 1. The Aramæan, spoken in Syria, Mesopotamia, and Babylonia, is subdivided into the Syriac and Chaldee dialects, sometimes called also the West and East Aramæan. 2. The Hebrew or Canaanitish dialect, Isa. 19:18, was spoken in Palestine, and probably with little variation in Phœnicia and the Phœnician colonies, as for instance, at Carthage and other places. The remains of the Phœnician and Punic dialects are too few and too much disfigured to enable us to judge with certainty how extensively these languages were the *same as* the dialect of Palestine. 3. The Arabic, to which the Ethiopic bears a special resemblance, comprises, in modern times, a great variety of dialects as a spoken language, and is spread over a vast extent of country; but so far as we are acquainted with its former state, it appears more anciently to have been limited principally to Arabia and Ethiopia.

These languages are distinguished from European tongues by several marked peculiarities: they are all, except the Ethiopic, written from right to left, and their books begin at what we should call the end; the alphabet, with the exception of the Ethiopic which is syllabic, consists of consonants only, above or below which the vowel-points are written; they have several guttural consonants very difficult of pronunciation to Europeans; the roots of the language are, in general, verbs of three letters, and pronounced, according to the various dialects, with one or more vowels; the verbs have but two tenses, the past and the future; and the pronouns in the oblique cases are generally united in the same word with the noun or verb to which they have a relation. These various dialects form substantially one language, of which the original home was Western Asia. That they have all diverged from one parent stock is manifest, but to determine which of them has undergone the fewest changes would be a difficult question. The language of Noah and his son Shem was substantially that of Adam and all the antediluvians. Shem and Heber were contemporary with Abraham, and transmitted, as we have good reason to believe their common tongue to the race of Israel; for it is not to be assumed that at the confusion of Babel no branch of the human family retained the primitive language. It does not appear that the descendants of Shem were among the builders of Babel, Gen. 10:8-10. The oldest records that are known to exist are composed in the Hebrew language. It flourished in its purest form in Palestine, among the Phœnicians and Hebrews, until the period of the Babylonish exile; soon after which it declined, and finally was succeeded by a kind of Hebræo-Aramæan dialect, such as was spoken in the time of our Saviour among the Jews. The West Aramæan had flourished before this for a long time in the east and north of Palestine; but it now advanced farther west, and during the period that the Christian churches of Syria flourished, it was widely extended. It is at present almost a dead language, and has been so for several centuries. The Hebrew may be regarded as having been a dead language, except among a small circle of *literati*, for about the space of two thousand years. Our knowledge of Arabic literature extends back very little beyond the time of Mohammed. But the followers of this pretended prophet have spread the dialect of the Koran over vast portions of the world. Arabic is now the vernacular language of Arabia, Syria, Egypt, and in a great measure of Palestine and all the northern coast of Africa; while it is read and understood wherever the Koran has gone, in Turkey, Persia, India, and Tartary.

The remains of the ancient Hebrew tongue are contained in the Old Testament and in the few Phœnician and Punic words and inscriptions that have been here and there discovered. The remains of the Aramæan are extant in a variety of books. In Chaldee, we have a part of the books of Daniel and Ezra, Dan. 2:4 to 7:28; Ezra 4:8 to 6:18, and 7:12-26, which are the most ancient of any specimens of this dialect. The Targum of Onkelos, that is, the translation of the Pentateuch into Chaldee, affords the next and purest specimen of that language. In Syriac, there is a considerable number of books and manuscripts extant. The oldest specimen of this language that we have, is contained in the Peshito, or Syriac version of the Old and New Testament, made perhaps within a century after the time of Christ. A multitude of writers in this dialect have flourished, many of whose writings are probably still extant, although but few have been printed in Europe. In Arabic, there exists a great variety of manuscripts and books, historical, scientific, and literary. A familiar knowledge of this and its kindred dialects throws much valuable light on the Old Testament Scriptures.

LAODICE'A, a large and opulent city of Asia Minor, the metropolis of Phrygia Pacatiana. It was situated on the river Lycus, not far above its junction with the Meander, and in the vicinity of Colosse and Hierapolis. Its earlier name was Diospolis; but after being enlarged by Antiochus II., it was called Laodicea. from his wife Laodice. About A. D. 65 or 66, this city, together with Hierapolis and Colosse, was destroyed by an earthquake, but was quickly rebuilt by Marcus Aurelius. It is now in ruins, and the place is called Eski-hissar, or the old castle. A Christian church was early gathered here. It was addressed by Paul in his letter to Colosse, and in another now lost, Col. 2:1; 4:13-16, though some think the "Epistle to the Ephesians" is the one alluded to. The church at Laodicea was probably visited by Paul, A. D. 63, and is one of the seven which received special messages from Christ after his ascension, Rev. 1:11; 3:14-22. We know little of its after-history, except that an important council was held there near the middle of the fourth century, and that some form of Christianity lingered there until the time of the Turks.

LAP'WING, supposed to mean the hoopoe, a beautiful migratory bird, of filthy habits and a loud, hoarse voice; pronounced unclean by Moses, Lev. 11:19. It is about the size of a thrush; its beak is long, black, thin, and a little hooked; its legs gray and short. On its head is a tuft of feathers of different colors, which it raises or lowers as it pleases.

Its neck and breast are somewhat reddish, and its wings and tail black, with white streaks.

LASE'A, a city near Fair-Havens, on the south side of Crete. Paul passed it on his voyage to Rome, Acts 27:8.

LATTICE. See HOUSE.

LAUD, to extol, by words of praise or in song, Rom. 15:11.

LA'VER, a large circular vessel, cast from the polished brass mirrors contributed by the Hebrew women, and placed between the door of the tabernacle and the altar of burnt-offering, with water for the necessary sacred ablutions, Ex. 30:18-21; 38:8; 40:7, 30-32.

For the temple of Solomon, besides the vast brazen sea for the use of the priests, (see SEA,) ten lavers were made for cleansing the sacrifices, 2 Chr. 4:6. Each laver contained about three hundred gallons, and was supported above a highly elaborate and beautiful base, 1 Kin. 7:27-39. They were stationed within the court of the priests, in front of the temple, five on each side. See TEMPLE.

LAW, in the Bible, signifies sometimes the whole word of God, Psa. 19:7-11; 119; Isa. 8:20; sometimes the Old Testament, John 10:34; 15:25, and sometimes the five books of Moses, which formed the first of the three divisions of the Hebrew Scriptures, Luke 24:44; Acts 13:15. The Pentateuch was probably "the law," a copy of which every king was to transcribe for himself and study, and which was to be made known to young and old, in public and in private, Deut. 6:7; 17:18, 19; 31:9-19, 26. In other places the Mosaic institutions as a whole are intended by "the law," in distinction from the gospel, John 1:17; Acts 25:8.

When the word refers to the law of Moses, careful attention to the context is sometimes requisite to judge whether the civil, the ceremonial, or the moral law is meant. The *ceremonial* or ritual laws, concerning the forms of worship, sacrifices, priests, purifications, etc., were designed to distinguish the Jewish nation from the heathen, and to foreshadow the gospel dispensation. They were annulled after Christ's ascension, Gal. 3:24; Eph. 2:15; Heb. 9; 10:1-22. The *civil* laws, Acts 23:3; 24:6, were for the government of the Jews as a nation, and included the ten commandments. The whole code was adapted with consummate wisdom to the condition of the Jews, and has greatly influenced all wise legislation in later years. Its pious, humane, and just spirit should characterize every code of human laws. The *moral* law, Deut. 5:22, Matt. 5:17, 18, Luke 10:26, 27, is more important than the others, from its bearings on human salvation. It was written by the Creator on the conscience of man, and sin has never fully erased it, Rom. 1:19; 2:12-15. It was more fully taught to the Hebrews, especially at mount Sinai, in the ten commandments, and is summed up by Christ in loving God supremely and our neighbor as ourselves, Matt. 22:37-40. It was the offspring of love to man, Rom. 7:10, 12; required perfect obedience, Gal. 3:10; James 2:10; and is of universal and perpetual obligation. Christ confirmed and enforced it, Matt. 5:17-20, showing its demand of holiness in the heart, applying it to a variety of cases, and supplying new motives to obedience, by revealing heaven and hell more clearly, and the gracious guidance of the Holy Spirit. Some have argued from certain passages of Scripture that this law is no longer binding upon Christians; that they "are not under the law, but under grace," Rom. 6:14, 15; 7:4, 6; Gal. 3:13, 25; 5:18; and the perversion of these passages leads men to sin and perish because grace abounds. Rightly understood, they harmonize with the declarations of the Saviour, Matt. 5:17. To the soul that is in Christ, the law is no longer the arbiter of his doom; yet it still comes to him as the divinely appointed teacher of that will of God in which he now delights, Psa. 119:97; Matt. 5:48; 11:30.

The word "law" sometimes means an inward guiding and controlling power. The "law in the mind" and the "law in the members," mean the holy impulses of a regenerated soul and the perverse inclinations of the natural heart, Rom. 7:21-23. Compare also Rom. 8:2; 9:31; James 1:25; 2:12.

LAW'YERS, men who devoted themselves to the study and explanation of the Jewish law, particularly of the traditionary or oral law. They belonged mostly to the sect of the Pharisees, and fell under the reproof of our Saviour for having taken from the people the key of knowledge. They were as the blind leading the blind, Matt. 32:35; Luke 10:25; 11:52. See SCRIBES.

LAZ'ARUS, I., a friend and disciple of Christ, brother of Martha and Mary, with whom he resided at Bethany near Jerusalem. Our Saviour had a high regard for the family, and often visited them; and when Lazarus was dangerously ill, word was sent to Christ, "Lord, behold, he whom thou lovest is sick." The Saviour reached Bethany after he had lain four days in his grave, and restored him to life by a word, "Lazarus, come forth." This public and stupendous miracle drew so many to Christ, that his enemies sought to put both him and Lazarus to death, John 11; 12:1-11. The narrative displays Christ as a tender and compassionate friend, weeping for and with those he loved, and at the same time as the Prince of life, beginning his triumph over death and the grave. Happy are they who, in view of their own death, or that of friends, can know that they are safe in Him who says, "I am the resurrection and the life;" and, "because I live, ye shall live also."

II. The helpless beggar who lay at the rich man's gate in one of Christ's most solemn and instructive parables. The one, though poor and sorely afflicted, was a child of God. The other, described as self-indulgent rather than vicious or criminal, was living without God in the enjoyment of every earthly luxury. Their state in this life was greatly in contrast with their real character before God, which was revealed in the amazing changes of their condition at death, Luke 16:19-31. See ABRAHAM'S BOSOM. Our Saviour plainly teaches us, in this parable, that both the friends and the foes of God know and begin to experience their doom immediately after death, and that it is in both cases unchangeable and eternal.

LEAD. There are early allusions to this well-known metal in Scripture. The Egyptians "sank as lead" in the Red sea, Exod. 15:10; Num. 31:22; Ezek. 27:12. Job refers to its use in preserving a permanent record of events, by being melted and poured into letters deeply cut in a rock, Job 19:24. Leaden tablets also were used by the ancients for similar records. This metal was employed, before the use of quicksilver was known, in purifying silver; and the process by which these metals are purged from their dross, illustrates God's discipline of his people, Jer. 6:29, 30; Ezek. 22:17-22.

LE'AH, the elder daughter of Laban, and the first wife of Jacob, though less beloved than her sister Rachel. She had, through life, the remembrance of the deceit by which her father had imposed her upon Jacob. She was the mother of seven children, among whom were Reuben — Jacob's first-born — and Judah, the ancestor of the leading tribe among the Jews, of the royal line, and of our Lord, Gen. 29:16-35; 30:1-21. She is supposed to have died before the removal of the family into Egypt, Gen. 49:31.

LEAS'ING, falsehood, Psa. 4:2; 5:6.

LEAV'EN, is sour dough which is kept over from one baking to another, in order to raise the new dough. Leaven was forbidden to the Hebrews during the seven days of the Passover, in memory of what their ancestors did when they went out of Egypt, they being then obliged to carry unleavened meal with them, and to make bread in haste, the Egyptians pressing them to be gone, Ex. 12:15, 19. They were very careful in cleansing their houses from it before this feast began, 1 Cor. 5:6. God forbade either leaven or honey to be offered to him in his temple, Lev. 2:11. The pervading and transforming effect of leaven is used in illustration of the like influence on society, exerted by the purifying principles of the gospel, or by false doctrines and corrupt men, Matt. 13:23; 16:6-12; 1 Cor. 5:6-8.

LEB'ANON, *white*, a long chain of mountains on the north of Palestine, so named from the whitish limestone of which they are composed, and in part perhaps from their snowy whiteness in winter. It consists of two main ridges running north-east and south-west, nearly parallel with each other and with the coast of the Mediterranean. See view in SIDON. The western ridge was called Libanus by the Greeks, and the eastern Anti-Libanus. Between them lies a long valley called Cœle-Syria, that is, Hollow Syria, and the "valley of Lebanon," Josh. 11:17, at present Bukkah. It opens towards the north, but is exceedingly narrow towards the south, where the river Litany, anciently Orontes, issues from the valley and flows west to the sea, north of Tyre. The western ridge is generally higher than the eastern, and several of its peaks are thought to be towards 10,000 feet high. One summit, however, in the eastern range, namely, mount Hermon, now called Jebel-esh-Sheikh, is higher still, and rises nearly into the region of perpetual ice. See HERMON. An Arab poet says of the highest peak of Lebanon, "The Sannin bears winter on his head, spring upon his shoulders, and autumn in his bosom, while summer lies sleeping at his feet."

The Hebrew writers often allude to this sublime mountain range, Isa. 10:34; 35:2, rising like a vast barrier on their north, Isa. 37:24. They speak of its sea of foliage agitated by the gales, Psa. 72:16; of its noble cedars and other trees, Isa. 60:13; Jer. 22:23; of its innumerable herds, the whole of which, however, could not atone for one sin, Isa. 40:16; of its excellent wine, Hos. 14:7, its snow-cold streams, Jer. 18:14, and its balsamic perfume, Hos. 14:5. Moses longed to enter the Holy Land, that he might "see that goodly mountain and Lebanon," Deut. 3:24, 25; and Solomon says of the Beloved, the type of Christ, "his countenance is as Lebanon," Song 5:15. "The tower of Lebanon which looketh towards Damascus," Song 7:4, is brought to recollection by the accounts given by modern travellers of the ruins of ancient temples, built of stones of vast size. Many such ruinous temples have been discovered in different parts of Lebanon, several of them on conspicuous points, high up in the mountains, where the labor of erecting them must have been stupendous.

At present, Lebanon is inhabited by a hardy and turbulent race of mountaineers. Its vast wilderness of mountains forms almost a world by itself. Its western slopes particularly, rising by a succession of terraces from the plain of the coast, are covered with vines, olives, mulberries, and figs; and occupied, as well as the valleys among the mountains, by numberless villages. Anti-Lebanon is less populous and cultivated. The chief inhabitants of Lebanon are Druses and Maronites; the former Mohammedan mystics, and the latter bigoted Romanists. Among them are interspersed many Greeks and Armenians.

For "cedar of Lebanon," see CEDAR.

LEBBE'US. See JUDAS II.

LEBO'NAH, Judg. 21:19, a town of Ephraim, near Shiloh, between Bethel and Shechem. Its name and site are preserved in the present village of Lubban.

LEEK, a bulbous vegetable resembling the onion. The Hebrews complained in the wilderness, that manna grew insipid to them; they longed for the leeks and onions of Egypt, Num. 11:5. Hasselquist says the *karrat*, or leek, is surely one of those after which the Israelites pined; for it has been cultivated in Egypt from time immemorial. The Hebrew word is usually translated "grass" in the English Bible. Its original meaning is supposed to be greens or grass.

LEES, or dregs, the refuse and sediment of wine. Wines that have been allowed to stand a long time on the lees, thereby acquire a superior color and flavor. Hence such wines are used as a symbol of gospel blessings, Isa. 25:6; also of a nation or community that, from long quiet and prosperity, has become rich and luxurious, and has settled down in carnal security, Jer. 48:11; Zeph. 1:12. To drink the dregs of the cup of God's wrath, Psa. 75:8, Isa. 51:17, is to drink it to exhaustion; that is, to suffer God's wrath without mitigation or end.

LE'GION. The number in a Roman legion varied at different periods, from three thousand to more than twice that number. In the time of Christ a legion contained six thousand, besides the cavalry. There were ten cohorts in each legion; which were divided each into three maniples or bands, and these into two centuries containing one hundred men each. In the Bible a legion means a number indefinitely large. The Saviour cured a demoniac who called himself "Legion," as if possessed by myriads of demons, Mark 5:9. The expression, "twelve legions of angels," Matt.

26 : 53, illustrates the immensity of the heavenly host, and their zealous devotion to Christ.

LEHA'BIM. See LIBYA.

LE'HI, *jaw-bone*, a place in Judah, where Samson was enabled to slay one thousand Philistines with the jaw-bone of an ass, and where, in answer to his petition, a fountain sprung up to relieve his thirst, Judg. 15:9–19. Probably the Hebrew word Lehi in ver. 19, should be left untranslated, as in the marginal reading: "God clave a hollow place that was in Lehi, and there came water thereout." This spring he called En-hakkore, the fountain of him that prayed. It continued to flow, and may even to this day be testifying that God hears the cry of his people, and can turn a dry land into springs of water for their use, Gen. 21:19; Num. 20:11.

LEM'UEL, the author of Proverbs 31. Some suppose it to be an enigmatical name for Solomon.

LEN'TILE, a species of pulse or bean. We find Esau longing for a mess of pottage made of lentiles, Gen. 25 : 34. Augustine says, "Lentiles are used as food in Egypt, for this plant grows abundantly in that country, which renders the lentiles of Alexandria so valuable that they are brought from thence to us, as if none were grown among us." In Barbary, Dr. Shaw says, "Lentiles are dressed in the same manner as beans, dissolving easily into a mass, and making a pottage of a chocolate color." See 2 Sam. 17:28; 23:11.

LEOP'ARD, a fierce wild beast of the feline genus, beautifully spotted with a diversity of colors; it has small eyes,

wide jaws, sharp teeth, round ears, a large tail; five claws on the fore feet, and four on those behind. It is swift, crafty, and cruel; dangerous to all domestic cattle, and even to man, Jer. 5:6; 13:23; Dan. 10:6; Hos. 13:7; Hab. 1:8. Its name, *leopard*, implies that it has something of the lion and of the panther in its nature. It seems from Scripture that the leopard could not be rare in Palestine. Its Hebrew name occurs significantly in several names of places; as Beth-nimrah, the haunt of leopards, Num. 32 : 36. So in Nimrah, Nimrim, and perhaps Nimrod the mighty hunter. Isaiah, describing the happy reign of the Messiah, says, chap. 11:6, "The leopard shall lie down with the kid, and the calf and the young lion and the fatling together." The spouse in the Canticles speaks of the mountains of the leopards, Song 4 : 8; that is to say, such as Lebanon and Hermon, where wild beasts dwelt.

LEP'ER, a person afflicted with leprosy. As it now exists, leprosy is a scaly disease of the skin, occurring in several distinct forms and with many degrees of severity; beginning with slight reddish eruptions, followed by scales of a greyish white color, sometimes in circles an inch or two in diameter, and at other times much larger; in many cases attacking only the knees and elbows, in others the whole body; usually not affecting the general health, but considered impossible of cure. It is said not to be infectious; but is communicated from father to son for several generations, gradually becoming less noticeable. It corresponds in the main with the disease the symptoms and treatment of which are so fully described in Lev. 13; 14. There is little doubt, however, that the ancient leprosy, in its more aggravated form, is to be regarded as a plague or judgment from God, Deut. 24:8. It was peculiarly dreaded among the Jews as unclean and infectious; and also as being a special infliction from Jehovah, as we know it to have been in the cases of Miriam, Num. 12:10, Gehazi, 2 Kin. 5:27, and Uzziah, 2 Chr. 26:16-23. No remedies were effectual. The sufferer was commended to the priest, not to the physician; and was separated from many of the privileges of society. We find that lepers associated chiefly with each other, 2 Kin. 7:8; Luke 17:12. The term, "the plague of leprosy," is applied not only to this disease in men, but to a similar infection sometimes sent into houses and garments, Lev. 14. The exact nature of this latter cannot be ascertained; but it bears the marks of a special aggravation, as a judgment from God, of some evil not unknown in that climate. It illustrates the awful result of moral corruption in society, uncounteracted by the grace of God. The disease in all its forms is a lively emblem of sin. This malady of the soul is also all-pervading, unclean, contagious, and incurable; it separates its victim from God and heaven; it proves its existence by its increasing sway and its fatal termination. But the Saviour has shown his power to heal the worst maladies of the soul by curing the leprosy with a word, Luke 17:12-19, and to admit the restored soul to all the privileges of the sons of God.

ELEPHANTI'ASIS, supposed by some to have been the disease of Job, and the "botch" or ulcer of Egypt, Deut. 28:27, 35, is a tuberculous malady somewhat akin to the leprosy, but more dreadful. Its name is derived from the dark, hard, and rough appearance of the skin; and from the form of the feet, swollen, and despoiled of the toes. This horrid malady infects the whole system; ulcers and dark scales cover the body; and the hair, beard, fingers, and all the extremities drop off. It is still met with in tropical countries, and was introduced into Europe by the crusaders; but after occasioning dreadful havoc, and the building of thousands of "hospitals for lepers," it disappeared or changed its form.

LES'BOS. See MITYLENE.

LET, sometimes used in the Bible in the old English sense, that is, to hinder, Isa. 43:13; Rom. 1:13.

LETTERS, Luke 23:38. The Hebrews have certain acrostic poems which begin with the letters of the alphabet, ranged in order. The most considerable of these is Psalm 119, which contains twenty-two stanzas of eight verses each, all acrostic; that is, the first eight begin with Aleph, the next eight with Beth, and so on. Psalms 25, 34, have but twenty-two verses each, beginning with the twenty-two letters of the Hebrew alphabet. Others, as Psalms 111, 112, have one-half of the verse beginning with one letter, and the other half with the next. Thus,

Blessed is the man who feareth the Lord,
Who delighteth greatly in his commandments.

The first half of the verse begins in the Hebrew with Aleph; the second with Beth. Psalms 37 and 145 are acrostic. The Lamentations of Jeremiah are also in acrostic verse, as well as the thirty-first chapter of Proverbs, from the eighth verse to the end. In John 7:15, the word "letters" means learning; the Jews said of Christ, Whence this man's qualifications to teach us the Scriptures, since he has not learned of the doctors of the law?

Paul speaks of "the letter" in distinction from "the spirit," Rom. 2:27, 29; 7:6; 2 Cor. 3:6; contrasting the mere word of the law and its outward observance, with its spiritual meaning, and cordial obedience to it through the Spirit of Christ.

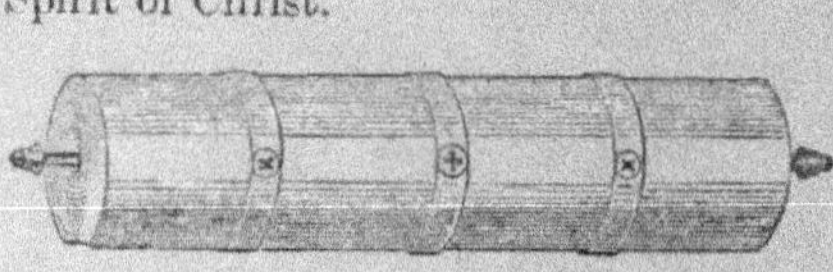

AN ANCIENT EPISTLE.

Epistolary correspondence seems to have been little practised among the ancient Hebrews. Some few letters are mentioned in the Old Testament, 2 Sam. 11:14; Ezra 4:8. They were conveyed to their destination by friends or travellers, Jer. 29:3; or by royal couriers, 2 Chr. 30:6; Esth. 8:10. The letter was usually in the form of a roll, the last fold being pasted down. They were sealed, 1 Kin. 21:8, and sometimes wrapped in an envelope, or in a bag of costly materials and highly ornamented. To send an open letter was expressive of contempt, Neh. 6:5. In the New Testament we have numerous examples of letters, from the pens of the apostles.

LE'VI, I., the third son of Jacob and Leah, born in Mesopotamia; and father of three sons, and of Jochebed the mother of Moses, Gen. 29:34; Ex. 6:16-20. For his share in the treacherous massacre of the Shechemites, Gen. 34, his father at death foreboded evil to his posterity, Gen. 49:5-7; but as they afterwards stood forth on the Lord's side, Moses was charged to bless them, Ex. 32:26-29; Deut. 33:8-11. The tribe of Levi was, according to Jacob's prediction, scattered over all Israel, having no share in the division of Canaan, but certain cities in the portions of other tribes. It was not the worse provided for, however, since God chose this tribe for the service of the temple and priesthood, and bestowed on it many privileges above the other tribes. All the tithes, first-fruits, and offerings, presented at the temple, as well as several parts of all the victims that were offered, belonged to the tribe of Levi. See LEVITES.

II. The apostle Matthew was also called Levi. See MATTHEW.

LEVI'ATHAN, Psa. 74:14; 104:26, an aquatic monster described in the book of Job, ch. 41. Probably the animal denoted is the crocodile, the terror of the Nile; as BEHEMOTH, in Job 40, is the hippopotamus of the same river.

The crocodile is a native of the Nile, and other Asiatic and African rivers; in some instances even thirty feet in length; of enormous voracity and strength, as well as fleetness in swimming; attacks mankind and the largest animals, with most daring impetuosity; when taken by means of a powerful net, will often overturn the boats that surround it; has proportionally the largest mouth of all monsters whatever; moves both its jaws alike, the upper of which has not less than thirty-six, and the lower thirty sharp, but strong and massy teeth; and is furnished with a coat of mail so scaly and callous as to resist the force of a musket-ball in every part, except under the belly. The general character of the LEVIATHAN, in fact, seems so well to apply to this animal, in modern as well as in ancient times the terror of all the coasts and countries about the Nile, that it is unnecessary to seek further. In several passages in the Bible, the king of Egypt appears to be addressed as leviathan, Isa. 27:1; Ezek. 29:3.

The following extract of a letter from an American gentleman in Manilla gives a graphic view of the strength and size of the crocodile: "My last operation in the sporting line, was no less than killing a crocodile, which for a year or two before had infested a village on the borders of the lake, taking off horses and cows, and sometimes a man. Having understood that he had killed a horse a day or two before, and had taken him into a small river, I proceeded to the spot, accompanied by my host, closed the mouth of the river with strong nets, and attacked the huge brute with guns and spears. After something of a desperate battle, we succeeded in driving him against the nets, where, being considerably exhausted by the wounds he had received from balls and lances, he got entangled, was dragged on shore, and the *coup de grace* given to him. He measured twenty feet in length, and from eleven to thirteen feet in circumference, the smallest part being eleven and the largest thirteen. The head alone weighed two hundred and seventy-five pounds. He had nearly the whole of the horse in him, and the legs, with the hoofs, were taken out entire."

LE'VITES. All the descendants of Levi may be comprised under this name, Ex. 6:16, 25; Josh. 3:3, (see LEVI;) but chiefly those who were employed in the lower services in the temple, by which they were distinguished from the priests, who were of the race of Levi by Aaron, and were employed in higher offices, Num. 3:6-10; 18:2-7. God chose the Levites for the service of his tabernacle and temple, instead of the first-born of all Israel, to whom such duties naturally belonged, and who were already sacred to God in memory of the great deliverance in Egypt, Ex. 13; Num. 3:12, 13, 39-51. In the wilderness, the Levites took charge of the tabernacle and its contents; and conveyed it from place to place, each of the three families having a separate portion, Num. 1:51; 4; 1 Chr. 15:2, 27. After the building of the temple they took charge of the gates, of the sacred vessels, of the preparation of the show-bread and other offerings, and of the singing and instrumental music, 1 Chr. 9; 23; 2 Chr. 29. They brought wood, water, etc., for the priests; aided them in preparing the sacrifices, and in collecting and disbursing the contributions of the people, 2 Chr. 30:16, 17; 35:1. They were also the temple guards, Neh. 13:13, 22; and the salutation and response in Psalm 134, are thought by Bishop Lowth to have been their song in the night. But besides their services in the temple, they performed a very important part in teaching the people, 2 Chr. 30:22, Neh. 8:7, among whom they were scattered, binding the tribes together, and promoting virtue and piety. They studied the law, and were the ordinary judges of the country, but subordinate to the priests, 2 Chr. 17:9; 19:8-11. God provided for the subsistence of the Levites, by giving to them the tithe of corn, fruit, and cattle; but they paid to the priests the tenth of their tithes; and as the Levites possessed no estates in land, the tithes which the priests received from them were considered as the first-fruits which they were to offer to the Lord, Num. 18:21-32. The payment of tithes to the Levites appears not to have been enforced, but depended on the good-will of the people; hence the special charges laid on their brethren, not to forget them, Deut. 12:12, 18, 19.

God assigned for the habitation of the Levites forty-eight cities, with fields, pastures, and gardens, Num. 35. Of these, thirteen were given to the priests, all in the tribes near Jerusalem. Six of the Levitical cities were appointed as cities of refuge, Josh. 20; 21. While the Levites were actually employed in the temple, they were supported out of the provisions kept in store there, and out of the daily offerings. The same privilege was granted to volunteers, drawn to Jerusalem by the fervor of their love to God's service, Deut. 12:18, 19; 18:6-8. The consecration of Levites was without much ceremony. See Num. 8:5-22; 2 Chr. 29:34.

The Levites wore no peculiar dress to distinguish them from other Israelites, till the time of Agrippa. His innovation in this matter is mentioned by Josephus, who remarks that the ancient customs of the country were never forsaken with impunity.

The Levites were divided into different classes: the Gershomites, Kohathites, and Merarites, Num. 3:17-20. They were still further divided into courses, like the priests, 1 Chr. 23-26. At first, they entered in full on their public duties at thirty years of age, Num. 4:3; 8:25; but David fixed the age for commencing at twenty years; and at fifty they were exempt, 1 Chr. 23:24-27. The different courses of porters, singers, guards, etc., were on duty in succession, one week at a time, 1 Chr. 23-26; 2 Chr. 23:4, 8; 31:17; Ezra 3:8-12. After the revolt of the ten tribes, a large portion of the Levites abandoned their cities in Israel, and dwelt in Judah, 2 Chr. 11:12-14; 13:9-11. After the captivity, numbers of them returned from beyond the Euphrates to Judea, Neh. 11:15-19; 12:24-31. In the New Testament they are not often mentioned, Luke 10:32; John 1:19; Acts 4:36. The "scribes" and "doctors," however, are supposed to have belonged chiefly to this class.

LEVIT'ICUS, the third book in the Pentateuch; called Leviticus, because it contains principally the laws and regulations relating to the Levites, priests, and sacrifices. The Hebrews call it "the priests' law." In the first section, the various bloody and unbloody sacrifices are minutely described: the burnt-offering, the meat, sin, peace, ignorance, and trespass offerings; the sins for which and the mode in which they were to be offered. The fulness of these details not only signified the importance of God's worship, but forbade all human additions and changes, that might lead to idolatry. The whole scheme was "a shadow of good things to come," typical of the Lamb "who through the eternal Spirit offered himself without spot unto God." Its best commentary is the epistle to the Hebrews.

A full account of the consecration of Aaron and his sons as priests, is followed by the instructive narrative of Nadab and Abihu. Then are given the laws respecting personal and ceremonial purifications, a perpetual memento of the defilement of sin, and of the holiness of God. Next follows a description of the great day of Expiation; after which the Jews are warned against the superstitions, idolatry, impurity, etc., of the Canaanites; and laws are given guarding their morals, health, and civil order. The observance of their distinguishing festivals is enjoined upon them; and laws are given respecting the Sabbath and the jubilee, vows and tithes. The warnings and promises in the latter part of the book point their attention to the future, and aim to unite the whole nation in serving their covenant God. The book is generally held to be the work of Moses, though he was probably assisted by Aaron. Its date is B. C. 1490. It contains the history of the first month of their second year after leaving Egypt.

LIB'ERTINES, Acts 6:9. This word is from the Latin libertinus, which signifies a freedman, that is, one who, having been a slave, either by birth or capture, has obtained his freedom; or one born of a parent who was a freedman. The "synagogue of the Libertines" stands connected with the Cyrenians and Alexandrians, both of whom were of African origin; it is therefore supposed by some, that the Libertines were of African origin also. It is, however, most probable that this word denotes Jews who had been taken captive by the Romans in war, and carried to Italy; and having there been manumitted, were accustomed to visit Jerusalem in such numbers as to erect a synagogue for their particular use; as was the case with Jews from other cities mentioned in the context. They originated the persecution against Stephen, which resulted in his martyrdom. See SYNAGOGUE.

LIB'NAH, a city in the western part of Judah, not far from Lachish, conquered by Joshua from the Canaanites, and assigned to the priests, Josh. 10:29, 30; 15:42; 21:13; 1 Chr. 6:57. Its inhabitants revolted against the idolatrous and cruel Jehoram, 2 Chr. 21:10. It was a strongly fortified place, and under its walls the Assyrian army was miraculously cut off, 2 Kin. 19:8, 9, 35.

LIB'YA, a country in the north of Africa, stretching along on the Mediterranean between Egypt and Carthage, and running back somewhat into the interior. The part adjoining Egypt was sometimes called Libya Marmarica; and that around Cyrene, Cyrenaica, from its chief city; or Pentapolitana, from its five cities, Cyrene, Apollonia, Berenice, Arsinoë, and Ptolemais. In these cities great numbers of Jews dwelt in the time of Christ; and they, with their Libyan proselytes, resorted to Jerusalem to worship, Acts 2:10. Libya received its name from the Lehabim or Lubim, Gen. 10:13; a warlike people, who assisted Shishak king of Egypt, and Zerah the Ethiopian, in their wars against Judea, 2 Chr. 12:3; 14:9; 16:8; Dan. 11:43. They were also allies of ancient Thebes, Nah. 3:9. Compare Jer. 46:9; Ezek. 30:5. Libya fell at length under the power of Carthage; and subsequently, of the Greeks, Romans, Saracens, and Turks.

LICE, the third plague of Egypt, Ex. 8:16; Psa. 105:31; peculiarly offensive to the priests, who were obliged to shave and wash their entire body every third day, lest they should carry any vermin into the temples. According to many interpreters, they were the small stinging gnats which abound in Egypt.

LIFE, in the Bible, is either natural, Gen. 3:17; spiritual, that of the renewed soul, Rom. 8:6; or eternal, a holy and blissful immortality, John 3:36; Rom. 6:23. Christ is the great Author of natural life, Col. 1:16; and also of spiritual and eternal life, John 14:6; 6:47. He has purchased these by laying down his own life; and gives them freely to his people, John 10:11, 28. He is the spring of all their spiritual life on earth, Gal. 2:20; will raise them up at the last day; and make them partakers for ever of his own life, John 11:25; 14:19.

LIGHT, one of the most wonderful, cheering, and useful of all the works of God; called into being on the first of the six days of creation, by his voice: "Let there be light;" and there was light. No object better illustrates whatever is pure, glorious, spiritual, joyful, and beneficent. Hence the beauty and force of the expressions, "God is light," 1 John 1:5, and "the Father of lights," Jas. 1:17; Christ is the "Sun of righteousness," and "the light of the world," John 1:9; 8:12. So also the word of God is "a light," Psa. 119:105; truth and Christians are lights, John

3:19; 12:36; prosperity is "light," Esth. 8:16; and heaven is full of light, Rev. 21:23-25. The opposite of all these is "darkness."

LIGN-ALOES. See ALOES.

LIG'URE, probably the same with the jacinth, a stone in the high-priest's breastplate, Ex. 28:19; 39:12, said to have been of a deep and brilliant red color, with a tinge of yellow, and transparent.

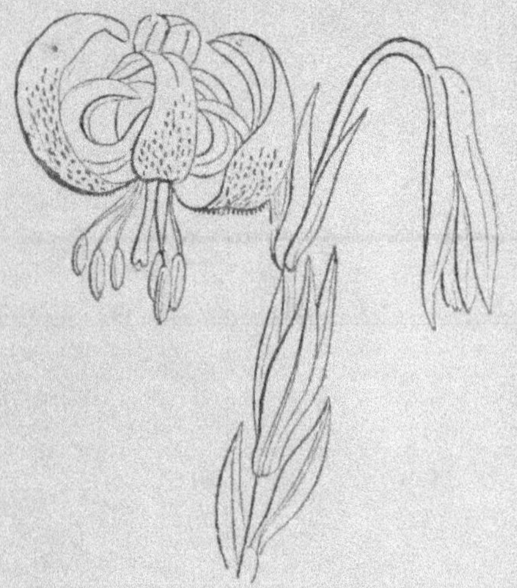

LILIUM CHALCEDONICUM.

LIL'Y. Of this queenly plant, several varieties are found among the wild flowers of Palestine, the profusion, beauty, and fragrance of which are the delight of travellers. The lily is a spring flower, and appears early in all parts of the Holy Land. It was introduced in the ornamental work of the temple, 1 Kin. 7:19-26; 2 Chr. 4:5. In Canticles it is often employed as a symbol of loveliness. More commonly it is applied to the bride and her various perfections: chap. 2:1, 2, where the bride speaks, ver. 1, the bridegroom answers, ver. 2, and the bride again responds, ver. 3. The bridegroom's lips are compared to lilies in chap. 5:13, and he is described as feeding among the lilies, chap. 2:16; 6:3; which typically represents Christ as delighting himself with the graces of his people. From the lily our Saviour has also drawn one of his most striking figures: "Consider the lilies of the field, how they grow;" "even Solomon in all his glory was not arrayed like one of these. If God so clothe the grass of the field, shall he not much more clothe you?" Matt. 6:28. We must be careful not to confound the lily of the valleys, Song 2:1, which means simply the lily growing in valleys, with our "lily of the valley," which belongs to another class of flowers.

LIN'EN, as is well known, is made of the fine fibres of flax, and was much used by the ancients. Four different words in Hebrew are translated in our Bible, "linen," "fine linen," and "silk:" PISHTAH, Judg. 15:14; Ezek. 44:17, 18; BAD, worn by the priests, Ex. 28:42; 39:28, and by king David, etc., 2 Sam. 6:14; SHESH, worn by Joseph when governor of Egypt, Gen. 41:42, and by the virtuous woman in Prov. 31:22, (see SILK;) and BUTZ, of which the veil of the temple and David's outer mantle were made, 1 Chr. 15:27; 2 Chr. 2:14; 3:14; 5:12. These words may indicate different qualities of linen, but are thought to mean in part cloth of different materials, particularly the two last. Some think BUTZ, in Latin *byssus*, denotes cotton cloth, and SHESH that made of hemp. See COTTON, and FLAX. Fine linen was sometimes made of snowy whiteness, and was a symbol of the purity of angels and of the redeemed church, Rev. 15:6; 19:8.

LINES, the cords used in measuring and settling the bounds of landed property, Psa. 16:6; Isa. 34:17.

LI'NUS, a Christian at Rome, whose salutation Paul sent to Timothy, 2 Tim. 4:21.

LI'ON, the well-known and noble king of beasts, frequently spoken of in Scripture. He often exceeds eight feet in length and four feet in height; and his majestic and dauntless aspect, his prodigious strength and agility, and his peculiar roar, make him the terror of the forests. Lions were common in Palestine, (see JORDAN,) and the Hebrews had seven different names for them, to distinguish the different ages, etc. Five of these occur together in Job 4:10, 11. See also Nah. 2:11, 12. The psalmist alludes to the stealthy creeping of the lion till he can spring upon his prey, when he says of the crafty wicked man, "He lieth in wait secretly as a lion in his den; .... he croucheth, and humbleth himself, that the poor may fall by

his strong ones." The Bible reader will remember the exploits of Samson and of David, Judg. 14:5, 6; 1 Sam. 17:34–36, the story of the disobedient prophet slain by a lion, 1 Kin. 13:28, and of the obedient Daniel, safe in the lions' den, Dan. 6; also the sublime image of Jehovah's care for his people, in Isa. 31:4.

"The Lion of the tribe of Judah," Rev. 5:5, is Jesus Christ, who sprung from the tribe of Judah and the race of David, and overcame death, the world, and the devil. It is supposed that a lion was the device of the tribe of Judah; whence this allusion, Gen. 49:9.

LIT'TER, a light, covered conveyance, resembling a sedan-chair, or a palanquin; borne by men, but oftener at the present day in Syria between two mules or camels. Solomon's chariot, Song 3:9, or bed as in the margin, is supposed to have been an elegant mule-litter. The Hebrew word translated litters in Isa. 66:20, is rendered wagons in Num. 7:3.

LIV'ER, Lev. 3:4. This organ in man was regarded by the ancients as the seat of the passions. Idolaters consulted the liver of the victim offered in sacrifice, for purposes of divination, Ezek. 21:21.

LIZ'ARD, a cold-blooded animal, with much resemblance to the serpent, but having four feet. Large numbers are

found in Syria, varying greatly in size, appearance, and place of abode; some dwelling partly in water, and others on the rocks of the desert, or among old ruins. Lizards were unclean by the Levitical law, Lev. 11:30.

LOANS. Jehovah, as the sole proprietor of the land occupied by the Jews, required them, as one condition of its use, to grant liberal loans to their poor brethren; and every seven years, the outstanding loans were to become gifts, and could not be reclaimed. If a pledge was taken on making a loan, it must be done with mercy and under certain benevolent restrictions, Exod. 22:25, 27; Deut. 15:1-11; 23:19, 20; 24:6, 10-13, 17. The great truth so prominent in this and similar features of the Mosaic laws, ought to be restored to its fundamental place in our theories of property; and no one who believes in God should act as the owner, but only as the steward of what he possesses, all of which he is to use as required by its great Owner. In the same spirit, our Saviour enjoins the duty of loaning freely, even to enemies, and without hope of reward, Luke 6:34, 35.

LO'CUST, a voracious winged insect, belonging to the genus known among naturalists as the Grylli, closely resembling the grasshopper, and a great scourge in oriental countries in both ancient and modern times. There are ten different names in the Hebrew Bible for insects of this kind; but some of these probably designate different forms or stages in life of the same species. The Bible represents their countless swarms as directed in their flight and march by God, and used in the chastisement of guilty nations, Deut. 28:38-42; 1 Kin. 8:37; 2 Chr. 6:28. A swarm of locusts was among the plagues of Egypt; they covered the whole land, so that the earth

was darkened, and devoured every green herb of the earth, and the fruit of every tree which the hail had left, Ex. 10:4-19. But the most particular description of this insect, and of its destructive career, in the sacred writings, is in Joel 2:3-10. This is one of the most striking and animated descriptions to be met with in the whole compass of prophecy; and the double destruction to be produced by locusts and the enemies of which they were the harbingers, is painted with the most expressive force and accuracy. We see the destroying army moving before us as we read, and see the desolation spreading. It should also be mentioned, that the four insects specified in Joel 1:4, the palmer-worm, the locust, the canker-worm, and the caterpillar, are strictly, according to the Hebrew, only different forms of locusts, some perhaps without wings, as mentioned below. The following extracts from Dr. Shaw and Mr. Morier, which are also corroborated by Niebuhr, Burckhardt, and other travellers, may serve as a commentary upon this and other passages of Scripture.

Dr. Shaw remarks, "Those which I saw, were much bigger than our common grasshoppers, and had brown spotted wings, with legs and bodies of a bright yellow. Their first appearance was towards the end of March, the wind having been some time from the south. In the middle of April, their numbers were so vastly increased, that in the heat of the day they formed themselves into large and numerous swarms, flew in the air like a succession of clouds, and as the prophet Joel expresses it, they darkened the sun. When the wind blew briskly, so that these swarms were crowded by others, or thrown one upon another, we had a lively idea of that comparison of the psalmist, Psa. 109:23, of being tossed up and down as the locust. In the month of May, these swarms gradually retired into the Metijiah and other adjacent plains, where they deposited their eggs. These were no sooner hatched, in June, than each of the broods collected itself into a compact body of a furlong or more square, and marching afterwards in a direct line towards the sea, they let nothing escape them; eating up every thing that was green and juicy, not only the lesser kinds of vegetables, but the vine likewise, the fig-tree, the pomegranate, the palm, and the apple-tree, even all the trees of the field, Joel 1:12; in doing which, they kept their ranks like men of war, climbing over, as they advanced, every tree or wall that was in their way; nay, they entered into our very houses and bedchambers like thieves. The inhabitants, to stop their progress, made a variety of pits and trenches all over their fields and gardens, which they filled with water; or else they heaped up therein heath, stubble, and such like combustible matter, which were severally set on fire upon the approach of the locusts. But this was all to no purpose, for the trenches were quickly filled up and the fires extinguished by infinite swarms succeeding one another, while the front was regardless of danger and the rear pressed on so close that a retreat was altogether impossible. A day or two after one of these broods was in motion, others were already hatched to march and glean after them, gnawing off the very bark and the young branches of such trees as had before escaped with the loss only of their fruit and foliage. So justly have they been compared by the prophet to a great army; who further observes, that the land is as the garden of Eden before them, and behind them a desolate wilderness."

Mr. Morier says, "On the 11th of June, while seated in our tents about noon, we heard a very unusual noise, that sounded like the rustling of a great wind at a distance. On looking up, we perceived an immense cloud, here and there semi-transparent, in other parts quite black, that spread itself all over the sky, and at intervals shadowed the sun. These we soon found to be locusts, whole swarms of them falling about us. These were of a *red* color, and I should suppose are the red predatory locusts, one of the Egyptian plagues. As soon as they appeared, the gardeners and husbandmen made loud shouts, to prevent their settling on their grounds. They seemed to be impelled by one common instinct, and moved in one body, which had the appearance of being organized by a leader, Joel 2:7."

The locust was a "clean" animal for the Jews, Lev. 11:22, and might be used for food. In Matt. 3:4, it is said of John the Baptist, that "his meat was locusts, and wild honey." They are still eaten in the East, and regarded by some as a delicacy, though usually left to the poorest of the people. Niebuhr remarks, "Locusts are brought to market on strings, in all the cities of Arabia, from Babelmandel to Basorah. On mount Sumara I saw an Arab who had collected a whole sackful of them. They are prepared in different ways. An Arab in Egypt, of whom we requested that he would immediately eat locusts in our presence, threw them upon the glowing coals, and after he supposed they were roasted enough, he took them by the legs and head, and devoured the remainder at one mouthful. When the Arabs have them in quantities, they roast or dry them in an oven, or boil them and eat them with salt. The Arabs in the kingdom of Morocco boil the locusts, and then dry them on the roofs of their houses. One sees there large baskets full of them in the markets."

Burckhardt also relates the fact in a similar manner: "The Bedaween eat locusts, which are collected in great quantities in the beginning of April, when they are easily caught. After having been roasted a little upon the iron plate on which bread is baked, they are dried in the sun, and then put into large sacks, with the mixture of a little salt."

In Rev. 9:7-10, there is a terrific description of symbolical locusts, in which they are compared to war-horses, their hair to the hair of women, etc. Niebuhr heard an Arab of the desert, and another in Bagdad, make the same comparison. They likened "the head of the locust to that of the horse; its breast to that of the lion; its feet to those of the camel; its body to that of the serpent; its tail to that of the scorpion; its antennæ, if I mistake not, to the locks of hair of a virgin; and so of other parts." In like manner, the Italians still call locusts little horses, and the Germans hay-horses.

LOD. See LYDDA.

LODGE. See GARDEN.

LOG, a Hebrew measure for liquids, containing five-sixths of a pint, Lev. 14:10, 12, 24.

LOINS. See GIRDLE.

LO'IS, a pious Jewess, whose "unfeigned faith" Paul traces in her daughter Eunice, and her grandson Timothy, 2 Tim. 1:5.

LOOK'ING-GLASS'ES, or rather, mirrors, were anciently made of metal, chiefly copper, Ex. 38:8; Job 37:18, melted and cast in a circular form, highly polished, and attached to an ornamental handle. Similar mirrors have been found in the ruins of ancient Egypt.

LORD. This name belongs to God by preëminence; and in this sense ought never to be given to any creature. Jesus Christ, as the Messiah, the Son of God, and equal with the Father, is often called Lord in Scripture, especially in the writings of Paul. The word LORD, in the English Bible, when printed in small capitals, stands always for JEHOVAH in the Hebrew. See JEHOVAH.

LORD'S-DAY. See SABBATH.

LORD'S SUPPER, called also "the breaking of bread," Acts 2:42; 20:7, and the communion of the body and blood of Christ, 1 Cor. 10:16, is one of the two simple ordinances of the Christian church; instituted by our Saviour in the most affecting circumstances on the Passover night in which he was betrayed, to be observed by his followers until his second coming. Bread and wine, the symbols of his body broken and his blood shed for our redemption, are to be tasted by each communicant, to keep in mind that great sacrifice, the foundation of all our hopes and the strongest motive to a holy and devoted life. In the Lord's supper the covenant is renewed between Christ and his people. It is also the visible token of Christian fellowship; and all true believers, and none but they, should claim to partake of it, 1 Cor. 5:6–8. In it Christians may expect and should seek to receive of the fulness of Christ, grace for grace, 2 Cor. 1:21, 22; Eph. 4:15, 16; while those who partake heedlessly incur great guilt, and may look for chastisement, 1 Cor. 11:20–34. The dogma of the Romish church, that the bread is changed into the very body and soul of Christ, which the priest offers anew in sacrifice, is contrary to the Scripture and to all the senses, as it is also to common-sense.

LOT, the son of Haran, and nephew of Abraham, followed his uncle from Ur, and afterwards from Haran, to settle in Canaan, Gen. 11:31; 12:4–6; 13:1. Abraham always had a great affection for him, and when they could not continue longer together in Canaan, because they both had large flocks and their shepherds sometimes quarrelled, Gen. 13:5–7, he gave Lot the choice of his abode. Lot chose the plain of Sodom, which appears then to have been the most fertile part of the land. Here he continued to dwell till the destruction of Sodom and the adjacent cities. He was a righteous man even in Sodom, 2 Pet. 2:7; but the calamities consequent upon his choice of this residence—his capture by eastern marauders, the molestation caused by his ungodly and vicious neighbors, the loss of his property in the burning city, the destruction of his sons-in-law and of his wife—if they do not prove that he regarded ease and profit more than duty, show that the most beautiful and fruitful land is not always the best; the profligacy of its citizens may sink it into the abyss of perdition, and endanger all who have any concern with it. Lot's wife, looking back with disobedient regrets, and arrested by the threatened judgment midway in her flight to the mountain, is an awful warning to all who turn their faces Zionward, but are unwilling to leave all for Christ, Gen. 19; Luke 17:32.

LOTS were often cast by the Jews, as well as other ancient nations, with the expectation, when God was appealed to, that he would so control them as to give a right direction in doubtful cases, Psa. 22:18; Prov. 16:33; 18:18. They were often used by the divine appointment. The portions of the twelve tribes were thus assigned to them; and hence each tribe's portion was called "the lot of its inheritance," Num. 26:55, 56; Psa. 125:3; Acts 8:21. The scape-goat was to be selected, and the order of the priests' service determined by lot, Lev. 16:8; 1 Chr. 24:5; 25:8. By the same means Achan, Jonathan, and Jonah were discovered, Josh. 7:14; 1 Sam. 14:41, 42; Jonah 1:7; and thus Matthias was designated by Christ to be an apostle in the place of Judas, Acts 1:26. A common mode of casting lots was by the use of pebbles, one or more of them being marked, and all of them being shaken together in some fold of a garment, an urn, or a helmet, before drawing, Prov. 16:33; John 19:24. As the use of lots by one who believes in the particular providence of God involves a solemn appeal to the Disposer of all events, they should never be used on trivial occasions; and in this day, a case can hardly occur when such an appeal would be warranted. See PURIM.

LOVE. GOD IS LOVE; AND HE THAT DWELLETH IN LOVE DWELLETH IN GOD, AND GOD IN HIM, 1 John 4:16. Love is a chief attribute of Jehovah, the length and breadth and height and depth of which are beyond comprehension, for they are infinite, Eph. 3:18, 19. Between the three Persons of the Godhead, love is unutterably full, perfect, and blissful; towards holy angels and Christians, God's love is an infinite fatherly complacency and affection; towards sinners, it is immeasurable compassion. It is shown in all his works and ways, and dictated his holy law, but is most signally displayed in the gospel, John 3:16. "Herein is love."

Holy love in man would make the whole heart and soul supremely delight in and obey God, and cordially and practically love all beings according to their character—the good with fellowship of soul, and the evil with a Christ-like benevolence. Such a love would meet and fulfil all the ends of the law, Matt. 22:37-40; Rom. 13:8-10. Without it, none can enter heaven; and as the affections of every unrenewed heart are all mixed with sin, being given to forbidden objects, or selfishly and unduly given to objects not forbidden, we must be "born again" in order to see God, John 3:3; 1 John 4:7, 19; 5:4.

LOWER PARTS OF THE EARTH, valleys, Isa. 44:23; also the grave, or the abode of disembodied spirits secluded from our view,

> "That undiscovered country from whose bourne
> No traveller returns."

Psa. 63:9; 139:15; Eph. 4:9.

LU'BIM. See LIBYA.

LU'CAS, the same with LUKE.

LU'CIFER, *light-bringer*, the Latin name of the morning-star, or "son of the morning." In the figurative language of Scripture, a brilliant star denoted an illustrious prince, Num. 24:17. Christ was given to men as the "bright and morning Star," Rev. 2:28; 22:16. The word Lucifer is used once only in the English Bible, and then of the king of Babylon, Isa. 14:12. It is now commonly, though inappropriately, given to the prince of darkness.

LU'CIUS of Cyrene, mentioned Acts 13:1, was one of the ministers and teachers of the Christian church at Antioch, and probably a kinsman of Paul, Rom. 16:21. He is supposed by some to be the same with the evangelist Luke; but of this there is no evidence.

LUD, a son of Shem, Gen. 10:22, and ancestor, it is thought, of the Lydians in Asia Minor.

LU'DIM, descendants of Mizraim, Gen. 10:13, dwelling in Africa, probably near Ethiopia; they were famous bowmen, Isa. 66:19, and are mentioned as soldiers with the Ethiopians, Libyans, and Tyrians, Jer. 46:9; Ezek. 27:10; 30:5.

LUKE, the evangelist, probably the same person who is called by St. Paul, "the beloved physician," Col. 4:14. The name Luke, or Lucas, Phile. 24, is the same as Lucanus in Latin. Luke was the writer of the gospel which bears his name, and of the Acts of the Apostles, having been the friend and companion of St. Paul in most of the journeys recorded in the latter book. Thus, in Acts 16:11, he first uses the word "we," and shows that he was with Paul at Troas and in his first Macedonian tour. After they reach Philippi, an interval of separation occurs; but they are again together at Philippi when Paul sails thence for Jerusalem, and from that time he continues with the apostle in his labors, voyages, and sufferings, to the close of his first imprisonment at Rome, Acts 17:1; 20:5, 6, 13-16; 21-28; Phile. 24; 2 Tim. 4:11. His personal history before and after this period of his companionship with Paul, is unknown, or rests on uncertain traditions. His own narrative contains the least possible mention of himself; yet we cannot doubt that he was eminently useful to the early church, by his learning, judgment, fidelity, and even his medical skill, besides leaving to the church universal the invaluable legacy of his writings.

LU'NATIC, a word formed from the Latin *luna*, the moon, and thus corresponding to the original Greek word and to the English "moonstruck;" applied to a class of persons mentally and often corporally diseased, who were believed to suffer most when the moon was full. Insanity, epilepsy, and morbid melancholy were among the frequent effects of demoniac possession, yet this possession existed independently of these effects, and was a more dreadful calamity. Lunatics are expressly mentioned in distinction from men possessed by evil spirits, Matt. 4:24; 17:15. See DEVILS.

LUST originally meant any longing desire, however innocent, Deut. 12:15; 14:26. But, in tacit acknowledgment of the depravity of man's passions, general usage soon attached the idea of guilt to the word; and now it usually denotes carnal, lascivious desire. In Gal. 5:17, we see that the aspirations of the heart renewed by the Holy Spirit, oppose and will subdue the native evil desires, 1 Cor. 15:57; but in the unrenewed heart these reign uncontrolled, lead to greater and greater outward sins, and secure eternal death, James 1:14, 15.

LUZ, the ancient name of a part at least of Bethel, Gen. 28:19; Josh. 16:2; 18:13; afterwards given to a smaller place founded by a refugee from Bethel, Judg. 1:26. See BETHEL.

LYCAO'NIA, a small province of Asia Minor, bounded north by Galatia, east by Cappadocia, south by Isauria and

Cilicia, and west by Phrygia. It appears to have been within the limits of Phrygia Major, but was erected into a Roman province by Augustus. The country is level, but not fertile, though peculiarly adapted to pasturage. Of its cities, Iconium, Derbe, and Lystra are mentioned in the New Testament, Acts 14:6. The "speech of Lycaonia," ver. 11, is generally supposed to have been a dialect of Greek, corrupted by a large mixture of Syriac. Lycaonia now forms part of the Turkish province of Caramania.

LY'CIA, a province in the south-west of Asia Minor, bounded west by Caria, east by Pamphylia, north by Phrygia and Pisidia, and south by the Mediterranean. The country is somewhat mountainous, though not barren. Of its cities, only Patara and Myra are mentioned in the New Testament, Acts 21:1, 2; 27:5.

LYD'DA, in Hebrew Lud or Lod, 1 Chr. 8:12; Ezra 2:33, and by the Greeks called Diospolis, was a city nine miles east of Joppa, on the way to Jerusalem. Here Peter healed Eneas, Acts 9:33, 34. It was destroyed not long after Jerusalem; but was soon rebuilt, and became the seat of a famous Jewish school. A Christian church was here organized, and was in existence A. D. 518. Lydda is often mentioned in the history of the crusades. It was situated in the midst of fine and extensive plains, the soil of which is a rich black mould, that might be rendered exceedingly fertile. It is at present only a miserable village called Ludd. The ruins of a stately church of the middle ages, called the church of St. George, preserve the name of a saint and martyr said to have been buried here in the third century. The English crusaders adopted him as the "patron" of England, and many fabulous legends are told of his exploits.

LYD'IA, a woman of Thyatira, residing at Philippi in Macedonia, and dealing in purple cloths. She was not a Jewess by birth, but had become a proselyte to Judaism and "worshipped God." She was led by the grace of God to receive the gospel with joy; and having been baptized, with her household, constrained Paul and his fellow-laborers to make her house their home while at Philippi, Acts 16:14, 40. See PHILIPPI.

LYSA'NIAS. See ABILENE.

LYS'IAS, or Claudius Lysias, commander of the Roman guard at Jerusalem during Paul's last visit there. In the honorable discharge of his duty, he repeatedly saved Paul from the malice of the Jews, Acts 21:27-40; 22; 23.

LYS'TRA, a city of Lycaonia, near Derbe and Iconium, and the native place of Timothy. Paul and Barnabas preached the gospel here; and having healed a cripple, were almost worshipped. Soon after, however, Paul was stoned there, Acts 14:6, 21; 16:1; 2 Tim. 3:11. It is now a small place called Latik.

M.

MA'ACAH, or MAACHAH, I., a city and region of Syria or Aram, 1 Chr. 19:6; somewhere near the foot of mount Hermon, and Geshur. The portion of Manasseh beyond Jordan reached to this country, like that of Og king of Bashan, Deut. 3:13, 14; but it does not appear to have become subject to Israel, Josh. 12:4-6; 13:13, except during the reign of David, Solomon, and Jeroboam II. The king of Maachah, with other Syrians, joined the Ammonites in a war with David, and were defeated and made tributary, 2 Sam. 10:6-8, 19.

II. A wife of David, and the mother of Absalom. She was a daughter of Talmai, king of Geshur in Syria, 2 Sam. 3:3.

III. The wife of Rehoboam and mother of Abijah, kings of Judah. She is called the "daughter" of Abishalom or Absalom, 1 Kin. 15:2; 2 Chr. 11:20-22. In 2 Chr. 13:2, she is called Michaiah, and is said to be the daughter of Uriel. She appears to have exerted a great influence over the members of the royal family; but was degraded from her high position, by Asa her grandson, for promoting idolatry, 2 Chr. 15:16.

Six others of the same name are mentioned, in Gen. 22:24; 1 Kin. 2:39; 1 Chr. 2:48; 7:16; 11:43; 27:16.

MACEDO'NIA, a large country lying north of Greece proper, bounded south by Thessaly and Epirus, east by Thrace and the Ægean sea, west by the Adriatic sea and Illyria, and north by Dardania and Mœsia. Its principal rivers were the Strymon and Axius. Its most celebrated mountains were Olympus and Athos: the former renowned in heathen mythology as the residence of the gods, lying on the confines of Thessaly, and principally within that state; the latter being at the extremity of a promontory which juts out into the Ægean sea, and noted in modern times as the seat of several monasteries, in which are many manuscripts supposed to be valuable. This region is believed to have been peopled by Kittim, Gen. 10:4; but little is known of its early history. The Macedonian empire is traced back some four hundred years before the famous Philip, under whom, and especially under his son Alexander the Great, it reached the summit of its power. Alexander, B. C. 336–323, at the head of Macedonians and Greeks united, conquered a large part of western and southern Asia. This power was foretold by Daniel, 8:3–8, under the symbol of a goat with one horn; and it is worthy of note that ancient Macedonian coins still exist, bearing that national symbol. After the death of Alexander, the power of the Macedonians declined, and they were at length conquered by the Romans under Paulus Æmilius, B. C. 168, who divided their country into four districts. The Romans afterwards divided the whole of Greece and Macedonia into two great provinces, which they called Macedonia and Achaia, B. C. 142, Rom. 15:26; 2 Cor. 9:2. See GREECE. In the New Testament the name is probably to be taken in this latter sense. Of the cities of Macedonia proper, there are mentioned in the New Testament, Amphipolis, Apollonia, Berea, Neapolis, Philippi, and Thessalonica. This country early received the gospel, A. D. 55, Paul having been summoned to labor there by a supernatural vision, Acts 16:9; 20:1. Its fertile soil is now languishing under the Turkish sway.

MA'CHIR, I., a son of Manasseh, Gen. 50:23. His posterity were active in the conquest of Gilead, Num. 32:39; Josh. 17:1; and in the war with Jabin and Sisera, Judg. 5:14.

II. A friend of Mephibosheth, the son of Jonathan, 2 Sam. 9:4, 5.

MACHPE'LAH, the field and cave purchased by Abraham for a family tomb. Sarah was first buried there, Gen. 23; and afterwards Abraham, Isaac, Jacob, with Rebekah, Leah, etc., Gen. 49:30; 50:13. See HEBRON.

MA'DAI, the third son of Japheth, ancestor of the Medes, etc., Gen. 10:2.

MADMAN'NAH, a city near Gaza, first assigned to Judah, and afterwards to Simeon, Josh. 15:31; 1 Chr. 2:49.

MAD'MEN, an unknown place in Moab, Jer. 48:2.

MADME'NAH, a town not far from Jerusalem, site not known, Isa. 10:31.

MAG'DALA, the ancient Migdal-el, in the border of Naphtali, Josh. 19:38; now a small Turkish village called Medjel. It lay near the shore of the sea of Galilee, at its most westerly point, three miles north-west of Tiberias; in the southern part of a small plain on which stood also Capernaum at the other end, and Dalmanutha in its immediate vicinity, Matt. 15:39; Mark 8:10. Mary Magdalene was born, or resided, at Magdala; and it was the seat of a Jewish school after Jerusalem was destroyed.

MA'GI, or WISE MEN, an appellation given among the Medes and Persians to a class of priests, wise men, philosophers, etc., who devoted themselves to the study of the moral and physical sciences, and particularly cultivated astrology and medicine. They alone performed the religious rites, and pretended to communicate to men secret things, future events, and the will of the gods. See MEDIA. As they thus acquired great honor and influence, they were introduced into the courts of kings and consulted on all occasions. They also accompanied the army in warlike expeditions; and so much importance was attached to their advice and opinions, that nothing was attempted without their approbation. A similar class of men existed in Babylon, Egypt, Arabia, etc. The book of Daniel shows in what high estimation they were held in Babylon. Daniel was appointed master of the wise men; but their jealousy of his wisdom and their hatred of his religion, as well as the terms in which they are spoken of in Isa. 47:13, 14, Dan. 2:9, 27, show that as a class they were destitute of true wisdom.

Not so those who came "from the East" to salute and adore the infant Jesus, Matt. 2:1–12. The captivity of the Jews beyond the Euphrates had dispersed through the East much knowledge of the true God; and these philosophers and astronomers, in their search after wisdom, had found and believed the prophecies respecting the Messiah, and were divinely guided to his presence at

Bethlehem. See STAR In them, the science and philosophy of the heathen world laid their homage at the feet of Christ. Compare Psa. 72:10, 11; Isa. 60:1-3.

MAG'IC means, in the Bible, all the superstitious ceremonies of magicians, sorcerers, enchanters, necromancers, spiritualists, exorcists, astrologers, soothsayers, interpreters of dreams, fortune-tellers, casters of nativities, etc., which are all forbidden by the law of God, whether practised to hurt or to benefit mankind. It was also forbidden to consult magicians on pain of death, Lev. 19:31; 20:6. See ENCHANTMENTS and SORCERERS.

MA'GOG. See GOG.

MA'HALATH, in the title of Psalms 53 and 88, is conjectured to refer to the tune or the instrument used in chanting these Psalms; or as Hengstenberg and Alexander suggest, to the spiritual malady which they lament.

MAHANA'IM, *two hosts,* a place so named because a host of angels here met the host of Jacob, on his return from Padan-aram, Gen. 32:1, 2. It lay north of the Jabbok and near Penuel, and afterwards became a Levitical city in the tribe of Gad, Josh. 21:38. It was apparently a town of some strength; for Ish-bosheth lived there during his short reign, and David took refuge there during Absalom's rebellion, 2 Sam. 2:8; 17:24, 27.

MA'HER-SHA'LAL-HASH-BAZ, *haste, spoil, speed to the prey,* the name given by Isaiah to one of his sons, for a prophetic intimation of the speedy victory of the Assyrians over Syria and Israel, Isa. 8:1-3.

MAH'LON, a son of Elimelech and Naomi, and the first husband of Ruth the Moabitess, Ruth 1.

MAKKE'DAH, a chief city of the Canaanites, near which five confederate kings were defeated, taken in the cave to which they had fled, and executed. It lay in the vicinity of Libnah, Azekah, and Lachish, south-west of Jerusalem, in the tribe of Judah, Josh. 10:10-28; 12:16; 15:41.

MAK'TESH, Zeph. 1:11, apparently in or near Jerusalem, and occupied by merchants; but we have no clue to its location.

MAL'ACHI, the last of the minor prophets, and of all the Old Testament writers; so little known, that it is doubted by some, though without sufficient reason, whether his name be a proper name, or only a generical one, signifying the angel of the Lord, that is, a messenger, a prophet, Hag. 1:13; Mal. 3:1. Malachi most probably prophesied about B. C. 416, in the latter part of the administration of Nehemiah, and after Haggai and Zechariah, at a time of great disorder among the priests and people of Judah, whom he reproves. He inveighs against the priests; reproves the people for having taken strange wives, for inhumanity to their brethren, for divorcing their wives, and for neglect of paying tithes and first-fruits. He seems to allude to the covenant that Nehemiah renewed with the Lord, together with the priests and the chief of the nation. In the latter part he foretells the coming of John the Baptist in the spirit and power of Elijah, Mal. 3:1; 4:5, 6; Matt. 11:10, 14; 17:10-13; Luke 1:17. He also foretells the two-fold coming of Christ, and the blessedness of those who fear and serve him. Thus the Old Testament closes with predictions of the Messiah, and the New Testament opens with the record of their fulfilment.

MAL'CHUS, the servant whose right ear was cut off by Peter and miraculously restored by Christ, in Gethsemane, Matt. 26:51. The seizure of the Saviour immediately after two manifestations of his divinity, Luke 22:51, John 18:6, evinces the blindness and obstinacy of mankind in sin.

MAL'LOWS, Job 30:4, supposed by Bochart to signify the plant called Orach, the Atriplex Halimus of Linnæus. It somewhat resembles lettuce, and its young leaves are used in the East, either green or boiled, as food, by the poor.

MAM'MON, a Chaldee word signifying *riches.* Our Saviour says we cannot serve God and mammon, Matt. 6:24. Wealth is as truly an idol to those who set their hearts on it, as Jupiter or Diana; and no idolater can enter heaven. He also charges us, from the example of the unjust steward, so to use worldly goods, which are generally sought and used sinfully—"the unrighteous mammon—" as to have God the Judge our friend, and receive the true riches in heaven, Luke 16:9, 11.

MAM'RE, I., an Amorite prince, brother of Eshcol and Aner. All three united their forces to aid Abraham in the rescue of Lot, Gen. 14. He gave his name to

II. The town where he dwelt, afterwards Hebron, in the suburbs of which was a large terebinth-tree, or grove, (see OAK,) called in the English Bible "the plain of Mamre." Here Abraham and his descendants often pitched their tents, Gen. 13 : 18; 18 : 1. The cave of Machpelah was adjacent to Mamre on the east, Gen. 23 : 17, 19; 49 : 30; and from the heights near by, Abraham could see the smoking plain of Sodom, Gen. 19:27, 28.

MAN OF SIN. See ANTICHRIST.

MAN'AEN, a foster-brother of Herod Antipas, but unlike him in character and end: Manaen was a minister of Christ at Antioch; Herod was guilty of the blood of both Christ and his forerunner, Acts 13 : 1. "One shall be taken, and another left."

MANAS'SEH, I., the eldest son of Joseph, born in Egypt. His descendants constituted a full tribe. This was divided in the promised land: one part having settled east of the Jordan, in the country of Bashan, from the river Jabbok northwards; and the other west of the Jordan, between Ephraim and Issachar, extending from the Jordan to the Mediterranean. It was far inferior to Ephraim in wealth and power, according to the prediction of Jacob, Gen. 41 : 50, 51; 48; Josh. 16; 17.

II. The son and impious successor of the good Hezekiah, king of Judah. He began to reign at twelve years old, B. C. 698, and reigned fifty-five years. For his shocking idolatries, tyranny, and cruelties, God suffered him to be carried as a prisoner to Babylon in the twenty-second year of his reign, probably by Esarhaddon king of Assyria. Here, however, he so humbled himself that God moved the Assyrians to restore him to his throne, as a tributary; and thenceforth he set himself to undo the evil he had done. He abolished the idols he had worshipped and the diviners he had consulted; accomplished many reforms for the spiritual and material good of his kingdom; repaired the defences of Jerusalem, enclosing with a wall new space on the west and Ophel on the south-east; and strengthened the walled cities of Judah. After a reign longer than that of any other king of Judah, he died in peace and was buried in Jerusalem, 2 Kin. 21; 2 Chr. 33.

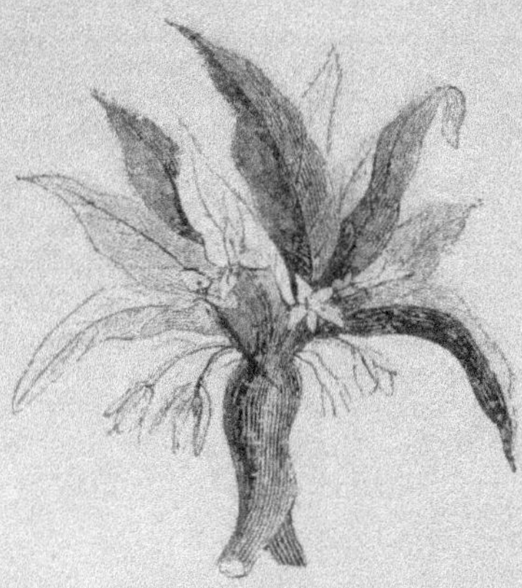

MAN'DRAKES, Hebrew Dudaïm, Gen. 30 : 14–16, Song 7 : 13, a plant to which was attributed, probably without reason, the power of rendering barren women fruitful. According to most of the ancient versions, it was the Atropa Mandragora of Linnæus, a plant of the genus belladonna, with a root like a beet, white and reddish blossoms, and fragrant yellow apples, which ripen from May to July. But this opinion is uncertain.

MA'NEH, a Hebrew weight of sixty shekels, Ezek. 45:12. See the TABLE at the end of the volume.

MAN'NA, the miraculous food given by God to the Israelites during their wanderings in the desert. It was a small grain, white like hoar-frost, round, and of the size of coriander-seed, Exod. 16; Num. 11. It fell every morning, with the dew, about the camp of the Israelites, and in so great quantities during the whole forty years of their journey in the wilderness, that it was sufficient to serve the entire multitude instead of bread, Ex. 16:35; Deut. 29:5, 6; Josh. 5 : 12. It is nowhere said that the Israelites had no other food. That numerous flocks and herds accompanied the camp of Israel is clear from many passages. Certainly the daily sacrifices were offered, and no doubt other offerings, affording animal food on which the priests and Levites subsisted, according to their offices.

When manna was first sent, the Israelites "knew not what it was," and "said one to another, MAN-HU, which means, What is it? Most interpreters think that from the frequent repetition of this inquiry the name MAN or manna arose.

Burckhardt says, that in the valleys around Sinai a species of manna is still found, dropping from the sprigs of several trees, but principally from the tamarisk, in the month of June. It is collected by the Arabs, who make cakes of it, and call it *honey of beyrouk*. See Ex. 16 : 31. Since his time it has been ascertained by Dr. Ehrenburg that the exudation of this manna is occasioned by an insect, which he has particularly described. Besides this substance and the manna of commerce, which is used as a laxative medicine, and is produced by the ash-trees of southern Europe, several other vegetable products in Arabia, Persia, etc., of similar origin and qualities, are known by the same name. It is in vain, however, to seek to identify with any of these the manna of the Israelites, which was evidently a special provision for them, beginning and terminating with their need of it. It was found, not on trees and shrubs, but on "the face of the wilderness" wherever they went; and was different in its qualities from any now known by that name, being dry enough to grind and bake like grain, but breeding worms on the second day. It was miraculous in the amount that fell, for the supply of millions; in not falling on the Sabbath; in falling in double quantities the previous day; and in remaining fresh during the Sabbath. By these last three peculiarities God miraculously attested the sanctity of the Sabbath, as dating from the creation and not from mount Sinai. Moreover, a specimen of manna was laid up in a golden vase in the ark of the covenant, in memory of a substance which would otherwise have perished, Heb. 9:4.

In Psa. 78 : 24, 25, manna is called "angels' food" and "corn of heaven," in token of its excellence, and that it came directly from the hand of God. The people gathered on an average about three quarts for each man. They who gathered more than they needed, shared it freely with others; it could not be hoarded up: and thus, as Paul teaches us, 2 Cor. 8 : 13–15, it furnishes for all men a lesson against hoarding the earthly and perishable gifts of God, and in favor of freely imparting to our brethren in need.

This great boon of God to the Israelites also offers many striking analogies, illustrative of "the true Bread" which came down from heaven to rebellious and perishing man, John 6:31–58; Rev. 2:17. Like the manna, Christ descends from above around the camp of his church in daily and abundant supplies, to meet the wants of every man.

MANO'AH, a native of Zorah, in the tribe of Dan, and the father of Samson, Judg. 13:14; 16:31. In the prediction of his son's birth and achievements, we see the Angel of the covenant, who appeared to Abraham, Gideon, etc., and who never slumbers nor sleeps, caring for his oppressed people. So too he appeared to Jacob, and would not tell his mysterious name, Gen. 32:29; Judg. 13:18; Isa. 9:6; Luke 13:34.

MAN'SLAYER. See REFUGE.

MAN'TLE. See GARMENTS.

MA'ON, a town in the edge of the hill-country of Judah, Josh. 15:55, near which Nabal lived and David took refuge from Saul, 1 Sam. 23:24, 25; 25:2. Dr. Robinson finds it in the ruinous place called Maîn, seven miles south by east from Hebron

MA'ONITES, called MEHUNIM in 2 Chr. 26:7, an Arabian tribe, named with the Amalekites and other foes of Israel. Their abode may have been near the place now called Maan, nearly east of Petra, on the Haj route from Damascus to Mecca. Uzziah defeated them.

MA'RAH, *bitterness*, a well near the Red sea, three days' journey from the point where the Israelites crossed it. The well was sweetened for the use of the distressed Hebrews by the miraculous efficacy imparted to the branches of a certain tree which Moses threw in, Ex. 15:23–25. No plant is now known possessed of such a quality. The name Amarah now marks the dry bed of a wintry torrent, a little south of which is a well called Hawara, which answers well to the description. Its water, after remaining a few seconds in the mouth, becomes exceedingly nauseous. The Arabs do not drink it, though their camels will. See also Ruth 1:20.

MA'RAN-A'THA, composed of two Syriac words, signifying "the Lord cometh." See ANATHEMA.

MARE'SHAH, a town in Judah, Josh. 15 : 44, fortified by Rehoboam, 2 Chr. 11 : 8, and the birthplace of Micah. In a valley near by, Asa defeated Zerah with an immense host of Ethiopians, 2 Chr. 14:9–13. It probably lay on the western border of Judah, just south of Eleutheropolis.

MARK, or MARCUS, the writer of one of the four gospels. See GOSPELS. There can be little doubt of the correctness of the general opinion of learned men, that he is the same person who is mentioned by the names of John and Mark in Acts 12:12, 25; 13:5, 13, and as the cousin and disciple of Barnabas, Col. 4:10. He was also the companion of Paul and Barnabas in their journey through Greece to Antioch, Perga, and Pamphylia, at which last place he left them and returned to Jerusalem, much to the dissatisfaction of Paul, Acts 13:5, etc.; 15:37-39. Yet he labored faithfully with Barnabas at Cyprus, and Paul mentions him, when in captivity at Rome, as one of those who were associated with him, Col. 4:10, 11; 2 Tim. 4:11; Phile. 24. He afterwards accompanied Peter also to Babylon. As he was the son of that Mary at whose house in Jerusalem the apostles were wont to convene, so it is probable that he was particularly instructed in the doctrines of Christianity by Peter, who on that account calls him *son*, 1 Pet. 5:13. Compare 1 Tim. 1:2 and 2 Tim. 1:2.

MAR'KET, in Greek AG'ORA, in Latin FO'RUM, a large open area in many ancient cities, especially of Greece and Rome, having the public market on one side only, the other sides of the area being occupied by temples, theatres, colonades, courts of justice, baths, and other public structures, the whole square often presenting a magnificent appearance. Here was the city exchange, the focus to which converged all the lines of public life. Hither laborers resorted in search of employment, Matt. 20:3-7, and children to pursue their sports, Luke 7:32. Here the ordinary assemblies of the people were held; here philosophers and statesmen met and debated; here laws were promulgated and news announced; hither men resorted for pleasure as well as for business. The most notable public men, and indeed all classes of citizens, here congregated; and what was done here was done before the whole city. Hence the proud Pharisees desired "greetings in the market-places," Matt. 12:38; and Paul resorted to the agora at Athens to meet and convince the philosophers, Acts 17:17; and the masters of the damsel at Philippi exorcised by Paul and Silas, "drew them into the market-place unto the rulers," Acts 16:19.

MAR'RIAGE, the union for life of one man and one woman, is an ordinance of the Creator for the perpetuity and happiness of the human race; instituted in Paradise, Gen. 1:27, 28; 2:18-24, and the foundation of no small part of all that is valuable to human society. By promoting parental love and the sense of responsibility, marriage most effectually promotes the health and happiness of children, and their careful education to virtue, industry, and honor, to right habits and ends, and to all that is included in the idea of *home*. God made originally but one man and one woman. The first polygamists were Lamech and those degenerate "sons of God," or worshippers of Jehovah, who "took them wives of all that they chose," Gen. 4:17; 6:2. On the other hand, Noah and his three sons had each but one wife: and the same appears to be true of all his direct ancestors back to Adam. So also was it with Job, Nahor, Lot, and at first with Abraham. See CONCUBINE. In after-times a plurality of wives became more common among the Hebrews, and the Scriptures afford numerous illustrations of its evil results, Gen. 16:30; Judg. 8:30; 2 Sam. 3:3-5; 1 Kin. 11:1-8; 2 Chr. 11:18-21; 13:21. In the time of Christ there is no mention of polygamy as prevalent among the Jews.

The Israelites were forbidden to marry within certain specified degrees, Lev. 18; 20; Deut. 27. Marriage with Canaanites and idolaters was strictly forbidden, Exod. 34:16; and afterwards with any of the heathen nations around them, especially such as were uncircumcised, Neh. 13. By the Levirate law, as it is termed, if a Jew died without children, his nearest brother or kinsman was bound to marry the widow, that her first-born son after this marriage might be reckoned the son and heir of the first husband, Gen. 38; Deut. 25:5-10; Matt. 22:23-26. The Saviour set his seal to marriage as a divine and permanent institution, aside from all the civil laws which guard and regulate, or seek to alter or annul it; forbidding divorce except for one cause, Matt. 5:32; 19:3-6, 9; and denouncing all breaches of marriage vows, even in thought, Matt. 5:28. Compare Heb. 13:4; Rev. 21:8.

Jewish parents were wont to arrange

with other parents as to the marriage of their children, sometimes according to the previous choice of the son, and not without some regard to the consent of the daughter, Gen. 21:21; 24; 34:4-6; Judg. 14:2, 3. The parties were often betrothed to each other long before the marriage took place. See BETROTHING. A dowry was given by the suitor to the parents and brethren of the bride, Ex. 22:16; Deut. 22:29; 2 Sam. 13:11, 11. The nuptials were often celebrated with great pomp and ceremony, and with protracted feasting and rejoicings. It was customary for the bridegroom to appoint a Paranymphus, or groomsman, called by our Saviour "the friend of the bridegroom," John 3:29. A number of other young men also kept him company during the days of the wedding, to do him honor; as also young women kept company with the bride all this time. The companions of the bridegroom are expressly mentioned in the history of Samson, Judg. 14:11, 20; Song 5:1; 8:13; Matt. 9:14; also the companions of the bride, Psa. 45:9, 14; Song 1:5; 2:7; 3:5; 8:4. The office of the groomsman was to direct in the ceremonies of the wedding. The friends and companions of the bride sang the epithalamium, or wedding song, at the door of the bride the evening before the wedding. The festivities of the wedding were conducted with great decorum, the young people of each sex being in distinct apartments and at different tables. The young men at Samson's wedding diverted themselves in proposing riddles, and the bridegroom appointed the prize to those who could explain them, Judg. 14:14.

The Jews affirm, that before Jerusalem was laid in ruins, the bridegroom and bride wore crowns at their marriage. Compare Isa. 61:10; Song 3:11, "Go forth, O ye daughters of Zion, and behold king Solomon with the crown wherewith his mother crowned him in the day of his espousals, and in the day of the gladness of his heart." The modern Jews, in some places, throw handfuls of wheat on the newly married couple, particularly on the bride, saying, "Increase and multiply." In other places they mingle pieces of money with the wheat, which are gathered up by the poor. The actual ceremony of marriage was very simple, consisting of little more than the reading of the marriage contract, Prov. 2:17, Mal. 2:14, and the nuptial blessing invoked by the friends, Gen. 24:60; Ruth 4:11, 12.

The wedding festivities commonly lasted seven days for a maid, and three days for a widow. So Laban says to Jacob, respecting Leah, "Fulfil her week," Gen. 29:27. The ceremonies of Samson's wedding continued seven whole days, Judg. 14:17, 18. These seven days of rejoicing were commonly spent in the house of the woman's father, after which they conducted the bride to her husband's home.

The procession accompanying the bride from the house of her father to that of the bridegroom, was generally one of more or less pomp, according to the circumstances of the married couple, and for this they often chose the night, as is still the custom in Syria. Hence the parable of the ten virgins that went at midnight to meet the bride and bridegroom, Matt. 25. "At a Hindoo marriage, the procession of which I saw some years ago," says Mr. Ward, "the bridegroom came from a distance, and the bride lived at Serampore, to which place the bridegroom was to come by water. After waiting two or three hours, at length, near midnight, it was announced, as if in the very words of Scripture, 'Behold, the bridegroom cometh; go ye out to meet him.' All the persons employed now lighted their lamps, and ran with them in their hands to fill up their stations in the procession; some of them had lost their lights, and were unprepared; but it was then too late to seek them, and the cavalcade moved forward to the house of the bride, at which place the company entered a large and splendidly illuminated area, before the house, covered with an awning, where a great multitude of friends, dressed in their best apparel, were seated upon mats. The bridegroom was carried in the arms of a friend, and placed in a superb seat in the midst of the company, where he sat a short time, and then went into the house, the door of which was immediately shut, and guarded by sepoys. I and others expostulated with the doorkeepers, but in vain. Never was I so struck with our Lord's beautiful parable as at this moment; 'and the door was shut.'"

Christianity invests the family institution with peculiar sacredness; makes true love its basis, and mutual preference of each others' happiness its rule ; and even likens it to the ineffable union between Christ and his church, Eph 5:22-33. Nowhere in the world is woman so honored, happy, and useful as in a Christian land and a Christian home. Believers are directed to marry "in the Lord," 1 Cor. 7 : 39. No doubt the restrictions laid upon the ancient people of God contain a lesson for all periods, and the recorded ill results of forbidden marriages among the Jews, if heeded, would prevent the serious evils which often result from union between a Christian and a worldling. As to the mutual duties of husband and wife, see Eph. 5:22-23; 1 Tim. 2:11, 12; 1 Pet. 3:1-7.

The Romish church puts dishonor on what the Holy Spirit describes as "honorable in all." It not only extols celibacy and virginity in the laity, but strictly refuses marriage to all its priests, bishops, etc., and in thus "forbidding to marry," fixes upon itself the name of anti-Christ, 1 Tim. 4 : 3. See BETROTHING, CONCUBINE, DIVORCE, GARMENTS, etc.

MARS'-HILL. See AREOPAGUS.

MAR'THA, sister of Lazarus and Mary, at Bethany. Though different from Mary in temperament, she was no less truly a devoted friend of Christ and beloved by him, John 11 : 5 His gentle reproof, Luke 10:38-42, does not imply that she was a stranger to renewing grace. Her affectionate care for the hospitable entertainment of Christ must not be forgotten, nor her promptness in hasting to meet him, nor her faith in his power, John 11:20-28; 12:1, 2. See MARY IV.

MAR'TYR, *a witness*, Matt. 18 : 16 ; Luke 24:48 ; in ecclesiastical history, "a witness, by the shedding of his blood, in testifying to the truth." Thus martyrs are distinguished from "confessors," properly so called, who underwent great afflictions for their confession of the truth, but without suffering death. The term "martyr" occurs only thrice in the New Testament, Acts 22 : 20; Rev. 2:13; 17:6. Since the time of Stephen, Acts 7 : 59 ; 22 : 20, myriads of martyrs have sealed the truth of Christianity by a painful death ; which they willingly endured through faith, rather than to deny Christ, and which they often eagerly desired as a special privilege. It is doubtless possible to be put to death as a Christian, without real love for Christ, 1 Cor. 13 : 3 ; but in general "the noble army of the martyrs" have borne a true and overwhelming testimony to the power and preciousness of faith in Christ ; and their blood witnesses before God against their foes, especially against that apostate church which is "drunken with the blood of the martyrs of Jesus," Rev. 17:6.

MA'RY, in Hebrew MIRIAM, I., "the mother of Jesus," Acts 1:14. Her amiable and lovely character, and her remarkable history in connection with the wonders relating to the birth of Christ, are recorded in the first two chapters of Matthew and Luke. The genealogy of the Saviour through her, in the line of David and Abraham, is preserved in Luke 3, to prove that he was born "as concerning the flesh" according to ancient prophecies. After the return from Egypt to Nazareth, she is but five times mentioned in the gospel history: three times with some appearance of reproval on the part of Christ, Matt. 12 : 46-50 ; Luke 2 : 49, 50 ; John 2 : 4 ; once when he commended her to the care of John, John 19 . 26 ; and lastly as among the disciples at Jerusalem after his ascension, Acts 1:14. Thenceforth, throughout the Acts of the Apostles, the Epistles, and the Revelation, no allusion is made to her. Manifestly the worship of Mary had not then commenced. The inventions of the Romish church in after-centuries are wholly destitute of foundation in Scripture, and subversive of the gospel. One of these unauthorized inventions is the alleged immaculate conception and spotless holiness of Mary. See Rom. 3 : 10, 23 ; Gal. 3 : 22 ; 1 John 1 : 8 ; and compare also the reproofs above alluded to, and her own confession of her need of a Saviour, Luke 1:47. Another unauthorized invention is her alleged virginity after the birth of Jesus, Matt. 1 : 25 ; Luke 2 : 7. No case can be found in Scripture where "first-born son" is used of an only child. In other passages the brethren, sisters, and mother of Christ are mentioned together, apparently as one family, Matt. 13 : 55, 56 ; and she was known as the wife of Joseph probably for almost thirty years, John 6 : 42. To adore her as the "queen of heaven," and the "mother of God," is, in the light of the Bible, blasphemous idolatry ; and to pray to her as divine, or even as a mediator with God, implies that she possesses the attribute of omnipresence, and degrades the only and sufficient Mediator, 1 Tim. 2 : 5; Heb. 4.16. She was "blessed" or signally favored "among women," as Jael was "blessed above women," Judg. 5 : 24; Luke 1 : 28; but Christ himself declares that a higher blessing belongs to those "that hear the word of God and keep it," Luke 11:27, 28.

II. The mother of Mark the Evangelist. She had a house in Jerusalem, where the followers of Jesus were wont to convene. Hither Peter, when delivered from prison by the angel, came and knocked at the gate, Acts 12:12. Many such hospitable Christian homes, and places of social prayer, even in troublous times, are for ever enshrined in the remembrances of the people of God.

III. The wife of Cleophas, and mother of James the Less and Joses, Matt. 27 : 56, 61; Luke 24 : 10; John 19 : 25. This last passage leaves it uncertain whether this Mary was sister to Mary our Lord's mother, or not. Some suppose that four persons are there named: Christ's mother, his mother's sister, Mary of Cleophas, and Salome. See MARY I. and JAMES III. She believed early on Jesus Christ, and accompanied him in some of his journeys, to minister to him, followed him to Calvary, and was with his mother at the foot of his cross. She was also present at his burial, prepared perfumes to embalm him, and was early at his sepulchre on the morning of his resurrection. See CLEOPHAS.

IV. The sister of Lazarus, whom our Lord raised from the dead. Her character presents a beautiful companion-picture to that of her more active and impulsive sister Martha. Contemplative, confiding, and affectionate, it was like heaven to her to sit at the feet of her adored Teacher and Lord, Luke 10 : 39–42. The character of the two sisters was well contrasted at the supper in Bethany, after the resurrection of Lazarus. No service was too humble for Martha to render, and no offering too costly for Mary to pour out, in honor of their Saviour, John 11; 12:1-8. This occurrence should not be confounded with that described in Luke 7:37–50.

V. The Magdalene, or native of Magdala on the sea of Galilee. She was foremost among the honorable women of substance who ministered unto Christ and his disciples, Matt. 28 : 1–10; Mark 15:47; 16:1–10; Luke 24 : 1–12; John 20 : 1, 2, 10–18. She was especially devoted to Christ, for his mercy in casting out from her seven evil spirits, Luke 8:2, 3. She was early at his tomb; and lingering there when the disciples had retired, she was the first to throw herself at the feet of the risen Saviour. There is no evidence that she was ever a profligate.

VI. A benevolent and useful Christian at Rome, saluted in Paul's epistle, Rom. 16:6.

MAS'CHIL is a term found as a title of thirteen Psalms, and imports one that instructs or makes to understand. Some interpreters think it means an instrument of music; but it more probably signifies an instructive song.

MA'TRIX, the womb. To "open the matrix," Ex. 13 : 12, 15, means, to be the first-born.

MAT'THEW, an apostle and evangelist, was son of Alpheus, a Galilean by birth, a Jew by religion, and a publican by profession, Matt. 9 : 9; 10 : 3; Luke 6 : 15. The other evangelists call him only LEVI, which was his Hebrew name, Mark 2 : 14; Luke 5 : 27; but he always calls himself Matthew, which was probably his name as a publican, or officer for gathering taxes. He does not dissemble his former profession; thus exalting the grace of Christ which raised him to the apostleship. His ordinary abode was at Capernaum, and his office probably on the main road, near the sea of Tiberias; here, in the midst of his business, he was called by Jesus to follow him, Matt. 9:9; Mark 2:14. It is probable that he had a previous knowledge of the miracles and doctrine of Christ.

For the GOSPEL OF MATTHEW, see GOSPEL.

MATTHI'AS, one of the disciples who continued with our Saviour from his baptism to his ascension, Acts 1 : 21–26, and was after the ascension associated with the eleven apostles. We know nothing further of him.

MAZ'ZAROTH, Job 38:32. Our translators properly suppose this word to denote the twelve signs of the zodiac, a broad circle in the heavens, comprehending all such stars as lie in the path of the sun and moon. As these luminaries appear to proceed throughout this circle annually, so different parts of it progressively receive them every month; and this progression seems to be what is meant by "bringing forth mazzaroth in his season," that is, Canst thou by thy power cause the revolutions of the heavenly bodies in the zodiac, and the seasons of summer and winter, in their regular succession?

MEALS. See EATING.

MEAS'URE. See the general table of Weights, Measures, and Money of the Hebrews, at the end of the Dictionary; also the particular names of each, as SHEKEL, TALENT, BATH, EPHAH, etc.

MEATS. "Meat" in the English Bible usually signifies "food," and not merely "flesh," Gen. 1:29, 30; Matt. 15:37. So in Luke 24:41; "Have ye here any meat?" literally, any thing to eat? The "meat-offerings" of the Jews were made of flour and oil, etc., Lev. 2. See OFFERINGS and SACRIFICES. As to the animal food used by the Jews, see CLEAN, and FOOD.

It does not appear that the ancient Hebrews were very particular about the seasoning and dressing of their food. We find among them roast meat, boiled meat, and ragouts. Moses forbade them to seethe a kid in its mother's milk, Ex. 23:19; 34:26—a precept designed to inculcate principles of humanity, and perhaps to prevent them from adopting an idolatrous custom of their heathen neighbors. The Jews were also forbidden to kill a cow and its calf in the same day; or a sheep, or goat, and its young one, at the same time. They might not cut off a part of a living animal to eat it, either raw or dressed. If any lawful beast or bird should die of itself or be strangled, and the blood not drain away, they were not allowed to taste of it. They ate of nothing dressed by any other than a Jew, nor did they ever dress their victuals with the kitchen implements of any but one of their own nation.

The prohibition of eating blood, or animals that are strangled, has been always rigidly observed by the Jews. In the Christian church, the custom of refraining from things strangled, and from blood, continued for a long time, being approved by the council held at Jerusalem, and recommended to the Gentile converts, Acts 15.

At the first settling of the church, there were many disputes concerning the use of meats offered to idols. Some newly converted Christians, convinced that an idol was nothing, and that the distinction of clean and unclean creatures was abolished by our Saviour, ate indifferently of whatever was served up to them, even among pagans, without inquiring whether the meats had been offered to idols. They took the same liberty in buying meat sold in the market, not regarding whether it were pure or impure according to the Jews; or whether it had been offered to idols or not. But other Christians, weaker, more scrupulous, or less instructed, were offended at this liberty, and thought the eating of meat which had been offered to idols was a kind of partaking in that wicked and sacrilegious offering. This diversity of opinion among the disciples called for the judgment of inspiration; and we find in several of Paul's epistles directions both for those who held such scruples, and for those who were free from them. The former, while in obedience to their own conscience they carefully abstained from the food in question, were charged to view with charity the conduct of those who did not share their scruples. The latter might freely buy and eat without guilt, since meat is in no wise injured as an article of food by being offered to an idol; yet whenever others would be scandalized, pained, or led into sin by this course, even they were required by the laws of Christian charity and prudence to abstain, Rom. 14:20-23; 1 Cor. 8; 10:19-33; Tit. 1:15. This principle is of general application in similar cases; and many in our own day might well adopt the generous determination of the self-denying apostle to partake of no questionable indulgence while the world stands, if it may be the occasion of sin to others.

MEDAD. See ELDAD.

ME'DAN, a son of Abraham and Keturah, Gen. 25:2. He is supposed to have settled in Arabia, near Midian his brother.

MED'EBA, a town east of the Jordan, in the tribe of Reuben, Josh. 13:9, 16. Near it the army of David gained a great victory, 1 Chr. 19:7. Long afterwards, it fell again into the hands of the Moabites its ancient masters, Num. 21:30; Isa. 15:2. Its ruins, on rising ground a few miles south-east of Heshbon, still retain the old name.

ME'DIA, called by the Hebrews MADAI, and supposed to have been peopled by the descendants of Madai the son of Japheth, Gen. 10 : 2, extended itself on the west and south of the Caspian sea, from Armenia and Assyria on the north and west, to Farsistan or Persia proper on the south; and included the districts now called Shirvan, Adserbijan, Ghilan, Masanderan, and Irak Adjemi. It covered a territory larger than that of Spain, lying between 32° and 40° of north latitude, and was one of the most fertile and earliest cultivated among the kingdoms of Asia. It had two grand divisions, of which the north-western was called Atropatene, or Lesser Media, and the southern Greater Media. The former corresponds to the modern Adserbijan, now, as formerly, a province of the Persian empire, on the west of the Caspian, surrounded by high mountains of the Tauritic range, except towards the east, where the river Kur, or Cyrus, discharges its waters into the Caspian. The Greater Media corresponds principally to the modern Irak Adjemi, or Persian Irak. Ecbatana was the ancient capital.

Media is one of the most ancient independent kingdoms of which history makes mention. After several centuries of subjugation under Assyria, the Medes rebelled under Arbaces in the time of Sardanapalus, and again in the time of Sennacherib, about 700 B. C. They became powerful, cultivated, and wealthy, Isa. 13 : 17, 18; 21 : 2, 3, and continued an independent kingdom until, under Cyrus, Media became united with Persia. In this way arose the Medo-Persian kingdom; and the "laws of the Medes and Persians" are always mentioned by the sacred writers together, Esth. 1:19, etc.; Dan. 6:8, 12, etc. So also the "Chronicles" of the Medes and Persians are mentioned together, Esth. 10 : 2. Indeed, from this time onward, the manners, customs, religion, and civilization of the Medes and Persians seem ever to have become more and more amalgamated. And in general it would seem, as we may gather from the ancient Zend writings, that the Medes, Persians, and Bactrians were originally the same people, having in common one language, the Zend, and one religion, the worship of Ormuzd, the highest being, under the symbol of fire. They also worshipped the stars, particularly the planets; and still more, the sun and moon. The priests of this religion, the Magi, were a Median race, to whom were intrusted the cultivation of the sciences, and the performance of the sacred rites. Among these, and as is supposed before the time of Cyrus, appeared Zerdusht, or Zoroaster, as a reformer, or rather as the restorer of the ancient but degenerated religion of light, whose disciples have maintained themselves even to the present day, in Persia and India, under the name of Guebres.

Media is first mentioned in the Bible as the part of Assyria to which the ten tribes were transported: at first, those beyond the Jordan, by Tiglath-pileser, 1 Chr. 5 : 26; and afterwards, about 721 B. C., the remainder of Israel, by Shalmaneser, 2 Kin. 17 : 6. The subsequent history of Media is involved in that of Persia. Both countries were subdued by Alexander of Macedon, 330 B. C.; and in the next century became tributary to the Parthians on their east, in connection with whom they are mentioned in Acts 2:9. See PERSIA.

ME'DIATOR, one who stands between two parties or persons as the organ of communication or the agent of reconciliation. So far as man is sensible of his own guilt and of the holiness and justice of God, he shrinks from any direct communication with a being he has so much reason to fear. Hence the disposition more or less prevalent in all ages and in all parts of the world, to interpose between the soul and its judge some person or thing most adapted to propitiate his favor—as a priestly order, an upright and devout man, or the smoke of sacrifices and the sweet savor of incense, Job 9:33. The Israelites evinced this feeling at mount Sinai, Deut. 5 : 23-31; and God was pleased to constitute Moses a mediator between himself and them, to receive and transmit the law on the one hand, and their vows of obedience on the other. In this capacity he acted on various other occasions, Exod. 32 : 30-32; Num. 14; Psa. 106:23; and was thus an agent and a type of Christ, Gal. 3 : 19. The Messiah has been in all ages the only true Mediator between God and man; and without Him, God is inaccessible and a consuming fire, John 14 : 6; Acts 4 : 12. As the Angel of the covenant, Christ was the channel of all communications between heaven and earth in Old Testament days; and as the Mediator of the new covenant, he does all that is needful to provide for a perfect reconciliation between God and man. He consults the honor of God by appearing as our Advocate with the blood of atonement; and through his sympathizing love and the agency of the Holy Spirit, he disposes and enables us to return to God. The believing penitent is "accepted in the Beloved"—his person, his praises, and his prayers; and through the same Mediator alone he receives pardon, grace, and eternal life. In this high office Christ stands alone, because he alone is both God and man, 1 Tim. 2:5. To join Mary and the saints to him in his mediatorship, as the antichristian church of Rome does, implies that he is unable to accomplish his own peculiar work, Heb. 8:6; 9:15; 12:24.

MEGID'DO, a town of Manasseh, though within the bounds of Issachar. It had been a royal city of the Canaanites, and they long retained a foothold in it, Josh. 12:21; 17:11; Judg. 1:27. It lay in the south-west border of the plain of Esdraelon, near the Kishon, which is probably intended by "the waters of Megiddo," mentioned in the song of Deborah and Barak as the scene of their victory, Judg. 5:19, 21. In the reign of Solomon, Megiddo was fortified, 1 Kin. 9:15. Here king Ahaziah died, and king Josiah was defeated, slain, and sorely lamented, 2 Kin. 9:27; 23:29; Zech. 12:11. Robinson identifies it with a village now called Leijun, the Legio of the Romans.

MELCHIZ'EDEK, *king of righteousness*, king of Salem, and also priest of the most high God, in which capacity he blessed Abraham, and received tithes at his hand, Gen. 14:18-20. Scripture tells us nothing of his father or mother, of his genealogy, his birth, or his death; he stands alone, without predecessor or successor, a royal priest by the appointment of God; and thus he was a type of Jesus Christ, who is "a priest for ever after the order of Melchizedek," and not after the order of Aaron, whose origin, consecration, life, and death, are known, Psa. 110:4; Heb. 7. See GENEALOGY.

It has been matter of great inquiry among commentators, who Melchizedek really was. He has been variously supposed to be the Holy Spirit, the Son of God, an angel, Enoch, and Shem. But the safest and most probable opinion is that which considers Melchizedek as a righteous and peaceful king, a worshipper and priest of the most high God, in the land of Canaan; a friend of Abraham, and of a rank elevated above him. This opinion, indeed, lies upon the very face of the sacred record in Gen. 14 and Heb. 7, and it is the only one which can be defended on any tolerable grounds of interpretation. See SALEM.

MEL'ITA. The name Melita was anciently applied to two islands; one in the Adriatic sea, on the coast of Illyricum, now called Meleda; the other in the Mediterranean, between Sicily and Africa, now called Malta. That the latter is the one on which Paul suffered shipwreck is evident both from the direction of the wind which blew him thither, (see EUROCLYDON,) and from the fact that he left the island in a ship of Alexandria, which had wintered there on her voyage to Italy, and after touching at Syracuse and Rhegium, landed at Puteoli, thus sailing on a direct course. The other Melita would be far out of the usual track from Alexandria to Italy; and in sailing from it to Rhegium, Syracuse also would be out of the direct course. The fact that the vessel was tossed all night before the shipwreck in the Adriatic sea, does not militate against this view, because the name Adria was applied to the whole Ionian sea, which lay between Sicily and Greece. See ADRIA. Acts 27:27; 28:1.

Malta is a rocky island, sixty-two miles south of Sicily, seventeen miles long and nine broad, and containing nearly one hundred square miles, and 100,000 inhabitants. At an early period it was seized by the Phœnicians; these were dispossessed by the Greeks of Sicily; they by the Carthaginians; and they in turn, 242 B. C., by the Romans, who held it in the time of Paul. After numerous changes, it fell at length into the hands of the English, who since 1814 have held undisputed possession of it. The name of "St. Paul's bay" is now borne by a small inlet on the north side of the island, opening towards the east, which answers well to the description in Acts 27. Here Paul was protected by the hand of God, amid perils on shore as well as in the sea. He remained here three months, and wrought many miracles.

MEL'ONS are common in the East, but do not differ particularly from ours. Watermelons grow luxuriantly in Palestine, even in dry and sandy soil. They are a delicious fruit in a hot climate, and were among the articles of food for which the Hebrews pined in the desert, Num. 11:5.

MEL'ZAR, the name or the official title of a butler or steward at the court of Nebuchadnezzar, Dan. 1:11-16.

MEM'PHIS, Hos. 9:6. See NOPH.

MEN'AHEM, the sixteenth king of Israel, previously general of the army of Zachariah. He was at Tirzah when he heard of his master's murder; and immediately marching against Shallum, who had shut himself up in Samaria, he captured and slew him, and then ascended the throne. He reigned in Samaria ten years, 771-760 B. C., and was a tyrannical and cruel idolater. Pul, king of Assyria, having invaded Israel during the reign of Menahem, obliged him to pay a tribute of a thousand talents, which Menahem raised by a tax on all his rich subjects of fifty shekels a head. He seems to have died a natural death; but his son and successor Pekahiah reigned only two years, and was the last of that dynasty, 2 Kin. 15:13-22. The name of Menahem is found on the Assyrian tablets recently discovered.

ME'NE, *he is numbered;* TE'KEL, *he is weighed;* UPHAR'SIN, *and they are dividing;* Chaldee words supernaturally traced on the wall at Belshazzar's impious feast, and significant of his impending doom, Dan. 5. The astrologers could not read them, perhaps because they were written in antique Hebrew characters; still less could they explain, even if they had dared to do it, what was so portentous. Daniel, however, received skill to understand and courage to declare their awful meaning; and the same night witnessed their fulfilment. Over how many proud heads, often found in scenes of ungodliness and revelling, the hand that has recorded their past history is even now preparing to record their doom.

MEPHIB'OSHETH, a son of Jonathan, also called Merib-baal, 1 Chr. 8:34. See ESHBAAL. Mephibosheth was very young when his father was killed in the battle of Gilboa, 2 Sam. 4:4, and his nurse was in such consternation at the news, that she let the child fall; and from this accident he was lame all his life. When David found himself in peaceable possession of the kingdom, he sought for all that remained of the house of Saul, that he might show them kindness, in consideration of the friendship between him and Jonathan. He gave Mephibosheth the estate of his grandfather Saul. Of a part of this, however, he was afterwards deprived by the treachery of his steward Ziba, and the hasty injustice, as it appears, of David towards an unfortunate but noble and loyal prince, 2 Sam. 9; 16:1-4; 19:24-30. David subsequently took care to exempt him from the number of the descendants of Saul given up to the vengeance of the Gibeonites, 2 Sam. 21:1-14, though another Mephibosheth, a son of Saul, was slain, ver. 8.

ME'RAB, the eldest daughter of king Saul, was promised to David in marriage, in reward for his victory over Goliath; but was given to Adriel, son of Barzillai the Meholathite, 1 Sam. 14:49; 18:17, 19. Merab had five sons by him, who were delivered to the Gibeonites, and hanged before the Lord, 2 Sam. 21:8, 9. The text intimates that the five men delivered to the Gibeonites were sons of Michal; but see ADRIEL.

MER'ARI, the youngest of Levi's three sons, born in Canaan, and head of a family of the Levites, Gen. 46:11; Ex. 6:16; Num. 3:17; 1 Chr. 6:1. In the journey through the wilderness they were charged with the framework of the tabernacle, to carry from one place of encampment to another, and there set it up, Num. 4:29-33; 7:8. Twelve cities were assigned to them beyond Jordan, Josh. 21:7, 34-40.

MER'CHANT, Gen. 23:16. The commodities of different countries were usually exchanged by traders of various kinds, in caravans or "travelling companies," Isa. 21:13, which had their regular seasons and routes for passing from one great mart to another, Gen. 37:25, 28. These merchants prospered by wandering, as ours do by remaining stationary. The apostle James reminds them to lay their plans in view of the uncertainty of life, and their need of divine guidance, James 4:13. Some of the maritime nations, as Egypt, and still more the Phœnicians, carried on a large traffic by sea, Isa. 23:2; Ezek. 27:28.

MER'CURY, a fabulous god of the ancient heathen, the messenger of the celestials, and the deity that presided over learning, eloquence, and traffic. The Greeks named him Hermes, interpreter, because they considered him as the interpreter of the will of the gods. Probably it was for this reason that the people of Lystra, having heard Paul preach, and having seen him heal a lame man, would have offered sacrifice to him as to their god Mercury; and to Barnabas as Jupiter, because of his venerable aspect, Acts 14:11, 12.

MER'CY, the divine goodness exercised towards the wretched and the guilty, in harmony with truth and justice, Psa. 85:10. The plan by which God is enabled to show saving mercy to men, for Christ's sake, is the most consummate work of infinite wisdom and love. The soul that has truly experienced the mercy of God will be merciful like him, Luke 6:36, compassionate to the wretched, Psa. 41:1, 2, and forgiving towards all, Matt. 5:7; 18:33.

MER'CY-SEAT, 1 Chr. 28:11, the cover of the Ark of the Covenant, which see. The Hebrew word means *a cover*, but contains an allusion to the covering or forgiving of sins, Psa. 32:1. In the New Testament it is designated by a Greek word meaning "the propitiatory," or "expiatory," Heb. 9:4, 5. It was approached only by the high-priest, and not without the blood of atonement, to show that the divine mercy can be granted only through the blood of Christ, Rom. 3:25.

LAKE MEROM, WITH MOUNT HERMON IN THE DISTANCE.

ME'ROM. The "waters of Merom," Josh. 11:5, or lake of Semechon, is the most northern of the three lakes supplied by the river Jordan. It is situated in the southern part of a valley formed by the two branches of mount Hermon. The lake is now called after the valley, the lake of Huleh. The lake proper is four or five miles long, and perhaps four broad, tapering towards the south. It is very shallow, and a large part of it is covered with aquatic plants. Thousands of water-fowl sport on its surface, and its waters abound in fish. On the north lies the plain of the Huleh, which is a dead level for a distance of six miles or more. Near the upper end of this, the three streams which form the Jordan unite. On the west side of the Jordan above the lake, a marsh extends up north as far as the junction of these streams, or even farther; while on the eastern side the land is tilled almost down to the lake. It is a splendid plain, and extremely fertile. All kinds of grain grow on it, with very little labor; and it still merits the praise accorded to it by the Danite spies: "We have seen the land; and behold, it is very good, ... a place where there is no want of any thing that is in the earth," Judg. 18:9, 10. Its rich soil is formed by deposit, and it seems to be partially submerged in the spring. Thus the lake and valley El-Huleh form an immense reservoir, and unite with the snows of Hermon to maintain the summer supplies of the Jordan. Near this lake Joshua defeated the kings of Northern Canaan, Josh. 11:1-8.

MER'IBAH, *strife*, I., a station of the Israelites between the Red sea and mount Sinai, where they murmured against the Lord, and a fountain gushed from the rock for their use, Ex. 17:1-7. It was also named Massah, *temptation*, when they tempted God there, Deut. 33:8; Heb. 3:8.

II. A similar miraculous fountain in the desert of Zin, near Kadesh, which see, Num. 20:13, 14. This was the scene of the transgression of Moses and Aaron, for which they were precluded from crossing the Jordan. It is called "the waters of Meribah," Deut. 33:8; Psa. 81:7; 106:32, and also Meribah-kadesh, Num. 27:14; Deut. 32:51; Ezek. 47:19.

MERO'DACH, an idol of the Babylonians, representing probably the planet Mars, Jer. 50:2. The names of Babylonish kings were also sometimes compounded with this name, as Evil-Merodach and Merodach-Baladan, Isa. 39:1, who is also called Berodach-Baladan in 2 Kin. 20:12.

ME'ROZ, an unknown place in Galilee, cursed in the song of Deborah and Barak for not joining with them against the foes of Israel, Judg. 5:23. Probably their vicinity to the scene of conflict, or the opportunity they had of rendering some special assistance, rendered their refusal peculiarly guilty.

ME'SHA, I., a place on the eastern frontier of the territory of Joktan, Gen. 10:30, supposed to have been in the region of Bassora, at the north-west end of the Persian gulf.

II. A king of Moab, who paid an enormous tribute to Ahab king of Israel, but revolted at his death, 2 Kin. 1:1; 3:4-27. Joram the son of Ahab, with the aid of Judah and Edom, made war upon him, and besieged him in his capital. Unable to force his way through the besieging host, king Mesha sought the aid of his gods by sacrificing his own son on the city wall; and the besiegers, horror-struck at this atrocious act, withdrew in terror, lest some curse should fall on them.

ME'SHACH. See ABED-NEGO.

ME'SHECH, or MESECH, Psa. 120:5, the sixth son of Japheth, Gen. 10:2, located near Tubal at the north-east corner of Asia Minor, in Iberia, and supposed by many to have been the father of the Muscovites. Meshech traded with Tyre in "the persons of men, and in vessels of brass," Ezek. 27:13; 32:26; 38:2.

MESOPOTA'MIA, *between the rivers*, the Greek name of the country between the Euphrates and the Tigris, called in Arabic, Al Jezira, the island. See ARAM II., and PADAN-ARAM. In its fullest sense, Mesopotamia extended from the Persian gulf to mount Taurus; but the name usually denotes only the tract above Babylonia, now called Diarbekr and celebrated for its exuberant fertility; while the part below, now Irak-Arabi, is sterile and without water. Mesopotamia was included in the territories of the Assyrian, Babylonian, Persian, Macedonian, and Roman empires successively, and belongs now to that of the Turks.

This region is associated with the earliest history of the human race both before and after the flood. Eden was not far off; Ararat was near to it on the north, and the land of Shinar on the south. The traveller here reaches what is truly "the old world," and is surrounded by objects compared with which the antiquities of Greece and Rome are modern novelties. This was the home of the patriarchs who preceded Abraham—Terah, Heber, Peleg, etc. Here Abraham and Sarah were born, and the wives of Isaac and Jacob, and most of the sons of Jacob, the heads of the twelve tribes. Mesopotamia is also mentioned in Scripture as the abode of the first oppressor of Israel in the time of the judges, Judg. 3:8–10; in the history of the wars of David, 2 Sam. 10:16; and as furnishing a delegation of Jews, and perhaps proselytes, to attend the Passover at Jerusalem, Acts 2:9.

MESSI'AH, or MESSI'AS, *anointed*, a title given principally, or by way of eminence, to that sovereign Deliverer promised to the Jews. They were accustomed to anoint their kings, high-priests, and sometimes prophets, when they were set apart to their office; and hence the phrase, "to anoint" for an employment, sometimes signifies merely a particular designation or choice for such an employment. Cyrus, who founded the empire of the Persians, and who set the Jews at liberty, is called, Isa. 45:1, "the anointed of the Lord;" and in Ezek. 28:14, the epithet "anointed" is given to the king of Tyre.

But, as we have already observed, MESSIAH is the designation given by the Hebrews, eminently, to that Saviour and Deliverer whom they expected, and who was promised to them by all the prophets. As the holy unction was given to kings, priests, and prophets, by describing the promised Saviour of the world under the name of Christ, Anointed, or Messiah, it was sufficiently evidenced that the qualities of king, prophet, and high-priest would eminently centre in him, and that he should exercise them not only over the Jews, but over all mankind, and particularly over those who should receive him as their Saviour. See CHRIST.

That Jesus Christ was the true MESSIAH of the Old Testament, the "Shiloh" of Jacob, the "Redeemer" of Job, the "Angel of the Covenant," is abundantly clear. The time of his appearance was predicted in Gen. 49:10; Dan. 9:20, 25; Hag. 2:7; Mal. 3:1. At the time when the Saviour actually came, and then only, could these predictions meet: then the seventy weeks of years were ended; and soon after, the sceptre was torn for ever from the hands of Judah, the only tribe that could then claim the headship of the Jews; and the temple in which the Messiah was to appear was annihilated. Then also the genealogical lists were extant, which proved the descent of Christ from the line predicted. Numerous and clear detached predictions respecting the birth, character, life, sufferings, and death of Christ, his resurrection, ascension, and kingdom, were all in him perfectly fulfilled, John 1:41; 4:25.

METHEG-AM'MAH, 2 Sam. 8:1; 1 Chr. 18:1. See GATH.

METHU'SELAH, son of Enoch, and father of Lamech. He lived 969 years, a longer life than any other on record, and died within the year before the deluge, Gen. 5:21, 22.

MI'CAH, I., the Morasthite, or of Maresheth, a village near Eleutheropolis, in the west of Judah; the seventh in order of the lesser prophets. He prophesied under Jotham, Ahaz, and Hezekiah, kings of Judah, for about fifty years, if with some we reckon from near the beginning of the reign of Jotham, to the last year of Hezekiah B. C. 750–698. He was nearly contemporary with Isaiah, and has some expressions in common with him. Compare Isa. 2:2 with Micah 4:1, and Isa. 41:15 with Micah 4:13. His bold fidelity served as a shield to the prophet Jeremiah a century afterwards, Jer. 26:18, 19; Mic. 3:12. He wrote in an elevated and vehement style, with frequent transitions. His prophecy relates to the sins and judgments of Israel and Judah, the destruction of Samaria and Jerusalem, the return of the Jews from captivity, and the punishment of their enemies. He proclaims the coming of the Messiah, "whose goings forth have been from of old, from everlasting," as the foundation of all hope for the glorious and blessed future he describes; and specifies Bethlehem in Judah as the place where He should be born of woman, Mic. 5:2, 3. The prediction was thus understood by the Jews, Matt. 2:6; John 7:41, 42.

II. An Ephraimite in the time of the judges, soon after Joshua, who stole eleven hundred shekels of silver from his mother, but restored them, and with her consent employed them in establishing a private sanctuary, with an image to be used in the worship of Jehovah, and with a Levite for his priest. Providence frowned on his idolatrous service, and a troop of Danites robbed him of his priest and of all his implements of worship, Judg. 17; 18.

MICAI'AH, I., a faithful and fearless prophet, consulted by king Ahab at the demand of Jehoshaphat as to the issue of their proposed campaign against the

Syrians. He was imprisoned to abide the event, which coincided with his predictions and probably secured his release, 1 Kin. 22:8–38. Ahab's conduct in this matter displays the amazing folly of sins against light.

II. A prince of Judah, who seconded the efforts of Jehoshaphat to instruct and reform the people of Judah, 2 Kin. 17:7–9.

MI'CHAEL. See ARCHANGEL.

MICHAI'AH, a young prince at the court of Jehoiakim, who communicated to the king's counsellors the solemn warnings of Jeremiah, Jer. 36:11–13.

MI'CHAL, the younger of Saul's two daughters, in love with David, and whom Saul reluctantly gave to him in marriage, 1 Sam. 14:49; 18:20–29. She saved her husband's life from assassins sent by her father, by a stratagem which gave him time to escape, 1 Sam. 19:14, 15. Her father then gave her in marriage to Phalti, 1 Sam. 25:44, from whom David some years after recovered her, 2 Sam. 3:12–21. When David brought the ark of God to Jerusalem, she conceived and expressed great disgust at his pious joy, and the affections of the king remained alienated from her till her death, 2 Sam. 6:16–23. Her hatred of unfashionable zeal in religion was stronger than her love of her husband and her God. She left no children.

MICH'MASH, a town of Benjamin, nine miles north by east of Jerusalem, Neh. 7:31; 11:31. It was a strong position, and lay on the north side of a deep valley; for which reasons perhaps Sennacherib, on his way to Jerusalem, left his heavy equipage there, Isa. 10:28, 29. In this deep valley, a little west of the town, are two steep hills or rocks, supposed to be the ones referred to in the account of Jonathan's achievement at "the passage of Michmash," 1 Sam. 13:23; 14:4. Dr. Robinson found here a village called Mukhmas, which appeared to be the remnant of a town of some size and importance.

MICH'TAM, prefixed to Psalms 16, 56–60, and meaning *golden*, *profound*, or as some think, *a writing* or *song*, as in Isa. 38:9.

MID'IAN, the fourth son of Abraham and Keturah, Gen. 25:2.

MID'IANITES, descendants of Midian, a nomade race in Arabia, numerous, and rich in flocks, herds, and camels, Isa. 60:6. The original and appropriate district of the Midianites seems to have been on the east side of the Elanitic branch of the Red sea, where the Arabian geographers place the city Madian, Acts 7:29. But they appear to have spread themselves northward, probably along the desert east of mount Seir, to the vicinity of the Moabites; and on the other side, also, they covered a territory extending to the neighborhood of mount Sinai. See Ex. 3:1; 18:1; Num. 22; 25; 31; Judg. 6–8. In Gen. 25:2, 4, compared with ver. 12–18, they are distinguished from the descendants of Ishmael, though elsewhere we find the two people intimately associated, so that they are called now by one name and now by the other. See Gen. 37:25, compared with verse 36. Their capital city was called Midian, and its remains were to be seen in the time of Jerome and Eusebius. It was situated on the Arnon, south of the city Ar, or Areopolis.

The Midianites were idolaters, and often led Israel astray to worship their gods. They also not unfrequently rendered the Hebrews tributary, and oppressed them. See Num. 22; 25; 31. Often when the Israelites had sown, and their harvest was nearly ready to be gathered in, the Midianites and Amalekites, children of the eastern desert, came down like locusts in countless swarms, with their cattle and tents and camels, to devour and carry off the fruits of the ground, and not only rob but destroy their owners. And often did the Jews, lacking the strength or the faith or the leadership necessary for effectual resistance, seek refuge in mountain-dens and caverns till the invaders retired. Gideon was their deliverer in one such period of oppression, Judg. 6; 7. The modern Ishmaelites still follow the ancient practice, and their violent incursions, robberies, and murders might be described in the same terms that were used with reference to their fathers by the historians of old.

MID'NIGHT. See HOUR.

MIG'DOL, *a tower*, a frontier town in Northern Egypt, towards the Red sea, Jer. 44:1; 46:14; Ezek. 29:10; 30:6. The Hebrews, on leaving Egypt, encamped between it and the sea, Exod. 14:2; Num. 33:7.

MIG'RON, a town in the vicinity of Ai and Gibeah, north of Michmash, now lost, 1 Sam. 14:2; Isa. 10:28.

MIL'COM. See MOLOCH.

MILE. The word *mile*, in Matt. 5:41, is spoken of the Roman milliare, or mile, which contained eight stadia, 1,000 paces, that is, about 1,614 yards, while the English mile contains 1,760 yards.

MILE'TUS, an ancient city, formerly the metropolis of all Ionia, situated on the western coast of Asia Minor, on the confines of Caria, just south of the mouth of the river Meander. It was the parent of many colonies, and was celebrated for a temple and oracle of Apollo Didymaeus, and as the birthplace of Thales, Anaximander, Democritus, and other famous men. The apostle Paul, on his voyage from Macedonia towards Jerusalem, spent a day or two here, and held an affecting interview with the Christian elders of Ephesus, who at his summons came nearly thirty miles from the north to meet him, Acts 20:15-38. He also revisited Miletus after his first imprisonment at Rome, 2 Tim. 4:20. There were Christians and bishops there from the fifth to the eighth century; but the city has long been in ruins, and its exact site can hardly be determined, so much is the coast altered around the mouth of the Meander.

MILK is often alluded to in the Bible, as a symbol of pure, simple, and wholesome truth, Heb. 5:12, 13; 1 Pet. 2:2; and in connection with honey, to denote fertility and plenty, Gen. 49:12; Num. 16:13; Josh. 5:6. The Jews and their neighbors used not only the milk of cows, but that of camels, sheep, and goats, Gen. 32:15; Deut. 32:14; Prov. 27:27. See BUTTER and CHEESE.

MILL. See CORN.

MIL'LO, I., probably a bastion of the citadel of Zion, at Jerusalem, mentioned in the history of David and Solomon, 2 Sam. 5:9; 2 Kin. 12:20; 1 Chr. 11:8; 2 Chr. 32:5.

II. The name of a family or of a fortress at Shechem; in the latter case, the "house of Millo" would mean the garrison of that fortress, Judg. 9:6.

MIL'LET, a kind of grain, of which there are several species cultivated in Italy, Syria, Egypt, and India. It is used partly green as fodder, and partly in the ripe grain for bread, etc. Ezekiel, 4:9, received an order from the Lord to make himself bread with a mixture of wheat, barley, beans, lentiles, and millet. "Durra," says Niebuhr, "is a kind

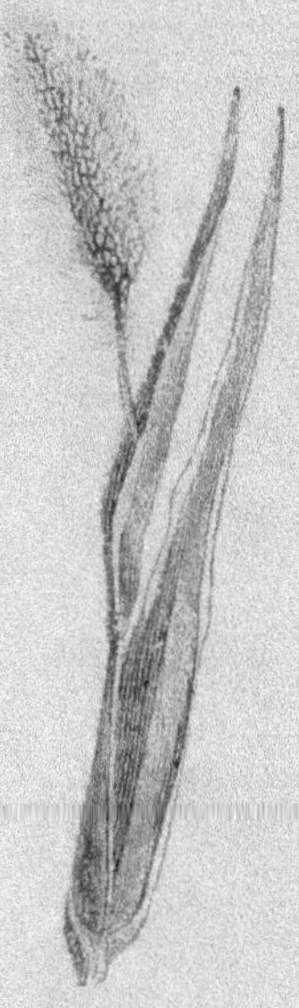

of millet, made into bread with camel's milk, oil, butter, etc., and is almost the only food eaten by the common people of Arabia Felix. I found it so disagreeable, that I would willingly have preferred plain barley bread." This illustrates the appointment of it to the prophet Ezekiel, as a part of his hard fare.

MIN'ISTER, one who attends or waits on another, Matt. 20:28; so Elisha was the *minister* of Elijah, 1 Kings 19:21; 2 Kings 3:11, and Joshua the *minister* of Moses, Ex. 24:13; 33:11. These persons did not feel themselves degraded by their stations, and in due time they succeeded to the office of their masters. In like manner, John Mark was minister to Paul and Barnabas, Acts 13:5. Angels are ministers of God and of his people, Psa. 103:21; Heb. 1:14. The term is applied to one who performs any function, or administers any office or agency: as to magistrates, Rom. 13:4, 6; to gospel teachers, Rom. 15:16; 1 Cor. 3:5; 4:1; and to teachers of error, 2 Cor. 11:15. Christ came to minister, not to be ministered unto; and is called in another sense a minister "of the circumcision," Rom. 15:8, and of the heavenly sanctuary, Heb. 8:2.

MIN'NI, a kingdom summoned to a war against Babylon, with Ararat and Ashchenaz, Jer. 51:27; supposed to denote Armenia, or a portion of it.

MIN'NITH, a town of the Ammonites

in the time of Jephthah, Judg. 11:33, four miles north-east of Heshbon. It furnished fine wheat for the market of Tyre, Ezek. 27:17.

MINT, a garden herb, sufficiently known. The Pharisees, desiring to distinguish themselves by a most scrupulous and literal observation of the law, gave tithes of mint, anise, and cummin, Matt. 23:23. Our Saviour does not censure this exactness, but complains, that while they were so precise in these lesser matters, they neglected the essential commandments of the law—making their punctiliousness about easy and external duties an excuse for disregarding their obligations to love God supremely, to be regenerated in heart, and just and beneficent in life.

MIR'ACLE, also called a sign, wonder, or mighty work, Acts 2:32; a work so superseding in its higher forms the established laws of nature as to evince the special interposition of God. A miracle is to be distinguished from wonders wrought by designing men through artful deceptions, occult sciences, or laws of nature unknown except to adepts. The miracles wrought by Christ, for example, were such as God only could perform; were wrought in public, before numerous witnesses, both friends and foes; were open to the most perfect scrutiny; had an end in view worthy of divine sanction; were attested by witnesses whose character and conduct establish their claim to our belief; and are further confirmed by institutions still existing, intended to commemorate them, and dating from the period of the miracles. Christ appealed to his mighty works as undeniable proofs of his divinity and Messiahship, Matt. 9:6; 11:4, 5, 23, 24; John 10:24–27; 20:29, 31. The deceptions of the magicians in Egypt, and of false prophets in ancient and in modern times, Deut. 13:1; Matt. 24:24; 2 Thess. 2:9; Rev. 13:13, 14, would not bear the above tests. By granting to any man the power to work a miracle, God gave the highest attestation to the truth he should teach and the message he should bring, 1 Kin. 18:38, 39; this is God's own seal, not to be affixed to falsehoods; and though the lying wonders of Satan and his agents were so plausible as to "deceive if possible the very elect," no one who truly sought to know and do the will of God could be deluded by them.

The chief object of miracles having been to authenticate the revelation God has made of his will, these mighty works ceased when the Scripture canon was completed and settled, and Christianity was fairly established. Since the close of the first century from the ascension of Christ, few or no undoubted miracles have been wrought; and whether a sufficient occasion for new miracles will ever arise is known only to God.

The following list comprises most of the miracles on record in the Bible, not including the supernatural visions and revelations of himself which God vouchsafed to his ancient servants, nor those numerous wonders of his providence which manifest his hand almost as indisputably as miracles themselves. See also PROPHECY.

OLD TESTAMENT MIRACLES.

The creation of all things, Gen. 1.
The deluge, comprising many miracles, Gen. 6–8.
The destruction of Sodom, etc., Gen. 19.
The healing of Abimelech, Gen. 20:17, 18.
The burning bush, Ex. 3:2–4.
Moses' rod made a serpent, and restored, Ex. 4:3, 4; 7:10.
Moses' hand made leprous, and healed, Ex. 4:6, 7.
Water turned into blood, Ex. 4:9, 30.
The Nile turned into blood, Ex. 7:20.
Frogs brought, and removed, Ex. 8:6, 13.
Lice brought, Ex. 8:17.
Flies brought, and removed, Ex. 8:21–31.
Murrain of beasts, Ex. 9:3–6.
Boils and blains brought, Ex. 9:10, 11.
Hail brought, and removed, Ex. 9:23, 33.
Locusts brought, and removed, Ex. 10:13, 19.
Darkness brought, Ex. 10:22.
First-born destroyed, Ex. 10:29.

The Red sea divided, Ex. 14:21, 22.
Egyptians overwhelmed, Ex. 14:26–28.
Waters of Marah sweetened, Ex. 15:28.
Quails and manna sent, Ex. 16.
Water from the rock, in Horeb, Ex. 17:6.
Amalek vanquished, Ex. 17:11–13.
Pillar of cloud and fire, Num. 9:15–23.
Leprosy of Miriam, Num. 12:10.
Destruction of Korah, etc., Num. 16:28–35, 46–50.
Aaron's rod budding, Num. 17:8.
Water from the rock, in Kadesh, Num. 20:11.
Healing by the brazen serpent, Num. 21:8, 9.
Balaam's ass speaks, Num. 22:28.
Plague in the desert, Num. 25:1, 9.
Waters of Jordan divided, Josh. 3:10–17.
Jordan restored to its course, Josh. 4:18.
Jericho taken, Josh. 6:6–20.
Achan discovered, Josh. 7:14–21.
Sun and moon stand still, Josh. 10:12–14.
Gideon's fleece wet, Judg. 6:36–40.
Midianites destroyed, Judg. 7:16–22.
Exploits of Samson, Judg. 14–16.
House of Dagon destroyed, Judg. 16:30.
Dagon falls before the ark, etc., 1 Sam. 5.
Return of the ark, 1 Sam. 6:12.
Thunder and rain in harvest, 1 Sam. 12:18.
Jeroboam's hand withered, etc., 1 Kin. 13:4, 6.
The altar rent, 1 Kin. 13:5.
Drought caused, 1 Kin. 17:6.
Elijah fed by ravens, 1 Kin. 17:6.
Meal and oil supplied, 1 Kin. 17:14–16.
Child restored to life, 1 Kin. 17:22, 23.
Sacrifice consumed by fire, 1 Kin. 18:36, 38.
Rain brought, 1 Kin. 18:41–45.
Men destroyed by fire, 2 Kin. 1:10–12.
Waters of Jordan divided, 2 Kin. 2:14.
Noxious waters healed, 2 Kin. 2:21, 22.
Children torn by bears, 2 Kin. 2:24.
Waters brought, 2 Kin. 3:16–20.
Oil supplied, 2 Kin. 4:1–7.
Child restored to life, 2 Kin. 4:32–35.
Naaman healed, 2 Kin. 5:10, 14.
Gehazi's leprosy, 2 Kin. 5:27.
Iron caused to swim, 2 Kin. 6:6.
Syrians smitten blind, etc., 2 Kin. 6:18, 20.
A man restored to life, 2 Kin. 13:21.
Syrians destroyed, 2 Kin. 19:35.
Hezekiah healed, 2 Kin. 20:7.
Shadow put back, 2 Kin. 20:11.
Pestilence in Israel, 1 Chr. 21:14.
Jonah preserved by a fish, Jonah 1:17; 2:10.

NEW TESTAMENT MIRACLES.

The star in the east, Matt. 2:3.
The Spirit like a dove, Matt. 3:16.
Christ's fast and temptations, Matt. 4:1–11.
Many miracles of Christ, Matt. 4:23, 24; 8:16; 14:14, 36; 15:30; Mark 1:34; Luke 6:17–19.
Lepers cleansed, Matt. 8:3, 4; Luke 17:14.
Centurion's servant healed, Matt. 8:5–13.
Peter's wife's mother healed, Matt. 8:14.
Tempests stilled, Matt. 8:23–26; 14:32.
Devils cast out, Matt. 8:28–32; 9:32, 33; 15:22–28; 17:14–18.
Paralytics healed, Matt. 9:2–6; Mark 2:3–12.
Issue of blood healed, Matt. 9:20–22.
Jairus' daughter raised to life, Matt. 9:18, 25.
Sight given to the blind, Matt. 9:27–30; 20:34; Mark 8:22–25; John 9:1–7.
The dumb restored, Matt. 9:32, 33; 12:22; Mark 7:33–35.
Miracles by the disciples, Matt. 10:1, 8.
Multitudes fed, Matt. 14:15–21; 15:35–38.
Christ walking on the sea, Matt. 14:25–27.
Peter walking on the sea, Matt. 14:29.
Christ's transfiguration, etc., Matt. 17:1–8.
Tribute from a fish's mouth, Matt. 17:27.
The fig-tree withered, Matt. 21:19.
Miracles at the crucifixion, Matt. 27:51–53.
Miracles at the resurrection, Matt. 28:1–7; Luke 24:6.
Draught of fishes, Luke 5:4–6; John 21:6.
Widow's son raised to life, Luke 7:14, 15.
Miracles before John's messengers, Luke 7:21, 22.
Miracles by the seventy, Luke 10:9, 17.
Woman healed of infirmity, Luke 13:11–13.
Dropsy cured, Luke 14:2–4.
Malchus' ear restored, Luke 22:50, 51.
Water turned into wine, John 2:6–10.
Nobleman's son healed, John 4:46–53.
Impotent man healed, John 5:5–9.
Sudden crossing of the sea, John 6:21.
Lazarus raised from the dead, John 11:43, 44.
Christ's coming to his disciples, John 20:19, 26.
Wonders at the Pentecost, Acts 2:1–11.
Miracles by the apostles, Acts 2:43; 5:12.
Lame man cured, Acts 3:7.
Death of Ananias and Sapphira, Acts 5:5, 10.
Many sick healed, Acts 5:15, 16.
Apostles delivered from prison, Acts 5:19.
Miracles by Stephen, Acts 6:8.
Miracles by Philip, Acts 8:6, 7, 13.
Æneas made whole, Acts 9:34.
Dorcas restored to life, Acts 9:40.
Peter delivered from prison, Acts 12:6–10.
Elymas struck blind, Acts 13:11.
Miracles by Paul and Barnabas, Acts 14:3.
Lame man cured, Acts 14:10.
Unclean spirit cast out, Acts 16:18.
Paul and Silas delivered, Acts 16:25, 26.
Special miracles, Acts 19:11, 12.
Eutychus restored to life, Acts 20:10–12.
Viper's bite made harmless, Acts 28:5.
Father of Publius, etc., healed, Acts 28:8, 9.

MIR'IAM, the sister of Moses and Aaron, probably the one who watched over Moses in the ark of bulrushes, Ex. 2:4, 5; Num. 26:59; Mic. 6:4. As a prophetess, she led the women of Israel in their song of worship and thanksgiving to God on the drowning of the Egyptians, Ex. 15:20, 21. Her jealous murmurs against Moses and his Cushite wife were punished by a temporary leprosy, Num. 12; Deut. 24:9; but she was forgiven and restored, and near the close of the wanderings of Israel, died at Kadesh-barnea, Num. 20:1.

MIR'ROR. See LOOKING-GLASS.

MISH'AEL, or ME'SHACH, a fellow-captive with Daniel in Babylon. See ABEDNEGO.

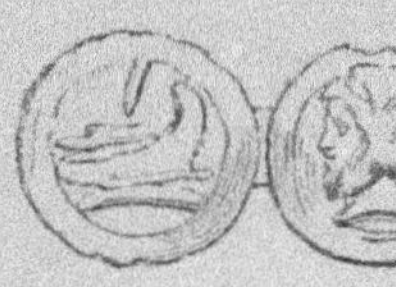

THE ROMAN AS.

MI'TE, a small piece of money, two of which made a *kodrantes*, or the fourth part of the Roman *as*. The *as* was equal to three and one-tenth farthings sterling, or about one and one-half cents. The mite, therefore, would be equal to about two mills, Luke 12:59; 21:2.

MI'TRE, the sacred turban or bonnet of the Jewish high-priest, made of a piece of fine linen many yards long, wound about the head, and having in front, secured with blue lace, a plate of pure gold on which was inscribed, "HOLINESS UNTO THE LORD," Ex. 28:4, 36-38; 39:28-31.

MIT'YLENE, the ancient capital of the island of Lesbos; a seaport on the east side of the island, towards Asia Minor. Paul touched there on his way from Greece to Jerusalem, Acts 20:14. The island is now called Mitelino; and the ruins of the city still exist near Castro.

MIZ'PAH, or MIZ'PEH, *a watch-tower*, I., a town in Gilead, Hos. 5:1; so named from the stone-heap cast up by Jacob and Laban, Gen. 31:49; supposed by many to be the place mentioned in the history of Jephthah, Judg. 10:17; 11:11, 29, 34.

II. A city of Benjamin, a central gathering-place of the tribes in the period of the judges, Josh. 18:26; Judg. 20:1, 3; 21:1. Here Samuel sacrificed and judged, and here Saul was designated as king, 1 Sam. 7:5-16; 10:17. It was fortified by Asa as a defence against Israel, 1 Kin. 15:22, was the residence of the governor, under Nebuchadnezzar, Jer. 40:6, and was reoccupied after the captivity, Neh. 3:19. Its name indicates that it occupied an elevated site, and it was near Ramah; hence Dr. Robinson identifies it with the modern place called Neby Samwil, four or five miles north-northwest of Jerusalem.

III. A town in the plain of Judah, Josh. 15:38.

IV. A valley near mount Hermon, towards Zidon, Josh. 11:3, 8.

MIZ'RAIM, a son of Ham, and father of various African races, Gen. 10:6, but particularly of the Egyptians, to whom his name was given. Mizraim is also the Hebrew word for Egypt in the Bible, and this country is still called Misr in Arabic.

MNA'SON of Cyprus, "an old disciple" with whom Paul lodged at Jerusalem, Acts 21:16.

MO'ABITES, descendants of Moab the son of Lot, Gen. 19:30-38. The land of Moab lay east and south-east of the Dead sea, and chiefly south of the river Arnon. At one period, however, it extended north as far as the Jabbok, and for a long time the region beyond the Jordan opposite Jericho retained the name of "the plains of Moab," Num. 22:1; Deut. 1:5; 29:1; Josh. 13:32. The Moabites had dispossessed a race of giants called Emim, Deut. 2:11, and had themselves been expelled by the Amorites from the territory north of the Arnon, Num. 21:13, 26; Judg. 11:13-18, which was again conquered by Moses, and assigned to the tribe of Reuben. On the approach of Israel from Egypt, the Moabites acted with great inhumanity, Num. 22-24; Deut. 2:8, 9; and though God spared them from conquest, he excluded them and their seed even to the tenth generation from the peculiar privileges of his people, Deut. 23:3-6. They were gross idolaters, worshipping Chemosh and Baal-peor with obscene rites, Num. 25, and sometimes with human sacrifices, 2 Kin. 3:27. See MOLOCH. At times, as in the days of Ruth, there was peace between them and Israel; but a state of hostility was far more common, as in the time of Eglon, Judg. 3:12-30; of Saul, 1 Sam. 14:47; of David, 2 Sam. 8:2, 12; of Joram and Jeroboam, 2 Kin. 3; 13:20; 14:25. They aided Nebuchadnezzar against the Jews, 2 Kin. 24:2; Ezek. 25:6-11; and after these began to be carried captive, appear to have regained their old possessions north of the Arnon, Isa. 15; 16. The Jewish prophets recorded many threatenings against these hereditary enemies of God and his people, Num. 24:17; Psa. 60:8; 83:6; Jer. 25:9-21; 48; Amos 2:1-3; and all travellers concur in attesting the fulfilment of these predictions. Desolation and gloom brood over the mountains of Moab, and its fruitful valleys are for the most part untilled. It is under Turkish government, but is inhabited chiefly by migratory Arabs, Zeph. 2:8, 9. Few travellers have ventured to traverse it in modern times. They describe it as abounding in ruins, such as shattered tombs, cisterns, walls, temples, etc., proving that it was once densely populated. See "Keith on Prophecy."

MOLE, a small animal, which burrows obscurely in the ground, Isa. 2:20. It is common in some parts of Palestine, and is mentioned as unclean in Lev. 11:30; or, according to Bochart, in ver. 29, in the word translated "weasel."

MO'LECH, MO'LOCH, or MIL'COM, *a king*, 1 Kin. 11:5, 7; Acts 7:43; supposed also to be intended by Malcham, or "their king," in Jer. 49:1; Amos 1:15; Zeph. 1:5, the name of a heathen deity, worshipped by the Ammonites. The Israelites also introduced the worship of this idol, both during their wanderings in the desert, and after their settlement in Palestine, 2 Kin. 23:10; Ezek. 20:26, 31. The principal sacrifices to Moloch were human victims, namely, children who were cast alive into the red-hot arms of his statue. See HINNOM. Compare Lev. 18:21; 20:2; Deut. 12:31; Psa. 106:37, 38; Jer. 7:31; 19:2-6; 32:35. According to some of these passages, Moloch would seem to be another name for Baal; and we find that the Phœnicians, whose chief god was Baal, and the Carthaginians their colonists, worshipped his image with similar horrid sacrifices, as the Romans did their god Saturn.

MON'EY. See next page.

MONTH. The Hebrew months were lunar months, that is, from one new moon to another. These lunar months were each reckoned at twenty-nine days and a half; or rather, one was of thirty days, the following of twenty-nine, and so on alternately: that which had thirty days was called a full or complete month; that which had but twenty-nine days was called incomplete. The new moon was always the beginning of the month, and this day they called new-moon day, or new month. The Hebrews usually designated the months only as first, second, etc.; and the names by which they are now known are believed to be of Persian origin, and to have been adopted by the Jews during the captivity. At the exodus from Egypt, which occurred in April, God ordained that that month—the seventh of the civil year—should be the first of the sacred year, according to which the religious festivals were to be reckoned; and from that time both these modes of numbering the months continued to be employed.

As the Jewish months were governed by the moon, while ours entirely disregard it, the two systems cannot wholly coincide. It is generally agreed, however, that their month Nisan answers most nearly to our April, Iyar to our May, etc., as in the following table.

Hebrew Months.	Nearly corresponding with our	Months of the Sacred Year.	Months of the Civil Year.	Seasons.
Abib, or Nisan, Ex. 12:2, 18. " 13:4. Esth. 3:7.	April.	1st	7th.	LATTER R.
Iyar, or Zif. 1 Kin. 6:1.	May.	2d.	8th.	
Sivan, Esth. 8:9.	June.	3d.	9th.	DRY SEASON.
Tammuz, Ezek. 8:14.	July.	4th.	10th.	
Ab.	August.	5th.	11th.	
Elul, Neh. 6:15.	September.	6th.	12th.	
Ethanim, or Tishri, 1 Kin. 8:2.	October.	7th.	1st.	EARLY R.
Marcheshvan, or Bul, 1 Kin. 6:38.	November.	8th.	2d.	RAINY SEASON.
Chisleu, Zech. 7:1.	December.	9th.	3d.	
Tebeth, Esth. 2:16.	January.	10th.	4th.	
Shebat, Zech. 1:7.	February.	11th.	5th.	
Adar, Esth. 3:7.	March.	12th.	6th.	

Twelve lunar months making but three hundred and fifty-four days and six hours, the Jewish year was short of the Roman by twelve days. To recover the equinoctial points, from which this difference of the solar and lunar year would separate the new moon of the first month, the Jews every three years intercalated a thirteenth month, which they called Veadar, the second Adar. By this means their lunar year nearly equalled the solar. See YEAR.

MON'EY was anciently weighed, and did not at first exist in the form of coins. The most ancient commerce was conducted by barter, or exchanging one sort of merchandise for another. One man gave what he could spare to another, who gave him in return part of his superabundance. Afterwards, the more precious metals were used in traffic, as a value more generally known and stated, and the amount agreed upon was paid over by weight, Gen. 23:16; 43:21; Ex. 30:24. Lastly they gave this metal, by public authority, a certain mark, a certain weight, and a certain degree of alloy, to fix its value, and to save buyers and sellers the trouble of weighing and examining the coins. The first regular coinage among the Jews is supposed to have been in the time of Simon Maccabæus, less than a century and a half before Christ. The coins were the shekel, and a half, a third, and a quarter of a shekel. The Jewish coins bore an almond rod and a vase of manna, but no image of any man was allowed. Compare Matt. 22:16-22. Many Greek and Roman coins circulated in Judea in New Testament times. See Tables at the end of the volume; also MITE, PENNY, SHEKEL.

Volney says, "The practice of weighing money is general in Syria, Egypt, and all Turkey. No piece, however effaced, is refused there: the merchant draws out his scales and weighs it, as in the days of Abraham, when he purchased his sepulchre. In considerable payments, an agent of exchange is sent for, who counts paras by thousands, rejects pieces of false money, and weighs all the sequins, either separately or together." This may serve to illustrate the phrase, "current money with the merchant," Gen. 23:16; and the references to "divers weights"—a large one to weigh the money received, and a small one for that paid out; and to "wicked balances," Deut. 25:13; Amos 8:5; Mic. 6:11. Our Saviour alludes to a class of "exchangers," who appear to have taken money on deposit, and so used it that the owner might afterwards receive his own with interest, Matt. 25 : 27. There were also money brokers who had stands in the outer court of the temple, probably to exchange foreign for Jewish coins; and to accommodate those who wished to pay the yearly half-shekel tax, Ex. 30 : 15, or to present an offering. They were expelled by the Lord of the temple, not only for obtruding a secular business within the house of prayer, but also for pursuing it dishonestly, Mark 11:15-17.

In 1 Tim. 6 : 10, Paul speaks of the "love of money" as a root of all evils; censuring not money itself, but the *love* of it—a prevailing form of human selfishness and covetousness. This passion, to which so many crimes are chargeable, may infest the heart of a poor man as well as that of the rich; for the one may have as much of "the love of money" as the other.

MOON. This beautiful and stately ruler of the night, Gen. 1 : 16, is one of the chief witnesses to mankind of the goodness, wisdom, and power of the Creator, Psa. 8 : 3; and as receiving all its light from the sun, and reflecting it on all around, it is a striking image of the church of Christ. In the clear sky of the East, the moon shines with peculiar brilliancy; and it was worshipped by most nations of antiquity, either directly, or as an idol-goddess under the name of Ashtoreth, Artemis, Diana, Hecate, Meni, Mylitta, Maja, etc. The Hebrews were specially cautioned against this form of idolatry, Deut. 4:19; 17:3; and yet fell into it, 2 Kin. 21 : 3; Isa. 65:11; Jer. 7:18; 8 : 2; 19 : 13; 44:17-25. See LUNATIC and NEW MOON.

MOR'DECAI, the uncle of Esther, who rose to dignity and honor in the court of Ahasuerus. See the book of Esther.

MORI'AH, the hill on which the temple of Jerusalem was built, 2 Chr. 3 : 1. See JERUSALEM. It seems to have been the same place where Abraham was about to offer up Isaac, Gen. 22 : 1, 2; and where David interceded for his people at the threshing-floor of Araunah, 2 Sam. 24:16-25.

MORTAR. This well-known utensil was employed by the Hebrews in preparing manna for use, Num. 11 : 8. Large iron mortars, for pounding grain, have been used by the Turks in the execution of criminals; but it is not known that the Jews ever practised this mode of punishment. To this day a favorite article of food in Syria is prepared by pounding meat for hours in an iron mortar, and adding grain and spice while the process of "braying" goes on, Prov. 27:22.

MO'SES, the name of the illustrious prophet and legislator of the Hebrews, who led them from Egypt to the promised land. Having been originally imposed by a native Egyptian princess, the word is no doubt Egyptian in its origin, and Josephus gives its true derivation—from the two Egyptian words, MO, *water*, and USE, *saved*. With this accords the Septuagint form, Mouses. The Hebrews by a slight change accommodated it to their own language, as they did also in the case of some other foreign words; calling it MOSHE, from the verb MASHA, to draw. See Ex. 2 : 10. Moses was born about 1571 B. C., the son of Amram and Jochebed, of the tribe of Levi, and the younger brother of Miriam and Aaron. His history is too extensive to permit insertion here, and in general too well known to need it. It is enough simply to remark, that it is divided into three periods, each of forty years. The first extends from his infancy, when he was exposed in the Nile, and found and adopted by the daughter of Pharaoh, to his flight to Midian. During this time he lived at the Egyptian court, and "was learned in all the wisdom of the Egyptians, and was mighty in words and in deeds," Acts 7:22. This is no unmeaning praise; the "wisdom" of the Egyptians, and especially of their priests, was then the profoundest in the world. The second period was from his flight till his return to Egypt, Acts 7 : 30, during the whole of which interval he appears to have lived in Midian, it may be much after the manner of the Bedaween sheikhs of the present day. Here he married Zipporah, daughter of the wise and pious Jethro, and became familiar with life in the desert. What a contrast between the former period, spent amid the splendors and learning of a court, and this lonely nomadic life. Still it was in this way that God prepared him to be the instrument of deliverance to His people during the third period of his life, which extends from the exodus out of Egypt to his death on mount Nebo. In this interval how much did he accomplish, as the immediate agent of the Most High.

The life and institutions of Moses present one of the finest subjects for the pen of a Christian historian, who is at the same time a competent biblical antiquary. His institutions breathe a spirit of freedom, purity, intelligence, justice, and humanity, elsewhere unknown; and above all, of supreme love, honor, and obedience to God. They moulded the character of the Hebrews, and transformed them from a nation of shepherds into a people of fixed residence and agricultural habits. Through that people, and through the Bible, the influence of these institutions has been extended over the world; and often where the letter has not been observed, the spirit of them has been adopted. Thus it was in the laws established by the pilgrim fathers of New England; and no small part of what is of most value in the institutions which they founded, is to be ascribed to the influence of the Hebrew legislator.

The name of this servant of God occurs repeatedly in Greek and Latin writings, and still more frequently in those of the Arabs and the rabbinical Jews. Many of their statements, however, are mere legends without foundation, or else distortions of the Scripture narrative. By the Jews he has always been especially honored, as the most illustrious personage in all their annals, and as the founder of their whole system of laws and institutions. Numerous passages both in the Old and New Testament show how exalted a position they gave him, Psa. 103:7; 105:26; 106:16; Isa. 63:12; Jer. 15:1; Dan. 9:11; Matt. 8:4; John 5:45; 9:28; Acts 7:20, 37; Rom. 10:5, 19; Heb. 3; 11:23.

In all that he wrought and taught, he was but the agent of the Most High; and yet in all his own character stands honorably revealed. Though naturally liable to anger and impatience, he so far subdued himself as to be termed the meekest of men, Num. 12:3; and his piety, humility, and forbearance, the wisdom and vigor of his administration, his unfailing zeal and faith in God, and his disinterested patriotism are worthy of all imitation. Many features of his character and life furnish admirable illustrations of the work of Christ—as the deliverer, ruler, and guide of his people, bearing them on his heart, interceding for them, rescuing, teaching, and nourishing them even to the promised land. All the religious institutions of Moses pointed to Christ; and he himself, on the mount, two thousand years after his death, paid his homage to the Prophet he had foretold, Deut. 18:15–19, beheld "that goodly mountain and Lebanon," Deut. 3:25, and was admitted to commune with the Saviour on the most glorious of themes, the death He should accomplish at Jerusalem, Luke 9:31.

Moses was the author of the Pentateuch, as it is called, or the first five books of the Bible. In the composition of them he was probably assisted by Aaron, who kept a register of public transactions, Ex. 17:14; 24:4, 7; 34:27; Num. 33:1, 2; Deut. 31:24, etc. Some things were added by a later inspired hand; as for example, the last chapter of Deuteronomy. The ninetieth Psalm also is ascribed to him; and its noble and devout sentiments acquire a new significance, if received as from his pen near the close of his pilgrimage.

MOTH. The common moth is an insect destructive to woollen cloths. The egg is laid by a small white miller, and produces a small shining worm; which by another transformation becomes a miller. Allusions to the moth, as devouring clothes, and as a frail and feeble insect, are frequent in Scripture, Job 4:19; 13:28; 27:18; Isa. 50:9; Hos. 5:12; Matt. 6:19, 20. See GARMENTS.

The insects called in general moths, of which the above is only one species, are exceedingly numerous. The main genus is called by naturalists *Phalœna*, and contains more than fifteen hundred species. Moths fly abroad only in the evening and night; differing in this respect from the tribe of butterflies, which fly only by day. Their larvæ, or the worms from which they spring, are active and quick in motion, mostly smooth, and prey voraciously on the food adapted to them; the common moth on cloths, others on furs, the leaves of plants, etc.

MOTH'ER. The Hebrew words AM and AB, mother and father, are simple and easy sounds for infant lips, like mamma and papa in English. See ABBA. "Before the child shall have knowledge to cry, My father, and My mother," Isa. 8:4. In addition to the usual meaning of "mother," AM sometimes signifies in the Bible grandmother, 1 Kin. 15:10, or some remote female ancestor, Gen. 3:20. It is put for a chief city, 2 Sam. 20 : 19; for a benefactress, Judg. 5 : 7; for a nation, as in the expressive English phrase, "the mother country," Isa. 3:12; 49:23. The fond affection of a mother is often referred to in Scripture; and God has employed it to illustrate his tender love for his people, Isa. 49 : 15. Mothers are endowed with an all-powerful control over their offspring; and most men of eminence in the world have acknowledged their great indebtedness to maternal influence. When Buonaparte asked Madame Campan what the French nation most needed, she replied in one word, "Mothers." The Christian church already owes much, and will owe infinitely more, to the love, patience, zeal, and self-devotion of mothers in training their children for Christ.

MOUNTAINS are among the most sublime and impressive of the Creator's works on earth, and form the noblest and most enduring monuments of great events. Most of the mountains of Scripture thus stand as witnesses for God—every view of their lofty summits, and every recurrence to them in thought reminding us of the sacred facts and truths connected with them. Thus mount Ararat is a standing memorial of the deluge—of man's sin, God's justice, and God's mercy. Mount Sinai asserts the terrors of the divine law. Mount Carmel summons us, like the prophet Elijah of old, not to "halt between two opinions;" but if Jehovah is God, to love and serve him. The mount of the Transfiguration still shines with the glory of the truths there taught, and mounts Ebal and Gerizim still echo the curses and the blessings once so solemnly pronounced from them. So mount Hor, Nebo, Lebanon, and Gilboa have been signalized by striking events; mount Zion, Moriah, and Olivet are covered with precious memories; and the mountains about Jerusalem and all other "everlasting hills" are sacred witnesses of the eternal power and faithfulness of God.

Judea was eminently a hilly country; and the sacred poets and prophets drew from the mountains around them many beautiful and sublime illustrations of divine truth. Thus a kingdom is termed a mountain, Psa. 30 : 7, especially the kingdom of Christ, Isa. 2 : 2; 11 : 9; Dan. 2 : 35. Thus also difficulty is a "great mountain," Zech. 4:7. A revolution is the "carrying of mountains into the midst of the sea," Psa. 46 : 3. God easily and speedily removes every obstacle—"hills melt like wax at the presence of the Lord," Psa. 97 : 5. The integrity of the divine nature is sure and lasting—"Thy righteousness is like the great mountains," Psa. 36:6. The eternity of God's love is pictured out by this comparison: "For the mountains shall depart, and the hills be removed; but my kindness shall not depart from thee, neither shall the covenant of my peace be removed, saith the Lord that hath mercy on thee," Isa. 54:10. When David wishes to express the stability of his kingdom, he says, "Lord, by thy favor thou hast made my mountain to stand strong," Psa. 30 : 7. The security and protection afforded by God to his people are thus beautifully delineated: "As the mountains are round about Jerusalem, so the Lord is round about his people from henceforth, even for ever," Psa. 125 : 2. When the prophet would express his faith in God, how pure it was, and what confidence it inspired, far above any assurance which could arise from earthly blessing or defence, he sings, "Truly in vain is salvation hoped for from the hills, and from the multitude of mountains: truly in the Lord our God is the salvation of Israel," Jer. 3:23.

The hills of Judea were anciently cultivated to the top, with scores of terraces, and covered with vines, olives, figs, etc. Hence the expression, alluding to the vine of God's planting, "The hills were covered with the shadow of it," Psa. 80 : 10; and others of the same kind. Travellers say it is a rare thing to pass a mountain, even in the wild parts of Judea, which does not show that it was formerly terraced and made to flow with oil and wine, though it may now be desolate and bare. Says Paxton, "There are many districts that are sadly encumbered with rock, yet the soil among these rocks is of a very superior kind: and were the rock somewhat broken up, the large pieces piled, and the small mixed with the soil, it might be made very productive. There is very striking proof of this in some districts, as that about Hebron, which abounds with rock, and yet is covered with the most productive vineyards. As to such a rocky country being so spoken of in the days of the patriarchs, I suppose that it was in truth, at that time, the finest of lands; that the rock which now lies bare in so many places, was then all covered with earth of the richest kind."

"Even in those parts where all is now desolate," remarks Dr. Robinson, "there are everywhere traces of the hand of the men of other days. . . . Most of the hills indeed exhibit the remains of terraces built up around them, the undoubted signs of former cultivation." Again, when travelling towards Hebron, he observes, "Many of the former terraces along the hill sides are still in use; and the land looks somewhat as it may have done in ancient times."

"We often counted forty, fifty, sixty, and even seventy terraces from the bottom of the valley up to the summit of the mountain. . . . What a garden of delights this must have been, when, instead of grass making green the surface, verdant and luxuriant vines were their clothing. . . . We could understand how the words of Joel shall yet be literally true, 'The mountains shall drop down new wine,' when every vine on these hills shall be hanging its ripe clusters over the terraces. In observing too the singular manner in which the most rocky mountains have at one time been made, through vast labor and industry, to yield an abundant return to the husbandman, we saw clearly the meaning of the promise in Ezekiel, 'But ye, O mountains of Israel, ye shall shoot forth your branches, and yield your fruit.'" Narrative of a Mission.

MOURNING. The Hebrews, at the death of their friends and relations, made striking demonstrations of grief and mourning. They wept, tore their clothes, smote their breasts, threw dust upon their heads, Josh. 7:6, and lay upon the ground, went barefooted, pulled their hair and beards, or cut them, Ezra 9:3, Isa. 15:2, and made incisions on their breasts, or tore them with their nails, Lev. 19:28; 21:5; Jer. 16:6; 48:37. The time of mourning was commonly seven days, 1 Sam. 31:11-13; but it was lengthened or shortened according to circumstances, Zech. 12:10. That for Moses and Aaron was prolonged to thirty days, Num. 20:29; Deut. 34:8; and that for Jacob to seventy days, Gen. 50:3.

During the time of their mourning, the near relations of the deceased continued sitting in their houses, and fasted, 2 Sam. 12:16, or ate on the ground. The food they took was thought unclean, and even themselves were judged impure. "Their sacrifices shall be unto them as the bread of mourners; all that eat thereof shall be polluted," Hos. 9:4. Their faces were covered, and in all that time they could not apply themselves to any occupation, nor read the book of the law, nor offer their usual prayers. They did not dress themselves, nor make their beds, nor uncover their heads, nor shave themselves, nor cut their nails, nor go into the bath, nor salute any body. Nobody spoke to them unless they spoke first, Job 2 : 11–13. Their friends commonly went to visit and comfort them, John 11 : 19, 39, bringing them food, 2 Sam. 3:35; Jer. 16:7. They also went up to the roof, or upon the platform of their houses, to bewail their misfortune: "They shall gird themselves with sackcloth; on the tops of their houses, and in their streets, every one shall howl, weeping abundantly," Isa. 15 : 3; Jer. 48:38. The mourning dress among the Hebrews was not fixed either by law or custom. We only find in Scripture that they used to tear their garments, a custom still observed; but now they tear a small part merely, and for form's sake, 2 Sam. 13:19; 2 Chr. 34:27; Ezra 9:3; Job 2 : 12; Joel 2 : 13. Anciently, in times of mourning, they clothed themselves in sackcloth, or hair-cloth, that is, in clothes of coarse brown or black stuff, 2 Sam. 3:31; 1 Kin. 21:27; Esth. 4:1; Psa. 35:13; 69:11.

They hired women to weep and wail, and also persons to play on instruments, at the funerals of the rich or distinguished, Jer. 9 : 17. In Matt. 9 : 23, we observe a company of minstrels or players on the flute, at the funeral of a girl of twelve years of age. All that met a funeral procession were accustomed to join them for a time, to accompany them on their way, sometimes relieving the bearers of the bier, and mingling their tears with those of the mourners, Rom. 12:15.

The custom of hiring women to weep and wail has come down to modern times. The following account of such a scene at Nablous, the ancient Shechem, is from Dr. Jowett. The governor of the city had died the very morning of Dr. Jowett's arrival. "On coming within sight of the gate, we perceived a numerous company of females, who were singing in a kind of recitative, far from melancholy, and beating time with their hands. If this be mourning, I thought, it is of a strange kind. It had indeed sometimes more the air of angry defiance. But on our reaching the gate, it was suddenly exchanged for most hideous plaints and shrieks, which, with the feeling that we were entering a city at no time celebrated for its hospitality, struck a very dismal impression upon my mind. They accompanied us a few paces; but it soon appeared that the gate was their station, to which, having received nothing from us, they returned. We learned, in the course of the evening, that these were only a small detachment of a very numerous body of 'cunning women,' who were filling the whole city with their cries, 'taking up a wailing,' with the design, as of old, to make the eyes of all the inhabitants 'run down with tears, and their eyelids gush out with waters,' Jer. 9:17, 18. For this good service, they would, the next morning, wait upon the government and principal persons, to receive some trifling fee."

Some of the Jewish forms of mourning are the appropriate and universal language of grief; others, to our modern and occidental taste, savor of extravagance. None of these were enjoined by their religion, which rather restricted than encouraged them, Lev. 10:6; 19:27; 21:1–11; Num. 6:7; Deut. 14:1. They were the established customs of the times. Sorrow finds some relief in reversing all the usages of ordinary life. Christianity, however, moderates and assuages our grief; shows us a Father's hand holding the rod, and the dark valley itself penetrated by the heavenly light into which it emerges, 1 Cor. 15 : 53–55; 1 Thess. 4:14–18; Rev. 7:13–17; 14:13.

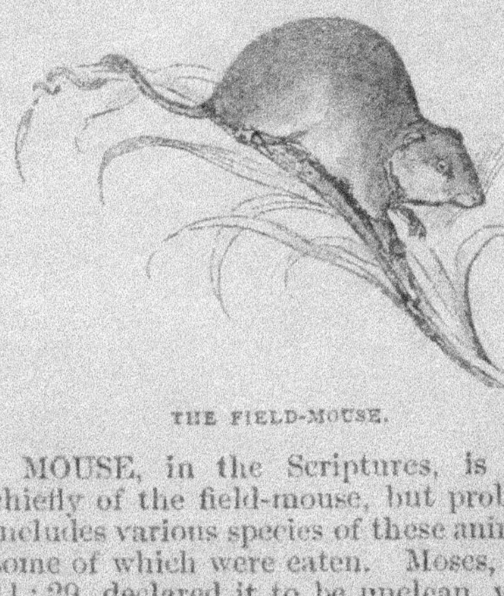

THE FIELD-MOUSE.

MOUSE, in the Scriptures, is used chiefly of the field-mouse, but probably includes various species of these animals, some of which were eaten. Moses, Lev. 11 : 29, declared it to be unclean, yet it was sometimes eaten; and Isaiah, 66:17, reproaches the Jews with this practice.

The hamster and the dormouse, as well as the jerboa, are sometimes used for food by the modern Arabs. Mice made great havoc in the fields of the Philistines, after that people had taken the ark of the Lord; which induced them to send it back with mice and emerods of gold, 1 Sam. 5:6, 9, 11; 6:4, 5. The field-mice are equally prevalent in those regions at the present day. See HAMATH.

MOUTH is sometimes used in Scripture for speaker, Ex. 4:16; Jer. 15:19. God spoke with Moses "mouth to mouth," Num. 12:8, that is, condescendingly and clearly. The law was to be "in the mouth" of the Hebrews, Ex. 13:9, often rehearsed and talked of. "The rod of his mouth," Isa. 11:4, and the sharp sword, Rev. 1:16, denote the power of Christ's word to convict, control, and judge; compare Isa. 49 : 2; Heb. 4 : 12. The Hebrew word for mouth is often translated "command," Gen. 45 : 21; Job 39:27; Eccl. 8:2; and the unclean spirits out of the mouth of the dragon, Rev. 16:14, are the ready executers of his commands.

MUL'BERRY-TREE. The word translated mulberry-tree signifies literally *weeping*, and indicates some tree which distils balsam or gum. The particular species is not known; though some think the poplar, or aspen, may be intended, 2 Sam. 5:23, 24; 1 Chr. 14:14, 15.

MULE, a mixed animal, the offspring of a horse and an ass. A mule is smaller than a horse, and has long ears, though not so long as those of an ass. It is a remarkably hardy, patient, obstinate, sure-footed animal, lives twice as long as a horse, and is much more easily and cheaply fed. Mules are much used in Spain and South America, for transporting goods across the mountains. So also in the Alps, they are used by travellers among the mountains, where a horse would hardly be able to pass with safety. There is no probability that the Jews bred mules, because it was forbidden to couple creatures of different species, Lev. 19 : 19. But they were not forbidden to obtain them from abroad and use them, 1 Kin. 10 : 25; Ezek. 27 : 14. Thus we may observe, especially after David's time, that mules, male and female, were common among the Hebrews; formerly they used only male and female asses, 2 Sam. 13:29; 18:9; 1 Kin. 1:33; 10:25; 18:5; Esth. 8:10, 14.

In Gen. 36 : 24, Anah is said to have found "mules" in the desert; but the Hebrew word here probably means hot springs. See ANAH.

MUNI'TIONS, implements of war. "Munitions of rocks" seems to mean, a rocky fortress or strong-hold. The strong tower of the righteous is impregnable and inaccessible to their foes, Isa. 33:16.

MUR'DER, the designed and malevolent taking of human life, was by the original appointment of God a crime to be punished by death. Cain, the first murderer, recognized it as such, Gen. 4:14. The ground for the death-penalty for murder is the eminent dignity and sacredness of man as a child of God, Gen. 9:5, 6. Like the Sabbath and marriage, it is a primeval and universal institution for mankind, and all nations have so recognized it, Acts 28 : 4. The Mosaic code reënacted it, Lev. 24:17; and while providing for the unintentional homicide a safe retreat, declares that deliberate murder must be punished by death, from which neither the city of refuge nor the altar of God could shield the criminal, Ex. 21 : 12-14; Num. 35 : 9-34; Deut. 19 : 1-13; 1 Kin. 2 : 5, 6, 28-34. Death was usually inflicted by stoning, upon the testimony of at least two witnesses, Num. 35 : 30. If a corpse were found in the open fields, and the murderer could not be discovered, the town nearest to the spot was obliged to purge itself by a solemn ceremony, lest it should become liable to the judgments of God, Deut. 21 : 1-9. In various ways God is represented as specially abhorring this crime, and securing its punishment, Deut. 32 : 43; 2 Sam. 21 : 1; Psa. 9 : 12; 55 : 23; Hos. 1 : 4; Rev. 22 : 15. Our Saviour instructs us that one may be guilty, in the sight of God, of murder in the heart, without any overt act, Matt. 5:21, 22; 1 John 3:15. Nothing is said specially in the law respecting self-murder, and only the cases of Saul, Ahithophel, and Judas are described in the Bible, 1 Sam. 31 : 4; 2 Sam. 17 : 23; Acts 1 : 18. Of all murders, that of the soul is incomparably the most awful, John 8:44, and many plunge not only themselves but others into the second death.

MUR'RAIN, a special mortality, wrought by miraculous agency, among the cattle of the Egyptians, while those of the Hebrews in the same region were unharmed, Ex. 9:3.

MU'SIC. The ancient Hebrews had a great taste for music, which they used in their religious services, in their public and private rejoicings, at their weddings and feasts, and even in their mournings. We have in Scripture canticles of joy, of thanksgiving, of praise, of mourning; also mournful elegies or songs, as those of David on the death of Saul and Abner, and the Lamentations of Jeremiah on the destruction of Jerusalem; so, too, songs of victory, triumph, and gratulation, as that which Moses sung after passing the Red sea, that of Deborah and Barak, and others. The people of God went up to Jerusalem thrice a year, cheered on their way with songs of joy, Psalms 84; 122; Isa. 30:29. The book of Psalms comprises a wonderful variety of inspired pieces for music, and is an inexhaustible treasure for the devout in all ages.

Music is perhaps the most ancient of the fine arts. Jubal, who lived before the deluge, was the "father" of those who played on the harp and the organ, Gen. 4:21; 31:26, 27. Laban complains that his son-in-law Jacob had left him, without giving him an opportunity of sending his family away "with mirth and with songs, with tabret and with harp." Moses, having passed through the Red sea, composed a song, and sung it with the Israelitish men, while Miriam, his sister, sung it with dancing, and playing on instruments, at the head of the women, Ex. 15:20, 21. He caused silver trumpets to be made, to be sounded at solemn sacrifices, and on religious festivals. David, who had great skill in music, soothed the perturbed spirit of Saul by playing on the harp, 1 Sam. 16:16, 23; and when he was himself established on the throne—seeing that the Levites were not employed, as formerly, in carrying the boards, veils, and vessels of the tabernacle, its abode being fixed at Jerusalem—appointed a great part of them to sing and to play on instruments in the temple, 1 Chr. 25. David brought the ark to Jerusalem with triumphant and joyful music, 1 Chr. 13:8; 15:16–28; and in the same manner Solomon was proclaimed king, 1 Kin. 1:39, 40. The Old Testament prophets also sought the aid of music in their services, 1 Sam. 10:5; 2 Kin. 3:15.

Asaph, Heman, and Jeduthun were chiefs of the music of the tabernacle under David, and of the temple under Solomon. Asaph had four sons, Jeduthun six, and Heman fourteen. These twenty-four Levites, sons of the three great masters of the temple-music, were at the head of twenty-four bands of musicians, which served in the temple by turns. Their number there was always great, but especially at the chief solemnities. They were ranged in order about the altar of burnt-sacrifices. As the whole business of their lives was to learn and to practise music, it must be supposed that they understood it well, whether it were vocal or instrumental, 2 Chr. 29:25.

The kings also had their music. Asaph was chief master of music to David. In the temple, and in the ceremonies of religion, female musicians were admitted as well as male; they generally were daughters of the Levites. Ezra, in his enumeration of those whom he brought back with him from the captivity, reckons two hundred singing men and singing women, 2 Sam. 19:35; Ezra 2:65; Neh. 7:67.

As to the nature of their music, we can judge of it only by conjecture, because it has been long lost. Probably it was a unison of several voices, of which all sung together the same melody, each according to his strength and skill; without musical counterpoint, or those different parts and combinations which constitute harmony in our music. Probably, also, the voices were generally accompanied by instrumental music. If we may draw any conclusions in favor of their music from its effects, its magnificence, its majesty, and the lofty sentiments contained in their songs, we must allow it great excellence. It is supposed that the temple musicians were sometimes divided into two or more separate choirs, which, with a general chorus, sung in turn responsive to each other, each a small portion of the Psalm. The structure of the Hebrew Psalms is eminently adapted to this mode of singing, and very delightful and solemn effects might thus be produced. Compare Psalms 24, 136, 148, 150.

Numerous musical instruments are mentioned in Scripture, but it has been found impossible to affix their names with certainty to specific instruments now in use. By a comparison, however, of the instruments probably held in common by the Jews with the Greeks, Romans, and Egyptians, a degree of probability as to most of them has been secured. They were of three kinds:

I. *Stringed instruments:*

1. KINNOR, "the harp," Gen. 4 : 21. Frequently mentioned in Scripture, and probably a kind of lyre.

2. NEBEL, "the psaltery," 1 Sam. 10:5. It appears to have been the name of various large instruments of the harp kind.

3. ASOR, signifying ten-stringed. In Psa. 92 : 4, it apparently denotes an instrument distinct from the NEBEL; but elsewhere it seems to be simply a description of the NEBEL as ten-stringed. See Psa. 33:2; 144:9.

4. GITTITH. It occurs in the titles of Psalms 8, 81, 84, etc. From the name, it is supposed that David brought it from Gath. Others conclude that it is a general name for a stringed instrument.

5. MINNIM, strings, Psa. 150:4. Probably another kind of stringed instrument.

6. SABECA, "sackbut," Dan. 3 : 5, 7, 10, 15. A kind of lyre.

7. PESANTERIN, "psaltery," occurs Dan. 3 : 7, and is supposed to represent the NEBEL.

8. MACHALATH. Found in the titles of Psalms 53 and 88; supposed to be a lute or guitar.

See illustrations in HARP.

II. *Wind instruments:*

9. KEREN, "horn," Josh. 6:5. Cornet.

10. SHOPHAR, "trumpet," Num. 10:10. Used synonymously with KEREN.

11. CHATZOZERAH, the straight trumpet, Psa. 98:6.

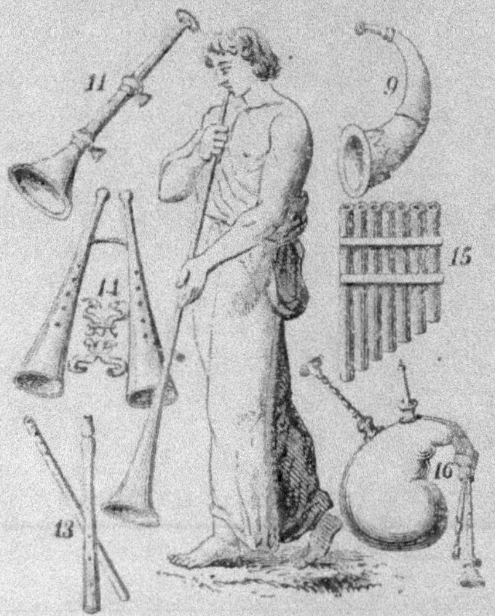

12. JOBEL, or KEREN JOBEL, horn of jubilee, or signal trumpet, Josh. 6 : 4. Probably the same with 9 and 10.

13. CHALIL, "pipe" or "flute." The word means bored through, 1 Sam. 10:5.

14. MISHROKITHA, Dan. 3 : 5, etc. Probably the Chaldean name for the flute with two reeds.

15. UGAB, "organ" in our version, Gen. 4:21. It means a double or manifold pipe, and hence the shepherd's pipe; probably the same as the syrinx or Pan's pipe; or perhaps resembling the bagpipe, numbered 16 in the cut.

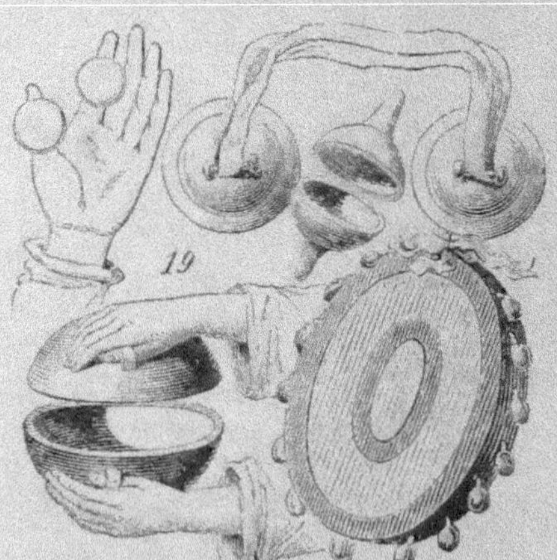

III. *Instruments which gave out sound on being struck:*

17. TOPH, Gen. 31:27, the tambourine and all instruments of the drum kind.

18. PHAAMON, "bells," Ex. 28 : 33. Attached to the hem of the high-priest's garment.

19. TZELTZELIM, "cymbals," Psalm 150 . 5. A word frequently occurring. There were probably two kinds, hand-cymbals and finger-cymbals.

20. SHALISHIM, 1 Sam. 18 : 6. In our version, "instruments of music." Margin, "three-stringed instruments." Most writers identify it with the triangle.

21. MENAANEIM, "cymbals," 2 Sam. 6:5. Probably the sistrum. The Hebrew word means to shake. The sistrum was generally about sixteen or eighteen inches long, occasionally inlaid with silver, and being held upright, was shaken, the rings moving to and fro on the bars.

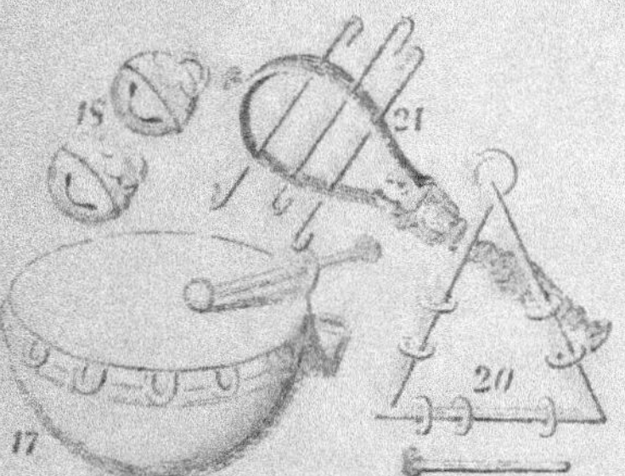

Further particulars concerning some of these may be found under the names they severally bear in our English Bible.

MUSTARD. A species of this annual shrub is found in Palestine, growing to the height of seven to nine feet, and with a stem one inch thick. Prof. Hackett, while examining a field of these plants, saw a bird of the air come and lodge in the branches before him, Matt. 13 : 31, 32; Mark 4 : 31, 32. Others suppose a tree is meant, called Salvadora Persica. It is found in Palestine, and bears berries containing small, mustard-like seeds. "A grain of mustard" was used proverbially to denote any thing extremely small, Matt. 17:20.

MUZZLE. See THRESHING.

MYRA, a town of Lycia, where Paul embarked for Rome, on board a ship of Alexandria, Acts 27:5.

MYRRH, a precious gum yielded by a tree common in Africa and Arabia, which is about eight or nine feet high; its wood hard, and its trunk thorny. It

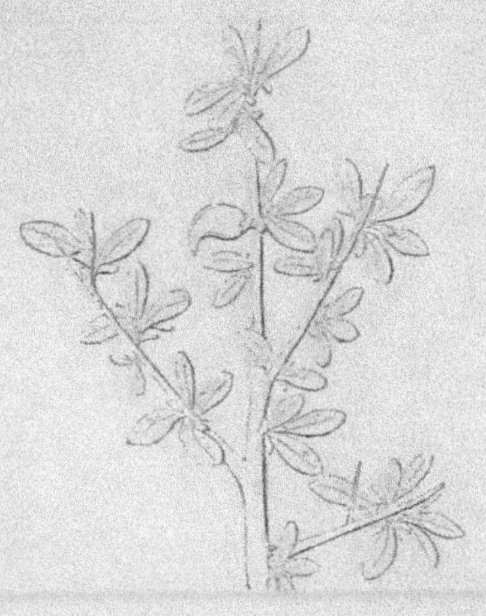

was of several kinds, and various degrees of excellence. The best was an ingredient in the holy ointment, Ex. 30 : 23. It was also employed in perfumes, Esth. 2:12; Psa. 45:8; Song 4 : 6; 5:5, 13; and in embalming, to preserve the body from corruption, John 19 : 39. The magi, who came from the East to worship Christ, offered him myrrh, Matt. 2:11.

In Mark 15 : 23, is mentioned "wine mingled with myrrh," which was offered to Jesus previous to his crucifixion, and intended to deaden the anguish of his sufferings. It was a custom among the Hebrews to give such stupefying liquors to persons who were about to be capitally punished, Prov. 31 : 6. Some have thought that the myrrhed wine of Mark is not the same as the "vinegar mingled with gall" of Matt. 27 : 34. They suppose the myrrhed wine was given to our Lord from a sentiment of sympathy, to prevent him from feeling too sensibly the pain of his sufferings; while the potation mingled with gall, of which he would not drink, was given from cruelty. But the other explanation is the more probable. See GALL.

MYRTLE, a beautiful and fragrant evergreen tree, growing wild throughout the southern parts of Europe, the north of Africa, and the temperate parts of Asia; principally on the sea-coast. The leaves are of a rich and polished evergreen; the flowers white, with sometimes a tinge of red externally; and the berries are of the size of a small pea, violet or whitish, sweetish, and with the

aromatic flavor which distinguishes the whole plant. These are used for spices in the Levant. It furnishes a useful tonic medicine, Neh. 8:15; Isa. 41:19; 55:13; Zech. 1:8, 10, 11.

MYS'IA, a province in the north-west corner of Asia Minor, bounded north by the Propontis, west by the Ægean sea, south by Lydia, and east by Bithynia. Paul preached in this country on his first journey to Europe, Acts 16:7, 8.

MYS'TERY means strictly a *secret*, and is so used when spoken of the heathen "mysteries" or secret rites, which were full of all manner of abominations. In the Scriptures the word "mystery" denotes those truths of religion which, without a revelation from God, would have remained unknown to man. Our Saviour says to his disciples, that they are peculiarly happy, because God has revealed to them "the mysteries of the kingdom of heaven," Matt. 16:17; 11:25; Luke 10:21-24. Paul explains the word in Eph. 3:1-9; and often speaks of the mystery of the gospel, of the mystery of the cross of Christ, of the mystery of Christ which was unknown to former ages, of the mystery of the incarnation, the resurrection, etc., Rom. 11:25; 1 Cor. 2:7-10; 4:1; 13:2; 15:51; 1 Tim. 3:9, 16. These, then, were called mysteries, not only because they included some things which stretch beyond all human thought, and others which would never have been known if the Son of God and his Holy Spirit had not revealed them, but also because they were not opened indifferently to every one; according to the advice of Christ to his apostles, "Give not that which is holy unto the dogs, neither cast ye your pearls before swine," 1 Cor. 2:14. In one place "mystery" seems to denote the whole cycle of God's secret plan in the administration of the gospel, gradually unfolded even to the end, Rev. 10:7; 11:15.

Mystery signifies also an allegory, that is, a mode of information under which partial instruction is given, a partial discovery is made, but there is still a cover of some kind, which the person who desires to know the whole must endeavor to remove. So the mystery of the seven stars, Rev. 1:20, is an allegory representing the seven Asiatic churches under the symbol of seven burning lamps. So the mystery, "Babylon the Great," is an allegorical representation of the spiritual Babylon, idolatry, spiritual fornication, etc., "I will tell thee the mystery of the woman;" that is, I will explain to thee the allegory of this figure, Rev. 17:5, 7.

N.

NA'AMAN, the highly esteemed general of Ben-hadad, king of Damascene Syria in the time of Joram king of Israel. He was afflicted with the leprosy; but was miraculously cured, on washing seven times in the Jordan, Lev. 14:7, according to the direction of Elisha, 2 Kin. 5; Luke 4:27. He had found all his honor and power valueless, and all physicians of no avail for his cure; was led to renounce his pride, and avail himself of the simple remedy prescribed; and being cured, was grateful not only to the prophet, but to the prophet's God. He frankly yielded to the evidence which proved that Jehovah was the living and true God; and took home with him two mule-loads of earth, for an altar to the Lord, Ex. 20:24. With respect to his attending Ben-hadad while in the temple of Rimmon, the prophet gave him no precise rule; discerning, we may suppose, a growing fear and love of God which would preserve him from all even outward homage to the idol.

NA'BAL, *foolish*, a descendant of Caleb, owner of a large property in lands and flocks, at Maon and Carmel in the south of Judah. He was under great obligations to David, for protecting him from the robbers of the desert; and yet, in the very hour most suggestive of a grateful generosity, he churlishly refused David's modest request of provisions for his needy troop. Indignant at this ingratitude and inhospitality, David was soon on his way to put him and his men to the sword. Happily, the discreet intervention of Abigail averted this catastrophe. Ten days after, the Lord smote him, and he died, 1 Sam. 25. See ABIGAIL.

NA'BOTH, an Israelite at Jezreel, who declined selling his ancestral vineyard to Ahab, Lev. 25 : 23, 24 ; and was in consequence murdered, on a false charge of blasphemy contrived by Jezebel the queen. Ahab took immediate possession of the coveted vineyard—perhaps as being legally forfeited to the government, construing blasphemy as treason ; or it may be, that the heirs were deterred from asserting their claim by a dread of the unscrupulous arts of Jezebel. Elijah, however, did not fear to denounce against the king and queen the vengeance of One "higher than they," 1 Kin. 21 ; 2 Kin. 9 : 24-26, 36 ; Eccl. 5:8.

NA'DAB, I., the oldest son of Aaron, slain by the Lord for presumptuously offering strange fire on the altar of burnt-offering, Lev. 10. See ABIHU.

II. Son of Jeroboam I. king of Israel. He succeeded his father, B. C. 954, and reigned but two years, being assassinated, while besieging Gibbethon, by Baasha, of the tribe of Issachar, who usurped his kingdom. Nadab did evil in the sight of the Lord ; and with him perished his children, and the race of Jeroboam, as God had foretold, 1 Kin. 15:25-30.

NA'HASH, I., a king of the Ammonites, defeated by Saul while besieging Ramoth-gilead, 1 Sam. 11. He, or as some think, his son of the same name, was on friendly terms with David, 2 Sam. 10:2.

II. The father of Zeruiah and Abigail, David's half-sisters, 2 Sam. 17:25 ; 1 Chr. 2 : 13-16. Nahash, however, may have been another name for Jesse ; or possibly the name of his wife.

NA'HOR, I., son of Serug, and father of Terah, Gen. 11:22-25 ; Luke 3:34.

II. Son of Terah, and brother of Abraham and Haran. He married Milcah his niece in Ur of the Chaldees, Gen. 11:26, 29, but seems to have transferred his residence to Haran, Gen. 24 : 10 ; 27:43. He had twelve sons, and among them Bethuel the father of Rebekah, Gen. 22:20-24.

NAH'SHON, or NAAS'SON, one of our Lord's ancestors, Matt. 1:4 ; Luke 3:32 ; chief of the tribe of Judah in the desert, Num. 1:7 ; 2:3 ; 7 : 12 ; and brother-in-law of Aaron, Ex. 6 : 23 ; Ruth 4 : 20 ; 1 Chr. 2:10.

NA'HUM, *consolation*, the seventh of the twelve minor prophets. The circumstances of Nahum's life are unknown, except that he was a native of Elkosh, which probably was a village in Galilee. His prophecy consists of three chapters, which form one discourse, in which he foretells the destruction of Nineveh in so powerful and vivid a manner, that he might seem to have been on the very spot. The native elegance, fire, and sublimity of his style are universally admired.

Opinions are divided as to the time in which Nahum prophesied. The best interpreters adopt Jerome's opinion, that he foretold the destruction of Nineveh in the time of Hezekiah, after the war of Sennacherib in Egypt, mentioned by Berosus. Compare Isa. 20 : 6, and Nah. 3 : 8. Nahum speaks of the taking of No-ammon, of the haughtiness of Rabshakeh, and of the defeat of Sennacherib, as things that were past. He implies that the tribe of Judah were still in their own country, and that they there celebrated their festivals. He notices also the captivity and dispersion of the ten tribes.

NAIL. The "nail" with which Jael killed Sisera was rather a tent-pin, such as is driven into the ground in order to fasten the cords of the tent, Ex. 27:19 ; Judg. 4:21, 22. Sometimes the Hebrew word is used for the wooden pins or iron spikes firmly inwrought into the walls of a building, Ezra 9 : 8 ; Ezek. 15 : 3. The word implies fixedness, Isa. 22:23 ; and a firm support, Zech. 10:4. Another Hebrew word describes the golden and ornamental nails of the temple, etc., 2 Chr. 3:9 ; Eccl. 12:11 ; Isa. 41:7 ; Jer. 10:4.

NA'IN, where Christ performed one of his chief miracles, in raising to life a widow's only son, Luke 7:11-17, was a small village in Galilee, three miles south by west of mount Tabor. It is now a petty hamlet, called Nein.

NAI'OTH, the abode of Samuel, and his pupils in a "school of the prophets,"

1 Sam. 19:18-24; 20:1. It appears to have been a suburb of Ramah; and David, having sought refuge there with Samuel, was pursued by Saul.

NA'KED, in the Bible, often means no more than "not fully dressed." So in John 21:7, Peter is said to have been "naked," that is, he had laid off his outer garment, and had on only his inner garment or tunic. See GARMENTS. So probably in Isa. 20:2; Mic. 1:8; Acts 19:16. Sometimes poorness and insufficiency of clothing are meant, as in James 2:15. So in Isa. 58:7; 2 Cor. 11:27. A nation is said to be "naked," when stripped of its defences, wealth, etc., Gen. 42:9; Ex. 32:25; 2 Chr. 28:19.

"Nakedness" is also put for shame. To "uncover the nakedness" denotes an unlawful or incestuous union, Lev. 20:19.

NAMES among the Hebrews were frequently significant; sometimes of a family trait, and sometimes of circumstances attending the birth of a child; often too they were assumed afterwards to commemorate some striking occurrence in one's history. Compare the cases of Ishmael, Esau, and Jacob, Moses, Ichabod, etc., Gen. 16:21; 25:25, 26; Ex. 2:10; 1 Sam. 4:21. Compound names were frequent; and often a part of the name of God, JAH, EL, JEHO, etc., was employed, as in Eliezer, Ex. 18:4, Samuel, Josiah, Adonijah. Sometimes a whole phrase was formed into a name; as Elioenai, *to Jehovah are mine eyes*, 1 Chr. 4:36. The New Testament names are chiefly ancient and family names perpetuated, Luke 1:61. The men of the East change their names for slight causes; and hence many persons occur in the Bible bearing two or more names, Ruth 1:20; 2 Sam. 23:8; John 1:42. Kings often changed the names of those to whom they gave offices, Dan. 1:6, 7; hence the honor and privilege implied in a "new name," Rev. 2:17. Many slight inflections of the same Hebrew name give it a very different appearance to an English eye, as Geshem and Gashmu, Neh. 6:1, 6. A Hebrew name was sometimes transferred to the Greek, with but little change: Elijah became Elias, or Elie. But sometimes it was exchanged for the Greek word of the same meaning, though very different in form: Thomas became Didymus, and Tabitha, Dorcas. The "name" of God is put for God himself, or for his perfections. To "raise up the name of the dead," is explained in Ruth 4; while to "put out" one's name, means to extinguish his family, Psa. 9:5.

NAO'MI, wife of Elimelech, and mother-in-law of Ruth. See RUTH.

NAPH'TALI, the sixth son of Jacob, by Bilhah, Rachel's handmaid, Gen. 30:8. We know but few particulars of the life of Naphtali. His sons were four, Gen. 46:24. The patriarch Jacob, when he gave his blessing, said, as it is in the English Bible, "Naphtali is a hind let loose; he giveth goodly words," Gen. 49:21. For an illustration of this passage, see HIND.

The tribe of Naphtali, called Nephtalim in Matt. 4:15, were located in a rich and fertile portion of northern Palestine; having Asher on the west, the upper Jordan and part of the sea of Tiberias on the east; and running north into the Lebanon range, some lower offshoots of which prolonged to the south formed the "mountains of Naphtali," Josh. 19:32-39; 20:7. They attended in force at the coronation of David, 1 Chr. 12:34; and are mentioned with honor in the wars of the Judges, Judg. 1:33; 5:18; 6:35; 7:23; as much reduced by the Syrians, 1 Kin. 15:20; and as among the first captives to Assyria, 2 Kin. 15:29; Isa. 9:1. Our Saviour spent much time in the southern part of this region, Matt. 4:13-15.

NARCIS'SUS, a Roman, many of whose household Paul salutes as Christians, Rom. 16:11. Two men of this name are mentioned in Roman histories of that time; one, executed three or four years before Paul wrote, was a favorite of the emperor Claudius; the other, of Nero his successor.

NA'THAN, I., a Hebrew prophet, Zech. 12:12, a friend and counsellor of David. He approved the king's purpose of building a temple to the Lord, but by divine direction transferred its accomplishment to Solomon, 2 Sam. 7:1-17. By a fine parable, pointedly applied, he convicted David of his guilt in respect to Uriah and Bathsheba, 2 Sam. 12; Psa. 51; and his bold fidelity here seems to have been appreciated by David, see NATHAN II., and is worthy of everlasting remembrance. Solomon was probably educated under his care, 2 Sam. 12:25; and was effectually aided by him in his peaceful succession to the throne, 1 Kin.

I. He wrote some memorials, long since lost, of both David and Solomon, 1 Chr. 29:29; 2 Chr. 9:29. How long he lived under the reign of Solomon is unknown; but two of his sons were high officers at court, 1 Kin. 4:5.

II. A son of David, by Bathsheba, 1 Chr. 3:5; 14:4; an ancestor of Christ, Luke 3:21. See GENEALOGY.

NATHAN'AEL, a disciple of Christ, probably the same as BARTHOLOMEW, which see. He was a native of Cana in Galilee, John 21:2, and was one of the first to recognize the Messiah, who at their first interview manifested his perfect acquaintance with Nathanael's secret heart and life, John 1:45–51. He was introduced by Philip to Jesus, who on seeing him pronounced that remarkable eulogy which has rendered his name almost another word for sincerity: "Behold an Israelite indeed, in whom is no guile." He was one of the disciples to whom Christ appeared at the sea of Tiberias after his resurrection, John 21:2; and after witnessing the ascension, returned with the other apostles to Jerusalem, Acts 1:4, 12, 13.

NAZARENE', an epithet applied to Christ, and usually translated "of Nazareth," as in Matt. 21:11; Acts 2:22; 4:10. It was foretold in prophecy, Psa. 22:7, 8, Isa. 53:2, that the Messiah should be despised and rejected of men; and this epithet, which came to be used as a term of reproach, showed the truth of these predictions, Matt. 2:23; Acts 24:5. Nazareth was a small town, in a despised part of Palestine. See GALILEE, and NAZARETH.

MODERN NAZARETH, SEEN FROM THE EAST.

NAZ'ARETH, a city of lower Galilee, about seventy miles north of Jerusalem, in the territory of the tribe of Zebulun. It was situated on the side of a hill overlooking a rich and beautiful valley, surrounded by hills, with a narrow outlet towards the south. At the mouth of this ravine the monks profess to show the place where the men of the city were about to cast Jesus from the precipice, Luke 4:29. Nazareth is about six miles west-north-west of mount Tabor, and nearly half way from the Jordan to the Mediterranean. It is said in the New Testament to be "the city of Jesus," because it was the place of his usual residence during the first thirty years of his life, Matt. 2:23; Luke 1:26; 2:51; 4:16. He visited it during his public ministry, but did not perform many miracles there because of the unbelief of the people, Matt. 13:54–58. It is not even named in the Old Testament, nor by Josephus; and appears to have been a small place, of no very good repute, John 1:46. The modern town, en-Nasirah, is a secluded village of about three thousand inhabitants, most of whom are Latin and Greek Christians. It lies about eight hundred feet above the level of the sea; and is one of the pleasantest towns in Syria. Its houses are of stone, two stories high, with flat roofs. It contains a mosque, a large Latin convent, and two or three chapels. The traditionary "mount of the Precipitation" is nearly two miles from the town, too remote to have answered the purpose of the enraged Nazarenes; while there were several precipitous spots close at hand, where the fall is still from thirty to fifty feet.

From the summit of the hill on the eastern slope of which Nazareth lies, is a truly magnificent prospect. Towards the north, the eye glances over the countless hills of Galilee, and reposes on the majestic and snow-crowned Hermon. On the east, the Jordan valley may be traced, and beyond it the dim heights of ancient Bashan. Towards the south, spreads the broad and beautiful plain of Esdraelon, with the bold outline of mount Tabor, and parts of Little Hermon and Gilboa visible on its eastern border, and the hills of Samaria on the south, while Carmel rises on the west of the plain, and dips his feet in the blue waters of the Mediterranean. Says Dr. Robinson in his "Biblical Researches in Palestine," "I remained for some hours upon this spot, lost in the contemplation of the wide prospect and of the events connected with the scenes around. In the village below, the Saviour of the world had passed his childhood; and although we have few particulars of his life during those early years, yet there are certain features of nature which meet our eyes now, just as they once met his. He must often have visited the fountain near which we had pitched our tent; his feet must frequently have wandered over the adjacent hills, and his eyes have doubtless gazed upon the splendid prospect from this very spot. Here the Prince of peace looked down upon the great plain, where the din of battles so oft had rolled, and the garments of the warrior been dyed in blood; and he looked out, too, upon that sea over which the swift ships were to bear the tidings of his salvation to nations and to continents then unknown. How has the moral aspect of things been changed! Battles and bloodshed have indeed not ceased to desolate this unhappy country, and gross darkness now covers the people; but from this region a light went forth, which has enlightened the world and unveiled new climes; and now the rays of that light begin to be reflected back from distant isles and continents, to illuminate anew the darkened land where it first sprung up."

NAZ'ARITE, under the ancient Hebrew law, a man or woman engaged by a vow to abstain from wine and all intoxicating liquors, and from the fruit of the vine in any form; to let the hair grow; not to enter any house polluted by having a dead body in it, nor to be present at any funeral. If by accident any one died in their presence, they recommenced the whole of their consecration and Nazariteship. This vow generally lasted eight days, sometimes only a month, and sometimes during their whole lives. When the time of Nazariteship expired, the person brought a number of sacrifices and offerings to the temple; the priest then cut off his hair and burnt it; after which he was free from his vow, Num. 6; Amos 2:11, 12. Perpetual Nazarites were consecrated as such by their parents from their birth, as was proposed by the mother of Samuel, 1 Sam. 1:11, and continued all their lives in this state, neither drinking wine, nor cutting their hair. Such were Samson and John the Baptist, Judg. 13:4, 5; Luke 1:15; 7:33.

As the cost of the offerings required at the expiration of the term of Nazariteship was very considerable for the poor, they were often relieved by persons not Nazarites, who assumed these charges for them for the sake of performing an act of piety and charity. Paul availed himself of this custom to disarm the jealousy of those who represented him as hostile to the faith of their fathers. He took four Christian Jews whose vow of Nazariteship was accomplished, assumed the expense of their offerings, and with them went through the customary services and purifications at the temple, Acts 21:20-26. There is also in Acts 18:18 an unexplained allusion to some similar vow made by Paul himself, or perhaps by Aquila, probably in view of some danger escaped or some blessing received.

NEAP'OLIS, now called Napoli, Acts 16:11, a maritime city of Macedonia, near the borders of Thrace, whither Paul came from the isle of Samothracia. From Neapolis he went to Philippi.

NEBAI'OTH, a son of Ishmael, Gen. 25:13, whose posterity occupied the pasture grounds of Arabia Deserta, Isa. 60:7, and ultimately possessed themselves of Edom. They are thought to have been the Nabathæans of profane history. See IDUMÆA.

NE'BO, I., a town in the vicinity of Bethel and Ai, Ezra 2:29; Neh. 7:33.

II. A city of Reuben, Num. 32:38, taken by the Moabites, who held it in the time of Jeremiah, Isa. 15:2; Jer. 48:1.

III. A mountain of Moab, whence Moses had a view of the promised land, and where he died. It is a summit of the range Abarim, "over against Jericho." Seetzen, Burckhardt, etc., identify it with mount Attarus, about ten miles north of the Arnon. Travellers do not observe any very prominent summit in the range immediately opposite Jericho; but it has not yet been fully explored, Deut. 32:49; 34.

IV. An idol of the Babylonians, Isa. 46:1. In the astrological mythology of the Babylonians, this idol probably represented the planet Mercury. It was also worshipped by the ancient Arabians. The extensive prevalence of this worship among the Chaldeans and Assyrians, is evident from the many compound proper names occurring in the Scriptures, of which this word forms part; as Nebuchadnezzar, Nebuzaradan, Nebushasban, Jer. 39:9, 13; and also in the classics, as Naboned, Nabonassar, Nabopolassar, etc.

NEBUCHADNEZ'ZAR, called in Jeremiah Nebuchadrezzar, the son and successor of Nabopolassar, succeeded to the kingdom of Chaldea about 600 B. C. He had been some time before associated in the kingdom, and sent to recover Carchemish, which had been wrested from the empire by Necho king of Egypt. Having been successful, he marched against the governor of Phœnicia, and Jehoiakim king of Judah, tributary to Necho king of Egypt. He took Jehoiakim, and put him in chains to carry him captive to Babylon; but afterwards he left him in Judea, on condition of his paying a large annual tribute. He took away several persons from Jerusalem; among others, Daniel, Hananiah, Mishael, and Azariah, all of the royal family, whom the king of Babylon caused to be carefully educated in the language and learning of the Chaldeans, that they might be employed at court, 2 Kin. 24:1; 2 Chr. 36:6; Dan. 1:1.

Nabopolassar dying, Nebuchadnezzar, who was then either in Egypt or in Judea, hastened to Babylon, leaving to his generals the care of bringing to Chaldea the captives taken in Syria, Judea, Phœnicia, and Egypt; for according to Berosus, he had subdued all these countries. He distributed these captives into several colonies, and in the temple of Belus he deposited the sacred vessels of the temple of Jerusalem, and other rich spoils. Jehoiakim king of Judah continued three years in fealty to Nebuchadnezzar, and then revolted; but after three or four years, he was besieged and taken in Jerusalem, put to death, and his body thrown to the birds of the air, according to the predictions of Jeremiah, chap. 22.

His successor, Jehoiachin, or Jeconiah, king of Judah, having revolted against Nebuchadnezzar, was besieged in Jerusalem, forced to surrender, and taken, with his chief officers, captive to Babylon; also his mother, his wives, and the best workmen of Jerusalem, to the number of ten thousand men. Among the captives were Mordecai, the uncle of Esther, and Ezekiel the prophet, Esth. 2:6. Nebuchadnezzar also took all the vessels of gold which Solomon made for the temple and the king's treasury, and set up Mattaniah, Jeconiah's uncle by the father's side, whom he named Zedekiah. Zedekiah continued faithful to Nebuchadnezzar nine years, at the end of which time he rebelled, and confederated with the neighboring princes. The king of Babylon came into Judea, reduced the chief places of the country, and besieged Jerusalem; but Pharaoh Hophra coming out of Egypt to assist Zedekiah, Nebuchadnezzar went to meet him, and forced him to retire to his own country. This done, he resumed the siege of Jerusalem, and was three hundred and ninety days before the place. In the eleventh year of Zedekiah, B. C. 588, the city was taken, and Zedekiah, being seized, was brought to Nebuchadnezzar, who was then at Riblah in Syria. The king of Babylon condemned him to die, caused his children to be put to death in his presence, and then bored out his eyes, loaded him with chains, and sent him to Babylon, 2 Kin. 24; 25; 2 Chr. 36.

During the reign of Nebuchadnezzar, the city of Babylon and the kingdom of Babylonia attained their highest pitch of splendor. He took great pains in adorning Babylon; and this was one great object of his pride. "Is not this," said he, "great Babylon, that I have built for the house of my kingdom, by the might of my power, and for the honor of my majesty?" But God vanquished his pride, and he was reduced for a time to the condition of a brute, according to the predictions of Daniel. See Dan. 1-4. An inscription found among the ruins on the Tigris, and now in the East India House at London, gives an account of the various works of Nebuchadnezzar at Babylon and Borsippa. Abruptly breaking off, the record says the king's heart was hardened against the Chaldee astrologers. "He would grant no benefactions for religious purposes. He intermitted the worship of Merodach, and put an end to the sacrifice of victims. *He labored under the effects of enchantment.*" Nebuchadnezzar is supposed to have died B. C. 562, after a reign of about forty years.

One of the famous structures ascribed to Nebuchadnezzar, and in which no doubt he took much pride, was the famous "hanging gardens," which he is said to have erected to gratify the wish of his queen Amytis for elevated groves such as she was accustomed to in her native Media. This could only be done, in a country so level as Babylonia, by constructing an artificial mountain; and accordingly the king caused one to be made, four hundred feet square and over three hundred feet high. The successive terraces were supported on ranges of regular piers, covered by large stones, on which were placed thick layers of matting and of bitumen and two courses of stones, which were again covered with a solid coating of lead. On such a platform another similar, but smaller, was built, etc. The various terraces were then covered with earth, and furnished with trees, shrubbery, and flowers. The whole was watered, from the Euphrates which flowed at its base, by machinery within the mound. These gardens occupied but a small portion of the prodigious area of the palace, the wall inclosing the whole being six miles in circumference. Within this were two other walls and a great tower, besides the palace buildings, courts, gardens, etc. All the gates were of brass, which agrees with the language used by Isaiah in predicting the capture of Babylon by Cyrus, Isa. 45:12. The ruins of the hanging gardens are believed to be found in the vast irregular mound called Kasr, on the east side of the Euphrates, eight hundred yards by six hundred at its base. The bricks taken from this mound are of fine quality, and are all stamped with the name of Nebuchadnezzar.

Another labor of this monarch was that the ruins of which are now called Birs Nimroud, about eight miles southwest of the above structure. See BABEL. The researches of Sir Henry Rawlinson have shown that this was built by Nebuchadnezzar, on the platform of a ruinous edifice of more ancient days. It consisted of six distinct terraces, each twenty feet high, and forty-two feet less horizontally than the one below it. On the top was the sanctum and observatory of the temple, now a vitrified mass. Each story was dedicated to a different planet, and stained with the color appropriated to that planet in their astrological system. The lowest, in honor of Saturn, was black; that of Jupiter was orange, that of Mars red, that of the sun yellow, that of Venus green, and that of Mercury blue. The temple was white, probably for the moon. In the corners of this long-ruined edifice, recently explored, were found cylinders with arrow-headed inscriptions, in the name of Nebuchadnezzar, which inform us that the building was named "The Stages of the Seven Spheres of Borsippa;" that it had been in a dilapidated condition; and that, moved by Merodach his god, he had reconstructed it with bricks enriched with lapis lazuli, "without changing its site or destroying its foundation platform." This restoration is also stated to have taken place five hundred and four years after its first erection in that form by Tiglath Pileser I., 1100 B. C. If not actually on the site of the tower of Babel mentioned in the Bible, and the temple of

Belus described by Herodotus, this building would seem to have been erected on the same general plan. Every brick yet taken from it bears the impress of Nebuchadnezzar. Borsippa would seem to have been a suburb of ancient Babylon.

NEB'UZAR-A'DAN, a general of king Nebuchadnezzar, and his agent in the sacking and destruction of Jerusalem, 1 Kin. 25:8–20; Jer. 39:9; 40:1; 52:12–30.

NE'CHO, or PHARAOH-NECHO, an Egyptian king, mentioned not only in Scripture, but by Herodotus, who says that he was son of Psammetichus, king of Egypt; and that, having succeeded him in the kingdom, he raised great armies, and sent out great fleets, as well on the Mediterranean as the Red sea; that he expended a vast sum and many thousands of lives in a fruitless effort to unite the Nile and the Red sea by a canal; and that he was the first to send a ship wholly around Africa. Josiah king of Judah being tributary to the king of Babylon, opposed Necho on his first expedition against Nebuchadnezzar, and gave him battle at Megiddo, where he received the wound of which he died; and Necho pressed forward, without making any long stay in Judea. On his return from the Euphrates, where he had taken and garrisoned the city of Carchemish, B. C. 610, he halted at Riblah in Syria; and sending for Jehoahaz, king of the Jews, he deposed him, loaded him with chains, and sent him into Egypt. Then coming to Jerusalem, he set up Eliakim, or Jehoiakim, in his place, and exacted the payment of one hundred talents of silver and one talent of gold. The accompanying cut, from the great "Tomb of the Kings" in Egypt, explored by Belzoni, is believed to represent four Jewish hostages or captives of distinction presented before Pharaoh-Necho. One of them may be meant for Jehoahaz. They were colored white; and with them were

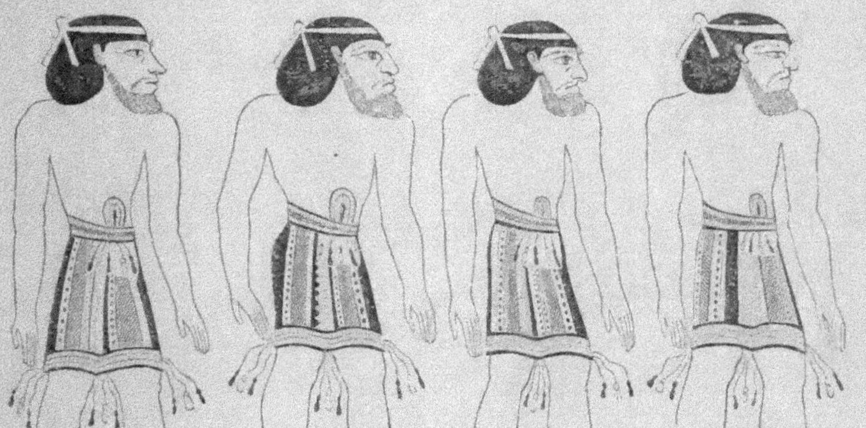

four red, four black, and four others white, supposed to represent Babylonians, Ethiopians, etc. They were led before the king, seated on his throne, by one of the hawk-headed figures so frequent on Egyptian monuments. Jeremiah, 46:2, acquaints us that Carchemish was retaken by Nabopolassar king of Babylon, in the fourth year of Jehoiakim king of Judah; so that Necho did not retain his conquests in Syria more than four years, 2 Kin. 23:29 to 24:7; 2 Chr. 35.20 to 36:6.

NECK. The phrases to "harden the neck," Prov. 29:1, and to be "stiffnecked," like a headstrong brute, illustrate the wilful obstinacy of sinners against the instructions and commands of God. The tyrants of ancient days sometimes put their feet on the prostrate necks of princes, in token of their subjugation, trampling them in the dust. Their mischief sometimes returned upon their own heads, Josh. 10:24; Psa. 18:40.

NEC'ROMANCER, one who pretended to discover unknown and future events by summoning and interrogating the dead, Deut. 18 : 10, 11, a crime punishable by stoning to death, Lev. 20 : 27. See SORCERER. No good reason can be given for believing that such pretended communications with departed spirits are less offensive to God now than in the time of Moses.

NEES'ING, translated sneezing in 2 Kin. 4 : 35; used in Job 41 : 18 to describe the violent breathing of the enraged leviathan, or crocodile.

NEG'INOTH, Hab. 3 : 19, a general name for Hebrew stringed instruments. Psalms 4, 6, 54, 55, and 76, are addressed to the leader of the music on that class of instruments.

NEHEMI'AH, the son of Hachaliah, was born at Babylon during the captivity. He was, according to some, of the race of the priests; according to others, of the royal family of Judah. He sustained the office of cup-bearer to the Persian king Artaxerxes Longimanus. Touched with the calamitous state of the colony of Jews which had formerly returned to Jerusalem, he besought the king of Persia to permit him to go to Jerusalem and aid in rebuilding it. He was accordingly sent thither as governor, in the twentieth year of Artaxerxes, about 444 B. C. He directed his attention chiefly to rebuilding the walls of the city. The enmity of the Samaritans, under which the colony had formerly suffered, was now increased; and under Sanballat, the governor of the country, they cast all possible hinderances in the way of the Jews. They even went so far as to attack the laborers at their work; so that Nehemiah had to cause them to labor with arms in their hands; yet in one year their task was completed. In this great work, and in his whole administration, his pious zeal and disinterestedness, his love for the people and city of God, and his prayerful reliance on divine aid were crowned with success. He had the coöperation of faithful friends, especially of Ezra, Neh. 8 : 1, 9, 13; 12 : 36, and instituted many excellent civil improvements. About 432 B. C., though perhaps not for the first time, he returned to his post at the court of Babylon, Neh. 2:6; 5:14; 13:6; but after a few years, was recalled to Jerusalem to reform certain growing irregularities—neglect of the temple service, breaches of the Sabbath, marriages with the heathen, etc. He required of those Jews who had married heathen wives, that they should either abandon them, or else themselves quit the country. This voluntary exile of a number of discontented priests, may have given occasion to the building of the temple on mount Gerizim, and the establishment of the Samaritan worship. See SANBALLAT.

The BOOK OF NEHEMIAH contains the history of all these transactions, written by himself near the close of his long life, B. C. 434. It is a sort of a continuation of the book of Ezra, and was called by some of the fathers the Second book of Ezra. Some portions of it, as chapters 8 and 9, and 12 : 1-26, appear to be compilations from public registers, etc. With it the historical books of the Old Testament close.

NE'HILOTH, supposed to mean flutes or wind instruments; found only in the title of the fifth Psalm, which is addressed to the leader of this class of instruments, as though intended to be sung with this accompaniment only.

NEHUSH'TA, wife of Jehoiakim, and mother of the young king Jechoniah, with whom she was probably associated in the government, as she is in the reproaches of Jeremiah, 2 Kin. 24:8; Jer. 13:18; 29:2.

NEHUSH'TAN, *brazen*, a name given by Hezekiah king of Judah to the brazen serpent that Moses had set up in the wilderness, Num. 21:8, and which had been preserved by the Israelites to that time. The superstitious people having made an idol of this serpent, Hezekiah caused it to be burned, and in derision gave it the name of Nehushtan, a mere piece of brass, 2 Kin. 18 : 4. Memorials, relics, and other outward aids to devotion which men rely upon, have the opposite effect; the visible emblem hides the Saviour it ought to reveal, John 3:14-16.

NEIGH'BOR. At the time of our Saviour, the Pharisees had restrained the meaning of the word "neighbor" to those of their own nation, or to their own friends; holding, that to hate their enemy was not forbidden by the law,

Matt. 5 : 43. But our Saviour informed them that the whole world were neighbors; that they ought not to do to another what they would not have done to themselves; and that this charity extended even to enemies. See the beautiful parable of the good Samaritan, the real neighbor to the distressed, Luke 10 29.

NER'GAL, one of the gods of the Cuthite heathen who were transplanted into Palestine, 2 Kin 17 30. This idol probably represented the planet Mars, which was ever the emblem of bloodshed Mars is named, by the Zabians and Arabians, *ill-luck*, *misfortune*. He was represented as holding in one hand a drawn sword, and in the other, by the hair, a human head just cut off; his garments were blood red, as the light of the planet is also reddish. His temple among the Arabs was painted red; and they offered to him garments sprinkled with blood, and also a warrior, (probably a prisoner,) who was cast into a pool. The name Nergal appears in the proper names Nergalsharezer, Neriglassar, Jer. 39:3, 13.

NETS are often referred to in Scripture, Prov. 1:17; Eccl. 7:26; Isa. 19:8, 9; Hab. 1:15, 16, particularly in connection with the first disciples of Christ, Matt. 4:18; 13 : 47–50; Luke 5 : 1–10. Before the invention of fire-arms, nets were much used in hunting and fowling, and possibly in catching men, as robbers, etc., Job 19 : 6; Psa. 140 : 5; Mic. 7:2. Among the ancient Romans there was a gladiatorial game, in which one man was armed with sword and shield, and his antagonist with a net, by casting which he strove to entangle the other so that he might easily dispatch him with his dagger.

NETH'ER, lower; as the lower stone of a handmill, Deut. 24 : 6; the foot of Sinai, Exod. 19 : 17; the regions of the dead, Ezek. 32:18.

NETH'INIM, *given*, or *consecrated*, a term first applied to the Lewites, Num. 8 : 19; but after the settlement in Canaan, to servants dedicated to the service of the tabernacle and temple, to perform the most laborious offices, as carrying of wood and water. At first the Gibeonites were destined to this station, Judg. 9 : 27; afterwards, other Canaanites who surrendered themselves, and whose lives were spared. Many of them appear to have been first assigned to David, Solomon, and other princes, and by them transferred to the temple service, 1 Kin. 9:20, 21; Ezra 2:58, 70; 8 : 20; Neh. 11 : 3. It is probable that they became proselytes, Neh. 10:28, and that many of them could cordially unite with David in saying, "I had rather be a doorkeeper in the house of my God, than to dwell in the tents of wickedness," Psa. 84:10. The Nethinim were carried into captivity with the tribe of Judah, and great numbers were placed not far from the Caspian sea, whence Ezra brought two hundred and twenty of them into Judea, Ezra 8:17.

NETO'PHAH, a town near Bethlehem, of which little more than the name is known, 2 Sam. 23:28, 29; 2 Kin. 25:23; Ezra 2:22; Neh. 7:26.

NETTLE, a well-known stinging plant, growing in neglected grounds, Isa. 34 : 13; Hos. 9 : 6. A different Hebrew word, in Job 30 : 7, Prov. 24 : 31, Zeph. 2 : 9, seems to indicate a larger species.

NEW MOON. The new moon was the commencement of each of the Hebrew months. See MONTH. The Hebrews had a particular veneration for the first day of every month, for which Moses appointed peculiar sacrifices, Num. 28:11-15; but he gave no orders that it should be kept as a holy day, nor can it be proved that the ancients observed it as such; it was a festival of merely voluntary devotion. It appears that even from the time of Saul, they made on this day a sort of family entertainment; since David ought then to have been at the king's table, and Saul took his absence amiss, 1 Sam. 20 : 5, 18. Moses implies that, besides the national sacrifices then regularly offered, every private person had his particular sacrifices of devotion, Num. 10 : 10. The beginning of the month was proclaimed by sound of trumpet, Psa. 81 : 3, and the offering of solemn sacrifices. But the most celebrated "new moon" was that at the beginning of the civil year, or first day of the month Tishri, Lev. 23:24. This was a sacred festival, on which no servile labor was performed, Amos 8 : 5. In the kingdom of the ten tribes, it seems to have been a custom of the people to visit the prophets at the new moons, for the purpose of carrying them presents, and hearing their instructions, 2 Kin. 4 : 23. Ezekiel says, 45 : 17, (see also 1 Chr. 23 : 31 ; 2 Chr. 8 : 13,) that the burnt-offerings offered on the day of the new moon were to be provided at the king's expense. The observance of this festival was discontinued soon after the establishment of Christianity, Gal. 4 : 9, 10, Col. 2 : 16, though the Jews take some notice of the day even now.

NIB'HAZ, a god of the Avites, 2 Kin. 17:31. Jewish interpreters say the name means *barker*, and affirm that this idol had the shape of a dog. Historical traces have also been found of the ancient worship of idols in the form of dogs among the Syrians. In the Zabian books, Nibhaz occurs as the "lord of darkness;" which, according to the character of the Assyrian-Chaldean mythology, would point to an evil planetary demon.

NICA'NOR, one of the first seven deacons, who were chosen and appointed at Jerusalem soon after the pentecostal descent of the Holy Ghost, Acts 6:1-6.

NICODE'MUS, a member of the Jewish Sanhedrim, at first a Pharisee, and afterwards a disciple of Jesus. He was early convinced that Christ came from God, but was not ready at once to rank himself among His followers. In John 3 : 1-20, he first appears as a timid inquirer after the truth, learning the great doctrines of regeneration and atonement. In John 7 : 45-52, we see him cautiously defending the Saviour before the Sanhedrim. At last, in the trying scene of the crucifixion, he avowed himself a believer, and came with Joseph of Arimathea to pay the last duties to the body of Christ, which they took down from the cross, embalmed, and laid in the sepulchre, John 19:39.

NICOLA'ITANS, heretical persons or teachers, mentioned in Rev. 2 : 6, 15. Whether they were the same as the Nicolaitans of the second century and later is very doubtful. Some suppose them to be followers of Nicolas the deacon, but there is no good evidence that he ever became a heretic.

NIC'OLAS, a proselyte of Antioch, that is, one converted from paganism to the religion of the Jews. He afterwards embraced Christianity, and was among the most zealous of the first Christians; so that he was chosen one of the first seven deacons of the church at Jerusalem, Acts 6:5.

NICOP'OLIS, a city where Paul spent probably the last winter of his life, having previously written to Titus, at Crete, to meet him there, Tit. 3:12. He is supposed to refer to the Nicopolis of Thrace, situated on the river Nestus, near the borders of Macedonia, and hence called, in the subscription to the epistle, Nicopolis of Macedonia. Others, however, suppose him to have meant Nicopolis in Epirus, which stood near the mouth of the Ambracian gulf, opposite to Actium, and which was built by Augustus in honor of his decisive victory over Antony.

NIGHT. The ancient Hebrews began their artificial day at evening, and ended it the next evening, so that the night preceded the day. This usage may probably be traced to the terms employed in describing the creation, Gen. 1:5, 8, 13, etc., "The evening and the morning were the first day" The Hebrews allowed twelve hours to the night, and twelve to the day; but these hours were not equal, except at the equinox. At other times, when the hours of the night were long, those of the day were short, as in winter; and when the hours of night were short, as at midsummer, the hours of the day were long in proportion. See HOURS.

The nights are sometimes extremely cold in Syria, when the days are very hot; and travellers in the deserts and among the mountains near Palestine refer to their own sufferings from these opposite extremes, in illustration of Jacob's words in Gen. 31 : 40, "In the day the drought consumed me, and the frost by night; and my sleep departed from mine eyes."

NIGHT-HAWK, an unclean bird, Lev. 11:16; Deut. 14:15. Its name seems to indicate voracity, and is therefore thought by many to point out the Syrian owl, a more powerful bird than the night-hawk, and exceedingly voracious; it sometimes attacks sleeping children.

NILE, the celebrated river of Egypt. It takes this name only after the junction of the two great streams of which it is composed, namely, the Bahr el Abiad, or White river, which rises in the mountains of the Moon, in the interior of Africa, and runs north-east till it is joined by the other branch, the Bahr el Azrek, or Blue river, which rises in Abyssinia, and after a large circuit to the south-east and south-west, in which it passes through the lake of Dembea, flows northwards to join the White river. This Abyssinian branch has in modern times been regarded as the real Nile, although the White river is much the largest and longest, and was in ancient times considered as the true Nile. The junction takes place about latitude sixteen degrees north. From this point the Nile flows always in a northerly direction, with the exception of one large bend to the west. About thirteen hundred miles from the sea it receives its last branch, the Tacazze, a large stream from Abyssinia, and having passed through Nubia, it enters Egypt at the cataracts near Syene, or Essuan, which are formed by a chain of rocks stretching east and west. There are here three falls; after which the river pursues its course in still and silent majesty through the whole length of the land of Egypt. Its average breadth is about seven hundred yards. In Lower Egypt it divides into several branches and forms the celebrated Delta; for which see under EGYPT. See also a view of the river in AMMON.

As rain very seldom falls, even in winter, in Southern Egypt, and usually only slight and infrequent showers in Lower Egypt, the whole physical and political existence of Egypt may be said to depend on the Nile; since without this river, and even without its regular annual inundations, the whole land would be but a desert. These inundations, so mysterious in the view of ancient ignorance and superstition, are caused by the regular periodical rains in the countries farther south, around the sources of the Nile, in March and later. The river begins to rise in Egypt about the middle of June, and continues to increase through the month of July. In August it overflows its banks, and reaches its highest point early in September; and the country is then mostly covered with its waters, Amos 8:8; 9:5; Nah. 3:8. In the beginning of October, the inundation still continues; and it is only towards the end of this month that the stream returns within its banks. From the middle of August till towards the end of October, the whole land of Egypt resembles a great lake or sea, in which the towns and cities appear as islands.

The cause of the fertility which the Nile imparts lies not only in its thus watering the land, but also in the thick slimy mud which its waters bring down along with them and deposit on the soil of Egypt. It is like a coat of rich manure; and the seed being immediately sown upon it, without digging or ploughing, springs up rapidly, grows with luxuriance, and ripens into abundance. See EGYPT.

It must not, however, be supposed that the Nile spreads itself over every spot of land, and waters it sufficiently without artificial aid. Niebuhr justly remarks, "Some descriptions of Egypt would lead us to think that the Nile, when it swells, lays the whole province under water. The lands immediately adjoining to the banks of the river are indeed laid under water, but the natural inequality of the ground hinders it from overflowing the interior country. A great part of the lands would therefore remain barren, were not canals and reservoirs formed to receive water from the river, when at its greatest height, which is thus conveyed everywhere through the fields, and reserved for watering them when occasion requires." In order to raise the water to grounds which lie higher, machines have been used in Egypt from time immemorial. These are chiefly wheels to which buckets are attached. One kind is turned by oxen; another smaller kind, by men seated, and pushing the lower spokes from them with their feet, while they pulled the upper spokes towards them with their hands, Deut. 11:10.

As the inundations of the Nile are of so much importance to the whole land, structures have been erected on which the beginning and progress of its rise might be observed. These are called Nilometers, that is, "Nile measures." At present there is one, one thousand years old and half in ruins, on the little island opposite Cairo; it is under the care of the government, and according to it the beginning and subsequent progress of the rise of the Nile were carefully observed and proclaimed by authority. If the inundation reached the height of twenty-two Paris feet, a rich harvest was expected: because then all the fields had received the requisite irrigation. If it fell short of this height, and in proportion as it thus fell short, the land was threatened with want and famine, of which many horrible examples occur in Egyptian history. Should the rise of the water exceed twenty-eight Paris feet, a famine was in like manner feared.

The annual rise of the river also varies exceedingly in different parts of its course, being twenty feet greater where the river is narrow than in Lower Egypt. The channel is thought to be gradually filling up; and many of the ancient outlets at the Delta are dry in summer and almost obliterated. The drying up of the waters of Egypt would involve its destruction as a habitable land to the same extent; and this fact is recognized in the prophetic denunciations of this remarkable country, Isa. 11:15; 19:1–10; Ezek. 29:10; 30:12.

The water of the Nile, although during a great part of the year turbid, from the effects of the rains above, yet furnishes, when purified by settling, the softest and sweetest water for drinking. Its excellence is acknowledged by all travellers. The Egyptians are full of its praises, and even worshipped the river as a god.

The Hebrews sometimes gave both to the Euphrates and the Nile the name of "sea," Isa. 19:5; Nah. 3:8. In this they are borne out by Arabic writers, and also by the common people of Egypt, who to this day commonly speak of the Nile as "the sea." It is also still celebrated for its fish. Compare Num. 11:5; Isa. 19:8. In its waters are likewise found the crocodile or leviathan, and the hippopotamus or behemoth. See EGYPT, and SIHOR.

NIM'RIM. See BETH-NIMRAH.

NIM'ROD, *rebellion, impiety*, a son of Cush and grandson of Ham, proverbial from the earliest times as a mighty hunter, Gen. 10:8–10; 1 Chr. 1:10. He seems to have feared neither God nor man; to have gathered around him a host of adventurers, and extended his conquests into the land of Shinar, where he founded or fortified Babel, Erech, Accad, and Calneh. According to one interpretation of Gen. 10:11, he also founded Nineveh and the Assyrian empire; though this is usually understood to have been done by Asshur, when expelled by Nimrod from the land of Shinar, Mic. 5:6. Nimrod is supposed to have begun the tower of Babel; and his name is still preserved by a vast ruinous mound, on the site of ancient Babylon. See BABEL.

WINGED AND HUMAN-HEAD LION, FROM THE RUINS OF NINEVEH.

NIN'EVEH, *dwelling of Ni'nus*, the metropolis of ancient Assyria, called by the Greeks and Romans "the great Ninus;" situated on the east bank of the Tigris, opposite and below the modern Mosul. Its origin is traced to the times near the flood. See NIMROD. For nearly fifteen centuries afterwards it is not mentioned. In the books of Jonah and Nahum it is described as an immense city, three days' journey in circuit, containing more than one hundred and twenty thousand young children, or probably six hundred thousand souls. It contained "much cattle," and numerous parks, gardens, groves, etc. Its inhabitants were wealthy, warlike, and far advanced in civilization. It had numerous strong-holds with gates and bars; and had multiplied its merchants above the stars; its crowned princes were as locusts, and its captains as grasshoppers. With this description agrees that of the historian Diodorus Siculus, who says Nineveh was twenty-one miles long, nine miles broad, and fifty-four miles in circumference; that its walls were a hundred feet high, and so broad that three chariots could drive upon them abreast; and that it had fifteen hundred towers, each two hundred feet high.

Nineveh had long been the mistress of the East; but for her great luxury and wickedness, the prophet Jonah was sent, more than eight hundred years before Christ, to warn the Ninevites of her speedy destruction. See also Isa. 14 : 24, 25. Their timely repentance delayed for a time the fall of the city; but about 753 B. C., the period of the foundation of Rome, it was taken by the Medes under Arbaces; and nearly a century and a half later, according to the predictions of Nahum, chap. 1–3, and Zephaniah 2:13, it was a second time taken by Cyaxares and Nabopolassar; after which it no more recovered its former splendor. Subsequent writers mention it but seldom, and as an unimportant place; so complete was its destruction, that for ages its site has been well-nigh lost, and infidels have even denied that the Nineveh of the Bible ever existed. The mounds which were the "grave" of its ruins, Nah. 1 : 14, were so covered with soil as to seem like natural hills. But since 1841, Layard, Botta, and others have been exploring its remains, so long undisturbed. The mounds chiefly explored lie at three corners of a trapezium about eighteen miles long, and twelve miles wide, and nearly sixty in circumference, thus confirming the ancient accounts of its vast extent. The recent excavations disclose temples and palaces, guarded by huge winged bulls and lions with human heads. The apartments of these buildings are lined with slabs of stone,

WARRIOR AND HORSES, FROM THE MOUND OF KHORSABAD, NINEVEH.

covered with sculptures in bas-relief, and inscriptions in arrow-headed characters which have been in part deciphered; and these sculptured memorials of the history and customs of the Assyrians, together with the various articles made of glass, wood, ivory, and metals, now brought to light after a burial of twenty-four centuries, furnish invaluable aid in the interpretation of Scripture, and most signally confirm its truth. Our surprise is equal to our gratification, when we behold the actual Assyrian account of events recorded in Kings and Chronicles. Not only do we find mention made of Jehu, Menahem, Hezekiah, Omri, Hazael, etc., and of various cities in Judea and Syria; but we discover Sennacherib's own account of his invasion of Palestine, and of the amount of tribute which king Hezekiah was forced to pay him; also pictures representing his capture of Lachish, 2 Kin. 18:14, and his officers, perhaps the railing Rabshakeh himself, presenting Jewish captives to the king, etc. (See cut and details in SENNACHERIB.) These mural tablets also furnish a graphic comment on the language of the prophet Ezekiel; and as he was a captive in the region of Nineveh, he had no doubt heard of, and had probably seen these very "chambers of imagery," as well as the objects they represent. We there find reproduced to our view the men and scenes he describes in chap. 23:6, 14, 15, etc.; 26:7-12: "Captains and rulers clothed most gorgeously," "portrayed with vermilion," "girded with girdles upon their loins," "exceeding in dyed attire upon their heads." The "vermilion" or red color is quite prevalent among the various brilliant colors with which these tablets were painted, Ezek. 23:14, 15. Here are "horsemen riding upon horses," "princes to look to" in respect to warlike vigor and courage; and their horses of high spirit, noble form, and attitudes, and decked with showy trappings. (See cut on previous page.) Here, in fine, are the idols, kings, and warriors of Nineveh, in various scenes of worship, hunting, and war; fortresses attacked and taken; prisoners led in triumph, impaled, flayed, and otherwise tortured; and sometimes actually held by cords

attached to hooks which pierce the nose or the lips, 2 Kin. 19:28, Isa. 37:29, and having their eyes put out by the point of a spear, 2 Kin. 25:7. For other cuts see NISROCH, SENNACHERIB, SHALMANEZER, and WAR.

The Christian world is under great obligations to Layard and Botta for their enterprising explorations, and to Rawlinson and Hincks for their literary investigations of these remains. To the student of the Bible especially these buried treasures are of the highest value, and we may well rejoice not only in this new accumulation of evidence to the truth of the history and prophecies of Scripture, but in the additional light thus thrown on its meaning. How impressive too the warning which these newly found memorials of a city once so vast and powerful bring to us in these latter days and in lands then unknown, to beware of the luxury, pride, and ungodliness that caused her ruin.

NISAN, a Hebrew month, nearly answering to our April, but varying somewhat from year to year, according to the course of the moon. It was the seventh month of the civil year; but was made the first month of the sacred year, at the coming out of Egypt, Ex. 12:2. By Moses it is called Abib, Ex. 13:4. The name Nisan is found only after the time of Ezra, and the return from the captivity of Babylon. See MONTHS.

NIS'ROCH, a god of the Assyrians, in whose temple, and in the very act of idolatry, Sennacherib was slain by his own sons, 2 Kin. 19:37. According to the etymology, the name would signify "the great eagle;" and the earlier Assyrian sculptures recently exhumed at Nineveh have many representations of an idol in human form, but with the head of an eagle, as shown above. Among the ancient Arabs also the eagle occurs as an idol. The other accompanying cut, representing a winged figure in a

circle, armed with a bow, is frequently met on the walls of ancient Nineveh in scenes of worship, and is believed to be an emblem of the supreme divinity of the Assyrians.

NI'TRE, not the substance used in making gunpowder, but natron, a mineral alkali composed of several salts of soda. It effervesces with vinegar, Prov. 25:28, and is still used in washing, Jer. 2:22. Combined with oil, it makes a hard soap. It is found deposited in, or floating upon, certain lakes west of the Delta of Egypt.

NO, or NO-AMMON. See AMMON.

NO'AH, *rest, comfort,* the name of the celebrated patriarch who was preserved by Jehovah with his family, by means of the ark, through the deluge, and thus became the second founder of the human race. The history of Noah and the deluge is contained in Genesis, ch. 5–9. He was the son of Lamech, and grandson of Methuselah; was born A. M. 1056, and lived six hundred years before the deluge, and three hundred and fifty after it, dying two years before Abram was born. His name may have been given to him by his parents in the hope that he would be the promised "seed of the woman" that should "bruise the serpent's head." He was in the line of the patriarchs who feared God, and was himself a just man, Ezek. 14:14, 20, and a "preacher of righteousness," 1 Pet. 3:19, 20; 2 Pet. 2:5. His efforts to reform the degenerate world, continued as some suppose for one hundred and twenty years, produced little effect, Matt. 24:37; the flood did not "find faith upon the earth." Noah, however, was an example of real faith: he believed the warning of God, was moved by fear, and pursued the necessary course of action, Heb. 11:7. His first care on coming out from the ark was to worship the Lord, with sacrifices of all the fitting animals. Little more is recorded of him except his falling into intoxication, a sad instance of the shame and misfortune into which wine is apt to lead. His three sons, it is believed, peopled the whole world; the posterity of Japheth chiefly occupying Europe, those of Shem Asia, and those of Ham Africa.

Numerous traces of traditions respecting Noah have been found all over the world. Among the most accurate is that embodied in the legend of the Greeks respecting Deucalion and Pyrrha. We may also mention the medals struck at Apamea in Phrygia, in the time of Septimus Severus, and bearing the name NO, an ark, a man and woman, a raven, and a dove with an olive-branch in its mouth. See ARK.

NOB, a city of priests, in Benjamin, near Jerusalem; its inhabitants were once put to the sword by command of Saul, for their hospitality to David, 1 Sam. 21:2; 22:9-23; Neh. 11:32; Isa. 10:32. Its site is unknown.

NOD, *wandering*, a region east of Eden, so named on account of the wanderings in it of the exiled Cain, Gen. 4:16.

NOPH, sometimes called also, in Hebrew, MOPH, Hos. 9:6, the ancient city of Memphis in Egypt. The ruins of it, though not to any great extent, are still found a few miles above Old Cairo, or Fostat, Isa. 19:13; Jer. 2:16; 44:1; Ezek. 30:13, 16.

Memphis was the residence of the ancient kings of Egypt till the times of the Ptolemies, who commonly resided at Alexandria. Here, it is supposed, Joseph was a prisoner and a ruler, and here Moses stood before Pharaoh. The prophets, in the places above referred to, foretell the miseries Memphis was to suffer from the kings of Chaldea and Persia; and threaten the Israelites who should retire into Egypt, or should have recourse to the Egyptians, that they should perish in that country. In this city they fed and worshipped the sacred bull Apis, the embodiment of their false god Osiris; and Ezekiel says, that the Lord will destroy the idols of Memphis, Ezek. 30:13, 16. Memphis retained much of its splendor till it was conquered by the Arabians in the eighteenth or nineteenth year of the Hegira, A. D. 641; after which it was superseded as the metropolis of Egypt by Fostat, now Old Cairo, in the construction of which its materials were employed. The pyramids, in which its distinguished men were buried, still survive; but the magnificent city, that stretched along for many miles between them and the river, has almost wholly disappeared.

NORTH. See EAST. The Babylonians and Assyrians are represented as coming from "the north," because they invaded Israel by a northern route, in order to avoid the desert, Jer. 1:14; 46:6, 24; Zeph. 2:13. "Fair weather," says Job, or golden weather, "cometh out of the north," Job 37:22. This is as true in Syria and Arabia now as it was three thousand years ago. A traveller there remarks, "Our friends, who have been long residents, informed us that we should have fair weather for our start on the morrow, as the wind was from the north. . . . . And so we have found it come to pass that the clouds of a golden hue always followed upon a north wind, and indicated a clear day; and as in the times of the Saviour, we could always say when it was evening, 'It will be fair weather, for the sky is red,'" Matt. 16:2.

NOSE. Several expressions in Scripture grew out of the fact that anger often shows itself by distended nostrils, hard breathing, and in animals by snorting, 2 Sam. 22:9; Job 39:20; Psa. 18:8. Gold rings hung in the cartilage of the nose, or the left nostril, were favorite ornaments of Eastern women, Prov. 11:22; Ezek. 16:12. Rings were inserted in the noses of animals, to guide and control them; and according to the recently discovered tablets at Nineveh, captives among the Assyrians were sometimes treated in the same way, 2 Kin. 19:28; Ezek. 38:4. See NINEVEH.

NOVICE, or neophite, one recently converted and received to the Christian church, 1 Tim. 3:6.

NUMBER, Isa. 65:11. See GAD III.

NUMBERS, THE BOOK OF, is so called because the first three chapters contain the numbering of the Hebrews and Levites, which was performed separately, after the erection and consecration of the tabernacle. The rest of the book contains an account of the breaking up of the Israelites from Sinai, and their subsequent wanderings in the desert, until their arrival on the borders of Moab. It was written by Moses, B. C. 1451, and is the fourth book of the Pentateuch. See EXODUS.

NURSE. The Bible contains various allusions to the tender and confidential relation anciently subsisting between a nurse and the children she had brought up, Isa. 49:22, 23; 1 Thess. 2:7, 8. See also the story of Rebekah, attended through life by her faithful and honored Deborah, the oak under which she was buried being called "The oak of weeping," Gen. 24:59; 35:8. The custom still prevails in the better families of Syria and India. Says Roberts in his

Oriental Illustrations, "How often have scenes like this led my mind to the patriarchal age. The daughter is about for the *first time* to leave the paternal roof; the servants are all in confusion; each refers to things long gone by, each wishes to do something to attract the attention of his young mistress. One says, 'Ah, do not forget him who nursed you when an infant;' another, 'How often did I bring you the beautiful lotus from the distant tank. Did I not always conceal your faults?' Then the mother comes to take leave. She weeps, and tenderly embraces her, saying, 'My daughter, I shall see you no more; forget not your mother.' The brother enfolds his sister in his arms, and promises soon to come and see her. The father is absorbed in thought, and is only aroused by the sobs of the party. He then affectionately embraces his daughter, and tells her not to fear. The female domestics must each *smell* of the poor girl, and the men touch her feet. As Rebekah had her *nurse* to accompany her, so, at *this* day, the *aya* (*nurse*) who has from infancy brought up the bride, goes with her to the new scene. She is her adviser, her assistant, and friend, and to her will she tell all her hopes and all her fears."

NYM'PHAS, a Christian at Laodicea, whom Paul salutes, together with the company of believers wont to worship at his house, Col. 4:15.

O.

OAK. As many as six varieties of the oak are found in Palestine. Dr. Robinson speaks of one at Hebron which had a trunk twenty-two and a half feet in circumference; and saw the crests and sides of the hills beyond the Jordan still clothed, as in ancient times, with magnificent oaks, Isa. 2:13; Zech. 11:2. The oak is often referred to in Scripture, Gen. 35:8; Isa. 44:14; Amos 2:9. There is, however, a second Hebrew word often translated "oak," which is supposed to denote the terebinth or turpentine-tree, called butm by the Arabs, Gen. 35:4; Judg. 6:11, 19; 2 Sam. 18:9, 14. It is translated "elm" in Hos. 4:13, and "teil-tree" in Isa. 6:13, in which passages the true oak is also mentioned. In many passages where "plain" or "plains" occurs, we should probably understand "terebinth," or "a grove of terebinths," Gen. 12:6; 13:18; 14:13; 18:1; Deut. 11:30; Judg. 9:6. This tree was found in all countries around the Mediterranean, and in Palestine grew to a large size. It was very long-lived. For many ages after Christ, a tree of this kind near Hebron was superstitiously venerated as one of those under which Abraham dwelt at Mamre. Under the welcome shade of oaks and other large trees many public affairs were transacted; sacrifices were offered, courts were held, and kings were crowned, Josh. 24:26; Judg. 6:11, 19; 9:6. See Grove.

OATH, a solemn affirmation, accompanied by an appeal to the Supreme Being. God has prohibited all false oaths, and all useless and customary swearing in ordinary discourse; but when the necessity or importance of a matter requires an oath, he allows men to swear by his name, Ex. 22:11; Lev. 5:1. To swear by a false god was an act of idolatry, Jer. 5:7; 12:16.

Among the Hebrews an oath was administered by the judge, who stood up, and adjured the party who was to be sworn. In this manner our Lord was adjured by Caiaphas, Matt. 26:63. Jesus had remained silent under long examination, when the high-priest, rising up, knowing he had a sure mode of obtaining an answer, said, "I adjure thee by the living God, that thou tell us whether thou be the Christ." To this oath, thus solemnly administered, Jesus replied that he was indeed the Messiah.

An oath is a solemn appeal to God, as to an all-seeing witness that what we say is true, and an almighty avenger if what we say be false, Heb. 6:16. Its force depends upon our conviction of the infinite justice of God; that he will not hold those guiltless who take his name in vain; and that the loss of his favor immeasurably outweighs all that could be gained by false witness. It is an act of religious worship; on which account God requires it to be taken in his name, Deut. 10:20, and points out the manner in which it ought to be administered, and the duty of the person who swears, Exod. 22:11; Deut. 6:13; Psa. 15:4; 24:4. Hence atheists, who profess to believe that there is no God, and persons who do not believe in a future state of reward and punishment, cannot consistently take an oath. In their mouths an oath can be only profane mockery.

God himself is represented as confirming his promise by oath, and thus conforming to what is practised among men, Psa. 95 : 11 ; Heb. 6 : 13, 16, 17. The oaths forbidden in Matt. 5 : 34, 35 ; Jas. 5:12, must refer to the unthinking, hasty, and vicious practices of the Jews ; otherwise Paul would have acted against the command of Christ, Rom. 1 : 9; Gal. 1:20; 2 Cor. 1:23. That person is obliged to take an oath whose duty requires him to declare the truth in the most solemn and judicial manner; though undoubtedly oaths are too often administered unnecessarily and irreverently, and taken with but slight consciousness of the responsibility thus assumed. As we are bound to manifest every possible degree of reverence towards God, the greatest care is to be taken that we swear neither rashly nor negligently in making promises. To neglect performance is perjury, unless the promise be contrary to the law of nature and of God ; in which case no oath is binding. See CORBAN, and VOWS.

A customary formula of taking an oath was, "The Lord do so to me, and more also ;" that is, the Lord slay me, as the victim sacrificed on many such occasions was slain, and punish me even more than this, if I speak not the truth, Ruth 1:17 ; 1 Sam. 3:17. Similar phrases are these : "As the Lord liveth," Judg. 8:19 ; "Before God I lie not," Rom. 9:1 ; "I say the truth in Christ," 1 Tim. 2:7 ; "God is my record," Phil. 1 : 8. Several acts are alluded to as accompaniments of an oath ; as putting the hand under the thigh, Gen. 24 : 2 ; 47 : 29 ; and raising the hand towards heaven, Gen. 14 : 22, 23 ; Deut. 32:40 ; Rev. 10:5.

OBADI'AH, I., the chief officer of king Ahab's household, who preserved the lives of one hundred prophets from the persecuting Jezebel, by concealing them in two caves and furnishing them with food, 1 Kin. 18:4.

II. The fourth of the minor prophets, supposed to have prophesied about 587 B. C. It cannot indeed be decided with certainty when he lived, but it is probable that he was contemporary with Jeremiah and Ezekiel, who denounced the same dreadful judgments on the Edomites, as the punishment of their pride, violence, and cruel insultings over the Jews after the destruction of their city. The prophecy, according to Usher, was fulfilled about five years after the destruction of Jerusalem.

III. Eight or ten others of this name are mentioned in 1 Chr. 3:21 ; 7:3 ; 8:38 ; 9 : 16, 44 ; 12 : 9. 27 : 19 ; 2 Chr. 17 : 7 ; 34:12 ; Ezra 8:9 ; Neh. 10:5.

O'BED, son of Boaz and Ruth, and grandfather of David, Ruth 4 : 17. See also the genealogies of Christ, Matt. 1:5 ; Luke 3:32.

O'BED-E'DOM, a Levite, whose special prosperity while keeper of the ark after the dreadful death of Uzziah encouraged David to carry it up to Jerusalem. Obed-edom and his sons were made doorkeepers of the tabernacle at Jerusalem, 2 Sam. 6:10-12 ; 1 Chr. 15:18-24 ; 16:38 ; 26:4-8, 15.

O'DED, a prophet of the Lord, who, being at Samaria when the Israelites under king Pekah returned from the war against Judah and brought 200,000 captives, went to meet them, and remonstrated with them ; so that the principal men in Samaria took care of the prisoners, gave them clothes, food, and other assistance, and carried the feeble on asses. Thus they conducted them to Jericho, 2 Chr. 28:9, etc.

OFFENCE'. This word answers to two different terms in the original, the one signifying a breach of the law, Rom. 5 : 15, 17, the other a stumbling-block or cause of sin to others, Matt. 5 : 29 ; 18 : 6-9 ; or whatever is perverted into an occasion or excuse for sin, Matt. 15:12; John 6:61 ; Rom. 9:33 ; Gal. 5:11.

OF'FERING. In the Hebrew, an offering, *minchah*, is distinguished from a sacrifice, *zebah*, as being bloodless. In our version, however, the word offering is often used for a sacrifice, as in the case of peace-offerings, sin-offerings, etc. Of the proper offerings, that is, the unbloody offerings, some accompanied the sacrifices, as flour, wine, salt ; others were not connected with any sacrifices. Like the sacrifices, some, as the first-fruits and tenths, were obligatory ; others were voluntary offerings of devotion. Various sorts of offerings are enumerated in the books of Moses. Among these are, 1. Fine flour, or meal ; 2. Cakes baked in an oven ; 3. Cakes baked on a plate or shallow pan ; 4. Cakes cooked in a deep vessel by frying in oil, (English version, "frying-pan," though some understand here a gridiron, or a plate with holes;) 5. First-fruits of the new corn, either in the simple state, or prepared by parching or roasting in the ear, or out of the ear. The cakes were kneaded with olive oil, or fried in a pan, or only dipped in oil after they were baked. The bread offered for the altar was without leaven; for leaven was never offered on the altar, nor with the sacrifices, Lev. 2:11, 12. But they might make presents of common bread to the priests and ministers of the temple. Honey was never offered with the sacrifices, but it might be presented alone, as first-fruits, Lev. 2:11, 12. Those who offered living victims were not excused from giving meal, wine, and salt, together with the greater sacrifices. Those who offered only oblations of bread or of meal, offered also oil, incense, salt, and wine, which were in a manner their seasoning. The priest in waiting received the offerings from the hand of him who brought them, laid a part on the altar, and reserved the rest for his own subsistence as a minister of the Lord. Nothing was wholly burned up but the incense, of which the priest retained none. See Lev. 2:2, 13, etc.; Num. 15:4, 5.

In some cases the law required only offerings of corn or bread, as when they offered the first-fruits of harvest, whether offered solemnly by the nation, or as the devotion of private persons. The unbloody offerings signified, in general, not so much expiation, which was the peculiar meaning of the sacrifices, as the consecration of the offerer and all that he had to Jehovah. Only in the case of the poor man, who could not afford the expense of sacrificing an animal, was an unbloody offering accepted in its stead, Lev. 5:11. See SACRIFICES.

OG, an Amoritish king of Bashan east of the Jordan, defeated and slain by the Israelites under Moses. He was a giant in stature, one of the last of the Rephaim who had possessed that region; and his iron bedstead, fourteen feet long, was preserved after his death as a relic. Ashtaroth-carnaim and Edrei were his chief cities; but there were many other walled towns, and the land was rich in flocks and herds. It was assigned by Moses to the half-tribe of Manasseh, Num. 21:33; 32:33; Deut. 1:4; 3:1-13; 4:47; 31:4; Josh. 2:10; 12:4; 13:30.

OIL was employed from the earliest periods in the East, not only for the purpose of consecration, but to anoint the head, the beard, and the whole person in daily life, Gen. 28:18. See ANOINTING. It was also universally used for food, Ezek. 16:13. Fresh and sweet olive oil was greatly preferred to butter and animal fat as a seasoning for food, and to this day in Syria almost every kind of food is cooked with oil. It had a place also among the meat-offerings in the temple, being usually mixed with the meal of the oblation, Lev. 5:11; 6:21. For lamps, also, pure olive oil was regarded as the best, and was used in illuminating the tabernacle. These many uses for oil made the culture of the olive-tree an extensive and lucrative business, 1 Chr. 27:28; Ezek. 27:17; Hos. 12:1. Oil was as much an article of storage and of traffic as corn and wine, 2 Chr. 32:28; Ezra 3:7. The best oil was obtained from the fruit while yet green, by a slight beating or pressing, Ex. 27:20; 29:40. The ripe fruit is now, and has been from ancient times, crushed by passing stone rollers over it. The crushed mass is then subjected to pressure in the oil-mill, Hebrew, *gath-shemen*. The olive-berries are not now trodden with the feet. This, however, seems to have been practised among the Hebrews, at least to some extent, when the berries had become soft by keeping, Mic. 6:15. Gethsemane, that is, *oil-press*, probably took its name originally from some oil-press in its vicinity. See OLIVE.

OINTMENTS were much used by the ancient Hebrews, not chiefly for medical purposes as among us, but as a luxury, Ruth 3:3; Psa. 104:15; Song 1:2; Matt. 6:17; Luke 7:46. Their perfumery was usually prepared in olive oil, and not in volatile extracts and essences. The sacred ointment is described in Ex. 30:22-33. The ointments of the rich were made of very costly ingredients, and their fragrance was highly extolled, Isa. 39:2; Amos 6:6; Matt. 26:7-9; John 12:5. See ANOINTING.

OLIVE. This is one of the earliest trees mentioned in Scripture, and has furnished, perhaps ever since the deluge, the most universal emblem of peace, Gen. 8:11. It is always classed among the most valuable trees of Palestine, which is described as a land of oil olive and honey, Deut. 6:11; 8:8; Hab. 3:17.

No tree is more frequently mentioned in the Greek and Roman classics. By the Greeks it was dedicated to Minerva, and employed in crowning Jove, Apollo, and Hercules. The olive is never a very large or beautiful tree, and seldom exceeds thirty feet in height: its leaves are dark green on the upper surface, and of a silvery hue on the under, and generally grow in pairs. Its wood is hard, like that of box, and very close in the grain. It blossoms very profusely, and bears fruit every other year. The flower is at first yellow, but as it expands, it becomes whiter, leaving a yellow centre. The fruit resembles a plum in shape and in color, being first green, then pale, and when ripe, black. It is gathered by shaking the boughs and by beating them with poles, Deut. 24:20, Isa. 17:6, and is sometimes plucked in an unripe state, put into some preserving liquid, and exported. It is principally valuable for the oil it produces, which is an important article of commerce in the East. A full-sized tree in full bearing vigor is said to produce a thousand pounds of oil, Judg. 9:8, 9; 2 Chr. 2:10. The olive delights in a stony soil, and will thrive even on the sides and tops of rocky hills, where there is scarcely any earth; hence the expression, "oil out of the flinty rock," etc., Deut. 32:13; Job 29:6. It is an evergreen tree, and very long-lived, an emblem of a fresh and enduring piety, Psa. 52:8. Around an old trunk young plants shoot up from the same root, to adorn the parent stock when living, and succeed it when dead; hence the allusion in describing the family of the just, Psa. 128:3. It is slow of growth, and no less slow to decay. The ancient trees now in Gethsemane are believed by many to have sprung from the roots of those which witnessed the agony of our Lord. The "wild olive-tree" is smaller than the cultivated, and inferior in all its parts and products. A graft upon it, from a good tree, bore good fruit; while a graft from a "wild" olive upon a good tree, remains "wild" as before. Yet, "contrary to nature," the sinner engrafted on Christ partakes of His nature and bears good fruit, Rom. 11:13-26.

OL'IVES, MOUNT OF, Ezek. 11:23, called also OLIVET, 2 Sam. 15:30, a ridge running north and south on the east side of Jerusalem, its summit about half a mile from the city wall, and separated from it by the valley of the Kidron. It is composed of a chalky limestone, the rocks everywhere showing themselves. The olive-trees that formerly covered it, and gave it its name, are now represented by a few trees and clumps of trees which ages of desolation have not eradicated. There are three prominent summits on the ridge; of these the southernmost, which is lower than the other two, is now known as the "Mount of Offence," originally the "Mount of Corruption," because Solomon defiled it by idolatrous worship, 1 Kin. 11:5-7; 2 Kin. 23:13. Over this ridge passes the road to Bethany, the most frequented road to Jericho and the Jordan. The sides of the mount of Olives towards the west contain many tombs, cut in the rocks. The central summit rises two hundred feet above Jerusalem, and presents a fine view of the city, and indeed of the whole region, including the mountains of Ephraim on the north, the valley of the Jordan on the east, a part of the Dead sea on the south-east, and beyond it Kerak in the mountains of Moab. Perhaps no spot on earth unites so fine a view, with so many memorials of the most solemn and important events. Over this hill the Saviour often climbed in his journeys to and from the holy city. Gethsemane lay at its foot on the west, and Bethany on its eastern slope, Matt. 24:3; Mark 13:3. It was probably near Bethany, and not as tradition says on the middle summit, that our

Lord ascended to heaven, Luke 24:50, Acts 1:12, though superstition has built the "Church of the Ascension" on the pretended spot, and shows the print of his feet on the rock whence he ascended! From the summit, three days before his death, he beheld Jerusalem, and wept over it, recalling the long ages of his more than parental care, and grieving over its approaching ruin. Scarcely any thing in the gospels moves the heart more than this natural and touching scene. No one can doubt that it was GOD who there spoke; his retrospect, his prediction, and his compassion alike proved it. See Luke 19:37-44, in connection with Matt. 23:35-38, spoken the next day. The same spot is associated with the predictions of his future judgments in the earth, Zech. 14:4. See view of the central summit in GETHSEMANE. Also SEPULCHRES.

O'MEGA, the last letter of the Greek alphabet. See letter A.

O'MER, a measure of capacity among the Hebrews; the tenth part of an ephah; a little more than five pints.

OM'RI was general of the army of Elah king of Israel; but being at the siege of Gibbethon, and hearing that his master Elah was assassinated by Zimri, who had usurped his kingdom, he raised the siege, and being elected king by his army, marched against Zimri, attacked him at Tirzah, and forced him to burn himself and all his family in the palace in which he had shut himself up. After his death, half of Israel acknowledged Omri for king, the other half adhered to Tibni, son of Ginath, which division continued four years. When Tibni was dead, the people united in acknowledging Omri as king of all Israel, who reigned twelve years, six years at Tirzah, and six at Samaria, 1 Kin. 16:8-28.

Tirzah had previously been the chief residence of the kings of Israel; but when Omri purchased the hill of Shomeron, 1 Kin. 16:24, he built there a new city, which he called Samaria, from the name of the previous possessor, Shemer or Shomer, and there fixed his royal seat. From this time Samaria was the capital of the kingdom of the ten tribes. It appears, under the name of Beth-Omri, on the stone tablets recently exhumed by Layard from the ruins of Nineveh.

ON. See HELIOPOLIS.

ONES'IMUS had been a slave to Philemon of Colosse, and had run away from him, and fled to Rome; but being converted to Christianity through the preaching of Paul, he was the occasion of Paul's writing the epistle to Philemon, Col. 4:9; Phile. 10.

ONESIPH'ORUS, a Christian friend of Paul at Ephesus, who came to Rome while the apostle was imprisoned there for the faith, and at a time when almost every one had forsaken him. This is supposed to have occurred during Paul's last imprisonment, not long before his death. Having found Paul in bonds, after long seeking him, he assisted him to the utmost of his power, and without regard to danger; for which the apostle implored the highest benedictions on him and his family, 2 Tim. 1:16-18; 4:19.

ON'ION, one of the vegetables of Egypt for which the Hebrews murmured in the desert, Num. 11:5. Hasselquist says that the onions of Egypt are remarkably sweet, mild, and nutritious. Juvenal, Pliny, and Lucian satirize the superstitious regard of the Egyptians for this bulb.

O'NO, a town of Benjamin, near Lydda, 1 Chr. 8:12; Ezra 2:33. The "plain of Ono" is supposed to denote a portion of the plain of Sharon near Ono, Neh. 6:2; 11:35.

ON'YCHA, an ingredient of the sacred incense, whose fragrance perfumed the sanctuary alone, Ex. 30:34. It is conjectured to mean the Blatta Byzantina of the shops; an article which consists of the cover or lid of a species of muscle, and when burnt emits a musky odor. The best onycha is found in the Red sea, and is white and large.

ON'YX, *a nail*, the eleventh stone in the high-priest's breastplate, Ex. 28:20. The modern onyx has some resemblance to the agate; and the color of the body of the stone is like that of the human nail; hence its name. The Hebrew word so translated is not known with certainty to signify the onyx; but denoted some valuable stone, Gen. 2:12; Ex. 25:7; 28:9-12, 20. A species of marble resembling the onyx was known to the Greeks, and may have been the "onyx-stones" stored up by David for the temple, 1 Chr. 29:2.

O'PHEL, a quarter of Jerusalem adjacent to the temple, and therefore occupied by the Nethinim, Neh. 3 : 26, 27; 11:21. It appears to have been enclosed by a wall, and fortified by a strong tower, 2 Chr. 27:3; 33:14; and is thought to be meant by the Hebrew OPHEL, translated "strong-hold," in Mic. 4:8. There can be little doubt that the name belongs to the lower ridge into which mount Moriah sinks, south of the area of the mosque. It is one hundred yards wide, and extends six hundred yards to the south, terminating in a bluff forty or fifty feet high above the pool of Siloam. It is separated from mount Zion on the west by the valley called Tyropœon, and is now devoted to the culture of olives, figs, and other fruit.

O'PHIR, I., one of the sons of Joktan, who settled in southern Arabia, Gen. 10:26-29.

II. A country to which the ships of Solomon traded, and which had for a long time been celebrated for the purity and abundance of its gold, Job 22 : 24; 28 : 16. "Gold of Ophir" was proverbially the best gold, Psa. 45 : 9; Isa. 13 : 12. The only passages which give us any information as to the location of Ophir are 1 Kin. 9:26-28; 10:11, 22; 22:48, with the parallel passages in 2 Chr. 8:18; 9:10, 21; 20:36, 37; from which it appears that the so called "ships of Tarshish" went to Ophir; that these ships sailed from Ezion-geber, a port of the Red sea; that a voyage was made once in three years; that the fleet returned freighted with gold, peacocks, apes, spices, ivory, algum-wood, and ebony. Upon these data interpreters have undertaken to determine the situation of Ophir; but they have arrived at different conclusions. Josephus places it in the peninsula of Malacca. Others have placed it at Sofala, in South Africa, where mines of gold and silver have been found, which appear to have been anciently and extensively worked. Others still suppose it to have been Southern Arabia.

OPH'RAH, I., a town of the Benjamites, located by Eusebius five miles east of Bethel; near which site stands the modern village Taiyibeh, on a conical hill, Josh. 18:23; 1 Sam. 13:17.

II. A town of Manasseh where Gideon resided; and where after his death his ephod was superstitiously adored, Judg. 6:11-24; 8:27.

OR'ACLE, a supernatural communication; applied to single divine revelations and to the entire word of God, Acts 7 : 38; Rom. 3:2; Heb. 5:12, etc. It is also spoken of the covering of the ark of the covenant; as if God there sat enthroned, and delivered his oracles, 2 Sam. 16 : 23. See MERCY-SEAT. In other places, it means the "Holy of Holies" in the temple, where the ark was placed, 1 Kin. 6:5, 16, 19; 8:6.

Strikingly unlike the true and living oracles of God were the famous counterfeit oracles of numerous heathen temples. The priests who pretended to convey to applicants the responses of their gods, often gave a reply capable of two opposite interpretations, when neither private information nor their own experience or sagacity gave them the clue to a safe answer. Thus Pyrrhus, king of Epirus, was encouraged to a war with Rome, by an oracle which was found after his defeat to foretell defeat as much as victory: Aio te, Aeacida, Romanos vincere posse.

O'REB, and ZE'EB, *raven* and *wolf*, two Midianite chiefs, captured after the victory of Gideon, and slain at the spots whither they had fled, and which were afterwards called, in memory of them, "the rock of Oreb" and the wine-press or cellar of Zeeb, Judg. 7 : 25. Their punishment foretells that of all God's enemies, Psa. 83:12; Isa. 10:26.

OR'GAN, Psa. 150 : 4, a wind instrument apparently composed of several pipes. It cannot, however, mean the modern organ, which was unknown to the ancients; but refers probably to the ancient *syrinx*, or pipes, similar to the Pandean pipes, a series of seven or more tubes of unequal length and size, closed at one end, and blown into with the mouth at the other, Gen. 4 : 21; Job 21:12. See MUSIC.

ORI'ON, Job 9:9, one of the brightest constellations of the southern hemisphere. The Hebrew *chesil* signifies, according to the best interpreters and the ancient versions, the constellation Orion, which, on account of its supposed connection with storms and tempests, Virgil calls "nimbosus Orion," stormy Orion. In Job 38:31, fetters are ascribed to him; and this coincides with the Greek fable of the giant Orion, bound in the heavens for an unsuccessful war against the gods.

OR'NAN. See ARAUNAH.

ORʹPAH, the Moabitess, Naomi's daughter-in-law, who remained with her people and gods, when Ruth followed Naomi and the Lord, Ruth 1:4–14. The one was taken, and the other left.

OʹSEE, the Greek form of HOSEA, Rom. 9:25.

OSʹPREY, a bird of the eagle kind, unfit for food, Lev. 11:13. It is thought to be the sea-eagle, or the black eagle of Egypt. See BIRDS.

OSʹSIFRAGE, *bone-breaker;* in Hebrew PERES, *to break;* an unclean bird of the eagle family, Lev. 11:13; Deut. 14:12. Some interpreters think the vulture is intended; others, a mountain bird like the lammergeyer of the Alps, which breaks the bones of wild goats by hunting them over precipices.

OSʹTRICH, the largest of birds, and a sort of connecting link between fowls and quadrupeds, termed by the Persians, Arabs, and by Greeks, the "camel-bird." It is a native of the dry and torrid regions of Africa and Western Asia. The gray ostrich is seven feet high, and its neck three feet long; it weighs nearly eighty pounds, and is strong enough to carry two men. The other species, with glossy black wings and white tail, is sometimes ten feet high. The beautiful plumes so highly valued are found on the wings, about twenty on each, those of the tail being usually broken and worn. There are no feathers on the thighs, or under the wings; and the neck is but scantily clothed with thin whitish hairs. The weight of the body and the size and structure of the wings show that the animal is formed for running rather than flying.

The ostrich is described in Job 39:13–18; and in various places where our translation calls it the "owl," Job 30:29; Jer. 50:39; or "daughter of the owl," Isa. 13:21; 34:13; 43:20; Mic. 1:8. In these and other passages it figures as a bird of the desert. Shy and timorous, it is occasionally driven by hunger to visit and ravage cultivated fields; but is usually found only in the heart of the desert, in troops, or small groups, or mingling familiarly with the herds of wild asses, gnus, and quaggas. Its food is often scarce and poor, plants of the desert "withered before they are grown up;" also snails, insects, and various reptiles; for it has a voracious and indiscriminating appetite, swallowing the vilest and the hardest substances. Job speaks particularly of the speed of the ostrich, "She scorneth the horse and his rider." So Xenophon, the biographer of Cyrus, says of the ostriches of Arabia, that none could overtake them, the baffled horsemen soon returning from the chase; and the writer of a voyage to Senegal says, "The ostrich sets off at a hard gallop; but after being excited a little, she expands her wings as if to catch the wind, and abandons herself to a speed so great, that she seems not to touch the ground. I am persuaded she would leave far behind the swiftest English courser."

She scoops out for herself a circular nest in the sand, and lays a large number of eggs; some of which are placed without the nest, as though intended for the nourishment of the young brood. The mother bird, with the help of the sun in the tropics, and of her mate in the cool nights, performs the process of incubation; but her timidity is such that she flies from her nest at the approach of danger, and as Dr. Shaw remarks, "forsakes her eggs or her young ones, to which, perhaps, she never returns; or if she does, it may be too late either to restore life to the one, or to preserve the lives of the others. Agreeably to this account, the Arabs meet sometimes with whole nests of these eggs undisturbed; some of them are sweet and good, others are addle and corrupted. They often meet with a few of the little ones no bigger than well-grown pullets, half starved, straggling and moaning about, like so many distressed orphans for their mother. In this manner the ostrich may be said to be 'hardened against her young ones, as though they were not hers; her labor,' in hatching and attending them so far, 'being vain, without fear,' or the least concern of what becomes of them afterwards. This want of affection is also recorded in Lam. 4:3, 'The daughter of my people is become cruel, like the ostriches in the wilderness;' that is, apparently by deserting her own children, and receiving others in return."

When the ostrich is provoked, she sometimes makes a fierce, angry, and hissing noise, with her throat inflated, and her mouth open; at other times she has a moaning and plaintive cry; and in the night the male repels prowling enemies by a short roar which is sometimes taken for that of a lion, Mic. 1:8.

OTH'NIEL, son of Kenaz, and first judge of the Israelites, delivering them from the tyranny of the king of Mesopotamia, and ruling them in peace forty years. His wife Achsa, daughter of his uncle Caleb, was the reward of his valor in taking the city of Debir, Josh. 15:17; Judg. 1:13; 3:9, 10.

OUCH'ES, sockets in which precious stones were set, Ex. 28:11, 25; 39:6.

OV'EN. See BREAD.

THE SCREECH-OWL; STRIX FLAMMEA.

OWL, a night bird of prey, unfit for food. Several species are found in Palestine, and are mentioned in the Bible; as in Lev. 11:17; Deut. 14:16; Isa. 14:23; 34:15; Zeph. 2:14. One of the words, however, translated "owl," probably means "OSTRICH," (which see;) and another, Lev. 11:17; Deut. 14:16; Isa. 34:11, the ibis or night-heron.

THE BULL OF SYRIA.

OX, the male of the beeve kind when grown, synonymous in the Bible with BULL; a clean animal, by the Levitical law; much used for food, 1 Kin. 19:21, and constituting no small part of the wealth of the Hebrews in their pastoral life, Gen. 24:35; Job 1:14; 42:12. Oxen were used in agriculture for ploughing, 1 Kin. 19:19; and for treading out the grain, during which they were not to be muzzled, 1 Cor. 9:9, but well fed, Isa. 30:24. The testing of a new yoke of oxen is still a business of great importance in the East, as of old, Luke 14:19. A passage in Campbell's travels in South Africa well illustrates the proverbial expression, "as a bullock unaccustomed to the yoke," Jer. 31:18: "I had frequent opportunities of witnessing the conduct of oxen when for the first time put into the yoke to assist in dragging the wagons. On observing an ox that had been in yoke beginning to get weak, or his hoofs to be worn down to the quick by treading on the sharp gravel, a fresh ox was put into the yoke in his place. When the selection fell on an ox I had received as a present from some African king, of course one completely unaccustomed to the yoke, such generally made a strenuous struggle for liberty, repeatedly breaking the yoke, and attempting to make its escape. At other times such bullocks lay down upon their sides or back, and remained so in defiance of the Hottentots, though two or three of them would be lashing them with their ponderous whips. Sometimes, from pity to the animal, I would interfere, and beg them to be less cruel. 'Cruel,' they would say, 'it is mercy; for if we do not conquer him now, he will require to be so beaten all his life.'"

The "wild ox," mentioned in Deut. 14:5, is supposed to have been a species of stag or antelope. See BULLS OF BASHAN.

P.

PA'DAN-A'RAM, *the plains of Aram or Syria,* Gen. 25:20; 28:2; 31:18, or simply PADAN, Gen. 48:7, *the plain,* in distinction from the "mountains" of Aram, Num. 23:7. See MESOPOTAMIA, and SYRIA.

PAL'ESTINE denotes, in the Old Testament, the country of the Philistines, which was that part of the Land of Promise extending along the Mediterranean sea on the varying western border of Simeon, Judah, and Dan, Ex. 15:14; Isa. 14:29, 31; Joel 3:4. Palestine, taken in later usage in a more general sense, signifies the whole country of Canaan, as well beyond as on this side of the Jordan; though frequently it is restricted to the country on this side that river; so that in later times the words Judea and Palestine were synonymous. We find also the name of Syria-Palestina given to the Land of Promise, and even sometimes this province is comprehended in Cœle-Syria, or the Lower Syria. Herodotus is the most ancient writer known who speaks of Syria-Palestina. He places it between Phœnicia and Egypt. See CANAAN.

PALM'ER-WORM. This old English term, meaning pilgrim-worm, is used in Joel 1:4; 2:25; Amos 4:9, like "canker-worm" and "caterpillar," for the locust in one or another of its various species or transitions. These insects are very destructive even before they reach the winged state. See LOCUST.

PALM-TREE, Ex. 15:27. This tree is called in Hebrew *tamar,* from its straight, upright, branchless growth, for which it seems more remarkable than any other tree; it sometimes rises to the height of a hundred feet. See TAMAR.

The palm is one of the most beautiful trees of the vegetable kingdom. The stalks are generally full of rugged knots, which render it comparatively easy to climb to the top for the fruit, Song 7:7, 8. These projections are the ves-

tiges of the decayed leaves; for the trunk is not solid like other trees, but its centre is filled with pith, round which is a tough bark, full of strong fibres when young, which, as the tree grows old, hardens and becomes ligneous. To this bark the leaves are closely joined, which in the centre rise erect, but after they are advanced above the sheath that surrounds them, they expand very wide on every side the stem, and as the older leaves decay, the stalk advances in height. With its ever verdant and graceful crown continually aspiring towards heaven, it is an apt image of the soul growing in grace, Psa. 92:12. The leaves, when the tree has grown to a size for bearing fruit, are six to eight feet long, are very broad when spread out, and are used for covering the tops of houses, and similar purposes.

The fruit, from which the palm is often called the date-tree, grows below the leaves in clusters sometimes weighing over fifteen pounds, and is of a sweet and agreeable taste. The diligent natives, says Mr. Gibbon, celebrate, either in verse or prose, the three hundred and sixty uses to which the trunk, the branches or long leaf-stalks, the leaves, fibres, and fruit of the palm are skilfully applied. A considerable part of the inhabitants of Egypt, of Arabia, and Persia, subsist almost entirely on its fruit. They boast also of its medicinal virtues. Their camels feed upon the date stone. From the leaves they make couches, baskets, bags, mats, and brushes; from the branches or stalks, cages for their poultry, and fences for their gardens; from the fibres of the trunk, thread, ropes, and rigging; from the sap is prepared a spirituous liquor; and the body of the tree furnishes fuel; it is even said that from one variety of the palm-tree, the *phœnix farinifera*, meal has been extracted, which is found among the fibres of the trunk, and has been used for food.

Several parts of the Holy Land, no less than of Idumæa, that lay contiguous to it, are described by the ancients to have abounded with date-trees. Judea particularly is typified in several coins of Vespasian by a disconsolate woman sitting under a palm-tree, with the inscription, JUDÆA CAPTA. In Deut. 34:3, Jericho is called the "city of palm-trees;" and several of these trees are still found in that vicinity; but in general they are now rare in Palestine. Palm wreaths, and branches waved in the air or strown on the road, are associated not only with the honors paid to ancient conquerors in the Grecian games and in war, but with the triumphant entry of the King of Zion into Jerusalem, John 12:12, 13, and with his more glorious triumph with his people in heaven, Rev. 7:9.

PAL'SY, or paralysis, strikes sometimes one side or portion of the body, and sometimes the whole; affecting the power of motion, or the power of sensation, or both. It is one of the least curable of diseases; but the Saviour healed it with a word, Matt. 4:24; 12:10; Mark 2:3-12. The "withered hand," Mark 3:1, was probably an effect of the palsy. There is also a palsy of the soul, which the Great Physician can heal, and he alone.

PAMPHYL'IA, a province of Asia Minor, having Cilicia east, Lycia west, Pisidia north, and the Mediterranean south. It is opposite to Cyprus, and the sea between the coast and the island is called the "sea of Pamphylia." The chief city of Pamphylia was Perga, where Paul and Barnabas preached, Acts 13:13; 14:24.

PAN'NAG, in Ezek. 27:17, is the Hebrew word for some unknown product of Palestine, which the Jews sold to the Tyrians. It is variously understood to mean millet, sweetmeats, a delicate spice, etc.

PA'PER, PAP'YRUS. See BOOK.

PA'PHOS, a maritime city on the western extremity of the isle of Cyprus. It had a tolerable harbor, and was the station of a Roman proconsul. About sixty furlongs from the city was the celebrated temple of Venus, who was hence often called the "Paphian goddess." The infamous rites in honor of this goddess continued to be practised hundreds of years after Paul and Barnabas introduced the gospel here, though their labors were blessed with some fruits, Acts 13:6-13. See ELYMAS.

PAR'ABLE, derived from a Greek word which signifies, to compare things together, to form a parallel or similitude of them with other things. What we call the Proverbs of Solomon, which are moral maxims and sentences, the Greeks call the Parables of Solomon. In like manner, when Job answers his friends, it is said he took up his "parable," Job 27:1; 29:1. In the New Testament the word parable denotes sometimes a true history, or an illustrative sketch from nature; sometimes a proverb or adage, Luke 4:23; a truth darkly or figuratively expressed, Matt. 15:15; a type, Heb. 9:9; or a similitude, Matt. 24:32. The parabolical, enigmatical, figurative, and sententious way of speaking, was the language of the Eastern sages and learned men, Psa. 49:4; 78:2; and nothing was more insupportable than to hear a fool utter parables, Prov. 26:7.

The prophets employed parables the more strongly to impress prince and people with their threatenings or their promises. Nathan reproved David under the parable of a rich man who had taken away and killed the lamb of a poor man, 2 Sam. 12. See also Judg. 9:7-15; 2 Kin. 14:9, 10. Our Saviour frequently addressed the people in parables, thereby verifying the prophecy of Isaiah, 6:9, that the people should see without knowing, and hear without understanding, in the midst of instructions. This result, however, only proved how inveterate were their hardness of heart and blindness of mind; for in no other way could he have offered them instruction more invitingly, clearly, or forcibly, than by this beautiful and familiar mode. The Hebrew writers made great use of it; and not only the Jews, but the Arabs, Syrians, and all the nations of the East were and still are admirers of this form of discourse.

In the interpretation of a parable, its primary truth and main scope are chiefly to be considered. The minute particulars are less to be regarded than in a sustained allegory; and serious errors are occasioned by pressing every detail, and inventing for it some spiritual analogy.

The following parables of our Lord are recorded by the evangelists.

Wise and foolish builders, Matt. 7:24–27.
Children of the bride-chamber, Matt. 9:15.
New cloth and old garment, Matt. 9:16.
New wine and old bottles, Matt. 9:17.
Unclean spirit, Matt. 12:43.
Sower, Matt. 13:3, 18; Luke 8:5, 11.
Tares, Matt. 13:24–30, 36–43.
Mustard-seed, Matt. 13:31, 32; Luke 13:19.
Leaven, Matt. 13:33.
Treasure hid in a field, Matt. 13:44.
Pearl of great price, Matt. 13:45–46.
Net cast into the sea, Matt. 13:47–50.
Meats defiling not, Matt. 15:10–15.
Unmerciful servant, Matt. 18:23–35.
Laborers hired, Matt. 20:1–16.
Two sons, Matt. 21:28–32.
Wicked husbandmen, Matt. 21:33–45.
Marriage-feast, Matt. 22:2–14.
Fig-tree leafing, Matt. 24:32–34.
Man of the house watching, Matt. 24:43.
Faithful and evil servants, Matt. 24:45–51.
Ten virgins, Matt. 25:1–13.
Talents, Matt. 25:14–30.
Kingdom divided against itself, Mark 3:24.
House divided against itself, Mark 3:25.
Strong man armed, Mark 3:27; Luke 11:21.
Seed growing secretly, Mark 4:26–29.
Lighted candle, Mark 4:21; Luke 11:33–36.
Man taking a far journey, Mark 13:34–37.
Blind leading the blind, Luke 6:39.
Beam and mote, Luke 6:41, 42.
Tree and its fruit, Luke 6:43–45.
Creditor and debtors, Luke 7:41–47.
Good Samaritan, Luke 10:30–37.
Importunate friend, Luke 11:5–9.
Rich fool, Luke 12:16–21.
Cloud and wind, Luke 12:54–57.
Barren fig-tree, Luke 13:6–9.
Men bidden to a feast, Luke 14:7–11.
Builder of a tower, Luke 14:28–30, 33.
King going to war, Luke 14:31–33.
Savor of salt, Luke 14:34, 35.
Lost sheep, Luke 15:3–7.
Lost piece of silver, Luke 15:8–10.
Prodigal son, Luke 15:11–32.
Unjust steward, Luke 16:1–8.
Rich man and Lazarus, Luke 16:19–31.
Importunate widow, Luke 18:1–8.
Pharisee and publican, Luke 18:9–14.
Pounds, Luke 19:12–27.
Good shepherd, John 10:1–6.
Vine and branches, John 15:1–5.

PAR'ADISE, a Greek word signifying a park, or garden with trees. The Hebrew word GAN, *garden*, is used in a similar way, Neh. 2:8; Eccl. 2:5; Song 4:13.

The Septuagint uses the word Paradise when speaking of the garden of Eden, in which the Lord placed Adam and Eve. This famous garden is indeed commonly known by the name of "the terrestrial paradise," and there is hardly any part of the world in which it has not been sought. See EDEN.

In the New Testament, "paradise" is put, in allusion to the paradise of Eden, for the place where the souls of the blessed enjoy happiness. Thus our Saviour tells the penitent thief on the cross, "To-day shalt thou be with me in paradise;" that is, in the state of the blessed, Luke 23:43. Paul, speaking of himself in the third person, says, "I knew a man that was caught up into paradise, and heard unspeakable words, which it is not lawful for a man to utter," 2 Cor. 12:4. And in Rev. 2:7; 22:14, the natural features of the scene where innocence and bliss were lost, are used to depict the world where these are restored perfectly and for ever.

PA'RAN, or EL-PARAN, Gen. 14:6, a large tract of desert country lying south of Palestine, and west of the valley El Arabah, which runs from the Dead sea to the gulf of Akaba. It was in and near this desert region that the Israelites wandered thirty-eight years. See EXODUS. It extended on the south to within three days' journey of Sinai, Num. 10:12, 33; 12:16, if not to Sinai itself, Deut. 33:2; Hab. 3:3. On the north, it included the deserts of Kadesh and Zin, Num. 13:3, 21, 27. Here Hagar and Ishmael dwelt, Gen. 21:14, 21; and hither David, and afterwards Hadad, retired for a time, 1 Sam. 25:1; 1 Kin. 11:18. Burckhardt found it a dreary expanse of calcareous soil, covered with black flints. Some cities and cultivated grounds, however, and considerable patches of pasture lands, were anciently found in this region. The north-east part is traversed from east to west by ranges of hills.

PARCHED GROUND, in Isa. 35:7, translated by Lowth "the glowing sand," by Henderson "the vapory illusion," and in German *sand-meer* and *wasserschein*, sand-sea and water-show, is understood to refer to the *mirage*, an optical illusion described by almost all travellers in tropical deserts. The inexperienced wanderer sees at a distance what he thinks is a beautiful sheet of water; and imagination clothes the farther shore with herbage, shrubbery, buildings, etc.; but on hasting towards it he finds the delightful vision recede and at length disappear, and nothing remains but the hot sands. Quintus Curtius long ago gave an account of this wonder in his Life of Alexander the Great. It is thus described in St. John's "Egypt and Nubia:"

"I had been riding along in a revery, when chancing to raise my head, I thought I perceived, desertwards, a dark strip on the far horizon. What could it be? My companion, who had very keen sight, was riding in advance of me, and with a sudden exclamation, he pulled up his dromedary, and gazed in the same direction. I called to him, and asked him what he thought of yonder strip, and whether he could make out any thing in it distinctly. He answered, that water had all at once appeared there; that he saw the motion of the waves, and tall palms and other trees bending up and down over them, as if tossed by a strong wind. This, then, was the mirage. My companion galloped towards it, and we followed him, though the Arabs tried to prevent us; and ere long I could with my own eyes discern something of this strange phenomenon. It was, as my friend had reported, a broad sheet of water, with fresh green trees along its banks; and yet there was nothing actually before us but parched yellow sand.

"Far as we rode in the direction of the apparition, we never came any nearer to it; the whole seemed to recoil, step for step, with our advance. We halted, and remained long in contemplation of the magic scene, until whatever was unpleasant in its strangeness ceased by degrees to affect us. Never had I seen any landscape so vivid as this seeming one; never water so bright, or trees so softly green, so tall and stately. We returned slowly to our Arabs, who had not stirred from the spot where we left them. Looking back once more into the desert, we saw the apparition gradually becoming fainter, until at last it melted away into a dim band, not unlike a thin mist sweeping over the face of a field."

The same phenomenon may be alluded to in the expression, "waters that fail," Jer. 15:18. It is ascribed to the unequal refraction of the rays of light, caused in some way by excessive heat. The Saviour and his proffered blessings are not, like earthly hopes, a deception and a mockery, but true waters of eternal life.

PARCH'MENT. See Book.

PAR'MENAS, one of the first seven deacons, Acts 6:5.

PAR'THIA is supposed to have been originally a province of Media, on its eastern side, which was raised into a distinct kingdom by Arsaces, B. C. 250. It soon extended itself over a great part of the ancient Persian empire, and is frequently put for that empire in Scripture, and other ancient writings. Parthia maintained itself against all aggressors for nearly five hundred years, and was not subjugated even by the Romans; but in A. D. 226, one of the descendants of the ancient Persian kings united it to his empire, and Persia resumed its former name and dynasty.

The Parthians were celebrated, especially by the poets, for a peculiarity of their mode of fighting on horseback, which consisted in discharging their arrows while they fled. They would seem to have borne no very distant resemblance to the modern Cossacks. It is said the Parthians were either refugees or exiles from the Scythian nations. Jews and proselytes from among them were present at Jerusalem at the Pentecost, Acts 2:9.

PARTI'TION, Eph. 2:14. See the various courts under Temple.

RED-LEGGED PARTRIDGE; PERDIX RUBRA.

PAR'TRIDGE, a well-known bird, three varieties of which are found in

Palestine. Saul's hunting of David like a partridge upon the mountain, 1 Sam. 26:20, may be illustrated by an occasional practice of the Arabs, who, observing that this bird becomes languid on being started several times in quick succession, at length rush suddenly in upon it and knock it over with their clubs. In Jer. 17:11, we may best render, As the partridge gathereth eggs which she hath not laid; the meaning being that she loses her toil, since the young birds, when hatched, forsake her.

PAR'VAIM, 2 Chr. 3:6, the region of fine gold; probably Ophir; or according to Gesenius, the East.

PASH'UR, I., the son of Immer, a priest and a chief officer in the temple; he violently opposed the prophet Jeremiah, and persecuted him even with blows and confinement in the stocks; but all recoiled on his own head, Jer. 20:1–6.

II. The son of Malchiah, an enemy of Jeremiah, and active in securing his imprisonment, Jer. 21:1; 38:1–6. Many descendants of this Pashur returned from captivity at Babylon, 1 Chr. 9:12; Ezra 2:38.

PASSION, Acts 1:3, *suffering;* the last sufferings and death of Christ. In Acts 14:15, James 5:17, "like passions" is nearly equivalent to "the same human nature."

PASS'OVER, Hebrew PESACH, Greek PASCHA, *a passing over*, a name given to the festival established and to the victim offered in commemoration of the coming forth out of Egypt, Ex. 12; because the night before their departure, the destroying angel, who slew the first-born of the Egyptians, *passed over* the houses of the Hebrews without entering them, they being marked with the blood of the lamb, which for this reason was called the Passover, Mark 14:12, 14, 1 Cor. 5:7, or the paschal lamb.

The month of the exodus from Egypt, called Abib by Moses, and afterwards named Nisan, was ordained to be thereafter the first month of the sacred or ecclesiastical year. On the fourteenth day of this month, between the two evenings, (see EVENING,) they were to kill the paschal lamb, and to abstain from leavened bread. The day following, being the fifteenth, reckoned from six o'clock of the preceding evening, was the grand feast of the Passover, which continued seven days, usually called "the days of unleavened bread," or "the Passover," Luke 22:1; but only the first and the seventh day were peculiarly solemn, Lev. 23:5–8; Num. 28:16, 17; Matt. 26:17. They were days of rest, and were called Sabbaths by the Jews. The slain lamb was to be without defect, a male, and of that year. If no lamb could be found, they might take a kid. They killed a lamb or a kid in each family; but if any family was not large enough to eat the lamb, they might associate another small family with them. The Passover was to be slain and eaten only at Jerusalem, though the remainder of the festival might be observed in any place. The lamb was to be roasted entire, and eaten the same night, with unleavened bread and bitter herbs; not a bone of it was to be broken; and all that was not eaten was to be consumed by fire, Ex. 12; John 19:36. If any one was unable to keep the Passover at the time appointed, he was to observe it on the second month; he that wilfully neglected it, forfeited the covenant favor of God; while on the other hand, resident foreigners were admitted to partake of it, Num. 9:6–14; 2 Chr. 30. The direction to eat the Passover in the posture and with the equipments of travellers, seems to have been observed only on the first Passover. Besides the private family festival, there were public and national sacrifices offered on each of the seven days of unleavened bread, Num. 28:19. On the second day also the first-fruits of the barley harvest were offered in the temple, Lev. 23:10.

Jewish writers give us full descriptions of the Passover feast, from which we gather a few particulars. Those who were to partake having performed the required purifications and being assembled at the table, the master of the feast took a cup of unfermented wine, and blessed God for the fruit of the vine, of which all then drank. This was followed by a washing of hands. The paschal lamb was then brought in, with unleavened cakes, bitter herbs, and a sauce or fruit-paste. The master of the feast then blessed God for the fruits of the earth, and gave the explanations prescribed in Ex. 12:26, 27, specifying each particular. After a second cup, with a second washing of hands, an unleavened cake was broken and distributed, and a blessing pronounced upon the Giver of bread. When all had eaten sufficiently of the food before them, a third cup of thanksgiving, for deliverance from Egypt and for the gift of the law, was blessed and drunk, Matt. 26:27; 1 Cor. 10:16; this was called "the cup of blessing." The repast was usually closed by a fourth cup and psalms of praise, Psa. 145:10; 136, etc.; Matt. 26:30.

Our Saviour partook of the Passover for the last time, with his disciples, on the evening with which the day of his crucifixion commenced, Matt. 26:17; Mark 14:12; Luke 22:7. The following day, commencing with the sunset three hours after his death, was the Jewish Sabbath, and was also observed as "a Passover," John 13:29; 18:28; 19:14, 31. Compare Matt. 27:62.

This sacred festival was both commemorative and typical in its nature and design; the deliverance which it commemorated was a type of the great salvation it foretold. The Saviour identified himself with the paschal lamb as its great Antitype, in substituting the Lord's supper for the Passover. "Christ our Passover is sacrificed for us," 1 Cor. 5:7; and as we compare the innocent lamb slain in Egypt with the infinite Lamb of God, the contrast teaches us how infinite is the perdition which He alone can cause to "pass over" us, and how essential it is to be under the shelter of his sprinkled blood, before the night of judgment and ruin overtakes us.

The modern Jews also continue to observe the Passover. With those who live in Palestine the feast continues a week; but the Jews out of Palestine extend it to eight days, according to an ancient custom, by which the Sanhedrim sent two men to observe the first appearance of the new moon, who immediately gave notice of it to the chief of the council. For fear of error, they kept two days of the festival.

As to the Christian Passover, the Lord's supper, it was instituted by Christ when, at the last Passover supper he ate with his apostles, he gave them a symbol of his body to eat, and a symbol of his blood to drink, under the form of bread and wine; prefiguring that he should give up his body to the Jews and to death. The paschal lamb which the Jews killed, tore to pieces, and ate, and whose blood preserved them from the destroying angel, was a type and figure of our Saviour's death and passion, and of his blood shed for the salvation of the world.

PASTOR, *shepherd*, one whose office it is to feed and guard the flock of Christ, Eph. 4:11; 1 Pet. 5:2. See SHEPHERD.

PASTURAGE. See SHEPHERD.

PATARA, a maritime city of Lycia in Asia Minor, at the mouth of the river Xanthus, celebrated for an oracle of Apollo, who was supposed to reside here during the six winter months, and the rest of the year at Delos. Paul, in passing from Philippi to Jerusalem, found here a ship for Phœnicia, in which he embarked, Acts 21:1.

PATE, Psa. 7:16, an obsolete word for head, or top of the head.

PATHROS, Isa. 11:11; Jer. 44:1, 15; Ezek. 29:14; 30:14, one of the three ancient divisions of Egypt, namely, Upper or Southern Egypt, which Ezekiel speaks of as distinct from Egypt, and the original abode of the Egyptians; as indeed Ethiopia and Upper Egypt really were. Its early inhabitants, called Pathrusim, were descendants of Mizraim, Gen. 10:14. See EGYPT.

PATMOS, an island of the Ægean sea, to which the apostle and evangelist John was banished by Domitian, A. D. 95, Rev. 1:9. It is a rocky and desolate island, about twenty-eight miles in circumference, with a bold and deeply indented shore; and was used by the Romans as a place of banishment for many criminals. It lies between Samos and Naxos, about forty miles west by south from the promontory of Miletus; and contains at present some four thousand inhabitants, mostly Greeks. Its principal port is a deep bay on the northeast side; the town lying on a high and steep hill, the summit of which is crowned by the old and castle-like monastery of St. John. Half way down the hill is a natural grotto, now covered by a Greek chapel, school, etc. In this cave, overlooking the sea and its islands towards his beloved Ephesus, tradition says that John saw and recorded his prophetic visions. The island is now called Patino; and the port Patmo, or San Giovanni di Patino.

PAUL, the distinguished "apostle of the Gentiles;" also called SAUL, a Hebrew name. He is first called Paul in

Acts 13:12; and as some think, assumed this Roman name according to a common custom of Jews in foreign lands, or in honor of Sergius Paulus, ver. 7, his friend and an early convert. Both names, however, may have belonged to him in childhood. He was born at Tarsus in Cilicia, and inherited from his father the privileges of a Roman citizen. His parents belonged to the tribe of Benjamin, and brought up their son as "a Hebrew of the Hebrews," Phil. 3:5. Tarsus was highly distinguished for learning and culture, and the opportunities for improvement it afforded were no doubt diligently improved by Paul. At a suitable age he was sent to Jerusalem to complete his education in the school of Gamaliel, the most distinguished and right-minded of the Rabbis of that age. It does not appear that he was in Jerusalem during the ministry of Christ; and it was perhaps after his return to Tarsus that he learned the art of tent-making, in accordance with a general practice among the Jews, and their maxim, "He that does not teach his son a useful handicraft, teaches him to steal," Acts 18:3; 20:34; 2 Thess. 3:8.

We next find him at Jerusalem, apparently about thirty years of age, high in the confidence of the leading men of the nation. He had profited by the instructions of Gamaliel, and became learned in the law; yielding himself to the strictest discipline of the sect of the Pharisees, he had become a fierce defender of Judaism and a bitter enemy of Christianity, Acts 8:3; 26:9-11. After his miraculous conversion, of which we have three accounts, Acts 9; 22; 26, Christ was all in all to him. It was Christ who revealed himself to his soul at Damascus, Acts 26:15; 1 Cor. 15:8; to Christ he gave his whole heart, and soul, mind, might, and strength; and thenceforth, living or dying, he was "the servant of Jesus Christ." He devoted all the powers of his ardent and energetic mind to the defence and propagation of the gospel of Christ, more particularly among the Gentiles. His views of the pure and lofty spirit of Christianity, in its worship and in its practical influence, appear to have been peculiarly clear and strong; and the opposition which he was thus led to make to the rites and ceremonies of the Jewish worship, exposed him everywhere to the hatred and malice of his countrymen. On their accusation, he was at length put in confinement by the Roman officers, and after being detained for two years or more at Cæsarea, he was sent to Rome for trial, having himself appealed to the emperor. There is less certainty in respect to the accounts which are given of Paul afterwards by the early ecclesiastical writers. Still, it was a very generally received opinion in the earlier centuries, that the apostle was acquitted and discharged from his imprisonment at the end of two years; and that he afterwards returned to Rome, where he was again imprisoned and put to death by Nero.

Paul appears to have possessed all the learning which was then current among the Jews, and also to have been acquainted with Greek literature; as appears from his mastery of the Greek language, his frequent discussions with their philosophers, and his quotations from their poets—Aratus, Acts 17:28; Menander, 1 Cor. 15:33; and Epimenides, Tit. 1:12. Probably, however, a learned Greek education cannot with propriety be ascribed to him. But the most striking trait in his character is his enlarged view of the universal design and the spiritual nature of the religion of Christ, and of its purifying and ennobling influence upon the heart and character of those who sincerely profess it. From the Saviour himself he had caught the flame of universal love, and the idea of salvation for all mankind, Gal. 1:12. Most of the other apostles and teachers appear to have clung to Judaism, to the rites, ceremonies, and dogmas of the religion in which they had been educated, and to have regarded Christianity as intended to be engrafted upon the ancient stock, which was yet to remain as the trunk to support the new branches. Paul seems to have been among the first to rise above this narrow view, and to regard Christianity in its true light, as a universal religion. While others were for Judaizing all those who embraced the new religion by imposing on them the yoke of Mosaic observances, it was Paul's endeavor to break down the middle wall of separation between Jews and Gentiles, and show them that they were all "one in Christ." To this end all his labors tended; and, ardent in the pursuit of this great object, he did not hesitate to censure the time-serving

Peter, and to expose his own life in resisting the prejudices of his countrymen. Indeed, his five years' imprisonment at Jerusalem, Cæsarea, and Rome arose chiefly from this cause.

The following chronological table of the principal events in Paul's life may be of use in directing and assisting inquiries into this most interesting portion of history. The different chronologies of Hug, Lardner, and Conybeare and Howson, are here presented side by side; and thus the table, while it shows the general agreement of chronologists, shows also that it is impossible to arrive at entire certainty in this respect.

	Hug.	Lard.	C. & H.
Paul's conversion, Acts 9. In the twenty-first year of Tiberius	36	36	36
He goes to Arabia, and returns to Damascus, Gal. 1:17; and in the third year escapes from Damascus, and visits Jerusalem, Acts 9:23-26, in the year	39	39	38
From Jerusalem he goes to Tarsus, Acts 9:30; and after several years of labor in Cilicia and Syria, Gal. 1:21, during which it is supposed most of the sufferings occurred which are mentioned in 2 Cor. 11:24-26, he went with Barnabas to Antioch in Syria, Acts 11:25, 26, where they labored during the year	44	43	44
From Antioch he is sent with Barnabas to Jerusalem, his second visit, to carry relief for the famine, and returns to Antioch, Acts 11:30	45	44	45
First great missionary tour, with Barnabas, from Antioch to Cyprus, Antioch in Pisidia, Iconium, Lystra, and Derbe; and returning through the same places and Attalia to Antioch, Acts 13:14, about two years, commencing	—	45	48
Third visit to Jerusalem, with Barnabas, to consult respecting circumcision, etc., and return to Antioch, Acts 15:2-30	53	50	50
Second missionary tour, from Antioch, through Cilicia, Derbe, Lystra, Phrygia, Galatia, Troas, Neapolis, Philippi, Thessalonica, Berea, Athens, and Corinth, Acts 15:35 to 18:1, where he finds Aquila	54	51	52
After eighteen months at Corinth, he makes his fourth visit to Jerusalem, by Cenchrea, Ephesus, and Cæsarea, and returns to Antioch, Acts 18:11-22, in	56	—	54
Third missionary tour, through Galatia and Phrygia, arriving at Ephesus, Acts 19:1, in	57	53	54
And after two years at Ephesus, going through Troas and Macedonia to Corinth, Acts 20:1	59	56	57
Fifth visit to Jerusalem, from Corinth, by Philippi, Troas, Miletus, Tyre, Ptolemais, and Cæsarea, Acts 20:3 to 21:15	60	58	58
After two years' imprisonment at Jerusalem and Cæsarea, he sails from Sidon, by Myra, Fair Havens, etc., to Malta, where he is shipwrecked; in the spring, he proceeds to Rome, Acts 21:17 to 28:16	63	61	61
Two years' imprisonment in Rome, and release, Acts 28:30	65	63	63
After laboring, as some think in Spain, Rom. 15:24, 28; also in Ephesus; Macedonia, 1 Tim. 1:3; Crete, Tit. 1:5; Asia Minor, 2 Tim. 1:15; and Nicopolis, Tit. 3:13, he is again a prisoner at Rome, joyfully awaiting martyrdom, though almost alone, 2 Tim. 2:9; 4:6-18	—	65	68

These various journeys of St. Paul, many of them made on foot, should be studied through on a map; in connection with the inspired narrative in Acts, and with his own pathetic description of his labors, 2 Cor. 11:23-29, wherein nevertheless the half is not told. When we review the many regions he traversed and evangelized, the converts he gathered, and the churches he founded, the toils, perils, and trials he endured, the miracles he wrought, and the revelations he received, the discourses, orations, and letters in which he so ably defends and unfolds Christianity, the immeasurable good which God by him accomplished, his heroic life, and his martyr death, he appears to us the most extraordinary of men.

The character of Paul is most fully portrayed in his epistles, by which, as Chrysostom says, he "still lives in the mouths of men throughout the whole world. By them, not only his own converts, but all the faithful even unto this day, yea, and all the saints who are yet to be born until Christ's coming again, both have been and shall be blessed." In them we observe the transforming and elevating power of grace in one originally turbulent and passionate—making him a model of manly and Christian excellence; fearless and firm, yet considerate, courteous, and gentle; magnanimous, patriotic, and self-sacrificing; rich in all noble sentiments and affections.

Epistles of Paul.—There are fourteen epistles in the New Testament usually ascribed to Paul, beginning with that to the Romans, and ending with that to the Hebrews. Of these the first thirteen have never been contested; as to the latter, many good men have doubted whether Paul was the author, although the current of criticism is in favor of this opinion. These epistles, in which the principles of Christianity are developed for all periods, characters, and circumstances, are among the most important of the primitive documents of the Christian religion, even apart from their inspired character; and although they seem to have been written without special premeditation, and have reference mostly to transient circumstances and temporary relations, yet they everywhere bear the stamp of the great and original mind of the apostle, as purified, elevated, and sustained by the influences of the Holy Spirit.

It is worthy of mention here, that an expression of Peter respecting "our beloved brother Paul" is often a little misunderstood. The words "in which" in 2 Pet. 3:16, are erroneously applied to the "epistles" of Paul; and not to "these things" immediately preceding, that is, the subjects of which Peter was writing, as the Greek shows they should be. Peter finds no fault, either with Paul, or with the doctrines of revelation.

The following is Lardner's arrangement of the epistles of Paul, with the places where they were written, and the dates:

EPISTLES.	PLACES.	A. D.
1 Thessalonians	Corinth	52
2 Thessalonians	"	52
Galatians	Corinth or Ephesus	end of 52 or beginning of 53
1 Corinthians	Ephesus	beginning of 56
1 Timothy	Macedonia	56
Titus	" or near it,	near end 56
2 Corinthians	"	about Oct. 57
Romans	Corinth	" Feb. 58
Ephesians	Rome	" April, 61
2 Timothy	"	" May, 61
Philippians	"	before end of 62
Colossians	"	" " 62
Philemon	"	" " 62
Hebrews	"	spring, 63

The arrangement of Hug is somewhat different; and some critics who find evidence that Paul was released from his first imprisonment and lived until the spring of A. D. 68, assign the epistles Hebrews, 1 Timothy, Titus, and 2 Timothy to the last year of his life. See TIMOTHY.

PAVE'MENT. See GABBATHA.

PEA'COCKS appear not to have been known in Palestine, until imported in the navy of Solomon, 1 Kin. 10:22; 2 Chr. 9:21. See TARSHISH.

PEARLS were ranked by the ancients among the most precious substances, Rev. 17:4, and were highly valued as ornaments for women. Their modest splendor still charms the orientals, and a string of pearls is a favorite decoration of eastern monarchs. The kingdom of heaven is compared to a goodly pearl, so superior to all others that the pearl merchant sold all that he had to secure it, knowing that he could obtain for it the highest price, Matt. 13:45, 46. The gates of heaven are described as consisting of pearls; "every several gate was one pearl," Rev. 21:21. The Saviour forbade his apostles to cast their pearls before swine, Matt. 7:6; that is, to expose the precious truths of the gospel unnecessarily to those who reject them with scorn and violence.

Pearls are a stony concretion in a species of oyster, found in the Persian gulf, on the coast of Ceylon, Java, Sumatra, etc., and in smaller quantities in various other places in both hemispheres. It is not known whether the pearl is a natural deposit, or the consequence of disease, or of the lodging of some foreign body, as a grain of sand, within the shells. The pearl-oyster grows in clusters, on rocks in deep water; and is brought up by trained divers, only during a few

weeks of calm weather in spring. The shell itself yields the well-known "mother of pearl."

PEEP, in Isa. 8:19, denotes the stifled, piping voice of necromancers.

PE'KAH, son of Remaliah, and general of the army of Pekahiah king of Israel. He conspired against his master, attacked him in the tower of his royal palace of Samaria, and having slain him, B. C. 758, he reigned in his place twenty years. In the latter part of his evil reign he formed an alliance with the Syrians of Damascus, and they attacked Ahaz king of Judah, who in turn sought the aid of Assyria. The result was, that Damascus was taken by Tiglath-pileser king of Assyria, and with it all the lands of Israel east of the Jordan and north of the sea of Galilee, their inhabitants being carried captive. Shortly afterwards Hoshea son of Elah conspired against Pekah, slew him, and reigned in his stead, 2 Kin. 15:25-38; 16:1-9; Isa. 7; 8:1-9; 17.

PEKAHI'AH, son and successor of Menahem king of Israel, was a wicked prince, and reigned but two years. Pekah, son of Remaliah, conspired against him, and killed him in his own palace, 2 Kin. 15:22-25.

PE'LEG, son of Eber, and fourth in descent from Shem. He was called Peleg, *division*, because in his time the earth was divided, Gen. 10:25; 11:16.

PEL'ETHITES are always mentioned together with the *Cherethites*, as constituting the king's body-guard, 2 Sam. 8:18; 22:23. The word, if not the name of a Jewish or a Philistine family, is supposed to signify *runners;* and thus they would seem to have been the royal messengers; just as the Cherethites, from a Hebrew word signifying *to cut off*, were the king's executioners. See CHERETHITES.

PEL'ICAN, Lev. 11:18, sometimes translated cormorant, Isa. 34:11; Zeph. 2:14; a voracious waterfowl, somewhat gregarious and migratory, frequenting tropical climates, and still found on the waters of Egypt and Palestine. It fully equals the swan in size, and resembles it in shape and color. Its plumage is of a grayish white, except the long feathers, which are black. Its great peculiarity is its broad, flat bill, fifteen inches long; and the pouch of the female under the bill, used for the temporary storage of food, and said to be able to hold fifteen quarts. When empty, this pouch is not seen; but when full, it presents a very singular appearance. The pelican is a dull, indolent, and melancholy bird; and its voice is harsh and dissonant, Psa. 102:6. Its Hebrew name is probably derived from its habit of emptying its pouch of the food stored in it, by compressing it against its breast. The young then receive their food from their mother's bill; and the current tradition that she tears her own breast to feed them with her blood, may have this origin. The pelican's bill also, terminating in a strong, curved, crimson tip and resting on the white breast, might seem to be tinged with blood.

PEN. The ancient pen was a stylus of hardened iron, Jer. 17:1, sometimes pointed with diamond, for writing on hard substances, like metallic plates; when waxen tablets were used, the stylus had one end made broad and smooth, for erasing errors, 2 Kin. 21:13. For parchment, cloth, and similar substances, a reed pen was used, or a fine hair pencil, with ink, Judg. 5:14; Job 19:24; Isa. 8:1; Jer. 36:23; 3 John 13.

PENI'EL, or PENU'EL, a town beyond the Jordan, and near the Jabbok; defended by a strong tower, which Gideon broke down because the men of Penuel refused to aid him against the Midianites, Judg. 8:8-17. It was restored by Jeroboam I., 1 Kin. 12:25. It received its name, *the face of God*, from Jacob's there wrestling with the Angel Jehovah face to face, Gen. 32:30.

PENIN'NAH, the second wife of Elkanah the father of Samuel. See HANNAH. Their story illustrates the evils of polygamy, 1 Sam. 1.

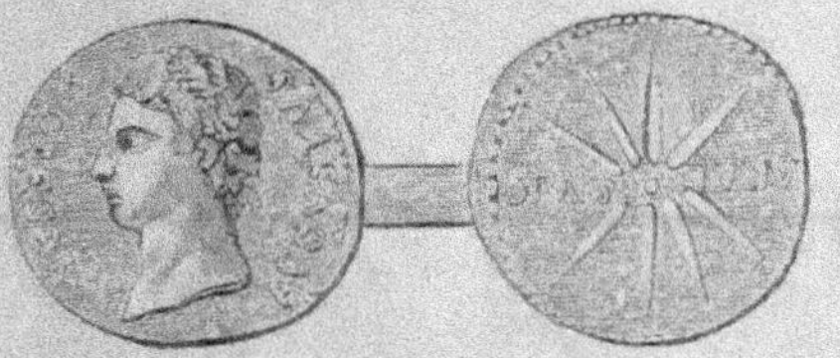

PEN'NY, the Greek drachma, or Roman denarius, equivalent to about fourteen cents. In reading the Scripture passages in which this word occurs, we should consider that the real value of money, to purchase labor or commodities, was far greater then than now; and also that even the nominal value of the drachma would be better expressed by "shilling," or "franc," than by "penny." Thus, "two hundred shillings' worth of bread would not suffice," Mark 6:37; "he took out two francs and gave them to the host," Luke 10:35. So in Rev. 6:6, "a measure of wheat for a penny" expresses to the English reader the idea of great plenty; whereas the original indicates a distressing scarcity. A drachma in Christ's time was good wages for a day's labor in a vineyard, Matt. 20:2.

PEN'TATEUCH, *the five books*, the books of Moses; that is, Genesis, Exodus, Leviticus, Numbers, Deuteronomy. See articles on those books, and also MOSES.

PEN'TECOST, *the fiftieth*, a feast celebrated the fiftieth day after the sixteenth of Nisan, which was the second day of the feast of the passover, Lev. 23:15, 16. The Hebrews call it the "feast of weeks," Ex. 34:22, because it was kept seven weeks after the passover. They then offered the first-fruits of their wheat harvest, which at that time was completed, Deut. 16:9, 10. These first-fruits consisted in two loaves of leavened bread, of five pints of meal each, Lev. 23:17. Besides this offering, there were special sacrifices prescribed for this festival, Num. 28:26-31.

The feast of Pentecost was instituted, first, to oblige the Israelites to repair to the temple of the Lord, and there acknowledge his dominion over their country and their labors, by offering to him the first-fruits of all their harvests. Secondly, to commemorate, and to render thanks to God for the law given from mount Sinai, on the fiftieth day after their coming out of Egypt. It was on the day of Pentecost, that the Holy Spirit was first poured out upon the apostles and the Christian church, Acts 2:1-3. On this occasion, as on the Passover seven weeks before, Judaism was at the same time honored and gloriously superseded by Christianity. The paschal lamb gave place to "Christ our Passover;" and the Jewish feast in memory of the giving of the law, to the gift of the Holy Spirit for "every nation under heaven," ver. 5. This gift was for the whole period of the gospel dispensation; and the mighty effects then produced foreshow the yet greater works the Spirit will perform in answer to prayer.

PE'OR, a mountain of Moab, from which Balaam surveyed the camp of Israel, Num. 23:28. It probably lay a few miles north-east of the Dead sea, but is not now recognized. This name and vicinity are also associated with an idol of the Moabites, Deut. 4:3. See BAAL.

PE'REZ-UZ'ZAH, 2 Sam. 6:8. See UZZAH.

PER'FUMES. The use of perfumes was common among the Hebrews and the orientals generally, before it was known to the Greeks and Romans. Moses also speaks of the art of the perfumer, in the English Bible "apothecary;" and gives the composition of two perfumes, of which one was to be offered to the Lord on the golden altar, Ex. 30:34-38, and the other to be used for anointing the high-priest and his sons, the tabernacle, and the vessels of divine service, Ex. 30:23-33. The Hebrews had also perfumes for embalming their dead. The composition is not exactly known, but they used myrrh, aloes, and other strong and astringent drugs proper to prevent infection and corruption. See EMBALMING, and OINTMENT.

PER'GA, a city of Pamphylia, Acts 13 : 13 ; 14 : 25. This is not a maritime city, but is situated on the river Cestrus, at some distance from its mouth, which has long been obstructed by a bar. It was one of the most considerable cities in Pamphylia; and when that province was divided into two parts, this city became the metropolis of one part, and Sidé of the other. On a neighboring mountain was a splendid temple of Diana, which gave celebrity to the city.

PER'GAMOS, now Bergamo, a city of Mysia, in Asia Minor, and the residence of the Attalian princes. There was here collected by the kings of this race a noble library of two hundred thousand volumes, which, after the country was ceded to the Romans, was transported to Egypt for Cleopatra, and added to the library at Alexandria. Hence the word parchment, from the Latin pergamentum, Greek pergamene; great quantities of this material being here used, and its manufacture perfected. Pergamos was the birthplace of Galen, and contained a famous temple of Esculapius the god of medicine, who was worshipped under the form of a living serpent. A Christian church was established here in the apostolic age, and was addressed by St. John, Rev. 1 : 11 ; 2 : 12. The modern city, called Bergamo, lies twenty miles from the sea on the north side of the river Caicus, and contains twelve thousand inhabitants. A large castle in ruins stands on the highest of three mountains which environ the town, and many remains of the ancient city still exist.

PER'IZZITES, Gen. 15:20, ancient inhabitants of Palestine, who had mingled with the Canaanites, or were themselves descendants of Canaan. They appear to have dwelt in the centre of Canaan, Gen. 34:30 ; Josh. 11:3 ; 17:15 ; Judg. 1:4, 5 ; but there were some of them on each side of the river Jordan, in the mountains, and in the plains. In several places of Scripture, the Canaanites and Perizzites are mentioned as the chief people of the country ; as in the time of Abraham and Lot, Gen. 13 : 7. Some remnants of this race existed in Solomon's day, and were subjected by him to a tribute of service, 1 Kin. 9:20. See CANAANITES.

PER'SIA, in Hebrew Paras, Ezek. 27 : 10, a vast region in Asia, the southwestern province of which lying between ancient Media on the north and the Persian gulf on the south, appears to have been the ancient Persia, and is still called Pharsistan, or Fars. The Persians, who became so famous after Cyrus, the founder of their more extended monarchy, were anciently called Elamites ; and later, in the time of the Roman emperors, Parthians. See PARTHIA.

The early history of the Persians, like that of most of the oriental nations, is involved in doubt and perplexity. Their descent is traced to Shem, through his son Elam, after whom they were originally named. It is probable that they enjoyed their independence for several ages, with a monarchical succession of their own ; until they were subdued by the Assyrians, and their country attached as a province to that empire. From this period, both sacred and profane writers distinguish the kingdom of the Medes from that of the Persians. It is not improbable that, during this period, petty revolutions might have occasioned temporary disjunctions of Persia from Assyria, and that the Persian king was quickly again made sensible of his true allegiance. When Media became independent, under Dejoces and then Phraortes, Persia became also subject to its sway, as a tributary kingdom. Media having vanquished her great rival Assyria, enjoyed a long interval of peace, during the reign of Astyages, son of Cyaxares. But his successor, Cyaxares the Second, united with the Persians against the Babylonians, and gave the command of the combined armies to Cyrus, who took the city of Babylon, killed Belshazzar, and terminated that kingdom 538 B. C.

Cyrus succeeded to the thrones of Media and Persia, and completed the union between those countries, which appear to have been in reality but two nations of the same race, having the same religion, (see MAGI and MEDIA,) and using languages near akin to each other and to the ancient Sanscrit. Previously to their union under Cyrus, Daniel speaks of the *law* of the Medes and Persians as being the same. The union was effected B. C. 536. The principal events relating to Scripture, which occurred during the reign of Cyrus, were the restoration of the Jews, the rebuilding of the city and temple, and the capture of Babylon, B. C. 539, Ezra 1 : 2. His dominion extended from the Mediterranean to the region of the Indus. Cambyses his successor, B. C.

529, added Egypt to the Persian realm, and the supremacy of Egypt and Syria was often in contest during subsequent reigns, Ezra 4:6. He was followed by Smerdis the Magian, B. C. 522, Ezra 4:7; Darius Hystaspis, B. C. 521, Ezra 5:6; Xerxes, the Ahasuerus of the book of Esther, B. C. 485; Artabanus, B. C. 465; Artaxerxes Longimanus, B. C. 464, Neh. 2:1; Xerxes II., B. C. 424; Sogdianus and Darius Nothus, B. C. 424; Artaxerxes Mnemon, B. C. 404; Artaxerxes Ochus, B. C. 364; Arses, B. C. 338; and Darius Codomanus, B. C. 335, who was subdued and slain by Alexander of Macedon, B. C. 330. In the seventh century Persia fell under the power of the Saracens, in the thirteenth it was conquered by Genghis Khan, and in the fourteenth by Tamerlane. Modern Persia is bounded north by Georgia, the Caspian sea, and Tartary; east by Affghanistan and Beloochistan; south by Ormus; and west by the dominions of Turkey. Its inhabitants retain to a remarkable extent the manners and customs of ancient Persia, of which we have so vivid a picture in Esther, Ezra, Nehemiah, and Daniel.

PER'SIS, a Roman lady, whom Paul salutes, Rom. 16:12, and calls his beloved sister.

PESTILENCE, or PLAGUE, in the Hebrew tongue, as in most others, expresses all sorts of distempers and calamities. The Hebrew word which properly signifies "the plague" is extended to all epidemical and contagious diseases. The prophets generally connect together the sword, the pestilence, and the famine, as three evils which usually accompany each other.

The glandular plague, which in modern times has proved so fatal in the East, is the most virulent and contagious of diseases. In the fourteenth century it overran Europe, Asia, and Africa, and 25,000,000 are estimated to have died of it within three years. Like the Asiatic cholera, it is one of the most appalling scourges sin has brought on this world; and may in this point of view correspond with the "plagues" referred to in the Bible, Ex. 9:14; 11:1; 1 Kin. 8:37.

PETER. This name in Greek signifies *a rock*, as does also the name Cephas in Syriac. Peter was one of the twelve apostles, and was also called Simon, Matt. 16:17, and Simeon, Acts 15:14. He was of Bethsaida, and was the son of Jonas, a fisherman, which occupation he also followed. After his marriage he resided at Capernaum, Matt. 8:14, Luke 4:38, though called at a later period to labor elsewhere as an apostle, and it would seem often accompanied in his journeys by his wife, 1 Cor. 9:5. When first introduced to Jesus by his brother Andrew, he received from Him the name of Peter, John 1:42, probably in reference to the boldness and firmness of his character, and his activity in promoting his Master's cause. He received his second call, and began to accompany Christ, at the sea of Galilee near his residence, and thenceforth learned to be a "fisher of men," Matt. 4:18-20; Luke 5:1-11. Many remarkable incidents are recorded in the gospels, which illustrate his character. Among these are, his attempt to walk on the water to meet Christ, Matt. 14:29; his avowal of the Messiahship and divinity of the Saviour, Matt. 16:16; his errors as to the design of Christ's incarnation, Matt. 16:22, 23; his warm attachment to the divine Teacher, John 6:67-69; his cutting off the ear of Malchus, John 18:10; his boastful determination to adhere to his Master under all circumstances, and his subsequent denial of Him with oaths, Matt. 26:74; Mark 14:29; John 13:37, 38; his poignant repentance, Matt. 26:75, and our Lord's forgiveness, after receiving an assurance of his love, which was thrice uttered as his denial of Christ had been, John 21:15-18. The death and resurrection of Christ, and the circumstances which accompanied them, led to a wonderful change in the apostle's mind, and thenceforward his bold and steadfast course is worthy of his name. On the day of Pentecost, he was one of the principal witnesses for the Saviour; in company with John he soon after healed a lame man at the temple gate, addressed the assembled crowd, was imprisoned, and fearlessly vindicated himself before the Sanhedrim, Acts 4:8-21. We find him afterwards denouncing the judgment of God on a guilty couple who had dared to lie to the Holy Ghost, Acts 5:1-11; visiting Samaria, and rebuking Simon the magician, Acts 8:5-24; healing Æneas and raising Dorcas to life at Lydda, Acts 9:32-43; seeing at Joppa a vision which prepared him to preach the gospel to the gentile Cornelius, Acts 10; imprisoned by Herod Agrippa, and delivered by an angel, Acts 12 : 3-19; and taking a part in the council at Jerusalem, Acts 15:7-11. The Bible gives us little information as to his subsequent labors; but it is probable that the three apostles who were most distinguished by the Saviour while upon earth continued to be favored as chief instruments in advancing his cause. Paul speaks of "James, Cephas, and John, who seemed to be pillars," Gal. 2:9. Yet in the same chapter we find him publicly reproving Peter for his wavering course in respect to the demands of Judaizing Christians, which he had been one of the first to repel at Jerusalem, Acts 15 : 9. He seems to have labored at Corinth, 1 Cor. 1 : 12; 3 : 22, and at Babylon, 1 Pet. 5 : 13. Papal writers affirm that he was the bishop of Rome. But the evidence is strongly against this assertion. Paul wrote to the Roman Christians, giving them directions and saluting the principal persons by name; he also wrote six letters from Rome; but in none of these letters, nor in the narrative in Acts, is there the slightest intimation that Peter was or had been at Rome. And as Peter never resided at Rome, he was never made the head of the church universal. Whatever honor and authority he received from Christ, in establishing the first institutions of Christianity and declaring what it enjoined and from what it released, Matt. 16 : 18, 19; the other apostles also received, Matt. 18 : 18; John 20 : 23; 1 Cor. 5:3, 5; Eph. 2 : 20; Rev. 21:14. There is no evidence that he had any supremacy over them, nor that he had any successor in that influence which was naturally accorded to him as one of the oldest, most active, and most faithful of those who had "seen the Lord."

Epistles of Peter. We have two epistles attributed to Peter by the common consent of the Christian church. The genuineness of the *first* has never been disputed; it is referred to as his accredited work by several of the apostolical fathers. It appears to have been addressed to Christian churches in Asia Minor, composed primarily of converted Jews and proselytes, but including many converts from paganism, 1 Pet. 4:3. It was written probably at Babylon on the Euphrates, 1 Pet. 5 : 13. See Babylon. Some, however, interpret this of Rome, and others of a petty town in Egypt called Babylon. The "fiery trials" through which the church was then passing are supposed to have been the persecutions in the latter years of Nero's reign, which terminated A. D. 68. Peter exhorts them to faith, obedience, and patience, in view of the truth of the gospel and the certainty of salvation in Christ.

The second epistle was addressed to the same persons as the former one; its general design being to confirm the doctrines which had been delivered in that, and to excite the Christian converts to a course of conduct becoming in every respect their high profession of attachment to Christ. This epistle was less confidently ascribed to the great "apostle of the circumcision," by the early church, than the first epistle. There is no sufficient ground, however, for doubting its canonical authority, or that Peter was its author, 2 Pet. 1:1, 18; 3:1. Compare also 1 Pet. 3:20; 2 Pet. 2:5. In many passages it resembles the epistle of Jude.

PHA'RAOH is properly an Egyptian word adopted into the Hebrew, and signifies *king;* so that when we find this name,* it means everywhere the king. Thus, also, Pharaoh Hophra is simply king Hophra. The above cut, from an Egyptian monument, represents a Pharaoh's daughter, probably Shishak's.

Of the kings of Egypt, there are not less than twelve or thirteen mentioned in Scripture, all of whom bore the general title of Pharaoh, except four. Along with this title, two of them have also other proper names, Necho and Hophra.

The following is their order. Some of them have been identified, by the labors of Champollion and others, with kings whose proper names we know from other sources, while others still remain in obscurity. Indeed, so brief, obscure, and conflicting are the details of Egyptian history and ancient chronology, that no name before that of Shishak can be regarded as identified beyond dispute.

1. PHARAOH, Gen. 12:15, in the time of Abraham, B. C. 1920. He was probably a king of the Theban dynasty.

2. PHARAOH, the master of Joseph, Gen. 37:36; 39–50; Acts 7:10, 13, B. C. 1728. Some suppose that the Pharaoh to whom Joseph became prime minister was the son of the one mentioned in Gen. 37:36.

3. PHARAOH, who knew not Joseph, and under whom Moses was born, B. C. 1571, Ex. 1:8; Acts 7:18; Heb. 11:23.

Very probably there was another Pharaoh reigning at the time when Moses fled into Midian, and who died before Moses at the age of eighty returned from Midian into Egypt, Ex. 2:11–23; 4:19; Acts 7:23.

4. PHARAOH, under whom the Israelites left Egypt, and who perished in the Red sea, Ex. 5–14; 2 Kin. 17:7; Neh. 9:10; Psa. 135:9; 136:15; Rom. 9:17; Heb. 11:27, B. C. 1491.

5. PHARAOH, in the time of David, 1 Kin. 11:18–22, B. C. 1030.

6. PHARAOH, the father-in-law of Solomon, 1 Kin. 3:1; 7:8; 9:16, 24, B. C. 1010.

7. SHISHAK, near the end of Solomon's reign, and under Rehoboam, B. C. 975, 1 Kin. 11:40; 14:25; 2 Chr. 12:2. From this time onward the *proper* names of the Egyptian kings are mentioned in Scripture. See SHISHAK.

8. ZERAH, king of Egypt and Ethiopia in the time of Asa, B. C. 930; called Osorchou by historians. See ZERAH.

9. SO, or *Sevechus*, contemporary with Ahaz, B. C. 730, 2 Kin. 17:4. See SO.

10. TIRHAKAH, king of Ethiopia and Egypt, in the time of Hezekiah, B. C. 720, 2 Kin. 19:9; Isa. 37:9. The *Tearcho* of Strabo, and the *Taracles* of Manetho. See TIRHAKAH.

11. PHARAOH NECHO, in the time of Josiah, B. C. 612. 2 Kin. 23:29, 30, etc.; 2 Chr. 35:20–24, etc. *Necho*, the son of Psammeticus. See NECHO.

12. PHARAOH HOPHRA, contemporary with Nebuchadnezzar. He was the grandson of Necho, and is the *Apries* of Herodotus. Zedekiah formed an alliance with him against Nebuchadnezzar, and he drove the Assyrians from Palestine, took Zidon and Tyre, and returned to Egypt with great spoil. He seems to have done nothing to prevent the subsequent destruction of Jerusalem, Jer. 37:1–5; 47:1; Ezek. 29–32. He reigned twenty-five years, and was dethroned by his army after an unsuccessful expedition against Cyrene, as was foretold, Jer. 44:30.

PHAR'ISEES, a numerous and dominant sect of the Jews, agreeing on some main points of doctrine and practice, but divided into different parties or schools on minor points; as for instance, the schools or followers of Hillel and Shammai, who were celebrated rabbins or teachers. The name is commonly derived from the Hebrew *pârash*, to separate, as though they were distinguished from the rest of the nation by their superior wisdom and sanctity. They first appeared as a sect after the return of the Jews from captivity. In respect to their tenets, although they esteemed the written books of the Old Testament as the sources of the Jewish religion, yet they also attributed great and equal authority to *traditional* precepts relating principally to external rites: as ablutions, fastings, long prayers, the distribution of alms, the avoiding of all intercourse with Gentiles and publicans, etc. See Matt. 6:5; 9:11; 23:5; Mark 7:4; Luke 18:12. In superstitious and self-righteous formalism they strongly resembled the Romish church. They were rigid interpreters of the letter of the Mosaic law, but not unfrequently violated the spirit of it by their traditional and philosophical interpretations. See Matt. 5:31, 43; 12:2; 19:3; 23:23. Their professed sanctity and close adherence to all the external forms of piety, gave them great favor and influence with the common people, and especially among the female part of the community. They believed with the Stoics, that all things and events were controlled by fate; yet not so absolutely as entirely to destroy the liberty of the human will. They considered the soul as immortal, and held the doctrine of a future resurrection of the body, Acts 23:8. It is also supposed by some that they admitted the doctrine of metempsychosis, or the transmigration of souls; but no allusion is made to this in the New Testament, nor does Josephus assert it. In numerous cases Christ denounced the Pharisees for their pride and covetousness, their ostentation in prayers, alms, tithes, and fasts, Matt. 6:2, 5, Luke 18:9, and their hypocrisy in employing the garb of religion to cover the profligacy of their dispositions and conduct; as Matt. 23; Luke 16:14; John 7:48, 49; 8:9. By his faithful reproofs he early incurred their hatred, Matt. 12:14; they eagerly sought to destroy him, and his blood was upon them and their children. On the other hand, there appear to have been among them individuals of probity, and even of genuine piety; as in the case of Joseph of Arimathea, Nicodemus, the aged Simeon, etc., Matt. 27:57; Luke 2:25; John 3:1. Saul of Tarsus was a Pharisee of the strictest sect, Acts 26:5; Gal. 1:14. The essential features of their character are still common in Christian lands, and are no less odious to Christ than of old.

PHAR'PAR, a river of Damascus. See in ABANA.

PHE'BE, or PHŒ'BE, a Christian woman of Cenchrea, the eastern port of Corinth, bearer of the epistle of Paul to the Romans, in which he commends her to their confidence and Christian love. She appears to have been a deaconess of the church, and to have had both the means and the disposition to do good abundantly. Paul says, "she hath been a succorer of many, and of me also," Rom. 16:1, 2. One who succors a faithful servant of Christ may thereby aid in the accomplishment of immeasurable good. The Holy Spirit presents the character and works of Phœbe as worthy of all imitation. Such mothers in Israel will be held in everlasting remembrance.

PHE'NICE, a city near the south coast of Crete, having a harbor, now called Lutro, opening to the south-east. Paul, on his voyage to Rome from Cæsarea, was unable to make this port, Acts 27:12.

PHENI'CIA, or PHENICE. See PHŒNICIA.

PHI'CHOL, apparently the title borne by the "captain of the host" of the king of Gerar, in the time of Abraham and Isaac, Gen. 21:22; 26:26.

PHILADEL'PHIA, a city of Lydia, in Asia Minor, where was one of the seven Asiatic churches, highly praised by Christ for its fidelity, Rev. 3:7-13. Philadelphia was so called from Attalus Philadelphus, king of Pergamos, by whom it was founded. It stood between the river Hermus and mount Tmolus, about twenty-eight miles south-east of Sardis. It suffered greatly by frequent earthquakes, and it was anciently matter of surprise that the city was not on this account abandoned. It is now a mean and ill-built town, of large extent, with a population of 12,000, including about 1,000 Greek Christians, who have a resident bishop and about twenty inferior clergy. There are five churches, and six mosques, one of which the native Christians believe to have been the church in which worshipped the primitive Christians whom John addressed.

PHILE'MON, a rich citizen of Colosse, in Phrygia, to whom Paul wrote an epistle, on occasion of sending back to him his servant Onesimus. Philemon, converted by the instrumentality of Paul, is exhorted to receive Onesimus as "a brother beloved." Paul was then a prisoner at Rome. His letter is universally admired for its delicacy, courtesy, and manliness. See ONESIMUS, and EPISTLE.

PHILE'TUS, a heretic, excluded from the church for denying the resurrection, and promoting infidelity, 2 Tim. 2:17, 18. See HYMENEUS.

PHIL'IP, I., THE TETRARCH, a son of Herod the Great, by his wife Cleopatra. In the division of Herod's kingdom, he was made tetrarch of Batanea, Trachonitis, and Auranitis, Luke 3:1. See HEROD I. From him the city of Cæsarea Philippi took its name.

II. HEROD PHILIP, another son of Herod the Great by Mariamne the daughter of Simon, not his favorite Mariamne. By Josephus he is called Herod. He lived a private life, having been disinherited by his father; and was the former husband of Herodias, Matt. 14:3. See HERODIAS.

III. THE APOSTLE, a native of Bethsaida, a disciple at first of John the Baptist, and one of the twelve who were earliest called to follow Christ, Matt. 10:3; John 1:43-48; Acts 1:13. He is several times mentioned in the gospels, John 6:5-7; 12:21; 14:8-10. Tradition says that he preached the gospel in Phrygia, and died at Hierapolis in Syria.

IV. The DEACON and EVANGELIST, Acts 6:5; 21:8; Eph. 4:11; a resident of Cæsarea, at least during one portion of his life, having four daughters who were endowed with the gift of prophecy, Acts 2:17; 21:8, 9. After the death of Stephen, when the Christians were driven from Jerusalem, except the apostles, he preached the gospel in Samaria with great success, and wrought many miracles. From the midst of these happy scenes he was called away to labor in a distant spot, with a single soul; but the gospel light was carried by the Ethiopian eunuch into the darkness of Africa, and is supposed to have there enlightened multitudes. In the narrative of Luke, Philip is incidentally distinguished from the apostles, Acts 8:1, 14, 16. He preached the gospel in the cities on the coast, from Ashdod to Cæsarea, where at a later period Paul and his companions were his guests for "many days," Acts 21 : 8–16. His subsequent history is unknown.

PHILIP'PI, a city of proconsular Macedonia, so called from Philip king of Macedon, who repaired and beautified it; whence it lost its former name of Dathos. It was constituted a Roman "colony" by Augustus, and as such possessed certain peculiar privileges, which made it a "chief city of that part of Macedonia." This expression, however, is supposed to mean, in Acts 16:12, that it was the first city the traveller met after landing at its port Neapolis, from which it lay ten miles north-west on an extensive plain. Here was fought the celebrated battle in which Brutus and Cassius were overthrown by Octavius and Antony, B. C. 42. Here, too, Paul first preached the gospel on the continent of Europe, A. D. 52, having been led hither from Troas by a heavenly vision. The first convert was Lydia; and the church which at once sprang up here was characterized by the distinguished traits of this generous and true-hearted Christian woman. Having cast out a spirit of divination from a young damsel here, Paul and Silas were seized and cruelly scourged and imprisoned. But their bonds were miraculously loosed, their jailor converted, and they permitted to pass on to Amphipolis. Luke appears to have remained here, and to have rejoined Paul when he again visited Philippi on his fifth journey to Jerusalem, A. D. 58, Acts 16 : 8–40; 20 : 3–6. The site is now strown with ruins.

Paul's EPISTLE TO THE PHILIPPIANS, written during his first imprisonment at Rome, A. D. 62, gratefully and warmly acknowledges the receipt of their gift by the hand of Epaphroditus, and their continued affection towards him; also their irreproachable Christian walk, and their firmness under persecution, Phil. 1 : 7, 28, 29; 2:12; 4:10–15. See also 2 Cor. 8:1, 2.

PHILIS'TINES, a celebrated people, who inhabited the southern seacoast of Canaan, which from them took the name of Philistia, Psa. 60 : 8; 108:9, or Palestine. They seem originally to have migrated from Egypt to Caphtor, by which some understand Crete, and others with the ancients Cappadocia, Gen. 10 : 14, and thence to have passed over to Palestine under the name of Caphtorim, where they drove out the Avim, who dwelt from Hazerim to Azzah, that is, Gaza, and dwelt in their stead, Deut. 2 : 23. The country they inhabited lay between the higher land of Judea and the Mediterranean, and was in the main a level and fertile territory. It resembles our own western prairies; and bears splendid crops year after year, though miserably cultivated and never manured.

The Philistines were a powerful people in Palestine, even in Abraham's time, B. C. 1900, for they had then kings and considerable cities, Gen. 20 : 2; 21 : 32; Ex. 13 : 17. They are not enumerated among the nations devoted to extermination with the seed of Canaan. Joshua, however, did not hesitate to attack them by command from the Lord, because they possessed various districts promised to Israel. But these conquests must have been ill-maintained, since under the judges, at the time of Saul, and at the beginning of the reign of David, the Philistines had their own kings and lords. Their state was divided into five little principalities, at the head of each of which was a "lord," namely, Gaza, Ashkelon, Ashdod, Gath, and Ekron—and they oppressed Israel during the government of the high-priest Eli, that of Samuel, and during the reign of Saul, for about one hundred and twenty years. Shamgar, Samson, Samuel, and Saul opposed them, and were victorious over them with great slaughter, at various times, but did not destroy their power, Judg. 3:14; 1 Sam. 4; 7; 14; 31. They maintained their independence till David subdued them, 2 Sam. 5 : 17; 8, from which time they continued in subjection to the kings of Judah, down to the reign of Jehoram, son of Jehoshaphat, when they revolted, 2 Chr. 21 : 16. Jehoram made war against them, and probably reduced them to obedience; for it is observed that they revolted again from Uzziah, who kept them under his sway during his whole reign, 2 Chr. 26:6, 7. During the unfortunate reign of Ahaz, the Philistines made great havoc in the territory of Judah; but his son and successor Hezekiah again subdued them, 2 Chr. 28 : 18; 2 Kin. 18 : 8. They regained their full liberty, however, under the later kings of Judah; and we see by the menaces uttered against them by the prophets Isaiah, Amos, Zephaniah, Jeremiah, and Ezekiel. that they brought many calamities on Israel, for which God threatened to punish them with great misfortunes, Jer. 47 ; Ezek. 25:15 ; Amos 1 : 6-8 ; Obad. 19 ; Zech. 9 : 5. See also Neh. 13 : 23. They were partially subdued by Esar-haddon king of Assyria, and afterwards by Psammetichus king of Egypt ; and there is great probability that they were reduced by Nebuchadnezzar, as well as the other people of Syria, Phœnicia, and Palestine, during the siege of Tyre. They afterwards fell under the dominion of the Persians ; then under that of Alexander the Great, who destroyed Gaza, the only city of the Philistines that dared to oppose him. They appear to have become entirely incorporated with the other inhabitants of the land under the Maccabees, and are no more mentioned as a distinct people. The ancient Philistines appear in sacred history as a warlike people, not strangers to the arts of life, Judg. 15:5 ; 1 Sam. 13 : 20 ; worshippers of Baal and Ashtoreth, under the names of Baal-zebub and Dagon ; having many priests and diviners, 1 Sam. 6 : 2 ; 2 Kin. 1 : 2 ; Isa. 2 : 6. They appear to have been of the race of Shem, their language being akin to the Hebrew, yet distinct from it, Neh. 13 : 24. Their land, once rich and covered with cities and towns, is now desolate, Zeph. 2:4-7.

PHILOS'OPHY, *love of wisdom*, in the New Testament means the vain and pernicious speculations of human reason ; the wisdom of this world, and "science falsely so called," 1 Cor. 1:18-27 ; 1 Tim. 6:20, in opposition to gospel truth. Paul cautioned the Colossians lest any man should spoil or plunder them through "philosophy," Col. 2:8 ; and it is one of the most melancholy proofs of the depravity of the human heart, that it has been able so to pervert that noble faculty, the reason. The loftiest human intellects have often been the blindest as to religious truth ; and the range and vigor of men's reasoning powers have been the measure, not of their knowledge and love of God, but of their pride, rebellion, and folly, Matt. 11 : 25 ; 1 Cor. 2 : 14 ; 3:18-20. In Athens, the Epicurean and Stoic philosophers made a jest of Paul's discourses ; and in many places of his epistles, he opposes the false wisdom of the age, that is, the pagan philosophy, to the wisdom of Jesus Christ, and the true religion, which to the philosophers and sophists seemed to be mere folly, because it was built neither on the eloquence nor the subtlety of those who preached it, but on the power of God, and on the operations of the Holy Ghost in the hearts and minds of believers ; and because it did not amuse and flatter man, but proved him a guilty rebel against God, in perishing need of a Saviour.

As there arose, under the influence of philosophy, several sects among the Greeks, as the Academics, the Peripatetics, and the Stoics, so also there arose among the Jews several sects, as the Essenes, the Pharisees, and the Sadducees. The Pharisees had some resemblance to the Stoics, the Sadducees to the Epicureans, and the Essenes to the Academics. The Pharisees were proud, vain, and boasting, like the Stoics ; the Sadducees, who denied the immortality of the soul, and the existence of spirits, freed themselves at once, like the Epicureans, from all solicitude about futurity : the Essenes were more moderate, more simple and religious, and therefore approached nearer to the Academics.

The danger against which Paul warned the church in his day still exists. Pride of intellect naturally allies itself with the atheism and impenitence of the heart, refuses to yield to the claims of revelation, and rejects whatever displeases its taste or rises above its comprehension. True wisdom, on the contrary, is humble and docile. "Whosoever shall not receive the kingdom of God as a little child, shall in no wise enter therein."

PHIN'EHAS. I., son of Eleazar, and grandson of Aaron the high-priest. His zealous and decided character was shown in the prompt execution of the profligate prince of Judah, and his companion a woman of Midian, in the plains of Moab, Num. 25. For this bold and timely service, the high-priesthood was secured to his family, also remaining faithful ; and except during an interval from Eli to Zadok, his posterity were at the head of the priesthood till the destruction of the temple. Phinehas led the host of Israel in the subsequent battle with the Midianites, Num. 31 : 6 ; Psa. 106 : 30, 31. He was at the head of the deputation sent to remonstrate with the tribes beyond the Jordan respecting the altar they had erected, Josh. 22:5–34. During the life of his father, he was superintendent of the Levites, Num. 3:32; and afterwards became the high-priest, Josh. 24:33, and as such communicated the will of God as to the punishment of the men of Gibeah, Judg. 20:28.

II. A son of Eli the high-priest. See HOPHNI.

PHŒNI'CIA, PHENICIA, or PHENICE, Acts 15:3, in its largest sense, designated a narrow strip of country extending nearly the whole length of the eastern coast of the Mediterranean sea, from Antioch to the borders of Egypt. But Phœnicia Proper was included between the cities of Laodicea in Syria and Tyre, and comprehended mainly the territories of Tyre and Sidon. Before Joshua conquered Palestine this country was possessed by Canaanites, sons of Ham, divided into eleven families, of which the most powerful was that of Canaan, the founder of Sidon, and head of the Canaanites properly so called, whom the Greeks named Phœnicians. Only these preserved their independence under Joshua, and also under David, Solomon, and the succeeding kings; but they were subdued by the kings of Assyria and Chaldea. Afterwards, they were successively subject to the Persians, Greeks, and Romans.

The Phœnicians were long renowned as a rich, cultivated, and powerful people. They were a confederacy of commercial cities, each of which with the adjacent territory was subject to its own king. Their coast was crowded with towns; and their fleets were the first to lose sight of the shores, traverse the whole Mediterranean, and establish their commerce and their colonies even on remote coasts of Europe and Africa. The productions of all known lands were exchanged in their markets, Ezek. 27. Carthage, the early rival of Rome, was a Phœnician colony; as were also Cadiz and Tarshish in Spain, Ezek. 38:13. Their language was almost identical with that of the Jews, and may be traced in the names of several Spanish cities. Solomon was indebted to them for aid in erecting the temple, and in building and navigating his ships. See TYRE. Their territory lay between the seashore and the summits of Lebanon; and being well watered and fertile, it produced at its various elevations a rich variety of agricultural products. Its inhabitants were worshippers of Baal and Ashtoreth.

At this day, Phœnicia is in subjection to the Turks, and belongs in the pashalic of Acre, not having had any national or native kings, or any independent form of government, for more than two thousand years. The name Phœnicia is not in the books of Hebrew Scripture; but only in the Maccabees and the New Testament. The Hebrew always reads Canaan, Isa. 23:11, margin. Matthew calls the same person a Canaanitish woman, 15:22, whom Mark calls a Syro-Phœnician, 7:26, that is, a Phœnician of Syria, because Phœnicia then made a part of Syria.

PHRYG'IA, an inland province of Asia Minor, bounded north by Bithynia and Galatia, east by Cappadocia, south by Lycia, Pisidia, and Isauria, and west by Mysia, Lydia, and Caria. It was called Phrygia Pacatiana, and also Phrygia Major, in distinction from Phrygia Minor, which was a small district of Mysia near the Hellespont, occupied by some Phrygians after the Trojan war. The eastern part of Phrygia Major was also called Lycaonia. This region was a high table land, fruitful in corn and wine, and celebrated for its fine breed of cattle and of sheep. Of the cities belonging to Phrygia, Laodicea, Hierapolis, Colosse, and Antioch of Pisidia, are mentioned in the New Testament. St. Paul twice travelled over it, preaching the gospel, Acts 2:10; 16:6; 18:23.

PHUT, or PUT, a son of Ham, Gen. 10:6, whose posterity are named with Cush and Ludim as serving in Egyptian armies, and as part of the host of Gog, Jer. 46:9; Ezek. 27:10; 30:5; 38:5; Nah. 3:9. In several of these passages Phut is translated Libyans. Josephus identifies them with the Mauritanians, in Northern Africa towards the west. See LIBYA.

PHYLAC'TERIES were little rolls of parchment, in which were written certain words of the law, and which were worn by the Jews upon their foreheads, and upon the left arm. The custom was founded on a mistaken interpretation of Ex. 13:9, 16, "And it shall be for a token upon thy hand, and for frontlets between thine eyes."

Leo of Modena informs us particularly about these rolls. Those worn upon the forehead have been described under the article FRONTLETS, which see. Those that were to be fastened to the arms were two rolls of parchment written in square letters, with an ink made on purpose, and with much care. They were rolled up to a point, and enclosed in a sort of case of black calf-skin. They then were put upon a square bit of the same leather, whence hung a thong of the same, of about a finger's breadth and a cubit and

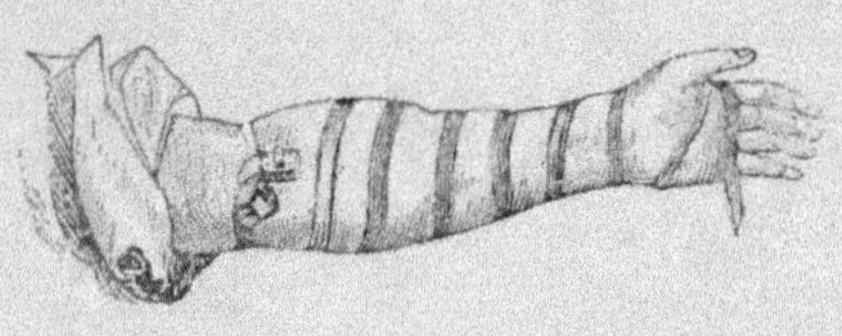

a half long. These rolls were placed at the bending of the left arm, and after the thong had made a little knot in the form of the letter Yodh (י,) it was wound about the arm in a spiral line, which ended at the top of the middle finger. They were called the Tephila of the hand.

The phylactery, from a Greek word signifying preservative, was regarded not only as a remembrancer of God's law, but as a protection against demons. It was probably introduced at a late period in the Old Testament history. Our Saviour reproaches the pride and hypocrisy of the Pharisees, shown in making their phylacteries broad as a sign of their superior wisdom and piety, Matt. 23:5. David, on the other hand, says, "Thy word have I hid in my heart, that I might not sin against thee," Psa. 119:11.

PHYSI'CIANS. The medical skill of the Egyptians was widely celebrated. Each physician confined his practice to diseases of a single class, and thus a large household would require the attendance of numerous physicians, Gen. 50:2. The Hebrews also had professional physicians, Ex. 21:19; Prov. 17:22; Matt. 9:12; Luke 4:23; 8:43. In the early ages they had little anatomical skill, partly on account of the ceremonial defilement caused by touching a corpse. They gave their attention to external rather than to internal injuries and diseases, Isa. 1:6; Ezek. 30:21; though they also prescribed for internal and mental disorders, 1 Sam. 16:16; 2 Chr. 16:12. They made use of salves, balms, and poultices, hyssop, oil baths, mineral baths, and river bathing, with many other remedies, Jer. 46:11. Many wickedly had recourse to amulets and enchantments.

PI-BE'SETH, a city of Egypt, called by the Greeks Bubastos, and containing a famous temple of the goddess Bubastis, who was compared to the Diana of Southern Europe. This temple was annually visited by immense multitudes. The ruins of Pi-beseth, on the eastern arm of the Nile near the ancient canal to Suez, consist of extensive mounds of bricks and broken pottery, Ezek. 30:17.

PIG'EONS. See DOVES.

PI-HAHI'ROTH, a place near the gulf of Suez, on its north-west side. It was the third and last encampment of the Hebrews, before crossing the Red sea, Ex. 14:2, 9; Num. 33:7. Its exact location cannot now be determined. See EXODUS.

PI'LATE, or PON'TIUS PI'LATE, was the fifth or sixth Roman procurator in the province of Judea, after the banishment of Archelaus. He was appointed A. D. 26, and continued in the province ten years, usually residing at Cæsarea. Pilate became odious both to the Jews and to the Samaritans for the severity and cruelty of his administration, Luke 13:1; and being accused by the latter before Vitellius, the governor of Syria, he was removed from his office and sent to Rome to answer to their accusations before the emperor. Before his arrival, Tiberius was dead; and Pilate is said to have been banished by Caligula to Vienna in Gaul, and there to have died by his own hand.

The character of Pilate is graphically described in the gospels. When Jesus had been condemned by the high-priest and the Sanhedrim, he was brought before Pilate the governor, without whose consent he could not be executed. Pilate saw in Jesus an innocent victim of Jewish malice, and desired to save him. Though dull and ignorant as to religious truth, he had some dim sense of the superiority of Christ's character, and feared to wrong him. All that he saw of Christ deepened this feeling; and he tried every method to soften the obduracy of the Jews. But he had not the firmness of character, the deep-rooted principle of justice, and the consciousness of rectitude necessary to carry him through; and after repeated efforts, Luke 23:7, 14-20; John 18:31, 38; 19:4-6, 9-12, 15, he at length gave way, and sacrificed a righteous man, rather than to provoke complaints against his administration and an investigation by the emperor. His washing of his hands, and his inscription upon the cross, only condemned himself. He would probably send a detailed report of his procedures to Tiberius; and the early fathers mention such an account as circulating in their day. The "Acts of Pilate," however, now in existence, are a subsequent fabrication. The Roman historian Tacitus, speaking of Christians, says, "The author of this name was Christ, who was capitally punished in the reign of Tiberius, by Pontius Pilate."

PIL'LAR sometimes means a monumental column, Gen. 35 : 20; 2 Sam. 18 : 18; or a column of cloud or smoke, Ex. 13 : 21; Judg. 20 : 40. The stately column which adorns and supports the front of a temple, Judg. 16 : 25–30; Job 9 : 6; 26 : 11, illustrates the position of prophets, Jer. 1:18, apostles, Gal. 2 : 9, believers, Rev. 3 : 12, and the church itself, respecting the truth, 1 Tim. 3:15.

PILLED, peeled, as a tree of its bark, Gen. 30:37.

PIL'LOWS were placed on the divans around an Eastern reception-room. The luxurious appliances mentioned in Ezek. 13 : 18, 19, were temptations to ease and voluptuousness; and emblems of similar soporifics for the conscience.

PINE, in Neh. 8 : 15, denotes some tree of a resinous nature. A different word in Isa. 41:19; 60:13, probably indicates the pine; a noble emblem of the promised prosperity of the church. Several varieties of pine abound upon mount Lebanon, the largest of which is the *sunobar kubar;* also found on several sandy plains of Palestine. Its wood is much used for beams and rafters.

PIN'NACLE, literally a wing; probably some part of the battlements on the outer wall of the temple, perhaps of Solomon's porch, accessible by stairs, Matt. 4 : 5, 6. Josephus describes a gallery constructed by Herod to overhang the deep valley of the Kidron, and says that the beholder on looking down from it would become dizzy. See TEMPTATION.

PIPE, a musical wind instrument, consisting of a tube with holes, like a flute or clarionet, 1 Sam. 10 : 5; 1 Kin. 1:40; Isa. 5 : 12; 30 : 29; Jer. 48 : 36; Matt. 9:23. The double pipe had two tubes, uniting in the mouth-piece; the tube played with the left hand emitting a few deep sounds, and serving as a base. The Scotch Deputation of Inquiry speak of overtaking among the hills of Judea "an Arab playing with all his might upon a shepherd's pipe made of two reeds. This was the first time we had seen any marks of joy in the land, for certainly 'all joy is darkened, the mirth of the land is gone,'" Isa. 24 : 11. See MUSIC.

PIS'GAH, a mountain ridge, the northern part of the Abarim range, east of the Dead sea; Nebo was one of its summits, Deut. 32:49; 34:1. It was in the southern part of the kingdom of Sihon, Num. 21:20; 23:24; and afterwards belonged to the Reubenites, Josh. 12 : 3; 13:20.

PISID'IA, a province of Asia Minor, separated from the Mediterranean by Pamphylia, lying on mount Taurus and the high table land north of it, and running up between Phrygia and Lycaonia as far as Antioch its capital. The Pisidians, like most of the inhabitants of the Taurus range, were an unsubdued and lawless race; and Paul in preaching the gospel at Antioch and throughout Pisidia, Acts 13:14; 14:24, was in peril by robbers as well as by sudden storms and floods in the mountain passes. Churches continued to exist here for seven or eight centuries.

PI'SON, one of the four rivers that watered Paradise, Gen. 2 : 11, 12, and which ran through all the land of Havilah, where excellent gold was found. It has, of course, been placed as variously as the garden of EDEN, to which article and EUPHRATES the reader is referred.

PIT, a reservoir, either natural or artificial, for water. Pits were sometimes used as dungeons, Gen. 37:20; Jer. 38:6; or being slightly covered, and baited, they served as traps to catch wild beasts, a device which illustrates the plots of designing men and women, Psa. 119:85; Prov. 22:14; 26:27; Ezek. 19 : 4. The word pit is also used to denote the grave, Psa. 28:1; 30:3, 9; and hell, Rev. 20:1

PITCH, Gen. 6 : 14, Ex. 2:3, translated "slime" in Gen. 11 : 3; 14 : 10, is properly bitumen or asphaltum, anciently found on and near the Dead sea, which was hence called the lake Asphaltites. It abounded in the vicinity of Babylon, and was used as fuel. The ark of Noah and that of Moses were rendered water proof by it; and the bricks of the tower of Babel were cemented with it. It is commonly found in a solid state; but being liquified by heat, and used as a mortar, it becomes as hard as the rocks it cements together. It is still thrown up by earthquakes from the bottom of the Dead sea, and floats to the shore sometimes in large masses. See SEA III.

PITHOM, one of the cities built by the children of Israel for Pharaoh in Egypt, during their servitude, Ex. 1:11. This is probably the Pathumos mentioned by Herodotus, which he places near Pi-beseth and the Pelusiac arm of the Nile, not far from the canal made by the kings Necho and Darius to join the Red sea with the Nile. See EGYPT.

PLAGUE. See PESTILENCE.

PLAIN. See CANAAN, and OAK.

PLAN'ETS, 2 Kin. 23:5. The Hebrew word means *inns* or *lodgings*, and is used with reference to the sun, denoting the twelve constellations of the zodiac, the houses of the sun in its annual apparent course round the heavens. These constellations are here spoken of as objects of idolatrous worship in Judah. Compare Gen. 37:9.

PLEDGE. The Jewish law protected the poor who were obliged to give security for a loan or the fulfilment of a contract. If a man pawned his robe, the usual covering for the cool nights, it must be returned on the same day, Ex. 22:26, 27. The creditor could not enter a house and take what he pleased; and the millstone being a necessary of life, could not be taken, Deut. 24:6, 10, 11. Compare Job 22:6; 24:3, 7. Idolaters sometimes disregarded these prohibitions, Amos 2:6-8. See LOANS. Pledges are necessary from the vicious, who cannot be trusted, Prov. 20:16.

PLEI'ADES, a cluster of seven stars in the neck of Taurus, or the Bull, one of the twelve signs of the zodiac. The sun enters Taurus about the middle of April; and the appearance of the Pleiades, therefore, marks the return of spring, Job 9:9; 38:31; Amos 5:8.

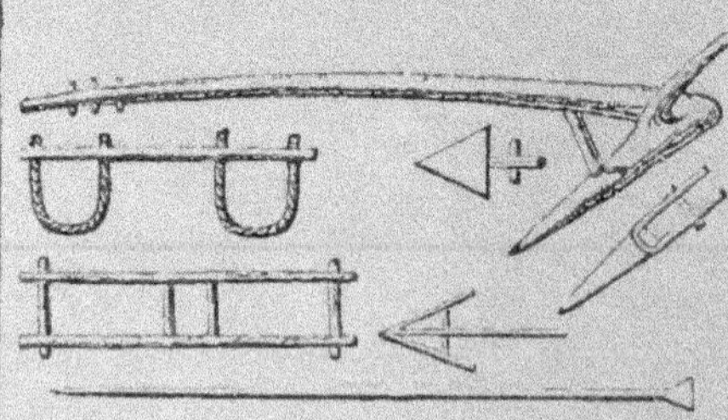

ANCIENT PLOUGH, YOKES, SHARES, AND GOAD.

PLOUGH, a slight and inefficient instrument in the East, but used from the earliest times, Gen. 45:6; Deut. 22:10; Job 1:14. See cut in MEROM. The plough now generally used in Syria consists substantially of but three parts: the beam or pole fastened to the yoke; the ploughshare; and the handle. The two latter parts, and even all three, are sometimes formed of a single branch of a tree with two limbs projecting in opposite directions. The ploughshare is

PLOUGHING AND SOWING; FROM AN ANCIENT EGYPTIAN PAINTING.

sometimes defended by a strip of iron, Isa. 2:4; Joel 3:10. As the handle was single, and with attention was easily managed by one hand, Luke 9:62, the ploughman brandished in the other a formidable goad, six or eight feet long, armed at the point with a pike, and at the heavy end, which was two inches thick, with a small iron spade for clearing the share from clay, Judg. 3:31; 1 Sam. 13:21; Acts 9:5. Ploughs were drawn by oxen, asses, and heifers, Deut. 22:10; Judg. 14:18; at this day camels and cows are also used in Palestine. Ploughing commenced soon after the autumnal rains had set in, towards the last of October.

POETRY OF THE HEBREWS. Of all the fine arts, poetry alone was cultivated among the Hebrews; and under the inspiration of the Almighty was carried to the highest degree of perfection. The poetry of this people was almost wholly lyric; whether didactic, elegiac, pastoral, or prophetic, it was still LYRIC. The essence of lyric poetry is the vivid expression of internal emotions. It is therefore subjective; in opposition to epic poetry, which treats of external objects, and is therefore objective. The chief subject of Hebrew poetry was religion, and then patriotism; which, under the theocracy, was very nearly allied to religion. The most obvious and striking characteristic of the poetry of the Hebrews is sublimity. Religious poetry was in ancient times almost peculiar to the Jews; the little that is found among other ancient nations is unworthy of comparison with it; as also is the Koran, which is an attempted imitation of the poetical parts of the Old Testament. The present prevailing views of the nature of Hebrew poetry were first developed by Bishop Lowth in his Lectures on the Poetry of the Hebrews.

Hebrew poetry differs from Hebrew prose in three respects: 1. In the peculiar poetical nature of the contents; of which the characteristics are sublimity, boldness, abruptness, lofty metaphors, personifications, etc. 2. In the peculiarities of the poetic dialect or diction, which, however, are not so striking as among the Greeks and Romans. 3. In rhythm, which differs from metre; the latter importing a measure of syllables or feet, the former a harmonious arrangement of words and members. It is the opinion of those best acquainted with the subject, that the Hebrews had no prosody, that is, no measure of syllables into poetic feet, as dactyles, trochees, and spondees. It is believed that the Hebrew poetry, much of which was designed to be sung or chanted, was characterized by a certain melodious flow and cadence which is now irrecoverably lost, together with the true pronunciation of the language.

But aside from this, the rhythm of Hebrew poetry consists in what is called its PARALLELISM, of which the fundamental principle is, that every verse must consist of at least TWO corresponding parts or members.

The parallelism of Hebrew poetry occurs either in the thought, or solely in the form. Of the former there are three kinds: namely,

1. Synonymous; where the two members express the same idea in different, but closely, and often literally, corresponding words: as for example,

What is man, that thou art mindful of him?
And the son of man, that thou dost visit him?
Psa. 8:4.

Why do the heathen rage?
And the people imagine a vain thing?
Psa. 2:1

He that sitteth in the heavens shall laugh;
The Lord shall have them in derision.
Psa. 2:4

Doth the wild ass bray when he hath grass?
Or loweth the ox over his fodder?
Job 6:5.

So also the song of Lamech, Gen. 4:23, and Job 7:1, etc.

2. Antithetical; where an antithesis of thought is expressed by corresponding members: as for example,

The house of the wicked shall be overthrown,
But the tabernacle of the upright shall flourish.
Prov. 14:11.

A soft answer turneth away wrath;
But grievous words stir up anger.
Prov. 15:1.

3. Synthetic; which is a mere juxtaposition; or rather, the thought is carried forward in the second member with some addition; the correspondence of words and construction being as before: as for example,

The law of the Lord is perfect, converting the soul:
The testimony of the Lord is sure, making wise the simple.
The statutes of the Lord are right, rejoicing the heart:
The commandment of the Lord is pure, enlightening the eyes.
The fear of the Lord is clean, enduring for ever.
The judgments of the Lord are true and righteous altogether.
Psa. 19:7, 8, 9.

Mere *rhythmical* parallelism is that in which no similarity or correspondence of thought exists; but the verse is divided by the *cæsura*, as it were, into corresponding numbers. This is the most imperfect species of parallelism, and may be compared with the hexameter, divided by the cæsura: as for example,

> Yet have I set my king
> Upon my holy hill of Zion.
> Psa. 2:6.

> Many there be which say of my soul,
> There is no help for him in God.
> Psa. 3:2.

This is most common in the book of Lamentations, where there is hardly any other species of parallelism.

Thus far we have had regard to the simplest and most perfect parallelisms of two members, such as are more usually found in the Psalms, Job, etc. But in the prophets and a few of the psalms, we find a less regular, and sometimes *compound* parallelism. Thus the parallelism is irregular when one member is shorter than the other; as Hosea 4:17:

> Ephraim is joined to idols;
> Let him alone.

Of *compound* parallelisms there are various kinds; as when the verse has three members either parallel with each other, as in Job 3:4, or two of them standing opposed to the third: as for example,

> For the ways of the Lord are right,
> And the just shall walk in them,
> But the transgressors shall fall therein.
> Hos. 14:9.

Or when the verse has four members, either compounded of two simple parallels, or the first line answering to the third and the second to the fourth, or all four nearly parallel to each other; as for example,

> The ox knoweth his owner,
> And the ass his master's crib;
> But Israel doth not know,
> My people doth not consider.
> Isa. 1:3.

> As the heaven is high above the earth,
> So great is his mercy towards them that fear him;
> As far as the east is from the west,
> So far hath he removed our transgressions from us.
> Psa. 103:11, 12.

> They have mouths, but they speak not;
> Eyes have they, but they see not;
> They have ears, but they hear not;
> Neither is there any breath in their mouths.
> Psa. 135:16, 17.

We may name Psalms 2 and 15 as affording examples of most of the species of poetic parallelism.

In the common manuscripts and editions of the Hebrew Bible, the members of the parallelisms in the poetical parts are not written or printed separately; but the accents serve to divide them. In other editions, however, the members are printed separately. It is matter of regret that this mode was not adopted in our English version; since in many cases the common reader has now no means of distinguishing whether what he reads is poetry or prose in Hebrew.

The preceding principles refer solely to the *rhythm* of Hebrew poetry. Besides this, there are other peculiarities; as for example, the *strophe*, as in Psa. 107, and in Psa. 42, 43, where verses 5, 11, and 5, are a burden or refrain, repeated at the end of each strophe. So also the *alphabetic* psalms and poems, (see LETTERS;) and the psalms of *degrees*, in which the chief words of each verse are taken up and repeated at the beginning of the next verse. See DEGREES.

More than a third of the Old Testament is poetry in Hebrew, including most of Job, the Psalms, Solomon's books, and the greater part of the prophets; technically, however, in the usage of the Jews, the three poetic books of the Old Testament are Job, Psalms, and Proverbs, which have a system of accentuation peculiar to themselves. Poetic fragments are also found here and there in the historical books, as in Gen. 4:23, 24; Ex. 32:18; Num. 21:14, 15, 18, 27-30; 23:7, 18; 24:3, 15. In the New Testament, also, many passages occur in which this Hebrew style seems to be transferred to the Greek, Matt. 8:20; Luke 1:46, 47; Rom. 11:33-35; Rev. 18; 19:1-3.

POLL, the head, Num. 2:47. To poll the head is to cut off the hair, 2 Sam. 14:25, 26; Ezek. 44:20

POL'LUX. See CASTOR.

POME'GRANATE, *grained apple*, the Punica Granatum of Linnæus; called also Malum Granatum, in French pomme granate, whence its English name. The tree grows wild in Persia and Syria, as generally in the south of Europe and north of Africa. It is low, with a straight stem, reddish bark, many and spreading branches, dark green lancet-formed leaves, and large and beautiful crimson blossoms. The fruit is of the size of an orange, of a tawny brown, with a thick, astringent coat, containing an abundance

of seeds, each enveloped in a distinct, very juicy, pink coat, whose flavor, in a wild state, is a pure and very strong acid; but in the cultivated plant, sweet and highly agreeable. The ripe pulp was eaten by itself, or with a sprinkling of sugar; or its juice was made into a sherbet. The value of the fruit and the beauty of the flower made the pomegranate welcome in gardens, Song 4:13; 6:7, 11; 8:2; Joel 1:12. It was abundant in Palestine, Num. 13:23; Deut. 8:8. Artificial pomegranates were used as ornaments on the robe of the high-priest, Ex. 28:33, and also as an architectural ornament, 1 Kin. 7:18.

POM'MELS, globular ornaments, affixed to the capitals of columns, 2 Chr. 4:12, 13.

PON'TUS, *the sea*, the north-eastern province of Asia Minor, bounded north by the Euxine sea, west by Galatia and Paphlagonia, south by Cappadocia and part of Armenia, and east by Colchis. It was originally governed by kings, and was in its most flourishing state under Mithridates the Great, who waged a long and celebrated war with the Romans, but was at length subdued by Pompey; after which Pontus became a province of the Roman empire. The geographer Strabo was born in Amasia, its capital; and one of its principal towns, Trapezus, still flourishes under the name of Trebizond. Many Jews resided there, and from time to time "went up to Jerusalem unto the feast," Acts 2:9. The devoted Aquila was a native of Pontus, Acts 18:2; and the gospel was planted there at an early period, 1 Pet. 1:1.

POOLS. See CISTERNS.

POOR, Psa. 12:5; 41:1-3, especially cared for in the Jewish dispensation, Ex. 23:6, Prov. 14:31, and even more so under the gospel, Matt. 25:42-45; Jas. 2:5. The slight offerings required of them by the law were as acceptable as the hecatombs of the rich, Lev. 5:7-13; Mark 12:41-44. The gleanings of the fields, the olive-trees, and the vines, were to be left for them, Lev. 19:9; Deut. 24:19; Ruth 2:2. Every seventh year, the spontaneous products of the ground were free to all, Lev. 25:7; and in the Jubilee their alienated inheritance returned to their possession. Compare also Lev. 25; Deut. 24. Neglect and oppression of the poor were severely reproved by the prophets, Isa. 10:2; Jer. 5:28; Amos 2:6; but charity to the poor was an eminent virtue among primitive Christians, Matt. 6:2-4; Luke 10:33-35; 19:8; Acts 9:36-39; 10:2; 11:29, 30.

POP'LAR, Gen. 30:37, Hosea 4:13, probably the white poplar, so called from the whiteness of the under side of the leaves. It is a beautiful and shady tree, common in Palestine and its vicinity. According to some, however, the storax-tree is intended.

PORCH. See HOUSE and TEMPLE.

POR'TERS kept the gates of private houses and of cities, 2 Sam. 18:26; 2 Kin. 7:10; Mark 13:34; John 10:3. The porters of the temple were Levites, at one period four thousand in number, divided into courses, 1 Chr. 16:42; 23:5. They stood on guard at every gate, and were on duty within the temple in their regular courses, 1 Chr. 26:1, 13, 19; 2 Chr. 8:14; 35:15. By night also they cheered the lonely hours with songs of praise, Psa. 134. We read, in 2 Cor. 23:2-19, of the faithful service they rendered in protecting Joash and slaying Athaliah.

POSSESSED'. See DEVIL.

POSTS, special messengers in the East, sent on occasions of importance, when they rode swiftly, and in many cases with fresh horses or dromedaries awaiting them at convenient distances, Esth. 8:10, 14. Job says, "My days are swifter than a post," Job 9:25. Foot-runners were also employed, 2 Sam. 18:22-27; and experienced runners will tire down and outrun a horse on long journeys. See FOOTMEN.

POT'IPHAR, a high officer of Pharaoh, who purchased Joseph of the Midianites, and made him master of his house, but afterwards imprisoned him on a false charge. He is supposed by some to have been the same "captain of the guard" who promoted Joseph in prison, Gen. 37:36; 39:40.

POTIPHE'RA, *belonging to the sun*, the priest of On, city of the sun, whose daughter Asenath was the wife of Joseph, Gen. 41:45. The name is found, in various forms, on ancient Egyptian monuments.

POTS, Job 41:20, applied in Scripture to a great variety of domestic vessels, of earthenware, iron, brass, and gold, used for cooking and serving food, etc., Judg. 6:19; 2 Kin. 4:40; Psa. 58:9; Eccl. 7:5; Heb. 9:4. In Psa. 68:13, "though ye have lain among the pots," the Hebrew word means originally cattle-folds; and in Psa. 81:6, "his hands were delivered from the pots," it refers to the baskets used by the Hebrews in the hard service exacted of them in Egypt, Ex. 1:14.

POTSHERDS, broken pieces of earthenware, Job 2:8, Isa. 30:14, fit types of the worthlessness and fragility of man, Psa. 22:15; Prov. 26:23; Isa. 45:9. The ruins of many of the most ancient cities in the world show little but such fragments of pottery covering the ground: it is usually coarse in grain, but well glazed. Such fragments are used by the poor in various ways, if not utterly broken into bits, Isa. 30:14. At this day it is common to find pieces of broken jars at eastern wells and pools, to drink from, and to see hot embers and coals carried in them from one spot to another.

POTTAGE. See Edom and Food.

POTTER, a maker of earthenware, Gen. 24:14, 15; Judg. 7:16, 19; Psa. 2:9. Ancient Egyptian paintings represent the potter turning and shaping, on his small and simple wheel made to revolve rapidly by the foot, the lump of clay which he had previously kneaded with his feet. A pan of water stands by his side, with which he kept the clay moist. After the body of the vessel was worked into shape and beauty, the handle was affixed to it, devices traced upon it, and after drying a little, it was carefully taken to the oven and baked. The potter's control over the clay illustrates the sovereignty of God, who made us of clay, and forms and disposes of us as he deems good: "O house of Israel, cannot I do with you as this potter? saith the Lord. Behold, as the clay is in the pot-

ter's hand, so are ye in my hand, saith the Lord," Jer. 18:1-6. "Shall the thing formed say to him that formed it, Why hast thou made me thus? Hath not the potter power over the clay, of the same lump to make one vessel unto honor and another unto dishonor?" Rom. 9:20, 21.

POTTER'S FIELD. See Aceldama.

POUND, a weight, and a sum of money, put, in the Old Testament, 1 Kings 10:17, Ezra 2:69, Neh. 7:71, for the Hebrew maneh, which see; and in the New Testament, for the Attic mina, which was equivalent to one hundred drachmæ, or about fourteen dollars.

POWER. For the use of this word in 1 Cor. 11:10, see Veil.

PRAYER is the offering of the emotions and desires of the soul to God, in the name and through the mediation of our Lord and Saviour Jesus Christ. It is the communion of the heart with God through the aid of the Holy Spirit, and is to the Christian the very life of the soul. Without this filial spirit, no one can be a Christian, Job 21:15; Psa. 10:4.

In all ages God has delighted in the prayers of his saints. From the promulgation of the law, the Hebrews did not intermit public worship daily in the tabernacle or the temple. It consisted in offering the evening and morning sacrifices, every day, accompanied with prayers by the priests and Levites in that holy edifice. Every day also the priests offered sacrifices, incense, offerings, and first-fruits for individuals; they performed ceremonies for the redemption of the first-born, or for purification from pollutions; in a word, the people came thither from all parts to discharge their vows and to perform their devotions, not only on great and solemn days, but also on ordinary days: but nothing of this was performed without prayer, 1 Chr. 23:30; Neh. 11:17; Luke 1:10. Compare also 1 Kin. 8:22, and the Psalms of David for temple worship.

Pious men were accustomed to pray thrice in the day, at fixed hours, Psa. 55:7; Dan. 6:10. See HOURS. Social, family, and secret prayer were all habitual with Bible saints; as well as brief ejaculations in the midst of their ordinary business, Neh. 2:4. No uniform posture in prayer is enjoined in the Bible; standing with the hands outspread, 1 Kin. 8:22, bowing the head, Gen. 24:26, kneeling, Luke 22:41, and prostration on the ground, Matt. 26:39, were all practised. Prayer should be offered with submission to God's will, fervently, perseveringly, and with a confiding reliance on God in Christ; it should be accompanied by humble confession and hearty thanksgiving, and with supplications for all living men, as well as for our friends and those nearest to us. Habitual prayer to God is a duty enjoined upon us by sound reason and by right affections; and he who lives without it thereby reveals the atheism of his heart. God requires all men thus to worship him, Ezek. 36:37; Matt. 7:1-11; Phil. 4:6; 1 Tim. 2:1-3; Jas. 1:5; and for neglecting this duty there can be no sufficient excuse. It is often said that prayer cannot alter the unchangeable purposes of God; but the great scheme of his providence embraces every prayer that shall be offered, as well as the answer it shall receive. It is objected that prayer cannot increase his knowledge of our wants, nor his readiness to supply them; and that in any case he will do what is for the best. But he deems it best to grant many blessings in answer to prayer, which otherwise he would withhold; "He will be very gracious unto thee at the voice of thy cry; when he shall hear it, he will answer thee." The words of David will be those of every truly praying man: "This poor man cried, and the Lord heard him, and delivered him out of all his troubles," Psa. 34:6.

False and formal religion makes a merit of its prayers, as though "much speaking" and "vain repetitions" could atone for heartlessness. Hypocrites also are wont to pray chiefly that they may have praise of men. These sins Christ reproves in Matt. 6:5-15, and gives to his disciples the form of the Lord's prayer as a beautiful model. In Eph. 6:18; 1 Thess. 5:17; 1 Tim. 2:8, Paul directs that believers should pray in all places and at all times, lifting up pure hands towards heaven, and blessing God for all things, whether in eating, drinking, or whatever they do; and that every thing be done to the glory of God, 1 Cor. 10:31. In a word, our Saviour has recommended to us to pray without ceasing, Luke 18:1; 21:36.

PREACHING, the public and oral inculcation of the truths of religion, especially of the gospel of Christ, Isa. 61:1; Acts 8:4; 2 Cor. 5:20; Eph. 3:8. Public instruction in religion was no doubt given in the earliest ages. Enoch prophesied, Jude 14, 15; and Noah was a preacher of righteousness, 2 Pet. 2:5. Frequent instances of religious addresses occur in the history of Moses, the judges, and the prophets; and these were to some extent in connection with the Jewish ritual, Neh. 8. The psalms sung in the temple conveyed instruction to the people. After the captivity, numerous synagogues were erected, in which the word of God was read and expounded from Sabbath to Sabbath. Under the gospel dispensation, the preaching of Christ crucified, by those whom he calls to be his ambassadors, is an established ordinance of prime importance—God's chief instrumentality for the conversion of the world, Mark 16:15; 1 Cor. 1:21; 2 Tim. 2:2; 4:2.

PREPARATION. The day on which our Saviour was crucified was called the "day of preparation," or "the preparation of the Passover," as preceding the Passover Sabbath, which commenced at sunset, Matt. 27:62; John 19:31.

PRETORIUM, a name given in the gospels to the house in which dwelt the Roman governor of Jerusalem, Mark 15:16. Here he sat in his judicial capacity, and here Jesus was brought before him. See GABBATHA. This was the palace built by Herod at Jerusalem, near the tower of Antonia, with which it had communication. It was a magnificent building, and inclosed a spacious court, Matt. 27:27; Mark 15:16; John 18:28, 33. Here the Roman procurators resided whenever they visited Jerusalem, their head-quarters being at Cæsarea, Acts 23:23; 25:1. The pretorium or palace of Herod (English translation, "judgment-hall") at Cæsarea is also mentioned in Acts 23:35. Paul speaks also of the pretorium (English translation, "palace") at Rome, in which he gave testimony to Christ, Phil. 1:13. Some think that by this he means the palace of the emperor Nero; and others, that he intends the place where the Roman Prætor sat to administer justice, that is, his tribunal. Others have maintained, with greater probability, that under the name of the pretorium at Rome, Paul would express the camp of the pretorian soldiers, whither he might have been carried by the soldier that always accompanied him, and who was fastened to him by a chain, as the manner was among the Romans.

PRESS, not only the vat in which the juice was trodden out from the grapes, but in some cases the whole place for the reception of wine, grapes, and orchard-fruit. It was often a room excavated in the ground; thus the husbandman "digged a wine-press" in his vineyard, Matt. 21:33. See also Prov. 3:10; Joel 3:13; Hag. 2:16. See WINE.

PREVENT, in the Bible means, not to hinder, but to precede, Psa. 59:10; 1 Thess. 4:15: to anticipate, Psalm 119:147, 148; Matt. 17:25; or to seize, 2 Sam. 22:6; Job 30:27.

PRICKS, the points with which ox-goads were armed, by kicking against which a refractory bullock only hurt itself the more. Hence a proverb, found in Greek and Latin as well as in Hebrew, applied to those who resist lawful authority, or the power of God, Acts 9:5; 26:14. Compare Job 15:25, 26. See OX.

PRIEST, one who officiated in the public worship of God, especially in making expiation for sin, being "ordained for men in things pertaining to God, to offer both gifts and sacrifices for sins." In the Old Testament, the priesthood was not annexed to a certain family till after the promulgation of the law by Moses. Before that time, the first-born of each family, the fathers, the princes, the kings, were priests in their own cities and in their own houses. Cain and Abel, Noah, Abraham, and Job, Abimelech and Laban, Isaac and Jacob, offered personally their own sacrifices. In the solemnity of the covenant made by the Lord with his people, at the foot of mount Sinai, Moses performed the office of mediator, and young men were chosen from among Israel to perform the office of priests, Ex. 24:5. But after the Lord had chosen the tribe of Levi to serve him in his tabernacle, and the priesthood was annexed to the family of Aaron, the right of offering sacrifices and oblations to God was reserved to the priests of this family, Num. 16:40. The punishment of Uzziah king of Judah is well known, who having presumed to offer incense to the Lord, was suddenly smitten with a leprosy, 2 Chr. 26:19. See also the case of Saul, 1 Sam. 13:7–14. However, it seems that on certain occasions the Hebrew prophets offered sacrifice to the Lord, especially before a constant place of worship was fixed at Jerusalem. See 1 Sam. 7:9, where Samuel, who was not a priest, offered a lamb for a burnt-sacrifice to the Lord. See also 1 Sam. 9:13; 16:5; 1 Kin. 18:31, 33.

The Lord having reserved to himself the first-born of Israel because he had preserved them from the hand of the destroying angel in Egypt, by way of exchange and compensation, he accepted the tribe of Levi for the service of his tabernacle, Num. 3:41. Thus the whole tribe of Levi was appointed to the sacred ministry, but not all in the same manner; for of the three sons of Levi, Gershom, Kohath, and Merari, the heads of the three great families, the Lord chose the family of Kohath, and out of this family the house of Aaron, to exercise the functions of the priesthood. All the rest of the family of Kohath, even the children of Moses and their descendants, remained among the Levites.

The high-priest was at the head of all religious affairs, and was the ordinary judge of all difficulties that belonged thereto, and even of the general justice and judgment of the Jewish nation, as being at the head of all the priests by whom this was administered, Deut. 17:8-12; 19:17; 21:5; 33:8, 10; Ezek. 44:24. He only had the privilege of entering the sanctuary once a year, on the day of solemn expiation, to make atonement for the sins of the whole people, Lev. 16:2, etc. He was to be born of one of his own tribe, whom his father had married a virgin; and was to be exempt from corporal defect, Lev. 21:13. In general, no priest who had any such defect could offer sacrifice, or enter the holy place to present the show-bread. But he was to be maintained by the sacrifices offered at the tabernacle, Lev. 21:17-22. The high-priest also received a tithe from the Levites, Num. 18:28.

God also appropriated to the high-priest the oracle of his truth; so that when he was habited in the proper ornaments of his dignity, and with the urim and thummim, he answered questions proposed to him, and God disclosed to him secret and future things. He was forbidden to mourn for the death of any of his relations, even for his father or mother; or to enter into any place where a dead body lay, that he might not contract or hazard the contraction of uncleanness, Lev. 21:10-12.

The priests served immediately at the altar. They slew and dressed the public sacrifices, or at least it was done by the Levites under their direction. Private offerers slew their own victims, except in the case of turtle-doves or young pigeons. But all offerings upon the altar, the sprinkling of blood included, were made by the priests alone. They kept up a perpetual fire on the altar of burnt sacrifices, and in the lamps of the golden candlestick in the sanctuary; they kneaded the loaves of show-bread, baked them, offered them on the golden altar in the sanctuary, and changed them every Sabbath-day. Compare Ex. 28:29; Lev. 8. Every day, night and morning, a priest, appointed by casting of lots at the beginning of the week, brought into the sanctuary a smoking censer of incense, and set it on the golden table, otherwise called the altar of incense, Luke 1:9.

The sacred dress of the priests consisted of the following articles: short linen drawers; a close-fitting tunic of fine linen or cotton, of woven work, broidered, reaching to the feet, and furnished with sleeves; a girdle of fine linen. Plain linen ephods are also ascribed to them, 1 Sam. 22:18; and a bonnet or turban, also of fine linen, in many folds. The priests always officiated with uncovered feet. The high-priest wore nearly the same dress with the priests, and four articles in addition: an outer tunic, called the robe of the ephod, woven entire, blue, with an ornamented border around the neck, and a fringe at the bottom made up of pomegranates and golden bells; an ephod of blue, and purple, and scarlet, and fine linen, with golden threads interwoven, covering the body from the neck to the thighs; having shoulder-pieces joined on the shoulders by clasps of gold in which were set onyx-stones graven with the names of the twelve tribes of Israel; and also a girdle of fine linen, woven with blue, purple, scarlet, and gold, passed several times round the body; a breastplate, attached at its four corners to the ephod, and likewise bearing the names of the twelve tribes on twelve precious stones; and the mitre, a high and ornamented turban having on the front a gold plate with the inscription, "HOLINESS TO THE LORD." Neither he nor the priests wore their sacred dresses out of the temple, as we infer from Ezek. 42:14; 44:17-19; Acts 23:5.

The Lord had given no lands of inheritance to the tribe of Levi, in the Land of Promise. He intended that they should be supported by the tithes, the first-fruits, the offerings made in the temple, and by their share of the sin-offerings and thanksgiving-offerings sacrificed in the temple; of which certain parts were appropriated to them. In the peace-offerings, they had the shoulder and the breast, Lev. 7:33, 34; in the sin-offering, they burnt on the altar the fat that covers the bowels, the liver, and the kidneys; the rest belonged to themselves, Lev. 7:6, 10. The skin or fleece of every sacrifice also belonged to them. When an Israelite sacrificed any animal for his own use, he was to give the priest the shoulder, the stomach, and the jaws, Deut. 18:3. The priest had also a share of the wool when sheep were shorn, Deut. 18:4. Thus, though the priests had no lands or inheritances, their temporal wants were supplied. God provided them houses and accommodations, by appointing forty-eight cities for their residence, Num. 35:1-7. In the precincts of these cities they possessed a thousand cubits beyond the walls. Of these forty-eight cities, six were appointed as cities of refuge for those who had committed casual and involuntary manslaughter. The priests had thirteen of these cities; the others belonged to the Levites, Josh. 21:10.

A principal employment of the priests, next to attending on the sacrifices and the temple service, was the instruction of the people and the deciding of controversies; distinguishing the several sorts of leprosy, divorce causes, the waters of jealousy, vows, causes relating to the law and uncleannesses, etc. They publicly blessed the people in the name of the Lord. In time of war their duty was to carry the ark of the covenant, to consult the Lord, to sound the holy trumpets, and to encourage the army, Num. 10:8, 9; Deut. 20:2.

The priesthood of Christ is the substance and truth, of which that of the Jews was but a shadow and figure. Christ, the everlasting priest according to the order of Melchizedek, abides for ever, as Paul observes; whereas the priests according to the order of Aaron were mortal, and therefore could not continue long, Heb. 7. The Lord, to express to the Hebrews what great favors he would confer on them, says he would make them kings and priests, Ex. 19:6; and Peter repeats this promise to Christians, or rather, he tells them that they are in truth what Moses promised to Israel, 1 Pet. 2:5, 9. See also Rev. 1:6. In an important sense every Christian offers himself a spiritual sacrifice, "acceptable to God through Jesus Christ;" but in the Christian church, there is no priest to make expiation for sin by a sacrifice but Christ alone, Heb. 9:11-26.

PRIS'CA, or PRISCIL'LA, the wife of Aquila. See AQUILA.

PROCH'ORUS, one of the seven original deacons, Acts 6:5, of whom nothing more is known.

PROGNOS'TICATORS, Isaiah 47:13, Chaldeans, who pretended to foretell future events by the varying aspects of the moon, or month by month.

PROM'ISE, used by Paul to denote the spiritual gifts of God, chiefly the Messiah, the Holy Spirit, and the fulness of gospel blessings, of which an assurance was given to Abraham and other saints in behalf of themselves, and of believers who should come after them, Romans 4:13, 14; Gal. 3:14-29. The "children of the promise" are either Isaac's posterity, as distinguished from Ishmael's; Jews converted to Christianity; or all true believers, who by faith lay hold on the promise of salvation in Christ. In Heb. 11:39, "promise" means the thing promised, Acts 1:4. The "exceeding great and precious promises" of God, include all good things for this life and the future; which are infallibly secured to his people in Christ, 2 Cor. 1:20; 1 Tim. 4:8; 2 Pet. 1:4. On the ground of the infinite merits of their Redeemer, infinite love, unbounded wisdom, and almighty power are pledged for their benefit; and having given them his only Son, God will with him freely give them every inferior blessing he sees to be desirable for them, Rom. 8:32.

PROPH'ECY, the foretelling of future events, by inspiration from God. It is very different from a sagacious and happy conjecture as to futurity, and from a vague and equivocal oracle, without any certain meaning. A true prophecy can come only from God; and is the highest proof of the divine origin of the message of which it is a part. A true prophecy may be known by these marks: being announced at a suitable time before the event it foretells; having a particular and exact agreement with that event; being such as no human sagacity or foresight could produce; and being delivered by one claiming to be under the inspiration of the Almighty. Many of the prophecies of Scripture foretold events ages before they occurred—events of which there was then no apparent probability, and the occurrence of which depended on innumerable contingencies, involving the history of things and the volitions of persons not then in existence; and yet these predictions were fulfilled at the time and place and in the manner prophesied. Such were the predictions respecting the coming and crucifixion of the Messiah, the dispersion and preservation of the Jews, etc. The Scripture prophecies are a scheme of vast extent, the very earliest predictions reaching down to the end of the world's history—a scheme gradually and harmoniously developed from age to age, and by many different persons, some of them not fully apprehending, and "searching diligently what the Spirit of Christ which was in them did signify," 1 Pet. 1:11, the whole manifestly the work of Jehovah, and marvellous in our eyes. A degree of obscurity rests on the prophetic writings, which patient and prayerful study alone can dispel; while those which are yet unfulfilled must await the coming of the events which will make all at length clear. Many predictions relating primarily to events and deliverances near at hand, were also designed of God as sure prophecies of yet more illustrious events in the future. For example, the general subject of the predictions in Matt. 24 is *the coming of Christ*, to judge his foes and deliver his friends. In penning a sketch of this subject, Matthew imitates a painter depicting from an eminence the landscape before him: the tower of the village church in the near foreground, and the mountain peak in the dim and remote horizon, rise side by side on his canvas. So in painting *the coming of Christ*, Matthew sketches first some features of his coming in the destruction of Jerusalem to occur within forty years, and in the next verse some distinctive features of his second coming at the end of the world; yet both belong to the same general view. Respecting the New Testament phrase, "This was done that it might be fulfilled," etc., see FULFILLED. For other meanings of "prophecy," see PROPHETS.

PROPHETS, a class of men of God, especially in the Old Testament dispensation, inspired to foretell future and secret events; and who also revealed the will of God as to current events and duties, and were his ambassadors to men. But the word is sometimes used in a wider sense: thus Aaron was Moses' prophet, Ex. 7:1, appointed to deliver to the people the messages that Moses received from God; the sacred musicians are said to prophecy, 1 Chr. 25:1; and Paul gives the name, according to the custom of the Greeks, to the poet Aratus, "a prophet of their own," Tit. 1:12. Scripture does not withhold the name of prophet from impostors, although they falsely boasted of inspiration. As true prophets, when filled by the energy of God's Spirit, were sometimes fervidly and vehemently agitated, similar motions were called prophesying when exhibited by persons who were filled with an evil spirit. Saul, being moved by an evil spirit, "prophesied in his house," 1 Sam. 18:10. In the New Testament, the "prophets" were a class of men supernaturally endowed, and standing next to the apostles. They seem to have spoken from immediate inspiration, whether in reference to future events or to the mind of the Spirit generally, as in expounding the oracles of God. See 1 Cor. 11:4, 5; 14:1, 30, etc. Thus it is said in Acts 13:1, that Judas and Silas were prophets; that there were in the church at Antioch certain prophets and teachers, that is, official instructors. God has set in the church, first apostles, then prophets, 1 Cor. 12:28. See also Eph. 2:20; Rev. 18:20; Acts 21:9.

The Old Testament prophets were special agents of Jehovah, raised up and sent as occasion required, to incite to duty, to convict of sin, to call to repentance and reformation, to instruct kings, and denounce against nations the judgments of God, 2 Kin. 17:13; Jer. 25:4. They aided the priests and Levites in teaching religion to the people, especially in the kingdom of Israel, from which the true priests of the Lord withdrew, 2 Kin. 4:23; and coöperated with the kings in public measures to promote piety and virtue. They were humble, faithful, self-denying, fearless men, 2 Kin. 1:8; Zech. 13:4; Matt. 3:4; aloof from the pleasures and luxuries of life, 2 Kin. 5:15; often persecuted, and slain, Matt. 23:34-37; Heb. 11:32-38; James 2:10; but exerting a powerful influence as witnesses for God. Some of them were called from the plough and the herd, 1 Kin. 19:20; Amos 7:14; Zech. 13:5. There were also "schools of the prophets," first mentioned in the time of Samuel, established at Gibeah, Naioth, Bethel, Gilgal, and Jericho, where young men were instructed in religion and prepared to guide in religious worship, 1 Sam. 10:5; 19:20; 2 Kin. 2:3, 5; 4:38. Many of the "sons of the prophets" here taught became not only religious teachers, but inspired prophets. Amos speaks of his own case as an exception, Amos 7:14, 15. There are several prophetesses mentioned in Scripture; as Miriam, Deborah, and Huldah; and in the New Testament, Anna, Elisabeth, and Mary, and the four daughters of Philip seem to have partaken for a time of prophetic inspiration.

The prophets received their messages from God, sometimes in visions, trances, and dreams. Compare Num. 24:2-16; Joel 2:28; Acts 10:11, 12; Rev. 1:10-20. These revelations were at times attended with overpowering manifestations of the Godhead; and at other times were simply breathed into the mind by the Spirit of God. Their messages were delivered to the kings, princes, and priests whom they most concerned, or to the people at large, in writing, or by word of mouth and in public places; often with miracles, or with symbolic actions designed to explain and enforce them, Isa. 20; Jer. 7:2; 19; Ezek. 3:10.

The Old Testament contains the inspired writings of sixteen of the Hebrew prophets; four of whom, Isaiah, Jeremiah, Ezekiel, and Daniel, are called the greater prophets, and the other twelve the minor prophets. Respecting the true chronological order of the prophets, there is in some cases great diversity of opinion. Below is given the arrangement preferred by some; while others, so far as the minor prophets are concerned, adhere to that given in the Hebrew Bible and our common version. See each name in its place, for further particulars.

1. Jonah, during the reign of Jeroboam II., king of Israel, which commenced 825 B. C.; or perhaps as early as Joash, the predecessor of Jeroboam.

2. Joel, under Uzziah king of Judah, nearly 800 B. C., before Amos and Hosea came upon the stage.

3. Amos, under Uzziah king of Judah, and during the latter years of Jeroboam II., king of Israel. About 787 B. C.

4. Hosea, under Uzziah, Jotham, Ahaz, and Hezekiah, kings of Judah, and under Jeroboam II. and his successors, kings of Israel. From about 785 to 725 B. C.

5. Isaiah, near the death of Uzziah king of Judah, and the beginning of the reign of Jotham, B. C. 758, to the reign of Manasseh, B. C. 697.

6. Micah, under Jotham, Ahaz, and Hezekiah, kings of Judah. Jotham began to reign B. C. 758, and Hezekiah died B. C. 697. Thus Micah was contemporary with Isaiah.

7. Nahum, in the latter part of the reign of Hezekiah, and after the expedition of Sennacherib. Between 710 and 700 B. C.

8. Zephaniah, soon after the beginning of the reign of Josiah, and before the destruction of Nineveh. About B. C. 630.

9. Jeremiah, in the thirteenth year of Josiah king of Judah, B. C. 628. Jeremiah continued to prophesy under Shallum, Jehoiakim, Jeconiah, and Zedekiah, to the taking of Jerusalem by the Chaldeans, B. C. 588. It is supposed he died two years afterwards, in Egypt.

10. Habakkuk, in Judah, near the beginning of the reign of Jehoiakim, about 610 B. C., and before the coming of Nebuchadnezzar.

11. Obadiah, near the fall and captivity of Jerusalem, B. C. 588, and before the desolation of Idumæa.

12. Ezekiel, carried captive to Babylon with Jeconiah king of Judah, 598 B. C. He began to prophesy about B. C. 590; and continued, under Nebuchadnezzar, till fourteen years after the final capture of Jerusalem B. C. 588.

13. Daniel, taken into Chaldea while young, B. C. 606, the fourth year of Jehoiakim king of Judah. He prophesied in Babylon to the end of the captivity, and probably finished about 534 B. C.

14. Haggai, returned from the captivity B. C. 536, and prophesied in the second year of Darius son of Hystaspes, B. C. 520.

15. Zechariah, prophesied in Judea at the same time as Haggai, B. C. 520, and seems to have continued after him.

16. Malachi, supposed to have prophesied about 416 B. C., in the latter part of the administration of Nehemiah at Jerusalem.

Christ, of whom all the prophets bore witness, Luke 24:27, 44; Acts 10:43; 1 Pet. 1:10, 11, is eminently THE PROPHET of his church in all ages, Deut. 18:15-19; Acts 3:22-24; revealing to them, by his inspired servants, by himself, and by his Spirit, all we know of God and immortality.

PROPITIA'TION, the offering which appeases the wrath of one against whom an offence has been committed. Christ is "the propitiation for our sins," Rom. 3:25, inasmuch as his sacrifice alone removes the obstacles which prevented the mercy of God from saving sinners, and appeases the just wrath of the law, 1 John 2 : 2; 4 : 10. The same Greek word is used in the Septuagint to denote an "atonement," Num. 5 : 8; a "sin-offering," Ezek. 44:27; and the covering of the ark of the covenant, Lev. 16 : 14; Heb. 9:5. See MERCY-SEAT.

PROS'ELYTE, in the Jewish sense, a foreigner who adopted the Jewish religion, a convert from heathenism to Judaism. The laws of the Hebrews make frequent mention of "the stranger that is within thy gates," Lev. 17 : 8–16; 24 : 16; Num. 15 : 14–16, and welcomed him to all the privileges of the people of God. Our Saviour rebukes the blind zeal of the Pharisees to make proselytes to ceremonial Judaism, without caring for the circumcision of the heart, Matt. 23 : 15; Rom. 2 : 28, 29. According to the later rabbins, there were two species of proselytes among the Jews. The first were called "proselytes of the gate," and were foreigners, either bond or free, who lived among the Jews and conformed to their customs in regard to what the rabbins call "the seven precepts of Noah;" that is, they abstained from injurious language in respect to God, from idolatry, homicide, incest, robbery, resistance to magistrates, and from eating blood, or the flesh of animals killed without shedding their blood. The other class were called "proselytes of justice;" that is, complete, perfect proselytes, and were those who had abandoned their former religion, and bound themselves to the observance of the Mosaic law in its full extent. These, according to the rabbins, by means of circumcision, baptism, and an offering, obtained all the rites of Jewish citizenship, Ex. 12:48, 49. This distinction, however, is not observable in the Bible. Proselytes were numerous in our Saviour's day, and were found in many places remote from Jerusalem, Acts 2 : 10; 8 : 27. Many converts to Christianity were gathered from among them, John 12 : 20; Acts 6 : 5; 13 : 43; 17:4.

PROV'ERBS, THE BOOK OF, a collection of pointed and sententious moral maxims, the fruit of Solomon's profound sagacity and unexampled experience, but above all, of the inspiration of God. Solomon is said to have uttered three thousand proverbs, 1 Kin. 4 : 32, B. C. 1000. The first nine chapters of Proverbs are written in an admirable poetic style, and are more continuous than the succeeding chapters, 10–22, which consist of separate maxims. Chapters 25–29 are proverbs of Solomon collected under the direction of king Hezekiah. Chapter 30 is ascribed to Agur, and affords examples of the enigmatic proverbs so popular in the East. Chapter 31, by "king Lemuel," is mainly a beautiful picture of female excellence. By whose care this book was compiled in its present form, is unknown; there is no book of the Old Testament, however, whose canonical authority is better attested. The New Testament contains frequent quotations and allusions to it, Rom. 12:20; 1 Thess. 5 : 15; Heb. 12 : 5, 6; Jas. 4 : 6; 1 Pet. 4:8; 2 Pet. 2:22. Its "winged words" are a rich storehouse of heavenly wisdom, and few questions can arise in actual life on which they do not shed light.

PROV'IDENCE, Acts 24 : 2, a superintending and forecasting care. The providence of God upholds and governs every created thing. Its operation is coëxtensive with the universe, and as unceasing as the flow of time. All his attributes are engaged in it. He provideth for the raven his food, and satisfieth the desire of every living thing. The Bible shows us all nature looking up to him and depending upon him, Job 38:41; Psa. 104; 145:15, 16; 147:8, 9; and uniformly declares that every occurrence, as well as every being, is perfectly controlled by him. There is no such thing as chance in the universe; "the lot is cast into the lap, but the whole disposing thereof is of the Lord," Prov. 16:23. Not a sparrow, nor a hair of the head, falls to the ground without his knowledge, Isa. 14:26, 27; Matt. 10:29, 30; Acts 17 : 24–29. Nothing that was not too minute for God to create, is too minute for him to preserve and control. The history of each man, the rise and fall of nations, and the progress of the church of Christ, reveal at every step the hand of Him who "worketh all things after the counsel of his own will."

PSALMS, THE BOOK OF. The Hebrew name for this book is TEHILLIM, praises, though many of the psalms are rather elegiac. Most of the psalms have the superscription *mizmôr*, a poem, song. This word is rendered in the Septuagint by *psalmos*, that is, a song sung to music, a lyric poem. The Greek *psalterion* means a stringed instrument; hence by a metaphor the book of Psalms is called Psalter. For the poetical characteristics of the Psalms, see POETRY.

CLASSIFICATION.—Some writers have classified the psalms according to their poetic character, into odes, elegies, etc. A preferable method is to divide them according to their contents. In this way they have been divided into six classes.

I. Hymns in praise of Jehovah; *tehillim* in the proper sense. These are directed to Jehovah as the God of all nature and the Creator of the universe, Psa. 8, 104; as the protector and patron of Israel, Psa. 20, 29, 33, or of individuals, with thanksgiving for deliverance from evils, Psa. 18, 30, 46, 47; or they refer to the more special attributes of Jehovah, Psa. 90, 139. These psalms express thoughts of the highest sublimity in respect to God, providence, redemption, etc.

II. Temple hymns; sung at the consecration of the temple, the entrance of the ark, etc., or intended for the temple service, Psa. 24, 132. So also "pilgrim songs," sung by those who came up to worship in the temple, etc.; as for example, the "songs of degrees," Psa. 120, etc. See DEGREES.

III. Religious and moral songs of a general character; containing the poetical expression of emotions and feelings, and therefore *subjective*: as for example, confidence in God, Psa. 23, 62, 125; devotedness to God, Psa. 16; longing for the worship of the temple, Psa. 42, 43; prayers for the forgiveness of sin, etc. To this class belong the seven penitential psalms, as they are termed, Psa. 6, 25, 32, 35, 38, 51, 130. Also didactic songs; the poetical expression of some truth, maxim, etc., Psa. 1, 34, 128; Psa. 15, 32, 50, etc. This is a numerous class.

IV. Elegiac psalms, that is, lamentations, psalms of complaint, generally united with prayer for help.

V. Messianic psalms, as 2, 22, 45, 69, 72, 110, etc.

VI. Historical psalms, in which the ancient history of the Israelites is repeated in a hortatory manner, Psa. 78, 105, 106, 114.

But it is impossible to form any perfect arrangement, because some psalms belong in part to two or more different classes. Besides the proper Messianic psalms, predictions of the Messiah are widely scattered through this book, and the attention of the devout reader is continually attracted by passages foretelling His character and His works. Not a few of these are alluded to in the New Testament; and it is unquestionable that the language and structure of many others not quoted were intended to bear witness to the Son of God. David himself was an eminent type of the Saviour, and many events of his life shadowed forth his Son and Lord. The mention of these in the inspired writings is not undesigned; the recorded trials and victories of David find in their reference to the Messiah their highest claim to a place in the sacred writings. Lord Bacon has remarked that many prophetic passages in the Old Testament are "of the nature of their Author, to whom a thousand years are as one day; and therefore they are not fulfilled punctually at once, but have springing and germinant accomplishment through many ages, though the height or fulness of them may refer to some one age."

INSCRIPTIONS.—With the exception of twenty-five psalms, hence called orphan psalms, all the rest have inscriptions of various kinds. They refer to the author, the occasion, different kinds of song, the melody or rhythm, the instrumental accompaniment, the choir who shall perform, etc. These are mostly very obscure, because the music and musical instruments of the Hebrews are almost unknown to us. They are of very high antiquity, if not as old as the psalms themselves; and in the Hebrew are not detached from the psalms, as in modern translations. They appear with numerous variations in the ancient Greek and Syriac versions. Many words in these inscriptions remain untranslated, and can only be conjecturally interpreted. See HIGGAION, MASCHIL, etc.

AUTHORS AND AGE OF THE PSALMS.—To David are assigned seventy-three psalms in the Hebrew, and in the Septuagint eleven more. Psalm 90 is ascribed to Moses. As to the authorship of the other psalms, much diversity of opinion has prevailed among biblical critics.

The whole collection of the Psalms appears to have first existed in five books, after the example, perhaps, of the Pentateuch. Each book closes with a doxology.

Book I.	comprises	psalms	1–41.
" II.	"	"	42–72.
" III.	"	"	73–89.
" IV.	"	"	90–106.
" V.	"	"	107–150.

One psalm occurs twice, Psa. 14; compare Psa. 53. Some occur as parts of other psalms; as for example, Psa. 70 forms also a part of Psa. 40. So also some psalms are repeated from other books of Scripture; thus Psa. 18 is the same with 2 Sam. 22. The final arrangement of the whole is generally referred to Ezra, 450 B. C.

These invaluable sacred songs exhibit the sublimest conceptions of God, as the creator, preserver, and governor of the universe; to say nothing of the prophetical character of many of them, and their relation to the Messiah and the great plan of man's redemption. They present us with the most perfect models of child-like resignation and devotedness, of unwavering faith and confidence in God. They are an inspired epitome of the Bible, for purposes of devotion; and are peculiarly dear to the people of God, as expressing every phase of religious experience. Luther, in his preface to the Psalter, has the following beautiful language: "Where canst thou find nobler words of joy, than in the psalms of praise and thanksgiving? There thou mayest look into the hearts of all good men, as into beautiful and pleasant gardens, yea, as into heaven itself. How do grateful and fine and charming blossoms spring up there, from every kind of pleasing and rejoicing thoughts towards God and his goodness! Again, where canst thou find more deep or mournful words of sorrow, than in the psalms of lamentation and woe? There thou mayest look again into the hearts of all good men, as upon death, yea, as if into hell. How dark and gloomy is it there, from anxious and troubled views of the wrath of God! I hold, however, that no better or finer book of models, or legends of saints and martyrs, has existed, or can exist on earth, than the Psalter. For we find here, not alone what one or two saints have done, but what the Head of all saints has done, and what all holy men still do; in what attitude they stand towards God and towards their friends and enemies; and how they conduct themselves in all dangers and sufferings. And besides this, all sorts of divine doctrines and precepts are contained in it. Hence it is that the Psalter is THE BOOK of all good men; and every one, whatever his circumstances may be, finds in it psalms and words suited to his circumstances, and which are to him just as if they had been put there on his very account, and in such a way that he himself could not have made or found or wished for better."

In Luke 24:44, the word "psalms" denotes one of the three divisions of the Hebrew Bible, the Hagiographa or devotional writings. See BIBLE. With regard to alphabetical psalms and psalms of degrees, see DEGREES, and LETTERS.

PSAL'TERY. See HARP, and MUSIC.

PTOLEMA'IS. See ACCHO.

PUB'LICAN, an officer of the revenue, employed in collecting taxes. Among the Romans there were two sorts of tax-gatherers: some were general receivers, who in each province had deputies; they collected the revenues of the empire, and accounted to the emperor. These were men of great consideration in the government; and Cicero says that among these were the flower of the Roman knights, the ornaments of the city, and the strength of the commonwealth. But the deputies, the under-collectors, the publicans of the lower order, were looked upon as so many thieves and pickpockets. Theocritus being asked which was the most cruel of all beasts, answered, "Among the beasts of the wilderness, the bear and the lion; among the beasts of the city, the publican and the parasite." Among the Jews, the name and profession of a publican were especially odious. They could not, without the utmost reluctance, see publicans exacting tributes and impositions laid on them by foreigners, the Romans. The Galileans, or Herodians, especially, submitted to this with the greatest impatience, and thought it even unlawful, Deut. 17:15. Those of their own nation who undertook this office they looked upon as heathen, Matt. 18:17. It is even said that they would not allow them to enter the temple or the synagogues, to engage in the public prayers or offices of judicature, or to give testimony in a court of justice.

There were many publicans in Judea in the time of our Saviour; Zaccheus, probably, was one of the principal receivers, since he is called "chief among the publicans," Luke 19:2; but Matthew was only an inferior publican, Luke 5:27. The Jews reproached Jesus with being a "friend of publicans and sinners, and eating with them," Luke 7:34; but he, knowing the self-righteousness, unbelief, and hypocrisy of his accusers, replied, "The publicans and harlots go into the kingdom of God before you," Matt. 21:31. Compare also the beautiful demeanor of the penitent publican in the temple, and the self-justifying spirit of the Pharisee, Luke 18:10-14.

PUB'LIUS, the prefect of Melita when Paul was shipwrecked on that island A. D. 60, Acts 28:7-9. Publius received the apostle and his company into his house, and entertained them with great humanity. The governor's father, dangerously sick, and many others ill of various diseases, were miraculously healed; and their hospitable care of Paul and his friends continued through the three wintry months of their stay, and furnished them abundant supplies on their departure.

PUL, I., an Assyrian king, about 765 B. C., when Assyria is first mentioned in Scripture after the time of Nimrod. He invaded Israel during the reign of Menahem, but was induced to retire by a present of a thousand talents of silver, equivalent to at least a million and a half of dollars, 2 Kin. 15:19, 20; 1 Chr. 5:26.

II. Isa. 66:19, a region remote from Judea, associated with Lud, and supposed by Bochart to be traceable in the island Philae in the Nile, near the confines of Egypt and Ethiopia.

PULSE, a general name for peas, beans, and all large or leguminous seeds.

PUN'ISHMENTS. The penalties inflicted in ancient times for various crimes and offences, varied in different nations, and at different times. Capital punishment for murder is generally agreed to have been permanently instituted at the origin of the human race; and Cain was only saved from it by a special interposition of God, Gen. 4:14, 15. It was reenacted, with reasons, after the deluge, Gen. 9:5, 6, and in the wilderness, Num. 35:9-34; and was early and widely recognized among mankind.

The mode of capital punishment usual among the Hebrews was stoning, Deut. 13:9, 10; 17:5; Josh. 17:25; John 8:7; but various other modes became known to them by intercourse with other nations: as decapitation, 2 Kin. 10:6-8; Matt. 14:8-12; precipitation from rocks, 2 Chr. 25:12; Luke 4:29; hanging, Josh. 8:29; Esth. 7:10; burning, Dan. 3; cutting asunder, Dan. 2:5; 3:29; Heb. 11:27; beating, on a wheel-like frame, Heb. 11:35; exposure to wild beasts, Dan. 6; 1 Cor. 15:32; drowning, Matt. 18:6; bruising in a mortar, Prov. 27:22; and crucifixion, John 19:18.

Minor punishments were scourging, Lev. 19:20; 2 Cor. 11:24; retaliation in kind for an injury done, Exod. 21:23-25; Deut. 19:19; imprisonment, 2 Chr. 16:10; Matt. 4:12; the stocks, Acts 16:24; banishment, Rev. 1:9; and personal torture, 2 Chr. 18:26; Isa. 50:6; Matt. 18:30; Heb. 11:37.

PU'RIM, *lots*, a Jewish festival instituted by Esther and Mordecai, during the reign of Ahasuerus king of Persia, in memory of the providential deliverance of the Jews from the malignant designs of Haman. The propriety of the name appears from the fact that the lot was cast in the presence of Haman for every day from the first month to the twelfth, before an auspicious day was found for destroying the Jews; and thus the superstition of Haman was made the means of giving them time to turn his devices against himself, Prov. 16:33; Esth. 3:7; 9:20-32. This festival was preceded by a day of fasting, and was observed by reading the book of Esther publicly in the synagogues, and by private festivities, mutual presents, alms, plays, and self-indulgence. Some think it is alluded to in John 5:1. It is still observed by the Jews, in the month of March.

PUR'PLE. The famous and costly Tyrian purple, the royal color of the ancients, is said to have been discovered by the Tyrian Hercules, whose dog having by chance eaten a shell-fish called Purpura, and returning to his master with his lips tinged with a purple color, occasioned the discovery of this precious dye. Purple, however, is much more ancient than this, since we find it mentioned by Moses in several places. Two kinds of purple are mentioned in the Old Testament: 1. ARGAMON, rendered in our version "purple," denoting a reddish purple obtained from a species of muscle or shell-fish found on the coasts of the

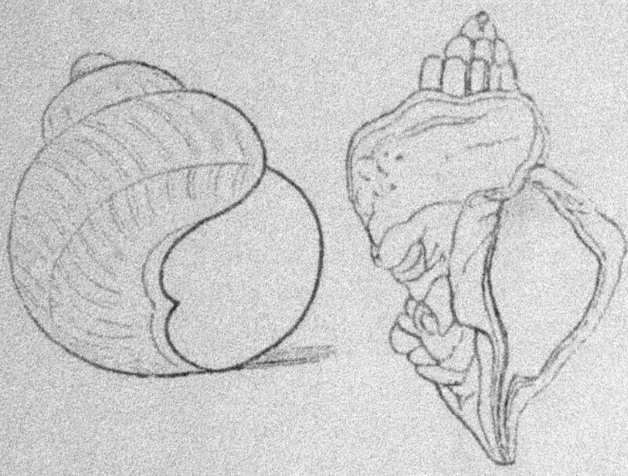

HELIX IANTHINA AND MUREX TRUNCULUS.

Mediterranean. 2. TECHELETH, rendered in the English Bible "blue." This was a bluish or cerulean purple, likewise obtained from another species of shell-fish. The "scarlet" or "crimson," for the two words denote essentially the same color, was produced from the coccus insect, *coccus ilicis*. All these were sacred colors among the Jews; and the latter was used for the high-priest's ephod, and for veils, ribbons, and cloths, Ex. 26:1, 4, 31, 36; 28:31; Num. 4:6–12; 15:38.

The "purple" of the ancients seems to have included many different tints derived originally from the shell-fish, and modified by various arts in which the Tyrians excelled. As each fish yielded but a few drops of coloring matter, the choicest purple bore a very high price. Purple robes were worn by the kings and first magistrates of ancient Rome, and Nero forbade their use by his subjects under pain of death. Our Saviour was clothed with a royal robe of purple, in mockery of his title, "The King of the Jews," John 19:2, 5. Compare also Judg. 8:26; Esth. 8:15; Prov. 31:22; Dan. 5:7; Luke 16:19. Moses used much wool dyed of a crimson and purple color in the work of the tabernacle, and in the ornaments of the high-priest, Ex. 25:4; 26:1, 31, 36; 39:1; 2 Chr. 3:14. The Babylonians also clothed their idols in robes of a purple and azure color, Jer. 10:9; Ezek. 23:15; 27:7, 16.

PUTE'OLI, *the wells*, now Pozzuoli, a maritime town in the Campania of Naples, on the northern side of the bay, eight miles north-west from that city. It was a Roman colony. Here Paul abode seven days, on his famous voyage and journey from Cæsarea to Rome, Acts 28:13.

PY'GARG, *white-rump*. This is properly the name of a species of eagle; but is applied, in Deut. 14:5, to a quadruped, apparently a species of gazelle or antelope. So the Syriac version and Targums. Both the Arabic versions refer it to a species of mountain goat.

Q.

THE QUAIL: COTURNIX COMMUNIS.

QUAILS. The oriental quail is a bird of passage, about the size of a turtle-dove, and nearly resembling the American partridge. Hasselquist states that it is plentiful near the shores of the Dead sea and the Jordan, and in the deserts of Arabia; and Diodorus affirms that it is caught in immense numbers about Rhinocolura, at the south-west corner of Palestine. Burckhardt also found great quantities of them in the regions south of the Dead sea. The flocks of quails, therefore, which came up to the camp of Israel, are entirely credible; and the miracle seems especially to have consisted in these immense flocks being directed to a particular spot, in the extreme emergency of the people, by means of "a wind from the Lord," Ex. 16:13; Num. 11:31; Psa. 78:27.

QUAR'TUS, a Christian residing at Corinth, but according to his name of Roman origin, whose salutation Paul sends to the brethren at Rome, Rom. 16:23.

QUATER'NION OF SOLDIERS, a detachment or division consisting of four men, Acts 12:4. The Romans detached a quarternion of four men for a night guard, and divided the night into four watches, so that each soldier should in his turn be on guard three hours. (See HOURS.) When therefore Herod, who adopted the Roman customs, is said to have delivered Peter to four quaternions of soldiers, it is to be understood that he was guarded by four men at a time, namely, two in the prison with him, and two before the doors, (compare ver. 6,) and that they were relieved every three hours by four others; making in all sixteen men.

QUEEN OF HEAVEN, a name given by the Hebrew idolaters to the moon, Jer. 7:18; 44:17, 18. See ASHTORETH.

QUICK, in the old English sense, means alive, or living. Num. 16:30; 2 Tim. 4:1; and quicken, to make alive. God bestows spiritual life on men dead in trespasses and sins, Eph. 2:5, through Christ the second Adam, who is a quickening Spirit, 1 Cor. 15:45.

QUICK'SANDS, Acts 27:17, probably the dangerous sandbanks and whirlpools in two gulfs on the African coast south of Malta; they were called the Greater and the Lesser Syrtis, and were much dreaded by ancient mariners. The course of the wind by which Paul and his companions were driven, threatened to cast them into the Lesser Syrtis.

R.

RA'AMAH, 1 Chr. 1:9, a region settled by Cushites, descendants of a grandson of Ham of the same name, Gen. 10:7. It is supposed to have adjoined the Persian gulf on its western shore towards the north, Ezek. 27:12.

RAAM'SES, or RAME'SES, a city built by the Hebrews during their servitude in Egypt, Ex. 1:11. It was situated in the land of Goshen; and appears to have been the capital of that country, Gen. 47:10. From it they commenced their united exodus from Egypt, Ex. 12:37; Num. 33:3, 5. It is thought to have been on the line of the ancient canal from the Nile to the Red sea, and some thirty-five miles north-west of Suez.

RAB, RAB'BI. The word RAB in Hebrew signifies chief; thus Nebuzaradan is the chief or captain of the guard, 2 Kin. 25:8, in Hebrew rab-tabbachim; so Ashpenaz is the rab, chief or master of the eunuchs, and Daniel of the magi, Dan. 1:3; 5:11. See RAB-MAG. At a later period, it was introduced as a solemn title of honor in the Jewish schools, meaning master, teacher, doctor. There were various distinctions and degrees; the term rab was accounted the least honorable; that of rabbi, signifying my master, being of higher dignity. Another form of the word was rabban or rabbon, from which comes also rabboni, John 20:16; this was regarded as the highest title of honor, and was never formally bestowed on more than seven persons, who all belonged to the celebrated school of Hillel, and were preëminently distinguished by their rank and learning. See GAMALIEL. The more common and usual appellation afterwards was rabbi; and this has descended among the Jews to the present day, Matt. 23:7, 8. It was a title often given to the Saviour both by his disciples and the people, Mark 9:5; 10:51; 11:21; John 1:38, 49; 4:31.

RAB'BATH, or RAB'BATH-AM'MON, afterwards called Philadelphia, the capital of the Ammonites, was situated near the southern source of the Jabbok, some twenty-two miles beyond Jordan. It was famous even in the time of Moses, Deut. 3:11; Josh. 13:25. When David declared war against the Ammonites, his general, Joab, laid siege to Rabbath-Ammon, where Uriah lost his life by a secret order of his prince; and when the city was reduced to the last extremity, Joab sent for David to hasten and go thither, to enjoy the honor of taking it, 2 Sam. 11; 12. From this time it became subject to the kings of Judah; but the kings of Israel subsequently became masters of it, with the tribes beyond Jordan. Towards the conclusion of the kingdom of Israel, Tiglath-pileser having taken away a great part of the Israelites, the Ammonites were guilty of many cruelties against those who remained; for which the prophets Jeremiah and Ezekiel pronounced very severe prophecies against Rabbath, their capital, and against the rest of the country; which probably had their completion five years after the destruction of Jerusalem, Jer. 49:1-3; Ezek. 21:20. Antiochus the Great afterwards took the city. It was long known to the Greeks and Romans as Philadelphia; but this name is now unknown in that vicinity, while the more ancient name still survives. It is now called

Amman, and is about fifteen miles southeast of Szalt, the ancient Ramoth-Gilead. Burckhardt found there extensive ruins, which he has described. He and numerous other travellers found it desolate, as had been foretold; it was literally "a stable for camels," "a couching-place for flocks," Ezek. 25:5.

RAB'BATH-MO'AB. See AR.

RAB'BI and RABBO'NI. See RAB.

RAB-MAG, a general officer of Nebuchadnezzar's army, at the taking of Jerusalem, Jer. 39:3. He was, as his name signifies, a chief of the Magi; a dignitary who had accompanied the king of Babylon in his campaign. See MAGI.

RAB'-SARIS, an officer sent with Rabshakeh and Tartan, to summon Hezekiah, 2 Kin. 18:17; Jer. 39:3. It signifies "the chief of the eunuchs." Such officers, high in honor and in trust, are found on the mural tablets of Nineveh so wonderfully preserved to this day; and in the Ottoman Porte of our own times the Kislar Aga, or chief of the black eunuchs, is one of the highest dignitaries. See SHALMANEZER.

RAB'-SHAKEH, chief butler or cupbearer, an officer sent from Lachish by Sennacherib king of Assyria, to summon Hezekiah to surrender; which message he delivered in a most audacious and insolent manner. The history is told in 2 Kin. 19:17, etc.; 2 Chr. 32:9, etc.; Isa. 36. See NINEVEH and SENNACHERIB.

RA'CA, a word derived from a Hebrew word signifying vain, trifling, brainless; otherwise, beggarly, worthless. It is thus translated by the Vulgate, in Judg. 11:3; in the English, "vain men." The word includes a strong idea of contempt. Christ says, Matt. 5:22, whoever shall say to his brother, "Raca," shall be condemned by the council, or sanhedrim. The term translated "fool" in the same passage, means vile and abandoned wretch.

RACE, Psa. 19:5; Eccl. 9:11. Various games were instituted among the Greeks and Romans, in honor of their gods, and with the design of training young men to personal vigor and activity, and to intrepidity and skill in war. These games were celebrated at stated places and times, with great pomp; renowned statesmen, legislators, and kings engaged in them; and it was deemed the highest of all honors to be crowned with a simple chaplet of laurel, olive, pine, or parsley, in the presence of the vast assemblage of witnesses who delighted to honor the victor. The preparatory training was very severe, and every weakening indulgence was forbidden. Among the most famous games were those celebrated on the Isthmus of Corinth, hence called the Isthmian games; and to these Paul alludes in his letters to Corinth, 1 Cor. 9:24–27. The foot-race was a game of the first rank; other games were the chariot-race, wrestling, boxing, leaping, and throwing the quoit or the jave-

lin. The foot-race well illustrates the Christian warfare, the sacrifices to be made, the diligent bringing the body under subjection, the laying aside every weight, the myriads of spectators lining the course, and among them those preriously crowned victors, the exhausting efforts required, (from which the word agonize is derived,) and the glorious prize, Phil. 3 : 13, 14 ; 2 Tim. 4 : 7, 8 ; Heb. 12:1.

RA'CHEL, *ewe* or *sheep*, Ruth 4 : 11, the younger sister of Leah, daughter of Laban, and the chosen wife of Jacob, though her sister was favored with more children. Rachel was the mother of Joseph and Benjamin, and died soon after the birth of the latter. See her history in Gen. 29–35. Her sepulchre, half an hour's walk north of Bethlehem, is shown unto this day, the spot being marked by a Mohammedan wely or tomb, a stone enclosure and a dome. The prophecy, Jer. 31 : 15, representing her as mourning over her posterity, the tribes of Ephraim, Manasseh, and Benjamin, is quoted in Matt. 2 : 18, in reference to the massacre at Bethlehem, in which undoubtedly many of her descendants suffered. It is supposed that one of the many places called Ramah was adjacent to Bethlehem.

RAGU'EL, Num. 10:29, or REUEL, Ex. 2:15, 18, 21, the Hebrew word being the same in both places. These passages represent him as the father of Hobab and Zipporah, and he is generally supposed to be the same as Jethro, Moses' father-in-law. Some, however, think he was Jethro's father, and that he is called the father of the others as being the head of the family. Compare Gen. 31 : 43 ; 2 Kin. 14:3 ; 16:2.

RA'HAB. The English word Rahab represents two different Hebrew words : I. RAHAB, a Canaanite woman of Jericho, who gave shelter to the two spies sent in thither by Joshua; and in return was spared, with all her kindred, when the city was taken and destroyed, Josh. 2 : 1–21 ; 6 : 17–25. Her faith, in doing this, is commended in Heb. 11:31 ; James 2:25. The Jews and many Christians endeavor to show that Rahab was only an honest innkeeper ; but more probably the designation of "harlot" given to her in our Bible is correct. If she had at some time led a dissolute life, she had evidently repented ; and she afterwards became a worshipper of Jehovah, and the wife of Salmon, a prince of the tribe of Judah, Ruth 4 : 21 ; Matt. 1 : 4. The penitent publican and sinner are always welcome to Christ ; and many such a one, through the renovating power of grace, will shine gloriously in heaven, while the unbelieving moralist will perish in his sins.

II. RAHAB, *pride, insolence*, a symbolical name for Egypt, Psa. 87:4 ; 89:10 ; Isa. 30 : 7 ; 51 : 9. In the last of these passages, Egypt is further symbolized as a ferocious sea-monster ; but it is doubtful whether the word Rahab itself is ever used to denote a sea-monster.

RAIN. In Scripture the "early" and the "latter" rain of Palestine is spoken of, Deut. 11:14 ; Hos. 6:3. The former falls in the latter part of October, the seed-time of Palestine ; and the weather then continues variable, with more or less rain the whole winter, until after the latter or spring rain in April. Afterwards, the weather becomes serene, and the crops ripen. The wheat harvest takes place in May ; by the middle of August, the fruits are gathered in ; and from that time to the coming of the first or October rains, prevail the scorching heats and droughts of summer. Nothing can more expressively represent spiritual blessings than copious showers of rain after this trying season is past, Deut. 32:2 ; Job 29:23 ; Isa. 44:3 ; Hos. 10:12.

It appears from meteorological records kept at Jerusalem, that the average annual fall of rain is fifty-six and a half inches ; the average fall in the United States is forty-five inches. It would seem therefore, that if the rains of Palestine could be preserved in pools and reservoirs, and employed in irrigating the ground during the summer, the old fertility might be restored ; it would be clothed again with verdure, and become like "the garden of the Lord."

RAIN'BOW, Genesis 9 : 13–15. This beautiful phenomenon is owing to the refraction of the beams of the sun in passing the drops of falling rain ; the rays are separated into the prismatic colors, and then reflected from the cloud opposite to the sun and the spectator. We need not suppose that the rainbow was unknown before the flood ; but God then appointed it to be the cheering seal of his covenant with the earth, which is as steadfast as the natural laws from which the rainbow springs.

RA'MAH, plural RA'MOTH, *an eminence ;* and hence many places in Palestine are named Ramah, Ramath, Ramoth, Ramathaim, etc. Sometimes the same place is called by one or other of these names indiscriminately, all signifying the same, 2 Kin. 8 : 28, 29. Sometimes Rama, or Ramoth, is joined to another name, to determine the place of such city or eminence; and it is sometimes put simply for a high place, and signifies neither city nor village.

I. The principal Ramah was a city of Benjamin, near Gibeah, towards the mountains of Ephraim, six miles from Jerusalem north, and on the road from Samaria to Jerusalem, Josh. 18:25; Judg. 19 : 13; Neh. 11 : 33. It was near the border line between Judah and Israel, and Baasha king of Israel caused it to be fortified, to obstruct the passage from the land of Judah into his own territory, 1 Kin. 15:17, 21, 22. It is also referred to in Isa. 10:29; Jer. 31:15; 40:1; Hos. 5 : 8. Dr. Robinson finds it in the modern village Er-Ram, on a conical hill a little east of the road above mentioned. The ruins are broken columns, a few bevelled stones, and large hewn stones, and an ancient reservoir on the south-west side. The village is almost deserted.

II. A city in mount Ephraim, called also Ramathaim-Zophim, or Ramah of the Zuphites, the place of Samuel's birth, residence, and burial, 1 Sam. 1 : 1, 19; 7 : 17; 8 : 4; 25 : 1; 28 : 3. Dr. Robinson suggests Soba, five miles west of Jerusalem, as its possible site. The resemblance of its name Ramathaim to Arimathea of the New Testament, together with intimations of early historians, have led to the general belief that these two places were identical. Arimathea, there is little doubt, lay on one of the hills east of Lydda, some twenty miles north-west of Jerusalem; and this site would meet most of the scriptural intimations as to the Ramah of Samuel. The chief difficulty is found in the account of Saul's first visit to Samuel, 1 Sam. 9:4-12; 10:2. The young prince "passed through the land of the Benjamites," going south or south-west, "and came to the land of Zuph" and the city where Samuel then was. After his interview with the prophet, and on his return home to Gibeah of Benjamin, he passed "by Rachel's sepulchre in the border of Benjamin at Zelzah." But the only "Rachel's sepulchre" we know of was near Bethlehem, many miles south of the direct road from Arimathea to Gibeah. Accordingly, if we suppose this interview took place at Arimathea, we seem obliged to suppose another Rachel's sepulchre between it and Gibeah; or, if "Rachel's sepulchre" was at Bethlehem, to infer that the city where Saul actually found Samuel, and at which the prophet had only that day arrived, 1 Sam. 9:10, was not his usual residence, but some place south or south-west of Bethlehem, only visited by him at intervals in his annual circuits as judge.

III. A city of Asher, Josh. 19:29.

IV. A city of Naphtali, Josh. 19 : 36. The site of both these places, visited by Dr. Robinson, is still called Rameh.

V. A city of Gilead, 2 Kin. 8 : 28, 29. See RAMOTH.

VI. A town belonging to Simeon, called Ramah of the south, Josh. 19 : 8; 1 Sam. 30:27.

RAMATHA'IM. See RAMAH.

RAME'SES. See RAAMSES.

RA'MOTH, a famous city in the mountains of Gilead; often called Ramoth-Gilead, and sometimes Ramath-Mizpeh, or the Watch-tower, Josh. 13 : 26. It belonged to Gad, was assigned to the Levites, and became one of the cities of refuge beyond Jordan, Deut. 4:43; Josh. 20:8; 21:38. It was famous during the reigns of the later kings of Israel, and was the occasion of several wars between these princes and the kings of Damascus, who had conquered it, and from whom the kings of Israel endeavored to regain it. Here Ahab died, Joram was wounded, and Jehu was anointed king of Israel, 1 Kin. 22; 2 Kin. 8 : 28, 29; 9:1-14; 2 Chr. 22:5, 6.

RA'VEN, Gen. 8:7, Lev. 11:15, a bird similar to the crow, but larger, and not gregarious. It feeds on dead bodies; and in its general characteristics resembles the crow of America. The eyes of its victim are the first part to be devoured, Prov. 30 : 17; and it drives away its young as soon as they can begin to shift for themselves, Job 38 : 41 ; Psa. 147 : 9. Elijah was miraculously fed by ravens, 1 Kin. 17:6.

REAR'WARD, the strong battalion that closed and guarded the rear of an army, Josh. 6:13; Isa. 52:12; 58:8.

REBEK'AH, a daughter of Bethuel, and sister of Laban in Mesopotamia, who became the wife of Isaac, and twenty years afterwards the mother of Jacob and Esau. The manner in which she was sought and obtained as the wife of Isaac, exhibits a striking picture of oriental manners and customs. Through her partiality for Jacob, she was tempted into the use of unjustifiable means to secure for him the inheritance, not having faith to leave to God the fulfilment of his own purposes, Gen. 25 : 22, 23. Her deceit led to disastrous results : Jacob fled from home ; and when he returned from Mesopotamia twenty years afterwards, his mother lay buried in the cave of Machpelah, Gen. 24-28 ; 49:31.

RECH'ABITES. Scripture acquaints us, Jer. 35 : 2-11, that Jonadab son of Rechab, in the time of Jehu king of Israel, laid an injunction on his posterity not to drink wine, not to build houses, not to plant vineyards, to have no lands, and to dwell in tents all their lives. This they continued to observe for above three hundred years; but in the last year of Jehoiakim king of Judah, Nebuchadnezzar coming to besiege Jerusalem, the Rechabites were forced to take refuge in the city, though still lodging in tents. During this siege, Jeremiah received orders from the Lord to invite them into the temple, and to offer them wine to drink. They refused to partake of it ; and their fidelity to their father's injunction was a severe reproof to the Jews for breaking their covenant with God. The Rechabites, originally from the land of Midian, are supposed to have retired to the desert at the captivity of the Jews ; and the divine promise concerning the perpetuity of the family, Jer. 35 : 19, was undoubtedly fulfilled, though it may now be impossible to distinguish them, as some profess to do, among the tribes of Central Arabia.

REDEEM'ER, a name given to Jesus Christ, the Saviour of the world, because he redeems mankind from the bondage and guilt of their sins, by dying in their place, and thus paying their ransom, Matt. 20 : 28 ; Gal. 3 : 13 ; Eph. 1 : 7 ; 1 Tim. 2:6 ; Tit. 2:14 ; 1 Pet. 1:18, 19 ; Rev. 5 : 9. In the law of Moses, Lev. 25:25, 48, this title is given to one who has the right of redemption in an inheritance, especially to a near kinsman, who may redeem it from a stranger or any Jew who had bought it. Such was Boaz, who, being one of the nearest relations of Elimelech, married Ruth the heiress of Elimelech, and thereby reëntered into the possession of her estate. Jeremiah redeemed the field of his nephew Hanameel, which was on the point of being sold to another, Jer. 32:7, 8. So Christ became a partaker of flesh and blood, that as our near kinsman he might redeem for us the heavenly inheritance, Job 19:25, 26.

The nearest kinsman was also called the redeemer of blood—in our English translation, the avenger, or revenger of blood ; and had a right to revenge the blood of his murdered kinsman, Num. 35 : 12, 19, 21 ; Deut. 19 : 6, 12. To protect the innocent from these avengers, or redeemers, God appointed cities of refuge throughout Israel. See REFUGE.

RECORD'ER, or remembrancer, a sort of registrar of affairs at the court of Judah, 2 Sam. 8:16 ; 1 Kin. 4:3 ; 2 Kin. 18:18.

RED SEA. See SEA.

RECONCILIA'TION, in Scripture, is the restoration of harmony between two persons at variance, by the removal of existing obstacles, 1 Sam. 29 : 4. Christ bids the man who has wronged his brother, to make peace with him, and secure his favor by confession and reparation, before presenting his gift at God's altar, Matt. 5 : 23, 24. In the far more important matter of peace with God, to make human salvation possible, a just God must be reconciled to the sinner, and the rebellious sinner be reconciled to God. This reconciliation is effected by the blood of the Lamb through the power of the Spirit, Rom. 5 : 10 ; 2 Cor. 5:19 ; Eph. 2:16.

REED, sometimes a stalk or rod of any plant, as of the hyssop, Matt. 27:48 ; John 19:29. Usually, however, the word *reed* denotes a reed or cane growing in marshy grounds, Job 40:21 ; Isa. 19:6 ; slender and fragile, and hence taken as an emblem of weakness, 1 Kin. 14 : 15 ; 2 Kin. 18 : 21 ; Isa. 36 : 6 ; Ezek. 29 : 6, and of instability, Matt. 11:7. "A bruised reed," Isa. 42 : 3, Matt. 12 : 20, is an emblem of a soul crushed and ready to sink in despair under a sense of its guilty and lost condition. Such a soul the Saviour will graciously sustain and strengthen. The *reed of spice*, or *good reed*, (English version, "sweet calamus," Exod. 30 : 23, "sweet cane," Jer. 6 : 20,) also called simply *reed*, (English version, "calamus" or "sweet cane,") Isa. 43 : 24, Song. 4 : 14, Ezek. 27 : 19, is the sweet flag of India, *calamus odoratus*. Reeds were anciently used as pens and as measuring-rods, Ezek. 40:5; 42:16. The Hebrew "reed" is supposed to have been about ten feet long.

REFUGE, Cities of. To provide security for those who should undesignedly kill a man, the Lord commanded Moses to appoint six cities of refuge, or asylums, that any one who should thus shed blood might retire thither, and have time to prepare his defence before the judges, and that the kinsmen of the deceased might not pursue and kill him, Ex. 21 : 13; Num. 35 : 11-34. Of such cities there were three on each side Jordan. On the west were Kedesh of Naphtali, Shechem, and Hebron; on the east, Golan, Ramoth-Gilead, and Bezer, Josh. 20 : 7, 8. These cities served not only for Hebrews, but for all strangers who resided in the country, Deut. 19 : 1-10. The Lord also commanded that when the Hebrews should multiply and enlarge their land, they should add three other cities of refuge. But this command was never fulfilled.

The custom of blood-revenge appears to have been an institution or principle very early introduced among the nomadic oriental tribes. So firmly was this practice established among the Israelites before their entrance into the promised land, and probably also even before their sojourning in Egypt, that Moses was directed by Jehovah not to attempt to eradicate it entirely, but only to counteract and modify it by the institution of cities of refuge. The custom of avenging the blood of a member of a family or tribe upon some member of the tribe or family of the slayer, still exists in full force among the modern Bedaweens, the representatives in a certain sense of the ancient Israelites in the desert. They prefer this mode of self-vengeance. Niebuhr informs us that "the Arabs rather avenge themselves, as the law allows, upon the family of the murderer; and seek an opportunity of slaying its *head*, or most considerable person, whom they regard as being properly the person guilty of the crime, as it must have been committed through his negligence in watching over the conduct of those under his inspection. From this time the two families are in continual fears, till some one or other of the murderer's family be slain. No reconciliation can take place between them, and the quarrel is still occasionally renewed. There have been instances of such family feuds lasting forty years. If in the contest a man of the murdered person's family happens to fall, there can be no peace until two others of the murderer's family have been slain." How far superior to this was the Mosaic institution of cities of refuge, where the involuntary homicide might remain in peace till the death of the high-priest, and then go forth in safety, while a really guilty person did not escape punishment.

Among most of the nations of antiquity, temples, and particularly the altars within them, were regarded as proffering an asylum for fugitives from violence. Among the Hebrews we find indications of the custom on the part of the culprit of fleeing to the Lord's altar. But this was not allowed to screen the guilty from deserved punishment, Ex. 21:14; 1 Kin. 2:28-34.

There is an appointed city of refuge for sinners exposed to the second death, and an altar of refuge sprinkled with atoning blood. Happy the soul that flees and is safe in Christ, ere it is overtaken by the avenging law of God.

REGENERA'TION, the new birth; that work of the Holy Spirit by which the soul, previously dead in sins, is created anew in Christ unto righteousness. It is expressed in Scripture by being born again and born from above, John 3:3-7; becoming a new creature, 2 Cor. 5:17; being quickened to a new life of holiness, Eph. 2:1; having Christ formed in the heart, Gal. 4:19; and being made partaker of the divine nature, 2 Pet. 1:4. The sole author of this change is the Holy Spirit, John 1:12, 13; 3:4; Eph. 2:8-10; and he effects it ordinarily by the instrumentality of gospel truth, 1 Cor. 4:15; Jas. 1:18; 1 Pet. 1:23. In this change the moral image of God is brought back into the soul, and the principle of supreme love to him and unselfish love to our neighbor is implanted. Regeneration, producing faith, is accompanied by justification, and by actual holiness of life, or sanctification begun, and completed when the "babe in Christ" reaches in heaven "the fulness of the stature of the perfect man" in Him. In Matt. 19:28, regeneration means Christ's making all things new. In Titus 3:5, "the washing of regeneration" denotes the purifying work of the Spirit in the new birth.

REHABI'AH, a grandson of Moses, and the only son of Eliezer; his numerous posterity are mentioned as betokening the divine favor, 1 Chr. 23:17.

RE'HOB, I., a Levitical city in Asher, Josh. 19:28; 21:31, on the northern border of the Holy Land, called also Beth-rehob, and lying in a valley south of Anti-Lebanon, not far north of Dan, Num. 13:21; Judg. 18:28. It was long governed by its own kings, Judg. 1:31, but in the time of David was rendered tributary, 2 Sam. 10:6, 8, 19. Some think there were two cities of this name in Asher.

II. The father of Hadadezer king of Zobah in Syria, 2 Sam. 8:3.

REHOBO'AM, the son and successor of Solomon, by Naamah, an Ammonitess, 1 Kin. 12; 14:21-31; 2 Chr. 10-12. He was forty-one years old when he began to reign, and was therefore born at the beginning of his father's reign. He ascended the throne about 975 B. C., and reigned seventeen years at Jerusalem. Under his reign the ten tribes revolted, and formed the kingdom of Israel under Jeroboam. The immediate cause of this schism was Rehoboam's headstrong folly in rejecting experienced counsellors, and claiming tyrannical power. He at once sought to recover the revolted tribes by force; and though directed by God not to make war, he did not long delay hostilities, and these continued during his whole reign. The people also fell into idolatry, and were punished in the fifth year of Rehoboam by an Egyptian army, which subjected them to a heavy tribute. See SHISHAK. Scripture leads us to trace the sins and misfortunes of Rehoboam in part to the influence of his heathen mother, 2 Chr. 12:13. The latter portion of his reign seems to have passed more quietly.

REHO'BOTH, I., a city of ancient Assyria, site unknown, Gen. 10:11.

II. A place in the wilderness south of Gerar and Beersheba, so named by Isaac on the occasion of his digging a well there, Gen. 26:22.

III. A city on the Euphrates, thought to be the modern Er-rahabeh, south of Carchemish, Gen. 36:37; 1 Chr. 1:48.

RE'HUM, an officer of the king of Persia, in Samaria, during the rebuilding of the temple; by an insidious letter to the king he procured an edict for the discontinuance of this work for a time, probably two years or more preceding 520 B. C., when it was resumed.

REINS, or KIDNEYS. The Hebrews often make the reins the seat of the affections, and ascribe to them knowledge, joy, pain, pleasure; hence in Scripture it is said that God searches the heart and tries the reins.

REM'PHAN, an idol, the same as Chiun. Compare Amos 5:26, and Acts 7:43. See CHIUN.

REPENT'ANCE, a change of mind, accompanied with regret and sorrow for something done, and an earnest wish that it was undone. Such was the repentance of Judas, Matt. 27:3; and so it is said that Esau found "no place of repentance" in his father Isaac, although he sought it with tears, Heb. 12:17; that is, Isaac would not change what he had done, and revoke the blessing given to Jacob, Gen. 27. God is sometimes said to "repent" of something he had done, Gen. 6:6; Jonah 3:9, 10; not that he could wish it undone, but that in his providence such a change of course took place as among men would be ascribed to a change of mind. But the true gospel repentance, or "repentance unto life," is sorrow for sin, grief for having committed it, and a turning away from it with abhorrence, accompanied with sincere endeavors, in reliance on God's grace and the influences of the Holy Spirit, to live in humble and holy obedience to the commands and will of God. This is that repentance which always accompanies true faith, and to which is promised the free forgiveness of sin through the merits of Jesus Christ, Matt. 4:17; Acts 3:19; 11:18; 20:12.

REPETI'TIONS in prayers, which our Saviour censures, Matt. 6:7, were short forms or particular expressions in prayer, which the Jews were accustomed to repeat a certain number of times. So Roman-catholics still repeat the Lord's prayer, Ave Marias, etc., a great number of times; and think that the oftener a prayer is repeated, the more meritorious and efficacious it is. The repeated cry of a soul in earnest is indeed welcome to God, Gen. 18; Matt. 26:44; Luke 18:1; but he regards the heart and not the lips; and the greater the number of prayers one repeats as a task by which to acquire merit, the greater his sin.

REPH'AIM; the Hebrew word is used in two distinct significations.

I. REPHAIM is used to comprehend all the gigantic races of the Canaanites, of whom there were several families. There were Rephaim beyond Jordan, at Ashtaroth Karnaim, in the time of Abraham, Gen. 14:5; also some in the time of Moses. Og king of Bashan was of the Rephaim. In the time of Joshua, some of their descendants dwelt in the land of Canaan, Josh. 12:4; 17:15, and we hear of them in David's time, in the city of Gath, 1 Chr. 20:4-6. The giant Goliath and others were the remains of the Rephaim, or of the kindred family of Anakim. Their magnitude and strength are often spoken of in Scripture. They appear to have excelled in violence and crime, and hence are monuments of divine justice.

II. REPHAIM, the shades or spirits of the departed, dwelling in Sheol or Hades, generally rendered in our version, "the dead," ("dead *things*," Job 26:5;) Psa. 88:10; Prov. 2:18; 21:16, etc.

THE VALLEY OF THE REPHAIM, OR GIANTS, was famous in Joshua's time, Josh. 15:8; 17:15; 18:16, and in the time of David, who here defeated the Philistines, 2 Sam. 5:18, 22; 1 Chr. 11:15; 14:9. It was a broad and fertile valley, Isa. 17:5, beginning near the valley of Hinnom, and extending several miles south-west from Jerusalem, when it contracted to a narrow passage leading off towards the Mediterranean. It was in Judah, but near the border of Benjamin.

REPH'IDIM, an encampment of the Israelites between the wilderness of Sin and mount Sinai, where the people murmured, and God gave them water from the rock. Here also the Amalekites attacked them, and were defeated, Ex. 17. It is thought to have been in the valley now called esh-Sheikh, a day's march north-west of Sinai, and near the western border of the Horeb group of mountains. See SINAI.

REP'ROBATE, rejected as not enduring the test of worthiness, Jer. 6:30. Some men are spoken of as reprobate even in this life, being hardened in sin and unbelief, Rom. 1:28; 2 Tim. 3:8; Tit. 1:16.

RE'SEN, an ancient Assyrian city, between Nineveh and Calah, Gen. 10:12. Its exact position cannot now be determined.

RESPECT' OF PER'SONS. The judges

of the Hebrews were directed to give sentence strictly according to truth and justice, without regard to the comparative wealth, influence, or other advantage of one party over the other, Lev. 19:15; Deut. 16:17, 19; Prov. 24:23. Thus God judges, not according to outward appearance or station, but according to the heart, Acts 10:34; Rom. 2:6–11. Thus ought men to estimate and treat their fellow-men; and to court the favor of the rich and influential is sharply censured in Scripture, Prov. 28:21; Jas. 2:1–9; Jude 16.

REST, in Acts 9:31, refers to the respite from persecution enjoyed by the Christians in Palestine, after the conversion of Saul of Tarsus, during the last two years of Caligula's short reign, A. D. 39 and 40, when the Jews were so harassed by the attempts of the emperor to force them to worship him as a god, that they forbore to afflict the followers of Christ.

RESTITU'TION, Job 20:10, 18. The repairing of wrongs done, and the restoring of what one has wrongfully taken from another, are strictly enjoined in Scripture, and are a necessary evidence of true repentance, Ex. 22:1–15; Neh. 5:1–13; Luke 19:8. Restoration should be perfect and just; replacing, so far as possible, all that has been taken, with interest, Lev. 6:1–6; 24:21. In Acts 3:21, the time of the "restitution of all things," is the time when Christ shall appear in his glory, and establish his kingdom as foretold in the Scriptures.

RESURREC'TION of CHRIST. This is of fundamental importance in Christianity, both historically and doctrinally. As a fact indisputably proved, it was the crowning demonstration of the truth of all Christ's claims, 1 Cor. 15:14–18. He had repeatedly foretold it; and his enemies were careful to ascertain that he was actually dead, and to guard his tomb for additional security. Yet he rose from the dead on the third day, and appeared on eleven different occasions to numerous witnesses, convincing even those who were the most doubtful, and after forty days ascended to heaven from the mount of Olives. To this all-important fact the apostles gave great prominence in their preaching, Acts 1:22; 2:24-32; 4:33; 10:40, 41. In its relation to Christian doctrine it stands as a rock of strength, assuring us of God's acceptance of the expiatory Sacrifice, of Christ's triumphant accomplishment of the work of redemption, and of his raising to immortal life the souls and bodies of his people. He was buried under the load of our offences; but he rose again, almighty to justify and save us. His dying proved the greatness of his love; his rising again shows that his love had secured its object.

RESURRECTION OF THE DEAD. It is the peculiar glory of the New Testament that it makes a full revelation of this great doctrine, which was questioned or derided by the wisest of the heathen, Acts 17:32. In the Old Testament also we find, though less frequently, the doctrine asserted; as for example, Isa. 26:19; Dan. 12:2. When our Saviour appeared in Judea, the doctrine of the resurrection of the dead was received as a principal article of religion by the whole Jewish nation except the Sadducees. Their denial of it rested on the assumption that at death the whole man, soul and body, perishes. "The Sadducees say that there is no resurrection, neither angel, nor spirit," Acts 23:8. Hence the refutation of this unscriptural assumption was a complete overthrow of the ground on which their denial of a future resurrection rested; for if the soul can survive the body, it is plain that God can give it another body. In this way our Lord met and effectually refuted them, Matt. 22:31, 32; Mark 12:26, 27.

The resurrection of Christ is everywhere represented in the New Testament as a pledge and an earnest of the resurrection of all the just, who are united to him by faith, 1 Cor. 15:49; 1 Thess. 3:14, in virtue of their union with him as their Head. He is "the resurrection and the life," John 11:25; they "sleep in Jesus," and shall be brought to glory "with him," 1 Thess. 4:13–17; 5:10; their "life is hid with Christ in God," Col. 3:3; and because he lives, they shall live also, John 14:19. The Scriptures also teach that there will be a resurrection of the unjust. But they shall be raised, not to be glorified with Christ, but to be judged by him, and sentenced to eternal punishment, Dan. 12:2; John 5:28, 29 compared with Matt. 35:31–46; Acts 24:15.

To cavillers against this doctrine in his own day, Christ replied, "Ye do err, not knowing the Scriptures, nor the power of God." The work is miraculous; and He who is omniscient and omnipotent will permit nothing to frustrate his designs. He has not revealed to us the precise nature of the spiritual body, nor in what its identity with the earthly body consists; but it will be incorruptible, fashioned like Christ's glorious body, Phil. 3:21, and a meet companion of the soul made perfect in his likeness.

REU'BEN, *behold, a son!* the eldest son of Jacob and Leah, so called in reference to the sentiment of his mother, "The Lord hath looked on my affliction," Gen. 29:32. Reuben, having defiled his father's concubine Bilhah, lost his birthright and all the privileges of primogeniture, the preëminence in the family being given to Judah, and the double portion to the two sons of Joseph, Gen. 35:22; 48:5; 49:3, 4, 8, 10; 1 Chron. 5:1, 2. He shared in his brothers' jealousy of Joseph, and yet interposed to save his life at Dothan with the design of restoring him privately to his father, Gen. 37:18–30. See also his well-meant proposal in Gen. 42:37. His tribe was never numerous or powerful in Israel. Dathan, Abiram, and On were members of it. It was the ninth of the tribes in the order of population when they entered Canaan, Num. 1:21; 26:7. Their inheritance was the fine pasture-land east of the Jordan, between the Arnon on the south and Gilead on the north; it is now called Belka, Num. 32; Josh. 22. We afterwards find them reproved by Deborah for remissness, Judg. 5:15, 16. Their position on the frontier exposed them to many assaults from the east, 2 Kin. 10:33; and they were among the first captives to Assyria, 1 Chr. 5:26, B. C. 740.

REVELA'TION, an extraordinary and supernatural disclosure made by God, whether by dream, vision, ecstasy, or otherwise, of truths beyond man's unaided power to discover. Paul, alluding to his visions and revelations, 2 Cor. 12:1, 7, speaks of them in the third person, out of modesty; and declares that he could not tell whether he was in the body or out of the body. Elsewhere he says that he had received his gospel by a particular revelation, Gal. 1:12.

For the BOOK OF REVELATION, see APOCALYPSE.

REVEN'GER, or AVENGER OF BLOOD, is a name given in Scripture to the man who had the right, according to the Jewish polity, of taking revenge on him who had killed one of his relations. If a man had been guilty of manslaughter involuntarily and without design, he fled to a city of refuge. See REFUGE.

RE'ZEPH, a city conquered by the Assyrians, 2 Kin. 19:12; Isa. 37:12. It is thought to have been afterwards called Rasapha, and to have stood some twenty-five miles west of the Euphrates towards Palmyra.

RE'ZIN, a king of Damascene Syria, who united with Pekah king of Israel to invade Judah, B. C. 742, 2 Kin. 15:37; 16:5–10; Isa. 7:1. Turning away from before Jerusalem, Rezin extended his conquests to the south as far as Elath; but was erelong conquered and slain by Tiglath-pileser king of Assyria, whose aid had been procured by king Ahaz. His people also were carried captive beyond the Tigris, Isa. 8:6; 9:11.

RE'ZON, the founder of a dynasty in Syria-Damascus in the time of David, and a great annoyance to Solomon, 1 Kin. 11:23–25. He had been an officer under Hadadezer king of Zobah.

RHE'GIUM, now Reggio, capital of the province of Calabria Ultra, in the kingdom of Naples, on the coast near the south-west extremity of Italy, eight miles south-east of Messina in Sicily. The ship in which Paul was on his way to Rome touched here, Acts 28:13, 14. Rhegium was a city of considerable note in ancient times. The modern city was nearly destroyed by an earthquake in 1783, and now contains about eighteen thousand inhabitants.

RHO'DA, *rose*, a young damsel in the household of Mary mother of John Mark, when Peter was miraculously released from prison, Acts 12:13.

RHODES, an island and a famous city in the Levant, the ancient name of which was Ophiusa. Its modern name alludes to the great quantity and beauty of the roses that grew there. The island is about forty miles long and fifteen wide; its mountains are well wooded, and its valleys highly fertile. The city of Rhodes, at the north-east extremity of the island, was one of the most celebrated of the Greek cities. It was famous for its brazen Colossus, which was one hundred and five feet high, made by Chares of Lyndus: it stood at the mouth of the harbor of the city, on sixty marble columns, and continued perfect only fifty-six years, being thrown down by an earthquake, under the reign of Ptolemy Euergetes king of Egypt, who began to reign B. C. 244. When Paul went to Jerusalem, A. D. 58, he visited Rhodes, Acts 21:1. Modern Rhodes is a Turkish walled town of 15,000 inhabitants, and considerable commerce. The air of Rhodes is proverbially pure, and its climate serene.

RIB'LAH, a city of Syria, in the country of Hamath, at the north-east extremity of Canaan, Num. 34 : 11. Its site is probably found in the modern village Ribleh, on the river Orontes, at the northern end of the great valley of Lebanon, El-Bukaa. Through this valley, by way of Hamath and Riblah, was the readiest access to Palestine from the north. At Riblah king Jehoahaz was taken and deposed by Pharaoh-necho; here also Nebuchadnezzar established his head-quarters when warring against Judah, 2 Kin. 23 : 33; 25 : 6, 20, 21; Jer. 39:5; 52:10.

RIGHT'EOUSNESS, rectitude, justice, holiness; an essential perfection of God's character, Job 36 : 3, Isa. 51:5-8, John 17 : 25, and of his administration, Gen. 18:25; Rom. 3:21, 22; 10:3. It is the wonder of grace that, as the righteous guardian of the law, he can acquit the unrighteous. "The righteousness of Christ" includes his spotless holiness, his perfect obedience to the law while on earth, and his suffering its penalty in our stead. It is called "the righteousness of God," because accepted by him, Rom. 3:25. "The righteousness of the law" is that perfect obedience the law demands; and "the righteousness of faith" is that imputed to the sinner who believes in Christ. With reference to personal character, righteousness is used both for uprightness between man and man, and for true religion, Gen. 18 : 23; Lev. 19 : 15; Isa. 60 : 17; Rom. 14:17; Eph. 5:9.

RIGHT-HAND, the most efficient member of the body, Matt. 5 : 30, and the ready executer of the behests of the will. Hence its use as a symbol of many of the strongest emotions of the inner man. The right-hand is significant of power, especially the almighty power of God, Ex. 15 : 6; Psa. 21 : 8; 77 : 10; of honor, Psa. 45 : 9; Matt. 25 : 31; Acts 7:55; of special benediction, Gen. 48:14; of fraternal love, Gal. 2:9; of hostility, Psa. 109:6; Zech. 3:1; and of allegiance, 1 Chr. 29 : 24. It was raised in the act

of prayer, and also in taking an oath, Gen. 14 : 22; hence the right-hand of a perjured man was "a right-hand of falsehood," Psa. 144 : 8. In regard to the points of the compass, the right-hand in Hebrew denotes the south, 1 Sam. 23:19; 24, as the left-hand means the north, Gen. 14:15. See EAST.

RIM'MON, *pomegranate*, I., a town of Palestine, near the frontier of Edom, Josh. 15 : 21, 32, Zech. 14 : 10, in the region assigned to the tribe of Simeon, Josh. 19:7; 1 Chr. 4:32; Neh. 11:29.

II. A town on a high chalky hill, a few miles east of Bethel, Judg. 20 : 45-47; 21 : 13. A village called Rummon still exists there.

III. A city of Zebulun, assigned to the Levites, Josh. 19 : 13; perhaps the same as Rimmono, 1 Chr. 6:77, which may be traced in the modern village Rimmaneh, north-west of mount Tabor.

IV. An unknown encampment of the Israelites in the desert, Num. 33:19.

V. An idol of the Syrians, 2 Kin. 5:18. See NAAMAN.

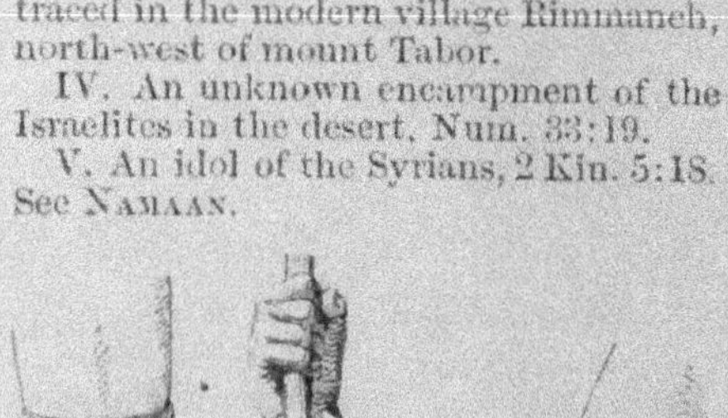

RINGS, ornaments for the ears, nose, legs, arms, or fingers. The antiquity of

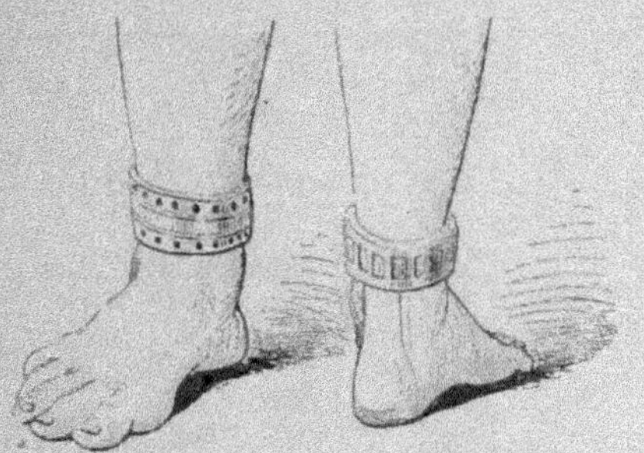

rings appears from Scripture and from profane authors. Judah left his ring with Tamar, Gen. 38 : 18. When Pharaoh committed the government of Egypt to Joseph, he gave him his ring from his finger, Gen. 41 : 42. After the victory of the Israelites over the Midianites, they offered to the Lord the rings, the bracelets, and the golden necklaces taken from the enemy, Num. 31 : 50.

The Israelitish women wore rings, not only on their fingers, but also in their

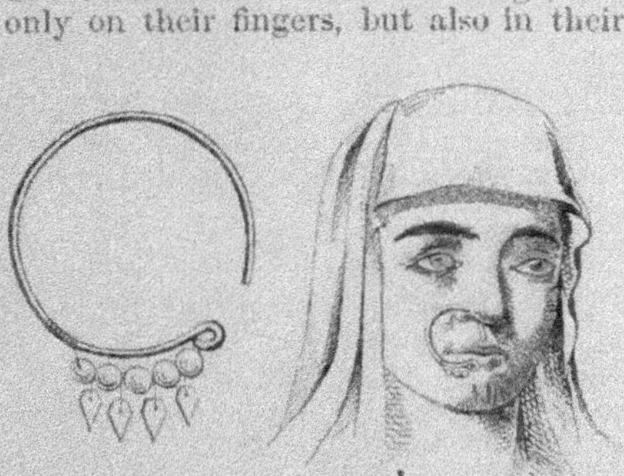

nostrils and their ears, and on their ankles. See BRACELETS. James distinguishes a man of wealth and dignity by the ring of gold on his finger, Jas. 2 : 2. At the return of the prodigal son, his father ordered a handsome apparel for his dress, and that a ring should be put on his finger, Luke 15:22.

The ring was used chiefly as a signet to seal with, and Scripture generally assigns it to princes and great persons; as the king of Egypt, Joseph, Ahaz, Jezebel, king Ahasuerus, his favorite Haman, Mordecai, king Darius, etc., 1 Kin. 21:8; Esth. 3:10; Jer. 22:24; Dan. 6:17. The patents and orders of these princes were sealed with their rings or signets, an impression from which was their confirmation. See SEAL.

RING-STREAKED, marked with circular streaks of various colors, Gen. 30 : 35.

RI'PHATH, a northern nation descended from a grandson of Japheth, Gen. 10:3, called Diphath in 1 Chr. 1:6. The name is traced in that of the Riphœan mountains, in Russia.

RIV'ER. This word answers in our Bible to various Hebrew terms, of which the principal are the following:

1. *Yeor*, an Egyptian word signifying *river*. It is always applied to the Nile and its various canals, except in Job 28:10; Dan. 12:5, 6, 7.

2. *Nahar*, applied, like our word *river*, to constantly flowing streams, such as the Euphrates. In our version this word is sometimes rendered "flood," Josh. 24:2, 3, etc.

3. *Nahal*, a torrent-bed, or valley through which water flows in the rainy season only, Num. 34:5, etc.; frequently rendered "brook," Num. 13:23; Job 6 : 15, etc. Such streams are to the orientals striking emblems of inconstancy and faithlessness. Flowing only in the rainy season, and drying up when the summer heat sets in—and some of them in desert places failing prematurely—they sadly disappoint the thirsty and perhaps perishing traveller who has looked forward to them with longing and with hope, Job 6:15-20; Jer. 15:18.

In some passages in our Bible the word "rivers" seems to denote rivulets or canals, to conduct hither and thither small streams of water from a tank or fountain, Ezek. 31 : 4. Such conduits were easily turned by moulding the soil with the foot; and some think this is the idea in Deut. 11 : 10; "where thou sowedst thy seed, and wateredst it with thy foot, as a garden of herbs." See also Prov. 21:1.

RIZ'PAH, a concubine of Saul, taken

after his death by the ambitious Abner. Her two sons were afterwards hung, with five other sons of Saul, to avenge the wrongs he had inflicted on the Gibeonites. With the most devoted maternal affection, Rizpah watched over their remains day and night, apparently from May to October; and David, being informed of her painful watchings, gathered the bones of all the family of Saul and gave them an honorable burial, 2 Sam. 3:7–11; 21:1–14.

ROBES. See GARMENTS.

ROD, an offshoot from the trunk of a tree, Gen. 30:37; Isa. 11:1; Ezek. 37:15–22. It also denotes a staff, used by one walking, Isa. 3:1; Ezek. 29:6; by a diviner, Hosea 4:12; by a surveyor, Psa. 74:2; by a shepherd, Lev. 27:32; Zech. 11:10–14; as an instrument of correction, Prov. 23:13; 29:15; as a sceptre, Esth. 8:4; Isa. 14:5; and as a symbol of power, Psa. 2:9, support and direction, Psa. 23:4.

ROE and ROEBUCK, not the animal still found in Scotland and Germany, but the oriental antelope or gazelle, the Antilopa Cervicapra, or Dorcas, of Linnæus. It is often referred to in the Bible, Deut. 12:15, 22; 14:5; 1 Kin. 4:23; Prov. 6:5; Song 2:7, 9, 17; 8:14; Isa. 13:14. It is about two and a half feet in height, of a reddish-brown color, with the belly and feet white, has long naked ears, and a short, erect tail. The horns are black, about twelve inches long, and bent like a lyre. It inhabits Barbary, Egypt, Arabia, and Syria, and is about half the size of a fallow-deer. It goes in large flocks, is easily tamed, though naturally very timid; and its flesh is reckoned excellent food.

There are no less than twenty-nine species of antelopes in all. This animal constitutes a genus between the deer and the goat. They are mostly confined to Asia and Africa, inhabiting the hottest regions of the old world, or the temperate zones near the tropics. None of them, except the chamois and the saiga, are found in Europe. In America only one species has yet been found, namely, the Missouri antelope, which inhabits the country west of the Mississippi. Antelopes chiefly inhabit hilly countries, though some reside in the plains; and some species form herds of two or three thousand, while others keep in small troops of five or six. These animals are elegantly formed, active, restless, timid, shy, and astonishingly swift, running with vast bounds, and springing or leaping with surprising agility; they frequently stop for a moment in the midst of their course to gaze at their pursuers, and then resume their flight. The greyhound, the fleetest of dogs, is usually outrun by them; and the sportsman is obliged to have recourse to the aid of the falcon, which is trained to the work, for seizing on the animal and impeding its motion, that the dogs may thus have an opportunity of overtaking it. In India and Persia a sort of leopard is made use of in the chase; and this animal takes its prey, not by swiftness of foot, but by its astonishing springs, which are similar to those of the antelope; and yet, if the leopard should fail in its first attempt, the game escapes.

The fleetness of this animal has been proverbial in the countries which it inhabits, from the earliest time, 2 Sam. 2:18; 1 Chr. 12:8; as also the beauty of its eyes; so that to say, "You have the eyes of a gazelle," is to pay a high compliment.

ROLL. See BOOK.

ROME, ROMANS. The city of Rome is in some respects the most celebrated on earth; as it was long the mistress of the heathen world, and has since been for many centuries the chief ecclesiastical capital of the nominal Christian world. It was situated on the river Tiber about fifteen miles from the Mediterranean, in the plain now called the Campagna di Roma. At the period of its greatest glory its walls were nearly twenty miles in circumference, and enclosed the famous seven hills of which their poets speak, Rev. 17 : 9. It surpassed all other cities in the magnificence of its structures, filled with paintings and sculptures; and contained, it is thought, two millions of inhabitants. Famous for its progress in the arts and in luxury, it was still more renowned for its conquests; and there was scarcely a nation then known whose spoils and captive princes had not contributed to swell the pomp and pride of the imperial city. The idols of all conquered nations were admitted among the thousands there worshipped; and the people were full of superstition, and in morals exceedingly corrupt. The painful representation of the sins of heathenism given by Paul in his letter to the Romans, 1 : 21–32, has been fully confirmed by their own writers.

Rome was founded by Romulus 752 B. C., and governed for a time by kings. After the expulsion of Tarquin, B. C. 509, it was governed by two consuls, elected annually; and this form of government continued several centuries, and indeed after the real power had passed into the hands of a sovereign. Julius Cæsar first acquired the sovereign power, though he refused the name of emperor. His nephew Octavius, afterwards Augustus, took the name of emperor about 30 B. C. In his reign our Saviour was born. The succeeding Roman emperors, who ruled over the larger part of the then known world, were mostly distinguished for their cruelties, debaucheries, and licentiousness; until Constantine embraced Christianity and made it the religion of his empire. By transferring the seat of his empire to Constantinople, A. D. 328, he gave a fatal blow to the power and influence of Rome; which thenceforth continued to be only the ecclesiastical metropolis of the western church. But as such she acquired afterwards, under the popes, an immense power, which still continues in Catholic countries; but which has received its death-wound through Protestantism, and the consequent enlightening of the popular mind. At the present day, Rome is rendered especially interesting by the magnificent ruins of its former greatness, temples, pillars, public baths, aqueducts, triumphal arches, and amphitheatres. It retains also its preëminence as a treasure-house of the fine arts. It has three hundred and sixty churches, among which is St. Peters, the largest in the world, and many others truly gorgeous. It contains also large libraries, including that of the Vatican; numerous galleries and museums full of the choicest paintings and sculptures, besides palaces, villas, schools, and hospitals. Yet it groans under priestly tyranny, and perpetuates the superstition, immorality, and misery of pagan Rome.

In the books of the Old Testament no direct allusion is apparently made to Rome, or to the Roman power, except in the prophetic visions of Daniel, 2:33, 40; 7:7, 19. Up to the time when the canon of the Old Testament was closed, before B. C. 400, the Romans had not so far extended their conquests as to bring them in contact with the Jews. But in the books of the Maccabees and in the New Testament they are often mentioned. See 1 Mac. 8. The first alliance between the Jews and Romans was made by Judas Maccabeus, B. C. 162. This was renewed by his brother Jonathan, B. C. 144. After this time, the Romans had much to do with Judea, not only under the Herods, but also when reduced to the form of a Roman province; until at last they utterly exterminated the Jews from the country. They took the city of Jerusalem not less than three times: first under Pompey, B. C. 63; again under Sosius, B. C. 33; and lastly under Titus, A. D. 70, when both the city and temple were destroyed. See JUDEA.

There were thousands of Jews resident at Rome, where a part of the city was anciently, as now, appropriated to them, and where they were usually allowed the free exercise of their national religion. Among these, and among the Romans themselves, the gospel was early introduced, perhaps by those who were at Jerusalem at the Pentecost, Acts 2:10. Under Claudius, about A. D. 50, both Jews and Christians were expelled from Rome; and among them apparently Aquila and Priscilla, Acts 18:2; Rom. 16:3. At the time of Paul's epistle, A. D. 58, the faith of the Christian church at Rome was everywhere celebrated, Rom. 1:8; 16:91. In A. D. 64, another fierce persecution against Christians in that city was instituted by Nero. These persecutions were followed by others more or less severe, with intervals of repose, making ten in all before the time of Constantine. At this period the corruption of doctrine and of practice, which had previously

RUINS OF THE COLISEUM, AT ROME.

appeared in the church, began to spread more rapidly; and by degrees the papal apostasy, with its fatal perversions of the truth as it is in Christ, became enthroned at Rome according to the predictions of Paul, Peter, and John.

The arena of the Coliseum, whose majestic ruins are now the most impressive monument of the ancient mistress of the world, was the theatre of many a conflict of Christian martyrs with wild beasts; and its sands drank the blood of thousands of unresisting victims, men, women, and children, who met a violent death—some tremblingly, some triumphantly, but all resolutely—rather than deny the Lord Jesus Christ. The Coliseum was erected for gladiatorial shows, by the labors of fifteen thousand men for ten years. It was an elliptical structure, 620 feet long and 513 broad; with an arena 290 feet by 180, surrounded by tiers on tiers of seats, the upper and outer circle being 160 feet from the ground. The vast amphitheatre is said to have contained seats for eighty thousand spectators; and its ruins will long stand, a melancholy proof of the cruelty of heathenism.

THE EPISTLE TO THE ROMANS was written by Paul during the three months he remained at Corinth, A. D. 58, before going to Jerusalem, Rom. 15:25. Compare Acts 20:2, 3, 16; Rom. 16:23; 1 Cor. 1:14; 2 Tim. 4:20. It is the most important, systematic, and argumentative of the epistles of Paul. Its immediate occasion seems to have been the misunderstanding which existed between Jewish and Gentile converts, not only at Rome, but everywhere. The Jew felt himself in privilege superior to the Gentile; who, on the other hand, did not allow this superiority, and was vexed by the assertion of it. In reference to this, in the first five chapters, the apostle proves that the entire human race is depraved and under condemnation—that neither Gentile nor Jew has any privilege of birth or personal merit, but that each receives all benefits through the mere sovereign grace of God, Christ alone being our *justification*. He then proceeds to exhibit Christ as our *sanctification;* and answers the objections made to the doctrine of gratuitous justification, that it tends to encourage sin, and that God has no right to treat mankind in this way. In chaps. 10, 11, he applies all this to the Jews. In the remainder of the epistle, which is hortatory, the apostle lays down many practical rules of conduct, which are of the highest moment to all Christians.

ROOF. See HOUSE.

ROOM is sometimes synonymous with seat or place, as in Luke 14:8-10; 20:46.

ROSE, the queen of flowers, highly esteemed in its native East for its fragrance, and the beauty of its form and colors. Several varieties of wild rose are still found in Palestine. The "rose of Sharon," sacredly associated with the heavenly Bridegroom, Song 2:1, Isa. 35:1, appears from the derivation of its Hebrew name to have been a bulbous plant; and is generally believed, in accordance with the ancient versions, to denote a plant of the Narcissus family, perhaps the meadow-saffron, which grows in rich profusion on the plain of Sharon.

RUBY. The oriental ruby is next in value, as a gem, to the diamond. Indeed, a ruby of this kind, above a certain size, is more valuable than a diamond of the same weight. The oriental ruby is a red variety of the sapphire; its color is usually between a vivid cochineal and crimson. The word "rubies" occurs several times in the English Bible, as Job 28:18; Prov. 3:15; 8:11; but the corresponding word in Hebrew is thought to denote red coral, or perhaps pearls; while the true ruby is more naturally designated by the "agate" or "carbuncle" of Isa. 54:12; Ezek. 27:16.

RUDE, 2 Cor. 11:6, artless and unpolished.

RUE, a well-known garden herb, having a strong odor and a bitter taste. Our Saviour reproaches the Pharisees with their superstitious affectation of paying the tithe of rue, which was not in reality subject to the law of tithe, while they neglected the more essential parts of the law, Luke 11:42.

RU'FUS, son of Simon the Cyrenian who was constrained to carry the cross on which the Saviour was to be crucified, Mark 15:21. If he is the same person whom Paul salutes in Rom. 16:13, as is probable, we may see in this instance the divine blessing abiding on the household of one who befriended Christ and bore his cross.

RUSH, translated bulrush in Isa. 58:5, flag in Job 40:21, and hook in Job 41:2; a plant growing in marshy ground or by water-courses, and used for chair-bottoms, baskets, mats, ropes, etc. The pith of a similar plant in Europe is used as the wick of a candle or rush-light. In Isa. 9:14; 19:15, a rush is put for the lowest of the people.

RUTH, a Moabitess, who, having returned with her mother-in-law Naomi to Judea, probably about the time of Gideon, soon afterwards married Boaz, a kinsman of Naomi. From this marriage descended David, and through him our Saviour Jesus Christ, Matt. 1:5.

THE BOOK OF RUTH contains this history, told in a most simple and affecting manner. The object of the writer, no doubt, was to trace the genealogy of king David. At the outset, he says that these events took place when the judges ruled in Israel—an intimation that in the time of the writer they had ceased to rule. At the close of the book the name of David is introduced; which shows that it was not written before his day, B. C. 1060. This book is inserted in our Bibles after the book of Judges, as a sort of sequel to it. Many of the ancient fathers made but one book of Judges and Ruth. The story of Ruth exhibits the frank and simple manners of the times, and the courtesy and charity of the Hebrew laws; gives an intimation of the future extension of the gospel to the Gentiles; and illustrates God's providential care of families, and the blessings which flow from filial piety and faith in God.

S.

SABACTHA'NI, *hast thou forsaken me*, a Syro-Chaldaic word, a part of our Saviour's exclamation on the cross, Matt. 27:46; the whole is taken from Psa. 22:1, where it is used prophetically.

SAB'AOTH, or rather Tsabaoth, *hosts* or *armies*. JEHOVAH SABAOTH is the Lord of Hosts; and we are to understand the word hosts in the most comprehensive sense, as including the host of heaven, the angels and ministers of the Lord; the stars and planets, which, as an army ranged in battle array, perform the will of God; the armies of earth, whose conflicts his providence overrules to the accomplishment of his own wise designs; the hordes of inferior creatures, as the locusts that plagued Egypt, the quails that fed Israel, and "the canker-worm and the palmer-worm, his great army," Joel 2:25; and lastly, the people of the Lord, both of the old and new cover nants, a truly great army, of which God is the general and commander, 2 Sam. 6:2; Psa. 24:10; Rom. 9:29; Jas. 5:4.

SAB'BATH, *rest*. God, having created the world in six days, "rested" on the seventh, Gen. 2 : 2, 3; that is, he ceased from producing new beings in this creation; and because he had rested on it, he "blessed" or sanctified it, and appointed it in a peculiar manner for his worship.

We here have an account of the ORIGINAL INSTITUTION of the day of rest. Like the institution of marriage, it was given to man for the whole race. Those who worshipped God seem to have kept the Sabbath from the first, and there are tokens of this in the brief sketch the Bible contains of the ages before the giving of the law at mount Sinai. Noah sent forth the raven from the ark, and the dove thrice, at intervals of seven days, Gen. 8. The account of the sending of manna in the desert proves that the Sabbath was already known and observed, Ex. 16 : 22-30. The week was an established division of time in Mesopotamia and Arabia, Gen. 29 : 27; and traces of it have been found in many nations of antiquity, so remote from each other and of such diverse origin as to forbid the idea of their having received it from Sinai and the Hebrews.

The REENACTMENT of the Sabbath on mount Sinai, among the Commandments of the Moral Law, was also designed not for the Jews alone, but for all who should receive the word of God, and ultimately for all mankind. Christ and his apostles never speak of the decalogue but as of permanent and universal obligation. "The Sabbath was made for man." The fourth commandment is as binding as the third and the fifth. Certain additions to it, with specifications and penalties, were a part of the Mosaic civil law, and are not now in force, Ex. 31 : 14; Num. 15 : 32-36. On the Sabbath-day, the priests and Levites, ministers of the temple, entered on their week; and those who had attended the foregoing week, went out. They placed on the golden table new loaves of show-bread, and took away the old ones, Lev. 24 : 8. Also on this day were offered particular sacrifices of two lambs for a burnt-offering, with wine and meal. The Sabbath was celebrated like the other festivals, from evening to evening, Num. 28:9, 10.

The chief obligation of the Sabbath expressed in the law, is to sanctify it, Ex. 20:8; Deut. 5:12: "Remember the Sabbath-day to sanctify it." It is sanctified by necessary works of charity, by prayers, praises, and thanksgivings, by the public and private worship of God, by the study of his word, by tranquillity of mind, and by meditation on moral and religious truth in its bearing on the duties of life and the hope of immortality. The other requirement of the law is rest: "Thou shalt not do any work." The ordinary business of life is to be wholly laid aside, both for the sake of bodily and mental health, and chiefly to secure the quiet and uninterrupted employment of the sacred hours for religious purposes. The spirit of the law clearly forbids all uses of the day which are worldly, such as amusements, journeys, etc., whereby one fails to keep the day holy himself, or hinders others in doing so.

The CHRISTIAN SABBATH is the original day of rest established in the garden of Eden and reënacted on Sinai, without those requirements which were peculiar to Judaism, but with all its original moral force and with the new sanctions of Christianity. It commemorates not only the creation of the world, but a still greater event—the completion of the work of atonement by the resurrection of Christ; and as he rose from the dead on the day after the Jewish Sabbath, that day of his resurrection has been observed by Christians ever since. The change appears to have been made at once, and as is generally believed under the direction of the "Lord of the Sabbath." On the same day, the first day of the week, he appeared among his assembled disciples; and on the next recurrence of the day he was again with them, and revealed himself to Thomas. From 1 Cor. 11:20; 14:23, 40, it appears that the disciples in all places were accustomed to meet statedly to worship and to celebrate the Lord's supper; and from 1 Cor. 16:1, 2, we learn that these meetings were on the first day of the week. Thus in Acts 20 : 6-11, we find the Christians at Troas assembled on the first day, to partake of the supper and to receive religious instruction. John observed the day with peculiar solemnity, Rev. 1:10; and it had then received the name of "The Lord's day," which it has ever since retained. For a time, such of the disciples as were Jews observed the Jewish Sabbath also; but they did not require this nor the observance of any festival of the Mosaic dispensation, of Gentile converts, nor even of Jews, Col. 2 : 16. The early Christian fathers refer to the first day of the week as the time set apart for worship, and to the transfer of the day on account of the resurrection of the Saviour. Pliny the younger, proconsul of Pontus near the close of the first century, in a letter to the emperor Trajan, remarks that the Christians were "accustomed on a stated day to meet together before daylight, and to repeat a hymn to Christ as God, and to bind themselves by a solemn bond not to commit any wickedness," etc. So well known was their custom, that the ordinary test question put by persecutors to those suspected of Christianity was, "Hast thou kept the Lord's day?" To which the reply was, "I am a Christian: I cannot omit it." Justin Martyr observes that "on the Lord's day all Christians in the city or country meet together, because that is the day of our Lord's resurrection, and then we read the writings of the apostles and prophets; this being done, the person presiding makes an oration to the assembly, to exhort them to imitate and to practise the things they have heard; then we all join in prayer, and after that we celebrate the sacrament. Then they who are able and willing give what they think proper, and what is collected is laid up in the hands of the chief officer, who distributes it to orphans and widows, and other necessitous Christians, as their wants require." See 1 Cor. 16 : 2. A very honorable conduct and worship. Would that it were more prevalent among us, with the spirit and piety of primitive Christianity!

The commandment to observe the Sabbath is worthy of its place in the decalogue; and its observance is of fundamental importance to society, which without it would fast relapse into ignorance, vice, and ungodliness. Its very existence on earth, by the ordinance of God, proves that there remains an eternal Sabbath in heaven, of which the "blest repose" of the day of God is an earnest to those who rightly observe it, Heb. 4:9.

"The second Sabbath after the first," Luke 6:1, should rather read, "The first Sabbath after the second day of the passover." Of the seven days of the passover, the first was a Sabbath, and on the second was a festival in which the fruits of the harvest were offered to God, Lev. 23 : 5, 9, etc. From this second day the Jews reckoned seven weeks or Sabbaths to the feast of Pentecost, Lev. 23:15, etc. Hence the first week or the first Sabbath which occurred after this second day, was called the first week or Sabbath after the second day.

The "preparation of the Sabbath" was the Friday before; for as it was forbidden to make a fire, to bake bread, or to dress victuals, on the Sabbath-day, they provided on the Friday every thing needful for their sustenance on the Sabbath, Mark 15:42; Matt. 27:62; John 19:14, 31, 42.

For "a Sabbath-day's journey," see JOURNEY.

SABBATICAL YEAR was to be celebrated among the Jews once every seven years; the land was to rest, and be left without culture, Exod. 23 : 10, 11; Lev. 25 : 1-7. God appointed the observance of the Sabbatical year, to preserve the remembrance of the creation of the world; to enforce the acknowledgment of his sovereign authority over all things, particularly over the land of Canaan, which he had given to the Hebrews; and to inculcate humanity on his people, by commanding that they should resign to servants, to the poor, to strangers and to brutes, the produce of their fields, of their vineyards, and of their gardens. Josephus and Tacitus both mention the Sabbatical year as existing in their day. See JUBILEE.

SABE'ANS. This word represents two distinct people, who, in accordance with the original Hebrew, might have been more properly called Sebæans and Shebæans.

I. The first denotes the inhabitants of the country called SEBA. This appears to have been the great island, or rather peninsula of Meroë, in northern Ethiopia, or Nubia, formed between the Nile and the Astaboras, now Athara. Upon this peninsula lay a city of the like name, the ruins of which are still visible a few miles north of the modern Shendy. Meroë was a city of priests, whose origin is lost in the highest antiquity. The monarch was chosen by the priests from among themselves; and the government was entirely theocratic, being managed by the priests according to the oracle of Jupiter Ammon. This was the Seba of the Hebrews, according to Josephus, who mentions at the same time that it was conquered by Cambyses, and received from him the name Meroë, after his sister. With this representation accord the notices of Seba and its inhabitants in Scripture. In Gen. 10:7, their ancestor is said to be a son of Cush, the progenitor of the Ethiopians. In Isa. 43:3, and Psa. 72 : 10, Seba is mentioned as a distant and wealthy country ; in the former passage, it is connected with Egypt and Ethiopia ; and Meroë was one of the most important commercial cities of interior Africa. These Sabeans are described by Herodotus as men of uncommon size. Compare Isa. 45:14. A branch of this family, it is thought, located themselves near the head of the Persian gulf; and the Sabeans mentioned in Job 1 : 15 were probably Cushites. See CUSH and RAAMAH.

II. The inhabitants of the country called SHEBA. The Sheba of Scripture appears to be the Saba of Strabo, situated towards the southern part of Arabia, at a short distance from the coast of the Red sea, the capital of which was Mariaba, or Mareb. This region, called also Yemen, was probably settled by Sheba the son of Joktan, of the race of Shem, Gen. 10:28; 1 Chr. 1:22.

The queen of Sheba, who visited Solomon, 1 Kin. 10; 2 Chr. 9; Matt. 12:42, and made him presents of gold, ivory, and costly spices, was probably the mistress of this region ; indeed, the Sabeans were celebrated, on account of their important commerce in these very products, among the Greeks also, Job 6 : 19; Isa. 60 : 6; Jer. 6 : 20; Ezek. 27 : 22; 38 : 13; Psa. 72 : 10, 15; Joel 3:8. The tradition of this visit of the queen of Sheba to Solomon has maintained itself among the Arabs, who call her Balkis, and affirm that she became the wife of Solomon.

Besides the Joktanite Sabæans, two others of the same name are mentioned in the Bible. 1. A son of Jokshan, and grandson of Abraham and Keturah, Gen. 10 : 28. 2. A grandson of Cush. It is possible that these descendants of the Ethiopian Sheba may have had their residence in Africa ; but the question of these two Shebas is obscure and difficult to determine. The Sebæans and Shebaans are both mentioned in the same prophecy, Psa. 72 : 10, as coming to lay their offerings at the feet of Christ.

SAB'TAH and SAB'TECHA, sons of Cush, Gen. 10 : 7. It cannot be decided whether they settled in Africa, Arabia, or south-eastern Asia.

SACK, SACK'CLOTH. SACK is a pure Hebrew word, and has spread into many modern languages. Sackcloth is a very coarse stuff, often of hair, Rev. 6:12. In great calamities, in penitence, in trouble, the Jews, etc., wore sackcloth about their bodies, Gen. 37:34; 2 Sam. 3:31; 1 Kin. 20:32; Matt. 11:21. The prophets were often clothed in sackcloth, and generally in coarse clothing, Matt. 3:4. The Lord bids Isaiah put off the sackcloth from about his body, and go naked, Isa. 20:2. Zechariah says, 13:4, that false prophets should no longer prophesy in sackcloth, (English translation, a rough garment,) to deceive the simple.

In times of joy, or on hearing good news, those who were clad in sackcloth cast it from them, and resumed their usual clothing, Psa. 30:11.

SACK'BUT. See MUSIC.

SAC'RIFICE, an offering made to God on his altar, by the hand of a lawful minister. A sacrifice differed from an oblation : it was properly the offering up of a life ; whereas an oblation was but a simple offering or gift. There is every reason to believe that sacrifices were from the first of divine appointment ; otherwise they would have been

a superstitious will-worship, which God could not have accepted as he did. See ABEL. Adam and his sons, Noah and his descendants, Abraham and his posterity, Job and Melchizedek, before the Mosaic law, offered to God real sacrifices. That law did but settle the quality, the number, and other circumstances of sacrifices. Every one was priest and minister of his own sacrifice; at least, he was at liberty to choose what priest he pleased in offering his victim. Generally, this honor belonged to the head of a family; hence it was the prerogative of the first-born. But after Moses this was, among the Jews, confined to the family of Aaron.

There was but one place appointed in the law for the offering of sacrifices by the Jews. It was around the one altar of the only true God in the tabernacle, and afterwards in the temple, that all his people were to unite in his worship, Lev. 17:4, 9; Deut. 12:5–18. On some special occasions, however, kings, prophets, and judges sacrificed elsewhere, Judg. 2:5; 6:26; 13:19; 1 Sam. 7:17; 1 Kin. 3:2, 3; 18:33. The Jews were taught to cherish the greatest horror of human sacrifices, as heathenish and revolting, Lev. 20:2; Deut. 12:31; Psa. 106:37; Isa. 66:3; Ezek. 20:31.

The Hebrews had three kinds of sacrifices:

1. The *burnt-offering* or *holocaust*, in which the whole victim was consumed, without any reserve to the person who gave the victim, or to the priest who killed and sacrificed it, except that the priest had the skin; for before the victims were offered to the Lord, their skins were flayed off, and their feet and entrails were washed, Lev. 1:1–17; 7:8. Every burnt-offering contained an acknowledgment of general guilt, and a typical expiation of it. The burning of the whole victim on the altar signified, on the part of the offerer, the entireness of his devotion of himself and all his substance to God; and, on the part of the victim, the completeness of the expiation.

2. The *sin-offering*, of which the *trespass-offering* may be regarded as a variety. This differed from the burnt-offering in that it always had respect to particular offences against law either moral or ceremonial, which were committed through ignorance, or at least not in a presumptuous spirit. No part of it returned to him who had given it, but the sacrificing priest had a share of it, Lev. 4–6; 7:1-10.

3. *Peace-offerings*: these were offered in the fulfilment of vows, to return thanks to God for benefits, (thank-offerings,) or to satisfy private devotion, (freewill-offerings.) The Israelites accordingly offered these when they chose, no law obliging them to it, and they were free to choose

among such animals as were allowed in sacrifice, Lev. 3; 7:11-34. The law only required that the victim should be without blemish. He who presented it came to the door of the tabernacle, put his hand on the head of the victim, and killed it. The priest poured out the blood about the altar of burnt-sacrifices: he burnt on the fire of the altar the fat of the lower belly, that which covers the kidneys, the liver, and the bowels. And if it were a lamb, or a ram, he added to it the rump of the animal, which in that country is very fat. Before these things were committed to the fire of the altar, the priest put them into the hands of the offerer, then made him lift them up on high, and wave them toward the four quarters of the world, the priest supporting and directing his hands. The breast and the right shoulder of the sacrifice belonged to the priest that performed the service; and it appears that both of them were put into the hands of him who offered them, though Moses mentions only the breast of the animal. After this, all the rest of the sacrifice belonged to him who presented it, and he might eat it with his family and friends at his pleasure, Lev. 8:31. The peace-offering signified expiation of sin, and thus reconciliation with God, and holy communion with him and with his people.

The sacrifices or offerings of meal or liquors, which were offered for sin, were in favor of the poorer sort, who could not afford to sacrifice an ox or goat or sheep, Lev. 5:10-13. They contented themselves with offering meal or flour, sprinkled with oil, with spice (or frankincense) over it. And the priest, taking a handful of this flour, with all the frankincense, sprinkled them on the fire of the altar; and all the rest of the flour was his own: he was to eat it without leaven in the tabernacle, and none but priests were to partake of it. As to other offerings, fruits, wine, meal, wafers or cakes, or any thing else, the priest always cast a part on the altar; the rest belonged to him and the other priests. These offerings were always accompanied with salt and wine, but were without leaven, Lev. 2.

Offerings in which they set at liberty a bird or a goat, were not strictly sacrifices, because there was no shedding of blood, and the victim remained alive.

Sacrifices of birds were offered on three occasions: 1. For sin, when the person offering was not rich enough to provide an animal for a victim, Lev. 5:7, 8. 2. For purification of a woman after childbirth, Lev. 12 : 6, 7. When she could offer a lamb and a young pigeon, she gave both; the lamb for a burnt-offering, the pigeon for a sin-offering. But if she were not able to offer a lamb, she gave a pair of turtles, or a pair of young pigeons; one for a burnt-offering, the other for a sin-offering. 3. They offered two sparrows for those who were purified from the leprosy; one was a burnt-offering, the other was a scape-sparrow, as above, Lev. 14:4, etc., 49-51.

For the sacrifice of the paschal lamb, see PASSOVER.

The perpetual sacrifice of the tabernacle and temple, Ex. 29 : 38-40, Num. 28 : 3, was a daily offering of two lambs on the altar of burnt-offerings; one in the morning, the other in the evening. They were burnt as holocausts, but by a small fire, that they might continue burning the longer. The lamb of the morning was offered about sunrise, after the incense was burnt on the golden altar, and before any other sacrifice. That in the evening was offered between the two evenings, that is, at the decline of day, and before night. With each of these victims was offered half a pint of wine, half a pint of the purest oil, and an assaron, or about five pints, of the finest flour.

Such were the sacrifices of the Hebrews—sacrifices of divine appointment, and yet altogether incapable in themselves of purifying the soul or atoning for its sins. Paul has described these and other ceremonies of the law "as weak and beggarly elements," Gal. 4:9. They represented grace and purity, but they did not communicate it. They convinced the sinner of his necessity of purification and sanctification to God; but they did not impart holiness or justification to him. Sacrifices were only prophecies and figures of the true sacrifice, the Lamb of God, which eminently includes all their virtues and qualities; being at the same time a holocaust, a sacrifice for sin, and a sacrifice of thanksgiving; containing the whole substance and efficacy, of which the ancient sacrifices were only representations. The paschal lamb, the daily burnt-offerings, the offerings of flour and wine, and all other oblations, of whatever nature, promised and represented the death of Jesus Christ, Heb. 9:9-15; 10:1. Accordingly, by his death he abolished them all, 1 Cor. 5:7; Heb. 10:8-10. By his offering of himself once for all, Heb. 10:3, he has superseded all other sacrifices, and saves for ever all who believe, Eph. 5 : 2; Heb. 9 : 11-26; while without this expiatory sacrifice, divine justice could never have relaxed its hold on a single human soul.

The idea of a substitution of the victim in the place of the sinner is a familiar one in the Old Testament, Lev. 16:21; Deut. 21 : 1-8; Isa. 53 : 4; Dan. 9 : 26; and is found attending all the sacrifices of animals, Lev. 4:20, 26; 5:10; 14:18; 16:21. This is the reason assigned why the blood especially, as being the very life and soul of the victim, was sprinkled on the altar and poured out before the Lord to signify its utter destruction in the sinner's stead, Lev. 17:11. Yet the Jews were carefully directed not to rely on these sacrifices as works of merit. They were taught that without repentance, faith, and reformation, all sacrifices were an abomination to God, Prov. 21:27; Jer. 6:20; Amos 5:22; Mic. 6:6-8; that He desires mercy and not sacrifice, Hos. 6:6; Matt. 9:13, and supreme love to him, Mark 12 : 33. "To obey is better than sacrifice, and to hearken than the fat of rams," 1 Sam. 15 : 22; Prov. 21 : 3; Matt. 5 : 23. See also the fiftieth Psalm. Then, as truly as under the Christian dispensation, it could be said, "The sacrifices of God are a broken spirit; a broken and a contrite heart, O God, thou wilt not despise," Psa. 51 : 17. The Jews, without these dispositions, could not present any offering agreeable to God; and he often explains himself on this matter in the prophets, Psa. 40:6; Isa. 1:11-14; Hos. 6:6; Joel 2:12-18; Amos 5:21, 22, etc.

The term sacrifices is sometimes used metaphorically with respect to the services of Christians; implying a giving up of something that was their own, and a dedication of it to the Lord, Rom. 12:1; Phil. 4:18; Heb. 13:15, 16; 1 Pet. 2:5.

SACRILEGE, any profanation or abuse of things peculiarly sacred to God; such as robbing the house of God, or making it a den of thieves, Matt. 21 : 12, 13; Rom. 2:2.

SAD'DUCEES. This name was applied in the time of Jesus to a portion or sect of the Jews, who were usually at variance with the other leading sect, namely, the Pharisees, but united with them in opposing Jesus and accomplishing his death, Matt. 16 : 1-12; Luke 20 : 27. The name would seem to be derived from a Hebrew word signifying *the just;* but the Talmudists affirm that it comes from a certain Sadoc, or Sadducus, who was the founder of the sect, and lived about three centuries before the Christian era. The Sadducees disregarded all the traditions and unwritten laws which the Pharisees prized so highly, and professed to consider the Scriptures as the only source and rule of the Jewish religion. They rejected the demonology of the Pharisees; denied the existence of angels and spirits; considered the soul as dying with the body, and of course admitted no future state of rewards and punishments, Matt. 22:23. While, moreover, the Pharisees believed that all events and actions were directed by an overruling providence or fate, the Sadducees considered them all as depending on the will and agency of man. The tenets of these free-thinking philosophers were not, in general, so acceptable to the people as those of the Pharisees; yet many of the highest rank adopted them, and practised great severity of manners and of life. Many members of the Sanhedrim were Sadducees, Acts 23 : 6-9; and so was the high-priest in the time of the apostles. The resurrection of Christ seems to have added bitterness to their hatred of Christianity, Acts 4:1; 5:17.

SAF'FRON, the common Crocus Sativus, a small bluish flower, whose yellow, thread-like stigmata yield an agreeable aromatic odor; and also the Indian saffron, Song 4:14. In the East these were used in making a highly valued perfume, and also as a condiment and a stimulating medicine.

SAINT, a holy person, a friend of God, either on earth or in heaven, Deut. 33:2. It is sometimes used of the pious Israelites, as Psa. 16 : 3; 34 : 9. Nothing is more frequent in Paul than the name of saints given to all Christians, Rom. 1:7; 8:27; 12:13; 15:25, 31; 16:2. In this acceptation it continued during the early ages of Christianity; nor was it applied to individuals declared to be saints by any other act of the church than admission to its membership, till various corruptions had depraved the primitive principles. The church of Rome assumes the power of making saints; that is, of announcing certain departed spirits as objects of worship, from whom the faithful may solicit favors—a notion worthy of the dark ages in which it originated.

SAL'AMIS, the chief city of the isle of Cyprus, visited by Paul and Barnabas, A. D. 48. This was the native isle of Barnabas, and many Jews resided there to whom the gospel had already been carried, Acts 4:36; 11:19, 20; 21:16. Paul's visit was signalized by the miracle wrought on Elymas, and by the conversion of the governor, Sergius Paulus, Acts 13:5-12. Salamis was a large city, situated on the east side of the island, and was afterwards called Constantia.

SALA'THIEL, 1 Chr. 3:17, or SHEAL'TIEL, father of Zerubbabel, Ezra 3 : 2; Neh. 12:1; Hag. 1:1; one of the ancestors of Christ, named in both the gospel genealogies, Matt. 1:14; Luke 3:27. See GENEALOGY.

SAL'CHAH, a city of Bashan, conquered by the Jews and assigned to Manasseh, Deut. 3:10; Josh. 12:5; 13:11. It was near the border of Gad, 1 Chr. 5 : 11, and where the boundary line between the two tribes ran out farthest into the desert. A town called Salchat still exists there, on the south-east border of the modern Hauran.

SA'LEM, *peace*, I., an ancient name of Jerusalem, Gen. 14 : 18, Heb. 7 : 1, 3, afterwards applied to it poetically, Psa. 76:2.

II. A city of the Shechemites, east of Sychar, Gen. 33:18.

SA'LIM, a town near Ænon and the Jordan, south of Bethshean, John 3:23.

SAL'MON, or SAL'MAH, 1 Chr. 2:11, a chief man of the tribe of Judah, husband of Rahab, and father of Boaz, Ruth 4:20; Matt. 1:4, 5; Luke 3:32. See ZALMON.

SALMO'NE, a promontory at the north-east extremity of the island of Crete, now cape Sidero, Acts 27:7.

SALO'ME, wife of Zebedee, mother of James the elder and John the evangelist, one of those holy women of Galilee who attended our Saviour in his journeys and ministered to him, Matt. 27:56. She requested of Jesus that her two sons James and John might sit one on his right hand and the other on his left hand in his kingdom, Matt. 20:20-23. Her conceptions as to the true nature of Christ's kingdom were no doubt changed by his crucifixion, which she witnessed "afar off," and by his resurrection, of which she was early apprized by the angels at the tomb, Mark 15 : 40; 16 : 1. Some infer, from comparing Matt. 27:56 and John 19:25, that she was a sister of Mary the mother of Jesus.

Salome was also the name of the daughter of Herodias.

SALT was procured by the Jews from the Dead sea, either from the immense hill or ridge of pure rock salt at its south-west extremity, or from that deposited on the shore by the natural evaporation. The Arabs obtain it in large cakes, two or three inches thick, and sell it in considerable quantities throughout Syria. Its well-known preservative qualities, and its importance as a seasoning for food, Job 6:6, are implied in most of the passages where it is mentioned in Scripture: as in the miraculous healing of a fountain, 2 Kin. 2:21; in the sprinkling of salt over the sacrifices consumed on God's altar, Lev. 2:13; Ezek. 43:24; Mark 9:49; and its use in the sacred incense, Ex. 30 : 35. So also good men are "the salt of the earth," Matt. 5 : 13; and grace, or true wisdom, is the salt of language, Mark 9 : 50; Col. 4 : 6. See also Ezek. 16 : 4. To sow a land with salt, signifies its utter barrenness and desolation; a condition often illustrated in the Bible by allusions to the region of Sodom and Gomorrah, with its soil impregnated with salt, or covered with acrid and slimy pools, Deut. 29 : 33; Job 39 : 9; Ezek. 47:11; Zeph. 2:9.

Salt is also the symbol of perpetuity and incorruption. Thus they said of a covenant, "It is a covenant of salt for ever before the Lord," Num. 18 : 19; 2 Chr. 13 : 5. It is also the symbol of hospitality; and of the fidelity due from servants, friends, guests, and officers, to those who maintain them or who receive them at their tables. The governors of the provinces beyond the Euphrates, writing to king Artaxerxes, tell him, "Because we have maintenance from the king's palace," etc., which in the Chaldee is, "Because we are salted with the salt of the palace," Ezra 4:14.

VALLEY OF SALT. This place is memorable for the victories of David, 2 Sam. 8 : 13; 1 Chr. 18 : 12; Psa. 60, and of Amaziah, 2 Kin. 14 : 7, over the Edomites. There can be little doubt that the name designates the broad deep valley El-Ghor, prolonged some eight miles south of the Dead sea to the chalky cliffs called Akrabbim. Like all this region, it bears the marks of volcanic action, and has an air of extreme desolation. It is occasionally overflowed by the bitter waters of that sea, which rise to the height of fifteen feet. The drift-wood on the margin of the valley, which indicates this rise of the water, is so impregnated with salt that it will not burn; and on the north-west side of the valley lies a mountain of salt. Parts of this plain are white with salt; others are swampy, or marked by sluggish streams or standing pools of brackish water. The southern part is covered in part with tamarisks and coarse shrubbery. Some travellers have found here quicksand pits in which camels and horses have been swallowed up and lost, Gen. 14 : 10; Zeph. 2 : 9. See JORDAN and SEA III.

SALUTATION. The usual formula of salutation among the Hebrews was Shâlom lekhâ, that is, Peace be with thee. The same expression is the common one among the Arabs to the present day: they say, Salam lekha, to which the person saluted replies, "With thee be peace," Gen. 29 : 6; Judg. 18 : 15, margin. Hence we hear of the Arab and Turkish Salams, that is, salutations. Other phrases of salutation are found in Scripture, most of them invoking a blessing: as, "The Lord be with thee;" "All hail," or, Joy to thee; "Blessed be thou of the Lord." These and similar phrases the orientals still use on all occasions with the most profuse and punctilious politeness. The letter of an Arab will be nearly filled with salutations; and should he come in to tell you your house was on fire, he would first give and receive the compliments of the day, and then say perhaps, "If God will, all is well; but your house is on fire." Their more formal salutations they accompany with various ceremonies or gestures; sometimes they embrace and kiss each other; sometimes an inferior kisses the hand or the beard of a superior, or bows low, with the hand upon the breast, and afterwards raises it to his lips or forehead. See Jacob's salutation of Esau, Gen. 43; and compare Gen. 19:1; 23:7; 42:6; 1 Sam. 25:53; 2 Sam. 1:2; John 20:26. The due and dignified performance of some of these ceremonious courtesies, especially when frequently recurring, requires much time; and hence, when the prophet sent his servant in great haste to lay his staff upon the dead child, he forbade him to salute any one, or answer any salutation by the way, 2 Kin. 4:29. For a similar reason, our Saviour forbade the seventy disciples to salute any one by the way, Luke 10:4, that is, in this formal and tedious manner, wasting precious time. Much of the oriental courtesy was superficial and heartless; but the benediction of Christ was from the heart, and carried with it what was "better than life." "My peace I give unto you; not as the world giveth, give I unto you," John 14:27.

SALVA'TION means, strictly, deliverance; and so it is used of temporal deliverance, victory, in Gen. 14:13; 1 Sam. 14:45. But as the spiritual deliverance from sin and death, through the Redeemer, Matt. 1:21, is a far greater salvation, so this word has come to be used mostly only in this moral and spiritual sense; and implies not only this deliverance, but also the consequences of it, namely, eternal life and happiness in the kingdom of our Lord, 2 Cor. 7:10; Eph. 1:13. It is most justly described as a "great salvation," Heb. 2:3.

The Hebrews rarely use concrete terms, as they are called, but often abstract terms. Thus, instead of saying, God saves them and protects them, they say, God is their salvation. So, a voice of salvation, tidings of salvation, the rock of salvation, the shield of salvation, a horn of salvation, a word of salvation, etc., are equivalent to a voice declaring deliverance; the joy that attends escape from a great danger; a rock where any one takes refuge, and is in safety; a buckler that secures from the attack of an enemy; a horn or ray of glory, of happiness and salvation, etc. Thus, to work great salvation in Israel, signifies to deliver Israel from some imminent danger, to obtain a great victory over enemies.

The "garments of salvation," Isa. 61:10, refer to the splendid robes worn on festival days. The expression is used figuratively to denote the reception of a signal favor from God, such as deliverance from great danger.

SAMA'RIA, I., one of the three divisions of the Holy Land in the time of our Saviour, having Galilee on the north and Judea on the south, the Jordan on the east and the Mediterranean on the west, and occupying parts of the territory assigned at first to Ephraim, Manasseh, and Issachar, Luke 17:11; John 4:4. It is described as having its hills less bare than those of Judea, and its valleys and plains more cultivated and fruitful. See CANAAN. Many gospel churches were early planted here, Acts 8:1, 25; 9:31; 15:3.

II. A city situated near the middle of Palestine, some six miles north-west of Shechem. It was built by Omri king of Israel, about 920 B. C., and named after Shemer the previous owner of the mountain or hill on which the city stood, 1 Kin. 16:23, 24. It became the favorite residence of the kings of Israel, instead of Shechem and Thirzah the former capitals. It was highly adorned with public buildings. Ahab built there a palace of ivory, 1 Kings 22:39, and also a temple of Baal, 1 Kin. 16:32, 33, which Jehu destroyed, 2 Kin. 10:18-28. The prophets often denounced it for its idolatry, Isa. 9:9; Ezek. 16:46-65. It was twice besieged by the Syrians, 1 Kin. 20; 2 Kin. 6:24; 7:1-20. At length Shalmanezer king of Assyria captured and destroyed the city, and removed the people of the land, B. C. 720, 2 Kings 17:3-6; Hos. 10:5-7; Mic. 1:1-6. See OMRI. The city was in part rebuilt by Cuthites imported from beyond the Tigris, but was again nearly destroyed by John Hyrcanus. The Roman proconsul Gabinius once more restored it, and called it Gabinia; and it was afterwards given by Augustus to Herod the Great, who enlarged and adorned it, and gave it the name of Sebaste, the Greek translation of the Latin word Augusta, in honor of the emperor. He placed in it a colony of six thousand persons, surrounded it with a strong wall, and built a magnificent temple in honor of Augustus. Early in the apostolic age it was favored by the successful labors of Philip and others, Acts 8:5-25; and the church then formed continued in existence several centuries, till the city of Herod was destroyed. Sebaste was afterwards revived, and is mentioned in the histories of the Crusades. It is now an inconsiderable village, called Sebustieh, with a few cottages built of stones from the ancient ruins.

The following is the account of the modern city, as given by Richardson: "Its situation is extremely beautiful, and strong by nature; more so, I think, than Jerusalem. It stands on a fine, large insulated hill, compassed all round by a broad, deep valley; and when fortified, as it is stated to have been by Herod, one would imagine that in the ancient system of warfare nothing but famine would have reduced such a place. The valley is surrounded by four hills, one on each side, which are cultivated in terraces to the top, sown with grain and planted with fig and olive trees, as is also the valley. The hill of Samaria rises in terraces to a height equal to any of the adjoining mountains.

"The present village is small and poor, and after passing the valley, the ascent to it is very steep; but viewed from the station of our tents, it is extremely interesting, both from its natural situation and from the picturesque remains of a ruined convent of good Gothic architecture.

"Having passed the village, towards the middle of the first terrace there is a number of columns still standing. I counted twelve in one row, besides several that stood apart, the brotherless remains of other rows. The situation is extremely delightful, and my guide informed me that they belonged to the serai or palace. On the next terrace there are no remains of solid building, but heaps of stone and lime, and rubbish mixed with the soil in great profusion. Ascending to the third or highest terrace, the traces of former buildings were not so numerous, but we enjoyed a delightful view of the surrounding country. The eye passed over the deep valley that compasses the hill of Sebaste, and rested on the mountains beyond, that retreated as they rose with a gentle slope, and met the view in every direction, like a book laid out for perusal on a writing-desk."

SAMARITANS, the inhabitants of Samaria. But in the New Testament this name is the appellation of a race of people who sprung originally from an intermixture of the ten tribes with gentile nations. When the inhabitants of Samaria and of the adjacent country were carried away by Shalmanezer king of Assyria, he sent in their place colonies from Babylonia, Cuthah, Ava, Hamath, and Sepharvaim, with which the Israelites who remained in the land became intermingled, and were ultimately amalgamated into one people, 2 Kin. 17:24-41. An origin like this would of course render the nation odious to the Jews. The new and mixed race indeed sent to Assyria for an Israelitish priest to teach them the law of Jehovah, and adopted in part the forms of the true religion; but most of them were but half converted from their native heathenism, Matt. 10:5; Luke 17:16-18. It was therefore in vain that, when the Jews returned from captivity and began to rebuild Jerusalem and the temple, the Samaritans requested to be acknowledged as Jewish citizens, and to be permitted to assist in their work, Ezra 4. In consequence of this refusal, and the subsequent state of enmity, the Samaritans not only took occasion to calumniate the Jews before the Persian kings, Ezra 4:4, Neh. 4, but also, recurring to the directions of Moses, Deut. 27:11-13, that on entering the promised land half of the people should stand on mount Gerizim to respond Amen to the blessings of the covenant pronounced by the Levites, they erected a temple on that mountain, and instituted sacrifices according to the prescriptions of the Mosaic law, although the original altar, according to the Hebrew Scriptures, stood on mount Ebal, Deut. 27:4; Josh. 8:30-35. Moreover, they rejected all the sacred books of the Jews except the Pentateuch. See SANBALLAT. From all these and other circumstances, the national hatred between the Samaritans and Jews, instead of being at all diminished by time, was, on the contrary, fostered and augmented, 2 Mac. 6:2; Luke 9:52, 53. Hence the name of Samaritan became among the Jews a term of reproach and contempt, John 8 : 48, and all intercourse with them was carefully avoided, John 4 : 9. The temple on mount Gerizim was destroyed by Hyrcanus about the year 129 B. C. ; but the Samaritans in the time of Christ continued to esteem that mountain sacred, and as the proper place of national worship, John 4 : 20, 21, as is also the case with the small remnant of that people who exist at the present day. The Samaritans, like the Jews, expected a Messiah, John 4 : 25, and many of them became the followers of Jesus, and embraced the doctrines of his religion. See Acts 8 : 1, etc. ; 9:31 ; 15:3.

It is well known that a small remnant of the Samaritans still exists at Nabulus, the ancient Shechem. Great interest has been taken in them by the learned of Europe ; and a correspondence has several times been instituted with them, which, however, has never led to results of any great importance. They have a copy of the Pentateuch, professedly made by Abishua the son of Phinehas, 1400 years before Christ. Several copies of this have been taken, the first in 1616, and compared with the received Hebrew text, with which it nearly coincides. There are various classes of different readings, but few or none in which the Samaritan does not appear to be a corruption of the original. Of late years the remnant of Samaritans at Nabulus have often been visited by travellers. They number about one hundred and fifty souls, and are devout observers of the law. They keep the Jewish Sabbath with great strictness, and meet thrice during the day in their synagogue for public prayers. Four times in each year, at the Passover, the Pentecost, the feast of Tabernacles, and the day of Expiation, they all resort to the site of their ancient temple on mount Gerizim to worship. See GERIZIM.

SA'MOS, an island of the Archipelago, on the coast of Asia Minor, opposite Lydia, from which it is separated by a narrow strait. The island was devoted to the worship of Juno, who had there a magnificent temple, fragments of which still exist. It was also celebrated for its valuable potteries, and as the birthplace of Pythagoras. The Romans wrote to the governor in favor of the Jews in the time of Simon Maccabæus, 1 Mac. 15:23. Paul landed here when going to Jerusalem, A. D. 58, Acts 20 : 15. It now contains about fifty thousand inhabitants ; and though ill-cultivated, is fruitful in oranges, grapes, and olives, and exports corn and wine.

SAMOTHRA'CIA, an island in the North-Ægean sea, on the coast of Thrace, nearly midway between Troas and Philippi. On his first visit to Europe, Paul anchored for the night on the north of the island, Acts 16:11. It was anciently called Samos ; and in order to distinguish it from the other Samos, the epithet Thracian was added. Samothracia contained a lofty mountain and a city of the same name, and was celebrated for its devotion to the heathen mysteries, particularly to those of Ceres and Proserpine. Hence the island received the epithet of "sacred," and was regarded as an inviolable asylum for all fugitives and criminals. It is now called by the Turks Semendrek.

SAM'SON, the son of Manoah, of the tribe of Dan, a deliverer and judge of the southern tribes of the Hebrews for twenty years, Judg. 13–16. His birth was miraculously foretold ; he was a Nazarite from infancy, and the strongest of men ; and was equally celebrated for his fearless and wonderful exploits, for his moral infirmities, and for his tragical end. His exploits were not wrought without special divine aid ; "the Spirit of God came mightily upon him," Judg. 13:25 ; 14:6, 19 ; 15:14 ; 16:20, 28. The providence of God was signally displayed in overruling for good the hasty passions of Samson, the cowardice of his friends, and the malice of his enemies. The sins of Samson brought him into great disgrace and misery ; but grace and faith triumphed in the end, Heb. 11:32. His story forcibly illustrates how treacherous and merciless are sin and sinners, and the watchful care of Christ over his people in every age. Compare Judg. 13:22 and Matt. 23:37.

SAM'UEL, *God hath heard*, 1 Sam. 1:20, a child of prayer, the celebrated Hebrew prophet and judge, Acts 3 : 24 ; 13 : 20. He was a Levite by birth, 1 Chr. 6 : 22–28, and the son of Elkanah and Hannah, at Ramah in mount Ephraim, north-west of Jerusalem. At a very tender age he was carried to Shiloh, and brought up beside the tabernacle under the care of Eli the high-priest. Having been conseerated to God from his birth, and devoted to Nazariteship, he began to receive divine communications even in his childhood, 1 Sam. 3; and after the death of Eli, he became established as the judge of Israel. He was the last and best of the Hebrew judges. We contemplate his character and administration with peculiar pleasure and reverence. The twelve tribes, when he assumed their charge, were in a low condition both morally and politically. He freed them from all foreign yokes, administered justice with vigor and impartiality, promoted education and true religion, united the tribes, and raised them higher in the scale of civilization. Their demand of a king, in view of the advanced age of Samuel and the vile character of his sons, showed a great want of faith in God and of submission to his will. Yet He granted them a king "in his wrath," Hos. 13 : 11. Samuel anointed Saul as their first king; and afterwards David, who in due time was to take the place of Saul already rejected by God. As long as he lived, Samuel exerted a paramount and most beneficial influence in Israel, even over Saul himself. He instituted the "schools of the prophets," which were long continued and very useful. He died at the age of ninety-eight, B. C. 1053, honored and lamented by all. Even after his death the unhappy Saul, forsaken by the God whom he had abandoned, sought the prophet's counsel through the agency of a pretended dealer with spirits. God was pleased to cause Samuel to appear, with a prophetic message to the king. In Psa. 99 : 6 he is ranked with Moses and Aaron. See also Jer. 15:1; Heb. 11:32.

The two BOOKS OF SAMUEL could not all have been written by him, because his death is mentioned in 1 Sam. 25, B. C. 1055. Thus far it is not improbable that he was the author, while the remaining chapters are commonly attributed to Nathan and Gad, B. C. 1018. Why Samuel's name is given to both books cannot be known. In the Septuagint they are called the First and Second Books of Kings. See KINGS. The two books comprise the history of Samuel, Saul, and David. They are quoted in the New Testament, Acts 13:22; Heb. 1:5, and alluded to in the Psalms, etc.

SANBAL'LAT, probably a native of Horonaim in the land of Moab, and a great enemy of the Jews. He may have received from the Persian government some authority over the Samaritans or imported Cuthites, as one of the governors west of the Euphrates. When Nehemiah came from Shushan to Jerusalem, Neh. 2 : 10, 19, B. C. 454, and began to rebuild the walls of Jerusalem, Sanballat, Tobiah, and Geshem taunted him, and sent to inquire on what authority he undertook this enterprise, and whether it were not a revolt against the king. Nehemiah nevertheless proceeded with vigor in his undertaking, and completed the walls of the city, Neh. 2:10; 4; 6.

Nehemiah being obliged to return to king Artaxerxes at Shushan, Neh. 13:6, B. C. 441, in his absence the high-priest Eliashib married his grandson Manasseh son of Joiada to a daughter of Sanballat, and allowed Tobiah, a kinsman of Sanballat, an apartment in the temple. Nehemiah, on his return to Jerusalem, (the exact year of which is not known,) drove Tobiah out of the temple, and would not suffer Manasseh the high-priest's grandson to continue in the city, nor to perform the functions of the priesthood. Manasseh being thus expelled, retired to his father-in-law Sanballat, who provided him the means of exercising his priestly office on mount Gerizim. See GERIZIM and SAMARITANS.

SANC'TIFY, to make holy, or to set apart for God, Gen. 2:3; Ex. 19:23. In the Old Testament, sanctification frequently denotes the ceremonial or ritual consecration of any person or thing to God: thus the Hebrews as a people were holy unto the Lord, through the covenant with its rites and atoning sacrifices, Ex. 31 : 13; and the Jewish tabernacle, altar, priests, etc., were solemnly set apart for the divine service, Lev. 8 : 10-12. In a similar sense, men "sanctified themselves" who made special preparation for the presence and worship of God, Ex. 19:10, 11; Num. 11:18; a day was sanctified when set apart for fasting and prayer, Joel 1:14; and the Sabbath was sanctified when regarded and treated as holy unto the Lord, Deut. 5 : 12. All such sanctifications were testimonials to the holiness of God, and signified men's need of moral sanctification, or the devotion of purified and obedient souls to his love and service.

In a doctrinal sense, sanctification is the making truly and perfectly holy what was before defiled and sinful. It is a progressive work of divine grace upon the soul justified by the love of Christ. The believer is gradually cleansed from the corruption of his nature, and is at length presented "unspotted before the throne of God with exceeding joy." The Holy Spirit performs this work in connection with the providence and word of God, John 14 : 26 ; 17 : 17 ; 2 Thess. 2 : 13 ; 1 Pet. 1 : 2 ; and the highest motives urge every Christian not to resist the Spirit of God, but to coöperate with him, and seek to be holy even as God is holy. The ultimate sanctification of every believer in Christ is a covenant mercy purchased on the cross. He who saves us from the penalty of sin, also saves us from its power ; and in promising to bring a believer into heaven, engages also to prepare him for heaven.

SANCTUARY, a holy place, devoted to God. It appears to be the name sometimes of the entire temple, Psa. 73 : 17 ; Heb. 9 : 1 ; sometimes of the "Holy place," where the altar of incense, the golden candlestick, and the show-bread stood, 2 Chr. 26 : 18 ; Heb. 9 : 2 ; and sometimes of the "Holy of Holies," the most secret and retired part of the temple, in which was the ark of the covenant, and where none but the high-priest might enter, and he only once a year on the day of solemn expiation. The same name was also given to the most sacred part of the tabernacle set up in the wilderness, Lev. 4 : 6. See TABERNACLE, and TEMPLE. The temple or earthly sanctuary is an emblem of heaven, Psa. 102:19 ; Heb. 9:1, 24 ; and God himself is called a sanctuary, Isa. 8 : 14, Ezek. 11 : 16, in reference to the use of temples as a place of refuge for fugitives, because he is the only safe and sacred asylum for sinners pursued by the sword of divine justice.

SAN'DALS, Mark 6:9. The ordinary oriental sandal is a mere sole, of leather or wood, fastened to the bottom of the foot by thongs, one passing around the great toe and over the fore part of the foot, and the other around the ankle. The sole was sometimes plaited of some vegetable fibre, or cut from a fresh undressed skin ; and the "shoe-latchet" or thong, and indeed the whole sandal, was often of very little value, Gen. 14 : 23 ; Amos 2:6 ; 8:6. Sandals are usually intended where "shoes" are spoken of in

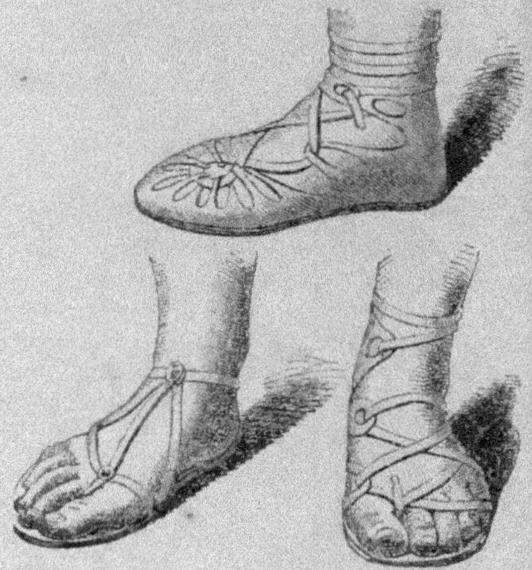

our version. Yet shoes are now worn in the East, and probably were used to some extent in Bible times. The Turks, Syrians, and Egyptians wear a light shoe,

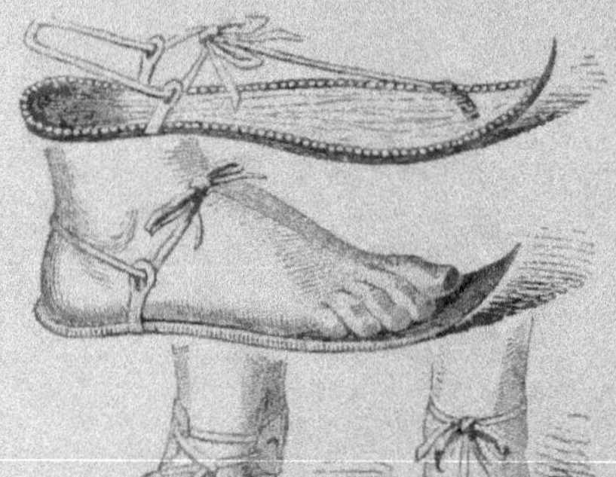

resembling our slipper, and sometimes a wooden shoe with a high heel. The Bedaween wears only a sandal.

The sandals of females were frequently much ornamented, Song 7 : 1, and probably resembled the slippers or light shoes of modern orientals, which cover the upper part of the foot, and are often made of morocco, or of embroidered work wrought with silk, silver, and gold, Ezek. 16:10. See BADGER'S SKINS.

It is not customary in the East to wear shoes or sandals in the houses ; they are always taken off on entering a house,

and especially temples and all consecrated places. Hence the phrase, "to loose one's shoes from off one's feet," Ex. 3:5; Deut. 25:9; Josh. 5:15. Visitors of the highest rank leave their slippers at the door; and on entering a Mohammedan mosque each worshipper adds his slippers to the pile in charge of the doorkeeper, unless attended by a servant. On the summit of mount Gerizim, the Samaritans who accompanied Dr. Robinson took off their shoes as they approached the site of their ruined temple. To bind on the sandals denoted preparation for a journey, Ex. 12:11; Acts 12:8. To bind on the sandals, to stoop down and unloose them, or to carry them until again needed, was the business of the lowest servants; a slave, newly bought, commenced his service by loosing the sandals of his new master, and carrying them a certain distance. Disciples sometimes performed this office for their master, and accounted it an honor; hence the expression of John the Baptist, that he was not worthy to loose or to carry the sandals of Jesus, Matt. 3 : 11; Mark 1 : 7. See also FOOT, with reference to washing the feet. The poor of course often went barefoot; but this was not customary among the rich, except as a sign of mourning, 2 Sam. 15 : 30; Isa. 20 : 2–4; Ezek. 24:17, 23. In the primitive days of the Israelitish commonwealth the custom, in transferring real estate, was, that the seller drew off his shoe and gave it to the buyer before witnesses, in confirmation of the bargain, Ruth 4:7–11. The loosing of a shoe of one who refused to marry the widow of his deceased brother, and spitting upon the owner's face, was a ceremony prescribed in the Jewish law, Deut. 25:7–10.

SANHE'DRIM, or BETHDIN, *house of judgment*, was a council of seventy senators among the Jews, usually with the addition of the high-priest as president, who determined the most important affairs of the nation. It is first mentioned by Josephus in connection with the reign of John Hyrcanus II., B. C. 69, and is supposed to have originated after the second temple was built, during the cessation of the prophetic office, and in imitation of Moses' council of seventy elders, Num. 11:16-24. The room in which they met, according to the rabbins, was a rotunda, half of which was built without the temple, that is, without the inner court of Israel, and half within, the latter part being that in which the judges sat. The Nasi, or president, who was generally the high-priest, sat on a throne at the end of the hall; the vice-president, or chief counsellor, called Ab-bethdin, at his right hand; and the sub-deputy, or Hakam, at his left; the other senators being ranged in order on each side. Most of the members of this council were priests or Levites, though men in private stations of life were not excluded. See SADDUCEES.

The authority of the Sanhedrim was very extensive. It decided causes brought before it by appeal from inferior courts; and even the king, the high-priest, and the prophets, were under its jurisdiction. The general affairs of the nation were also brought before this assembly, particularly whatever was in any way connected with religion or worship, Mark 14:55; 15:1; Acts 4:7; 5:41; 6:12. Jews in foreign cities appear to have been amenable to this court in matters of religion, Acts 9:2. The right of judging in capital cases belonged to it, until this was taken away by the Romans a few years before the time of Christ, John 18:31. The Sanhedrim was probably the "council" referred to by our Lord, Matt. 5:22. There appears also to have been an inferior tribunal of seven members, in every town, for the adjudication of less important matters. Probably it is this tribunal that is called "the judgment" in Matt. 5:22.

SAPPHI'RA. See ANANIAS I.

SAP'PHIRE, a gem next in hardness and value to the diamond, and comprising, as varieties, all those precious stones known by the name of oriental gems, namely, the oriental ruby, oriental topaz, and oriental emerald, Job 28:6. In general the name of sapphire is given to the blue variety, which is either of a deep indigo blue, or of various lighter tints, Ex. 24:10, and sometimes gradually passes into perfectly white or colorless, which, when cut, may almost pass for a diamond, Ex. 28:18; 39:11; Rev. 21:19.

SA'RAH, or SARA, the wife of Abraham, the daughter of his father by another mother, Gen. 20:12. Most Jewish writers, however, and many interpreters, identify her with Iscah, the sister of Lot, and Abraham's niece, Gen. 11:29; the word "daughter," according to Hebrew usage, comprising any female descendant, and "sister," any female relation by blood. When God made a covenant with Abraham, he changed the name of Sarai, or my princess, into that of Sarah, or princess; and promised Abraham a son by her, which was fulfilled in due time. The most prominent points of her history as recorded in the Bible are, her consenting to Abraham's unbelieving dissimulation while near Pharaoh and Abimelech; her long-continued barrenness; her giving to Abraham her maid Hagar as a secondary wife; their mutual jealousy; and her bearing Isaac in her old age, "the child of promise," Gen. 12-23. She appears to have been a woman of uncommon beauty, and a most exemplary and devoted wife. Her docility is eulogized in 1 Pet. 3:6, and her faith in Heb. 11:11. See also Isa. 51:2; Gal. 4:22-31. Sarah lived to the age of one hundred and twenty-seven years. She died in the valley of Hebron, and Abraham came to Beer-sheba to mourn for her, after which he bought a field of Ephron the Hittite, wherein was a cave hewn in the rock, called Machpelah, where Sarah was buried, Gen. 23:9.

SAR'DIS, now called Sart, a city of Asia Minor, formerly the capital of Crœsus king of Lydia, proverbial for the immensity of his wealth. It was situated at the foot of mount Tmolus on the north, having a spacious and delightful plain before it, watered by several streams that flow from the neighboring hill and by the Pactolus. It lay upon the route of Xerxes to Greece; and its inhabitants were noted for their profligacy, Rev. 3 : 4. It is now a pitiful village, but contains a large khan for the accommodation of travellers, it being the road for the caravans that come out of Persia to Smyrna with silk. The inhabitants are for the most part shepherds, who have charge of the numerous flocks and herds which feed in the plains.

To the southward of the town are very considerable ruins still remaining, chiefly those of a theatre, a stadium, and two churches. The height on which the citadel was built is shattered by an earthquake. There are two remarkable pillars, remnants, it is thought, of an ancient temple of Cybele, built only three hundred years after Solomon's temple. These ruins, and the countless sepulchral mounds in the vicinity, remind us of what Sardis was, before earthquake and the sword had laid it desolate.

The Turks have a mosque here, formerly a Christian church, at the entrance of which are several curious pillars of polished marble. Some few nominal Christians still reside here, working in gardens, or otherwise employed in such like drudgery. The church in Sardis was reproached by our Saviour for its declension in vital religion. It had a name to live, but was really dead, Rev. 3:1-6.

SAR'DIUS, or SAR'DINE, a species of precious stone of a blood-red, or sometimes of a flesh-color. It is more commonly known by the name of carnelian, Ex. 28:17; Rev. 4:3.

SAR'DONYX; as if a sardius united to an onyx; a species of gem exhibiting the reddish color of the carnelian and the white of the chalcedony, intermingled either in shades or in alternate circles, Rev. 21:20.

SAREP'TA. See ZAREPHATH.

SAR'GON, Isa. 20:1-4, one of the later Assyrian kings, who sent his general, Tartan, with an army against Ashdod, and took it. The north-west palace at Nimroud in the ruins of Nineveh was built by him. There is some doubt whether he is or is not to be identified with one of the kings elsewhere mentioned in Scripture; and some regard him as having reigned for about three years between Shalmaneser and Sennacherib. Others think he was the same as Shalmaneser, which see.

SA'RON. See SHARON.

SA'TAN signifies, properly, *adversary*, *enemy*, 1 Kin. 11 : 14, Psa. 109:6, and is so applied by Jesus to Peter, Matt. 16:23; Mark 8:33. Hence it is used particularly of the grand adversary of souls, the devil, the prince of the fallen angels, the accuser and calumniator of men before God, Job 1 : 7, 12; Zech. 3 : 1, 2; Rev. 12:10. He seduces them to sin, 1 Chr. 21 : 1; Luke 22 : 31; and is thus the author of that evil, both physical and moral, by which the human race is afflicted, especially of those vicious propensities and wicked actions which are productive of so much misery, and also of death itself, Luke 13 : 16; Heb. 2 : 14. Hence Satan is represented both as soliciting men to commit sin, and as the source, the efficient cause of impediments which are thrown in the way of the Christian religion, or which are designed to diminish its efficacy in reforming the hearts and lives of men, and inspiring them with the hope of future bliss, Matt. 4 : 10; John 13 : 27; Rom. 16 : 20; Eph. 2 : 2. See DEVIL.

The "synagogue of Satan," Rev. 2:9, 13, probably denotes the unbelieving Jews, the false zealots for the law of Moses, who at the beginning were the most eager persecutors of the Christians. They were very numerous at Smyrna, to which church John writes.

SAT'YRS, in Greek mythology, were imaginary demons, half men and half goats, believed by the superstitious to haunt forests and groves. The Hebrew word translated satyrs in Isa. 13 : 21; 34 : 14, means hairy, shaggy creatures, such as wild goats, or perhaps monsters of the ape family. It is translated "goats" in Lev. 4:24, and "devils" in Lev. 17 : 7. The gambols of these wild animals on the ruins of Babylon mark it as an uninhabited and lonely waste. See APE.

SAUL, the son of Kish, of the tribe of Benjamin, the first king of the Israelites, anointed by Samuel, B. C. 1091, and after a reign of forty years filled with various events, slain with his sons on mount Gilboa. He was succeeded by

David, who was his son-in-law, and whom he had endeavored to put to death. His history is contained in 1 Sam. 10–31. It is a sad and admonitory narrative. The morning of his reign was bright with special divine favors, both providential and spiritual, 1 Sam. 9:20; 10:1–11, 24, 25. But he soon began to disobey God, and was rejected as unworthy to found a line of kings; his sins and misfortunes multiplied, and his sun went down in gloom. In his first war with the Ammonites, God was with him; but then follow his presumptuous sacrifice, in the absence of Samuel; his equally rash vow; his victories over the Philistines and the Amalekites; his sparing Agag and the spoil; his spirit of distracted and foreboding melancholy; his jealousy and persecution of David; his barbarous massacre of the priests and people at Nob, and of the Gibeonites; his consulting the witch of Endor; the battle with the Philistines in which his army was defeated and his sons were slain; and lastly, his despairing self-slaughter, his insignia of royalty being conveyed to David by an Amalekite, 1 Sam. 31; 2 Sam. 1; 1 Chr. 10:13, 14. The guilty course and the awful end of this first king of the Hebrews were a significant reproof of their sin in desiring any king but Jehovah; and also show to what extremes of guilt and ruin one may go who rebels against God, and is ruled by his own ambitious and envious passions.

SAUL was also the Hebrew name of the apostle Paul.

SAV'IOUR is a term applied preëminently to our Lord Jesus Christ, because, as the angel expressed it, he came to "save his people from their sins," Matt. 1:21. He was therefore called JESUS, which signifies *Saviour*, John 4:42; Acts 4:15; 5:31.

SA'VOR, an agreeable taste or odor, or that quality of objects which appeals to the sense of smell or of taste, Matt. 5:13. The sacrifice of Noah and that of Christ were acceptable to God, like the odor of a sweet incense to a man, Gen. 8:21; Eph. 5:2. The chief savor of the apostles' teaching was Christ crucified; and this teaching was welcomed by some to their eternal life, and rejected by others to their aggravated condemnation, 2 Cor. 2:15, 16.

SCAPE-GOAT, Hebrew AZAZEL, a word used only in connection with the ceremonies of the great Day of Atonement, Lev. 16:8. 10, 26, as to the derivation and meaning of which there has been great diversity of opinion. The safest and best interpretation is, that the goat itself symbolically bore away the sins of God's people from His presence and remembrance, Psa. 103 : 12. See EXPIATION.

SCAR'LET, a color much prized by the ancients, Ex. 25 : 4 ; 26 : 1, 31, 36. It is assigned as a merit of Saul, that he clothed the daughters of Israel in scarlet, 2 Sam. 1 : 24. So the diligent and virtuous woman is said to clothe her household in scarlet, Prov. 31:21. The depth and strength of the color are alluded to in Isa. 1 : 18 ; and it is used as a symbol of profligacy in Rev. 17 : 3, 4. This color was obtained from the Coccus Ilicis of Linnæus, a small insect found on the leaves of a species of oak, the Quercus Cocciferus, in Spain and the countries on the eastern part of the Mediterranean, which was used by the ancients for dyeing a beautiful crimson or deep scarlet color, and was supposed by them to be the berry of a plant or tree. It is the Kermez of the Materia Medica. As a dye it has been superseded in modern times by the cochineal insect, Coccus Cactus, which gives a more brilliant but less durable color. See PURPLE.

SCEP'TRE, a "rod" or decorated staff, sometimes six feet long, borne by kings and magistrates as a symbol of authority, Gen. 49 : 10 ; Num. 24 : 17 ; Esth. 4:11 ; 5:2 ; Isa. 14:5 ; Zech. 10:11. See ROD.

SCE'VA, a Jew at Ephesus, a leader among the priests, perhaps the head of one of the twenty-four courses. His seven sons pretended to practise exorcism, and presumed to call on evil spirits to come out from persons possessed, in the name of Jesus. Their ignominious discomfiture by a man possessed by an evil spirit, promoted the cause of the gospel at Ephesus, Acts 19:14-16.

SCHISM, a rent or fissure ; generally used in the New Testament to denote a division within the Christian church, by contentions and alienated affections, without an outward separation into distinct bodies, 1 Cor. 1:10-12 ; 12:25, 26. The sin may lie on the side of the majority, or of the minority, or both. It is a sin against Christian love, and strikes at the heart of Christianity, John 17:21 ; Rom. 12:4-21.

SCHOOL'MASTER, 1 Cor. 4 : 15, Gal. 3:24, 25, in Greek Paidagogos ; a sort of attendant who took the charge of young children, taught them the rudiments of knowledge, and at a suitable age conducted them to and from school. Thus the law was the pedagogue of the Jews, watching over the childhood of the nation, and at length conducting them through its types and prophecies to Christ. When a Jew came to a believing knowledge of Christ, this office of the law ceased.

Little is known respecting the schools of the Jews, nor when and how far they took the place of domestic instruction, Deut. 6 : 7-9 ; 11 : 18-20. It is probable that elementary education was under the charge of the ministers of religion, as well as the instruction of those of riper years. At the time of Christ, it would appear that the Jews in general were able at least to read and write.

SCOR'PION, Luke 10 : 19, one of the largest and most malignant of all the insect tribes. It somewhat resembles the lobster in its general appearance, but is much more hideous. Those found in Southern Europe seldom exceed two inches in length ; but in tropical climates it is no uncommon thing to meet with them five or six times as long. They live upon other insects, but kill and devour their own species also. Maupertuis put about a hundred of them together in the same glass, and in a few days there remained but fourteen, which had killed and devoured all the rest. He inclosed a female scorpion in a glass vessel, and she was seen to devour her young as fast as they were born. There was only one of the number that escaped the general destruction by taking refuge on the back of its parent ; and this soon after revenged the cause of its brethren, by killing the old one in its turn. Such is the terrible nature of this insect ; and it is even found that when placed in circumstances of danger, from which it perceives no way of escape, it will sting itself to death. The passage most descriptive of the scorpion is Rev. 9:3–10, in which it is to be observed that the sting of these creatures was not to produce death, but pain so intense that the wretched sufferers should seek death, ver. 6, rather than submit to its endurance. Dr. Shaw states that the sting of scorpions is not always fatal, the malignity of their venom being in proportion to their size and complexion. The poison is injected by means of a sharp curved sting at the end of the six-jointed tail. It occasions great pain, inflammation, and hardness, with alternate chills and burning. These animals frequent dry and hot places, and lie under stones and in the crevices of old ruins. The Jews encountered them in the wilderness, Deut. 8:15, and a range of cliffs across the hot valley south of the Dead sea, called Acrabbim, or scorpions, appears to have been much infested by them. The scorpion of Judea, when curled up, greatly resembled an egg in size and shape; hence the comparison and the contrast in Luke 11:11, 12. The scorpions which the haughty Rehoboam threatened to use instead of whips, 1 Kin. 12:11, were probably scourges armed with knobs like the joints of a scorpion's tail; and like the sting of that animal, occasioned extreme pain.

SCOURGE, or WHIP. The punishment of scourging was very common among the Jews. Our Saviour was subjected to this barbarous and ignominious torture, which was at times so severe as to end in death, John 19:1. Moses limits the number of stripes to forty, which might never be exceeded, Deut. 25:1–3. The Jews afterwards, in order to avoid in any case exceeding forty, and thus breaking the law, were accustomed to give only thirty-nine stripes, or thirteen blows with a scourge of three thongs. There were two ways of giving the lash: one with thongs or whips, made of rope-ends, or straps of leather sometimes armed with iron points; the other with rods or twigs. The offender was stripped from his shoulders to his middle, and tied by his arms to a low pillar, that he might lean forward, and the executioner the more easily strike his back; or, according to the modern custom in inflicting the bastinado, was made to lie down with his face to the ground, Deut. 25:2. Paul informs us, 2 Cor. 11:24, that at five different times he received thirty-nine stripes from the Jews; and in the next verse, shows that correction with rods was different from that with a whip; for he says, "Thrice was I beaten with rods." The bastinado with rods was sometimes given on the back, at others on the soles of the feet.

SCRIBE, in the earlier Hebrew writings, was one skilled in writing and accounts, Ex. 5:6; Judg. 5:14; Jer. 52:25; the person who communicated to the people the commands of the king, like the modern Secretary of State, 2 Sam. 8:17; 20:25. In the later times of the Old Testament, especially after the captivity, and in the New Testament, a scribe is a person skilled in the Jewish law, a teacher or interpreter of the law. So Ezra was "a ready scribe in the law of Moses," Ezra 7:6; 1 Chr. 27:32. The scribes of the New Testament were a class of men educated for the purpose of preserving and expounding the sacred books. They had the charge of transcribing them, of interpreting the more difficult passages, and of deciding in cases which grew out of the ceremonial law, Matt. 2:4, and were especially skilled in those glosses and traditions by which the Jews made void the law, Matt. 15:1–6. Jewish writers speak of them as the schoolmasters of the nation; and one mode in which they exercised their office was, by meeting the people from time to time, in every town, for the purpose of holding familiar discussions, and raising questions of the law for debate. Their influence was of course great; many of them were members of the Sanhedrim, and we often find them mentioned in connection with the elders and chief priests, Matt. 5:20; 7:29; 12:38; 20:18; 21:15. Like the Pharisees, they were bitterly opposed to Christ, and joined with the priests and counsellors in persecuting him and his followers, having little knowledge of Him concerning whom Moses and the prophets did write. The same persons who are termed scribes, are in parallel passages sometimes called lawyers and doctors of the law, Matt. 22:35; Mark 12:28. Hence "scribe" is also used for a person distinguished for learning and wisdom, 1 Cor. 1:20.

SCRIP, a bag or wallet, in which travellers carried a portion of food, or some small articles of convenience, 1 Sam. 17:40; Matt. 10:10.

SCRIPTURE, or SCRIPTURES, *the writings*, that is, by eminence: the inspired writings, comprising the Old and New Testaments. See BIBLE.

SCYTHIANS, wandering tribes in the immense regions north and north-east of the Black and Caspian seas. They are said by Herodotus to have made an incursion into South-western Asia and Egypt, some seven hundred years before Christ; and it was perhaps a fragment of this host, located at Bethshean, which gave that city its classical name Scythopolis. In Col. 3:11, "Scythian" appears to signify the rudest of barbarians.

SEA. The Hebrews give the name of sea to any large collection of water, Job 14:11; as to the lakes of Tiberias and Asphaltites, and also to the rivers Nile and Euphrates, Isa. 11:15; 18:2; 21:1; Jer. 51:36, 42. The principal seas mentioned in Scripture are the following:

I. The GREAT SEA, the Mediterranean, called also the hinder or Western sea. Indeed, the Hebrew word for sea, meaning the Mediterranean, is often put for the west. The Great sea is 2,200 miles long, and in the widest part 1,200 miles in width. In many places it is so deep as to give no soundings. It is little affected by tides, but is often agitated by violent winds. The prevailing direction of the wind in spring is from the south-east and south-west, and from the north-east and north-west the rest of the year.

II. The RED SEA, Ex. 10:19; 13:18; Psa. 106:7, 9, 22, derived its name from Edom, which lay between it and Palestine; or from the hue of the mountains on its western coast, or of the animalculæ which float in masses on its surface. It lies between Arabia on the east and north-east, and Abyssinia and Egypt on the west and south-west, and extends from the straits of Babelmandel to Suez, a distance of about 1,400 miles, with an average width of 150 miles, and a depth of 1,800 feet. At the northern end it is divided into the two gulfs of Suez and Akaba, anciently called the gulf of Heroöpolis and the Elanitic gulf. The first of these is 190 miles in length, and the second 100 miles. Between these gulfs lies the celebrated peninsula of mount Sinai. That of Akaba is connected with the Dead sea by the great sand valley El Arabah, described under the article JORDAN. It is only these gulfs of the Red sea that are mentioned in Scripture. The Israelites, in their exodus out of Egypt, miraculously crossed the western gulf south of Suez, and then, after many years of sojourning and wandering in the deserts of the peninsula and north of it, they came to Ezion-geber, at the extremity of the eastern gulf. See EXODUS and WANDERINGS. In Zech. 10:11, both the Red sea and the Nile appear to be mentioned.

III. The DEAD SEA, also called The Salt sea, Gen. 14:3; The sea of the Plain, Deut. 4:40; The Eastern sea, Zech. 14:8; by the Greeks and Romans, lake Asphaltites; and by the modern

THE DEAD SEA; AND THE CONVENT OF SANTA SABA, ON THE BROOK KIDRON.

Arabs, The sea of Lot. It lay at the south-east corner of the Holy Land, and receives the waters of the Jordan from the north, and of the Arnon and several smaller streams from the east. It is over forty miles long, and eight or nine miles wide, and lies as in a chaldron between bare limestone cliffs, which rise on the west side 1,200 or 1,500 feet above its surface, and on the east side 2,000 feet or more. At the south end is a broad and low valley, overflowed after the annual rains. The general aspect of the region is dreary, sterile, and desolate; but at a few points there are brooks or fountains of fresh water, which in their way to the sea pass through spots of luxuriant verdure, the abode of birds in great numbers.

The waters of the Dead sea are clear and limpid, but exceedingly salt and bitter. Their specific gravity exceeds that of all other waters known, being one-fifth or one-fourth greater than that of pure water. They are found by repeated analyses to contain one-fourth their weight of various salts, chiefly the chlorides of magnesium and sodium. Salt also is deposited by evaporation on the shore, or on garments wet in the sea. In the bed of the sea it is found in crystals, and near the shore in incrustations deposited on the bottom. No fish can live in these acrid waters, and those which are brought down by the Jordan quickly die. Compare Ezek. 47 : 8–10, where the healing of this deadly sea, and its abounding in fish, as well as the new fertility and beauty of the dreary wilderness between it and Jerusalem—by means of the healing power of the Kidron flowing from beside the altar of God—forcibly illustrate the healing and renovating power of gospel grace. A person unacquainted with the art of swimming floats at ease upon the surface of lake Asphaltites, and it requires an effort to submerge the body. The boats of Lieut. Lynch met with a gale on entering it from the Jordan; and "it seemed as if the bows, so dense was the water, were encountering the sledge-hammers of the Titans, instead of the opposing waves of an angry sea."

At times, and especially after earthquakes, quantities of asphaltum are dislodged from the bottom, rise and float on the surface, and are driven to the shores, where the Arabs collect them for various uses. Sulphur is likewise found on the shores, and a kind of stone or coal, called Musca by the Arabs, which on being rubbed exhales an intolerable odor. This stone, which also comes from the neighboring mountains, is black, and takes a fine polish. Maundrell saw pieces of it two feet square, in the convent of St. John in the Wilderness, carved in bas-relief, and polished to as great a lustre as black marble is capable of. The inhabitants of the country employ it in paving churches, mosques, courts, and other places of public resort. In the polishing its disagreeable odor is lost. When placed by Mr. King upon hot coals, a strong stench of sulphur issued from it, and it soon began to blaze. The blaze rose four or five inches high, and continued about two minutes.

An uncommon love of exaggeration is observable in all the older narratives, and in some of modern date, respecting the nature and properties of the Dead sea. Chateaubriand speaks of a "dismal sound proceeding from this lake of death, like the stifled clamors of the people ingulfed in its waters," and says that its shores produced a fruit beautiful to the sight, but containing nothing but ashes; and that the heavy metals float on the surface of the sea. Others allege that black and sulphureous exhalations are constantly issuing from the water, and that birds attempting to fly across it are struck dead by its pestiferous fumes. These legends are corrected by more reliable accounts, which show that the birds fly over or float upon the sea uninjured; that no vapor is exhaled from its surface, except that caused by the rapid evaporation of its waters under the hot sun; and that the low level and excessive heat of the valley of the Jordan and the Dead sea account for the diseases prevailing there, without imagining any more fearful cause. The "apples of Sodom" above referred to by Chateaubriand, and described by Josephus and others, answer, with some exaggerations, to fruits now growing around the Dead sea.

In 1848, Lieut. Lynch of the United States' navy passed down the Jordan from the sea of Tiberias, with two metallic boats, and spent three weeks in a survey of the sea of Sodom. He found it nearly 1,300 feet deep, and its surface more than 1,300 feet below the level of the Mediterranean. From the eastern side, some eight miles from the south end, a low promontory projects three-fourths of the way towards the western cliffs, and sends up a point five miles towards the north. Below this point the lake becomes suddenly shallow, the southern bay not averaging more than twelve or fifteen feet in depth, Josh. 15:2. This lower part is believed to cover the sites of the cities destroyed by fire from heaven, Sodom, Gomorrah, Admah, and Zeboim. The vale of Siddim was once a smiling plain, well watered, and like a garden of the Lord, Gen. 13:10; it is now, and for all future ages, a monument of his just indignation, Deut. 29:23, and an awful warning to reckless sinners that the day of the Lord will come upon them also suddenly and without remedy, Matt. 10:15; 11:22–24; 2 Pet. 2:4–9; Jude 7. The bottom of the shallow bay is a deep slimy mud, Gen. 14:10. On its south-west border lies a mountain or ridge composed chiefly of rock-salt, and called Usdum or Sodom, between which and the sea stands a round pillar of salt forty feet high, reminding one of Lot's wife. At present the Dead sea has no perceptible outlet, and the waters poured into it by the Jordan are probably evaporated by the intense heat of the unclouded sun, or in part absorbed in the earth. It is thought by some that the northern and principal part of the sea was the product of some convulsion of nature, long before that which destroyed Sodom and formed the south bay; that the Jordan at first flowed into the Red sea through the remarkable crevasse which extends from its sources to the gulf of Akabah; and that at some period beyond the reach of history, its bed and valley sunk down to their present level and formed the Dead sea. Lieutenant Lynch in sounding discovered a ravine in the bed of the sea, corresponding to the channel of the Jordan in its valley north of the sea. See Jordan.

IV. The sea of Tiberias or of Galilee; the lake of Gennesareth, or of Cinnereth, Num. 34:11, is so called from the adjacent country, or from some of the principal cities on its shores. It resembles, in its general appearance, the lake of Geneva in Switzerland, though not so large. The Jordan passes through it from north to south. It is twelve or fourteen miles long, six or seven miles in breadth, and 165 feet deep. Its waters lie in a deep basin, surrounded on all sides by rounded and beautiful hills, from 500 to 1,000 feet high, except the narrow entrance and outlet of the Jor-

SEA OF GALILEE, FROM THE NORTH-WEST COAST; WITH MAGDALA AND TIBERIAS.

dan at either end. Its sheltered location protects it in some degree from the wind, but it is liable to sudden squalls and whirlwinds, and many travellers on its shores have met with violent tempests—reminding them of those encountered by Christ and his disciples. A strong current marks the passage of the Jordan through the middle of the lake, on its way to the Dead sea. The volcanic origin of the basin of this lake is strongly inferred from numerous indications, such as the black basaltic rocks which abound, frequent and violent earthquakes, and several hot springs. According to Lieut. Symonds, it is 328 feet below the level of the Mediterranean. Lieut. Lynch makes it 653 feet below. Its waters are clear and sweet, and contain various kinds of excellent fish in great abundance. The appearance of the sea from the hills on the western shore is far less grand and more beautiful than that of the Dead sea. It should be seen in spring, when the hills around it are clothed with grain and festooned with flowers. The towns that once crowded its shores with a teeming population, the groves and shrubbery that covered its hills, and the boats and gallies that studded its surface are gone. But the sea remains, hallowed by many scenes described in the gospels. The Saviour of mankind often looked upon its quiet beauty and crossed it in his journeys; he stilled its waves by a word, and hallowed its shores by his miracles and teachings. Here several of the apostles were called to become "fishers of men," and in its waters Peter sank trembling and crying, "Lord, save me," Matt. 4 : 18; 14 : 22; Luke 8 : 22; John 21:1.

"How pleasant to me thy deep blue wave,
O sea of Galilee,
For the glorious One who came to save
Hath often stood by thee.

O Saviour, gone to God's right hand,
Yet the same Saviour still,
Graved on thy heart is this lovely strand
And every fragrant hill."

M'CHEYNE.

V. SEA OF WATERS OF MEROM. See MEROM.

The BRAZEN OR MOLTEN SEA, made by Solomon for the temple, was a circular vessel at least fifteen feet in diameter, which stood in the court of the temple, and contained three thousand baths, according to 2 Chr. 4 : 5, or two thousand baths according to 1 Kin. 7:26. Calmet supposes this may be reconciled by saying

that the cup or bowl contained two thousand baths, and the foot or basin a thousand more. It was supported by twelve oxen of brass, and was probably the largest brazen vessel ever made—an evidence of the skill of the workers in metal at that period. It contained from 16,000 to 24,000 gallons, and was supplied with water either by the labor of the Gibeonites, or as Jewish writers affirm, by a pipe from the well of Etam, so that a constant flow was maintained. This water was used for the various ablutions of the priests, 2 Chr. 4 : 6 ; a perpetual and impressive testimony from God of the necessity of moral purification in the inexhaustible fountain of Christ's grace. The preceding engraving must be chiefly imaginary.

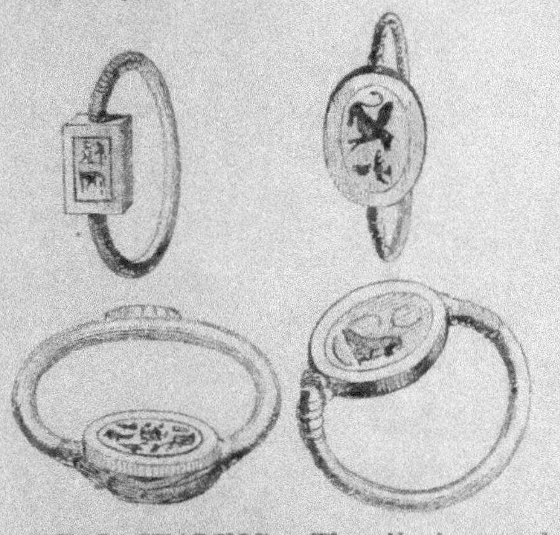

SEAL, SEALING. The allusions and references to seals and sealing are frequent in the sacred writings. Seals or signets were in use at a very early period, and they were evidently of various kinds. Some were used as a substitute for signing one's name, the owner's name or chosen device being stamped by it with a suitable ink on the document to be authenticated. Seals to be used for this purpose, with or without the sign manual, appear to have been worn by the parties to whom they respectively belonged. The seal of a private person was usually worn on his finger, or his wrist, or in a bracelet, being small in size, Jer. 32:10 ; Luke 15 : 22 ; Jas. 2:2. See RINGS. The seal of a governor was worn by him, or carried about his person in the most secure manner possible. The royal seal was either personal, to the king, or public, to the state ; in other words, the seal of the king and the seal of the crown, 2 Sam. 1:10 : the first the king retained ; the latter he delivered to the proper officer of state. So far modern usages enable us to comprehend clearly the nature of this important instrument. The impress of the royal seal on any document gave it the sanction of government, 1 Kin. 21:8 ; and a temporary transfer of the seal to another hand conveyed a plenary authority for the occasion, Esth. 3:10, 12 ; 8:2. Instead of wax, clay was sometimes used to take the impression of a seal, probably on account of the heat of the climate, Job 38 : 14. The seal was a token of possession and of careful preservation, Deut. 32 : 34 ; Job 9 : 7 ; 14 :17. A portion of clay covering the lock or opening of a door, etc., guarded it from being opened clandestinely, Song 4 : 12 ; Dan. 6 : 17 ; Matt. 27 : 66. Travellers in the East have met the same custom in modern times. The cord around a book, box, or roll of parchment was often secured with a seal, Isa. 8 : 16 ; Rev. 5 : 1. The Holy Spirit seals Christians, impressing his image upon them as a token that they are his, Eph. 1:13, 14 ; 4:30. See So.

SEA'SONS. See CANAAN.

SE'BA. See SABEANS.

SE'BAT, the first month of the Jewish civil year, and the eleventh of the ecclesiastical year—from the new moon of February to that of March. See MONTH. They began in this month to number the years of the trees they planted, the fruits of which were esteemed impure till the fourth year, Zech. 1:7.

SE'CRET. See MYSTERY.

SECT, from a Latin word answering to the Greek word *hæresis*, which latter our translators have in some places rendered "sect," in others, "heresy." As used in the New Testament, it implies neither approbation nor censure of the persons to whom it is applied, or of their opinions, Acts 5:17; 15:5. Among the Jews, there were four sects, distinguished by their practices and opinions, yet united in communion with each other and with the body of their nation: namely, the Pharisees, the Sadducees, the Essenes, and the Herodians. Christianity was originally considered as a new sect of Judaism; hence Tertullus, accusing Paul before Felix, says that he was chief of the seditious sect of the Nazarenes, Acts 24:5; and the Jews of Rome said to the apostle, when he arrived in this city, "As concerning this sect, we know that everywhere it is spoken against," Acts 28:22. See HERESY.

SECUN'DUS, a disciple at Thessalonica, who accompanied Paul in some of his journeys, Acts 20:4.

SEDI'TION, a popular tumult, Acts 24:5, or a religious faction, Gal. 5:20. The same Greek word is translated "insurrection," in speaking of Barabbas, Mark 15:7, and "dissension" in Acts 15:2.

SEED, Gen. 1:11; often used figuratively in Scripture, Dan. 9:1; 1 Pet. 1:23; 1 John 3:9. There was an injunction in the Mosaic law against sowing a field with mingled seed of diverse kinds, Lev. 19:19. The "precious seed" is often committed to the ground with many fears; but the harvest, at least in spiritual things, shall be a season of joy, Psa. 126:5, 6.

SEER, one supernaturally enlightened to see things which God only can reveal; applied to certain Hebrew prophets, 1 Sam. 9:9; 2 Chr. 29:30; 33:18, 19; Isa. 29:10; 30:10. Compare Num. 24:3, 4.

SEIR, I., a mountain of Judah, near Kirjath-jearim, Josh. 15:10.

II. A Horite, one of the primitive rulers of the country south and south-east of the Dead sea, Gen. 36:20; Deut. 2:12.

III. A mountainous tract lying between the southern extremity of the Dead sea and the eastern gulf of the Red sea. Mount Hor formed part of Seir, and is the only part that retains its original name. See IDUMÆA.

VIEW OF PART OF THE MAIN VALLEY OF PETRA.

SE'LA, the name of a place mentioned in 2 Kin. 14:7, where it is said that Amaziah king of Judah slew ten thousand men of Edom, in the valley of Salt, and took Sela by war, and called the name of it JOKTHEEL, subdued by God. Sela, in Hebrew, signifies a rock, and answers to the Greek word Petra; whence it has been reasonably inferred that the city bearing the name of Petra, and which was the celebrated capital of Arabia Petræa, is the place mentioned by the sacred historian. It is also mentioned in Isa. 16 : 1, and may be intended by the word Sela, translated rock, in Judg. 1:36; Isa. 42:11. The ruins of this place were in modern times first visited by Burckhardt, 1812, and attest the splendor of the ancient city. He says, "At the distance of a two long days' journey northeast from Akabah, is a rivulet and valley in the Djebel Shera, on the east side of the Arabah, called Wady Mousa. This place is very interesting for its antiquities and the remains of an ancient city, which I conjecture to be Petra, the capital of Arabia Petræa, a place which, as far as I know, no European traveller has ever visited. In the red sand-stone of which the valley is composed are upwards of two hundred and fifty sepulchres, entirely cut out of the rock, the greater part of them with Grecian ornaments. There is a mausoleum in the shape of a temple, of colossal dimensions, likewise cut out of the rock, with all its apartments, its vestibule, peristyle, etc. It is a most beautiful specimen of Grecian architecture, and in perfect preservation. There are other mausolea with obelisks, apparently in the Egyptian style, a whole amphitheatre cut out of the rock, with the remains of a palace and of several temples. Upon the summit of the mountain which closes the narrow valley on its western side, (mount Hor,) is the tomb of Haroun, or Aaron. It is held in great veneration by the Arabs." That this was indeed the ancient Sela or Petra is established by various concurring proofs; Josephus, Eusebius, and Jerome affirm that the tomb of Aaron was near Petra; and the location and ruins correspond with the notices given in the Bible, and by Pliny and Strabo.

Subsequent travellers, especially Laborde, have given minute and graphic descriptions of this wonderful city, with drawings of the principal ruins. The valley of Petra, 2,200 feet above the great valley El-Arabah, is about a mile long from north to south, and half a mile wide, with numerous short ravines in its sides, making its whole circuit perhaps four miles. It is accessible through ravines at the north and the south; but the cliffs which define it on the east and west are precipitous, and vary from two hundred to one thousand feet in height. The main passage into the city is on the east, and begins between cliffs forty feet high and fifty yards apart, which soon

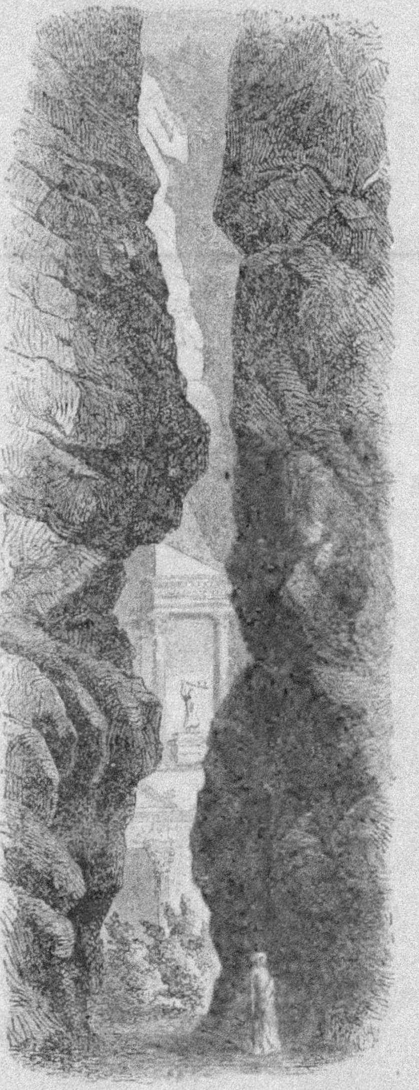

GORGE IN PETRA, WITH A PART OF EL-KHUSNEH.

become higher, nearer, and full of excavated tombs. This winding ravine is a mile long, and gives entrance to a small brook; its sides at one place are but twelve feet apart and two hundred and fifty feet high. At the termination of this narrow gorge you confront the most splendid of all the structures of Petra, el-Khusneh, the temple mentioned by Burckhardt, hewn out of the face of the opposite cliff. Here you enter a wider ravine, which leads north-west, passes the amphitheatre in a recess on the left, and at length opens on the great valley of the main city towards the west. The tombs excavated in these, and in all the side gorges, are without number, rising range above range; many of them are approached by steps cut in the rock, while others are inaccessible, at the height of nearly four hundred feet. The theatre was so large as to accommodate more than three thousand persons. The palace, called Pharaoh's house by the Arabs, is the chief structure not excavated in the mountain that survives in any good degree the ravages of time; it was evidently a gorgeous building. Most of the valley is strown with the ruins of public edifices and with fragments of pottery. The brook flows through the valley towards the west, and passes off through a narrow gorge like that by which it entered. One of the finest temples, the Deir, stands high up in a ravine on the west side. It is hewn out of the solid rock; its front is one hundred and fifty-two feet in length and height; and its lower columns, half projecting from the rock, are eight feet in diameter. A singular charm is thrown over the whole by the beauty of the stone from which these various structures are wrought. It is a fine and soft sandstone, variegated with almost every variety of hues, red, purple, black, white, azure, and yellow, the deepest crimson and the softest pink blending with each other, while high above the sculptured monuments the rocks rise in their native rudeness and majesty. The whole strange and beautiful scene leaves on the spectator's mind impressions which nothing can efface.

Petra was an ancient city, a strong fortress, and for many ages an important commercial centre. It was the chief city among scores which once filled that region. Yet the prophets of God foretold its downfall, and its abandonment to solitude and desolation, in terms which strikingly agree with the facts. "Thy terribleness hath deceived thee, and the pride of thy heart, O thou that dwellest in the clefts of the rock, that holdest the height of the hill: though thou shouldest make thy nest as high as the eagle, I will bring thee down from thence, saith the Lord," Jer. 49:7-22. See also Isa. 34:5-15; Ezek. 35; Joel 3:19; Amos 1:11, 12; Obad. 3-16. When its ruin took place we are not informed. There were Christian churches there in the fifth and sixth centuries, but after A. D. 536 no mention is made of it in history.

SE'LAH, a musical term which occurs seventy-three times in the Psalms, and is found also in Hab. 3:3, 9, 13. It usually occurs at the end of a period or strophe, but sometimes at the end only of a clause. This difficult word, it is now generally believed, was a direction for a meditative pause in the singing of a psalm, during which perhaps there was an instrumental interlude.

SELEU'CIA, a fortified city of Syria, situated on the seacoast, a little north of the mouth of the Orontes. It stood near mount Pierius, and was therefore sometimes called Seleucia Pieria, and sometimes Seleucia by the sea, in order to distinguish it from other cities of the same name, of which there were not less than seven or eight in Syria and the vicinity. They were all thus named from Seleucus Nicator. Paul and Barnabas embarked here for Cyprus, on their first missionary tour, Acts 13:4.

SEN'ATE, Acts 5:21. See SANHEDRIM.

SE'NIR, a name given to mount Hermon by the Amorites, Deut. 3:9; 1 Chr. 5:23; Ezek. 27:5. See HERMON.

SENNACH'ERIB, king of Assyria, son and successor of Shalmaneser, began to reign B. C. 710, and reigned but a few years. Hezekiah king of Judah having shaken off the yoke of the Assyrians, by which Ahaz his father had suffered under Tiglath-pileser, Sennacherib marched an army against him, and took all the strong cities of Judah. Hezekiah, seeing he had nothing left but Jerusalem, which he perhaps found it difficult to preserve, sent ambassadors to Sennacherib, then besieging and destroying Lachish, to make submission. Sennacherib accepted his tribute, but refused to depart, and sent Rabshakeh with an insolent message to Jerusalem. Hezekiah entreated the Lord, who sent a destroying angel against the Assyrian army, and slew in one night 185,000 men. Sennacherib returned with all speed to Nineveh, and turned his arms against the nations south of Assyria, and afterwards towards the north. But his career was not long; within two or three years from his return from Jerusalem, while he was paying adorations to his god Nisroch, in the temple, his two sons Adrammelech and Sharezer slew him and fled into Armenia. Esar-haddon his son reigned in his stead, 2 Kin. 18; 19; 2 Chr. 32.

A most remarkable confirmation of the above Bible history has been found in the long buried ruins of ancient Nineveh. The mound called Kouyunjik, opposite Mosul, has been to a good degree explored, and its ruins prove to be those of a palace erected by this powerful monarch. The huge stone tablets which formed the walls of its various apartments are covered with bas-reliefs and inscriptions; and though large portions of these have perished by violence and time, the fragments that remain are full of interest. One series of tablets recounts the warlike exploits of Sennacherib, who calls himself "the subducer of kings from the upper sea of the setting sun to the lower sea of the rising sun," that is, from the Mediterranean to the Persian gulf.

The most important of these mural pages to Bible readers, are those recounting the history of his war against Syria and the Jews, in the third year of his reign. Crossing the upper part of mount Lebanon, he appears to have conquered Tyre and all the cities south of it on the seacoast to Askelon. In this region he came in conflict with an Egyptian army, sent in aid of king Hezekiah; this host he defeated and drove back. See 2 Kin. 19:9; Isa. 37. The inscription then proceeds to say, "Hezekiah king of Judah, who had not submitted to my authority, forty-six of his principal cities, and fortresses and villages dependent upon them, of which I took no account, I captured, and carried away their spoil. The fortified towns, and the rest of his towns which I spoiled, I severed from his country, and gave to the kings of Askelon, Ekron, and Gaza, so as to make his country small. In addition to the former tribute imposed upon their countries, I added a tribute the nature of which I fixed." Compare 2 Kin. 18:13;

FROM THE PALACE OF SENNACHERIB, KOUYUNJIK, NINEVEH.

Isa. 36:1. He does not profess to have taken Jerusalem itself, but to have carried away Hezekiah's family, servants, and treasures, with a tribute of thirty talents of gold and eight hundred talents of silver. The amount of gold is the same mentioned in the Bible narrative. The three hundred talents of silver mentioned in Scripture may have been all that was given in money, and the five hundred additional claimed in the Ninevite record may include the temple and palace treasures, given by Hezekiah as the price of peace.

In another apartment of the same palace was found a series of well preserved bas-reliefs, representing the siege and capture by the Assyrians of a large and strong city. It was doubly fortified, and the assault and the defence were both fierce. Part of the city is represented as already taken, while elsewhere the battle rages still in all its fury. Meanwhile captives are seen flayed, impaled, and put to the sword; and from one of the gates of the city a long procession of prisoners is brought before the king, who is gorgeously arrayed and seated on his throne upon a mound or low hill. They are presented by the general in command, very possibly Rabshakeh, with other chief officers. Two eunuchs stand behind the king, holding fans and napkins. Above his head is an inscription which is thus translated: "Sennacherib the mighty king, king of the country of Assyria, sitting on the throne of judgment at the gate of the city Lachisa; I give permission for its slaughter." The captives are stripped of their armor, ornaments, and much of their clothing, and are evidently Jews.

Little did Sennacherib then anticipate the utter ruin of his own proud metropolis, and still less that the ruins of his palace should preserve to this remote age the tablets containing his own history, and the image of his god Nisroch so incapable of defending him, to bear witness for the God whom he blasphemed and defied. See NINEVEH, NISROCH, SHALMANESER, and SO.

SE'PHAR, "a mountain of the East," a boundary of the Joktanite tribes, Gen. 10:30. It is perhaps the same as mount Sabber in South-western Arabia.

SEPH'ARAD, a place in Asia Minor near the Bosphorus, to which Jewish captives were conveyed, Obad. 20.

SEPHARVA'IM. When Shalmaneser king of Assyria carried away Israel from Samaria to beyond the Euphrates, he sent people in their stead into Palestine, among whom were the Sepharvaim, 2 Kin. 17:24, 31. That Sepharvaim was a small district under its own king, is apparent from 2 Kin. 19:13; Isa. 37:13. It may, with most probability, be assigned to Mesopotamia, because it is named along with other places in that region, and because Ptolemy mentions a city of a similar name, Sipphara, as the most southern of Mesopotamia.

SEP'TUAGINT, *the seventy*, is the name of the most ancient Greek version of the Old Testament, and is so called because there were said to have been seventy translators. The accounts of its origin disagree, but it should probably be assigned to the third century before Christ. This ancient version contains many errors, and yet as a whole is a faithful one, particularly in the books of Moses; it is of great value in the interpretation of the Old Testament, and is very often quoted by the New Testament writers, who wrote in the same dialect. It was the parent of the first Latin, the Coptic, and many other versions, and was so much quoted and followed by the Greek and Roman fathers as practically to supersede the original Hebrew, until the last few centuries. The chronology of the Septuagint differs materially from that of the Hebrew text, adding, for example, 606 years between the creation and the deluge. See ALEXANDRIA.

TOMBS HEWN IN THE ROCK, PETRA.

SEP'ULCHRE, a place of burial. The Hebrews were always very careful about the burial of their dead. Many of their sepulchres were hewn in rocks: as that

OTHER TOMBS, ETC., IN PETRA.

of Shebna, Isa. 22:16; those of the kings of Judah and Israel; and that in which our Saviour was laid on Calvary. These tombs of the Jews were sometimes beneath the surface of the ground; but were often in the side of a cliff, and multitudes of such are found near the ruins

"TOMB OF ABSALOM," ROCK TOMBS, AND GRAVES IN THE KIDRON VALLEY.

of ancient cities, 2 Kin. 23:16; Isa. 22:16. Travellers find them along the bases of hills and mountains in all parts of Syria; as on the south side of Hinnom, the west side of Olivet, at Tiberias, in Petra, in the gorge of the Barada, and in the sea-cliffs north of Acre. The tombs, as well as the general graveyards, were uniformly without the city limits, as is apparent at this day with respect to both ancient and modern Jerusalem, 2 Kin. 23:6; Jer. 26:23; Luke 7:12; John 11:30. See ACELDAMA. The kings of Judah, almost exclusively, appear to have been buried within Jerusalem, on mount Zion, 1 Kin. 2:10; 2 Kin. 14:20; 2 Chr. 16:14; 28:27; Acts 2:29. Family tombs were common, and were carefully preserved, Gen. 50:5–13; Judg. 8:32; 2 Sam. 2:32; 1 Kin. 13:22. Tombstones with inscriptions were in use, Gen. 35:20; 2 Kin. 23:16, 17. Absalom was buried under a heap of stones. 2 Sam. 18:17. In many ancient heathen nations, a king was buried under a vast mound, with his arms, utensils, horses, and attendants, Ezek. 32:26, 27; and the pyramids of Egypt are believed to be the tombs of kings, each having but one or two apartments, in one of which the stone coffin of the builder has been found.

It was thought an act of piety to preserve and adorn the tombs of the prophets, but was often an act of hypocrisy; and our Saviour says that the Pharisees were like whited sepulchres, which appeared fine without, but inwardly were full of rottenness and corruption, Matt. 23:27–29; and Lightfoot has shown that every year, after the winter rains were over, the Hebrews whitened them anew. In Luke 11:44, Christ compares the Pharisees to "graves which appear not," so that men walk over them without being aware of it, and may thus contract an involuntary impurity. A superstitious adoration of the tombs and bones of supposed saints was then and is now a very prevalent form of idolatry; and our Saviour tells the Jews of his day they were as guilty as their fathers, Luke 11:47, 48: they built the sepulchres of the prophets, their fathers slew them; the hypocritical idolatry of the sons was as fatal a sin as the killing of the prophets by their fathers. These worshippers of the prophets soon afterwards showed that they allowed the deeds of their fathers, by crucifying the divine Prophet whom Moses had foretold. In Syria at the present day the tomb of David on mount Zion and that of Abraham at Hebron are most jealously guarded, and any intruder is instantly put to death; while almost all the laws of God and man may be violated with impunity. Deserted tombs were sometimes used as places of refuge and residence by the poor, Isa. 65:4; Luke 8:27; the shepherds of Palestine still drive their flocks into them for shelter, and wandering Arabs live in them during the winter. See BURIAL.

Maundrell's description of the sepulchre north of Jerusalem—supposed by many to be the work of Helena queen of Adiabene, though now known as "the tombs of the kings,"—may be useful for illustrating some passages of Scripture:

"The next place we came to was those famous grots called the sepulchres of the kings; but for what reason they go by that name is hard to resolve; for it is certain none of the kings, either of Israel or Judah, were buried here, the holy Scriptures assigning other places for their sepulchres. Whoever was buried here, this is certain, that the place itself discovers so great an expense, both of labor and treasure, that we may well suppose it to have been the work of kings. You approach to it at the east side through an entrance cut out of the natural rock, which admits you into an open court of about forty paces square, cut down into the rock with which it is encompassed instead of walls. On the west side of the court is a portico nine paces long and four broad, hewn likewise out of the natural rock. This has a kind of architrave, running along its front, adorned with sculpture, of fruits and flowers, still discernible, but by time much defaced. At the end of the portico, on the left hand, you descend to the passage into the sepulchres. The door is now so obstructed with stones and rubbish, that it is a thing of some difficulty to creep through it. But within you arrive in a large fair room, about seven yards square, cut out of the natural rock. Its sides and ceiling are so exactly square, and its angles so just, that no architect, with levels and plummets, could build a room more regular. And the whole is so firm and entire, that it may be called a chamber hollowed out of one piece of marble. From this room you pass into, I think, six more, one within another, all of the same fabric with the first. Of these the two innermost are deeper than the rest, having a second descent of about six or seven steps into them. In every one of these rooms, except the first, were coffins of stone placed in niches in the sides of the chambers. They had been at first

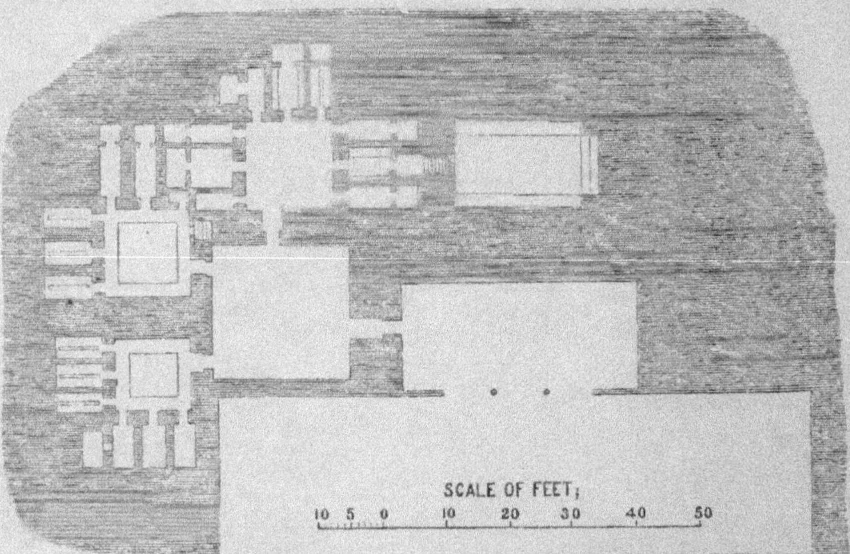

PLAN OF THE "TOMBS OF THE KINGS."

covered with handsome lids, and carved with garlands; but now most of them were broken to pieces by sacrilegious hands."

SE'RAH, a daughter of Asher, thrice named among those who migrated to Egypt, Gen. 46:17; Num. 26:46; 1 Chr. 7:30. Why she was thus distinguished is unknown, but the rabbis have many fables respecting her.

SERAI'AH, the name of six persons, alluded to in the following passages: 2 Sam. 8:17; 2 Kin. 25:18; Ezra 7:1; Jer. 36:26; 40:8; 51:59. The last is termed "a quiet prince," or as in the marginal reading, "chief chamberlain." He bore to the Jews in Babylon a message from the prophet Jeremiah.

SER'APHIM, *burning ones*, celestial beings surrounding the throne of God. Compare Deut. 4:24; Heb. 12:29. They appear to be distinguished from the cherubim, Ezek. 1:5-12. The prophet Isaiah, 6:2, 3, represents them as reverently adoring the triune God, and burning with zeal to fly and execute his will. Each one had six wings, with two of which he covered his face, with two his feet, and with the two others he flew. They cried to one another, and said, "Holy, holy, holy is the Lord of hosts; the whole earth is full of his glory!"

SER'GEANTS, Acts 16:35, properly Roman lictors, public servants who bore a bundle of rods, sometimes with an axe in the centre, before the magistrates of cities and colonies as insignia of their office, and who executed the sentences which their masters pronounced.

SER'GIUS PAU'LUS, proconsul or governor of the isle of Cyprus, was converted under the ministry of Paul, A. D. 48, Acts 13:7.

SER'PENTS. These reptiles, unclean among the Hebrews, Lev. 11:10, 41, are widely diffused through the world, but are most numerous and venomous in tropical climates. About one-sixth part of all that are known are supposed to be poisonous. These are distinguished by having two hollow poison-fangs in the upper jaw, and are usually of slower motion than most snakes. Venomous serpents were abundant in Egypt and Arabia, and seven different kinds are mentioned in the Hebrew scriptures, some of which are identified with existing species. See ADDER, ASP, COCKATRICE, and VIPER.

THE COBRA DI CAPELLO.

The serpents mentioned in Num. 21; Isa. 14:29; 30:6, and by whom multitudes of the Israelites were destroyed in the desert north of the gulf of Akabah, were probably called "fiery" and "flying" with reference to the agonizing heat caused by their poison, and the rapidity of their darting motion. Herodotus indeed speaks of winged serpents as appearing every spring on the Arabian border of Egypt; but he did not see them, nor are there any to be met with in modern times. The serpent of brass, made and erected on a pole by Moses, had no healing virtue in itself, but was a test of the penitence and faith of the people. The author of Ecclesiasticus says of the Israelites, "They were troubled for a small season that they might be admonished, having a sign of salvation to put them in remembrance of the commandment of thy law. For he that turned towards it was not saved by the thing that he saw, but by thee, that art the Saviour of all." Our Saviour himself shows that the brazen serpent was a type of Him, John 3:14, 15. The believing view of Christ is salvation to the soul infected by the fatal poison of sin. Respecting the brazen serpent, see NEHUSHTAN. Hezekiah destroyed a true and most sacred relic; Rome, on the contrary, fabricates false relics and adores them. See CHARMERS.

Interpreters have largely speculated concerning the nature of the serpent that tempted Eve. Some have thought that serpents originally had feet and speech; but there is no probability that this creature was ever otherwise than it now is. Its subtle, crafty malignity is often alluded to in the Scriptures, Gen. 3:1; Matt. 10:16; 23:33. Besides, it cannot be doubted but that by the serpent we are to understand the devil, who employed the serpent as a vehicle to seduce the first woman, Gen. 3:13; 2 Cor. 11:3; Rev. 12:9.

SE'RUG, a descendant of Shem, and an ancestor of Abraham, Gen. 11:20-23; Luke 3:35. Jewish tradition says he was the first of his line that fell into idolatry, Josh. 24:2.

SER'VANT. This word sometimes denotes a man who voluntarily dedicates himself to the service of another. Thus Joshua was the servant of Moses; Elisha of Elijah; and Peter, Andrew, Philip, and Paul were servants of Jesus Christ. The servants of Pharaoh, of Saul, and of David, were their subjects in general, and their court officers and counsellors in particular. The Philistines, Syrians, and other nations were servants of David, that is, they obeyed and paid him tribute. The servants of God are those who are devoted to his service and obey his holy word.

In its primary sense, the word usually means in the Bible either a hired servant, or one whose service was the property of his master for a limited time and under various restrictions. Joseph is the first whom we read of as sold into bondage, Gen. 37:27, 28. The households of some of the early patriarchs contained many servants, who were apparently treated with kindness and justice; the highest trusts were sometimes confided to them, and they might inherit their master's estate, Gen. 14:11-16; 15:2-4; 24:1-10. They shared the religious privileges of the household, Gen. 17:9-13, 27; 18:19, and were not transferred to other masters.

At the establishment of the Hebrew commonwealth, involuntary servitude was everywhere prevalent; and so far as it existed among the Jews, Moses sought to bring it under the restrictions demanded by religion and humanity. The mildest form of bond-service was that of a Hebrew in the house of another Hebrew. He might become bound to this service in various ways, chiefly through poverty, Ex. 21:7; Lev. 25:39-47; to acquit himself of a debt he could not otherwise pay, 2 Kin. 4:1; to make restitution for a theft, Ex. 22:3; or to earn the price of his ransom from captivity among heathen. This form of service could not continue more than six or seven years; unless, when the Sabbatical year came round, the servant chose to remain permanently or until the Jubilee with his master, in token of which he suffered his ear to be bored before witnesses, Ex. 21:2, 6; 25:40. The Hebrew servant was not to be made to serve with rigor, nor transferred to any harder bondage; he had an appeal to the tribunals, a right to all religious privileges, the power of demanding release on providing a pecuniary equivalent, and a donation from his master at his release, Lev. 25:47-55; Deut. 15:12-18. Compare also 2 Chron. 28:10, 11; Neh. 5:1-13; Jer. 34:8-22. The law likewise provided for the deliverance of a Hebrew, who was in bondage to a resident foreigner, Lev. 25:47-54.

From the heathen around and among them, especially from their captive enemies and the remains of the Canaanites, the Hebrews obtained many servants. These were protected by law, Deut. 1:16, 17; 27:19, and might become proselytes, attend the festivals, enjoy religious instruction and privileges, Ex. 12:44; Deut. 12:18; 29:10-13; 31:10-13. The servant who was mutilated by his master was to be set free, Ex. 21:26, 27; the refugee from foreign oppression was to be welcomed, Deut. 23:15, 16; and kidnapping or man-stealing was forbidden on pain of death, Exod. 21:16; Deut. 24:7; 1 Tim. 1:10.

Roman slavery, as it existed in the time of Christ, was comparatively unknown to the Jews. The Romans held in bondage captives taken in war, and purchased slaves. Their bondage was perpetual, and the master held unquestioned control of the person and life of his slaves. Yet large numbers were set free, and in many instances Roman freedmen rose to the highest honors.

The allusions of the Bible to involuntary servitude, imply that it is an evil and undesirable condition of life; yet the bondman who cannot obtain his freedom is divinely exhorted to contentment, 1 Cor. 7:20-24. Meanwhile the Bible gives directions as to the mutual duties of masters and servants, Eph. 6:5-9; Col. 3:22; 4:1; Tit. 2:9; Phile.; 1 Pet. 2:18; and proclaims the great truths of the common origin of all men, the immortality of every human soul, and its right to the Bible and to all necessary means of knowing and serving the Saviour—the application of which to all the relations of master and servant, superior and inferior, employer and employed, would prevent all oppression, which God abhors, Deut. 24 : 14 ; Psa. 103 : 6 ; Isa. 10:1-3 ; Amos 4:1 ; Mal. 3:5 ; Jas. 5:4.

SETH, the first son of Adam after the death of Abel, Gen. 4:25, 26 ; 5:3, 6, 8, and ancestor of the line of godly patriarchs.

SEV'EN. As from the beginning this was the number of days in the week, so it often has in Scripture a sort of emphasis attached to it, and is very generally used as a round or perfect number. Clean beasts were taken into the ark by sevens, Gen. 7. The years of plenty and famine in Egypt were marked by sevens, Gen. 41. With the Jews, not only was there a seventh day Sabbath, but every seventh year was a sabbath, and after every seven times seven years came a jubilee. Their great feasts of unleavened bread and of tabernacles were observed for seven days ; the number of animals in many of their sacrifices was limited to seven. The golden candlestick had seven branches. Seven priests with seven trumpets went around the walls of Jericho seven days, and seven times seven on the seventh day. In the Apocalypse we find seven churches mentioned, seven candlesticks, seven spirits, seven stars, seven seals, seven trumpets, seven thunders, seven vials, seven plagues, and seven angels to pour them out.

Seven is often put for any round or whole number, just as we use "ten," or "a dozen ;" so in Matt. 12 : 45 ; 1 Sam. 2 : 5 ; Job 5 : 19 ; Prov. 26 : 16, 25 ; Isa. 4:1 ; Jer. 15 : 9. In like manner, seven times, or seven-fold, means often, abundantly, completely, Gen. 4:15, 24 ; Lev. 26:24 ; Psa. 12:6 ; 79:12 ; Matt. 18 : 21. And seventy times seven is a still higher superlative, Matt. 18:22.

SHAAL'BIM, a town of Gad, long held by the Amorites, Josh. 19 : 42, Judg. 1 : 35, but in the time of Solomon the head-quarters of one of his commissaries, 1 Kin. 4:9.

SHAD'OW sometimes denotes intense darkness and gloom, Psa. 23 : 4, and sometimes a cool retreat, Isa. 33 : 2, or perfect protection, Psa. 17:8 ; Isa. 49:2 ; Dan. 4 : 12. The long shadows cast by the declining sun are alluded to in Job 7:2 ; Jer. 6:4. The swift, never ceasing motion of a shadow is an emblem of human life, 1 Chr. 29:15 ; Psa. 102:11.

SHA'DRACH, the Chaldean name given to Ananias at the court of Nebuchadnezzar, Dan. 1:7. See ABED-NEGO.

SHAL'ISHA, a district adjoining mount Ephraim on the west, 1 Sam. 9 : 4. Baal-shalisha is placed by Eusebius fifteen miles from Lydda, towards the north.

SHAL'LUM, I., son of Jabesh, or a native of Jabesh, who treacherously killed Zechariah king of Israel, and usurped his kingdom, B. C. 772. He held it only one month, when Menahem son of Gadi killed him in Samaria. Scripture says that Shallum was the executioner of the threatenings of the Lord against the house of Jehu, 2 Kin. 15:10-15.

II. See JEHOAHAZ II.

III. The husband of Huldah the prophetess in the time of Josiah, 2 Kin. 22:14.

Others of this name are alluded to in Num. 26:49 ; 1 Chr. 2:40 ; 9:17, 19, 31 ; Ezra 2:42 ; 7:2 ; 10:24, 42 ; Neh. 3:12 ; 7:45.

SHALMANE'SER, king of Assyria, between Tiglath-pileser and Sennacherib. He ascended the throne about B. C. 728, and reigned fourteen years. Scripture reports that he came into Palestine, subdued Samaria, and obliged Hoshea to pay him tribute ; but in the third year, being weary of this exaction, Hoshea combined secretly with So king of Egypt to remove the subjection. Shalmaneser brought an army against him, ravaged Samaria, besieged Hoshea in his capital, and notwithstanding his long resistance of three years, 2 Kin. 17 ; 18 : 9-12, he took the city and dismantled it, put Hoshea into bonds, and carried away most of the people beyond the Euphrates. He thus ruined the kingdom of Samaria, which had subsisted two hundred and fifty-four years, from B. C. 975 to 721. The bas-relief copied in the next page was found on a fine Assyrian obelisk of black marble, six and a half feet high, and covered on all sides with inscriptions. It was discovered in the ruins of the north-west palace at Nimroud, and is believed from various evidences to represent Shalmaneser receiving tribute from the Jews subdued by his arms. Hezekiah king of Judah successfully resisted him, 2 Kin. 18 : 7 : but he appears to have ravaged

Moab, Isa. 10:9; 15, 16, 23; and is said in Josephus to have conquered Phœnicia, with the exception of insular Tyre, which he besieged in vain for five years.

SHAM'BLES, 1 Cor. 10:25, a public meat-market.

SHAM'GAR, son of Anath, the third judge of Israel, after Ehud and shortly before Barak, in a time of great insecurity and distress, Judg. 3:31; 5:6. Scripture only says he defended Israel, and killed six hundred Philistines with an ox-goad. See PLOUGH.

SHAM'MAH, I., one of the three chief of David's thirty heroes, who shared with David and Eleazar the honor of the exploit recorded in 2 Sam. 23:11, 12; 1 Chr. 11:12-14. Another feat is described in 2 Sam. 23:13-17.

II. A brother of David, 1 Sam. 16:9; 17:13; elsewhere called Shimeah, 2 Sam. 13:3, 32; 1 Chr. 2:13.

Others of this name are mentioned, Gen. 36:13, 17; 2 Sam. 23:25, 33; 1 Chr. 11:27; 27:8.

SHA'PHAN, I., a scribe or secretary under king Josiah, to whom he read from the newly found autograph roll of the book of the law, 2 Kin. 22:12; Jer. 29:3; 36:10; Ezek. 8:11.

II. The father of Ahikam, 2 Kin. 22:12; 25:22; Jer. 26:24.

SHA'PHAT, I., the father of Elisha, 1 Kin. 19:16.

II. A descendant of David, 1 Chr. 3:22.

III. A chief herdsman of David in Bashan, 1 Chr. 27:29.

SHAREZ'ER, I., a son of Sennacherib, who assisted in slaying his father, Isa. 37:38.

II. A delegate sent to Jerusalem with Regemmelec and others, probably soon after the return from the Babylonish captivity, to inquire of the priests at Jerusalem whether a certain fast was still to be observed, Zech. 7:2; 8:19.

SHAR'ON, I., a plain adjoining the seacoast of Palestine between Carmel and Joppa, about sixty miles in length and of variable width, expanding inland as it stretches from the promontory of Carmel towards the south. It contains some sandy tracts, but the soil is in general highly productive, and the plain was of old famous for its beauty and fertility, 1 Chr. 27:29; Song 2:1; Isa. 33:9; 35:2; 65:10. It contained a town of the same name, called Saron in Acts 9:35. The whole plain was once thickly populated, but is now comparatively uninhabited. The heat of summer is excessive, and the climate somewhat unhealthy. All travellers describe the view of the plain from the tower of Ramleh as one of surpassing richness and beauty. The frowning hills of Judah on the east confront the glittering waters of the Mediterranean on the west. Towards the north and south far as the eye can reach spreads the beautiful plain, covered in many parts with fields of green or golden grain. Near by are the immense olive-groves of Ramleh and Lydda, and amid them the picturesque towers, minarets, and domes of these villages; while the hill-sides towards the north-east are thickly studded with native hamlets. The uncultivated parts of the plain are covered in spring and the early summer with a rich profusion of flowers.

II. A town in the tribe of Gad, in the district of Bashan beyond the Jordan, 1 Chr. 5:16.

SHA'VEH, a valley north of Jerusalem, called also the King's Dale, Gen. 14:17; 2 Sam. 18:18.

SHA'VING. The Jews shaved their beards and hair in time of mourning, repentance, or distress, Job 1:20, Jer. 48:37, and in certain ceremonial purifications, Lev. 14:9; Num. 8:7. At other times they wore them long, like other oriental nations—except the Egyptians, who kept their beards shaved, as we learn from Herodotus and from antique monuments. Hence Joseph shaved before he was presented to Pharaoh, Gen. 41:14. See BEARD.

SHEAL'TIEL. See SALATHIEL.

SHE'AR-JASH'UB, *the remnant shall return*, Isa. 7:3; 10:21, the name of one of Isaiah's sons; supposed to have had a prophetic meaning, like Maher-shalal-hash-baz.

SHE'BA, I., son of Raamah, Gen. 10:7. His posterity are supposed to have settled near the head of the Persian gulf. See CUSH and RAAMAH.

II. Son of Joktan, of the race of Shem, Gen. 10:28. See SABEANS II.

III. Son of Jokshan, and grandson of Abraham by Keturah, Gen. 25:3. He is supposed to have settled in Arabia Deserta.

IV. A turbulent Benjamite, who after the death of Absalom made a fruitless effort to excite a rebellion in Israel against David. Being pursued, and besieged in Abel-beth-maachah, near the southern part of Lebanon, he was beheaded by the people of the city, 2 Sam. 20.

SHEBA, QUEEN OF. See SABEANS II.

SHE'BAT, the fifth month of the Jewish civil year, and the eleventh of the ecclesiastical year, from the new moon of February to that of March, Zech. 1:7. See MONTH.

SHEB'NA, steward of king Hezekiah's palace, Isa. 22 : 15, afterwards his secretary, 2 Kin. 18:18, 37.

SHE'CHEM, I., a Canaanite prince, at the town of the same name, who abducted Dinah the daughter of Jacob, and was soon afterwards treacherously slain, with many of his people, by Simeon and Levi, Gen. 34.

II. A city of central Canaan, between the mountains Gerizim and Ebal, thirty-four miles north of Jerusalem; called also Sychar and Sychem, Acts 7:16. It is first mentioned in the history of Abraham, who here erected his first altar in Canaan, and took possession of the country in the name of Jehovah, Gen. 12:6; 33:18, 19; 35:4. Jacob bought a field in its neighborhood, which, by way of overplus, he gave to his son Joseph, who was buried here, Gen. 48 : 22; Josh. 24:32. After the conquest of Canaan it became a Levitical city of refuge in Ephraim, and a gathering-place of the tribes, Josh. 20 : 7; 21 : 21; 24 : 1, 25; Judg. 9. Here Rehoboam gave the ten tribes occasion to revolt, 1 Kin. 12. In its vicinity was Jacob's well or fountain, at which Christ discoursed with the woman of Samaria, John 4:5. See also Acts 8 : 25; 9 : 31; 15 : 3. After the ruin of Samaria by Shalmaneser, Shechem became the capital of the Samaritans; and Josephus says it was so in the time of Alexander the Great. At the present day it is also the seat of the small remnant of the Samaritans. See SAMARITANS. It was called by the Romans Neapolis, from which the Arabs have made Napolose, or Nabulus.

VIEW OF NABULUS AND MOUNT GERIZIM FROM THE NORTH-WEST.

The valley of Shechem extends several miles north-west between mount Ebal and mount Gerizim, and is about five hundred yards wide; so that in the pure and elastic air of Palestine the two mountains are within hailing distance of each other, one circumstance among thousands evincing the exact truthfulness of Bible narratives, Deut. 27:11-14; Judg. 9:7. The winter rains which fall in the eastern part of the valley find their way to the Jordan, while in the western part are numerous springs, forming a pretty brook which flows towards the Mediterranean. "Here," says Dr. Robinson, "a scene of luxuriant and almost unparalleled verdure burst upon our view. The whole valley was filled with gardens of vegetables and orchards of all kinds of fruits, watered by several fountains which burst forth in various parts and flow westward in refreshing streams. It came upon us suddenly, like a scene of fairy enchantment. We saw nothing to compare with it in Palestine." The modern town has several long and narrow streets, partly on the base of mount Gerizim. It does not appear to extend so far to the east as the ancient city did. The houses are high, and well built of stone, and covered with small domes. Nabulus is thought to contain eight thousand inhabitants, all Mohammedans except five hundred Greek Christians, one hundred and fifty Samaritans, and as many Jews. The rocky base of mount Ebal on the north of the valley is full of ancient excavated tombs. On mount Gerizim is the holy place of the Samaritans, and the ruins of a strong fortress erected by Justinian. At the foot of these mountains on the east lies the beautiful plain of Mukhna, ten miles long and a mile and a half wide; and where the valley opens on this plain, Joseph's tomb and Jacob's well are located, by the unanimous consent of Jews, Christians, and Mohammedans. The former spot is now covered by a Mohammedan Wely, or sacred tomb; and the latter by an arched stone chamber, entered by a narrow hole in the roof, and the mouth of the well within is covered by a large stone. The well itself is one hundred and five feet deep, and is now sometimes dry. It bears every mark of high antiquity.

The following extract is from Dr. Clarke's description of this place: "There is nothing in the Holy Land finer than a view of Napolose from the heights around it. As the traveller descends towards it from the hills, it appears luxuriantly embosomed in the most delightful and fragrant bowers, half concealed by rich gardens, and by stately trees collected into groves, all around the bold and beautiful valley in which it stands. Trade seems to flourish among its inhabitants. Their principal employment is in making soap; but the manufactures of the town supply a very widely extended neighborhood, and are exported to a great distance upon camels. In the morning after our arrival, we met caravans coming from Grand Cairo, and noticed others reposing in the large olive plantations near the gates.

"The sacred story of events transacted in the fields of Sychem, from our earliest years is remembered with delight; but with the territory before our eyes where those events took place; and in the view of objects existing as they were described above three thousand years ago, the grateful impression kindles into ecstasy. Along the valley we beheld 'a company of Ishmaelites coming from Gilead,' Gen. 37:25, as in the days of Reuben and Judah, 'with their camels bearing spicery and balm and myrrh,' who would gladly have purchased another Joseph of his brethren, and conveyed him as a slave to some Potiphar in Egypt. Upon the hills around, flocks and herds were feeding, as of old; nor in the simple garb of the shepherds of Samaria was there any thing repugnant to the notions we may entertain of the appearance presented by the sons of Jacob. It was indeed a scene to abstract and to elevate the mind; and under emotions so called forth by every circumstance of powerful coincidence, a single moment seemed to concentrate whole ages of existence.

"The principal object of veneration is Jacob's well, over which a church was formerly erected. This is situated at a small distance from the town, in the road to Jerusalem, and has been visited by pilgrims of all ages, but particularly since the Christian era, as the place where our Saviour revealed himself to the woman of Samaria. The spot is so distinctly marked by the evangelist, and so little liable to uncertainty, from the circumstance of the well itself and the features of the country, that, if no tradition existed for its identity, the site of it could hardly be mistaken. Perhaps no Christian scholar ever attentively read the fourth chapter of John, without being struck with the numerous internal evidences of truth which crowd upon the mind in its perusal. Within so small a compass it is impossible to find in other writings so many sources of reflection and of interest. Independently of its importance as a theological document, it concentrates so much information, that a volume might be filled with the illustration it reflects on the history of the Jews and on the geography of their country. All that can be gathered on these subjects from Josephus seems but as a comment to illustrate this chapter. The journey of our Lord from Judea into Galilee; the cause of it; his passage through the territory of Samaria; his approach to the metropolis of this country; its name; his arrival at the Amorite field which terminates the narrow valley of Sychem; the ancient custom of halting at a well; the female employment of drawing water; the disciples sent into the city for food, by which its situation out of the town is obviously implied; the question of the woman referring to existing prejudices which separated the Jews from the Samaritans; the depth of the well; the oriental allusion contained in the expression, 'living water;' the history of the well, and the customs thereby illustrated; the worship upon mount Gerizim; all these occur within the space of twenty verses."

THE FAT-TAILED SYRIAN SHEEP.

SHEEP. Of the Syrian sheep, according to Dr. Russell, there are two varieties: the one called Bedaween sheep, which differ in no respect from the larger kinds of sheep among us, except that their tails are somewhat longer and thicker; the others are those often mentioned by travellers on account of their extraordinary tails; and this species is by far the most numerous. The tail of one of these animals is very broad and large, terminating in a small appendage that turns back upon it. It is of a substance between fat and marrow, and is not eaten separately, but mixed with the lean meat in many of their dishes, and also often used instead of butter. A common sheep of this sort, without the head, feet, skin, and entrails, weighs from sixty to eighty pounds, of which the tail itself is usually ten or fifteen pounds, and when the animal is fattened, twice or thrice that weight, and very inconvenient to its owner.

The sheep or lamb was the common sacrifice under the Mosaic law; and it is to be remarked, that when the divine legislator speaks of this victim, he never omits to appoint that the rump or tail be laid whole on the fire of the altar, Ex. 29 : 22; Lev. 3 : 9. The reason for this is seen in the account just given from Dr. Russell; from which it appears that this was the most delicate part of the animal, and therefore the most proper to be presented in sacrifice to Jehovah.

The innocence, mildness, submission, and patience of the sheep or lamb, rendered it peculiarly suitable for a sacrifice, and an appropriate type of the Lamb of God, John 1 : 29. A recent traveller in Palestine witnessed the shearing of a sheep in the immediate vicinity of Gethsemane; and the silent, unresisting submission of the poor animal, thrown with its feet bound upon the earth, its sides rudely pressed by the shearer's knees, while every movement threatened to lacerate the flesh, was a touching commentary on the prophet's description of Christ, Isa. 53:7; Acts 8:32–35.

There are frequent allusions in Scripture to these characteristics of the sheep, and to its proneness to go astray, Psa. 119 : 176; Isa. 53 : 6. It is a gregarious animal also; and as loving the companionship of the flock and dependent on the protection and guidance of its master, its name is often given to the people of God, 2 Kin. 22:17; Psa. 79:13; 80:1; Matt. 25 : 32. Sheep and goats are still found in Syria feeding indiscriminately together, as in ancient times, Gen. 30:35; Matt. 25 : 32, 33. The season of sheep-shearing was one of great joy and festivity, 1 Sam. 25:2, 8, 36; 2 Sam. 13:23.

Sheep-cotes or folds, among the Israelites, appear to have been generally open houses, or enclosures walled round, often in front of rocky caverns, to guard the sheep from beasts of prey by night, and the scorching heat of noon, Num. 32:16; 2 Sam. 7:8; Jer. 23:3, 6; John 10:1–5. See SHEPHERD.

SHEEP-MARKET, John 5 : 2. The original might with at least equal propriety be rendered sheep-gate; and a gate so called is mentioned in Neh. 3:1-32; 12:39. It was adjacent to the temple, and was so named from the number of sheep introduced through it for the temple service. Dr. Barclay thinks the "sheep-market" was an enclosure for sheep and other animals designed for sacrifice, outside the temple area on the east.

SHEK'EL. The shekel was properly and only a weight. It was used especially in weighing uncoined gold and silver: "The land is worth 400 shekels of silver; . . . Abraham weighed to Ephron the silver—in the audience of the sons of Heth," Gen. 23:15, 16. In such cases the word shekel is often omitted in the Hebrew, as in Gen. 20:16; 37:28, where our translators have supplied the word "pieces," but improperly, because coined money was not then known. See MONEY. Between the sacred shekel, Ex. 30:13, and the shekel after the "king's weight," 2 Sam. 14:26, there would seem to have been a difference; but this difference cannot now be determined, and many think the phrase "shekel of the sanctuary" simply means a full and just shekel, according to the temple standards. The first coin which bore the name of shekel was struck after the ex-

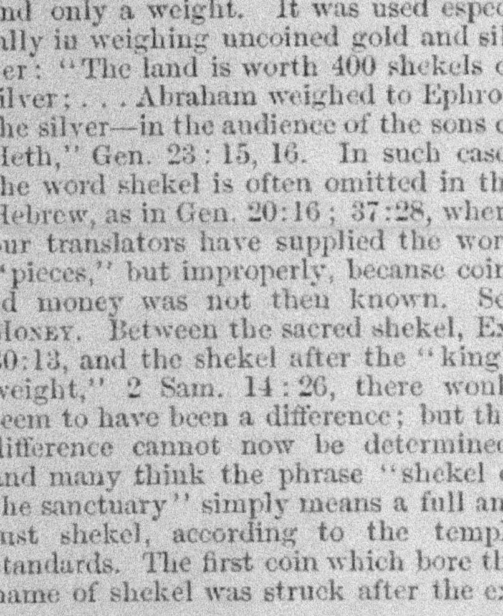

ile, in the time of the Maccabees, 1 Mac. 15:6, and bore the inscription, Shekel of Israel. Böckh, whose authority in matters pertaining to ancient weights and measures is very high, fixes it proximately at 274 Paris grains. It is the coin mentioned in the New Testament, Matt. 26:15, etc., where our translators have rendered it by "pieces of silver."

SHEM, a son of Noah, Gen. 5:32; 6:10, always named before Ham and Japheth, as the eldest son; or, as some think, because he was the forefather of the Hebrews. In Gen. 10:21, the word elder may be applied to Shem, instead of Japheth. He received a blessing from his dying father, Gen. 9:26, and of his line the Messiah was born. He had five sons, and their posterity occupied the central regions between Ham and Japheth, and peopled the finest provinces of the East. The languages of some of these nations are still called the Shemitic languages, including the Hebrew, Chaldee, Syriac, Arabic, Ethiopic, etc.; but in this general class are found several languages spoken by nations descended from Ham.

SHEMAI'AH, I., a prophet of Israel, by whom God forbade Rehoboam to endeavor to coerce the ten tribes back to their allegiance, and called the king and his court to repent at the invasion of Shishak. He is said to have written the history of Rehoboam's reign, 1 Kings 12:22-24; 2 Chr. 12:5-8, 15.

II. A Levite, who made a registry of the twenty-four priestly classes, 1 Chr. 15:8, 11; 24:6.

III. A false prophet among the exiled Jews in Babylon, who opposed the prophet Jeremiah, and incurred divine judgments on himself and his family. For his name, Nehelamite, the marginal reading is *a dreamer*, Jer. 29:24-32.

IV. A false prophet in the pay of Sanballat and Tobiah, who sought to terrify Nehemiah into the cowardly and forbidden step of taking refuge within the temple, Num. 3:38; Neh. 6:10-14.

SHE'MER, the former owner of the hill on which Omri built Samaria, 1 Kin. 16:24.

SHEM'INITH, in the titles of Psa. 6, 12, and in 1 Chr. 15:21. It means properly the eighth, and seems to have been not an instrument, but a *part* in music, perhaps the lowest.

SHE'NIR. See HERMON.

SHEPHATI'AH, the name of seven distinguished Jews, alluded to in the following passages: 2 Sam. 3:4; 1 Chr. 12:5; 27:16; 2 Chr. 21:2; Ezra 2:4, 57; Neh. 11:4; Jer. 38:1.

SHEP'HERD, or PASTOR. Abel was a keeper of sheep, Gen. 4:2, as were the greater number of the ancient patriarchs. When men began to multiply, and to follow different employments, Jabal son of Lamech was acknowledged as father, that is, founder of shepherds and nomads, Gen. 4:20. A large part of the wealth of ancient patriarchs consisted in flocks and herds, the care of which was shared by their sons, daughters, and servants. Rachel the bride of

Jacob was a shepherdess, Gen. 29:6; his sons, the fathers of the tribes of Israel were shepherds, and so was David their king, Psa. 78:70-72. The employment is highly honored in the Bible, Luke 2:8-20. In the time of the kings, the "chief herdsman" occupied a post of some importance, 1 Sam. 21:7; 2 Kin. 3:4; 1 Chr. 27:29-31. In Palestine and its vicinity, besides those who united the keeping of flocks and herds with the tillage of the ground, there were and still are numbers of nomades or wandering shepherds confining themselves to no settled home. These dwellers in tents often had a wide range of pasture grounds, from one to another of which they drove their flocks as occasion required, Gen. 37:12-17. In the vast deserts east and south of Palestine they found many spots which in winter and spring were clothed with verdure, Ex. 3:1; Psa. 65:12. But the heat of summer withered these "pastures of the wilderness," and drove the shepherds and their flocks to seek for highlands and streams. There are many indications in Scripture of the conscious strength and independence of the ancient shepherd patriarchs, of the extent of their households, and the consideration in which they were held, Gen. 14:14-24; 21:22-32; 26:13-16; 30:43; Job 1:3.

God sometimes takes the name of Shepherd of Israel, Psa. 80:1; Jer. 31:10; and kings, both in Scripture and ancient writers, are distinguished by the title of "Shepherds of the people." The prophets often inveigh against the "shepherds of Israel," that is, the kings, who feed themselves and neglect their flocks; who distress, ill-treat, seduce, and lead them astray, Ezek. 34:10. In like manner Christ, as the Messiah, is often called a shepherd, Zech. 13:7, and also takes on himself the title of "the Good Shepherd," who gives his life for his sheep, John 10:11, 14, 15. Paul calls him the great Shepherd of the sheep, Heb. 13:20, and Peter gives him the appellation of Prince of shepherds, 1 Pet. 5:4. His ministers are in like manner the pastors or under-shepherds of the flock, Jer. 3:15; 23:3; Eph. 4:11.

In John 10:1-16, our Saviour says the good shepherd lays down his life for his sheep; that he knows them, and they know him; that they hear his voice, and follow him; that he goes before them; that no one shall force them out of his hands, and that he calls them by their names. These, however, being all incidents taken from the customs of the country, are by no means so striking to us as they must have been to those who heard our Lord, and who every day witnessed such methods of conducting this domesticated animal. Modern travellers in the East meet with many pleasing confirmations of the truth of Scripture in respect to these particulars; they see the shepherd walking before his flock, any one of which will instantly run to him when called by its own name. The hireling, or bad shepherd, forsakes the sheep, and the thief enters not by the door of the sheepfold, but climbs in another way. See SHEEP. The Bible applies many of the excellences of the faithful shepherd in illustration of the Saviour's care of his flock. The shepherd was responsible for each member of the flock intrusted to him, Gen. 31:39; Ex. 22:12; John 10:28; he had need of great courage and endurance, Gen. 31:40; 1 Sam. 17:34, 35; John 10:15; he exercised a tender care towards the feeble, and carried the lambs in his arms, Gen. 33:13; Isa. 40:11; Mark 10:14, 16; and searched for the lost sheep, bringing it back from the "land of drought and the shadow of death" into green pastures and by the still waters, Psa. 23; Luke 15:4-7.

SHESHACH, a poetical name for Babylon, signifying, as some judge, house or court of the prince, Jer. 25:26; 51:41.

SHESHBAZ'ZAR. See ZERUBBABEL.

SHETH'AR-BOZ'NAI. See TATNAI.

SHIB'BOLETH, *a stream*. In a war between the Ephraimites and the men of Gilead under Jephthah, the former were discomfited, and fled towards the fords of the Jordan. The Gileadites took possession of all these fords, and when an Ephraimite who had escaped came to the river side and desired to pass over, they asked him if he were not an Ephraimite. If he said, No, they bade him pronounce *shibboleth*; but he pronouncing it *sibboleth*, according to the dialect of the Ephraimites, they killed him. In this war there fell 42,000 Ephraimites, Judg. 12. This incident should not be passed over without observing, that it affords proof of dialectical variations among the tribes of the same nation, and speaking the same language, in those early days. There can be no wonder, therefore, if we find in later ages the same word written different ways, according to the pronunciation of different tribes. That this continued, is evident from the peculiarities of the Galilean dialect, by which Peter was discovered to be of that district, Mark 14:70.

SHIELD, a piece of defensive armor. God is often called the shield of his people, Gen. 15:1; Psa. 5:12; 84:11, as are also princes and great men, 2 Sam. 1:21; Psa. 47:9. See ARMOR.

SHIGGAION, Psa. 7, title, and SHIGGIONOTH, Hab. 3:1; probably song, or song of praise; perhaps some particular species of ode.

SHILOH, I. This term is used, Gen. 49:10, to denote the Messiah, the coming of whom Jacob foretells in these words: "The sceptre shall not depart from Judah, nor a lawgiver from between his feet, until Shiloh come; and unto him shall the gathering of the people be;" that is, until the time of Christ, Judah's self-government as a tribe should not cease. It must be admitted, however, that the literal signification of the word is not well ascertained. Some translate, "The sceptre shall not depart from Judah till he comes to whom it belongs." Others, with more probability, till the coming of the Peacemaker, or of the One desired.

II. A famous city of Ephraim, about ten miles south of Shechem, and twenty-four north of Jerusalem. Here Joshua assembled the people to make the second distribution of the Land of Promise; and here the tabernacle of the Lord was set up, when they were settled in the country, Josh. 18:1; 19:51. The ark and the tabernacle continued at Shiloh, from B. C. 1444 to B. C. 1116, when it was taken by the Philistines, under the administration of the high-priest Eli. In honor of the presence of the ark, there was "a feast of the Lord in Shiloh yearly;" and at one of these festivals the daughters of Shiloh were seized by a remnant of the Benjamites, Judg. 21:19-23. At Shiloh Samuel began to prophesy, 1 Sam. 4:1, and here the prophet Ahijah dwelt, 1 Kin. 14:2.

SHIMEI, I., a Benjamite kinsman of Saul, who insulted king David when fleeing before Absalom, and humbled himself on David's return. On both occasions David spared and forgave him; but when dying he cautioned Solomon against a man who knew no restraints but those of fear. Shimei gave his parole never to leave Jerusalem; but broke it by pursuing his fugitive servants to Gath, and was put to death on returning, 2 Sam. 16:5-14; 19:16-23; 1 Kin. 2:8, 9, 36-46.

II. An officer under David, and perhaps under Solomon, 1 Kin. 1:8; 4:18.

III. A distinguished family at Jerusalem, Zech. 12:13.

SHINAR, a level region of indefinite extent around Babylon and the junction of the Euphrates and Tigris, Gen. 10:10; 11:2; 14:1; Josh. 7:21, Heb., garment of Shinar; Isa. 11:11; Dan. 1:2; Zech. 5:11. See MESOPOTAMIA.

SHIP. The ships of the ancients were very imperfect in comparison with modern ones. Navigators crept carefully along the shores, from one headland or prominent point to another, making a harbor if practicable every night; and when out of sight of land, being ignorant of the compass and quadrant, they guided their course by the sun and certain stars. Even in St. Paul's time, vessels passing from Palestine to Italy, sometimes wintered on the way! Acts 27:12; 28:11. The ancient ships were in general small, though a few large ships are on record. They were often highly ornamented both at the prow and the stern; and the figurehead or "sign," by which the vessel was known. was sometimes an image of its tutelar divinity. They were usually propelled by oars, often in several "banks" or rows one above another, as well as by sails. In

PART OF A WAR-GALLEY, FROM AN ANCIENT BAS-RELIEF.

war, the galley tried to pierce and run down its antagonist. The Phœnicians were celebrated for their ships and their extensive commerce, as appears from Ezekiel's description, ch. 27, as well as from numerous ancient historians. Though Joppa and in Christ's time Cesarea were Jewish ports, 2 Chr. 2:26, Jonah 1:3, yet the Jews were never a maritime people, and most of their foreign navigation would appear to have been carried on by the aid of Phœnicians, 1 Kin. 9:26; 10:22; 22:49, 50. Paul's graphic and faithful description of his voyage and shipwreck in Acts 27, discloses many of the peculiarities of ancient navigation. For the "ships of Tarshish," see TARSHISH.

SHIPH'RAH and PU'AH, midwives in Egypt, who through the fear of God spared the newborn sons of the Hebrews, contrary to the orders of the king. God rewarded their kindness to his people, though condemning no doubt the untruthfulness of their excuse to the king. He "made them houses," that is, probably gave each of them a numerous family, Ex. 1:15-21.

SHI'SHAK, a king of Egypt, who declared war against Rehoboam king of Judah in the fifth year of his reign. He

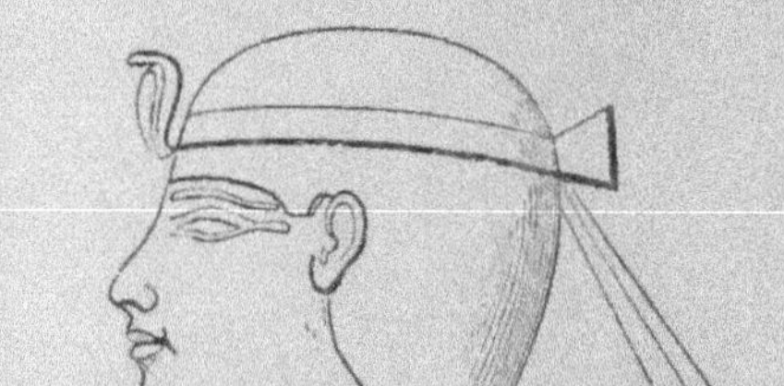

SHISHAK, FROM A THEBAN TEMPLE.

entered Judah, B. C. 971, with an innumerable multitude of people out of Egypt, the countries of Lubim, of Suchim, and of Cush, captured the strongest places in the country, and carried away from Jerusalem the treasures of the Lord's house and of the king's palace, as well as the golden bucklers of Solomon. Jeroboam having secured the friendship of Shishak, his territories were not invaded, 1 Kin. 11 : 40 ; 14 : 25, 26 ; 2 Chr. 12:2-9. Shishak is generally believed to have been the Sesonchis of secular history, the first king of the twenty-second or Bubastine line. He dethroned the dynasty into which Solomon married, 1 Kin. 3:1, and made many foreign conquests. In the palace-temple of Karnak in Egypt, the walls of which are yet standing, Sesonchis is represented in a large bas-relief, dragging captive kings in triumph before the three chief Theban gods. Each country or city is personified, and its name written in an oval

above it. One of these figures, with Jewish features, has an inscription which Champollion interprets, "kingdom of Judah." Several other symbols are thought to denote as many walled towns of Judah, captured by Shishak. See Pharaoh.

SHIT'TAH, and SHIT'TIM, a valuable kind of wood, of which Moses made the greater part of the tables, altars, and planks belonging to the tabernacle. Jerome says, "The wood is hard, tough, smooth, without knots, and extremely beautiful ; so that the rich and curious make screws of it for their presses. It does not grow in cultivated places, nor in any other places of the Roman empire, but only in the deserts of Arabia." It is thought he means the black acacia,

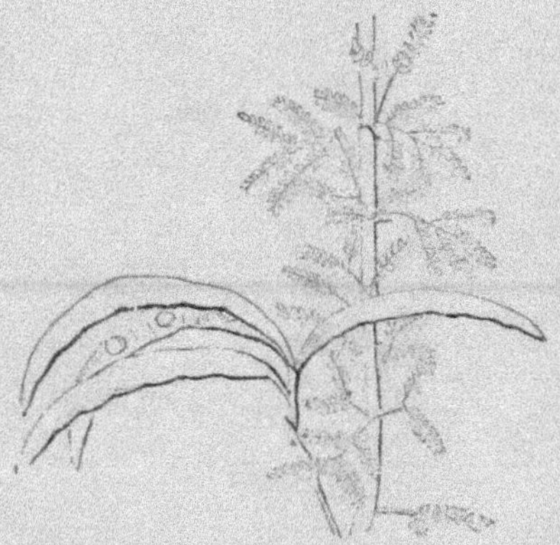

the Acacia Seyal, which is found in the deserts of Arabia, and the wood of which is very common about mount Sinai and the mountains which border on the Red sea, and is so hard and solid as to be almost incorruptible.

SHOES. See Sandals.

SHOSHAN'NIM-E'DUTH, *lilies of testimony*, Psa. 60 ; 80. See Shushan.

SHRINE. See Diana.

SHU'LAMITE, *peaceful*, in Hebrew a feminine name, corresponding to Solomon as Julia does to Julius. It is the figurative name of the bride in Solomon's Song, 6 : 13 ; and the bridegroom is represented by Solomon, also meaning peaceful.

SHU'NEM, a city of Issachar, Josh. 19 : 18. The Philistines encamped at Shunem, in the great field or plain of Esdraelon, 1 Sam. 28 : 4 ; and Saul encamped at Gilboa. Abishag, king David's nurse, was of Shunem, 1 Kin. 1:3 ; so also was the woman whose son Elisha restored to life, 2 Kin. 4 : 8-37. Eusebius and Jerome place it five miles south of Tabor ; and it is now recognized in a poor village called Solam, on a declivity at the north-west corner of the smaller valley of Jezreel.

SHUR, a city on the north-east border

of Egypt, not far from the modern Suez, Gen. 16:7; 20:1; 25:18; 1 Sam. 15:7; 27:8. It gave its name to the desert between it and Canaan, towards the Mediterranean, Ex. 15:22.

SHU'SHAN, I., Psa. 60, title; plural SHOSHAN'NIM, Psa. 45, 69, titles; the name of a musical instrument. The word signifies a lily, or lilies; and if the instrument were so named from its similarity to this flower, we might understand the cymbal. Or it may denote a melody, so named for its pleasantness, or, as some suppose, the pleasantness of the subject matter of the song, as in the title to Psalm 45.

II. The capital city of Elam, or Persia, Gen. 14:1, Dan. 8:2, on the river Ulai. It was the winter residence of the Persian kings, after Cyrus, Esth. 1:5; and is deeply interesting as the scene of the wonderful events narrated in the book of Esther. Here Daniel had the vision of the ram and he-goat, in the third year of Belshazzar, Dan. 8. Nehemiah was also at Shushan, when he obtained from Artaxerxes permission to return into Judea, and to repair the walls of Jerusalem, Neh. 1:1.

The present Shouster, the capital of Khusistan, in long. 49 East, lat. 32 North, on the river Karun, a branch of the Shat-el-Arab, has been generally believed to be the ancient Shushan, the Susa of the Greeks; but Mr. Kinneir rather thinks the ruins about thirty-five miles west of Shouster are those of that ancient residence of royalty, "stretching not less, perhaps, than twelve miles from one extremity to the other. They occupy an immense space between the rivers Kerah and Abzal; and like the ruins of Ctesiphon, Babylon, and Kufa, consist of hillocks of earth and rubbish, covered with broken pieces of brick and colored tile. The largest is a mile in circumference, and nearly one hundred feet in height; another, not quite so high, is double the circuit. They are formed of clay and pieces of tile, with irregular layers of brick and mortar, five or six feet in thickness, to serve, as it should seem, as a kind of prop to the mass. Large blocks of marble, covered with hieroglyphics, are not unfrequently here discovered by the Arabs, when digging in search of hidden treasure; and at the foot of the most elevated of the pyramids (ruins) stands the tomb of Daniel, a small and apparently a modern building, erected on the spot where the relics of that prophet are believed to rest." Major Rennell coincides in the opinion that these ruins represent the ancient Susa. The desolation of the place, abandoned to beasts of prey, agrees with the prediction in Ezek. 32:24.

The preceding statements are confirmed by Loftus, who with Col. Williams visited and in part explored these ruins in 1851–2. Shush, he says, abounds in lions, wolves, lynxes, jackals, boars, etc. During nine months of the year the country is burnt up by the most intense heat, though exceedingly rich and beautiful in the rainy season. His excavations in the great mound disclosed the ruins of a vast palace, commenced apparently by Darius, carried on by Xerxes, and finished by Artaxerxes Mnemon. It is altogether probable that this was the scene of the festival described in Esther 1. The "pillars of marble" may perhaps be even now traced in the ruined colonnade forming a great central court; the huge columns were fluted and highly ornamented, and one of the capitals measured was twenty-eight feet high.

SIB'MAH, a city of Reuben, Num. 32:38; Josh. 13:19. Isaiah, 16:8, 9, speaks of the vines of Sibmah, which were cut down by the enemies of the Moabites; for that people had taken the city of Sibmah, Jer. 48:32, and other cities of Reuben, after this tribe had been carried into captivity by Tiglath-pileser, 2 Kin. 15:29; 1 Chron. 5:26. Jerome says that between Heshbon and Sibmah there was hardly the distance of five hundred paces.

SID'DIM. See SEA III.

SI'DON, in the Old Testament ZIDON, now called Saida, was a celebrated city of Phœnicia, on the Mediterranean sea, twenty miles north of Tyre and as many south of Beyroot. It is one of the most ancient cities in the world, Gen. 49:13, and is believed to have been founded by Zidon, the eldest son of Canaan, Gen. 10:15; 49:13. In the time of Homer, the Zidonians were eminent for their trade and commerce, their wealth and prosperity, their skill in navigation, astronomy, architecture, and for their manufactures of glass, etc. They had then a commodious harbor, now choked with sand and inaccessible to any but the smallest vessels. Upon the division of

Canaan among the tribes by Joshua, Great Zidon fell to the lot of Asher, Josh. 11:8; 19:28; but that tribe never succeeded in obtaining possession, Judg. 1:31; 3:3; 10:12. The Zidonians continued long under their own government and kings, though sometimes tributary to the kings of Tyre. They were subdued successively by the Babylonians, Egyptians, Seleucidæ, and Romans, the latter of whom deprived them of their freedom. Many of the inhabitants of Sidon became followers of our Saviour, Mark 3:8, and he himself visited their coasts, Matt. 15:21-28; Mark 7:24-31. Many of them also resorted to him in Galilee, Luke 6:17. The gospel was proclaimed to the Jews at Sidon after the martyrdom of Stephen, Acts 11:19, and there was a Christian church there, when Paul visited it on his voyage to Rome, Acts 27:3. It is at present, like most of the other Turkish towns in Syria, dirty and full of ruins, though it still retains a little coasting trade, and has five thousand inhabitants. It incurred the judgments of God for its sins, Ezek. 28:21-24, though less ruinously than Tyre. Our Saviour refers to both cities, in reproaching the Jews as more highly favored and less excusable than they, Matt. 11:22. Saida occupies an elevated promontory, projecting into the sea, and defended by walls. Its environs, watered by a stream from Lebanon, are famous for their beautiful gardens, and fruit-trees of every kind.

SIGN, a token, pledge, or proof, Gen. 9:12, 13; 17:11; Ex. 3:12; Isa. 8:18. Also a supernatural portent, Luke 21:11; and a miracle, regarded as a token of the divine agency, Ex. 4:7-9; Mark 8:11. The "signs of heaven" were the movements and aspects of the heavenly bodies, from which heathen astrologers pretended to obtain revelations, Isa. 44:25; Jer. 10:2. See SHIP.

SIG'NET, a ring for sealing. See RING, and SEAL.

SI'HON, king of the Amorites at Heshbon, on refusing passage to the Hebrews, and coming to attack them, was himself slain, his army routed, and his dominions divided among Israel, Num. 21:21-34; Deut. 2:26-36.

SI'HOR, *black* or *turbid*, the Nile. In Isa. 23:3, and Jer. 2:18, this name must necessarily be understood of the Nile. In Josh. 13:3; 1 Chr. 13:5, some have understood it of the little river between Egypt and Judah.

SI'LAS, Acts 15:22, and SILVA'NUS, 2 Cor. 1:19, the former name being a contraction of the latter; one of the chief men among the first disciples at Jerusalem, Acts 15:22, and supposed by some to have been of the number of the seventy. On occasion of a dispute at Antioch, as to the observance of legal ceremonies, Paul and Barnabas were chosen to go to Jerusalem, to advise with the apostles; and they returned with Judas and Silas. Silas joined himself to Paul; and after Paul and Barnabas had separated, Acts 15:37–41, A. D. 51, he accompanied Paul to visit the churches of Syria and Cilicia, and the towns and provinces of Lycaonia, Phrygia, Galatia, and Macedonia. He was imprisoned with him at Philippi, joined him at Corinth after a brief separation, bringing, it is supposed, the donation referred to in 2 Cor. 11:9, Phil. 4:10, 15, and probably went with him to Jerusalem, Acts 16:19, 25; 17:4, 10, 14; 18:5; 1 and 2 Thess. 1:1. He appears always as a "faithful brother," well known and praised by all the churches, 2 Cor. 1:19; 1 Pet. 5:12.

SILK, in the time of the Ptolemies, came to Greece and Rome from the far east of China, etc., by the way of Alexandria, and was sold for its weight in gold. It sometimes came in the form of skeins, and was woven into a light and thin gauze. It is mentioned in Rev. 18:12, and probably in Ezek. 16:10, 13. In Gen. 41:42 and Prov. 31:22, the word rendered *silk* in our version is the same that is elsewhere correctly rendered *fine linen*. It is not known how early or extensively the Jews used it.

FOUNTAIN AND POOL OF SILOAM.

SILO'AM, John 9:7, 11, or SHILOAH, Neh. 3:15; Isa. 8:6; a fountain and pool at the base of the hill Ophel, near the opening of the Tyropœon into the valley of the Kidron on the south of Jerusalem;

> "Siloah's brook, that flowed
> Fast by the oracle of God."
>
> MILTON.

The pool is now an artificial stone reservoir, fifty-three feet long, eighteen feet wide, and nineteen feet deep. Steps lead to the bottom of the pool, three or four feet above which the water flows off south-east to water the cultivated grounds in the valley below. The fountain is in an arched excavation in the foot of the cliff above the pool; and the small basin here is connected by a winding passage cut through the solid rock under the hill Ophel, with the "Fountain of the Virgin" eleven hundred feet north on the

UPPER POOL, OR FOUNTAIN OF THE VIRGIN.

east side of mount Moriah. See BETHESDA. This passage was traversed throughout by Dr. Robinson. The water flowing through it is tolerably sweet and clear, but has a marked taste, and in the dry season is slightly brackish. It is thought to be derived from the reservoirs under the ancient temple area, and in part from mount Zion. It runs "softly," Isa. 8:6, but ebbs and flows in the "Fountain of the Virgin," and less perceptibly in that of Siloam, at irregular intervals. Thus the water rose more than a foot in the upper fountain, and fell again within ten minutes, while Dr. Robinson was on the spot. He once found a party of soldiers there washing their clothes, John 9:1–11, and it is in constant use for purposes of ablution. At Siloam also the water is used for washing, watering animals, etc.

Nothing is known respecting the "tower" near Siloam, the fall of which killed eighteen men. The ancient city wall is believed to have enclosed this pool. Christ teaches us by the above incident that temporal calamities are not always proofs of special guilt, Luke 13 : 4, 5, though the utmost sufferings ever endured in this world are far less than the sins of even the best of men deserve, Lam. 3:39.

SILVA'NUS. See SILAS.

SIL'VER, one of the precious metals, and the one most commonly used as coin among all nations. It is first mentioned in Scripture in the history of Abraham, Gen. 13:2; 20:16; 23:16, and was used in constructing the tabernacle, Ex. 26:19, 32, and afterwards the temple, 1 Chr. 29 : 4. In employing it as a medium of trade, the ancient Hebrews weighed it out, instead of having coins. In the times of the New Testament there were coins. See SHEKEL, and MONEY.

SIM'EON, I., one of the twelve patriarchs, the son of Jacob and Leah, Gen. 29 : 33; Ex. 6 : 15. Some have thought he was more guilty than his brethren in the treatment of Joseph, Gen. 37 : 20; 42 : 24; 43 : 23; but he may have been detained as a hostage because he was one of the eldest sons. The tribes of Simeon and Levi were scattered and dispersed in Israel, in conformity with the prediction of Jacob, on account of their sacrilegious and piratical revenge of the outrage committed against Dinah their sister, Gen. 34; 49 : 5. Levi had no compact lot or portion in the Holy Land; and Simeon received for his portion only a district dismembered from Judah, with some other lands the tribe overran in the mountains of Seir, and in the desert of Gedor, 1 Chr. 4:24, 39, 42. The portion of Simeon was west and south of that of Judah, having the Philistines on the north-west and the desert on the south, Josh. 19:1–9. The tribe was reduced in numbers while in the wilderness, from 59,300 to 24,000, Num. 1 : 23; 26 : 14; very probably on account of sharing in the licentious idolatry of Moab, with Zimri their prince, Num. 25, or for other sins. They are little known in subsequent history. We find them faithful to David, 1 Chr. 12 : 25, and afterwards to Asa, 2 Chr. 15 : 9, and in general absorbed by Judah. Moses omits this tribe in his dying benedictions, Deut. 33; but its place in Israel is restored by a covenant-keeping God, Ezek. 48 : 24; Rev. 7 : 7.

II. A venerable saint at Jerusalem, full of the Holy Spirit, who was expecting the redemption of Israel, Luke 2:25–35. It had been revealed to him that he should not die before he had seen the Christ so long promised; and he therefore came into the temple, prompted by inspiration, just at the time when Joseph and Mary presented our Saviour there, in obedience to the law. Simeon took the child in his arms, gave thanks to God, and blessed Joseph and Mary. We know nothing further concerning him.

III. Surnamed NI'GER, or the Black, Acts 13:1, was among the prophets and teachers of the Christian church at Antioch. Some think he was Simon the Cyrenian; but there is no proof of this.

IV. The apostle Peter is also called Simeon in Acts 15 : 14, but elsewhere Simon.

SI'MON, I., one of the twelve apostles. See PETER.

II. The Canaanite, or Zelotes, one of the twelve apostles. See ZELOTES.

III. One of the "brethren" of Jesus, Matt. 13:55; Mark 6:3. He is by some supposed to be the same with the preceding Simon Zelotes. See JAMES III.

IV. The Cyrenian, who was compelled to aid in bearing the cross of Jesus, Matt. 27:32, probably on account of his known attachment to His cause. He was "the father of Alexander and Rufus," Mark 15 : 21; and from the cordial salutation of Paul, Rom. 16:13, it would seem that the family afterwards resided at Rome, and that their labor of love was not forgotten by God.

V. A Pharisee, probably at Capernaum, who invited Jesus to dinner at his house, Luke 7:36–50.

VI. The leper; that is, who had been a leper; a resident of Bethany, with whom also Jesus supped, Matt. 26 : 6; Mark 14:3. Compare John 12:1–11.

VII. The tanner; a disciple who dwelt at Joppa, and in whose house Peter lodged, Acts 9:43; 10:6, 17, 32.

VIII. The sorcerer of Samaria; often called Simon Magus, that is, the Magician. See SORCERER. This artful impostor, by the aid of some knowledge of philosophy, medicine, physics, and astronomy, acquired an ascendency over the people of Samaria. But the preaching and miracles of Philip brought great numbers to Christ, and convinced even Simon that a real and great power attended the gospel. He coveted these spiritual gifts of the apostles for selfish ends, and sought them by joining the church and afterwards offering to purchase them with money. Peter took the occasion to expose his hypocrisy by a terrible denunciation, Acts 8:9-24. There are various doubtful traditions as to his subsequent course. The sin of trafficking in spiritual things, called Simony after him, was more odious to Peter than to many who claim to be his especial followers.

IX. The father of Judas Iscariot, John 6:71; 13:2, 26.

SIMPLE and SIMPLICITY are sometimes used in the Bible in a good sense, denoting sincerity, candor, and an artless ignorance of evil, Rom. 16 : 19; 2 Cor. 1:12; 11:3; sometimes in a bad sense, denoting a heedless foolishness both mental and moral, Prov. 1 : 22; 9:4; 14:15; 22:3; and sometimes in the sense of mere ignorance or inexperience, 2 Sam. 15:11; Prov. 1:4; 21:11.

SIN, I., any thought, word, desire, action, or omission of action, contrary to the law of God, or defective when compared with it.

The origin of sin is a subject which baffles all investigation; and our inquiries are much better directed when we seek through Christ a release from its penalty and power, for ourselves and the world. Its entrance into the world, and infection of the whole human race, its nature, forms, and effects, and its fatal possession of every unregenerate soul, are fully described in the Bible, Gen. 6 : 5; Psa. 51 : 5; Matt. 15 : 19; Rom. 5:12; Jas. 1:14, 15.

As contrary to the nature, worship, love, and service of God, sin is called ungodliness; as a violation of the law of God and of the claims of man, it is a transgression or trespass; as a deviation from eternal rectitude, it is called iniquity or unrighteousness; as the evil and bitter root of all actual transgression, the depravity transmitted from our first parents to all their seed, it is called "original sin," or in the Bible, "the flesh," "the law of sin and death," etc., Rom. 8:1, 2; 1 John 3 : 4; 5 : 17. The just penalty or "wages of sin is death;" this was threatened against the first sin, Gen. 2 : 17, and all subsequent sins: "The soul that sinneth it shall die." A single sin, unrepented of and unforgiven, destroys the soul, as a single break renders a whole ocean cable worthless. Its guilt and evil are to be measured by the holiness, justice, and goodness of the law it violates, the eternity of the misery it causes, and the greatness of the Sacrifice necessary to expiate it.

"Sin" is also sometimes put for the sacrifice of expiation, the sin-offering, described in Lev. 4:3, 25, 29. So, Rom. 8:3; and in 2 Cor. 5 : 21, Paul says that God was pleased that Jesus, who knew no sin, should be our victim of expiation: "For he hath made him to be sin for us, who knew no sin; that we might be made the righteousness of God in him."

For the sin against the Holy Ghost, see BLASPHEMY.

II. A desert of Arabia Petræa, near Egypt, and on the western arm of the Red sea. Ex. 16 : 1; 17:1; Num. 33:12. To be distinguished from the desert of Zin. See ZIN.

III. An ancient fortified city, called "the strength of Egypt," Ezek. 30 : 15, 16. Its name means *mire*, and in this it agrees with Pelusium and Tineh, the Greek and modern names of the same place. It defended the north-east frontier of Egypt, and lay near the Mediterranean, on the eastern arm of the Nile. Its site, near the village of Tineh, is surrounded with morasses; and is now accessible by boats only during a high inundation, or by land in the driest part of summer. A few mounds and columns alone remain.

SINAI, a mountain, or mountain range, in Arabia Petræa, in the peninsula formed by the two arms of the Red sea, and rendered memorable as the spot where the law was given to Israel through Moses, Ex. 19:1 to Num. 10:33. As this mountain has been almost unknown in modern times, until recently, and is of such importance in Scripture history, we shall enter into some details respecting it.

The upper region of Sinai forms an irregular circle of thirty or forty miles in diameter, possessing numerous sources of water, a temperate climate, and a soil capable of supporting animal and vegetable life; for which reason it is the refuge of all the Bedaweens when the low country is parched up. This, therefore, was the part of the peninsula best adapted to the residence of nearly a year,

PLAIN ER-RAHAH, AND CONVENT OF ST. CATHARINE.

during which the Israelites were numbered, and received their laws from the Most High. In the highest and central part of this region, seven thousand feet above the level of the sea, rises the sacred summit of Horeb or Sinai. The two names are used almost indiscriminately in the Bible, the former predominating in Deuteronomy. Some have thought there were two adjacent summits, called, in the time of Moses, Horeb and Sinai; and indeed the monks give these names to the northern and southern heights of the same ridge, three miles long. But the comparison of all the Scripture passages rather shows that HOREB was the general name for the group, and SINAI the name of the sacred summit.

In approaching this elevated region from the north-west, Burckhardt writes, "We now approached the central summits of mount Sinai, which we had had in view for several days. Abrupt cliffs of granite, from six to eight hundred feet in height, whose surface is blackened by the sun, surround the avenues leading to the elevated region to which the name of Sinai is specifically applied. These cliffs inclose the holy mountain on three sides, leaving the east and north-east sides only, towards the gulf of Akaba, more open to the view. At the end of three hours, we entered these cliffs by a narrow defile about forty feet in breadth, with perpendicular granite rocks on both sides. The ground is covered with sand and pebbles, brought down by the torrent which rushes from the upper region in the winter time."

The general approach to Sinai from the same quarter is thus described by Mr. Carne: "A few hours more, and we got sight of the mountains round Sinai. Their appearance was magnificent. When we drew near, and emerged out of a deep pass, the scenery was infinitely striking; and on the right extended a vast range of mountains, as far as the eye could reach, from the vicinity of Sinai down to Tor, on the gulf of Suez. They were perfectly bare, but of grand and singular form. We had hoped to reach the convent by daylight; but the moon had risen some time when we entered the mouth of a narrow pass, where our conductors advised us to dismount. A gentle yet perpetual ascent led on, mile after mile, up this mournful valley, whose aspect was terrific, yet ever varying. It was not above two hundred yards in width, and the mountains rose to an immense height on each side. The road wound at their feet along the edge of a precipice, and amid masses of rock that had fallen from above. It was a toilsome path, generally over stones placed like steps, probably by the Arabs; and the moonlight was of little service to us in this deep valley, as it only rested on the frowning summits above. Where is mount Sinai? was the inquiry of every one. The Arabs pointed before to Jebel Moosa, the mount of Moses, as it is called; but we could not distinguish it. Again and again point after point was turned, and we saw but the same stern scenery. But what had the beauty and softness of nature to do here? Mount Sinai required an approach like this, where all seemed to proclaim the land of miracles, and to have been visited by the terrors of the Lord. The scenes, as you gazed around, had an unearthly character, suited to the sound of the fearful trumpet that was once heard there. We entered at last on the more open valley, about half a mile wide, and drew near this famous mountain."

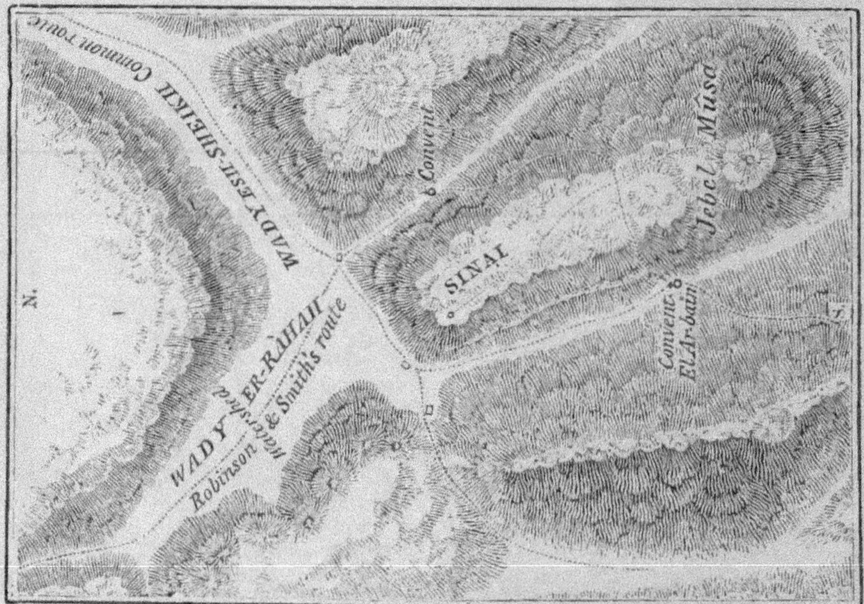

The elevated valley or plain Er-Rahah, here and above referred to, is now generally believed to be the place where the Hebrews assembled to witness the giving of the law. It is two miles long from north-west to south-east, and on an average half a mile wide. The square mile thus afforded is nearly doubled by the addition of those portions of side valleys, particularly Esh-Sheikh towards the north-north-east, from which the summit Ras-Sufsafeh can be seen. This summit, which Dr. Robinson takes to be the true Sinai, rises abruptly on the south side of the plain some fifteen hundred feet. It is the termination of a ridge running three miles south-east, the southern and highest point of which is called by the Arabs Jebel Mûsa, or Moses' Mount. Separated from this ridge by deep and steep ravines, are two parallel ridges, of which the eastern is called the Mountain of the Cross, and the western, Jebel Humr. The convent of St. Catharine lies in the ravine east of the true Sinai; while mount Catharine is the south peak of the western ridge, lying south-west of Jebel Mûsa, and rising more than one thousand feet higher. From the convent, Dr. Robinson ascended the central and sacred mountain, and the steep peak Ras-Sufsafeh. "The extreme difficulty," he says, "and even danger of the ascent, was well rewarded by the prospect that now opened before us. The whole plain Er-Rahah lay spread out beneath our feet; while wady Esh-Sheikh on the right and a recess on the left, both connected with and opening broadly from Er-Rahah, presented an area which serves nearly to double that of the plain. Our conviction was strengthened that here, or on some one of the adjacent cliffs, was the spot where the Lord descended in fire and proclaimed the law. Here lay the plain where the whole congregation might be assembled; here was the mount which might be approached and touched; and here the mountain brow where alone the lightnings and the thick cloud would be visible, and the thunders and the voice of the trump be heard, when the Lord came down in the sight of all the people upon mount Sinai. We gave ourselves up to the impressions of the awful scene; and read with a feeling which will never be forgotten the sublime account of the transaction and the commandments there promulgated, in the original words as recorded by the great Hebrew legislator."

The plain Er-Rahah is supposed to have been reached by the Hebrews from the shore of the Red sea, south of the desert of Sin, by a series of wadys or broad ravines winding up among the mountains in an easterly direction, chiefly wady Feiran and wady Esh-Sheikh. The former commences near the Red sea, and opens into the latter, which making a circuit to the north of Sinai, enters the plain at its foot from the north-northeast. For several miles from its termination here, this valley is half a mile wide. By the same northern entrance most travellers have approached the sacred mountain. Its south side is less known. To the spectator on Jebel Mûsa, it presents no trace of any plain, valley, or level ground to be compared with that on the north; yet some writers maintain that the Hebrews received the law at the southern foot of Sinai. See map, in the article EXODUS.

In many of the western Sinaite valleys, and most of all in El-Mukatteb, which enters wady Feiran from the north-west, the more accessible parts of the rocky sides are covered by thousands of inscriptions, usually short, and rudely carved in spots where travellers would naturally stop to rest at noon; frequently accompanied by a cross and mingled with representations of animals. The inscriptions are in an unknown character, but were at first ascribed to the ancient Israelites on their way from Egypt to Sinai; and afterwards to Christian pilgrims of the fourth century. Recently, however, many of them have been deciphered by Prof. Beer of Leipzig, who regards them as the only known remains of the language and characters once peculiar to the Nabathaeans of Arabia Petræa. Those thus far deciphered are simply proper names, neither Jewish nor Christian, preceded by some such words as "peace," "blessed," "in memory of."

The giving of the law upon mount Sinai made it one of the most memorable spots on the globe. Here, moreover, God appeared to Moses in the burning bush, Exod. 3 and 4; and six centuries later, sublimely revealed himself to the prophet Elijah when fleeing from the fury of Jezebel, 1 Kin. 19. There are frequent allusions in Scripture to the glorious and awful delivery of the Law, Judg. 5:5; Psa. 68:8, 17; Hab. 3:3. In the New Testament, the dispensation proclaimed on Sinai is contrasted with the gospel of the grace of God, Gal. 4:24, 25; Heb. 12:18-29.

SI'NIM, Isa. 49:12, a people very remote from the Holy Land, towards the east or south; generally believed to mean the Chinese, who have been known to Western Asia from early times, and are called by the Arabs Sin, and by the Syrians Tsini.

SI'NITES, a Canaanite tribe, probably near mount Lebanon, Gen. 10:17; 1 Chr. 1:15.

SI'ON, I., a name given in Deut. 4:48 to one of the elevations of the mountain ridge called Hermon, which see.

II. The Greek or New Testament form of Zion, which see.

SIR'ION. See Hermon.

SIS'ERA, a general in the army of Jabin king of Hazor, sent by his master against Barak and Deborah, who occupied mount Tabor with an army. Being defeated, he fled on foot, and was ingloriously slain by Jael, Judg. 4, 5. See Jael.

SIS'TER. In the style of the Hebrews, "sister" has equal latitude with "brother." It is used, not only for a sister by natural relation, from the same father and mother, but also for a sister by the same father only, or by the same mother only; or for any near female relative, Gen. 12:13. See Brother.

SITH, an obsolete word, meaning since, Ezek. 35:6.

SI'VAN, the third Hebrew ecclesiastical month, and the ninth of the civil year, beginning with the new moon of our June, Esth. 8:9.

SLAVE, Jer. 2:14; Rev. 18:13. See Servant.

SLIME. See Pitch, and Sea III.

SLING, an instrument much used in war before the invention of fire-arms. It was a formidable weapon in hands like those of David and the Benjamites, Judg. 20:16; 1 Sam. 17:48-50; 1 Chr. 12:2; 2 Chr. 26:14.

SMITH, an artificer in brass, iron, etc., first mentioned in Gen. 4:22. The art of the smith is one of the essentials of civilization; and without it a nation was peculiarly defenceless in time of war, Judg. 5:8; 1 Sam. 13:19-22; 2 Kin. 24:14. Workers in silver and in copper were distinguished from each other, Acts 19:24; 2 Tim. 4:14.

SMYR'NA, a celebrated Ionian city, situated at the head of a deep gulf on the western coast of Asia Minor, forty miles north by west of Ephesus. It was one of the richest and most powerful cities of that region, and was frequented by great numbers of Jews. A Christian church was established there at an early day, and was one of the seven churches addressed by Christ in the Revelation of John, 1:11; 2:8-11. It is still a prosperous commercial city, being visited by many foreign ships, and by numerous caravans of camels from the interior. Its population is nearly 150,000; of whom one-half are Turks, one-fourth Greeks, and the remainder chiefly Armenians, Jews, and Franks. So many of its inhabitants are not Mohammedans, that it is called by the Turks Giaour Izmir, or Infidel Smyrna. It has a deep and capacious harbor, well protected except towards the west by the hills which rise to a great height in the rear of the city, inclosing it on three sides. On these hills lie the scanty remains of the ancient city; among which is the ground-plot of the stadium, where is said to have occurred the martyrdom of Polycarp—the pupil of the apostle John, and very probably "the angel of the church in Ephesus," Rev. 2:8. Smyrna has been often devastated by earthquakes and conflagrations; multitudes perished there of the cholera in 1831, and 60,000 died of the plague in 1824; yet its fine situation secures a prompt recovery from every disaster. It is now the seat of important missionary efforts, and enjoys the ordinances of a Protestant church.

SNAIL, in Lev. 11:30, is probably a sort of lizard; and in Psa. 58:8, the common slug or snail without a shell, which "melteth" away by depositing its slime wherever it passes.

SNOW is often alluded to in Scripture, for its whiteness, Ex. 4 : 6; Num. 12 : 10; 2 Kin. 5 : 27; Psa. 51 : 7; Isa. 1:18, and for its cleansing qualities, Job 9 : 30. The expression in Prov. 25 : 13, "as the cold of snow in the time of harvest," alludes to its use in preparing cool drinks for the reapers; while on the other hand, in Prov. 26 : 1, "snow in summer," that is, a fall of snow, being unseasonable and unnatural, is compared to honors inappropriately lavished on a fool. Snow from Anti-Lebanon is still sold at Damascus and Beyroot in the summer, and even conveyed to Egypt. It rarely fell of any great depth in the latitude of Palestine, or remained long on the ground except in elevated spots, 2 Sam. 23:20. Like every other wonder of nature, it is ascribed to the hand of God, Psa. 147:16, 17.

SO, king of Egypt, made an alliance with Hoshea king of Israel, and promised him assistance; but was unable to prevent Shalmaneser king of Assyria from taking Samaria and subverting the kingdom, B. C. 721, 2 Kin. 17 : 4. See PHARAOH. So is believed to have been the Servetus or Sabaco II. of secular history, the second king of the Ethiopian or twenty-fifth dynasty, and the predecessor of Tirhakah. A singular fact has been brought to light by the recent explorations at Nineveh, corroborating the Scripture record the more forcibly, because unexpected and direct. The Bible shows that Egypt and Assyria, though remote, were often in conflict during the height of the Assyrian power, and that So was at war with Shalmaneser. After war comes the treaty of peace; and as the Bible prepares us to suppose such treaties were made, the Assyrian ruins furnish evidence of their existence. In the remains of Sennacherib's palace recently disentombed, a small room was found which seems to have been a hall of records; and among the seals it contained was the seal of So, well known to students of Egyptian antiquities. It was impressed, as was then the custom, on a piece of fine clay, which also bore the impress of a royal signet of Assyria; thus showing the probability that such a treaty between the two nations had here been deposited. If so, when the two monarchs affixed their seals to a document which like themselves has turned to dust, the Most High by their act affixed an additional seal to his holy word, which is true and abideth for ever.

SOAP, Mal. 3 : 2, Hebrew, borith, *the cleanser;* in Jer. 2 : 22 distinguished from nitre, which see. It is well known that the ancients used certain vegetables and their ashes for the purpose of cleansing linen, etc. The ashes of seashore plants contain barilla or carbonate of soda, and those of poplar and other inland plants contain carbonate of potash. Combined with oil or fat these alkalies produced soap; but it is not known in what forms the Jews used them.

SO'COH, or SHO'CHOH, I., 1 Kin. 4:10, a town in the plain of Judah, near Azekah, famous for a battle of David and Saul with the Philistines, 1 Sam. 17 : 1; against whom Rehoboam fortified it, and by whom it was afterwards taken, 2 Chr. 11:7; 28:18.

II. A town in the mountains of Judah, south by west of Hebron, Josh. 15:48. Dr. Robinson found traces of both these sites, under the name of Suweikeh, or Shaukeh.

SOD'OM, one of the cities of the plain, and for some time the dwelling-place of Lot, Gen. 13 : 10-13; 14:12. Its crimes and vices were so enormous, that God destroyed it by fire from heaven, with three neighboring cities, Gomorrah, Zeboim, and Admah, which were as wicked as itself, Gen. 19. The plain of Siddim in which they stood was pleasant and fruitful, like an earthly paradise; but it was first burned, and afterwards mostly overflowed by the waters of the Dead sea or lake of Sodom. See JORDAN, and SEA III. The prophets, in denouncing woes upon other countries, mention the destruction of Sodom and Gomorrah, and intimate that these places shall be desert and dried up and uninhabited, Jer. 49 : 18; 50 : 40; that they shall be covered with briers and brambles, a land of salt and sulphur, where can be neither planting nor sowing, Deut. 29 : 23; Amos 4:11. Throughout Scripture the ruin of Sodom and Gomorrah is represented as a most signal effect of God's anger, and as a mirror in which those living at ease in sin and lust may see their own doom. The name is given in Rev. 11 : 8, to the great and corrupt city of antichrist. "Sodomites" were men addicted to the beastly lusts alluded to in Gen. 19; 1 Kin. 14:24; Rom. 1:26, 27.

SOL'OMON, *peaceful*, the son and successor of David, born of Bathsheba, B. C. 1033. The prophet Nathan called him Jedidiah, "beloved of the Lord," 2 Sam. 12:25, and he was a child of promise, 1 Chr. 22:9, 10. At the age of eighteen he received from David the throne which his brother Adonijah had endeavored to usurp. Scripture records his earnest and pious petition for wisdom from above, that he might govern that great people well; and the bestowal of that wisdom, with numerous other blessings in its train, Matt. 6:33. His unequalled learning and sagacity soon became renowned throughout the East, and continue so even to this day. In every kind of temporal prosperity he was preëminently favored. His unquestioned dominion extended from the Euphrates to the "river of Egypt;" Palmyra in the desert and Ezion-geber on the Red sea were in his possession. He accomplished David's purpose by erecting a temple for Jehovah with the utmost magnificence. Many other important public and private works were executed during his reign. He established a lucrative commerce with Tyre, Egypt, Arabia, India, and Babylon, by the fruits of which he himself first and chiefly, and indirectly the whole land, were greatly enriched. He was the wisest, wealthiest, most honored, and fortunate of men. But through the temptations connected with this flood of prosperity, he became luxurious, proud, and forgetful of God; plunged into every kind of self-indulgence; allowed his wives, and at length assisted them, in their abominable idolatries; and forfeited the favor of God. Yet divine grace did not forsake him; he was reclaimed, and has given us the proofs of his repentance and the fruits of his experience in his inspired writings. His reign continued forty years, B. C. 1015–975, and was uniformly peaceful, and favorable to the people, if we except the evils of a corrupt example and an excessive taxation. His history is less fully recorded than David's by the sacred historians, 1 Kin. 1:11; 2 Chr. 1–9; but we may learn much respecting him from his writings, especially from the book of Ecclesiastes. Nothing could more emphatically teach us the weakness of human nature, even when accompanied with the utmost learning and sagacity, the perils of prosperity, or the insufficiency of all possible earthly good to satisfy the wants of man.

The writings of Solomon covered a wide range in the natural sciences, as well as in philosophy and morals. "He spake three thousand proverbs; and his songs were a thousand and five: and he spake of trees—of beasts, and of fowl, and of creeping things, and of fishes," 1 Kin. 4:32, 33.

SOLOMON'S POOLS, Eccl. 2:6. Among these may perhaps be included the ancient structures now so called, two or three miles south-west of Bethlehem. These are three large reservoirs lying one above and beyond another in a narrow valley. They are built of large stones, and plastered within; and the water collected in them, and in several fountains in the vicinity, was conveyed in an aqueduct to Bethlehem and Jerusalem. The upper pool is 380 feet in length, the middle pool 423, and the lower one 582. Their average breadth is 200 feet, and their depth 38 feet. At present they contain comparatively little water; yet they are of incalculable importance to Bethlehem, and might easily be made so to Jerusalem. The aqueduct crosses the valley of Hinnom below the south-west corner of the city wall, winds south around mount Zion, and turns north again into the city towards the Haram area.

SOLOMON'S PORCH. See TEMPLE.

SOLOMON'S SONG, called also CANTICLES, and SONG OF SONGS, B. C. 1012. This highly figurative and beautiful poem has always held a place in the canonical Scriptures, and of course was a part of the Bible in the time of Christ; it was so regarded by the early Christians, and appears in the ancient catalogues, manuscripts, and versions. Numerous and very different opinions have been held as to the subject and plan of this poem; but that its design is to set forth the spiritual love and mutual communion between Christ and his people, is evident from its harmony, when so understood, with the large class of Scripture passages which represent God and particularly Christ as the husband of the church, and employ the marriage relation in its various aspects to illustrate the relation between the Saviour and his people. Thus Psalm 45 is a Messianic nuptial song. See also Isa. 54:5; 62:5; Jer. 3; Ezek. 16; Hos. 1-3; 2 Cor. 11:2; Eph. 5:23-32; Rev. 19:7-9; 21:2-9.

In the exposition of this beautiful poem we must remember the difference between eastern and western nations. Modern conventional rules and notions are not the standard to which its plan, its images, or its phraseology should be brought. The veiling of spiritual fervor and enjoyment under the symbol of love is common among oriental nations, and commentators have quoted portions of Eastern allegorical songs which bear no small resemblance to this inspired allegory. Many Christians, deeply imbued with the spirit of the gospel, have found great delight and benefit in reading it. Jonathan Edwards says, "I found an inward sweetness that would carry me away in my contemplations. This I know not how to express otherwise than by a calm, delightful abstraction of the soul from all concerns of the world; and sometimes a kind of vision of fixed ideas and imaginations of being alone in the mountains or some solitary wilderness, far from mankind, sweetly conversing with Christ, and rapt and swallowed up in God. The sense I had of divine things would often of a sudden kindle up an ardor in my soul that I knew not how to express. While thus engaged, it always seemed natural to me to sing or chant forth my meditations, or to speak my thoughts in soliloquies with a singing voice."

Dr. John Brown of Haddington, in the introduction to his admirable paraphrase of this book, says, "If understood of the marriage and fellowship between Christ and his people, it will appear most exalted, instructive, and heart-warming. Its majestic style, its power on men's conscience to promote holiness and purity, the harmony of its language with that of Christ's parables and the book of Revelation, the sincerity of the bride in acknowledging her faults, and its general reception by the Jewish and Christian church, sufficiently prove it inspired of God. To such as read it with a carnal and especially with a wanton mind, it is the savor of death unto death, as the mind and conscience of such are defiled; but to such as have experienced much fellowship with Christ, and read it with a heavenly and spiritual temper of mind, it will be the savor of life unto life. The speakers in it are, Christ, Believers, and the Daughters of Jerusalem," or companions and friends of believers.

SON sometimes denotes a grandson, or any remote descendant, Gen. 29:5; 2 Sam. 19:24. At other times a son by adoption is meant, Gen. 48:5; or by law, Ruth 4:17; or by education, 1 Sam. 3:6; 20:35; or by conversion, as Titus was Paul's "son after the common faith," Tit. 1:4. And again it denotes a mental or moral resemblance, etc., Judg. 19:22; Psa. 89:6; Isa. 57:3; Acts 13:10. In a similar sense men are sometimes called sons of God, Luke 3:38; Rom. 8:14.

SON OF GOD, a peculiar appellation of Christ, expressing his eternal relationship to the Father, Psa. 2:7; Dan. 3:25; Luke 1:35; John 1:18, 34. Christ always claimed to be the only-begotten Son of the Father, Matt. 4:3; 8:29; 27:54; John 3:16-18; and the Jews rightly understood him as thus making himself equal with God, John 5:18; 10:30-33.

SON OF MAN, a title of Christ, assumed by himself in his humiliation, John 1:51. It was understood as a designation of the Messiah, according to Old Testament predictions, Psa. 80:17; Dan. 7:13, 14; but appears to indicate especially his true humanity or oneness with the human race. It is applied to him more than eighty times in the New Testament.

SOOTHSAYER. See SORCERER.

SOP, John 13:26, a small portion of bread, dipped in sauce, wine, or some other liquid at table, Ruth 2:14. Modern table utensils were unknown or little used by the ancients. The food was conveyed to the mouth by the thumb and fingers, and a choice morsel was often thus bestowed on a favored guest. Similar customs still prevail in Palestine. Jowett says, "There are set on the table in the evening two or three messes of stewed meat, vegetables, and sour milk. To me the privilege of a knife, spoon, and plate was granted; but the rest helped themselves immediately from the dish, in which five Arab fingers might be seen at once. Their bread, which is extremely thin, tearing and folding up like a sheet of paper, is used for rolling together a large mouthful, or sopping up the fluid and vegetables. When the master of the house found in the dish any dainty morsel, he took it out with his fingers, and put it to my mouth."

SOP'ATER, a Berean Christian, and one of those who attended Paul from Greece into Asia Minor, Acts 20 : 4. He is supposed to have been the kinsman of Paul called Sosipater in Rom. 16:21.

SOR'CERER, one who practised sorcery; nearly synonymous with magician, soothsayer, or wizard. This was a class of persons who dealt in incantations and divinations, and boasted of a power, in consequence of their deep science and by means of certain rites, to evoke the spirits of the dead from their gloomy abodes, and compel them to disclose information on subjects beyond the reach of human powers. They pretended also that, by means of certain herbs and incantations, they were able to expel demons, Acts 13:6, 8. Those persons also who devoted themselves to the general studies above mentioned, often abused their knowledge and deceived the common people, by pretending to foretell the destinies of men from the motions and appearances of the planets and stars, and to cure diseases by repeating certain phrases, etc. Of this class appears to have been Simon the sorcerer, mentioned in Acts 8 : 9, 11. Females who practised such arts were called sorceresses and witches, Mal. 3:5; Rev. 22:15. See DIVINATION, ENCHANTMENTS, and MAGIC.

SO'REK, a valley in which Delilah resided, not far from Zorah and Eshtaol, Judg. 16:4. In winter and spring it was the channel of a brook, flowing northwest from Judah, by the region of Dan and the Philistines, into the Mediterranean. Jerome mentions a village of Sorek in that vicinity. The same Hebrew word, translated "choice" and "noble" in Gen. 49 : 11, Isa. 5 : 2, Jer. 2 : 21, is the name of a vine bearing small grapes, but very sweet and almost without seeds. This vine may have given the valley its name.

SOSIP'ATER. See SOPATER.

SOS'THENES, the chief of the synagogue at Corinth, who was beaten by the Gentiles when the Jews carried Paul before Gallio the proconsul, Acts 18:17. He appears to have been the leader of the Jews in this attempt to destroy Paul. Whether he was converted, and is identical with the "Sosthenes our brother" in 1 Cor. 1:1, is unknown.

SOUL. The ancients supposed the soul, or rather the animating principle of life, to reside in the breath, and that it departed from the body with the breath. Hence the Hebrew and Greek words which, when they refer to man, in our Bibles are translated "soul," are usually rendered "life" or "breath" when they refer to animals, Gen. 2 : 7; 7:15; Num. 16:22; Job 12 : 10; 34 : 14, 15; Psa. 104:29; Eccl. 12:7; Acts 17:25.

But together with this principle of life, which is common to men and brutes, and which in brutes perishes with the body, there is in man a spiritual, reasonable, and immortal soul, the seat of our thoughts, affections, and reasonings, which distinguishes us from the brute creation, and in which chiefly consists our resemblance to God, Gen. 1 : 26. This must be spiritual, because it thinks; it must be immortal, because it is spiritual. Scripture ascribes to man alone understanding, conscience, the knowledge of God, wisdom, immortality, and the hope of future everlasting happiness. It threatens men only with punishment in another life, and with the pains of hell. In some places the Bible seems to distinguish soul from spirit, 1 Thess. 5 : 23; Heb. 4:12: the organ of our sensations, appetites, and passions, allied to the body, from that nobler portion of our nature which most allies man to God. Yet we are to conceive of them as one indivisible and spiritual being, called also the mind and the heart, spoken of variously as living, feeling, understanding, reasoning, willing, etc. Its usual designation is the soul.

The immortality of the soul is a fundamental doctrine of revealed religion. The ancient patriarchs lived and died persuaded of this truth; and it was in the hope of another life that they received the promises. Compare Gen. 50:33; Num. 23 : 10; 1 Sam. 28:13-15; 2 Sam. 12:23; Job 19:25, 26; Eccl. 12:7; Heb. 11 : 13-16. In the gospel "life and immortality," and the worth of immortal souls, are fully brought to light, Matt. 16 : 26; 1 Cor. 15 : 45-57; 2 Tim. 1 : 10. To save the souls of men, Christ freely devoted himself to death; and how does it become us to labor and toil and strive, in our respective spheres, to promote the great work for which He bled and died!

SPAIN comprehended, in ancient usage, the modern kingdoms of Spain and Portugal, that is, the whole Spanish peninsula. In the time of Paul, it was subject to the Romans, and was frequented by many Jews. For the supposed origin of its name, see CONEY. In Rom. 15 : 24, 28, Paul expresses his intention of visiting Spain ; and many conjecture that he did so between his first and second imprisonments at Rome, about A. D. 64-66.

SPAN, Lam. 2 : 20, the distance from the extremity of the thumb to that of the little finger, when stretched apart ; some nine inches.

SPAR'ROW, a small bird, the Passer Domesticus of naturalists, with quill and tail feathers brown, and its body gray and black, resembling the small "chirping-bird" of America. It is a general inhabitant of Europe, Asia, and Africa ; is bold and familiar in its habits, and frequents populous places. It builds under the eaves of houses, and in similar situations ; feeds on seeds, fruits, and insects ; and lays five or six eggs of a pale ash color, with brown spots. The Hebrew name Tzippor includes also other small chirping birds, feeding on grain and insects, and classed as clean, Lev. 14 : 4 ; among others the thrush, which may be alluded to in Psa. 102 : 7, a bird remarkable throughout the East for sitting solitary on the habitations of men and warbling in sweet and plaintive strains. A sparrow is of course of comparatively little value ; and it is therefore a striking exemplification of God's providence to say that he watches even over the sparrow's fall, Matt. 10 : 29. These birds are still very numerous, troublesome, and cheap in Jerusalem, Luke 12 : 6, and flit in great numbers around the mosque of Omar, on the site of the ancient temple, within the precincts of which they built their favored nests of old, Psa. 84:3.

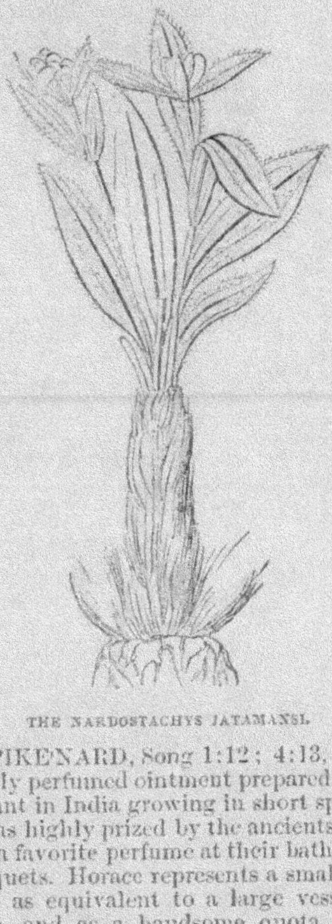

THE NARDOSTACHYS JATAMANSI.

SPIKE'NARD, Song 1:12 ; 4:13, 14, a highly perfumed ointment prepared from a plant in India growing in short spikes. It was highly prized by the ancients, and was a favorite perfume at their baths and banquets. Horace represents a small box of it as equivalent to a large vessel of wine, and as a handsome quota for a guest to contribute to an entertainment. It was kept closely sealed, sometimes in alabaster boxes ; and to unseal and open it was called breaking the box, Mark 14 : 3. The evangelists speak of it as diffusing a rich perfume ; and as "precious," and "very costly," a pound of it being worth more than three hundred denarii, or over forty dollars, John 12:3-5. See ALABASTER, and PENNY.

SPI'DER, a well-known insect, remarkable for the thread which it spins, and with which it forms a web of curious texture, but so frail that it is exposed to be broken and destroyed by the slightest accident. To the slenderness of this filmy workmanship Job compares the hope of

the wicked, 8 : 14. So also in Isa. 59 : 5, it is shown that the works of sinners are utterly inadequate to cover or protect them. In Prov. 30 : 28, it is said in our version that "the spider taketh hold with her hands, and is in kings' palaces;" but the Hebrew employs here a different word, which signifies, according to the best interpreters, a species of lizard frequent in Palestine.

SPIRIT is a word employed in various senses in Scripture.

I. For THE HOLY SPIRIT, the third person of the Holy Trinity, who inspired the prophets, animates good men, pours his unction into our hearts, imparts to us life and comfort; and in whose name we are baptized and blessed, as well as in that of the Father and the Son. When the adjective Holy is applied to the term Spirit, we should always understand it as here explained; but there are many places where it must be taken in this sense, although the term Holy is omitted. See HOLY SPIRIT.

II. BREATH, respiration; or the principle of animal life, common to men and animals: this God has given, and this he recalls when he takes away life, Eccl. 3:21. See SOUL.

III. The RATIONAL SOUL which animates us, and preserves its being after the death of the body. That spiritual, reasoning, and choosing substance, which is capable of eternal happiness. See SOUL.

The "spirits in prison," 1 Pet. 3 : 19, it is generally thought, are the souls of antediluvian sinners now reserved unto the judgment-day, but unto whom the Spirit preached by the agency of Noah, etc., 2 Pet. 2 : 5, when they were in the flesh. Thus Christ "preached" to the Ephesians, whom he never visited in person, Eph. 2:17.

IV. An ANGEL, good or bad; a soul separate from the body, Mark 14:26. It is said, Acts 23 : 8, that the Sadducees denied the existence of angels and spirits. Christ, appearing to his disciples, said to them, Luke 24:39, "Handle me, and see; for a spirit hath not flesh and bones, as ye see me have."

V. The DISPOSITION of the mind or intellect. Thus we read of a spirit of jealousy, a spirit of fornication, a spirit of prayer, a spirit of infirmity, a spirit of wisdom and understanding, a spirit of fear of the Lord, Hos. 4:12; Zech. 12:10; Luke 13:11; Isa. 11:2.

VI. The RENEWED NATURE of true believers, which is produced by the Holy Spirit, and conforms the soul to his likeness. Spirit is thus the opposite of flesh, John 3 : 6. This spirit is vitally united with, and in some passages can hardly be distinguished from the "Spirit of Christ," which animates true Christians, the children of God, and distinguishes them from the children of darkness, who are animated by the spirit of the world, Rom. 8:1-16. This indwelling Spirit is the gift of grace, of adoption—the Holy Spirit poured into our hearts—which emboldens us to call God "Abba, *my Father*." Those who are influenced by this Spirit "have crucified the flesh, with its affections and lusts," Gal. 5:16-25.

"Distinguishing or discerning of spirits" consisted in discerning whether a man were really inspired by the Spirit of God, or was a false prophet, an impostor, who only followed the impulse of his own spirit or of Satan. Paul speaks, 1 Cor. 12:10, of the discerning of spirits as being among the miraculous gifts granted by God to the faithful at the first settlement of Christianity.

To "quench the Spirit," 1 Thess. 5:19, is a metaphorical expression easily understood. The Spirit may be quenched by forcing, as it were, that divine Agent to withdraw from us, by irregularity of life, frivolity, avarice, negligence, or other sins contrary to charity, truth, peace, and his other gifts and qualifications.

We "grieve" the Spirit of God by withstanding his holy inspirations, the impulses of his grace; or by living in a lukewarm and incautious manner; by despising his gifts, or neglecting them; by abusing his favors, either out of vanity, curiosity, or indifference. In a contrary sense, 2 Tim. 1 : 6, we "stir up" the Spirit of God which is in us, by the practice of virtue, by compliance with his inspirations, by fervor in his service, by renewing our gratitude, and by diligently serving Christ and doing the works of the Spirit.

SPOIL, booty taken in war, in which all the soldiers were permitted by David to share, whether actually engaged in battle or not, 1 Sam. 30:21–35. A portion of what was thus gained was devoted to the Lord of hosts as early as the time of Abraham, Gen. 14 : 20 ; and under the Mosaic legislation a definite rule for this purpose was established, Num. 31 : 26–47 ; 1 Chr. 26 : 27. Christ "spoiled" principalities and powers when by his atoning work he triumphed over Satan and his hosts, and deprived them of their power to injure his people, Col. 2 : 15. Paul warns Christians not to permit human philosophy, tradition, etc., to "spoil" them, that is, to rob them of Scripture truths and spiritual blessings, Col. 2:8. See PHILOSOPHY.

STA'CHYS, a disciple of Paul, by whom he is honorably mentioned, Rom. 16:9. From his name it would seem that he was a Greek, though residing at Rome.

STACTE, one of the four ingredients composing the sacred perfume, Exod. 30 : 34, 35. Some think the gum called storax is intended ; but it is generally understood to be the purest kind of myrrh ; and as the Hebrew properly signifies *a drop*, it would seem to refer to myrrh as distilling, dropping from the tree of its own accord, without incision. So Pliny, speaking of the trees whence myrrh is produced, says, "Before any incision is made, they exude of their own accord what is called Stacte, to which no kind of myrrh is preferable."

STAR. Under the name of stars, the Hebrews comprehended all the constellations, planets, and heavenly luminaries, except the sun and moon. The psalmist, to exalt the power and omniscience of God, says, "He telleth the number of the stars ; he calleth them all by their names," Psa. 147 : 4 ; God being described as a king taking a review of his army, and knowing the name of every one of his soldiers. Christ is called "the Morning Star," which is the brightest of the heavenly train, and ushers in the day, Rev. 22 : 16. Compare Num. 24:17. To express a very extraordinary increase and multiplication, Scripture uses the similitude of the stars of heaven, or of the sands of the sea, Gen. 15:5; 22 : 17 ; 26 : 4 ; Ex. 32 : 13. In times of disgrace and public calamity, it is said the stars withhold their light ; they are covered with darkness ; they fall from heaven, and disappear. These figurative and emphatic expressions, which refer to the governing powers of nations, are only weakened and enervated by being explained.

In the pure atmosphere of Judea and the East the stars shine with peculiar brilliancy, and seem as if hanging midway in the heavenly canopy, while the eye penetrates the ether far beyond them. The beauty and splendor that men observed in the stars ; the great advantages they derived from them ; the wonderful order apparent in their courses ; the influence ascribed to their returns, in the production and preservation of animals, fruits, plants, and minerals, have induced almost all heathen nations to impute to them life, knowledge, power, and to pay them a sovereign worship and adoration. The Israelites also needed to be warned against this sin. "Learn not the way of the heathen," says God, "and be not dismayed at the signs of heaven ; for the heathen are dismayed at them," Jer. 10:2. See IDOLATRY.

STAR IN THE EAST. It is a fact of great interest, that when the Saviour appeared, not only were the Jews eagerly expecting the Messiah, but many in various heathen lands were cherishing similar hopes : in part through the diffusion of the Hebrew prophecies ; in part through the felt need of a Saviour ; and in part perhaps through direct divine intimations. The eastern magi apparently were not only apprized of the coming birth of a royal and divine being in Judea, but were miraculously guided to Bethlehem by a meteoric light, appearing in the right direction for their course, Matt. 2 : 9. The fanciful theory of the distinguished astronomer Kepler, that the conjunction of the planets Jupiter and Saturn six years before the common Christian era may have constituted the "star in the east," does not appear to meet the terms of the inspired narrative. See MAGI.

STEPH'ANAS, a Christian of Corinth, whose family Paul baptized, the first convert to the gospel in Achaia, probably about A. D. 52, 1 Cor. 1:16. He was forward in the service of the church, and came to Paul at Ephesus, 1 Cor. 16 : 15, 17.

STE'PHEN, one of the seven deacons first chosen by the church at Jerusalem, and distinguished among them as "a man full of faith and of the Holy Ghost." He seems from his name to have been a Hellenistic Jew, (see GRECIANS,) and to have been chosen in part as being familiar with the language, opinions, and customs of the Greeks, Acts 6 : 1–6. His mighty works and unanswerable arguments roused the bitterest hostility against him, and he was brought before the Sanhedrim for trial, on the charge of blasphemy and heresy. His speech in his own defence, probably recorded only in part, shows historically that Christianity was the true development of the religion of Moses, fulfilling all its types and prophecies; and that the opponents of Christianity were but the children and imitators of those who had always opposed true religion. His enraged hearers hurried him to death, a judicial tribunal becoming a riotous mob for the occasion. Compare John 18 : 31. With Christlike magnanimity he forgave his murderers, and "fell asleep" amid their stones, with his eyes upon the Saviour "standing at the right hand of God," as if rising from his throne to protect and receive the first martyr of his church, Acts 7. The results of Stephen's death illustrate the saying of Tertullian, "The blood of the martyrs is the seed of the church," Acts 8 : 1, 4; 11 : 19-21. Augustine observes that the church owes the conversion and ministry of Paul to the prayer of Stephen. Paul, himself a Cilician, Acts 6 : 9; 22 : 3, had undoubtedly felt the force of his arguments in the discussions which preceded his arrest; and long afterwards alluded to his own presence at the martyr's death, Acts 22 : 19, 20—that triumph of Christian faith and love which has taught so many martyrs and Christians how to die. Yet nothing he heard or witnessed availed for his conversion, till he saw the Saviour himself, Acts 9. The scene of Stephen's martyrdom is placed by modern tradition on the east side of Jerusalem, near the gate called after his name. Earlier traditions located it more to the north.

STOCK, the trunk of a tree, Job 14:8, or a reproachful name for the idols carved out of it, Jer. 2:27; Hos. 4:12. The stocks in which Paul and Silas were fastened, Acts 16 : 24, were an instrument well known in Europe and America until

recent times; consisting of two beams, the upper one movable, with grooves between them large enough to receive the ancles of the prisoner. The arms also were sometimes confined. Stocks were frequently erected in market-places, that the insults of the populace might be added to the pain of confinement, Job 13:27; Jer. 20:2.

STO'ICS, a set of fatalistic heathen philosophers, so named from the Greek word signifying porch, or portico, because Zeno its founder, more than three centuries before Christ, held his school in a porch of the city of Athens. They placed the supreme happiness of man in living agreeably to nature and reason; affecting the same stiffness, patience, apathy, austerity, and insensibility as the Pharisees, whom they much resembled. They were in great repute at Athens when Paul visited that city, Acts 17 : 18.

STONE. The allusion in Rev. 2 : 17 may be to the practice at the Olympic games of giving the successful competitor a white stone, inscribed with his name and the value of his prize; or to the mode of balloting with black and white stones on the question of the acquittal of an accused person, or his admission to certain privileges; if the stones deposited in the urn by the judges were all white, the decision was favorable. In early ages, flint-stone knives were in common use, instead of steel, Ex. 4:25; Josh. 5:2. It was also customary to raise a heap or mound of stones in commemoration of any remarkable event, Gen. 31:46; Josh. 4:5-7; 7:26; 8:29; 2 Sam. 18:17. The same custom still prevails in Syria, and passing travellers are wont to add each one a stone to the heap. See CORNER-STONE.

STON'ING was a punishment much in use among the Hebrews, and the rabbins reckon all crimes as being subject to it, which the law condemns to death without expressing the particular mode. They say that when a man was condemned to death, he was led out of the city to the place of execution, and there exhorted to acknowledge and confess his fault. He was then stoned in one of two ways; either stones were thrown upon him till he died, or he was thrown headlong down a steep place, and a large stone rolled upon his body. The former was the usual mode; and the witnesses were required to cast the first stones, Deut. 17:5-7; for which purpose they sometimes threw off their outer garments, Acts 7:58. To the latter mode it is supposed there is a reference in Matt. 21:44. So also in Luke 4:29, where compare NAZARETH.

STORK. Its Hebrew name signifies kindness or mercy, and its Greek name natural affection, probably because of the tenderness which it is said to manifest towards its parents—never, as is reported, forsaking them, but feeding and defending them in their decrepitude. In modern times, parent storks are known to have perished in the effort to rescue their young from flames; and it has been a popular, but perhaps ill-founded opinion, that in their migratory flights, the leader of the flock when fatigued is partially supported by others as he falls into the rear. In Jer. 8:7, allusion is made to the unerring instinct of the stork as a bird of passage, and perhaps to its lofty flight: "The stork in the heavens knoweth her appointed times." Moses places it among unclean birds, Lev. 11:19; Deut. 14:18. The psalmist says, "As for the stork, the fir-trees are her house," Psa. 104:17. In the climate of Europe, she commonly builds her nest on some high tower or ruin, or on the top of a house; but in Palestine, where the coverings of the houses are flat, she builds in high trees.

The stork has the beak and legs long and red; it feeds on field-mice, lizards, snakes, frogs, and insects. Its plumage would be wholly white, but that the extremities of its wings, and some small part of its head and thighs, are black. It sits for the space of thirty days, and lays but four eggs. Storks migrate to southern countries in August, and return in the spring. They are still the object of much veneration among the common people in some parts of Europe and Asia.

STRAIT, narrow, and difficult to pass, Matt. 7:13, 14. This word should not be confounded with straight. To be "in a strait," is to have one's way beset with doubts or difficulties, to be at a loss, 1 Sam. 13:6; 2 Sam. 24:14; Phil. 1:23.

STRAN'GER is sometimes used in a special sense, easily understood from the context. It usually denotes a foreigner, one who is not a native of the land in which he resides, Gen. 23:4. The Mosaic law enjoined a generous hospitality towards foreign residents, saying, "Thou shalt love him as thyself," Lev. 19:33, 34; Deut. 10:18, 19; 24:17; 27:19. They were subject to the law, Ex. 20:10, Lev. 16:29, and were admitted to many of the privileges of the chosen people of God, Num. 9:14; 15:14. The strangers whom David collected to aid in building the temple, 1 Chr. 22:2, probably comprised many of the remnants of the Canaanite tribes, 1 Kin. 9:20, 21. Hospitality to strangers, including all travellers, was the duty of all good citizens, Job 31:32; Heb. 13:2.

STREETS, in the towns and cities of Palestine, are supposed to have been comparatively narrow and ill graded, on account of the unevenness of their sites, and the little use of wheel-carriages. They were wider, however, than in many modern cities, Luke 14 : 21, and terminated in large public areas around the gates, Neh. 8 : 1. Josephus says that those of Jerusalem were paved. They were named, like our own streets, Acts 9:11, and often resembled the bazaars of modern eastern cities, the shops of the same kind being in the same street and giving it its name, as the bakers' street, Neh. 3 : 31, 32; Jer. 37:21, and the valley of the cheesemongers. Here, and especially at the prominent points and corners, men loved, as the Turks do now, to spread their piece of carpet and sit, 1 Sam. 4:13; Job 29:7; and here at the hours of prayer they performed their devotions, Matt. 6:5.

STRONG DRINK. See WINE.

SUC'COTH, *booths*, I., a spot in the valley of the Jordan and near the Jabbok, where Jacob set up his tents on his return from Mesopotamia, Gen. 33:17. Joshua assigned the city subsequently built here to the tribe of Gad, Josh. 13:27. Gideon tore the flesh of the principal men of Succoth with thorns and briars, because they returned him a haughty answer when pursuing the Midianites, Judg. 8:5. It seems to have lain on the east side of the Jordan; but may possibly have been on the west side, at the place now called Sakût. Compare 1 Kin. 7 : 46; Psa. 60:6.

II. The first encampment of the Israelites, on their way out of Egypt, Ex. 12 : 37.

SUC'COTH BE'NOTH, *tents of the daughters*, 2 Kin. 17:30, an object of idolatrous worship among the Babylonians: an idol; or as some think, tents or booths, in which the Babylonian females prostituted themselves to Mylitta, the Assyrian Venus.

SUK'KIIM, allies of Shishak in his invasion of Judah, 2 Chr. 12 : 3; probably from regions south-east of Egypt.

SUM'MER. See CANAAN.

SUN, the great luminary of day, which furnishes so many similitudes to the Hebrew poets, as well as those of all nations, Judg. 5 : 31; Psa. 84 : 11; Prov. 4 : 18; Luke 1 : 78, 79; John 8 : 12. For the idolatrous worship of the sun, see BAAL.

SUPERSTI'TION and SUPERSTI'TIOUS, Acts 17:22 and 19:25, are not to be understood offensively. Paul found the Athenians "much addicted to devotion," such as it was: perhaps "religion" and "religiously inclined" may better express the sense of the original.

SUP'PER, see EATING, and LORD'S SUPPER. For the suppers, or love-feasts, which used to accompany the celebration of the Lord's supper, see FEASTS.

SURE'TY, one who makes himself personally responsible for the safe appearing of another, Gen. 43:9 and 44:32, or for the full payment of his debts, etc., Prov. 22:26. Christ is the "surety of a better testament;" that is, in the glorious and complete covenant of grace he engages to meet all the claims of the divine law against his people, that they may be absolved, and enriched with all covenant blessings, Heb. 7 : 22. Hence his obedience unto death, Isa. 53:5, 12.

SWAL'LOW, the well-known bird of passage, which is so common both in our country, in Europe, and in the East, Psa. 84:3; Isa. 38:14; Jer. 8:7. See CRANE, and SPARROW.

SWAN. This bird is mentioned only in Lev. 11 : 18, and Deut. 14:16; and it is there quite doubtful whether the Hebrew word means a swan. The Septuagint calls it the ibis, and the purple hen, a water-fowl.

SWEAR'ING. See OATH.

SWINE, a well-known animal, forbidden as food to the Hebrews, who held its flesh in such detestation that they would not so much as pronounce its name, Lev.

11:7; Deut. 14:8. The eating of swine's flesh was among the most odious of the idolatrous abominations charged upon some of the Jews, Isa. 65 : 4; 66 : 3, 17. The herd of swine destroyed by evil spirits in the sea of Gennesaret, Matt. 8:32, are supposed to have been kept by Jews for sale to the Gentiles around them, in defiance of the law. The beautiful and affecting parable of the prodigal son shows that the tending of swine was considered to be an employment of the most despicable character; it was the last resource of that depraved and unhappy being who had squandered his patrimony in riotous living, Luke 15:14-16. The irreclaimably filthy habits of this animal illustrate the insufficiency of reformation without regeneration, 2 Pet. 2 : 22; as its treading in the mire any precious thing which it cannot eat, illustrates the treatment which some profligates give to the gospel, Matt. 7:6.

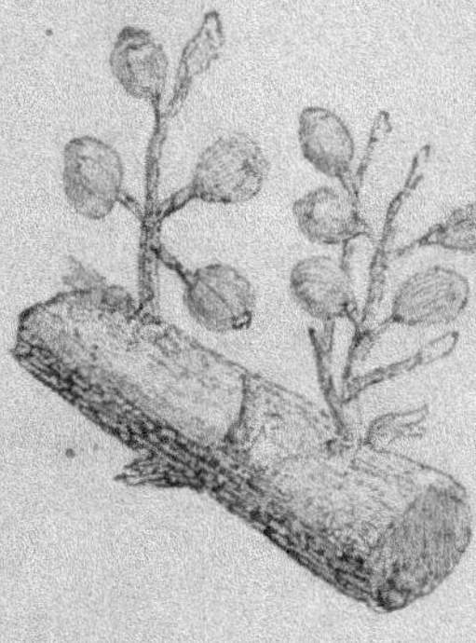

SYC'AMORE, or SYCAMINE, Luke 17:6, a curious tree, which seems to partake of the nature of both the mulberry and the fig, the former in its leaf, and the latter in its fruit. Hence its name in Greek, meaning the mulberry-fig. The sycamore is thus described by Norden: "I shall remark that they have in Egypt divers sorts of figs; but if there is any difference between them, a particular kind differs still more. I mean that which the sycamore bears, that they name in Arabic *giomez*. It was upon a tree of this sort that Zaccheus got up, to see our Saviour pass through Jericho, Luke 19 : 4. This sycamore is of the height of a beech, and bears its fruit in a manner quite different from other trees. It has them on the trunk itself, which shoots out little sprigs in form of a grape-stalk, at the end of which grows the fruit, close to one another, much like bunches of grapes. The tree is always green, and bears fruit several times in the year, for I have seen some sycamores which had fruit two months after others. The fruit has the figure and smell of real figs, but is inferior to them in the taste, having a disgustful sweetness. (Compare Amos 7:14.) Its color is a yellow, inclining to an ochre, shadowed by a flesh color; in the inside, it resembles the common fig, excepting that it has a blackish coloring, with yellow spots. This sort of tree is pretty common in Egypt. The people, for the greater part, live on its fruit."

The sycamore has a very large trunk, which breaks up into five or six stout branches not many feet above the ground; it is planted by the roadside, and often where two ways meet; and sends its enormous roots deeply into the ground in every direction, so that few trees can compare with it in steadfast firmness. The power that could say to it, "Be thou plucked up by the root, and be thou planted in the sea," and it should obey, must be of God, Luke 17:6. From 1 Kin. 10 : 27; 1 Chr. 27 : 28, and 2 Chr. 1 : 15, it is evident that this tree was quite common in Palestine, as well as in Egypt; and from its being joined with the vines in Psa. 78 : 47, as well as from the circumstance of David's appointing a particular officer to superintend the plantations of them, it seems to have been as much valued in ancient as in modern times. From Isa. 9 : 10, we find that the timber of the sycamore was used in the construction of buildings; and notwithstanding its porous and spongy appearance, it was of extreme durability. Describing the catacombs and mummies of Egypt, Dr. Shaw states that he found the mummy chests, and the little square boxes containing various figures, which are placed at the feet of each mummy, to be both made of sycamore wood, and thus preserved entire and uncorrupted for at least three thousand years.

SY'CHAR, or SY'CHEM. See SHECHEM.

SYE'NE, a city on the southern frontiers of Egypt, towards Ethiopia, between Thebes and the cataracts of the Nile, and now called Assouan. Pliny says it stands in a peninsula on the eastern shore of the Nile; that it was a mile in circumference, and had a Roman garrison. "From Migdol," the tower, "unto Syene," denotes the whole length of Egypt from north to south, Ezek. 29:10; 30:6. Few remains of the ancient city are now extant. In its vicinity are quarries of the Egyptian granite called Syenite, which furnished the material for numerous obelisks and colossal statues.

SYN'AGOGUE, a word which primarily signifies an assembly; but, like the word church, came at length to be applied to the buildings in which the ordinary Jewish assemblies for the worship of God were convened. From the silence of the Old Testament with reference to these places of worship, many commentators and writers on biblical antiquities are of opinion that they were not in use till after the Babylonish captivity; and that before that time, the Jews held their social meetings for religious worship either in the open air or in the houses of the prophets. See 2 Kin. 4:23. In Psa. 74 : 8, it is at least very doubtful whether the Hebrew word rendered *synagogues*, refers to synagogue-buildings such as existed after the captivity. Properly the word signifies only places where religious assemblies were held. In the time of our Saviour they abounded. Synagogues could only be erected in those places where ten men of age, learning, piety, and easy circumstances could be found to attend to the service which was enjoined in them. Large towns had several synagogues; and soon after the captivity their utility became so obvious, that they were scattered over the land, and became the parish churches of the Jewish nation. Their number appears to have been very considerable; and when the erection of a synagogue was considered a mark of piety, Luke 7 : 5, or a passport to heaven, we need not be surprised to hear that they were multiplied beyond all necessity, so that in Jerusalem alone there were not fewer than 460 or 480. They were generally built on the most elevated ground, and consisted of two parts. The westerly part of the building contained the ark or chest in which the book of the law and the sections of the prophets were deposited, and was called the temple by way of eminence. The other, in which the congregation assembled, was termed the body of the synagogue. The people sat with their faces towards the temple, and the elders in the contrary direction, and opposite to the people; the space between them being occupied by the pulpit or reading-desk. The seats of the elders were considered more holy than the others, and are spoken of as "the chief seats in the synagogues," Matt. 23:6. The women sat by themselves in a gallery secluded by lattice-work.

The stated office-bearers in every synagogue were ten, forming six distinct classes. We notice first the Archisynagogos, or ruler of the synagogue, who regulated all its concerns and granted permission to address the assembly. Of these there were three in each synagogue. Dr. Lightfoot believes them to have possessed a civil power, and to have constituted the lowest civil tribunal, commonly known as "the council of three," whose office it was to judge minor offences against religion, and also to decide the differences that arose between any members of the synagogue, as to money matters, thefts, losses, etc. To these officers there is perhaps an allusion in 1 Cor. 6:5. See also JUDGMENT. The second office-bearer was "the angel of the synagogue," or minister of the congregation, who prayed and preached. In allusion to these, the pastors of the Asiatic churches are called "angels," Rev. 2; 3.

The service of the synagogue was as follows: The people being seated, the "angel of the synagogue" ascended the pulpit, and offered up the public prayers, the people rising from their seats, and standing in a posture of deep devotion, Matt. 6 : 5; Mark 11 : 25; Luke 18 : 11, 13. The prayers were nineteen in number, and were closed by reading the execration. The next thing was the repetition of their phylacteries; after which came the reading of the law and the prophets. The former was divided into fifty-four sections, with which were united corresponding portions from the prophets; (see Acts 13:15, 27; 15:21:) and these were read through once in the course of the year. After the return from the captivity, an interpreter was employed in reading the law and the prophets, Neh. 8 : 2-8, who interpreted them into the Syro-Chaldaic dialect, which was then spoken by the people. The last part of the service was the expounding of the Scriptures, and preaching from them to the people. This was done either by one of the officers, or by some distinguished person who happened to be present. The reader will recollect one memorable occasion on which our Saviour availed himself of the opportunity thus afforded to address his countrymen, Luke 4 : 20 ; and there are several other instances recorded of himself and his disciples teaching in the synagogues. See Matt. 13 : 54 ; Mark 6 : 2 ; John 18 : 20 ; Acts 13 : 5, 15, 44 ; 14 : 1 ; 17 : 2-4, 10, 17 ; 18 : 4, 26 ; 19 : 8. The whole service was concluded with a short prayer or benediction.

The Jewish synagogues were not only used for the purposes of divine worship, but also for courts of judicature, in such matters as fell under the cognizance of the Council of Three, of which we have already spoken. On such occasions, the sentence given against the offender was sometimes, after the manner of prompt punishment still prevalent in the East, carried into effect in the place where the council was assembled. Hence we read of persons being beaten in the synagogue, and scourged in the synagogue, Matt. 10 : 17 ; Mark 13 : 9 ; Acts 22 : 19 ; 26 : 11 ; 2 Cor. 11 : 24. To be "put out of the synagogue," or excommunicated from the Jewish church and deprived of the national privileges, was a punishment much dreaded, John 9:22 ; 12:42 ; 16 : 2. In our own day the Jews erect synagogues wherever they are sufficiently numerous, and assemble on their Sabbath for worship ; this being conducted, that is, the reading or chanting of the Old Testament and of prayers, in the original Hebrew, though it is a dead language spoken by few among them. Among the synagogues of Jerusalem, now eight or ten in number, are some for Jews of Spanish origin, and others for German Jews, etc., as in the time of Paul there were separate synagogues for the Libertines, Cyrenians, Alexandrians, etc., Acts 6:9.

SYN'TYCHE, and EUO'DIAS. Phil. 4 : 2, 3, women eminent for virtue and good works in the church at Philippi. Paul exhorts them to persevere, or rather, to act harmoniously together in their Christian labors, as all should do who are "in the Lord."

SYR'ACUSE, now Siracasa, a large and celebrated city on the eastern coast of Sicily, furnished with a capacious and excellent harbor. The city, founded 734 B. C., was opulent and powerful, and was divided into four or five quarters or districts, which were of themselves separate cities. The whole circumference is stated by Strabo to have been one hundred and eighty stadia, or about twenty-two English miles. Syracuse is celebrated as having been the birthplace and residence of Archimedes, whose ingenious mechanical contrivances during its siege by the Romans, 200 B. C., long delayed its capture. Paul passed three days here, on his way from Melita to Rome, in the spring of A. D. 63, Acts 28 : 12. Population anciently 200,000 ; now 11,000.

SYR'IA, in Hebrew ARAM, a large district of Asia, lying, in the widest acceptation of the name, between the Mediterranean, mount Taurus, and the Tigris, and thus including Mesopotamia, that is, in Hebrew, Syria of the two rivers. See ARAM II. Excepting the Lebanon range, it is for the most part a level country. In the New Testament, Syria may be considered as bounded west and north-west by the Mediterranean and by mount Taurus, which separates it from Cilicia and Cataonia in Asia Minor, east by the Euphrates, and south by Arabia Deserta and Palestine, or rather Judea, for the name Syria included also the northern part of Palestine. The valley between the ridges of Lebanon and Anti-Lebanon was called Cœle-Syria, which appellation was also sometimes extended to the adjacent country on the east. At the time of the Jewish exile, Syria and Phœnicia were subject to the king of Babylon, and they afterwards were tributary to the Persian monarchs. After the country fell into the hands of the Romans, Syria was made the province of a proconsul ; to which Judea, although governed by its own procurators, was annexed in such a way, that in some cases an appeal might be made to the proconsul of Syria, who had at least the power of removing the procurators from office. Syria is now in the possession of the Turks. Its better portions have been thickly populated from a very early period, and travellers find traces of numerous cities wholly unknown to history.

SY'RO-PHŒNI'CIA is Phœnicia properly so called, but during the period when by conquest it was united to the kingdom of Syria, it prefixed to its old name Phœnicia, that of Syria. The Canaanitish woman is called a Syro-phœnician, Mark 7 : 26, because she was of Phœnicia, then considered as part of Syria. Matthew, who is by some supposed to have written in Hebrew or Syriac, calls her a Canaanitish woman, Matt. 15 : 22, because that country was really peopled by Canaanites, Zidon being the eldest son of Canaan, Gen. 10 : 15. See PHŒNICIA.

T.

TA'ANACH, a Canaanite royal city, Josh. 12:21, in the territory of Issachar, but assigned to Manasseh, Josh. 17 : 11; 21:25. There is still a small place called Taanuk on the south border of the plain of Esdraelon, four miles south-east of the site of Megiddo, which is usually named with Taanach, Judg. 1:27 ; 5:19 ; 1 Kin. 4:12.

TA'BER, to beat the tabret, a small drum or tambourine. The word is used in Nah. 2 : 7 of women beating their breasts in sign of grief.

TAB'ERAH, *burning*, so named on account of the fire which fell upon the Israelites for their murmurings while encamped here, Num. 11 : 1-3 ; Deut. 9:22.

TAB'ERNACLE, a tent, booth, pavilion, or temporary dwelling. For its general meaning and uses, see TENT. In the Scriptures it is employed more particularly of the tent made by Moses at the command of God, for the place of religious worship of the Hebrews, before the building of the temple. The directions of God, and the account of the execution of them, are contained in Exod. 25, and the following chapters. This is usually called the tabernacle of the congregation, or tent of assembly, and sometimes the tabernacle of the testimony.

The tabernacle was of an oblong rectangular form, thirty cubits long, ten broad, and ten in height, Ex. 26:15-30 ; 36 : 20-30 ; that is, about fifty-five feet long, eighteen broad, and eighteen high. The two sides and the western end were formed of boards of shittim wood, overlaid with thin plates of gold, and fixed in solid sockets or vases of silver. Above, they were secured by bars of the same wood overlaid with gold, passing through rings of gold which were fixed to the boards. On the east end, which was the entrance, there were no boards, but only five pillars of shittim wood, whose chapiters and fillets were overlaid with gold, and their hooks of gold, standing in five sockets of brass. The tabernacle thus erected was covered with four different kinds of curtains. The first and inner curtain was composed of fine linen, magnificently embroidered with figures of cherubim, in shades of blue, purple, and scarlet ; this formed the beautiful ceiling. The next covering was made of fine goats' hair ; the third of rams' skins or morocco dyed red; and the fourth and outward covering of a thicker leather. See BADGERS' SKINS. We have already said that the east end of the tabernacle had no boards, but only five pillars of shittim wood; it was therefore closed with a richly embroidered curtain suspended from these pillars, Ex. 27:16.

Such was the external appearance of the sacred tent, which was divided into two apartments by means of four pillars of shittim wood overlaid with gold, like the pillars before described, two cubits and a half distant from each other; only they stood in sockets of silver instead of brass, Ex. 26 : 32; 36 : 36; and on these pillars was hung a veil, formed of the same materials as the one placed at the east end, Exod. 26:31-33; 36:35; Heb. 9:3. The interior of the tabernacle was thus divided, it is generally supposed, in the same proportions as the temple afterwards built according to its model; two-thirds of the whole length being allotted to the first room, or the Holy Place, and one-third to the second, or Most Holy Place. Thus the former would be twenty cubits long, ten wide, and ten high, and the latter ten cubits every way. It is observable, that neither the Holy nor the Most Holy place had any window. Hence the need of the candlestick in the one, for the service that was performed therein.

The tabernacle thus described stood in an open space or court of an oblong form, one hundred cubits in length, and fifty in breadth, situated due east and west, Ex. 27 : 18. This court was surrounded with pillars of brass, filleted with silver, and placed at the distance of five cubits from each other, twenty on each side and ten on each end. Their

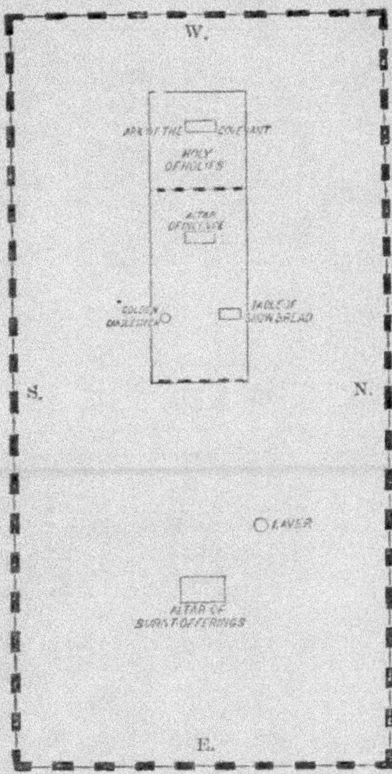

sockets were of brass, and were fastened to the earth with pins of the same metal, Exod. 38 : 10, 17, 20. Their height was probably five cubits, that being the length of the curtains that were suspended on them, Ex. 38:18. These curtains, which formed an enclosure round the court, were of fine twined white linen yarn, Ex. 27 : 9; 38 : 9, 16, except that at the entrance on the east end, which was of blue and purple and scarlet and fine white twined linen, with cords to draw it either up or aside when the priests entered the court, Ex. 27 : 16; 38 : 18. Within this area stood the altar of burnt-offerings, and the laver with its foot or base. This altar was placed in a line between the door of the court and the door of the tabernacle, but nearer the former, Exod. 40 : 6, 29; the laver stood between the altar of burnt-offering and the door of the tabernacle, Ex. 38 : 8. In this court all the Israelites presented their offerings, vows, and prayers.

But although the tabernacle was surrounded by the court, there is no reason to think that it stood in the centre of it. It is more probable that the area at the east end was fifty cubits square; and indeed a less space than that could hardly suffice for the work that was to be done there, and for the persons who were immediately to attend the service. We now proceed to notice the furniture which the tabernacle contained.

In the Holy Place, to which none but priests were admitted, Heb. 9:6, were three objects worthy of notice: namely, the altar of incense, the table for the show-bread, and the candlestick for the lights, all of which have been described in their respective places. The altar of incense was placed in the middle of the sanctuary, before the veil, Ex. 30:6-10; 40:26, 27; and on it the incense was burnt morning and evening, Ex. 30:7, 8. On the north side of the altar of incense, that is, on the right hand of the priest as he entered, stood the table for the show-bread, Ex. 26:35; 40:22, 23; and on the south side of the Holy Place, the golden candlestick, Ex. 25:31-39. In the Most Holy Place, into which only the high-priest entered once a year, Heb. 9:7, was the ark, covered by the mercy-seat and the cherubim.

The gold and silver employed in decorating the tabernacle are estimated at not less than a million of dollars. The remarkable and costly structure thus described was erected in the wilderness of Sinai, on the first day of the first month of the second year, after the Israelites left Egypt, Ex. 40:17; and when erected was anointed, together with its furniture, with holy oil, ver. 9-11, and sanctified by blood, Ex. 24:6-8; Heb. 9:21. The altar of burnt-offerings, especially, was sanctified by sacrifices during seven days, Ex. 29:37; while rich donations were given by the princes of the tribes for the service of the sanctuary, Num. 7.

We should not omit to observe, that the tabernacle was so constructed as to be taken to pieces and put together again, as occasion required. This was indispensable; it being designed to accompany the Israelites during their travels in the wilderness. With it moved and rested the pillar of fire and of cloud. As often as Israel removed, the tabernacle was taken to pieces by the priests, closely covered, and borne in regular order by the Levites, Num. 4. Wherever they encamped, it was pitched in the midst of their tents, which were set up in a quadrangular form, under their respective standards, at a distance from the tabernacle of two thousand cubits; while Moses and Aaron, with the priests and Levites, occupied a place between them.

How long this tabernacle existed we do not know. During the conquest it remained at Gilgal, Josh. 4:19; 10:43. After the conquest it was stationed for many years at Shiloh, Josh. 18:1; 1 Sam. 1:3. In 2 Sam. 6:17, and 1 Chr. 15:1, it is said that David had prepared and pitched a tabernacle in Jerusalem for the ark, which before had long been at Kirjath-jearim, and then in the house of Obed-edom, 1 Chr. 13:6, 14; 2 Sam. 6:11, 12. In 1 Chr. 21:29, it is said that the tabernacle of Moses was still at Gibeon at that time; and it would therefore seem that the ark had long been separated from it. The tabernacle still remained at Gibeon in the time of Solomon, who sacrificed before it, 2 Chr. 1:3, 13. This is the last mention made of it; for apparently the tabernacle brought with the ark into the temple, 2 Chr. 5:5, was the tent in which the ark had been kept on Zion, 2 Chr. 1:4; 5:2.

Feast of Tabernacles. This festival derives its name from the booths in which the people dwelt during its continuance, which were constructed of the branches and leaves of trees, on the roofs of their houses, in the courts, and also in the streets. Nehemiah describes the gathering of palm-branches, olive-branches, myrtle-branches, etc., for this occasion, from the mount of Olives. It was one of the three great festivals of the year, at which all the men of Israel were required to be present, Deut. 16:16. It was celebrated during eight days, commencing on the fifteenth day of the month Tishri, that is, fifteen days after the new moon in October; and the first and last days were particularly distinguished, Lev. 23:34-43; Neh. 8:14-18. This festival was instituted in memory of the forty years' wanderings of the Israelites in the desert, Lev. 23:42, 43, and also as a season of gratitude and thanksgiving for the gathering in of the harvest; whence it is also called the Feast of the Harvest, Ex. 23:16; 34:22. The season was an occasion of rejoicing and feasting. The public sacrifices consisted of two rams and fourteen lambs on each of the first seven days, together with thirteen bullocks on the first day, twelve on the second, eleven on the third, ten on the fourth, nine on the fifth, eight on the sixth, and seven on the seventh; while on the eighth day one bullock, one ram, and seven lambs were offered, Num. 29:12-39. On every seventh year, the law of Moses was also read in public, in the presence of all the people, Deut. 31:10-13; Neh. 8:18. To these ceremonies the later Jews added a libation of water mingled with wine, which was poured upon the morning sacrifice of each day. The priests, having filled a vessel of water from the fountain of Siloam, bore it through the water-gate to the temple, and there, while the trumpets and horns were sounding, poured it upon the sacrifice arranged upon the altar. This was probably done as a memorial of the abundant supply of water which God afforded to the Israelites during their wanderings in the desert; and perhaps with reference to purification from sin. 1 Sam. 7:6. This was accompanied with the singing of Isa. 12: "With joy shall ye draw water from the wells of salvation;" and may naturally have suggested our Saviour's announcement while attending this festival, "If any man thirst, let him come unto me and drink," John 7:37, 38. The first and eighth days of the festival were sabbaths to the Lord, in which there was a holy convocation, and in which all labor was prohibited, Lev. 23:39; Num. 29:12, 35; and as the eighth was the last festival day celebrated in the course of each year, it appears to have been esteemed as peculiarly important and sacred.

TA'BLE. See BREAD, and EATING.

TAB'ITHA. See DORCAS.

TA'BOR, an isolated mountain of Galilee, on the north-eastern side of the plain of Esdraelon, an arm of which extends beyond the mountain in the same direction. It is of limestone formation, conical in form, and well wooded, especially on the north side, with fine oaks and other trees and odoriferous plants. It rises 1,350 feet above the plain at its base, which is 400 feet above the Mediterranean, and by a winding path on the north-west side one may ride to its summit in an hour. There is a small oblong

MOUNT TABOR, FROM THE PLAIN OF ESDRAELON.

plain on the summit, surrounded by a larger but less regular tract, perhaps a mile in circumference. The prospect from mount Tabor is extensive and beautiful. Dr. Robinson and many others speak of it as one of the finest in Palestine; and Lord Nugent declared it the most splendid he could recollect having ever seen from any natural height. See Jer. 46:18. Its general features are the same as those of the view from the heights of Nazareth, five miles to the west. See NAZARETH. Glimpses of the Mediterranean appear over the high grounds which intervene. In the plain at the southern base of the mountain are the sources of the brook Kishon, and the villages Endor and Nain, famous in Bible history. Besides the fertile expanse of Esdraelon, and mounts Carmel, Gilboa, etc., on its borders, the view embraces a portion of the sea of Galilee in the north-east; and towards the north the mountains of Galilee, with the town of Safed crowning the highest of them all, recalling the proverb which it is said to have first suggested, "A city that is set on a hill cannot be hid." Still farther to the north and east, the snow-crowned head of Hermon overlooks the fifty miles which intervene. Psa. 89:12.

On the summit of Tabor a fortified town anciently stood, probably of the same name, 1 Chr. 6:77. This was in existence, and was garrisoned by the Romans in the time of Christ, which conflicts with the tradition that makes Tabor the scene of the transfiguration.

Ruins of ancient walls enclose the area on the summit; and at various points there are remains of fortifications and dwellings, some of which are of the age of the crusaders, and others of more ancient date. Tabor lay on the borders of Issachar and Zebulun, Josh. 19:12, 22. The host of Barak encamped upon it, before the battle with Sisera, Judg. 4:6, 12, 14. At a later day it appears to have been desecrated by idolatry, Hos. 5:1.

TAB'RET, Gen. 31:27, Isa. 5:12, a sort of small drum or tambourine, played as an accompaniment to singing. See TIMBREL.

TACH'ES, golden and brazen clasps, uniting the separate curtains of the tabernacle, Ex. 26:6, 11.

TAD'MOR, or TA'MAR, *a palm-tree*, 1 Kin. 9:18, a city founded by Solomon in the desert of Syria, on the borders of Arabia Deserta, towards the Euphrates, 2 Chr. 8:4. It was remote from human habitations, on an oasis in the midst of a dreary wilderness; and it is probable that Solomon built it to facilitate his commerce with the East, as it afforded a supply of water, a thing of the utmost importance in an Arabian desert. It was about one hundred and twenty miles north-east of Damascus, more than half the distance to the Euphrates. The original name was preserved till the time of Alexander, who extended his conquests to this city, which then exchanged its name Tadmor for that of Palmyra, both signifying that it was a "city of palms." It submitted to the Romans about the year 130, and continued in alliance with them during a period of one hundred and fifty years. In the third century the famous queen Zenobia reigned here over all the adjacent provinces, till conquered and carried captive to Rome by Aurelian. When the Saracens triumphed in the East, they acquired possession of this city, and restored its ancient name. It is still called Thadmor. Of the time of its ruin there is no authentic record; but it is thought, with some probability, that its destruction occurred during the period in which it was occupied by the Saracens.

Of its appearance in modern times, Messrs. Wood and Dawkins, who visited it in 1751, thus speak: "It is scarcely possible to imagine any thing more striking than this view. So great a number of Corinthian pillars, mixed with so little wall or solid building, afforded a most romantic variety of prospect." Volney observes, "In the space covered by these ruins, we sometimes find a palace, of which nothing remains but the court and walls; sometimes a temple, whose peristyle is half thrown down; and now a portico, a gallery, a triumphal arch. If from this striking scene we cast our eyes upon the ground, another almost as varied presents itself. On which side soever we look, the earth is strowed with vast stones half buried, with broken entablatures, mutilated friezes, disfigured reliefs, effaced sculptures, violated tombs, and altars defiled by the dust." Most of the edifices the ruins of which are above described, date from the first three centuries of the Christian era; while shapeless mounds of rubbish, covered with soil and herbage, contain the only memorials of the Tadmor of Solomon. The city was situated under and east of a ridge of barren hills, and its other sides were separated only by a wall from the open desert. It was originally about ten miles in circumference; but such have been the destructions effected by time, that the boundaries are with difficulty traced and determined.

TAHAP'ANES, Jer. 2:16, or TAHPAN'HES, Jer. 43:7, 9, or TEHAPH'NEHES, Ezek. 30:18, the name of an Egyptian city, for which the Seventy put Taphne, and the

Greek historians Daphne. This city lay in the vicinity of Pelusium, towards the south-west, on the western bank of the Pelusiac branch of the Nile, and is therefore called by Herodotus the Pelusiac Daphne. To this city Johanan and many of the Jews retired, after the destruction of Jerusalem by the Chaldeans, taking with them the prophet Jeremiah, Jer. 43:7-9; 44:1. That Tahapanes was a large and important city, is apparent from the threats uttered against it by Ezekiel, 30:18. According to some, Hanes, in Isa. 30:4, is an abbreviated name of the same city.

TALE sometimes means a number, verified by counting, Ex. 5:8, 18; 1 Chr. 9:28.

TAL'ENT. This was a weight used among the Jews, Greeks, and Romans, but varying exceedingly in different countries and in different parts of the same country. The Jewish talent is usually estimated at about 125 pounds troy weight, though others estimate it a little less than 114 pounds troy. The common Attic talent was equal, on the usual estimate, to about 56 lbs. 11 oz. troy. In the New Testament, *a talent* is a denomination of money, which was anciently reckoned by weight. The value of the talent, therefore, varied in different countries, in proportion to the different weights of the talent. The Jewish talent appears, from Ex. 38:25, 26, to have been equal to 3,000 shekels; and as the shekel is estimated at about fifty cents, the value of the talent would be about 1,500 dollars. The Attic talent is usually reckoned at about 225 pounds sterling, or 1,000 dollars, though others make it only about 860 dollars. The talent spoken of in the New Testament is probably the Jewish, and is used only of an indefinitely large sum, Matt. 18:24; 25:14-30.

TAL'MAI, king of Geshur, on the borders of Palestine and Syria. David married Maacha his daughter, the mother of Tamar and Absalom. The latter avenged the wrongs of his sister Tamar by the murder of Amnon, and then took refuge at the court of his grandfather, where he remained three years, 2 Sam. 3:3; 13 and 14.

TA'MAR, *a palm-tree*, I., a Canaanitish woman, mother of Pharez and Zarah, Gen. 38.

II. A daughter of David. See TALMAI.

III. A daughter of Absalom, 2 Sam. 14:27.

TAM'MUZ, a Syrian idol, mentioned in Ezek. 8:14, where the women are represented as weeping for it. It is generally supposed that Tammuz was the same deity as the Phœnician Adonis, and perhaps the Egyptian Osiris. The fabled death and restoration of Adonis, supposed to symbolize the departure and return of the sun, were celebrated at the summer solstice first with lamentation, and then with rejoicings and obscene revels.

TAP'ESTRY, cloth for hangings and bed-covers, covered with ornamental needlework, Prov. 7:16.

TAP'PUAH, I., now Teffuh, a town among the hills north-west of Hebron, Josh. 12:17; 15:53.

II. Another city of Judah, south-west of Hebron, Josh. 15:34.

III. A town on the line of Ephraim and Manasseh, Josh. 16:8.

IV. A descendant of Caleb, 1 Chr. 2:43.

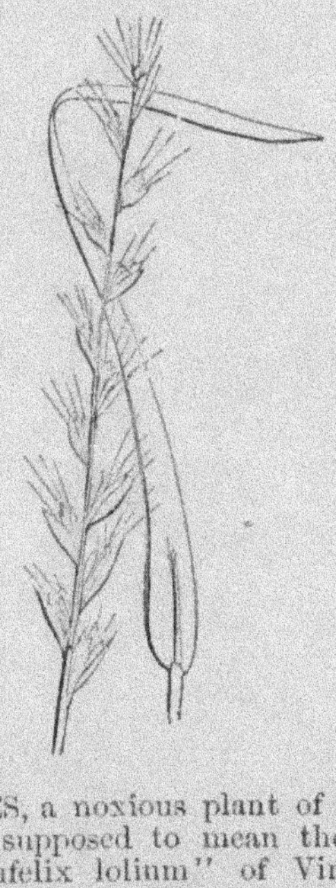

TARES, a noxious plant of the grass family, supposed to mean the darnel, the "infelix lolium" of Virgil, now called Siwan or Zowan by the Arabs. It grows among the wheat everywhere in Palestine, and bears a great resemblance to it while growing, so much so that before they head out the two plants can hardly be distinguished. The grains are found two or three together in a dozen small husks scattered on a rather long head. The Arabs do not separate the darnel from the wheat, unless by means of a fan or sieve after threshing, Matt. 13 : 25-30. If left to mingle with the bread, it occasions dizziness, and often acts as an emetic.

TAR'GET, 1 Sam. 17:6, a small round shield. The same word in verse 45 is translated a shield, and elsewhere a javelin. See ARMOR.

TAR'SHISH, I., the second son of Javan, Gen. 10:4.

II. Tartessus, an ancient city between two mouths of the Guadalquiver, in the south of Spain. It was a Phœnician colony, and was the most celebrated emporium in the west to which the Hebrews and Phœnicians traded. That Tarshish was situated in the west is evident from Gen. 10:4, where it is joined with Elisha, Kittim, and Dodanim. See also Psa. 72 : 10. According to Ezek. 38 : 13, it was an important place of trade; according to Jer. 10 : 9, it exported silver, and according to Ezek. 27 : 12, 25, silver, iron, tin, and lead to the Tyrian markets. They embarked for this place from Joppa, Jonah 1:3, 4. In Isa. 23:1, 6, 10, it is evidently represented as an important Phœnician colony. It is named among other distant states, in Isa. 66 : 19. All these notices agree with Tartessus.

In some of these passages, however, Tarshish may be used as a general expression, applicable to all the distant shores of Europe; and thus the custom may have arisen of designating as "ships of Tarshish" any large merchant ships bound on long voyages in any direction. The English term Indiaman is very similarly used. Whether the ships fitted out by Solomon at Ezion-geber on the Red sea, sailed around Africa to Tarshish in Spain, or gave the name of Tarshish to some place in India or Ethiopia, as the discoverers of America gave it the eastern names India and Indians, cannot now be determined, 1 Kin. 10:22 ; 22:48, 49 ; 2 Chr. 9:21 ; 20:36 ; Isa. 23 : 1, 14 ; 60:9.

TAR'SUS, the name of a celebrated city, the metropolis of Cilicia, in the south-eastern part of Asia Minor ; situated six miles from the Mediterranean, on the banks of the river Cydnus, which flowed through and divided it into two parts. Tarsus was distinguished for the culture of Greek literature and philosophy, so that at one time, in its schools and in the number of its learned men, it was the rival of Athens and Alexandria. In reward for its exertions and sacrifices during the civil wars of Rome, Tarsus was made a free city by Augustus. It was the privilege of such cities that they were governed by their own laws and magistrates, and were not subjected to tribute, to the jurisdiction of a Roman governor, nor to the power of a Roman garrison, although they acknowledged the supremacy of the Roman people, and were bound to aid them against their enemies. That the freedom of Tarsus, however, was not equivalent to being a Roman citizen, appears from this, that the tribune, although he knew Paul to be a citizen of Tarsus, Acts 21 : 39, yet ordered him to be scourged, 22 : 24, but desisted from his purpose when he learned that Paul was a Roman citizen, 22:27. It is therefore probable that the ancestors of Paul had obtained the privilege of Roman citizenship in some other way, Acts 9:30 ; 11:25 ; 22:3. It is now called Tarsous; and though much decayed and full of ruins, is estimated to contain a population in summer of 7,000, and in winter of 30,000, chiefly Turks. During the excessive heat of summer, a large part of the people repair to the high lands of the interior.

TAR'TAK, an idol, introduced by the Avites into Samaria, 2 Kin. 17:31.

TAR'TAN, an Assyrian general, sent to Jerusalem with Rabshakeh by Sennacherib, 2 Kin. 18:17 ; and perhaps the same who captured Ashdod in the reign of Sargon, Isa. 20:1.

TAT'NAI, a governor of Samaria under Darius, whose administration was characterized by great justice and moderation towards the Jews, Ezra 5 and 6, B. C. 519.

TAV'ERNS, THREE, a village thirty-three miles south of Rome, mentioned by Cicero, and still called Tre Taverne. See APPII FORUM.

TEARS. Small urns or lachrymatories, of thin glass or simple pottery, and containing the tears of mourners at funerals, used to be placed in the sepulchres of the dead at Rome and in Palestine, where they are found in great numbers on opening ancient tombs. This custom is illustrative of Psa. 56:8, which shows that God is ever mindful of the sorrows of his people. In Rev. 7:17 he is represented as tenderly wiping all tears from their eyes, or removing for ever all their griefs.

TE'BETH, Esth. 2:16, the tenth month of the Hebrew sacred year, commencing with the new moon in January.

TEHAPH'NEHES. See TAHAPANES.

TEIL-TREE, the lime or linden. See OAK.

TEKO'A, Jer. 6:1, a city of Judah, now in ruins, situated on an extended height, twelve miles south of Jerusalem. Here originated the wise woman who was Joab's agent, 2 Sam. 14:2, and Amos the prophet, Amos 1:1. It was inhabited by Christians in the time of the crusades. The wilderness of Tekoa, mentioned in 2 Chr. 20:20, inclines towards the Dead sea.

TEL-A'BIB, a place on the river Chebar in Mesopotamia, where a colony of captive Jews was located, Ezek. 3:15. A town called Thallaba is still found in that region.

TE'MA, an Ishmaelite tribe and district, in the north of Arabia Deserta towards Damascus, Gen. 25:15. It is associated with Dedan, Isa. 21:14; Jer. 25:23, and was famous for its caravans, Job 6:19. The region is still called Tema by the Arabs.

TE'MAN, *south*, a city and region in Eastern Idumea, settled by Teman the grandson of Esau, Gen. 36:11, 15, 42; Amos 1:12; Hab. 3:3. The men of Teman, Gen. 36:34, like others of the Edomites, had the reputation of great wisdom, Jer. 49:7, 20; Obad. 8, 9. Compare the sayings of Eliphaz the Temanite in the book of Job.

TEM'PLE, a building hallowed by the special presence of God, and consecrated to his worship. The distinctive idea of a temple, contrasted with all other buildings, is that it is the dwelling-place of a deity; and every heathen temple had its idol, but the true and living God dwelt "between the cherubim" in the Holy of Holies at Jerusalem. Hence, figuratively applied, a temple denotes the church of Christ, 2 Thess. 2:4; Rev. 3:12; heaven, Psa. 11:4; Rev. 7:15; and the soul of the believer, in which the Holy Spirit dwells, 1 Cor. 3:16, 17; 6:19; 2 Cor. 6:16.

After the Lord had instructed David that Jerusalem was the place he had chosen in which to fix his dwelling, that pious prince began to realize his design of preparing a temple for the Lord that might be something appropriate to His divine majesty. But the honor was reserved for Solomon his son and successor, who was to be a peaceful prince, and not like David, who had shed much blood in war. David, however, applied himself to collect great quantities of gold, silver, brass, iron, and other materials for this undertaking, 2 Sam. 7; 1 Chr. 22.

The place chosen for erecting this magnificent structure was mount Moriah, Gen. 22. 2, 14; 2 Chr. 3:1, the summit of which originally was unequal, and its sides irregular; but it was a favorite object of the Jews to level and extend it. The plan and the whole model of this structure was laid by the same divine architect as that of the tabernacle, namely, God himself; and it was built much in the same form as the tabernacle, but was of much larger dimensions. The utensils for the sacred service were also the same as those used in the tabernacle, only several of them were larger, in proportion to the more spacious edifice to which they belonged. The foundations of this magnificent edifice were laid by Solomon, in the year B. C. 1011, about four hundred and eighty years after the exodus and the building of the tabernacle; and it was finished B. C. 1004, having occupied seven years and six months in the building. It was dedicated with peculiar solemnity to the worship of Jehovah, who condescended to make it the place for the special manifestation of his glory, 2 Chr. 5-7. The front or entrance to the temple was on the eastern side, and consequently facing the mount of Olives, which commanded a noble prospect of the building. The temple itself, strictly so called, which comprised the Porch, the Sanctuary, and the Holy of Holies, formed only a small part of the sacred precincts, being surrounded by spacious courts, chambers, and other apartments, which were much more extensive than the temple itself. It should be observed that the word temple does not always denote the central edifice itself, but in many passages some of the outer courts are intended.

From the descriptions which are handed down to us of the temple of Solomon, it is utterly impossible to obtain so accurate an idea of its relative parts and their respective proportions, as to furnish such an account as may be deemed satisfactory to the reader. Hence we find no two writers agreeing in their descriptions. The following account may give a general idea of the building.

The Temple itself was seventy cubits long; the Porch being ten cubits, 1 Kin. 6:3, the Holy place forty cubits, ver. 17, and the Most Holy place, twenty cubits, 2 Chr. 3:8. The width of the Porch, Holy, and Most Holy places was twenty cubits, 2 Chr. 3:3, and the height over the Holy and Most Holy places was thirty cubits, 1 Kin. 6:2; but the height of the porch was much greater, being no less than one hundred and twenty cubits, 2 Chr. 3:4, or four times the height of the rest of the building. The Most Holy place was separated from the Sanctuary by an impervious veil, Luke 23:45, and was perhaps wholly dark, 1 Kings 8:12, but for the glory of the Lord which filled it. To the north and south sides, and the west end of the Holy and Most Holy places, or all around the edifice, from the back of the porch on one side, to the back of the porch on the other side, certain buildings were attached. These were called side chambers, and consisted of three stories, each five cubits high, 1 Kin. 6:10, and joined to the wall of the temple without. Thus the three stories of side chambers, when taken together, were fifteen cubits high, and consequently reached exactly to half the height of the side walls and end of the temple; so that there was abundance of space above these for the windows which gave light to the temple, ver. 4.

Solomon's temple appears to have been surrounded by two main courts: the inner court, that "of the Priests," 1 Kin. 6:36; 2 Chr. 4:9; and the outer court, that "of Israel;" these were separated by a "middle wall of partition," with lodges for priests and Levites, for wood, oil, etc., 1 Chron. 28:12. The ensuing description is applicable to the temple courts in the time of our Lord.

The "court of the Gentiles" was so called because it might be entered by persons of all nations. The chief entrance to it was by the east or Shushan gate, which was the principal gate of the temple. It was the exterior court, and by far the largest of all the courts belonging to the temple, and is said to have covered a space of more than fourteen acres. It entirely surrounded the other courts and the temple itself; and in going up to the temple from its east or outer gate, one would cross first this court, then the court of the Women, then that of Israel, and lastly that of the Priests. This outmost court was separated from the court of the women by a wall three cubits high of lattice work, and having inscriptions on its pillars forbidding Gentiles and unclean persons to pass beyond it, on pain of death, Acts 21:28; Eph. 2:13, 14. From this court of the Gentiles our Saviour drove the persons who had established a cattle-market in it, for the purpose of supplying those with sacrifices who came from a distance, Matt. 21:12, 13. We must not overlook the beautiful pavement of variegated marble, and the "porches" or covered walks, with columns supporting magnificent galleries, with which this court was surrounded. Those on the east, west, and north sides were of the same dimensions; but that on the south was much larger. The porch called Solomon's, John 10:23, Acts 3:11, was on the east side or front of this court, and was so called because it was built by this prince, upon a high wall rising from the valley of Kidron.

The "court of the Women," called in Scripture the "new court," 2 Chr. 20:5, and the "outer court," Ezek. 46:21, separated the court of the Gentiles from the court of Israel, extending along the east side only of the latter. It was called the court of the women because it was their appointed place of worship, beyond which they might not go, unless when they brought a sacrifice, in which case they went forward to the court of Israel. The gate which led into this court from that of the Gentiles, was "the Beautiful gate" of the temple, mentioned in Acts 3:2, 10; so called, because the folding-doors, lintel, and side-posts were all overlaid with Corinthian brass. The worshipper ascended to its level by a broad flight of steps. It was in this court of the women, called the "treasury," that our Saviour delivered his striking discourse to the Jews, related in John 8:1-20. It was into this court also that the Pharisee and the publican went to pray, Luke 18:10-13, and hither the lame man followed Peter and John, after he was cured—the court of the women being the ordinary place of worship for those who brought no sacrifice, Acts 3:8. From thence, after prayers, he went back with them, through the "Beautiful gate" of the temple, where he had been lying, and through the sacred fence, into the court of the Gentiles, where, under the eastern piazza, or Solomon's porch, Peter preached Christ crucified. It was in the same court of the women that the Jews laid hold of Paul, when they judged him a violater of the temple by taking Gentiles within the sacred fence, Acts 21:26–29.

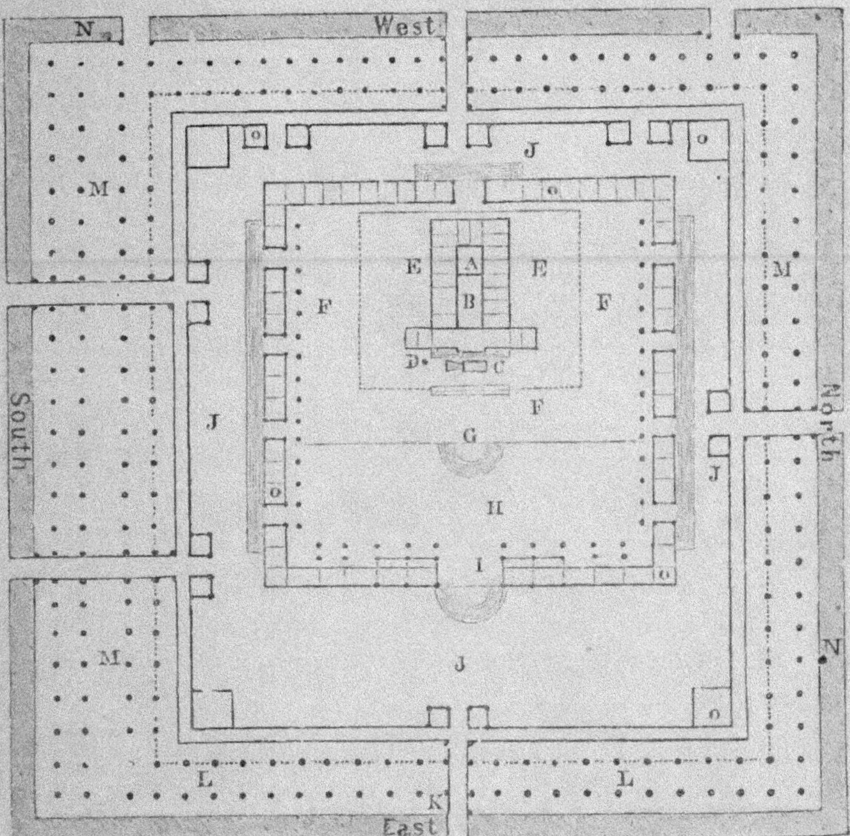

PLAN OF THE TEMPLE IN THE TIME OF CHRIST.

A. The Holy of Holies.
B. The Holy Place.
C. The Altar of Burnt offerings.
D. The brazen Laver.
E. The court of the Priests.
F. The court of Israel.
G. The gate Nicanor.
H. The court of the Women.
I. The gate Beautiful.
J. The court of the Gentiles.
K. The Eastern or Shushan gate.
L. Solomon's Porch, or colonnade.
M. The Royal Porch.
N. The outer Wall.
o. Apartments for various uses.

The "court of Israel" was separated from the court of the women by a wall thirty-two and a half cubits high on the outside, but on the inside only twenty-five. The reason of which difference was, that as the rock on which the temple stood became higher on advancing westward, the several courts naturally became elevated in proportion. The ascent into this court from the east was by a flight of fifteen steps, of a semicircular form, and the magnificent gate Nicanor. On these steps the Levites stood in singing the "songs of degrees." The whole length of the court from east to west was one hundred and eighty-seven cubits, and the breadth from north to south, one hundred and thirty-five cubits. In this court, and the piazza which surrounded it, the Israelites stood in solemn and reverent silence while their sacrifices were burning in the inner court, and while the services of the sanctuary were performed, Luke 1:8-11, 21, 22.

Within this court, and surrounded by it, was the "court of the Priests;" one hundred and sixty-five cubits long and one hundred and nineteen cubits wide, and raised two and a half cubits above the surrounding court, from which it was separated by pillars and a railing. Within this court stood the brazen altar on which the sacrifices were consumed, the molten sea in which the priests washed, and the ten brazen lavers for washing the sacrifices; also the various utensils and instruments for sacrificing, which are enumerated in 2 Chr. 4. It is necessary to observe here, that although the court of the Priests was not accessible to all Israelites, as that of Israel was to all the priests, yet they might enter it for three several purposes: to lay their hands on the animals which they offered, or to kill them, or to wave some part of them.

From the court of the Priests, the ascent to the temple was by a flight of twelve steps, each half a cubit in height, which led into the sacred porch. Of the dimensions of this in Solomon's temple, as also of the Sanctuary and Holy of Holies, we have already spoken. It was within the door of the porch, and in the sight of those who stood in the courts immediately before it, that the two pillars, Jachin and Boaz, were placed, 2 Chr. 3:17; Ezek. 40:49.

SIDE VIEW OF THE TEMPLE, IN PART AFTER DR. BARCLAY.

In this profile view of the Temple and its precincts from the south, *n n* is the outer southern wall of the temple area; *a* is a part of the royal buildings on mount Zion; *b* is the Tyropœon bridge, connecting Zion with the south portico of the temple; *o* and *p* are gates leading subterraneously to the area above; *q* is a gate to the substructions; *l* is the tower Ophel; and *m* the Red heifer bridge over the Kidron.

Within, towards the north, is shown a section of the temple area; *c* representing the western cloister; *d* the *hil* or sacred fence; *e* the high wall in the rear of the temple; *f* the Holy House; *g* the great altar of burnt offerings; *h* a covered colonnade in the court of the priests; *i* the gate Nicanor in front of the court of Israel; *j* the gate Beautiful in front of the court of the women; and *k* the eastern cloister, Solomon's porch.

The temple of Solomon retained its pristine splendor but thirty-three years, when it was plundered by Shishak king of Egypt, 1 Kin. 14:25, 26; 2 Chr. 12:9. After this period it underwent sundry profanations and pillages from Hazael, Tiglath-pileser, Sennacherib, etc., 2 Kin. 12; 16; 18; and was at length utterly destroyed by Nebuchadnezzar king of Babylon, B. C. 588, after having stood, according to Usher, four hundred and twenty-four years, three months, and eight days.

After lying in ruins for fifty-two years, the foundations of the second temple were laid by Zerubbabel, and the Jews who had availed themselves of the privilege granted by Cyrus and returned to Jerusalem, Ezra 1:1-4; 2:1; 3:8-10. After various hinderances, it was finished and dedicated twenty-one years after it was begun, B. C. 515, Ezra 6:15,

16. The dimensions of this temple in breadth and height were double those of Solomon's. The weeping of the people at the laying of the foundation, therefore, Ezra 3:12, 13, and the disparaging manner in which they spoke of it, when compared with the first one, Hag. 2:3, were occasioned by its inferiority not in size, but in glory. It wanted the five principal things which could invest it with this: namely, the ark and mercy-seat, the divine presence or visible glory, the holy fire on the altar, the urim and thummim, and the Spirit of prophecy. In the year B. C. 163, this temple was plundered and profaned by Antiochus Epiphanes, who ordered the discontinuance of the daily sacrifice, offered swine's flesh upon the altar, and completely suspended the worship of Jehovah, 1 Mac. 1:46, 47, etc. Thus it continued for three years, when it was repaired and purified by Judas Maccabaeus, who restored the divine worship, and dedicated it anew.

Herod, having slain all the Sanhedrim, except two, in the first year of his reign, B. C. 37, resolved to atone for it by rebuilding and beautifying the temple. This he was the more inclined to do, both from the peace which he enjoyed, and the decayed state of the edifice. After employing two years in preparing the materials for the work, the temple of Zerubbabel was pulled down, B. C. 17, and forty-six years before the first Passover of Christ's ministry. Although this temple was fit for divine service in nine years and a half, yet a great number of laborers and artificers were still employed in carrying on the outbuildings all the time of our Saviour's abode on earth. His presence fulfilled the predictions in Hag. 2:9; Mal. 3:1. The temple of Herod was considerably larger than that of Zerubbabel, as that of Zerubbabel was larger than Solomon's. For whereas the second temple was seventy cubits long, sixty broad, and sixty high, this was one hundred cubits long, seventy broad, and one hundred high. The porch was raised to the height of one hundred cubits, and was extended fifteen cubits beyond each side of the rest of the building. All the Jewish writers praise this temple exceedingly for its beauty and the costliness of its workmanship. It was built of white marble, exquisitely wrought, and with stones of large dimensions, some of them twenty-five cubits long, eight cubits high, and twelve cubits thick. To these there is no doubt a reference in Mark 13:1; Luke 21:5: "And as he went out of the temple, one of his disciples saith unto him, Master, see what manner of stones, and what buildings are here!" Luke says, "goodly stones." See a description of the ornaments of one of its gates under VINE.

This splendid building, which rose like a mount of gold and of snow, and was once the admiration and envy of the world, has for ever passed away. According to our blessed Lord's prediction, that "there should not be left one stone upon another that should not be thrown down," Mark 13:2, the whole structure above ground was completely demolished by the Roman soldiers, under Titus, A. D. 70. The temple area is now occupied by two Turkish mosques, into which, until recently, neither Jew nor Christian was permitted to enter. Beneath the vast area of El-Haram still exist immense arched ways and vaults of unknown date; also a large and deep well, and other indications that the temple always possessed a copious and perennial supply of water, derived perhaps in part from Gihon by Hezekiah's aqueduct, and in part from Solomon's pools, and flowing off through the fountain of the Virgin and the pool of Siloam. In the outer walls of the present area are

seen at several places stones of vast size, evidently belonging to the ancient walls.

Near the south-west corner certain huge stones mark the beginning of an arch, a part of the stately bridge which anciently connected the temple area with mount Zion; and a little north of this spot is the celebrated wailing-place of the Jews. See WALL.

In the time of the kings, a regular guard of Levites was always on duty at the temple, 1 Chr. 26; 2 Chr. 23:19. During the supremacy of the Romans there was a Roman garrison in the strong tower of Antonia, which, with its various courts and fortifications, adjoined the temple area on the north, and was connected with it by passages both above and under ground, John 18:12; Acts 4:1; 5:26; 21:31–40.

The utmost veneration and love were always cherished towards the temple by pious Jews, Psa. 84. All the people also, from various motives, gloried in it, many with a bigoted and idolatrous regard. Hence the charge of blaspheming the temple, which was found the most effectual means of enraging the populace against Christ and his followers, Matt. 26:61; 27:40; John 2:19, 20; Acts 6:13; 21:27–30.

TEMPT, to make trial of, Luke 10:25, and usually to present inducements to sin. Satan is the great tempter, seeking thus most effectually to destroy men's souls, 1 Chr. 21:1; Job 1 and 2; Matt. 4:1; 1 Thess. 3:5. Men are also led into sin by their own evil inclinations and by other men, James 1:14, 15. God, being holy and desirous of men's holiness, does not thus tempt them, James 1:13; but he makes trial of them, to prove, exercise, and establish their graces, Gen. 22:1; James 1:2, 3. Christ stands ready to support his people under any possible temptation, 1 Cor. 10:13; Heb. 2:18; 4:15; 2 Pet. 2:19. Yet they are not to rush into temptation unbidden, Luke 11:4. Men tempt God by presumptuously experimenting on his providence or his grace, or by distrusting him, Ex. 17:2, 7; Isa. 7:12; Matt. 4:7; Acts 5:9; 15:10. Sore afflictions are often called temptations or trials, as they are frequently the occasions of sin, Matt. 6:13; Luke 8:13; 22:28; James 1:12; 1 Pet. 1:6, 7.

Christ, at the outset of his public ministry, was violently assailed by the tempter, who thus displayed his effrontery and his blindness, hoping perhaps that the human soul of the Redeemer would be left unaided by his divinity, Matt. 4. The temptations are to be understood as real transactions, and not as visions. The tempter was baffled, and left him for a season, to meet a like rebuff on every future assault, Luke 4:13; 22:53; John 14:30. The Saviour triumphed, and paradise was regained.

TENT. Dwelling in tents was very general in ancient times among Eastern nations, Gen. 4:20; their way of life being pastoral, locomotion became necessary for pasturage, and dwellings adapted for such a life became indispensable, Isa. 38:12. The patriarchs Abraham, Isaac, and Jacob dwelt in tents, Gen. 18:1; Heb. 11:9; and on the exodus of the Israelites from Egypt, throughout their peregrinations until they obtained the promised land, and to some extent afterwards, they adopted the same kind of habitation. See BOOTHS. Hence the expression, "Every man to his tents, O Israel," etc., Judg. 7:8; 2 Sam. 20:1; 2 Kin. 8:21. Indeed, the people of the East, men, women, and children, lived very much in the open air, as is obvious from the New Testament narratives. And the same is true of them at the present day. The Midianites, the Philistines, the Syrians, the descendants of Ham, the Hagarites, and the Cushanites are mentioned in Scripture as living in tents. But the people most remarkable for this unsettled and wandering mode of life are the Arabs, who from the time of Ishmael to the present have continued the custom of dwelling in tents. Amid the revolutions which have transferred kingdoms from one possessor to another, these wandering tribes still dwell in tents, unsubdued and wild as was their progenitor. This kind of dwelling is not, however, confined to the Arabs, but is used throughout the continent of Asia. The word *tent* is formed from the Latin, "to stretch;" tents being usually made of canvas stretched out, and sustained by poles with cords secured to pegs driven into the ground. The "nail of the tent" with which Jael pierced the head of Sisera was such a tent-pin, Judg. 4:21. See also Isa. 33:20; 40:22; 54:2. The house of God, and heaven, are spoken of in Scripture as the tent or tabernacle of Jehovah, Psa. 15:1; 61:4; 84:1; Heb. 8:2; 9:11; and the body as the tabernacle of the soul, taken down by death, 2 Cor. 5:1; 2 Pet. 1:13. Says Lord Lindsay, "There is something very melancholy in our morning flittings. The tent-pins are plucked up, and in a few minutes a dozen holes, a heap or two of ashes, and the marks of the camels' knees in the sand, soon to be obliterated, are the only traces left of what has been for a while our home." "Often," says M'Cheyne, "we found ourselves shelterless before being fully dressed. What a type of the tent of our body! Ah, how often is it taken down before the soul is made meet for the inheritance of the saints in light." A tent is also put for its inmates, Hab. 3:7; Zech. 12:7.

Tents are of various colors; black, as the tents of Kedar, Psa. 120:5; Song 1:5; red, as of scarlet cloth; yellow, as of gold shining brilliantly; white, as of canvas. They are also of various shapes; some circular, others of an oblong figure, not unlike the bottom of a ship turned upside down. In Syria, the tents are generally made of cloth of goats' hair, woven by women, Exod. 35:26. Those of the Arabs are of black goats' hair. Some other nations adopt the same kind, but it is not common. The Egyptian and Moorish inhabitants of Askalon are said to use white tents; and D'Arvieux mentions that the tent of an Arab emir he visited was distinguished from the rest by its being of white cloth. An Arab sheikh will have a number of tents, for himself, his family, servants, and visitors; as in patriarchal times Jacob had separate tents for himself, for Leah, Rachel, and their maids, Gen. 31:33; Judg. 4:17. Usually, however, one tent suffices for a family; being divided, if large, into several apartments by curtains.

TENTH-DEAL, that is, *tenth part*, corresponding to the Hebrew *assaron*, or the tenth part of an ephah. It may therefore be the same as the omer, about five pints, Lev. 23:17.

TE'RAH, the son of Nahor, and father of Nahor, Haran, and Abraham, Gen. 11:24, begat Abraham at the age of seventy-two years, in Ur of the Chaldeans. Upon Abraham's first call to remove into the land of promise, Terah and all his family went with him as far as Haran, in Mesopotamia, about B. C. 1918, Gen. 11:31, 32. He died there the same year, aged two hundred and seventy-five years. Scripture intimates plainly that Terah had fallen into idolatry, or had for a time mingled some idolatrous practices with the worship of the true God, Josh. 24:2, 14; and some think that Abraham himself at first did the same thing; but that afterwards God, being gracious to him, convinced him of the vanity of this worship, and that he undeceived his father Terah.

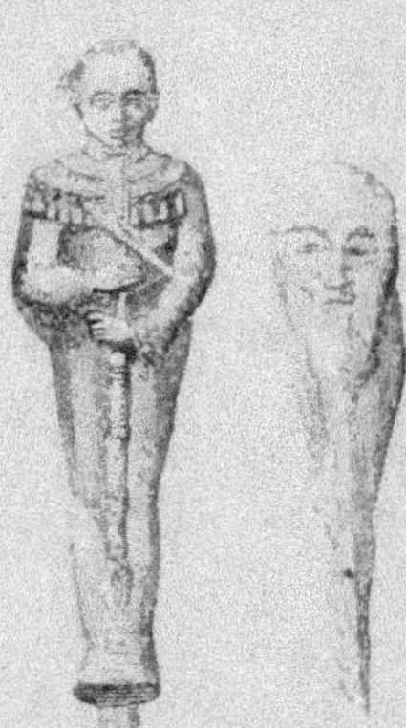

TER'APHIM, small idols or superstitious figures, from the possession, adoration, and consultation of which extraordinary benefits were expected. See margin 2 Kin. 23:24; Ezek. 21:21. The Eastern people are still much addicted to this superstition of talismans. The ancient teraphim appear to have been household gods, and their worship was sometimes blended with that of Jehovah, Judg. 17. They seem in one case to have resembled the human form in shape and size, 1 Sam. 19:13, 16. The images of Rachel, Gen. 31:19, 30, were teraphim. So Judg. 17:5; 18:14, 20; Hos. 3:4.

TER'EBINTH. See OAK.

TER'TIUS, a Christian whom Paul employed as his amanuensis in writing the epistle to the Romans, Rom. 16:22.

TER'TULLUS, a Roman orator or advocate, whom the Jews employed to bring forward their accusation against Paul, before the Roman procurator at Cæsarea, probably because they were themselves unacquainted with the modes of proceeding in the Roman courts, Acts 24:1, 2.

TES'TAMENT, in Scripture, usually signifies covenant, and not a man's last will, Matt. 26 : 28. Both meanings are blended, however, in Heb. 9 : 16, 17. Paul speaks of the new testament, or covenant, in the blood of the Redeemer; and calls the law the old covenant, and the gospel the new covenant, 1 Cor. 11:25; 2 Cor. 3 :6, 14; Heb. 7: 22; 10; 12:24. See BIBLE, and COVENANT.

TESTIMONY, the whole revelation of God, testifying to man what he is to believe, do, and hope, Psa. 19:7; 119:88, 99; 1 Cor. 1 : 6; Rev. 1 : 2. The two stone tables of the law were a visible "testimony" or witness of God's covenant with his people; and hence the ark of the covenant was called sometimes the testimony, or the ark of the testimony, Ex. 25:22; 34:29. See ARK.

TE'TRARCH is strictly the ruler of the fourth part of a state or province; but in the New Testament it is a general title applied to those who governed any part of a kingdom or province, with an authority subject only to that of the Roman emperor. Thus Herod the Great and his brother were at one time, in early life, constituted tetrarchs of Judea by Antony. At the death of Herod the Great, he left half his kingdom to Archelaus, with the title of ethnarch; while the other half was divided between two of his other sons, Herod Antipas and Philip, with the title of tetrarchs. See HEROD I. and II. In the same manner Lysanias is also said to have been tetrarch of Abilene, Luke 3:1. It is Herod Antipas who is called the tetrarch in Matt. 14:1; Luke 3:19; 9:7; Acts 13:1. As the authority of the tetrarch was similar to that of the king, so the general term king is also applied to Herod, Matt. 14:9; Mark 6:14.

THADDE'US, a surname of the apostle Jude. See JUDAS II.

THAM'MUZ. See TAMMUZ.

THEBES. See AMMON.

THE'BEZ, an Ephraimite town near Shechem, at the siege of which Abimelech was killed, Judg. 9 : 50-55; 2 Sam. 11:21.

THEFT, Ex. 20:15, Prov. 22 : 22, under the Mosaic law, was punished by exacting a double or a quadruple restitution, which was secured if necessary by the sale of the goods or services of the thief to the requisite amount, Exod. 22 : 1-8, 23; 2 Sam. 12 : 6; Prov. 6 : 30, 31; Luke 19 : 8. A night-robber might lawfully be slain in the act; and a man-stealer was to be punished by death, Ex. 21:16; 22:2.

THEOPH'ILUS, *friend of God*, an honorable person to whom the evangelist Luke addressed his gospel, and the Acts of the Apostles, Luke 1 : 3; Acts 1 : 1. We can only say of him, in general, that most probably he was a man of some note, who lived out of Palestine, and had abjured paganism in order to embrace Christianity.

THESSALO'NIANS, EPISTLE TO THE, I. and II. These were the earliest of Paul's epistles, and were written from Corinth, in A. D. 52 and 53. In the first epistle, Paul rejoices over Timothy's good report of the faith of Christians at Thessalonica; and confirms them against the persecutions and temptations they would meet, by discussing the miraculous testimony of God to the truth of the gospel, 1:5-10; the character of its preachers, 2:1 to 3:13; the holiness of its precepts, 4 : 1-12; and the resurrection of Christ and his people, 4:13 to 5:11. The remainder of the epistle consists of practical exhortations.

In the second epistle, he corrects certain errors into which they were falling, particularly respecting the second coming of Christ. This, he shows, must be preceded by the career of "the man of sin," "the son of perdition," "whose coming is after the working of Satan, with all power and signs and lying wonders;" who usurps divine authority over the church, and "opposeth and exalteth himself above all that is called God." The exact fulfilment in the Romish church of these predictions, at first so contrary to human anticipations, proves that the apostle wrote by inspiration.

THESSALONI'CA, a city and seaport of the second part of Macedonia, at the head of the Thermaic gulf. When Æmilius Paulus, after his conquest of Macedonia, divided the country into four districts, this city was made the capital of the second division, and was the station of a Roman governor and questor. It was anciently called Therma. It was inhabited by Greeks, Romans, and Jews, from among whom the apostle Paul gathered a numerous church. There was a large number of Jews resident in this city, where they had a synagogue, in which Paul, A. D. 52, preached to them on three successive Sabbaths. Some of the Jews, and many of the Gentiles, embraced the gospel; but the rest of the Jews determined to maltreat the apostle, and surrounded the house in which they believed he was lodging. The brethren, however, secretly led Paul and Silas out of the city, towards Berea, and they escaped from their enemies, Acts 17. Thessalonica, now called Saloniki, is at present a wretched town, but has a population of about 70,000 persons, one-third of whom are Jews.

When Paul left Macedonia for Athens and Corinth, he left behind him Timothy and Silas, at Thessalonica, that they might confirm those in the faith who had been converted under his ministry. He afterwards wrote to the church of the Thessalonians two epistles. See PAUL.

THEU'DAS, an insurgent Jew, mentioned by Gamaliel, A. D. 33, as of the preceding generation, Acts 5:36, 37, and therefore not to be confounded with a Theudas of A. D. 44, mentioned by Josephus. The period following the death of Herod the Great was full of revolts. Theudas was also a common name, answering to the Hebrew Matthew, under which name Josephus speaks of an unsuccessful reformer who was burnt in the latter part of Herod's reign.

THIGH. The mode of taking an oath, alluded to in Gen. 24:2-9; 47:29-31, was significant of the swearer's obligation to obedience. Jacob's thigh was disabled by the Angel, to show the patriarch that his prevalence was through his faith and prayer, not through force, Gen. 32:25-31. Smiting the thigh was a gesture of self-condemnation and grief, Jer. 31:19; Ezek. 21:12. Warriors wore their swords upon the left thigh, unless left-handed, in readiness for use, Judg. 3:15-21; Psa. 45:3; Song 3:8; so too they may have borne their names and titles, not only on their shields, but on their swords, or on the robe or mailed coat covering the thigh, Rev. 19:16. "Hip and thigh," Judg. 15:8, seems to mean utterly and irrecoverably.

THIS'TLES, and THORNS. Under these terms, together with brambles, briers, and nettles, are included numerous troublesome plants, many of them with thorns, well fitted to try the husbandman's patience, Gen. 3:18. Plants of this class were a symbol of desolation, Prov. 24:31, and were often used as fuel, Psa. 58:9; Eccl. 7:6; Isa. 33:12. They also served for hedges, Hos. 2:6. A petty village on the plain of Jericho is now protected against Arab horsemen by a hedge of thorny Nubk branches. Dr. Eli Smith, visiting the plain where Gideon once threatened to tear the flesh of the princes of Succoth with thorns and briers, noticed such plants there of remarkable size, some of the thistles rising above his head on horseback, Judg. 8:7. Few of the Hebrew terms can now be affixed with certainty to particular varieties among the many found in Syria. The plant of which the thorny

crown of the Saviour was made, with the design to mock rather than to torture him, is supposed to have been the Zizyphus Spina Christi, a common tree with dark and glossy leaves, having many small and sharp spines on its round and pliant branches, Matt. 27:29; John 19:2, 3. Paul's "thorn in the flesh," 2 Cor. 12:7-10, may have been some bodily infirmity, unfavorable to the success of his public ministrations. Compare Gal. 4:13, 14; 2 Cor. 10:10.

THOM'AS, the apostle, Matt. 10:3, called in Greek Didymus, that is, *a twin*, John 20:24, was probably a Galilean, as well as the other apostles; but the place of his birth, and the circumstances of his calling, are unknown, Luke 6:13-15.

He appears to have been of an impulsive character, sincerely devoted to Christ, ready to act upon his convictions, and perhaps slow to be convinced, as he at first doubted our Lord's resurrection, John 11:16; 14:5, 6; 20:19–29. Several of the fathers inform us that he preached in the Indies; and others say that he preached in Cush, or Ethiopia, near the Caspian sea.

There are nominal Christians in the East Indies, who bear the name of St. Thomas, because they report that this apostle preached the gospel there. They dwell in a peninsula of the Indus, on this side the gulf.

THORNS. See THISTLES.

THREE. The phrase, "three days and three nights," Matt. 12:40, was equivalent in Hebrew to the English "three days;" the Jews employing the expression "a day and a night" to denote our "day" of twenty-four hours. Nor did "three days," 1 Sam. 30:13, literally "this third day," according to their usage, necessarily include the whole of three days, but a part of three days, a continuous period including one whole day of twenty-four hours, and a portion of the day preceding it and the day following it. Compare Gen. 7:12, 17; 1 Sam. 30:12, 13.

THRESHING was anciently and is still performed in the East, sometimes with a flail, Ruth 2:17; Isa. 28:27; sometimes by treading out the grain with unmuzzled oxen, Deut. 25:4, but more generally by means of oxen dragging an uncouth instrument over the sheaves of grain. See CORN. The instrument most used in Palestine at this time is simply two short planks fastened side by side and turned up in front, like our common stone-sledge, having sharp stones or irons projecting from the under side, Isa. 28:27; 41:15; Amos 1:3. The Egyptian mode is thus described by Niebuhr: "They use oxen, as the ancients did, to beat out their corn, by trampling upon the sheaves, and dragging after them a clumsy machine. This machine is not, as in Arabia, a stone cyl-

inder, nor a plank with sharp stones, as in Syria, but a sort of sledge, consisting of three rollers fitted with irons, which turn upon axles. A farmer chooses out a level spot in his fields, and has his corn carried thither in sheaves, upon asses or dromedaries. Two oxen are then yoked in a sledge; a driver gets upon it, and drives them backward and forward upon the sheaves; and fresh oxen succeed in the yoke from time to time." By this operation, the straw is gradually chopped fine and the grain released. Meanwhile the whole is repeatedly turned over by wooden pitchforks with three or more prongs, and in due time thrown into a heap in the centre of the floor. The machine thus described is called a *noreg*, and answers to the Hebrew *morag* mentioned in 2 Sam. 24 : 22; 1 Chron. 21:23.

When the grain is well loosened from the straw by the treading of oxen, with or without one of the instruments above mentioned, the whole heap is next thrown with forks several yards against the wind, which blowing away the chaff, the grain falls into a heap by itself, 2 Kin. 13:7; and if necessary, the process is repeated. For this purpose the threshing-floors are in the open air, Judg. 6 : 37, and often on high ground, like that of Araunah on mount Moriah, 1 Chr. 21:15, that the wind may aid more effectually in winnowing the grain, Jer. 4 : 11, 12, which is afterwards sometimes passed through a sieve for farther cleansing. The ground is prepared for use as a threshing-floor by being smoothed off, and beaten down hard. While the wheat was carefully garnered, the straw and chaff were gathered up for fuel; a most instructive illustration of the day of judgment, Matt. 3:12.

THRONE, an established emblem of kingly dignity and power, used by sovereigns on all state occasions. That of Solomon was of ivory, overlaid with gold; having six broad steps, every one guarded by a golden lion at each end, 1 Kin. 10:18-20. Heaven is called God's throne, and the earth his footstool, Isa. 66 : 1. His throne is also sublimely described as everlasting, and as built upon justice and equity, Psa. 45:6; 97:2. See also Isa. 6 : 2-4; Ezek. 1. Christ is on the throne for ever, as the King of heaven, Psa. 110:1; Heb. 1 : 8; Rev. 3 : 21; and his faithful disciples will partake of his kingly glory, Luke 22:30; Rev. 4:4; 5:10. He forbade men lightly to swear by heaven or its throne, as they were thus irreverent to God, Matt. 5:34; 23:22.

THUM'MIM. See URIM.

THUN'DER and lightning are significant manifestations of the power of God, and emblems of his presence, Ex. 19:16; 1 Sam. 2:10; 12:17; Psa. 18:13. Thunder is poetically called "the voice of the Lord" in the sublime description of a thunder-storm in Psalm 29:

"The voice of the Lord is upon the waters;
The God of glory thundereth;
The Lord is upon many waters.
The voice of the Lord is powerful;
The voice of the Lord is full of majesty.
The voice of the Lord breaketh the cedars;
Yea, the Lord breaketh the cedars of Lebanon," etc.

See also Job 37:1-5; 40 : 9; Jer. 10:13. In illustration of Psa. 29:9, Moffat, while describing the thunder-storms of South Africa, says that the antelopes flee in consternation; and that he has observed the Bechuanas starting off early on the morning following such a storm in quest of young antelopes prematurely born. In Psa. 78 : 48, "hot thunderbolts" means lightning.

THYATI'RA, a city of Lydia, in Asia Minor, a Macedonian colony, anciently called Pelopia and Euhippia, now Ak-hissar. It was situated on the confines of Lydia and Mysia, near the river Lycus, between Sardis and Pergamos. It was the seat of one of "the seven churches," Rev. 1 : 11; 2 : 18, 24. The art of dyeing purple was particularly cultivated at Thyatira, as appears from an inscription recently found there; and it still sends to Smyrna, sixty miles south-west, large quantities of scarlet cloth, Acts 16 : 14. Ak-hissar is a poor town, with six thousand inhabitants, chiefly Turks.

THY'INE-WOOD, Rev. 18 : 12, the wood of the Thyia or Thuja Articulata of Linnæus, an aromatic evergreen tree, resembling the cedar, and found in Libya, near mount Atlas. The wood was used in burning incense, and under the name of citron-wood was highly prized by the Romans for ornamental wood-work. It yields the sanderach resin of commerce.

TIBE'RIAS, a city of Galilee, founded by Herod Antipas, and named by him in honor of the emperor Tiberius. A more ancient and greater city, perhaps Chinneroth, seems previously to have flourished and gone to ruin near the same site, on the south. Tiberias was situated on the western shore of the lake of Gennesareth, about two hours' ride from the place where the Jordan issues from the lake. In the vicinity of the city were hot springs, which were much celebrated. The lake is also sometimes called, from the city, the sea of Tiberias, John 6:1, 23; 21:1. See SEA IV. After the destruction of Jerusalem, Tiberias was celebrated as the seat of a flourishing school of Jewish learning. The crusaders held it for a time, and erected a church, in which the Arabs have since housed their cattle. Modern Tubariyeh lies on a narrow undulating plain between the high table-land and the sea. It was half destroyed by an earthquake in 1837, and has a population of only twenty-five hundred souls, nearly one-third of whom are Jews. The walls are little more than heaps of ruins, the castle is much shattered, and the place has an aspect of extreme wretchedness and filth. As the Arabs say, "The king of the fleas holds his court at Tubariyeh." South of the town are numerous remains of the ancient city or cities, extending for a mile and a half, nearly to the hot springs. The waters of these springs are nauseous and salt, and too hot for immediate use, 136° to 144°; but the baths are much resorted to for the cure of rheumatic diseases, etc.

TIBE'RIUS, CLAU'DIUS DRU'SUS NE'RO, the second emperor of Rome, was the son of Livia, and stepson of Augustus; and being adopted by that emperor, he succeeded to his throne, A. D. 14. He was at first moderate and just, but soon became infamous for his vices and crimes, and died A. D. 37, after a cruel reign of twenty-two and a half years. It was in the fifteenth year of his reign that John the Baptist commenced his ministry; and the crucifixion of Jesus took place in the third or fourth year after, Luke 3:1. This emperor is several times casually mentioned under the title of Cæsar, Luke 20:22-25; 23:2; John 19:12. His subjects were commanded to pay divine worship to his images.

TIB'NI, an unsuccessful competitor with Omri the general, for the throne of Israel, during three years after the death of Elah, 1 Kin. 16:18-23.

TI'DAL, apparently the chief of several allied tribes, with whom he joined Chedorlaomer in the invasion of the vale of Siddim, mount Seir, etc., and was defeated by Abraham, Gen. 14:1-16.

TIG'LATH-PILE'SER, king of Assyria, was invited by Ahaz king of Judah to aid him against the kings of Syria and Israel, 2 Kin. 16:7-10. This he did, but exacted also a heavy tribute from Ahaz, so as to distress him without helping him, 2 Chr. 28:20, 21. From the kingdom of Israel, also, he carried off the inhabitants of many cities captive, and placed them in various parts of his kingdom, B. C. 740, 1 Chr. 5:26; 2 Kin. 15:29, thus fulfilling unconsciously the predictions of Isaiah, 7:17; 8:4. He is supposed to be meant by Jareb, *the pleader*, in Hos. 5:13; 10:6. He reigned nineteen years at Nineveh, and was succeeded by his son Shalmaneser.

TILE, a broad and thin brick, usually made of fine clay, and hardened in the fire. Such tiles were very common in the region of the Euphrates and Tigris, (see BABYLON,) and offered to the exiled prophet Ezekiel the most natural and obvious means of depicting the siege of Jerusalem, Ezek. 4:1. Great numbers of similar rude sketches of places, as well as of animals and men, are found on the tiles recently exhumed from the ancient mounds of Assyria, interspersed among the wedge-shaped inscriptions with which one side of the tile is usually crowded. At Nineveh Layard found a large chamber stored full of such inscribed tiles, like a collection of historical archives, Ezra 6:1. They are usually about a foot square, and three inches thick.

TIM'BREL, an instrument of music, early and often mentioned in Scripture, Gen. 31:27; Job 21:12. The Hebrews called it *toph*, under which name they comprehended all kinds of drums, tabors, and tambourines. We do not find that the Hebrews used it in their wars, but only at their public rejoicings, Ex. 15:20; Isa. 24:8; and it was commonly employed by the women, Psa. 68:25. It consisted, and still consists, of a small circular rim or hoop, over which a skin is drawn. The rim is also hung with small bells. The timbrel is used as an accompaniment to lively music, being shaken and beaten with the knuckles in time. After the passage of the Red sea, Miriam, sister of Moses, took a timbrel, and began to play and dance with the women, Exod. 15:20. The daughter of Jephthah came to meet her father with timbrels and other musical instruments, Judg. 11:34. See MUSIC.

TIME. Besides the ordinary uses of this word, the Bible sometimes employs it to denote a year, as in Dan. 4:16; or a prophetic year, consisting of three hundred and sixty natural years, a day being taken for a year. Thus in Dan. 7:25; 12:7, the phrase "a time, times, and the dividing of a time" is supposed to mean three and a half prophetic years, or 1,260 natural years. This period is elsewhere paralleled by the expression, "forty-two months," each month including thirty years, Rev. 11:2, 3; 12:6, 14; 13:5.

TIM'NA, a secondary wife of Eliphaz the son of Esau, a name which recurs in the records of the Idumæan tribes, Gen. 36:12, 22, 40; 1 Chr. 1:36, 51.

TIM'NAH, TIM'NATH, and THIM'NATHAH, an ancient city of the Canaanites, Gen. 38:12–14; on the borders of Judah and Dan after the conquest, Josh. 15:10; 19:43. It was for a long time subject to the Philistines, and Samson's wife was a Timnite, Judg. 14:1–5; 2 Chr. 28:18. Its deserted site, now called Tibneh, lies three miles south-west of Zorah.

TIM'NATH-SE'RAH, or TIM'NATH-HE'RES, Judg. 2:9, a town in Ephraim, which yielded to Joshua a home, an income, and a burial-place, Josh. 19:50; 24:30. The site the Jewish leader is supposed to have chosen, now called Tibneh, lies in a rough and mountainous region on the road from Gophna to Antipatris.

TIM'OTHY, a disciple of Paul. He was of Derbe or Lystra, both cities of Lycaonia, Acts 16:1; 14:6. His father was a Greek, but his mother a Jewess, 2 Tim. 1:5; 3:15. The instructions and prayers of his pious mother and grandmother, and the preaching of Paul during his first visit to Lystra, A. D. 48, resulted in the conversion of Timothy and his introduction to the ministry which he so adorned. He had witnessed the sufferings of Paul, and loved him as his father in Christ, 1 Tim. 1:2; 2 Tim. 3:10, 11. When the apostle returned to Lystra, about A. D. 51, the brethren spoke highly of the merit and good disposition of Timothy; and the apostle determined to take him along with him, for which purpose he circumcised him at Lystra, Acts 16:3. Timothy applied himself to labor in the gospel, and did Paul very important services through the whole course of his preaching. Paul calls him not only his dearly beloved son, but also his brother, the companion of his labors, and a man of God; observing that none was more united with him in heart and mind than Timothy, Rom. 16:21; 1 Cor. 4:17; 2 Cor. 1:1; 1 Tim. 1:2, 18. Indeed, he was selected by Paul as his chosen companion in his journeys, shared for a time his imprisonment at Rome, Heb. 13:23, and was afterwards left by him at Ephesus, to continue and perfect the work which Paul had begun in that city, 1 Tim. 1:3; 3:14. He appears to have possessed in a very high degree the confidence and affection of Paul, and is therefore often mentioned by him in terms of warm commendation, Acts 16:1; 17:14, 15; 18:5; 19:22; 20:4; 2 Tim. 3:10; 4:5.

EPISTLES TO TIMOTHY. The first of these Paul seems to have written subsequently to his first imprisonment at Rome, and while he was in Macedonia, having left Timothy at Ephesus, 1 Tim. 1:2, A. D. 64. The second appears to have been addressed to Timothy in north-western Asia Minor, during Paul's second imprisonment and in anticipation of martyrdom, A. D. 67. This dying charge of the faithful apostle to his beloved son in the gospel, the latest fruit of his love for him and for the church, we study with deep emotions. Both epistles are most valuable and instructive documents for the direction and admonition of every Christian, and more especially of ministers of the gospel. With the epistle to Titus, they form the three "pastoral epistles," as they are called.

TIN, a metal known and used at an early period, Num. 31:22, and brought by the Tyrians from Tarshish, Ezek. 27:12. In Isa. 1:25 it means the alloy of lead, tin, and other base admixtures in silver ore, separated from the pure silver by smelting.

TIPH'SAH, the ancient Thapsacus, an important city on the western bank of the Euphrates, which constituted the north-eastern extremity of Solomon's dominions, 1 Kin. 4:24. The ford at this place being the last one on the Euphrates towards the south, its possession was important to Solomon in his design to attract the trade of the East to Palestine. Hence the building of Tadmor on the desert route. Perhaps the same city is meant in 2 Kin. 15:16, though some understand here a city of the same name near Samaria.

TI'RAS, a son of Japheth, supposed to have been the forefather of the ancient Thracians, Gen. 10:2.

TIRES, or "little moons," are thought to have been ornaments for the neck, worn not by women only, Isa. 3:18, but by men, and even on the necks of camels, Judg. 8:21, 26. Some suppose the tire, in Ezek. 24:17, was an ornamented headdress.

TIRHA'KAH, king of Ethiopia, or Cush, and of Egypt. This prince, at the head of a powerful army, attempted to relieve Hezekiah, when attacked by Sennacherib, 2 Kin. 19 : 9, but the Assyrian army was routed before he came up, Isa. 37:19, B. C. 712. He is undoubtedly the Taracus of Manetho, and the Tearcho of Strabo, the third and last king of the twenty-fifth or Ethiopian dynasty. It is supposed that he is the Pharaoh intended in Isa. 30:2 ; and that Isa. 19 depicts the anarchy which succeeded his reign. He was a powerful monarch, ruling both Upper and Lower Egypt, and extending his conquests far into Asia and towards the "pillars of Hercules" in the west. His name and victories are recorded on an ancient temple at Medinet Abou, in Upper Egypt; whence also the representation above given of his head was copied by Rosselini.

TIRSHA'THA, perhaps meaning severe or august, a title of honor borne by Zerubbabel and Nehemiah as Persian governors of Judea, Ezra 2 : 63; Neh. 7 : 65.

TIR'ZAH, *pleasant*, Song 6 : 4, a city of the Canaanites, Josh. 12 : 24, and afterwards of the tribe of Manasseh or Ephraim; and the royal seat of the kings of Israel from the time of Jeroboam to the reign of Omri, who built the city of Samaria, which then became the capital of this kingdom, 1 Kin. 15 : 21, 33 ; 16 : 6, 23 ; 2 Kin. 15:14, 16. Its exact location is unknown.

TISH'BITE, from Tishbe in the tribe of Naphtali, where Elijah was born, 1 Kin. 17 : 1. It is mentioned in one of the apocryphal books.

TISH'RI, or TIS'RI, the first month of the Jewish civil year, and the seventh of the ecclesiastical; called, in 1 Kin. 8 : 2, Ethanim, which see; and answering nearly to our October. On the first day of Tishri the feast of Trumpets occurred; on the tenth, the great day of Expiation; and on the fifteenth, the feast of Tabernacles commenced.

TITHE, *a tenth*, the proportion of a man's income devoted to sacred purposes from time immemorial, Gen. 14 : 20; 28 : 22. This was prescribed in the Mosaic law, Num. 31 : 31. A twofold tithe was required of each Jewish citizen. The first consisted of one-tenth of the produce of his fields, trees, flocks, and herds, to be given to God as the sovereign Proprietor of all things and as the King of the Jews, Lev. 27: 30-32 ; 1 Sam. 8 : 15, 17. The proceeds of this tax were devoted to the maintenance of the Levites in their respective cities, Num. 18 : 21-24. A person might pay this tax in money, adding one-fifth to its estimated value. The Levites paid a tenth part of what they received to the priests, Num. 18:26-28. The second tithe required of each landholder was one-tenth of the nine parts of his produce remaining after the first tithe, to be expended at the tabernacle or temple in entertaining the Levites, his own family, etc., changing it first into money, if on account of his remoteness he chose to do so, Deut. 12:17-19, 22-29 ; 14:22-27. Every third year a special provision was made for the poor, either out of this second tithe or in addition to it, Deut. 14:28, 29. These tithes were not burdensome; but the pious Israelite found himself the richer for their payment, though it does not seem to have been enforced by any legal penalties. The system of tithes was renewed both before and after the captivity,

2 Chr. 31:5, 6, 12; Neh. 10:37; 12:44; 13:5; but they were not always regularly paid, and hence the divine blessing was withheld, Mal. 3:8–12. The Pharisees were scrupulously exemplary in paying their tithes, but neglected the more important duties of love to God and man, Matt. 23:23.

The principle of the ancient tithes, namely, that ministers of the gospel and objects of benevolence should be provided for by the whole people of God, according to their means, is fully recognized in Scripture as applicable to the followers of Christ. He sent his servants forth, two and two, without provisions or purses, to receive their support from the people, since "the laborer is worthy of his hire," Matt. 10:9–14; Luke 10:4–8, 16. Paul also reasons in the same way, 1 Cor. 9:13, 14; Gal. 6:6. For purposes of piety and beneficence, he directed the Corinthians, and virtually all Christians, to lay aside from their income, on the first day of the week, as the Lord had prospered them, 1 Cor. 16:2. There is no reason to doubt that the early Christians gave more freely of their substance than did the ancient Jews, Acts 4:34–36; 2 Cor. 8:1–4.

TITTLE, a very small particle; literally, a small horn; the minute tip at the extremity of some Hebrew letters, Matt. 5:18. In transcribing the Hebrew Scriptures, the Jews exacted the utmost accuracy. Every page and every line must contain just so much; and the most trivial defect vitiated the whole roll, and compelled the scribe to begin his task anew. Yet the extreme care thus expressed for the perfect integrity of the letter of God's word is but a feeble illustration of the Saviour's care for the same word—every truth, every threatening, and every promise has the most perfect guarantee possible: "It is easier for heaven and earth to pass, than one tittle of the law to fail," Luke 16:17.

TITUS, a distinguished Christian minister of Greek origin, Gal. 2:3; converted under the preaching of Paul, Tit. 1:4, whose companion and fellow-laborer he became, 2 Cor. 8:23. He joined Paul and Barnabas in the mission from Antioch to Jerusalem, Acts 15:2; Gal. 2:1; and subsequently was sent to Corinth and labored with success, 2 Cor. 8:6; 12:18. He did not rejoin the apostle at Troas, as was expected, but at Philippi, 2 Cor. 2:12, 13; 7:6; and soon after resumed his labors at Corinth in connection with a general effort for the relief of poor Christians in Judea, taking with him Paul's second epistle, 2 Cor. 8:6, 16, 17. Some eight or ten years later, we find him left by the apostle at Crete, to establish and regulate the churches of that island, Tit. 1:5. Here he received the EPISTLE TO TITUS from Paul, then at Ephesus, inviting him to Nicopolis, Tit. 3:12; whence he went into the neighboring Dalmatia, before Paul was finally imprisoned at Rome, 2 Tim. 4:10. Tradition makes him labor for many years in Crete, and die there at an advanced age. His character seems to have been marked by integrity, discretion, and a glowing zeal. He was trusted and beloved by Paul, whose epistle to him is similar in its contents to the first epistle to Timothy, and was probably written not long after it, A. D. 65.

TOB, a district beyond Jordan, where Jephthah took refuge when expelled from Gilead, Judg. 11:3, 5. Its location is not known.

TOBI'AH, an Ammonite prince, in league with Sanballat and the Samaritans against the pious Jews, who were rebuilding the ruined temple, Neh. 2:10; 4:3. His threats and treachery were employed in vain. During Nehemiah's absence, Tobiah was unlawfully established by some of the chief men of Judah, his relatives, in a fine apartment of the new temple; but was ignominiously expelled on the governor's return, Neh. 6:17–19; 13:1–9.

TOGAR'MAH, a descendant of Japheth, Gen. 10:3, supposed to have given his name to the region of Asia afterwards called Armenia, Ezek. 38:15, 16. It was celebrated for its horses and mules; and the men of Togarmah, like the modern Armenians, were an industrious, peaceable, and trafficking people, Ezek. 27:14.

TOI, king of Hamath in Syria, sent his son to rejoice with David on his victories over Hadadezer king of Zobah, 2 Sam. 8:9–11; 1 Chr. 18:9.

TO'LA, I., the eldest son of Issachar, and head of a family, Gen. 46:13; Num. 26:23.

II. Of the tribe of Issachar, judge of Israel, at Shamir in mount Ephraim, for twenty-three years after the death of Abimelech, Judg. 10:1, 2.

TOMB. See SEPULCHRE.

TO'PAZ, a precious stone of wine-yellow color, with occasional pale tinges of green or red. It was one of the twelve gems in the high-priest's breastplate, Exod. 28 : 17 ; 39 : 10, and was a highly prized product of Cush, or Southern Arabia, Job 28:19 ; Ezek. 28:13.

TO'PHET. See HINNOM.

TORMENT'ORS. The Greek word usually denotes men who had charge of instruments of torture, by which unwilling witnesses were compelled to testify, and the agonies of execution in some cases were protracted. The same men, however, were keepers of prisons and jails ; and it is probably with reference only to their office as jailers that the word is used in Matt. 18:34.

TOR'TOISE, Lev. 11:29. The Hebrew word rather denotes a species of lizard, so named in the original for its slowness of motion.

TOWERS were erected not only in the outer walls and on the heights within cities, Judg. 9 : 47–49, Psa. 48:12, Luke 13 : 4, but along the frontiers of a country, at points where the approach of an enemy could be descried at a distance, Judg. 9:17 ; Isa. 21:6–9 ; Ezek. 33:2–6. A tower afforded a refuge to the surrounding inhabitants, in case of invasion ; and often, when most of a city was subdued, the tower or citadel remained impregnable. So God is a strong and safe protector of his people, Psa. 18 : 2 ; 61 : 8 ; Prov. 18 : 10. A slight tower or look-out was often erected for the keeper of a vineyard or flock, 2 Chr. 26:10 ; Isa. 5:2 ; Mic. 4:8 ; Matt. 21:33 ; and travellers in Palestine see them in use at this day.

TRACHONI'TIS, in the time of Christ, was, as its name imports, a rugged province, lying on the north-east border of Palestine, south of Damascus, between the mountains of Arabia Deserta on the east, and Iturea, Auranitis, and Batanea on the west and south, Luke 3:1. Herod the Great subdued the robbers that infested it ; and after his death it was governed by Philip his son, and then by Herod Agrippa.

TRADI'TION, Col. 2 : 8, Tit. 1 : 14, a doctrine, sentiment, or custom not found in the Bible, but transmitted orally from generation to generation from some presumed inspired authority. In patriarchal times, much that was valuable and obligatory was thus preserved. But tradition has long been superseded by the successive and completed revelations of God's will which form the inspired Scriptures, the only perfect and sufficient rule of belief and practice. With this, even before the time of the Saviour, Isa. 8:20, all traditions were to be compared, as being of no value if they conflicted with it, added to it, or took from it, Rev. 22:19. The Jews had numerous unwritten traditions, which they affirmed to have been delivered to Moses on mount Sinai, and by him transmitted to Joshua, the judges, and the prophets. After their wars with the Romans under Adrian and Severus, in view of their increasing dispersion over the earth, the Jews desired to secure their traditions by committing them to writing. Accordingly Rabbi Judah "the Holy," composed the Mishna, or second law, the most ancient collection of the Hebrew traditions, about A. D. 190–220. To this text two commentaries were afterwards added : the Gemara of Jerusalem, probably about A. D. 370 ; and the Gemara of Babylon, A. D. 500 ; forming, with the Mishna, the Talmud of Jerusalem and that of Babylon. The contents of these voluminous works poorly remunerate the student for the laborious task of reading them. Our Saviour severely censured the adherents of such legendary follies in his own day, and reproached them with preferring the traditions of the elders to the law of God itself, and superstitiously adhering to vain observances while they neglected the most important duties, Matt. 15 : 1–20 ; Mark

7:1-13. The traditions of the Romish church, with less apology than the ancient Jews had before the New Testament was written, are still more in conflict with the word of God, and still more deserving of the Saviour's condemnation.

In 2 Thess. 2:15; 3:6, "tradition" means inspired instructions from the lips of those who received them from God, and were authorized to dispense them in his name. These apostolic sayings were obligatory only on those who received them as inspired directly from the apostles. Had any of them come down to our times, the only means of endorsing them must be by showing their agreement with the word of God, since inspiration and miracles have ceased.

TRANCE, a state of the human system distinguished from dreaming and revery; it is one in which the bodily senses are locked up and almost disconnected from the spirit, which is occupied either with phantasms, as in trances produced by disease, or, as in ancient times, with revelations from God. Numerous instances are mentioned in Scripture: as that of Balaam, Num. 24:4, 16; those of Peter and Paul, Acts 10:10; 22:17; 2 Cor. 12:1-4. Compare also Gen. 2:21-24; 15:12-21; Job 4:13-21.

TRANSFIGURATION, Matt. 17:1-9; 2 Pet. 1:16-18. This remarkable event in the life of Christ probably took place on Hermon or some other mountain not far from Cæsarea Philippi; the tradition which assigns it to Tabor not being sustained. See TABOR. The whole form and raiment of the Saviour appeared in supernatural glory. The Law and the Prophets, in the persons of Moses and Elijah, did homage to the Gospel. By communing with Christ on the theme most momentous to mankind, his atoning death, they evinced the harmony that exists between the old and new dispensations, and the sympathy between heaven and earth; while the voice from heaven in their hearing gave him honor and authority over all. Besides its great purpose, the attestation of Christ's Messiahship and divinity, this scene demonstrated the continued existence of departed spirits in an unseen world, furnished in the Saviour's person an emblem of humanity glorified, and aided in preparing both him and his disciples for their future trials.

TREASURES. Kings were wont to store their possessions and guard what they most valued in well-fortified cities, hence called treasure-cities, Ex. 1:11; 1 Chr. 27:25; Ezra 5:17. "Treasures in the field," Jer. 41:8, were provisions, etc., buried, as is the custom in many parts of the world, in subterranean pits. Numerous ruined granaries of this kind are still found in the vicinity of Beth-shean. The "pilgrim fathers" in like manner found heaps of corn buried in the ground by the Indians. In consequence also of the great insecurity of property in the East, it seems to have been usual from the earliest times to hide in the ground gold and jewels; and the owners being killed or driven away, or forgetting the place of deposit, these hidden treasures remain till chance or search brings them to light. They are much sought for by the Arabs at this day, and are believed by them to be the object travellers from the West have in view in exploring ancient ruins, Job 3:21; Prov. 2:4; Matt. 13:44. But a few years since, some workmen digging in a garden at Sidon, discovered several copper pots, filled with gold coin from the mint of Philip of Macedon and his son Alexander, unmixed with any of later date. This lost treasure, worth many thousands of dollars, had remained apparently undisturbed over two thousand years.

TREES were frequently used as types of kings, or men of wealth and power, Psa. 37:35; Isa. 2:13; Dan. 4:10-26; Zech. 11:1, 2. The "tree of knowledge of good and evil" bore the forbidden fruit, by eating of which Adam fatally increased his knowledge—of good by its loss, of sin and woe by actual experience, Gen. 2:9, 17. The "tree of life" may have been both an assurance and a means of imparting life, a seal of eternal holiness and bliss, if man had not sinned. Compare Rev. 22:2.

TRENCH, a passage of approach to the walls of a besieged city, like a deep ditch; the earth thrown up constituting a wall. The Redeemer, weeping over Jerusalem a few days before he was crucified under its walls, said, "The days shall come upon thee, that thine enemies shall cast a trench about thee, and compass thee round, and keep thee in on every side." Luke 19:43. The Romans fulfilled this prediction by enclosing the entire city of Jerusalem by a wall, that the Jews might neither escape nor be relieved from without. In 1 Sam. 26:5, "trench" appears to mean the circle formed by camp equipage. See CAMP.

TRES'PASS, an injury done to another, with more or less culpability. The Mosaic law required a trespasser not only to make satisfaction to the person injured, but by an offering at the altar to reconcile himself to the divine Governor, Lev. 5; 6:1-7; Psa. 51:4. Christ repeatedly declares, that in order to be forgiven of God, we must be forgiving to men, Matt. 6:14, 15, and that no brother must have aught against us, Matt. 5:23, 24.

TRIBE. Jacob having twelve sons, who were heads of so many families, which together formed a great nation, each of these families was called a *tribe*. But this patriarch on his death-bed adopted Ephraim and Manasseh, the two sons of Joseph, and would have them also to constitute two tribes in Israel, Gen. 48:5. Instead of twelve tribes, there were now thirteen, that of Joseph being two. However, in the distribution of lands by Joshua under the order of God, they reckoned but twelve tribes and made but twelve lots; for the tribe of Levi, being appointed to the sacred service, had no share in the distribution of the land, but received certain cities to dwell in, with the first-fruits, tithes, and oblations of the people. Each tribe had its own leaders and tribunals; and the whole twelve, in their early history, constituted a republic somewhat resembling the United States. In the division made by Joshua of the land of Canaan, Reuben, Gad, and half of Manasseh had their lot beyond Jordan, east; all the other tribes, and the remaining half of Manasseh had their distribution on this side the river, west.

The twelve tribes continued united as one state, one people, and one monarchy, till after the death of Solomon, when ten of the tribes revolted from the house of David, and formed the kingdom of Israel. See HEBREWS.

TRIB'UTE. Every Jew throughout the world was required to pay an annual tribute or capitation-tax of half a shekel, about twenty-five cents, in acknowledgment of God's sovereignty and for the maintenance of the temple service, Ex. 30:12-15. It was with reference to this that Christ says, in effect, Matt. 17:25, 26, "If this tribute be levied in the ame of THE FATHER, then I, THE SON, am free." In other New Testament passages, tribute means the tax levied by the Romans. On the question of paying tribute to foreigners and idolaters, Matt. 22:16-22, Christ gave a reply which neither party could stigmatize as rebellious, or as unpatriotic and irreligious. By themselves using Cæsar's currency, both parties acknowledged the fact of his supremacy. Christ warns them to render to all men their dues; and above all, to regard the claims of Him whose superscription is on every thing, 1 Cor. 10:31; 1 Pet. 2:9, 13.

TRO'AS, a maritime city of Mysia, in the north-west part of Asia Minor, situated on the Ægean coast, at some distance south of the supposed site of ancient Troy. The adjacent region, including all the coast south of the Hellespont, is also called Troas, or the Troad. The city was a Macedonian and Roman colony of much promise, and was called Alexandria Troas. The Turks call its ruins Eski Stamboul, the old Constantinople. Its remains, in the centre of a forest of oaks, are still grand and imposing. The apostle Paul was first at Troas for a short time in A. D. 52, and sailed thence into Macedonia, Acts 16:8-11. At his second visit, in A. D. 57, he labored with success, 2 Cor. 2:12, 13. At his third recorded visit he tarried but a week; at the close of which the miraculous raising of Eutychus to life took place, Acts 20:5-14, A. D. 58. See also 2 Tim. 4:13.

TROGYL'LIUM, the name of a town and promontory of Ionia, in Asia Minor, between Ephesus and the mouth of the Meander, opposite to Samos. The promontory is a spur of mount Mycale, Acts 20:15.

TROOP, Isa. 65:11. See GAD III.

TROPH'IMUS, a disciple of Paul, a Gentile and an Ephesian by birth, came to Corinth with the apostle, and accompanied him in his whole journey to Jerusalem, A. D. 58, Acts 20:4. When the apostle was in the temple there, the Jews laid hold of him, crying out, "He hath brought Greeks into the temple, and hath polluted this holy place;" because, having seen him in the city accompanied by Trophimus, they imagined that he had introduced him into the temple. Some years afterwards, Paul writes that he had left him sick at Miletus, 2 Tim. 4:20. This did not occur at Paul's former visit to Miletus, since Trophimus went with him to Jerusalem; nor on the voyage to Rome, for they did not go near Miletus. It is therefore one of the circumstances which prove that Paul was released, and revisited Asia Minor, Crete, Macedonia, and perhaps Spain, before his second imprisonment and death. Of Trophimus nothing farther is known.

TROW, an old word for think, Luke 17:9.

TRUM'PET. The Lord commanded Moses to make two trumpets of beaten silver, for the purpose of calling the people together when they were to decamp, Num. 10:2. They used these trumpets to proclaim the beginning of the civil year, of the sabbatical year, Lev. 23:24, Num. 29:1, and of the jubilee, Lev. 25:9, 10. See MUSIC.

The feast of Trumpets was kept on the first day of the seventh month of the sacred year, which was the first of the civil year, called Tishri. The beginning of the year was proclaimed by sound of trumpet, Lev. 23:24; Num. 29:1; and the day was kept solemn, all servile business being forbidden. In addition to the daily and the monthly sacrifices, Num. 28:11-15, a solemn holocaust was offered in the name of the whole nation, of a bullock, a ram, a kid, and seven lambs of the same year, with offerings of flour and wine, as usual with these sacrifices. Scripture does not mention the occasion of appointing this feast.

TRYPHE'NA, and TRYPHO'SA, female disciples at Rome, apparently sisters, and very useful in the work of evangelization, Rom. 16:12.

TU'BAL, a son of Japheth, Gen. 10:2; supposed to have been the originator of the Tybareni, who occupied the northeastern part of Asia Minor. They were a warlike people, and brought slaves and copper vessels to the market of Tyre, Isa. 66:19; Ezek. 27:13; 32:26; 38:2; 39:1.

TU'BAL-CAIN, son of Lamech and Zillah, inventor of the art of forging metals, Gen. 4:22.

TUR'TLE-DOVE, or TURTLE, the Columba Turtur; a distinct bird from the common dove or pigeon, smaller and differently marked, and having a soft and plaintive note, Isa. 59:11; Ezek. 7:16. It is a bird of passage, Jer. 8:7,

leaving Palestine for a short trip to the south, and returning early in spring, Song 2:12. It is timid and fond of seclusion, and pines in captivity, Psa. 11:1. The law allowed it as a burnt or sin-offering by the poor, Lev. 1:14; 5:7; Matt. 21:22, and in several cases of purification, etc., Lev. 12:6-8; 14:22; Num. 6:10; Luke 2:24. Before the giving of the law, Abraham offered birds, which were a turtle and a pigeon; and when he divided the other victims he left the birds entire, Gen. 15:9.

TYCHI'CUS, a disciple employed by the apostle Paul to carry his letters to several churches. He was of the province of Asia, and accompanied Paul in his journey from Corinth to Jerusalem, Acts 20:4. He carried the epistle to the Colossians, that to the Ephesians, and the first to Timothy. The apostle calls him his dear brother, a faithful minister of the Lord, and his companion in the service of God, Eph. 6:21, 22; Col. 4:7, 8; 2 Tim. 4:12, and had intentions of sending him into Crete, in the absence of Titus, Tit. 3:12.

TYPE, in Greek *tupos*, a word denoting some resemblance, and translated "figure" in Rom. 4:15, "ensample" in Phil. 3:17, "manner" in Acts 23:25, and "form" in Rom. 6:17. So also Moses was to make the tabernacle according to the type or model he had seen in the mount, Acts 7:44. In the more general use of the word, a scriptural type is a prophetic symbol, "a shadow of good things to come," Heb.

10:1, "but the body is Christ," Col. 2:17. The typical character of the old dispensation is its most distinguishing feature. For example, the paschal lamb and all the victims sacrificed under the law were types of the Lamb of God, and illustrated his great atonement; showing that guilt deserved death, and could only be atoned for by the blood of an acceptable sacrifice. But they were also intended to foretell the coming of their great Antitype.

The Old Testament types include persons, officers, objects, events, rites, and places. Thus Adam and Melchizedek, the prophetic and the priestly office, manna and the brazen serpent, the smitten rock and the passage over Jordan, the Passover and the Day of Atonement, Canaan and the cities of refuge are scriptural types of Christ.

However striking the points of resemblance which an Old Testament event or object may present to something in the New Testament, it is not properly a type unless it was so appointed by God, and thus has something of a prophetic character. Due care should therefore be taken to distinguish between an illustration and a type.

TYRAN'NUS, the name of a person at Ephesus, in whose school Paul publicly proposed and defended the doctrines of the gospel, Acts 19:9. By some he is thought to have been a Greek sophist, a teacher of rhetoric or philosophy, converted to Christianity; while others suppose him to have been a Jewish doctor or rabbi, who had a public school.

TYRE, or TY'RUS, *a rock*, the celebrated emporium of Phœnicia, the seat of immense wealth and power, situated on the coast of the Mediterranean, within the limits of the tribe of Asher, as assigned by Joshua, Josh. 19:29, though never reduced to subjection. Tyre was a "daughter of Zidon," but rapidly gained an ascendency over this and all the other cities of Phœnicia, which it retained with few exceptions to the last. It is mentioned by neither Moses nor Homer; but from the time of David onward, reference is frequently made to it in the books of the Old Testament. There was a close alliance between David and Hiram king of Tyre, which was afterwards continued in the reign of Solomon; and it was from the assistance afforded by the Tyrians, both in artificers and materials, that the house of David, and afterwards the temple, were principally built, 2 Sam. 5:11; 1 Kin. 5; 1 Chr. 14; 2 Chr. 2:3; 9:10. The marriage of Ahab king of Israel with Jezebel, a royal princess of Phœnicia, brought great guilt and endless misfortunes on the ten tribes; for the Tyrians were gross idolaters, worshippers of Baal and Ashtoreth, and addicted to all the vices of heathenism. Secular history informs us that Tyre possessed the empire of the seas, and drew wealth and power from numerous colonies on the shores of the Mediterranean and Atlantic. The inhabitants of Tyre are represented in the Old Testament as filled with pride and luxury, and all the sins attendant on prosperity and immense wealth; judgments are denounced against them in consequence of their idolatry and wickedness; and the destruction of their city by Nebuchadnezzar is foretold, which is also described as accomplished, Isa. 23:13; Ezek. 26:7; 27; 28:1-19; 29:18. After this destruction, as it would seem, the great body of the inhabitants withdrew to "insular Tyre," on an island opposite the former city, about thirty stadia from the main land. This had been a sort of port or suburb of the main city, but was soon enlarged into a new Tyre, and became opulent and powerful; it was fortified with such strength, and possessed resources so abundant, as to be able to withstand the utmost efforts of Alexander the Great for the space of seven months. It was at length taken by him in 332 B. C., having been first united to the mainland by an immense causeway, made of the ruins of the old city, the site of which was thus laid bare, in remarkable fulfilment of prophecy: "And they shall lay thy stones and thy timber and thy dust in the midst of the water;" "and thou shalt be no more; though thou be sought for, yet shalt thou never be found again," Ezek. 26:12, 21. The ships of Tyre returned from long voyages to find it not only taken but "devoured with fire," Isa. 23:1, 14; Zech. 9:4. After many subsequent reverses of fortune, and various changes of masters, Tyre at last fell under the dominion of the Romans, and continued to enjoy a degree of commercial prosperity, though the deterioration of its harbor, and the rise of Alexandria and other maritime cities, have made it decline more and more. Our Saviour once journeyed into the region of Tyre and Sidon, Matt. 15:21; and a Christian church was here established before A. D. 58, Acts 21:3-7. Compare Matt. 11:21, 22. The church prospered for several centuries, and councils were held here; and during this period Tyre was still a strong fortress, as it was also in the age of the crusaders, by whom it was only taken twenty-five years after they had gained Jerusalem. Since its reconquest by the Turks, it has been in a ruinous condition, and often almost without inhabitants. At present it is a poor town, called Sur, slightly defended by its walls, and having a population of less than three thousand. It occupies the east side of what was formerly the island, one mile long and half a mile from the shore, thus enclosing two so-called harbors separated by Alexander's causeway, which is now a broad isthmus. The only real harbor is on the north; but even this is too shallow to admit any but the smallest class of vessels. It is filled and the north coast of the island lined with stone columns, whose size and countless number evince the former magnificence of this famous city. But its old glory is gone for ever, and a few fishermen spread their nets amid its ruins, in the place of the merchant princes of old.

U.

U'LAI, or EULÆ'US, a river which ran by the city Shushan, in Persia, on the bank of which Daniel had a famous vision, Dan. 8:2, 16. It was the Choaspes of the Greeks, and is now called the Kerkhah; but appears to have had in ancient times a second channel, still traceable, nine hundred feet wide and twenty feet deep, and flowing along the east side of Shushan. The two channels emptied their waters through the river now called the Karun into the Shat-el-Arab, the united stream of the Euphrates and Tigris, twenty miles below their junction at Korna.

UN'BELIEF of the testimony of God makes him a liar, and is a sin of the greatest enormity. It is the work of a depraved and guilty heart; for no one without this bias could reject the abundant witness God furnishes of the truth of his word, Psa. 14:1. Especially is unbelief towards an offered Saviour an unspeakable crime, justly sealing the condemnation of him who thus refuses to be saved, John 5:18; 1 John 5:10.

UNCLEAN'. See CLEAN.

UNC'TION, *anointing*, 1 John 2:20, 27, the special communication of the influence of the Holy Spirit by Christ to believers, leading them into all truth and holiness.

UNDERGIRD', passing a cable several times under and around a ship and tightening it on deck, to prevent the working and parting of the timbers and planks in a gale, Acts 27:17. The process is called frapping, and has been resorted to in various instances in modern times.

U'NICORN, *one-horned*, corresponding to the word Monoceros, by which the original Hebrew REEM is translated by the Seventy. The Hebrew word means *erect*, and has no reference to the number of horns. Most interpreters now understand it of the wild buffalo of the Eastern continents, the Bos Bubalus of Linnæus, resembling the American buffalo, but having larger horns and no dewlap. This animal has the appearance of uncommon strength. The bulk of his body, and his prodigious muscular limbs, denote his force at the first view, Num. 23:22. His aspect is ferocious and malignant, and at the same time stupid. His head is of a ponderous size; his eyes diminutive; and what serves to render his visage still more savage, are the tufts of frizzled hair which hang down from his cheeks and the lower part of his mouth, Job 39:9-12; Psa. 22:21.

Wild buffaloes occur in many parts of Africa and India, where they live in great troops in the forests, and are regarded as excessively fierce and dangerous animals. The hunters never venture in any numbers to oppose these ferocious animals face to face; but conceal themselves in the thickets or in the branches of the trees, whence they attack the buffaloes as they pass along.

In Egypt, as also in Southern Europe, the buffalo has been partially domesticated in comparatively modern times. Travellers also find it in parts of Syria, Persia, and India. It is less docile than the ox, retaining a remnant of ferocity and untractability, together with a wild and lowering aspect. It is commonly driven and guided by means of a ring in the nose. To the ancient Hebrews, however, it seems to have been known only in its wild state, savage, ferocious, and often immensely large.

UPHAR'SIN, *and they are dividing*, a Chaldee word, an active plural form with the conjunction prefixed: while PERES or PHARES, from the same root, is a passive participle, and means *divided*, Dan. 5:25, 28.

U'PHAZ, a region producing fine gold, Jer. 10:9; Dan. 10:5. In Hebrew it differs from Ophir by only one letter; and it is thought to denote the same region.

UR, the country of Terah, and the birthplace of Abraham, Gen. 11:28, 31; 15:7. It is usually called "Ur of the Chaldees," Neh. 9:7; Acts 7:4; and is located, with strong probability, in the north-west part of Mesopotamia. The city of Orfah, to which the Jews make pilgrimages as the birthplace of Abraham, is a flourishing town of 30,000 inhabitants, seventy-eight miles south-west of Diarbekir. Some, however, place Ur in Lower Chaldea, at extensive ruins now called Warka, in latitude 31° 19' N., longitude 45° 40' E.

UR'BAN, a Roman disciple, Paul's companion in Christian labors, Rom. 16:9.

URI'AH, a Hittite in David's army, renowned for his valor. To save Bathsheba Uriah's wife from death for adultery, and secure her for himself, David caused Uriah to be exposed to death, 2 Sam. 11; 12:9; 23:39; 1 Kin. 15:5.

URI'JAH, I., a high-priest in the time of king Ahaz. He is called a faithful witness by Isaiah, 8:2; but erred in constructing and using at the king's request an altar unlike that prescribed in the law, Ex. 27:1-8; 38:1-7; 2 Kin. 16:9-12.

II. A faithful prophet, from Kirjath-jearim in Judah, in the time of Jehoiakim. He confirmed the predictions of Jeremiah against Judah; and having fled to Egypt for refuge from the enraged king, and been sent back by Pharaoh-necho on demand, he was wickedly slain and dishonorably buried, Jer. 26:20-23. Compare 2 Kin. 24:4.

U'RIM AND THUM'MIM, *lights and perfections*, or light and truth; a divinely appointed means of "inquiring of the Lord," its name being expressive perhaps of the truth of his revelations. It would appear, though not certainly, to have been made known to the Jews at some time prior to its first mention in Scripture, Ex. 28:30. It had some connection with the high-priest's breastplate, Lev. 8:8, and perhaps is to be understood as present when the ephod is mentioned, being worn on the outside of it, Num. 27:21; 1 Sam. 23:9, 11; 2 Sam. 2:1. It is spoken of in the following additional passages, Deut. 33:8; Josh. 7:6, 15; 1 Sam. 28:6; and last of all in Ezra 2:63; Neh. 7:65. Some think it was the precious stones on the sacred breastplate, which made known the divine will by casting an extraordinary lustre. Compare Ex. 39:8-14; Lev. 8:8. Others assert that they were the words Manifestation and Truth, written upon two precious stones, or upon a plate of gold. Various in fact are the conjectures upon this subject, and Moses has nowhere spoken of the Urim and Thummim in such terms as to remove the obscurity. When this oracle was to be used in inquiring of the Lord, if at Jerusalem, the high-priest put on his robes, and going into the Holy Place, stood before the curtain that separated the Holy Place from the Most Holy Place; then, turning his face directly towards the ark and the mercy-seat, upon which the divine presence rested, he proposed the subject respecting which he desired "light and truth." See BREASTPLATE.

US'URY, as employed in our version of the Bible, means only interest. When our translation was made, the word usury had not assumed the bad sense which it now has. The Jews might require interest of foreigners, Deut. 23:19, 20, but were forbidden to receive it from each other, Ex. 22:25, Psa. 15:5; being instructed to lend money, etc., in a spirit of brotherly kindness, "hoping for nothing again," Deut. 15:7-11; Luke 6:33-35. The exacting of usury is often rebuked, Neh. 5:7, 10; Prov. 28:8; Ezek. 22:12-14. The Mosaic code was adapted to a non-commercial people, but its principles of equity and charity are of perpetual and universal obligation.

UZ, the land in which Job dwelt, Job 1:1; Jer. 25:20; Lam. 4:21. The Seventy call it Ausitis. It appears to have been a region in Arabia Deserta, between Palestine, Idumæa, and the Euphrates, and most probably not far from the borders of Idumæa. It is uncertain whether its inhabitants were descendants of Uz the son of Aram, Huz the son of Nahor, or Uz the Horite, Gen. 10 : 23 ; 22 : 21 ; 36:28. They appear to have had much knowledge of the true God and the principles of virtue and religion.

UZAL, a son of Joktan, located in Arabia Felix, Gen. 10:27.

UZ'ZAH, a son of Abinadab, who fell dead while conducting the ark from Kirjath-jearim towards Jerusalem, 2 Sam. 6; 1 Chr. 13. In his person God chastised the prevalent irreverence, which was intimated in the rude jolting along of the ark by oxen, exposed both to sight and to touch, while the law required it to be carefully covered by the priests, and then borne by staves on the shoulders of the Levites, who were not to look upon or touch the ark itself on pain of death, Ex. 25:14; Num. 4 : 5, 15, 19, 20. Perhaps Uzzah was not even a Levite. Compare 1 Chr. 15:2, 13.

UZZI'AH, or AZARIAH, king of Judah. See AZARIAH.

V.

VAL'LEY. With respect to the general features of the Holy Land, see CANAAN; and for descriptions of some of its numerous valleys, see JERUSALEM, JEZREEL, JORDAN, REPHAIM, SHECHEM, and SODOM. "The valley of the shadow of death," is an expression denoting an extremely perilous and cheerless condition of the soul, Psa. 23 : 4, and may have been suggested by the psalmist's experience with his flock in some of the deep, narrow, and dark ravines of Syria. Thus the entrance to Petra is by a long winding defile, between rugged precipices in some spots not more than twelve or fourteen feet apart and two or three hundred feet high, and almost excluding the light of day. See view in SELA. A similar pass south of mount Carmel is now known as the "Valley of Deathshade."

VAN'ITY does not usually denote, in Scripture, self-conceit or personal pride, 2 Pet. 2 : 18, but sometimes emptiness and fruitlessness, Job 7 : 3; Psa. 144 : 4; Eccl. 1. It often denotes wickedness, particularly falsehood. Deut. 32:21; Psa. 4:2; 24:4; 119:37, and sometimes idols and idol-worship, 2 Kin. 17 : 15; Jer. 2:5; 18:15; Jonah 2:8. Compare Paul's expression, "they turned the truth of God into a lie," Rom. 1:25. "In vain," in the second commandment, Ex. 20 : 7, is unnecessarily and irreverently. "Vain men," 2 Sam. 6 : 20; 2 Chr. 13 : 7, are dissolute and worthless fellows.

VASH'TI, the queen of Persia, divorced by Ahasuerus or Xerxes her husband for refusing to appear unveiled before his revelling company, Esth. 1.

VEIL, an indispensable part of the outdoor dress of Eastern ladies, who live secluded from the sight of all men except their own husbands and their nearest relatives. If an Egyptian lady is surprised uncovered, she quickly draws her veil over her face, with some exclamation like, "O my misfortune." To lift or remove one's veil was to insult and degrade her, Gen. 24:65; Song 5:7; 1 Cor. 11:5, 10. The custom of wearing veils, however, has not been prevalent at all times. Sarah the wife of Abraham, and Rebekah and her companions at the well do not appear to have worn them, Gen. 12:14, 15; 21:16. Compare also Gen. 38 : 14, 15; Prov. 7 : 13. See ABIMELECH.

Veils were of different kinds. Those now worn in Syria and Egypt may be divided into two classes, the one large and sometimes thick, the other small and of lighter materials. The usual indoor veil is of thin muslin, attached to the headdress, and falling over the back, sometimes to the feet. A similar veil is added to the front of the headdress on going abroad, partially covering the face and hanging low. The other veil, to be worn in the street, is a large mantle or sheet, of black silk, linen, or some coarse material, so ample as to envelope the whole person and dress, leaving but one of the eyes exposed, Song 4 : 9. Such was the veil worn by Ruth, 3:15, translated "mantle" in Isa. 3:22. Many women wear no other veil than this. The Greek word translated "power" in 1 Cor. 11 : 10, probably means a veil, as a token of her husband's rightful authority and her own subordination. This was to be worn in their Christian assemblies "because of the angels;" that is, because of the presence either of true angels, or of the officers of the church, who being unaccustomed to see the unveiled faces of women, might be distracted by them in the discharge of their public duties.

For the "veil of the temple," see TABERNACLE and TEMPLE.

VEN'GEANCE, in Deut. 32 : 35, Rom. 12:19, Heb. 10 : 30, Jude 7, means retributive justice—a prerogative of God, with which those interfere who seek to avenge themselves. So also in Acts 28 : 4; though many suppose that the islanders meant the goddess of justice, Dike, whom the Greeks and Romans regarded as a daughter of Jupiter, and feared as an independent, just, and unappeasable deity.

VERMIL'ION, a brilliant red color, resembling scarlet, Jer. 22 : 14; Ezek. 23:14. The vermilion now used is a sulphuret of mercury.

VETCH'ES. See FITCHES.

VI'ALS. See CENSER.

VINE. Of this valuable and familiar plant there are several varieties, the natural products of warm climates, where also it has been cultivated from the earliest times. Hence the early and frequent mention of its products in Scripture, Gen. 9 : 20; 14 : 18; 19 : 22; Job 1 : 18. The grape-vine grew plentifully in Palestine. Deut. 8 : 8, and was particularly excellent in some of the districts. The Scriptures celebrate the vines of Sibmah and Eshcol; and profane authors mention the excellent wines of Gaza, Sarepta, Lebanon, Sharon, Ascalon, and Tyre. See SOREK. The grapes of Egypt, Gen. 40 : 11, being small, we may easily conceive of the surprise which was occasioned to the Israelites by witnessing the bunch of grapes brought by the spies to the camp, from the valley of Eshcol, Num. 13 : 23. The account of Moses, however, is confirmed by the testimony of several travellers; and even in England a bunch of Syrian grapes has been produced which weighed nineteen pounds, was twenty-three inches in length, and nineteen and a half in its greatest diameter. At the present day, although the Mohammedan religion does not favor the cultivation of the vine, there is no want of vineyards in Palestine. Besides the large quantities of grapes and raisins which are daily sent to the markets of Jerusalem and other neighboring places, Hebron alone, in the first half of the eighteenth century, annually sent three hundred camel loads, or nearly three hundred thousand pounds weight of grape juice, or honey of raisins, to Egypt.

In the East, grapes enter very largely into the provisions at an entertainment, and in various forms contribute largely to the sustenance of the people. See GRAPES. To show the abundance of vines which should fall to the lot of

Judah in the partition of the promised land, Jacob, in his prophetic benediction, says of this tribe, he shall be found

> Binding his colt to the vine,
> And to the choice vine the foal of his ass;
> Washing his garments in wine,
> His clothes in the blood of the grape.
> Gen. 49:11.

In many places the vines spread over the ground and rocks unsupported. Often, however, they are trained upon trellis-work, over walls, trees, arbors, the porches and walls of houses, and at times within the house on the sides of the central court. Thus growing, the vine became a beautiful emblem of domestic love, peace, and plenty, Psa. 128:3; Mic. 4:4.

The law enjoined that he who planted a vine should not eat of the produce of it before the fifth year, Lev. 19:23-25. Nor did they gather their grapes on the sabbatical year; the fruit was then left for the poor, the orphan, and the stranger, Ex. 23:11; Lev. 25:4, 5, 11. See also Lev. 19:10; Deut. 24:21. At any time a traveller was permitted to gather and eat grapes in a vineyard, as he passed along, but was not permitted to carry any away, Deut. 23:24. Another generous provision of the Mosaic code exempted from liability to serve in war a man who, after four years of labor and of patience, was about to gather the first returns from his vineyard, Deut. 20:6.

Josephus describes a magnificent and costly vine of pure gold, with precious stones for grapes, which adorned the lofty eastern gate of the Holy Place. It was perhaps in view of this that our Saviour said, "I am the true Vine;" and illustrated the precious truth of his oneness with his people, John 15:1-8.

In the expression, "The vine of Sodom," Deut. 32:32, there does not seem to be an allusion to any then existing degenerate species of vine. The writer means rather to say that their vine, that is figuratively their corrupt character, instead of yielding good grapes, bears only poisonous fruit, like that for which the shores of the Dead sea have always been famed—such as "the apples of Sodom," for example, said to be beautiful without, but nothing but shreds or ashes within.

For the "wild grapes" in Isa. 5:2, 4, see under GRAPES.

The Jews planted their VINEYARDS most commonly on the side of a hill or mountain, Jer. 31:5, (see MOUNTAIN,) the stones being gathered out, and the space hedged round with thorns, or walled, Isa. 5:1-6; Psa. 80; Matt. 21:33. Vineyards were sometimes rented for a share of their produce, Matt. 21:33, 34; and from other passages we may perhaps infer that a good vineyard consisted of a thousand vines, and produced a rent of a thousand silverlings, or shekels of silver, Isa. 7:23, and that it required two hundred more to pay the dressers, Song 8:11, 12. In these vineyards the keepers and vine-dressers labored, digging, planting, propping, and pruning or purging the vines, John 15:2, gathering the grapes, and making wine. They formed a distinct class among cultivators of the ground, and their task was sometimes laborious and regarded as menial, 2 Kin. 25:12; 2 Chr. 26:10; Song 1:6; Isa. 61:5. Scripture alludes to the fragrance of the "vines with the tender grapes," Song 2:13, and draws from the vineyard many illustrations and parables, Judg. 9:12; Matt. 20:1; 21:28. The vineyard of Naboth, 1 Kin. 21, has become a perpetual emblem of whatever is violently taken from the poor by the rich or the powerful. The deserted hut or tower, in which a watchman kept guard during the season of ripe grapes, Psa. 80:12, 13, Song 2:15, becomes, when all are gathered, an apt image of desolation, Isa. 1:8. A beautiful allegory in Psalm 80 represents the church as a vineyard, planted, defended, cultivated, and watered by God.

The VINTAGE followed the wheat harvest and the threshing, Lev. 26:5; Amos 9:13. The "first ripe grapes" were gathered in June, or later on elevated ground, Num. 13:20; and grapes continued to be gathered for four months afterwards. The general vintage, however, was in September, when the clusters of grapes were gathered with a sickle, and put into baskets, Jer. 6:9, carried and thrown into the wine-vat or wine-press, where they were probably first trodden by men, and then pressed, Rev. 14:18-20. It was a laborious task, lightened with songs, jests, and shouts of mirth, Jer. 25:30; 48:33. It is mentioned as a mark of the great work and power of the Messiah, that he had trodden the figurative wine-press alone, and of the people there was none with him, Isa. 63:1-3; Rev.

19:15. The vintage was a season of great mirth, Isa. 16:9, 10, and often of excesses and idolatry, Judg. 9:27; while the mourning and languishing of the vine was a symbol of general distress, Isa. 24:7; Hab. 3:17; Mal. 3:11. Of the juice of the squeezed grapes were formed wine and vinegar. See PRESS.

Grapes were also dried into raisins. A part of Abigail's present to David was one hundred clusters of raisins, 1 Sam. 25:18; and when Ziba met David, his present contained the same quantity, 2 Sam. 16:1; 1 Sam. 30:12; 1 Chron. 12:40. Respecting other uses of the fruits of the vine, see GRAPES, HONEY, VINEGAR, and WINE.

VINEGAR, *poor or sour wine*, the produce of the second or acetous fermentation of vinous liquors. The term sometimes designates a thin, sour wine, much used by laborers and by the Roman soldiers, Num. 6:3; Ruth 2:14; 2Chr. 2:10; John 19:29. See GALL. In other places it denotes the common sharp vinegar, which furnished the wise man with two significant illustrations, Prov. 10:26; 25:20.

VINEYARD. See VINE.

VIOL, Isa. 5:12, Amos 6:5, a stringed instrument of music, resembling the psaltery. See MUSIC.

VIPER, a genus of serpents noted for the virulence of their poison, which is said to be one of the most dangerous in the animal kingdom. Hence the viper is a symbol of whatever is most evil and destructive, Job 20:16; Isa. 30:6. As such the term was applied by Christ and by John to certain classes of the Jews, Matt. 3:7; 12:34; 23:33; Luke 3:7. Paul's escape from the bite of a viper in Malta led the people to believe that he was a god in human form, Acts 28:3. A species of viper in Northern Africa, though little more than a foot long, is called the most formidable serpent there; and Hasselquist speaks of a viper in Cyprus, whose bite produces a universal gangrene, and occasions death within a few hours. See SERPENTS.

VISION, a supernatural presentation of certain scenery or circumstances to the mind of a person either while awake or asleep, Isa. 6; Ezek. 1; Dan. 8; Acts 26:13. See DREAM.

VOW, a promise made to God of doing some good thing or abstaining from some lawful enjoyment, under the influence of gratitude for divine goodness, of imminent danger, the apprehension of future evils, or the desire of future blessings. To fulfil a vow binding one to sin, was to add sin to sin; but no considerations of inconvenience or loss could absolve one from a vow, Psa. 15:4; Mal. 1:14. Jacob, going into Mesopotamia, vowed the tenth of his estate, and promised to offer it at Beth-el, to the honor of God, Gen. 28:20-22. Moses enacted several laws for the regulation and execution of vows. "If thou shalt forbear to vow, it shall be no sin in thee; that which is gone out of thy lips thou shalt keep and perform," Deut. 23:21, 23; Eccl. 5:4, 5. The vows of minors, etc., were not binding without the consent of the head of the family, Num. 30. A man might devote himself or his children to the Lord, Num. 6:2. Jephthah devoted his daughter, Judg. 11:30-40; and Samuel was vowed and consecrated to the service of the Lord, 1 Sam. 1:11, 27, 28. If men or women vowed themselves to the Lord, they were obliged to adhere strictly to his service, according to the conditions of the vow; but in some cases they might be redeemed, Lev. 27. These self-imposed services were more in keeping with the ancient dispensation, in which outward sacrifices and observances had so large a share, than with enlightened Christianity. See CORBAN, and NAZARITES.

VULGATE is the name of the Latin version of the Scriptures used by the church of Rome. The Old Testament was a very close translation of the Greek Septuagint, not of the Hebrew. It was made at a very early period by an unknown author. A part of this version was afterwards revised by Jerome, and some of the books retranslated from the Hebrew.

VUL'TURE, a large bird of prey, belonging to the genus *hawks*, and including a great many species. It is pronounced unclean by Moses, Lev. 11:14; Deut. 14:13. See BIRDS. The vulture has a naked or downy head, a bare neck and long wings, and is disgusting to every sense, especially to the smell. It is a carrion bird, though not exclusively, and has extraordinary powers of vision. Scarcely can an exhausted camel fall on its route and die, before numbers of these filthy scavengers show themselves in the distance, hastening to the spot, Job 28:7.

W.

WA'FER, a thin cake made of fine flour, Exod. 16:31, and used in various offerings, anointed with sweet oil, Exod. 29:2, 23; Lev. 2:4; 7:12; Num. 6:15.

WA'GES. The law and the gospel both require the full and prompt payment of a just equivalent for all services rendered according to agreement, Lev. 19:13; Jer. 22:13; Jas. 5:4. Eternal death is the wages or just recompense of sin; while eternal life is not a recompense earned by obedience, but a sovereign gift of God, Rom. 6:22, 23.

WAG'ONS were sent by Joseph to convey his father's family into Egypt. The same vehicle, translated "cart" in 1 Sam. 6:7, was employed to transport some of the sacred utensils, Num. 7:3, 6. and in one instance the ark itself. In these latter cases it was drawn by oxen. It was probably of simple structure, with two solid wheels. Such carts are sometimes used in Syria in removing agricultural produce, Amos 2:13; but vehicles of any kind are little used, and travellers and merchandise are borne on the backs of camels, horses, and mules. See CART.

WALK is often figuratively used to denote a man's mode of life, or his spiritual character, course, and relations, Ezek. 11:20. He may walk as a carnal, or as a spiritual man, Rom. 8:1; with God, or in ignorance and sin, Gen. 5:24; 1 John 1:6, 7; in the fire of affliction, Isa. 43:2, or in the light, purity, and joy of Christ's favor here and in heaven, Psa. 89:15; Rev. 3:4.

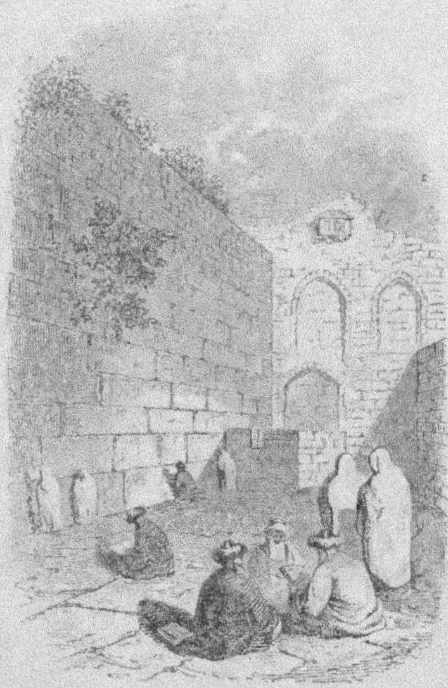

WALLS. The walls of dwellings in the East were of very different materials, from mere clay, or clay and pebbles, to durable hewn stone. See the latter part of the article HOUSE. As to city walls, see BABYLON, CITY, and JERU-

SALEM. The accompanying cut shows a portion of the western wall of the sacred area, Haram-es-Sherîf, at Jerusalem. The huge stones in its lower part are believed by the Jews, and with good reason, to have formed a part of the substructions of their ancient temple, and to be near the site of the Holy of Holies. Hence they assemble here every Friday, and more or less on other days, to weep and wail with every token of the sorest grief, and to pray for the coming of the Messiah. In former years they had to pay a large price for this melancholy privilege. A little beyond this spot, towards the south, is the fragment of an immense arch of forty-one feet span, one of five or six which supported a lofty causeway, from mount Zion to the temple area at its southern portico, 1 Kin. 10:5; 1 Chr. 26:16, 18. Some of the stones in this part of the wall are twenty to twenty-five feet long.

WANDERINGS OF THE ISRAELITES. See EXODUS. The following tabular view of their various encampments, so far as they are recorded in Exodus, Numbers, and Deuteronomy, is from Dr. Robinson's Biblical Researches. The "great and terrible wilderness" between mount Sinai and Palestine is still known by the Arabs as Et-Tyh, or *the Wanderings*.

I. FROM EGYPT TO SINAI.

EXODUS XII.–XIX.	NUMBERS XXXIII.
From Rameses, 12:37.	From Rameses, verse 3.
1. Succoth, 12:37.	Succoth, ver. 5.
2. Etham, 13:20.	Etham, ver. 6.
3. Pi-hahiroth, 14:2.	Pi-hahiroth, ver. 7.
4. Passage through the Red sea, 14:22; and three days' march into the desert of Shur, 15:22.	Passage through the Red sea, and three days' march in the desert of Etham, ver. 8.
5. Marah, 15:23.	Marah, ver. 8.
6. Elim, 15:27.	Elim, ver. 9.
7.	By the Red sea, ver. 10.
8. Desert of Sin, 16:1.	Desert of Sin, ver. 11.
9.	Dophka, ver. 12.
10.	Alush, ver. 13.
11. Rephidim, 17:1.	Rephidim, ver. 14.
12. Desert of Sinai, 19:1.	Desert of Sinai, ver. 15.

II. FROM SINAI TO KADESH THE SECOND TIME

NUMBERS X.–XX.	NUMBERS XXXIII.
From the desert of Sinai, 10:12	From the desert of Sinai, ver. 16.
13. Taberah, 11:3; Deut. 9:22.	
14. Kibroth-hattaavah, 11:34.	Kibroth-hattaavah, ver. 16.
15. Hazeroth, 11:35.	Hazeroth, ver. 17.
16. Kadesh, in the desert of Paran, 12:16; 13:26; Deut. 1:2, 19. Hence they turn back and wander for thirty-eight years, Num. 14:25-36.	
17.	Rithma, ver. 18.
18.	Rimmon-parez, ver. 19.
19.	Libnah, ver. 20.
20.	Rissah, ver. 21.
21.	Kehelathah, ver. 22.
22.	Mount Shapher, ver. 23.
23.	Haradah, ver. 24.
24.	Makheloth, ver. 25.
25.	Tahath, ver. 26.
26.	Tarah, ver. 27.
27.	Mithcah, ver. 28.
28.	Hashmonah, ver. 29.
29.	Moseroth, ver. 30.
30.	Bene-jaakan, ver. 31.
31.	Hor-hagidgad, ver. 32.
32.	Jotbathah, ver. 33.
33.	Ebronah, ver. 34.
34.	Ezion-gaber, ver. 35.
35. Return to Kadesh, Num. 20:1.	Kadesh, ver. 36.

III. FROM KADESH TO THE JORDAN.

NUMBERS XX., XXI; DEUT. I., II., X.	NUMBERS XXXIII.
From Kadesh, Num. 20:22.	From Kadesh, ver. 37.
36. Beeroth Beene jaakan, Deut. 10:6.	
37. Mount Hor, Num. 20:22; or Mosera, Deut. 10:6; where Aaron died.	Mount Hor, ver. 37.
38. Gudgodah, Deut. 10:7.	
39. Jotbath, Deut. 10:7.	
40. Way of the Red sea, Num. 21:4; by Elath and Ezion-gaber, Deut. 2:8.	
41.	Zalmonah, ver. 41.
42.	Punon, ver. 42.
43. Oboth, Num. 21:10.	Oboth, ver. 43.
44. Ije-abarim, Num. 21:11.	Ije-abarim, or Iim, ver. 44, 45.
45. The brook Zered, Num. 21:12; Deut. 2:13, 14.	
46. The brook Arnon, Num. 21:13; Deut. 2:24.	
47.	Dibon-gad, ver. 45; now Dhibân.
48.	Almon-diblathaim, ver. 46.
49. Beer (well) in the desert, Num. 21:16, 18.	
50. Mattanah, 21:18.	
51. Nahaliel, 21:19.	
52. Bamoth, 21:19.	
53. Pisgah, put for the range of Abarim, of which Pisgah was part, 21:20.	Mountains of Abarim, near to Nebo, ver. 47.
54. By the way of Bashan to the plains of Moab by Jordan, near Jericho, Num. 21:33; 22:1.	Plains of Moab by Jordan, near Jericho, ver. 48.

SIEGE OF A CITY: FROM THE NIMROUD PALACE, NINEVEH.

WAR, one of the evil fruits of the fall, and an appalling manifestation of the depravity of mankind, Gen. 6:11-13; Isa. 9:5; Jas. 4:1, 2, often rendered apparently inevitable by the assaults of enemies, or commanded by God for their punishment. See AMALEKITES and CANAAN. By this scourge, subsequently to the conquest of Canaan, God chastised both his own rebellious people and the corrupt and oppressive idolaters around them. In many cases, moreover, the issue was distinctly made between the true God and idols; as with the Philistines, 1 Sam. 17:43-47; the Syrians, 1 Kin. 20:23-30; the Assyrians, 2 Kin. 19:10-19, 35; and the Ammonites, 2 Chr. 20:1-30. Hence God often raised up champions for his people, gave them counsel in war by Urim and by prophets, and miraculously aided them in battle.

Before the period of the kings, there seems to have been scarcely any regular army among the Jews; but all who were able to bear arms were liable to be summoned to the field, 1 Sam. 11:7. The vast armies of the kings of Judah and Israel usually fought on foot, armed with spears, swords, and shields; having large bodies of archers and slingers, and comparatively few chariots and horsemen. See ARMS. The forces were arranged in suitable divisions, with officers of tens, hundreds, thousands, etc., Judg. 20:10; 1 Chr. 13:1; 2 Chr. 25:5. The Jews were fully equal to the nations around them in bravery and the arts of war; but were restrained from wars of conquest, and when invaders had been repelled the people dispersed to their homes. A campaign usually commenced in spring, and was terminated before winter, 2 Sam. 11:1; 1 Kin. 20:22. As the Jewish host approached a hostile army, the priests cheered them by addresses, Deut. 20:2; 1 Sam. 7:9, 13, and by inspiring songs, 2 Chr. 20:21. The sacred trumpets gave the signal for battle, Num. 10:9, 10; 2 Chr. 13:12-15; the archers and slingers advanced first, but at length made way for the charge of the heavy-armed spearmen, etc., who sought to terrify the enemy, ere they reached them, by their aspect and war-cries, Judg. 7:18-20; 1 Sam. 17:52; Job 39:25; Isa. 17:12, 13. The combatants were soon engaged hand to hand; the battle became a series of duels; and the victory was gained by the obstinate bravery, the skill, strength, and swiftness of individual warriors, 1 Chr. 12:8; Psa. 18:32-37. See Paul's exhortations to Christian firmness, under the assaults of spiritual foes, 1 Cor. 16:13;

THE CATAPULT, A MACHINE FOR THROWING HEAVY DARTS.

Eph. 6:11-14; 1 Thess. 3:8. The battles of the ancients were exceedingly sanguinary, 2 Chr. 28:6; few were spared except those reserved to grace the triumph or be sold as slaves. A victorious army of Jews on returning was welcomed by the whole population with every demonstration of joy, 1 Sam. 18:6, 7. The spoils were divided after reserving an oblation for the Lord, Num. 31:50; Judg. 5:30; trophies were suspended in public places; eulogies were pronounced in honor of the most distinguished warriors, and lamentations over the dead.

In besieging a walled city, numerous towers were usually erected around it for throwing missiles; catapults were prepared for hurling large darts and stones. Large towers were also constructed and mounds near to the city walls, and raised if possible to an equal or greater height, that by casting a movable bridge across access to the city might be gained. The battering-ram was also employed to effect a breach in the wall; and the crow, a long spar with iron claws

at one end and ropes at the other, to pull down stones or men from the top of the wall. These and similar modes of assault the besieged resisted by throwing down darts, stones, heavy rocks, and sometimes boiling oil; by hanging sacks of chaff between the battering-ram and the wall; by strong and sudden sallies, capturing and burning the towers and enginery of the assailants, and quickly retreating into the city, 2 Chr. 26:14, 15. The modern inventions of gunpowder, rifles, bombs, and heavy artillery have changed all this. See BATTERING-RAM.

As the influence of Christianity diffuses itself in the world, war is becoming less excusable and less practicable; and a great advance may be observed from the customs and spirit of ancient barbarism towards the promised universal supremacy of the Prince of peace, Psa. 46:9; Isa. 2:4; Mic. 4:3.

"Wars of the Lord" was probably the name of an uninspired book, long since lost, containing details of the events alluded to in Num. 21:14, 15.

WARD, or GUARD. To put "in ward" was to place under guard, or in confinement, Gen. 40:3; Lev. 24:12. Ward also seems to mean a guard-room, Neh. 12:25, Isa. 21:8, and the guards themselves, Acts 12:10, or any small band, 1 Chr. 25:8; 26:16.

WASH'ING. Various ceremonial washings were enjoined in the Mosaic law, both upon priests, Exod. 30:19-21, and upon others, Lev. 12-15; Heb. 9:10. These were significant of spiritual purification through the Saviour's blood, Tit. 3:5, Rev. 1:5, as well as of that holiness without which none can see God. To these the Jews added other traditional ablutions, Mark 7:2-4; and regarded it as an act of impiety to neglect them, as Christ frequently did, Luke 11:38. The washing of the hands before and after meals, Matt. 15:2, called for by their custom of feeding themselves with their fingers, is still practised in Syria. See cut in BED. Where there is a servant in attendance, he pours water from a pitcher over his master's hands, holding also a broad vessel underneath them, 2 Kin. 3:11; Psa. 60:8. See FOOT and SANDALS. "Washing the hands" was a protestation of innocence, Deut. 21:6; Matt. 27:24; and has given rise to the proverbial saying common among us, "I wash my hands of that."

WATCH, a division of the night. See HOURS.

WATCH'ER, Dan. 4:13, 17, 23, a figurative designation of heavenly beings, apparently angels, as seen by Nebuchadnezzar in his dream.

WATCH'MEN are of as early a date as cities, robbers, and wars, Exod. 14:24; Judg. 7:19. Jerusalem and other cities had regular guards night and day, Song 3:1-3; 5:7, to whose hourly cries Isaiah refers in illustration of the vigilance required by God in his ministers, Isa. 21:8, 11, 12; 62:6. At this day the watchmen of Jerusalem "keep not silence," nor do they "hold their peace day nor night;" especially at night and when danger is apprehended, they are required to call to each other every few minutes, and the cry passes from one to another entirely around the city walls. Those of Sidon also do the same. Watchmen always had a station at the gate of a city and in the adjacent tower, 2 Sam. 18:24-27; 2 Kin. 9:27; also on hill-tops overlooking a large circuit of terraced vineyards, whence they could "see eye to eye," and "lift up the voice" of warning or of cheer, Isa. 52:7, 8; and their responsible office, requiring so much vigilance and fidelity, illustrates that of prophets and ministers, Jer. 6:17; Ezek. 33:1-9; Heb. 13:17.

WA'TER. See CISTERNS, and WELLS. In Isaiah 35:7, the Hebrew word for "parched ground" that shall become a pool of water, is the same with the Arabic term for the mirage, a peculiar optical illusion by which travellers in hot and dry deserts think they see broad lakes and flowing waters; they seem to discern the very ripple of the waves, and the swaying of tall trees on the margin in the cool breeze; green hills and houses and city ramparts rise before the astonished sight, recede as the traveller advances, and at length melt away in the hot haze. Not so the blessings of the gospel; they are no alluring mockery, but real waters of everlasting life, Isa. 55:1; John 4:14; Rev. 22:1. Compare Isa. 29:8; Jer. 15:18.

WA'TER-SPOUTS are well-known phenomena in the Levant, and are supposed to be produced by whirlwinds. A dense, black, funnel-shaped cloud is seen depending from the sky, and sometimes moving rapidly over the sea, from which at times a similar cone ascends to meet the upper one. Where they unite, the column may be three or four feet thick; and when they break, torrents of water descend. The word occurs in Psa. 42:7, where, however, the psalmist probably alludes to cataracts of water.

WAX, to grow or become, Ex. 22:24; Isa. 50:9; Luke 13:19.

WEA'SEL, one of the unclean animals, Lev. 11 : 29. Several varieties of weasels are found in and around Palestine; but in the verse above probably the common mole is intended.

WEAV'ING, an art very early practised by all nations, and exhibited on the ancient monuments of Egypt, Gen. 41 : 42. See FLAX. It is usually performed by women, 2 Kin. 23 : 7; Prov. 31:13, 19. The distaff, the shuttle, and the weaver's beam and pin are mentioned, Judg. 16 : 14; 1 Sam. 17:7; Job 7 : 6; Prov. 31 : 19. The Jews say that the high-priest's tunic was made without a needle, being "woven from the top throughout;" thus also "the High-priest of our profession" was clothed, John 19:23.

WED'DING. See MARRIAGE.

WED'DING-GAR'MENT. See GARMENTS.

WEEKS, or successive periods of seven days each, were known from the earliest times among nations remote from each other in Europe, Asia, and Africa, Gen. 29:27. See SABBATH. The Hebrews had only numeral names for the days of the week, excepting the Sabbath; the names now current among us being borrowed from Saxon mythology. The Jews called Sunday "one of the Sabbath," that is, the first day of the week. Monday was "two of the Sabbath." A prophetic week and a week of years were each seven years; and a week of sabbatical years, or forty-nine years, brought round the year of jubilee. In John 20:26, the disciples are said to have met again after "eight days," that is, evidently after a week, on the eighth day after our Lord's resurrection. See THREE.

For the "Feast of Weeks," see PENTECOST.

WEEP'ING. See FUNERAL.

WEIGHTS. The Hebrews weighed all the gold and silver they used in trade. The shekel, the half shekel, the maneh, the talent, are not only denominations of money, of certain values in gold and silver, but also of certain weights. The weight "of the sanctuary," or weight of the temple, Ex. 30:13, 24; Lev. 5:5; Num. 3 : 50; 7:19; 18 : 16, was perhaps the standard weight, preserved in some apartment of the temple, and not a different weight from the common shekel; for though Moses appointed that all things valued by their price in silver should be rated by the weight of the sanctuary, Lev. 27 : 25, he makes no difference between this shekel of twenty gerahs and the common shekel. Ezekiel, 45 : 12, speaking of the ordinary weights and measures used in traffic among the Jews, says that the shekel weighed twenty gerahs: it was therefore equal to the weight of the sanctuary. See the TABLES OF WEIGHTS AND MEASURES at the end of the volume.

WELLS and SPRINGS. By those living in a temperate climate, where the well or the aqueduct furnishes to every house a supply of water practically inexhaustible, no idea can be formed of the extreme distress caused by thirst, and of the luxury of relieving it by drinking pure water—a luxury which is said to excel all other pleasures of sense. One must reside or travel in a Syrian climate to realize the beauty and force of the allusions of Scripture to "water out of the wells of salvation," "cold water to a thirsty soul," "the fountain of living waters," and many others. The digging of a permanent well or the discovery of a spring was a public benefaction, and its possession was a matter of great importance. Its existence at a given spot decided the nightly resting-place of caravans, the encampment of armies, and the location of towns, 1 Sam. 29 : 1; 2 Sam. 2 : 13. Hence BEER, the Hebrew name for a well or spring, forms a part of many names of places, as Beeroth, Beer-sheba. See also EN. So valuable was a supply of water, that a field containing a spring was a princely dowry, Judg. 1 : 13–15, and a well was a matter of strife and negotiation between different tribes. Thus we read that Abraham, in making a treaty with king Abimelech, "reproved him because of a well of water which Abimelech's servants had violently taken away," and the ownership of the well was sealed to Abraham by a special oath and covenant, Gen. 21 : 25–31. A similar transaction occurred during the life of Isaac, Gen. 26:14–33. In negotiating with the king of Edom for a

THE WELL OR FOUNTAIN AT NAZARETH.

passage through his territory, the Israelites said, "We will go by the highway; and if I and my cattle drink of thy water, then I will pay for it," Num. 20:17–19. Still stronger is the expression in Lam. 5:4: "We have drunk our own water for money;" that is, we bought it of our foreign rulers, though we are the natural proprietors of the wells that furnished it. The custom of demanding pay for water of the traveller is still found in some parts of the East; while in many other towns a place is provided where cold water and sometimes bread are offered gratuitously to the stranger, at the expense of the village, or as an act of charity by the benevolent, Mark 9:41. In case of a hostile invasion, nothing could more effectually harass an advancing army or the besiegers of a city, than to fill with stones the wells on which they relied, 2 Kin. 3:25; 2 Chr. 32:3.

Wells are sometimes found in Palestine furnished with a well-sweep and bucket, or a windlass; and in some cases there were steps leading down to the water, Gen. 24:15, 16; but usually the water is drawn with pitchers and ropes; and the stone curbs of ancient wells bear the marks of long use. They were often covered with a large flat stone, to exclude the flying sand and secure the water to its owners, and also for the security of strangers, who were liable to fall into them unawares—a mischance which very often occurs in modern Syria, and against which the beneficent law of Moses made provision, Ex. 21:33, 34. This stone was removed about sunset, when the females of the vicinity drew their supply of water for domestic use, and the flocks and herds drank from the stone troughs which are still found beside almost every well. At this hour, the well was a favorite place of resort, and presented a scene of life and gayety greatly in contrast with its ordinary loneliness, Gen. 24:11–28; 29:1–10; Ex. 2:16–19; 1 Sam. 9:11. Wells, however, were sometimes infested by robbers, Judg. 5:11; and Dr. Shaw mentions a beautiful spring in Barbary, the Arabic name of which means, "Drink, and away!" a motto which may well be inscribed over even the best springs of earthly delight. See CISTERN.

The cut above given presents a view of "The Fountain of the Virgin" at Nazareth, so called from the strong probability that the mother of our Lord was wont to draw water from it, as the women of Nazareth do at this day. It is a copious spring, just out of the village;

and the path that leads to it is well worn, as by the feet of many generations. All travellers in Palestine mention the throngs of females that resort to it, with their pitchers or goat-skins on the shoulder or head, and loitering to gossip or gaily returning in companies of two or three. Every day witnesses there what might almost be described in the very words of Gen. 24:11: "And he made his camels to kneel down without the city, by a well of water, at the time of the evening, even the time that women go out to draw water. And behold, Rebekah came out, with her pitcher upon her shoulder; and she went down to the well, and filled her pitcher, and came up." It is an uncommon sight to see "a man bearing a pitcher of water," Mark 14:13.

Jacob's well, at the eastern entrance of the charming valley of Shechem, is still in existence, though now little used and often nearly dry. It is covered by a vaulted roof, with a narrow entrance closed by a heavy rock. Around it is a platform, and the remains of a church built over the spot by the empress Helena. Close at hand is mount Gerizim, which the woman of Sychar no doubt glanced at as she said, "Our fathers worshipped in this mountain." On the west is the broad and fertile plain of Mukhna, where the fields were "white already to the harvest." The woman intimated that the well was "deep," and had no steps. Actual measurement shows it to be seventy-five feet deep, and about nine feet in diameter. Dr. Wilson, in 1842, sent down with ropes a Jew named Jacob, to explore the well and recover a Bible dropped into it by Rev. Mr. Bonar three years before. This was found, almost destroyed by lying in water. As the traveller stands by this venerated well and thinks of the long series of men of a hundred nations and generations who have drunk of its waters, thirsted again, and died, he is most forcibly affected by the truth of Christ's words to the Samaritan woman, and made to feel his own perishing need of the water "springing up into everlasting life," John 4.

WHALE, the largest known inhabitant of the sea, Job 7:12, put by our translators for a Hebrew word including all the huge marine monsters, as in Gen. 1:21. In Ezek. 32:2, referring to Egypt and the Nile, it doubtless means the crocodile; as also in Psa. 74:13; Isa. 27:1; 51:9; Ezek. 29:3, where it is translated "dragon." The "great fish" that swallowed Jonah cannot be named with certainty. The Greek word in Matt. 12:40 being also indeterminate. Whales, however, were anciently found in the Mediterranean, and sharks of the largest size.

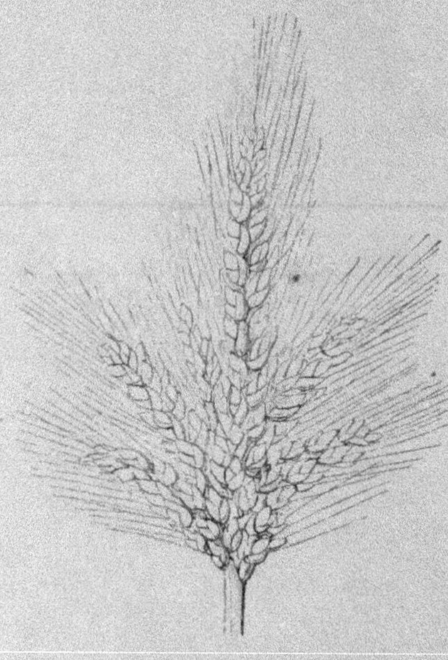

TRITICUM COMPOSITUM.

WHEAT is the principal and most valuable kind of grain for the service of man, and is produced in almost every part of the world, Gen. 30:14; Deut. 8:8; Judg. 6:11; Matt. 13:25; 1 Cor. 15:37. It is often intended where the word corn is used. See CORN. The Egyptian wheat, Triticum Compositum, has six or seven ears on one head; so that it presented its usual appearance in this respect in Pharaoh's dream, Gen. 41:5-7. The "meat-offerings" of the Mosaic service, Lev. 2, were all made of wheaten flour.

WHEEL, Psa. 83:13, translated "rolling thing" in Isa. 17:13. Mr. Thomson, for many years a missionary in Syria, thinks the wild artichoke may here be referred to. This plant sends out numerous stalks or branches of equal length in all directions, forming a globe a foot in diameter. These globes become rigid and light as a feather in autumn, and thousands of them fly rolling and bounding over the plains, the sport of every wind. This "rolling thing" furnishes the modern Arabs with a current proverb and a curse.

WHIRLWINDS were very frequent in the deserts of Arabia, Job 37 : 9 ; 38 : 1 ; Nah. 1:3, and travellers in the East have encountered many. Most of them are not formidable, Isa. 17:13 ; but one now and then occurs, sudden, swift, and awful in its devastating course ; houses and trees are no obstruction in its way, and the traveller is buried alive under the pillar of sand it raises and bears along, like a water-spout at sea, Job 1:19 ; Isa. 21 : 1. The sudden and resistless judgments of God are well compared to whirlwinds, Psa. 58:9 ; Prov. 1:27 ; Isa. 66 : 15. One of the Hebrew words thus translated sometimes denotes only a powerful and tempestuous gust of wind, Jer. 23:19 ; 30:23 ; Zech. 9:14. See WINDS.

WIDOW. A custom was prevalent in patriarchal times, Gen. 38, and was afterwards confirmed by the Mosaic law, Deut. 25 : 5-10, that a widow without children, in order to preserve the family name and inheritance, should marry the brother of her deceased husband ; or, he failing, his nearest kinsman, Ruth 3:12, 13 ; 4:1-11 ; Matt. 22:23-30. The high-priest was forbidden to marry a widow, Lev. 21 : 14. The humanity and justice of true religion are shown in the Bible, as might be expected, by numerous indications that God and the friends of God sympathize with the sorrows, supply the wants, and defend the rights of the widow, Exod. 22 : 22-24 ; Deut. 16 : 11 ; 24:17, 19 ; Psa. 68:5 ; Isa. 1:17 ; 10:2 ; Jer. 22 : 3 ; Matt. 23 : 14. The apostolic church was not negligent in providing for widows, Acts 6 : 1-3 ; 1 Tim. 5 : 16 ; and James makes this duty an essential part of true piety, Jas. 1 : 27. Heathenism, on the contrary, makes those who have been slaves to a husband's caprices during his life, either victims upon the funeral pile at his death, or forlorn and hopeless sufferers under destitution and contempt. The duties of Christian widows are specified in 1 Tim. 5:3-16.

WILDERNESS. See DESERT.

WILLOW, a very common tree, which grows in marshy places, Job 40 : 22, Isa. 44 : 4, with a leaf much like that of the olive. God commanded the Hebrews to take branches of the handsomest trees, particularly of the willows of the brook, and to bear them in their hands before the Lord, as a token of rejoicing, at the feast of Tabernacles, Lev. 23 : 40. The "weeping willow," memorable in connection with the mourning Hebrew captives, Psa. 137 : 2, is a native of Babylonia, and hence is named Salix Babylonica. The "brook of the willows," Isa. 15 : 7, on the southern border of Moab, flows into the south-east extremity of the Dead sea.

WIMPLE, a veil or hood ; but the Hebrew signifies, properly, a broad and large mantle or shawl. See VEIL. Thus, in Ruth 3:15, Boaz gives Ruth six measures of barley, which she carries away in her mantle, rather than veil, as in the English translation. So in Isa. 3:22.

WINDS, Matt. 24 : 31. The winds which most commonly prevail in Palestine are from the western quarter, more usually perhaps from the south-west, Luke 12:54. Not unfrequently a north wind arises, Job 37 : 9, which, as in ancient days, is still the sure harbinger of fair weather ; illustrating the truth of the observation in Prov. 25 : 23, "The north wind driveth away rain." For the tempestuous wind called EUROCLYDON, see that article.

But the wind most frequently mentioned in the Bible is the "east wind," which is represented as blasting and drying up the fruits, Gen. 41 : 6 ; Ezek. 17:10 ; 19 : 12, and also as blowing with great violence, Psa. 48:7 ; Ezek. 27:26 ; Jonah 4:8. It is also the "horrible tempest," literally the glow-wind, of Psa. 11 : 6. This is a sultry and oppressive wind blowing from the south-east, and prevailing only in the hot and dry months of summer. Coming thus from the vast Arabian desert, it seems to increase the heat and drought of the season, and produces universal languor and debility. Rev. Dr. Eli Smith, who experienced its effects during the summer, at Beyrout, describes it as possessing the same qualities and characteristics as the Sirocco, which he had felt at Malta, and which also prevails in Sicily and Italy ; except that the Sirocco, in passing over the sea, acquires great dampness. This wind is called by the Arabs the Simoom, by the Turks the Samiel, and by the Egyptians the Camsin; and has long been regarded as a pestilential wind, suddenly overtaking travellers and caravans in the deserts, and almost instantly destroying them by its poisonous and suffocating breath. But late and judicious travellers find no evidence that this wind is laden with any poisonous influence. It is indeed oppressively hot and dry, rapidly evaporating the water in the ordinary skin bottles, stopping the perspiration of travellers, drying up the palate and the air passages, and producing great restlessness and exhaustion. As it often blows with a terrible roaring and violence, it carries dust and fine sand high up into the air, so that the whole atmosphere is lurid, and seems in a state of combustion, and the sun is shorn of his beams, and looks like a globe of dull smouldering fire. Both men and animals are greatly annoyed by the dust, and seek any practicable shelter or covering. The camels turn their backs, and hide their heads from it in the ground. It is often accompanied by local whirlwinds, which form pillars of sand and dust, rising high above the ground and moving with swiftness over the plain. Such a tempest may have suggested some features in the prophetic descriptions of the day of God's power: "wonders in the heavens and in the earth, blood and fire and pillars of smoke: the sun shall be turned into darkness, and the moon into blood," Joel 2:30, 31; Acts 2:19, 20.

Dr. Thomson describes another variety of hot winds or siroccos, often more overwhelming than those just mentioned. The sky is covered with clouds, and pale lightnings play through the air; but there is no rain, thunder, or wind. The heat, however, is intolerable; every traveller seeks a refuge, the birds hide themselves in the thickest shades, the fowls pant under the walls with open mouths, and no living thing is in motion.

WINE. The vine being natural to the soil of Canaan and its vicinity, wine was much used as a beverage, especially at festivals, Esth. 1:7; 5:6; Dan. 5:1-4; John 2:3. As one of the staple products of the Holy Land, it was employed for drink-offerings in the temple service, Ex. 29:40; Num. 15:4-10; it was included among the "first-fruits," Deut. 18:4, and was used in the celebration of the Passover, and subsequently of the Lord's supper, Matt. 26:27-29. Together with corn and oil it denoted all temporal supplies, Psa. 4:7; Hos. 2:8; Joel 2:19.

The word "wine" in our Bible is the translation of as many as ten different Hebrew words and two Greek words, most of which occur in but a few instances. The two most frequently used, Yayin and its Greek equivalent Oinos, are general terms for all sorts of wine, Neh. 5:18. Without minute details on this subject, we may observe that "wine" in Scripture denotes,

1. The pure juice of the grape, fermented, and therefore more or less intoxicating, but free from drugs of any kind, and not strengthened by distilled liquors.

2. Must, the fresh juice of the grape, unfermented or in process of fermentation. For this the Hebrew employs the word *tîrôsh*, English version, *new wine.* Wine, as a product of agriculture, is commonly mentioned by this name along with corn and oil, Gen. 40:11; Exod. 22:29; Deut. 32:14; Luke 5:37, 38.

3. Honey of wine, made by boiling down must to one-fourth of its bulk. This commonly goes, in the Old Testament, by the name *debhash, honey;* and only the context can enable us to determine whether honey of grapes or of bees is to be understood, Num. 18:12; Prov. 9:2, 5.

4. Spiced wine; made stronger and more inviting to the taste by the admixture of spices and other drugs, Song 8:2.

5. Strong drink, Hebrew *shechar.* This word sometimes denotes pure strong wine, as Num. 28:7; or drugged wine, as Isa. 5:22; but more commonly wine made from dates, honey, etc., and generally made more inebriating by being mingled with drugs.

See also, in connection with this article, FLAGON, MYRRH, and VINEGAR.

The "wine of Helbon" was made in the vicinity of Damascus, and sent from that city to Tyre, Ezek. 27:19. It resembled the "wine of Lebanon," famous for its excellence and fragrance, Hosea 14:7. See HELBON.

Great efforts have been made to distinguish the harmless from the intoxicating wines of Scripture, and to show that inspiration has in all cases approved the former alone, and condemned the latter, directly or indirectly. It is not necessary, however, to do this in order to demonstrate that so far as the use of wine leads to inebriation it is pointedly condemned by the word of God. Sin and shame are connected with the first mention of wine in the Bible, and with many subsequent cases, Gen. 9 : 20; 19 : 31–36 ; 1 Sam. 25 : 36, 37 ; 2 Sam. 13:28 ; 1 Kin. 20:12–21 ; Esth. 1:10, 11 ; Dan. 5:23 ; Rev. 17 : 2. It is characterized as a deceitful mocker, Prov. 21 : 1 ; as fruitful in miseries, Prov. 23 : 29–35 ; in woes, Isa. 5:22 ; in errors, Isa. 28:1–7 ; and in impious folly, Isa. 5 : 11, 12 ; 56 : 12 ; Hos. 4 : 11. The use of it is in some cases expressly forbidden, Lev. 10 : 9 ; Num. 6 : 3 ; and in other cases is alluded to as characteristic of the wicked, Joel 3 : 3 ; Amos 6 : 6. Numerous cautions to beware of it are given, 1 Sam. 1:14 ; Prov. 23:31 ; 31:4, 5 ; 1 Tim. 3:3 ; and to tempt others to use it is in one passage made the occasion of a bitter curse, Hab. 2 : 15. On the other hand, whatever approval was given in Palestine to the moderate use of wine, can hardly apply to a country where wine is an imported or manufactured article, often containing not a drop of the juice of the grape ; or if genuine and not compounded with drugs, still enforced with distilled spirits. The whole state of the case, moreover, is greatly modified by the discovery of the process of distilling alcohol, and by the prevalence of appalling evils now inseparable from the general use of any intoxicating drinks. Daniel and the Rechabites saw good reason for total abstinence from wine, Jer. 35:14 ; Dan. 1 : 8 ; and the sentiment of Paul, on a matter involving the same principles, is divinely commended to universal adoption, Rom. 14 : 21 ; 1 Cor. 8 : 13.

For "wine-press," see PRESS, and VINE.

WIN'NOW. See FAN, and THRESHING.

WIN'TER. See CANAAN.

WISE MEN FROM THE EAST. See MAGI, and STAR.

WIST, knew ; the past tense, from an obsolete present wis, Ex. 16 : 15. Wot and wotteth, meaning know and knoweth, Gen. 21 : 26 ; 39 : 8, and to wit, meaning to know, Gen. 24 : 21, are also from the same Saxon root. "Do you to wit," 2 Cor. 8 : 1, means, make you to know, or inform you. "To wit," in 2 Cor. 5:19, means, that is to say.

WIT. See WIST.

WITCH and WIZ'ARD. Our best exposition of these terms as found in the Bible is in the narrative of the witch of Endor. She was widely known as "one that had a familiar spirit" or an attendant demon, and was thereby professedly able to summon departed souls from the spirit world and converse with them. From this it appears that the essential character of witchcraft was a pretended *commerce with demons and the spirits of the departed.* In this respect it is identical with modern witchcraft and with spiritualism ; and all the condemnation pronounced against witchcraft in the Bible falls equally on these and every similar system of professed commerce with ghosts and demons.

To this practice the ancient witches and wizards joined the arts of fortune-telling and divining, and a professed knowledge and control of the secret powers of the elements, heavenly bodies, etc. In order to give color and concealment to their pretended commerce with spirits, they made use of drugs, fumigations, chemical arts, incantations, and every mysterious device to awe and impose upon a superstitious people. Their unlawful arts were near akin to the others forbidden in Deut. 18:10, 11: "There shall not be found among you any one that maketh his son or his daughter to pass through the fire, or that useth divination, or an observer of times, or an enchanter, or a witch, or a charmer, or a consulter with familiar spirits, or a wizard, or a necromancer." It would appear from this catalogue that all forms of superstition were as prevalent in the East in the days of Moses as they now are. Those familiar with the Syria and Arabia of our days inform us that old and young of all sects universally believe in the potency of "the evil eye," of incantations, charms, amulets, serpent-charming, and exorcism ; and that these superstitions exert a prodigious influence on oriental life. Even modern mesmerism has its counterpart among the pretended magic arts of the East, practised, like many other existing superstitions, from time immemorial.

Such follies and knaveries are all strictly forbidden in the Bible, and many of them in the Jewish dispensation were punishable with death. They are all *idolatrous*—ignoring the only true God, and seeking help from foreign sources. They are sure to prevail in proportion as men lose a calm trust in the Almighty, and an intelligent loving obedience to his will. He that fears God needs fear nothing else; while he that, like king Saul, departs from God, finds help and comfort nowhere. See ENDOR, and SORCERER.

WITHE, Judg. 16:7, a band made by plaiting together willow or some other pliable twigs or stalks.

WIT'NESS, one who testifies to any fact from his own personal knowledge. Under the Mosaic law, two witnesses under oath were necessary to convict a person charged with a capital crime, Num. 35 : 30; and if the criminal was stoned, the witnesses were bound to cast the first stones, Deut. 17 : 6, 7; Acts 7 : 58. The Greek word for witness is MARTYR, which see. The apostles were witnesses, in proclaiming to the world the facts of the gospel, Acts 1 : 8, 22; 2:32; 2 Pet. 1:12, 16-18; and Christ is a "faithful witness," in testifying to men of heavenly things, John 3 : 12; Rev 1 : 5. The heroes of the ancient church are "witnesses" to the power of true faith, Heb. 12:1.

WOE is sometimes used in our Bibles where a softer expression would be at least equally proper: "Woe to such a one!" is in our language a threat or imprecation of some calamity, natural or judicial, to befall a person; but this is not always the meaning of the word in Scripture. We find the expression, "Woe is me!" that is, Alas for my sufferings! and, "Woe to the women with child, and those who give suck!" that is, Alas for their redoubled sufferings in times of distress! If in the denunciatory language of Christ, we should read, "Alas for thee, Chorazin! Alas for thee, Bethsaida!" we should do no injustice to the general sentiments of the passage.

Yet in many cases the word woe is used in a fuller and more awful sense, expressing an inspired denunciation and foreshadowing of God's wrath upon sinners; as when we read, "Woe to those who build houses by unrighteousness, and cities by blood;" woe to those who are "rebellious against God," etc., in numerous passages, especially of the Old Testament, Hab. 2:6, 9, 12, 15, 19; Zeph. 3:1.

WOLF, a ferocious wild animal, the Canis Lupus of Linnæus, belonging to the dog genus. Indeed, it closely resembles the dog; and it is only by a few slight differences of shape that they are distinguished. Wolves never bark, but only howl. They are cruel, but cowardly animals; they fly from man, except when impelled by hunger; in which case they prowl by night in great droves through villages, and destroy any persons they meet, Jer. 5 : 6; Ezek. 22:27; Hab. 1:8. They are swift of foot, strong enough to carry off a sheep at full speed, and an overmatch for ordinary dogs. In severe winters, wolves assemble in large troops, join in dreadful howlings, and make terrible devastations. They are the peculiar object of terror to shepherds, as the defencelessness and timidity of the sheep render it an easy prey to wolves, Luke 10 : 3; John 10 : 12. So persecutors and false teachers have been "grievous wolves" to the flock of Christ, Matt. 10 : 16; Acts 20 : 29. The wolf inhabits the continents of Europe, Asia, Africa, and America. Driven in general from the populous parts of the country, he is yet everywhere found in large forests and mountainous regions.

WOMAN is spoken of in Scripture as the beloved and honored companion and helpmeet, not the servant, of man, Gen. 2 : 23, 24, created as the necessary completion of man, Gen. 2 : 18; and though subordinate in sphere, Gen. 3 : 16; 1 Cor. 11 : 3, 8, 9; 14 : 34, 35; 1 Tim. 2 : 11–14, yet specially qualified for that sphere, and as necessary in it as man in his. Man and woman are indeed essentially one, the natural qualities of each so responding to those of the other as to lay the foundation of the most tender and abiding unity. The Bible thus raised the Jewish woman high above the women of heathenism; and the Old Testament contains some of the finest portraitures of female character. But still greater is the contrast between the women of heathenism and those of Christianity: the former with mind and soul undeveloped, secluded, degraded, the mere toys and slaves of their husbands; the latter educated, refined, ennobled, cheering and blessing the world. Christianity forbids a man to have more than one wife, or to divorce her for any cause but one, Matt. 5:32; 19:3-9; declares that bond and free, male and female, are all one in Christ, Gal. 3:28; and that in heaven they are no more given in marriage, but are as the angels of God, Matt. 22:33. If woman was first in the Fall, she was honored in the exclusive parentage of the Saviour of mankind; and women were the truest friends of Christ while on earth. The primal curse falls with heaviest weight on woman; but the larger proportion of women in our churches may indicate that it was the purpose of God to make his grace to man "yet more abound" to her who was the first in sinning and suffering.

In the East, women have always lived in comparative seclusion, not appearing in public unless closely veiled, not mingling in general society, nor seeing the men who visit their husbands and brothers, nor even taking their meals with the men of their own family. Their seclusion was less in the rural districts than in towns, and among the Jews than among most other nations. They were chiefly engaged in domestic duties, Prov. 31; among which were grinding flour, baking bread, making cloth, needlework, etc. The poor gleaned the remnants of the harvest; the daughters of the patriarchs joined in tending their fathers' flocks, Gen. 29:9; Ex. 2:16; and females of all classes were accustomed to draw water for family use, bearing it in earthen pitchers on their shoulders often for a considerable distance, Gen. 24:15-20; John 7:28.

WORD, one of the titles of the second person of the Trinity, indicating perhaps that by his acts and teachings God is revealed, somewhat as thought is by words, 1 John 1:1; 5:7; Rev. 19:13. "The word of the Lord" was a common phrase in the Old Testament, always denoting some revelation of Jehovah. Long before the coming of Christ, the Jewish paraphrasts of the Bible used "THE WORD" in the passages where JEHOVAH occurred in the original; and the term was familiar to Jewish writers as the name of a divine being, the Son of God. To show its true meaning and its application to our Saviour, was of great importance to John, the last of the inspired writers, in whose later years certain errors as to the person of Christ, borrowed from Eastern philosophy, had begun to creep into the Christian church. He describes "THE WORD" as a personal and divine Being, self-existent, and coëxistent from eternity with the Father, yet distinguished from him as THE SON, the creator of all created things, the source of all life and light to men, and in the fulness of time incarnate among men, John 1:1-3, 14. John's gospel is full and clear respecting the divinity of Christ, John 20:31.

WORLD, the earth on which we dwell, 1 Sam. 2:8; its inhabitants, John 3:16, or a large number of them, John 12:19. In several places it is equivalent to "land," meaning the Roman empire, or Judea and its vicinity, Luke 2:1; 4:3; Acts 11:28. It also denotes the objects and interests of time and sense, Gal. 6:14; 1 John 2:15.

WORM'WOOD, Lam. 3:15, an intensely bitter and poisonous plant, a symbol for whatever is nauseous and destructive, Deut. 29:18; Jer. 9:15. The fruits of vicious indulgence are "bitter as wormwood," Prov. 5:3; and injustice and oppression are like wormwood and gall, Amos 5:7; 6:12. The Chaldee paraphrase calls it "the wormwood of death." In Rev. 8:10, 11, the star called Wormwood seems to denote a mighty prince, or power of the air, the instrument, in its fall, of sore judgments on large numbers of the wicked. Compare Dan. 10:20, 21; Isa. 14:12.

WOR'SHIP OF GOD, both spiritual and visible, private and public, by individuals, families, and communities, is not only a self-evident duty for all who believe in God, but is abundantly commanded in his word. See PRAYER. The stated assembling of all people for united worship on the Sabbath, in continuance of the temple and synagogue services enjoined by God and practised by Christ, is a most manifest duty. The very name church, meaning assembly, implies it; and the preaching of the gospel, the great means for promoting Christianity, requires it. The directions of Paul, not to forsake the "assembling of ourselves together," to read his epistles "in all the churches," and to join in "psalms and hymns and spiritual songs," and his rules for securing the highest spiritual edification of all when they came together in the church, all indicate the established law of Christianity.

"Worship" is sometimes used of the form of homage paid by subjects to kings, or of honor to one held entitled to it, Dan. 2 : 46; Luke 14 : 10. In the East, this is still often rendered by prostrating the body and touching the forehead to the ground, Gen. 33 : 3; Matt. 18:26.

"Will-worship," Col. 2 : 23, is a term descriptive of such forms of adoration and service as are not prescribed in God's word, but are offensive in his sight. Such are the masses and penances of Popery.

WRITING. See Book.

Y.

YEAR. The Hebrews always had years of twelve months. But at the beginning, as some suppose, they were solar years of twelve months, each month having thirty days, excepting the twelfth, which had thirty-five days. We see, by the enumeration of the days of the deluge, Gen. 7 and 8, that the original year consisted of three hundred and sixty-five days. It is supposed that they had an intercalary month at the end of one hundred and twenty years, at which time the beginning of their year would be out of its place full thirty days. Subsequently, however, and throughout the history of the Jews, the year was wholly lunar, having alternately a full month of thirty days, and a defective month of twenty-nine days, thus completing their year in three hundred and fifty-four days. To accommodate this lunar year to the solar year, (365 days, 5 hours, 48 minutes, and 47.7 seconds,) or the period of the revolution of the earth around the sun, and to the return of the seasons, they added a whole month after Adar, usually once in three years. This intercalary month they call Ve-adar. See Month.

The ancient Hebrews appear to have had no formal and established era, but to have dated from the most memorable events in their history; as from the exodus out of Egypt, Exod. 19 : 1; Num. 33:38; 1 Kin. 6:1; from the erection of Solomon's temple, 1 Kin. 8 : 1; 9 : 10; and from the Babylonish captivity, Ezek. 33:21; 40:1. See Sabbatical year, and Jubilee.

The phrase, "from two years old and under," Matt. 2 : 16, that is, "from a child of two years and under," is thought by some to include all the male children who had not entered their second year; and by others, all who were near the beginning of their second year, within a few months before or after. The cardinal and ordinal numbers are often used indiscriminately. Thus in Gen. 7:6, 11, Noah is six hundred years old, and soon after in his six hundredth year; Christ rose from the dead "three days after," Matt. 27 : 63, and "on the third day," Matt. 16 : 21; circumcision took place when the child was "eight days old," Gen. 17 : 11, and "on the eighth day," Lev. 12:3. Compare Luke 1 : 59; 2:21. Many slight discrepances in chronology may be thus accounted for.

YESTERDAY and TO-DAY, in Heb. 13 : 8, are used in a general sense for time past and present. Christ is eternally the same. The life and knowledge of man are comparatively only "of yesterday," Job 8:9.

YOKE, a symbol of subjection and servitude, 1 Kin. 12 : 4; an iron yoke, of severe oppression, Deut. 28:48. The ceremonial law was a yoke, a burdensome restriction, Acts 15 : 10; Gal. 5 : 1. The withdrawing or breaking of a yoke denoted a temporary or an unlimited emancipation from bondage, Isa. 58 : 6, Jer. 2:20, and sometimes the disowning of rightful authority, Jer. 5 : 5. The iron yoke imposed by our sins, none but God can remove, Lam. 1 : 14; but the yoke of Christ's service is easy and light, Matt. 11:29, 30.

Z.

ZA'ANAN, Mic. 1 : 11, supposed to be the same as Zenan, Josh. 15 : 37, a town in the plain country of Judah.

ZAANAN'NIM, Josh. 19 : 33, a town in the north of Naphtali, near Kedesh and the foot of Anti-Lebanon, Judg. 4:11.

ZA'BAD, the name of four persons, 1 Chr. 2:36; 7:21; 2 Chr. 24:26; Ezra 10:27.

ZA'BUD, a son of Nathan the prophet, the confidential friend and adviser of king Solomon, probably having shared with him the instructions of the venerable prophet, 1 Kin. 4:5.

ZACCHE'US, *just*, from the Hebrew Zaccai, Neh. 7:14, a worthy tax-gatherer at Jericho, who in order to see Christ took a position in a sycamore-tree, by which He was about to pass. The Saviour drawing near and knowing his heart, called him to come down, and proposed to become his guest. As he held office under the Romans, he was called "a sinner" by the Jews, Luke 19:1-10. He showed sincere penitence and faith in the Saviour, who in turn promised him salvation as a child of Abraham by faith, Gal. 3:7, as he also seems to have been by birth. The "house of Zaccheus" now shown on the plain of Jericho is probably the remnant of a fort built in the tenth century, or even more recently.

ZACHARI'AH king of Israel succeeded his father Jeroboam II., 773 B. C., and reigned six months. He did evil in the sight of the Lord, and Shallum son of Jabesh conspired against him, killed him in public, and reigned in his stead. Thus was fulfilled what the Lord had foretold to Jehu, that his children should sit on the throne of Israel to the fourth generation, 2 Kin. 14:29; 15:8-11.

ZACHARI'AS, I., a person mentioned in Matt. 23:35, Luke 11:51, and most probably designating the son of the high-priest Jehoida, or Barachias, who was stoned to death by order of king Joash for publicly rebuking the king, his court, and the people for their growing corruptions, 2 Chr. 24:20-22. Some suppose the prophet Zechariah to be intended; but history gives no account of his death. Others refer it to a Zacharias the son of Baruch, who was put to death just before the destruction of Jerusalem; but it seems unnatural and unnecessary to suppose that Christ here spoke prophetically.

II. A priest belonging to the eighth course or class, called that of Abia, 1 Chr. 24, the husband of Elisabeth, and father of John the Baptist. His residence, when not on duty, was in the hill-country south of Jerusalem. He is known to us by his pious and blameless life; his vision of Gabriel in the temple, promising him a son in his old age; his hesitancy in believing, for which he was visited by a temporary dumbness; his miraculous restoration at the circumcision of his son; and his noble and prophetic song of praise, Luke 1:5-25, 57-79.

ZA'DOK, the son of Ahitub, and father of Ahimaaz, high-priest of the Jews in the reigns of Saul and David. See ABIATHAR.

Others of this name are mentioned in 2 Kin. 15:33; 1 Chr. 6:12; Ezra 7:2; Neh. 3:4; 13:13.

ZAL'MON, or SALMON, Hebrew Tzalmon, a height in Samaria near Shechem, Judg. 9:48, perhaps a part of mount Ebal; apparently the same that in Psa. 68:14 is spoken of as covered with new-fallen snow.

ZALMUN'NA and ZE'BAH, Midianitish kings, defeated and slain by Gideon, Judg. 8:5.

ZAMZUM'MIM, a race of giants east of the Jordan, defeated by Chedorlaomer, Gen. 14:5, and exterminated by the Ammonites, who possessed their territory until themselves subdued by Moses, Deut. 2:20, 21. See AMMONITES, and ZUZIM.

ZANO'AH, the name of two towns in Judah, Josh. 15:34, 56. The inhabitants of one of them aided in rebuilding Jerusalem, Neh. 3:13; 11:30.

ZAPH'NATH-PAANE'AH, *saviour of the world*, an Egyptian name given by Pharaoh to Joseph, in commemoration of the salvation wrought through him, Gen. 41:45.

ZA'RED. See ZERED.

ZAR'EPHATH, Obad. 20, a Phœnician seaport on the Mediterranean between Tyre and Zidon, usually subject to Tyre. During a famine in Israel, the prophet Elijah resided here, with a widow whose cruse of oil and barrel of flour were supplied and whose child was restored to life by miracle. Her noble faith in God is worthy of everlasting remembrance; and her generous self-forgetfulness, of universal imitation, 1 Kings 17:9-24. The place was afterwards called by the Greeks Sarepta, Luke 4:26, and is now known as Sarafend, a large village on the hills adjoining the seacoast.

ZAR'ETAN, called also Zartanah and

Zarthan, 1 Kin. 4 : 12 ; 7 : 46 ; a town on the west side of the Jordan, near Beth-shean and north of Succoth. The reflux of the Jordan at the crossing of the Israelites was marked as far north as Zaretan, Josh. 3:16. See ZEREDA.

ZEB'EDEE, the husband of Salome, and father of James and John the apostles. He was a fisherman in comfortable circumstances, on the west shore of the sea of Galilee, and readily spared his two sons at the call of the Saviour, Mark 1:19, 20. His wife also attended Christ, and ministered to him of her substance. See SALOME. His son John was personally known to the high-priest, and was charged by the dying Saviour with the care of His mother, John 18 : 15, 16 ; 19 : 26.

ZEBO'IM, I., one of the four royal cities in the vale of Siddim, destroyed by fire from heaven. See SODOM. Eusebius and Jerome mention a town by this name in their day, on the western shore of the Dead sea.

II. A valley and town of the Benjamites, east of Michmash, 1 Sam. 13 : 18 ; Neh. 11:34.

ZE'BUL, a governor of the city of Shechem, who labored adroitly to preserve the city for Abimelech his master, the son of Gideon, Judg. 9.

ZEB'ULUN, I., or ZABULON, Rev. 7:8, the sixth son of Jacob and Leah, born in Mesopotamia, Gen. 30 : 20. Moses gives us few particulars respecting him. His tribe was respectable for numbers, Num. 1 : 30 ; 26 : 26 ; and its portion in the Holy Land accorded with the prediction of Jacob, Gen. 49 : 13, extending from the Mediterranean sea at Carmel to the sea of Gennesaret, between Issachar on the south, and Naphtali and Asher on the north and north-west, Josh. 19 : 10. His posterity are often mentioned in connection with Issachar, his nearest brother, Deut. 33 : 18. They were entangled with the Phœnicians on the west, Judg. 1:30, Isa. 8 : 23, and took part with Barak and Gideon in the defence of the country against its oppressors, Judg. 4 : 10 ; 5 : 18 ; 6 : 35. Elon, one of the judges of Israel, was a Zebulunite, Judg. 12:11, 12. The inhabitants of this region in the time of Christ were highly favored by his instructions—Nazareth and Cana, Capernaum, Magdala, and Tiberias being all in these limits.

II. A city in the border of Asher, but probably belonging to Zebulun, Josh. 19:27.

ZECHARI'AH, I., son of Berechiah, and grandson of Iddo the priest ; called the son of Iddo in Ezra 5 : 1 ; 6 : 14, and his successor in the priesthood, Neh. 12:4, 16, perhaps because Berechiah was then dead. Zechariah is the eleventh of the minor prophets. He returned from Babylon with Zerubbabel, and began to prophesy while yet young, Zech. 2:4, in the second year of Darius son of Hystaspes, B. C. 520, in the eighth month of the holy year, and two months after Haggai. These two prophets, with united zeal, encouraged the people to resume the work of the temple, which had been discontinued for some years, Ezra 5:1.

Zechariah's prophecies concerning the Messiah are more particular and express than those of most other prophets, and many of them, like those of Daniel, are couched in symbols. The book opens with a brief introduction ; after which six chapters contain a series of visions, setting forth the fitness of that time for the promised restoration of Israel, the destruction of the enemies of God's people, the conversion of heathen nations, the advent of Messiah the Branch, the outpouring and blessed influences of the Holy Spirit, and the importance and safety of faithfully adhering to the service of their covenant God. Chapter 7 relates to commemorative observances. Chapters 9–11 predict the prosperity of Judah during the times of the Maccabees, together with the fate of Persia and other adjacent kingdoms. The remaining three chapters describe the future destiny of the Jews, the siege of Jerusalem, the triumphs of Messiah, and the glories of the latter day when "Holiness to the Lord" shall be inscribed on all things.

II. A wise and faithful prophetic counsellor of king Uzziah, whose death was the beginning of calamities to Judah, 2 Chr. 26 : 5, 16, perhaps the same who was the father-in-law of Ahaz, 2 Chr. 28:27 ; 29:1.

III. A son of Jeberechiah, associated with Urijah the high-priest by Isaiah as a "faithful witness," Isa. 8 : 1 ; 2 Chr. 29:13.

IV. A son of Jehoiada. See ZACHARIAS I.

ZEDEKI'AH, I., the twentieth and last king of Judah, son of Josiah and

Hamutal, and uncle to Jeconiah his predecessor, 2 Kin. 24:17, 19; Jer. 52:1. When Nebuchadnezzar took Jerusalem, he carried Jeconiah to Babylon, with his wives, children, officers, and the best artificers in Judea, and put in his place his uncle Mattaniah, whose name he changed to Zedekiah, and made him promise with an oath that he would maintain fidelity to him. He was twenty-one years old when he began to reign at Jerusalem, and he reigned there eleven years. He did evil in the sight of the Lord, committing the same crimes as Jehoiakim, 2 Kin. 24:18-20; 2 Chron. 36:11-13. Compare Jer. 29:16-19; 34; 38:5; Ezek. 17:12, 14, 18. In the ninth year of his reign, he revolted against Nebuchadnezzar, trusting to the support of Pharaoh-hophra king of Egypt, which proved ineffectual, and despising the faithful remonstrances of Jeremiah, Jer. 37:2, 5, 7-10. In consequence of this the Assyrian marched his army into Judea, and took all the fortified places. In the eleventh year of his reign, on the ninth day of the fourth month, (July,) Jerusalem was taken, 588 B. C. The king and his people endeavored to escape by favor of the night; but the Chaldean troops pursuing them, they were overtaken in the plain of Jericho. Zedekiah was taken and carried to Nebuchadnezzar, then at Riblah, in Syria, who reproached him with his perfidy, caused his children to be slain before his face, and his own eyes to be put out; and then loading him with chains of brass, he ordered him to be sent to Babylon, 2 Kin. 25; Jer. 39; 52; Ezek. 19. All these events remarkably fulfilled the predictions of Jeremiah and Ezekiel, in the chapters previously referred to. Compare also, with respect to Zedekiah's blindness, Jer. 34:3; Ezek. 12:13.

II. A false prophet, exposed by Micaiah when urging Ahab to fight with the Syrians, 1 Kin. 22:11-37. His fate is foreshadowed in ver. 25.

III. Another false prophet, denounced by Jeremiah, Jer. 29:21, 22.

ZELOPH'EHAD, a descendant of Joseph, whose death in the wilderness, leaving five daughters and no sons, led to the establishment of a law that in such cases daughters should inherit the patrimony of their father; but they were not to marry out of their tribe, Num. 26:33; 27:1-11; Josh. 17:3, 4.

ZELO'TES, *a zealot;* in general, one passionately and fanatically ardent in any cause. After the time of Christ, the name Zelotæ was commonly applied to an association of private individuals who without authority or law sought to enforce their own views of the law. In their opinion it was a high crime to pay tribute to the Romans, and rebellion was the duty of every patriotic Jew. Beginning with moderation, they became more and more violent; and during the Roman war and the siege of Jerusalem by Titus, their excesses and crimes under the pretext of zeal for the Lord are described by Josephus as truly appalling; so that they acquired the appropriate name of Sicarii, or assassins. As the germ of this body seems to have existed in our Lord's day, some suppose that the apostle Simon Zelotes was so called from his having once belonged to it. The name Canaanite, or more properly Cananite, from the Hebrew *kana*, has the same meaning with Zelotes, Matt. 10:4; Mark 3:18. Little more is known respecting Simon.

ZE'NAS, a pious lawyer, and a friend of Paul, who, writing from Nicopolis during the last year of his life, commends him and Apollos, then at Crete on a journey, to the kind offices of Titus, Tit. 3:13. His name is Greek, and his profession may have been Greek civil law, rather than Jewish law.

ZEPHANI'AH, I., a Kohathite, in the seventh generation from Levi, 1 Chron. 6:36.

II. A priest, high in the sacred order, during the troublous times of king Zedekiah, who often communicated with Jeremiah by his agency. He was among the captives slain by the king of Babylon at Riblah, 2 Kin. 25:18-21; Jer. 21:1; 29:25, 29; 37:3; 52:24-27.

III. The ninth in order of the minor prophets, of the tribe of Simeon. He prophesied in the early part of king Josiah's reign, before the reforms of that good king were instituted, 2 Chr. 34:3; Zeph. 1:4, 5. This would fix his date about 630 B. C., and the destruction of Nineveh, foretold in Zeph. 2:13, occurred in 625 B. C. His prophecy contains two oracles, in three chapters, directed against idolaters in Judah, against surrounding idolatrous nations, and against wicked rulers, priests, and prophets. It closes with cheering promises of gospel blessings. His style and manner are like those of Jeremiah, during whose early years they were contemporary. His subsequent history is unknown.

ZEPH'ATH, a Canaanitish city afterwards called Hormah, one of the "uttermost cities of Judah southwards," afterwards assigned to Simeon, Josh. 12 : 14; 15:30; 19: 4. The name is supposed to be traceable in Sufah, a long and rough pass leading from the south up into the mountains of Judah. It was at Zephath that the Israelites were repulsed in attempting to ascend from Kadesh, Num. 14 : 40-45; 21 : 3; Deut. 1 : 44; Judg. 1 : 17.

ZEPHA'THAH, a valley near Mareshah, south-west of Jerusalem, where Asa defeated Zerah the Cushite, 2 Chr. 14 : 10.

ZE'RAH, I., the son of Reuel, and grandson of Esau, Gen. 36:13, 17.

II. Son of Judah and Tamar, Gen. 38:30; called Zara in Matt. 1:3.

III. Son of Simeon, and founder of the Zarhites, Num. 26 : 13; called Zohar in Gen. 46:10.

IV. A Cushite king who invaded Judah with an immense army in the reign of Asa, 2 Chr. 14:9-13. It is not agreed by interpreters whether he came from Southern Arabia or from Egypt and Ethiopia. Many, however, follow Champollion, who identifies him with Osorchon and Osoroth of the Egyptian monuments and history, the son and successor of Shishak.

ZE'RED, or Zared, a brook, or the valley through which it flows into the south-east part of the Dead sea, probably by Kir Moab, now Kerak, Num. 21 : 12; Deut. 2:13, 14.

ZERE'DA, or Zered'athah, a city of Manasseh, near Beth-shean, 1 Kings 11:26; 2 Chr. 4:17; supposed to be the same with Zere'rath, Judg. 7 : 22, and perhaps Zaretan.

ZE'RESH, the wife of Haman, haughty and revengeful like him, and destined to see him and her ten sons hanging on the gallows she had designed for Mordecai the servant of God, Esth. 5:10-14; 6:13; 7:10; 9:13.

ZERUB'BABEL, or Zorob'abel, son of Salathiel, of the royal race of David, called "Sheshbazzar the prince of Judah" in Ezra 1 : 8. Zerubbabel, as his name imports, was born in Babylon, and was the leader of the first colony of Jews which returned from the Babylonish captivity, 536 B. C. Cyrus committed to his care the sacred vessels of the temple, with which he returned to Jerusalem, Ezra 1 : 11. He is always named first, as being chief of the Jews that returned to their own country, Ezra 2 : 2; 3 : 8; 5:2; Hag. 1:1; 2:1-9, 21-23. He laid the foundations of the temple, Ezra 3:8, 9, Zech. 4 : 9, and restored the worship of the Lord, and the usual sacrifices. When the Samaritans offered to assist in rebuilding the temple, Zerubbabel and the principal men of Judah refused them this honor, since Cyrus had granted his commission to the Jews only, Ezra 4 : 2, 3. They procured from the Persian court an order that the work should cease; and it was not resumed until the second year of Darius son of Hystaspes, 521 B. C. We know nothing further of his history, except that from him both Joseph and Mary descended, Matt. 1:13; Luke 3:27.

ZERUI'AH, sister of David, and mother of his famous generals, Joab, Abishai, and Asahel, 1 Chr. 2 : 16. Her husband is unknown.

ZI'BA, a rich steward of Saul, whom David charged with similar duties towards Mephibosheth, son of Jonathan, 2 Sam. 9 : 2-10. By a false representation David was induced to transfer to Ziba the lands he had given to Mephibosheth, but afterwards divided them between the two, being convinced that he had acted hastily, and unable to decide with certainty for either, 2 Sam. 16:1-4; 19:24-30.

ZICH'RI, a valiant Ephraimite prince, general of Pekah king of Israel in the war with Ahaz, 2 Chr. 28:7. He is perhaps the man called "Tabeal's son," Isa. 8:6, whom Rezin and Pekah proposed to make king of Judah.

ZI'DON. See Sidon. The word Zidonians often includes all the Phœnicians, as well as the inhabitants of Zidon.

ZIF, the second month of the Hebrew year, also called Iyar, and nearly corresponding to our May, 1 Kin. 6:1.

ZIK'LAG, a city of Judah and Simeon, on the borders of the Philistines, Josh. 15:31; 19:5, who held it until the time of Saul, when Achish king of Gath gave it to David. Hither many other refugees from Judah resorted, and David was thus enabled to aid Achish, and to chastise the Amalekites who had sacked Ziklag during his absence, 1 Sam. 27:1-6; 30; Neh. 11:28.

ZIL'LAH, Gen. 4:19. See LAMECH.

ZIL'PAH, the maid of Leah, who became the secondary wife of Jacob, and the mother of Gad and Asher, Gen. 29:24; 30:9–13.

ZIM'RI, I., a prince of the tribe of Simeon, slain by Phinehas for his heaven-daring crime on the plains of Moab, Num. 25:14.

II. A general of half the cavalry of Elah king of Israel. He rebelled against his master, killed him, and usurped his kingdom. He cut off the whole family, not sparing any of his relations or friends; whereby was fulfilled the word of the Lord denounced to Baasha the father of Elah, by the prophet Jehu. Zimri reigned but seven days; for the army of Israel, then besieging Gibbethon, a city of the Philistines, made their general, Omri, king, and came and besieged Zimri in the city of Tirzah. Zimri, seeing the city on the point of being taken, burned himself in the palace with all its riches, 1 Kin. 16:1–20; 2 Kin. 9:31.

III. Others of this name are mentioned in 1 Chr. 2:6; 8:33–36.

ZIN, a desert on the south border of Canaan, and the west of Edom, Num. 34:1–4. It formed part of the great wilderness of Paran, Num. 13 : 26; and in its north-east corner was Kadesh-barnea, memorable for the death of Miriam, the mission of the twelve spies into Canaan, the murmuring of the Israelites, the rock flowing with water, and the unholy passion of Moses, Num. 13 : 21; 20 : 1–13; 27: 14.

MOUNT ZION; WITH THE MOSQUE OF DAVID, PART OF THE SOUTH WALL OF THE CITY, AND THE VALLEY OF HINNOM.

ZI'ON, or SION in the New Testament, the highest and southernmost mount of Jerusalem, rising about twenty-five hundred feet above the Mediterranean, and from two to three hundred feet above the valleys at its base. It was separated from Akra on the north and Moriah on the north-west by the valley Tyropœon; and had the valley of Gihon on the west, that of Hinnom on the south, and that of the Kidron on the south-east. It was a fortified town of the Jebusites till subdued by David, and thenceforward was often called "the city of David," 2 Sam. 5 : 7; 1 Kin. 8 : 1. He seems to have greatly delighted in its beauty and strength, and to have loved it as a type of the church of the Messiah: "Beautiful for situation, the joy of the whole earth, is mount Zion, on the sides of the north, the city of the great King." "Walk about Zion, and go round about her; tell the towers thereof; mark ye well her bulwarks; consider her palaces, that ye may tell it to the generation following:" "The kings were assembled, they passed by together; they saw it, and so they marvelled; they were troubled, and hasted away," Psa. 48:2, 12, 13. A mosque near its southern brow now covers the "tomb of David" so called, most jealously guarded by the Mohammedans, 1 Kin. 2:10; 11:43; 22:50. This mount, together with Moriah and Ophel, was enclosed by the first wall, and fortified by citadels, 1 Chr. 11:5. Upon it were erected the magnificent palaces of Solomon and long afterwards of Herod. It was finely adapted for the purposes of military defence, and so strongly was it fortified at the time of its capture by the Romans, that the emperor exclaimed, "Surely we have had God for our aid in the war; for what could human hands or machines do against these towers?" Great changes have occurred on its surface, and a considerable portion of it lies outside of the modern wall on the south, and is occupied by cemeteries, or "ploughed as a field," according to Jer. 26:18; Micah 3:12. Two rabbis, we are told, approaching Jerusalem, observed a fox running upon the hill of Zion, and Rabbi Joshua wept, but Rabbi Eliezer laughed. "Wherefore dost thou laugh?" said he who wept. "Nay, wherefore dost thou weep?" demanded Eliezer. "I weep," replied the Rabbi Joshua, "because I see what is written in the Lamentations fulfilled; because of the mount of Zion, which is desolate, the foxes walk upon it." "And therefore," said Rabbi Eliezer, "do I laugh; for when I see with my own eyes that God has fulfilled his *threatenings* to the very letter, I have thereby a pledge that not one of his *promises* shall fail; for He is ever more ready to show mercy than judgment."

"Zion," and "the daughter of Zion," are sometimes used to denote the whole city, including especially Moriah and the temple, Psa. 2:6; 9:11; 74:2; Isa. 1:8; Joel 2:23, and sometimes figuratively for the seat of the true church on earth and in heaven, Jer. 8:19; Heb. 12:22; Rev. 14:1. See JERUSALEM.

ZIPH, a city of Judah, four miles south-east of Hebron; near it were wild fastnesses in which David for a long time lay hid, 1 Sam. 23:14, 15.

ZIPPORAH, daughter of Jethro, wife of Moses, and mother of Eliezer and Gershom. When Moses fled from Egypt into Midian, and there stood up in defence of the daughters of Jethro, priest or prince of Midian, against shepherds who would have hindered them from watering their flocks, Jethro took him into his house, and gave him his daughter Zipporah in marriage, Ex. 2:15–22; 4:25; 18:2–4.

ZIZ, THE CLIFF OF, the pass near Engedi, by which the Moabites and Ammonites ascended from the shore of the Dead sea, having followed the southern and western coast to this point, 2 Chr. 20:16. The same route is still traversed by the Arabs.

ZO'AN, a very ancient city of Lower Egypt, Num. 13:22, on the east side of the Tanitic arm of the Nile, and called by the Greeks Tanis, now San. It was a royal city, Isa. 19:11, 13; 30:4, and gave its name to the level country around it, in which were wrought the first mighty works of God by Moses, Psa. 78:12, 43. Vast heaps of ruined temples, obelisks, sphinxes, etc., attest the ancient grandeur of this city, and its ruin according to prophecy, Ezek. 30:14.

ZO'AR, a city on the south-east side of the Dead sea, was destined, with the other four cities, to be consumed by fire from heaven; but at the intercession of Lot it was preserved, Gen. 14:2; 19:20–23, 30. It was originally called Bela; but after Lot entreated the angel's permission to take refuge in it, and insisted on the smallness of this city, it had the name Zoar, which signifies small.

ZO'BAH, a country of Syria, whose king carried on war with Saul and David, 1 Sam. 14:47; 2 Sam. 8:3; 10:6. It seems to have lain near Damascus, and to have included the city Hamath conquered by Solomon, 2 Chr. 8:3, but also to have extended towards the Euphrates, 2 Sam. 8:3.

ZO'HAR, a Hittite, Gen. 23:8. Also a son of Simeon, Gen. 38:30, and a descendant of Judah, 1 Chr. 4:7.

ZO'HELETH, a large rock near the well En-rogel, in the valley adjoining Jerusalem on the south-east, where the adherents of Adonijah assembled in rebellion, 1 Kin. 1:9.

ZO'PHAR, one of Job's three friends, a native of some unknown place called Naamah. He appears but twice in the dialogue, once less than his two associates, whose general sentiments he shares, with perhaps more severity of judgment against Job, Job 2:11; 11; 20.

ZO'RAH, a city of Danites within the limits of Judah, 2 Chr. 11:12, called also Zoreah, Josh. 15:33; 19:40. Samson was a Zorite, or Zorathite, Judg. 13:2, 25; 1 Chr. 2:54; 4:2. It is now recognized in a secluded mountain village called Surah, on the edge of the hills north of Beth-shemesh. The road followed by Samson in going to Timnath leads down through rocky gorges, very likely to be haunted by wild beasts. It was here that he slew the lion, without the help of any weapon, Judg. 14:5-7.

ZOROB'ABEL. See ZERUBBABEL.

ZUPH, plur. ZOPHIM, an Ephrathite, ancestor of Samuel, and the region in mount Ephraim which he inhabited, 1 Sam. 1:1; 9:5; 1 Chr. 6:35. See under RAMAH II.

ZUR, a Midianitish prince, whose daughter was slain by Phinehas, Num. 25:15-18, and who was himself subsequently slain in war with the Israelites, Josh. 13:21.

ZU'ZIM, taken by the Chaldee and Septuagint version as an appellative for stout and valiant men. They dwelt east of the Jordan in the time of Abraham, when they were subdued by Chedorlaomer and his allies, Gen. 14:5, and are supposed to have been the same race of giants called Zamzummim in Deut. 2:20.

CHRONOLOGICAL INDEX TO THE BIBLE.

COMPILED BY JOSEPH ANGUS, D.D.

PERIOD I

FROM THE CREATION, B. C. 4004, TO THE DEATH OF NOAH, 2006 YEARS.

DATE AND PLACE.	EVENT OR NARRATIVE.	BIBLE REFERENCE.
B. C. 4004.	The creation,	Gen. 1; 2:4-7.
	Institution of the Sabbath,	Gen. 2:1-3.
	Creation of Adam and Eve, briefly described in chap. 1, recapitulated,	Gen. 2:8-25.
4004.	The fall of man,	Gen. 3:1-13
Eden.	Connection of the first sin with man's subsequent state,	Rom. 5:14. 1 Cor. 15.
Eden.	First promise of a Saviour; expulsion from Eden,	Gen. 3:14-24.
4003-2, Near Eden.	Birth of Cain and Abel,	Gen. 4:1, 2.
3875.	Sacrifice first mentioned; Abel's accepted,	Gen. 4:3-7.
3875.	Cain's crime and curse,	Gen. 4:8-15.
3875-3504, Nod.	Cain builds Enoch; his descendants; Lamech's speech, etc.,	Gen. 4:16-24.
3874. Near Eden.	Birth of Seth and of Enos; world and church distinguished,	Gen. 4:25, 26.
3769.	Genealogy from Adam to Noah; the line of the Messiah,	Gen. 5.
3074.	Adam dies, aged 930 years,	Gen. 5:5.
2468.	Wickedness of the world; God determines to destroy it after a respite of 120 years; Noah preaches, (2 Pet. 2:5,)	Gen. 6.
2468.	Covenant renewed with him; he builds an ark as God commanded,	Gen. 6:18.
2348.	Noah enters the ark; the Deluge, A. M. 1656,	Gen. 7.
2347,	The waters abate; Noah leaves the ark,	Gen. 8.
Armenia, or *Ararat*, Gen. 8:4.	God's covenant renewed with Noah,	Gen. 9:1-17.
Togarmah, Ezek. 27:14.	Noah and his sons; his prediction concerning them,	Gen. 9:18-27.
2247, A. M. 1757.	Babel; confusion of tongues; dispersion,	Gen. 11:1-9.
B. C. 2233.	Genealogies of Noah's sons; Nimrod founds the Babylonian or Assyrian empire,	Gen. 10.
Shinar, or *Irak Arabi*.	Genealogy from Shem to Terah; the line of the Messiah,	Gen. 11:10-28.
1998.	Death of Noah,	Gen. 9:28, 29.

PERIOD II.

FROM THE DEATH OF NOAH TO THE BIRTH OF MOSES 417 YEARS.

DATE AND PLACE	EVENT OR NARRATIVE.	BIBLE REFERENCE.
B. C.	I. JOB.	
Uz, in Eastern Idumæa.	The exact date of Job is not known. There is good reason, however, for placing his history before that of Abraham. Chapters 19:25–27; 32:23–28, are direct references to the work of the Messiah,	Job 1–42.
	II. ABRAHAM.	
1996, Ur, *Orfa*	Birth of Abraham; marries Sarai; leaves Ur and his idolatrous kindred, (Josh. 24:2,)	Gen. 11:27–32.
1922, Haran, *Charræ, Harran.*	Terah, Lot, and Sarai; death of Terah,	See Acts 7:2–4.
1921, Canaan.	Leaves Haran at God's command with Sarai and Lot,	Gen. 12:1–9.
1921.	Great blessings promised him,	Gen. 12:1–9. See Acts 3:25. Rom. 4. Gal. 3:16.
1920.	Visits Egypt; dissimulates,	Gen. 12:10–20.
1918.	Returns to Canaan; Lot in Sodom,	Gen. 13:1–13.
1917, Hebron.	Promises renewed; goes to Mamre,	Gen. 13:14–18.
1913, Siddim, *El Ghor.*	Chedorlaomer; Lot taken and rescued,	Gen. 14.
	Melchizedek blesses Abram,	Gen. 14.
1912, Hebron.	Covenant of God with Abram,	Gen. 15.
1910.	Hagar; Ishmael born,	Gen. 16.
1897.	Covenant renewed; names changed; circumcision,	Gen. 17.
	Abraham entertains angels, one of whom is the Angel of the covenant; Sodom; Lot's wife; Lot's incest,	Gen. 18; 19:1–36; 19:4–11 30–36.
1896, Gerar.	Abraham leaves Hebron; dissembles with Abimelech,	Gen. 20.
Land of Moab.	Moab and Ben-ammi born,	Gen. 19:37, 38.
	Isaac born; Ishmael sent away; covenant with Abimelech,	Gen. 21:1–34.
Moriah, (site of the temple.)	Trial of Abraham's faith,	Gen. 22:1–19
Machpelah, near Hebron.	Death and burial of Sarah,	Gen. 23.
	Account of Nahor's family,	Gen. 22:20–24.
1856, Beersheba.	Abraham sends his servant to Haran; Laban receives him; marriage of Isaac,	Gen. 24.
1850.	Abraham marries Keturah; children by her,	Gen. 25:1–6.
1836, Lahai-roi.	Birth of Esau and Jacob; their character,	Gen. 25:19–28.
1821, Beersheba.	Abraham dies; Isaac and Ishmael bury him in the cave of Machpelah,	Gen. 25:7–11.

PERIOD II.—CONTINUED.

DATE AND PLACE.	EVENT OR NARRATIVE	BIBLE REFERENCE.
B. C.	III. ISAAC AND JACOB.	
1804, Lahai-roi.	Esau sells Jacob his birthright; Isaac leaves Canaan,	Gen. 25:29-35.
1804.	Covenant confirmed to Isaac at Gerar,	Gen. 26:1-5.
1804, Beersheba.	Isaac dissembles; covenant with Abimelech,	Gen. 26:6-33.
1796.	Esau marries two Hittite women,	Gen. 26:34, 5.
1773.	Death of Ishmael; descendants,	Gen. 25:12-18.
1760, Beersheba.	Jacob obtains his father's blessing, and flees from Esau,	Gen. 27; 28:1-5.
1760, Padan-aram.	Jacob's vision at Luz; the promises continued to him; stays with Laban his uncle,	Gen. 28:10-22; 29:1-14.
1760, Arabia.	Esau marries a daughter of Ishmael,	Gen. 28:6-9.
1753.	Jacob marries Leah and Rachel,	Gen. 29:15-30.
1752-1745, Padan-aram, *Al Jezirah.*	Jacob's children: Reuben, Simeon, Levi, and Judah, by Leah; Dan and Naphtali, by Bilhah, Rachel's maid; Gad and Asher, by Zilpah, Leah's maid; Issachar, Zebulun, and Dinah, by Leah; Joseph, by Rachel,	Gen. 29:31-35; 30:1-24.
1745.	Jacob's bargain with Laban; he becomes rich.	Gen. 30:25-43.
1739, Galeed.	Jacob, returning to Canaan, is pursued by Laban; their covenant,	Gen. 31.
1739, Succoth. See Josh. 13:27.	Jacob's vision at Mahanaim; wrestles with an angel at Penuel; reconciled to Esau; settles at Succoth,	Gen. 32; 33:1-17.
1736, Shechem.	Jacob removes to Shalem, Gen. 33:18-20; birth of sons of Judah,	Gen. 38:1-5.
1732	Dinah defiled by Shechem; slaughter of Shechemites by Simeon and Levi,	Gen. 34.
thel, Luz, *Beit-in.*	Jacob removes; purges his household of idols; the promises renewed to him; his name changed to Israel,	Gen. 35:1-15.
	Rachel dies on the birth of Benjamin,	Gen. 35:16-20.
1729, Hebron.	Sin of Reuben; Jacob abides with Isaac,	Gen. 35:21-27.
1729.	Esau's descendants,	Gen. 36.
	IV. JOSEPH, ETC.	
1728, Dothan.	Joseph's two dreams; envy of his brethren; sold to the Ishmaelites and to Potiphar in Egypt,	Gen. 37.
1726, Timnath.	Er and Onan slain by God; incest of Judah and Tamar; Pharez, a progenitor of Messiah, born.	Gen. 38:6-30.
1719, Egypt.	Joseph advanced, tempted, falsely accused, and imprisoned,	Gen. 39.
1718.	Pharaoh's butler and baker imprisoned; Joseph interprets their dreams,	Gen. 40
1716.	Death of Isaac at Mamre,	Gen. 35:28, 29.
1715.	Joseph interprets Pharaoh's dreams; his elevation,	Gen. 41:1-49.
1712, 1711.	Birth of Joseph's two sons, Manasseh and Ephraim.	Gen. 41:50-52.
1708.	Commencement of the seven years' famine,	Gen. 41:53-57.
1707.	Joseph's ten brethren come to buy corn; Simeon a pledge,	Gen. 42.

PERIOD II.—CONTINUED

DATE AND PLACE.	EVENT OR NARRATIVE.	BIBLE REFERENCE.
B. C. 1706.	They come again to buy corn; Joseph makes himself known to them; sends for his father,	Gen. 43-45.
1706.	Jacob and his family arrive; settle in Goshen; Jacob meets Pharaoh,	Gen. 46:8-25; 47:1-12.
1704-1701	Joseph, by giving corn to the Egyptians, increases the wealth of the king,	Gen. 47:13-26.
1689, Egypt.	Jacob blesses Ephraim and Manasseh,	Gen. 47:27-31; 48.
1689.	Jacob's predictions concerning his sons and Judah; his death,	Gen. 49.
Machpelah.	Joseph and his brethren bury their father,	Gen. 50:1-13.
1689.	Joseph shows kindness to his brethren,	Gen. 50:14-21.
1635, Egypt.	Joseph predicts the return to Canaan; charges them to carry up his bones there; his death,	Gen. 50:22-26.
1577, Egypt.	The Israelites multiply; a new king oppresses them,	Exod. 1:1-21; 15-21.
1573.	Pharaoh orders the male children to be cast into the river,	Exod. 1:22.

PERIOD III.

FROM THE BIRTH OF MOSES, B. C. 1571, TO HIS DEATH, 120 YEARS.

DATE AND PLACE.	EVENT OR NARRATIVE.	BIBLE REFERENCE.
B. C.	I. TO THE EXODE.	
1571-1532.	Birth, exposure, rescue, and early life of Moses,	Ex. 2:1-10.
1531, Midian.	Moses, having killed an Egyptian, flees; marries Zipporah, daughter of Jethro; Gershom born,	Ex. 2:11-22.
1531, Egypt.	The Israelites groan for their bondage,	Ex. 2:23-25; Psa. 88.
1491, Horeb, (Acts 7:30.)	God appears to Moses in a burning bush; appoints him and Aaron to bring the Israelites out of Egypt,	Ex. 3; 4:1-17.
1491, Egypt, (Acts 7:31.)	Moses leaves Midian; meets Aaron; they deliver their message,	Ex. 4:18-31.
	Moses and Aaron demand the release of the Israelites; Pharaoh refuses,	Ex. 5.
1491.	God renews his promise by his name Jehovah,	Ex. 6:1-13.
1491.	Descendants of Reuben, Simeon, and of Levi, from whom came Moses and Aaron,	Ex. 6:14-27.
1491.	Moses and Aaron again sent; confirm their message by a miracle; magicians imitate them,	Ex. 6:28-30; 7:1-13.
1491.	Pharaoh refuses to let Israel go; eight plagues,	Ex. 7:14-25; 8; 9; 10:1-20.
1491.	The Passover instituted,	Ex. 12:1-20.
1491.	The ninth plague, three days darkness,	Ex. 10:21-27.
1491.	Israelites bidden to ask gold of the Egyptians; Pharaoh threatened with the death of the firstborn,	Ex. 11:1-8; 10:28, 29; 11:9, 10.

PERIOD III.—CONTINUED.

DATE AND PLACE.	EVENT OR NARRATIVE.	BIBLE REFERENCE.
B. C. 491.	The Passover eaten, the same day of the same month on which Christ our Passover was sacrificed for us; the firstborn slain,	Ex. 12:21–30.
1491, Rameses.	The exodus of Israel from Egypt, A. M. 2513,	Ex. 12:31–36, and 40–42.
	II. JOURNEYS OF THE ISRAELITES.	
1491, Succoth, Eccl. year 1.	First journey. Passover reinforced. Firstborn commanded to be set apart. Joseph's bones removed,	Ex. 12:37–39, 43–51; 13:1–19; Num. 33:1–5.
1 mon., 1 day. Etham.	Second journey. Israel guided by a pillar of cloud and fire,	Ex. 13:20–22; Num. 33:6.
1491, Pihahiroth; that is, mouth of pass.	Third journey. Pharaoh pursues,	Ex. 14:1–9; Num. 33:7.
Marah.	Fourth journey. Passage of the Red sea. See 1 Cor. 10:1, 2. Destruction of Pharaoh's army. Song of Moses. The bitter waters sweetened,	Ex. 14:10; 15:26; Num. 33:8.
Elim, *Wady Ghurundel.*	Fifth journey,	Ex. 15:27; Num. 33:9.
Red sea.	Sixth journey,	Num. 33:10.
2 mon., 15 day. Desert of Sin.	Seventh journey. People murmur for bread. Quails and manna. Directions on manna. See John 6:31, 49; Rev. 2:17,	Ex. 16:1–36; Num. 33:11.
Dophkah.	Eighth journey,	Num. 33:12.
Alush.	Ninth journey,	Num. 33:13.
Rephidim.	Tenth journey. Water given from the rock in Horeb, (1 Cor. 10:4.) Joshua defeats Amalek, while Moses prays,	Ex. 17:1–16; Num. 33:14.
3 mon., 15 day. Sinai.	Eleventh journey. Preparation for giving of the law,	Ex. 19:1–25; Num. 33:15.
1491. 3 mon., 15 day. Sinai.	Moral law given. Divers laws (chiefly judicial) enjoined. The angel promised as a guide to the Israelites,	Ex. 20:23.
	The people promise obedience; the blood of the covenant sprinkled on them. Moses and others have a vision of God's glory. Moses remains forty days and forty nights in the mount,	Ex. 24.
	Ceremonial law given. The tabernacle and its furniture, the priests and their garments, etc. The Sabbath again enjoined. Daily sacrifice and incense. Rom. 8:3; Rev. 8:3, 4. Tables of the law given to Moses,	Ex. 25–31.
	Idolatry of the calf; the tables broken; the people punished; the tabernacle removed out of the camp. Moses intercedes for the people, and asks to see God's glory,	Ex. 32:33.
Eccl. year 1. 6 mon., Sinai.	The tables renewed; the name of the Lord proclaimed; God makes a covenant with Israel. Moses stays on the mount forty days and forty nights; his face shines,	Ex. 34.

PERIOD III.—CONTINUED.

DATE AND PLACE.	EVENT OR NARRATIVE.	BIBLE REFERENCE.
B. C. 1491.	Offerings of the people for the tabernacle. Bezaleel and others prepare the tabernacle and its furniture,	Ex. 35-39.
1490. Eccl. year 2. 1 mon., 1 day.	Moses commanded to rear the tabernacle and to anoint it, and to sanctify Aaron and his sons,	Ex. 40:1-16; (John 1:14; 2:19-21. Col. 2:9.)
1490. Eccl. year 2. 1 mon., 1 day.	The tabernacle set up. The glory of the Lord fills it. The Israelites directed by the cloud,	Ex. 40:17-38.
	Laws on various sacrifices and offerings,	Lev. 1-7.
	Consecration of Aaron and his sons as priests,	Lev. 8.
1 mon., 8 day.	The offerings of Aaron. Fire consumes the sacrifice,	Lev. 9.
	The offerings of the princes accepted,	Num. 7.
	Destruction of Nadab and Abihu,	Lev. 10.
	Of the great day of atonement, and of the scape-goat,	Lev. 16; see Heb. 9; 5:1.
1 mon., 14 day	The second Passover celebrated. Some allowed to observe it in the second month,	Num. 9:1-14.
	Laws on meats and purifications,	Lev. 11-15.
	Miscellaneous laws, moral, ceremonial, and judicial. Shelomith's son stoned for blasphemy,	Lev. 17-22; 24.
	Laws concerning festivals, etc.,	Lev. 23; 24.
	Prophetic promises and threatenings,	Lev. 26.
	Laws of vows, devotions, and tithes,	Lev. 27.
2 mon., 1 day.	The tribes numbered; their order,	Num. 1; 2.
	The Levites appointed to the service of the tabernacle instead of the firstborn; their duties,	Num. 3; 4.
	Institution of various ceremonies. The law of the Nazarites. The form of blessing,	Num. 5; 6.
	Consecration of the Levites; their age and period of service,	Num. 8.
	Use of the silver trumpets,	Num. 10:1-10.
	Manner in which the cloud guided the people,	Num. 9:15-23.
	Arrival of Jethro with Moses' wife and sons. He advises Moses to appoint judges to assist,	Ex. 18:1-26.
1491. 2 mon., 20 day	Twelfth journey. Order of the march,	Num. 10:11, 12, (33:16,) 28.
Wilderness of Paran, *El Tyh.*	Moses entreats Hobab to accompany Israel; Jethro returns to Midian,	Num. 10:29-32; Ex. 18:27.
	The form of blessing on the removal and resting of the ark,	Num. 10:33-36.
	The burning at Taberah. People murmur for flesh; Moses complains of his charge; seventy elders appointed as a council to assist him; quails given in wrath,	Num. 11:1-34.
Hazeroth.	Thirteenth journey. Miriam smitten with leprosy for sedition,	Num. 11:35; (33:17,) 12:15.
5 mon. to 7 mon. Kadesh Barnea, or En-Mishpat.	Fourteenth journey. Spies sent to search the land; ten of them bring an evil report; Caleb and Joshua faithful,	Num. 12:16; (33:18,) 13.

PERIOD III.—CONTINUED.

DATE AND PLACE.	EVENT OR NARRATIVE.	BIBLE REFERENCE.
B. C. 1490. Eccl. year 2. 7 mon., 6 day.	Israel murmurs at the report of the spies; God threatens; Moses intercedes; condemned to wander forty years,	Num. 14:1-39; Psa. 90.
	The people, going up against the will of God, are discomfited,	Num. 14:40-45.
	Laws of offerings; the sabbath-breaker stoned,	Num. 15.
	The rebellion of Korah, etc.; earthquake, fire, and plague inflicted; Aaron approved as high-priest by the budding of his rod,	Num. 16; 17.
	The charge and portion of the priests and Levites,	Num. 18.
	Water of purification; how to be made and used,	Num. 19.
1490-1452. Eccl. year 2-40.	The next seventeen journeys (15th to 31st) of the Israelites, being their wandering in the wilderness nearly thirty-eight years,	Num. 33:19-35.
1452.	Thirty-second journey; Death of Miriam,	Num. 20:1; 33:36.
Eccl. year 40. 1 mon.	The people murmur for water; Moses and Aaron transgressing, not to enter Canaan,	Num. 20:2-13.
1490, Kadesh.	Edom refuses a passage to the Israelites,	Num. 20:14-21.
Mount Hor.	Thirty-third journey; Aaron dies; Arad attacks Israel, and is defeated,	Num. 20:22 to 21:3; 33:37-40.
Zalmonah.	Thirty-fourth journey; the people murmur; fiery serpents are sent; the brazen serpent set up,	(See John 3:14;) Num. 21:4-9; (33:41.)
Punon, Oboth, Iim.	Thirty-fifth, thirty-sixth, and thirty-seventh journeys,	Num. 21:10, 11; 33:42-44.
Dibon-gad.	Thirty-eighth journey,	Num. 33:45.
	The Israelites stop at Zared, Arnon, and Beer,	Num. 21:12-18.
	Sihon the Amorite opposes their passage; defeated,	Num. 21:21-32.
	Og of Bashan attacks them; defeated,	Num. 21:33-35.
Almon-diblathaim.	Thirty-ninth journey,	Num. 33:46.
Abarim.	Fortieth journey,	Num. 21:18-20; 33:47.
Plains of Moab by Jordan.	Forty-first journey; account of Balaam and Balak,	(Luke 1:78; Rev. 22:16; 1 Cor. 15:25;) Num. 22:1-41; (33:48;) 23; 24.
	Forty-second journey; idolatry of Baal-Peor; zeal of Phinehas,	Num. 25:1-18; (33:49.)
	Third numbering of the people,	Num. 26.
	The daughters of Zelophehad; laws of inheritance,	Num. 27:1-11; 36.
	Laws of offerings, vows, etc.,	Num. 28-30.
1451.	The slaughter of Midian; Balaam slain,	Num. 31.
Eccl. year 40.	Territories given to Reuben, Gad, and part of Manasseh, on the east of Jordan,	Num. 22.

PERIOD III.—CONTINUED.

DATE AND PLACE.	EVENT OR NARRATIVE.	BIBLE REFERENCE.
B. C. 1451.	Directions for the Israelites on their entering Canaan; borders of the land described; forty-eight cities for the Levites, of which six are to be cities of refuge; the laws on murder, - -	Num. 33:50-56; 34; 35.
	III. THE REVIEW AND CLOSING CHARGE OF MOSES.	
Eccl. year 40.	Moses reviews the history of the Israelites, introducing some new particulars, - - - - - - - - - - - - - - -	Deut. 1:4.
11 mon., 1 day.	The moral law repeated and enforced, - - - - - - - -	Deut. 5:9; 10:1-5, 10-22; 11.
	The ceremonial law repeated, with injunctions against idolatry etc., - - - - - - - - - - - - - - - - - - -	Deut. 12-16; 17:1.
Plains of Moab by Jordan.	The judicial law repeated and explained. Christ foretold as the Prophet to whom they are to hearken, -	Deut. 17:2-20; 18-26.
	Moses directs Israel, after entering Canaan, to write the law on stones, and to recite its blessings and curses upon mount Gerizim and mount Ebal, -	Deut. 27.
	Prophetic promises and curses, - - - - - - - - - - - - - - -	Deut. 28.
	Concluding appeal to the Israelites, - - - - - - - - - - -	Deut. 29; 30.
	IV. JOSHUA'S APPOINTMENT—DEATH OF MOSES.	
Eccl. year 40. 11 mon.	Joshua appointed to succeed Moses, - - - - - - - - - - -	Num. 27:12-23.
	Moses encourages the people and Joshua; charges the priests to read the law publicly every seventh year, -	Deut. 31:1-13.
	God's charge to Joshua; Moses writes a song of witness; completes the writing of the law, and delivers it to the Levites, with a prediction of the disobedience of Israel, - - - - - - - - - - - - - - - -	Deut. 31:14-29.
	Moses recites his song, and exhorts Israel to set their hearts upon it, -	Deut. 31:30; 32:1-47.
	Moses ascends mount Nebo to view the land of Canaan, and to die, -	Deut. 32:48-52.
	Moses prophetically blesses the tribes, - - - - - - - - - -	Deut. 33.
1451.	Moses views the promised land; his death, burial, and character, -	Deut. 34.

PERIOD IV.

FROM THE ENTRANCE INTO CANAAN TO THE DEATH OF SOLOMON, 475 YEARS.

DATE AND PLACE.	EVENT OR NARRATIVE	BIBLE REFERENCE.
	I. CONQUEST OF CANAAN, 7 YEARS. (TO THE JUDGES, 25 YEARS.)	
B. C. 1451.	God's charge to Joshua,	Josh. 1:1-9.
Eccl. year 41.	Spies sent to Jericho; Rahab receives them,	Josh. 2.
1 mon., 1 day.	Joshua reminds Reuben, etc., of their engagement, (cf. Num. 22;) they promise obedience. The Israelites directed concerning the passage of the Jordan. God encourages Joshua,	Josh. 1:10-18; 3:1-13.
10 day.	Passage of the Jordan, (A. M. 2551;) a memorial erected; the Canaanites alarmed,	Josh. 3:14-17; 4; 5:1.
1451, Gilgal.	Circumcision renewed; the Passover; manna ceases,	Josh. 5:2-12.
	The Captain of the Lord's host appears to Joshua; miraculous capture of Jericho; a curse on the rebuilder of it,	Josh. 6:1; 5:13-15; 6:2-27.
	The Israelites discomfited through Achan's sin; he is destroyed,	Josh. 7.
	Capture of Ai by stratagem,	Josh. 8:1-29.
Gilgal.	The Gibeonites obtain a league with Joshua,	Josh. 9.
	Conquest of several kings in succession,	Josh. 10.
1450-1445.	The rest of the conquests,	Josh. 11.
1444, Ebal and Gerizim.	The law written on a stone altar, (cf. Deut. 27,) and proclaimed to all the people,	Josh. 8:30-35.
	Reuben, etc., return to their land on the eastern side of Jordan; they erect an altar of memorial; Israel offended, ask an explanation,	Josh. 22.
	II. GENERAL DIVISION OF THE LAND.	
1444.	Enumeration of conquests,	Josh. 12.
	Land not yet conquered,	Josh. 13:1-6.
	Joshua divides the land; the nine tribes and a half receive their portions by lot; the Levites not to receive land,	Josh. 13:7-14; 14:1-5.
	Inheritance of Reuben, etc., on the eastern side of Jordan,	Josh. 13:15-33.
Hebron, Kirjath Arba, Josh. 21:11.	Inheritance of Caleb,	Josh. 14:6-15; 15:13-19.
	Lot of Judah,	Josh. 15:1-12, 20-63.
	Lots of Ephraim and half of Manasseh,	Josh. 16; 17.
1444, Shiloh.	The tabernacle set up,	Josh. 18:1.
	Lots of the other tribes; Joshua's inheritance,	Josh. 18:2-28; 19.
	Cities of refuge appointed,	Josh. 20.
	Levitical cities,	Josh. 21.

PERIOD IV.—CONTINUED.

DATE AND PLACE.	EVENT OR NARRATIVE.	BIBLE REFERENCE.
	III. LAST ACTS OF JOSHUA, ETC.	
B. C. 1427, Shechem,	Joshua's charge to the elders of Israel,	Josh. 23.
Sychar N. T.	Joshua addresses the tribes and renews the covenant,	Josh. 24:1-28.
1426, Shechem.	Death and burial of Joshua,	Josh. 24:29-31.
	Burial of Joseph's bones, etc.,	Josh. 24:32, 33.
	IV. INTERREGNUM AND GOVERNMENT OF JUDGES, 330 YEARS.	
	Conquests after Joshua's death,	Judg. 1:1-26.
	Nations not subdued by Israel,	Judg. 1:27-36.
1425, Bochim.	The angel of the Lord rebukes the Israelites for not driving out the Canaanites,	Judg. 2:1-5.
	Commencement of idolatry in Israel,	Judg. 2:6-13
1413.	Account of Micah and his image,	Judg. 17.
	A party of Danites, having robbed Micah of his image, establish themselves in Laish, (afterwards Dan.) and set up idolatry,	Judg. 18.
1406, Gibeah, *Jeba.*	History of the Levite and his concubine; slaughter of the Benjamites, etc.,	Judg. 19; 20; 21.
	The captivities of Israel for idolatry, and their deliverances by judges,	Judg. 2:14-23; 3:1-4.
1402-1394.	Captivity of the eastern Israelites for eight years to Mesopotamia; Othniel judge,	Judg. 3:5-11.
1354-1336.	Captivity of the eastern Israelites for eighteen years to Moab; Ehud judge,	Judg. 3:12-30.
	Captivity of the western Israelites to the Philistines; Shamgar judge,	Judg. 3:31.
1316-1296.	Captivity of the northern Israelites for twenty years to the Canaanites; Deborah judge; song of Deborah and Barak,	Judg. 4; 5.
1256.	Captivity of the eastern and northern Israelites for seven years to Midian,	Judg. 6:1-6.
Bethlehem.	The history of Ruth, an ancestress of the Messiah,	Ruth 1-4.
1249, Shechem.	Gideon judge; is visited by the Angel of the covenant, and delivers Israel from Midian; refuses to be made king,	Judg. 6:7-40; 7; 8.
1235-1232.	Usurpation of Abimelech; Jotham's fable,	Judg. 9.
1232-1188.	Tola and Jair judges,	Judg. 10:1-5.
1206-1188.	The Philistines and Ammonites oppress Israel for eighteen years; Jephthah; his vow,	Judg. 10:6-18; 11.
1187.	Slaughter of Ephraim by the Gileadites,	Judg. 12:1-6.
182-1157.	Ibzan, Elon, and Abdon judges,	Judg. 12:7-15.
1156-1116.	The Philistines oppress Israel forty years,	Judg. 13:1.
1156.	Birth of Samson,	Judg. 13:2-25.
1155, Shiloh.	Birth of Samuel; Hannah's song,	1 Sam. 1; 2:1-11.
	The wickedness of Eli's sons,	1 Sam. 2:12-21.
1143.	Call of Samuel,	1 Sam. 3.

PERIOD IV.—CONTINUED.

DATE AND PLACE.	EVENT OR NARRATIVE.	BIBLE REFERENCE.
B. C. 1136–1117.	Marriage of Samson; his exploits,	Judg. 14; 15:1-19; 16:1-3.
	Judgment on Eli's house,	1 Sam. 2:22-36, 22-25.
1116, Gaza.	Capture and death of Samson,	Judg. 15-20; 16:4-31.
1116, Ebenezer.	Israel twice defeated by the Philistines; ark taken and Eli's sons slain; death of Eli,	1 Sam. 4; 19-22.
Ashdod, Azotus, Acts 8:40; *Esdud.*	The ark placed in the house of Dagon; removed to Ekron, (*Akir,*) then to Bethshemesh, (*Ain Shems,*) thence to Kirjath-jearim, where it remains till removed by David,	1 Sam. 5; 6; 7:1, 2.
1112, Mizpeh.	Samuel judge; he moves the Israelites to repentance; the Philistines discomfited,	1 Sam. 7:3-17.
1095, Ramah, in Ephraim.	Samuel appoints his sons judges; their corrupt government; the Israelites ask for a king; God bids Samuel hearken to them,	1 Sam. 8.
	V. THE REIGN OF SAUL, 40 YEARS.	
1096, Ramah.	Samuel privately anoints Saul as king, and gives him three signs,	1 Sam. 9; 10:1-16.
Mizpeh.	Saul chosen and proclaimed king,	1 Sam. 10:17-27.
Gilgal, S. E. of Jericho.	Saul rescues Jabesh-Gilead; is inaugurated as king; Samuel's address to Israel,	1 Sam. 11; 12.
1094.	Saul gathers an army against the Philistines; he disobeys Samuel, and is warned of his rejection from the kingdom,	1 Sam. 13:1-15.
	The Philistines discomfited; Saul's rash oath endangers Jonathan; the people rescue him; Saul's victories; his family,	1 Sam. 13:16-23; 14.
1080.	Saul smites the Amalekites; spares Agag and the best of the spoil; denounced by Samuel,	1 Sam. 15.
1064. Bethlehem.	Samuel secretly anoints David, at Bethlehem, as future king,	1 Sam. 16:1-13.
	David's victory over Goliath; Jonathan loves David,	1 Sam. 17:1-40, 55, 56, 41-54, 57, 58; 18:1-4; Psa. 9.
1063.	David's victories; Saul's melancholy; he attempts to kill David	1 Sam. 18:5-9; 16:14-23; 18:10-16.
1062, Gibeah, Naioth.	David marries Saul's daughter; Saul makes various attempts to kill him; David flees to Samuel; Saul sends after him,	1 Sam. 18:17-30; 19:1-3; Psa. 11; 1 Sam. 19:4-24; Psa. 59.
1062.	David's covenant with Jonathan,	1 Sam. 20.
1061, Nob and Gath.	David flees to Ahimelech, (where his lie costs the lives of the priests of the house of Eli,) then to Achish; feigns madness,	1 Sam. 21; Psa. 56; 34.

PERIOD IV.—CONTINUED.

DATE AND PLACE.	EVENT OR NARRATIVE.	BIBLE REFERENCE.
B. C. 1062, Adullam.	David flees again, joined by several followers, -	1 Sam. 22:1; Psa. 142; 2 Sam. 22:1, 2; 1 Chr. 12:8-18; 2Sam. 23:13-17; 1Chr. 11:15-19.
Nob.	David goes to Mizpeh, then to Hareth; slaughter of the priests by Saul,	1 Sam. 22:3-19; Psa. 52, 109, 17, 140; 35, 64.
Keilah.	Abiathar joins David; David defeats the Philistines,	1 Sam. 23:1; 22:20-23; 23:6, 2-5, 7-12; Psa. 31.
1060, Ziph.	Saul pursues David; an invasion obliges him to return,	1Sam. 23:13-23; Psa. 54; 1Sam. 23:24-28.
1059, Engedi, Hazezon Tamar,	Saul pursues David; David spares Saul's life; Saul confesses his fault,	1Sam. 23:29; 24; Psa. 57, 58, 63.
1058, Ziph.	Death of Samuel; David and Nabal,	1 Sam. 25.
	David again spares Saul's life,	1 Sam. 26.
1057.	David flees to Achish, 1 Sam. 27:1-7; Psa. 141; several resort to him,	1 Chr. 12:1-7.
	David makes an excursion on the Amalekites, and repairs to Gath with the booty,	1 Sam. 27:8-12.
1056.	The Philistines prepare for war, and advance to Shunem; David accompanies them; Saul consults the witch of Endor,	1 Sam. 28.
	David dismissed from the army of the Philistines; on his way back to Ziklag he is joined by several,	1 Sam. 29. 1 Chr. 12:19-22.
	On his return to Ziklag, David finds that it had been sacked by Amalek, and his family taken; he pursues Amalek, and smites them,	1 Sam. 30.
Gilboa, *Djebal Gilbo.*	Saul, defeated in battle and his sons slain, kills himself,	1 Sam. 31; 1 Chr. 10:1-14.
Ziklag, (16 m. s. w. of Gath?)	An Amalekite pretends to have slain Saul, and is put to death by David,	2 Sam. 1:1-16.
	David's lament over Saul and Jonathan,	2 Sam. 1:17-27.
	VI. THE REIGN OF DAVID, 40 YEARS.	
1056, Hebron. Acts 13:21.	David acknowledged as king of Judah,	2 Sam. 2:1-7.
	Ishbosheth proclaimed king of Israel,	2 Sam. 2:8-11.
1054.	Civil war ensues; David waxes stronger; Abner and Ishbosheth treacherously slain,	2 Sam. 12:32; 3; 4.
1049, Hebron, Jerusalem.	David made king over all Israel; his troops; he dispossesses the Jebusites of the hill of Zion, and dwells there,	2 Sam. 5:1-3; 23:8-12, 18-39; 5:4, 5, 6-10; 1 Chr. 11:1-3; 12:23-40; 11:10-14, 20 26-47, 4-9.

PERIOD IV.—CONTINUED.

DATE AND PLACE.	EVENT OR NARRATIVE.	BIBLE REFERENCE.
B. C. 1048.	Hiram of Tyre congratulates David; David's family; he twice defeats the Philistines, - - - -	2 Sam. 5:11-25, 13-17; 1 Chr. 14:1-17.
1046, from Kirjath Jearim to house of Obed-edom, thence to Zion, Psa. 132.	David removes the ark; Uzzah, not being a Levite, smitten for touching the ark, (see Num. 4:15,) - - - -	2 Sam. 6:1-11; 6:12-23; Psa. 68, 132, 105, 96, 106; 1 Chr. 13:1-4, 5-14; 15:1-16:43, 5-24.
	David forbidden to build the temple; great blessings promised him; his prayer and thanksgiving, - - - -	2 Sam. 7; 1 Chr. 17; Psa. 2, 45, 22, 16, 118, 110.
1041.	Victories over Philistia, Moab, Syria, and Edom,	2 Sam. 8; 1 Chr. 18; Psa. 60. 108.
	David's kindness to Mephibosheth, - - - -	2 Sam. 9.
1038-1037, Medeba.	David defeats Ammon and Syria, - - - -	2 Sam. 10; 1 Chr. 19; Psa. 20, 21.
1036 and 1034, Jerusalem.	Siege of Rabbah; David's adultery and murder, - - - -	2 Sam. 11:1; 11:2-12, 23; 26-31; 1 Chr. 20:1, 3; Psa. 51, 32, 33, 103.
1033.	Birth of Solomon; Amnon, David's eldest son, forceth his sister Tamar, David's only daughter; David fails to punish this injury, - - - -	2 Sam. 12, 24, 25; 13:1-22.
1031.	Absalom kills Amnon, and flees, - - - -	2 Sam. 13:23-39.
1028.	Absalom brought back, and restored to his father's presence, - - - -	2 Sam. 14:1-7, 15-17, 8-14, 18-33.
1025.	Absalom raises a revolt against David, - - - -	2 Sam. 15:1-12.
1024.	David and his followers flee; Zadok and Abiathar sent back with the ark; Hushai desired by David to join himself to Absalom to circumvent Ahithophel's counsels, - - - -	2 Sam. 15:13-27; Psa. 3.
1024, Bahurim.	Ziba's treachery to Mephibosheth; Shimei curses David, - - - -	2 Sam. 16:1-14; Psa. 7.
Jerusalem.	Hushai defeats Ahithophel's counsel; Ahithophel hangs himself, - - - -	2 Sam. 16:15-23; 17:1-26.
Mahanaim, 65 miles N. E. of Ephraim.	David furnished with provisions, chiefly by Barzillai, - - - -	2 Sam. 17:27-29; Psa. 42, 43, 55, 4, 5, 62, 143, 144, 70, 71.
	Absalom defeated and slain by Joab, - - - -	2 Sam. 18.
Jerusalem.	David returns; Shimei pardoned; Mephibosheth exposes Ziba's treachery; David's gratitude to Barzillai, - - - -	2 Sam. 19; 20:3.

PERIOD IV.—CONTINUED.

DATE AND PLACE	EVENT OR NARRATIVE.	BIBLE REFERENCE.
B. C. 1023.	Revolt of Sheba, (at Abel,)	2 Sam. 20:1, 2, 4–26.
1021.	The three years' famine,	2 Sam. 21:1–14.
1019.	Last wars with the Philistines; David's praise for victories, his enemies subdued,	2 Sam. 21:15–22; 22:2-51; 1 Chr. 20:4–8; Psa. 18.
1018.	David, in pride, numbers Israel; the plague,	2 Sam. 24:1-9; 10–25; 1 Chr. 21:1–5; 27:23, 24; 21.6, 7, 8–30.
1016, Jerusalem.	David prepares materials, and instructs Solomon as to the building of the temple,	1 Chr. 22.
	Adonijah's rebellion; Solomon anointed and proclaimed David's successor; Adonijah submits,	1 Kin. 1:1–4.
	David arranges the courses of the priests, etc.,	1 Chr. 23–26.
	Arrangement of the state officers,	1 Chr. 27:1–22, 25–34.
	David calls a solemn assembly, and exhorts both them and Solomon to the work of the temple; the offerings of the princes and people; David's thanksgiving; Solomon acknowledged as king,	1 Chr. 28:11–21; 29:1–25; Psa. 72, 91, 145.
	David's final charge to Solomon; directs Joab and Shimei to be put to death; David's last words; his death,	1 Kin. 2:1–9; 2 Sam. 23:1–7; 1 Chr. 29:26–30; 1 Kin. 2:10, 11.
	Psalms of David, of which the date and occasion are not known,	Psa. 6, 8, 12, 19, 23, 24, 28, 29, 38–41, 61, 65, 69, 78, 86, 95, 101, 104, 120–122, 124, 131, 133, 139.
	VII. THE REIGN OF SOLOMON, 40 YEARS.	
1016, Gibeon, *Jib*, 17 m. N. W. of Gilgal.	Solomon's burnt-offering; God giving him a choice, he asks for wisdom; wealth and honor added to him,	1 Kin. 2:12; 3:4–15; 2 Chr. 1:1–5, 6–12.
1015, Jerusalem.	Solomon's wise judgment,	1 Kin. 3:15–28; 2 Chr. 1013.
	Adonijah and Joab put to death; Abiathar deposed; Shimei not to leave Jerusalem,	1 Kin. 2:13–38.
Tyre, *Tsur.*	Solomon obtains materials and men for the building of the temple,	1 Kin. 5:1–18; 2 Chr. 2:1–18.
1012, Jerusalem.	Shimei put to death for going to Gath,	1 Kin. 2:39–46.
	Solomon marries Pharaoh's daughter,	1 Kin. 3:1–3.

PERIOD IV.—CONTINUED.

DATE AND PLACE.	EVENT OR NARRATIVE.	BIBLE REFERENCE.
B. C. 1012–1005, 1 Kin. 6:1–37.	The building of the temple,	1 Kin. 6:1–8, 15–36; 7:13–50; 6:9–14, 37, 38; 7:51; 2 Chr. 3:1–9, 3, 4, 22, 10–14; 3:15 to 4:22; 5:1.
1005, Jerusalem.	The dedication of the temple,	1 Kin. 8:1–11, 62–64, 12–61, 65, 66; 2 Chr. 5:2–14; 7:4–7; 6; 7:3, 8, 10; Psa. 47, 97–100, 135, 136.
1002.	Other buildings of Solomon; God makes a covenant with him,	1 Kin. 7:1–12; 9:1–9; 2 Chr. 7:11–22.
	Acquisitions of Solomon; he carries out David's arrangements for the temple services,	1 Kin. 9:10–14, 15–25; 2 Chr. 8:1–10, 12–16.
1001, Jerusalem.	Pharaoh's daughter brought by Solomon to his new palace,	1 Kin. 9:24; 2 Chr. 8:11.
	Solomon's song,	Song 1–8.
	The greatness of Solomon,	1 Kin. 4:1–28, 2–19; 10:26; 9:26–28; 10:14–25, 27–29. 2 Chr. 9:26, 25; 1:14; 8:17, 18; 9:13–21, 24; 1:15–17; 9:27, 28.
	The wisdom of Solomon,	1 Kin. 4:29–33; 2 Chr. 9:22; Prov. 1–31; 5; 6:24–35; 7.
993, Jerusalem.	Solomon's fame; visit of the queen of Sheba,	1 Kin. 4:34; 10:1–13; 2 Chr. 9:23, 1–12.
980–977.	Solomon's wives seduce him into idolatry; Hadad and Rezon stirred up against him,	1 Kin. 11:1–25.
977.	Ahijah predicts to Jeroboam the division of the kingdom; Solomon seeks to kill Jeroboam, who flees into Egypt,	1 Kin. 11:26–40.
	Solomon writes Ecclesiastes, or the Preacher, probably as an expression of repentance,	Eccl. 1–12; 3–11:8.
976, Jerusalem.	Death of Solomon; Rehoboam his son succeeds,	1 Kin. 11:41–43; 2 Chr. 9:29–31.

PERIOD IV.—CONTINUED.

DATE AND PLACE.	EVENT OR NARRATIVE.	BIBLE REFERENCE.
B. C.	**VIII. DIVISION OF THE KINGDOM.**	
976, Shechem.	On the accession of Rehoboam, the people, headed by Jeroboam, demand a relaxation of burdens,	1 Kin. 12 : 1-5; 2 Chr. 10:1-5.
	Acting upon the advice of the young men instead of the old men, Rehoboam refuses the request of the people,	1 Kin. 12:6-15; 2 Chr. 10:6-15.
	Ten tribes revolt; Judah and Benjamin adhere to Rehoboam, and form the kingdom of Judah,	1 Kin. 12:16-19; 2 Chr. 10:16-19.
*	The ten tribes make Jeroboam their king, and form the kingdom of Israel,	1 Kin. 12-20.

PERIOD V.

FROM THE DEATH OF SOLOMON TO THE CLOSE OF THE OLD TESTAMENT CANON.*

I. HISTORY OF THE TWO KINGDOMS.

JUDAH.	B. C.	ISRAEL.
REHOBOAM king 17 years, 1 Kings 14:21, *f. p.*, (*Judah;*) 2 Chr. 12:13, *f. p.*, (*reigned.*)	976	*JEROBOAM* king 22 years; he establishes himself at Shechem, 1 Kings 12:25.
Rehoboam, preparing to attack the ten tribes, is forbidden by Shemaiah, 1 Kin. 12:21-24; 2 Chr. 11:1-4.		
Rehoboam fortifies his kingdom; the priests and Levites of Israel resort to him; Rehoboam's family, 2 Chr. 11:5-23.	974	Jeroboam, having set up golden calves at Dan and Bethel, is reproved by a man of God, 1 Kin. 12:26-33; 13:1-10.
		Seduced by an old prophet of Bethel, the man of God disobeys the word of the Lord, and is slain by a lion, 1 Kin. 13:11-32.
Rehoboam and Judah's idolatry, 1 Kin. 14:22-24; 2 Chr. 12:1.	973	These calves borrowed from Egypt, where Jeroboam had resided.
Shishak plunders Jerusalem, 1 Kin. 14:25-28; 2 Chr. 12:2-12.	972	Twice warned by the man of God and by Ahijah, yet persisting in his idolatry.
Character and death of Rehoboam, 1 Kin. 14:21, *l. p.* 29-31; 2 Chron. 12:13, *l. p.* 14-16.		The step seemed politic. It seemed a form of worship something like that established at Jerusalem, and attracted the tribes, but in the end it proved the ruin of the kingdom.
ABIJAH, or ABIJAM, king 3 years, 1 Kin. 15:1, 2, 6; 2 Chr. 13:1, 2.	958	
Abijah defeats Jeroboam in battle, 2 Chr. 13:3-21. His heart not perfect.		

* The names of new kings are here printed in capitals; and if founders of new dynasties, in italic capitals.

PERIOD V.—CONTINUED.

JUDAH.	B. C.	ISRAEL.
	957	Ahijah denounces Jeroboam, 1 Kin. 13:33, 34; 14:1–18.
Character and death of Abijah. ASA king 41 years, 1 Kin. 15:3–10; 2 Chr. 13:22; 14:1.	956	
	955	Jeroboam's death. NADAB king 2 years, 1 Kin. 14:19, 20; 15:25, 26.
	953	Nadab slain at Gibbethon. *BAASHA* king 24 years, 1 Kin. 15:27–34.
Asa puts away idolatry, and strengthens his kingdom, 1 Kin. 15:11–15; 2 Chr. 14:2–8; 15:16–18.	951	
Asa's victory over the Ethiopians, 2 Chr. 14:9–15.	944	
Moved by Azariah, Asa makes a solemn covenant with God, 2 Chr. 15:1–15, 19.	942	
Asa bribes Ben-hadad king of Syria to attack Baasha, 1 Kin. 15:16–22.	941	Baasha, attempting to build Ramah, is attacked by the king of Syria, 2 Chr. 16:1–6.
Asa, reproved by Hanani for applying to Ben-hadad, puts him in prison, 2 Chr. 16:7–10. His idolatrous alliance with Syria, and his imprisonment of the prophet, after all his reformations, prove his ruin.		
	931	Baasha denounced by Jehu; his death. ELAH king 2 years, 1 Kin. 16:1–8.
	930	Elah slain. *ZIMRI* king 7 days; destroys Baasha's house. Omri elected king. Zimri destroys himself, 1 Kin. 16:9–20.
	926	*OMRI* king 12 years, including 6 years' civil war with Tibni. Samaria built, 1 Kin. 16:21–26.
	917	Omri dies. AHAB king 22 years. Jericho rebuilt by Hiel, who reaps Joshua's curse, 1 Kin. 16:27–34. 1 Kin. 16:25. Compare Mic. 6:26; 1 Kin. 16:34; Josh. 6:26.
Asa's death. JEHOSHAPHAT king 25 years; his piety and prosperity, 1 Kin. 15:23, 24; 22:41–47; 2 Chr. 16:11–14; 17:1; 20:31–33; 17:2–19; compare ver. 6 and 20:33. His great error is his alliance with Ahab, whose daughter Athaliah his son Jehoram marries. Hence his expedition to Ramoth, which nearly cost him his life.	914	
	910 to 906	Elijah prophesies a famine; raises the widow's son; his trial with the prophets of Baal. Elisha a prophet, 1 Kin. 17–19.
	902 and 901	Ben-hadad besieges Samaria. The Syrians twice defeated. Ahab denounced, 1 Kin. 20.
	900	Ahab seizes Naboth's vineyard. Elijah denounces him, 1 Kin. 21.
Jehoshaphat visits Ahab, and joins with him in battle against the Syrians, 2 Chr. 18.	898	Ahab makes war on Syria, and is slain, as Micaiah predicted. AHAZIAH king, 1 Kin. 22:1–35, 36–40, 51–53. Ver. 39. See Amos 3:15.
Jehoshaphat reproved by Jehu for joining with Ahab. He visits his kingdom, and exhorts the judges, etc., to be faithful, 2 Chr. 19; Psa. 82.		Psa. 82 placed here from internal evidence, (Towns.)

PERIOD V.—CONTINUED

JUDAH.	B. C.	ISRAEL.
Overthrow of Moab, etc. Jehoram regent, 2 Chr. 20:1–30; Psa. 115; 46.	897	Psa. 115 and 46. The schools of the prophets, (Naioth,) 1 Sam. 10:10; 19:20; 2 Kin. 2:2, seem to have trained at this time a large number of religious teachers.
Jehoshaphat joins Ahaziah. Being reproved, and his ships wrecked, he refuses to join in a subsequent expedition, 1 Kin. 22:48, 49; 2 Chr. 20:35, 37.		
Afterwards joins Joram against Moab. and is saved only by a miracle, 2 Kin. 3. On 2 Chr. 20:13; see Joel 2:18.		Ahaziah falling sick and sending to inquire of Baalzebub, is denounced by Elijah. JEHORAM, or JORAM, his brother, king 12 years, 2 Kin. 1; 3:1–3. Elijah translated. Elisha acknowledged as his successor; his miracles, 2 Kin. 2.
	894	Joram, joined by Jehoshaphat and the king of Edom, defeats Moab, 2 Kin. 3:4–27. Elisha multiplies the widow's oil; promises a son to the Shunammite, 2 Kin. 4:1–17.
2 Kin. 9:2, 13. Read, therefore, in 1 Kin. 19:16, grandson; and by Elijah anointing Jehu, understand ordering Elisha to do it. Jehu was anointed to exterminate the house of Ahab.	893	Naaman healed, 2 Kin. 5.
	892	Elisha causes iron to swim; discloses the Syrian king's purpose, and smites his army with blindness, 2 Kin. 6:1–23.
Jehoram begins to reign in concert with Jehoshaphat, 2 Kin. 8:16. 2 Chr. 21:5. Three dates are given for the beginning of Jehoram's reign: B. C. 897, when he was regent during his father's absence, 2 Kin. 1:17; 3:1; 891, 2 Kin. 8:16; and 889.	891	Ben-hadad besieges Samaria; severe famine ensues; plenty restored by the sudden flight of the Syrians, 2 Kin. 6:24–33; 7.
	890	Elisha raises to life the widow's son; other miracles, 2 Kings 4:18–44; 8:1, 2.
Death of Jehoshaphat. JEHORAM, or JORAM, king 8 years; his wicked and troubled reign. Elijah's letter, written before his translation, brought to him, 1 Kin. 22:45, 50; 2 Kin. 8:17–22; 2 Chr. 20:34; 21:1–18.	889 to 887	2 Kin. 4:44. This is Elisha's twelfth miracle, Elijah having wrought six. Townsend places 4:18 after 4:17; but there is clearly an interval of two years or so between them.
Ahaziah begins to reign as viceroy to his father, 2 Kin. 9:29.	886	
Death of Jehoram. AHAZIAH king one year; his evil reign, 2 Kin. 8:23–27; 2 Chr. 21:19, 20; 22:1–4.	885	Return of the Shunammite. Hazael kills Ben-hadad, and becomes, as Elisha predicted, king of Syria, 2 Kin. 8:3–15.
Ahaziah joins Joram against Hazael, and afterwards visits him at Jezreel, 2 Kin. 8:28, 29.	884	Joram being wounded in battle by the Syrians, retires to Jezreel, 2 Chron. 22:5, 6. Jehu anointed, 2 Kin. 9:1–13.
Ahaziah slain by Jehu, 2 Chr. 22:7–9.		Joram slain by Jehu, 2 Kin. 9:14–28.
ATHALIAH usurps the throne 6 years. Joash the son of Ahaziah rescued, 2 Kin. 11:1–3; 2 Chr. 22:10–12.	883	*JEHU* king 28 years; slays Jezebel, Ahab's sons, Ahaziah's brethren, and Baal's worshippers, 2 Kings 9:30–37; 10:1–31.

PERIOD V.—CONTINUED.

JUDAH.	B. C.	ISRAEL.
JEHOASH, or JOASH, king 40 years. Athaliah slain, 2 Kings 11 : 4-12; 2 Chr. 23-24:3.	877	
	860	Hazael oppresses Israel, 2 Kin. 10:32, 33.
Joash repairs the temple, 2 Kin. 12:4-16; 2 Chr. 24:4-14.	855	Death of Jehu. JEHOAHAZ king 17 years. 2 Kin. 10:34-36; 13:1, 2.
Death of Jehoiada, 2 Chr. 24:15, 16.	850	History of Jonah. Jon. 1-4.
	849 842	Israel given over by God to Hazael and Ben-hadad, and delivered, 2 Kin. 13:1-7.
	841	Jehoash begins to reign in concert with Jehoahaz, 2 Kin. 13:10.
Joash and the people fall into idolatry; Zechariah, reproving them, is slain in the temple-court, (*cf.* Matt. 23:35.) The Syrians invade Judah, 2 Chr. 24:17-24; 2 Kin. 12:17, 18.	840	
Joash slain by his servants. AMAZIAH king 29 years, 2 Kin. 12:19-21; 14 : 1-6; 2 Chron. 24 : 25-27; 25:1-4.	838	Death of Jehoahaz. JEHOASH, or JOASH, king 16 years. He visits Elisha, who promises three victories. Hazael dies, 2 Kin. 13 : 8, 9, 11, 14-19, 22-24.
	838	Elisha dies. A corpse thrown into Elisha's sepulchre revives, 2 Kin. 13:20, 21.
	836	Jehoash thrice beats the Syrians, 2 Kin. 13:25.
Amaziah hires an army of Israelites to assist him against Edom, but at a prophet's command he sends them back, 2 Chr. 25:5-10.	827	The Israelites, who had been dismissed by Amaziah, plunder the cities of Judah as they return, 2 Chr. 25:13.
Amaziah smites the Edomites and worships their gods, 2 Chron. 25 : 11; 2 Kin. 14:7; 2 Chr. 25:12, 14-16.		
Amaziah provokes the king of Israel to battle, and is taken prisoner by him, 2 Kin. 14:8-14.	826	Jehoash defeats the king of Judah, and plunders the temple, 2 Chron. 25:17-24.
	823	Death of Jehoash. JEROBOAM II. king 41 years; he reigns wickedly, 2 Kin. 13:12, 13; 14:15, 16, 23, 24.
	822	Jeroboam restores the coast of Israel, according to the word of Jonah, 2 Kin. 14:25-27.
Amaziah slain. UZZIAH, or AZARIAH, king 52 years. During the days of Zechariah he reigns well, 2 Kin. 14 : 17-22; 15 : 1-4; 2 Chr. 25:25; 26:15.	808 to 800	
	801	Hosea makes his first appeal to the ten tribes, Hos. 1-3.
Amos 7 : 10-19, Lightfoot and others place after 2 Kin. 14 : 28.	793	Amos denounces judgment against the surrounding nations, and against Israel and Judah, Amos 1-9.

PERIOD V.—CONTINUED.

JUDAH.	B. C.	ISRAEL.
On the increase of Uzziah's army, Joel foretells the overthrow of Judah, Joel 1–3.	787	1:3, see 2 Kin. 16:9; ver. 6, see 2 Kin. 18:8; 1:8, see 2 Chron. 26:6; ver. 11, see Num. 20:14; 5:27, see 2 Kin. 10:32; 17:6.
	783	Death of Jeroboam, 2 Kin. 14:28, 29. *An interregnum for eleven years.* State of Israel during the interregnum. Hosea denounces judgment, Hos. 4.
The three children have names given to them, indicating the *place* of the wickedness of the house of Ahab, (ver. 4; see 1 Kin. 21:1;) their punishment, *not finding mercy* in calamity; and their rejection, *no longer the people* of God. They are, however, to be gathered again under the Messiah, their one Head, ver. 11; ver. 7, see 2 Kin. 19:35.	771	ZECHARIAH, fourth from Jehu, king six months. Shallum slays him, 2 Kin. 15:8–12.
	770	*SHALLUM* king one month. Menahem slays him, 2 Kin. 15:13–15. *MENAHEM* king 10 years, 2 Kings 15:16–18.
	769	Pul of Assyria, coming against Israel, is bribed to return, 2 Kin. 15:19, 20.
Uzziah struck with leprosy for invading the priest's office. Jotham regent, 2 Kin. 15:5; 2 Chr. 26:16–20, 21.	765	
	761	Death of Menahem. PEKAHIAH king 2 years, 2 Kin. 15:21–24.
2 Kin. 15:5, several, that is, lone or separate.	759	Pekahiah slain by Pekah. *PEKAH* king 20 years, 15:25–28.
Isaiah designated in a vision to the prophetic office. He prophesies of Christ's kingdom, and of judgment on the people for their sins, Isa. 1:1; 6:2–5.	757	Isa. 1:1. Isa. 7–10:4. On the order, compare 7:1 with 2 Kin. 16:5. Isa. 1:2–31. On order, see ver. 7, 8, compared with 2 Chr. 28:6–9. Isa. 6:1, see John 12:41.
Death of Uzziah. JOTHAM king 16 years; his prosperity, 2 Kin. 15:6, 7, 32–35; 2 Chr. 26:22, 23; 27:1–6.	756	Isa. 6:13, see 2 Kin. 25:12. Isa. 2:19, see Rev. 6:15. 2 Chr. 27:2, see chap 26:19. Isa. 7:8, see 2 Kin. 17:24.
Micah reproves the wickedness of Judah, Mic. 1, 2.	753	Reign of Ahaz,------------15 years. " Hezekiah,-------29 " " Manasseh II.,---21 " 65 " Isa. 7:16, see 2 Kin. 15:29.
Judah begins to be afflicted by Syria and Israel. Death of Jotham, 2 Kin. 15:36–38; 2 Chr. 27:7–9. AHAZ king 16 years, 2 Kin. 16:1–4; 2 Chr. 28:1–4. Invasion of Pekah and Rezin. Isaiah prophesies on the occasion, denouncing Ahaz's intended alliance with Assyria, 2 Kings 16:5; Isa. 7–9; 10:1–4. Isaiah prophesies the ruin of Damascus and of the ten tribes, Isa. 17.	742	Isa. 8:1, a man's pen, that is, common writing; see Rev. 13:18; 21:17. Mic. 1:5, see 1 Kin. 16:32. Mic. 1:13, see Jer. 34:7. Isa. 17 see 2 Kin. 16:9; 18:11.
Judah devastated by Syria and Israel; the latter restore their captives, by advice of Oded, 2 Chr. 28:5–15.	740	
Ahaz, being assailed by enemies, hires Tiglath-pileser the king of Assyria	740	Tiglath-pileser ravages Gilead, Galilee, and Naphtali, and carries cap-

PERIOD V.—CONTINUED.

JUDAH.	B. C.	ISRAEL.
against them. Obadiah and Isaiah, 2 Kin. 16:6-9; 2 Chr. 28:16, 21, 17-20; Obad.; Isa. 1:2-31; 28.		tive their inhabitants to Assyria, 2 Kin. 15:29. Isa. 5:21, see 2 Sam. 5:20.
Sacrilege and idolatry of Ahaz, 2 Chr. 28:22-25; 2 Kin. 16:10-18; Hosea 5, 6.	738	Pekah slain by Hoshea, 2 Kin. 15:30, 31.
		Anarchy for nine years.
	730	*HOSHEA* king 9 years. Shalmaneser king of Assyria invades his territory
Death of Ahaz, 2 Kings 16:19, 20; 2 Chr. 28:26, 27; Isa. 14:28-32. HEZEKIAH king 29 years, 2 Kings 18:1, 2; 2 Chr. 29:1. Reformation by Hezekiah, 2 Kings 18:3-6; 2 Chr. 29:2-36; 30, 31. Moab denounced, Isa. 15, 16. Micah supports Hezekiah's reformation, Mic. 3-7. See Jer. 26:18; Mic. 3:9.	726	and makes him a tributary, 2 Kin. 17:1-3. Isa. 14:28-32, against Philistia, see 2 Chr. 26:6. Ahab, who subdued them, was dead; but a cockatrice out of that nest, Hezekiah, was still to bite them, 2 Kin. 18:8. Isa. 15. The destruction of Moab by Shalmaneser foretold. They are exhorted to renew their tribute, 16:1. See 2 Kings 3:4.
	723	Hoshea attacked and imprisoned by Shalmaneser for not giving the tribute. Hosea predicts the captivity of the ten tribes, and exhorts to repentance, 2 Kin. 17:4; Hos. 7-14.
Hezekiah's prosperity, 2 Kin. 18:7, 8.	723	Shalmaneser besieges Samaria, 2 Kin. 17:5; 18:9.
	721	The ten tribes carried into captivity unto Assyria, 2 Kings 17:6-23; 18:10-12.
Prophecy of the restoration of the ten tribes, of the punishment of Egypt, and conversion of Egypt and Assyria, Isa. 18, 19.		

II. HISTORY OF JUDAH TO THE CAPTIVITY, 114 YEARS.

DATE AND PLACE.	EVENT OR NARRATIVE.	BIBLE REFERENCE.
B. C. 715.	Tyre denounced, Isa. 23. Prophecy concerning the invasion by Assyria,	Isa. 10:5; 14:27.
714.	The desolation and recovery of Judea predicted, etc.,	Isa. 24; 26:17, 18; 27.
713, Judea.	Isaiah predicts the invasion by Assyria and the destruction of Babylon. Sennacherib comes up against Judah, but being pacified by a tribute, retires. Isaiah denounces Egypt, and warns Jerusalem,	Isa. 22:1-14; 21; 2 Kin. 18:13-16; 2 Chr. 32:1-8; Isa. 36:1; 20; 29-31.

PERIOD V.—CONTINUED.

DATE AND PLACE.	EVENT OR NARRATIVE.	BIBLE REFERENCE.
Jerusalem.	Sickness of Hezekiah; his song of thanksgiving. Isaiah predicts the blessings of Christ's kingdom, and judgments of the enemies of Zion,	2 Kin. 20:1-6, 8, 9-11, 7; Isa. 38:1-6, 22, 7, 8, 21, 9-20; 2 Chr. 32:24; Isa. 32-35.
712.	Nineveh denounced by Nahum,	Nah. 1-3.
712, Jerusalem.	Hezekiah showing in pride to the ambassadors from Babylon his treasures, Isaiah predicts the Babylonian captivity,	2 Kin. 20:12-19; Isa. 39; 2 Chr. 32:25, 26.
711, Judea.	Second invasion of Sennacherib; destruction of his army,	2 Kin. 18:17-37, 26-28; 19:1-37. Psa. 44, 73, 75, 76; Isa. 36:2, 11-22; 37:1-38; 2 Chr. 32:9-21-23.
710-699.	Various prophecies of Isaiah,	Isa. 40-66; 57:3-9.
697, Jerusalem.	Hezekiah's wealth; his death. MANASSEH king fifty-five years; his awful impiety; judgment denounced by God's prophets,	2 Kin. 20:20, 21; 21:1-16; 2 Chr. 32:27-33; 33:1-10.
	Isaiah predicts the captivity of Shebna,	Isa. 22:15-25.
678, Samaria.	The heathen nations, who had been transplanted to Samaria in place of the Israelites, being plagued by lions, make a mixture of religions,	2 Kin. 17:24-41.
677, Babylon.	Manasseh taken captive by the king of Assyria; his conversion and restoration; he puts down idolatry,	2 Chr. 33:11-17.
642, Jerusalem.	Death of Manasseh. AMON king two years; his impiety,	2 Kin. 21:17-22; 2 Chr. 33:18-23.
640.	Amon slain by his servants. JOSIAH king thirty-one years,	2 Kin. 21:23-26; 22:1, 2; 2 Chr. 33:24, 25; 34:1, 2.
634.	Josiah vigorously puts down idolatry,	2 Chr. 34:3-7.
628.	Jeremiah called; he expostulates with the Jews, on account of their sins,	Jer. 1:2; 3:1-5.
623, Jerusalem.	Josiah provides for the repair of the temple. The Book of the Law having been found, Josiah consults Huldah; he causes it to be read publicly, and renews the covenant,	2 Kin. 22:3-20; 23:1-3, 4-20; 2 Chr. 34:8, 28-33.
623.	Zephaniah exhorts to repentance,	Zeph. 1, 2, 3.
622, Jerusalem.	A most solemn celebration of the Passover by Josiah,	2 Kin. 23:21-27; 2 Chr. 35:1-19.
612.	Jeremiah reproves the backsliding of the people, and bewails the coming captivity,	Jer. 3:6-11, 12-25; 4-6.
612.	Habakkuk predicts judgment,	Hab. 1-3.
611.	Jeremiah exhorts the people to repentance, and laments their approaching calamities,	Jer. 7-10.

PERIOD V.—CONTINUED.

DATE AND PLACE.	EVENT OR NARRATIVE.	BIBLE REFERENCE.
B. C. 610.	Jeremiah reminds the people of the covenant of Josiah,	Jer. 11; 15, 12.
609, Megiddo and Jerusalem.	Josiah slain in battle with the king of Egypt. Jeremiah and the people lament him. JEHOAHAZ king three months,	2 Kin. 23:29, 30, 28, 30 *l. p.*, 31, 32; 2 Chr. 35:20–27; 36:1, 2.
Riblah.	Jehoahaz deposed and imprisoned by Pharaoh-Necho, and subsequently taken to Egypt. JEHOIAKIM king eleven years,	2 Kin. 23:33–37; 2 Chr. 36:3–5.
	Jeremiah delivers various predictions, and appeals to the Jews respecting the captivity and destruction of Jerusalem,	Jer. 13–19.
	Jeremiah predicts the fate of Pashur, Jer. 20: of Shallum, that is, Jehoahaz, and Jehoiakim,	Jer. 22:1–23.
608.	Apprehension and arraignment of Jeremiah,	Jer. 26.
606.	Jeremiah predicts the overthrow of the army of Pharaoh-Necho king of Egypt, by Nebuchadnezzar,	Jer. 46:1–12.
	The obedience of the Rechabites to their father contrasted with the disobedience of the Jews,	Jer. 35.
	Jeremiah predicts the captivity of the Jews for seventy years, and the subsequent judgment on Babylon,	Jer. 25.
Jerusalem.	Jeremiah desires Baruch to write his prophecies on a roll, and then to read it publicly in the temple,	Jer. 36:1–8; 45.
606.	Nebuchadnezzar takes Jerusalem, and puts Jehoiakim in fetters, intending to take him to Babylon, but afterwards releasing him, makes him a tributary, and spoils the temple,	2 Kin. 24:1; 2 Chr. 36:6, 7; Dan. 1:1, 2.
	Nebuchadnezzar orders the master of his eunuchs to select and send to Babylon some of the royal family and nobility, to stand in the king's palace. Daniel, Hananiah, Mishael, and Azariah, (otherwise called Belteshazzar, Shadrach, Meshach, and Abednego,) are taken there,	Dan. 1, 3, 4, 6, 7.

III. FROM THE FIRST CAPTURE OF JERUSALEM, B. C. 606, TO THE DECREE OF CYRUS, FOR THE RESTORATION OF THE JEWS, B. C. 536—70 YEARS.

DATE AND PLACE.	EVENT OR NARRATIVE.	BIBLE REFERENCE.
	EVENTS AT JERUSALEM, WITH CONTEMPORANEOUS EVENTS AT BABYLON.	
B. C. Babylon.	Daniel meets with kindly treatment,	Dan. 1:5, 8–17.
605.	Baruch again reads the prophetic roll; Jehoiakim burns it,	Jer. 36:9–32.
603.	Jehoiakim rebels against Nebuchadnezzar,	2 Kin. 24:1 *l. p.*, 24.

PERIOD V.—CONTINUED.

DATE AND PLACE.	EVENT OR NARRATIVE.	BIBLE REFERENCE.
B. C. Babylon.	Daniel before Nebuchadnezzar,	Dan. 1:18-21.
	Interprets Nebuchadnezzar's dream, Dan. 2; describing the Babylonian, 32, Medo-Persian, 32-39, Macedo-Grecian, 32-39, and Roman empires, 33, 40-43, with Messiah's kingdom, 34, 35, 44, 45.	
599.	Death of Jehoiakim. JEHOIACHIN or JECHONIAH king three months,	2 Kin. 24:5-9; 2 Chr. 36:8, 9; Jer. 22:24-30; 23.
599.	Second capture of Jerusalem by Nebuchadnezzar. Jehoiachin is carried to Babylon, with many of his subjects. ZEDEKIAH or MATTANIAH king eleven years,	2 Kin. 24:10-19; 2 Chr. 36:10-12; Jer. 52:1, 2; 24.
597.	Predictions of the duration of the captivity,	Jer. 29:1-14, 16-20, 15, 21-32.
	Of the restoration of the Jews,	Jer. 30, 31.
595.	Predictions against the surrounding nations. Hananiah the false prophet denounced,	Jer. 27, 28, 48, 49.
	Prophecies against Babylon,	Jer. 50, 51.
Babylon.	Ezekiel's vision in Babylon; his commission, Ezek. 1-3:1-21. He prophesies of the miseries of Jerusalem,	Ezek. 3:22-27; 4-7.
594.	Visions of the idolatries which occasioned the captivity,	Ezek. 8, 10, 11.
Babylon.	Various predictions against the false prophets, Jerusalem, and the Jewish nation,	Ezek. 12-19; 16; 18:5-18.
593.	Prophecies addressed to the elders of the Jews,	Ezek. 21-23.
Jerusalem.	Zedekiah's rebellion and wickedness,	Jer. 37:1, 2; 2 Kin. 24:20; 2 Chr. 36:13; Jer. 52:3.
	The wickedness of priests and people, (the cause of the captivity, ver. 15, 16,) with a summary account of the judgments that followed,	2 Chr. 36:14-21.
590.	Nebuchadnezzar lays siege to Jerusalem for the third time,	2 Kin. 25:1; Jer. 39:1; 52:4; 37:3, 4.
Babylon.	Ezekiel foretells the destruction of Jerusalem,	Ezek. 24.
Jerusalem.	Capture of the city foretold. The people, at Jeremiah's word, release their Hebrew bond-servants,	Jer. 34:1-10.
589.	Jeremiah shut up in prison; his predictions there,	Jer. 32, 33.
Babylon.	Ezekiel in Babylon, prophesies against Egypt, Ezek. 29:1-16, and against Tyre,	Ezek. 26. See Isa. 23.
Jerusalem.	The Chaldeans raise the siege to march against the approaching Egyptian army. Jeremiah predicts the destruction of the Philistines,	Jer. 37:5; 47.
	On the departure of the Chaldean army, the people recall their bond-servants, for which Jeremiah denounces them, and predicts the speedy return of the Chaldeans,	Jer. 34:11-22; 37:6-10

PERIOD V.—CONTINUED.

DATE AND PLACE.	EVENT OR NARRATIVE.	BIBLE REFERENCE.
B. C. 588.	Jeremiah reimprisoned; continues to denounce Zedekiah; he is put into the dungeon of Malchiah,	Jer. 37:11-21: 21; 38; 39:15-18.
	Ezekiel, in Babylon, again prophesies against Egypt and Nineveh,	Ezek. 30:20-26; 31.
	Jerusalem finally taken. Zedekiah carried to Babylon. Jeremiah delivered,	2 Kin. 25:2, 4-7; Jer. 52:5-7; 39:2-7, 11-14.
	Nebuzaradan burns the temple, and carries away the people, leaving a few poor persons to till the land,	2 Kin. 25:8-21; Jer. 52:12-30; 39:8-10. Psa. 74, 79, 83, 94.
	Jeremiah bewails the desolation of his country,	Lam. 1-5.
	Gedaliah appointed governor. Jeremiah and many others attach themselves to him,	2 Kin. 25:22-24; Jer. 40:1-16.
	Ishmael slays Gedaliah, and attempts to carry away the people to the Ammonites; Johanan intercepts him; the people, fearing the Chaldeans, flee into Egypt, contrary to the command of God,	2 Kin. 25:25, 26; Jer. 41-43:1-7.
	Jeremiah prophesies against Egypt and the idolatrous Jews,	Jer. 43:8-13; 46:13-28; 44.
	Brief summary of the captivities by Nebuchadnezzar,	Jer. 52:28-30.
	REMAINDER OF THE HISTORY OF THE JEWS IN CAPTIVITY—BABYLON.	
Babylon	Ezekiel predicts the utter desolation of Judea,	Ezek. 33:21-33.
587.	Predictions against Ammon, Moab, Edom, Philistia, Tyre, and Egypt,	Ezek. 25, 27, 28, 32.
	Ezekiel appeals to the captives,	Ezek. 33:1-20.
	Evil rulers denounced; restoration of the Jews promised; predictions of Messiah's kingdom,	Ezek. 34-37, 17, last clause.
	Prophesies of the church and its enemies, and of the conversion of the Jews,	Ezek. 38, 39.
573.	Ezekiel's vision of the future temple,	Ezek. 40-48.
572.	Last prediction against Egypt,	Ezek. 29:17-21; 30:1-19.
570.	Nebuchadnezzar sets up an image,	Dan. 3.
569.	Daniel interprets Nebuchadnezzar's second dream,	Dan. 4:1-27.
568-563.	The fulfilment of Nebuchadnezzar's dream, in his madness, and subsequent recovery,	Dan. 4:28-37.
561.	Evil-Merodach king of Babylon releases Jehoiachin,	2 Kin. 25:27-30; Jer. 52:31-34.
558.	Daniel's first vision of the living creatures,	Dan. 7.
556.	Belshazzar's feast. Babylon taken,	Dan. 5.
	Daniel's vision of the ram and he-goat,	Dan. 8.
538.	Daniel's prayer for the restoration of Jerusalem. Prophecy of the seventy weeks,	Dan. 9; Psa. 102.
537.	Daniel cast into the den of lions,	Dan. 6.

PERIOD V.—CONTINUED.

DATE AND PLACE.	EVENT OR NARRATIVE.	BIBLE REFERENCE.
B. C. 536.	Decree of Cyrus for the rebuilding of the temple, and restoration of the Jews to their own country,	2 Chr. 36:22, 23; Ezra 1:1-4; Psa. 126, 85.
Jerusalem and Babylon.	Psalms conjectured to have been written during the distresses and afflictions of the church, chiefly in the Babylonish captivity,	Psa. 10, 13-15, 25-27, 36, 37, 49, 50, 53, 67, 77, 80, 89, 92, 93, 123, 130, 137.

IV. FROM THE DECREE OF CYRUS, B. C. 536, TO THE FINAL PROPHECY OF THE OLD TESTAMENT, B. C. 397, ABOUT 139 YEARS.

DATE AND PLACE.	EVENT OR NARRATIVE	BIBLE REFERENCE.
B. C.	FROM THE RETURN OF THE JEWS TO THE DEDICATION OF THE SECOND TEMPLE.	
536, Jerusalem.	Return of the Jews. Cyrus restores the vessels of the temple. An altar set up,	Ezra 1:5-11; 2; 3:1-7; Psa. 87, 107, 111-114, 116, 117, 125, 127, 128, 134.
535, Jerusalem.	Foundation of the second temple, under the direction of Zerubbabel,	Ezra 3:8-13; Psa. 84, 66.
534.	The building of the temple interrupted by the Samaritans,	Ezra 4:1-5, 24; Psa. 129.
Babylon.	The last vision of Daniel,	Dan. 10-12.
520, Jerusalem.	Building of the temple resumed. Haggai and Zechariah incite the people to the work, and exhort them to repentance,	Ezra 4:24; 5:1; Hag. 1:1-11; Ezra 5:2; Hag. 1:12-15; 2:1-9; Zech. 1:1-6; Hag. 2:10-23; Zech. 1:7-21; 2; 6; 2:5.
519	The building of the temple again interrupted, and resumed,	Ezra 5:3-17; 6:1-13; Psa. 138; Zech. 7, 8.
516.	Dedication of the second temple,	Ezra 6:14-22; Psa. 48, 81, 146-150.

PERIOD V.—CONTINUED.

DATE AND PLACE.	EVENT OR NARRATIVE.	BIBLE REFERENCE.
	FROM THE OPPOSITION TO THE JEWS IN THE REIGN OF XERXES TO THE DEATH OF HAMAN.	
486.	Opposition in the reign of Xerxes,	Ezra 4:6.
464.	Opposition in the reign of Artaxerxes Longimanus,	Ezra 4:7-23.
462, Susa.	Artaxerxes, or Ahasuerus, divorces Vashti his queen,	Esth. 1.
458.	Ezra commissioned to visit Jerusalem,	Ezra 7:2-14.
457.	Artaxerxes makes Esther queen,	Esth. 2:1-20.
Jerusalem.	Ezra comes to Jerusalem; causes the people to put away their heathen wives,	Ez. 8 10, 18-44.
	Concluding prophecies of Zechariah,	Zech. 9-14.
Susa.	Mordecai discovers the conspiracy against Ahasuerus,	Esth. 2:21-23.
453, 452.	Plot of Haman to destroy the Jews, and its defeat. The feast of Purim,	Esth. 3-10.
	FROM THE FIRST COMMISSION OF NEHEMIAH TO THE CLOSING OF THE OLD TESTAMENT CANON.	
445, Susa.	Nehemiah receives a commission from Artaxerxes to visit Jerusalem, and rebuild the wall,	Neh. 1; 2:1-8.
Jerusalem.	Nehemiah arrives at Jerusalem. Sanballat strives to hinder the work; the builders work under arms,	Neh. 2:9-20; 3; 4.
	Nehemiah relieves the Jews oppressed by usury; his own generosity,	Neh. 5.
	The wall completed by the Jews, and dedicated,	Neh. 6; 12:27-43.
Susa.	Nehemiah returns to Persia,	Neh. 7:1-4.
Jerusalem.	Second commission of Nehemiah, and reformation,	Neh. 7:6-73; 8; 9; 10; 11; 12:1-9, 44-47; 13:1-3; Psa. 1, 119.
433.	Malachi prophesies against the corruptions introduced during the second absence of Nehemiah,	Mal. 1, 2, 3:1-15.
428.	Further reformation by Nehemiah,	Neh. 13:4-31.
397.	Final prophecy of the Old Testament,	Mal. 3:16-18; 4.
	Detached genealogies, etc., inserted probably at the completion of the canon,	1 Chr. 1-9; Neh. 12:10-26.

PERIOD VI.

OLD AND NEW TESTAMENTS CONNECTED.

PALESTINE.

B. C.	
413	Jehoiada high-priest.
373	Johanan high-priest.
351	Ochus king of Persia plants Jews near the Caspian.
341	Jaddua high-priest.
332	Alexander, having destroyed Tyre, visits Jerusalem; plants Jews in Alexandria.
324	Alexander dies; his kingdom divided.
321	Onias high-priest.
320	Ptolemy Lagus captures Jerusalem; plants Jews in Alexandria and Cyrene.
312	Seleucus obtains Syria; era of the Seleucidæ.
306	The dominions of Alexander formed into four kingdoms, as foretold by Daniel.
300	Simon the Just high-priest.
292	Eleazar high-priest.
285	Version of the Seventy commenced at Alexandria.
251	Onias II. high-priest.
246	Ptol. Euergetes offers sacrifices at Jerusalem.
216	Ptolemy Philopater, prevented from entering the Holy of Holies, attempts to destroy the Jews in Alexandria, but is miraculously prevented.
203	Antiochus the Great obtains Palestine.
200	The sect of the Sadducees founded.
199	Scopas, an Egyptian general, recovers Judea to the king of Egypt.
198	Antiochus regains Judea.

PERSIA, SYRIA, AND EGYPT.

B. C.	
405	Artaxerxes Mnemon, Persia.
401	Death of Cyrus the younger.
381	Artaxerxes Ochus, Persia.
350	Egypt recovered by Persians.
335	Darius Codomanus, Persia.
331	Alexander defeats Persia on the Granicus, 334; at Issus, 333; at Arbela, the Persian empire ends.
324	Ptolemy Lagus, Egypt.
312	Seleucus I., Nicator, Syria.
312	Empire of Seleucus from Antioch to India.
291	Seleucus on the Tigris built.
285	Dionysius (Alex.) determines solar year.

B. C.	EGYPT.	B. C.	SYRIA.
285	P. Philadelphus.	280	Antiochus I.
		261	Anti. II. Theos.
247	P. Euergetes I.	246	Sel. II. Callinic.
		226	Sel. III. Keraunus.
222	P. Philopater.	223	Ant. III. the Great.
205	P. Epiphanes.		
190	First Roman army in Asia.		
		187	Sel. IV. Philop.

EUROPE.

B. C.	
404	Euclid.
401	Retreat of the Ten Thousand.
397	Zeuxis.
389	Plato.
363	Mantinea, death of Epaminondas.
356	Birth of Alexander.
345	Aristotle.
338	Demosthenes.
334	Apelles.
295	Epicurus.
281	Theocritus.
280	Pyrrhus king of Epirus enters Italy.
268	[Berosus,
261	Manetho, Egyptians.]
264	First Punic war.
258	Regulus prisoner.
236	Archimedes.
220	Plautus.
224	Colossus of Rhodes overthrown.
220	Hannibal.
218	Second Punic war.
216	Battle of Cannæ.
210	Zeno.
202	Hannibal defeated in Africa by Scipio Africanus.

195	Onias III. high-priest.			175	Ant. IV. Epiph.	190	Scipio Asiaticus
176	Heliodorus, attempting to plunder the temple, is prevented by an angel.	181	P. Philometor.	164	Ant. V. Eupator.		
				162	Demetr. Soter defeated and slain by		
170	Antiochus Epiphanes takes Jerusalem, slays 40,000 persons, and profanes the temple.						
167	Antiochus persecutes the Jews.			150	Alexander Balas		
165	Judas Maccabæus purifies the temple, and institutes the feast of dedication.						
161	Judas Maccabæus slain; his brother Jonathan succeeds.						
149	Onias builds a temple in Egypt like that in Jerusalem.					149	Third Punic war, lasts three years.
144	Jonathan, murdered by Tryphon, is succeeded by Simon his brother, who is made ruler by Demetrius.	146	P. Physcon.	146	Demet. Nicator	148	Carthage destroyed.
		144	P. Physcon.	144	Ant. VI. Theos.	148	Corinth destroyed.
141	The sovereignty and priesthood confirmed by the Jews to Simon and his posterity.			143	Tryphon.		
				139	Ant. VII.		
135	The Pharisees.			130	Demet. Nic. II.	136	Scipio Nasica.
135	Simon murdered; John Hyrcanus his son succeeds him.			127	Alexander.	133	Tiberius Gracchus
				123	Ant. VIII.		
130	John Hyrcanus throws off the Syrian yoke, and makes himself independent. He destroys the temple on mount Gerizim.	110	P. Lathyrus.				
110	The Essenes.			111	Ant. IX.	111	Jugurthine war, (five years.)
107	Aristobulus succeeds his father Hyrcanus, and assumes the title of king.			108	Ant. VIII. and IX.		
				93	Philip and Ant. X.		
106	Alexander Jannæus succeeds his brother Aristobulus, and reigns for twenty-seven years.	88	P. Alexander.	92	Demetrius Euc.	100	Julius Cæsar born.
						88	Civil war. Marius and Sylla.
79	Jannæus dies. Alexandra his wife succeeds, and makes her son Hyrcanus high-priest, and favors the Pharisees.	81	P. Auletes?	83	Tigranes of Armenia.	81	Cicero's first oration.
				69	Ant. XI.		
70	Alexandra dies. Hyrcanus succeeds, but is forced to yield the crown to his younger brother Aristobulus.					71	Spartacus.
						69	Lucullus defeats Mithridates and Tigranes.
65	Pompey the Great reduces Syria to a Roman province. Hyrcanus endeavors to regain the crown.	55	P. Auletes.	65	Pompey makes it a Roman province.		

PERIOD VI.—CONTINUED.

B. C.	PALESTINE.	B. C.	SYRIA AND EGYPT. EGYPT.	B. C.	SYRIA.	B. C.	EUROPE.
63	Pompey, appealed to by Hyrcanus and Aristobulus, decides for the former; he takes Jerusalem, and makes Judea tributary.		ROMAN GOVERNORS.			63	Catiline conspiracy.
						60	First triumvirate; Pompey, Cæsar, Crassus.
57	Aristobulus and his son Alexander, raising disturbances, are vanquished by Gabinius the Roman governor of Syria.	55	Gabinius.		ROMAN GOVERNORS.	60	Catullus.
						57	Sallust.
						50	Cornelius Nepos, Varro.
54	Crassus plunders the temple.	51	Cleopatra.	51	Bibulus.	49	Battle of Pharsalia.
47	Antipater, being appointed by Julius Cæsar procurator of Judea, makes his son Herod governor of Galilee, and Phasael of Jerusalem.			50	Q. M. Scipio.	46	Cæsar reforms calendar.
				47	S. Cæsar.	44	Cæsar slain. Diodorus Siculus.
				43	Cassius.	42	Battle of Philippi.
44	Walls of Jerusalem rebuilt.			38	Ventidius.		
43	Antipater poisoned; Herod and Phasael revenge his death.						
40	The Parthians, having taken Jerusalem, slay Phasael, and place Antigonus son of Aristobulus upon the throne. Herod flies to Rome, and is appointed king of Judea.			39	Parthians invade Syria, 50; and are fiercely expelled by Vent.	44	Second triumvirate; Octavius, Antonius, Lepidus.
37	Herod takes Jerusalem, beheads Antigonus, and is established as king of Judea; reigns thirty-four years.					36	Lepidus expelled the triumv.
						33	War between Oct. and Ant.
						31	Battle of Actium.
35	Herod makes Aristobulus, brother of his wife Mariamne, high-priest, but afterwards murders him.	30	Made a Roman province by Octavius.	34	Plancus.	27	Octavius emperor, with title of Cæsar Augustus.
				27	Messala C.	31	Mæcenas.
25	Herod rebuilds Samaria, and calls it Sebaste.					29	Horace.
22	Herod begins to build Cæsarea. Trachonitis, Auranitis, and Batanea, are added to his dominions.			22	Agrippa.	27	Propertius.
						25	Livy.
						21	Tibullus.
17	Herod, after two years' preparation, begins to rebuild and enlarge the temple.			13	S. Saturninus and T. Volumnius.	20	Ovid.
6	Zacharias receives the announcement respecting the birth of John the Baptist. The canon of the New Testament begins.					5	Dion. Halicarnassus.

CHRONOLOGICAL INDEX TO THE BIBLE.

PERIOD VII.

FROM THE BIRTH OF JESUS CHRIST TO THE END OF THE FIRST CENTURY.

DATE AND PLACE.	EVENT OR NARRATIVE.	BIBLE REFERENCE.
A. D. 1.	Nativity of Jesus Christ, (four years before the common era,)	Luke 2:1-16.
12.	Jesus visits Jerusalem,	Luke 2:41-52.
18.	Augustus Cæsar followed by Tiberius.	
26.	Pilate sent from Rome as governor of Judea,	Luke 3:1.
29.	John the Baptist begins his ministry,	Matt. 3:1.
30.	Jesus baptized by John,	Matt. 3:1.
33.	Jesus Christ was crucified, and rose from the dead,	Matt. 27; 28.
34.	Ananias and Sapphira struck dead,	Acts 5.
35.	Stephen stoned, and the church persecuted,	Acts 6; 7.
36.	Saul converted,	Acts 9; 13:9.
37.	Tiberius dies, and is followed by Caligula.	
38.	Conversion of the Gentiles,	Acts 10.
41.	Caius Caligula succeeded by Claudius.	
42.	Herod Agrippa made king of Judea.	
44.	James beheaded by Herod; Peter liberated by an angel,	Acts 12:1-19.
54.	Claudius Cæsar followed by Nero.	
63.	Paul sent a prisoner to Rome,	Acts 26; 28.
65.	The Jewish war begins.	
67.	The Roman general raises the siege of Jerusalem, by which an opportunity is afforded for the Christians to retire to Pella beyond Jordan, as admonished by Christ,	Matt. 24:16-20.
68.	Paul suffers martyrdom at Rome by order of Nero,	2 Tim. 4:6, 7
69.	Vespasian made emperor by his army.	
70.	Jerusalem besieged and taken by Titus Vespasian, according to the predictions of Christ; when 1,100,000 Jews perished, by famine, sword, fire, and crucifixion; besides 97,000 who were sold as slaves, and vast multitudes who perished in other parts of Judea,	Luke 19:41-44.
71	Jerusalem and its temple razed to their foundations,	Matt. 24:2.
79.	Vespasian dies, and is succeeded by Titus. Herculaneum and Pompeii destroyed by an eruption of Vesuvius.	
81.	Titus dies, and is succeeded by Domitian.	
95.	John banished to the isle of Patmos, by Domitian,	Rev. 1:9.
96.	John writes the Revelation.	
96.	Domitian succeeded by Nerva.	
97.	John liberated from exile. New Testament canon closed.	
98.	Nerva dies, and is succeeded by Trajan.	
100.	John, the last surviving apostle, dies, about one hundred years old.	

TABULAR VIEW OF THE PROPHETS,

SHOWING THE PERIODS DURING WHICH IT IS SUPPOSED THEIR PROPHECIES WERE DELIVERED.

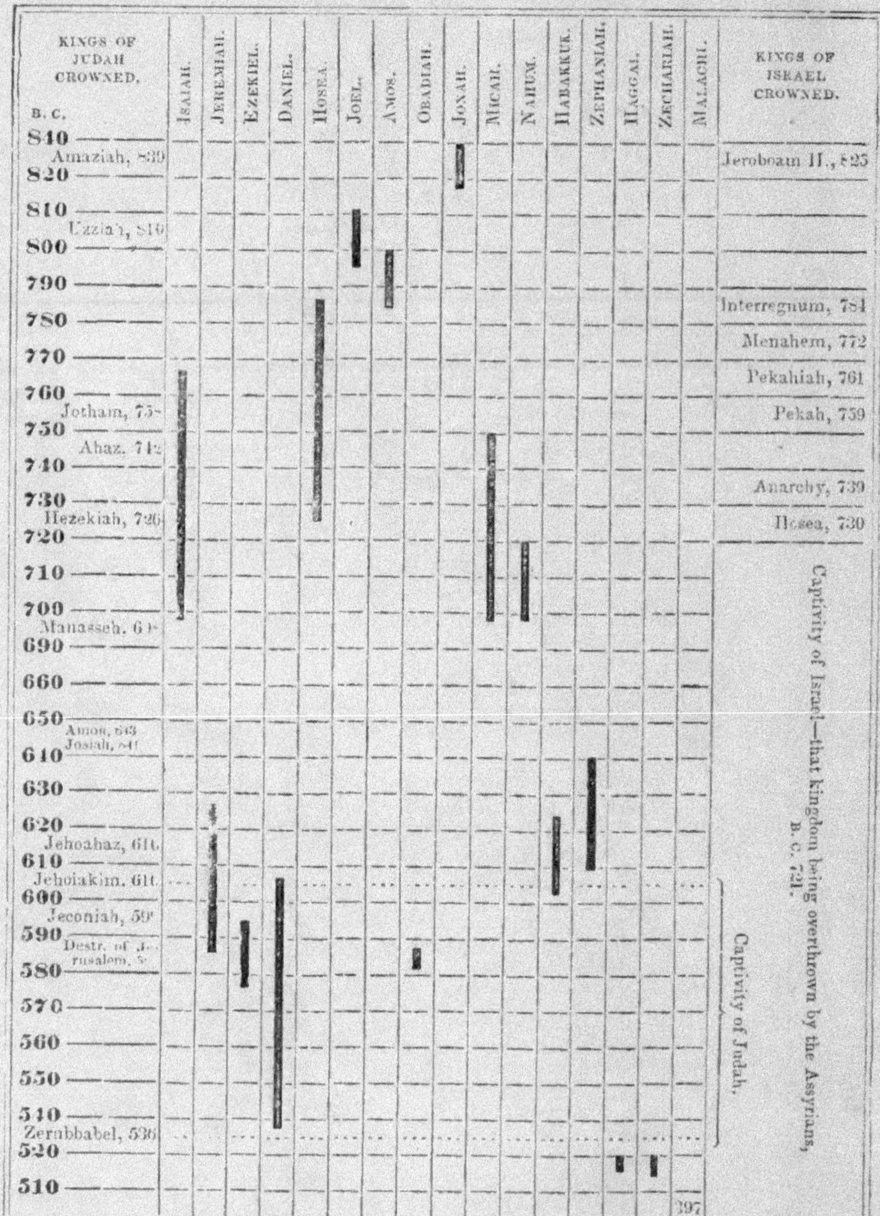

CHRONOLOGICAL TABLE OF THE PATRIARCHS, FROM ADAM TO MOSES, 2,500 YEARS.

This table exhibits the years of the birth and death of the patriarchs; the comparative length of their lives; who of them were alive at the same period; and the rapid decrease in the length of life after the deluge. Thus, Lamech the father of Noah was born A. M. 874, and died A. M. 165 ; he was contemporary with Adam fifty-six years, and he died but five years before the flood. Shem was born nearly one hundred years before the flood, and lived many years after both Abraham and Isaac were born. Eber outlived six generations of his descendants, including Abraham.

YEARS FROM THE CREATION.		100	200	300	400	500	600	700	800	900	1000	1100	1200	1300	1400	1500	1600	1700	1800	1900	2000	2100	2200	2300	2400	2500
Adam	1									930																
Seth		130									1042															
Enos			235									1140					DELUGE A. M. 1656.									
Cainan				325									1235													
Mahalaleel				395									1290													
Jared					460										1422											
Enoch							622			987																
Methuselah							687										1656									
Lamech									874								1651									
Noah											1056										2006					
Shem																1558						2158				
Arphaxad																	1658				2096					
Salah																	1693					2126				
Eber																		1723				2187				
Peleg																		1757		1996						
Reu																		1787			2026					
Serug																			1819		2049					
Nahor																	DELUGE B. C. 2348.		1849	1997						
Terah																			1878		2083					
Abraham																					2008	2183				
Isaac																						2108	2288			
Jacob																						2168		2315		
Levi																							2255	237		
Kohath																							2288		2421	
Amram																								2367		2504
Moses																									2433	2553
YEARS BEFORE CHRIST.	4000	3900	3800	3700	3600	3500	3400	3300	3200	3100	3000	2900	2800	2700	2600	2500	2400	2300	2200	2100	2000	1900	1800	1700	1600	1500

TABLES

OF

WEIGHTS, MEASURES, AND MONEY, MENTIONED IN THE BIBLE.

DRAWN CHIEFLY FROM THE TABLES OF DR. ARBUTHNOT.

---

1. JEWISH WEIGHTS, REDUCED TO ENGLISH TROY WEIGHTS.

	lbs.	oz.	pen.	gr.
The gerah, one twentieth of a shekel,	0	0	0	12
Bekah, half a shekel,	0	0	5	0
The shekel,	0	0	10	0
The maneh, 60 shekels,	2	6	0	0
The talent, 50 manehs, or 3,000 shekels,	125	0	0	0

---

2. SCRIPTURE MEASURES OF LENGTH, REDUCED TO ENGLISH MEASURE.

	Eng. ft.	Inches.
A digit,	0	0.912
4 = A palm,	0	3.648
12 = 3 = A span,	0	10.944
24 = 6 = 2 = A cubit,	1	9.888
96 = 24 = 8 = 4 = A fathom,	7	3.552
144 = 36 = 12 = 6 = 1.5 = Ezekiel's reed,	10	11.328
192 = 48 = 16 = 8 = 2 = 1.3 = An Arabian pole,	14	7.104
1920 = 480 = 160 = 80 = 20 = 13.3 = 10 = A measuring line,	145	11.04

---

3. THE LONG SCRIPTURE MEASURES.

	Eng. miles.	Paces.	Feet.
A cubit,	0	0	1.824
400 = A stadium, or furlong,	0	145	4.6
2000 = 5 = A sabbath-day's journey,	0	729	3
4000 = 10 = 2 = An eastern mile,	1	403	1
12000 = 30 = 6 = 3 = A parasang,	4	153	3
96000 = 240 = 48 = 24 = 8 = A day's journey,	33	172	4

NOTE.—5 feet = 1 pace; 1,056 paces = 1 mile.

4. SCRIPTURE MEASURES OF CAPACITY FOR LIQUIDS, REDUCED TO ENGLISH WINE MEASURE.

	Gal.	pints.
A caph,	0	0.625
1.3 = A log,	0	0.833
5.3 = 4 = A cab,	0	3.333
16 = 12 = 3 = A hin,	1	2
32 = 24 = 6 = 2 = A seah,	2	4
96 = 72 = 18 = 6 = 3 = A bath, ephah, or firkin,	7	4.50
960 = 720 = 180 = 60 = 30 = 10 = A kor, choros, or homer,	75	5.25

---

5. SCRIPTURE MEASURES OF CAPACITY FOR THINGS DRY, REDUCED TO ENGLISH CORN MEASURE.

	Bu.	Pks.	Gal.	Pints
A gachal,	0	0	0	0.141
20 = A cab,	0	0	0	2.833
36 = 1.8 = An omer, or gomer,	0	0	0	5.1
120 = 6 = 3.3 = A seah,	0	1	0	1
360 = 18 = 10 = 3 = An ephah,	0	3	0	3
1800 = 90 = 50 = 15 = 5 = A letech,	4	0	0	1
3600 = 180 = 100 = 30 = 10 = 2 = A homer, or kor,	8	0	0	1

---

6. JEWISH MONEY, REDUCED TO THE ENGLISH AND AMERICAN STANDARDS.

	£	s.	d.	$	cts.
A gerah,	0	0	1.3687	0	02.5
10 = A bekah,	0	1	1.6875	0	25.09
20 = 2 = A shekel,	0	2	3.375	0	50.187
1200 = 120 = 50 = A maneh, or mina Hebr.,	5	14	0.75	25	09.35
60000 = 6000 = 3000 = 60 = A talent,	342	3	9	1505	62.5
A solidus aureus, or sextula, was worth	0	12	0.5	2	64.09
A siclus aureus, or gold shekel, was worth	1	16	6	8	03
A talent of gold was worth	5475	0	0	24309	00

In the preceding table, silver is valued at 5*s.* and gold at £4 per ounce.

---

7. ROMAN MONEY, MENTIONED IN THE NEW TESTAMENT, REDUCED TO THE ENGLISH AND AMERICAN STANDARDS.

	£	*s.*	*d.*	*far.*	$	cts.
A mite,	0	0	0	0.75	0	00.343
A farthing, about	0	0	0	1.50	0	00.687
A penny, or denarius,	0	0	7	2	0	13.75
A pound, or mina,	3	2	6	[illegible]	13	75

ALPHABETICAL INDEX

OF

TOPICS TO BE NOTICED IN READING THE BIBLE.

The inspired writings are infinitely rich in truth, and each verse is so connected with the rest that an intelligent inquirer may easily extend his investigations from one passage over the whole of Scripture. Without attempting to exhaust topics of inquiry, we mention the following. The letters may be prefixed to each verse, or not, according to the taste of the reader.

A. What *analogies* between sensible and spiritual things may be here traced?

a. What prophecy is here *accomplished?* where found? when written? what rule of interpretation is illustrated?

B. What *blessing* is here sought or acknowledged, or promised, and why?

C. What *custom* is here referred to?

c. What trait of *character* is here given? good or bad? belonging to our natural or our renewed state? what advantages are connected with it?

D. What *doctrine* is here taught? how illustrated? what its practical influence?

d. What *difficulty* is here found in history or in doctrine? how explained?

E. What *evangelical* or other *experience* is here recorded?

e. What *example* is here placed before us? of sin or of holiness? lessons?

F. What *facts* are here related? what doctrine or duty do they illustrate? do you commend or blame them, and why?

f. What is here *forbidden?* in thought, word, or deed?

G. What is the *geographical* position of this country, or place? and what its history?

H. What facts of *natural history* or of *general history* are here referred to or illustrated?

I. What *institution* or ordinance is here mentioned? on whom binding? what its design? what its connection with other institutions?

i. What *instructions* may be gathered from this fact, or parable, or miracle?

K. What *knowledge* of human nature, or want of knowledge, is here displayed?

L. What *Levitical* institute is here mentioned? why appointed?

M. What *miracle* is here recorded? by whom wrought? in whose name? what were its results? what is hereby taught?

N. What is worthy of notice in this *name?*

O. What *obligation* or duty is here enforced? how? and from what motives?

P. What *promise* is here given? to whom?

p. What is the meaning of the *parable* here given? what truth as to God, Christ, man, "the kingdom," is taught?

Q. What important *question* is here proposed? what is the true answer?

R. What prophecy is here *recorded?* is it fulfilled? how? when?

S. What *sin* is here exposed?

s. What *sect* is here introduced? mention its tenets.

T. What *type* is here traced?

t. What *threatening?* when inflicted?

U. What *unjustifiable* action of a good man? what *unusual* excellence in one not pious?

W. What *woe* is here denounced; what *warning* given? against whom, and why?

X. What is here taught of the work, character, person of Christ?

x. What sublimity of thought or of language is here? what inference follows?